HEATHER GRAHAM

THREE COMPLETE CIVIL WAR NOVELS

One Wore Blue

And One Wore Gray

And One Rode West

WINGS BOOKS

New York • Avenel, New Jersey

ABOUT THE AUTHOR

HEATHER GRAHAM lives in an old Mediterranean house in Coral Gables, Florida, with her husband, Dennis, whom she met while in high school, and their five children—Jason, Shayne, Derek, Bryee-Annon, and Chynna.

Years ago she began visiting Civil War sites, becoming more and more aware each time of the poignancy of a nation fighting against itself—brother fighting brother. This Civil War trilogy is a special labor of love for that time, with empathy for its anguish, and respect for its valor and heroes.

This omnibus was originally published in separate volumes under the titles:

One Wore Blue, copyright © 1991 by Heather Graham Pozzessere
And One Wore Gray, copyright © 1992 by Heather Graham Pozzessere
And One Rode West, copyright © 1992 by Heather Graham Pozzessere

This edition contains the complete and unabridged texts of the original editions. They have been completely reset for this volume.

This 1995 edition is published by Wings Books,
distributed by Random House Value Publishing, Inc.,
40 Engelhard Avenue, Avenel, New Jersey 07001,
by arrangement with Dell Publishing, a division of
Bantam Doubleday Dell Publishing Group, Inc.

Random House
New York · Toronto · London · Sydney · Auckland

Printed and bound in the United States of America

Library of Congress Cataloging-in-Publication Data

Graham, Heather.
  [Novels. Selections]
  Three complete Civil War novels / Heather Graham.
    p.   cm.
  Contents: One wore blue — And one wore gray — And one rode west.
  ISBN 0-517-14888-9 (hard)
  1. United States—History—Civil War, 1861–1865—Fiction. 2. War stories,
American. I. Title.
PS3557.R198A6   1995
813'.54—dc20
                                                        95-31186
                                                          CIP

8 7 6 5 4 3 2 1

CONTENTS

One Wore Blue

This book is dedicated with many, many thanks to some of the wonderful people we've come to know in Harpers Ferry and Bolivar, West Virginia.

To Mrs. Shirley Dougherty, who has bewitched, intrigued, entertained and taught us so many times with the "Harpers Ferry Myth and Legends" Tour (Ghost Tour!)

To Dixie, for being the gentleman that he is, but especially for his kindness that very first time we came.

To Mr. and Mrs. Stan Hadden for their hospitality and their charm, and for the wonderful Civil War flavor of Stan's "Eagle."

To many of the National Park Service guides for their own love of history, for their enthusiasm, for their patience.

And it is dedicated to Harpers Ferry itself, a town where the mists still hover over the Shenandoah and Potomac rivers, where the mountains rise into the distance, where the past and present seem to collide, and, as Jason says, where a haunting quality seems to settle over the streets by the darkness of the night, and a restless spirit still remains. Perhaps they still walk here, men in blue, and men in gray.

Lastly, but very especially, it is dedicated to my editor, Damaris Rowland, with tremendous gratitude for the enthusiasm and support she has unwaveringly given this project. Damaris, thank you.

PART 1

John Brown's Body

KIERNAN

*K*iernan's world, it seemed, had split in two.

One side was blue, and one side was gray.

Ever since it began to come apart, everything had changed. All that had been beautiful in life had begun to fade. A way of life that had been full of charm and wit and easy grandeur had passed away. They were holding on to it tightly, but it was gone. The world was split apart, and families were split apart—like Camerons.

One wore blue, and one wore gray.

One had been her childhood friend back in Tidewater Virginia. He and Kiernan had tramped through fields together, they had been chastised together. They had told their dreams to each other during long lazy days when they had lain by pleasant, bubbling springs beneath powder-blue skies.

And the other Cameron brother had been her hero. As a child, she had adored him. As a woman, she had loved him. And when the world had changed, she had hated him—fiercely, desperately, as passionately as she had loved him. She had her beliefs, and she had her loyalties.

It was just that she had loved him so long. . . .

Even when she had stood before the altar with another man and promised to love and honor and cherish that man until death did them part, she had loved him.

Almost as much as she had hated him.

She had told him that she hated him the day that she walked away from him.

But he had been destined to ride back into her life that day, Kiernan would later realize.

Jesse. Jesse Cameron.

The one who wore blue.

It began very late in the afternoon of that autumn day in 1861, when the breeze was cool, when the mountains seemed the most gentle.

They came against the beautiful fall colors of the twilight. They were like a great wave, cresting and falling, rising again. Beneath the dying sun they seemed to weave and undulate. A piece of metal—a belt buckle, a sword—would catch a ray of the fading light, and it would flash and shimmer. They came onward still, visible almost like a writhing snake one moment, then disappearing into shadow the next. When they disappeared, the peace, the tranquillity of the coming night in the Blue Ridge Mountains, seemed to deny that they could exist. Here, where fall came so gently and so beautifully, where those last rays of sun and the coming shadow fell upon oaks and rolling fields of green and amber, here at Montemarte, they could not possibly exist.

But they did.

And still they came. Men marching, and more men on horseback. Rows and rows of soldiers.

Kiernan Miller could see them on the distant mount as she stood by the old oaks in the summer garden of Montemarte. In the dim light, it was difficult to see what color they wore. But even as she watched them, she felt panic and dismay rise within her. Her hand flew to her throat, as if she could swallow her despair.

The Confederates had pulled out of the nearby town of Harpers Ferry—she knew that. They had blown up the munitions there and pulled out. They were still near—she knew that too—but they had no large numbers, and so the horde slowly but surely rising toward her had to be Yanks.

As they came closer, she could see the blue uniforms—standard Federal issue. Union Army. They weren't deserters or guerrilla fighters.

There could be only one reason for them to be riding toward Montemarte.

To burn it to the ground.

She stood very still, only her bright, beautiful green eyes betraying the depths of her tension. The night breeze rippled through the gold and honey-rich fire of her hair. Her slim form was as straight as the old oaks. In better times, she might have been a picture of elegance, for the breeze also touched upon the fullness of her fine gown—white eyelet over a full silver-blue skirt and a low-cut bodice with French puff sleeves. It was a beautiful gown, right out of the pages of Godey's Lady's Book. She didn't know why she bothered to dress for evenings anymore, except that she had found herself plunged into a new world, and she was fighting to hang on to the traditions she knew so well.

The Yankees were coming.

She wanted to scream, and she wanted somewhere to run. She wanted to cast this information upon one of the many gallants she had known in her life. And she wanted one of them to stand up and sweep her up and promise her that everything would be all right, that she would be cherished and protected.

But there was nowhere to run, and no one to run to. Inside the house, the children would have seen the men by now. They would be coming to her. She would have to have something to say to them. It was doubtful that she could save the house—Miller firearms had already been used too successfully against the Union. She had to save her charges, though, and the slaves dependent upon her.

But the Yankees were coming. . . .

A cavalry unit was leading, with infantry in the back, she realized. There must have been a hundred soldiers.

Suddenly, even as they headed nearer and nearer her, the party split. Half now headed toward her, and half toward the Freemont estate down the hill.

"Kiernan! Yankees! For the love of God, Yankees!"

Kiernan swung around. Patricia, her twelve-year-old sister-in-law, stood on the front porch, her fingers clenched into her skirt.

It was curious how very lovely Patricia Miller looked. She, too, had dressed for dinner. Her blond hair hung in a single braid down her back, and her muslin gown filled with soft lilac flowers. She was framed by the house, the gracious and elegant house that looked so very beautiful and welcoming in the twilight.

Montemarte sat upon the hill on the outskirts of Harpers Ferry. Like others in the area, the Millers had found their riches in the production and manufacture of arms, and Montemarte was a monument to those riches. It was not a plantation home but a magnificent manor. There were stables for the horses that had once been the Miller family pride. There were gardens to feed the household, and there were gardens for beauty, but there were no fields for income—just the manor with its classic white Greek columns, and the stables and outbuildings.

"Kiernan—"

"I know, I know!" Kiernan told her softly. "The Yankees are coming." With a sigh she squared her shoulders and fought off a last temptation to burst into tears. She lifted her skirts and hurried for the porch. "Patricia, they're going to want to burn the house."

"No! They can't! What will we do? Where will we go?" Patricia asked, tears in her wide brown eyes.

Despite its beauty, Montemarte was just a house, Kiernan told herself. Their home, yes, but still just a creation of brick and wood and mortar and plaster. They were not destitute; she could bring the Miller children to her father's home, deep in Tidewater Virginia, on the peninsula, where the Yankees would dare not come lest they met up with Stonewall Jackson or General Lee.

She knew why Patricia was so desperate. The war had scarcely begun, but already Patricia had lost everyone. If it hadn't been for Kiernan's reckless marriage to Patricia's brother, not even Kiernan would be here now for the children.

"Don't worry," she told Patricia. "We'll be fine, whatever happens."

"Like hell!" snapped a voice, and Kiernan's eyes quickly rose to meet those of Patricia's twin brother, Jacob Miller. Brown-eyed and tow-headed like Patricia, he was already very tall and very straight, and he carried his father's old rifle. He gazed at Kiernan with hurt and with knowledge that shouldn't have been seen in eyes so very young. "Bad things are happening in a lot of places, Kiernan. Lots of bad things. You'd best get yourself and Patricia hid somewhere." There was a catch in his throat. " 'Tricia's young yet, but when them Yanks see you—"

"Jacob," Kiernan said, and lowered her head to hide a smile. He meant to defend her honor—to the death. She had heard some of the same stories about the invading Union Army that he had, but she couldn't believe that fifty men, riding with such discipline, were coming to dishonor one lone woman. "We're going to be all right. They're coming because of the Miller Firearms Factories. It's revenge, I'm afraid, but nothing more."

"Kiernan—"

She set her hand upon the rifle, lowering it. "Jacob Miller, you can't take on an entire Union cavalry company. In memory of your parents and Anthony, I have to make sure that you grow up and live to a ripe old age. Do you understand?"

"They're going to burn us out."

"Probably, yes."

"And you want to just surrender the place to them?"

"No, Jacob." She offered them both a grave smile. "I want to make the evening as wretched for them as we possibly can. I want you both to go back inside. One of you sit in the library and read a book. One of you go and make sure that Janey has started supper. I'll stay and meet them on the porch, and when they order us to go, we'll go. But on our own sweet time, and with lots of dignity."

Jacob still looked as if he wanted to start shooting. Dear God, the twins had always listened to her in the past! She prayed that Jacob wouldn't pick this moment to defy her.

"Jacob, please, for the love of God. Help me now. I swear I won't bear the sight of any more blood right now. They won't want to hurt you."

"All Yanks ever want to do is hurt southerners!" Jacob claimed, a catch in his throat. He was still just a child. He didn't want to be hurt.

He also didn't want to be a coward. He was the man of the house now, and a man stood up for what was his.

"That's not true," she said. But she herself wasn't certain anymore. War had changed everything. It had ravaged the land, it had torn apart families.

There had once been a time when they in the South had believed that the North would just let them secede, let them go their separate way.

That time was long past.

There had also been a time when they had all thought that the southern soldiers wouldn't need more than a few weeks to whop the North.

That time was also long past, no matter how brilliant the southern generals were, no matter how valiant her men, no matter how gallantly they rode their horses and wielded their swords. It had really started that long-ago day at nearby Harpers Ferry, when John Brown had made his move to seize the arsenal. The old fanatic had been captured and tried. He had committed treason and murder, and he had been condemned to hang.

And he had promised them all, on the day of his hanging, that the land would run red with blood.

"No one is going to hurt you. Put the rifle away."

"I want it close at hand," Jacob said stubbornly.

He turned to put it away. Thankfully, she thought, he wasn't going to throw away his life in a foolhardy quest for valiance.

"Thank you," Kiernan told him, smiling.

But the Yankees were still coming.

"Go in!" she commanded them. "Quickly—now!" She didn't want them to hear her voice quavering.

She clenched her hands before her. She didn't want them to see her fingers trembling.

Suddenly, Janey was on the porch with them. Plump and aging, her anxiety shone in her ink-dark eyes. "Miz Kiernan! The Yankees are coming!"

"Janey, I know that," Kiernan said, surprised at just how calm she managed to sound. "Go back in and start supper."

"Supper's on this minute, Miz Kiernan. But didn't you hear me? The—"

"Yes, yes, the Yankees are coming. Go on in, all of you. This is a house where dignity has always resided. We will go on with our lives. I will wait to greet the— er, visitors. You all go in and go about your business."

They stared at her, all three of them, as if she had gone crazy. But then Patricia—bless her—lifted her little nose, turned about, and walked regally into the house. After a moment, Jacob followed her.

"It don't make sense!" Janey said. Kiernan stood her ground on the porch, and Janey sniffed. "I said that it don't make sense. You want me to go make supper so that they can burn supper to the ground too! You ought to be high-tailing it out of here right now, missy, and that's a fact! They get their hands on you, and they might not just burn the house!"

"Janey, nothing is going to happen to me. Those are obviously not guerrilla troops. Watch them march. I'm not going to be—"

"Maybe they aren't gonna rape you," Janey said bluntly. "But you're the last adult remaining of the Miller family, and after the damage done by Miller fire-arms, why, they just might want to send you to some northern prison camp, and as I hear it, they aren't mighty nice places to be!"

"Don't be ridiculous, Janey," Kiernan said firmly. "They don't do horrible things to women in the North." A tinge of unease swept through her. They didn't, did they? She wasn't sure, but it didn't matter. She had to stand her ground.

"I wouldn't count on that, Miz Kiernan!"

She and Janey were good friends, even if Janey's status was that of a slave at the moment. Anthony's will had freed her, but all kinds of paper work still had to be done to make her freedom a fact. It didn't matter. Janey would never leave her. Not when they needed each other so very badly.

But for the moment, Kiernan raised her voice just slightly and used the tone she had learned all the long years back home. "Janey, I said to go in."

Janey sniffed one more time and started into the house. "Dear Lord, give me strength! These old bones are too old to be trotting up into a snow-covered northern city to take care of the fool mistress in some jail!"

Janey paused in the doorway, sniffed once more for good measure, and started in. "Can't see why I'm cooking no supper that no human body's gonna get to sink teeth into! Supper's gonna be char-broiled tonight, that it is!"

The door closed with a slam.

Kiernan stood still on the porch and felt the breeze move about her again, lift her hair, and rustle her skirt. The enemy was still coming.

Like the undulating wave of a deep-blue ocean—relentless, unstoppable, they came. And she waited still, silent, her heart pounding, her breath coming too quickly, despite her determination to appear calm.

The Yanks were coming to burn down her home. There would be no help—the deed would be done in retaliation for every rifle ever manufactured by the family into which she had married, the Millers.

She wondered why she was remaining. Why she didn't just run. She couldn't possibly stop them.

Then she knew that she was staying for her belief, for Virginia, for the Con-federacy, and for herself, her soul. She couldn't bend to the enemy, now or ever. She couldn't run, and she couldn't bend.

She watched the movement of the enemy troops. The first horses in front broke loose and came galloping up the rise upon which she stood. Her heart thundered. She didn't move.

A moment later, a handsome bay was drawn up before her by a rugged-looking cavalryman with a dark moustache and beard that didn't entirely hide his sneer.

"You must be Mrs. Miller, ma'am."

"I am," Kiernan said.

"Ma'am, I'm Captain Hugh Norris, and I reckon you'd best be out of the place right quick. I've orders to torch the house."

"Whose orders?" she demanded.

"Why, the orders of General—"

"Your general has no jurisdiction here."

"Ma'am, the Union is here. Your Confederates have left you. And I'm going to burn this place to the ground, so you'd best get your kin and help out of here. Lady, you ain't smelt nothing bad until you've smelt burning flesh!"

Kiernan fought very hard to remain still, staring at the man, determined not to give in to his demand.

"Then you'll just have to give me time, sir."

"I'm torching her in ten minutes, Mrs. Miller." He was gleeful. Obviously, his task appealed to him.

"I don't know, sir. I think it would create an awfully bad image if it was found out that Union officers burned down houses with women and children still in them. You will just have to bide your time, sir."

Norris stared at her in a fury. His bay pranced to and fro before the porch steps. Suddenly, he nudged the bay and brought it leaping up to the porch, very close to her. Kiernan raised her chin and didn't take a step back despite the heavy hooves of the bay.

"Lady, let me tell you something. The day of the great southern high-brow belle is over. Real soon, you won't dare be talking to a man like that! So take your time. I won't burn you down. I'll just drag you out. Then it'll look like the darned Yank saved your hide despite your determination for suicide!"

"I think not, sir," she told him. She was insane! What was she going to do? What *could* she do?

She needed to be rescued. She needed the whole southern cavalry under Jeb Stuart to come riding in. She needed a horseman, a hero in butternut and gray.

"Sergeant! Set some tinder!" Norris commanded.

One of his men leaped down from his horse. He called out in turn to several of the men, and they quickly joined him, collecting dried twigs and sticks and winding them with dried hay of their own to stuff into the latticed nooks and crannies at the base of the porch. Kiernan watched them, powerless to stop them, yet suddenly so furious, she wanted to tear into the men, to scratch their eyes out, to tear their hair out by the handfuls.

But she managed to stand still and silently, condemning, upon the porch.

"Damn you!" Norris thundered. Suddenly, he raced his horse down the steps and out before his men.

"Prepare to light your torches, men!" he called out.

Kiernan remained still even as they set fire to the torches.

"Prepare to fire the house!"

They couldn't burn it with her standing there—she was determined! The men in blue looked at her nervously, then looked at their commander, then looked back to her again.

They started forward.

A cry bellowed out, loud, harsh, and full of authority.

"Halt!"

A rider was coming from behind the others, taking the path from the town in the valley below that the others had taken.

He rode with no discipline. He rode like one born and bred to sit upon a horse, with reckless, absolute ease upon his steed. He rode as if he knew the hills and mountains and valleys and more. He rode as if he knew the very muscle and heart of his mount.

The silver horse raced, churning up dirt and grass, and its rider was heedless of the speed. Distance was swiftly breached.

"Norris, halt!"

The order rang out with unmistakable authority, and at the sound of it, a faint recognition and unease stirred in Kiernan's blood.

Captain Hugh Norris swore under his breath and rode down to meet the approaching rider.

A man who also wore blue.

Dark blue, deep dark blue, the blue of the Union Army. His uniform, too, was cavalry, trimmed in gold braid. His hat was blue, pulled low over his forehead and topped with a tall plume.

Not a hundred feet from the house, he drew up as Hugh Norris confronted him. And the new arrival produced a piece of paper beneath the captain's nose.

An argument ensued, low-voiced, intense. The men with the burning torches waited uneasily. Countless gazes swept over Kiernan, and she realized that few of these men relished burning down a house.

Even those with eyes that mirrored the death that they had seen. They waited, as she waited.

Someone had come and halted the destruction of her house and of her world.

A Yank. A man in blue.

Not just any Yank, she was beginning to fear.

The two men broke apart.

"Douse your torches!" the new arrival ordered with his indomitable tone of command. He was instantly obeyed. The men thrust their burning torches to the ground.

The new arrival came riding up to the porch on his silver horse. He tilted back his plumed hat, and steel-blue eyes met hers.

The unease that had tinged the base of her spine now swept through her. Her heart skipped a beat, then slammed hard against the wall of her chest.

A Yank had come. . . .

Not just any Yank.

Jesse Cameron. The one Yank she had known most of her life. The Yank she despised the most. The one she had loved once upon a time. The one who now sent her heart and mind into a tumult.

It had been a long time since she had seen him. A long, long time since she had thrown her heart at his feet. Since he had ignored her every plea.

Since he had ridden north, wearing blue.

He hadn't changed.

Or maybe he had. His eyes were every bit as hard as ever, but they seemed to hold an even greater wisdom, a weariness; and a certain ruthlessness. Tiny new lines were etched around them. If anything, his jaw was more firmly set. He was clean shaven, baring the sharp planes and angles of his face. It was a rugged face, but handsome still, for its hard lines were tempered by the dark arches of his brow and the startling color of his eyes. It was given sensuality by the fullness of his mouth—a mouth that was grim and taut now as he stared at her.

"Hello, Kiernan."

She didn't want to admit that she knew him. No, she didn't want to remember that she knew him. She didn't want to remember the last time that she had seen him, and most of all, she despised the fact that she was seeing him now.

With him the victor for the moment, and she the enemy, her life and limb threatened.

She didn't respond. He shrugged, but she was certain that his eyes glittered and that his temper was somewhat frayed. "Mrs. Miller, as of this moment, I'm taking over this property for use as my headquarters, for hospital and surgical space as is necessary, as of this moment. You will kindly inform your household."

Kiernan gritted down hard on her teeth.

He had ridden in to save her home, she realized, to keep the manor from being burned to the ground. She had prayed for a hero in gray.

The house was being saved by a man in blue.

She'd rather eat dirt, she determined, lifting her chin.

"Captain Norris has plans to burn the place, Captain Cameron. I'm afraid you'll have to seek your headquarters elsewhere."

He stared hard at her. He dismounted from his horse and strode up the steps to the porch. He paused, just feet from her. He was tall, over six foot two, and broad-shouldered in his cavalry shirt and skirted cloak. He was dangerous. Jesse had always been dangerous.

As dangerous as the currents that now seemed to riddle the air with him so close—vital, electric. She felt a sudden heat, and it seemed to crackle on the breeze that swept between them.

Jesse could always bring about that kind of tension.

He spoke softly, so softly that his words couldn't possibly carry to the other soldiers, who still formed a ring around the front of the house, watching them.

"I'm trying to save your home and your neck, Mrs. Miller," he told her tensely.

"My neck hasn't been threatened, Captain Cameron," she snapped back.

"Keep talking, Mrs. Miller, and it will be!" he promised her. "Now shut up, and the manor can remain standing."

"Will you really be taking it over?"

"Yes."

"Then I'd rather see it burn."

"I'm sure you would, Kiernan. Common sense was never your strong suit. But what of young Jacob Miller and his sister?"

"Jacob wouldn't want a Yankee turncoat like you living in the house, either, Captain Cameron."

"You'd rather it burned?"

"Yes."

He smiled at last and then started to laugh. He laughed so hard that she wanted to throw herself at him and hit him, despite their audience. He turned away and went down the steps.

Fear swept through her. Montemarte wasn't actually hers—it belonged to Jacob and Patricia. She really had no right to recklessly bring about its destruction. But still, she couldn't seem to swallow her pride.

"Captain Cameron!" she called to him sharply. He paused, his back stiff and straight. "Will you—will you burn it now?"

He turned back to her, setting his left foot on a step and leaning an elbow on his knee. "Well, Mrs. Miller, I probably should do just that. But I am sorry to disappoint you. I'm afraid that I can't burn it now. I had to threaten and cajole and just about turn handstands to get the general to turn the place over to me. You see, Millers aren't real popular among the Union men. Lots and lots of them have had friends and kin killed by Miller firearms. They'd like to see the total destruction of Miller property and Miller people."

"That shouldn't be difficult now, considering that the majority of the Millers are dead—thanks to the Union Army."

"I assure you, several hundred Union men died the same—thanks to the Confederate Army."

"They were on Virginia soil!"

He shrugged, and when he spoke again, he seemed to drop all pretense for the moment. "I didn't start the war, Kiernan."

"But we're on opposite sides."

"So fight me!" he warned her softly. "But I'm moving in, with my staff. Take your little charges and run to your own home. You'll be safe enough there for a while. I probably won't be able to salvage everything in the house, but at least I can keep it standing."

"I don't want any favors from you," she said heatedly. "And I'll be damned if I'll run away from a passel of bad-mannered Yanks."

His brow shot up with surprise. "You're staying?"

She lifted her chin. "Stonewall Jackson will bring his army in here and wipe out the lot of you," she promised. "I might as well wait for him to come. And keep your men from looting the house blind."

"You haven't been asked to stay, Mrs. Miller."

"Are you planning on having your men throw me and the children out—bodily?"

"Heavens no, Mrs. Miller. It's war, and I have managed to send men into battle. But I'm a merciful commander—I wouldn't dream of sending them in after you."

"Then I'm staying."

"Maybe not. I didn't say that I wouldn't come in after you myself."

"What a fine point of valor, Captain Cameron!" she drawled with dripping sarcasm.

"Go home, Kiernan," he told her softly. She hated that tone of voice, hated the way that it washed over her so warmly. The way that it seemed to stroke her, inside and out, and bring back memories.

"This is my home now," she reminded him. "And Jackson will come back. Or Lee will come back. Some southern general will come for this land again, and you will be routed."

"That's highly possible, Kiernan." He stared at her and shrugged. "Fine. Stay. But I'm taking over the house. Be forewarned."

"Forewarned, sir? I'll be looking over your shoulder. I'll be making sure that you treat Reb prisoners with the same care that you would give to your own injured."

Fire flashed in his eyes, an absolute fury. She knew how to set a knife against Jesse's spine because she knew Jesse. She knew his passion for medicine. Casting out the suggestion that he might treat Rebel prisoners with less than his full commitment was like a slap in the face.

But other than the flare of his eyes, he gave no hint of emotion. He arched a brow to her. As always, his control infuriated her.

He took a step closer, and his voice lowered to an even more dangerous tone. He was so near that she could breathe in the scent of him. He didn't touch her, but still she felt his warmth and both the anger and the sensuality of his words. His words were a warning.

"I thought you'd run because of me, Mrs. Miller, like you did before. I won't mind your being around. I'll enjoy it. You're the one who promised never to suffer life with a Yank, remember?"

"I won't be suffering a life with you!" she snapped quickly. "I'll be surviving in spite of you. I'll fight you every step of the way. And the South will win."

"Maybe the battles, but never the war," he told her, and for a moment she wondered if they were speaking about the conflict of nations or the tumult that raged between them.

He stared at her for a several seconds. The wind ruffled her hair, and she was suddenly very cold. It was all she could do to keep from shivering as he stared at her with his steel and smoldering eyes.

"The Confederates will come back!" she vowed to him.

"They very well might," he responded. For a moment, her will was locked within his gaze, within the heat and tension, riddled with it, shaking with it. There was too much between them—too much hatred, too much passion, too many currents that sizzled and slashed like lightning. "But until your Rebs come back, Mrs. Miller," he warned her, "it's going to be share and share alike."

He swept off his hat and bowed to her with mock gallantry. Then he turned and started back down the steps, calling orders to his men.

Kiernan spun around and tore into the house. Patricia caught her in the hallway.

"Are they going to burn the house down, Kiernan?" she asked anxiously.

"No! No!"

"Then what?" Jacob demanded, arriving in the foyer from the kitchen.

"They're using it as a headquarters."

"As a headquarters! As a place to plan how to kill more of our people?" Jacob asked.

Kiernan shook her head. How she hated Jesse! How she wished that he'd never come!

She'd prayed for a hero in gray. She'd prayed that the house could survive.

And the house had been saved—by an enemy in blue! An enemy she had known long and well.

"Captain Cameron is a—a doctor," she said.

"Cameron!" Jacob said.

"Yes," Kiernan answered. "It's Jesse. Jesse stopped them from burning the place. But he's taking it over."

Jacob stared at her, then swung around in silence. She heard him leave by the rear of the house. Patricia stared at Kiernan a moment longer, then turned and raced after her brother.

Kiernan tore up the stairs.

The twins would have to tend to themselves for the moment. She needed time. She was desperate for time.

Jesse had come.

She threw open the door to her room and threw herself upon her bed, burying her face in her pillow. She wanted to plot, to plan, to reason—but only one thought kept racing in her head. Jesse was here, Jesse was here.

She hated him so very much. And yet she had never stopped loving him. Even when she stood before an altar and swore to love, honor, and cherish another man, she had never stopped loving him.

But not as much as she hated him for wearing blue—when all of his family had donned gray.

When she had fought for the life they had always known, for Virginia, for love, honor, and family.

She rolled over and stared at the ceiling.

If only it were *Daniel* Cameron who had come. The brother who wore gray.

Not so long ago, they had all dressed in blue. The Camerons had both come riding into Harpers Ferry during John Brown's raid.

Jesse had come to her rescue then.

Back when the world had still seemed sane.

How very much had happened since then!

October 16, 1859
Harpers Ferry, Virginia
Near Midnight

"*A* shot's been fired!"

Kiernan bolted upright in her bed. Lacey Donahue, her gray hair covered in a nightcap, was carrying a candle to the foot of Kiernan's bed, and hovering over her in distress.

Half awake, Kiernan struggled to understand what was happening. "A shot? Fired by whom?"

"I don't know!" Lacey murmured.

"When? Where?"

"I don't know, but I know that I heard it!" Lacey swore.

"Lacey, I didn't hear a thing," Kiernan assured her.

What Lacey wanted was companionship, Kiernan realized as her plump hostess curled up on the foot of her bed. "There's something going on in the streets. I woke up and there were people out there!" Lacey said.

"Lacey, out where? These are public streets—" Kiernan began, but Lacey nervously interrupted her.

"No, no, dear! There are strangers running around with guns. No, wait, they're not running around—they're sneaking around. Oh, Kiernan, you must know what I mean. They are people with no right to be out there!"

Kiernan leaped out of bed and hurried to the window, drawing back the frilled curtains. To the far left she could see the Potomac and the railroad crossing over to Maryland. A little closer, she could see the buildings of the armory. The moon was out, and the street was gently lit.

"I don't see anything," she said.

"Step back!" Lacey warned her. "Don't let anyone see you there!"

Kiernan hid a smile and moved back. She looked out, thinking that she loved the night and the beauty of the mountains and valleys here where the Shenandoah and the Potomac rivers came together. There was a beautiful story about the Indian maiden Shenandoah, who had loved her brave, Potomac, too deeply and too well. And when they were parted, it was her tears that had formed the rivers.

Kiernan's home was in the Tidewater region of Virginia, far down on the peninsula, right on the James River, and not at all far the from the original Jamestown settlement. Virginia was a big state, and she'd come a long way to reach Harpers Ferry, several days' ride. But the country was beautiful. She loved all of it. From the low-lying land along the James to Williamsburg, to Richmond, Fredericksburg, and all the way over here, where they were in the point of the state that joined Maryland, and where one actually had to look to the south to face Washington, D.C. She loved the peninsula where she lived. But at night, when the moon beat gently down upon the town, with the Blue Ridge Mountains rising all around and the waters rushing between, she didn't think that any place could be more beautiful.

Or more peaceful, like tonight.

Lacey was just nervous, Kiernan thought. Her husband, Thomas, was away with Kiernan's father and Andrew Miller and his son, Anthony Miller. They were looking for a site farther south on which to build a second factory. Since the federal armory was at Harpers Ferry, Andrew Miller wanted to stay in production there, but he also wanted to expand and explore new possibilities. And he wanted to be away from the ever-watchful eye of the federal government to do that.

The political situation was not an easy one at the moment. Southerners were swearing that if Abraham Lincoln was elected president, there would be war. Discontent was sweeping the country. If it did come to war, the federal government would have to take an immediate interest in Harpers Ferry because of the armory.

Kiernan was fascinated by politics. She knew she wasn't supposed to be—her aunt Fiona had told her it was a most unladylike trait, and that she would pay for it somewhere down the line. Her father had chastised her, too, mainly because Aunt Fiona had done so.

But Kiernan was an only child, and she had been her father's companion and his best friend as she grew up, except for the time she had gone away to Lady Ellen's Finishing School for Girls. She knew her father's mind very well, and she thought that he had been right when he warned his friend Andrew Miller that no one really knew what Virginia would do in the end.

"South Carolina is the one screaming states' rights the loudest, Andrew," he had stated at the dinner table. "Why, the majority of the Founding Fathers were Virginians! Washington, Jefferson, Madison, Monroe—all Virginians. Patrick Henry—a Virginian. Why, Virginia is the very heart and soul of this country. It has never been proved that a state can secede!"

"If Lincoln is elected," Andrew had argued back, "then South Carolina will secede. And once she leaves the Union, I promise you, her sister cotton and tobacco and slave states will follow suit. You mark my words."

Kiernan wondered if it would happen, or if the uproar was just the political climate of the day. The real trouble was out in the wilds of the West. Abolitionists were racing out westward to Missouri and Nebraska and Kansas—"bleeding Kansas" as they called it, for all the bloodshed. There was a war going on in the West already. Proslavery men and abolitionists were at one another so viciously, it had become a string of raids and murders rather than battles. Slaveholders were racing out, too. Everybody was trying to claim the new states for their own side.

Horrible things were happening, really horrible things, things that made some of the stories about Indians seem tame. A war was already going on between the slaveholding factions and those determined that Nebraska would be a free state. Cities had been attacked. Unarmed men, women, and children had died. Among the abolitionists, one name stood out: John Brown. Even in Virginia, they had heard stories about him, about the way he had taken his followers into Missouri, ripped unarmed men from their houses, and butchered them then and there in front of their loved ones. Retaliation, he had claimed it was.

But it was murder, Kiernan thought, horrible, heinous murder. She was grateful that such things didn't happen in Virginia, even this far west in the mountains. She was convinced that anyone who was running around killing people in either Kansas or Missouri ought to be prosecuted.

The problems weren't just in the West, she knew. A woman named Harriet Beecher Stowe had written a book called *Uncle Tom's Cabin,* and in it she had created the cruelest human being who could be imagined to own and persecute slaves.

But it wasn't always like that! Kiernan wanted to shout to the newspapers. Most of the slaveowners she knew were good people, determined to enforce good conditions for their slaves, seeing to it that they received proper religious training. There were *some* cruel men, she had to admit, but none she knew were as bad as Simon Legree!

Most southerners didn't even own slaves. The problem really had to do with the economy. The South was a cotton kingdom, and slaves were necessary to work the plantations. That didn't mean that everyone was happy about it. Why, Jefferson, when he wrote the Declaration of Independence, wanted all men to be free—including the slaves—when he had been a slaveholder himself. Other statesmen had convinced him that the Declaration would never get past the Continental Congress if it contained such a clause, for the very reason that the South still needed slaves today—the economy.

But whether a master or mistress was a good person or a bad person wasn't the point in the long run, the way Kiernan saw it. The point was freedom. She couldn't begin to imagine being owned by anyone. Her father was a wonderful man. No master could be kinder, or more gentle. But he was an old-time Virginian—the son, grandson, and great-grandson of planters. Her view on the slavery question was not the same as his, or that of any of their neighbors or business associates.

Kiernan didn't know Lacey Donahue's thoughts on the subject, but Lacey and her husband, Thomas, owned no slaves. They had no servants living in the house at all, for that matter. Her maid was an Irish girl who came in every morning, and Thomas, a lawyer, had a clerk and an assistant who came in every day to his office below the living floors of this three-storied house right on the main street of town.

The women were very much alone in the house tonight. That was surely why little bumps in the night and the idea of people walking about in the street bothered Lacey. She was a sweetheart. Childless, she clung to her husband. To the best of Kiernan's knowledge, Lacey and Thomas had never been separated before, but Thomas and Andrew Miller and Kiernan's father were all planning on investing in the new armory together.

Kiernan was aware, too, that her father and Andrew Miller were interested in another alliance—a marriage between her and Anthony. She cared for Anthony, cared for him deeply. He was tall and almost gaunt, with golden hair and mahogany eyes and the most charming and elegant manner imaginable. He was dedicated to his father, and to Virginia. He was bright and fun, a wonderful dancer, a man quick to plan a picnic with her or a daring horse race with a friend.

Maybe she did love Anthony. They had everything in common, and she enjoyed him tremendously. Yet for reasons she didn't understand herself, she waited and stalled about marrying him. She didn't mind flirting with him in the least, and she loved dancing with him and being with him, it was just . . .

She had dreamed of love being something different, something that would make her whole body tremble. She would feel a vast excitement knowing that she would see the man she loved, of feeling a rush of heat and fever every time that he was near.

Feelings she tried to push to deep corners of her heart and mind plunged forward despite her best efforts.

She wanted love to feel the way she had once felt about Jesse Cameron.

Oh, but that was so long ago! she thought. When she had been a very little girl, she had thought that the sun rose and set on him. No man had ever sat a horse better. No man had ever managed to shoot quite so well, or tease a little girl so gallantly.

Jesse was ten years her senior. She had just been leaving her dolls behind when he had first returned from West Point in his uniform. No one had been as fascinating as Jesse in that uniform. No one had ever had quite such an effect upon her. He was always cordial when he saw her, his flashing blue eyes filled with humor and affection when he greeted her in his husky Virginia drawl. "Mornin', Miss Mackay. I swear, but you do grow more lovely by the day." Naturally, he teased her. He was always surrounded by girls, the belles of the South—and the North.

Or at least he had teased her until recently, she thought. Not that she saw him very often. He had come out of West Point to move on to medicine, and he had been spending an awful lot of time in Washington. And then she had spent time with her father, and with Anthony Miller.

Now she had to remind herself that her feelings for Jesse had been a childhood infatuation and nothing more. Their families had been friends for decades. Jesse's brother Daniel had been one of her best friends, and he had admitted to her that Jesse had often laughed at her mischief-making and said that she was a "wayward little dickens," and that any man had best watch out when she was in the vicinity.

Of course, she'd never *really* been a "wayward dickens." Jesse had overreacted. She had simply been careful to stand up against some of the pranks that others played around her. In school one day Tristan Tombey had tried to get her attention by dipping her hair in an inkwell. Well, she'd just gotten back at Tristan. Admittedly, she'd flirted with him, teased him, smiled, tugged upon his heartstrings. But that had been the only way to attach the inkwell to his suspenders so that every single thing he was wearing and his body could be coated in ink. As it happened, Jesse had just been on his way home, passing by the schoolyard, when Tristan had first put up his fuss.

Jesse had laughed, but he'd also pulled her up on his horse and insisted on taking her home. "Miss Mackay, you are an outrageous little flirt, and I pity the poor young lad who falls for you next!" Jesse had told her firmly.

Then he'd taken her home, and despite her outraged protests, he'd laughingly told the entire story to her father. She'd gotten into horrible trouble, of course, but Jesse had still been amused. On his way out he had taken hold of her chin, and those striking eyes of his had lit like blue fire into her own. "Take heed,

Miss Mackay, you're too young to be practicing such a talent for flirtation. Someday, some poor soul may fight back."

"A gallant southern gentleman?" she had taunted sweetly in turn. "Such as yourself? To cause a lady—oh, no! a child!—distress?"

"Ah, but men will not always be gallant southern gentlemen," he had warned her. And with a tousle of her hair, he had left.

And she had been furious.

But even then, she had dreamed about him, about those blue eyes of his, and about the deep, husky taunt of his voice.

Because Jesse didn't always tease. Once before, she had determined to go swimming down in one of the creeks and on her way she'd come across little Cissy Wade, one of Old Man Evan Turner's slave children, and on an impulse, she'd talked the skinny, frightened-looking little girl into coming with her. When they'd come back, Kiernan had been astounded by Evan Turner's fury with Cissy. Kiernan had confidently explained that it had been all her fault, but Turner had taken a cane to Cissy and warned Kiernan—rich little lady that she might be—that she'd get the same if she didn't run along. Poor farmers needed what slave help they had.

Well, Kiernan hadn't run. She'd stayed to see Turner strike Cissy. And she understood why her papa had always called Turner white trash, but that hadn't helped any. She'd heard Cissy scream, and she'd come running for help, though she knew she'd never reach Papa in time to do Cissy any good.

As soon as she had hit the roadway home, she had nearly plowed right into Jesse on one of the Camerons' beautiful black racing horses. He dismounted and caught her before she could race on.

"Kiernan! What now? Who did you tempt into doing what?"

She didn't care if Jesse teased her or not. There were tears in her eyes. Jesse held her shoulders and tried to shake free. "I took Cissy swimming. Just down to the creek, just for an hour. And he's beating her! Old Man Turner is beating her with a cane. Jesse, he's going to kill her!"

Jesse stepped back with a weary look in his eyes.

"Kiernan, Turner *owns* Cissy. By law, he can beat her."

"He'll kill her!"

"Kiernan, you should have thought about Cissy's position before you invited her along."

"I just wanted her to have some fun. He works her so hard. She always looks so very tired. I didn't mean to hurt her. I'd never hurt her! Oh, I'd like to tear his hair out!"

"A few more years on you, Miss Mackay, and you'd probably try," he said lightly. Then he added, "All right, all right. Go on home, Kiernan. I'll do what I can."

She hadn't gone home. She'd followed Jesse back to Turner's farm, and she'd hid back in the bushes. Jesse had ridden in on the action, dismounted from his horse, and stripped the cane right out of Turner's hands. Old Man Turner swung around, but even though Jesse hadn't quite reached twenty, he was very tall and broad-shouldered and Turner wasn't about to wrestle with him. Still, he had his say.

"You ain't got no right, boy, you ain't got no right. Even if you do come from Cameron money!"

"You're going to beat this child to death, Turner!" Jesse had exclaimed.

"She's mine, and she was a runaway."

"She wasn't any runaway, and you know it!" Jesse said angrily.

Turner's voice lowered, and the two of them argued onward.

At the end of it all, Jesse produced a large wad of money, and suddenly Cissy, dazed and silent now except for her sniffles, was on the back of Jesse's horse.

Jesse had bought her from Turner. A week later, the Camerons bought the rest of her family—her mother, her father—a rickety old field hand—and her baby brother.

Maybe it was then that her infatuation really began.

Ah, but Jesse could still infuriate her! He treated her like a child!

When her father had staged her coming-out ball, she'd thought that Jesse was off with the military, either in Washington or out in the West fighting Indians. It had been a wonderful night for her. She was tied into an incredible corset, wearing what seemed like a million petticoats. For the first time her father allowed her a fashionable adult gown with a daring, daring bosom. Her hair was curled and elegantly piled on top of her head. She felt beautiful and very grown-up—and more. She felt very confident with herself as a woman, and she had the time of her life flirting, smiling, and dancing. The young men flocked to her, and it was wonderful. She knew that she must never really torment a young swain, but it was certainly proper enough to be a very charming flirt, and she couldn't help but enjoy her power.

That is, she had enjoyed it until she saw Jesse. He had been leaning in a doorway watching her, and she realized that he had been watching her for quite some time. There was a very irritating amusement in his eyes and in his lopsided smile.

And then he came to her to claim a dance and swept her into his arms, even though she had promised the dance to someone else.

"Ah, but you are growing up to fulfill your every promise of beauty, Miss Mackay!" he had assured her. But his blue gaze had still been alight with laughter, even when he had bent over her hand and brushed it with a kiss. The kiss brought a flush to her cheeks, and she wanted to kick him even as she felt palpitations pulsing beneath her breast, right in the area of her heart. "So who are you out to dazzle tonight?" he asked.

"The world, Jesse Cameron," she told him sweetly. But when he laughed again and released her, she had been careful to accidentally tread upon his toes with her new leather pumps.

Jesse could go hang! She had outgrown Jesse Cameron, outgrown that kind of infatuation, she told herself firmly that night in 1859 at Harpers Ferry. She wasn't in awe of Jesse anymore. She had grown up—and she had grown up with definite opinions, so she was probably—to Jesse—more than ever a "wayward little dickens."

Jesse could be amusing and polite. He could even be charming—when he chose to be so, she thought. He never minced his words or opinions, and he had never given a fig for popular thought. He was incapable of bending or compromising, she reminded herself. If she married him, he would surely never accept her advice the way Anthony did.

Nor would he tolerate indecisiveness on the question. Jesse would demand all or nothing if he demanded anything.

Anthony was by far the more civil man.

Jesse was really nothing compared to Anthony.

It was the feeling she had had for Jesse that she remembered. The excitement when he was near, the wild, challenging excitement, the shivers, the tremors. It was that feeling she missed with Anthony. It wasn't Anthony's fault. She simply wasn't a child anymore, so naturally she did not feel those things.

"Look! Oh, Kiernan! Someone's moving down there again!" Lacey called.

Kiernan hadn't been paying attention. By the time she looked, whoever had moved—if he had moved—had disappeared.

"Lacey, I'm sorry. I just don't see anything."

"You're not trying!" Lacey told her.

"All right, all right, I'll keep my eyes open this time, I promise," Kiernan assured her.

A moment later, they heard the whistle from the night train. It was about one thirty.

"Everything is all right. The midnight train has come through," Kiernan said.

Lacey shivered emphatically. "I tell you, something is going on tonight."

A fierce chill swept through Kiernan. She still hadn't seen a thing, but she suddenly sensed that maybe Lacey's fears were based on something real.

Kiernan looked from Lacey back to the window. She blinked, certain that she had seen a movement by the shadowy buildings. Little pricks of unease danced up and down her spine. Lacey was right—there was something going on.

But it didn't affect them, she thought. Surely they were safe in Lacey's home.

She turned back to her hostess once again. "Lacey, have we got a gun in the house?"

Lacey slowly shook her head, and Kiernan almost laughed. They were alone because the men were off to find a spot for a new weapons-productions plant, and they hadn't a single firearm in the house.

"Oh, Kiernan! Do you think we're in trouble?"

"Of course not," Kiernan told her. "Maybe it's just a late meeting down there or an inspection going on or something of that sort."

"Then why would they sneak around? And why would I have heard a shot?"

Kiernan shrugged. She wanted to assure Lacey, but she herself was now convinced that something wasn't right. The people below did seem to be slinking, or making movements that just weren't right.

"I'm sure we're in no danger," she told Lacey. After all, why would they be? It was a big town. And as two women alone, they certainly offered no one any kind of a threat. Lacey and Thomas lived comfortably, but they weren't particularly wealthy, so there were no great treasures in the house.

But whoever had come into Harpers Ferry hadn't come for wealth or riches. Kiernan knew that, just as she knew that something was happening.

"Why don't we go down and have a glass of sherry?" she suggested.

"We can't see the town from downstairs," Lacey told her.

Kiernan smiled. "Then we'll bring the sherry up here. How's that?"

That suggestion appealed to Lacey. The two women lit the candle by

Kiernan's bedside and hurried downstairs to the parlor by Thomas's office for the sherry.

They must look like a pair of wraiths, Kiernan thought. She had on a lace-trimmed white cotton gown that seemed to float as she moved, and Lacey wore a pale blue gown, an eerie color in the night. Harpers Ferry already had ghost stories. It was said that down by the old Harper house, a ghost could often be seen in the windows. It was supposed to be Mrs. Harper, watching over the gold her husband had supposedly buried somewhere in the yard. Some said that George Washington, who had been determined that this would be the site for the armory, still walked the streets upon occasion, checking out his interests.

And there were the Indians, of course. Potomac and Shenandoah were still shedding their tears.

Back in the guest room, Kiernan poured them each a glass of sherry. They took up sentinel in rockers on either side of the window, sipping the drink. Lacey seemed happy enough, either content that they were safe, or enjoying their impromptu party.

Kiernan was growing increasingly more uncomfortable. There *was* movement out there, by the firehouse, and by the armory buildings. And the night was passing swiftly. Looking out at the sky and toward the mountains and the rivers, Kiernan thought that the first pink streaks of day would soon reach delicately over the water.

Lacey was telling her about a party she had attended in Washington recently, marveling at how quickly the railroad had taken her into the capital city. Kiernan swallowed more sherry. She had just begun to relax when she heard a fierce pounding on the door below.

She and Lacey leaped out of their chairs at the same time, staring at each other.

"What do we do?" Lacey cried.

"Ignore it!" Kiernan suggested.

"What if someone is trying to help us?"

"What if someone is trying to hurt us?"

Wide-eyed, they continued to stare at each other.

And then they heard the glass of the office door below shatter as it crashed open. Lacey yelped, and Kiernan managed to swallow back a scream. It wouldn't help to let anyone know where they were.

"Lacey, we need something, anything! Why is there not a single weapon in this house!"

"I don't know, I don't know—we never needed a weapon in the house!" Lacey countered, wringing her hands.

Barking at poor Lacey wouldn't help a thing, Kiernan realized. She was just as terrified herself.

Then they heard footsteps coming up the stairs.

Kiernan saw a parasol in the corner of the room. She dived for it, wondering what earthly good it would do her. But she couldn't just stand there and accept whatever happened. She couldn't allow anyone to come in and harm poor dear Lacey. She would have to fight.

With a parasol!

They heard the door to Lacey's bedroom across the hall being thrown open and footsteps moving about.

"Hide!" Kiernan whispered to Lacey.

"Where?" Lacey demanded.

There was nowhere to hide. It was a pleasant, comfortable room, warmed by Lacey's special touches, but it was small and sparsely furnished. There was the bed, a wardrobe, the two padded rockers, and a nightstand.

"Slip under the bed!" Kiernan suggested, then realized that Lacey could not slip her round form into any such space.

"*You* hide, Kiernan Mackay," Lacey told her. Her command was heroic, for Kiernan could see the frantic race of Lacey's pulse above the ruffles at her throat.

"I'd never leave you alone—" Kiernan began, but the question suddenly became moot as the door to the room burst open.

Two men stood before them, and both were armed. One aimed a Colt at Lacey's heart, and the taller of the two, a bearded black man, held a rifle pointed straight at Kiernan.

Her own heart leaped with fear, and she forced herself to stand tall and indignant.

"Who in God's name are you, and how dare you burst into a private residence to threaten vulnerable women!" she cried out with vehemence that surprised her. Her hands were clammy. She'd never been more frightened in her life.

"We're soldiers for freedom, miss," the shorter, white man told her. "And you're Kiernan Mackay, the daughter of John Mackay, slaveholder."

"I am Kiernan Mackay," she acknowledged coldly. "And you—"

"We're the revolution. It's starting here, tonight. The country will rise here, this very night."

She swallowed hard, realizing that he was talking about a slave revolution.

Such things had happened in the Caribbean and South America, she knew. Slaves had risen against their masters and mistresses, and the carnage had been horrible. People had been butchered in their beds—little children, anyone.

But she couldn't believe that that could happen here. Certainly not in Lacey's home—when Thomas had always made it clear that he would never own another human being.

"You have no right to come here!" she said. "Revolution, indeed! You'd hurt anyone in your reckless endeavors."

"We don't mean no harm to Mrs. Donahue," the man said, frightening Kiernan further. He knew them both! He knew that it was Lacey's house, and he had known that Kiernan would be in it. Whatever was going on had been well organized. "But Miss Mackay, you're to come with us."

"No," she said flatly.

Lacey wedged her plump body between Kiernan and the men in the doorway. "You'll not touch this girl, you ruffians! I don't know what you think you're going to do with a young woman—"

"Nothing evil, ma'am," the tall black man assured her. "We've come under the guidance of John Brown, and John Brown comes under the guidance of the Lord. But the war has begun, and Miss Mackay is to come with us—a hostage for John Brown."

John Brown. Her blood simmered hotly, then chilled to ice. John Brown had ruthlessly butchered men. He was a fanatic, and he did believe that he killed men in the name of God. She badly wanted to disdain these men, but she was very frightened. Surely John Brown didn't wage war upon women and children!

"We don't want to hurt you," the short white man told Kiernan. "If you'll come along quietly . . ."

She didn't want them to hurt her either. But if she went with them, what then?

She shook her head slowly. "No, I can't come with you. I'm not dressed."

"That's right!" Lacey said. "You can't take a young woman out on the streets like this!" Lacey played for time because Kiernan was playing for time. But what good was time going to do them? If they meant to harm her, Kiernan wasn't going to allow them to do so without a fight. She still held the parasol. She wrapped her hands tightly around it. But what good was a parasol against guns?

"Miss Mackay, you're to come now. If you resist us any longer, I'll truss you up like a Christmas turkey, and Cain here"—the short man indicated his tall black companion—"will carry you over his shoulder."

She must not be tied up, Kiernan thought. If she had any chance at all of escape, she couldn't be tied up. "All right. I'll walk down the stairs," she said.

"Wait!" Lacey cried. "If Kiernan goes, you'll have to take me too."

"No, Mrs. Donahue, we don't want you!" Cain, the black man, spoke emphatically.

"Lacey, please stay here," Kiernan said, staring at Lacey and praying that the woman would understand that she would be better off without her.

"But Kiernan—"

"Lacey, please."

Lacey stepped back, her small mouth pursed indignantly. She was holding up rather well, Kiernan decided.

Better than I am at this moment, she thought.

"Miss Mackay." Cain stepped back politely for her to pass by. Kiernan did so, walking by him. She still held the parasol. She was wonderfully dressed, she thought to herself, with her laced and smocked white cotton nightgown and small blue parasol. She wasn't even wearing shoes.

"Fine," she said curtly. She stepped past them and started down the stairs. If she could leave the house ahead of them, perhaps she could run. These men seemed to know a lot, but they couldn't possibly know this town as she did—the alleys, and where the trails led almost straight up to the heights.

She moved quickly, but they were right behind her.

She came into the parlor. In the growing light of dawn, she could see the poker by the fire. A much better weapon than a parasol! she thought.

Not that it could stop a bullet either.

She hurried through the parlor to the office. The shattered glass lay before the door. She stopped in her tracks.

"Gentlemen, since you won't allow me shoes, I'd appreciate it very much if you could sweep up the glass before we proceed."

"What!" the white man demanded belligerently.

"My feet," Kiernan said flatly. "If you want to impress the rest of the world, you shouldn't have your hostages bleeding and in pain."

"There's no need to hurt the girl now," Cain said.

The other shrugged. "Oh, hell!"

The two of them stepped around her to collect the broken glass. Kiernan waited until they were bent over at their task, then turned and fled back through the parlor for the back-porch door.

She could hear swearing behind her. When she reached the back door, she found it bolted. Swearing to herself, she slid the bolt and rushed through.

She stood on the back step for a moment, surveying her options. She was almost dead center in the town, and the cliffs rose high above her. The Roman Catholic church jutted out almost straight above her, and the climbing pathway to Jefferson's Rock and the cemetery were straight above that. She knew the area well—knew that a treacherous path hewn out of the foliage led precariously up the path.

She could leap from the steps and run quickly around the house for the street.

Or she could run for the footpath up the hill and try to disappear into the jutting cliff and dirt and the foliage that clung tenaciously to it.

The footsteps were close.

She threw the parasol behind her and raced across the yard, painfully aware that she was barefoot. She found the overgrown path up the steep cliff and began to climb, hoping that the foliage would fall back around her and hide her. She grabbed for bushes, for handholds as well as footholds, moving as quickly as she could.

"She's started up!" one of them shouted.

"Stop, or I'll shoot!" his companion warned her.

Was it an idle threat? She had a feeling that the two of them had been ordered to bring her back alive. She kept climbing.

An expletive rang out in the cool dawn.

And then someone was following her, climbing up behind her.

"Kiernan!"

Her name was called from the street. She could hear the sound of horse's hooves. Someone was out there, calling to her in a husky rich voice.

But she was still being followed.

"I'll kill the bitch!" she heard.

She kept climbing, nearly mindless as her desperation grew.

"Climb, Kiernan, climb!"

She didn't need the husky warning. She could only pray that the rider in the street had dismounted and was following her own pursuer.

Her breath came quickly, and her heart hammered. She was gaining ground, though—of that she was certain. If she could reach the crest, she could race to the church. Perhaps she could wake Father Costello—perhaps he was already awake and at prayer. Maybe the church would provide a refuge.

As she reached the crest, her nightgown caught on a branch. Gasping for breath, she paused to tug it free.

Then hands fell upon her shoulders. She screamed as she was dragged to the ground. She struggled fiercely, seeing the hard-lipped white man atop her. She screamed again. His hand fell flat over her mouth, and she tried to bite. His fist went up in the air, and she knew that it would connect shortly with her jaw.

But it didn't.

Instead, the man's eyes went very wide. Kiernan was dimly aware that a leather-gloved hand had clamped onto the man's wrist. Someone was behind him. The rider, tall and fierce, dragged her attacker from her.

She heard a wicked-sounding blow connect with the man's body.

But she screamed anew, for the earth beneath her had broken under the conflict. She couldn't catch herself, and she started to fall over the side of the cliff, above sheer rock.

"Kiernan!"

For a moment she saw him, tall and in uniform, dark in the shadows, holding on to her attacker.

He thrust the man away and pitched forward to come rolling after her.

His body covered her, and his weight threw them both far to the left and back to the trail. They tumbled endlessly together back to the yard.

They landed with her on top. Coughing, dizzy, she tried to rise. And stared down into endlessly blue eyes.

"Jesse!" she gasped. "Jesse Cameron!"

He smiled his lazy, taunting smile. "Hello, Miss Mackay. It's been a while, hasn't it? But then, a man never knows quite when he'll run into you, eh, Kiernan?"

Two

"When you'll run into me?" Kiernan repeated. It was too incredible that he was there. She was straddled over him in her white nightgown with its lace and smocking, now torn and disheveled. Her hands rested upon his chest, and her hair trailed over the navy blue of the uniform cavalry shirt he was wearing. His hair, like her own, was in reckless disarray, dark strands trailing over his forehead. "Oh, my God, it's Jesse!"

"In the flesh," he agreed.

She suddenly cuffed him upon the broad chest. "And rude and abrasive at that!"

He slipped his hands around her waist, lifting her to his side. She should have risen instantly, Kiernan thought, mortified, but he had only moved her in order to rise to his feet. Once he was up, he reached for her hands, pulling her up before him. "Kiernan—"

"What are you doing here?" she demanded. "How can you be here?"

"The night train spread the word," Jesse said. "I was sharing a late whiskey with a general friend, and he ordered me here to tend to any wounded. Troops will be here soon."

"What's going on?"

"Kiernan, that will have to wait. I have to find that man."

"Jesse, he knew *who* I was and *where* I was!"

"I know."

"But what—"

"Get back into the house." He strode away, picking up his hat where it lay in the dirt.

"What if he comes again? There were two of them."

He strode back to her, pulling a Colt six-shooter from the holster that hung on his hip. "You know how to use this?"

She nodded. He grinned at her and touched her cheek. "He's probably long gone by now. Get back into the house, Kiernan, and stay there until I get back. All right?"

She nodded slowly. A quivery warmth spread through her limbs. She stretched out her fingers and clenched them tightly again.

Jesse Cameron was back in her life. He'd ridden in just when she needed him most. He could have captured the man, except that he had thrown himself upon her to save her from a deadly fall.

In his dark clothing, he blended into the foliage, even as the sun unerringly began to rise. She heard rustling and knew that he had found his way back up the cliff. But she was certain, as he had been, that the man was long gone. The cliff rose all the way to Jefferson's Rock, where Thomas Jefferson had surveyed the area, and on to the cemetery; it was hard, rugged ground. But there were numerous other ways down, and even a stranger to the area would have found them by now.

She felt her cheeks grow warm, and she pressed her hands to them tightly. Jesse. He shouldn't have been there, but he was. He lacked Anthony's manners, perhaps, but manners weren't necessary to save her life.

She turned and quickly hurried back toward the house. Lacey was waiting for her by the back door. "Kiernan! Oh, thank heaven! What happened? Who was that man in the yard? Why, I almost came out with the rolling pin, except that you were on top of him and you seemed to know him. Really, Kiernan, that wasn't at all proper behavior if you did know him—or if you didn't," Lacey mused worriedly. "But then, what difference does it make? You're back here, and you're safe—and you do know him, don't you, dear?"

"Yes. Oh, Lacey, something very big is going on. You know him too. It was Jesse—Jesse Cameron, one of our neighbors back home."

"What's he doing here?"

"An alarm went on via the night train. He didn't explain everything. Some general sent him here. There will be troops soon."

"But why?" Lacey began. "Oh dear, yes! He's a doctor, isn't he? Still serving in the military. Oh, my goodness!" She stared at the Colt in Kiernan's hand. "Can't we put that thing away somewhere?"

"I think I'd like to have it close."

"Those men aren't coming back," Lacey said with confidence.

"How can you be sure?"

"Come with me." Lacey led Kiernan through the house to the front, where the shattered glass still lay before the door. "Look," Lacey said, pointing through the door.

Kiernan looked down the street. A crowd had gathered outside the arsenal buildings now. Armed men were milling in the streets. Someone was in charge, and shouting was going on.

"It's all out in the open now," Lacey murmured.

Kiernan heard footsteps on the wooden sidewalk to their right and swung around quickly. One of Lacey's neighbors, Mr. Tomlin, was hurrying along. He carried a rifle and was speaking to his sixteen-year-old, Eban, who followed behind him. "Give me some more o' them nails, boy." He stopped in front of Lacey and Kiernan. "Don't that beat all, ladies? We produce guns here, and just when you want it, there ain't no ammunition to be bought. But heck, that's all right. We'll nail 'em just the same, eh?" He winked at Kiernan, and she saw that he was loading his rifle with nails.

"Mr. Tomlin," she murmured, "what are you doing?"

"There's a rebellion in the streets, Miss Mackay, ain't you seen?" He stared at her for the first time and saw her torn and ragged gown and the tufts of grass that stuck to her hair. "Bejesu, Miss Mackay, are you all right?"

Kiernan nodded as Lacey answered for her.

"She's fine now! But she wasn't so terribly fine an hour ago!"

"They tried to take you! They tried to take you too!" Eban Tomlin said, staring at Kiernan with awe.

"Who else did they try to take?" Kiernan demanded tensely.

"Try? Why, they got all kinds of people. They got the mayor! And the master armorer. And they even rode five miles out and got Colonel Lewis Washington, George Washington's kin! They say as how Colonel Lewis had things belonging to George, and John Brown wanted those things," Eban said excitedly. " 'Course, Brown come in here calling himself 'Isaac Smith,' but it didn't take no time for someone to guess who it really was!"

"Oh, my Lord!" Lacey breathed.

"And they got more. Reckon they got at least twenty people hostage, maybe more."

"Lacey heard shots," Kiernan said.

"Hell, yes!" Eban said. His father's look of warning brought a flush to his face. "Sorry, ladies. Yes, there's been shooting. And it just beats all, it sure does. Old John Brown, he wants to free the world. Well, ladies, he comes into Harpers Ferry and shoots down poor Hayward Shepherd, the free black man at the railroad station. Guess they didn't want no alarm going out. But then the train came through, and he let that train go on by, and it seems they know what's going on down here as far as Washington and beyond. You'd best get back inside now, ladies. There's all manner o' ruckus going on in the streets now. Some o' those people out there get a little scared and get a gun and shoot up everything in sight."

Kiernan glanced at his nail-filled rifle. "Yes, I know," she murmured.

He tipped his hat to them. "Come on, boy," he told Eban.

Kiernan headed back into the house, and Lacey followed after her. "We'll sit tight, Kiernan. News will come to us. I'm so glad you want to stay in the house!"

"Lacey, I'm not staying in the house. I'm going to get dressed as quickly as possible!"

She tore into the kitchen and pumped up water to bring to her room. She started up the stairs, smiling as she passed Lacey.

"Oh dear, oh dear!" Lacey wailed.

"I'll be all right. I've got a Colt with real bullets, and I know how to use a gun."

Lacey stood at the foot of the stairs calling up to her. "Kiernan, dear, please! Heaven only knows what's really going on!"

Kiernan dumped the water into her wash bowl. She whisked off her torn nightgown and slipped quickly into a chemise and pantalets and a petticoat. She hesitated, then decided that in the midst of a revolution, she could dispense with a corset. Clad in her undergarments, she turned back to the water and scrubbed herself quickly.

"Kiernan—are you listening to me? Oh!" Lacey murmured suddenly.

Rinsing her mouth out, Kiernan wondered what had brought that quick exclamation to Lacey's lips. She looked up, then froze.

Jesse was back. He stood in the doorway, leaning casually against the frame, a lazy smile curving his lip as he watched her.

Color flooded through her, rising from her toes to her hairline. What did he think he was doing? No gentleman in the world would come upon a lady in a state of undress and stare at her so.

But Jesse would. Despite her rising fury, she also felt a sweet, exciting sensation ripple through her. Damn him! He was still one of the most handsome men she had ever seen, with his coal-black hair and wicked blue eyes and lazy, sensual smile.

"Jesse—"

"Well now, darlin'," he drawled softly, and those eyes of his raked over her thoroughly with laughter, humor, and something else. Then his eyes landed upon her own. "You've grown up while I've been away."

She should have blushed to kingdom come. She probably had a right to throw a screeching fit or hysterics. But the sense of danger and excitement rippling through her demanded that she stare him down. If he wanted an innocent feminine reaction from her, she decided, he wasn't going to get it.

"Captain Cameron, if you don't mind"—she faced him, her hands set disapprovingly upon her hips—"I'd appreciate it if you'd wait below until I'm decent to receive company."

He laughed. "Kiernan, you must be the most decent thing I've seen in a month of Sundays. Isn't it just like a woman? The town is in the grip of history, and you're worried about being seen in your knickers."

"I don't wear knickers, Captain Cameron."

"All right, then, petticoats."

"Jesse—"

"Come on down as soon as you consider yourself decent. I can't stay long. In fact, I may not be able to stay long enough to—"

"Don't move!" Kiernan commanded him. She strode across the room to the wardrobe and quickly found a white cotton day dress with flounces and a sophisticated black pattern. She pulled it over her head just as Lacey reached the doorway to chastise Jesse.

"Captain Cameron, what do you think you're doing?"

"Ah, Mrs. Donahue, I've known Kiernan since she was squalling around in diapers."

"But Captain Cameron, I'm responsible for her welfare, and she isn't in diapers any longer."

The dress fell over her head. Kiernan's eyes met Jesse's, and she felt the sizzle in them just as he replied softly to Lacey, "No, ma'am. She isn't in diapers any longer at all."

She couldn't speak for a moment, and his eyes remained on hers. He, too, was silent. Kiernan felt electricity sweep through the air between them like invisible lightning. Not even Lacey spoke to break the tension between them.

Then Kiernan discovered that she could move. She walked toward Jesse, facing him as she turned her back to Lacey. "Would you be a dear and get the buttons, please?"

Lacey quickly began to button up the long row of tiny pearls that served as buttons for the dress while Kiernan continued to stare at Jesse.

"I take it, Jesse, that you did not find the man."

"No, I'm afraid he's joined his companions."

"Companions?"

"The people in the street say John Brown has a force of about twenty men with him."

"What about the other man?"

"I didn't see him, Kiernan. I wish I could have kept my hands on the one. But . . ." his voice trailed away. He was worried, she thought. "I could have kept my hands on him, or you. I chose you," he said lightly.

"Oh!" Lacey breathed. Of course it had been true. If he hadn't thrown himself upon her, she would have pitched down the rock instead of rolling down the trail. But the way he made it sound . . .

"Lacey, he had to break my fall," Kiernan said with what dignity she could muster.

"Oh," Lacey repeated, this time understanding.

But Jesse wasn't going to let her understand anything. His eyes raked over Kiernan like blue flames, taunting her, and his smile was overtly sensual. "You've definitely grown up," he told her. "You're sophisticated and elegant." Then he ruined the handsome compliment by reaching over to remove a twig from her hair. "And almost domesticated."

She snatched the twig out of his hand, then smiled, fighting for control. The excitement stirring in her was exhilarating. She wanted it to take her somewhere, even if she wasn't sure where.

Even if the world was in revolt all around her.

"I'll never be domesticated, Captain. Barnyard animals are domesticated."

"So they are. Let me see, Kiernan. What is a lady such as yourself—untamable?"

"I'm not a wild horse, Jesse."

"Horses need to be broken to the saddle, Kiernan. Women upon occasion also need to be tamed."

"And have you tamed many women?" she demanded.

"A few," he admitted, lazily slouching against the doorframe.

"Well, Captain Cameron, I cannot be broken or tamed!"

"Kiernan, Captain—!" Lacey began, distressed.

Jesse didn't seem to realize that Lacey, still buttoning Kiernan's dress, was even there—or else he didn't mind. He laughed lightly. "I don't remember making such an offer," he drawled.

Lacey inhaled sharply. "Captain, this isn't at all proper."

"Jesse, you never do make offers or say anything concrete," Kiernan said, inadvertently as mindless of Lacey as Jesse was. He had that effect upon her. No, he had it on everyone. He could make people laugh, he could make them furious, he could make them relax.

And he could create an excitement, a tension that demanded awareness of itself.

"It's all insinuation," she told him, keeping her brittle smile intact. She wanted to hit him!

"Captain, Kiernan, please!" Lacey implored. "I must protest! This just isn't proper."

"That's because nothing at all is proper about Jesse," Kiernan said sweetly.

"Now I protest!" Jesse said. "I can be extremely proper, Mrs. Donahue, when the occasion warrants. But Kiernan and I are very old friends. Actually, Mrs. Donahue," he whispered conspiratorially, moving very close to her and offering her his most charming smile, "I even saw Kiernan buck naked when she was a little thing."

"Oh dear, oh dear!" Lacey breathed as she buttoned Kiernan furiously.

"Never!" Kiernan snapped.

"Oh, yes," Jesse assured Lacey charmingly. "As a child, she used to love to strip off every blessed bit of clothing and jump into the lake."

"You're absolutely despicable to remember such things, Jesse," Kiernan told him sweetly, "and to bring them up!"

"Ah, but you speak of my fond memories!" he protested, as if he were wounded.

The last of her tiny buttons was done up. "Really?" She challenged him with a superior air. "Lacey, I'm quite certain he hasn't thought a thing about me for the last year or so until the moment he came after me."

"Came to your rescue," he reminded her.

"Humility is his greatest asset," she murmured with dripping sarcasm.

Jesse grinned. "Her kind and gentle ways are surely Kiernan's greatest attributes!" he countered.

"Oh dear, what is going on here, Captain?" Lacey interjected. "This just is not proper, not with Kiernan practically engaged."

"Engaged?" His brows lifted with surprise. A flurry swept Kiernan's heart at his obvious interest. "Who's the lucky man? Ah, never mind, I know. It's young Anthony Miller, the arms heir, I do imagine. Well, there's a nice mannered pup for you, Kiernan."

"Anthony is the very soul of propriety," she assured him angrily.

"Indeed. I imagine you maneuver him about with the twitch of your little finger," Jesse agreed. He was laughing at her, she thought, and once again she wanted to hit him. But there also seemed to be a bit of an edge in his voice. Could he possibly be jealous?

"He is completely charming," she said sweetly.

"Then you *are* engaged? My congratulations."

"No," Kiernan admitted. "We're not engaged yet."

"He's madly in love with her!" Lacey said.

"And well the lad should be!" Jesse stated, still laughing. "Beauty, grace— and a mind like a whip!"

Kiernan kept her smile intact. "If you'll excuse me, I'm going to size up the situation in town myself."

She swirled around, but he caught her arm. "Kiernan, stay in. Come downstairs, and I'll tell you both what I know."

He didn't wait for an answer but went downstairs ahead of her. Kiernan shrugged to Lacey, who was concerned that she had completely failed to chaperone a young and innocent woman.

Kiernan wished she could have told Lacey that anyone would have failed with Jesse around. And she was furious with herself because he always had the ability to lead her along, then step back. The older, wiser, very masculine—male!

Times have changed, she wanted to shout at him. I'm very much grown up now, and I can hold my own in any battle!

But she wondered if she really could hold out in a battle with him.

She gritted her teeth. She could—and she would!

Jesse found his way into the parlor with Lacey and Kiernan following behind. The teasing was gone from his eyes and his manner as he politely waited for both women to perch upon the loveseat. He pulled up a chair before them and straddled it backward to face them very seriously.

"What I've managed to get so far is that John Brown has been planning this raid for months. He was over in Sandy Hook, Maryland, laying out his strategy. He must have hoped that many more people would rise to fight against slaveholders with him. I imagine that he wanted a revolution to start here, with slaves rising against their masters and slaying them in the streets. He really believes that only a bloodbath can cleanse the land."

"My God!" Lacey gasped.

Kiernan watched Jesse, shaking, imagining the scene that Jesse had so bluntly painted. "Are you sure it won't come to that?" she demanded.

"No," he said flatly, "it's not going to come to that. John Brown is already holed up."

"There's been bloodshed," Kiernan whispered.

He arched a brow. "You heard?"

"A neighbor came by. Loading up his shotgun with nails," Kiernan said. "Oh!" she exclaimed passionately. "What right has this man to come to Virginia? How dare he think to command our lives!"

"He dares," Jesse murmured. He quit looking at her for a moment. He seemed to look beyond her, to the future that stretched before them all.

He seemed worried by what he saw there.

"It seems that the townfolk had their own way of dealing with the events that happened," he said. "A man was killed right away."

"Hayward Shepherd, at the station," Lacey said, her eyes round. "He was a good soul, a gentle man."

"Gentle men get caught up in the deeds of others," Jesse mused.

"There's more?" Kiernan asked.

He returned her gaze steadily. "Yes. One of the hostages has been shot."

"No!" Lacey murmured.

"I'm afraid so. A local farmer named Turner has been killed."

They were all still for a moment. Then Lacey burst out, "Oh, my dear God, Kiernan! What if—"

"Lacey, I'm fine," Kiernan reminded her gently. She stared steadily at Jesse. "They—er, they don't usually shoot women anyway, do they?"

"Of course not," Jesse told her. But watching him, Kiernan shivered inside. She might have been one of the hostages.

"They still have—people?"

"Yes. Mayor Beckham, among them. Colonel Lewis. Mr. Allstadt, the armorer."

"What will happen now?" Lacey asked worriedly.

Jesse smiled. "The cavalry will ride in, Mrs. Donahue," he said, rising. "Actually, Jefferson Davis, the secretary of war, has ordered Lieutenant Colonel Robert E. Lee to bring in troops. They'll handle things, ma'am. I've got to go now. There are some people I have to see, and things I have to do before I meet up with those troops."

"Wait, don't go yet, Captain Cameron!" Lacey implored, jumping to her feet. Kiernan cast her a quick glance. She could have sworn that Jesse had very much unsettled Lacey. Then Lacey smiled, looking down at her hands. Lacey might be unsettled, but she was also charmed.

And she didn't want to be left alone in the midst of all that was happening.

"Mrs. Donahue, honestly, you're going to be all right," he told her. "John Brown and his men are holed up in the firehouse down by the armory. You'll be safe from him. I'm not sure about some of your gun-toting neighbors. Just stay off the streets."

"But what if those people come back for Kiernan?"

"They've tangled with Kiernan once. I don't think they'll be willing to do so again." He winked at Kiernan over Lacey's head, and she had to smile again.

"Coffee!" Lacey said. "Just stay for a cup of coffee. Breakfast. I make a very good plate of ham and eggs and sausage. And very good corn muffins. You must have a little time," Lacey argued.

To Kiernan's surprise, Jesse agreed, pulling out his pocket watch. "All right. I've got an hour, Mrs. Donahue. No more."

Kiernan stood to join Lacey in the kitchen. "I'll help you," she said.

"No!" Lacey gasped. She had been worried about Jesse's sense of propriety upstairs, but now she was determined to keep him just as long as she could—even if that meant leaving Kiernan to flirt with him.

But he was no longer in his taunting mood, Kiernan realized as Lacey left. He wandered to one of the front-facing windows, pulled back the drape, and stared out broodingly.

Kiernan felt a quickening in her heart. "Jesse, what's wrong? Are you lying to make Lacey feel better? Are we in serious trouble here? Do you think that a full-scale revolt will break out?"

He turned back to her and shook his head slowly. "No, Kiernan, I'm not lying. John Brown can't expect any more help. If he could, it would already have come his way. No, I'm afraid that Mr. Brown is doomed."

Kiernan snapped, irritated, "The man is a murderer. He *should* be doomed. Are you in sympathy with him?"

Again, Jesse shook his head. "No, I can't condone what he's done. If I were judge or juryman, I'd have to condemn him to death. And if he isn't killed when the troops ride in, I'm sure he will hang."

"Then what's wrong?" she asked him.

He looked at her again, really looked at her. "You were always an intuitive little thing," he told her softly. He felt warmth—startling, deep—ripple through him. So often she had read his mind and his thoughts. He remembered coming home from West Point determined to go on to medical school. He had stopped to pay his respects to her father, and she had been sitting at the piano. And she had looked up and smiled when he had come into the room. "Are you going to tell your pa that you want to be a doctor more than a planter?" His interest in medicine was no real surprise to anyone—he had always been fascinated by the field. But he was the eldest son of a very prosperous cotton and tobacco planter. He'd made the decision to go on to medical school himself, without leaving the military. He wanted to combine his interest in medicine with the military, and he thought that he could do very well. He hadn't explained it all to his father, his sister, or even to Daniel yet. But when Kiernan had looked at him that day, he knew that she understood.

"Intuitive," Jesse murmured again now, his smile curving ruefully. "Either that, or you've always known me."

Kiernan wanted to know him—very much, at that moment. She wanted to know him better than anyone else in the world knew him. In fact, she wanted to rise and rush over to the window to him and feel him put his arms around her and hold her close. But she was afraid—she didn't know why—of the emotions she was reading in his eyes, in his manner.

"So what *is* wrong?" she repeated, curling her fingers into the sofa.

"I'm not sure, Kiernan. It won't end here—that's what I'm afraid of, I think. That these events will go on and on. The bloodshed between the abolitionists and the proslavery men will not end out in Kansas. The cry for states' rights will go on, and the split between people will drive more and more deeply into the land itself. I won't like the way our world begins to move. I love my life the way that it is. I love Cameron Hall, and my brother and my sister, and the sloping grass and the James River and—" He broke off, then shrugged, and she realized that he had let her glimpse far more of himself than he had intended.

"Nothing is going to change," Kiernan said quickly. "Cameron Hall has stood for centuries now! And Daniel will always be near." She smiled. "We're all Tidewater people. We'll all remain that."

"Ah—not if you marry this mountain man, this Anthony of yours," he said. He was teasing her again—and he was doing it because he didn't want her to pursue the conversation in the direction it had been going.

Still, she flushed just slightly. "I haven't made up my mind to marry Anthony," she said.

"Why not?" he demanded.

Kiernan rose and strode across the room to the other window. She wanted to offer him a charming smile and tell him that it was none of his business.

But the truth suddenly flooded through her, and she didn't want to tell him the truth either.

That she had been waiting for him. Always.

She lifted her chin, smiled at him, and decided to offer a half-truth. "I'm not sure that I love him."

"Ah. Is there someone that you do love?" he asked softly. But he suddenly seemed angry, both with her and with himself. "Never mind, don't answer that," he told her.

"I didn't intend to. My feelings are none of your business," she snapped quickly.

"Kiernan, I—" He took a step toward her, then paused. When he stepped toward her again, she was stunned when he suddenly pulled her into his arms, pulled her hard against him. His fingers threaded through her hair at her nape, and she almost protested the pain, except that she could feel his passion. He gazed down at her with intensity. "Kiernan, you don't understand. The world is going to change, and I'm afraid that I'm going to disappoint you. I wish that I could make you understand." He stared at her searchingly. "Kiernan!" He shook her slightly. Her head fell back farther, and her eyes met his—not with alarm, but with surprise and curiosity, and with a flame to challenge his words. "Oh, hell!" he whispered. He cupped her chin, and she felt the rough texture of his palm and fingers, his stroke gentle and provocative as he deftly moved his thumb against the softness of her flesh. He lowered his head and kissed her.

It was like no other kiss she had ever known.

Anthony had kissed her, brushed his lips against hers. It had been pleasant enough. She had considered the experience with a certain amusement.

But now she knew that his pleasant touch had been oh, so tepid.

This was fire—sweet, savage fire. He asked no permission, gave her no chance for the least hesitance. His lips molded over hers, claiming them completely, giving fire and heat and passion and demanding it in return. He kissed her the way no gentleman should ever kiss a lady.

But Jesse had never pretended to be a gentleman. Not with her.

And with the moist searing heat of his lips against hers, she wanted to be no lady.

He pulled her ever closer against him. Her hooped petticoats rose to her rear as her body pressed decadently close to his. His tongue wedged through the barrier of her lips and teeth and delved wickedly into the dark and secret recesses of her mouth. It seemed to enter deeper into the secret chambers of her soul and body. The excitement she had always felt when he was near took soaring flight. Her heart hammered, her limbs felt weak—and the heat was part of her now, urging her to slip her arms around his neck, to taste the kiss, to give way to the sweet, evocative passion.

Still he kissed her, his tongue playing with hers, his lips commanding, his body so close, so tight. She could feel so many raw, exhilarating sensations, the shape and form of him, the feel of his clothing, the heat and desire that lay beneath it. She could feel herself molding the length of his form. Longings that were reckless and wild crept into her mind and heart, winding throughout her like a serpent—the serpent that had brought Adam and Eve to the brink of damnation in Eden.

Jesse . . .

His lips were coercive, moving against hers, molding them so hotly. His tongue flicked here and there.

Ah, if this was damnation, let the fires begin! She would gladly have abandoned all for him. She would have walked naked with him into a field of green grass and flowers and lain down beside him. . . .

He broke the kiss at last, just lifting his lips from hers. The warmth of his breath stirred an even deeper quivering within her as his whisper touched her. "If he can't kiss you like this, Kiernan, don't marry him."

"What?" she demanded sharply. Furious, she tried to pull away. She raised a hand to strike him, but he caught it, and his laughter, husky and rich, rang out.

"If he can't kiss you like that, sweetheart, don't marry him."

"Bastard!" she charged him, struggling to be free.

But he pulled her tight once again. "Hold out for the best there is, Kiernan. You should have it. Make sure that there's fire. Maybe there'll be ice, too, but hold out for the extremes, for the best, the brightest. Don't accept anything lukewarm. Because you're fire and ice, and you're the brightest and the best, Kiernan."

"Kiernan! Captain!" Lacey called to them, hurrying to the parlor doorway. "Breakfast."

His eyes remained locked on hers. Then at last he released her.

Kiernan took a quick swing, slapping him hard against the cheek.

"Oh dear!" Lacey wailed.

"You don't play fair," Jesse told Kiernan, smiling slowly as he raised a hand to his reddening cheek.

"Fair! Jesse Cameron, you—"

"Ah, ah, careful, Kiernan. Watch out for Mrs. Donahue's tender ears," he warned her quickly, laughing at her again. Both his hands touched her shoulders as he set her aside to move past her. "She can swear like a mule driver when she wants to, Mrs. Donahue."

"I can kick just like a mule too," she snapped, seething.

"Now, both of you—" Lacey began.

"*Can* you?" Jesse interrupted, his hands suddenly on Kiernan's shoulders again. "Miss Mackay, I don't suggest you try it with me."

"Oh, and what *will* do, Jesse?"

"You don't want to know, Kiernan."

"Fine gentleman you are, Jesse."

He grinned. "Ladies aren't supposed to kick like mules, Kiernan."

"And gentlemen don't—" She broke off. She wanted to tell him that an honorable gentleman would never ever have stolen a kiss like the one he had just stolen.

"Gentlemen don't what, Kiernan?"

"I'd move to safety, Jesse," she warned him sweetly.

He laughed again. "Take care, Kiernan, with me. Test your powers on that charming almost-fiancé of yours, but not on me. Anything you start, Kiernan, I'll finish."

"Really!" Lacey implored. "If we could all just sit down and have breakfast—"

"Don't dare *me*, Jesse."

"I made griddle cakes!" Lacey wailed.

Jesse released Kiernan and turned to Lacey. He bent down to kiss her cheek. "I have a feeling I'm persona non grata at the moment, Mrs. Donahue. Thanks for the invitation. You be a good dear and keep yourself safe in the house, eh? I've got to go."

"But Captain Cameron—"

"Behave, Kiernan," he warned, suddenly very stern as he stared at her over Lacey's head. "Please be careful. I'll be outside town to meet the troops tonight. And I promise you, the streets are wild."

"These people are my neighbors!" Lacey murmured.

"Yes, and I'm sure you'll both be fine," Jesse agreed. "But for my peace of mind, stay in, all right?"

He started out. Kiernan glanced at Lacey briefly, then went racing after him. She still wanted to kick him, hard.

She called to him. "Captain!"

Startled by her use of his title, he swung and waited, a coal-dark brow inquisitively arched.

"Are you coming back, Jesse?"

He nodded. "I'll come in with the troops, Kiernan."

"Be careful, Jesse," she warned him.

He grinned and took a step back toward her. She shrank away quickly. "Oh, no, Captain! Keep your distance. You don't play fair."

He shook his head suddenly. "No, Kiernan, you're the one who doesn't play fair." He smiled, but she sensed that he was serious too.

"What do you mean?" she asked. She felt warm again, flushed, with subtle rivers of excitement running through her veins.

"Kiernan, you always wanted to make all the rules. That's not fair."

"Don't they say that all's fair in love and war?" she murmured. She didn't want to make all the rules. She just wanted to keep her heart safe.

"That's what I'm afraid of," he told her huskily. He touched her again, just her hands, meeting her eyes. "Love—and war."

"I don't understand."

"And I can't explain. But you take care, Kiernan. I'll be back soon."

He kissed her again, just brushing her lips with his own. And still she felt his touch like a sweep of staggering warmth.

She met the blaze of his cobalt-blue eyes just briefly, and then he was gone.

Three

During the long morning, Kiernan waited in the house. It was obviously that Jesse had appalled Lacey—but Lacey seemed equally upset that Kiernan had somehow driven him away when he had promised to stay for breakfast. "I felt so much safer with the captain in the house!" she said nervously, sitting at the breakfast table. There was still a great commotion in the streets. But the events now taking place were happening far down by the armory and firehouse, so they couldn't see terribly much. They heard shots being fired, and still there were many shouts. The drama unfolding seemed to put an almost tangible tension in the air—Kiernan could feel it, even in the house.

"He wouldn't have left us if he felt that we'd be in any danger, Lacey," Kiernan assured her.

Lacey clapped her hands together. "How delightfully romantic! You mean, he would have defied duty to stay with two ladies?"

"No, not Jesse," Kiernan said wryly. "He would have packed up the two ladies and dragged them along with him." She wished he had dragged her along with him. She couldn't bear sitting still when so very much was going on. The town was at war! She didn't know what she could do, but she felt she should be doing something.

"Oh, dear," Lacey said with a sigh. "Just how well do you know this young man?"

"I've known him all my life," Kiernan admitted. "We grew up together over in the Tidewater." She was eating her third stack of griddle cakes. She wasn't the least bit hungry, but she had eaten and eaten, exclaiming over the deliciousness of the food, to assuage Lacey. After all, Lacey blamed Kiernan for the fact that the captain was not wolfing down a good portion of the meal.

"What will happen when Anthony returns?" Lacey asked worriedly.

"What do you mean, what will happen?" Kiernan asked her.

"Well, he's—he's very much in love with you, dear! When he sees Jesse Cameron—"

"He knows Jesse Cameron, Lacey. You know Jesse, Lacey!" She counted on her fingers. "You met him at my coming-out ball, the barbecue at the Stacys' in Richmond, and oh, yes! I believe you both were at Anthony's sister's birthday party two years ago up at Montemarte."

"Yes, I met him. But you know him so well."

"Anthony knows him very well," Kiernan asserted with an amused smile. "They're all good friends—Jesse, his brother Daniel, Anthony, and a number of others who were at West Point during the same years. And they've met socially time and time again, both at Cameron Hall and out here at Montemarte."

Lacey was disgruntled. "How amazing that the captain stumbled upon you in the nick of time."

"I don't think he stumbled on me," Kiernan assured her. "He must have known that I was up here. I wrote to Daniel Cameron recently, so Jesse knew that I'd be in Harpers Ferry with you while Papa and your husband and Anthony and his father were on their business trip. He heard about the attack in Washington after John Brown's men let that night train come through. He was ordered down to tend to the wounded. Despite appearances, he does have his own peculiar sense of honor. He would have felt he owed it to my father to see to my welfare."

"Hmph!" Lacey stated.

"And what does that mean?"

"It means that there's no fool like an old fool, but I'm not an old fool, Kiernan Mackay. That man came here for a great deal more than a sense of obligation to your father."

Kiernan's heart was beating too hard, and a flush was warming her cheek. She chewed her griddle cake and sipped her coffee quickly. "We fight like cats and dogs, Lacey. Surely you noticed."

"I noticed a great deal," Lacey said sagely.

Kiernan shrugged. She didn't know how to explain to Lacey that maybe, just maybe, she was in love with Jesse. Or that if she was, it didn't mean anything. It wasn't because Jesse didn't care about her—she was sure that he did. She had felt it in his kiss. Jesse knew women—his was a practiced, arrogant, masterful kiss. He could elicit emotion from a woman even if he himself felt no more than longing, of that she was certain. Jesse knew how to seduce.

She could still feel the warmth of his mouth where he had kissed her. She could taste and breathe the sensation, and hunger for more, hunger to explore everything that had always been forbidden.

But he hadn't offered her anything. All he had said was that she shouldn't marry Anthony if he couldn't kiss her like that. What did Jesse himself want?

And why had it seemed that he was in pain? Talking about love and war, then telling her what scared him.

Why should all of it scare him? Nothing had ever seemed to frighten Jesse before. He had stayed with the cavalry, and he had fought Indians out in the new territories in the West. If war came, and if Virginia seceded, she'd stand behind him. She'd agonize when he rode away, but they were both Tidewater Virginians—fierce, independent, and loyal, passionate lovers of their land and the Tidewater region.

Maybe he wanted to know if she was in love with Anthony. Maybe he himself wasn't ready to settle down.

But maybe he didn't really care a whit for her. After all, she was a young woman to taunt and tease and practice seduction upon. Maybe she had only dreamed that he was waiting for her to grow up.

She knew through rumor that he'd had his share of affairs. Jesse had a way about him. There was something in his eyes. Even if he was as silent about his personal life as a man could be, one could sense things.

"What will poor Anthony say?"

For Lacey, it was almost as if his name were Poor Anthony.

"Say about what, Lacey?" Kiernan asked with a weary sigh.

"Everything that has happened. He'll be so upset that you were threatened by those horrible men. And he'll be very upset that he wasn't here to rescue you. And he'd be very upset if he knew—"

"But Lacey, poor Anthony won't know anything," Kiernan said. "Jesse will ride away with the troops tomorrow, and by the time Anthony and the other men return, this will all be history. We won't tell them that I was threatened."

"But Kiernan, Anthony has a right to know. And everyone in town will know what happened here!" She waved a handkerchief before her. "And your father—"

"Lacey, please. There's no reason to worry Papa needlessly. They'll know what happened here, but they will also know that we're fine. And I'm not engaged to Anthony. I haven't figured out what I want to do yet." She smiled at Lacey.

"But your father *has* to know! You were nearly taken a hostage because—"

"Because my father is a wealthy man."

"A slaveowner," Lacey corrected.

"Like many Virginians!" Kiernan protested.

"Like most wealthy Virginians. Why, you know as well as I do that very few of the poorer farmers own even one slave, young lady. And not all wealthy Virginians are slaveowners, at least not in the western counties," Lacey stated. Lacey opposed slavery, Kiernan knew. Not violently, not the way that John Brown did. But in her own quiet way, she was very much against the institution.

"Lacey, please, there's no reason for Papa to know anything. I'm fine. Nothing happened to me in the end."

"Because of Jesse Cameron's timely arrival."

"Yes, because of his timely arrival," Kiernan admitted. She smiled, and began to clear their dishes. Lacey decided to let it be—for the moment. But several hours later, as they sat in the parlor together, she began anew.

"Kiernan, I just worry so."

"And you really shouldn't. In fact, you absolutely mustn't. I think I'll take a little walk," Kiernan said suddenly. She would go out and find out what was going on. She couldn't bear to sit and wait any longer.

"But you can't go out there! You promised Captain Cameron you wouldn't go!"

"I didn't promise anybody anything, and I don't owe Captain Cameron any allegiance!" she said firmly.

"But Kiernan—"

"I have Jesse's Colt, Lacey, and I know how to use it. I can't stand it anymore, not knowing what's going on out there." She leaped up and squeezed Lacey's cheeks together with her thumb and forefinger. Lacey's mouth made a big round O and a sound escaped her, but she couldn't protest further as Kiernan planted a kiss upon her forehead. "Don't worry! I'll be fine. I'll be careful, and I know how to shoot. And I have real live ammunition in the gun—which is apparently much more than anyone else has."

She hurried from the kitchen to the parlor. Lacey called after her, but she moved quickly, finding the Colt on the mantel. She felt a twinge of guilt about defying Lacey, but that couldn't be helped. Momentous things were happening, and she had to understand what they were.

"I'll be back soon!" she called, then she hurried out to the street. She looked up and saw that the sun was already beginning its descent. In another few hours, darkness would fall over them again.

There was no one before the house, but down the street to her left, a crowd had gathered before the firehouse—out of range of shot, it seemed. Militiamen were surrounding the firehouse, she realized, and the citizens of Harpers Ferry were surrounding the militia.

Things seemed fairly quiet and subdued, but still, an air of electric tension seemed to have settled upon the town.

People were talking about how the townfolk had battled John Brown until he'd had no choice but to take refuge in the firehouse.

Kiernan hurried down the street. When a hand fell upon her shoulder, she nearly jumped sky-high and swung around. Dr. Bruce Whelan, white-haired with a drooping moustache, stared at her sternly with a pair of clear, dove-gray eyes.

"Doc Whelan—"

"I was told to look out for you, young lady," he said gruffly.

"What?"

"Captain Cameron came through to help with the wounded." He waved a hand in the air. "People were all kind of cut up, what with firing shotguns filled with whatever debris they came across. There's been a heap of death today, young lady. A heap of death."

"Jesse doesn't have the right—" she began.

"Yes, Jesse does. He said that he come upon you in a bit of trouble, Kiernan Mackay."

Her heart sank. If Doc Whelan knew about last night, her father would know. He'd be loath to leave her alone ever again. Anthony and his father would be loath to leave her, but she really did love her independence.

"Nothing catastrophic happened—"

"You might be in grave danger at this very moment!" he corrected her. "Jesse said you managed a good fight on your own, but hell, girl! Not even a man can stand up against a bullet. And now John Brown has his hostages holed up with him in the firehouse. Colonel Lewis Washington is in there, girl! They're saying that Brown wanted to have the sword Frederick the Great gave to George Washington and the pistol Lafayette gave him, and so they've taken that fine brave gentleman. And Mr. Allstadt, his neighbor, and his young son. You could have been among them!"

She gritted her teeth. Jesse must have described her flight from her pursuer with full dramatic license, she thought.

"But I am all right."

"And you should be off the streets."

"Doc Whelan, the whole town is on the streets!"

"The whole town is out here, right. But the things happening to the whole town haven't been good! Kiernan, Mr. Beckham has been killed."

She gasped, thinking of the kindly mayor. He had been such a gentle man!

"And young lady, when Mayor Beckham was killed, a lynch mob broke into the Wager Hotel and seized one of the raiders who had been taken prisoner. They dragged him on out to the bridge and shot him up on either side of the head. Half the maniacs in this town are still pumping bullets into the body."

"My Lord," Kiernan breathed.

"Go home, Kiernan."

"I will, soon. I promise."

"There's more, young lady. There was shooting all around, what with the various militias coming in. Seems like there were about twenty raiders to begin with. Some of them were wounded and killed. Some were shot trying to escape across the river. It just isn't a good day to be out, and I do mean it."

"I know, Doc Whelan. Really, I do."

He tried to look stern, but then he shrugged. "Don't imagine I could get you to go home if I talked myself blue in the face. So be careful, and head back in by nightfall. Hell, some assistance could still come this way before we get federal troops in here to deal with this." He stared at her for a moment. "Too bad Captain Cameron isn't around. I reckon he'd get you back inside." He grinned, then laughed out loud. "He'd pick you right up over his shoulder and see you back to the house." He grinned again and started on his way. He paused to laugh again—no, to cackle—then he started down the street once more.

The shooting was over for the moment, Kiernan realized. She hurried onward.

Jesse wasn't about, but she wasn't going to be told what she could and couldn't do.

Jesse Cameron was a lot closer than Kiernan thought.

Colonel Baylor of one of the militia companies had taken matters under control as best he could. Negotiations hadn't gone very well between the townsfolk and the raiders holed up in the firehouse. Two of Brown's men had been shot under a white flag of surrender. One had crawled back into the firehouse, and one had been killed, his body mutilated by the people.

But someone had asked for a doctor, and Jesse was regular army. He was sent in with one of Baylor's militiamen, a man called Sinn.

The firehouse was a brick structure, about thirty-five by thirty feet. The doors were heavy wood, and they were soundly battened down. Under a white flag of truce, Jesse and Sinn approached the firehouse. The doors opened briefly, and they were let in.

Jesse had been with the cavalry in Kansas, and he'd heard about the doings of old "Ossawatomie" Brown for years, but he'd never met the man.

When he did now, he was startled, physically moved, by the fires burning in the old man's eyes. He'd never seen anything like it. Brown's face was haggard, aged, and lined. It was full of character, with a long beard and thick bushy brows. But that blaze in his eyes was arresting. He was a murderer, a cold-blooded one, Jesse was convinced.

But he was also convinced that he had never before seen a man who so truly believed that he committed murder for God's own cause.

"The cavalry is here," Brown commented.

Jesse shook his head. "I'm a doctor. I've come to see to your wounded."

"Then take a look at the boy."

The boy was on the ground, to the far left of the entrance and the old fire engines. Jesse nodded and strode over to his side.

He was a handsome young man, no more than twenty. As soon as Jesse stooped down beside him, he knew that that the boy was going to die. He was gut-shot, and badly. There wasn't a thing that any man could do to save him.

Sinn was getting ready to address Brown with terms from Colonel Baylor, but Brown, with his fire-edged eyes, was watching Jesse. "He's my son, Oliver."

Jesse nodded again. The young man's pain-filled eyes touched his father's. "It hurts, Pa. Can't you shoot me?"

"You'll get over it," Brown said.

Jesse stiffened. He could swear that despite this abrupt answer, the old man cared deeply for the boy.

He opened his surgical bag and found bandaging to bind up what he could of the fatal wound. The lad's eyes were on him now. He pulled out a syringe and a bottle of morphine. At least he could ease the lad's pain. He set the needle just beneath the boy's skin and administered the drug.

"Thanks, mister," he breathed. There were tears in his eyes.

His eyes closed, and he moaned again. "If you must die," Brown suddenly thundered, "die like a man!"

Jesse's gaze snapped to the old man's. For a long moment they stared at each other. Brown saw the condemnation in Jesse's gaze.

He seemed sorry for his harsh words, but that blaze was still about his eyes. He didn't mind offering up his own life for his cause, nor his own flesh and blood.

Sinn told John Brown that he'd murdered Mayor Beckham when the man had been unarmed.

Brown gave his attention to Sinn. "That, sir, was regrettable."

Jesse had done all that he could. He saw that the hostages and the other wounded were gathered in the rear of the firehouse.

He recognized Colonel Washington immediately. Washington nodded his way, tall and straight. Jesse saluted him, and Washington returned the salute.

"We'll see you soon, sir," Jesse said to him.

Washington offered him a half grin. "Either that, or in hell, Captain!"

Brown and Sinn broke off in their negotiations. "Captain!" Sinn said to him. "Are you ready, sir?"

"A moment."

Jesse saw to the others, though he could do little for them under the circumstances. He bandaged what he could and set a few limbs on splints, removed a nail from an arm muscle, and gave some advice for staying still until real medical help could be given.

"A man doesn't need to be in good health to hang," one of the raiders said dryly.

"Hang?" the lean young farmer Jesse had been helping said.

"Sure, for treason," he was told.

His eyes went wide, and he searched out old John Brown.

"Was this treason, sir?"

"Sure was," John Brown answered.

"Heck, I didn't want to be guilty of treason," the young farmer said. "I just wanted to free the slaves." He gripped Jesse's arm. "I just wanted to free the slaves. We didn't mean nothing else."

Jesse nodded, thinking the man might not live to hang anyway. "I understand exactly what you meant." He could have told him that innocent people had been killed, but he decided not to. He was a doctor, not a judge, and if John Brown thought he knew what God intended, Jesse sure as hell didn't.

"Captain?" Sinn called to him.

He closed his bag with a snap, straightened, and joined Sinn at the door. The two men exited the firehouse.

Jesse felt the searing eyes of old John Brown boring into him. He turned back.

Indeed, the man was watching him with his blazing gaze.

A coldness crept along Jesse's spine. He wasn't afraid of John Brown, he knew that. He was afraid that John Brown foretold some kind of doom.

The heavy doors closed behind them, and he and Sinn went back to report to Baylor.

Then he was free once again to ride through a town gone mad.

Kiernan saw Eban at the edge of the crowd and circled around until she could reach him.

"Eban, what's happening?" she demanded.

"Some of the hostages have escaped," he told her.

"Oh, how wonderful!" she exclaimed. Then she asked softly, "Has anyone else been—"

"No more of the hostages have been killed," Eban told her. "But you should have seen what they did to Daingerfield Newby."

"Who?"

"He was a free black man. I hear tell he joined up with John Brown because no matter how he tried to earn the money to buy his wife and family, her master kept raising her price. The poor man was shot down with anything you could imagine and left there in the alley." He pointed up the hill a little way. "I hear they let the hogs get ahold of him then."

"Oh!" Kiernan gasped. She felt ill. Yet something drew her to the spot—maybe she couldn't quite believe that people she knew so well had been driven to such violence. But she walked uphill toward the alley, then paused with horror.

Blood still stained the alley. It was on the ground, and splashed against the wall.

Hogs were still rooting around the alley. She backed away, feeling ill.

Daingerfield Newby would never buy his wife and children.

"Miss Mackay!" Eban stood behind her. "Are you all right?"

She nodded. Pieces of burned nails lay at her feet, and she bent down and picked one up. The citizens had fired these at the poor man. She stared at Eban, and he was instantly on the defensive. "For pity's sake, Miss Mackay. John Brown's men killed Mr. Turner, just 'cause he owned slaves. They meant to rouse all the slaves in the area against us. They meant to have us murdered in our beds! But we stopped them. We fought back with nothing, and we holed them up in that firehouse. We're going to get them. But it's too late for Turner. They put a gun right up to his head and pulled the trigger and killed him. And they killed Hayward! They're supposed to be so good and kind and all-loving to the black men, but they come in here and shoot down a free black man themselves. It's frightening, Miss Mackay, darned frightening. We fought back, that's all we done. We fought back."

Kiernan nodded again. Who was to be condemned in this madness? John Brown? But John Brown seemed to believe that God whispered in his ear and gave him his orders.

"Is Brown still in the firehouse?" Kiernan asked.

"He is, Miss Mackay." Eban tilted his hat to her. "And he's still got hostages. No one knows what he intends to do. The militia have been talking with him. If they rush him, he might kill the captives. We're at a standstill now, waiting on Washington, D.C., and the federal military."

A chill rushed through her, and she was suddenly very afraid. Many militia units had been called in, it seemed. People were grouped in the streets. She could still hear shots and wild cries.

And in that awful alley the blood still lingered.

She was afraid, with the kind of fear that Jesse had been talking about himself feeling.

We didn't start this tragedy, she thought, trying not to imagine the mutilated body of the black freeman. John Brown had ridden into town and awakened the terror of a peaceful people. But John Brown hadn't started the debate on slavery. She couldn't blame him for that.

She could blame him for bringing it and all this horror and bloodshed to Virginia.

" 'Scuse me, Miss Mackay," Eban told her. "I'm going to find out what's going on."

Kiernan stayed at the edge of the crowd as the day waned. The sun began to set in earnest. She learned that Colonel Robert E. Lee had a detachment of marines stationed just outside of town, and that he'd be taking over from the militia soon enough.

She wondered if Jesse was with Lee.

She heard shots again, by the firehouse. The crowd was shoving. Before she knew it, she was being pushed nearer and nearer the firehouse.

Suddenly she nearly tripped over the body of a man, a man so filled with shot that he must have been heavy with the lead. His face and body were ruined beyond recognition.

She was pushed again as the crowd gathered nearer. She was almost shoved upon the man. She looked down at sightless holes where eyes had been, and she started to scream, panic growing within. Another shot was fired into the body. The young farmer who had aimed the rifle seemed heedless of the crowd around the dead man.

"No!" Kiernan screamed again. She had to get away from those horrible sightless eyes.

Suddenly, she was swept up high into strong arms. She looked up, her horror mirrored in her gaze.

Deep blue eyes stared sternly down upon her. Jesse. Jesse wasn't with Lee at all. He was here.

With her.

Come to her rescue once again.

Her arms locked around his neck, despite the fury in his eyes.

"Jesse," she whispered.

"Make way!" he demanded, and the crowd parted. His long strides brought them quickly through the crowd and to his waiting roan horse.

He set her atop it, then leaped up behind her. Within seconds they were cantering down the street, and the clean wind was blowing against her cheeks and washing away the scent of tragedy and blood.

And the chill that had seeped into her was warmed away by the heat of the arms around her.

Four

He didn't take her back to Lacey's house.

The well-trained roan quickly traveled through the town of Harpers Ferry, climbing the hill to Bolivar Heights with what should have been frightening speed.

She wasn't frightened—not with Jesse.

She felt the muscled heat of his chest hard against her back as she rode, and the events of the past two days seemed to fade away. Nothing could happen to her now that Jesse's arms were around her.

He didn't stop in the town of Bolivar, but climbed up to the woods atop one of the hills. He spurred his horse all the way to the top, where the tall trees looked down at a great distance on the little cleft of land where the Shenandoah met the Potomac and old Harper had started his ferry service across the river. The townspeople seemed tiny now, and the buildings looked tiny, too, like toys.

Jesse leaped down from his horse and reached up for her. She set her hands on his shoulders and slid down into his arms. She was trembling, and he kept his arms tight around her.

"Oh, Jesse, the things they're doing down there are so horrible!"

His hands moved gently, soothingly, over her hair. "It's all right. It will all be over soon enough. A tempest in a teapot." He stroked her cheek, meeting her eyes, then spun her around so she could see down the far distance of the cliff. Again, the people and buildings were like toys. The white rushing waters of the rivers could be seen, meeting. "Today will end. Shenandoah and Potomac will continue to shed their haunting tears, and the mountains will be beautiful again." His arms were about her, his fingers entwined at her waist and over her belly. He must have felt that she had ceased to tremble.

His tone suddenly changed, and he swung her around so that she faced him again.

"And I told you not to leave the house!"

"Damn you, Jesse, you're not my father!"

He uttered an oath beneath his breath, and she placed her hands upon his arms. She broke free of his touch, backing away from his tall, muscular form, a form that suddenly seemed threatening.

"If you'd stayed inside, you'd never have been exposed to all this!"

"But Jesse, so many people are down there! So many people I know are pumping lead and debris into a man's body!"

"And with any luck, they won't pump it into one another," Jesse said. He came toward her again. She couldn't back away any farther on top of the mountain cliff.

"Jesse—"

"You little fool!" he said heatedly. "You could have gotten hurt!"

"The whole town could have been hurt."

"Some people *were* hurt! The mayor was killed, gunned down unarmed."

"Jesse—"

He was really angry. But when he stopped before her again, his fingers gripping her upper arms and pulling her close, she couldn't think of another argument. He stared down into her eyes, and his were alive with cobalt fire. Her heart suddenly seemed to flutter like butterfly wings against her ribs, and a weakness seized hold of her knees. She was just as angry as he, she told herself, and that anger made her weak.

"Jesse—" she started, but his mouth touched hers, smothering her whisper. His touch was both fierce and coercive, a sweep of dazzling fire, stealing away both breath and reason. Her fingers curled on his chest, her lips parted, fascinated, to the pressure of his. The hot sultry fever of his kiss pervaded her, touched her mouth, and stole and curled through her body like slow-moving nectar—or lava. Her senses seemed so very much alive. Her flesh burned to the slightest brush of his hand. His body against hers was hard but like the fever inside her, so very hot, and pulsing, and alive. The closer she drew herself against him, the more she knew about the fever that threatened to consume them both. For even as she tasted the texture of his tongue, she felt the pressure of hips hard against hers, and the fever of that touch that should have been so forbidden to her did nothing but entice and seduce her into a longing for further discovery.

His lips parted from hers, touched them again, parted, and touched—sweet, open-mouthed, hotter, and hotter. Her mind began to reel. She shouldn't be here with him. She should be scandalized, horrified.

There was someone else in her life. . . .

Someone with whom things had never been like this.

Still, she had to draw away, she had to stop.

"Jesse . . ." His name was barely a whisper on the breeze, yet he heard it. He suddenly emitted a soft oath and drew away from her. To Kiernan's surprise, he nearly thrust her from him. He walked away, placing a booted foot high on a rock as he leaned upon an elbow to stare out at the valley below them.

Her mouth was still damp from his touch. She could still feel the touch. He seemed to be a knot of fury again.

"Damn you, Kiernan!" he swore, spinning around to stare at her. "If you would just do what you're told now and then!"

"Jesse, you've no right—"

"Your father isn't here, and your precious beloved Anthony isn't here either. Where the hell is he?"

She flushed, feeling her temper rise, and dizziness assailed her again. She should never, never allow Jesse to touch her. He was as volatile as a forest blaze, erupting in passion, erupting in anger.

"You know where Anthony is," she began as primly as possible.

"Never mind, never mind," he said suddenly. He strode back to her. "Just listen to me and stay the hell inside, away from the melee out there, will you? Look what you've done to us!"

"Me!"

"Kiernan—"

Her eyes narrowed, and she took a wild swing at him. He caught her wrist and their eyes met in a flame, and then he smiled slowly, ruefully.

"I'll take you back to Lacey's."

"I'd prefer to walk!"

"It's a very long walk."

"I'd prefer a very long walk."

He shook his head. "Sorry." Before she knew it, she was up in his arms and upon the big roan, Pegasus. And he was up behind her, his arms wrapping around her.

He nudged Pegasus, and the roan took them down the face of the mount.

Kiernan's temper waned with the warmth of his arms around her. By the time he had delivered her to the front of Lacey's house, she was aware only of a sense of desolation and loss. He dismounted from Pegasus to help her down, and she knew that he was leaving her. She should have been scandalized and horrified that he had kissed her so, touched her so, but she wasn't. It was simply what came between the two of them. There had been something just and sweet and right about it, and she refused to be ashamed of it.

"Stay in," he commanded her curtly.

She smiled, allowing her lashes to fall over her eyes. "Captain Cameron, I am my own keeper."

"Kiernan—"

"But I choose to stay in," she told him hastily. "Oh, Jesse, people are behaving so horribly!"

"Yes," he told her simply, "they are." He mounted Pegasus once again and looked down at her. "Things might get worse, and it's getting dark. So please . . ."

She curtsied to him regally, then turned and fled into the house.

The shattered glass had been swept up, but where the office door pane had been, there was a big hole. She decided to patch up the door with some canvas and spend the evening reassuring Lacey. She needed to stem her own feelings of guilt for having deserted her.

"Who's there?"

She heard the sharp call as she opened the door. "It's me, Lacey. I'm back."

"Oh, and just in time!" Lacey appeared in the doorway, holding a candle high against the darkening shadows of the night. "Thank heaven! I was getting so worried!"

"Everything's fine, Lacey. Well, not really fine. Let's go into the parlor, and I'll tell you about it."

Lacey nodded, her eyes wide, and preceded Kiernan into the parlor. Kiernan told her about the events in town, but she did so very carefully, softening the violence. Still, Lacey was horrified, and very nervous.

She insisted on serving Kiernan a cup of tea, then on making supper, so Kiernan went into the storage closet and found some canvas and a hammer and nails and set about doing a makeshift job of repairing the door.

The two women ate a quiet supper, all the while aware of the drama down the street.

"Didn't the captain say that he'd be back?" Lacey asked Kiernan anxiously.

"Well, he may make it. Then again, he may not."

"He should be looking after you," Lacey insisted.

Kiernan smiled ruefully. "No, Lacey, remember? Poor Anthony is supposed to be looking after me."

Lacey had the good grace to blush. "Never mind. Oh, I wish that this night would pass!"

"I don't think needlework will do it tonight," Kiernan murmured. In fact, nothing was going to ease the evening for her. She was torn between the horror of the sights she had seen, and the pulsing magic that returned to her lips when she thought of Jesse.

It had been a forbidden kiss, because of Anthony.

"How about some cards?"

"Hearts?" Kiernan said.

"Good heavens, no! Poker!" Lacey shocked her, and Kiernan burst into laughter. "Lacey! How very decadent. Wouldn't your husband be shocked?"

Lacey sniffed. "And what about your father, young lady? You know how to play."

"I grew up in my father's company," Kiernan reminded her, grinning broadly. "Get the cards and shuffle, Mrs. Donahue. You're on. We'll play for pennies."

"Done!" Lacey agreed.

Playing did help to pass the time. Something about the taboo aspect of the game for ladies made it exciting. It would always be a secret between them that they had passed the night so.

The hour grew late. Jesse didn't return.

Finally, Lacey yawned and admitted that she was exhausted. "But how will I sleep?" she demanded.

"Nothing is going to happen," Kiernan assured her.

But Lacey was still nervous, so Kiernan suggested that they put on their nightgowns and bunk in together. Lacey enjoyed that idea. "We'll sleep with Jesse's Mr. Colt right by our bedside," Kiernan said cheerfully.

"The bed in your room is nice and big. We should both be comfortable in it!" Lacey agreed. But when they were settled, she moaned again.

"I shall never be able to sleep!"

But to Kiernan's amusement, Lacey closed her eyes as peacefully as a babe soon after they crawled into bed. It was early still, Kiernan thought, and that was why she couldn't seem to close her own eyes. Or maybe she was frightened. She had come close to being kidnapped that morning, and she very well could have been one of those hostages still being held by John Brown.

John Brown must be desperate by now, she thought, with his few followers holed up in the firehouse. He must realize that his grand revolution wasn't coming. The countryside had not been stirred to great revolt.

The United States Army was coming for him, and in the morning, he would have to face the fire. Would he kill the hostages because of his despair?

Or could the bloodshed be kept down? Kiernan fervently hoped that it could.

She wondered what John Brown looked like, and she wondered if he could really rationalize murder into a crusade. But then she remembered *Uncle Tom's Cabin* and how furious she had been when she read the book.

Then again, she had to admit that some people were cruel and took much better care of their horses and their dogs than their slaves. She tossed about in bed. Then suddenly Lacey inhaled deeply with a shake, and exhaled with a long, low snore.

It was the end of trying to sleep.

She stood up and wandered over to the window. To her amazement, two men were standing below the window. They were both tall and dark in the shadows of the night. For a moment she held her breath.

One of them stepped forward and stooped low, plucking a pebble from the ground. He looked up and tossed it high toward the window. Just before she stepped back, Kiernan released her bent-up breath, smiling. The face that had turned upward toward hers was familiar.

Jesse was back.

The pebble landed with a little crack on the window. Kiernan stared down below.

Now both faces were upturned to hers. Jesse was with his brother Daniel, and both were dressed in the uniforms of the United States cavalry. Both were wearing their handsome plumed hats, and both were grinning broadly at her. They were very much alike. Like Jesse, Daniel had the ebony-dark hair and near cobalt-blue eyes that ran in the Cameron family. His features, too, were similar— handsome, well defined. His mouth was full and sensual. He was several years younger than Jesse, though, and his shoulders were not quite as broad. His manner was lighter—dramatically gallant. He was Kiernan's good friend, and she loved him, while Jesse . . . ah, Jesse!

"Sh!" She brought her finger to her lip and shook her head when she realized that Daniel had a pebble, too, and was about to throw it up to her.

She threw open the window and called down softly, "Stop the rocks!"

"Then come down and let us in!" Daniel called. "There's a nip in the air."

"It's downright cold," Jesse corrected, casting his brother a wry glance.

Kiernan looked quickly over to Lacey, who was still sleeping soundly.

Kiernan waved to the Cameron brothers—a wave that promised she'd be right down. Daniel grinned and gave her a thumbs-up sign. Jesse's easy smile curved into his lip.

Kiernan left the room behind, raced down the stairs to the back, and threw open the door.

Daniel was just on the other side of it. He swept her up high into his arms and swung her around as he came into the narrow hallway. "My Lord, Kiernan!" he teased, setting her down at last. "Every time I see you, you get prettier, more grown up, more sophisticated, more elegant. More—"

"Voluptuous?" Jesse suggested.

Kiernan quickly cast him a glance. As he leaned in the doorway, there was definite amusement in his suggestion. His eyes flickered over her, and his glance instantly warmed her.

His eyes could do things to her that actually seemed indecent.

Yes, he had always liked to tease her. This afternoon, though, he hadn't teased. He had gotten caught in his own fire, she realized, and that was why he had grown so very angry with her.

They both realized it, she knew, as their eyes met and held.

"Yes, voluptuous," Daniel said. He laughed. "Forgive us, Miss Mackay," he said, stepping back and sweeping off his hat to hold it to his heart. "We army men do have our failings. Days on the trail, and all that."

Kiernan tore her eyes from Jesse's at last. "Days on the trail, indeed! Jesse came straight from a bar in Washington. What about you?"

"I was at a party at a friend's house when a messenger came from Jeb Stuart." Stuart was a dashing young cavalry commander and a good friend of both Camerons. "He knew that Jesse had already been sent in, and that Jesse was concerned about you when he heard about the ruckus here."

"That's what I imagined," Kiernan said, looking from one to the other. "You're both going to be with the troops challenging John Brown in the morning? Christa will be worried sick." Christa was their sister, a year younger than Kiernan, the last of the immediate Cameron clan. Like Kiernan, she had trailed after Daniel as a child, and the three of them had always been very close.

And a bit in awe of Jesse, although Daniel denied it. Now the brothers were thick as thieves, and no brothers could offer each other greater loyalty or friendship.

"You wouldn't have some apple pie here somewhere, would you? And some hot coffee for a frozen soul?"

"We do happen to have apple pie," Kiernan admitted to Daniel. "And I'll make coffee. But don't try to side-step the situation, Daniel Cameron." She swirled around and headed for the kitchen, the brothers following behind her. They both took seats at the kitchen table and spread their long legs beneath it, as she started the coffee and placed the pie and plates and Lacey's embroidered napkins before them.

"What's going to happen in the morning?" she asked stubbornly.

"They'll ask John Brown to surrender," Jesse answered flatly.

"And if he doesn't?"

Jesse shrugged, cutting pieces of pie as she stood over him. "We'll storm the firehouse, I imagine."

"And there's no danger in that? The both of you? You've really no right to risk both your lives that way. I'm telling you—"

"And I told you not to leave the house today," Jesse interrupted suddenly, waving the pie spade before her nose.

"The whole town was out on the streets, Jesse," she told him.

"The whole town," Daniel laughed, "including Doc Whalen. He told me that you were out on the street, and he'd heard tell Jesse had already gotten his hands on you."

Kiernan quickly lowered her eyes. "Indeed, he had," she said sweetly.

"Whalen's suggestion, so I heard," Jesse murmured, "was that you should be trussed like a turkey over a shoulder and taken to a woodshed. I wasn't nearly as crude."

"You were barely short of it!" Kiernan responded quickly.

Jesse raised a brow to her, and she felt a hot flush rise over her body.

"Do I detect a note of tension here?" Daniel asked.

"No!" Jesse and Kiernan snapped simultaneously.

"Oh, excuse me!" Daniel said, and grinned.

"I wasn't at all crude," Jesse said.

Kiernan leaped up to see how the coffee was doing, but she suddenly felt a clamp of steel upon her arm.

"This time," he told her softly.

"This time?" She arched a brow. Storms were brewing between them, she could feel it. She felt tension hot and sweet on the air. She wanted to do battle with him. She wanted to argue and fight—

And touch him.

"Hey! The coffee is boiling over!" Daniel cried out. Jesse's eyes still burned into hers. He released her wrist slowly, and she tore her gaze from his at last and hurried to salvage the coffee.

Daniel started talking and he kept talking, eating his pie with relish.

Kiernan and Jesse drank their coffee, listened, and watched each other warily. Thankfully, Daniel didn't seem to need much help with the conversation.

Jesse stood up suddenly. "We've got to get back," he said.

Daniel nodded regretfully. "Yes." He stood up and pulled Kiernan to her feet and kissed her cheek then hugged her tightly again. "Tomorrow, Kiernan, please stay in until it's all over!" he begged her.

"She'll stay in," Jesse said with an edge. "I can guarantee it."

"Oh?" Kiernan said sweetly.

"Yes. Because I'll be around tomorrow. And I will see to it, even if I have to carry you around like a sack of potatoes."

"Sir, your gallantry is overwhelming!" Kiernan drawled.

"I call it as I see it," Jesse told her.

"I can't imagine your being so cavalier if my father were here!"

He arched a dark brow and grinned. "Kiernan, I would be the same no matter who was here, and you know it." He paused a second, his grin spreading. "Including the saintly Anthony!" He turned around, heading out. Daniel grinned and followed him. Kiernan hurried along the hall behind them to the rear door.

"Please take care!" she urged Daniel on the back porch. Their horses were tethered in back beneath a tree by the uphill trail, sheltered by the cliffs.

He paused. "I promise."

Jesse reached his horse and mounted smoothly. The roan trotted over to the steps, and he smiled down to her. "Am I to take care, too, Miss Mackay?"

"Of course, Jesse," she said coolly. "I'd be deeply grieved to see anything happen to you. For Christa's sake."

"Only for Christa's sake?"

"You *are* a good neighbor," she said sweetly.

He laughed and dipped low from the horse's back to find her hand.

He kissed it lightly. "How very sweet and honorable, Miss Mackay!" He freed her hand. "Now, please make sure that you keep your very sweet and honorable derriere indoors tomorrow!" he charged her firmly.

"Jesse, darlin', you do have the manners of an orangutan. Someone should take a horsewhip to you—sir!" she told him sweetly.

"I mean it, Kiernan."

"So do I."

"I'll find you if you're out, I swear."

"A promise, Jesse, or a warning?"

"A threat—and take it that way," he advised. Then he smiled and lifted his hand to his hat in salute.

The big roan swirled, and he was off into the night.

"Jesse, take care!" she whispered softly. It was far too late. He was gone, and he never heard her words.

Standing next to her in the moonlight, Daniel was still watching her. He shrugged, laughter in his eyes. "He has his way," he told her, offering no explanation and certainly no apology.

"Yes, he does. Oh, Daniel, do take care. Both of you."

"We will," Daniel promised her. He hugged her again, then leaped up onto his mount, as comfortable on horseback as his brother was. He lifted his hat and waved to her. "Scrape up a good dinner for us tomorrow night, eh?"

"I promise!" she called. "Daniel!"

"Yes?"

"See that you—that you and Jesse come to me as soon as you can!"

"I will."

He waved, and rode into the night after his brother.

Kiernan shivered fiercely, then hurried back inside. There was certainly no comfort in this night. She was suddenly very much alone. All the warmth had gone from the evening, and it was very chilly indeed.

And like Jesse, she was afraid.

Of love—and war.

Five

esse hadn't ridden more than a minute or two before Daniel was beside him, watching him and about to say something.

Because of the way that they had left Kiernan, he thought.

No, because of the way that *he* had left Kiernan.

It was probably a good thing that Daniel hadn't been around during the day,
Jesse reflected. He'd be fielding questions right and left if he had.

But now he was in for some brotherly concern no matter what, Jesse realized.

"You're awfully quiet, Jess," Daniel told him.

"Reckon so," Jesse murmured. He knew darned well that Daniel wasn't
going to leave an answer like that alone.

"Because of tomorrow and John Brown? Or because of Kiernan?"

Jesse cast him a quick glance and discovered that his brother's eyes were
dancing. Maybe Daniel had seen a lot more over the years than Jesse had imagined. Maybe there was more to see than he had even seen himself.

Who was he kidding? There had always been something about Kiernan. Even
as a child, she'd had the most extraordinary eyes, green eyes that defied and
challenged and laughed and dared.

By ten, she'd had a certain way of walking. Jesse remembered feeling darned
sorry for her father because she had become such a brazen little piece of Tidewater baggage so quickly. Kiernan was beautiful, and Kiernan could steal the heart
and soul and taunt the body. But she was also proud and stubborn, and no one
was ever going to sway her mind.

She could play and she could tease, but she did so only within the bounds of
propriety. Naturally, she liked attention. She could flirt with the best of them,
but she was certainly no sweet and naive creature—she had her opinions about
life and about her place within it, and she never minded voicing them.

He knew her so well, Jesse thought, because he'd watched her for years from
Cameron Hall. He'd watched with definite amusement when she was little.
She'd always had her way. She was sometimes gentle, sometimes kind, but always
proud, and always inquisitive about the world around her. She had been quick to
test her powers, and she had been very quick to realize that she was a woman in a
society where women were born to be revered. She was just as quick to understand her father's business, but she still loved to dance and to ride, casting aside
her cloak of innocent femininity when necessary, donning it again when it was
convenient. She was a little witch in her own way, Jesse thought. But she was all
woman, with a mind like a whip and a heart like steel.

Jesse had retained some of his amusement as he watched her grow older. But
at her coming-out party, she had been stunning, so stunning that she had taken
his breath away. And maybe that night he realized that he had always been
waiting for her.

Anthony Miller had seemed to be just perfect for her. He was the son of the perfect family—southern, aristocratic, rich. And he was more—he was the perfect gentleman. Anthony Miller was handsome and could be charming. He was quick to compliment her and quick to be at her side to fulfill her slightest whim.

Actually, Jesse had to admit, he liked Anthony Miller. There wasn't a thing wrong with Anthony Miller. At Montemarte he had mastered all the things a young man was supposed to master. He was cordial, proper, a loyal son to his father, a fine young man with a code of ethics and all the right ingredients of southern chivalry.

It was just that he wasn't right for Kiernan. Kiernan would run him ragged in a matter of months.

Jesse grinned, realizing that he considered himself to be the only man right for Kiernan. When he had watched her play with others, he had always thought that he was the right one for her. The one to love and understand her, the one to let her win upon occasion, yet the one who knew her ways enough to stand firm when she wanted or needed a steadying hand.

A certain tension gripped him. Until today, he had never known just how much he felt that way. Until he had touched her with the breeze stirring by them on the top of the cliff and he had felt the lightning and the longing that swept through them both, he had not known.

He had not known how hungrily he would crave her, how the desire would grow to be something unimaginable. Yes, he was the man to tame her, to seize the fire and the flame, and to watch it burn in beauty.

The right man for her . . .

Except that suddenly he wasn't right for her anymore. She believed passionately in causes, in her sense of loyalty, of right and wrong.

Maybe he was wrong himself about the things that the future might bring. Congress had been fighting and squabbling about many issues for years. South Carolina had wanted to secede once before, and old Andy Jackson had had to go down and assert that a union was a union.

But maybe Jesse wasn't wrong. Maybe the nightmare he felt brewing before them was destiny, and it really would be a storm that no man would be able to stop. Jesse couldn't condone the actions of a fanatic like John Brown, but it was hard not to listen to some of the things that the man had to say.

John Brown was going to die one way or the other. But things wouldn't end here in Harpers Ferry.

He couldn't say certain things to Kiernan. He could try to tell her that Anthony wasn't right for her—he wasn't hard enough, he wasn't strong enough, dammit, he just wasn't passionate enough. But Jesse himself had nothing to offer her, nothing that she would want.

Anthony, too, was caught up in her spell, Jesse thought. Few men could be immune to her. Her sweet backside should be met with a hickory stick for what she was doing to Anthony Miller. She didn't love Anthony, Jesse was convinced of it. But Anthony was everything that she *should* want—the perfect southern gentleman again—and she was definitely entertaining herself with him.

Waiting, Jesse thought wryly with humor. There were times back home when he was convinced that she watched him just as he watched her. There were times when he was convinced that they had been made to be together, bred to be together. And maybe it was something even deeper than that. He felt it when he touched her, he tasted it when he kissed her. Something sweet and electric and so volatile that it had to be older than time itself.

He caught himself in his thinking and unconsciously he squared his shoulders and straightened on his horse. He was wrong, dead wrong, to be thinking about Kiernan so. The world was revolving differently these days. His world was moving on an uneven axis, a very precarious axis. He was very much afraid that the world he knew and loved was coming to an end. He wasn't sure where he stood, but he was becoming more and more aware that he was going to have to choose sides soon. He would have to choose by his conscience. A number of the people he loved dearly would hate him for making that choice. He would have to learn to live with their hatred.

But a man couldn't betray himself, then learn to live with his own betrayed heart and mind and soul. It couldn't be done.

Kiernan might be the one to hate him the most fiercely when he made up his mind. There would be no areas of gray for Kiernan.

Then again, it could all unfold differently from what he was imagining, he told himself. Maybe South Carolina would not vote to secede. Maybe none of the other southern states would want to go with her. Hell, Virginia had provided four of the first five presidents of the United States. Maybe Virginia would not pull out of the Union. A number of the state's western counties had no wish whatsoever to pull out.

"Well?" Daniel said.

"Well, what?"

"What's bothering you? The situation or the girl?"

"Both," Jesse said briefly.

Daniel was silent for a moment, then said lightly, "Seems to me like there's been something brewing between the two of you for a long, long time. Seems to me like—"

"Seems to me like it isn't your business, brother," Jesse cautioned him lightly.

But Daniel laughed. "I've known you both all my life. You're my blood and she's a whole lot of my spirit, so I reckon I've a right to my say."

"You reckon so," Jesse said dryly.

Daniel grinned. "Do something!" he told Jesse. "Marry her, before she does decide to marry Anthony Miller."

Jesse sighed with exasperation. "I can't marry her."

"Why the hell not?"

"She wouldn't be happy."

"Oh? And she's going to be happy with Anthony Miller? Well, hell, all right, if you say so."

"She shouldn't marry Miller. She doesn't love him," Jesse said flatly.

"Lots of people marry people they don't love," Daniel commented. "And some of them do damned well. Just like Kiernan might. She and Miller have everything in common to make it right. They've the same background, the same loyalties. But then, so do the two of you."

"Yeah," Jesse murmured, "so do the two of us." But conviction was missing from his voice. He didn't know how to explain what he was feeling to Daniel, because they, too, came from the same background. They should have shared loyalties. He turned to his brother, determined to say as much as he could. "Daniel, there's going to be a war."

"It's not going to be a war, Jesse. It will be a skirmish at best. After today, old John Brown can't be in very good shape. He's had men killed, and he's had men wounded. It won't be much of a battle. If he doesn't surrender, it'll be over in a matter of minutes."

Yes, old John Brown did have men sick and wounded. He'd seen young Oliver Brown, and he couldn't forget his father's words to him. *Die like a man.* He saw the light, all right. Old John Brown saw the light.

"Brown's frightening," Jesse said out loud. "He's just about the most frightening man I've ever met in my life."

"Damn, Jesse, that man did get to you!" Daniel was silent for a moment, watching him. "Hell, Jesse, you can't think that the old fanatic should get away with this."

Jesse shook his head vehemently. "No, I don't. As far as I'm concerned, he committed murder in Kansas, and he committed murder here. Hell, I'm no judge or jury, but it sure does look like what he did here was treason as well." He thought of the young followers of Brown who had suddenly seemed to realize that what they were doing could be construed as treason. "Daniel, I just don't know how to describe it. There's a light in his eyes. He knows he's going to die, and he knew his son was going to die. But it's like he's on a holy mission."

"He's a fanatic, and he should hang."

"I'd be the first to say that he should," Jesse agreed, and exhaled slowly. "But you should meet that old man, Daniel. He's frightening, I swear it."

"I've never seen you afraid of anything, Jess," Daniel commented.

Jesse grinned. "Then you didn't always see real good, brother. Every living man has been afraid at some time in his life. I'm not afraid of going up against a man in battle, and I don't even think I'm afraid of dying. But I've been afraid."

"Of what?"

"Of things that I can't touch, things out of my reach, things I can't even understand. Things that I can't get my hands on, and things that I can't stop from happening."

Daniel stared at him. For a long moment, Jesse thought his brother was going to make a joke. But then, as Daniel's eyes met his, he realized that his brother knew exactly what he was talking about.

"Only time will tell, Jesse. Only time will tell."

"Yeah, I guess so." They were alike in so many ways. Back at Cameron Hall, they'd grown up with the same rights and wrongs drilled into them. They both had a sound sense of ethics and loyalty and honor. And both of them would follow it.

But the paths that they followed might be completely different.

"We're blood, Jesse, no matter what."

Daniel had reined in and now extended his hand across the chasm between them. Jesse took his brother's hand. "Blood, Daniel. No matter what."

"It's a pact."

"It's a pact."

They held hands in the road, their eyes meeting, their grips firm. Then Daniel grinned. They hadn't come to an impasse yet. "Jesse, you're awfully damned grim tonight."

"It was a grim day." He thought about Kiernan, and his voice softened. "Most of it."

"Do you know what you need? A drink!" Daniel announced, convinced.

Jesse grinned slowly. "Well, what the hell. You must be right. What I need is a drink."

"And since we're still both officially on leave, it seems like a right good thing to do with the rest of the evening," Daniel told him. He kicked his horse to quicken his pace.

It was a peculiar set of circumstances that had brought them both to Harpers Ferry, just as it was a peculiar set of circumstances that had brought their West Point commander, Brevet Lieutenant Colonel Robert E. Lee, and their old West Point and army friend, Lieutenant Jeb Stuart, in on a situation that was being manned by U.S. marines. When word of the raid had reached Washington, all that President Buchanan had on hand had been this navy unit under Israel Green. Green had immediately headed out from Washington with his troops.

Jeb had been visiting relatives in north Virginia when he was summoned to the war department. Jeb had invented a new way to attach a saber to a belt. He was interested in selling his patent, and the government was interested in buying it. He'd been waiting when all of a sudden things had started to happen. He was sent out to Arlington House to bring back Lee.

Jesse had already been sent the night before. The old general, Winfield Scott, had heard something about the goings-on, and while things had still been rumor at that time—and Brown had only identified himself with the alias of "Smith"— the old war horse had known that real trouble was afoot. Daniel, on the other hand, had been with Jeb. Stuart had volunteered to come with Lee as an aide, and Daniel had volunteered to come with Stuart as an aide.

Now, the two brothers rode to the Wager Hotel for their drink. Since neither of them was officially attached to the troops, they were at their liberty to choose their own accommodations, and they chose the hotel. They were due to meet up with Lee and Jeb by six the next morning.

When they reached the Wager, the situation was being boisterously discussed in the hotel's barroom. "Let's have that drink upstairs, shall we?" Jesse demanded of his brother.

"Sounds like a good place to me."

They left their horses to be stabled, and Jesse retired straight to their room. Daniel bought a bottle of good Kentucky bourbon and brought it up. They shared a drink while Daniel brought Jesse up to date on what was happening at Cameron Hall.

The Tidewater plantation home itself was actually Jesse's, since he was the oldest son. But the family's land holdings were vast, and there were a number of other fine structures built on the Cameron land, so they shared the responsibility for it. It was unspoken but understood to their family of three—Jesse, Daniel, and Christa—that whenever one of them married, he or she was welcome to make their home on the family estate.

In fact, Jesse thought, Daniel knew the land a lot better than he himself did. Daniel was closer to it. Jesse loved Cameron Hall, and he loved his family history. But he wondered if he loved it as much as Daniel did.

And then again, he wondered if he could ever give it up. No one had asked him to, not yet.

After a while, he and Daniel fell silent. It was a comfortable silence. Then Daniel yawned.

"I still don't get it, Jess."

"What don't you get?"

"You and Kiernan. Why don't you just sweep her up on that steed of yours and carry her away?"

He'd done that, Jesse mused, he'd done that very thing just that afternoon. He could have ridden on forever with her. He could have kissed her, and he could have let the kiss become more. If he ever kissed her again, he thought, it *would* become more. He wasn't Anthony Miller, he wasn't the gentleman he should be, and he was suddenly certain that none of the standard rules could come into play between Kiernan and himself.

"I want her to make a choice," Jesse said.

Daniel snorted. "Between you and Anthony Miller?"

"There's nothing wrong with Anthony Miller," Jesse heard himself saying. He almost grinned in the pale moonlight that settled over the room.

"I like Anthony just fine," Daniel said. "But I repeat—what's the choice?"

Jesse grinned broadly. He took a long swig on the bourbon and handed the bottle back to Daniel. "Thanks, brother." He inhaled deeply. "Hell, there may be lots of choices soon. Let's get some sleep. Morning's going to come soon enough."

Morning did come soon enough.

By seven-thirty, the storming troops lined up in position in front of the firehouse. Lee, following both diplomacy and procedure, offered the militia units first crack at storming John Brown's position. The militia commanders declined. Too many of the militia were family men. Federal troops were paid to risk their lives.

The marine commander, Israel Green, told Lee with ceremony and honor that his marines would be proud to enter the fray. John Brown was to be offered one last chance to surrender. Jeb Stuart brought Lee's terms to Brown.

Jesse accompanied Jeb Stuart when he brought the terms to Brown. Jeb read Lee's order, which first identified Lee and his command under President Buchanan of the United States. Then it demanded the release of the hostages and went on to advise Brown that he couldn't possibly escape. If he would surrender himself and restore the armory property, Colonel Lee would keep them safe until he was given further orders from the president. If Brown did not surrender, Lee could not vouch for his safety.

Old John Brown opened the firehouse door a four-inch crack. He told Jeb that he wanted his freedom to take his followers back across the river to Maryland.

There was an uproar from the hostages inside. "Have Lee amend his terms!" someone cried out.

Then there was another call from the prisoners. "Never mind us! Fire!"

Jesse grinned. He recognized the voice—it was Colonel Lewis Washington. The spirit of revolution did live on, Jesse thought.

Jesse couldn't hear what happened next, but Stuart and Brown spoke for some time. Then Brown shouted out, "Lieutenant, I see we can't agree. You have the numbers on me, but you know we soldiers aren't afraid of death. I would as lief die by a bullet as on the gallows."

"Is that your final answer, Captain?" Jeb demanded.

There was a silence for just a moment. The sun was rising, beautiful in the morning sky. Jesse could hear the chirps and cries of birds.

He glanced around. His old West Point teacher, the gentlemanly and indomitable Robert Lee, stood at some distance by a pillar of one of the buildings.

He wasn't armed. He looked upon the situation as one of little consequence, one that the marines would handle quickly and efficiently.

That was all it was, Jesse told himself. Lee was right. Why did Jesse himself insist on making more of it?

"Yes," Brown announced flatly.

Stuart stood back and waved his hat. It was the signal to Israel Green to bring in his troops, with bayonets only to reduce the risk of injuring the hostages.

The marines began to pound on the heavy doors with sledgehammers. The wood shuddered and groaned and splintered, but did not give. A halt was called, and a battering ram was formed. A ragged hole was dug into the doors, and the men burst through. Jesse followed.

It was over quickly. The marines stepped in with their silver bayonets flashing. After Colonel Washington greeted them all and identified Brown, Green struck Brown, who fell.

The raiders swept the firehouse with gunfire. A marine clutched his stomach near the doorway and fell. Smoke began to fill the firehouse. A few more marines rushed the place, and one of the raiders was instantly killed. Another, wounded, was dragged outside.

Colonel Washington pulled on his gloves before leaving the firehouse. Jesse was behind him, helping one of the hostages out, when Washington was greeted by a friend. "Lewis, old fellow, how do you feel?"

"Hungry as a hound and dry as a powder horn!" Jesse heard the disheveled Washington say, and he grinned again, touched by the man's spirit and pride.

That's it, he thought to himself, that is the grandeur we've created here in Virginia. We have bred such men!

It was, he realized, part of what he was afraid of losing.

More went on, but Jesse could no longer heed any man who was walking and well. His duty was first to the civilians and then to the marines—and then to the raiders.

Jesse learned later from Jeb Stuart that John Brown had been taken to a room at the Wager. Assembled to question him were Lee, Stuart, Senator Mason, Virginia's governor Henry Wise, an Ohio congressman, Colonel Washington, and Congressman Faulkner of Virginia.

They quizzed him for hours, Jeb said. John Brown wouldn't incriminate others, but he was damned forthright about himself and his determination. He said that he had only meant to free the slaves, that he'd meant no harm to others. When he was reminded that innocents had died, he had assured them that no man or woman of any innocent nature had been harmed to his knowledge. Jeb admitted that Brown was an extraordinary man. A fanatic, a doomed man, but also much more.

While Brown was being quizzed, Jesse did what he could for the wounded. Another of John Brown's sons, a boy named Watson, lay dying during the long afternoon. There was nothing that any man could do, but Watson, too, was grilled endlessly for his part in the affair.

A boy named Anderson lay on the grass, waiting to die. As the boy continued to breathe, a man walked by him and callously remarked that it was taking him a long time to die. But eventually, his death silenced the voices of his tormenters.

At last a pit was dug, and the dead were buried, except for Anderson's body. He was claimed by doctors from Winchester. Jesse gritted his teeth when he learned that the boy had been stuffed headfirst into a barrel, then rammed and packed down so hard that blood and bone and sinew all seemed to crack alike.

It wasn't so bad that the body of a boy who hadn't understood that he was involved in treason was going to medical science. It just seemed horrible that any human being could be so abused, so stripped of his dignity in death.

For Jesse, it was the final straw. He'd done what he could do. He'd seen to the wounded, he'd stormed in with the troopers, and he'd tended the wounded again.

He didn't want to see any more at Harpers Ferry. A place that had always been beautiful and peaceful to him would never be the same again. Something about the misuse of Anderson's body had been the final straw. When they had rolled that barrel away and he had come too late to do a damned thing about it, something inside of him had seemed to snap. A tempest raged in him like something he hadn't begun to imagine.

He mounted his horse. He probably should have looked for Daniel, but he didn't know where his brother was. He was angry, but had no outlet to vent the anger.

And he felt curiously as if he had been hurt, and he didn't know why he felt that way.

All in all, he was like a tempest brewing.

It was the best time in the world for him to stay away, far away, from Kiernan.

But he didn't. He discovered himself riding for Lacey's house.

Kiernan hadn't expected to see Jesse that early in the day. She had ventured out that afternoon when she had heard that it was all over, that the firehouse had been stormed, that John Brown was now a captive. But she hadn't gone far. She'd seen what people had done to the wounded and slain raiders the day before. Although she was appalled and horrified by the innocent lives that had been lost at Harpers Ferry because of the raiders, she couldn't help being disturbed by some of the things done to them in retaliation.

She was a Virginia lady, she had told herself, gazing at her reflection in the glass that morning. She was delicate and protected and tender, and she wasn't supposed to be exposed to anything evil.

But she knew that she was anything but delicate, and she had never allowed herself to be overprotected. What had happened was simply horrible, and she didn't want to see more.

She was sitting in the parlor, reading a newspaper from a nearby Maryland press, when she heard a tumultuous pounding on the rear door. She started, alert and wary for a moment. The attempt to kidnap her and take her hostage remained with her, and she wasn't immune to a sense of unease if anything resembling danger threatened.

But kidnappers did not knock at a door, certainly not so violently. Lacey had ventured out, when all was well, to hear the latest on what was happening at the hotel.

Kiernan rose and hurried to the door, throwing it open quickly since the pounding threatened to tear it from its hinges.

Jesse stood before her. His plumed hat was pulled at a rakish angle over his forehead. He was in uniform, a shoulder-skirted regulation cape around his shoulders.

"Jesse!" she murmured, and stepped back. She could barely see his eyes, shadowed as they were by the brim of his hat. She sensed a deep tension about him, an energy even greater than that which he usually exuded. "I wasn't expecting you or Daniel yet. I've nothing ready. Oh, but come in—I'm so sorry! I didn't mean to be rude. I'm sure there's something to drink, and—"

He moved through the doorway, his presence powerful. He swept his plumed hat from his head, and she saw his eyes at last. They were dark and seemed filled with a whirlwind emotion.

"I don't need anything to drink," he told her.

"Then—"

"Ride with me," he said briefly.

Kiernan stared at him. He was in a dangerous mood, she sensed. She shook her head uncertainly. "Jesse, Lacey isn't here. She's gone down—"

"Leave her a note," he commanded.

She should have told him right where to go for so commanding her. No lady would ever do such a thing, but she had never pretended to be the perfect lady around Jesse.

"Jesse, I should tell you to go straight to hell!" she whispered softly to him.

He set a hand against the doorframe and moved closer against her. His face was just inches away. "But you're not going to, are you?"

Despite his arrogance, there was something almost desperate about his words.

For the first time, she realized, Jesse needed her, really needed her, as an adult.

As a woman.

She lifted her chin. "I'll come with you, Jesse," she said. "This time."

He didn't smile, didn't even seem to note her taunt. He took it fully for granted that she would come with him. But she realized that, equally, she needed to be with him.

"I'll be right with you," she murmured. In the kitchen she wrote Lacey a note, saying only that she was with Jesse. She ran up to her room for a cape and hurried back down.

Jesse was still by the rear door, pacing the small area of the rear entry like a caged lion. Kiernan felt a fierce shiver seize hold of her. He ceased moving at last, not realizing that she had returned, and stared out into the small rear yard at the golds and grays of the autumn afternoon. A lowering sun cast its gentle rays upon the rock and shale of the mountain cliffs. He stared, she thought, but he didn't see.

"Jesse," she said softly.

His dark blue gaze shot quickly to her. He opened the door for her, and his eyes followed her as she left the house. He didn't speak.

His sleek roan stood waiting in the yard. Jesse lifted her up onto the horse, then mounted behind her with smooth agility. She thought that in his present mood they would race again, but he walked the horse from the yard, then reined in.

"What is it, Jesse?" she asked him.

"I don't know where to go," he admitted, an edge of raw frustration to his voice.

Kiernan should remain silent, she knew, absolutely silent. Jesse's present state of mind couldn't be good for either of them.

But something of his wild, reckless, and even tormented mood was entering into her heart and, like the dark winds of a storm, into her soul and body. "Head west along the river," she told him.

They passed quietly out of town and headed down the pike that lined the water. They passed the old mill and kept riding until they were several miles out of town. They could hear the rush of the white water passing over the rapids, but they couldn't see it through the abundance of foliage and trees growing on the strip of land between the road and the river.

"Turn here," Kiernan advised him.

Jesse might have missed the narrow, overgrown trail heading toward the water if Kiernan hadn't pointed it out. But he didn't question her wisdom in taking it. He knew they were near Montemarte, the Millers' estate.

A small wooden fishing shack sat almost on the water with a dock that stretched out over the rocks. In the dim twilight, the shack was almost invisible.

Kiernan felt Jesse hesitate, felt a greater heat building inside him. "Anthony's?" he inquired dryly.

"His father's," she replied flatly. He'd come to her for a place to go, and she had been generous enough to offer this quiet haven.

He nudged the horse forward. At the shack he dismounted and reached up to her. She slipped down into his arms, but he released her quickly and walked down to the water by the shack. The water was low. He set one shiny black boot upon a rock and stared out at the ever-moving water.

Kiernan ignored him and hurried into the shack. There wasn't much there. It was rebuilt every summer after the waters of the river rose and receded. There was a fireplace and a pot for making coffee and a skillet for frying whatever fish might be caught. There was a rough-hewn table and four chairs, and one sleigh bed shoved into the far corner of the room. There was a ledge with a handy supply of whiskey and tobacco and a few glasses.

She and Anthony had last been there, Kiernan thought, at the end of summer, not long ago. In a pleasant twilight, the other men had debated politics, but Anthony had dropped out to teach her the proper way to fish.

It had been nice. Not exciting, just a pleasant twilight to while away . . .

She dragged a chair over to stand upon to reach up for the whiskey. Jesse might well want a drink once he came into the shack.

But as she stood upon the chair, the door burst open.

Jesse stood in the doorway. The dying orange glow of the afternoon framed him with his low-brimmed plumed hat and his shoulder-skirted navy cape.

In the coming twilight, with the hectic rush of the water tearing over the rapids behind him, she felt his recklessness, his energy, his tempest, more certainly than she had ever felt it before.

She stopped reaching for the glasses and rubbed her palms over her skirt, watching him, sensing the passion and heat and need within him. Her mouth was dry. Her heart pounded. Her blood seemed to race through her system as swiftly and wildly as the water rushed over and around the ancient rocks.

Jesse didn't want a drink, she realized.

Jesse wanted her.

Six

Suddenly, he slammed the door shut behind him and advanced upon her, his long strides bringing him to stand before the chair. She was silent, staring down into the cobalt depths of his eyes.

She'd thought that he'd have so much to say, that he would speak and she would listen, that she would soothe the anguish that swept his soul. She'd thought there would be many words to share.

But there were no words. He reached out to her, wrapping his arms around her. The tempest and the passion and the heat in his arms were so great that she instinctively wound her own arms around him, and for a long moment, his head lay against her breast. Indeed, she thought, she soothed him.

But his was a wildness that did not seek to be soothed.

His hands wound around her waist, and he lifted her from the chair. She slid slowly, evocatively, against the length of his body. She felt again all the things that she had felt in that previous touch.

Felt his body, the hot corded tension. Felt the deep power of his chest, the hardness of his thighs. Felt the taut demand of his hips and the unyielding strength of that which lay within his loins.

His lips touched hers hungrily. He did not seek to slowly seduce—there was nothing leisurely about his kiss. His lips took and consumed hers, ravaged them. He did not seek a subtle entry to her mouth. Instead, his tongue plunged between her lips and teeth and demanded the sweetness of her mouth.

His arms held her with magic, with fire and fervor and tempest, with something that entered deep into her body and demanded a response.

He broke away and stared down at her in the shadows cast by the dying sun. For a long, long moment she didn't move. They stared at each other, caught up in the heedless, swirling excitement that hurtled and slammed between them. Feelings raced through Kiernan, hungers and yearnings, and dark forbidden things.

She had imagined them before. She'd tasted hints of aching and wonder in his arms before.

He began to kiss her again.

She closed her eyes and swept her arms around his neck. She met his kiss as a new-found thirst and desire brought a trembling to her lips.

She was learning swiftly what to do with those lips.

An innate sensuality blossomed and grew within her, there in the wooden shack, in the late afternoon of a day that had been beset by blood as dark as the crimson of the dying sun.

Their lips met again and again, open-mouthed, in hungry, wet kisses, kisses that melded their lips and their bodies, that brought the searing heat from that sweet touch to burn deep into the heart of unleashed desire.

Kiernan knew what she was doing all the while. She knew before his lips trailed from hers to touch her earlobes and her cheeks, to slide provocatively along the narrow column of her throat, to rest against her pulse and travel onward along the length of her collarbone.

The touch of his fingers upon her shoulder sent her cape falling to the floor. And his lips fell against the naked flesh of her throat once again.

The things he did with his tongue . . .

She felt that she was falling, that his touch had already entered into her body. She trembled as her senses reeled. The warmth was so sweet, entering, like nectar that caressed her inside and out. She concentrated so on the wonder of the sensation that she barely realized that Jesse had found the tiny hooks and buttons at the back of her gingham day gown, and that she was slowly losing it as he slipped it downward to her waist.

His fingers lifted the delicate strap of her chemise, and his mouth pressed against the spot where it had been. That same wet warmth was placed over the fine silk where it molded the very tip of her breast. He caressed and nurtured the flesh beneath the fabric, wet against the hardening bud of her nipple.

Like lightning it moved, the searing ecstasy of the sensation. It touched her breast, and like his kiss, it touched so much more. It spread like the summer rays of the sun, spiraling down to her stomach and beyond, entering low into intimate places between her thighs—shocking places.

"Oh, Jesse!"

She whispered his name at last—not with protest but with wonder. She discovered herself swept up into his arms, held tight against the rough fabric of his cavalry cape. As he carried her to the bed, she didn't care.

She didn't care about the dust that had settled upon the woolen blanket and down mattress. The room was surely cold, but she felt no chill. None of it mattered. She had mused and pondered and imagined, as any young woman might, this first time with flowery, chivalrous phrases, with soft candlelight and the scent of roses on the air.

But none of that mattered, none of it at all.

It didn't even matter that no words of God's blessing had made them man and wife.

She was with Jesse, and she trusted him as much as she desired him. Perhaps therein lay the beauty of this tryst in the cold and rugged cabin in the woods.

When he saw the dust, he set her upon her feet, swept his cape from his shoulders, and laid the garment with the soft lining upward upon the sleigh bed. Then he turned back to her, and again he paused, and she realized that he was trembling too.

He lifted a ringlet of her hair from her shoulders, and she saw the slight movement in his fingers. He buried his face against it, then she was in his arms once more, tasting his kiss, tasting all the sweet and mysterious and haunting things that it promised.

He found more hooks, and she felt her gown whisper down to her feet, leaving her in the bone of her corset, her delicate chemise, her petticoat, and her pantalets.

He was an experienced lover, she thought. Despite his haste and fire, he was at ease with the complexity of her clothing. He could kiss and tease and tantalize, his lips never leaving her flesh. Her petticoat crumpled to her feet. The softness of her chemise was stripped away, the material rustling over her naked flesh, as sensual as his touch. Still his mouth and the moist searing heat of it kept her in wonder as he cast aside the restriction of her stays, tossing the bone far from them.

Her shoulders and breasts were naked to his gaze.

He paused briefly to just stare at her. In the twilight, his eyes reflected flames, flames that smoldered and elicited both desire and shyness, a need to be known, and a need to hide. But before she could react fully to the fires that blazed in his eyes, she was within his arms again.

There were words at last, words that touched her flesh in hot whispers. They told her that she was beautiful. Words of poetry—

And words of raw hunger.

She found herself swept up again and laid both fiercely and tenderly upon the satin lining of his cape. He lay quickly down beside her. The brush of his fingers and the warmth of his tongue raged over the mounds of her breasts, explored contours and creamy skin, and set fire to the pebblelike peaks of rouge and crimson that tautened instantly at his touch.

She had thought before that his kiss could enter deeply into her. Now it seared a trail so hot that it denied her all thought. All she knew was longing. She arched against the palm of his hand as he pulled the tie to her pantalets. A flush —soft pink in the twilight of the shack—flooded her cheeks. But she felt the husky tenor of his delighted laughter, and when his lips found hers again, his whispers eased her from embarrassment.

He had wanted her so very long. He had waited, and he had known, he had always known, just as he had known the summer gales that swept the Tidewater, that one day they would come to this.

Her pantalets were shed, her shoes were tossed aside.

And her stockings were removed more erotically than she had ever imagined clothing could leave the human body. The stroke of his fingers, feather-light against her thighs, moved upwards toward that center of flame.

His shoulders were broad and bronzed in the light, his chest dusted with a heavy spattering of dark hair. He was well muscled but whipcord lean, so taut in the belly, lean in the hips . . .

And passionate within the dark nest of his loins.

She saw him completely for only seconds because he crawled over her and straddled her hips. She gasped as his sex touched her, as hard as steel but as hot as fire against her flesh. With almost the curl of a smile to his lips, his face was still very tense. He stared at her again. She felt shuddering within him and knew that no matter how badly he wanted her, he would pull back now if she wished it.

The sun suddenly fell farther. Red light flooded into the shack, washing away the shadows. His flesh was toned red, and when she lifted her own hand, she saw that it too was caught in that glowing reflection.

Like a reflection of blood.

She started to shiver, suddenly very afraid. But she wasn't afraid of Jesse. She wanted to hold him tighter than ever.

"Jesse," she whispered.

"It isn't right," he told her. "I shouldn't have you here. I shouldn't have swept you away, I should never have touched you. Your father would have a right to take a rifle to my heart this very moment."

She blinked away the illusion of the red light. The shivering stopped. Her soul was on fire, her body was on fire. She wanted to touch his flesh, to run her fingers over the muscled breadth of his shoulders, to test the tight ripples in his belly, to press her lips against his chest. Most of all, she wanted to appease the longing inside her. She wanted the emptiness to be filled.

She reached out and touched his cheek. She spoke a truth that she never thought she would utter.

"I love you, Jesse."

A soft oath escaped him, and she was swept back into his arms. She felt the fervor of his kiss, and the heat and fire began to build and spread anew within her. Hungrily he feasted upon her breasts.

And hungrily she tasted him in turn, twisting, turning, to press her lips to his shoulders, his throat, and softly, wetly, drew patterns down the rippling muscles of his chest.

He shifted upon her suddenly. The thrust of his knee parted her thighs, and the weight of his body spread her further. She felt the erotic touch of his hands again. His fingers caressing, exploring, ever more boldly. She felt him touch her intimately in the very place where she seemed to feel the spiraling heat most deeply.

A cry tore from her lips and she surged against him. And still he touched her, more deeply, more intimately.

Tantalizing . . .

He had created a tempest within her, and she rocked and undulated against his touch. A spark glowed deeply inside her, and each sweet stroke of his sent the fire burning more and more brightly.

Again he shifted, and it seemed that all of his body parted her. Incredibly, impossibly, he demanded more from her, and he gave more to her. His kisses lingered upon the softness of her upper thighs.

She must protest, she knew that she must—just as she knew that her cheeks were flooded with color. She tried to whisper his name, but the word wouldn't come.

She couldn't protest. The feelings were too exquisite, the longings too intense.

Then he took his boldness a step further, and she felt the searing moist heat of his kiss, of his tongue, against the most intimate of virgin flesh. Nothing, not the wind, not the fire, not the ice of winter, could ever cause such sensation. She gasped and sought to rise, but his fingers curled around hers.

The ecstasy was so sweet that it was anguish. She could bear no more of it. She was faint, she was dizzy, she was trembling, and she knew that she must reach some promised explosion or perish soon for the longing and the soaring.

It was then that he took her, when she needed him so desperately. The pain came swift and staggering. She cried out with it, stunned, her fingers tightening upon his flesh.

But so quickly it was gone!

She had been empty, and now she was filled. His kisses held her while the thrust of his body entered within her, deep, deeper. A velvet blade cut her in two, brought agony, a certainty that she could never bear the intrusion.

But his kiss, his touch, his slow, shattering movement—all these brought her feelings and senses reeling into play again. The agony receded, and the sweetly soaring ecstasy came to the fore once again.

He moved so slowly, thrusting against her until she cried out, then rose again. Then once more he moved, slowly, achingly slowly . . .

Until she discovered that she was rising against him. Until the need within her was so rich and so great that she could not bear his absence. Oh, how it grew, this need! And still he took care, planting kisses upon her breasts as he moved. She arched against him, thrust and writhed against him.

Suddenly his arms wrapped tightly around her, and she knew that Jesse would wait no more. She arched against him, and he willingly availed her of her longing, bearing down upon her deep and hard and fast, creating a rhythm that flew with a pulsing beat. She lost all sense of what was around her. She heard the water beating over the rock, and the sound swept into her. She hungered, she wanted, she ached. She needed all that she received, but she reached, and she did not know why she reached. The sweetness, the ecstasy filled her until she thought that she must die with it, that she must explode, and still he moved. . . .

Then it seemed that she *did* die, and that her senses *did* explode. Shattering light burst all around her, the rays fell from the sun, a thousand stars seemed to burst and shimmer down upon her all in one. She could not move, for the stars disappeared and the world went briefly black, and when she could see again, the stars were still cascading down upon her. Warmth radiated through her body and to her limbs, sweet nectar filled with warmth. Her body was racked with shudders.

And then she felt Jesse. He went deadly taut above her, muscles bunching and constricting, and he moved against her once again, thrusting so very deeply.

A sweet warmth burst from within him, showering into her. To her amazement, it brought a new flow of ripples within her own body, tantalizing, wonderful little aftershocks of splendor.

His weight rested briefly upon her until he rolled to his side. His arms curled around her, and he brought her with him. She leaned her cheek against the sweat-sleek flesh of his chest, and her lashes closed over her eyes. She had never felt such exhaustion.

She had never known such wonder.

Jesse was silent, stroking her hair. She herself couldn't speak because she couldn't think what to say. It had been one thing to share such absolute intimacy in the heat of the moment, but now, in memory, much of it made her blush. And now, as the cold night air settled over her and darkness began to replace the multitude of colors of the sunset, she realized that she should not have done this. Her father would be horrified; indeed, any man or woman within her world would be horrified.

She'd never really even kissed Anthony.

And Anthony would have never even thought of making love to her like this. It would not be proper. If she married Anthony, they would probably go through years together with neither of them ever knowing the other as intimately as she now knew Jesse.

And yet doing this couldn't be wrong. She loved Jesse. She had told him so. He had given her every opportunity to stop what had happened between them.

She shivered from the briskness of the air. "Cold?" Jesse asked her.

"Very," she whispered.

He pulled her close and kissed her forehead, then balanced his weight to roll over her and leap lightly to the floor. Naked and comfortable in his nakedness, he walked over to the fire and knelt low. "There's kindling," he murmured. He strode back to his pants for his striker, and within a few minutes he had a warm fire going. Kiernan had not waited for that warmth to draw his navy cavalry cape around herself. She wasn't sure if she was ashamed of her own behavior or not, but she simply couldn't be as comfortable in front of Jesse as he was in front of her. When he returned, she was sitting up and watching him somewhat nervously.

He smiled. His dark hair was totally disheveled and fell in an ebony lock over his forehead. He seemed younger than the man who had carried her here in such a tempest. His smile was crooked and wicked, yet broad and filled with both humor and tenderness.

"I saw you reaching for the liquor when we came in. Need a drink now?"

"Yes," she said. "No—I mean, I don't need a drink. I really shouldn't be drinking whiskey. Ladies don't . . ." She paused and her voice trailed away, and then she looked up at Jesse. "Oh, Jesse, ladies don't ever do what I did here today, do they? Ever."

He found a glass and wiped the rim carefully, then splashed whiskey into it. He took a long sip himself, then came to sit beside her. He drew her close to him, and the roughness of his cheek rubbed against her forehead when he spoke. "Only the very greatest ladies could love so deeply and so well," he told her. He offered her the whiskey. She sipped it and coughed and choked, and he patted her upon the back, smiling.

"Don't! Oh, please don't laugh at me!" she implored him.

"Kiernan, I would never laugh at you. Lord, sweetheart, today has been the most tender day in all of my life, and I will thank you for it always."

He seemed sincere, and she discovered that she could no longer meet his eyes. She stared at her hands. His were so large and so bronzed—the palms roughened from constant riding, but the fingers so long and precise and dedicated to his medical calling—very dark against the whiteness of her own.

Those fingers curled around hers. "I think that this has been coming all our lives."

"I am practically engaged to another man," she murmured.

"Ah, yes. Poor Anthony," Jesse said dryly. She didn't like the tone of his voice. He rose and reached for his long johns and then his trousers with their yellow piping. He pulled them on and headed to the fire, poking it to stoke up the flame. The firelight played upon his chest. For a few moments she dared to survey him. She relished the play of gold and orange and fire that danced over his flesh. In his very masculine way, he was beautiful, toned and hard and beautiful.

He had held her in his arms, he had held her against his flesh, and he had given her so very much. She had no experience, yet she was shrewdly convinced that she had been seduced by a rare man, that what she had touched was indeed a form of magic. And without Jesse, she might never touch that magic again.

She could never have shared this experience with any man but Jesse, she thought. Never. Maybe she had always known it.

"There's no reason to be rude about Anthony," she murmured, drawing the cape more tightly about her as if it were a shield of respectability.

"No," he said, sounding bitter. "There's no reason to be rude about Anthony."

"Jesse, I hadn't seen you in months, and suddenly—"

"And suddenly I was back in your life," he interrupted. His voice was quiet, thoughtful.

"You came to me this afternoon," she began, but she didn't finish. This time he strode back to the bed and came down on one knee before her, taking her hand.

"Yes, I came in a tempest to steal you away like the wind. And you came with me," he murmured, and brushed aside her hair.

She smiled. "Yes, I came with you," she told him. She let the cape fall to reach for that straying lock of black hair upon his forehead, and she smoothed it back. She didn't want to talk about Anthony again. She didn't want to hear or say words that might dispel the closeness between them. She didn't want the magic broken.

She didn't want there to be anything else in the world except for the night, and the two of them.

Anthony was surely in her past now. Jesse, despite his recklessness and stubborn streak and even the wildness that sometimes brewed in his heart, was a man of extreme honor. There was no question that he would marry her. But that was the future. Anthony would have to be dealt with first, gently. And there was her father. He might be difficult to handle. He'd be appalled that she'd come so close to one man while nearly engaged to another. But it would all work out. It was just a matter of diplomacy.

She didn't want diplomacy now. She didn't want anything to spoil the memory of this night.

"Jesse, what was it? Why were you so upset?"

"I had no right to come for you. Really, I didn't."

"But what was wrong?"

He shrugged and sat up beside her, folding his legs beneath himself and pulling her close. "What was right?" he murmured.

"John Brown is in custody. It's over."

"It's not over. Don't you see? It will never really be over, and nothing will be the same again."

"I don't know what you're talking about."

"You saw only some of what people were doing. You didn't see it all." He stood again and paced to the fire. He stared into the flames. "Kiernan, in the West, I saw terrible things. The Indians did terrible things to the white men—a number of which they learned from the white men, I might add. Because the white men were doing terrible things to the Indians. I saw things just as horrible here. People weren't just shot, Kiernan. They were abused. Atrocities were committed here."

She understood him, yet she didn't understand him. She had felt a vague sense of horror herself, but Jesse's seemed deeper, seemed to touch something within him that she didn't comprehend, or seemed to relate to something that he knew and that she did not.

"Jesse, John Brown attacked these people. He shot the mayor, one of the nicest, most gentle men I have ever met. People reacted."

"Yes, but people reacted badly to people all the way around," he murmured.

"Jesse, you're scaring me. I don't understand you."

"That's what I'm afraid of. You'll never understand me."

"Then tell me what you mean!" Kiernan flared.

He shook his head. "I don't know what I'm saying myself, Kiernan."

But suddenly, she did. She leaped up, pulling his cape along with her, and stared at him hard. "John Brown is a fanatic," she said flatly, staring at him. "And so is that Lincoln. If he wins the election, the country is going to split. It's going to split right in two."

"You don't know that, Kiernan."

"Yes—yes, I do. Because of sectionalism, Jesse, and because of the economy. And because there is a way of life for us, and a way of life for them."

"You can't pull a country apart, Kiernan."

Kiernan was suddenly more frightened than she had ever imagined she could be. She'd had everything in her hands. She'd had Jesse. She'd made love with him. She should never have done it, but she'd never been conventional, and neither had Jesse. It had been the most beautiful thing in the world, and her future had been bright, as beautiful as the blazing stars that had touched her in the aftermath of his touch.

And now it was slipping away from her. It was as if she had held water in the cup of her palm, then suddenly opened up her fingers. It was all trickling away.

"Jesse, you're a Virginian!"

He stiffened. "You can't tear it apart, Kiernan. You just can't tear it apart."

She spun away from him. Half blinded by the tears that stung behind her lashes, she hurried about the shack, looking for her strewn clothing.

She couldn't handle the corset alone. She needed his help, but she couldn't bear accepting it.

Suddenly he was behind her. "Don't touch me!" she snapped.

"It's too late for that," he murmured, a hint of amusement touching the tension in his voice.

"Let go!" She tried to wrench free, but he had her ribbons. As she pulled to free herself, he pulled harder and she jerked back against him.

"Stand still!"

She had little choice but to let him finish tying the garment. But once he was finished, she pulled free again, hurriedly finding the rest of her clothing. She felt his eyes upon her, but she didn't want to look his way. At last she had to. "I'm going, Jesse."

"When I'm ready."

"I'll walk back."

"No, you'll ride back with me."

"Jesse—"

"You came with me. I'll take you back."

He started moving at last, his eyes on hers while he grabbed his shirt off the floor. Her gaze nearly fell from his, but she forced herself to meet him with her growing fury.

How could he argue against the rights of the southern states? How could he argue against her father, against his own brother, against his own way of life?

It didn't matter, she tried to tell herself. It *couldn't* matter.

But it did. She felt as if she were being buffeted in a tumult, dragged down the rocks of the river. People were already talking about war.

If it came to war, would Jesse be on the wrong side of it?

He tucked his shirt into his pants, sat, and pulled on his boots.

Then with a mocking curl to his lip, he swept up his hat and set it low upon his head, then reached for his cape.

The cape on which they had lain together.

She swirled around, heading for the door. He caught her arm, jerking her back. "I thought you said you loved me."

"I can't love a traitor."

"I'm not a traitor."

"You're on the wrong side."

"There are no damned sides!"

"Then swear!" she told him suddenly. "Swear that you would be on the right side—"

"What would the right side be, Kiernan? Tell me that, please, will you?"

She paused, staring at him. She wanted to burst into tears and throw herself into his arms. She wanted to forget it all and to lie down now before the fire beside him. She wanted to see the flames upon their naked flesh as they made love again.

She wanted him to love her and for him to be the man she had always wanted. The man who lived the life she knew so well—the Virginian.

She wanted him to be with her, no matter what.

"My side is the right side, Jesse," she told him rigidly. She waited for him to agree, to promise that he would always be with her.

But he was silent as his cobalt eyes bored into hers. She spun around again, tears about to fall. And once again he caught her, spinning her around to face him. "Kiernan, marry me. You're going to be my wife. You *have* to."

"I don't have to do anything, Jesse Cameron."

"Do you think you can run back to Anthony Miller after this?"

"I don't need to run anywhere, Jesse. But Anthony's loyalties lie with mine."

He swore savagely. One last time he wrenched her against him. She tried to twist from his hold, but he caught her chin and held her face to his, and he kissed her again. He kissed her ruthlessly and passionately until he forced a response. He lifted his head from hers. "Don't play foolish games with our lives, Kiernan!" he warned her.

She broke free from his hold and hurried outside. He was quickly behind her, his arms sweeping around her waist when she would have gone on. Before she could voice more than an oath, she was sitting upon his roan once again, and he was mounting behind her.

"Where are you taking me now?" she demanded.

"Home!" he snapped.

He did not walk the roan. He gave the animal free rein, and the hungry horse galloped into Harpers Ferry.

He urged the horse to the front of Lacey's house. Still furious, Kiernan slid down from the horse on her own.

"Kiernan!"

She stopped and swung around. Jesse would have to come around to siding with Virginia. She would have to make him understand that he must.

He jumped off his mount and headed toward her. But a rakish grin suddenly slashed across his handsome features.

"What?" She backed away, afraid that he would touch her again.

He did, pulling her against him although she struggled against his hold. She went rigidly still and repeated, "*What,* damn you?"

His voice was low, husky, soft. "I warned you before not to marry him if he couldn't kiss you as I did. Now I can warn you that you'll never have anything like you had tonight with him. Not in a thousand years, Kiernan."

She broke free, lifting her hand to slap him. He caught it and chuckled softly.

"Kiernan—"

"Go to hell, Jesse," she told him. She pulled her hand free and spun around, heading for the house.

"Kiernan, I cannot change my conscience!"

She kept walking, calling back to him, "And I cannot change mine!"

She felt his silence, felt the tension of it.

Then she heard the sound of his horse's hoofbeats as he rode away, and she swirled around again.

"Jesse!" she whispered in anguish.

But it was too late—he was gone.

She stood in misery. The night wind suddenly picked up, and it was cold. So very cold.

As cold as a world without Jesse.

Seven

Kiernan didn't see Jesse again that night, nor did Daniel make it back. She heard a report of a slave rebellion in Pleasant Valley and that Jesse and Daniel had ridden out there with Lee and Stuart.

There was still nervousness in town that the nearby slaves would rise and rebel—even if it was too late for them to join John Brown's cause.

Kiernan knew that she should be worried, too, but she was far too involved in her own inner conflict to dwell on fears that might be unfounded.

She spent the evening trying with all of her heart to be calm. She tried to enjoy the dinner that Lacey made in case the Camerons managed to come back.

But the truth of it was Kiernan could hardly stand sitting there with Lacey. Just being polite was the most difficult thing she had ever done. Her mind didn't stop racing for an instant, and at the first opportunity, she begged exhaustion and hurried up to her bedroom.

And there she went into a frenzy of washing her face, which alternately seemed to burn with shame and grow cold with chills of wonder. She went over every minute detail of what had happened, and she began to wonder how on earth she had been so brazen. Then she reminded herself that it had been Jesse, that she loved Jesse.

Ultimately, no matter how she chastised herself, a sweet quivering started up deep inside her, and she knew she could be certain of one thing.

She wanted to be with him again.

But she was angry, too, furious that he seemed to be living on a different plane of reality. It occurred to her she had told Jesse she loved him—but he never said those words to her.

Jesse had said that he would marry her. No, he had said that she *must* marry him! His duty called, she thought wryly. Perhaps there was more of his upbringing in him than he cared to admit. But she would never marry him if he thought it was necessary because of what had happened between them. She would only marry him if he loved her.

And if he loved Virginia.

She wondered if she was wrong to feel so passionately about her state. It was not proper for her to care as much as she did about the politics of the day. It was not an admirable feminine trait, her father warned her often enough. But she and Anthony shared the same passions. He did not mind what she had to say, for he agreed wholeheartedly.

She couldn't marry Anthony, she knew, had probably always known. Not while Jesse existed in her life.

A warmth swept over her that brought her to a renewed and different trembling. What if there were . . . complications from today? She had been innocent until that afternoon, but she wasn't naive. She could be carrying Jesse's child at this very moment.

To her amazement, the idea did not bring horror or shame to her. Instead, excitement seized hold of her, and she knew that she would love to have Jesse's child.

Because she loved Jesse.

And perhaps, if she were in the family way, she would be able to forget their differences, no matter how devastating they seemed now.

She hugged her pillow close to her body. She walked to the window, wondering if he would appear beneath it again. But he did not, and the cold of the evening swept around her. She closed the window and stepped back. She lay back on her bed, again hugging her pillow to herself.

At last, she slept.

If the day ended in a tumult, her night was haunted by the sweetest of dreams.

Kiernan had barely opened her eyes when she heard Lacey calling to her excitedly, "Kiernan! Come down. We've company!"

She leaped up, her hands shaking. It was Jesse, she was certain, and Daniel. They'd come back for breakfast.

She washed hastily and searched through the gowns she had brought. She decided on a soft green gown with a sweeping wide skirt and a green velvet jacket. The sleeves were elegantly large beneath the elbows, while the jacket was snugly fitted. She struggled a bit with her corset since Lacey was not available to help her, and a sudden nervousness caused her to fumble. How would she greet him today? Would it be different to see him?

Yes, it would never be the same again.

At last she was dressed. She picked up her brush to do something dignified and elegant with her hair, but she hadn't time and besides, her fingers were trembling. She brushed it out over her shoulder, then swept it into a simple coil at her nape. Its honey color was caught by rays of light and glistened with gold highlights. She stared at her reflection and bit her lips for color. Her cheeks were already flaming. Her eyes, brilliant with her reckless excitement, were flashing like emeralds.

She couldn't blush so!

She was furious at him, she reminded herself, and she had to remain furious at him.

She gave her hair one last pat, then spun around with her skirt swirling and headed for the stairs. She forced herself to walk slowly and came down the staircase with commendable decorum.

Her heart was thundering. Jesse was back.

But Jesse was not back. Her heart swung heavily against the wall of her chest as she reached the landing in the parlor.

"Kiernan!"

It was Anthony who called her name, and it was Anthony and his father and her father and Lacey's husband who had all come back this morning.

Her father, whom she loved dearly. His misty gray eyes rested upon her, damp with emotion, and his wrinkled and weathered cheeks split into a glad smile of appreciation. She knew instantly that he had heard of the trouble at Harpers Ferry and that he had worried himself sick over her.

"Papa!" she whispered.

Although she had really been longing for Jesse, she ran to her father.

She didn't reach him. Anthony said her name again and stepped forward. She found herself plummeting into Anthony's arms as he rushed toward her.

"Kiernan, oh, sweet Kiernan! You're here, you're well, you're unhurt!"

She looked up at him. Anthony Miller was a handsome man with golden hair that had a tendency to curl. His eyes were a soft brown like the hue of mahogany. His features were lean and finely honed.

And his concern for her was real and deep. She read it in the anguish that tightened his face and burned in his eyes. She would have pulled away from him except that guilt suddenly and swiftly tore through her. She couldn't marry him, she knew that, but she couldn't hurt him either.

She set her hands upon his arms and smiled, then reached for his cheek to reassure him. "I'm fine, Anthony. Absolutely fine." She had never realized how deeply he cared for her until now, when she was going to hurt him so deeply.

"Oh dear, there's the door again!" Lacey murmured, and hurried to see to the rapping.

Anthony didn't release Kiernan.

He pulled her closer, crushing her to his chest. His chin rested upon the top of her head, and she felt his trembling as his fingers smoothed over her hair, cradling her head. There couldn't have been a more tender picture of concern.

It was then that she heard Jesse's voice.

"Excuse us. It seems that we're interrupting."

She pulled back quickly, meeting Anthony's eyes first, then turning to see Jesse and Daniel. Jesse was greeting Kiernan's father, but his eyes were on her, blazing blue orbs of condemnation.

Damn him! He must realize that she couldn't possibly be cruel to Anthony!

"Jesse, my son, you're not interrupting us in any way!" Kiernan's father told him, taking his hand and clapping him on the back. "I've not had a chance to greet my own daughter yet, what with young love and all, but you lads are lways welcome."

"Indeed," Jesse said pleasantly, smiling at her expectantly. "Young love. How touching."

She wanted to throttle him. He stood shaking her father's hand, staring at her.

Lacey was suddenly back in the room, bearing a silver tray with small wine-glasses upon it. "My very best blackberry wine, gentlemen. And lady!" She acknowledged Kiernan with a wide, brimming smile. "We must celebrate, every-one being here and well and beneath my roof!"

"Hear, hear!" Daniel said, laughing and availing himself quickly of a glass.

Kiernan wasn't sure how or when, but at last she was disengaged from An-thony. She hugged her father fiercely, realizing that she was heartily glad to see him again.

But then she found herself uncomfortably close to Jesse. His head bent low, he whispered to her.

"Haven't quite told him that you're not marrying him?"

She lifted her chin, smiling, trying to appear every bit as casual as Jesse did.

"Why, Captain Cameron, I haven't even begun to make up my mind about such things as yet!"

"Perhaps you should. Soon."

"Perhaps you should see to your own affairs, Captain. To my mind, they are in grave disarray."

"Perhaps *I* should ask your father for your hand. Perhaps we should bare our souls before him—and about the other things that have recently been bared."

She swung around, seeing amusement in his eyes.

And a warning.

"You wouldn't dare."

"Kiernan, I'd dare anything, you know that."

"But you won't, please. For my sake."

He inhaled sharply, watching her, and she knew that she had hit the proper note with him. Jesse *would* dare anything. But pleading with him had a different effect.

For the moment, she was safe.

Safe? But she loved him!

And she hated him for the stand he was taking.

Lacey soon had everyone seated. John Mackay and Thomas Donahue and Andrew and Anthony Miller all demanded to hear the details of everything that had happened in their absence.

"It was right distressing to be in the mountains hearing about the things going on down here," John Mackay said. "Right distressing. Word was so vague. One minute, the whole town was up in arms. The next minute, it was nothing but a little bitty skirmish. Daughter," he told Kiernan, shaking his head, "I'll not be so quick to leave you alone again, ever."

"Pa, I'm just fine," Kiernan said.

"Thanks to Captain Cameron," Lacey murmured vaguely. Kiernan froze. Lacey looked up and realized that everyone was staring at her. "Oh, I am sorry!" she said with distress.

"Lacey Donahue, what are you talking about?" John Mackay demanded. He was on his feet facing Lacey, who looked as if she were about to cry. John swung around on Kiernan. "Young lady, what is she talking about?" He didn't wait for Kiernan to answer, but swung on Jesse. "By the soul of my dear friend, your departed father, young man, I demand an answer."

Jesse shrugged and looked at Kiernan, giving her the option to answer.

"Oh, Pa, it was nothing, really. A few of those scoundrels surprised Lacey and me, and they decided that I would make a good hostage."

"Lord!" Anthony exclaimed in horror.

"But nothing happened!" Kiernan insisted. "Jesse came along, and they took off. It was nothing, really."

"Nothing, really! Why young woman, I do hope you displayed a proper gratitude to Jesse."

"John," Jesse murmured. His eyes were on Kiernan again, and she didn't much like either the amusement or the hint of danger within them. "I assure you, Kiernan displayed a gratitude unequal to any I have ever known."

Damn him! Her cheeks were flaming, but she determined to fight fire with fire. She smiled sweetly for her father. "Indeed, Father, I thanked him fully. After all, Jesse was such an incredible . . . gentleman."

"One cannot say enough for your daughter's strength and courage and . . . passion, sir!"

Oh, if only she could throw something!

But suddenly Anthony stood up and faced Jesse. "Captain, I am in your debt. I am ever so beholden to you!" Emotion trembled in his voice.

Jesse looked at Anthony, and for a long moment Kiernan thought that he would explode with some damning words.

But he did not.

Beholden indeed, Jesse thought. Anthony, you poor fool, you owe me nothing. I took what was dear to you on your very own property, and now we are both here playing to her whimsy.

He leaned back, sipped his drink, and replied casually, "Kiernan and I are old friends, Anthony. I happened along at the right time." He sat forward, and his eyes met Kiernan's again. "Heaven might have found some pity for Mr. Brown after all, had he managed to seize Kiernan." He smiled to take the sting—and the truth!—from his words. "Perhaps we'd never have needed to storm the place had he snared Kiernan. She'd have given him a political tongue-lashing and sent him running instantly to surrender!"

John Mackay roared with laughter, while Anthony looked uncertain. Kiernan cast daggers upon Jesse with her eyes, and Lacey hastily refilled the glasses.

Kiernan's father sobered. "Still, Jesse Cameron, in truth, we are in your debt.

FIX

All ended well here, but you young people do not remember the Nat Turner rebellion in the Tidewater region back in '31. Fifty were killed then, dragged from their beds and murdered. Women and children. Bless the good Lord that a like thing did not happen here."

They were all silent. Kiernan glanced at Jesse, and he watched her very soberly.

Jesse, I *am* grateful for everything! she thought. And I do love you.

But there was no way to let him know her thoughts. Nor did she want to—he was holding himself away from her and from everything that he should profess to love.

His somber eyes did not leave hers as talk continued.

Though he was invited, Jesse declined dinner. He swept his hat off to wish them all a good day.

There was nothing that Kiernan could do then but watch him leave the house. She felt a touch on her shoulder. It was Anthony. He put his arm around her. "My God, Kiernan, you're safe!" he whispered. "It is all that I prayed for, night and day, since we heard the news. I vowed my life for yours, but there was no way to give it."

I can't marry you, Anthony, she thought. The words were in her heart and on her lips.

But she couldn't say them, not now. She forced a smile, and feeling ill, she returned inside with Anthony.

Daniel Cameron had remained. He told them that their trip to Pleasant Valley the night before had yielded no sign of rebellion. "Just sleepy farmers and slaves who were afraid of John Brown more than they were intrigued by him."

"So it's really over with then," John Mackay said with satisfaction.

"All but the trial and the hanging," Daniel said.

The men continued talking, and Kiernan realized that Daniel was watching her closely.

She pleaded exhaustion and fled from them all, upstairs to the haven of her room.

In the morning she learned that Jesse had been called back to Washington.

Kiernan didn't see Jesse again until John Brown's trial, which began on October 27.

Brown had been brought to Charles Town, which lay a few miles from Harpers Ferry, the day after his capture. He and four other captured raiders were arraigned on the twenty-fifth, and the next day they were indicted for treason against the Commonwealth of Virginia, for conspiring with slaves to rebel, and for murder. Each defendant pleaded not guilty, and each asked for a separate trial.

The trials began with Brown's.

John Mackay was determined to attend, as were Anthony and Andrew Miller and Thomas Donahue.

They all frowned upon Kiernan's attending, and she wasn't sure if she wanted to be there herself.

But she knew that Jesse would be there. She was certain that the prosecution would demand that he be on hand if they needed him as a witness.

Anthony had remained very kind. She did love him, she realized, as a very dear and important friend, one whom she would never injure, if it was in her power to avoid it. There would one day be a way to talk him. But for now she managed to evade his determination to propose an engagement. When he pressed her, she came up with the excuse that she hadn't received all the education that she desired.

"Kiernan," he had told her politely one evening, "we are not getting any younger."

He didn't mean *we*—he meant *her*. For some reason, men were allowed to marry at any age they chose. He was, as always, unerringly tactful in reminding her that she was already eighteen, several years older than most women in her social class were when they married.

"Then Anthony, perhaps you should look elsewhere."

"We'll speak of it later," he assured her quickly. "Kiernan, take your time, study where you will. All the more will you grace my house."

"Anthony, I am not sure—"

"There is no other woman I could want."

"Anthony," she said in a rush, "I'm not sure that I love you."

"But I love you. Enough for both of us. Kiernan, nothing that you can say will dissuade me."

Not even the fact that I have slept with another man? she wondered in silence.

Or that I love that other man? Have always loved him?

She knew that she had to speak the truth. But she didn't know how to do it without wounding him.

When they arrived at the Charles Town courtroom, she knew that she should have been more decisive. Anthony was escorting her when she looked across the room and saw that Jesse had already arrived—and that he was watching her upon Anthony's arm.

It was amazing that he had spotted her so quickly, she thought. The courtroom was packed.

There was a tremendous commotion, but then Judge Parker brought the court to order.

John Brown, still suffering from his wounds, was brought in on a cot. Kiernan stared at him, searching for something in the man to confirm what she had heard. She was not disappointed. His eyes did burn. As they moved about the courtroom, she felt a distinct unease.

The prisoner had barely come in and order had just been called when one of his defense attorneys began to make a plea for him. He read a telegram from A. H. Lewis of Ohio who stated that there were many instances of insanity within Brown's family. Clemency was the suggestion.

It was an intriguing defense stratagem, Kiernan thought, one that might well save the man's life.

Except that John Brown wasn't about to allow it. He stood, rising from his cot with considerable dignity, and denied that he was insane.

He would not be sent to an institution; he would not have his life salvaged. He had known what he was doing, and he believed in the right of it.

Watching him, Kiernan was startled by the pity she felt for the man. He frightened her, and yet she was sorry for him. She could not admire him, yet she could admire his conviction.

As the day dragged on, proof of his treason was read out time and time again, and she believed more and more that he truly thought himself a servant of God, and that although he had shed blood, he regretted that blood must darken the land.

She left the courtroom that first day with a great deal of confusion. And in that confusion, she wanted to see Jesse.

She saw him sooner than she had expected. As she was leaving the courtroom on Anthony's arm, she ran right into him. He stepped back, and lifted his hat to her and to Anthony. "Kiernan, Anthony. What a pleasure."

His voice was edged with sarcasm, and his eyes held a distinctively mocking light when they fell upon her.

Anthony shook Jesse's hand and greeted him enthusiastically, and then her father was there and Andrew Miller and Thomas Donahue, and the men became quickly involved in conversation. Before she knew it, they had invited Jesse to dinner with them.

Well, she had wanted to see him. But not with half of the world present, and the only conversation that of the trial.

She held her breath, waiting to see if Jesse would decline the invitation.

He did not. "I'd enjoy the companionship," he said, and turned to Kiernan. "And of course, the presence of such a fine lady."

They met in two hours in the restaurant of the hotel where they were staying. Eager as she was to see Jesse alone, Kiernan was hard pressed to remain graciously with the others for long as they spoke outside the courtroom. She tried to respond appropriately to their conversation, she tried to remain calm and demure lest her father grew suspicious. But the first second that she could, she excused herself and bolted for her room. In the short time she had before dinner, she ordered a bath and scrubbed her hair with perfumed shampoo. With furious energy, she towel-dried her honey-colored tresses. Then she dressed in an elegant peach and yellow gown with draping white linen sleeves and tore down to the dining room, hoping to meet Jesse before the others arrived.

The place was a madhouse with all the people in town attending the trial. Kiernan looked anxiously about but did not see Jesse. The tuxedoed maître d' of the restaurant found her, and bowing low, he informed her that Captain Cameron had reserved a room for their party.

She reached the doorway and saw Jesse standing by one of the chairs, sipping a full drink. He was in full dress uniform, dark, handsome, exciting. Her heart was suddenly still as she watched him.

He sensed that she was there and turned to her. Their eyes met, and for a moment, her need to rush into his arms seemed to be overwhelming. In only a second, her heart and limbs would have taken flight.

"Ah, here you are, Cameron, Kiernan. Jesse, I do say, what a fine thing you've done for us all, thinking to reserve this privacy!"

She didn't move. Her heart sank, and her limbs did not take flight. Anthony was behind her, setting his hands tenderly upon her shoulders. Though Jesse's eyes continued to meet hers, he spoke casually to Anthony.

"I was expecting that there might be a crowd and thought of reserving space."

Then her father came in, and Andrew and Thomas. Kiernan found herself seated in between Anthony and her father, and across from Jesse.

"Well, Jesse," John Mackay demanded, making a broad motion as he unfolded his napkin and set it upon his lap. "What did you think of the proceedings today? Brown could easily have grabbed hold of that insanity plea, by Jove! There's a madman if I've ever seen one."

"Sir, he's a fanatic, certainly. If that makes him a madman, I'm not certain."

"Bah!" Andrew Miller said irritably. "He's mad. And dangerous. And a fool. He thinks that he has the word of the Lord in his ears! Well, let me tell you, the Lord says otherwise. In the Bible the good Lord said, 'Slaves, obey your masters.' Isn't that right, Captain Cameron?"

Kiernan stared at Jesse, praying that he wouldn't be difficult at the dinner table.

Jesse shrugged. "Mr. Miller, I'm afraid that I wasn't a very good Bible student."

"What are you saying, sir?" Andrew Miller, his face flushed, demanded. "You don't think that Brown will hang—or that he deserves to?"

"Oh yes, he'll hang," Jesse said. "And by any law, he deserves to do so."

Andrew settled back. Lacey's husband, Thomas, looked acutely uncomfortable. He was Andrew's friend and a strong advocate of states' rights, but he didn't believe in slavery himself.

Jesse leaned forward. "Gentlemen, we've a lady present at the table. I suggest we cease to discuss politics for the duration of the meal."

Kiernan was deeply annoyed when her father literally snorted, "Kiernan? Why, Jesse, you know my girl as well as anyone!"

Jesse smiled at her. "Probably better," he offered pleasantly.

"Then you know she's not in the least offended by talk of politics."

"My, my," Kiernan murmured sweetly, "it must be the company I keep!" She side-kicked her father. He yelped and stared at her and frowned warningly, but she continued to smile sweetly. "Humor me, Father," she said. "Let's do cease with all of this for a while."

There were plays to discuss, their land, the military itself, the trip that the men in partnership had taken into the mountains. The food offered by the hotel was very good, but Kiernan barely tasted hers. She grew restless as coffee was served to them in elegant silver pitchers. The meal would end soon. Maybe then she'd have a chance to talk to Jesse.

But it wasn't to be. Jesse barely touched his coffee. He stood and told them that he had an appointment for a drink with an old army friend and bade them good night, bowing handsomely to Kiernan.

The trial lasted two and half more days. Kiernan sat through the entirety of it. She listened to John Brown, and she listened to the witnesses. She was torn. What had happened had been horrible—John Brown had committed murder. He had come with hundreds of pikes with which to arm slaves. If he had created an insurrection, hundreds of people might have been brutally murdered in cold blood.

Yet there was something about the man. He would not be quickly forgotten.

On October 31, closing arguments were given. The case was handed over to the jury at one-thirty in the afternoon.

The jury deliberated for forty-five minutes. The verdict came in. John Brown was guilty on all three counts. Old Ossawatomie Brown was going to be hanged by the neck until dead.

Kiernan had expected shouts and cries from the crowd that so often upon the steps of the courthouse had shouted threats and insults upon the man.

But there was silence, dead silence.

Brown himself merely adjusted the pallet on his cot and stretched out upon it.

Kiernan looked across the courtroom. Jesse took his eyes from Brown and stared at her. He seemed sad—no, stricken, almost anguished. She felt his stare like a touch. But people stood all around them. In seconds, they were lost to each other in the crowd. "Daughter, it's done. Let's go," her father told her. She was led from the courtroom on his arm.

With the trial over, Kiernan knew that Jesse would be riding back to Washington. But she had to see him alone one last time.

She didn't know when she would see him again.

He would be joining them for dinner again, as he had every night, but sitting through those meals with the others in attendance had been pure misery. She would have escaped those occasions if she could have. No matter how polite Jesse was, how careful with his words, he still refused to lie about his convictions about the political situation. Sometimes his comments were nearly traitorous to the life that they led, traitorous for a Tidewater Virginian.

When he wasn't creating tension at the table, he was watching her and Anthony with that rueful twist of his lip and pained and bitter mockery in his eyes.

This last night, Kiernan dressed carefully for dinner. She chose a gown with a soft underskirt and an overskirt and bodice of deep blue velvet. The sleeves and low-cut bodice were trimmed lightly with fur against the chill of the night. She swept her hair back cleanly but allowed tendrils of golden-red curls to escape the coil and frame her face. She stepped back from her hotel room mirror and surveyed her image.

Anthony was right—she *was* growing older. Her eyes seemed very old. But she wasn't displeased with her image. The gown was beautiful, and it displayed an ample amount of bosom and shoulder without being too daring. The color was perfect for her, and the gown was perfect for a proper evening out with her father and friends.

And it was perfect for reminding Jesse that she was a grown-up woman, one with whom he had made love.

She wasn't going to mind dinner that night, she determined. She was going to find a chance to tell him that she needed to see him alone.

She hurried down to the dining room they had shared every evening. To her dismay, her father and Andrew were already seated. Thomas Donahue came in immediately behind her. A smile crinkled his pleasant, weathered old face, and he paused to tell her that she was a beautiful sight for old and weary eyes. She smiled in turn. Thomas was very dear.

When Anthony arrived, he brushed her cheek with a kiss and pulled back her chair.

"I wonder where Jesse has gotten himself to," John Mackay said to no one in particular.

"There's a lot of military brass around," Anthony said, unknowingly defending his rival. "Perhaps he has been waylaid."

Their waiter arrived with a message on a small silver tray. John took the message and crumpled it in his hand. "The boy's running late. He says that we should go ahead and order, and he'll be along as soon as he can."

Kiernan jumped out of her chair, so restless that she could no longer bear it. She had to see Jesse.

All eyes turned to her.

"There's a chill in the air," she told her father regally. "If you gentlemen will just excuse me—"

But Anthony was up too. "If you need a wrap, Kiernan, I would be delighted to fetch it for you."

"Oh, thank you, Anthony, but I'm not sure that I left the stole I want in my room. I might have left it in the sofa by the registrar. Stay, please." She gave him one of her most charming smiles, then added, "Really, you gentlemen go on and talk without me. I'll be just a few minutes."

Her father's blue eyes were downright suspicious, but Kiernan ignored them. She left the room and moved quickly through the dining room beyond.

She knew that she'd have to have a wrap when she returned, so she raced upstairs to her room and grabbed the stole, which was on the foot of her bed—exactly where she knew it would be. She raced back down the main stairway and outside to the huge veranda that surrounded the hotel.

It was quiet out there. All the conversation was going on inside. The night was cool and beautiful.

She looked down the street, into the darkness of the night. Jesse was staying at a different hotel and would arrive from the north.

But when would he come?

She gazed across the road to the livery stable, and with a sudden spurt of energy she flew down the few steps from the porch to the road and hurried across the street.

To her amazement, she discovered him coming around the side of the stable. There was foliage all about, and she might not have recognized him in the darkness, except that she knew him so well—his walk, the tilt of his hat.

"Jesse!"

She breathed out his name, and he saw her. Before she knew what she was doing, she raced along the trail toward him.

She threw herself into his arms, pressed her lips to his with a starved hunger, and nearly burst with the sweet fervor of the kiss he gave her in return, his tongue filling her mouth, his passion robbing her of breath and reason. As he held her against him, she felt their hearts beating like the wings of eagles. She felt the coolness of the night and the soaring heat between them. Slowly, he eased her down to her feet and stared into her eyes. She flushed and lowered her face.

"Where's poor Anthony?" he asked her.

"In—in the restaurant."

"Did you tell him that you're not going to marry him?"

"I tried to."

"Tried?"

"He can be very stubborn."

"Just tell him that you're going to marry me."

She looked up at him, searching his eyes. Her fingers wound around the button of his cape. "But I'm not going to marry you, Jesse. Not until you see things the right way."

"Your way?" he quizzed. He arched a brow and spoke very softly. He bent down and pressed a kiss to the corner of her mouth. He rubbed his tongue lightly, slowly, across her lower lip, caught it between his teeth, then kissed it very tenderly. She pressed against him, savoring the warmth of him and the sheer luxury of touching him. "The right way is your way?" he repeated.

"Yes, my way," she murmured. "Oh, Jesse—"

Suddenly, swiftly, he set her aside. "So now what, Kiernan? You flirt and tease and torment poor Anthony until I come around to your way of thinking?"

Her eyes narrowed sharply, furiously. "Who is to say that I am tormenting him, Jesse? Dear Lord, he's a better man than you, so it seems!"

She was suddenly seized so tightly that she could scarcely breathe. "In what way, Kiernan? Is he a better man when he kisses you, touches you? Have you decided to test your greatest powers upon Anthony too?"

"Let go of me, you arrogant Yank!" she spat out. "How dare you suggest such things! Anthony is far too noble—"

"Anthony is far too besotted a fool, Kiernan," Jesse said bluntly. "He hasn't been making love to you in dark corners. He allows you to dangle him along at your whim and asks for nothing in return but one of those devastating smiles. Well, I'm not Anthony, Kiernan. I love you, but my mind is my own, and I cannot change what I see as right or wrong for you or for anyone else. Do you understand that?"

She understood that he was rejecting her—and his own life-style—because of something that might or might not happen in the future.

She tried to wrench free of him, torn by the pain. "Don't you ever touch me again, Jesse Cameron!"

"Touch you? Why, Miss Mackay! Do correct me if I'm wrong, but I could have sworn that you came soaring across the earth to land in my arms."

"How very, very rude of you to put it so."

"That, too, is because I am not the driveling Anthony."

Once again, he pulled her closer, so close that she could feel the hot whisper of his breath, so very close that she could feel the excitement of his body. Enter her . . . warm her, stir her.

"Kiernan, I love you. I am the man for you, the only one to know you and to love you. But you won't rule me. Do you understand? I'd give you everything that I can give you, but there are certain things that I cannot give. When you're ready to accept me for what I am, for what I believe, come to me." He smiled at her then, a smile that was bittersweet, anguished, and crooked with a wry humor that mocked himself as well as her. "If you're lucky, I'll be waiting."

"Oh!" she cried, but he was holding her too tightly against him for her to injure him. "You bastard!"

"I know," he agreed. He kissed her again, her hard, with passion and insinuation. He kissed her so long and so completely that she felt that she had been ravished there on the streets. He kissed her until she had no breath, until her limbs were powerless, until the hot fires of desire raced ruthlessly through her.

Then he set her down. "Until then, little girl," he demanded harshly, "torment me no longer!"

He tipped his hat and walked on by her. Kiernan was left to look after him in amazement.

For a moment she felt as if he had given her a physical blow, a strike to the cheek—no, to her heart.

Then her pride raced to her salvation, and she swept past him. With her back to him she said icily, "Please inform my father that I've retired for the evening because I'm feeling ill."

He caught her arm and pulled her back. His eyes were light, and his smile was tender.

"No. He'd never believe that you were suddenly ill. You're simply not the type for vapors, Kiernan."

"Fine!" she snapped. "We'll dine!" She strode on before him, pausing only once to swirl back around. "Don't wait for me, Jesse. My loyalties are fierce."

She preceded him across the street, and they dined. The conversation was easy-flowing and polite, and anyone in the room would have said that it was a comfortable dinner among good friends.

And then it ended. Jesse rose and bade the men good night, telling them that he was riding back to Washington that evening.

He paused by Kiernan. He lifted her hand to his lips, and his eyes met hers. "Good evening, Kiernan," he told her softly. "It's been a pleasure."

"Indeed, it has, Captain," she said with regal dignity. She withdrew her hand and kept her eyes steady upon his. "Good-bye, Captain," she said flatly.

He nodded, pulled the brim of his plumed hat low, and exited the room in long strides.

Moments later, she heard the thunder of his horse's hooves as he rode out of town.

And out of her life.

Eight

Kiernan would not attend the hanging—Jesse knew that. She wouldn't even be allowed, and if she were, she would not come. He had no chance of seeing her there.

And he shouldn't see her. They had both laid their positions on the line. He couldn't compromise on this. If he saw her, he would want her, want to insist that she forget Anthony, that she marry him and cling to him as a wife should. And accept whatever he chose to do in the future.

He'd already asked her to marry him. He couldn't force her to do so. Even if he wished a thousand times over that he could kidnap her and force his will upon her, he knew it would never work. Anthony would feel honor-bound to challenge him in some way, and he had no desire to hurt Anthony.

But she didn't love Anthony. Jesse knew that she was in love with him—she had told him so.

He'd never meant to touch her. But when he had seen her standing upon the chair and looking down upon him in the shack along the river, he felt as if he had always meant to touch her.

Maybe he'd been in love before that day. But seeing her in the sunfire light of that shack, seeing the gold of her hair and the sparkling emerald of her eyes, the softness of her flesh, and breathing the scent of her he knew he'd never be free of her again. He could deny that he was like Anthony, but it wasn't true. She haunted his days, as she haunted Anthony's, and she was a tempest in his nights.

He'd had no right to her, knowing that his conscience came between them. But in his arrogance he had thought that she wouldn't be able to stay away, that she would love him more than any belief or ideal once they had been together.

He had been wrong.

Still, he came back to Charles Town. He was stationed in Washington, and he had plenty of leave time as the day set for John Brown's hanging drew near. So he determined that he would ride out and attend. He had been there at the beginning of the drama involving old John Brown. He might as well be there at the end.

It was December 2, 1859. The day was cold, but clear.

Since the trial, a number of restrictions had been placed on Charles Town. Many feared that an escape plot was being hatched outside the city, and a proclamation had been handed out that visitors would be arrested for trying to enter Charles Town. Only the military were allowed to the immediate execution site.

But that didn't keep civilians from the Charles Town streets, or from following the events as closely as they could. People came out in masses to see old John Brown head out for his hanging.

Jesse rode into the town alone with his military pass and remained upon Pegasus, keeping his distance from the general fanfare. A curious mood of a celebration was stirring much of the crowd, along with a somber element too. John Brown had committed murder, and he had committed treason, but he had comported himself well in court. Jesse sensed that he would become a martyr in the North. Even Governor Wise, after questioning him about the raid, said that he was "the gamest man I ever saw."

"Cameron!"

Jesse was startled to hear his name called, and he turned to see Anthony Miller. Miller was with his local militia unit, but he broke away from them to ride to Jesse's side. A broad grin was spread across his face as he offered Jesse his hand. "Come for the hanging, eh?"

Jesse shook his hand, then shrugged. "I've come to see the end, I guess."

"And a damned good thing it is," Anthony announced flatly. Jesse didn't have a response to that, but Anthony didn't seem to need one. "There are a number of interesting folks here for this. One of our esteemed senators, over there. And that man with the Richmond Grays is an actor. I've seen him perform —he's excellent. His name is Boots or something like that. Booth, that's it. John Booth. If you ever get a chance, you should see him perform. Yes, there are lots of interesting people gathered here."

"Any of my neighbors?" Jesse asked. He wanted to know about Kiernan. She wouldn't be at the hanging, but she could be in town. He couldn't bring himself to ask.

"You mean John Mackay?"

He meant Kiernan Mackay.

"Yes."

Anthony shrugged. "No, I'm not expecting John." Anthony tilted his hat back. "Kiernan's gone and gotten this idea she needs more education. What a girl like that needs with more education, I'll never know. I just want to get married and end all this back-and-forth business. I guess I could never make you understand just how badly. But she's got it in her head to go to Europe for a while. Says there's a fine finishing school in London." He shook his head, confused and hurt. "John's on the coast, seeing her off."

Jesse nodded. His heart leaped to his throat, then slammed down hard against his chest.

So she wasn't with Anthony. She wasn't a complete fool. She was heading across the ocean to watch things from a distance.

"When is she coming back?"

"I imagine in about a year."

A year. So much could happen in a year.

"Excuse me," Anthony went on, "I've got my troops over there. You're welcome to join us. There'll be a dinner at my father's house later."

"Thanks, but I've got to ride back to Washington tonight," Jesse told him.

He couldn't get into a party mood after a hanging. Whether a man deserved to die or not, it was an ugly way to meet one's maker.

And still, he understood the way a lot of the folks felt. John Brown had attacked them. He had come into Harpers Ferry to create an insurrection. When he had gone after the slaveholders in the West, he had murdered them in cold blood, dragging the men from their beds, slaying them with swords before their loved ones. The battle in Kansas and Missouri had been an ugly one. John Brown had shown no mercy. It was fitting that he should die.

But still, he really believed in the freedom for all men that he preached.

"You're not one of those—" Anthony began. "You're not one of those people who think that Brown should be set free?"

Jesse looked at him steadily. "He broke the law," Jesse said. "He committed murder and treason. No, Anthony, I'm not one of those—people—who think that."

Anthony grinned, abashed. "Sorry. I didn't mean to imply that you were one of those bleeding-heart abolitionists. Hell, you've got slaves yourself back at Cameron Hall."

Yes, he did, Jesse thought. A number of them. Cameron Hall was still a working plantation, and he understood the economic position of the South as well as anyone.

They had freed a number of their slaves, though, he and Daniel and Christa. He'd discussed the issue with his father several years ago, before his death. They'd agreed they wouldn't buy any new slaves at auctions. If a slave married a slave from another plantation, they'd purchase the wife or child. They'd also establish a way for the men and women to earn their freedom and hope that they'd want to stay on as paid workers.

But it was compromise, Jesse realized. All compromise, and he was guilty of it. Washington and Jefferson had made the same compromise. They'd believed in freeing slaves. Jefferson had wanted the slaves freed when he'd written the Declaration of Independence.

But he'd been convinced that he'd never get the states together if he tried to do such a thing.

All these years later the situation hadn't improved.

"It's been good to see you, Jesse," Anthony told him. "Don't forget, you're welcome anytime."

"Thanks, Anthony."

Anthony lifted his hat again and rode off. Jesse watched him go.

He felt the sun on his face and looked up, hearing the movement of restless cavalry horses. The troops were well disciplined, even if there was a tremendous amount of fanfare.

His mind wandered to Kiernan.

She was gone, Jesse thought. Kiernan was gone, to where he couldn't reach her. It was just as well.

Jesse waited, feeling the sun on him. He felt a little bit numb.

At the appointed time, John Brown appeared. He was brought along in a horse-drawn cart, his hands bound behind him. He rode in silence, sitting straight with quiet dignity.

He sat upon his own coffin.

He stepped from the cart with dignity and walked to the gallows the same way.

A hush fell over the military crowd. Sheriff John W. Campbell pulled a white linen hood over the prisoner's head, then set the noose around his neck. The jailor asked Brown to step forward onto the trap.

"You must lead me," Brown said, his voice steady, "for I cannot see."

The jailor availed him and adjusted the noose.

"Be quick," Brown said.

A hatchet stroke sprang the trap, and with an awful sound, the body dropped through.

John Brown was dead.

There was complete silence. Suddenly, the voice of a militiaman broke the silence.

"So perish all such enemies of Virginia! All such enemies of the Union! All such enemies of the human race!"

Jesse felt no such sense of elation. By due process of law, John Brown had been hanged on a beautiful winter morning.

Brown had said little enough at the moment of his execution, but Jesse couldn't forget some of the things that the man had said and written earlier— especially the words he had written to one of his guards not long before his date with the hangman.

"The crimes of this guilty land: will never be purged away; but with blood."

John Brown was dead. It was over.

It was just beginning.

Jesse turned his horse.

And in his heart, he rode north.

PART 2

A House Divided

Nine

Near Cameron Hall,
Tidewater, Virginia
December 20, 1860

Kiernan sat on her dapple-gray mare high atop the forested ridge overlooking Cameron Hall.

The morning sun had just risen. Dewdrops played upon the sweeping lawn like a carpet of diamonds. The main house, regal with its soaring white columns, stood in the center of the manicured portion of the property. Behind the house were handsome gardens that in the summer were filled with the scent of roses. The house was one of the oldest in Tidewater Virginia, the original structure having been built soon after the Indian massacre of 1622. Jesse's great-great-great—she really wasn't sure how many greats—grandparents had lovingly laid the first brick and set their names upon it. They had built with beauty and a deep affinity for their new land.

The house had weathered the ravages of time to remain one of the most gracious plantation homes on the James River.

There was a wide breezeway, and on pleasant days, the doors on both ends of the house were cast open so that the soft cool air from the river whispered throughout the wide-open hallway and into the house. The porches became an extension of the hallway, open, inviting, touched by the breeze.

Two large wings had been added to the house just after the Revolution, and they extended gracefully to either side. The kitchen, smokehouse, laundry, bakehouse, stables, and slave quarters entended from the right of the house toward the cliff, from which Kiernan now looked upon the activity of the busy plantation. Close to where she sat upon her mare, near a copse of trees and foliage and the river's edge, was the family cemetery. Camerons had been buried there ever since Lord Cameron, who had built the place, and his beloved Jassy had been tenderly laid to rest by their heirs. Now handsome monuments stood in the plot, enclosed by an ornate wrought-iron fence, with beautifully sculpted angels and madonnas and renditions of Christ. The cemetery itself was beautiful and graceful and spoke of a rich heritage.

From where she sat her horse, Kiernan could see past the sloping lawns that fell from the left side of the house and to the numerous fields beyond, fields of the stuff that had built the South: cotton and tobacco.

No one could ask for a finer home or a more prestigious heritage. The sons of Cameron Hall had always been held up to gentlemen of the state and beyond as fine prospects for their daughters. It was a home that any woman would envy. From her sentinel upon the mount, Kiernan thought it embodied everything stately and gracious and beautiful in the world. How she had missed it during her year abroad! With a tinge of shame she realized that she loved Cameron Hall more than she loved her own home nearby. It too, was beautiful, built of brick and mortar and stone, and it was gracious and pleasant. But it was barely fifty years old. It hadn't weathered the centuries as Cameron Hall had. It didn't have the personality of its James River neighbor. It didn't seem to live and breathe and be so much a part of this world.

She breathed in deeply. The air was sweet with the scents of early morning bread-baking and ham-smoking. The air that came in from the river was decidedly cold today, but she didn't care. She knew the dampness and the cold of winter, just as she knew the humidity and heat of summer. This was home. She had been away a long time, and this morning she wasn't at all sure why she had tormented herself for so long.

At first, leaving had seemed to be the only way to escape marriage to Anthony without being downright cruel.

It had also been a way to escape Jesse. His assignment had been Washington when she left, and that had been far too close. She knew that Jesse had wanted his assignment to be close to home when he was just out of West Point. His father had still been living then, and his father had been military all of his life.

Then Jesse had traveled with the cavalry out west and had spent time fighting Indians at the tail end of the action in Mexico.

And he had spent time in "bleeding Kansas" as the government tried to put some kind of restraint on the horror there. Kiernan had known a great deal of what was going on in his life then. She and Daniel had always been good correspondents. He had felt the need to put things on paper to her, and she had been more than willing to keep him advised about things back home. She had always scanned his missives for information about Jesse. She had always known what he was doing.

And she knew now.

The year she had spent in Europe had been a tense one on this side of the Atlantic—electric, frightening. In London she had avidly sought every piece of information about the states that she could find. She had read political commentaries by the dozens.

Old John Brown had become a martyr. The northern abolitionists had rallied to make sure that his death would never be forgotten. They sang, "John Brown's body lies a-moulderin' in his grave." And Harriet Beecher Stowe's *Uncle Tom's Cabin* continued to fan the flames of fury.

But the worst thing that had happened had been the election of Abraham Lincoln. The South just couldn't stomach it.

Before the election, Kiernan had hoped that the political climate would quiet down, that various sections of the country would manage to live with their differences—as they had been doing since the Revolution.

But as soon as she had heard the results, she had come home. She had arrived in time to discover that South Carolina was planning a convention and that it would vote on the matter of secession. Other states were following that example—Florida, Mississippi, and Tennessee, just to name a few. The feeling was that South Carolina would secede. So would the other states.

So far, though, Virginia seemed to be watching the action. Careful, cautious, dignified, the homeland of so many of the founding fathers, Virginia would watch.

Many Virginia sons, however, were not so cautious. Young men and old men everywhere were forming up into new militia units. Rich men were buying up horses and designing uniforms and purchasing arms. Poor men were seeking to serve beneath them.

If it came to war, they would be prepared.

Many of the South's finest were either enlisted men or commissioned officers in the United States Army—Robert E. Lee and Jeb Stuart, among others.

And the Cameron brothers.

Daniel had written that he had been considering resigning his position, but neither he nor Jesse had done so as yet. Few men had resigned their positions. It remained to be seen just how many would. And of course, it remained to be seen what South Carolina and the other states would do.

The sun rose further into the sky as Kiernan sat upon her mare, surveying the scene below her. She had headed for home the moment that she had heard about the presidential election. From the time her ship had left the London docks, she had felt a growing excitement. Every step of the way, she had wondered why she had ever left home at such a crucial time. London was fascinating, her school for young ladies was entertaining, but she realized the moment she arrived that she had outgrown school. It had been a time of waiting for her, a time for reflecting.

And a time for dreams, for she had not managed to leave Jesse behind. She had been disappointed the previous November to discover that she was not in the family way. Such a situation might have swayed her hand. *Would* have, she thought, a small smile tugging at her lips. Her father would have had Jesse walking down the aisle at gunpoint had it been necessary. But it was not necessary.

How had she slept through so very many nights, when all she could do was remember him? She thought endlessly of him, reliving all that had happened between them. She had met many young men in London, some of them titled, some of them very rich. She had played the games by all the right rules that a young woman should play, and she had tried to fall out of love with Jesse and into love with someone else. She watched as many of her friends were married off according to the dictates of their parents, and she had been extremely grateful for her father's leniency. But none of it mattered. She didn't need a wealthy man, for her father was a wealthy man. She was unimpressed by titles, and she was, in truth, far more fond of Anthony and Daniel than she was of any of the young men she met in London drawing rooms or chose as escorts for a night of London theater.

Perhaps Jesse was right about her, she mused. She had enjoyed the flirting. She had enjoyed having young men flock about her and marvel at her soft Virginia accent, lose their voices when they spoke with her, and turn beet-red in their attempts to be charming in turn. It had been fun to test her power, she reflected.

Except that she had returned to her small school bedroom every evening to feel a painful ache where she should have felt triumphant. Games could never again be as innocent as they once had been. If she tormented others, it was because she was tormented herself.

She was very afraid that she would be tormented until the day that she died. Jesse had done that to her.

She sighed softly and heard the whisper of her breath join with that of the breeze.

What now? What could she do? Stay in love with Jesse, hold Anthony off indefinitely, pray that he would find someone else himself?

Or give up her own beliefs?

No. She could never give up her passion for this place, for this land. Surely, surely, Jesse would never really be able to do that either.

Now that events were growing critical, Jesse would have to change his heart and his mind. This very place, Cameron Hall, could be in jeopardy. Everything that he loved.

"My, my. To what do we owe this fine pleasure?"

Kiernan nearly leaped from her side-saddle when she heard the husky drawl. Her heart thudded against her rib cage as she turned quickly with surprise. It was Jesse. She knew it long before she saw his face. She would know his voice anywhere, she had heard it in her dreams a thousand times, she had felt the sensual whisper along her spine in long cold nights when she had fought hard against the memories of that she had sworn she would forget.

She looked at his face. She wondered how he had come upon her so silently, or if she had simply been so lost in her reflections that her senses had betrayed her.

He stood some distance from her, having dismounted from his horse, the fine huge roan, Pegasus. He had bred Pegasus at Cameron Hall, and he had brought him into the cavalry with him. Pegasus was impeccably trained, but no horse standing nearly seventeen hands high could tiptoe through brush.

And neither could Jesse—but there he was, indisputably, almost upon her. Tall, striking, standing still in the tall grass, the breeze lifting his hair and pulling upon the cotton of his white open-necked shirt. He was dressed as a civilian in buff-colored breeches and high black boots, dressed as the master of Cameron Hall. His hair seemed exceptionally dark, and his eyes, even at this distance, seemed exceptionally blue. He held Pegasus's reins and stood with his feet planted firm, his legs apart upon the incline of the mound, as a slow smile curved his lip.

"So you've come home," he said softly.

"And so have you."

His lashes fell over his eyes and his smile was broad when he raised his gaze to her once again. "I'm not supposed to be here?"

"I—I did think that you were in Washington."

"Please, don't let the rudeness of my presence destroy your visit. Is my sister expecting you?"

She shook her head. "No one is expecting me."

She had changed—and then again, she hadn't, Jesse thought. She appeared more sophisticated than ever. Surely her riding habit was the latest in French fashion. The cut of the green velvet creation was a very tailored one, but the sharp-angled brim of her green-feathered bonnet lent both femininity and elegance to the outfit. Beneath the closely fitted jacket of the ensemble she wore a laced shirt that added to the very feminine grace of the habit, despite its almost masculine cut.

She wore it well. Seated atop the dapple-gray mare, she was the very height of sophistication and beauty. In fact, she was stunning. Her eyes defied the emerald splendor of the dew-kissed grasses. Her hair, entwined in rich braids and pinned at her nape, took up the colors of the sun and shone with a fiery splendor. And she seemed older, and perhaps wiser, for there was a curious sadness about her gaze.

Watching her, Jesse felt the pain that he thought he had buried come to life again. He clenched and unclenched his fingers, and a heat like the radiating play of the sun upon naked flesh in summer came upon him. It was bittersweet to see her, to have her here before him, to remember what it had been to touch her.

Surely there was no difference among women, he told himself. One was surely the same as the other in the darkness.

But it wasn't true at all. No woman felt the same as Kiernan did, even in the dark. No woman carried the same sweet scent, no one whispered or sighed the same.

With dark fury, he suddenly wished with all his heart that she had married Anthony. He might have purged her from his dreams and his life if only she had done so.

"What are you doing here, Kiernan?" he said suddenly, fiercely.

She stiffened upon her mount. "It's wonderful to see you too, Jesse," she said coolly.

"You're trespassing."

"My Lord, your manners haven't improved—" she began, but he dropped the roan's reins and strode toward her with long steps. She started to back her mare away, but his hands were already upon the mare's bridle, holding her steady. Before she knew it, he was reaching up to her.

"Jesse, what do you think you're—"

She fell silent, for she knew what he was doing. He was lifting her down and into his arms. All the winter's cold was instantly dispelled as he wrapped her tightly into his embrace. He kissed her hard and savagely, suffusing her body with all the warmth of his own, and with the memory of all the splendor.

His hand gently moved over her chin, exploring bone structure and texture. But his eyes were savage as his thumb caressed the softness of her cheek, and his body was rock hard as it pressed against hers. She was caught between the man and the horse, and she was vulnerable to the ferocity of his power.

"My God, I have missed you!" he whispered. "You can't imagine what it's been like. In every drawing room where I have been a guest I've listened to the sound of rustling silk, and I've prayed that I could turn and see you there. And every damned night I've lain awake and thought of you, and even when I've slept, my dreams have been plagued by you. Every time I touched a woman's hair, it seemed coarse in my hands because it was not yours, it wasn't the color of fire, and it did not have the sheen of satin and the feel of velvet and silk. Words whispered have never been the same, you witch! Damn you. Damn you a thousand times over!"

She stared into his eyes, and she felt the heat and the hatred within them.

And she felt so much more. She felt the need in his touch. She felt the hunger and tension in the body pressed so closely to hers. And when he ruthlessly lowered his mouth to hers once again, she parted her lips by instinct and responded with a sweet memory that swept away the time that lay between them.

She was back in his arms again. Nothing else mattered.

She broke away from him, aware of the fires that had been ignited between them. Desire that lay dormant when he was not near rose to the surface of her being. It felt as if her heart beat for him, as if her every breath was for him, as if her limbs flamed for him, as if she were split apart by the fires that burned and radiated from deep within her. She needed desperately to be with him.

She moistened her lips and met his hot gaze. She struggled for breath, then for the sound to make a whisper. "Where can we go?"

He grinned broadly, and she realized that he had voiced that question a year before.

And that she had taken him to the haven.

"I'll show you," he replied softly.

They left the horses in the field atop the mount as he caught her hand and brought her running swiftly down the slope. It seemed in only seconds that they were racing by the cemetery and plunging into the dense foliage that lined the river to the left of the docks. They scurried through a trail of brush and trees until they came to a copse wherein stood an elegant white gazebo, a summer cottage. Like the manor, it was built with a breezeway. Octagonal in shape, its etched-glass doors would welcome the breezes from the river if opened, and yet warm the place against the damp chills of winter. She should have known the place. She had come there often enough as a child.

Now Jesse opened the double doors, which had been closed against the December cold. He led her inside, closed the door again, and leaned against it. For a long time he stood staring at her, and she was suddenly afraid of why she had come, and at the same time she felt a growing pleasure and longing sweep through her. He looked so damned good. The white of his shirt emphasized the bronze of his face and throat. The simple cotton enhanced the structure of his shoulders and torso and arms. His face seemed more lined, she thought, etched more deeply around his eyes. But he seemed more handsome to her than ever, grave, taunting, demanding. They were both growing older, and Jesse was growing even more sensual.

And more determined, she thought briefly.

She would soon be in his arms. And they would stand together, now that he had come home.

"Jesse—"

He swore something unintelligible that held a note of anguish, then strode toward her once again. "No, dammit, I do not want to talk!" He swept the elegant little hat from her head, and before she could stop him, his fingers were in her hair, freeing it from the pins. He spread it out to frame her face, and his lips and mouth touched hers again with such fervor that decency seemed lost, and the fierce flames of desire were awakened. Was it right to love so deeply and so desperately? Kiernan didn't know—she only knew that she lost her soul within his arms, that she sought to touch his tongue with her own, that she was surrendering to the simple ecstasy of his lips upon hers, caressing, seeking, touching again and again.

There was no chaise, no bed, no lounge within the gazebo. But a cloth lay over a wrought-iron table. Jesse swept it up and laid it out upon the floor, then returned for her.

Not even the wildest fires of raw desire could strip away the cold within the summer house. And so he did not seek to divest her of her clothing.

He swept her up and carried her to the cloth, and he bore her down upon it as her eyes met his with the emerald blaze of her longing, and her fingers curled into the ebony hair at his nape. When she was upon the floor, she felt the wetness of his kiss again, warmly raging, touching her lips, drawing away, his tongue seeking, his teeth catching her lower lip lightly, and then again, his tongue meeting hers just outside their parted mouths, and their lips closing finally around the exotic hunger of the kiss.

Velvet still encased and enclosed her, bringing her warmth, a warmth that melted into the growing heat of her body as she thirsted for his touch. His touch came so sweetly. Her velvet jacket was loosened, her breasts spilled free in a froth of lace and silk undergarments. Her skirt was loosed, the ribbon tie of her pantalets was freed. Beneath the textures of the fabrics, his hands roamed freely. His palm began a sultry movement beneath the velvet of her skirt to caress the naked flesh of her hip, of her buttock, of her thigh. Warm velvet brushed against her as his touch traveled on. A heightening expectation, sweet and sensual, then raw and erotic, snaked through her, for with his touch, his kiss never ceased. Always it was there against a part of her. When his lips left hers, it was only for his mouth to form and cover seductively the rouge pinnacle of her breast. His tongue teased the tautening peak, then his lips formed again to suckle upon it deeply, sending startling waves of moist sweet heat rippling through her body to soak her with shattering desire that centered bluntly at the point between her thighs.

With his touch he found that point. With bold, excruciating precision, he stroked her where she most longed to be stroked, centered in upon all the shocking heat and sweet nectar and stroked. Stroked until gasps escaped her throat and she undulated to the rhythm of his hand. The velvet of her skirt bunched high atop of her hip, then she felt the rock-hard point of his erection burn erotically against her naked belly. She reached down to touch him. Her finger closed around his surging hardness and heat and vital life, and she almost pulled away, startled by the searing power and that very masculine life and power and pulse. His fingers closed around hers, holding her there. His kiss caught her lips again, and as his lips played wickedly with hers, she became fascinated with him and explored that living steel, trembling as she stroked and caressed, discovered the dark nest of hair at his groin, the soft sacs within it, and again, the driving rod of his sex. His hoarse cries and whispers drove her on until he was suddenly atop her, and the cry within her own body was answered by the hard and thundering thrust of his shaft deep, deep inside her, seeming to touch to her womb and to her heart.

Bringing with it splendor.

And so if winter winds blew around the summer cottage, the cold inside was dispelled. Her every dream from far-away England was answered, her nights of loneliness, her time of waiting, the endless days when desire had lain dormant because the man to fuel the fires of that desire had been denied her—by her own choice, perhaps.

But time was swept away now, and the world was eclipsed. She had barely seen his face again, she had heard so very few of his words. But here she was again, swept into the rhythms of his passions, caught up in the desperate and heady desire of the excitement that sparked between them. Oh, where was discipline, where was conscience, where was honor, and dear Lord, what had happened to restraint?

In his arms, she did not know, nor could she care. The sweet winter's scent of the river came in along with the breeze, mingled with the subtle scent that belonged only to her lover. Movement went on constantly, exquisitely, the twist and spiral of his body, the taunt when he was away, the gratification when he came again, growing wet and sleek and surging harder and faster with each thrust. She realized suddenly that whimpering sounds, soft eager cries, were coming from her, and that she surged in a likewise frenzy to have more of him, to join with him, to meld their bodies completely. And then suddenly, with one stroke, the wonder burst upon her. The delicious crest was met, and she went stiff, feeling heady, searing pleasure burst forth over all of her body. She shuddered as it swamped her again and again. She drifted as Jesse moved again, and then once more, then fell atop her as the sweetness from him pervaded all of her.

He fell to her side and pulled her against him. For a moment he was still, but then he held a tendril of her hair and brought it against his face, breathing deeply.

"Oh, Jesse," she whispered.

"I wonder," he murmured, "how I lived without you."

She twisted into his arms, delighted just to be held against him, to luxuriate in the warmth and the tenderness that he offered. "Oh, Jesse, is it always like this?" she asked.

He pressed a kiss against her forehead. "No. It is never like this."

"What are we going to do?" she demanded.

To her dismay, he gently eased himself free from her and stood. He absently buttoned his shirt, stuffed the ends into his breeches, and buttoned up his pants. Kiernan sat up, and with far greater difficulty, she rearranged her own clothing.

He strode to where the windows looked toward the house. Through the foliage the back porch with its regal and gracious columns could barely be seen. But as he looked more closely, his eyes grazed over the tops of some of the beautiful monuments within the family graveyard.

"I love this place," he said suddenly, passionately. "My God, I love this place."

I love you, Jesse. She almost said the words, except that she had said them before. She knew that he loved her too. And so she spoke as he did, and her words, too, were true.

"I love it, too, Jesse," she said softly.

He turned to her suddenly, his hands planted firmly on his hips. His hair was rakishly disarrayed, and he appeared very much the man he was, older and wiser than many she knew, perhaps even world-weary. He was strikingly appealing, sensual, bold, sexual, hard—very much the master of his world.

"Then marry me," he said.

To her own dismay, her eyes fell and she started to shiver. She loved Jesse, she wanted to marry him. She wanted to live with him here as lady of Cameron Hall, and she wanted to grow old sipping cool drinks with him upon the porch in the summer, watching their children grow.

She couldn't speak at first. Then she murmured, "What if there is war?"

"There is no war right now."

"Lincoln will soon be president," she said.

"Why the damned hell did you ever have to know anything about politics!" he demanded savagely. "It's a despicable trait in a woman."

She cried out in protest, rising upon her knees. "Oh, Jesse! You don't mean that, you've never meant it before—"

"Well, maybe I mean it now," he muttered. He stared at her again. "Marry me."

She rose, straightening her skirt. She walked to him and leaned against his chest and felt the beat of her heart. Yes! Yes, I'll marry you, there is nothing that I want more in all the world! The words were on the tip of her tongue, aching to be spoken.

"Oh, Jesse!" she murmured miserably. She turned entreating green eyes up to his. "Promise me that you'll be with me, that you'll always be with me!"

His lip curved. "Right or wrong. On your side."

"Oh, Jesse! This *is* your side!"

He smiled a bittersweet smile and lowered his lips to kiss her tenderly, his fingers curving with a tender touch around her skull.

Suddenly, he pulled back, frowning. For a moment she didn't understand, then she too heard the sound of hoofbeats.

"Jesse, Jesse! Confound it, where the hell are you?"

It was Daniel's voice, sounding both excited and anxious. Kiernan stepped back quickly, smoothing her hair, her eyes downcast.

Jesse instinctively stepped before her, shielding her, then strode to the breezeway doors of the summer house.

"Daniel, I'm here. What is it?"

Convinced that she was as put-together as it was possible for her to be, Kiernan stepped up to Jesse's side. Daniel was riding through the trees, as excellent a horseman as his brother. His blue eyes were alive with fire. He opened his mouth to speak, but then he saw Kiernan.

"Kiernan! You're home and you're here!" He leaped down from his horse, and before she knew it, she was in his arms and he was swinging her around, then giving her a sound kiss upon her lips. Jesse watched from the doorway, bemused as he always seemed to be when they met, a dignified figure watching the meeting of children.

"Yes, I'm home!" She laughed and hugged him in return. "I told you I was coming home."

"Yes, but I didn't know that you were here already."

He suddenly stared from her to Jesse, and then back to her again. He must have noticed that her hair was somewhat disarrayed.

But whatever he thought or whatever he knew, he kept it to himself. Before he could speak again, Jesse was striding toward them both, saying, "Daniel, what is it? What brought you racing down here?"

"Oh, oh my Lord. It's happened!"

"What's happened?"

"Secession, Jesse. Secession! South Carolina has just voted herself out of the Union."

Ten

*W*ord of the vote for secession in South Carolina spread through Virginia like wildfire. The decision had been made on December 20, and by that evening, the bells throughout Charleston were ringing to herald a brand-new era for the state. It was not much of a surprise. Ever since the election of the Republican president—and Lincoln was adamantly against the institution of slavery—it had seemed that little else could be expected to happen.

Other conventions were planned throughout the South. As Christmas Day 1860 arrived, tensions were high, and excitement was rampant.

Jesse and Kiernan were both quiet.

On Christmas Eve, Kiernan came to Cameron Hall's Christmas party. Guests came from miles and miles around, including Anthony and his family. It was the first time that Kiernan had seen Anthony since her return to Virginia, and when she greeted him, she tried very hard to be warm. Anthony had not changed during the past year. He seemed to believe that she had now sown whatever feminine wild oats she may have had to sow. His eagerness, his tenderness, were apparent in his eyes.

She saw him first in the open breezeway. Christmas Eve was cold that year, but the doors had been thrown open because the many people present at the affair created an astonishing warmth within the house. Flames burned brightly in every fireplace throughout the stately manor. Cameron Hall had been decked for the occasion with holly boughs and bayberry candles and beribboned wreaths. Mulled wine simmered upon the hearths, and the sweet smell of cinnamon filled the air.

Kiernan had arrived early with her father, and was hugged enthusiastically by Christa and Daniel. Jesse had taken her shoulders and placed a perfunctory kiss upon her cheek, and their eyes had met. There had been little that they could say before others.

They had been able to say little to each other since Daniel had first brought the news of the secession. Daniel had been with them when they returned to Cameron Hall to tell Christa, and Daniel had insisted upon accompanying her home to tell her father the news.

Excitement over the news ran very, very high. The only one subdued about events was Jesse.

"They insist in South Carolina that it will be a peaceful split," Daniel had informed them.

"There will be no peace," Jesse said quietly.

"Well, now it is up to the other states to choose sides," Daniel mused. They all knew it didn't matter much what the others did—all that mattered was the choice Virginia made.

Kiernan had had no further opportunity to speak with Jesse alone. Others arrived at the Christmas Eve party just after she did.

It was a joyous occasion. Even though speculation and excitement rose with an ever-increasing fervor, it was still Christmas Eve, a warm and poignant occasion. The guests arrived in beautiful apparel, the men in distinguished frock coats and elegant tuxedos, the ladies in every manner of velvet and silk and fur. And despite the cold, bosoms were bared as daringly as fashion would allow. Fiddles and flutes joined the music of the pianoforte, which had been brought into the huge hallway, and reel after reel was played for dancers who knew no exhaustion.

When Anthony and his family arrived, Kiernan was in the breezeway with Christa. Christa, the last of the Camerons, was a beauty with the family blue eyes and raven hair set against a cream complexion and fine delicate features. She had a will to match that of both her brothers. Christa whispered against Kiernan's cheek to let her know that Anthony had arrived, then swept by her in her velvet and taffeta skirts to greet the Millers herself. Anthony and his father were there, as well as Patricia and Jacob, his younger sister and brother. Kiernan stayed back, watching the four Camerons converge on the breezeway, welcoming the new arrivals. The Millers had come a long way. They would be guests of the estate and probably stay until the new year.

Anthony was, as ever, perfectly polite. But after he had shaken hands with Jesse and Daniel and kissed Christa on the cheek, his gaze swiftly roamed over the crowd and came to rest upon her.

She felt pinned down by the cast of his eyes, captured in some mockery of circumstance. The tenderness in his gaze was almost unbearable. He moved swiftly through the crowd of dancers and diners and merrymakers to reach her side.

Even as he walked, Kiernan knew that Jesse was watching him, watching her.

Anthony reached her side and touched her shoulders with trembling fingers.

He pulled her close and offered the most proper and still emotional kiss upon her cheek. He was loath to set her free. "Kiernan, I've missed you so very much. Are you home now for good? I hope so. Things are happening quickly now. There may be war. You can't go running around the world anymore. You have to stay home—and marry me. Let me make an announcement this Christmas, Kiernan. Please, let that be your gift to me!"

She stared into the warm brown of his eyes and felt the tension in his arms upon her. "Oh, Anthony!" she told him miserably. "I can't. I just can't!"

Disappointment darkened his eyes and he swallowed hard, but he spoke softly and quickly again. "I've rushed you again. Forgive me."

She wanted to scream at him. *He* didn't need to be forgiven—*she* did. But she couldn't tell him that she was in love with another man. Perhaps she should— perhaps that would end it. But she couldn't put still more pain into that dark gaze of his.

Not even with Jesse watching.

Or maybe *because* Jesse was watching. Maybe Jesse needed to remember that there were other men who could love her—men who did not betray their own kind.

"I'd love to dance, Anthony," she told him. She looked over his shoulder and gave Jesse a brilliant smile, then moved into Anthony's arms.

It was Christmas, and it was a party. She danced with Anthony, and Andrew, and Anthony's young brother, Jacob. She danced with her father, and she danced with Daniel, and she danced with any number of the other guests.

Handsome men, young Virginians, planters, military friends of the Camerons, neighbors—dashing, exciting young men. She flirted outrageously.

Jesse danced, too, with his own sister and with Andrew's pretty sister, Patricia.

Then he danced with Elizabeth Nash, the steel heiress from Richmond. Then he danced with Charity McCarthy, the widow of a senator, still residing in Washington.

She lived very near where Jesse was stationed, Kiernan found herself thinking bitterly.

Jesse danced with Charity again. In the arms of a Virginia militia lieutenant, Kiernan watched Jesse again with the sable-haired, very elegant Charity.

The woman's head was cast back as she laughed, revealing an ample expanse of her shoulders and breast and the diamond locket she wore to emphasize her natural assets. Jesse's hand was upon her waist, and his eyes seemed caught within hers. It seemed, too, that nothing in the world mattered to him except for the elegant woman in his arms.

"I am in love."

"What?"

Startled, Kiernan looked back at the young lieutenant with whom she was dancing. He was a very good-looking boy, with ash-blond curls, warm hazel eyes —and cheeks that barely needed shaving. He smiled sweetly at her. "I'm in love. Truly, Miss Mackay, you are the most beautiful woman I have ever seen. Dare I hope that we might become better acquainted?"

She was probably a year older than he, Kiernan thought. She stared at him blankly, then realized that Jesse was sweeping by again with the widow from Washington. She flashed the boy a smile. "I do cherish my friends, sir. And I'd be delighted to count you among them."

A few minutes later she was startled by a firm hand upon her arm, and she was swept into Jesse's arms. His eyes flashed a dangerous, wicked blue, as hot as they had ever been. They stared arrogantly into her own.

"What now, Miss Mackay? Another conquest? Is it not enough that young Mr. Miller must trip over his tongue every time you are near? Would you have another young man panting on the whisper of a promise? Or have you taken love up as sport?"

Her hand went rigid, and she would have slapped him. But his hold upon her was tight, and his words were quick and harsh. "No, no, careful, love! Imagine, what would they all think if you suddenly slapped your host upon the dance floor? Your father would be aghast—I would be forced to tell him the truth about our relationship. Anthony would be horrified and honor-bound to come to your rescue to salvage your honor. He would be forced to challenge me. And in the duel I'd have to try damned hard to stay alive and at the same time manage not to kill the poor young fool. Is that what you want, Kiernan? The two of us—or three or more of us—fighting over you?"

She still wanted to strike him. But more than anything, she wanted to cry. She lowered her eyes and shook her head. "No. No, that's not what I want." She looked up at him again, her eyes damp. "What I want is you, Jesse."

He smiled, a slow, somewhat painful grin that curled his lip in self-mockery. "But you have had me, Kiernan. And you have me still."

They whirled around the dance floor once again. Kiernan knew where he was taking her. They whirled to the open doorways and then beyond. He slipped off his handsome frock coat to set it about her shoulders as they moved down the porch. They could hear the sounds of laughter and singing from the slave quarters. Delicious aromas wafted on the air from the smokehouse and the kitchen and the bakehouse. That sweet smell that was Christmas was on the air, a smell of cinnamon, cloves, bayberry, holly, mulling wine, rum, and fruitcake, and so many other special scents.

Kiernan felt as if she were going to cry again. She lifted her arms and encompassed the scene, the porch, the winter garden, the lawn sweeping down to the river, the stables and other appendixes to the beautiful estate, the graveyard with its long history. "This!" she whispered. "This is what I want."

He smiled, sitting up atop a latticed railing at the far end of the porch and drawing her close. "This? The hall? You could have married Daniel long ago for this."

She blushed. "No, I don't mean the hall, although I do love it." She turned to him very seriously. "Jesse, I want you. And I want the life that we have always led. I want the river, and I want the land, and I want years of Christmases just like this one. I want the elegance—"

"You know how much work a plantation is!" he reminded her sharply.

Yes, she did know. It was dawn-to-dusk work, no matter how many slaves a man or woman owned. It was constant supervision of a massive household. The laundry, candles, beeswax, baking, sewing, cleaning, buying, harvesting, and always listening to problems, solving them, and starting all over again. But Kiernan had never minded. She had been her father's hostess since she was a child, and she had learned so very much that way.

And all the work was for moments like these, moments when she could look out upon the river.

"I want this," she murmured. "I want you and me and this. I want to grow old throwing such parties, and sitting upon this porch. And watching my grandchildren tumble down the lawn. I want to be buried in that little graveyard, with a headstone that says Cameron."

"Then marry me," Jesse interrupted. "If I can promise you nothing else, I think I could see to it that you are interred in that plot with a Cameron headstone."

She pulled away from him and glanced at him sharply. "You're laughing at me, Jesse."

"No," he told her softly, "I am not."

His eyes were dark, a dusky blue. He watched her with a combination of tenderness and warmth. For a moment, she thought that they shared everything. He understood exactly how she felt. He loved the things that she loved and he loved her.

Maybe it was just the moment itself that they shared. But she felt compelled to move closer to him and to watch him with growing wonder as he bent down and just touched her lips with his own, lightly, gently, oh, so tenderly, so sweetly.

They broke away, watching each other.

It was then that she heard the sharp sound of a man clearing his throat. Jesse looked up over her head, and Kiernan spun around with dread.

It was her father. A blush suffused her cheeks, and she wondered what he had seen.

He had seen enough. He was staring hard at Jesse.

"Kiernan, get in the house," John Mackay advised her firmly.

"Papa—" she began to protest.

"Kiernan, your father asked you to go inside," Jesse reminded her firmly, his eyes upon John.

She had never been in terror of her father. She loved him, loved him dearly. He had always been a good, giving, and even tender parent. They were, after all, all the family that each other had. But his eyes, which were usually such a soft and gentle blue, were now as hard as steel. She wanted to protest, but she looked from him to Jesse and back to him, then to Jesse once again. Neither seemed to be paying her any heed.

"Papa, Jesse—"

They both turned on her. Their words were unanimous. "Go inside, Kiernan."

Trembling and furious that both would order her about so, she gritted her teeth, inched her chin up, and headed for the doors, decrying her sex.

But she paused just inside the doors and tried to listen to their words, her heart seeming to spin within her chest.

She heard Jesse's voice first, assuring John that his intentions were entirely honorable. He had, in fact, asked Kiernan to marry him. As yet, she had not agreed, and that was why Jesse had not yet come to John.

Her father was curiously silent.

"Mr. Mackay," Jesse began again. "I assure you—"

"I know, Jesse, I know. You have grown up honorable, and five years ago I would have welcomed your suit. I would have deplored my daughter's handling of young Miller. I cannot fault her behavior now, for she has refused an engagement with him. But I have to tell you, Jesse, that if you came to me now, I could not give you my blessing."

Kiernan could not see Jesse, but she knew that he was stiffening, that he was standing very tall, that his backbone was rigid, that his temper was held in check out of respect for her father.

"You won't be here much longer, will you?" her father asked softly.

Jesse was very quiet. "I don't know, Mr. Mackay."

"It will depend which way the wind blows, won't it?" John asked him.

Again, Jesse was quiet.

"Perhaps you should stay away from her until we know," John suggested.

"That will be difficult, sir," Jesse said.

"And why is that?"

"Because I love her, you see."

"Indeed," John said quietly. "Then, sir, I must ask you for prudence. Let things go on as they have been. We'll watch the wind."

"All right, Mr. Mackay," Jesse agreed. "We'll watch the wind."

Kiernan was still at the doorway when her father came bursting back through it. He stared at her, and his shaggy brow went flying up. "Hmpf!" he exclaimed. "I should have suspected you were there!"

She looked anxiously to the porch, but her father caught her arm and pulled her back into the hallway and into the dance in progress. "I should have kept you in Europe a bit longer, eh, daughter? I've been warned that a beautiful woman is trouble, and trouble you're proving to be!"

"Papa!" she wailed.

He winked at her, softening his words. But when the music died, he said, "Bid Christa and Daniel and Jesse good-bye. And be especially polite to young Anthony—his father and I are business partners. Then we'll be going."

"But it's early!"

"I have a feeling that it's already too late," John Mackay said with a weary sigh. "You'll do as you're told this once, daughter. Now I mean it—run along."

Much as she was unaccustomed to his giving her orders, she knew that he meant his words. The party had barely begun, but it did not matter—they would leave.

She hugged and kissed Daniel, fought for regal control as she said good-bye and thank you to Jesse, and was as demure and charming as her father could have wanted when she bade good night to Anthony. She would see them all again, soon, she knew. Her father would hold a twelfth-night dinner at their home.

But she was suddenly very much afraid. It was one thing to hold Jesse off by her own desire and determination. But now that her father was involved . . .

Her father had seen the same torment in Jesse that she knew he had about the political situation that faced them all.

She loved Jesse. But was her love stronger than whatever might happen in the country? Could she ever really be Jesse's enemy?

Yes, she could, she thought, and was more bitter because of that love.

Yet she could not believe that when the time was really upon them, that Jesse could leave his home—that he could leave her—because of a misguided disagreement with Virginia's political stance.

She did not want him to be torn away from her. She wanted to hold him, to hold him as tightly as she could.

And so before she left, she found Christa. She dared to take her friend, Jesse's sister, into her confidence.

"Christa, please ask Jesse to meet me at the summer cottage tomorrow, at dusk."

Christa's eyes grew large and wide. "All right, Kiernan."

"And please—"

"I won't say anything to anyone else, Kiernan. I promise."

Kiernan smiled. The two girls hugged one another, then Kiernan hurried out, not wanting to risk her father's temper.

In the carriage, John Mackay stared at her. "So it's been Jesse Cameron all along, has it?"

"Yes, Papa," she said primly.

"You love him, huh?"

"Yes!"

"Do you love him enough?"

"Enough?" She flushed, and suddenly she found herself defending Jesse's position. "Virginia has not seceded, sir. We are not at war."

Her father wagged a finger at her. "You listen to me, missy. Virginia will secede, and there will be a war. Jesse knows that. That's the only reason he hasn't pressed you. If he weren't the man that he is, if he didn't love you enough to know your own heart better than you do yourself, he would have been at my door long ago. You mark my words, young lady, guard your heart.''

She'd guard her heart, all right.

But she would still meet him at the summer cottage tomorrow. She had a Christmas gift for him.

He arrived at the cottage at exactly noon and saw that Kiernan had come before him, for a fire had been lit. He could see the smoke drifting softly from the chimney. He smiled. She wouldn't worry about the smoke attracting attention. She knew he came here often, and that his family respected his privacy.

He entered, and for a moment he blinked, trying to adjust to the dim light in the room. All that gave it luminescence was the fire that played in the grate. The room was bathed in a very pale glow of gold, otherwise touched in shadow.

And then he saw her.

She was only a few feet away from the fire, upon the floor. But the floor was not bare—it was covered in fur.

And like the floor, she was covered in fur. A beautiful white fox was draped over the length of her. Her hair, loose and free and set to shine like fire from the glow of the blaze, rippled and waved over the fur.

Then, as he stood, she let the fur fall. She was naked, naked in the achingly soft and sensual pool of the fur.

"Merry Christmas," she whispered. Her emerald eyes were green in the glow, the eyes of a cat, mysterious, haunting, compelling.

He paused—God in heaven, he didn't know how he did so, but he did—and allowed his eyes to rake over her, to relish and savor, to savage and adore the woman that he thought he knew so well. He knew the sweet scent of that glorious golden hair, knew its feel between his fingers. He knew those eyes, the elegant shape of her face. He knew the taste of her flesh, the curve of her hip, the fullness of her breast. He knew the length and shape of her thighs, knew the musky sweet secret femininity between her legs. He knew so very much about her . . . but not as much as he thought he knew.

She rose. She seemed to glide from the elegant cocoon of fur, like Venus sweeping from Poseidon's shell. She stood before him, sensual, exciting, sweeping his breath away. The boldness to her movement was belied by the sudden shyness in her eyes, by their uncertainty as her gaze met his.

A soft, tender question curved her lips, lips that were full, shapely, moist, waiting to be kissed.

She stretched her arms out to him, wanting him, arms soft and creamy, heightened the beauty of her breasts as they rose. Alabaster, touched by the tiny blue lines of veins, crested by nipples as rouge as a rose in winter. His eyes swept lower still, taking in the golden nest at her thighs, the curve of her hip.

A cry, ragged, hoarse, tore from his lips, and she was within his arms. He tore his clothes from his body, and soon he was next to her before the fire.

Upon their knees, they met one another. The fire glowed over their bodies, making his shoulders sleek, making the curves of her body, her breasts, her hips gleam. Their fingers met and meshed, and then their lips caressed and parted and caressed again.

Soon their bodies were dampened and slickened by the torrents of kisses and caresses that they shared and exchanged. The fire glowed upon them still.

It glowed until he pressed her back upon the fur and sank hard within her. The winter's cold became summer with its heat.

After the blaze had swept through, the fire still played within the grate, and the glow remained to warm them.

Mississippi seceded from the Union on January 9, Florida seceded on the tenth, and Alabama on the eleventh.

The four states needed only Georgia for the seceded territory to stretch from North Carolina's southern border to the Mississippi.

Joseph E. Brown, Georgia's strongly secessionist governor, asked his legislature to call for a convention. Speeches were made by visitors from the already-seceded states.

On January 19, Georgia became the fifth state to secede from the Union. Louisiana seceded on the twenty-sixth, and Texas on February 1.

By the end of the month, Jesse and Daniel had both ridden back to join their units. Virginia had made no move to leave the Union.

Her legislature had suggested that a convention be held in Washington, at the Willard Hotel, in the hope of preventing war. It convened on February 4 and was known as the Washington Peace Convention.

But delegates from the lower South were conspicuously absent. On the same day, they were holding their own convention in Montgomery, Alabama, to form a new government, a Confederacy of seceded states.

So while peace was discussed in the North, the Confederacy was becoming a reality. The Confederate delegates rushed to perform important tasks to solidify their own union before Abraham Lincoln could take office. In Montgomery, Jefferson Davis—once President Buchanan's secretary of war, the man in charge of that department when John Brown had raided Harpers Ferry—was elected to the highest office of the new Confederacy.

The Confederate Constitution was ratified. The "stars and bars" was adopted as the flag. An army was authorized. The laws of the United States were also adopted, with exceptions regarding states' rights and the instituion of slavery. The Mississippi River was declared open for navigation, Texas was admitted to the Confederacy. The provisional government authorized loans, contracts, and treasury notes—and prepared for war.

Much of this went on while the Washington Peace Convention was still playing with hope at the Willard Hotel.

At home, Kiernan waited, wishing desperately that she could be where all the action was taking place. She read every newspaper she could get her hands on, and she waited.

Virginia remained steady for the moment, and both Cameron brothers remained with their regiments. Kiernan heard frequently from Daniel, who was eager to explain his position. "My heart lies with this new Confederacy," he wrote, "with the states and the people with whom we have so very much in common. I think that I am a southerner, a Confederate—a Rebel, if you will! But first and foremost, I am a Virginian, and I will abide by the will of the state I love so dearly. Actually," he went on to admit, "I believe that I have stolen that sentiment from Colonel Lee, but then, you know how we both admire him, and he expresses what we feel." The letter rambled on. It ended with a postscript. "Jesse sends his love."

His love—and his silence, Kiernan thought.

Throughout the South, major events were taking place.

In Florida, warlike actions had begun even before the state had seceded. Militia had been trained. In Pensacola, Federal troops had been forced off the mainland forts of McRee and Barrancas to Fort Pickens in the harbor. Fort Marion at St. Augustine had been seized, and Alabama and Florida troops had taken over the navy yard at Pensacola. Southern military leaders wanted to attack Fort Pickens, but they also wanted to avert war, and so they waited.

Similar events were taking place throughout the Confederacy. In South Carolina, Brigadier General Pierre Beauregard watched the Union troops at Fort Sumter and feared that Washington would send reinforcements.

Everywhere, the tension increased.

And still Kiernan waited. Anthony no longer plagued her with his constant, patient proposals, for he had hurried home. He had left his position with his local militia, for many of its members were pro-Union, as were many of the western counties of the state. Politically, Anthony was everything that Kiernan longed for Jesse to be—passionately, loyally, unshakably sympathetic to their cotton and tobacco neighbors.

Anthony scarcely even wrote, though his words were passionate when he did. He and his father were recruiting and arming a unit of cavalry. They were busy buying horses and designing uniforms.

Then, in early April 1861, Kiernan's time of waiting came to an end.

Christa came riding by to tell her with a great deal of jubilation that both her brothers were soon coming home. "I'm so delighted! They've both gotten leave to come for my birthday. I wanted to tell you as soon as I heard from the both of them. Thank goodness Daniel is such a wonderful correspondent!"

"Yes, thank goodness," Kiernan agreed.

"Oh, I can't wait to see them!"

"Neither can I," Kiernan told her fervently. "Oh, neither can I!"

Two days later, Christa was back. She met Kiernan on her porch and did not dismount from her horse. She smiled mischievously. "A soldier just stopped by, a friend of Jesse's who resigned his commission."

"Oh?" Kiernan said, her heart thundering.

Christa laughed. "Well, it seems that Jesse is capable of writing after all. He sent me a note, and in it is a request for you."

"Yes?"

Christa handed her an envelope. Kiernan raised a brow to her, then reached for the letter inside.

Her eyes scanned the brief but affectionate passages to Christa, asking about the house, servants, the weather, and Christa's state of mind and health.

The last paragraph referred to her.

Christa, please see Kiernan for me. And ask her to meet me at the summer cottage. Dusk, the night of the sixteenth.

"What do I tell him?" Christa asked her.

Kiernan lowered her lashes swiftly, not wanting Christa to see the wild elation within her eyes. She fought for control, then raised her eyes to Christa's once again and smiled demurely. "Tell him I'll be there."

Christa smiled and started to turn her horse away. Then she paused, turning back. "Oh, I forgot. There's a postscript on the back. He says that it might be cold. He suggests you wear fur."

Kiernan smiled and lowered her head quickly. She folded her hands before her, but despite her best efforts, her voice was filled with a soft tremor.

"Tell him . . . tell him I'll wear fur."

She turned and ran back into the house, unable to look into Christa's eyes any longer.

She'd wear fur. It was what Jesse wanted.

Jesse was coming home.

Eleven

ooking out from the breezeway doors of the gazebo, Jesse could see the monuments of the cemetery and beyond in the evening light. The lawn sloped up to the house, and the garden was just coming out from its winter's cloak of green to flower again.

It had been a beautiful day.

April in Virginia was often a whimsical month. Sometimes a dead heat lay over the coastal land. The heavy humidity of summer came creeping in early, and the nights were sultry and warm. Sometimes, it was just the opposite. The day could be bitterly cold, and it was even possible for a light spattering of wet snow to fall, the kind that could chill you to the bone.

Then sometimes, it was just beautiful, everything that came with the promise of spring. The sun would shine throughout the day, hot and radiant, throwing a bold new yellow light over the soft new grass that was just bursting through the old. The first of the spring flowers would be bathed in that light, their colors the brighter for it. But the heat of the sun was softened and tempered by the coolness of the air coming in from the river, and it was easy to walk, easy to breathe, easy to love to be alive. Newborn foals frolicked and played in the fields, and the horses bred from Arabian stock whipped their tails up incredibly high and seemed to dance within their paddocks.

It had been one of those days today. A cool day, tempered by a warm sun. The night coming on was a gentle and balmy one. The whisper of the breeze was itself sensual, seeming to wrap around him as he waited in the summer house.

He wondered if she would come.

The wire services were alive with the latest developments between the Union and the new-formed Confederacy.

In the early hours of April 12, the southern troops under General Beauregard in Charleston had fired upon the Union position at Fort Sumter in Charleston harbor.

Major Robert Anderson had been in command at Sumter, with Captain Abner Doubleday his second in command. Beauregard had set up batteries in Charleston because South Carolina was offended by the Federal troops sitting on its sovereign territory. The Federals had been asked to surrender, but Anderson, expecting supplies from Washington, had refused. He'd had only sixty-six cannon, many of them unmounted, and he was short of powder-bag cartridges.

At 3:20 A.M., hostilities came to a head. One last demand for a surrender was made and refused, and the Federals were warned that they would soon be fired upon.

And so they were. Two hours later, a Confederate shell broke over Fort Sumter, and the shelling continued. Anderson gave Doubleday the honor of firing the first Union shot at seven, and the uneven contest began.

It went on all through the day. By nightfall, the shelling slackened, but by dawn of the thirteenth, it came again. Anderson and Doubleday kept their men low to the ground against the smoke inhalation. The supply ship Anderson had awaited came—but it was held in the harbor by the Confederate artillery.

Soon after noon, a Confederate shell blew away the fort's flagstaff. Secessionist Colonel Wigfall rowed out to Sumter, having seen the flag go down, and demanded a surrender of the fort.

Anderson, having no way to fight, conceded. To that point, he had not lost a man.

Surrender ceremonies were planned for the next day, and Anderson asked and received permission from Beauregard to salute the American flag before hauling it down. The hundred-gun salute brought about the death of a Union soldier when the fiftieth gun exploded.

Throughout South Carolina, there was tremendous jubilation. Union forces had been thrust away.

In Virginia, the situation was at a crucial peak. A legislature would now decide the fate of the state. Lincoln had made a call to arms. War seemed imminent.

It seemed impossible for Virginia to take up arms against her sister states.

Would Kiernan come? Jesse wondered again in the summer cottage.

Even as the question plagued his mind, he saw movement in the foliage beyond, and then she burst into the clearing and raced into the gazebo.

She closed the doors behind her, leaning against them. Her eyes touched his, filled with life and a blazing green excitement. Her breast rose and fell swiftly with the force of her breathing. Her hair was free and wild, tumbling around her shoulders and down her back in a sweep of sunlit waves.

The fur she wore rimmed an elegant gold cape that swept evocatively around her body.

"Jesse!"

She whispered his name, and then she was in his arms. He quickly discovered that beneath the cape she wore a simple cotton day dress and nothing more. As he slipped the tie on the cape and it fell softly to the floor, he felt her hands upon him, tugging his shirt free from his breeches. He felt her fingers upon his naked flesh and marveled at the touch, shuddering as the hot fires of desire snaked through him.

In the days to come, he would remember this night, remember it with aching poignancy, and he would tremble anew, thinking of all that he had held in his arms.

For in all the long years when they had watched each other and waited, when he had wondered at the beauty she would be when she grew up, he had never imagined this.

He knew that she was his. He had been her first lover, the first to touch her, to teach her. And she had learned to give so very much to him. She had never questioned propriety, she had simply loved him. And in that, he had never known a feeling more exquisite, never known a power so great. She was sensual, elegant, beautiful, and in his life, he had never imagined a love so great.

She stroked his back, her fingers playing upon muscle and sinew. She rose against him, the soft curves of her body haunting and evocative beneath the simple cotton of her dress as she pressed against his naked chest. She nibbled against his lower lip, then rose to meet him in a wild and sweet open-mouthed kiss that drove every demon known to man to tear into his groin and his blood. He had stripped her of the gown and borne her down upon the fur that had offered them so sweet and heady a haven before.

In the days to come, he would indeed remember this evening! Remember the feel of her lips, moist and searing warm, moving over his body, the feeling of soft, exhilarating fire, wet upon his chest, trailing patterns, circling his nipples where her teeth teased and played. He felt the flow of her hair following the taunt of her lips, soft velvet to bring him to an ever-greater need. And still she loved and teased and taunted him with tender kisses upon his flesh, exotic, erotic, decadent kisses upon his flesh, moving lower and lower against him until, incredibly, she touched the pulsing fullness of his sex with her mouth.

Lightly at first, with kisses that were so soft and sweet that they tormented him nearly to hell. He grabbed hold of her, unable to bear the bursting desire, when suddenly she closed her sweet caress hard around him, and in all his life he had never felt so searing an explosion of desire.

He drew her to him. The hot blood surged and raced throughout his body, and he pressed her down hard into the velvet-soft fur upon the floor. His fingers became entangled in her hair, and he ravished her with burning kisses as her long legs wound erotically around his hips, and he swept inside her, thrusting deeply into the welcoming, sheathing warmth.

When the sweetness of the tempestuous climax claimed them both, he scarce let the cool breeze of the night whisper over them before he turned upon her again, fiercely, needing the night. In the coming darkness, he smiled down into the misty beauty of her eyes and began to make love to her again.

Kissing, caressing, finding sweetly erotic places, the pulse at her throat, the lobe of her ear. He shimmied his body down the length of her hers, and his kisses grew slow and sultry upon her naked flesh, teasing her breasts, loving them tenderly, demanding their fullness. Still his body caressed hers as he moved again, kissing the point at the back of her knee, the softness of her thighs, and the beckoning warmth of the sweet petals between them. She cried out, and he caressed her still, stroked her, whispered to her. But she was up on her knees to meet him, her lips searing his, her fingers entwined about his nape, curling into his hair. Windswept yearnings became a tempest in the tranquil quiet of the night. The end burst upon Jesse with shattering volatility, drawing everything from him. The world spun as he stared down at her, her lashes fallen over her eyes, her hair a tangle about them both, her delicate, beautiful features flushed and damp. Her eyes opened to his, and he kissed her again and fell to her side, pulling her close.

"Oh, Jesse," she murmured.

"I was afraid that you wouldn't come," he told her.

"Why?"

He kissed her forehead. "Never mind. Let's not get into it. I don't want to argue with you."

Even as he tried to pull her close, she stiffened.

"Why, Jesse?"

He leaned up on an elbow. "Because war is imminent. I'm sure you've heard about Fort Sumter."

She blinked, staring at him. "Yes, I've heard about Fort Sumter. The wire services carried little else. Jesse, the Virginia legislature is meeting on the matter of secession."

"I know," he said quietly.

He wondered what it was in his tone that she heard. She pushed away from him, shaken, hugging her arms about herself in the sudden coolness that came once they had parted.

"Jesse, what is the matter with you?" she cried. "How can you turn against everything that—"

"I've not turned against anything!" he said irritably. He pushed up and stood, staring down at her. "Kiernan, it's never been anything but one way with you. You've never even looked at the big picture. Not once."

"What big picture?" she demanded. Her eyes were open wide now, and very dangerous in their luster.

He sighed.

He wanted life to go on, too, exactly the way it had been. He loved Virginia, he loved his home. He could never explain to her just how much. He and Daniel and Christa used to walk down and set flowers on the graves of their parents, and when his sister and brother were gone, Jesse had stayed, closing his eyes, thinking of the past that had been theirs, the times and trials that the house had weathered, the triumphs, the agonies.

He loved the James River. He loved to watch the steamers come in, and he loved to hear the singing and the chanting as the slaves loaded the bales of cotton onto the decks of the ships.

Why in God's name did she think that he was turning against everything he loved? Couldn't she understand? There was something greater at stake than slavery and states' rights. They were all Americans.

" 'A house divided against itself cannot stand,' " he quoted softly.

"What?"

"It's something that Lincoln said a few years ago," he told her, "in Illinois, after he was nominated for senator."

He could tell from her reaction that she didn't have much interest in Abraham Lincoln.

"It's true, Kiernan. My God, we aren't even a century old as a nation. Americans bested the English, some of the finest soldiers in the world, because they joined together. Because Virginia stood up for Massachusetts."

"Because we had help from the French," Kiernan murmured dryly.

"Because we stood together," Jesse said flatly. "We're *one* country. And we can be great because of the farmlands of the South and the industry in the north."

"You want to fight against Virginia."

"I want to fight *for* Virginia."

She leaped up, facing him, very beautiful and dignified in her nakedness. Her fingers wound into fists at her side as she faced him. "Jesse, you talk about a house divided against itself! Cameron Hall is your house. Virginia is your house. I am part of your house! Don't you see? You're against slavery? So are a lot of people! Maybe, eventually, we'll manage to free our own slaves! Without being told to do so by fanatics. Damn you, Jesse, *you* still own slaves. You haven't figured out how to change the world yourself!"

"My slaves will be freed!" he told her passionately. But then he curbed his anger, swallowing down a taste of pain and bitterness. "Kiernan, I love Virginia."

"Then what will you do if Virginia secedes?"

"I don't know," he told her flatly. He took a step toward her. Even after the hours they had shared together, she stepped away from him. Anger spilled from him again, and he pulled her back into his arms. "I love you, Kiernan!"

Tears filled her eyes as they met his. "Do you love me enough, Jesse?"

"Damn you!" He exploded. "Do *you* love *me* enough?"

She jerked free from him and spun around for her clothing. She snatched up her dress and started away from him again, but he caught her arm and pulled her hard against his chest. He kissed her, sweetly, savagely. He refused to let her go when she fought his hold. He kissed her until her lips parted to his, until she offered up a surrender to at least that demand. The hair on his chest chafed against the softness of her breasts, and he felt the hardening of her nipples against his flesh. She twisted her lips free from his at last.

"Let me go, Jesse."

"No, not tonight."

"Please."

"I can't," he told her. "Dammit, Kiernan, don't ask me to let you go tonight!"

Suddenly, the force she had exerted against him was gone. She rested her cheek against his chest, and he felt the dampness of her tears.

He swept her up into his arms and carried her back to the furs.

He kissed away her tears, and she curled into his arms again. They made love, slowly, tenderly. The night around them was achingly sweet.

When they rose at last, Jesse was the one to move first. He rose and dressed and helped her into her things.

"I'll take you home," he told her.

"I know my way."

"I'll take you home," he insisted.

He set her in front of him on Pegasus, and when they reached her mare tethered under trees, he kept Kiernan with him and led the mare along.

When they neared her house, she stirred. "Jesse, you should leave me here. My father—"

"I'm taking you home, Kiernan."

As it was, John Mackay was waiting on his front porch. It, too, was broad and handsome, with its brick facade, its pillars tall and regal. John Mackay sat with his pleasant, lined face in repose, his pipe in his mouth, a tumbler of whiskey in his hand.

"Though you might be bringing her home, Jesse," John said. "Else I might have worried about the time."

"I'd not have let her come alone, sir."

"I'm sorry, Papa," Kiernan began.

"It's all right. I knew you were safe with Jesse."

Someone else might not have considered her safe in Jesse's company. But Mackay was a different man. Even if he suspected that his daughter and Jesse were lovers, her life and her happiness mattered more to him. He was indeed a rare man, created within a rare breed.

"I'll just go in so you two can say good night," John offered.

Jesse dismounted from Pegasus and reached up to lift her down. She leaned against him and accepted the tender kiss he placed upon her lips.

She lowered her head against him.

"I love you, Kiernan."

"I love you, too, Jesse," she said. But then her emerald eyes, brimming with dampness and fire, rose to meet his. "But if Virginia secedes and you don't resign your commission in the Federal army, I won't see you again. Ever."

She pulled away from his arms and raced for the door.

There was nothing he could do but watch her go.

Jesse awoke the next morning with an incredible headache.

A great deal of the pain was his own fault. After he left Kiernan, he'd come home and spent the better part of the night with a bourbon bottle and Daniel, discussing times recently past, and times long past. Christa had found them down in the den in the first faint hours of daylight. Being a good Cameron, she had shared a sound swig of bourbon with them—and then ordered them both up to bed.

His headache was his own fault. And it was a damned mean and nasty one. It wasn't helped a bit by the screeching and shouting and carrying-on that was coming from outside the house.

Staggering from the bed with a sheet wrapped about his waist, he stumbled across the room to the wide double doors. They led to a balcony that looked out over the rear porch and the gardens and all the way down to the river. He saw that Daniel was outside, greeting two riders. One of them was Anthony Miller, a fact that seemed to make the pounding in his head all the fiercer. The other was a closer neighbor from the Williamsburg area, Aaron Peters.

The two had ridden in, whooping and hollering. Having listened to them, Daniel suddenly swept his hat from atop his head and threw it high into the air. A thunderous war whoop escaped him, as if he were out west joining in with the Cheyenne or Sioux.

"What the hell?" Jesse muttered. The sound of his own voice hurt him.

He pulled on his breeches and his boots and drew a shirt from the heavy armoire in the corner of his room. Suddenly, he stopped. He ran his hands over the armoire, then stood back to look at the room.

It was the master's room of Cameron Hall. He hadn't taken it over until several years after his father's death. As the oldest son, he had inherited the hall. Not that it had meant anything in the years gone past. He had been involved in his medical career and the service, and Daniel had been just as avid a horse soldier. They came from a long line of fighters. The first Cameron on the Virginian shore had battled the Indians, survived the massacre, and lived on to create a dynasty. Camerons had battled pirates, and his grandfather had fought for the fledgling colonies in the American Revolution.

Jesse moved his hand over the armoire. It had stood where it did now as long as Jesse could remember, just like the big master bed and the elegant glass-paned doors that led out to the porch. The desk had held the Cameron ledgers for years and years.

He moistened his lips, feeling a cold sweat break out on his skin. A feeling of dread was already falling over him.

He slipped on his shirt and hurried from the room. Again he paused, for though he rarely gave the portrait gallery at the top of the stairway much attention, he now felt as if each and every Cameron were staring down at him. He paused and studied the pictures. Lord Jamie Cameron, and his beautiful barmaid bride, the indomitable Jassy. His grandmother, Amanda, cool and elegant, accused of being a Tory spy, but standing by her husband in the end. And Eric Cameron, a slight twitch of amusement to his lips, his eyes painted a startling deep blue. He seemed to question Jesse—to dare him to hold to his own faith.

And then there was his father. The portrait had been painted late, when he was older, his hair was snow white, his eyes still a startling blue. There was something wise in the gaze that seemed to follow him. Something, too, that seemed to warn him that there could be no course for him except the one he believed in most deeply.

"But I would betray you all!" he whispered. He realized that the whisper hurt his head, and that he was in worse shape than he had imagined if he was talking to his long-dead ancestors.

He came down the stairs and strode through the breezeway. A larger grouping of men had gathered on the porch by then.

Anthony Miller cried out, shooting a gun off into the air.

"For the love of God!" Jesse exclaimed. "Will someone tell me what is going on here?"

"Hell, yes! It's secession, Jesse! Old Abe Lincoln up there in the North is begging the states for troops. Well, Virginia will not take arms against her southern brethren. The legislature has voted her out! Hell, Jesse, we're seceded! We're out of the Union!"

Jesse felt a churning in the pit of his stomach. No one seemed to notice his discomfort. They were all shooting off their guns like a pack of fools, talking about whopping the Yanks in a matter of weeks if the Yanks thought to fight about anything at all.

He sank down into a whitewashed wrought-iron chair. Christa, sitting there too, looked at him and reached out to pour hot coffee into his cup.

"Jesse?"

"Thanks," he muttered to her. He looked out onto the yard. Even Daniel was behaving like a fool, throwing his plumed hat up into the air and letting out a cry like a banshee.

"Jesse, Daniel's going to resign his commission today."

Jesse nodded blankly, sipping his coffee black.

"Jesse, there's more news," she said in a rush, her beautiful eyes dark on his. "Lincoln sent an emissary from Washington across the river to Arlington House."

Arlington House was Colonel Robert E. Lee's home. The message had come to him through his wife, who was George Washington's step-great-grandchild. Her father had built Arlington House, and she possessed many fine household items and furniture that had belonged to the first president. It was a beautiful and graceful home, where Colonel Lee had raised his children. It was on a mount and looked right across the river over to Washington, D.C. It was a very strategic location.

Jesse leaned back. "And?" he asked Christa.

She spoke in a rush. "Lincoln was ready to offer Colonel Lee command of the federal field forces, Jesse. Why, everybody knows that he's one of the finest soldiers in the field, even Lincoln. But, Jesse"—she paused, leaning forward—"Jesse, Lee refused him. He was against secession—at least, that's what Daniel told me. But now that Virginia has seceded, Lee has tendered his resignation. Jesse, everyone is doing so."

He nodded blankly and looked at her with a lopsided smile. "Christa, why did you let the two of us drink so much last night? By God, but I am in pain this morning!"

He rose and stretched and stared at the men still caterwauling on his property. Someone had just trampled over a rose bush.

"Excuse me," Jesse muttered. He strode back inside, and entered the parlor. The April morning was chilly, and Christa had seen to it that a fire was set against the cold.

He leaned against the mantel, feeling curiously numb now that secession had come.

Someone suddenly burst in on him. He swirled around to see the young, anxious, and highly flushed face of Anthony Miller.

"Oh! Sorry, Jesse. I didn't mean to interrupt you. You look like a man seeking solitude. But, hell—you should be out there celebrating with us!"

Jesse stared at Anthony, at the wild exhilaration in his eyes. Suddenly, raw anger ripped through him. "Anthony, there has been firing. There's going to be a war. What the hell is there to celebrate in that?"

Anthony stared at him blankly, then flushed. "Hell, Jesse. I never took you for a coward."

"Don't make the mistake of taking me for one now," Jesse warned him sharply.

Anthony lifted his hand to his hair. "Captain Cameron, I apologize. I'll leave you, sir, to your own deliberations." He swung around, but then paused, looking back. "You know her mighty well, Jess. Think she'll marry me now? What with war being on the brink? I'm banking on her finding a little romance in it all. I'll be her soldier-boy, marching away to war—well, riding. It's a cavalry unit we've recruited." He grinned with a boyish appeal. It should have been difficult to be angry.

But Jesse still felt slow burning fury.

"Do I think that *who* will marry you now, Miller?"

"Why, sir, I refer to your good neighbor here in the Tidewater region, Miss Mackay. Kiernan."

There was something so painstakingly eager on Anthony's face that Jesse looked back to the fire. "You don't want to marry her, Anthony."

A silence followed his words. Then the sharp sound of Anthony's voice queried him again. "Cameron, I demand you explain yourself, sir!"

Jesse gazed at Anthony, who was as straight as a poker. What was he to tell the misguided sap? That the girl he adored was in love with Jesse himself? But was she so much in love with him anymore?

"There's nothing to explain, Anthony. Forget it."

But Anthony wasn't about to forget it. He came striding across the room, pulling off his riding gloves in his agitation. He faced Jesse at the fireplace. "I demand, Captain Cameron, that you explain yourself!"

"And I'm telling you, there is nothing to explain."

"You have cast aspersions upon the woman I love!"

"I cast no aspersions upon her! I merely suggested that she might not be— that she might not be the woman that you want to marry!"

"Because she has meant something to you, sir? How dare you suggest any impropriety on her part!"

"I did no such thing!" Jesse snapped irritably. "If anyone suggested such a thing, Anthony, I'm afraid it was you."

Anthony took a wild swing at him. Instinctively, Jesse ducked, but Anthony swung again. This time Jesse dropped low and swung beneath him, turning back to come up with his right fist flying in self-defense. He caught Anthony square in the jaw, and the younger man landed hard by the mantel.

Anthony rubbed his jaw, staring at Jesse. Jesse gritted his teeth and walked over to him, offering him a hand. "Ask her to marry you. Maybe war *will* change her mind."

But Anthony's anger had risen too high. He eschewed the hand offered to him and rose. "I reckon we're not even going to be on the same side in that war, are we, Cameron?"

"I won't celebrate bloodshed. That's the only decision I've made so far."

"She won't go with you because she doesn't want you," Anthony stated aggressively.

Jesse lifted his hands, clearly stating he wanted no part of a fight.

But Anthony's glove came flashing across his face in a stinging blow. Startled, he touched his cheek and stared at the younger man as if he had gone insane.

"What the hell—?"

"I'll meet you, sir, with pistols. By the old chapel in the glen, this evening, at dusk."

"What?"

"I said—"

"I know what you said! Damnation, Anthony, no one meets with pistols anymore!"

"Then let it be swords!"

Jesse swore softly. "Jesus, Anthony, I don't want to kill you."

Anthony bit down on his lip as if he regretted his hasty challenge.

Again, Jesse tried to dissuade him. "Anthony, there is no one in this room except you and me. No one saw what happened here. Let's not meet with pistols or swords."

Anthony worked his mouth as if he were about to agree, but then he stiffened. "I have my honor, sir!"

"God in heaven!" Jesse began.

"What's going on in here?" a soft voice suddenly demanded. Jesse looked past Anthony to see that Christa had come into the room, and Daniel and the others were behind her.

"Why, Mr. Cameron and I have just agreed upon a meeting with pistols over a personal and private matter."

"What?" Daniel demanded increduously.

"Aaron, I'd look kindly upon it if you'd agree to be my second. Daniel, I'll naturally assume that you'll stand for your brother," Anthony said.

Jesse threw up his hands in exasperation. "What the hell is this desire for bloodshed?" he demanded.

"Sir, I will meet you at dusk!" Anthony insisted. "The challenge was mine, therefore the choice of weapons is yours."

"Well, why not bring everything that you have?" Jesse drawled sarcastically. "Let's do this up well!"

"This is not a matter to be taken lightly!"

"Very well, then, Anthony. Meet me at dusk!" Jesse said with disgust. He bowed low to Anthony with an elegant, cavalier mockery, then looked upward. "God help me, for I do not seek to kill this poor fool!" he muttered.

Anthony turned crimson, but Jesse ignored him. With everyone staring at him, he swore a sudden, savage oath and strode swiftly from the room.

Twelve

Few people were as thrilled by the vote for secession as Kiernan's father. John Mackay was totally convinced that the southern cause was right. When the colonies had felt unjustly treated by England, they had broken away. They had fought a revolution and gained their independence. He saw the present southern situation as very much the same.

Oddly enough after a sleepless night, Kiernan rose early. She spent time in the laundry advising Julie on how to remove a custard stain from one of her father's favorite shirts. There were several deer and a wild hog to be properly preserved, so she had then spent time in the smokehouse. There was plenty to keep her busy. But no matter how preoccupied Kiernan became, she couldn't keep her mind off Jesse.

By the time her celebrating father remembered that she was down at the smokehouse, it was late in the afternoon.

She heard a gunshot and looked up at old Nate, who was hanging a slab of the venison. She hurried around the structure, wiping her hands on her apron and smoothing back some tendrils of hair that were escaping the bun at her nape. She looked up to see her father on horseback, racing up and down the path through the manor house appendixes. At one end he stopped, turned, and saw Kiernan. A broad grin split his weathered face, and his misted blue eyes came alight.

"They've done it, girl! They've voted us out! Virginia is out of the Union!"

His pistol exploded in the air again. A nearby chicken squawked in panic. Nate looked at Kiernan.

She wiped her hands nervously on her apron again. "We're out?" she repeated to her father.

"Indeed, we are, missy! Let them hothead Yanks breathe hard and threaten and ramble on about sedition now! The heart of the country, the heart of the revolution, is southern!"

He turned his horse away and raced back toward the house. From her distance, Kiernan could see that riders awaited him by the front porch. His old cronies had come by with the news, she thought. They'd retire now to his den and drink themselves into being heroes.

She sighed softly and reminded herself that her father had been a military man, West Point like so many of the others, and that he had served in Mexico. She smiled softly. He had been very handsome and dignified in his uniform.

A uniform he would never wear again.

But Jesse!

It had reached the crisis stage for Jesse, she realized, and the blood drained from her face. She had told him not to see her again, but she suddenly realized that it was imperative that she see him. She had to convince him to resign his commission with the Union Army.

She smoothed back her fallen hair again and pressed her palms over her apron. She was a mess, she thought. Beneath her apron she wore a simple gingham dress and a single petticoat, and her hair was sodden and limp from the smokehouse, and she probably smelled like a good old country ham. Her heart beating furiously, she had to hurry back to the house and bathe before going to Cameron Hall. It would be one of the most important occasions of her life.

"Nate, just finish here, please," she advised him. He was one of her father's few free black men, a talented worker who had earned the money to buy himself from John Mackay by tinkering on the side. But Nate had liked his home, he had liked John Mackay, and so he had stayed on. Now, looking at Kiernan, he rolled his eyes as if wondering at the strange ways of the gentry, then nodded solemnly. He made Kiernan smile, and she waved as she left him, but her smile faded as she ran quickly for the house. An instinct was warning her that she hadn't much time.

A half-dozen horses were standing in her yard, their reins hanging, and she surmised that the men had gone in for a drink to celebrate the occasion. She had heard church bells ringing earlier, and she now realized that they must have heralded the final vote in the legislature.

As Kiernan started to run up the brick steps, she heard her name cried out. "Kiernan!"

She turned to see Christa was riding up, bareback and wild. Christa leaped from her horse with little concern for her skirts or for ladylike dignity and raced to her. "You've got to come! Now!"

Kiernan felt the blood drain from her face. A trembling swept raggedly through her body. Something had happened, something horrible.

"Jesse—" she voiced his name. There had been an accident. He was hurt, he was dead. "Oh, my God! He's dead?"

"He's not dead!" Christa told her quickly. "Not yet, anyway. Kiernan, you've got to stop them."

"Stop who, from doing what?"

"Jesse and Anthony—"

"Anthony?"

"He and Andrew were in Williamsburg on business when the news came in from Richmond. He rode straight out to tell Daniel. And then he and Jesse got into a confrontation."

"What? What was it? Over what?"

Christa shook her head, her blue eyes bright. "I don't know!" she wailed. "Neither one of them will say anything at all! They're just planning to have a duel."

"A duel!" Kiernan exclaimed.

"Yes! Oh, I thought that I could shame the two of them out of it at first. I thought they could not be serious! Jesse tried to refuse to fight, but Anthony insisted that his honor would be tarnished if Jesse refused to satisfy his demand. I don't even know what it's over. One moment everyone was throwing their hats in the air, and the next moment I came inside to find Jesse and Anthony at each other's throats. I can't explain any more, Kiernan. We have to go. I haven't been able to stop them, and Daniel hasn't been able to stop them. You have to come and do what you can!"

"Oh, Lord!" Kiernan breathed in misery. Was this over her? What had Jesse said to Anthony? Had he told him about their affair? But Jesse would not have done that. What was it then? Jesse's determination that secession was a mistake? No, the lines were clearly drawn now. If Jesse believed in something different, Anthony would have felt honor-bound to allow him that belief.

He wouldn't kill Jesse unless they came face to face on a battle line.

"Kiernan, come!"

Kiernan tugged off her apron and looked at the assortment of horses in front of her. Her father's big stallion, Riley, was eating grass just down the walk. After Christa took a leap and remounted her horse, she offered Kiernan a hand. "You haven't time to get your mare. Ride with me!"

"I'll take Riley."

Christa arched a brow. Riley could be deadly. John Mackay's pride and joy was big and powerful and had a will of his own.

"You'll break your neck!" Christa warned her.

"I need to be there!" Kiernan told her. She leaped up onto Riley, her skirt swinging. She was a good enough rider to handle him, and for all his temperament, she'd never seen a faster horse. John Mackay had won money on him time and time again.

She looked to Christa. "Where?"

"In the glen past our property, down by the old burned-out church."

Kiernan nodded and nudged Riley. He set off like lightning. Christa cried out something from behind her, but Kiernan didn't hear.

Her heart was thundering as loudly as Riley's hooves against the ground. The reckless pace and the seething energy within the massive stallion seemed to join with the shivering that had set up inside of her. She ducked down low against the horse, riding tightly against him, heedless of the wind and brush that sped past her as she reached the road. She careened by a wagon and tore past a group of revelers. Christa was far behind her.

She had to reach them. She couldn't let either of them die, not for her! There had to be a way to reason with them.

She could remind them that they could shoot one another in battle soon enough.

Jesse couldn't die—but she couldn't bear life herself if he were to kill Anthony. Anthony loved her, and Anthony was willing to die for her. This was her fault because she'd never told him the truth. She'd put him off, and she'd put him off, but she had never explained that she didn't love him.

She saw the trail off to the glen and plunged down it, unaware of the branches that reached out to snare tendrils of her hair. She raced on—and heard a shot.

Riley heard it too. Startled, the stallion came to a stop, then reared up on his hind legs, standing almost straight up. Kiernan struggled to remain seated. "You overgrown fraidycat!" she yelled at the horse desperately, clinging to its neck. "Get down!"

He did, but when Riley reared once again, she went flying off.

She landed softly, with tears stinging her eyes. She had to get to the copse where the shot had come from! But if Riley went off without a rider, there would be all hell to pay. Her father would have her blood.

Blood! Dear God, a shot had been fired!

Riley suddenly went trotting into the bushes.

She leaped to her feet and raced after him. As she did so, she heard hoofbeats charge by on the trail. "Wait!" she cried out, but the rider did not hear her, or give her heed. Growing more and more desperate, she charged after Riley.

The horse had paused to munch a long clump of grass. She lunged for Riley's reins. He pulled back, snorting, his dark brown eyes wild. But her strength was great in her growing panic. She managed to subdue the horse and mount him again.

Returning to the trail, she raced again until she reached the copse by the old church. She pulled in hard on the reins.

Someone was lying on the ground with two men beside him. Daniel was one, she realized, and the other man she barely knew, but she thought his name was Aaron.

And the one on the ground . . .

She screamed and leaped down from her father's wayward stallion and ran over the cool, shaded earth.

Her heart slammed hard against her chest. It was Jesse! If he was dead, her world was over, and she wanted to die herself.

Daniel looked up at her and saw the raw terror in her eyes. His smile reassured her. "Just a wound," he said quickly. "A flesh wound."

She fell down to the earth upon her knees. It wasn't Jesse. Jesse was nowhere to be seen. The man stretched out on the ground was Anthony Miller, and his shirt and sleeve were soaked in blood.

"Oh, my God!" she breathed.

His dark, deer-brown eyes opened to hers, and he tried to smile. "Kiernan." Then his eyes shut again.

"Anthony!" she cried.

"It's all right," Daniel told her softly. "Jesse gave him a shot of morphine."

"What?" she whispered.

Daniel rose, drew her to her feet, and placed his hands on her shoulders. He pressed her away from the fallen man. "It's all right, Kiernan."

"Jesse—"

"Jesse is fine. He allowed Anthony to take the first shot, and then he just clipped him in the arm. His shooting arm. Anthony wanted to take another shot, but Jesse told him there would be plenty of fighting soon enough. Anthony said that he still wasn't satisfied."

"So what happened then?" Kiernan cried.

Daniel grinned. "I gave Anthony a good pop to the jaw. He fell, and Jesse came over and looked at his arm and gave him a shot against the pain and advised that we just wrap it up real good. Anthony is going to be fine."

"Oh!" she whispered, then she hurried back to Anthony, falling down by his side, determined to see to the truth of it for herself. She ripped up the fabric of his white shirt and found that the wound that had soaked his clothing had already been carefully and neatly bandaged.

She looked up at Daniel. "Jesse tended to him here?"

"Yes," Daniel said, and added wryly, "my brother has to be one of the very few men who would bring his own medical bag to a duel."

He was trying to make her smile, but she couldn't. "Jesse saw to his arm and gave him morphine?"

"Yes, after I slugged him. I didn't want to slug him—I had to, or he would never have let Jesse tend to the wound. Jesse had to dig a bit for the bullet— that's why the morphine."

"Buy why did Jesse leave him like this? Why didn't he—"

"Because someone else has to take care of Anthony now. Aaron's brother has gone for a wagon. He'll take Anthony into Williamsburg, where he can be seen again by a doctor." He paused for a minute. "And because Jesse is leaving."

She felt as if she had been physically struck, slammed across the face and the chest. She stood dead still, staring at Daniel. "Leaving? What do you mean, leaving?"

"Leaving, Kiernan. I don't know when he'll be back."

"But I don't understand!"

"I've resigned my commission, Kiernan. I've written and posted my letter. But Jesse isn't resigning. He has decided that in all good conscience, he can't."

"No!"

Tears were forming behind her eyes, tears she wouldn't allow herself to shed. "Where is he?"

"Probably at the house."

She twirled around, clutching her stomach, and leaped up atop Riley. She slammed her heels hard against his side. The horse seemed to leap into the air, and then they were running again, tearing through the foliage.

She took the shortcut through the fields, through the rows and rows of spring planting. She passed the workers in the fields, felt the sun upon her face, and felt the harsh wind against her as she rode.

The stallion was hot and lathered by the time she reached the back steps.

"Jesse!" she screamed and raced up the steps.

Jigger, the Camerons' very proper black butler, met her at the breezeway door.

"Where's Captain Cameron, Jigger?" she demanded.

"Which one, Miss Mackay?" he asked politely.

"Doctor Cameron! Jesse!"

"Why, he done packed up, Miss Mackay. He won't be coming back to the house." Her face must have crumpled along with her heart, because Jigger spoke quickly. "You might still catch him down by the graveyard, Miss Mackay. He said there were still a few folks he wanted to say good-bye to."

She twirled upon the top step and looked down the sloping lawn, over the garden, and to the cemetery.

Pegasus was standing beneath one of the heavy oak trees just outside the wrought-iron gates.

Jesse stood within, she saw. His plumed hat was in his hands, and his head was bowed.

"Jesse!" she shrieked, and tore down the steps, across the expanse of lawn, her heart beating furiously, creating a thunder in her ears. She ran and ran, sobs tearing from her lips.

He looked up as she neared him and smiled slowly—slowly, tenderly, wistfully, and with an aching bitterness.

"Kiernan." Her name on the breeze seemed a caress.

"Jesse!" She suddenly stopped dead still. He was on one side of the wrought-iron fence, she on the other. Her heart slammed against her chest. Her anguish must have been naked in her eyes.

"I did my best, Kiernan. God knows, I didn't want to hurt him." He shrugged. "I didn't tell him anything about us. I guess he sensed something, I don't know. But he'll be all right."

She nodded jerkily. She didn't want to hear about Anthony now. She knew that he was all right.

"Jesse, you can't ride away," she told him.

"I have to ride away." His smile took on a wry twist. "I don't want to fight a duel with every friend and acquaintance I ever had."

"Jesse!" she cried it out with pain, with anguish, with all her love.

He said softly, "Are you going to kiss me good-bye?"

He was really leaving. The crucial moment had come. He loved his home, but not enough.

And he loved her, but not enough.

"Jesse, if you leave this place now, I will hate you forever!"

He stiffened. "Kiernan, if I stayed here now, you could never really love me, for I would not be able to abide myself."

"I hate you, Jesse Cameron! I swear, I hate you with all my heart! And I will despise you forever. No rebel enemy will ever loathe you as completely as I do now!"

He was silent for a long while. The river breeze rustled by the trees. He raised his head to look toward the river, and then the foliage, and then the house.

He glanced down to the graves of his mother and father one last time.

Then he turned and strode from the cemetery. He walked to the oak and picked up Pegasus' reins.

Then he strode back to her and pulled her into his arms with a force to deny her any thought of protest. His lips burned her lips—no, burned into her being, like a brand of memory that would last a lifetime and beyond. It was a brief reminder of all the sweet passion that had been between them.

He was leaving. She broke free and slammed her hands against his chest, shaking, her voice trembling. "I hate you Jesse Cameron! I'll take arms against you myself if I ever see you in the South again!" She raised a hand high again to strike him, to scratch out at him, to hurt him the way he was hurting her.

He caught her arm. "I'm sorry," he whispered. His blue eyes were intent upon hers. "For I will love you the rest of my life."

He released her and walked past her, leading Pegasus.

Suddenly weak, she sank down to the ground, her back to him. She heard a soft, feminine cry and a rustle of silk and realized that Christa and Daniel had come up behind them.

"Good-bye, Jesse. Take care."

"I'm a doctor, Christa. I'll try to save what lives I can," Jesse told her.

Kiernan, listening, closed her eyes tight, and the tears squeezed out. She heard Christa sob softly.

Jesse walked to his brother. Kiernan turned at last. Jesse waved a hand out to encompass the place, the house, the James River, the grand docks, the fields, the cemetery—and her.

"Take care of things, Daniel."

"I will."

They embraced tightly, two brothers. It was Daniel's face that she saw, clenched tight, his jaw hard against the tears, twisted in pain.

Damn Jesse. Damn him!

Jesse released Daniel and looked back to her one more time.

"Kiernan—"

She turned away, bowing her head.

She heard his footsteps as he walked again. Heard his easy movement as he leaped atop Pegasus. Heard the hoofbeats as the horse rode away.

She looked up, her tears blinding her. "I hate you, Jesse. . . . I love you, Jesse," she whispered almost in silence.

Moments later, Christa came and tried to force her to rise. She shook her head vehemently. Then Daniel was by her side, but she didn't hear his words.

"Leave me, please!" she pleaded with both of them.

Though she knew that Daniel would not leave her, that he would be near, she felt alone as the darkness fell over the trees.

She felt numb.

But she wasn't going to remain so, she swore to herself. She would get over Jesse. She would hate him the way she should hate an enemy.

If he ever did come back, she would take arms against him.

Her heart seemed to cry out as she sat in the growing dampness and dark of night, her head bowed before the old cemetery.

The pain washed over her, and she allowed it to.

Then she felt numb again.

At last she rose and furiously told herself that her strength was greater than his.

"Come on," Daniel said. "I'll take you home."

She looked at him and wiped the last tears from her cheeks, shaking. "How can you be so calm, Daniel? He's a traitor! He's a Yankee, a damned Yankee."

He smiled awkwardly. "But he's my brother."

"And what if you meet on a battle line?"

"Then he's still my brother!" Daniel snapped heatedly. He sighed. "And my enemy. Hell, Kiernan, I don't like what he's done one bit. But I understand it. When the lines are drawn and there is no more neutral territory, a man has to fight for what he believes is right. And if he doesn't, he ain't no use to anybody. I understand him, and I forgive him."

"Well, I don't understand him," Kiernan said icily, "and I will never forgive him!" She added softly, "Never."

She turned from Daniel and started for the house.

He followed after her.

"Kiernan, I'll take you—"

She swung around. "Thank you, Daniel, but no. I will stand on my own from now on."

She smoothed her fingers over her gingham skirt, squared her shoulders, and walked toward the house.

Someone had tethered Riley to a ring by the columns. She slipped the tie and mounted the stallion.

She looked out to the river, then to the house.

And then she rode away, very proud, very straight, and very much alone.

When she reached her house, her father was waiting for her once again. He was waiting upon the porch in the white-wood swing, watching the path for her.

She stiffened. He would be furious with her. She had caused a duel between two men. Thank God Anthony hadn't been killed or seriously injured.

He stood up when he saw her. He walked down the steps and looked up at her while she was still mounted. He scanned her weary, tear-stained face and reached up to help her dismount.

"A bad day, eh, girl?"

"Oh, Papa!" she whispered.

He looked into her eyes, smoothing back her hair. "I've heard, Kiernan, I've heard all about it."

He led her up the steps, calling for someone to come and take Riley. He sat her down and slipped an arm around her, and in a moment he was pressing a glass to her lips.

"Brandy," he said.

She looked at him through damp eyes. "You hate it when I drink."

"Take a sip now. I've a dozen things to be mad with you for, girl, a dozen more this day. But I'm not mad, and I wouldn't think of punishing you, for it seems to me that you've punished yourself enough already."

She took a sip, then more than a sip. Shuddering, she swallowed it all down.

"You were right about Jesse."

He rocked quietly for a minute. "I like Jesse Cameron. Always have, always will."

"I hate him."

"Yes. Well, maybe that's for the best."

"I don't ever, ever want to see him again."

John Mackay didn't say a word to her. He just sat with his arm around her, rocking on the swing.

The night passed on as they sat there. John spoke at last.

"Ah, Kiernan, time will tell, eh? Many a young man we'll not see again. For honor is a splendid thing. But blood and death are forever. And if there's anything in this world I'm certain of, Kiernan, it's that we're headed for war."

The swing creaked upon its hinges, and her father drew her close.

"War."

Thirteen

Events suddenly moved very quickly in the Old Dominion. Virginia had officially passed her ordinance of secession on April 17, and within a week, the Confederate vice president, Alexander Stephens, arrived in Richmond to negotiate a military alliance between the Confederacy and Virginia. Stephens alluded to the possibility of Richmond becoming the Confederate capital, and the Virginia delegates quickly reached an agreement with him.

In May, the Confederate government dismantled its offices in its first capital, Montgomery, and moved to Richmond. They had chosen Richmond as a capital because of its close proximity to the approaching conflict. Only a hundred miles lay between Washington, D.C., and the new heart of the Confederacy.

John Mackay, staunch Confederate that he was, watched the happenings in his home state and shook his head. "It's a mistake," he told Kiernan. "Mark my words. It's too close to the conflict. Northern armies will cross that hundred miles. There will be a bloodbath. Why, they're already screaming, 'On to Richmond!' in the North. They are determined that the Confederate Congress will not convene this month."

Kiernan, listening to him at the dinner table, smiled bitterly. "But Pa, I hear the Southern boys are going to tear up those Yanks in a matter of weeks. I'm quite sure that Richmond will be safe."

He narrowed his eyes on her. "You're one of the most ardent little rebels around."

"I am," she assured him. She moved her fingers up and down her water glass idly. "I've listened to some of Daniel's friends. They're spoiling for a fight, like little boys. They think that they're bigger and stronger and that they can just beat the Yanks up and then everything will be fine."

John reached across the table and patted her hand. "We've the very best horsemen, and the very best marksmen. And the very best military leaders. How can we lose?"

But one of their very best men was in the North.

She had vowed that she was no longer going to think of Jesse. It was July, and he'd been gone a long time now. They had been quiet months for Kiernan, easy months in the Tidewater region. A hot, lazy summer was coming on.

As Kiernan had watched the events taking shape around her, she had avoided Cameron Hall. It was too painful to go there. As it was, her nights had been torture. Due to the pain that Jesse caused her, she really began to hate him. She prayed that the pain would ease. She had even avoided Daniel and Christa.

But they were her friends and her closest neighbors, and she couldn't stay away forever. Daniel, a cavalry captain, had recently left for the Confederate Army. Troops were gathering at an important railway station, Manassas Junction, and Daniel was with them.

Anthony was with those troops, too, or would be soon. The army was still being organized, and Anthony's company had yet to move in from the western side of the state.

She didn't know where Jesse was.

She tried very hard to convince herself that she didn't care. At some moments she actually felt numb, and she relished those moments.

The conflict moved ever closer.

Alexandria, just across the Potomac from Washington, was occupied. It was the Union's backyard, and it had surprised no one when forces marched in. The first Union casualty had occurred there. The very popular young colonel Ephraim Elmer Ellsworth had spotted a Confederate flag atop the Marshall House hotel. He climbed to the roof to tear it down. Coming down the stairs, he was shot to death by the hotel's proprietor. The proprietor, in turn, was shot to death by one of Ellsworth's men.

Kiernan felt sorrow that a Union man had been killed. From what she read, he had been a handsome, gallant, and giving man—and a very close personal friend to Abe Lincoln. His body had lain in state at the White House before it was sent home to upstate New York for burial.

Ellsworth, like John Brown, became a martyr in the North, stirring men to cry out and clamor for more bloodshed.

It seemed very sad.

But it also seemed very sad that Robert E. Lee, after refusing an offer from the North and accepting a commission in the Confederacy, had been forced to leave his home. She could imagine Lee and his wife talking through the night of the decision that he'd been forced to leave. He would have known that the Federals couldn't possibly let him be there at Arlington House. And so his wife and his children had been uprooted along with him. The enemy now tramped through the halls where his children had played.

So much seemed so very sad.

Perhaps the duel between Jesse and Anthony had been fought over her, but it never would have happened without the prospect of war. And if not for the prospect of war, she would have married Jesse. No questions of honor would have been raised. Jesse would never have had to tell his brother good-bye, and he would never have had to walk away from his home.

But she wouldn't waste her time thinking about Jesse. If anything, she would worry about Anthony.

She had gone into Williamsburg to see him the day after the duel. She cared very much about him, but she had to admit to herself that it was guilt that forced her to visit him rather than deep affection.

In Williamsburg, she had felt more guilty than ever, because Anthony had assured her that he was fine, that his pride was wounded more than anything else.

He had told her again that he loved her, that he'd fight a thousand duels for her, that he'd die over and over again for her.

But Jesse, who claimed to love her too, would not even remain to fight in his own state for her. He claimed that as a doctor, he wanted to save lives, but lives could be saved on this side of the conflict just as well.

She had been thinking about Jesse when Anthony had demanded, "Well, Kiernan?"

"Well?"

"Will you marry me now? Or will you at least think about it? I'll march soon enough, now that Virginia has seceded, I know that. We'll be going off to whip those boys in blue. Let me carry the memory of your love into battle with me!"

"Anthony, I don't—"

He pressed his finger against her lip. "Don't say no to me, please. Tell me that you'll think about it. Let me live on that hope."

She hadn't had the heart to tell him no.

It would not be only Anthony against Jesse. It would be Daniel against Jesse too. Brother against brother.

But that was war. And as Kiernan's father had told her, war was coming. Everyone spoke of it. Everyone seemed to long for it. "On to Richmond!" As her father had said, the North was very determined to swiftly end the rebellion. Patriotism ran high on both sides.

One morning in July, John Mackay lifted his head and quickly folded up the paper he had been reading at the table. He frowned. "Listen!" he told her.

She didn't hear anything at first, but then she heard horses, a large group of them, coming down the long drive.

John stood quickly, and Kiernan followed him to the door. Suddenly, she heard a loud Rebel cry, and the sounds of pounding hooves came closer and closer.

"What is it?" Kiernan asked.

"Seems to be a Rebel company," John replied, grinning. "But what it is doing on my front lawn, I surely don't know."

He strode out onto the porch, Kiernan following him.

There was, indeed, a Rebel company on their lawn. They were a handsome lot, even if they moved with a wild confusion, their horses prancing everywhere. They were dressed in butternut and gray, the handsome new uniforms of the South. The uniforms didn't seem to be government issue, but ones specifically designed and lovingly hand-sewn for this particular company. The Rebs wore cavalry hats, just like those in the Union cavalry, except that these were gray. Gray, pulled low, and finely plumed.

There were about twenty-five in the company, tramping across the lawn, reckless, loud, and constantly cheering.

"What in the Lord's good name—" John Mackay began. But a rider broke away from the melee and trotted toward them. He pushed back his hat.

"Anthony!" Kiernan gasped.

He grinned broadly at her. He was wonderfully, engagingly handsome with his warm, dancing brown eyes, his golden curls beneath the fine plumed hat, and his perfectly curved moustache and finely clipped beard. He sat his horse so well, and his smile, so endearing, touched her that night as it had never touched her before. She did not love Anthony. And she could never love anybody with the wild and desperate passion with which she had loved Jesse.

As he stood before her that night, so gallant and so comical, she laughed in delight as she had not laughed in some time.

Not since Jesse had left.

"Mr. Mackay!" Anthony called, and he grinned at Kiernan again. "Despite your daughter's very inappropriate laughter at such a fine pack of soldiers for the Confederacy, I have come to ask you for her hand in marriage. No, sir! Your pardon, I take that back! I have come to beg you for her hand in marriage!"

John Mackay's brow shot up.

"Well, son, if you're going to be begging and pleading, I'm the wrong one to be doing it to!"

Anthony grinned, and he leaped down from his horse. The men of his company quit their wild prancing and brought their horses to a standstill behind his, as disciplined now as they had been unruly just seconds before.

Anthony walked toward the steps to Kiernan, pausing with a booted foot atop the first step. He reached for her hand. "We're riding even now for Manassas Junction. We will barely arrive when we were ordered to. But all these fine fellows know how deeply I pine for you. I have told them, of course, that you have moments of heartlessness. I have told them that you have refused me for years. But the last time I spoke with you, you didn't actually refuse me. So you see, we decided to waylay our journey just a bit—"

"Just a bit!" Kiernan exclaimed. "You've ridden well over a hundred miles out of your way! You came all the way over here to the peninsula!"

He grinned again. "Yes. So it would be churlish for you to refuse me still again!"

He walked up the last step and pulled her close against him. "Kiernan, I've no time, no time at all. Not even a night to spend with you, not a day to take you anywhere, not even home. But I've got a preacher with me—Captain Dowling is also Father Dowling of Charles Town—and if you would consent to be my wife this night, I promise that I'll come back for you. And I'll take you anywhere in the world that you want to go once this skirmish is over. I'll take your kiss into battle, and with the sweet promise of you in my future, I swear I shall lead these fine gents to sure victory."

Kiernan stared at him blankly for several moments. She felt numbness steal over her.

Yes. Yes, marry him, marry Anthony. She had known him so long, and she did care for him very deeply. And she owed him, because she had led him on in a way, when she had known in her heart she loved Jesse.

She didn't love Anthony, but he loved her enough for both of them he had told her once.

Marry him, marry him, marry him, she told herself. Erase forever the hope that Jesse will come back.

"Anthony," her father answered for her, "this has been a cavalier and highly romantic deed on your part, but perhaps it might be best to wait until—"

"Yes!" Kiernan exclaimed.

"What?" Anthony and her father voiced the word simultaneously.

Anthony, she realized, had not really dared to hope. Her father, she thought, knew her too well.

"I said yes!" Kiernan exclaimed.

"Kiernan," John said, frowning, "this is so fast."

"Nonsense, Papa, we've known each other for years. Anthony has been asking me for years! And he's about to ride away into battle—" She broke off, for his troops were shouting and whooping, cheering her on.

"It seems that I'm outvoted here," John murmured. He stared at Anthony. "Young man, give me a moment alone with my daughter."

He drew her into the house, closing the door so they could have privacy in the hallway. He set his hands upon her shoulders.

"Daughter, do you know what you're doing?"

"Yes, Papa, I do."

"You were in love with Jesse Cameron."

She didn't blink. She stared steadily into his eyes. "I hate Jesse Cameron," she said flatly.

"That's what scares me," John told her. "There's a very thin line between love and hate. All these years, young lady, I never forced your hand, never arranged a marriage, so that you could fall in love and marry the man of your choice."

"But if you had arranged a marriage for me, you would have arranged it with Anthony," she reminded him.

He sighed softly. "Kiernan, don't do this."

"Papa, I must!"

"You're always too passionate, Kiernan, too reckless."

"Papa, don't stop me, please. He's riding into battle. He came miles and miles out of his way."

"And he's riding out again as soon as you say the word. I won't stop you, Kiernan, but listen to me first. If you marry him tonight, he will ride back into your life. You will be his wife, and when he returns for you, you will go to his home. You will share his bed at night, and you will take care of his family. Do you understand that?"

She shivered deep inside. Images of Cameron Hall flashed through her mind. She had always dreamed that she would be the lady of the hall.

"Yes," she told her father.

"You really want to do this?"

"Yes, with all my heart."

John sighed softly again, then opened the door. Anthony was waiting on the porch, handsome and dignified in his new uniform, straight and tall. Only his eyes betrayed his anxiety.

"Seems my daughter is now all-fired determined, Anthony. All these years, and we have to have a wedding here tonight with the supper dishes barely off the table. Well, then, it's what you both want. Come in, men, come in."

A cry went up like nothing Kiernan had ever heard before. Anthony let out a whoop and threw off his hat and plucked her up high into his arms. She stared down into his eyes, and she was glad.

It was just that she felt cold and numb.

"Lieutenant Miller, let's get to it!" one of his men advised. Suddenly the gray-clad soldiers were filing into her house, and her feet were back on the ground.

Anthony's adoring eyes were still staring into her own. "Thank you!" he told her.

She tried to smile, but her lips would not move. She stared at him gravely until her father caught her arm, pulling her back into the house. "Anthony, come on."

She remembered very little of the ceremony. Her father stood by her side and slipped her hand into Anthony's. Captain Dowling—Father Dowling of Charles Town—said all the proper words while Anthony's men stood witness behind them.

Her father had pulled a handful of daffodils from a vase, and she curled her fingers around them as she listened to the words. Anthony had to nudge her to repeat her vows, but she did so. She repeated them firmly, even if she was so cold that she didn't know what she said.

Then the same cries went up in the air, and Jubilee, her father's housekeeper, who had been very much a mother to Kiernan, started to cry. Father Dowling said that the groom could kiss his bride, and she was in Anthony's arms.

He kissed her.

And then she knew that she had made a big mistake. His kiss was filled with love and warmth. It was tender and restrained.

And it was little else. It wasn't demanding, passionate, or filled with fever. It wasn't a kiss to cause the world to cease spinning, a caress to warm her inside and out. It did not touch her blood or reach into her limbs, or into the very center of her being. It wasn't hot and wet and reckless and . . .

It wasn't Jesse's kiss.

Tears stung her eyes, but she swore that she would not shed them. She forced herself to curl her arms around Anthony's neck, to return his kiss, to try to give him a hint of the love that he was so determined to give to her.

The war whoops and hollering continued. The men stamped the floor. She heard the pop of a champagne cork.

She allowed herself to break away from the kiss, and she forced herself to keep her eyes upon Anthony's. She hadn't really thought this out at all. She didn't love him.

But she would be a good wife to him, she swore. She'd be a wonderful mother to his little brother and sister, she'd keep the house while he went to war, and she'd learn what she could about his business. She'd be good for him, she really would. She'd make up for the fact that she'd love another man until the day that she died.

But Anthony would never know that, she vowed.

"Kiernan, I love you. If I died tonight, I'd die happy, knowing that you love me."

She forced a smile to her lips. Her father brought them both champagne and shook Anthony's hand, and he welcomed him as his son-in-law.

It felt as if her cheek were kissed a hundred times as each of Anthony's men filed by her. Her father's supply of champagne, cool from the wine cellar, was drunk, and Jubilee managed to get out enough pies and cakes and breads and smoked meat to create something of a wedding feast.

It all went by so fast. Then a nervous private urged the company on. The troops filed out until only Anthony was left, holding her hands in the hallway.

"You've made me the happiest man on earth," he told her. He pulled her against him again and kissed her. She tried very hard to return his emotion, to fight the tears that stung her eyes.

"Take the greatest care, Anthony."

"I will. I'll come for you as soon as I can. Oh, Kiernan, thank you! I love you so very much."

He kissed her one last time, then released her, looking over her head to her father and thanking him.

"Care for her for me, sir."

She sensed her father's smile. "I've been doing so all these years, young man. I reckon I can manage awhile longer."

Anthony grinned, and he was gone.

Her father came up behind her, setting his arm upon her shoulder as they watched Anthony and his company ride away. They were beautiful—all of them, Kiernan thought, all young, and elegant in their new plumage, excellent horsemen.

God protect them all, she thought.

"Well, Mrs. Miller?" her father said. He spun her around to face him. She lifted her chin. She was close to tears, but she knew she had to smile.

"I'm happy, Papa. Honest to God, I'm happy. I'll be good to him, honest I will."

He lifted a brow. "Most men don't want a wife to be good to them, Kiernan. They want a wife to love them."

She lowered her head quickly. "Papa, I care very much for him." She raised her eyes to his. "He was so handsome tonight, wasn't he? Handsome and gallant and wonderful!"

"Handsome and gallant and wonderful."

And that, John Mackay agreed, young Anthony Miller had been. Everything was right about the boy. He liked his new son-in-law just fine.

But handsome and gallant and wonderful didn't mean everything. The real measure of a man was inside him. While one man might not be any worse or any better than another, it was largely the qualities inside of him that made him what he was.

She was still in love with Jesse Cameron. John Mackay understood that better than she did herself at that moment. He still liked Jesse himself. There was something special about Jesse Cameron, and something special about the way he and Kiernan connected.

But Jesse was gone with an enemy army, and it was best that Kiernan learn to forget him.

She was on the right track, John determined wryly. She was married now, legally wed, forever bound.

He hoped she understood that.

"I'm tired, Papa. I'm going up to bed," she told him.

He studied her eyes, nodded, and kissed her cheek. She smiled brilliantly and hurried away.

But later, he passed by her room and heard her sobbing softly.

Not a good sign for a bride of less than four hours, he thought. He sighed. Anthony Miller was a good man. And he'd be good to Kiernan. They'd get on well enough, which was what most people did anyway.

But his heart went out to her as he stood outside her bedroom door. She was his only child, and he loved her with all his heart. He prayed for her happiness. When Anthony came for her, when they lived together, when there were little children at her feet, perhaps then she would find the happiness that seemed determined to elude her now.

But Kiernan never had to lie in the bed she had made for herself. Manassas saw to that.

In his hospital tent at Bull Run, Jesse was up to his elbows in blood.

The wounded, the already dead, and the dying were arriving with frightening speed. He was probing a ball from an artillery man's shoulder when suddenly a cry went out that they should evacuate quickly.

The ball wasn't quite out. Jesse gritted his teeth and stood his ground, even as shells exploded nearly overhead.

"Captain Cameron! Did you hear me?" a young sergeant demanded.

"I heard you! And I promise you, son, if there's ever a ball in your shoulder, I'll see that it's out before I hightail it and run, all right?" He looked up, motioning to his orderlies. "Get the rest of these men out of here, and onto the wagons—fast!"

He paused, then set back to his task. Another shell exploded, ripping along his nerves, but he held steady. He could hear the troops racing by him.

They had taken the offensive here at Bull Run. Military leaders had advised Lincoln to use patience, but the northern populace had been clamoring for action. The attack had been sound enough. Under the command of Brigadier General Irvin McDowell, Lincoln had ordered that the troops advance.

But the strategy had not gone smoothly from the start.

Jesse's corps had started out with the campaign on the sixteenth of July. McDowell's army had been thirty-five thousand strong, marching out of Washington with colorful Zouaves in the front.

But two days of confusion and straggling and an incredibly slow pace had followed. They had entered Centreville, Virginia, a town directly east and north of Bull Run, which was a lazy, sluggish stream.

But behind that stream was Confederate General Beauregard and his army, with twenty-two thousand Confederates waiting to defend the vital railroad position at Manassas Junction.

On the day of their arrival, McDowell ordered a reconnaissance probe. That resulted in a skirmish with two Confederate brigades at Blackburn's Ford.

The skirmish resulted in two more days of confusion, days in which McDowell resupplied his poorly disciplined troops and created his battle plan. Finally, at about 2:00 A.M. on the twenty-first, McDowell had his twelve-thousand-man flanking column marching down the Warrenton Pike from Centreville.

McDowell's plan had been sound enough, Jesse thought. But his troops were still not an army—they were an untrained, inexperienced mob. It seemed painfully clear now that Confederates had been warned of the plan. Beauregard had been reinforced by troops from the west under Confederate General Joseph E. Johnston.

The battle had grown heated by midmorning, when a Confederate colonel led his troops against the Union attack force. Jesse heard from the wounded coming in that reinforcements for the Rebs as well as the Union forces had come piecemeal, as the Confederate and Union generals alike sent men scrambling from the Confederate right to bolster the sagging left flank.

One of Jesse's orderlies, a longtime army man and Virginian from Powhatan County by the name of Gordon Gray, told him dolefully that it had been their own statesmen who bolstered up the day for the Rebs. "Colonel Bartow and General Lee were up there, heading things up. But the Rebs are just as raw and green and scattered as most of these new recruits we got here ourselves. Then that eccentric college professor from the Virginia Military Institute stood up there with his troops—Jackson. Thomas Jackson, Brigadier General Jackson. And he held still up there on the hill. General Lee tried to rally his troops, and his cry went up—'Look! There's Jackson standing like a stone wall. Rally around the Virginians!' " Gordon shook his head sadly. "And by God, they did. Jackson's men on the hill started our troops running, and they've been running ever since."

The Federals had regrouped, and savage fighting had continued. Men had streamed into the field hospital. But now, it seemed, they were being beaten back at last.

Shells were exploding one right after another.

Jesse pulled the ball cleanly from the soldier's shoulder and quickly set to bandaging the wound. The soldier opened pained and opiate-glazed eyes to Jesse. "Am I going to live?" he asked.

"Maybe to the ripe old age of a hundred," Jesse told him.

The soldier grinned. Corporal Gordon Gray appeared to help him scramble over to the wagon where a score of wounded waited. The wagon started off. A shell that exploded overhead missed the wagon by inches.

Gordon forgot his military etiquette. "Jesse, come on!"

Jesse quickly and efficiently closed up his bag and gave orders to save what they could of the field hospital. His cots and bandages and surgical equipment were quickly packed and loaded unto another waiting wagon. Pegasus was tethered to the rear of it. A veteran of many confrontations in the West, the seasoned war horse awaited Jesse's command.

Jesse mounted Pegasus to follow the wagon.

Soon he was part of the Union retreat.

And it was a retreat. Soldiers ran pell-mell from the action. Haphazard shots were fired.

In front of them, Jesse could see the carriages of the darn fool civilians who had ridden out from Washington to watch the rebellious little Confederates get their comeuppance.

Those Confederates had proven themselves not so easy to beat.

Jesse had never expected that it would be easy. He knew too many of the men who fought for the South.

He gritted his teeth, seeing an overturned carriage. "Hold up!" he called to the wagon. He leaped off Pegasus and hurried to the carriage. A civilian man was caught beneath one of the broken wheels. "Gordon! Come quickly. Help me!"

They extricated the man from the debris. Jesse was sure he had a broken leg, but there was nothing that he could do about it now. Thankfully, the man fell unconscious after he was pulled out. He wouldn't feel the pain as the wagon jolted back to Washington.

It was the last time the man would watch a battle for sport, Jesse reckoned.

It had been a grim day all around. He closed his eyes and thought of all the wounded who had passed through his tent.

He winced when he thought of all those who had died before he'd had a chance to touch them. Hundreds lay on the field today.

Well, they had all wanted war.

Pegasus stopped suddenly without a signal from Jesse. The wagon had stopped, and Pegasus, fine animal that he was, had stopped along with it.

They had come across another hospital wagon, and the driver was calling out to him.

"Captain Cameron! There's another field tent up ahead. It's out of artillery range for the moment. The doc there was killed by a shell. Think you can bandage up a few men who won't make the march back without a little help?"

Jesse nodded. "Corporal, bring my bag," he called to his corporal.

He walked into the tent and looked with dismay at the scared and filthy faces of the men who could sit or stand. He looked with deeper dismay at those unconscious on the ground and on the few cots. The uniforms hadn't been standardized yet, so along with the regular army blue, there were any number of outfits upon the men.

He walked to a cot where a sheet covered a man.

"Oh," said the soldier who had stopped him. "Those are Rebs. Someone brought them here by mistake. Seems they were cavalry and with the dust and powder on them, they looked a lot like the Union boys. Why don't you see to them last?"

Jesse felt his heart beating hard. Reb cavalry—the injured could be any number of men he knew.

Hell, there were hundreds of Reb cavalry men that he didn't know.

He looked across the field tent at the two orderlies who seemed to be doing their best to make order out of the chaos, to make the injured men as calm and comfortable as possible.

"Take me around to whoever needs help first. Don't go by their uniforms. Just take me to the men with the worst injuries."

"You're going to mess with the Rebs—" the annoyed soldier began.

"Damned right, Private. I'm here to save lives, and I'm not going to ask a pack of questions first. Understand?"

He didn't receive an answer. One of the orderlies stepped forward quickly. Jesse began to look at the men. He was appalled by the number that he found dead already. The tent was a nightmare. The men were gut-shot, they were blinded. Their limbs were so badly battered that Jesse knew amputation was the only way out. But for the moment, he did patch-up jobs. He had no time to do more. He bandaged the men up just enough to enable them to get back to Washington.

He turned in time to see the second orderly pull a sheet over one of the Rebs. He felt his heart quicken. He'd tried hard to be impartial. He couldn't do it anymore.

A cavalry officer could be his brother.

"He's dead, Captain," the orderly said. "Trust me. I've been weeding out the dead ones all day."

Jesse ignored the orderly.

He walked over to the shrouded body. A hot feeling of sickness and apprehension swept through his body. Don't let it be Daniel, God, help me. It can't be Daniel.

He snatched the cover back, and a deep, startled sound escaped him.
The man was dead.
It wasn't Daniel.
It was Anthony Miller.

The Confederates were indisputably able to claim the victory at Bull Run. The Union troops had flown like the green recruits they were, leaving the field uncontested.

But both sides had suffered badly. A *Harper's Weekly* correspondent Jesse saw soon after he finished patching up what men he could told him he estimated the North had probably lost close to five hundred, with maybe twelve hundred wounded. It was hard to make a count and might be hard for some time in all the confusion. Close to twelve hundred men were missing, too, but who knew what "missing" men were lost and shell-shocked and what "missing" men were flat-out deserting now that they knew war wasn't going to be a glorious triumph.

The South had lost, too, the correspondent was convinced. Maybe close to four hundred had been killed, and fifteen hundred wounded—but not nearly so many were "missing." Jesse got what information he could out of the men and learned what he could about the southern troops. He found out nothing about his own brother, but the correspondent knew someone who had said that Jeb Stuart had been leading cavalry damned admirably, and a parlay with him might still be possible.

Jesse didn't seek permission from a superior officer. In the confusion that reigned, he wasn't about to go through military red tape to confer with Stuart, an enemy officer. He sent out Private Gibbs into the recent battle zone with a white flag and a message. It took Gibbs some time, but he managed to reach Stuart and arrange a meeting.

Jesse met his old school chum on a ridge where the left flank had fought.

Bodies littered the ground. Trees and grass had been mowed down from the hail of bullets and artillery. Stuart, an incredible horseman, came galloping upon the field with neither fear nor suspicion. Jesse didn't gallop to meet him, for the body of Anthony Miller was on a litter affixed to his saddle by splints.

The two soldiers—Confederate and Union—met.

Jeb nodded to him gravely. "Jesse. It's a damned sorry thing, but it's good to see you alive."

"You, too," Jesse agreed. "Daniel—"

"Your brother's company was under me. He's fine.. He didn't receive so much as a nick."

"Thanks," Jesse told him.

"We can't meet long," Jeb warned him.

"I know," Jesse said. "But I found someone who was once an old friend among our dead and wounded, Jeb. I reckoned you could see him returned to his father for burial."

Jeb arched a brow and looked to the sheeted bundle in the litter. He leaped down from his mount and came around, lifting the sheet.

He looked up at Jesse. "Jesu," he murmured. "I can't take him to his father. Andrew Miller was with Johnston's army. He was killed, too, not far from here, in the early stages of the battle."

Jesse felt his throat tighten. Father and son together in one day? Two bodies would have to be received by the children. All that remained of the Miller family now were Anthony's younger brother and sister, he thought.

"By God," Jeb muttered, "I'll have to deliver both of these bodies to his wife."

"His wife?" Jesse tensed.

Jeb looked up at him. "You didn't know? Anthony married Kiernan Mackay."

"No," Jesse said. "I didn't know." Hot arrows pierced him. She had finally married him. She hadn't loved him, but she had married him.

I'm actually jealous, Jesse thought in amazement. How the hell can I envy a dead man?

Jeb was looking at him again. "It was good of you to come out here like this, Jesse. I'll see to it that Anthony makes it home. I'll see to it that Kiernan knows you got him back to me."

Jesse shook his head. "No, keep my name out of it, please. Give Daniel my best, though."

Jeb smiled with a slow, wry curve to his lip. He knew Jesse's situation. Jeb's own father-in-law was a colonel with the Union Army, and would certainly receive quick advancement now with the war under way.

Jeb knew what it was like to have a family split. "I'll see to it that he gets your regards."

Jesse dismounted from his horse and released the litter contraption. "Take care, Jeb."

"You, too, Jesse."

Jesse mounted and rode along the bloodstrewn trail. His heart had never felt quite so heavy. He hadn't returned the body of a one-time friend.

He had returned the body of a husband to a wife.

To Kiernan.

Fourteen

A week later, Kiernan stood in the railway station at Harpers Ferry still numb. From head to toe, she was dressed in black. She was now a widow, and she was still in disbelief that Anthony was dead.

Daniel had ridden down the peninsula and brought the news to her.

She had been too shocked at first to truly understand what had happened to her. From the night Anthony had married her and left her, she had dreaded his coming back. She had dreaded lying in bed with him, she had been certain that she could never begin to give him what she had given to Jesse so freely.

And now . . .

Her father left her alone after they received the news. John was busy mourning himself for Anthony's father. Andrew had been one of John best friends, as well as his business partner. Now that fine older gentleman was dead.

"He was too old to go to war!" John said, shaking his head. But he realized that his daughter didn't even hear him. She was silent, numb.

It was summer. Something had to be done with the bodies, even if Daniel had taken it upon himself to see that they were put in fine mahogany coffins. Those coffins had to be interred soon.

Within a day, the Millers' lawyer appeared at the Mackays' door. He explained the circumstances to John.

John Mackay in turn sat Kiernan before him and tried to explain the situation to her.

Andrew and Anthony were dead. Young Jacob Miller and his sister Patricia were the heirs to Montemarte. Anthony, always a gentleman in every manner, had adjusted his will before leaving home to ride to battle—and to try to acquire a wife. Kiernan had been left a sum of gold and a share of the rifle works, which now made her her father's business partner.

With the death of both Andrew and Anthony, she had also been left in charge of the children.

With lost eyes she stared at her father. "Kiernan, do you understand? You must care for them. You must protect their home for them. Kiernan, their lives are in your hands." She didn't answer him, and he sighed. "We can have them brought down here. It will be rough on them to lose everyone and then to be uprooted so cruelly too. But if you can't deal with the situation—"

"No!" she protested, instantly standing. The guilt weighed on her terribly. She hadn't loved Anthony, yet she had married him. She hadn't wanted to sleep with him—and he was dead.

The very least that she could do was to care for his family. That would be no difficulty. She knew the children well, she enjoyed them. She knew the Miller household well enough, and it was a fine one.

It was just so far from her own home. But the next morning, dressed in black and with the coffins in tow, she was ready to travel to Harpers Ferry and Montemarte. John Mackay would have accompanied her, but she insisted that she could manage alone. Thomas and Lacey Donahue were wired to meet her at the station with the children. She would manage well enough.

And so she came back to Harpers Ferry, a little more than a year and a half after John Brown had tried to seize the armory.

As she stood in the railway station in her black, she looked around and found that the place had changed, pathetically changed. It was very empty. Quiet lay over the streets like a pall. The whisper of the breeze seemed the only sound.

She heard the clip-clop of horses' hooves and the wheels of a carriage. Thomas Donahue stepped down from the carriage and hurried across the platform to reach her.

"Kiernan!"

A big, kind gentleman, he took her into his arms and held her warmly.

She hugged him fiercely in return, then looked at him with wide eyes. "Thomas, what happened here?"

"I'll get you to the house," he told her. "We'll talk there." He lifted her baggage up onto the carriage.

The stationmaster had already been ordered to bring the coffins up to the Episcopal church. There would be a service first thing in the morning.

Thomas clucked to the horses and the carriage was off, bringing them around to the house. Lacey was on the steps to meet her and hugged her warmly. She looked at Kiernan very sadly, then clucked like an old mother hen and brought her inside. "I was going to have the children brought here, but then I thought that we should wait. Have some tea, then Thomas can see you up to the house. The children are fine, of course. They are with dear Janey out at Montemarte, and she's been supervising the dears for so long now—well, everyone is fine, of course, but anxious for you. Oh, Kiernan!" Tears welled up in her eyes. "It is so good that you have come!"

She hugged her again. Kiernan found herself before the fire with Thomas while Lacey went into the kitchen to prepare tea.

"Thomas, what has happened here?" she asked him. "It is so terribly desolate!"

Thomas sucked on his pipe, studying the fire. "It's been bad here, you know." He shrugged and screwed up his face in thought. "Let's see—the vote for secession happened in April. We had a Rebel soldier at the telegraph office and Union boys at the arsenal. It's hard to keep track of things, they change so quickly. On the eighteenth, southern forces marched in. The Yanks had destroyed what they could of the armory before leaving. A local man, an Irishman named Donovan, had shouldered a musket to guard the place, and when the Rebs marched in, poor Donovan was very nearly lynched for his Yankee sympathies.

"It's been a hard road here, Kiernan, what with folks split in their beliefs, some for the old government, some for the new. It was tough with the Rebel soldiers in town—young, green fellows for the most part, brash, and impressed with their own importance. 'Course, they were all Virginians in here then, and I've heard tell that we're the most tolerant of the folk, and that if it had been soldiers from the Gulf states, Donovan would be as dead as a doornail by now. Harpers Ferry is between the hawk and the buzzard, I do tell you!

"Let me see, the Rebs were here a few months. Jeb Stuart came in to form up a cavalry corps—a friend of yours was with him and stopped by, young Daniel Cameron. He was as fine and cavalier a soldier as ever, but I tell you, Kiernan, even though it was our southern boys in here, it was still the downfall of the town. The strutting militia fellows were pulled out and a fine man, a colonel named Jackson—he's a general now, distinguished himself at Bull Run, he did, the one they're calling "Stonewall"—he came in, and things were better. But the town was tainted somehow. Suddenly everyone either was a spy or was thought a spy. There's been black-marketing and the like ever since. With all the soldiers in —well, women of the weaker persuasion have flourished."

"Everyone seems to be gone!" Kiernan murmured.

"Oh, there's still folks about, though not so many. Things got worse. There were cries of 'Yanks!' every other day. One day there was a horrible hailstorm— yes, ma'am, a hailstorm—and the troops all went marching out to meet up with a supposed attack. They came back frozen and wet and soaked through, and their brand-new uniforms a wreck. The machinery in the rifle workshops has all been dismantled and sent south to Fayettesville, in South Carolina. The Miller place was dismantled along with the one-time federal works—but the Rebs did leave payment for that. The Millers' lawyer put it all aside and has taken good care of it. You've still got some control of the place your Pa and Andrew and me set up a year or so ago down in the valley. We can talk on that later."

He fell silent, a sad old man. Kiernan prompted him onward. "What happened then?"

"Let's see. Jackson left, and General Joe Johnston was put in command. Then on June fourteenth, the Rebs started blowing things up. They blew the railroad bridge and the arsenal buildings, and they retreated up the valley. Some Mississippi and Maryland troops came through at the end of the month, and they finished off the bridge. Then on the Fourth of July, there was a lively skirmish. Yanks said they won, Rebs said they won. But at nightfall, the Yanks were firing across the river from Maryland Heights, and they killed a civilian. Then things got worse. A Union general, Patterson, was after the Reb Joe Johnston's troops, but Johnston gave him the slip to make it on over to Bull Run and throw in his lot with Beauregard. Patterson pulled back here to Harpers Ferry. I tell you, Kiernan, whatever prowess the Union soldiers might lack on the battlefield, they do not lack in foraging! They ravaged this town. If it wasn't tied down, they took it. Why, some of the boys have told me that they even stole a tombstone out of the Methodist cemetery!" He paused, and exhaled slowly. "Well, they've gone now. There still seem to be some sharpshooters up on the heights yet, and we get some Confederates running around in town—mostly up on the heights this side—to return their fire. But the town—well, she's been wounded. Sometimes I think it's been a mortal blow."

Kiernan stood up and came to his side, setting an arm around his shoulder and laying her cheek against it. "I'm so sorry, Thomas."

He patted her hand absently. "I'm sorry for you, Kiernan. So quickly a bride, so swiftly a widow. Anthony was a very fine young man."

"I know," Kiernan said.

"Here's tea!" Lacey announced, bustling through from the kitchen. She offered Kiernan a wry grin. "It's not much, but it's all I could muster. There's some fine cold chicken, Kiernan. Those Yanks carried off nearly every feathered creature in town, but Janey sent this one over when Thomas told her you were coming. She wants you to know, too, how happy she is to have you coming."

Janey would have thought of something like that, Kiernan thought. She remembered briefly that Janey had been freed by Anthony's will, but that paper work still had to be taken care of. She would get to it quickly, she promised herself. She felt a chill steal over her. There was so much. . . .

There was the beautiful home in the mountains, Montemarte. Anthony had loved Montemarte very much. It was old, like Cameron Hall. It was beautiful, it was graceful. It had been built nearly a century ago. It belonged to Jacob now—Jacob, a boy of twelve.

She owed it to Anthony to protect that heritage for him.

There was Patricia, too, and there was the business, the Miller Firearms factories.

She suddenly felt weary. She wondered if she was competent to deal with it all.

You will be competent! she commanded herself sternly. You will! After everything that you did to that poor man!

"Kiernan, dear?" Lacey repeated. "Are you all right? Of course, you're not. I keep forgetting that poor Anthony has barely grown cold, that we've not even gotten his body into the ground."

"It's all right, Lacey," Kiernan said. She smiled. She and Thomas sat down to the meal that Lacey had worked so hard and so anxiously to prepare. Kiernan did her best to do justice to the meal. She pushed most of her food around, but her tea was very hot and sweet, and she suspected that Lacey had braced it with a touch of something a bit stronger.

"Was everything all right?" Lacey asked her.

"Everything was wonderful," Kiernan assured her. She smiled, still holding her teacup.

"I'll get more tea!" Lacey told her.

The town had changed drastically since she had last been here, Kiernan thought. When John Brown had conducted his raid, there had been several thousand people in town. It had been a prosperous place. And now?

The silence was oppressive. As darkness approached, it seemed to fall even more heavily. No light seemed to flicker into the house from outside. No street lamps were lit, and inside the house, no light was lit.

Thomas Donahue must have sensed her question, for he explained softly to her, "Can't have too much light. The Yanks over there shoot at anything. We keep it dark."

"Oh," Kiernan murmured.

Thomas leaned close to her. "Kiernan, you've got to take grave care."

"Why is that?" she asked him, her eyes widening.

"Well, Miller firearms have been provided for many a fighting man. Andrew managed to get his stock and himself out of town before the Yanks could come for him. Now Andrew and Anthony are dead, but down in the valley, our employees are still manufacturing arms at a startling rate for the Rebs. The Yanks might still decide to come in for the house."

"Montemarte?" she inquired, startled.

"Montemarte," Thomas said.

"But that would be wanton destruction of property!" Kiernan protested.

Thomas smiled bitterly. "Watch the war unfold, Kiernan. There has already been wanton destruction of property. I'm not saying that anything *will* happen, I'm just warning you that you've got to take care, and be prepared."

She straightened her shoulders, though her heart was sinking.

She didn't want to be here. She wanted to go home to her father. She wanted to endure the war in Tidewater Virginia. She wanted to know what was happening to Daniel.

And no matter how she despised him, she wanted to know of any word from Jesse.

But she had married Anthony, and her place was here now.

"I'll manage," she told Thomas. She realized that her voice was harsh, and she squeezed his hand to take away the sting of it. But when he looked at her, she knew that he saw the tears that she held back, and that he understood.

He pushed back his chair. "Seems I ought to be taking you out to Montemarte now."

She rose. She kissed Lacey and promised that they would see each other again very soon.

She followed Thomas out to the carriage.

It wasn't a long ride to Montemarte, not more than twenty minutes.

But that night, the ride was far too short.

Thomas drew the wagon up before the house and helped her out.

There was a light in the window. They were far away from the snipers up on Maryland Heights.

Thomas took her arm and led her up the walk. She wondered how the children would react to her. For a moment, an uneasy fear curled in her chest and constricted her throat. She was such a sham! Their brother's widow. Oh, if they only knew! She'd had no right to marry him. They would look into her eyes, and they would know, and they would despise her for the hypocrisy they saw.

She slowed her pace and stared up at the beautiful facade of the house.

"Kiernan?" Thomas said worriedly.

She walked forward, her knees trembling.

For the dear Lord's sake! She was about to meet children!

Children could see so clearly.

They might even see that she was in love with a Yankee soldier—a man their brother had challenged in a duel, a man who had shot their brother.

Maybe they would see her as the woman who had caused that duel.

God, what a coward, she railed silently against herself. She kept walking.

Suddenly, the door burst open. In a blur of motion, someone was running against her.

A soft body catapulted into hers. Instinctively, she stooped low, opening her arms.

Patricia Miller, just turned twelve, easily threw herself into Kiernan's arms. And Kiernan just as easily wrapped her arms around the little girl, who was so woefully dressed in gray.

"You've come! You've come to be with us. Jacob said that you wouldn't, that you wouldn't feel you'd been married long enough to be obliged. But I knew you'd come." Patricia pulled away from her, her warm, tear-stained eyes ardently upon Kiernan's. "I knew that you'd come. I always knew why Anthony loved you so much. You'll stay, won't you? You won't leave us too?"

Kiernan returned her stare, and warmth flooded through her.

Patricia was a child who had lost her father and her older brother on the same day. She was hurt and lost and alone, and suddenly, standing there upon the porch, she gave something back to Kiernan—something that Kiernan had lost, or perhaps even something that she had never had.

"Yes, of course, I'll stay."

"You're my sister now, aren't you?" Patricia demanded.

"Yes, I'm your sister now. And you and Jacob and I are going to do very well together." She looked past Patricia. Jacob, twelve, was his sister's twin, but he was already sprouting up to be a man and was not so quick to hand over his love and trust. Kiernan would not force him to do so.

"Hello, Jacob," she said.

His brown eyes, so like Anthony's, were grave. "Hello, Kiernan."

What was missing in Jacob's greeting was made up for in Janey's. The black woman had stepped through the doorway too. "Oh, Miz Kiernan! It is good to have you home!"

Janey hugged her fiercely.

Home.

But it wasn't her home!

She had made her bed . . .
Yes, now it was hers.
Home.

In the morning, Kiernan sat between Jacob and Patricia in the Episcopal church and listened while words were spoken over the bodies of Anthony and Andrew Miller.

The reverend spoke of Anthony's grieving widow, and she realized he meant her.

For the first time she realized that, whether or not she had loved Anthony as she should, she had lost a very dear friend. She would never hear his laughter again, never see the sincerity in his warm dark eyes. Tears welled in her own, and a feeling of pain and loss moved through her with a startling severity. Anthony was dead. The dead did not rise, not here on earth. She would never see him again.

The reverend spoke on about the valor and the courage of these men who had been so swift to give their lives to the great southern cause. The Millers were beloved in this country, and the reverend's words were impassioned and earnest. He spoke of the loss of life, of youth and beauty, and of dreams, and as he did so, Kiernan closed her eyes and saw Anthony as she had seen him that last night. So exuberant, so tender, so excited, and as the reverend had said, so beautiful in his youth and gallantry and courage. Now, that was all gone. All that was left of the fine young man was a mangled body to lie and rot in a graveyard.

Either it was the realization that Anthony was dead and gone, or it was the sudden knowledge, deep, swift and sure, that the bloodshed had just begun. But suddenly the numbness left her, and her tears trailed down her cheeks in silent streams. At last she was able to grieve.

The bodies were placed in a fine black hearse and drawn uphill by an ebony gelding to the cemetery. Behind it, in Thomas Donahue's black-draped carriage, the Donahues, Kiernan, Jacob, and Patricia followed. Up at the crest of the hill, in the old cemetery, Anthony and his father were laid to rest in a gated family plot with their kin.

Dust to dust, ashes to ashes . . .

As they stood by the grave site, even Jacob's fingers curled around hers.

The Confederate flag that had draped Andrew's coffin was handed over to Patricia. The one that draped Anthony's was given to Kiernan. She and Patricia stepped forward to toss summer roses into the ground atop the coffins.

Soon those roses would die, she thought.

Dust to dust . . . like the men beneath them.

The funeral was over.

All that had to be endured now was the meal back at Montemarte. When they returned to the house, there was frightfully little on the tables, but there were very few people there.

The war had already stripped Harpers Ferry and Bolivar and the surrounding countryside of much of their population.

Still, Kiernan thought that she should speak to Janey about the poor spread that had been put on the table for the mourners.

Janey looked at her with dark eyes that were weary and sad. "Miz Kiernan, I put out everything I could manage."

"Janey, if you needed help, you should have gotten it!"

Janey was quiet for a minute.

"Janey?"

"Well, Miz Kiernan, this place never was a plantation, not like your home back in the Tidewater region."

"Well, of course not, but—"

"We have gardens here. Chickens, a cow, and a few pigs. We used to have two more house slaves and ten to tend to the stables and the grounds."

"That's what I mean. If you needed help—"

"That's what I've been trying to tell you, Miz Kiernan. Outside the house, there's Jeremiah and his sons David and Tyne left, and there's me left inside. Mr. Andrew and Mr. Anthony were gone when the Union troops were here. All but Jeremiah's family and me done gone and run off." She lifted her hands expressively. "Mr. Andrew were never a hard man on nobody—he never whipped a man that I know of—but that taste of freedom was too strong. They just run off. Now, if we were on the Maryland side of the river, the law would probably have gone after them all. But this is Virginia, and it's a state in rebellion, and no one were going to try to give slaves back to a southern man, especially not the man who owns the Miller Firearms Factories."

Kiernan looked at Janey, and her heart sank. The huge house had to be taken care of. The gardens and the livestock . . . and they had to eat.

But everyone was gone—everyone but Janey and a man named Jeremiah and his sons. However was she going to manage?

She felt hysteria rise within her. She didn't belong here, she should be home. She hated the empty mountain roads, the shell-shot streets in town, and the darkness and the depression that had settled over the area. She hated the Yankees for killing Anthony and Andrew, and most of all she hated Jesse.

It was all his fault.

No, she couldn't hate him, she couldn't even think about him anymore. She couldn't afford to pray for his life, and she didn't dare let herself realize that she was grateful she hadn't heard about his death.

She inhaled and exhaled quickly. She heard the voices of the mourners speaking softly and gently to Jacob and Patricia. There weren't many of them—the food would suffice. They would do very well there at Montemarte—she would see to it that they did.

There were things to be grateful for.

"Janey, thank you for not running off."

Janey smiled, a proud, handsome woman. "I am a free woman, Miz Kiernan. I love those children like my own, and they love me. Why would I run off?"

"Thank you just the same," Kiernan said. "Because I need you very badly. Tomorrow, I'll go and tell Jeremiah the same." She started to walk away, but turned back. "Janey, I've been in something of a fog lately, I'm afraid. Do you know if Mr. Andrew made any considerations for Jeremiah in his will?"

"I don't think so, Miz Kiernan."

"Then you can tell Jeremiah that I will see to it myself that he is legally made a free man."

Janey smiled broadly. "He'll like that just fine—indeed, he will."

To her complete dismay, Kiernan realized that she was very near hysterical tears. "Oh, Janey!" she murmured. Suddenly, she was in the other woman's arms.

"It's gonna be all right, Miz Kiernan. We're gonna make it."

Yes, Kiernan decided, they were going to make it. And not just make it—she was going to do a damned good job of it.

She pulled away from Janey. "We'll make it just fine, Janey. I know we will. Let's get through the rest of today, shall we?"

By evening, the last of their guests, including Thomas and Lacey, had gone. Jacob insisted on seeing himself to bed. Kiernan tucked in Patricia, staying with her while the little girl clung to her. When Patricia's arms at last went limp around her, Kiernan eased herself away. She left Patricia's room and walked across the hallway to the guest room she had chosen for herself.

She hadn't taken Anthony's room. There was still way too much of Anthony about the room—his combs, his shaving equipment, his clothing, diplomas, papers, and memorabilia. Wandering there, she had felt too much as if he were still alive.

She would never be able to sleep there.

One day, Jacob would grow up and marry. He would be the one to take over his father's room, the big master room with the heavy four-postered bed that looked big enough to sleep six.

She had taken the guest room that looked south over the mountains to the back. It was a peaceful view.

She stood by the window, her hands shaking. Leaning against the window frame, she looked out into the darkness and remembered the day Jesse had left. She had been bitterly miserable. But it had been easy to be miserable then. She had had a home where everything had been taken care of for her.

Now she was here, where everything could only be taken care of by her.

She couldn't fret over it any longer, she decided, and morning would come early. She dressed in a cool nightgown and crawled beneath the covers of her bed. The sheets were crisp and comfortable against her skin. The night breeze carried the scent of jasmine upon it. Tears stung her eyes again, but she blinked them away. She told herself that she had to sleep.

And to her amazement, she did.

Eight weeks later, down on her hands and knees in the garden, Kiernan cried out with soft elation as she studied the tomato vines. Janey, plucking the perfectly ripe red orbs behind her, paused and looked behind her.

"They're beautiful!" she exclaimed, flushing, and then laughed as Janey smiled at her pleasure. Kiernan had turned her attention to lovingly tending the garden, and she was amazed by the perfection of the fruit she was growing.

"I've never seen such fine tomatoes in all my born days," Janey assured her.

Kiernan stood up and took a bow. "My lettuce is equally exquisite," she assured Janey. She noticed that Jacob, who still had not warmed to her, was up on the step watching her. He was smiling.

"Exquisite?" he asked her politely, and a smile that reminded her very much of his brother's smile curved his lip.

"Entirely," she told him. Taking two tomatoes from a vine, she tossed the first one over to him. "Catch!"

His reflexes were good, and he caught the tomato. But his smile suddenly faded, as did Kiernan's, as he heard the sound of hoofbeats.

Kiernan swung around. Riders were coming, three of them, dressed in Union blue.

They must be from the 13th Massachusetts, she thought. Harpers Ferry had been quiet—dead quiet—since she had come. Neither army had occupied the area, and the snipers from both sides kept to their action in the heart of town.

But Union General Nathaniel Banks—whom even the most stalwart of the Confederate sympathizers regarded as a gentleman—had moved on, leaving only a few troops at Sandy Hook, the Maryland point across the river.

The people hated the 13th Massachusetts. They had harassed and shot at the people and had taken everything that they had ever owned from them. Kiernan had not met up with any of those Yanks, but she had heard about them from Lacey.

She was certain that these three men were from Sandy Hook. They were the only Yanks in the area.

It was too late to get a gun, too late to do anything but stand and wait.

"Kiernan," Jacob said nervously.

"There are only three men. Just stand your ground."

"Kiernan, you've been supplying lots of men out of the factory in the valley!" Jacob reminded her with a wisdom well beyond his years. "What if—"

"If they meant real harm, there would be more of them," she said.

"If they try to touch this house, I'll kill them with my bare hands!" Jacob claimed.

One of the men suddenly let out a loud shot and came tearing down on them. Kiernan's eyes widened with horror and she almost shrieked and turned away.

The rider halted and leaped down. He was young, maybe twenty, and his face was riddled with pimples. "Tomatoes, eh? Well, we'll take them. And anything else that you have, you Rebel-lovin' Confederates." He stepped forward, placing a hand on Kiernan's shoulders. She wrenched free, never having known such deep hatred as she knew that moment.

"You won't touch a thing on this property!" she swore.

"I'll have me those tomatoes, sure as the mornin' comes!" he told her.

She still held the one tomato in her hands. If he wanted it so damned badly, he was going to get it. She backed away and hurled it into his face it with force that surprised even herself.

He swore, and to Kiernan's sudden alarm, he pulled his pistol.

A shot rang out. Her hand instantly flew to her throat, and she wondered, dazed, if she had been hit.

But she had not.

It was the Union soldier sinking down to her feet who had been hit. He clutched a bloody stain at his abdomen that spread to engulf his lower body even as he fell.

Fifteen

Jacob screamed to Kiernan as the fire that had been aimed against the Yankee was returned by his two companions. Instinctively, she fell flat, looking around her.

The barrage of fire was coming from more horsemen, these clad in gray, who were coming up the rise of the lawn. There were two of them, Kiernan dimly realized.

The fight did not last long. Even as she lay flat upon the grass, frozen and numb, the gunfire around her ceased.

The three Yankees lay dead.

There was no question of seeing to their wounds or discovering if they still breathed. The first man lay with his glazed eyes open to the heaven above. The second wore a clean hole through his temple, and the third had been caught in the heart.

She stared at them all, a scream rising in her throat, bile forming in her stomach.

Kiernan looked up. Jacob was by her side, helping her to her feet, even as the two Rebs came riding up. The first instantly leaped off his horse. He was a man of her father's age, white-haired, white-bearded, with fine, weathered features. "Mrs. Miller, are you all right?"

The courteous voice, the trembling in the man's tone, brough the first realization to her that she might easily have been killed by either side. She almost fell to the ground, but she felt Jacob's arm of support and she knew that she couldn't fall apart in front of him. Janey was running to her side too. Patricia would have heard the shots from inside, and she would soon be running out. Jeremiah and the boys were out back feeding the hens and choosing a fryer for the night, but they had heard the shots. It was no time to fall apart.

"I'm fine," she told the man. She glanced back to the bodies on her lawn, then stared straight at the Reb soldier again. "I—thank you. It seems that you came upon us just in time."

The second Rebel, a younger man, had also dismounted from his horse and was inspecting the dead. He spat out a stream of juice from his chewing tobacco, and his voice was laced with disgust when he spoke. "These boys ain't no regular troops. There ain't been none of this regiment around here in months. Looks like a group of deserters to me. Not even guerrillas—just plain old deserters."

He looked from his commander to Kiernan and started to spit again. "Oh, pardon me, ma'am."

Kiernan lifted her arms in a gesture that said he must make himself comfortable.

What was a little tobacco spit after the blood and . . . the blood and innards of a man still warm upon her lawn. The Reb was telling her something very serious. Kiernan looked curiously to him, trying to understand.

"Yanks is still men for the most part, Mrs. Miller," he told her. "My youngest son is bearing arms up there for the 47th Maryland artillery corps, and I can tell you that he may be a ferocious fighter and he may be waving a flag for Abe Lincoln, but if he needed food or to use someone's home—in the South or in the North—he'd be wiping his boots clean before he entered and he'd be saying 'please' and 'thank you' all the while. He was raised right, and so were most of them northern boys. But on both sides you got no-good-no-accounts, too, and that's what you had here, young lady. Them's what you got to watch out for."

"Then I do thank you, indeed, for coming along at the right time," Kiernan told him. "I don't even know your names to thank you properly." She paused. "But you know me."

"Course, we do, ma'am." He lifted his hat to her. "You're old Andrew's daughter-in-law, Anthony's wife. And your rifle works are keeping a lot of boys in good supply. Whatever we can do for you, we'll always be glad to do. My name is Geary, Sergeant Angus Geary. This here is T.J. Castleman, one of the finest sharpshooters you ever will meet."

"Are you stationed near here?" Kiernan asked. "Is a Rebel army moving back in?"

"Well, now, ma'am, we're not exactly moving back in, but we're not exactly moving out either. We've got ourselves an intriguing job, it seems, harassing Union forces in the Shenandoah Valley. We're up and down it seems, sometimes in the mountains, sometimes down low."

"We're with Stonewall—General Thomas Jackson, that is. The finest commander ever drew breath this or any other side of the border."

"Well," Kiernan told Sergeant Geary, flashing a quick glance to his sharpshooting companion, "since you did a great deal to improve my day, I'd very much like to do something for yours. Can we offer you gentlemen a home-cooked meal?" She realized, even as the words left her mouth, that she was inviting them to dinner over three corpses. "Oh," she murmured, certain that she herself could not eat, "perhaps we could—er, get these men onto a wagon, and I could have Jeremiah drive them into town, and they could be sent back—"

"No ma'am, I don't think that that would be a right good idea," T.J. Castleman told her. "Don't you worry none. Sarge and I will see to these Yanks."

She opened her mouth, but no sound left it. Angus spoke to her again. "You see, Mrs. Miller, if we send them back, the Yanks will know we caught up with them, and they'll know just whereabout we caught up with them too. As far as Yanks go, we need them to think that you're just living over here somewhere on the Rebel side just as sweet and quiet as can be. Like as not, sooner or later, someone might decide that this fine house shouldn't stand no more. But till that day comes—" He broke off and shrugged. "You got any weapons in the house?"

Jacob grinned and replied for her. "What do you think, Sarge? Sure, we got a gun in the house. We got a cabinet full of some of my pa's best, and I've got my very own rifle, handmade for me. And I got a fine supply of shells too."

"Well, that's good, boy, that's real good. 'Cause if you ever see a few stragglers like this again, you shoot, and you shoot to kill. But mark my next words just the same—if you see a whole army heading your way, you stand aside. If the army comes, they won't come to hurt you. They'll just rip up the place a bit. 'Course if you shoot at them, they'll have to shoot at you. And even if one Reb is

worth ten Yanks"—he winked at Kiernan—"there just isn't any way for one Reb
to take on a whole company or a brigade. You understand, Mrs. Miller?"

"Yes," Kiernan said, studying the man's fine gray eyes. She understood completely. She wouldn't let Jacob foolishly kill himself taking on a regular unit.

She understood, too, that there were deserters and some less-than-honorable
guerrillas from both sides who might just come by. And if they came by, then
they might as well shoot, because if they didn't, there was a good chance that
they would die anyway.

"Sarge, I'll take care of the bluebellies," T.J. said. He spat out a wad of
tobacco juice, then looked at Kiernan guiltily again. She shook her head, almost
smiling.

"Please, sir, you must be comfortable here. We're very grateful."

He grinned to her in turn. She thought that he had the good rugged sense of
a mountain man, and that, along with the Virginia gentry who knew so much
about horses and guns and riding and the terrain, the fine solid citizens like T.J.
were the ones who were going to win the war.

"That meal sounds real fine to me," he told her.

She didn't dare look at the corpses again. She took Janey by the elbow.
"Let's go on in and see if Jeremiah has gotten hold of one of those chickens yet.
Then we'll get something on the table mighty quick."

Kiernan never asked what they did with the Yank bodies—she didn't really want
to know. She was certain, though, that they had seen to it that the bodies were
well away from the house.

Certain that the two men didn't have much time, Kiernan saw to it that they
ate within the hour. She was excited at this prospect of company. Not that she'd
really been deprived or lonely. Thomas and Lacey had been up to see her several
times, and she'd been into town often enough. The foreman of the rifleworks in
the valley had been up to see her, and she had sat through her first business
meeting with him.

But this was different. She knew almost nothing about the rifleworks, and
Thomas was as worthy a partner as her own father, so she had done more
listening than anything else, and she had asked them both to assure her that the
majority of their sales were to either the Confederate government or to private
concerns wishing to equip military companies they were raising on their own.

Bull Run, the first major engagement of the war, had shown everyone that
Virginia—so slow to pull away from the old government—was going to pay for
her alliance with the new. Their land, it already seemed to be apparent, was
going to be the major battlefield.

Having Sergeant Angus and T.J. in the house was the first time she herself
was involved in the war effort. She suddenly deeply and desperately wanted to be
involved. It seemed to be the only way to survive it all.

She thought about it during the meal. She couldn't eat a thing herself, but
she was glad that T.J. and Angus seemed to enjoy every single mouthful as well
as the house, and the snowy table linen, and the silverware.

Janey had been against the use of the good family silverware. To convince her
that they must put it on the table tonight, Kiernan promised her they would
bury it very soon, what with rogue Rebels and rogue Yanks in the area.

She trusted both T.J. and Angus implicitly. She was glad that she did, for T.J.

—much more evidently than the world-worn Angus—showed his awe and pleasure at the beauty of the simple things within the house—the fine lace drapes, the beautifully hewn English furniture, the crystal sconces, and the elegant tableware. When the meal was finished, she played old Irish ballads and lively Virginia reels for them on the spinet. Jacob danced with his sister, and then sweet Patricia politely urged T.J. to be her partner. To teach T.J., Kiernan bowed low to Angus and became his partner.

Then it seemed that Angus became serious very quickly, realizing that they had been gone a long time.

He thanked Kiernan and the family, and he promised them that he'd guard them whenever he could.

"We're often near, in the valley," he said, looking directly at her. "In fact, if you've ever a need for us that you might be knowing in advance, you might want to look in that ancient old oak back by the ruins of the old Chagall estate. Do you know where that is?" he asked Kiernan.

She nodded, meeting his eyes. "I rode there once, long ago, with Anthony."

"Well, you keep us in mind," Angus said.

When the two Rebs departed, Kiernan was delighted to see that Angus had left his hat. With a brief word to the twins and Janey, she went flying after him. She found Angus just about to dismount from his horse—evidently, the grinning T.J. had waited to inform him that he was hatless until he was about to ride away.

"Ah, Mrs. Miller, I'll be thanking you again!" he told her.

Kiernan handed him his hat and stepped back, smiling, shielding her eyes from the sun that was slipping into the earth.

"I owe you the thanks, sir," she reminded him. She stepped forward again. It wasn't necessary to whisper—the twins couldn't possibly hear her—but she felt compelled to speak as softly as she could and get as close to the gentleman as she could be. "I'd like to do something that I might be really thanked for myself," she said. Angus stared at her, sternly. "Did I misunderstand something?" she demanded. "Didn't you tell me about the oak because I might be able to bring you information?"

T.J. and Angus exchanged a quick glance. Angus looked down at his hands, then at her. "Yes," he admitted. "Not that I had any right to do so, ma'am. You've already given far and above the call of duty, what with a brave young lad of a husband dead and in the ground. And with the rifleworks."

"I'd like to be a spy," she said frankly.

Angus winced. "Spying is a dangerous trade, Mrs. Miller."

Dangerous, yes. But the mere thought of it made her feel alive.

Male spies, if caught, were hanged, she reminded herself.

She gritted her teeth. Not even Yankees hanged women.

Not yet.

She had no intention of getting caught. She wasn't even sure what she could do.

She smiled at Angus, for he looked very concerned. "Angus, I'm probably a prime target because of the rifleworks anyway. I won't do anything horrible—I don't think that I'd be able to do anything horrible, I don't know any Yankees that well. What I can do is make sure that anything I hear gets to that old oak as soon as possible."

Angus looked to T.J., and T.J. shrugged. "We need her, Sarge," T.J. drawled. "There's too many folks in these woods who are for the Yanks, and too many folks who just don't really show what they're feeling deep inside. Mrs. Miller, ma'am, don't you risk nothing, but if you hear tell of anything that you think we should know, why, exercise one of those fine horses of yours down by that old oak. I think that would serve us well enough, don't you, Sarge?"

Angus swept his hat up on his head. "Mrs. Miller, we would be forever and deeply indebted."

Kiernan smiled, and she waved as they rode away.

It wasn't long before she made her first trip out to the old oak at the ruins of the Chagall estate.

It wasn't that she had learned anything that was a major secret. It was just that she had some early information on something that everyone would soon know about. And that was because Thomas had been learning things from one of the railroad employees.

The mill on Virginius Island had been partially destroyed by a Union colonel to prevent the Confederates from making use of it. The proprietor of the mill, Mr. Herr, had long been suspected of very heavy Federal leanings. There was quite a quantity of grain within the mill, and Herr had offered it to the Federal officials in Maryland.

Thomas told Kiernan that men from the 3rd Wisconsin regiment would be "supervising" the able-bodied men left in Harpers Ferry as they loaded the grain onto ships, since currently no bridge was left over the Potomac. Supposedly, citizens would receive recompense for their efforts. Thomas said that it was most unlikely that anyone would ever be recompensed for any of these activities.

Thomas had been glum generally. Bullet holes extended over the length and breadth of his house because Union troops shot at anything that moved or seemed to move from their point on Maryland Heights. The once-vibrant town of Harpers Ferry was becoming a ghost town where nothing dared appear by night. As winter approached, the early darkness decreed that some lights must be lit against the early shadows of the evening—which could endanger them all. Kiernan realized that Thomas had loved his town more than either government, and that in his eyes, there could be no winners or losers—his town was dying.

She did her best to cheer him up, then rode home. She wasn't sure why, but she took a roundabout trail. It was a beautiful way to ride. October was new, and the mountains were covered in their most beautiful foliage. The rivers, dangerous for the unwary, were nevertheless beautiful too. The water was high at this time of year, but in places the rushing water still danced over the rocks in a cool white fury, and leaves still fell upon the water, adding a spray of muted, lulling color.

Before she knew it, she had come to a halt before the trail that led down to the fishing shack on the water. She almost allowed her horse to carry her down that trail, for she was feeling very nostalgic. It had been almost two years since John Brown had raided Harpers Ferry.

And almost two years since she had led Jesse here.

She bit hard into her lip. She hadn't thought much about Jesse lately—or maybe she had never really stopped thinking about him, maybe she'd just forced him into the back of her mind. But suddenly everything came rushing back to her. She remembered how upset he had been that day, how the events had seemed to cast his very soul to the devil . . .

And how he had come to her because of it.

He had known, she thought. Somehow, Jesse had known that their world would come to this.

A house divided.

Not even love could change what had come. Angus had spoken proudly of his Yankee son. Harpers Ferry was split in two. Virginia herself was split. What southern mother wouldn't love her northern child? Daniel had not ceased to love his brother.

And I loved you so deeply, she thought of Jesse.

But that was in the past, just as that day of sweet tempest and tender torment they had spent upon the river was past. Their love had never had a chance.

She turned her horse and rode away. But she was too restless to return home to the children, which perhaps was why she headed up to the ruins of the Chagall estate and the oak tree there. Kiernan dismounted from her horse in the high grass and stared over at the estate. It had probably once been very beautiful. The remains of its driveway were overgrown with weeds and long grasses, but four Doric pillars still stood, scorched, but defying time. She stared at the house and felt the whisper of a chill wind that foreboded winter. She shivered and pulled her cape closer about herself, then she turned to the oak.

It was an ancient tree, split once by lightning, big and heavy still. Within its wide gnarly trunk was a deep hole—a perfect place for a message.

Except, she had no paper or anything with which to write her message.

A fine spy she was going to make, she thought.

But even as she stood there, she heard a rustling in the trees. She was about to leap upon her horse in panic and ride like the wind for home, but a voice called out to her quickly.

"Mrs. Miller!"

She paused and watched as T.J. came sauntering out of the bushes, a blade of grass between his teeth, just as cool and calm as a man could be on a lazy autumn's day.

"Hello, ma'am. Reckon you've got something to say to us, is that right?"

"I don't really know," she admitted, but she told him what she knew about the wheat.

He nodded when she was finished. "We've heard something about it already. Thanks for the confirmation. We'll take this one to the militia, I think, and see how those boys feel about the situation. Thank you kindly, ma'am. Thank you kindly. You doing all right, you and those children?"

"Yes, we're doing very well, thank you."

He nodded. "Better ride on home, then. Don't pay to be a woman alone these days, and it's just as well that I don't be seen with you now."

Kiernan mounted her horse and bade him good-bye. He lifted a hand to her, still standing beneath the oak, that blade of grass in his mouth.

She wondered if he'd run out of chewing tobacco.

"Kiernan! Kiernan!"

Late on the afternoon of October 16, Kiernan was out back laughing with

Jeremiah. Young David was rushing around the hen coop trying to procure the eggs of a suddenly indignant chicken.

Kiernan's laughter faded as soon as she heard her name called, and she rushed around to the front of the house. To her amazement, Thomas Donahue was there. And he was mounted on his carriage horse, which was unusual since Thomas hated to ride.

"Thomas! What is it? Come on down, come inside. We'll have you some tea or coffee—or something stronger—quick as a wink, I promise."

Thomas shook his head, refusing to dismount. "I've got to warn a few more folks. Seems the Virginia militia isn't happy about the Yanks making the folks in town load that wheat. There've been rumors that Colonel Ashby is on his way in to put a stop to it all."

"Oh?" Kiernan's heart was hammering.

"Well, the Yanks are coming after the Rebs. Ashby is supposed to be up on Bolivar Heights. The Yanks are going to engage him there. Get those young ones inside and under cover, Kiernan. Who knows where bullets may fly. You hear?"

"Yes, Thomas, thank you!"

Thomas turned his mount around, and Kiernan shouted for Patricia and Jacob and the others. "We're going to spend some time in the basement," she told them. "Patricia, gather up some blankets. Jacob, why don't you bring your rifle down? Janey, we can almost make a picnic out of it. Why don't you see what we have in the larder?"

"Miz Kiernan, does this mean that I don't have to fight with that chicken no more?" David asked.

She smiled. David was eight, precocious, a whirlwind of energy. He worked as hard as any adult, and he was smart, for Patricia frequently read to him. Patricia had never voiced her opinion on slavery to Kiernan, and Kiernan often wondered if the younger Millers had an opinion one way or the other. But Patricia, motherless herself for so long, had adopted David, and David certainly had prospered for it.

"No, David, you don't have to fight with that chicken anymore," Kiernan assured him. "You just help Patricia. And we'll all get down to the basement."

"Miz Kiernan?"

Jeremiah's elder son, Tyne, was no boy. Nearly twenty, he was at least six feet two inches tall, ebony black, muscled, sleek, and handsome. Kiernan imagined that he would have made a fine African prince, for he stood with pride that no bondage could break.

"Tyne?" she said.

He lowered his voice. "No bluebelly is gonna have any cause to pay heed to me, nor any Reb for that matter. A good field hand stays in a field. You take the young 'uns down to that basement. If you say so, I'll keep my eyes open here."

Kiernan paused. He could run off on her. But he could have run off on her months ago. Besides, she had promised Jeremiah and his sons their freedom.

She nodded. "All right, Tyne."

She herded the rest of her charges into the basement as Tyne had urged.

They had not been down very long before they heard the first shots—and then the sound of the cannon, booming.

As Kiernan wrapped her arm around Patricia, holding her close against the sounds of battle, she realized that it was two years ago exactly that John Brown had come to Harpers Ferry.

In time, the sounds of the shots died away. Kiernan was just rising when the door to the basement opened. She looked up the steps, feeling her heart leap to her throat.

"Miz Kiernan?"

She dared to breathe again. It was Tyne.

"Is it over?"

"Seems to be. It's been mighty quiet for a spell now. I seen some bluebellies heading back toward town and the river, and I seen the boys in gray lookin' as if they was retreating toward Charles Town. They was actin' as if they'd done won the battle, so it's hard to tell what's really goin' on."

"None of them came toward the house?" Kiernan asked him, hurrying up the stairs.

"None that I could see."

She exhaled slowly, then hurried past Tyne to the front of the house. Her fingers curled around one of the pillars. There was a bullet mark in it, and she shivered. She had known that the fighting would be close. She hadn't known how close.

She noticed a body far down in the grass. She walked from the porch and started to run. She came to the body and fell down in her knees beside it.

It was a Yankee. He had fallen on his stomach.

She bit her lip, knowing that if he was injured, she would have to help him. She turned him over.

She didn't have to help him. His sightless eyes were staring heavenward.

Young eyes—oh, so very young. Once a soft blue, like a cloudy sky, set in a young face. He had barely begun to shave.

It was a handsome face. One that had probably won many a sweetheart, one his sisters would have adored.

"Oh, God!" she breathed.

Tyne was behind her. She swallowed hard. She really couldn't start crying hysterically over a Yankee soldier.

Had she caused his death? No, the Rebels had known about the grain and the mill before she had told T.J. Rebels and Yanks were dying everywhere now—it was a war, for the love of God! She couldn't stop them from dying.

Not even Jesse could stop them from dying.

Jesse. Jesse could be lying like this in blue on some other woman's lawn. He was a doctor, but he never stayed out of the action. He'd ridden with his troops in the West when he should have been in a hospital field tent.

"We've got to—we've got to return him," Kiernan said. This was no deserter —he was a brave young man who had died in battle. "Get rid of his tobacco first," Tyne advised her. Kiernan couldn't move. Tyne stooped down and rifled through the soldier's blood-soaked clothing. He found a pouch of tobacco and a pipe and handed them to Kiernan. "He's just a boy. Too young to be smokin'. His mama probably wouldn't like it real well."

Kiernan nodded.

"I'll get the wagon," Tyne told her.

She nodded again.

She sat with the dead Yank until Tyne returned with Albert, the mule, hitched to the wagon. He lifted the dead man and placed him in the wagon. Kiernan rose from her knees at last and came around to look at the dead soldier who was scarcely more than a boy.

A plaid blanket was balled up in a corner of the wagon. Kiernan laid it gently across the man.

Tyne had been silent. "He's the enemy, Miz Kiernan."

She glanced at him, wondering how serious he was. The Yanks were the ones trying to free the black people.

"My enemy, but not yours, Tyne."

Tyne shrugged, adjusting the blanket. "Well, I'll tell you, Miz Kiernan, I've heard that Abe Lincoln is a mighty good man. Tall and gentle and ugly as sin, but a mighty good man nonetheless. But I hear tell, too, that even though he wants to free the black man, he wants for him an island somewhere, a republic of black men. And I kinda got a hankerin' for Virginia. Some of those folks up north, they don't want the southern folk beatin' us black folk down here, and that's a mighty fine thing for them to be wantin' too. But some of them same folk have a notion that if they rub up next to a black man, why, some of that color is gonna to come off. They're afraid that it might be dirt. Now I may be a lucky man for a slave, Miz Kiernan. But I been around white folk all my life who don't think that taking my hand is gonna make their own dirty. So I'm with you, Miz Kiernan, one way or the other."

"Thank you, Tyne," she told him.

His mouth curled at the corner. "I never did have to pick cotton, Miz Kiernan. I might feel a whole lot different if I'd been a 'field nigger,'" he told her wryly.

She nodded. Tyne was a proud man. She understood that. She had her own pride.

She started to climb into the wagon.

"You don't need to come, Miz Kiernan. I can take care of this for you."

"Tyne, you can't bring him anywhere alone. You're—"

"Miz Kiernan," he told her, grinning. "A black man wouldn't wanta bring a dead Reb back to his regiment, oh, no! But if'n I bring this bluebelly in, I'll be all right. They're the ones fightin' to free us, remember?"

She smiled, lowered her head, and nodded. Tyne crawled up into the wagon and picked up the whip.

"Tyne!" she called.

"Yes, Miz Kiernan?"

"Ride gently with him, please."

"Yes ma'am, I will."

He flicked the whip, and the wagon rolled away. She watched it for a while and then started back for the house.

She sat on the swing for a while and felt the coolness of the autumn breeze. She was amazed by how very calm she felt. She was coming to terms with life, she thought. She would never get over the pain of seeing men die, but she was living in the midst of war, and she was surviving it. Constant gunshots riddled the town far below her home, but she was surviving.

Neither side really had the manpower to hold Harpers Ferry. The heights around the town made it impossible to hold.

She shivered suddenly, remembering that Harpers Ferry was a ghost town. Whether the blue or gray could hold it or not, it was an important railway stop, and they would both be impelled to come back, again and again.

She sighed softly. She would weather it.

And with that thought, she felt surprisingly calm.

She was still calm that night when Tyne returned to tell her there were still Yanks around, and that a number of citizens were being arrested for harboring Rebels.

She wasn't harboring anyone.

That night, when she first slept, her dreams were peopled by dead men. The Yanks who had died on her lawn drifted by, like Irish death-ghosts. The pale blue eyes of the boy today haunted her.

And then she was turning over the blue-clad Yank's body again, and she started to scream.

Because it was Jesse's body.

She awoke with a start and reminded herself that Jesse was out of her life.

But she lay awake for a long, long time.

When she slept again, it was dreamlessly. And she slept late, well into the morning. She went for a ride in the afternoon, and when she returned, she spent time in the stables with Tyne and Jeremiah and David, grooming the horses and mules and deciding which animals did and didn't need new shoes. There were still some Yankees around, near town, she didn't know how many.

But she was very calm. She had her life under the very best control that she could, given the circumstances.

But it was that very evening, in the deceptively peaceful beauty of the autumn night, that the massive blue column of soldiers came riding into her life.

And Jesse Cameron.

The one who wore blue.

Interlude

JESSE

October 17, 1861
Washington, D.C.

"Jesse, can I talk to you?"

From his desk at the hospital in Washington, Jesse looked up. Captain Allan Quinn, 14th Northern Virginia Cavalry, Union Army, stood in front of him. Jesse's first thought was to recall which of Quinn's men were in his wards, and in his mind he quickly went through the names of the ones who were there. He knew the unit—he had ridden with most of them when he had chosen regular cavalry duty. Many from the unit had been with him in the West.

Just as Daniel had been, and Jeb, and some of the others.

Looking at Quinn, Jesse breathed an inward sigh of relief. Two of Quinn's boys were here, fallen in skirmishes, but both of them were doing well. One had been an amputation, and at the time, it had disturbed Jesse greatly because he suspected that the operation would not have been necessary had he been able to tend to the wound earlier. But the cavalryman was doing well now, and he had told Jesse that he'd been grateful to lose an arm rather than a leg. He could ride just fine one-armed, but he'd not have fared so well with only one leg.

The other man had suffered a head wound, but it had been a clean one. A bullet had whizzed by, ripping hair and skin but miraculously leaving bone and brain intact. He, too, was doing well.

But not as well as he might have been doing if medical attention had been more readily available to him.

Jesse didn't like being in Washington. He wanted a hospital closer to the action. By the time the injured were reaching him here, many had received haphazard attention that only complicated the injury. He disagreed with many a man on his own side about the proper way to attend to wounds. A doctor in the West with whom he had worked had proved to his satisfaction that using the same sponges on different men hastened the onset of infection. Most physicians scoffed at the idea, but Jesse had watched his patients carefully. Clean sponges saved lives—just as a good shot of alcohol could sometimes help, inside and out, when nothing else was available.

Something suddenly told Jesse that Quinn hadn't come to talk about his wounded. An uneasy feeling crept over him. He'd known Quinn a long time, and Quinn knew a lot about his life.

"Jess."

"What is it? What's wrong?" Jesse asked tensely. "Have you heard something about my brother?"

Quinn, who was Jesse's own age, was probably destined to rise far in the military. He shrugged. "No, Jesse, I haven't heard anything about Daniel. I'm not even certain that anything is wrong at all. Well, it's going to be wrong, I guess."

By then Jesse was on his feet, his pen clutched tight in his hand. "Then tell me what *might* be wrong, or what it is that's *going to be* wrong."

"Lots of skirmishing going on."

"Yes, I know that. Allan, will you tell me what—"

"Jesse, there was a battle near Harpers Ferry yesterday, up on Bolivar Heights."

Jesse's fingers curled tightly around the pen he still held.

Kiernan. Kiernan would have been very near the battle.

He broke out in a cold sweat. "Any civilians caught up in it?" he asked hoarsely.

"No, Jesse, it's not that. She—er, Mrs. Miller wasn't caught by a ball or anything like that."

Jesse dropped the pen and clenched his hands together tightly behind his back as a sensation of relief flooded over him. She was all right.

Kiernan. Damn her!

Damn, but he'd tried hard not to think of her! It had been over between them, over before it had ever begun.

She had told him that she'd hate him, that she'd be his worst enemy. And she'd married Anthony, who was now dead.

Kiernan was out at Montemarte. Jesse knew it because Christa still wrote him. Christa was as ardent a Confederate as any, but she had never ceased to write him. She didn't write about the war, she didn't condemn him, and she didn't try to sway him. She just wrote about people, places, and events. She had told him that Kiernan went out to take care of her sister- and brother-in-law at Montemarte, near Harpers Ferry.

He had thought of writing Kiernan and telling her that it was a damned fool place to be, but she wouldn't have wanted to hear it from him. She probably wouldn't have even opened a letter from him.

She would be so much better off back home. Harpers Ferry was destined to be in a tug-of-war, and that tug-of-war would affect the nearby countryside.

It already had. And his heart was beating too damned hard.

And Quinn was in the same position that he was. Quinn was a Virginian too. Sometimes it was damned confusing. A number of states had regiments fighting on both sides of the line. Quinn had moved in the same social circles as Jesse, and Quinn knew that Kiernan Mackay was important to him. Hell, Jesse thought wearily, half of the world has probably heard about that insane duel between him and Anthony.

He looked across at his friend. "Quinn, what are you trying to tell me?" he demanded. "There was a battle, but it's over. And Kiernan Miller is all right, no civilians were hurt. Then—?"

"Have you ever met up with Captain Hugh Norris?"

Jesse frowned. Norris—yes, he had met the man at Manassas. He was from Maryland, and he was very bitter about the numerous "traitors" from his own state. He seemed to have a mean streak in him a mile long.

"I've met him."

"His brother was killed at Bull Run, and he's convinced that the Millers were responsible."

Jesse's brows shot up. "The Millers were responsible for the battle at Manassas?" Anthony and Andrew would have enjoyed hearing about their own importance in that one, Jesse reflected wryly.

"No," Allan said. "This Norris thinks that a Miller firearm might have killed his brother because his brother died near the left flank, and the southern troops there were mostly from the western counties of Virginia."

"You can blame it on whoever you want, I guess," Jesse said. Tension began to ripple along his spine. Norris was out there, Kiernan was out there. It was a little more than an hour's journey by train—when the trains were running. Otherwise, it was a very long ride.

Quinn continued. "I heard talk from some fellows who just rode in that Norris has a command there and that he has received some sort of blessing to burn down the Miller estate, Montemarte. I know that you and Anthony had some differences before he died, but—well, I know, too, that you were neighbors with the Mackay plantation. The way I see it, Anthony and his father are dead. There's just his widow and those children out there now, and for the life of me, I can't see how God can be on our side if we burn widows and children out of their homes. I can't interfere—I've got my assignment here, guarding the capital. But Jesse, you've got a lot of freedom, and General Banks is out there, and Banks thinks highly of you. Maybe you can do something."

Jesse's mouth was dry. They'd be burning down lots of houses before the war ended, he thought. Both sides were already well versed in destruction, determined to keep important supplies and resources out of each other's hands.

But Quinn was right. At this stage, there was little reason to burn a widow out of her house.

Even if that widow did have some control over the Miller Firearms Factories. He had to convince someone of that.

"Thanks, Quinn," he said briefly, then lifted his hat from his desk, and hurried along the corridor. Colonel Sebring was his immediate superior, and Sebring was a reasonable man.

Jesse burst into his office. "Sir, I need to take some operations closer to the field. Now. And I know right where I want to take them."

Sebring looked up from his desk, startled. He leaned back, a bushy brow arching. "Now?"

"Now, sir. I'm requesting permission to leave within the hour. We've discussed this—"

"Oh," Sebring said. "You've heard about the incident at Bolivar Heights. It was a skirmish, Jesse. Nothing major. You're one of the best physicians we've got —no one stands up to battle conditions like you do, and no one works as well in the horrid conditions—"

"That's exactly why I shouldn't be in Washington, sir!"

Sebring leaned back. "I gather, son, that you want to take over the Miller estate—what's it called, Montemarte?"

It was Jesse's turn to be startled. Sebring was definitely a wise old coot. Montemarte was well known, and the Millers were well known. But Jesse had never imagined that Sebring might know about his involvement with either.

"Captain Norris is out there now, determined to burn the place down. I can see no reason for it. The factories are deep in the valley. And it wouldn't be good politics either. A number of the counties in western Virginia are unhappy about being in the Confederacy. They're holding a referendum on it next week. They may eventually secede from the state, form their own state, and move back into the Union. If we go around burning down their homes, it will never happen, sir."

Sebring watched Jesse and twirled the curl on his snow-white mustache.

"I need you here, Jesse. But maybe that's selfish on my part. I've got civilian doctors by the score here."

"Colonel," Jesse reminded him, his teeth on edge, "I could ride regular cavalry, it would be my right—"

"Oh, hold your pants, young man!"

"I can't, sir. Norris is in or near Harpers Ferry. I'm all the way out here."

Colonel Sebring grinned. "You've got a point, you've got a point." He was quiet for a moment, then reached for his pen to write out orders. "I'll be sending you the most shot-up and torn of the men in the vicinity. And I'll also be sending you a few who just need a little convalescence but can fight. And"—he paused, wagging a finger at him—"when it's necessary to pull out, we pull out. You understand?"

"Yes, sir, I understand."

Jesse took the orders Sebring handed to him and started to leave.

"Oh, Jesse," Sebring said.

He turned back.

"Don't let your personal life interfere any more with your military life."

Jesse paused. "If I'd allowed it to interfere, sir, I'd be on the other side."

Sebring shrugged. "You've got me there, son."

Jesse started moving again, but one more time, Sebring stopped him.

"Captain!"

Jesse turned back.

"You watch out for that girl too. There's some who think she might be watching us mighty keenly—and passing on everything that she knows."

"What?" Jesse demanded, startled.

"You heard me right, Jesse. You keep an eye on her. We haven't shot any women yet that I know of, but who knows what this war might come to?"

Jesse nodded and hurried out before Sebring could stop him again.

He wondered how Sebring knew so much about events in Harpers Ferry.

Kiernan might well be watching the Union—it would be just like her. But it seemed that the Union was watching her too.

Damn, she'd be better off, much better off, if she'd just go home, back to Tidewater Virginia.

But she wasn't going to go home—he knew that. There were no guarantees that any part of Virginia was going to be particularly safe now anyway. Virginia, after all, bordered the capital.

With raw anxiety, Jesse was determined to get out there quickly.

He felt as if he owed Anthony something too. He wasn't sure why—or maybe he was.

He'd had Anthony's wife.

But maybe he could save Anthony's house for his family.

And Kiernan, the little fool. He didn't know what the Union would do with women either. He did know that one Washington socialite, the very beautiful widow, Rose Greenhow, was imprisoned. She was suspected of having used her charm and contacts to procure information for General Beauregard that had brought about the rout at Bull Run.

There was talk that she would be brought up on charges of treason. There was only one penalty for treason—death.

"Oh, damn her!" Jesse said the words aloud. With long strides he returned to his desk to issue orders about his current patients to his clerk and, within minutes, he was out of the hospital.

He hitched a train ride for himself and Pegasus for a good part of the way out of Union Station. Once he was seated, he leaned back.

He was going to see Kiernan again. His heart raced, and a wildfire surged through him. It seemed so long ago that he'd seen her last. The chasm between them had never been greater. She had sworn to be his enemy, and she would not let him touch her in any way.

All he could do was watch out for her.

He gritted his teeth tightly together. He might not make it in time. By the time he arrived, the house might be nothing but ashes. And Kiernan might be on her way into the Shenandoah Valley, far from his reach. She could head for Richmond, she could head for home. Or she could choose to remain.

Was she spying?

I'm going to stop you if you are, he thought. I'm going to stop you for your own good.

Hell, the South didn't need her—not now. The South was doing damned well.

At Manassas Junction, the Union had learned what Jesse had known all along —that the South would not be easy to beat.

Through the long hot nights of the summer, while he had tended to the men and boys wounded here, he had remembered the sight of that battlefield. There was nothing like war. Men who had been healthy and whole had been shot, torn, ripped, ragged and bleeding, lying atop one another in fields of dirt and blood— maimed, crying, dying.

No, there was nothing at all like war.

Manassas had been the true test. Since then, both sides had been learning warfare, learning in life those tactics that they had read about in books at the military academies. When to attack, and when to fall back. How to flank your enemy, how to encircle him. How to fight an army that outnumbered your own. How to win.

The common soldier didn't need to know how to do any of these things. He had only to follow orders and to march without blinking into the thunderous volley of fire from his enemy. And when the volley was over, the soldier had to know when to thrust his bayonet so that his enemy might die, and he might stay alive.

The art of warfare was for the generals and the colonels. The South was filled with brilliant military men. Colonel Lee was a general now—recently put in charge of all of the men in western Virginia, Jesse had heard. And Stuart, his old friend, was General Jeb now. Jackson, that fine gentleman from the Virginia Military Institute, had been called "General Stonewall" ever since Manassas. The South was indeed in a strong position.

Manassas had been a fine test, and the test was still going on. The war was young, and men were still mastering the arts of it. In August, in the rolling hill country southwest of Springfield, Missouri, the battle of Wilson's Creek had been fought. Like Manassas, it had been a clear victory for the Confederacy. The Union leader had been killed, and his troops had withdrawn. They had not just retreated—they had left most of the state to the Rebs.

In Virginia, men were skirmishing and battling in various pockets. The South had yet to invade the North, but Washington remained ringed by forces. There had been confrontations in a number of places. Union forces had moved against Confederates at Big Bethel, and there had been skirmishing at Piggot's Mill, Wayne Court House, and Blue's House, among others. The action had kept the hospitals filled.

The Rebs were doing all right. They didn't need any help from Kiernan.

Jesse left the train in Maryland and rode until he reached General Banks with his orders from Colonel Sebring.

Banks frowned, wondering what Jesse was talking about at first. Then he remembered that he had given his captain permission to burn the house. "The Millers are hard-core Rebels, Captain Cameron. I've done my best to deal justly and properly with the civilian populations around here, but Captain, the Millers are an exception."

"But the Miller men are dead, sir. The adults, that is. There's a boy living there, a widow, and a little girl. The house would be absolutely perfect for a hospital. Sir, dammit, I can save more of your troops!"

Banks stared at Jesse, startled. Jesse wondered for a minute if he was going to be court martialed, but then Banks smiled. "Go on. Convince me."

Jesse reminded him that western Virginia might come back to the Union fold and that kind treatment of the people—even Rebs like the Millers—might have an influence next week, when it came time for people to vote. Banks's grin kept growing. At the end, Banks nodded, reaching for his pen. "You've sold me, Captain. The place is yours." He frowned for a minute. "Just keep your eye on—"

"I know, sir. Keep my eye on Mrs. Miller. I've been warned." And I know her, he added in silence. I know her very well.

Banks assigned him two orderlies and a small company of guards for his operations. But before the men could be assembled, Jesse was on the road again, very aware of the desperate need to hurry. When he reached the soldiers on the outskirts of Harpers Ferry, he learned that Norris and his men were already on their way to Montemarte.

It was then that Jesse started to race up the cliffs and ragged terrain, anxious to beat Norris.

There was no scent of fire on the air. That was a good sign.

At last he burst upon Montemarte. He saw the ring of soldiers in blue surrounding the place. He saw Norris, mounted, shouting orders.

And he saw the lit torches, ready to be set to the kindling planted about the porch.

Even as he raced onward, he saw Kiernan.

She stood upon the porch, tall, slim, and regal, the very essence of everything beautiful and graceful and charming in the world, her world, their world, the world that they had both known. The sunlight from the dying day caught the tendrils of her hair, and it seemed ablaze itself, a color deeper, richer, more alive than even the true fires that threatened her existence.

She was dressed beautifully, elegantly, as if she had just stepped away from tea. White lace lay over a gown of silver blue, a gown with full, sweeping skirts, its bodice cut to reveal the elegant length of her throat and just a hint of the fullness and roundness of her breasts. Her eyes were magnificent—burning, blazing emerald. With every inch of flesh and bone and beauty, she was defiant. As she stood there, the men began to move toward the house with their burning torches.

"Halt!" Jesse roared. He leaned closer to Pegasus and raced harder to reach the house. "Norris, halt!" he thundered.

Norris saw him at last. He pulled his horse around and came toward Jesse, but by then, Jesse had nearly reached the house. He reined in hard, meeting up with Norris upon his bay.

"What the hell do you think you're doing?" Norris demanded furiously. "I've got permission to—"

"Not anymore. Read, Norris," Jesse told him, producing his orders.

"A hospital!" Norris bit out heatedly.

"The place is mine. Do you understand?" Jesse demanded.

"You bastard!" Norris hissed suddenly. "I'll get you for this, Cameron!"

Jesse arched a brow to him while Pegasus pranced nervously beneath him. "You'll get me for this? For setting up a hospital? What the hell is the matter with you, Norris?"

Norris rode close to him. "I'll tell you what's the matter. This place should burn! And *she* should burn. They should all burn, right down to the ground!"

"There are children in there."

"They'll grow up to be Rebs! And they'll kill more of us on the battlefield."

"Andrew Miller is dead, Norris. And Anthony Miller is dead. That's enough."

"You watch yourself, Cameron. You just watch yourself!" Norris warned furiously.

"I always do, Norris," Jesse told him. "Douse your torches!" he ordered loudly to the men. He stared at Norris again. "And you watch yourself, Norris. I've chosen a medical command this time, but I was cavalry a long, long time before that. And I know what I'm doing."

"You threatening me?"

"I'm telling you that I know how to watch out for myself."

"Reb-lover! Or are you a Reb?" Norris demanded.

"Get the hell out of my way," Jesse snarled, "before I forget that we're on the same side."

He rode past Norris and reined in right before the porch.

She stood there still, as regal as ever, like a princess, not about to forget her station in life.

"Hello, Kiernan," he said softly.

Her eyes swept over him, cold and filled with disdain. Gone, long gone, was the girl he had once known, the girl he had loved.

She was a stranger now, distant, as cold as the frost of the coming winter.

She didn't respond to him in any way. He gritted his teeth, feeling his temper flare. He wanted to shout at her in fury. He wanted to shake that cold superiority from her eyes and make her understand. "Mrs. Miller, as of this moment I'm taking over this property for use as my headquarters, for hospital and surgical space as is necessary. You will kindly inform your household."

Her gaze swept chillingly over him once again, but at last, she spoke. "Captain Norris has plans to burn the place, Captain Cameron. I'm afraid you'll have to seek your headquarters elsewhere."

That was the final straw. He wanted to do more than shake her. He wanted to draw her over his knee as if she were still a child and paddle some sense into her. He'd half-killed himself to reach her in time, and she was telling him that she'd rather see her house burned than see him in it.

Before he knew what he was doing, he had dismounted and was striding up the steps. His fingers itched to touch her. Somehow, he restrained himself. He spoke through clenched teeth. "I'm trying to save your home and your neck, Mrs. Miller," he told her.

"My neck hasn't been threatened, Captain Cameron."

"Keep talking, Mrs. Miller, and it will be! Now shut up, and the manor can remain standing."

She delicately arched one brow, watching him. "Will you really be taking it over?"

"Yes."

Her lip curled. "Then I'd rather see it burn."

It took every ounce of his self-control to refrain from wrenching her shoulders around to force her to understand the gravity of her position. He fought to speak in a level tone.

"I'm sure you would, Kiernan. Common sense was never your strong suit. But what of young Jacob Miller and his sister?"

"Jacob wouldn't want a Yankee turncoat like you living in the house, either, Captain Cameron."

"You'd rather it burned?"

"Yes."

He stared at her, and he thought of the reckless speed with which he had come here, so desperate to salvage her home for her.

And she'd rather see it burned than see him touch it. He could have killed her.

Instead, he started to laugh. Hard. He turned away from her, starting down the steps.

"Captain Cameron!"

He paused. She was suddenly hurrying down the steps to him. Her breathing was hard. Her breasts were rising and falling with agitation, and for a moment, all he could remember was the feel of the woman in his arms, and the look of those green eyes when they were drenched with passion. She was still so damned regal.

But there was a chink within that armor of hers. She didn't really want the house to burn. She just wanted him to know how very much she hated him.

"Will you—will you burn it now?" she asked him.

He set his foot on a step and leaned an elbow casually upon it. "Well, Mrs. Miller," he told her, "I probably should do just that. But I am sorry to disappoint you. I'm afraid that I can't burn it now. I had to threaten and cajole and just about turn handstands to get the general to turn the place over to me. You see, Millers aren't real popular among the Union men. Lots and lots of them have had friends and kin killed by Miller firearms. They'd like to see the total destruction of Miller property and Miller people."

"That shouldn't be difficult now, considering that the majority of the Millers are dead—thanks to the Union Army."

"I assure you, several hundred Union men died the same—thanks to the Confederate army."

"They were on Virginia soil!" she said, her eyes narrowing.

"I didn't start the war, Kiernan."

"But we're on opposite sides."

He felt his temper snap.

He loved her so much. . . .

And they were enemies. No words that she had ever spoken had shown him that as clearly as the look in her eyes today.

"So fight me!" He managed to say the words softly. "But I'm moving in, with my staff. Take your little charges and run to your own home. You'll be safe enough there for a while. I probably won't be able to salvage everything in the house, but at least I can keep it standing."

"I don't want any favors from you!" she snapped. Again, the fire was in her eyes. Her breasts rose and fell with her rapid breathing. "And I'll be damned," she continued, "if I'll run away from a passel of bad-mannered Yanks!"

His heart seemed to slam against his ribs—and his groin.

"You're staying?"

Her chin shot up, and she might have been the Queen of England. "Stonewall Jackson will bring his army in here and wipe out the lot of you," she promised. "I might as well wait around for him to come. And keep your men from looting the house blind."

"You haven't been asked to stay, Mrs. Miller."

"Are you planning on having your men throw me and the children out—bodily?"

"Heavens no, Mrs. Miller. It's war, and I have managed to send men into battle. But I'm a merciful commander—I wouldn't dream of sending them in after you."

She ignored his sarcasm completely. She almost smiled in cool, calculating challenge. "Then I'm staying."

"Maybe not," he told her heatedly. "I didn't say that I wouldn't come in after you myself."

"What a fine point of valor, Captain Cameron!"

"Go home, Kiernan!"

"This is my home now. And Jackson will come back. Or Lee will come back. Some southern general will come for this land again, and you will be routed."

She was probably right about that, Jesse determined. Stonewall would claim the area again—and again. Or Lee would come back, or someone.

He couldn't hold it long. But when the Union was here, he had to manage to be here too.

He stared at her—at the pride in her stance, at the beauty in her face, at the fire within her eyes and the passion.

And the fury and the hatred.

And still, he wanted nothing more than to strip away the silver finery of her dress and hold her beneath him and take the fury and the tempest into his arms. To lie with her, to bed her again.

His gaze raked up and down her, and then he shrugged and spoke as casually as he could. "That's highly possible, Kiernan. Fine. Stay. But I'm taking over the house. Be forewarned."

"Forewarned, sir?" Her fury was ragged in her voice. "I'll be looking over your shoulder. I'll be making sure that you treat Reb prisoners with the same care that you would give to your own injured."

Oh, how he itched to seize her throat! But she had intended to reach into his soul, and he would never let her know how easily she could do so. He stepped closer to her. "I thought you'd run because of me, Mrs. Miller, like you did before. I won't mind your being around. I'll enjoy it. You're the one who promised never to suffer life with a Yank, remember?"

"I won't be suffering a life with you! I'll be surviving in spite of you!"

He smiled slowly, watching her. Fine, challenge me! You will not win, Kiernan, so help me God, you will not win!

"I'll fight you every step of the way. And the South will win."

"Maybe the battles, but never the war," he said quickly.

He realized that he wasn't talking about the great conflict between the North and the South. He was talking about the two of them.

Suddenly, the tension was so great that it was nearly unbearable. He felt her heat, felt the raw desperation and fury and determination in her.

And he felt the sizzle of the fire that had always burned between them. Dear Lord, he wanted her! And the memories of the things that had once been between them were suddenly naked in her eyes.

Damn, but I will have you again! he vowed in silence. Perhaps she didn't fully remember. She'd been Anthony's wife.

A black wave of unreasoning anger washed over him. He'd been warned to keep his personal life out of the military.

And here he was, growing heedless of the forces around him, heedless of the autumn day.

Wanting her. Wanting to take her until he could erase the touch of a dead man. Wanting her to remember only him, and hating that dead man for ever having touched her. Hating the emotions that touched him, but still wanting her. Wanting her so badly that he could have swept her into his arms right now and had her, there on the lawn, despite the troops, despite—honor.

"The Confederates will come back!" she cried out suddenly.

"They very well might," he told her. "But until your Rebs come back, Mrs. Miller, it's going to be share and share alike."

He swept off his hat and bowed low to her with a mocking gallantry, with all the fury that still churned within him.

Then he turned very quickly on his heel and walked away from her, shouting orders to the men who still waited. His words came out normally, no matter what thoughts that raced through his mind.

Damn her, damn her, damn her!

It was, indeed, war.

PART 3

War

Sixteen

*D*espite her insistence that she would stay in the house, Kiernan disappeared for much of his moving-in process.

The Miller housekeeper greeted him when he stepped into the hall of Montemarte. He didn't see her at first in the shadows, and for a moment, it was as if the autumn twilight played tricks on his eyes. He could remember the hallway from better times. It stretched from the entry to the rear of the house, much like the breezeway at Cameron Hall. There was a fine spinet set at the end of the hallway, and there were groupings of elegant furnishings. Dead center in the hall was a fireplace. It was warm and inviting. During their balls and entertainments, the Millers had always ordered the furniture pulled back. Dancers in silks and satins and taffetas had waltzed through the evenings. He could almost hear the rustle of skirts now.

"So, Yankee, you're here."

The words made him start. He stared into the shadows and saw the woman. She was tall and handsome, ramrod stiff with graying hair. He remembered her vaguely. She had always held an important place in this household, since Andrew's wife had died soon after the birth of Anthony's younger sister and brother.

She knew him. She'd welcomed him and Daniel and Christa, and she'd accompanied her young charges to Cameron Hall.

She knew him by name. Yet she seemed to prefer calling him "Yankee" at the moment.

He set his hands on his hips and stared across the room at her. Janey—that was her name.

"I see," he said. "You would just as soon the place be burned down too."

She looked at him, then shook her head. "No, not me. I like a roof over my head. I like this roof just fine. But if you think I'm going to welcome you here, Yank, you're wrong."

He shrugged. "Fine. Don't welcome me, but listen to me. If there's anything of real value—"

"We done buried the silver a long time ago, Yank."

"Good. But see that handsome spinet there? It just might be better off up in the attic."

"I hear you loudly, Yank," Janey assured him. "I'll see to some moving right away."

"Good." He started for the stairs. He had to find a place for himself to sleep at night, and he wanted a room with good light so that he could maintain an office in it too.

Halfway up the stairs, he realized that Janey was on his heels. He paused and turned back, and she almost bumped into him. "I'll give you a tour, Yank."

"Oh?"

"That way I can warn you where not to sleep."

They reached the second floor, and Janey hurried on by him. "Not there— that's young Master Jacob's room." She went on down the hallway. "And this one is Patricia's room." She started onward again, but Jesse stopped. A doorway was open to a very large room with windows that faced the east and the rising sun. The massive bed in the room looked comfortable and, after the rush he'd gone through that day, very inviting. There was a desk across from it, and a very large armoire off to the side by the windows. It was perfect.

But it was a master bedroom, he thought. Anthony's room? Or Andrew's room?

Had it ever been Kiernan's room? Had she ever slept with her husband in it?

"Yankee, are you comin'?" Janey demanded.

He ignored her and voiced his own question. "Is this Mrs. Miller's room?"

Janey paused, her jaw twisting, and she hesitated to give him an answer. She spoke at last. "No, this ain't nobody's room right now. Used to be Master Andrew's room, and it would have been Master Anthony's room, except he done got himself killed. So there's no one in there right now. But it'll be Master Jacob's room one day—"

"I'm not moving in for eternity, Janey," Jesse told her, "just for the duration."

"The duration of what?" she demanded.

"The war."

She snickered. "You ain't gonna hold this property even that long, Yank."

"Right. But even if we lose this place, we'll be back for it. The Union will keep fighting for this area. I won't be here long enough for Jacob to grow up, get married, and bring home a bride—I hope," he added under his breath. "This will be just perfect."

Janey turned and started to walk away. Somewhat amused, Jesse called her back.

"What is it, Yank?"

"Where *does* Mrs. Miller sleep?"

Janey's eyes narrowed sharply. "What do you want to know that for, Yank?"

"So that I don't put injured men on her bed," Jesse replied dryly.

Janey inhaled and exhaled with a long sigh. She pointed to the door next to his own. "There's her room. So you'll be all set. The healthy folk will be at this end, far down the hall, and you can put your injured in the rooms closer to the stairs. There's five more on this floor. The one over there will be big enough for a ward. The others can accommodate two or three men."

"Thank you for that information, Janey."

Once again, she started to leave him.

"Oh, Janey?"

"Yes, sir, Master Yank?" Janey slung the field-hand accent at him with fake, wide-eyed innocence. He almost smiled. The woman was as feisty as her mistress.

"Where did Master Anthony sleep?"

Janey paused, and he thought she was hiding a smile. "Why, Yank? He ain't sleepin' there no more, so you don't have to worry about puttin' no injured man in his bed."

"Curiosity," he admitted.

Janey pointed across the hall to the room that she had said was large enough for a ward.

Kiernan wasn't sleeping in the room that had been her husband's.

Had she ever slept in his room? Jesse wanted to know, but he couldn't ask Janey any more questions. Not if he wanted her to keep answering his questions now.

"Thank you," he told her.

"I'm not gonna cook for Yanks," she said flatly.

"I have a company cook," he told her. She left, and started down the stairs. But before Jesse had stepped into the room he intended to make his own, she was back.

"Ain't gonna be no Yanks in my kitchen. I'll cook for the household, same as always. You can eat at the table if Miz Kiernan says—"

"No, Janey," he corrected her. "I've taken over the house. And I dine late. At least eight o'clock because I need all the daylight hours. If Mrs. Miller wants to dine at that time of day, then she—and the children—may join me."

Janey looked as if she wanted to stamp a foot on the floor, but she didn't. Instead, she walked away, and Jesse inspected his new room at last.

Apparently, Kiernan had no interest in fighting him for the dining room. Nor did she fight him on much else during the days in which he took charge of the Montemarte mansion.

After looking over his sleeping quarters, Jesse had found two black men downstairs moving the spinet. One was elderly, and Jesse didn't like to see him huffing and puffing over the heavy furniture. He told them both to wait, rolled up his sleeves, and joined them in moving the spinet up the stairs, followed by several other large pieces.

He wasn't trying to salvage Miller furniture. He needed the space for the cots that would be arriving in the morning.

He didn't speak much with the two men, but he noted that their dark eyes were on him as they worked together. He learned that they were father and son, that the elder was named Jeremiah, and the younger, Tyne. Jeremiah was growing old. Tyne, on the other hand, was young and as strong as an ox.

From Tyne, Jesse learned that they were the only ones who remained on the estate—the two of them, another son, David, and Janey.

He also realized that they were loyal. Whatever came in the future, they would not be leaving Kiernan. That gave him a feeling of some relief. Irritably, he wondered why. After all, if everyone deserted her, then Kiernan might be inclined to travel farther south and keep herself safe.

Neither Kiernan nor the children dined with him at eight-thirty that evening.

Janey, however, presented him with a well-seasoned chicken pot pie. It was one of the best-tasting dishes he had eaten since Virginia seceded from the Union.

He was exhausted by the time he climbed upstairs to strip down and stretch out on his bed, so exhausted that he should have slept instantly.

He didn't.

He knew that she was there, just behind the wall. He could leave his room and burst in on hers, and he could force her into his arms, and . . .

No, dammit, he wouldn't do it, ever. The choice had to be hers.

He groaned, turned over, and slept at long last, wondering if he was strong enough to let the choice remain hers. She had told him often enough that she would despise him if he went north.

He had ridden north, and he was wearing blue.

Sometime in the night, he finally slept.

Downstairs in the dining room, he breakfasted alone. Janey served him a stack of hotcakes while he read the most recent issue of *Harper's Weekly*, brought to him by one of his new company, a man who had taken up residence in a tent on the lawn along with his fellow soldiers.

"Where is Mrs. Miller this morning?" he asked Janey.

"Why, she done gone into town, Yankee."

"I see," he said to her. He complimented her on her coffee, then went out to supervise the setup of his hospital facilities in the large entry hallway. Cots had arrived, bandages, and his surgery equipment contained in his special black bag —the one he refused to ride into battle without, the one with all his field instruments.

By afternoon, Montemarte had been transformed.

By early evening, the first of Jesse's patients had arrived.

A middle-aged soldier who had weathered the war in Mexico and a great deal of action in the West was carried in by his company just as twilight came. Skirmishing was going on in the woods to the west of them. There would be more patients soon.

Jesse hadn't expected help from the household at Montemarte, and he didn't really need it. He had a company of twenty able-bodied soldiers to do his bidding, and two of his men were excellent orderlies.

But Tyne happened to be on the porch when the wounded soldier arrived, and Tyne helped carry him up and into the surgery he had created from the Miller's downstairs office. Absently, Jesse told Tyne that it was necessary to keep the man still while he inspected his leg.

Later, after he had dug out the ball, found that the break was clean, and set the splint, he realized he had given Tyne orders through the whole operation, and that the powerful Negro had silently given him some of the finest help he had ever received in the operating theater.

Nor had he expected anything from Kiernan. She had insisted that she wouldn't leave, but she gave him a very wide berth. When he finished with his patient at last, cleaned up, and came down to the dining room, Janey informed him that Miz Kiernan had retired for the evening, as had the children.

In the morning he was surprised to discover that Kiernan had been in to see his patient. Speaking with the bedridden veteran, Jesse asked him how he had passed his night.

"Right fine, Captain, right fine."

"How's the pain?"

"It's there, but it could be worse."

The man was a grizzled old soldier with salt-and-pepper hair and a fine dark beard. He grinned. "Well, I was feeling the worse for it, but then I woke up, and there, sure as rain, was this angel. She was just standing over me, and when I opened my eyes, she asked me how I was feeling. Why, I told her that I thought that I'd died and gone right on up to heaven, she were that purty. Hair like gold and fire, and eyes greener than me old Pa's tales about Ireland! She brought me a whiskey, and I swallowed it down, and I slept like a babe right after that."

"Whiskey, eh?"

"Whiskey it were."

Jesse wondered if he'd dare drink anything Kiernan offered him if he were bedridden himself—the whiskey might be laced with rat poison. It surprised him that she had been so decent to this Yank in her house.

But maybe she reserved her real hatred for Yanks like him—Yanks who she felt should be wearing the colors of the Confederacy.

He couldn't afford to think about it for long. The men Colonel Sebring was sending him to convalesce were arriving, and he had to go over all their files. By nightfall, the large upstairs room was full.

He had yet to see Kiernan again.

Still, he knew that she was about. She visited his patients.

To each and every one of them, she was an angel. She never told them that she was anything but the stoutest of Rebels, but when he slept, she awoke and carried water to his injured crew, whiskey if they needed it. She even wrote a few letters. She might despise Jesse, but just as Tyne was providing him with excellent help in the surgery, Kiernan was proving to be an excellent matron for his ward.

He stayed awake purposely one night to catch her in the act of nursing. He heard her light footsteps hurrying down the hall. He rose and came silently into the hallway in his breeches and bare feet.

He watched her with the men. There were six of them now. She listened to their battle stories, and she retorted to all of them that they should have known that one Rebel was worth ten Yankees. None of the injured seemed to take it ill from her.

She might have called them rats and locusts, and they still wouldn't have taken it ill, Jesse decided wryly. She was simply too beautiful as she tended to them. Her smile was beautiful, her hair was beautiful, floating about her shoulders. She did look like an angel, for she wore a very proper white flannel nightgown and robe, and both drifted about her with her every movement like the white tunic and wings of the sweetest angel.

He felt his pulse beating in his throat, and he longed with all his heart to leap upon her in the darkness of the hallway, and sweep her away the minute she left the sickroom.

But he did not. He moved against the shadows of the doorway, and he clenched his teeth tightly while he allowed her to pass, unaccosted.

Her scent drifted by him.

Swearing, he returned to his bedroom. He didn't sleep. The next day, he was exhausted, and he dragged himself through the day, glad that no soldiers in his care were in need of surgery that day.

The next night, he forced himself to sleep. But he thought that he heard her laughter in his dreams, and he damned her in silence for not having run away, far, far away, after he arrived.

*   *   *

Several days after his arrival, his routine began to change.

It was late at night, not late enough for Kiernan to have begun her nocturnal wanderings, but late enough for him to have eaten dinner, made a last round of the patients, and retired to his room. But he wasn't in bed. Stripped down to a white shirt and his regulation breeches, he was going through the reports he intended to send Colonel Sebring.

His desk faced the windows for the light of the morning and faced away from the door that entered into the room.

He heard the door open and expected it to be Janey. She was careful to keep a certain distance from him, but she was also careful to see to his needs. She cooked him substantial meals daily, and she instructed his men in the use of the laundry for the best output on sheets and bandages. She was remarkable in her management of time and labor, and he realized that it was becoming very easy to depend on her. Despite her avowals that she was only doing her best to keep the house in order for the rightful residents, she often went above and beyond what was necessary for that. At night, when she knew that his candle was burning and that he was still working, she often made him coffee.

He didn't look up when he heard the door close and felt the presence in the room. She didn't like him to thank her—that made it seem too much as if she had actually done something for him.

"Just put it on the desk, will you, please, Janey?"

A moment later he realized that there was silence and that nothing had come to his desk. He frowned, set down the sheet of paper he was writing on, and turned at last.

Janey was not in the doorway at all. It was the boy, Jacob. Tall, lean, with golden-blond curls and wide dark eyes, he was a younger version of Anthony Miller. Right now, he seemed very much like his brother, for he was holding one of his family's special pistols, a six-shooter, and it was aimed at Jesse's heart.

The boy would know how to shoot, Jesse thought. Coming from this family, he would know how to shoot. They were at point-blank range from each other.

Maybe Jacob Miller hadn't seen enough fighting yet to want to pull the trigger. His fingers were shaking, and it was taking him both hands to hold the pistol. His face, in the soft candlelight of the room, was chalk white.

Jesse leaned back in his chair.

"Do you really want to pull that trigger?" he asked Jacob softly.

The boy was silent for so long that Jesse began to wonder if he had heard him or not.

"I want you out of my house," Jacob said at last. "Dead is one way to go."

Jesse lowered his eyes, hiding a smile. Yes, dead was one way to leave. He shouldn't be smiling. A nervous lad might easily shoot him down, where Indians and Jayhawkers and Rebs had not managed to do so.

And Jacob was deadly serious.

"If you shoot me, you must know that one of my men may get a little crazy and shoot you back, even if you are just twelve."

"Nearly thirteen."

"A rotten age to die."

"You brought a whole passel of Yanks here!" Jacob accused him. "You killed my brother!"

Jesse wondered where Jacob had gotten such information. He realized he was talking in a broad sense, that anyone in blue was responsible for killing Anthony Miller.

"I—I don't care if I *am* shot down by a Union company," he told Jesse. "Just as long as I take one bluebelly with me."

"Right," Jesse said. "But what about Patricia? And Kiernan? Once I'm gone, this house is tinderwood."

Jacob blinked once. "They'll go east," he said. "They'll go to Kiernan's father."

It was what he himself wanted, Jesse thought wryly. "Jacob, if you would just—"

"You know Kiernan better than I do," Jacob said suddenly. "You probably know her better than my brother did."

"I lived next to her all of my life, Jacob."

"You wanted my brother dead!" Jacob accused him.

Jesse stood up. The gun in Jacob's hand waved at him, but he was suddenly too angry to let the boy get away with his words. Reason wasn't working. "You're damned wrong, Jacob Miller. I've never wanted any man dead." Hand outstretched, he started across the room. "Now give me that pistol, and go back—"

He broke off, throwing himself down and at Jacob's legs as, to his amazement, the boy actually fired the gun. A bullet grazed Jesse's arm, then hit the desk somewhere. Blood suddenly drenched the sleeve of his white shirt, but he knew he was all right. He had Jacob down on the ground beneath him, and the gun was wrenched from his hands.

"What did you want to go do a damned fool thing like that for?" Jesse demanded furiously.

"I didn't mean to!" Jacob gasped. "Honest to God, I didn't really mean to!"

The door to the room suddenly burst open. Corporal O'Malley, a fresh-faced Irishman hailing from Manhattan, on night duty with the patients, stood there, his rifle loaded and aimed.

"Captain Cameron—"

"I'm fine, Corporal," he called over his shoulder.

"But Captain—"

"I said I'm fine. We had a little accident here."

O'Malley seemed to assess the situation, then grinned and started out of the room. But in his place, another arrival rushed past him in a panic.

Kiernan was dressed in her angel attire, Jesse noted, the chaste white that drifted and wafted around her, that covered her from throat to foot, that made her the most sensual creature he had ever seen.

Angel, indeed. An angel sent from hell to torment his every waking moment and beyond.

But for once, there was nothing in her shimmering green eyes besides fear. Was it fear for his safety? he wondered briefly.

He remembered that he was sitting on top of one of her charges, and that she'd be concerned.

"Jesse, what—oh, my God! Jacob!"

She rushed forward, but Jesse put up a warning hand, his eyes narrowing, and she came to a halt, staring at them both, her lower lip caught between her teeth.

"Jesse, don't hurt him!" she pleaded. "Jesse, please, for the sake of our friendship—"

" 'Jesse'? What the hell happened to 'Captain Cameron'? he scolded her. "Friendship? What friendship? I'm a Yank, remember? You'd rather see this house burn to the ground than see me in it, remember? Jacob was only trying to help you, Mrs. Miller."

Her face was suddenly whiter than the boy's, if that was possible. Jesse rose to his feet, pulling Jacob up along with him with his good hand. Kiernan issued another gasp. "Your arm! Let him go. Let me see to it—"

"Mrs. Miller, it breaks my heart to turn down an offer of tender ministrations from you, but I believe I'll do just that. Now, excuse us."

He had Jacob by the shirt collar and was starting for the door.

"Jesse—"

He stopped, furious with her. "It's 'Captain Cameron' to you, ma'am, and if you will excuse me, the lad and I have a few things to discuss."

She started almost as if he had slapped her. He ignored her and pulled Jacob along the hallway and to the stairs, then down to the ground floor. He made his way through the cots waiting in the entry hall to the left, to what had been a Miller office but was now his surgery, with big windows that faced the east. He paused to light a lamp. He realized then that Kiernan had followed.

"Jesse—"

"Captain Cameron!"

"Captain Cameron, then!" she snapped, the angel's sweet tone leaving her voice. He smiled. Even now, pretense was so quickly stripped away with her. "He's just a boy, he didn't—"

"He's a big boy, and he did," Jesse told her flatly. "Out." He left Jacob in the center of the room and walked right into Kiernan, forcing her to back up. It was a damned good thing that he had his own anger.

Because it felt good to touch her body, to feel the soft fabric brushing him, to feel the curve of her breasts touching his chest as he forced her back.

"Damn you! I won't leave him here with you!" she cried, and her fists slammed against his chest.

He plucked her swiftly up and off her feet. For one wild moment, her eyes met his, and he remembered all those other times that he had held her so. Fire raged through his loins and tore into his limbs, and still her eyes met his. He felt a shudder rake through her body, and her lashes lowered.

When her gaze met his again, it was all fury. "Let me down, Yank, let me—"

He did let her down. He deposited her flatly outside the door, slammed it in her face, and locked it.

He turned, hearing her pounding on it and calling his name, then any name that seemed to come to her mind.

He looked at Jacob, who now stood wide-eyed in the center of the room, staring at him.

Jesse smiled. "Well, we're alone at last." Feeling a certain sweet satisfaction—even though all the fires of hell were still tormenting him—Jesse strode across the room to the cabinet where he had kept a set of his medical instruments and a supply of bandages. "Here, you can patch this arm up for me. You did it—you might as well fix it."

He paused, glancing toward the door. The house was well built. Kiernan was still swearing away and pounding on the wood.

He ignored her.

Jacob stared at him. His eyes strayed toward the door, then met Jesse's again. Jesse returned the look, as if to assure Jacob that he had no intention of paying heed to Kiernan. "Now, to my wound. You might cause me pain cleaning it out. Think I'll have a drink. Yes, there's a whiskey bottle over there. Want a shot?"

"I—er, I'm not old enough," Jacob told him blankly.

"Sure you are. If you're old enough to run around pointing pistols at men, you're old enough to share a small drink."

Several bottles and glasses stood on a cherrywood table that he had wedged close to the desk to leave as much room as possible in the room. He poured out two shots of whiskey and handed one to Jacob. He swallowed down his own, then studied the boy as he took a sip. Jacob winced, but he didn't cough, and he swallowed down all of the amber liquid.

"You've had whiskey before," Jesse said.

"Once or twice," he admitted. "Pa gave me some the day Virginia voted out of the Union."

"Mm," Jesse murmured. "Well, let's see if it's steadied your hand."

From a basin he poured out fresh water. He ripped off his shirt sleeve and inspected his wound. "Let's see. Do we need to sew it up?"

"Sew?" Jacob said, and swallowed hard.

"Sew," Jesse said. "Maybe just a stitch or two."

He had been hit in the left arm, and for that he was grateful—he needed his right arm. He easily washed away the blood on the wound, and it probably would have been all right without any stitches. But it seemed like a good time for Jacob to learn something, something that might make all the difference for him in the future.

Jesse went through his bag and produced a needle and sutures. He threaded the needle and brought it over to Jacob. "Here, start right here. Just two of them, small and neat. Don't worry about tying them off. I've got one hand left —I'll help you."

"Sew it—just like that?"

"Yep."

"Don't you need something for the pain?"

"It's just two stitches, and I'll take another shot of whiskey. It wouldn't be a good idea for me to go too far under the influence of liquor in this house, do you think?"

Jacob flushed. He had the needle in his hand. His eyes sought Jesse's once again.

"I've had stitches before. Go on, sew."

Jacob was in far more pain than he was, Jesse decided as the needle touched his flesh. He locked his teeth and braced himself hard against the pain. The needle went through his flesh and back out again, then quickly, very quickly, it went in and out again. What Jacob's touch lacked in experience, it made up for with speed.

A cold sweat had broken out on Jacob's brow. Jesse told him where to hold the suture, and he tied it off. He swallowed down another shot of whiskey and poured a little portion over the wound, wincing at the sting. "Don't know why, but it's good for it," he told Jacob, who was staring at him once again.

Jacob remained silent—and obviously scared. Jesse leaned back against the desk and watched him. "Let's get one thing straight here and now. You're on one side of this war, and I'm on the other. I don't expect you to change sides— I've been given the best arguments in the world, and I'm not changing sides. It's a war. That's what happens in war. But I want you to understand one thing. I didn't want your brother's death, not in any way. I admired him, and in better times, I considered him a friend."

Jacob looked down at his feet, then looked up at Jesse and shrugged. "Yeah, well, I—I guess I know that."

"You do?"

Jacob shrugged, shoving his hands into his pockets. "Anthony told me he challenged you to a duel. He wouldn't tell me what it was about—only that his temper had kind of gone and that it had been real stupid on his part. He said that you wouldn't kill him. He said you were a right good man, that there was only one thing wrong with you."

"What was that?"

"That you were a Yank, of course."

"Oh," Jesse said softly.

"I—I didn't really mean to kill you," Jacob told him.

"I didn't think you did. I never met a Miller who couldn't handle a firearm. If you'd wanted me dead now, I'd be dead," Jesse said.

"Yeah, maybe," Jacob said with a flush.

"I came here because I owe your brother," Jesse said. "We may not be on the same side, Jacob, but I came here fighting for you."

Jacob nodded.

"I'm not asking for surrender. I just want to call a truce in this house," Jesse told him. He offered Jacob his hand.

Jacob stared from his hand to his eyes. "That's it? I shot you, and that's it?"

"Yep. I'd like your word that you won't try to shoot me again."

Jacob shook his hand, still looking into his eyes. "You've got my word. That's enough for you?"

"Yep. I never had reason to doubt a Miller before."

A small smile touched Jacob's face. He nodded. "No, we don't lie. We never lie," he said proudly. He swallowed hard and studied Jesse's face again. "Thank you," he said.

Those two words must have cost him a great deal, Jesse decided. "There's nothing to thank me for. Now, we probably should go up to bed."

"Yes, sir," Jacob said to him. He started for the door, then turned back. "You came here because you felt you owed something to Anthony?"

"Yes," Jesse said.

Jacob gazed at him innocently. "That's funny. I could have sworn that you came here for Kiernan."

His eyes were steady on Jesse's. Jesse kept his eyes steady too.

"Yes, that too," he admitted.

Jacob grinned again, lowered his head, and said good night. He opened the door, and Kiernan nearly came tumbling into the room.

She had given up her pounding sometime before, and she was tired out. But her gaze raced quickly over her young charge, her fear and concern evident. "Jacob, are you all right?"

"I'm fine. I learned how to do sutures, Kiernan." He held her shoulders and kissed her cheek, then walked past her up the stairs.

Kiernan, exhausted, leaned against the wall, her eyes closed.

Then those emerald orbs shot open and gazed upon him with glittering fury and reproach. "You left me out there thinking—you left me terrified and worried sick!"

"You shouldn't have been terrified or worried sick," Jesse said dryly. "You've known me all your life, and you know damned well that I'd never do injury to a child."

"No!" she protested, her eyes still flashing their emerald fire. "I don't know you at all. Because the man I thought I knew would never have walked away from the graveyard at Cameron Hall that day."

Pain was mingled with the anger of her voice. He wanted to touch her. He took a step toward her. "Kiernan—"

She straightened, pushing away from the wall. She smiled at him, a regal, elegant, very superior smile.

"It's Mrs. Miller to you, Captain Cameron. Mrs. Miller."

She swung around and left the room, her head high, her hair flowing, the angel-white fabric of her gown floating behind her.

He followed her out to the stairway and watched her run up the steps.

He smiled suddenly, then wondered how he could be smiling while everything inside of him ached at the same time.

Sadly, the same conclusive and useless thought that had plagued him since he had come plagued him again.

Damn her.

Damn her sweet, beautiful, elegant, little hide.

Seventeen

During the following week, Jesse had Jacob for a dinner companion. By the end of the week, Jacob's sister, Patricia, had joined them. Kiernan kept her distance.

For a woman who so detested Yankees, Kiernan was spending a fair amount of time with them. She no longer waited until the wee hours of the night to move among them. Afternoons, when he looked in on the wards, he usually found her there.

In the midst of the pain and injury and the growing cold of the coming winter, she was the sweetest breath of spring. She smelled delicious. She was dressed elegantly. She moved with a rustle of silk, with that sweet fragrance, with her beauty, her hair always smoothed beneath a net, her fingers thin and delicate upon a pen as she wrote a letter, or upon a cloth as she soothed a man's brow.

They were all in love with her.

"Ain't she just the most glorious thing that ever lived and breathed, Doc?" an old soldier asked him one day as Jesse looked carefully over his chart.

Jesse cocked a brow and grunted. Yes, she was glorious, he thought dryly. But the old coot had never seen her angry.

Of course, the injured men never did see her angry. They saw her in full skirts, with her demure smile, and they heard her laughter and her teasing tones.

One afternoon, it was almost as if she were holding court. She was seated on a chair in the middle of the beds in the large ward. She wore a beautiful yellow day dress with a lace overlay that covered the bodice to the collar and the sleeves to mid-elbow. A beautiful brooch highlighted her throat at her collar. Her skirt flowed around her. Her eyes were alive and dancing, and her accent was thicker and richer than he'd ever heard flow from her ruby lips before.

The men were enthralled.

"It's not that I don't think highly of you gents," she drawled softly. "It's just that I most earnestly do believe that two of our boys have the speed and the fighting ability of about ten of ya'll."

"Why, that ain't true at all, Miz Miller," a young soldier protested. "We just ain't had all the right opportunities."

"And we haven't got generals like Stonewall or Lee," the grizzled fellow said sagely.

"Men fight very hard to protect their own land."

"We can still outfight the Rebs," another lad offered.

Watching silently from the doorway, Jesse realized that the soldier speaking had just come into Montemarte the day before yesterday with his arm all torn up by shrapnel. Jesse had been sent the soldier to see if he couldn't save the arm. He'd spent hours in the surgery, removing bits of metal and ball.

"You just wait and see, Miz Miller," he was saying now. "When our boys are the ones with the element of surprise, they'll take the Rebs. Why, we've got some boys going down into the valley in just a few days' time. They'll whomp the few troops old Stonewall has sitting there."

"Whomp 'em?" Kiernan asked, laughing sweetly.

"Why, sure. We'll have surprise on our side—and better numbers, too, probably."

"Well, we'll just see then, won't we?" she asked. She stood, and moved among them. "Why, Billy Joe Raily, I declare, your skin looks nice and white and so healthy today. That bit of yellow tinge is all gone." She stroked the man's cheek with the back of her hand.

Billy Joe looked as if he were just about to burst. Kiernan had her bedside manner down pat. A touch, and poor Billy Joe was probably trying hard not to climax.

Jesse imagined that he was saving his men from their battle wounds—so they could die of heart attacks from the excitement Kiernan caused them.

She stooped to place a wet cloth on another brow, then turned and saw him. And stopped dead still.

For a moment, the demure mask of the very sweet belle slipped. She was every bit as beautiful, but her face suddenly appeared sharp and weary, and her eyes bore a trace of wariness. She straightened, still staring at him, and set the cloth upon the table. Then she turned around to sweep the room with her gaze.

"Good afternoon, boys," she wished them, serene and innocent. The mask was back in place.

She swept by Jesse.

He breathed in the sweet scent of the woman and her perfume, and he listened to the rustle of silk.

Later that afternoon, near twilight, he looked out of his bedroom window and saw her in front of the house. She had changed into a dark velvet riding habit that had been fashioned more for utility than for elegance. As he watched, she hurried toward the stables.

He dropped the letter he had just received from Washington, grabbed his wool, shoulder-skirted frock coat, and hurried downstairs. By the time he reached the porch, she was just riding out, careful to skirt around the tents of his men and the bivouac on the front lawn.

Jesse hurried toward the stables himself. Old Jeremiah was seated on a chair by the door, leaning back and dozing. But when Jesse strode by him, he opened his eyes wide, then hurried after Jesse.

"Where you goin' there, Master Jess?"

"Riding."

"Don't seem to me like no good time to go ridin'. It's gonna be dark soon enough."

Right before Pegasus's stall, Jesse paused. "Oh, really? You should have thought to stop your mistress then."

"What?"

"Kiernan just left. Mrs. Miller just rode away from here," Jesse said impatiently.

"Did she now?"

"Jeremiah, you're trying to tell me that you didn't see Mrs. Miller riding out, when you were sitting right here?"

"Come to think of it—"

"Right, come to think of it," Jesse muttered. He drew Pegasus's bridle from its hook and moved around to the horse's head.

"Want me to saddle him up for you, Master Jess?"

"No, thanks," Jesse said. "If I let you do it, I have a feeling I'd be sitting here all night waiting for you to finish."

"Why, Master Jess—"

"Step aside, Jeremiah," Jesse said. He pushed on Pegasus's neck, backing him out of the stall. He quickly threw a blanket and his saddle over the horse's back and cinched and tightened the girth. Then leaped upon the horse and looked down at Jeremiah.

"Don't fret too much, Jeremiah. She's way ahead of me."

Jeremiah stepped back; he had no choice. Jesse set his heels to Pegasus, and they started off.

He didn't skirt around his own encampment and made up some time by riding through it. Still, when he reached the place where Kiernan had disappeared into the trees, he reined in. He studied the ground, but it was bone dry, and there were few prints. One trail seemed to have more broken foliage along it, so he urged Pegasus in that direction.

Mentally, he drew a picture of the area. Harpers Ferry was far below, with Maryland Heights, the mounts and hills and crests and valleys, all around. He thought of the manors and the plantations in the region, places where he had attended balls and fêtes and where he had hunted with friends.

He remembered that the trail before him led to the ruins of the Chagall estate.

"All right, Pegasus, let's see what she's up to," Jesse murmured. He tightened his thighs, urging the horse forward.

Some mornings when Kiernan awoke, she still prayed that she would discover that it had all been a horrible nightmare.

Jesse had never come to the house. None of the Yanks had ever come. The war had yet to touch them, and a dozen injured men were not living in her house.

At first, nothing could conceivably have been worse than having Jesse in the next room. Surely not even the fires of hell could bring so much torment as having him so near. She had not slept, just knowing that he was there. Hearing his footsteps across the wooden floor, imagining the movements that he made— she could picture his face because she knew him so well. He would be weary coming in from surgery. He would cast off his coat or his jacket, sit back in the chair at the desk, and prop his booted heels up upon it. He would sink down, close his eyes, and press his temple between his thumb and his forefinger. Then, slowly, his hand would fall, his eyes would open, and he would rise.

She could hear him moving about the room, stripping down. His boots falling to the floor, his shirt over a chair, his breeches, his belt. Then she would hear his weight as he fell upon his bed, and she would picture him again, fingers laced behind his head, his eyes upon the darkened shadows on the ceiling.

In the silence that followed she could imagine no greater anguish than lying awake and seeing him in her mind's eyes, just feet apart from her. He was her enemy now. They had no future together. Jesse had donned blue and gone his own way, and she could never change him. She had sworn to hate him.

And she had sworn to herself that she hated him.

And she did, completely. But love died hard, she realized, no matter what color cloth covered a man.

And now she was Anthony's widow. She had married Anthony, and Anthony was dead, and it had not been that long ago, and she should have been in deepest mourning.

But none of that mattered when Jesse was in a room. No matter how deep her fury, no matter how desperate her situation, when he came near, smoldering sparks came alive, furnaces blazed. Her hatred was intense—and so, too, was her longing.

It was not simply Jesse's arrival that tormented her. It was the men who camped out on the lawn. It was the men who lay in Anthony's room across the hall. Yankees. Sick Yankees, hurt Yankees.

When she had first heard a man screaming in the surgery, she had simply stayed in her bedroom, her hands clamped over her ears. She could have sworn that the victim had died. But there he was that night, alive and well, and with a gentle smile when he saw her looking in on him. He, too, was the enemy.

But how could she wish him dead?

Then the others came. They were men with lean faces and blue eyes and brown eyes, and men with weary and worn faces. Some wore whiskers, and some did not. They, too, were the enemy. They were the same as any man, and as often as not in this region, they had kinfolk on the other side, and they prayed not so much to live as to not encounter their own loved ones at the other end of their rifles. She wanted to ignore their suffering; but she discovered that she could not bear it.

She also discovered that Jesse's patients were a fine way to learn the movements of the Union troops. They had all come in from skirmishes in the countryside nearby, and the information they had was invaluable.

She had already left a message at the oak for foraging Confederates to vacate a place before Yankees with superior numbers could surprise them. Now she had a second opportunity to do so. It pleased her greatly. It seemed, at the very least, some recompense for the anguish of having Jesse in the house and the agony of hearing the screams that came from the surgery.

Night was coming quickly this evening, she realized, riding harder as she neared the Chagall estate. She reined in, seeing the pillars of the burned-out place, white and black and ghostly in the pale moonlight that had replaced the rays of the day's dying sun.

The wind rustled through the trees, and haunting shadows fell over the terrain. Movements seemed to flutter all about her, and for a moment she held still, as a shiver of fear danced up and down the length of her spine.

She had been a fool to come so late at night, she thought. But there was little to fear, she told herself. The Rebs would not hurt her, and the Yanks were already living in her house.

And still . . .

The breeze was very cool, and the night seemed to have eyes.

She leaped off her horse and raced to the old oak. Just as she neared the tree, a shadow stepped out from behind it.

The shadow of a man, and not of a man . . .

Tall, dark, pitch-black, and menacing, the moonlight caught him in a strange silhouette, throwing his shadow far and wide across the tree and all the overgrown lawn before the house.

Kiernan screamed, reeling back, her hand flying to her mouth. Instinctively, she turned to run. She heard a shout, but in her panic, it meant nothing. She tore across the weeds and grass and fallen branches, desperate to reach her horse. The wind rose again, rustling through the trees with sudden vengeance.

She could feel him, the shadow on her back, hounding her. She ran faster, gasping, screaming desperately for every breath, running so hard that her lungs ached and threatened to burst, her legs cramped and burned, and her heart hammered.

Just feet away from her horse, the shadow devoured her. She was swept off her feet, and she screamed again in a wild panic. She felt herself falling and hitting the hard earth, the shadow on top of her.

She fought it, swinging out, kicking, screaming, slamming hard again and again against the blackness and the hard bulk as panic overwhelmed her.

"Kiernan!"

At last, her name penetrated her terrified senses. She went rigidly still.

"Kiernan!"

Jesse! It was Jesse. She should have known. She should have recognized the angle of his hat, even in a distorted silhouette. She should have known the feel of him, the scent of him. . . .

But when she had left the house, he was in his room! He had just finished surgery, he'd probably received messages from Washington, and he should have been involved in all that was going on in his hospital.

How had he reached the oak ahead of her?

"Jesse!" Sanity was returning to her. The wind was high, and it whistled and rustled through the trees like something alive. The moonlight came down upon them fully now, and his face was clear above her own. It was a handsome face with clear, defined features, a rugged face, with fine character lines around his eyes. It was a face she knew so well.

Suddenly, she worried that somebody might be in the area—Angus or T. J. or one of their neighbors. If they saw Jesse straddled over her like this, they might . . .

Kill him.

"Jesse, get off me, you fool!"

"Why, Kiernan?" he demanded. His voice was harsh, his eyes were nearly obsidian in the night. His touch was steel.

"Why?" she repeated, incredulous. "Because you've got me pinned to the ground! Because you just scared me half to death. Because I hate, loathe, and despise you. Because you're the enemy. Because you're goddamned wearing blue!"

His eyes glittered in the darkness. His hands pinned her wrists above her head. He was so close to her. She felt the warmth of his breath, sensed the heat and tension in him, felt the rippling of his muscles. It didn't matter what she said. He ignored her.

"What the hell are you doing out here?"

"What the hell is it to you?" she spat. She stiffened in agony beneath him, praying that he would move, and quickly. He wasn't hurting her; he was just holding her with his thighs, with his weight, with the taut ring of his fingers around her wrists.

"What are you doing out here?" he thundered again.

"I came for a ride!"

"At night?"

"Yes, it's night, isn't it? Bright boy. That must be why you Yanks do so well in battle."

"Stop it!" he commanded her.

"Stop what?"

"Stop acting like that!"

"Acting! I'm not acting, Captain. This is war, remember?" She stared up at him, growing very cold against the damp earth, hating him, and suddenly afraid as she saw a ruthless glimmer in his eyes that was as cold as the night. Had his grasp slackened just a bit? She strived with all her strength to kick him. He swore, and she gasped out, rolling hard to elude his touch.

But he was right with her. Before she had moved six inches, he was on top of her again, splayed over her this time. He held her wrists together with one hand and lifted her chin with his free thumb. "I'll ask you again. What are you doing out here?"

"I came for a ride. What are *you* doing out here?"

"Following you."

"Jesse, I'm not going to tell you anything—"

"Kiernan, they shoot spies!"

"Go to hell, Jesse. I'm not a spy! And if I—"

"Bitch!" he swore suddenly. He rose to his feet, drawing her up before him. His hands were so tight on hers that she almost cried out with the pain. He pulled her so tautly against him that she could scarcely bear it. His fingers wound into her hair, tight and painful. She met his gaze.

"You used my men. You acted like an angel of mercy, but you didn't care in the least that they suffered. You'd just as soon see them dead, right? But you moved among them from that very first night for whatever little tidbit you might pick up from them—men so very grateful for the least little bounty that you offered!"

He was shaking, trembling with his rage. He had her pulled so flush against him that she could feel the beat of his heart. The heat of his words and his anger touched her lips, almost like a kiss.

"Jesse, damn you, I didn't—"

"Damn you! Don't lie to me!"

"Fine, fine!" she cried out. Tears stung her eyes from the pressure of his fingers upon her hair. She could not look away. "I'd use them anytime, Jesse, and I'd use you. You're the enemy. My God, how many times do you have to be told that? I hate you, Jesse, and I hate them! They're invading my land! They've taken over my house! They've killed my friends and my people! What the hell do you want from me?"

He was dead silent as the wind rustled through the trees again and as the night drifted all around him. He swore an oath, still furious, still shaking, his fingers curling around her shoulders. "What do I want out of you?" he repeated savagely. His teeth flashed white in the moonlight. "What do I want out of you? I want to curl my fingers around your throat. I want—"

He became still again. But only a second passed before his lips were suddenly on hers, hard and nearly as savage as her words. His mouth formed, hot and demanding upon hers, igniting an instant blaze within her, a combustion that rocketed the night, that seized hold of all her senses and left her powerless to resist.

It had been so long . . .

So long since he had held her so, so long since she had felt the world tremble beneath her feet, felt joy erupt in her heart and in her limbs and in the deepest, inner core of her body. She could not resist, for she was melded to his form, so tight against him that they might have been one. His arms were so powerful around her. His tongue ringed her lips and forced entry to the sweetest depths of her mouth.

He held her and kissed her. With each passing second the hot, sultry seduction of his mouth and tongue took her deeper and deeper into a no man's land of longing and memory. Bright tears flooded her eyes as the thing that she could never deny to herself sprang into her thoughts.

She loved him.

No war could change that, no color could cover that blindness. She loved him, and she wanted him.

No! She'd never been a wife to Anthony in any sense. At the very least, she could be a decent widow.

She wrenched free from the seduction of his touch. "Jesse. No, damn you!" she cried out, and stepped back a foot, wiping her mouth with the back of her hand as if she could erase what had happened.

"Kiernan—"

"No! Never! Not here, not now! Not near Anthony's house, dear Lord!"

"Kiernan!" His voice was hard and rugged and rasping as he took a step forward.

"I'm a widow, Jesse! Anthony's widow!" she stressed.

He went dead still, his fingers knotted tightly into fists and clenched at his side. "Damn you, Kiernan," he muttered.

"Don't touch me again!" she whispered. "Don't touch me. If he was ever your friend, if you ever had any respect for him. Jesse, this is his home, his land."

"And it was *his* home, *his* land, where we first made love!" Jesse exploded.

It was like a slap in the face—because it was true.

She spun around, anxious to reach her horse. But she didn't get very far before he caught hold of her elbow and spun her back around to face him.

"Where are your widow's weeds, Kiernan? Where is your black, where the hell is your mourning?"

In dismay, she stared at him. She had shed her mourning colors only a few months after she had come. Black had been so hot when she had been working in the garden. They hadn't done laundry frequently enough to clean them.

She had loved Anthony in a way, but she had never managed to feel like his widow, and it had been easy to slip.

Jesse smiled a mocking smile and took a step back. "What a love affair it must have been!" he taunted.

She took a wild swing at him. He caught her arm and wrenched her up against him once more. She felt the awful thundering of her heart when she thought he was going to kiss her again.

"Let me go, Jesse."

He held her still. She couldn't best his strength. His lips would touch hers again, and she would be lost.

"He was your friend, Jesse. He fought you, but he always admired you."

He was stiff, as rigid as steel. He held her in silence, his teeth grating, his jaw clenched. When he spoke, it was through clenched teeth. His eyes were dark upon hers, his features taut. "Damn you, Kiernan! Damn you."

But she was free. She looked at him, quickly backing away from him, hoping that her tears would not fall and that she would not betray her own emotions.

She turned and fled and mounted her horse and galloped all the way home.

He was behind her all the way, but he did not try to catch her again. At the house, she did not dare to look at him again.

She left her horse with Jeremiah, who was worried, and who cried after her. She would not stop. She fled to the house and to her room.

Once again that night, she listened. She listened to his footsteps in the room next to her own. She listened to the creaking of his chair as he sat. She heard his boots fall, heard the very weariness as he shed his clothing and fell into his bed.

She closed her eyes tight, clenching down on her jaw. It would be so easy to rise and walk the few steps down the hall. So easy to open the door and drift in white, like the white of a bride, to his bed.

And lie down beside him.

And feel his arms and the night breeze against her naked flesh.

She buried her face in the pillow.

Trying to hate him . . .

And hating herself.

It was morning before she realized that she had not left her message in the oak. The information she had learned from the Yanks might save a number of lives.

She dressed in a simple gingham and brown day dress in case Jesse happened to notice her moving about the house. Very carefully, she folded her written message and slipped it low into her bodice and left her room. Knowing that she had to take grave care, she went first to the ward and spoke with the men. Corporal O'Malley was there with an assistant, speaking with the men and looking over bandages and braces and splints. Kiernan swept among them all, offering smiles and assurances, pouring water and providing what little amenities that she could to make them more comfortable.

One moment, she felt as if twin darts of fire were burning into her back, and she turned.

Jesse stood in the doorway watching her. He had accused her of caring nothing for the men, and he had said that spying was her only reason to be among them.

He'd never have believed that she wanted nothing from them that morning, that she had learned that she cared for any man's suffering, no matter what color he wore.

But Jesse would never believe that. The look he gave her now condemned her a thousand times over. It made her shake inside and want to cry out.

She turned quickly from him and changed the cool cloth on the forehead of the soldier who had asked her assistance. When she turned back again, Jesse was gone.

She lingered with the men for another hour. She heard Corporal O'Malley say something about finding Tyne to help Jesse get ready in surgery.

It was time for her to leave.

She hurried downstairs and out of the house. Glancing back, she was certain that no one stood at a window to watch her departure. She ran to the stables.

But when she opened the door, she found two soldiers standing there, staring at her.

"Gentlemen?" she demanded.

The first, Private Yeager, shook his head. "Don't try to sweet-talk us, Mrs. Miller."

"Sweet-talk you, sir?" she said sharply, her brow rising.

"You're carrying information to the Rebs," the second soldier, Sergeant Herrington, said flatly.

"Don't be absurd!" she lied. "Get out of my way."

She started forward, but Yeager stood directly in front of her. "Hand it over, Mrs. Miller. You're carrying a message."

"Get out of my way!" She stepped around him.

To her amazement, he pulled her back. His eyes were bright. "You're carrying a message, and I want it."

"Don't you dare handle me like that!" she cried imperiously.

"I'll handle you—" he began, but then his voice broke. He was staring over her shoulder. His hold went slack, and Kiernan spun around.

Jesse stood dead set in the doorway, his arms folded across his chest, his eyes implacable.

"What's going on here, Sergeant?"

Sergeant Herrington cleared his throat. "Sir, she's carrying notes to the Rebels. We're convinced of it."

Jesse arched a brow and looked at Kiernan. "Are you carrying secret missives to Rebel soldiers, Mrs. Miller?"

"No," she lied flatly.

Jesse looked to the two men. "She denies the charge, men."

"Well, just you let me—let me—" Herrington began.

"Let you what?" Jesse asked.

"Search her!" Herrington spat out with relish.

Kiernan gasped. "Captain! You cannot let this orangutan touch me!"

"Madam, such a comparison is insulting to orangutans."

"Captain—"

"We are soldiers in the Union Army, gentlemen. I cannot let you search a lady. And as gentlemen, men of honor, you are obliged to accept her word. You may return to your posts."

Herrington cast her a furious stare and walked out, the hapless Private Yeager at his heels.

Kiernan's heart sank. She certainly couldn't ride away now. She started after them, but Jesse slammed the door in her face before she could go.

Startled, she looked at him—and her heart began to beat hard, for there was fire in his eyes, and they were alone, very alone, in the stables.

"Are you carrying a message, Kiernan?" he quizzed her softly.

"You'll never know, will you?" she asked sweetly. "Now, if you'll excuse me—"

He shook his head. "I certainly will not excuse you." He took a step toward her, and she backed away.

"Jesse, what are you doing?"

"I'm going to find out if you're carrying a message."

"What?" she cried. "You can't!" She took another step back, a step that landed her in a freshly broken bale of hay, and she fell back into it.

Jesse stood above her, his long legs straddled over her own as he stared down at her.

"Jesse, you wouldn't dare!"

"I've told you before, I dare anything."

"You just said that a gentleman in the Union Army couldn't do such a thing! You wouldn't allow those men—"

"Ah, but Kiernan, you told me long ago that you considered me no gentleman. And I told those men that *they* couldn't." He smiled wickedly. "I certainly didn't say that *I* couldn't . . . or *wouldn't.*"

To Kiernan's astonishment and rising horror, he was suddenly down upon the hay.

Upon her.

Eighteen

His knee lay at an angle over her thigh. He leaned upon one elbow at her side, while his left arm was braced around her waist. She stared at him furiously. "Jesse, I always knew you were no gentleman, but—"

"Kiernan, let's not go through this again. I want the message."

"There is no message."

"There is. You can give it to me, or I can take it."

He was serious, she decided. But she couldn't just hand over proof that she had been using her association with the hospitalized men to aid the Confederacy. Why in the Lord's name hadn't she waited until she reached the tree before she wrote down her message?

Because he might have followed her, she thought dully, and she never would have had a chance to write it down.

"Jesse," she said very softly, her eyes on his with what she hoped was open honesty, "I'm asking you to stop this. It's totally undignified. It dishonors all— all that we ever were to one another," she added with a note of pathos.

"And what is that, Kiernan?" he asked softly. His knuckles brushed softly over her cheeks, and she was amazed by the warmth that filled her with that touch. The warmth spread the length and breadth of her, the rake of his knuckles was so tender. His lips were close to hers, and the weight of his body was painfully familiar.

She had to seduce him into letting her go free, she reminded herself. She reached up and brushed back a lock of his hair, a dark lock that dangled rakishly upon occasion, no matter how much she knew he tried to subdue it. She smoothed it back and allowed the tips of her fingers to stroke his face in turn.

"Jesse, let me up, please. I have to get away. There are times when I just have to ride away. Don't you understand?"

He caught her fingers and planted a kiss upon them. He held them still, fascinated. Another kiss fell, and another. She felt the hot, sultry movement of his tongue upon them.

"Jesse . . ."

"I understand," he murmured. "There are Yankees in your house. Yankees." He repeated the word, looked into her eyes, smiled, and shivered. "Ugh."

She almost snatched her hand away. She gritted her teeth and pouted. "Jesse, be serious, please."

"I'm very serious," he promised her. He eased back, curling his fingers around hers, allowing both their hands to rest upon her chest, just above the rise of her breasts. "Let's see, you need to ride away because there are Yankees in your house."

"That's right, Jesse."

"You've been good to those poor, sick Yankees."

"Yes, I have. I tend to them daily."

"And now you want to ride away with all the little goodies, tidbits of information, that those poor sick Yankees with their tongues hanging out have given you, right?"

"Right." Her own reply stunned her—she had been so entranced by the cadence of his voice. "No—wrong! Oh, Jesse, you're confusing me so!"

"Like hell I am!" To her great irritation, he grinned. "Ah, Mrs. Miller, it is the dramatic stage's loss that you never tried your hand at acting."

"Jesse, you get off me!" she cried out, twisting frantically to be free from him. But this was one fight that he did not intend to lose. Before she knew it, her hands were slammed down high atop her head. He straddled her and grabbed her wrists together to hold them tightly with one hand. His fingers wound around her wrists hard, pinning them above her head.

And then his free hand was on her, on her breast. His fingers touched her bare flesh, delving with purpose into her clothing. She squirmed in wild desperation that only seemed to entangle them more fully. Buttons gave way, and her breasts seemed to spill forth over the ties of her corset and the soft, now-mangled material of her chemise.

"Jesse, you bastard!"

Her voice broke as the ties of her corset suddenly gave, and her note fell free. Still holding her with one hand, Jesse unfolded the missive with the other, holding it out to read quickly in silence.

His eyes fell upon hers, a bright, hard blue.

"You wouldn't dream of spying, Kiernan?" he asked politely.

"Jesse, you've got what you wanted. Now get off me!"

But he didn't move. His eyes raked over her in the light and shadow of the stables. Her hair, freed now, was tousled and tangled with the hay. Her face was so flushed, her eyes so wide.

And her breasts, naked, spilling forth.

She gritted down hard on her teeth, trying to force his eyes back to hers, for she could feel her nipples hardening beneath his scrutiny. As she lay exposed, she could not hide her emotions.

"I haven't gotten what I wanted at all," he told her.

"You must be insane!" she cried out. He was going to touch her again, she knew it. His hand was touching her clothing. "No!" she breathed, and closed her eyes. God, don't let him touch me, because he'll know how very much I want him. "Please!" she whispered.

But she felt the ties coming together, not apart. The velvet of her bodice was being pulled closed, covering her nakedness, not revealing it.

She opened her eyes. He was watching her still, with a dark and brooding tension. No violence remained, no breath of ruthlessness as he touched her cheek again.

"I could arrest you."

"Then arrest me," she told him.

"I don't want to. I want you to stop doing what you're doing."

"I'm lying on a stable floor in misery. I want to stop doing that myself," she murmured bitterly.

He smiled and sank back on his haunches, lifting her up beneath him. It felt so good, for those few moments, to have his arms around her.

"Kiernan, you can't win this war, you just can't. Do you know that you're suspected as far away as Washington?"

"You—you were warned about me?" she said in dismay.

He nodded. "Don't you see? I can't let you go on doing what you're doing. And I definitely can't let you use my men."

She tossed her head back. "Then arrest me, Jesse."

"Surrender the fight. You've no right being in this war!"

"I have every right to be in this war. This is my home—Virginia is my home. I cannot—I will not—surrender, ever," she assured him passionately.

"Kiernan—"

"No!" She pulled away from him. He didn't try to stop her when she rose and turned away, adjusting her clothing. She swirled back around. "*You* surrender! You've no right being in this war!"

"What?" He, too, was on his feet. "What are you talking about?"

"You've no right being in this war. I'm fighting for my home, but you're making war on yours. What are you fighting for? Some absurd ideal? What ideal? The U.S. Congress says you're fighting to subdue the states in rebellion! Do you think you're fighting to end slavery? But slavery hasn't been abolished in most northern states. What are you trying to do? Why in God's name do you keep this up? You've seen the men come in to you day after day, broken, bleeding, dying! Why the hell are you on their side?"

"Because the Union has to stand!" he shouted back. "It has to stand together. Don't you see that? The halves are nothing without the whole!"

"No, no, I don't see it at all!" she cried back. Why did she always come so damnably near tears every time they got into one of these fights? She had lost this battle with him long before. "Damn you, Jesse!" she cried out. She had to get past him. She couldn't burst into tears, she didn't dare let him come close to her again. "You've got your message, your proof. Arrest me, hang me, do whatever it is you want to do. But let me out of here now! I cannot bear what you've done! I cannot bear to talk with you, to try to reason with you."

He exhaled with exasperation. "You're under house arrest, Kiernan."

"Fine. It doesn't matter. You fool, don't you know that Jackson or someone else will come back here? You'll be beaten, Jesse, because the Rebs are more disciplined. And because they're fighting for their homes."

She gasped when his hands landed hard upon her shoulders again, and he gave her a shake that sent her head falling back and her hair cascading all around, and forced her eyes to meet his.

"Yes! Jackson will come back, or he'll send another commander. And yes, the South can fight. They can ride, and they can shoot. They've been born and bred to horses and guns. And my God, yes, they're good—they run circles around us all the time. But in the end, Kiernan, we'll win. We'll win because there simply are more of us. And we'll win because we have more factories, and more clothing, and more power."

Suddenly, she was more afraid than she had ever been. It had never occurred to her that the South could lose.

She broke free from him, staring at him hard. Her tears were hot behind her eyes now. "I hate you, Jesse!" she reminded him.

To her surprise, he smiled a slow, anguished, crooked smile. "I know," he said, and added very softly, "and I still love you."

"But not enough! Not enough!" she whispered desperately.

He reached for her. "Kiernan—"

"No! For the love of God, let me go!"

He freed her, and she tore away, nearly blinded by her tears as she ran back to the house as quickly as she could.

The next morning she awoke to a tremendous commotion. Rising, she hurried to the window and looked out.

Men were arriving. Two horse soldiers were leading a caravan with a wagon, and beyond the wagon, more men followed. They didn't march like men going off to battle—they came slowly, hanging upon one another, limping men aided by ones with bloodied bandages around their arm.

They were a company of wounded, she realized.

Even as she watched, Jesse came out into the yard. He called out, and she saw that Tyne was hurrying to join him. Janey was out there, too, and then Jeremiah, and then David, and even Jacob.

The cool morning air drifted by her, and a numbness settled around her. They were all Yankees. Bluebellies. They had left behind any number of Rebel dead and wounded.

She heard a cry of agony, and the numbness drifted from her shoulders like a cloak. They were in pain, all of them. They would die, some of them.

She looked away, swallowing hard. She couldn't worry about them, she just couldn't. Every time Jesse patched them up, they just went back to the war, back to killing more men of the Confederacy. More Virginians.

But then Jesse was shouting orders, and everyone was running about to follow them. As she watched, he moved through the men who were able to stand, quickly assessing their wounds. Little David was hurrying about with water for them all, and as Jesse saw each man, he called to Janey to see that the man was sent either to a room or to the hallway to await surgery. He disappeared into the wagon for a moment, then reappeared and addressed Corporal O'Malley. "We've two dead in the wagon, Corporal. See to them, will you?"

"Right, sir!" O'Malley agreed.

A sick sensation stirred in Kiernan's belly, and she hurried across the room to douse her face in her wash water. Then she felt better.

She dressed quickly, then hurried downstairs. The commotion was still going on, men limping here and there, stretchers being borne in by men who were still largely whole. As she came through the great hall, she suddenly stopped dead still. There weren't only Yankees in her hallway.

Three of the men who had been carried in were dressed in gray.

"Mrs. Miller!"

A faint, husky voice called out to her. Her heart leaped to her throat, and she moved quickly through the cots and beds to reach the fallen soldier in gray.

He was in bad shape, she thought. There was blood on the gray wool of his uniform at his stomach, and blood covered most of his left leg. His hair was matted, and his face was covered in mud. She stared at him for a long horrified moment before she recognized him.

"T.J.!" she cried, and curled her fingers over his, looking at him anxiously.

She saw that David was moving among the men with a water pitcher, and she called to him.

"David, come quickly!"

He obeyed, and she poured out a cup of water and lifted T.J.'s head so that he could drink. She ripped off the bottom of her skirt to get a cloth to clean away the mud upon his face.

"Oh, T.J.!" she murmured.

His eyes opened to hers. "Don't let them chop me up, Mrs. Miller. Don't let them stick their saws on me."

"T.J.—" she began, but his eyes had closed. His breathing was shallow. She placed her hand upon his heart and found that its beat was slow and weak. "Oh, T.J., don't die on me!" she pleaded.

He needed help, and he needed it badly. Suddenly, his fingers wound around hers. "Let it be, Mrs. Miller. Some of those"—he paused, moistening his cracked lips—"some of those Yank sawbones boast that they can kill more Rebs on their operating tables than the soldiers can in the fields. If they just forget me, I can die in peace."

"You're not going to die, and this Yankee sawbones isn't like the others," Kiernan promised him quickly. "T.J., he'll help you, I swear he will."

But he didn't answer her. His eyes were already closed again.

Kiernan looked across the room desperately. So many men, and they all seemed badly hurt. She saw Janey by one of the wounded men, and she hurried over to him.

"Where's Jesse?"

Janey stared at her, amazed to see her.

"Janey! Where's Jesse?"

Janey indicated the office. "In surgery. He ain't gonna want to talk to you right now, Miz Kiernan."

Kiernan ignored her and hurried to the office, bursting in. For a moment she paused in the doorway, horrified. The man on the operating table was tossing and screaming, thrashing about wildly. Jesse was shouting to Tyne to subdue him and trying to administer a dose of morphine.

The man had nothing left of his foot or lower leg, nothing but pulp that could not be recognized as human flesh.

"Jesse . . ." His name came out a whisper.

He looked up, saw her, and suddenly summoned her. "Kiernan, quick—I need you."

"But Jesse—"

"I need you!"

Suddenly, she was beside him and the maimed man. He gave her an instant medical lesson, showing her the different saws that he needed for an amputation, telling her to staunch the flow of blood instantly and to keep all the sponges and bandages clean.

She looked around. There had to be someone else to help. She was going to pass out.

But there was no one. Corporal O'Malley was stitching up men with minor injuries. Jeremiah was assisting him. Janey was doing her best with the chaos in the hallway.

"Jesse, I can't do this," she breathed, but he didn't seem to hear her. He was telling Tyne to use his mighty shoulders and arms to brace the man, and whether Kiernan wanted to be there or not, she was. The man was quickly prepped, and Jesse was demanding his instruments, scalpel, saw, and bone saw.

She did it. Somehow, she did it. She handed him his instruments as he demanded them, and she caught the bloodied things when he finished. She followed his every order as he packed and bandaged the leg just below the knee, where he had sewn the flesh as carefully as he dared, to give the man a chance to walk with a false limb later.

Tyne carried away the severed calf.

Then she thought she would pass out.

But Jesse shouted for water, insisted upon washing his hands, then demanded to know who was next. She remembered that this was why she had come.

"Jesse, there's a man out there very badly wounded. He needs you quickly."

"O'Malley will see that he's brought in next."

"Jesse"—she paused—"Jesse, he's a Reb."

He stared at her for a moment. "Corporal O'Malley?" Jesse called out. His eyes were still on her. "O'Malley, which man needs me the most?"

O'Malley, tying off a stitch in the hallway, looked up. "I guess the Reb is the next worst off. The worst off of them that's still alive, that is."

"See that he's brought in," Jesse ordered.

Janey saw that the man just out of surgery was taken to a bed. Jesse spread out a clean sheet on the table, and in a minute, O'Malley and a man with a bandaged head were bringing in T.J.

"Hey, Captain!" the stranger complained. "Why the Reb? I've got an awful headache, here."

"Private Henson, I'm sure you do. But it's a superficial wound, and you're going to be just fine. I'll be with you soon enough." He looked down at T.J. "This boy is going to die if I don't get to him soon. He might die anyway."

"He should die—he's a Reb," the man said. "Doc, you shouldn't try to save him."

"Private, when I took an oath to save lives, they didn't allow me to make any distinctions in the color of the uniform a man happens to be wearing. I'll get to you soon enough, and I'll see that you have some time to get over that headache."

Private Henson's brow shot up, but he no longer argued with Jesse. He turned and left with Corporal O'Malley at his heels.

"Jesse," Kiernan breathed.

He looked across the table at her. "You just stay right where you are. No, wash your hands first, and my instruments. Keep doing what you're doing. You're doing it fine."

He started on T.J. Tyne helped him rip off the uniform that covered the wounds. First Jesse sponged and cleaned the blood from T.J.'s gut, and then he began to demand things from her again—a clamp, and then a probe. She gritted her teeth hard as he searched the battered flesh for bits and pieces of metal. He seemed satisfied, then demanded more things from her—a clamp, a needle, sutures. As she stood silently before him, he began to sew. She lowered her head, then she felt his eyes on her, blue and inquisitive. "Are you going to faint?"

"I would have done so by now," she snapped at him.

He smiled and turned back to his work. He ordered T.J.'s breeches ripped away so that he could get to the leg.

"Jesu," he murmured. "I don't know . . ."

T.J. chose that moment to rouse from his drugged stupor. A hand wound around Jesse's wrist, and Jesse and Kiernan both looked at T.J.'s white face.

"Doc, don't take it."

"Soldier, I don't know—"

T.J. fought desperately to remain conscious. "Doc, I was gut-shot. You don't even know that I can make it now."

"Reb, you weren't that shot up inside. None of your major organs were torn. I did a good job taking out the metal. I can't promise that any man will make it, but soldier, you should."

"Sweet Jesus, Doc, don't take my leg! I'm begging you not to take my leg. Mrs. Miller, don't let him!"

Jesse looked across the table at Kiernan.

"Please," she whispered.

He shrugged. "All right, Reb, I'll try," he said. But T.J., it seemed, had already drifted under again. He had put his faith in Kiernan and surrendered to the morphine.

"Tyne," Jesse ordered, "get hold of him. Kiernan, let's rip up these trousers the rest of the way."

They started on his leg. T.J. screamed when the probe first touched his flesh, then he was silent. So was Jesse, dead silent as he worked. Kiernan responded instantly as he ordered clamps, and sponges, then the probe, then a scalpel, then a sponge.

It seemed to go on endlessly. She sponged up blood and more blood, and she gnawed holes in her lower lip, but she didn't falter.

In time, Jesse sewed and swabbed the blood one last time, then wrapped the limb in clean white bandages. Kiernan watched his hands as he worked, watched the artistry. He moved confidently, competently, with skill and decision—and more. Even his most determined touch was compassionate and gentle.

He finished with T.J., his last orders being to bathe down his shoulders and face. Kiernan covered him in a clean sheet. Jesse leaned over the injured Reb one last time.

"Will he live?" Kiernan whispered.

"He's breathing now," Jesse told her. "Like I told him, I can't promise any man."

Kiernan nodded. Jesse was still staring at her. "Friend of yours?" he asked.

"Yes."

He was still watching her. She felt a flush creep up her cheeks.

"Just a friend," she told him.

A slow curl touched the corner of Jesse's lip, and his eyes caught hold of hers. "I wasn't implying anything, Mrs. Miller."

He turned away before she could respond, calling to Corporal O'Malley to see that the Reb was made comfortable in a ward and that the next patient be brought in.

He looked at Kiernan. "Are you staying?"

She couldn't bear any more of the blood and the screams. She had never meant to come.

But she was staying.

She had already discovered that Yanks were men, too, men who could be broken, torn, hurt, made to bleed in anguish. They were men with families, mothers, fathers, sisters, brothers, and lovers.

They were men who might go back and kill more Rebs. But at the moment, they were men who were hurt. Jesse hadn't hesitated to mend up a Rebel soldier. He had taken an oath to save lives, and that was what he did.

She was here now. She would help him. "I'll stay," she told him quietly.

He looked at her for a moment. "Good," he said briefly. "I can use it." He glanced to Tyne. "She's good, isn't she?"

Tyne, who had kept silent during the time they worked together, grinned. "She's mighty good." He looked at Kiernan. "We had three men fall flat down on their faces last week, Miz Kiernan. Soldier boys. You outdone them all," he told her.

The day wasn't over yet, Kiernan decided. They might yet see her flat on her face.

No, she told herself. She wasn't going to pass out in front of Jesse.

But as the hours wore on, she survived. She discovered she had an instinct for working with Jesse. She sensed just what he would need, and when. Work between them narrowed down to a very few words, and time passed very quickly.

Yankees came and went. The two other Rebel soldiers were treated. Their wounds were very minor. The last of the patients came into the surgery, then went out.

Tyne left with the bloodstained laundry. Jesse scrubbed his hands, and Kiernan sank into Andrew Miller's big swivel desk chair, exhausted.

"How are you?" Jesse asked her.

She felt his eyes on her, but she was too tired to care. Yet she felt more than the exhaustion. She felt a strange exhilaration along with it. She had mattered that day, had mattered very much. She had worked until she was bone tired, but the work had been good.

Even if she had been saving Yankees.

She understood something of what Jesse must feel as a doctor. Life—human life—was sacred.

It didn't matter what color uniform a man wore.

"I'm fine," she said very softly.

"Are you sure?" he queried, his voice equally quiet, and curious. He walked to where she sat and leaned over her, his hands upon the arms of the chair.

She smiled. "I'm tired. I think that I'm more tired than I've been in my whole life."

Jesse nodded, watching her. She'd never seen his eyes look so blue. "It was a darned rough day. You should never have had to see half of what you saw today."

No, she shouldn't have had to see the naked male limbs, and she shouldn't have had to see the dirt and the blood.

Once upon a time, the lady she had been trained to be would have fainted dead away at the thought.

But time had a way of changing things.

"I'm all right, really," she told him. She searched out his eyes. "I even feel . . . good," she admitted. "Is that very strange?"

He shook his head, smiling. "It is good to save lives, very good. And I'm glad that you feel that way." He straightened. "But we were lucky today. We didn't lose anyone."

"Do you lose men often, Jesse?"

"Often enough. Cannons and rifles and bayonets are made to kill. And often enough, they do."

She was silent—he was right. She was happy because she had not had to feel life slip away beneath her fingers.

"I've got to make rounds and see how our patients are faring," he told her. "Get yourself a stiff drink, and go to bed. You'll feel even better."

He left her. She started to drift off to sleep in the chair, but then she heard a soft and soothing voice—Janey's. "Chile, you are done worn out. Come on into the kitchen, I've a hot bath for you. And chicken soup. It's been a long day. Lord, yes, a long day."

Kiernan allowed herself to be led into the kitchen. Once undressed, she sank into the hot bath and found it close to heaven.

Soap had never smelled so sweet. Water had never encompassed her so gently, and heat had never touched her limbs so kindly. She sighed and relaxed. When she emerged, Janey was ready with a towel and chicken soup and a stiff brandy. Kiernan devoured both.

"I really did all right," she murmured out loud to Janey.

"Yes, you did, Miz Kiernan. Yes, you did. Now, get on up to bed, because you'll be feelin' it in the mornin'."

Kiernan knew that she was right. Drowsy, she thanked Janey and gave her a fierce hug. She was hugged just as tightly in return. She wrapped her flannel robe about herself and left the kitchen.

The men on cots in the great hall were quiet now. The house was quiet. The hour had grown very late. Kiernan moved quietly among them, heading for the stairway.

"Goodnight, Mrs. Miller," Corporal O'Malley called to her.

She nodded to him and hurried up the stairs.

At the top she suddenly remembered T.J. She didn't know where they had taken him, but she was closest to the ward that had been Anthony's room, so she hurried in there.

The lights were dim; the men seemed to be sleeping. She heard a soft moan, but when she tiptoed over to the cot from where the sound had come, she found that the occupant was sleeping. She tiptoed away again, ready to leave the room.

"Mrs. Miller!" one of the Yanks called to her softly, a man who had been with them awhile.

"Yes?"

"Are you looking for the Rebs?"

"Yes. Yes, I am."

"They're down the hall, in the boy's room. He's bunking in with his sister. Doc needed the space, and the boy didn't mind none. Neither did the little girl."

"Thank you," Kiernan told him.

She hurried out and down the hallway. She opened the door to Jacob's room —then backed away from what she saw.

Jesse was bent over one of the Rebs. She started to turn, but he said softly to her, "Come in, Kiernan."

He couldn't have seen her in the dark, but she came in, closing the door behind her. She leaned against it for a moment, then Jesse beckoned her forward. He was seeing to T.J.

T.J. was still. Eyes closed, he was as still as . . .

Death.

"Oh, God!" she breathed.

Jesse looked at her, startled, then shook his head, smiling. "Kiernan, he's doing very well."

"Oh!" She felt weak, but she couldn't faint now, she couldn't possibly, not after the day she had been through.

"He's sleeping soundly."

"His leg—?"

"Only time will tell."

She nodded, and clenched her nails into her palms to fight the dizziness that assailed her. She wanted to tell him that she was grateful, but she was suddenly afraid to talk.

She turned quickly. "Good night, Jesse," she said quickly.

"Good night," he responded.

Next, Kiernan looked in on the children. Curled together on Patricia's bed, they were sleeping sweetly.

She returned to her own room. It seemed like aeons since she had left it, but it had only been that morning.

She stared out at the moonlight for a while then slipped beneath her sheets. She was so exhausted, she should have fallen asleep easily.

But sleep eluded her. All that she could think of was the long day.

And Jesse.

She tried very hard to sleep. She tried to remember Anthony's face, and that she was his widow, and that this was his house.

All that she could see was Jesse.

She rose and quietly left her room, walked quickly down the few feet of hallway to his room, and before she dared to think about what she was doing, she opened the door, entered the room, and closed the door behind her.

Jesse was in bed.

But he wasn't asleep, and he hadn't been asleep. He was sitting up in bed, his shoulders and chest naked. His fingers were laced behind his head and he leaned back against the fine oak frame of the big bed. In the darkness and shadow, his eyes were upon her.

Moonlight danced palely within the room. It touched his shoulders and chest, casting them in a bronzelike light. It did not touch his features and gave away nothing of the emotion in his eyes.

"Well, Mrs. Miller," he said softly. "What are you doing here?"

She left the doorway and walked across the room to stand beside his bed. "I wanted you to know that I'm grateful, very grateful, for what you did for T.J."

He stretched his arm out to her, turning his hand palm out, waiting for her to take it. She hesitated, then took it.

And then she found herself pulled down next to him, and before she knew it, his arms were around her and she was rolled down into the depths of the big master bed, lying on the pillow at his side while he braced himself over her, running his fingers gently through her hair.

"I want you to know," he told her huskily, "that I would have tried to save him whether you asked me to or not." He watched her expectantly.

Warmth, a sweet searing explosion of it, suddenly seemed to streak through her. She knew why she had come, she knew why she wanted to be here. She stared into the blue eyes that were so very intent upon her own. Those eyes held so much care and so much wisdom. They were the eyes of a man who could not be denied for the simple measure of what he was inside.

"There's no need for you to be grateful," he said harshly.

Despite his tone, she smiled. She wound her arms around his neck. "I'm not that grateful," she murmured. "I mean—well, I *am* grateful, but I'm not here only because I'm grateful."

"Then?"

"I'm here because . . ."

"Because?"

"Because I want you to hold me."

He returned her smile, slowly. The moonlight played upon his rugged features, and his smile was crooked and sensual.

"Gladly," he whispered.

His arms encompassed her, he kissed her.

Nineteen

*I*f the taste of his kiss was bittersweet, it was made up for by the simple ecstasy of feeling his arms around her again. So many nights she had lain awake, tortured by memory. So many times she had remembered him when he had been far away from her.

War still raged, and it would go on tomorrow.

But for Kiernan, it would stop this night.

His lips upon hers were ardent, fevered. She felt a trembling deep within him as he fought to leash the passion that ignited swiftly between them. The wanting within him touched her as no aphrodisiac could, sending erotic tongues and laps of fire to dance and sweep over her flesh and through her limbs.

She returned his kiss, eager for it, met the fever of his tongue, gasped and sought him again and again when he broke away to circle her lips erotically, slowly, with the bare rim of his tongue, taking her mouth with the fullness of his own, pulling away again.

His tongue moved over her throat, slowly sliding along the length of it.

She gasped, her eyes closed, as she heard the rending of fabric. He ripped her gown cleanly so that it fell open, baring all her flesh to him.

But she did not open her eyes, for she felt that slow burning touch of his kiss, of his tongue, again. Centering upon her collarbone, it moved again, drawing a hot wet pattern between her breasts, moving sensually over that valley. Her breasts ached to be touched so, to be licked and caressed by the force of his mouth. But he did not touch them.

Rather, he continued the hot slide of his tongue onward over her abdomen. She shivered slightly, for when his mouth did not touch her, she was cold. But she could not move—she could only lie still in the greatest, sweetest fascination.

His kiss moved over her belly, and his tongue entered the cavity of her navel, played there, danced there. Suddenly, she was aware of his whisper against her flesh, a whisper that told her how sweetly she smelled, how wonderfully she tasted. The scent of the lilac from her bath still haunted her flesh, haunted his senses.

Then he was silent, and the searing-hot, wet slide of the tip of his tongue traveled ever more downward. Downward, until she thought she would scream. Her entire body awakened, and both cold and steaming, it was near agony in the tempest, sweet and hungry, that seized her—the wanting, the knowing, the needing.

That searing hot dampness was suddenly within her, deep within her, pervading her. An invasion so sweet, it brought a shattering sensation to burst throughout her. A cry welled within her, touched her lips, but never escaped her.

For he was suddenly atop her, his arms around her, and his lips were hot and hungry and molded over hers, smothering any sounds of ecstasy that might have escaped her. The bare bronze sleekness of his body was pressed taut to hers, seeming to meld with it.

His eyes upon her, he held himself above her and watched her eyes as he began his body's own riveting invasion of hers, coming deeper, deeper, deeper.

A soft whisper of desperation tore from her lips, and she buried her face against his throat, pulling tighter and tighter against him, arching, twisting, feeling him with all her length, inside and out. He was slow, torturously slow, pressing her back and watching her eyes again as he moved against her, seeming to burn inside her until he touched her womb, her heart, her very soul.

Then slowness was wickedly abandoned. Even in the darkness his eyes were startlingly blue upon her, and his smile was as wicked as the storm that he promised. He was suddenly a tempest, a whirlwind. He moved like lightning and swept her into his rhythm. Night breezes moved about, but the heat seemed consuming. Slick and warm, she clung to him, tasting him, kissing his lips, his shoulders, his lips again. She reached for things that, even now, she barely understood. Things intangible, elusive, as raw as the bare earth, as mystical as the clouds in a night sky. Things that made her hunger, and wonder. For it was splendor to be held so, and it was an even greater splendor for which she reached.

And then he was nearly still, rigid and taut. He moved slowly, slowly, then with startling speed, touched all of her inside again. He withdrew and filled her once again, hard.

Again she almost cried out. But his lips were there, and he kissed her, his tongue ravishing her mouth to steal sound away while the pulsing shaft of his body moved as hard and hot as molten steel deep, deep into her, one long, slow, last time, sinking, staying there.

All that she had reached for came cascading down upon her. Great waves of sensation rushed over her, swirled around her, settled into her. Warmth, dampness, and the sweet liquid heat of his fulfillment entered into her and brought with it a new sensation of ecstasy, a shuddering that seized hold of her.

The trembling remained for long, long moments.

She felt his swift movement as he withdrew from her at last, felt the hot slick wetness of their passion trail across her belly and thighs as he fell to her side, enveloping her in his arms.

She felt the breeze in the room, so cold against her naked flesh. She shivered violently, and he pulled her closer against him, bringing the covers over them both.

Little objects in the room suddenly seemed to stand out in the shadows and moonlight. Andrew Miller's desk, his bed frame, the windows that looked out onto his lawn. Andrew Miller's. One day they would have been Anthony's.

And hers.

But she was lying here tonight with Jesse. "Oh, God," she breathed suddenly.

"What is it?" Jesse asked.

"I've got to go."

She tried to leap up, but his arms suddenly wound more tightly around her. "Why?"

She was pinned down. His knee lay over her thighs, and his arm braced her. He didn't intend to let her go.

"Jesse—"

"Why? How can you say that now, after everything that we've just shared?" Fury riddled his question. His features were taut, his jaw nearly locked.

"We have to forget it—" she tried to begin.

They were the wrong words. He pounced on her, and his hand moved over her. "Mrs. Miller, I promise you, I will never forget it. I will never forget the feel of your flesh, the taste of it. Nor the taste or texture of the bud of your breast in my mouth, the feel of your tongue against my own, the scent of your soap, the scent of you as a woman. I promise you that I will not forget the way you move against me." He ran his fingers lightly over the sheen of her shoulder. "I won't forget anything at all, Mrs. Miller. I won't forget your eyes, I won't forget lying between your thighs, I won't forget tasting—"

"Stop it, Jesse!" she nearly shrieked.

"What? It's all right to do it, but not to talk about it?" he demanded. "Or does it go deeper than that?"

"Jesse, I'm a widow!" she reminded him desperately.

His hold upon her eased, then tightened again. "Fine, Mrs. Miller. You are a widow. But he couldn't have given you what I give you. Damn you, Kiernan, you came to me! Don't be a hypocrite. Quit denying me!"

"I'm not denying you!" He had to let go of her because she was shaking in fury. "How could I ever deny you? You had me when I should have been his! You had me first, on his property, when I should have been his fiancée. And now when I'm his widow—Jesse, this is his house!"

He released her. "My Lord. I'm in worse shape with him dead. I'm battling a ghost!"

"It's his house, Jesse!"

"So it's all right if we find a bale of hay in a barn?"

"No, it's his barn, his family—"

"You were never in love with him!" he suddenly thundered.

"Sh!" She pressed her fingers frantically against his lips. He was rigid in his fury. "Please, Jesse?"

He was still, but his jaw remained twisted, his limbs hard, the tension of his body radiating through her like the heat of the sun.

"Jesse, I have to go!" She tried to draw the remnants of her nightgown around her, but his hand was upon her arm again, drawing her back.

"Look at me," he told her.

She met the searing blue of his stare.

"Admit to me that you were never in love with Anthony."

"Jesse—"

"Admit it!"

"You're hurting me!"

"I'm going to hurt you worse!"

"Damn you!" Tears stung her eyes. "All right, all right. You know that I was never in love with him. Why do you have to hear me say it?"

"Why do you have to pretend that there was something between you?" he pressed on furiously. "Did you lie here with him in this bed? Is that what brought on your sudden fit of guilt?"

"It's none of your business, Jesse."

"It is! I'm making it my business!"

"Jesse—"

"You didn't love him. Why the hell did you marry him?"

"Because he wasn't a Yankee!" she spat out, suddenly as furious as he.

His hold on her slackened. She slipped from it, rolled quickly, and leaped to her feet. Holding her gown together, she stared at him and repeated, "Anthony was never a Yankee!"

She turned to flee, but Jesse didn't let her go. In a flash he was up, naked and menacing. He had caught her by both of her arms and dragged her back up against him. "No, he was never a Yankee. But he was never the man for you either. And he's dead now, Kiernan. I didn't want him dead, but he is. Hundreds of men are dead. Maybe thousands by now—I don't really know. But don't pretend that you were in love with him. Not to me!"

"Maybe you can take over his house," Kiernan charged him in a heated whisper, "but you cannot take over his widow! I won't let you—I swear I won't let you!"

She tried to wrench free, but he held her too tight, and his fingers wound harder about her wrists as she struggled. She went still suddenly and met his mocking gaze.

"I already have," he reminded her.

"Let me go, Captain Cameron!" she snapped.

"No!" He was suddenly very earnest. "You listen to me, Kiernan. I have feelings for Anthony, that's one of the reasons why I came here. I know about guilt. I thought that at least I could save his house, his family—something for him. And I've done that, Kiernan, at least so far. It might be a long, long war. You've done what's right too. Jacob and Patricia need you, and they have you. You've loved them and cared for them, and Anthony would have been pleased and proud."

"He'd have been damned pleased and proud to walk in and find me in bed with you, right?" she inquired with a sizzling taunt, her dazzling eyes piercing his, her head cast back imperiously.

"*You* came to *me*," he reminded her curtly.

Hot color covered her cheeks. "Jesse, let me pass."

"No! Not until you admit that you never had with him what you've had with me. Guilt can't change that! And guilt can't keep me away anymore, Kiernan."

"Jesse—"

"Tell me!"

"You bluebellied son of a bitch!" she exploded. "No, I never had anything with Anthony like I have with you. I never had anything at all with him! He married me and rode away the same night."

"What?" he asked incredulously.

"You heard me! Now let me—"

He pulled her close and started to kiss her, a hard, ravishing kiss. She struggled fiercely against him, trying to free her lips, her arms. She didn't win, but he suddenly drew his head away.

"Tell me that you won't want me ever again, Kiernan."

"Will you just let me go!" She tried hard to kick the fine display of naked masculine flesh before her, and she was suddenly very desperate and very determined.

But he dodged all her blows, then spun her around and pulled her hard and flat against his body. "Tell me, Kiernan." The sound of his voice, the hot whisper of it, bathed her ear and her throat. Even as she hated him, she felt the sweet fire of wanting ignite within her all over again. His fingers just edged over her breasts, and his hand moved downward as he held her taut against him.

"Jesse—" She jerked within his arms, trying to stamp on his feet but managing only to dislodge most of what remained of her torn nightgown.

"Oh, shut up, Kiernan!" he commanded her with throaty laughter. He lifted her by her upper arms, and even as she stared down at him, her eyes wide with alarm, he tossed her into the air and she fell flat upon the bed once again, her nightgown lost completely.

Her eyes narrowed in fury. "Jesse, you—"

He dived down upon her, and his lips were upon hers.

She struggled, but the warmth of his kiss was undeniable. Something languid and sweet swept slowly through her. She touched his hair, feeling the texture of it, only then realizing that her hands were free.

She was free.

But by then, she did not want to go. She did want what he had to give her.

He made love to her a second time that night, and she made love to him in return.

Later, she awoke and felt the probe of his sex at her buttocks as they lay curled with his arms around her. He made love to her so, and when it was over, she drifted to sleep again, content to feel his arms around her.

She was still at war—at war with Jesse.

But she was too tired to fight at the moment.

She awoke as dawn was coming through the windows, and then she was upset. As his arm curled around her, she pleaded, "Jesse, I have to go now. The children."

Some emotion passed through his eyes. He understood, she knew. He released her.

"Your gown," he began, his tone almost apologetic.

"I've got it. I'll wear a sheet," she said quickly, wrapping herself up in one even as she spoke. She prayed that she wouldn't meet anyone in the hallway as she hurried toward the door.

"Kiernan!"

She turned back. His hair was tousled, his shoulders very bronze against the white of the sheets, his eyes very blue.

She wondered if she would ever stop loving him.

"Jesse, I have to go."

"Kiernan, I want you to marry me."

"I can't marry you, Jesse!"

"Why the hell not?" he demanded irritably.

"You're a Yankee! I didn't marry you before because you're a Yankee. And I won't marry you now for the same reason. Don't you understand?" Why was he always able to bring her so dangerously close to tears? "I'll never marry you, Jesse! Never!"

She spun around and tore out of his room, almost carelessly, desperate not to meet anyone.

There was no one in the hallway. She could hear sounds in the ward—the "hospital" day was beginning.

Shaking, she sat on her own bed, the sheet pulled about her tightly. She looked out at the dawn breaking through her windows. It would be a beautiful day.

No one, no one but herself or Jesse, would be any the wiser about the night that they had passed together.

But how would she survive the days to come? Wanting him, loving him, having him so very near, knowing he was just beyond a doorway.

And that she had to stop seeing him.

She sat in torment for a long, long time. But in the end, her dilemma did not matter. It was taken care of for her.

By nightfall, new orders had come for Jesse. He had been commanded to move out.

Kiernan washed and dressed and began to move about the house with its many rooms of injured soldiers. Corporal O'Malley was very pleased that they hadn't lost anyone during the night. " 'Course, that don't put any of the men in the clear, but living is a darned good sign, if you'll pardon my language. Don't you think so, Mrs. Miller?"

"Oh, I've come to pardon quite a bit," Kiernan assured him.

"Even the Reb who was hurt bad is doing fine. But then again, if they send him to a prison camp—oh, I'm sorry, again. I keep forgetting where your sympathies lie, Mrs. Miller. You're so good to all of us. A couple of the boys say you spy on us, but I know real compassion when I see it, and that's what you've got, ma'am, that's what you've got."

Real compassion? But I *was* spying, she wanted to cry out.

It didn't matter. Maybe O'Malley needed his few illusions, and maybe she was one of them.

"Thank you, Corporal. But I am a Confederate," she told him, "and this morning, I think I will see to the Rebs."

She smiled at him and hurried down the hallway. T.J. was awake, sitting up in his bed. Patricia was already up and about and perched on a stool by T.J.'s side, writing a letter for him. She gave Kiernan a brilliant smile. "Kiernan, they told me yesterday that T.J. might die, but look at him! He's doing very well!"

T.J.'s gaze met Kiernan's. They both knew that it was too soon for the little girl's hopes to be so raised.

"It's good to see you doing so well," she said, and coming to the bed, she soaked a cool cloth in water and set it upon his forehead. He was scarcely warm. That, too, was a good sign, she knew.

T.J. grasped her hand warmly. "You saved my leg."

"T.J., you can't be certain. You mustn't—"

"Look at it!" He was too excited to realize that he shouldn't be exposing his masculine limbs to a lady and a little girl, even though that lady had been present for far worse. He lifted away the sheet so that she could see his leg, and she was amazed. The stitches were very neat. There was no sign of swelling, and barely any discoloration. She remembered Jesse working on it the day before, and she felt a strange shaking take hold of her. He was very, very good.

"Still," she warned, "you know that infection may set in during the days to come."

He nodded. His fingers were shaking, and he wound them together in his lap to still them. "I wanted to die," he told her. "When I realized that I'd been picked up by the Yanks, I was so damned afraid of what a Yankee sawbones might do to me that I wanted to die. But he's good. Hell, he's brilliant."

"Yes, he's very good."

"Too bad he's a Yank."

"That's what my brother says about Jesse," Patricia said airily, studying the pen. " 'Course, he really shouldn't be one at all."

T.J. looked surprised, and he glanced from Kiernan to Patricia. "Sounds like you've known him awhile."

"We have. We've been out to his place a number of times, and before the war, Jesse was welcome here. He didn't have to take the place over then. I love Jesse," she said enthusiastically, then reddened. "Oh. I love him as much as you're allowed to love a Yank."

T.J. grinned. "Don't worry, Patricia. You can't love a word—you can love a person, a man. It's all right."

She looked worriedly from T.J. to Kiernan, hoping that it really was all right. "They would have burned my father's house down if it hadn't been for him. Jacob didn't care at first, but even my brother likes him now. We don't know him half as well as Kiernan does."

T.J.'s eyes shot to Kiernan's. In seconds, she was certain T.J. understood everything there was to understand about her relationship with Jesse.

He wasn't going to say anything, though.

Patricia leaped off her seat when one of the other men turned over and let out a soft croak for water.

Kiernan leaned close to T.J. "War is funny, isn't it?" she said softly. "I'd been trying to reach you with information about Union troops making a foray into the valley."

T.J. closed his eyes and spoke wearily. "There's always someone near the oak," he said. "The war is over for me now. I imagine I'll be spending it in a camp."

"Maybe not."

The masculine words spoken behind Kiernan sent shivers racing along her spine.

She had absolutely no idea just how long Jesse had been standing there. Was it long enough for him to hear what she had told T.J.?

She spun around. His eyes were fire when they touched hers, but he had come to see T.J. He pulled back the sheets and looked at the leg, then inspected the wound in T.J.'s gut. He seemed pleased. He pulled the sheet back up over his patient.

"I'd have liked more time," he murmured, "a lot more time. But I've been called back to Washington."

Stunned, Kiernan stared at him. Just that morning she had been praying for a way . . .

But this wasn't it. The Yankee patients would be all right. They'd receive careful passage back to Washington. But what would happen to T.J., and these other two?

A prison camp would kill T.J.

And where would Jesse be?

"Jesu, Doc," T.J. said. "I won't stand a snowball's chance in hell!"

Jesse was silent, contemplative. "We'll see, soldier," he said at last.

He nodded to Kiernan, then left the room.

During the day she tried to see Jesse alone. She was more than willing to plead for a miracle to save T.J.

But she couldn't even get close to Jesse. He was a whirlwind of activity. Wagons had come for his patients, and he had to make sure that every one of them was as comfortably prepared for travel as possible, bandaged and bedded down for a journey across the river.

Corporal O'Malley advised her about the sudden hurry.

The area didn't really belong to anyone at the moment, either the Rebs or the Yanks. Sharpshooters and skirmishes were the rule of the day here. But a rumor had reached Washington through spies working for a man named Pinkerton— who was organizing something called the Secret Service—that Stonewall Jackson was coming in somewhere nearby with a major troop movement.

Jesse was very important to the Union because he had a way of making men live. He was going to be promoted with his new orders to full colonel.

There was no stopping him. Whenever she came near Jesse, he immediately put her to work preparing patients for the trip. She didn't mind the labor. She had helped him stitch up most of the patients the day before, and she couldn't help but care about them.

After working late into the night, she still had not managed to speak to Jesse. Not until midnight had the last of the injured Yanks been bedded down in wagons to move back to Washington.

And now, the house seemed empty.

Patricia and Jacob had fallen asleep on the steps of the front porch, and Tyne and Jeremiah had long since carried them up to bed. With the last soldier bedded down, Jeremiah had gone to his quarters to find his own rest. Tyne and Corporal O'Malley were still with the Rebs, and Janey was in the kitchen.

Alone in the great hall, Kiernan stared about at the emptiness and felt the sound of silence.

She heard a slight noise and turned. Jesse, in his full blue uniform, leaned against the doorway to what had been his surgery, watching her.

"You must be very happy."

She shrugged. She wasn't happy at all.

"I don't suppose I can get you to leave the area?"

She shook her head. "The Rebs won't hurt me," she murmured.

"Personally, I don't think the Rebs are coming right now. They've got other things to do," he said flatly. "It's deserters and stragglers I'm thinking about."

She smiled. "We've had them before, and we handled them. Well"—she paused—"T.J. handled them for me, actually. But I'm prepared now. I'm a good shot, and Jacob is a great shot."

"I've left word with General Banks that I might need the house again. He'll see that none of his troops threaten it again."

"Thank you," she murmured awkwardly.

"I've only one thing left to attend to," he murmured. He started across the empty hallway, his booted heels clicking harshly on the floor.

He headed upstairs to the Rebels. There was a wagon waiting outside to take them away.

Kiernan tore after him and caught him halfway up the stairs, her skirts sweeping wildly around as she tried to stop him.

"Jesse, you can't let T.J. be taken to a camp! You just can't! He'll die there, and you know it."

He paused, a curious smile curving his lip. "Kiernan, you are so damned beautiful, and you plead so elegantly with me. But it's always over some other man!"

"Jesse, please!"

"Kiernan, get out of my way. Please."

"Jesse, I won't—"

"Kiernan, you fool! You're the one who gave that boy information he could use against the Union troops!"

"But I didn't!"

"You might have jeopardized everything."

"Jesse—"

"Kiernan, move!" He picked her up by the waist, and for a moment he held her above him. The air crackled between them, and when she met his eyes, the sweetest memories of the night came flooding back to her.

She felt the tension and the passion in his touch.

He set her down, very gently.

"Excuse me."

He walked past her, reached the room where T.J. was lying, and entered it. He leaned over T.J., checking the texture and temperature of his skin, looking into his eyes.

"How're you feeling, Reb?"

"Good as can be expected, Yank."

"Jesse!" Kiernan started into the room.

"Corporal O'Malley, stop her! That's an order!" Jesse said.

O'Malley caught her just before she could fling herself at Jesse.

"If she can't shut up, remove her from the room!"

"Yes, sir!" O'Malley said unhappily.

Held back by O'Malley, Kiernan bit hard on her lower lip and held still.

"Soldier, you know that this war is over for you now, right?" Jesse demanded.

"Yes, sir, I reckon it is."

"You're a Virginian, right?"

"Yes, sir."

"A man of your word?"

"Always, Doc."

Jesse nodded. "That's what I thought. I've drawn up papers for you and these boys."

"I can't be a Yank, sir."

"You don't have to be a Yank, soldier. The document just promises that you won't take up arms against the Union again. Can you live with that?"

T.J. smiled slowly and exhaled a long breath. "Yes, sir, I can live with that. So can the boys."

"One more thing. Anything Mrs. Miller told you dies in this room. Is that understood?"

He turned and looked at Kiernan, then spoke to T.J. again. "Have I your word?"

"Yes, sir, you have my word."

"Kiernan?"

His blue eyes blazed into her like blades of fire, demanding, always demanding.

She was trembling. Jesse meant to leave T.J. and the two other Rebs here with her, free to go home as soon as they could.

"You—you have my word," she breathed.

"Good. Damn, it was nice not to have to argue with you for once! O'Malley, I guess it's safe to let this Reb go. Get signatures from these other soldiers, and I guess we'll be out of here. Gentlemen, good luck to you," he said, doffing his hat to T.J. and the two other men. Then he strode out of the room.

Kiernan was still for a minute, then she turned and went after him. He was gone from the stairway, and for a moment, she thought that he had left without even saying good-bye to her.

She heard sounds coming from the office that had been his surgery, and she realized that he was gathering the last of his personal instruments. She crossed the great hall quickly and opened the door to the office.

His greatcoat was already over his shoulders. His back was to her, but she knew that he realized she had entered the room. He had cleaned his instruments, and he was repacking them in a large black leather bag. It was a fine surgeon's bag, with his initials embossed into it with large bold script.

He picked up the instruments she had come to know yesterday: Bullet forceps, bone forceps, dissection forceps. Gnawing forceps. Bone scraper. Capital saw, chain saw, metacarpal saw, bone file. Different scissors and scalpels and tourniquets.

All went back into the bag.

Kiernan walked to the rear and collected his suture materials, the black silk thread, his curved and straight needles. She brought them to him and watched him pack them into his bag. His hands brushed hers, and he glanced at her.

She stayed before him, silent. He turned away and reached for the last of his anesthetics, the chloroform and ether, then his pain killers, the opium and morphine.

He hesitated, then turned back to his bag and produced the small syringe he had used for injecting morphine. "I'm leaving you this for T.J. I'll write a prescription for you. Be very careful with the dosage. I'll leave you this too: powdered sassafras, to lower his body temperature if it starts to rise. Keep his bandages clean, and treat the wounds with simple cerates. Can you manage?"

She nodded. "I'll manage."

He closed his case. "Well, then. That's the last of it." His hands moved over the leather. "It's handsome, isn't it? Daniel bought it for me as a Christmas gift a few years ago. I never imagined that I'd be using the amputation instruments so frequently. And I never imagined that I'd be looking at it and wondering where Daniel might be."

"Jesse—"

He turned and faced her. "I have to go. I swore when I received permission to come that I would pull out promptly when I was ordered to do so."

"Jesse, thank you," she said quickly. How was it that they had been so very close last night, yet now she could barely muster words and sounds? He was leaving again, riding away. And once again, there seemed to be nothing at all that she could do about it. "Thank you for T.J.," she said quickly, "and for Jacob. For the house."

"But not for you?" he said softly.

She wanted so very much to run to him. He stood so tall and straight, striking and dark, with his sharp blue eyes, his slouch hat low over his forehead, his greatcoat emphasizing the breadth of his shoulders. He was leaving.

She didn't know when she would see him again, if ever.

"Come here, Kiernan. Please. I'm leaving—what danger can I be to you?"

She walked across the room to him, and he raised her chin with his thumb and forefinger. His lips touched hers gently, tenderly, poignantly. Then his mouth rose, and he whispered softly above hers, "Take care, Kiernan. Take care."

She stared at him, willing the tears in her eyes not to fall. He smiled with a bittersweet curve to his lip. "Still can't wish a Yankee well, eh, Kiernan? Well, that's all right. I understand."

He released her, lifted his bag, and started for the door. He did not turn back.

She closed her eyes. She heard the door shut softly, heard his booted footsteps ringing as they crossed the empty hallway.

She came to life. She ran across the room, threw open the door, and raced out to the porch.

Jesse was just mounting Pegasus. The few men who waited to ride escort with him were down by the end of the sloping lawn, standing sentinel in the moonlight.

"Jesse!"

Mounted on Pegasus, he waited. Kiernan ran breathlessly across the lawn.

"Jesse—" She paused before Pegasus. Jesse waited patiently, his eyes still filled with tenderness, with weariness, with sorrow.

"Jesse, take care," she whispered. "Please, take care of yourself."

He smiled, his lip curling into the slow grin that she loved so very much.

He touched the brim of his hat. "Thank you, Kiernan. I'll do that." He started to urge Pegasus forward. She suddenly rushed forward, touching Jesse's calf, pressing her face against his knee. "Don't die, Jesse, please don't die."

He reached down and touched her hair, then stroked her cheek. "I won't die," he promised her. She looked up at him. "I love you, Kiernan," he said.

She was silent, afraid to speak. He smiled again, aware that she could not reply. Then he nudged Pegasus forward and cantered across the field to join his men.

"I love you, Jesse!" she cried softly.

But it was too late—he was gone.

She had no right to love a Yankee, she told herself fiercely.

But then she remembered what T.J. had told Patricia earlier, and she realized that it wasn't a Yankee that she loved.

She loved Jesse.

She loved a man.

And once again, that man was riding away.

PART 4

A Separate
Peace

Twenty

*K*iernan didn't think she'd ever seen a drearier time than the winter that followed.

Much of Harpers Ferry and the surrounding countryside had been devastated by both armies. The Union soldiers had destroyed munitions and food supplies, and the Rebs had come back and destroyed everything that could be used by the Union troops.

The exchange seemed never ending.

Things seemed to be the very bleakest in the heart of the town. The continual Union sharpshooter fire from Maryland Heights—returned by Rebs up on Loudoun Heights—had nearly stripped the streets of human habitation. Harpers Ferry had once been a thriving town with a population of six thousand. But so many people had fled the devastation that it was now a ghost town, with only a few hundred dazed but dogged souls remaining.

Thomas and Lacey Donahue came out to Montemarte on Christmas Day. Kiernan had done her very best to make it, if not a joyous occasion for the twins, at the very least a pleasant one. It was a difficult day, for it was the first Christmas they would spend without their father or brother.

She couldn't help feeling a pull of nostalgia herself, for just last Christmas she had met Jesse at the summer cottage at Cameron Hall, and just last Christmas she had been filled with dreams. Everybody had thought back then that the South would whop the North, and that it would all be over very soon.

No one had realized just how tenacious Abe Lincoln could be, and no one had imagined that John Brown's prophecy about the land being soaked in blood would prove so true.

Christmas was a quiet day. After church, Jeremiah killed one of their last big chickens, and Janey cooked it up with cranberries and turnip greens and sweet potatoes. Lacey had brought along an apple pie, and the meal was delicious. T.J. was still with them, healing nicely, spending more and more time outdoors. Kiernan often found him looking off into the distance, as if seeking out the war with his eyes. But he wasn't going back, he had told her. He'd given his word, and if his word didn't mean anything, what were they fighting for?

When dinner was over, they exchanged gifts—little things that year, all made by hand, socks for T.J. and Thomas, handkerchiefs for Kiernan and Lacey, a chemise cut down from one of Kiernan's own for Patricia, and a sheath for Jacob for his hunting knife. Then Kiernan and the twins accompanied Thomas and

Lacey to their home in town. Kiernan planned to stay over in Harpers Ferry to witness certain documents for them.

But she didn't go to their house with them right away. She asked Thomas to let her off on High Street for a minute, and he obliged her. She stood in the center of the once-busy thoroughfare and felt the cold and the emptiness. Dead leaves rustled on the ground as she looked down the steep incline and at the windows of the homes and shops along the street. Everything was silent.

Depression weighed down upon her, and she realized that she was probably standing on Union soil. Harpers Ferry was one of the counties that was determined to form its own state. A lot of Union soldiers had been around when the vote had been taken, but there were still plenty loyal to the old government hereabouts. There'd be a new constitution soon, and a new state soon enough, she reckoned.

She hugged her arms close to her chest and shivered.

A new order to things had arrived, she admitted to herself at last.

And there was another admission she had to make. She was going to have Jesse's baby.

Just last year, she hadn't thought it would be so horrible. Last year, she simply would have married Jesse.

But this year she was Anthony's widow, and she should still have been wearing black. And Jesse was gone, fighting the war. She might never see him again. Even if he had been standing in front of her right then, she didn't think that she could tell him she was with child. Even to tell him might be to surrender.

People around here would ostracize her cruelly. People everywhere, for that matter, might feel obliged to do so.

She didn't really care about people in general, but she did care about Patricia and Jacob.

There was nothing to be done, she thought. She couldn't leave the twins, although they might prefer to come home with her.

But she would have to tell her father. He would offer her no cruel words. He would never think of throwing her out into the world. And he would, she was certain, love the baby too. But he would be very disappointed in her. His fine old shoulders would sag with the weariness and weight of what she had done.

The cold of the day touched her cheeks, making them numb. She clenched her teeth and welcomed the cold inside her. She needed that numbness. She didn't have to say anything to the twins yet. When the time came, she would.

Resolute, she walked down the street to the Donahue house.

By February, the newly formed state of West Virginia had written itself a constitution. Kiernan listened while Thomas and T.J. discussed the meaning of it all, but for Kiernan it had no meaning at all. When the Union was in residence, they held the town and the area. When the Confederates were around, it was as southern as pecan pie.

The Union was still destroying the town. A few soldiers had rowed over from Maryland Heights early in the month, and one had been killed by Rebs trying to return. The Union had retaliated, and troops under Major Tynsdale destroyed the section of town where he suspected the Rebs hid. Earlier, Tynsdale had accompanied John Brown's wife down from Pennsylvania acting as a protector, and he had been with her to see that her husband's remains were brought home for burial.

Tynsdale now had those who remained in the town whisper. For John Brown had prophesied the destruction of the town, and now, a little more than two years after his death, the destruction had come—implemented by Tynsdale.

At the end of February, General Banks was in possession of the town. Kiernan didn't breathe very easily with so many soldiers so close, but no one disturbed them, which she was certain was Jesse's doing.

One day while she was out in the laundry, she found T.J. behind her, ready to take the heavy basket she was carrying. He set it down for her, then leaned in the doorway, watching her. She stared at him and finally demanded, "All right, T.J. What is it?"

He pulled out his corncob pipe and lit it, taking his time. "Mrs. Miller, this ain't none of my business, and it ain't my place to say anything, but you're working too hard."

"We all have to work, T.J., if we want to keep eating and wearing clothes."

"But you're working *too* hard"—he hesitated a second—"if you want that young 'un you're carrying to make it healthy and well into this world."

She felt the color fade from her face. Instinctively, protectively, she clutched her stomach. "Is it so very obvious?" she asked worriedly.

T.J. shook his head. "No, not when you're wearing your big, er"—T.J. flushed himself—"your petticoats and all. It's just that I know you, and I see you sick, and I see you very tired. I see you just stare out the window, with eyes as sad and weary and bleak as the winter itself. You helped me, just like that Yankee doc helped me, and I'd like to help you in return."

"No one can help me, T.J. I'm not sick at all anymore. I feel very well. But thank you." She was silent, biting her lower lip. "Do you think I have some time left before I have to tell the children?"

T.J. nodded. "Just don't come out with those big baskets no more, Mrs. Miller. You call me."

"I will, T.J. Thank you."

"You know," he began. "I'm sure the Yank would be more than willing—"

"I don't want to hear it, T.J.," Kiernan said stubbornly.

"He'd marry you."

"I still have the children, T.J. They'd never live among the people who killed their father and brother!"

"I think you're mistaken, Mrs. Miller. I think they have a better perspective on this war than you think."

"That may very well be," Kiernan told him. "Let's just see how things go, shall we? I need some time."

But she wasn't to have much time. The next week she went into town with the children to see what supplies they could purchase. It wasn't easy, for she received her income from the rifle works in Confederate currency, and when the Yankees were in residence, no one wanted to accept it. Still, she was able to do some shopping. One good thing about the Yanks being around was that the strict blockade that went on all winter had been lifted, and northern goods were in abundance.

But as she was leaving a shop, she was stunned when a flying missile struck her in the chest. Patricia, at her side, screamed, and for a wild moment of panic,

Kiernan thought she had been hit by a bullet, for a red stain was spreading out on her breast.

She realized that it was a tomato.

"Yankee lover! Whore!" came a call from a window.

She spun around, but it was too late. The tomato hurler hated Yankees, but he didn't feel like getting caught by one.

"Kiernan!" Patricia cried in dismay. "Why—"

"Let's get out of here," Jacob said very angrily. "Kiernan, get between us. If they throw anything else, they'll have to hit me first!"

"If he hits me again, I'll throw it back at him!" Kiernan declared. She was furious, but she was shaking, too, and very close to tears.

"Let's go!" Jacob insisted.

She allowed him to lead her along. At the Donahues' house, Lacey tried to clean up Kiernan's dress and assure herself that Kiernan wasn't hurt. Thomas watched in silence from the fireplace. A while later, he walked to the doorway to pick up his rifle, and Kiernan realized with alarm that he was about to go after the man who had offended her.

She flew up and over to him. "Thomas, no!"

"Kiernan, that man had no right to dishonor a lady!"

"Thomas, please don't go after him." If he were to die because of her—for her honor, or lack of it—she didn't think that she could bear it. "Thomas, you can't go after anyone. I—I *have* been seeing a Yankee, or I *was* seeing one. Please, Thomas, put down the gun."

Lacey gasped. "Do you mean Captain Cameron? Kiernan!" she began.

"That's enough, Lacey!" Thomas said quickly—the children were in the house. His eyes were on Kiernan. "The man still had no right!"

"Please, please, Thomas. Put the gun down. I have to take the children home before the sharpshooters get started. Please promise me that you'll put the gun down."

He sighed at long last and set his rifle down. "All right, Kiernan."

She smiled at him and called to Patricia and Jacob.

They were both silent as she drove the carriage back to Montemarte. When they arrived, Jeremiah was there to take the carriage from her, and she hurried into the house.

Dusk was just falling. She sat in a rocker in Andrew's office—or Jesse's surgery, all scrubbed down now, the cots and bandages gone, no trace of blood remaining. She sat and stared out at the coming darkness.

She felt someone enter the room. Somehow, she knew it was Jacob.

"You're going to have a baby, right?" he demanded.

She nodded, still rocking, still staring.

"It isn't my brother's baby, is it?"

She turned to look at him at last. "Oh, Jacob. I'm so very sorry."

Jacob stood stiffly by the door. His brown eyes seemed to be touched by so much pain, and so much wisdom. He was too young to have that kind of wisdom.

"What are you going to do?" he asked her.

"I don't know yet."

"Are you going to—to leave Patricia and me?"

"No, Jacob, I'd never leave you, I promise you that. Unless, of course . . ."

"Unless what?"

"Unless you wanted me to."

He was silent again. "No. No, I don't want you to leave us. I reckon I don't want to go into town too often, but I don't want you to leave us." He sighed, and his shoulders fell as if he carried the weight of the world upon them. "We'll get by, Kiernan. I know we will."

"Thank you."

He hesitated a minute. "You know, you could marry that Yank." No matter how well Jacob had come to know Jesse, he still seemed to find it necessary to keep his distance.

Kiernan shrugged. "I don't even know where he is, Jacob. I swore to him once that I'd never marry him."

"But you're in love with him, aren't you?"

"Jacob, I—"

"You are. I saw the way he looked at you when he was here. And I saw the way that you looked at him." Jacob frowned suddenly. "He never—I mean, he didn't—he didn't *make* you do anything, did he?"

She shook her head, trying not to smile. Jacob could be so very fierce. What a fine man he was going to be one day!

"No," she said softly, "Jesse never forced me to do anything."

"Well, whatever, we will get by," he promised her. To her surprise, he walked across the room and set his arms around her shoulders. He hugged her briefly, then left her, and she sat alone in the darkness.

Jesse, she thought. Where was he tonight? She prayed that he was warm and safe from danger, and then she wondered what she would do if he were here right now, sitting with her.

He was a Yankee, and he was never going to change. She certainly could not change him—at least, not his sense of right and wrong and his loyalty.

For his part, he had never asked her to change. He had understood that she had her convictions. But she wasn't certain anymore herself, either about right or wrong, or about their fine southern cause. All she knew was that war killed and maimed, and that it was bitter and painful, no matter what the color of the soldiers' uniforms.

But could she marry him now?

Yes, she decided she could. But only if he wanted her, really wanted her. Not because of the baby, and not because of honor. Love, finally, must be enough.

And she would marry him only if he came to her, of course. She still couldn't quite swallow her pride enough to court a Yankee.

She was so calm, she thought, as a slow smile curved her lip. Not so very long ago, the mere thought of her present position would have been scandalous, a horror within the society that had been hers since birth. Her situation would have made matrons whisper and pull their children aside on the sidewalk when she came by.

Hers was the type of situation that would make those who considered themselves very righteous throw things at her, like tomatoes. It was every father's nightmare.

It was not simply that she was expecting a child. Surely any number of hasty marriages took place, and of course, whispering went along with them.

But Kiernan's scandal went beyond that. She was the widow of a fine southern soldier who had laid down his life at Manassas. She was expecting the child of a Yank, and her husband had not even been dead a year.

But Jacob loved her, despite everything. He meant to stand by her. That was what mattered now. If she only had sure knowledge that Jesse was alive and well.

Suddenly, she felt a fluttering deep within her abdomen. She thought that she had imagined it, but then it came again.

Despite everything, a thrill burst through her as sweet as any she had ever known. Her baby was alive and well and moving. Her baby was real. Her baby, Jesse's baby, their flesh and blood.

Conceived in war . . .

But conceived in love.

"And I will love you, little one!" she vowed vehemently. "I will love you enough to make up for everything!"

She smiled. She was suddenly glad that Jacob knew. Patricia would be all right if Jacob was all right. Both twins could help her now, and she might even begin to live with enthusiasm, with hope.

The fluttering movement came inside her again, the quickening. She wrapped her arms tenderly over her abdomen, and she started to cry softly, tears of a curious joy.

Daniel Cameron had been in the Shenandoah Valley, running spying and harassment raids with a crack company of horse soldiers. Now, in March 1862, his most recent orders had been to move east—Lincoln had put a General named McClellan in charge of his eastern army, and McClellan was planning a huge assault on Richmond by moving up through the peninsula—the Tidewater region.

Daniel had been living in a state of tension ever since the orders had come. For one thing, he was certain that Jesse was with McClellan's army. For another, this campaign was also going to bring the battle frighteningly close to home. He was anxious, damned anxious to be a part of it. If Union soldiers came anywhere close to Cameron Hall, he'd be on the doorstep waiting for them.

It wasn't just his home that concerned him so. Christa was there alone. And John Mackay was near, too, alone what with Kiernan caring for the Miller children in Harpers Ferry. Kiernan was doing well enough. Daniel hadn't heard from Jesse, and he hadn't heard from Kiernan, which was strange—they had once been such avid correspondents. But time was scarce these days; he'd barely had time to get notes off to Christa. Christa kept him advised, because Jesse wrote to her too.

Seated at his desk in his field tent, Daniel felt his fingers tighten around his pen. War was so damned strange. All his life, he'd followed his brother, followed him to West Point, followed him to Kansas. He hadn't attended medical school like Jesse—he'd never had Jesse's calling for it. But otherwise, they'd been as close as brothers could be.

But now he hadn't seen him, hadn't heard a word from him in over a year. If he did see Jesse, he was supposed to shoot him.

Jesse wouldn't be riding into battle, Daniel knew. He would be taking his skill into field hospitals. Daniel knew that Jesse was trying his best to save lives in this war, but he had been a cavalry soldier for years. There was no telling that he might not mount up in the heat of things and come riding into battle himself—maybe even against orders.

That was Daniel's biggest fear. Not death, not capture, not loss—just meeting his brother in battle.

He sighed, crumpling up the orders he had been writing and starting over again. Suddenly, there was a fracas outside his tent. For a moment, he thought the canvas structure was going to fall over. As he stared at the support pole in amazement, he heard his name called.

"Captain Cameron! Captain Cameron!"

"What the hell is going on here?" he demanded with a roar, leaping up at last.

His aide, Corporal Beal, came through the opening, following an indignant young lad with handsome blond curls and dark eyes. Corporal Beal nearly had his hands upon the boy's nape, but the lad seemed tough. He eluded Beal and strode to Daniel's desk, saluting him quickly.

"Captain Cameron," the boy began.

"Captain Cameron," Beal interrupted, "this wild young pup wouldn't listen when I said that you were busy, that we had to pull out. He ran right past me, and when I caught up to him, why, he took a swing at me and I had to take one back, but he's a scamp, he is, wild and—"

"It's all right, Corporal Beal," Daniel said. He took his seat behind his field desk, frowning as he recognized Jacob Miller. "Jacob's an old friend of mine."

"I done told him we were moving out in a hurry—"

"The Union hasn't done anything in a hurry yet, Corporal. I think I can spare a few minutes for an old friend." He smiled, his gaze on Jacob. "You can leave us now."

"He could be a spy," Beal warned dourly.

"Not this one. The boy is as loyal as they come. Right, Jacob?"

To his surprise, Jacob reddened, but he replied, "Yes, sir, Captain Cameron."

"You can't trust no one these days," Beal muttered, "not no one, not no how!" Daniel grinned at Jacob, and Beal sniffed again, but he left them at last.

"You haven't turned Yank, have you, boy?" Daniel asked. He indicated the folding field chair opposite his desk, and Jacob took a seat.

"No, I haven't turned Yank."

"You're not trying to join the army?"

"No, not yet."

"That's a relief," Daniel told him. "Does Kiernan know that you're out here?" He stiffened suddenly. He'd heard rumors that Kiernan had been giving good information to the troops in the valley. But she wouldn't allow a child this age to engage in espionage, would she?

Still, the war had made people do all kinds of things.

"Did she give you a message for me?"

"No, no!" Jacob protested. His hat was in his hands, and he twisted it between his fingers, looking down at it. "No, in fact"—he paused, looking up at Daniel—"she'd probably have my hide if she knew that I was here."

"Oh." Puzzled, Daniel leaned forward. "Then . . . ?"

"This is a matter of the strictest confidence," Jacob said, sitting very straight.

"The strictest," Daniel agreed somberly.

"I'd like you to get through to your brother, sir. I know he's a Yank and you're a Reb, and that you probably don't talk to each other much anymore. But I want you to let him know that . . ."

"That?"

"That he's going to be a father."

For a moment, Daniel was stunned. Then he said, "Oh!" very softly, and leaned back in his chair. It shouldn't be such a surprise. Anybody who knew Jesse and Kiernan could feel the electricity in the air when they were near each other. If anyone had seen what Jesse meant to Kiernan, it was Daniel himself. And if anybody knew Jesse's heart, well, that was Daniel, too. That the two of them had consummated those feelings, even in war, wasn't that much of a surprise.

He leaned forward. "Is Kiernan well?" he asked Jacob.

"Just fine. But—but she'll never let him know. Don't you see?"

"Proud, huh?"

"Very. And, well, he's—"

"A Yankee."

"Right," Jacob agreed miserably. He looked at Daniel anxiously once again. "Can you get a message through to him?"

Daniel nodded. "Yes, I can."

"You have to be very, er . . ."

"Discreet?"

"Yes."

"I'll write to my sister," Daniel said, "and she'll get through to him. No others will be involved—unless I can think of something else, equally discreet. Do you trust me?"

"Yes, sir, I do."

"Good. Then you'd better be on your way. You don't want Kiernan to start worrying about you."

Jacob Miller saluted him, slammed his slouch hat back down over his head, and started out. Then he looked back. "Maybe you could not mention my name? No, wait—never mind. That wouldn't be very honorable, would it? Go ahead and use my name in this if you want. Make sure you let him know that Patricia and I are all right with this thing. Your brother is a darned good man, sir, except that he's a Yank."

"I've felt that myself, Jacob," Daniel assured him.

Jacob grinned at that, and then he was really gone. Daniel sat back and drummed his fingers on his desk.

It occurred to him that he was going to be an uncle, and he grinned.

"Why, you little hellions!" he thought fondly of his brother and Kiernan.

But his smile faded. This was war. He wasn't at all sure that anybody could do the right thing by anybody else.

He'd try, though. He'd sure as hell try.

Twenty-one

*I*t was late afternoon when Thomas Donahue came riding up to Montemarte at a gallop. It was a fast pace for Thomas—he didn't like his old bones to rattle, he had told Kiernan often enough. Seeing him come so quickly, a sweep of dread instantly wove through her.

She raced out onto the porch. The Yankees were heading out to the house again, it was about to be burned, something horrible had happened, the war had been lost.

"Kiernan!" Thomas wheezed as he dismounted. She ran to him, offering him support. "You've got to go home."

"Home! What's happened?"

"It's your father, Kiernan."

"Oh, God! Oh, no!" She felt faint. Black waves washed before her eyes. "He's not . . . he's not—"

"He's sick, Kiernan, very sick. Christa Cameron managed to get a letter through with an employee of the railroad. She thinks you should come right home. But she's also aware that it's a long and dangerous journey right now. She wanted you to know that she'd be with him, that she'd take care of him. That she'd do everything in the world for him that she could."

"But she wouldn't be me!" Kiernan whispered. "And if Papa is very sick . . ."

No, she thought suddenly. War was awful, and it already had taken so very much from her and from everyone. She wouldn't let it keep her away from her father too.

She stood very straight. "I'm going home, Thomas."

"But there's troops aplenty on all these roads!" Thomas warned her. "Troops in blue and troops in gray, and I don't know which are more dangerous."

"I'll be all right. Who would disturb a woman in my—er, delicate condition?"

Thomas hesitated. He didn't want to tell her that she was still very beautiful, and that war does strange things to good men and worse things to bad men.

"I'll come with you," Thomas offered.

"You'll do no such thing. You hate to travel, and I'll be moving very quickly. I'll bring Janey and Tyne with me." She couldn't bring T.J.—she'd have to leave him and Jeremiah and David at Montemarte. But the twins would come with her too. She couldn't leave them. She had promised she wouldn't.

"I can't talk you out of this, can I?" Thomas said.

"No." On her tiptoes, Kiernan gave him a kiss. Then she shooed him on his way home and hurried for the stairs, calling for Janey to help her pack. Patricia ran into her room, and Kiernan told her to hurry and pack for the trip. She was in a whirlwind of motion, getting her things together. Janey helped her, then ran to the kitchen to find Tyne and Jeremiah and see that the wagon was readied.

When she had finished with her clothing, Kiernan hurried back down the stairs to the office and went through the medicines that Jesse had left. Her father was sick—but with what? She stared at the bottles with their neatly printed labels and decided to take them all.

Her fingers were trembling, but she was determined to leave then and there, just as soon as the children were ready.

She was going home.

She touched her stomach and felt a strange excitement sweep through her. The baby could be born at home, in Tidewater Virginia.

Suddenly she was very glad, if breathless. She pulled out the swivel chair and sat. The baby began to move vigorously inside her, as if caught up in the frenzy of her emotion.

Home, she was going home.

The door to the office suddenly swung open, and Jacob appeared. Kiernan looked up at him and realized that she hadn't seen him all day.

"Where have you been?" she asked.

"We're going on a trip?" he asked incredulously.

She nodded. "We have to. My father is ill, Jacob. I have to go home. I want you to come with me."

"But I just—"

"You just what?"

"Nothing. Of course, I'll come with you. I'd never let you go alone," Jacob said. He turned around. "I just hope he can find us now," he murmured.

"Pardon?" Kiernan called after him, trying to rise. It was becoming very hard to do. "Jacob?"

But Jacob was gone, and an hour later, when they were ready to ride out, she didn't remember that she had been questioning him.

All that was on her mind was that her father was very sick.

She was going home.

It was nearly dawn, and the day was going to bring more fighting, Jesse knew.

He was with George B. McClellan's troops on the peninsula, moving toward Richmond.

So far, the Peninsula Campaign had been a lesson in confusion.

McClellan had taken his troops to the tip of the peninsula. There, during the first week of April, a Confederate line had stretched from the York across the peninsula to the Warwick River.

The Union had laid siege there for a month, a slow and overly cautious siege, giving Confederate General Joseph Johnston time to join Confederate General Magruder and shore up his troops. On May 4, McClellan began a grand assault, but Johnston had already moved up the peninsula. On May 5, the Union vanguard overtook the Confederate rear guard, and action followed at Williamsburg. There had been more and more fighting. The Union took Norfolk, and the Confederate ironclad *Virginia* was destroyed. The James River was opened to the Union, but on May 15, at Drewry's Bluff, seven miles outside Richmond, the Confederates were able to employ river obstructions.

Rains washed over the Chickahominy River, and two Union corps were isolated near the villages of Seven Pines and Fair Oaks Station. On the Confederate side, General Johnston suffered a severe wound.

General Robert E. Lee was put in command.

McClellan remained cautious.

Jesse had it on good word from scouts whom he trusted that they should never have been in their present position. There'd been only seventeen thousand Confederates on that defense line at Yorktown when they'd started their Peninsula Campaign. Now they were facing far greater numbers.

It was ceasing to matter to Jesse. They came in, and he did the best he could to patch them up. He watched them die after he had done his best to make them live. He realized that every day more would come to him. His promotion to full colonel hadn't changed anything. Now he was responsible for other doctors as well as for his own patients.

Very early one morning, Jesse was bandaging the arm of the scout, a man with dark, soulful eyes, a drooping moustache, and a weary knowledge about him—Sergeant Flicker.

"There will be action aplenty this morning, Colonel," Flicker said.

"Oh? I heard we were away from the main body of Confederates."

"Hell, no—there's cavalry out there! Our best intelligence says there's no Rebs out there, but our boys've been trading all night with fellows dressed in gray who look a whole lot like Rebs to me."

Jesse arched a brow at him. It was common knowledge that Union "intelligence" tended to be either exaggerated or dead-out wrong.

But cavalry!

His heart thudded. His brother could be out there.

The thought had just crossed his mind when an enlisted man came running into his tent. "Colonel Cameron. Sir!"

"Yes, what is it?" Jesse demanded.

"Reb to see you, sir!"

"What?" Jesse demanded.

The soldier hesitated at his tone of voice. "Sir—"

"For the love of God, spit it out, will you?"

The soldier grimaced. "We were passing some fine Virginia tobacco over for a pound or two of decent coffee, sir."

Jesse grinned. The man shouldn't have been admitting this to him, but trading went on all the time. Men in blue and gray often talked all night, then fired at and killed one another at daybreak.

"It's all right—keep going. There's a Reb to see me?"

"Claims to be your brother, sir!"

"And there's cavalry near us? Then, soldier, he most certainly is my brother. Where are the Rebs?"

"Right across the stream. We got the message from a little boat a Reb whittled out of a tree branch. We'll probably start fighting real soon, but since it's not quite daylight yet, the major can make sure there's no firing till you both get back to your right sides. The Reb says that if you'll see him, he'll be waiting just downstream."

"Hell, yes—I'll see him!" Jesse announced. He donned his overcoat against the coolness of the morning air and followed the man out of his tent. The Union troops were already dug into their positions for the morning, ready for trench warfare. Jesse hurried down the line toward the stream.

"Make way!" The soldier leading him along called out. "The colonel here has got some kinfolk to see!"

Men made way for him. He passed by Colonel Grayson, in charge of the infantry unit on the front of the line. He saluted, and Grayson returned the motion. "Don't take long out there. I've orders to start shells flying by the first real light."

"Thanks," Jesse told him. He kept walking, leaping out from the trenches to hurry along the stream. Surrounded by the mist rising from the water, he could already see the figure of his brother. He wore an overcoat and a plumed hat, both of a gray color that seemed one with the mist of the morning.

"Daniel?" Jesse called. His footsteps moved faster. He was running.

"Jess!"

Suddenly he stood dead still in front of his brother. They looked very much alike, he knew. He was older, but Daniel might have been a mirror image of himself in the mist—except that one wore blue and one wore gray.

Daniel might have been thinking the same thing. For a long moment they stared at one another gravely. It had been a long, long year, and they had both changed in that time.

And yet they hadn't changed that much at all. Jesse took a step forward, and they embraced, and he saw that they were both trembling.

"Daniel," he said, stepping back. "Damn, it's good just to see you well and alive."

Daniel grinned. "You too, Jess."

"It's been a long time."

"Too long for brothers, Jess."

"Been home recently?"

Daniel nodded. "Christa's fine. I've been worried, though, what with the Union troops on the peninsula. I'm not real popular with some of the Union troops. My boys and I have done a fair amount of harassing of Union troops. I'm worried about Cameron Hall."

"Cameron Hall?" Jesse exclaimed. "Why would Union troops want to burn the hall? Legally, it's mine, not yours."

"Well, Jess, it's in Virginia, and it's in the Confederacy, and I'm part of that Confederacy. I reckon that's the way they see it, I don't know. I've told Christa to go stay with John Mackay until it's over. Mackay's been ill, and he can use her over there. I don't know if word's gotten through to Kiernan yet about her father."

"Mackay is ill?"

"I'm afraid so."

"What is it?"

"Something in his lungs. But Jesse—"

"I wonder if I can get a leave, get to him. You all are giving us such a pounding here—"

"Jesse, stop. You've got to listen to me."

"There's more?"

"Kiernan is—"

"Oh, Lord!" Jesse breathed, gripping his brother's arm. "What's happened? What's wrong with her? Where is she?"

"Jesse—"

"Daniel, if there's anything—"

"Jesse, I'm trying to tell you!" Daniel exploded. "She isn't ill! She's going to have your child!"

He might have been hit by bricks, he was so stunned. Of all the things he had expected that morning, the last was the information that he was going to be a father.

"But how—"

"Jesse, you know damned well how!" Daniel said, grinning with a mild rebuke.

"How do you know?" Jesse demanded.

"Jacob Miller came to see me right before we headed out this way. He thought you should know. He also thought you should know that he and his sister think you're all right—for a Yank. I told him that I felt the same way myself. Jesse, you've got to marry her."

"Daniel, I've been *trying* to marry her!"

"Hey!" came a loud shout from Jesse's lines. "Tell the Reb to get his head down, and you get back here, Colonel Cameron. The fightin's about to commence!"

"Get back, Daniel," Jesse said. He embraced his brother fiercely one last time.

"Hey! Hey, sir! The firing is going to start!"

"Keep your head down!" Jesse ordered Daniel.

"Yeah—and I'll expect to hear about a wedding!" Daniel retorted.

"Is she still at Montemarte?"

"I don't know, she might be on her way home. Jesse, damn you, now you get back, and keep your head down!" Daniel said. Jesse nodded, and they both turned away, hurrying back to their lines.

The first firing started the minute Jesse stepped back down into the trenches. It went on for hours.

Jesse worked mechanically through the day. There were long spells when it seemed that his mind was completely empty, numb. Shells exploded overhead, and screams and screeches could be heard constantly. At one point his field hospital seemed overrun by the Rebs, but then they were repulsed, and the Union managed to move forward bit by bit.

The wounded poured in.

Five doctors worked under Jesse, and all five worked feverishly. He searched for bullets with his bare fingers and bit down hard on his jaw every time he saw that there was no way to save a man's life but to remove a mangled limb.

At least he had chloroform and ether. He had heard that the surgeons on the other side had run out. It was difficult to believe in the field tent that they were lucky in any way, but Jesse believed that they were. He had sufficient help to make the operations successful, a man to deliver the anesthetic and make sure that the patients were receiving enough air along with it, a man to secure the patient, a man to hold the limb, and a surgeon to carefully sever flesh, then muscle, then bone.

By the end of the day, he was weary of it, and weary of war. He wanted to go back to treating influenza and stomach disorders. He wanted to deliver a baby.

He wanted to deliver his own. Jesu, Kiernan! There were other things out there in the world. It had been a day just like this when she had stood by his side, the perfect assistant. She had never blanched, she had never failed him.

She had promised that she would never marry him.

You *will* marry me! he thought furiously.

Calling to an orderly, he had the last of his patients taken on a stretcher from the field surgery and proximity to the field to a wagon. Then he was listening intently.

The firing had stopped. The battle was over.

He stepped out of the tent. It was nearly dusk, and it was quiet on this side of the stream, and quiet on the other.

A soldier was hurrying past. Jesse caught hold of his arm. "What's happened?"

"We got beat back in most places, Colonel. We're pulling out of here now. Setting up camp due east. There's still some wounded right across the stream. But be careful, sir. There's still Rebs around."

"Order my men out except for Corporal O'Malley. Tell them to break down into the wagons, but leave the canvas standing and leave behind my instrument bags. If I find anyone, O'Malley can assist me."

"Yes, sir, Colonel Cameron. Don't forget there's still Rebs out there."

"Thanks. Don't forget I rode regular cavalry for years."

"Yes, sir!" The soldier grinned. "Is that all, sir?"

Jesse nodded, then hurried to the stream. He crossed through the water, and it was so cold that he could feel it even through his high black boots.

Then he stood still. The scene before him was one of contrast. The stream itself was peaceful, with its cool water dancing over rocks and fallen branches.

But by that stream lay the bodies of the fallen. Jesse looked from the blood-red skies of the coming dusk to the devastation in human life spread before him.

He went from man to man. Bodies covered in blue were intertwined with bodies clothed in gray. He bent down and sought pulses on both.

"Jesse!"

He was startled to hear his name called. Standing, he looked around the field. He felt a shudder rip through him.

An officer was calling to him, a cavalry officer in gray.

Daniel.

He ran across the field and fell to his knees at his brother's side. Daniel's hand was clutched low over his gut. His fingers were sticky with blood.

"Damn you, Daniel!" Jesse swore. "I told you to keep your head down."

"I did keep my head down!" Daniel insisted. "He shot me in the gut!" He tried to smile but winced and went white, and his eyelids fell as he lost consciousness.

Jesse ripped open his brother's frock coat and shirt. A quick probe with his fingers told him that the bullet was still in Daniel's body. He had to remove it as soon as possible. And he had to suture some of the blood vessels. But Daniel was weak. He'd lost a lot of blood and was losing more and more of it as minutes passed by.

"I've got to get you to the field tent."

"Yank, you touch the captain again," a voice suddenly warned him, "and you'll need a field tent yourself!"

Jesse turned around, inwardly damning himself. He should have been listening, he should have been paying attention. But his brother was wounded, and he hadn't heard the approach of the two Rebel soldiers who were now aiming their rifles at him.

"He needs help," Jesse said.

"Well, he don't need it from no Yank! We've come for him—he's our captain."

"You can't take him. If he's not helped right away, he'll die."

"Hell, you'd kill him if we gave you a chance! But we ain't gonna give no Yankee surgeon that chance. Get your hands off him, and we'll let you live. We've got some fine southern prisons."

"You fools!" Jesse swore suddenly. Ignoring them, he hefted his brother into his arms and faced the two. "He's my brother! And I'm a damned good surgeon, and I won't let my own flesh and blood die! I'm taking him. So shoot me!"

The two men looked at each other, then stared at Jesse.

"Tom," one said, "the captain does have a Yank brother who's a surgeon."

The other man asked suspiciously, "How do we know that you're his brother?"

"Hell, just look at me!" Jesse swore with exasperation, and started walking forward. "I haven't time for this."

He heard the click of a gun. He scarcely hesitated. Daniel was rousing.

"Daniel, will you tell these blind soldiers of yours that I'm your brother?"

Daniel grimaced. "Boys, he's my brother! Oh, hell, Jess! Are you taking me back to the Union lines?"

"Yep." He didn't add that he had no choice if he was going to live.

"Captain!" the soldier called Tom called.

"Get on back, boys. Jesse'll patch me up right as rain, and I'll be back myself then."

The Rebels still wouldn't let Jesse pass. Tom stubbornly stood his ground.

"Supposin' you save the captain, Doc. They'll take him to one of your Yankee camps. Maybe they'll try him and shoot him as a spy. Maybe one of those other Yank sawbones will get his hands on him—"

"You think I'm going to let them take my brother to a prison camp!" Jesse exploded.

The men stared at him for a minute. "How you gonna stop 'em?" Tom asked.

Jesse could feel his brother's blood, warm and wet against him. "I give you my word, I won't let them take my brother. Now, either shoot me, and shoot to kill, or let me pass. He's bleeding, and he needs help fast."

This time, the men let him pass.

Jesse bore Daniel's weight across the stream. Daniel's eyes were half open.

"Am I going to make it, Jess?"

"You sure are. I won't let you die."

"If you think I'm going to die, will you try to get me home? I sure would like to go home, Jess."

"So would I," Jesse told him. "So would I."

He had never felt the yearning to be at Cameron Hall so strongly. He wanted to be home, and he wanted Kiernan to be there. He wanted to hold her in his arms, to touch the beauty of new life, to sit before a fire with her, to stare out upon the river. He could almost see it.

Daniel groaned, and the image was dispelled. His throat tightened until he almost choked on it.

God, if you ever let me save a life, please, let it be this life, he prayed.

The last daylight faded as he carried his brother into his hospital field tent and tenderly laid him down.

Twenty-two

*K*iernan didn't think she'd ever been on a longer or more grueling journey than the one she took that April.

Rains had washed away much of the roads. The war had kept them from being repaired.

She often climbed down from the wagon to walk as Tyne and Jacob set their shoulders to help the horses pull it over a deep pock or scar. They had to stop for fallen trees and move them, and they had to stop from sheer exhaustion. With no accommodations nearby, they slept in the wagon, the four of them together, huddled tight for warmth.

There were continual stops for the soldiers.

Just as they had come down the drive from Montemarte, Thomas had returned and given Kiernan a pass that he had procured from a Yankee colonel. It would get her through the Yankee lines, he had assured her.

She thanked Thomas heartily. It had not even occurred to her that she might need such a document. But during the journey, it had stood to her advantage a number of times.

Northern Virginia was a very curious place these days, she realized quickly. Yanks were here, Rebs were there, and towns of total devastation lay in between.

It was not possible for them to take a direct route. They were on the road for a week before they reached Richmond, where they learned that the armies were engaged in a number of serious battles right on the outskirts of the city. Yanks had come from the peninsula in huge numbers. All along the frontiers of the southern capital, the magnificent boys in gray were repelling the invaders.

"On to Richmond!" the Yankees cried.

But the southern boys, commanded by the genteel and remarkable Robert E. Lee, were holding them back. Jeb Stuart's cavalry had actually ridden right around the enemy.

The tension in the city was crackling. She had never imagined that Richmond could be anything like it was now—so vastly overcrowded. The roads were filled with soldiers—and politicians. Prices had skyrocketed with the influx of so many people. Janey went off to buy food and came back grumbling that she hadn't even enough money for a potato.

Kiernan, exhausted and overwhelmed by all they had learned in Richmond, stood by the wagon and told Janey not to worry. "Spend whatever you have to spend. We'll rest tonight here and try to make home by tomorrow night."

"Miz Kiernan," Tyne told her, "you ain't been listening. The soldier boys been fightin' right outside the city. There's a defense ring around it. They ain't gonna let us through."

"They're letting us through," Kiernan said stubbornly. "All I want is to go home!" she exclaimed. "And they're not going to stop me—the Rebels or the Yankees!"

She took Patricia and Jacob to a restaurant near the beautiful capitol building while Tyne and Janey went to see about accommodations for the evening.

She remembered the restaurant well. She and her father had come here often enough in earlier years. Now there was a crowd in the front, waiters in line to get in. She managed to get close enough to see inside.

At least it hadn't changed. The tables were covered in snowy-white cloths, the silver and crystal were elegant, and a violinist played while the diners ate and chatted. Entering the restaurant, Kiernan realized they were hardly dressed for the elegance of the place, which had persevered despite the war. Her voluminous cape hid her condition amazingly well, and the children somehow managed to present themselves at their best despite their days upon the road.

She was dismayed by the line of people waiting for tables. The sight of them all nearly made her burst into tears, she was so exhausted. Worrying about John Mackay had taken its toll on her, and sleeping in the wagon had not been easy. She was always uncomfortable these days with so much weight to carry about. But she was also determined, and usually, no matter what, she was able to remain calm.

But this long line to eat a decent meal was nearly her undoing.

"Why, Mrs. Miller!"

A man was coming across the room toward them. He was tall and lean and dressed in an impeccable dove-gray frock coat and white ruffled shirt. Kiernan could have sworn she had never seen him before, but he seemed to know her.

She glanced at Jacob anxiously. "Who is that?"

"I'm not sure!" Jacob whispered back. "Maybe he's one of your business partners."

"Business!" she exclaimed suddenly. Patricia, exhausted too, opened her innocent brown eyes wide to Kiernan. Kiernan just smiled. "Miller Firearms," she murmured. "They'll get us home."

"Mrs. Miller!"

The man was upon them. A spark of life invaded Kiernan's system, and she extended her hand for the man to kiss. "I saw you last in Charles Town," the man said, "at the trial of the detestable John Brown. You were still Miss Mackay back then. I heard about your husband, and I'm so very sorry. Still, everything is still moving smoothly here in Richmond. Andrew Miller, Thomas Donahue, and your father picked the perfect site for their operation in the Shenandoah Valley!"

"Yes, they were very clever, Mr. . . . ?"

"Norman. Niles Norman, Mrs. Miller, at your service. If there's anything at all that I could do for you—"

"Why, actually, sir, there is. My throat is parched, and the poor children have been standing for ages. You see, I'm trying to reach my father right now. He's quite ill, I'm afraid. We've taken a loathsome journey in a wagon, what with the railroads being so dangerous, to be with him. And now—well, we're famished, and exhausted, and . . ."

She allowed her hand to flutter in the air and a tear to moisten her eye.

Jacob looked at her with a cocked brow.

Niles Norman was immediately at her service.

They didn't have to wait a moment longer. Niles knew someone in the right place, and soon they were sitting. A few minutes later, a beautiful rack of lamb sat before them with mint jelly and sweet potatoes and green pole beans dripping with sweet-cream butter.

Kiernan didn't think that food had ever tasted quite so good.

Niles Norman remained with them, chatting about the war. The Yankees were breathing right down their necks in Richmond, but they weren't afraid, not a bit. General Lee would keep them out.

Kiernan smiled sweetly. "Then we shouldn't have any problem getting through down on the peninsula, should we?"

Niles Norman frowned. "Now, Mrs. Miller, it just doesn't seem to be the right time—"

"But it has to be, Mr. Norman. I must get through!"

She brought her handkerchief to her eyes. In seconds Norman was assuring her that he would get her a pass; after all, she was part owner of Miller Firearms, and where might confederate boys be without those arms?

Jacob continued to stare at her with questioning eyes. She kicked him beneath the table, and Niles Norman fluttered nervously about her.

She gave him a sweet and dazzling smile.

Although accommodations in the city were extremely scarce, Niles Norman found them two rooms, with space for Tyne and Janey too. When Niles said good night to Kiernan, he cleared his throat several times, then told her that he would love to see her again. Surely, the time wasn't right, but . . .

"Mister," Jacob snorted, "you just don't know how wrong the time is!" he proclaimed.

"Jacob!" Kiernan protested warningly.

It was Jacob's turn for a sweet and innocent smile. "Sorry, Mr. Norman, sir. But trust me. Kiernan is not ready for anything at the moment."

"What in God's name did you think you were doing?" Kiernan demanded furiously of Jacob after Niles Norman left them at last.

Jacob planted his hands on his waist, staring her down. "You were flirting!"

"I had to flirt!" she responded, astonished. "How else were we going to get anything done?"

"Seven months gone with another man's child—"

"Jacob!" Kiernan gasped. She was suddenly so furious that she could hardly stand it. She almost slapped him. Tears threatened at the back of her eyes, and she clenched her fingers tightly and stepped back rather than take a chance of striking Jacob.

"Even *you* are defending Jesse!" she whispered. "Dammit!" She was so weary, and the baby was so heavy, and as much as she loved the life building within her, her pregnancy was a strain. She couldn't help resenting Jesse at that moment. "You're defending him, and he's a Yankee! The Yankee who took over your house!"

"He's the father of your child," Jacob reminded her. "And I know that it would matter very much to him that you flirted. I—I know it, because I know him!" After his first faltering, Jacob was now firm in his conviction. "I know him, and so—well, you just haven't got any right to flirt like that!"

She hadn't any right to flirt—because of Jesse? Oh, if it weren't for Jesse—if it weren't for the foolish fact that she loved him despite all odds—she wouldn't be in this predicament now.

No, no—she wanted her baby.

"You've no right—no right at all, young Mr. Miller—to tell me what I can and cannot do," she snapped to Jacob. She was wrong to fight with him, but she was too tense and weary to try to explain. And she was frightfully close to tears. She couldn't fall apart now. She was too close to home.

"Oh, please! Stop it, both of you!" Patricia implored.

Kiernan swung around to look at Patricia, startled by her words.

"Jacob is—" Patricia hesitated, not quite as bold as her brother. "Jacob is only standing up for Captain Cameron. And Kiernan, you do love the captain, don't you?"

Kiernan swallowed hard, then nodded. "I have loved him a very long time," she admitted in a soft whisper. "Long before the war. If the war hadn't come along when it did, I probably would have married him. But you must understand about Anthony."

"We do understand," Jacob interrupted her with quiet dignity, and offered her a crooked smile. "You have been a very good widow to him. You would have been a good wife."

He kissed her cheek and went on into the bedroom where he would sleep. Kiernan looked after him, and then Patricia slipped an arm around her. And then the tears did slip down her cheek.

"Kiernan!" Patricia whispered with alarm. "What—?"

"I love you. I love you both," she said, and quickly wiped away her tears, bringing Patricia into the bedroom they would share.

They set off in the morning.

Tyne snapped the reins over the horses' backs, and the wagon moved down the pike. They had barely left behind the city with its fine red-brick row houses when they were stopped by a sentry. Kiernan produced the Confederate pass that Niles Norman had procured for her, and the soldier scratched his head.

"Mrs. Miller, with all due respect, ma'am, there's fighting out there."

"The fighting is out past Williamsburg, isn't it?" she asked.

"Yes, ma'am."

"Then that's the way I'm going," she said sweetly.

Reluctantly, the soldier agreed to let them pass. A quarter-mile down the road, though, Kiernan asked Tyne to pull in on the reins. The wagon rolled to a stop, and she turned back to talk to the twins.

"I've no right to bring you both through this. I'll take you back to Richmond, then I'll come through myself."

"We can't take the time," Jacob said stubbornly. "What if your father . . ." He let the words trail away meaningfully.

"My father may already be dead, Jacob. And it won't help him to endanger you." If John were dead, she thought, she wouldn't be able to bear it.

But she would have to bear it. No matter what happened, she must survive it, and she must make herself be strong—for Jacob, for Patricia, and for the baby.

"We're going with you," Patricia said. "We're not afraid of Yankees. We've already lived with them, remember?"

"Yes, I remember."

"You should," Jacob said softly. He was grinning. He seemed to have become Jesse's champion—and to enjoy taunting her about her transgressions.

"How nice of you to remind me," she said sweetly, gritting her teeth. "Tyne, let's go forward."

Down the road, they met another Confederate sentry. They were given another warning.

An hour later, they moved past a scene of utter devastation. Fighting had just preceded them. Patricia cried out at the sight of a body on the road before them, and Kiernan quickly forced the little girl to lay her head against her shoulder and close her eyes. She had to grit her teeth herself as they moved onward.

"Come on, good Lord Jesus!" Tyne prayed. Kiernan looked from Patricia's blond head to the road. There were more sentries up ahead, dressed in blue. Troops, scores of them, marched along the road. Tyne pulled in on the reins, and Kiernan felt her heart beat furiously.

"We're going to be all right!" she assured Tyne and the children. But she was shaking. She'd seen Yankees before. As Jacob had been kind enough to remind her, she'd seen them rather close.

But she'd never seen so many.

"Halt!" A voice commanded.

Tyne pulled in on the reins, and a footsoldier strode over to the wagon. A young man looked up to Kiernan. "Lady, where do you think you're going?"

"Home," she told him. "I'm trying to go home. And you're in my way."

"There's been fighting all around here, ma'am, and all down the peninsula."

Her heart slammed hard against her chest. She prayed that she still had a home to go to.

"You have to let me by."

"I'm sorry, ma'am. I can't do that."

"But why?"

"Darkie," the soldier said, addressing Tyne, "draw that wagon over there. Lady, I'm afraid that you and the children will have to come with me to see the general. Come right along."

There was no choice. She stepped down from the wagon, helping Patricia. She reached for Jacob, but he eluded her touch.

"You must behave here," she warned him.

He arched a brow at her.

"Jacob—"

"Lady, you must follow me now," the soldier told her.

"Lead onward, sir. I'm following."

She pulled her hood farther down over her forehead, more as a cover against the stares directed their way than against the coolness of the rain-dampened morning. The soldier led them past rows and rows of marching men—tired men, wounded men, men who marched covered in mud and bandages. Some limped along, using their rifles as crutches.

"Burial detail, halt!" an officer commanded.

They moved past the soldiers performing the weary task of laying their own to rest on foreign soil. They passed by men who seemed to be at leisure. Some were in the grass with their mess kits, gnawing on hardtack, lying back and chewing blades of grass. A number of men had bandaged heads, and feet, and arms—and some had bandages where there should have been limbs.

Kiernan's heart hammered hard, her muscles contracted. Deep within her womb, the baby suddenly moved, violently, swiftly—as if it, too, had seen the ravages of battle and turned against them.

The men watched her walk along with Jacob and Patricia. Some smiled and tipped their hats. Some were appreciative, some were curious, and some were just weary.

And some looked at her as if she were the enemy as much as any gray-clad man they faced in battle.

Kiernan hurried along, putting an arm around Patricia's shoulder. Suddenly, the soldier leading her came to a stop outside a large tent.

"You wait here, ma'am," he told her, and left her standing with Patricia and Jacob. Jacob stared across the road to where a number of injured Yanks sat on their coats in the field.

"Jacob, please be careful here. I know you hate them, but we've got to get by them."

Jacob arched a brow at her, indicating a fellow on the ground who was missing his left calf and foot and his right hand.

"It's hard to hate a man who looks like that, Kiernan," he said softly.

"Kiernan, how long will we have to be here?" Patricia asked urgently.

"I don't know," she answered honestly.

The Yanks were being rather rude, she decided, leaving her standing out here. Her back was killing her. The cape she was wearing grew warm as the sun rose high in the sky, but if she removed it, her condition would become very apparent. She wondered if it mattered, if any of these men cared one way or another that she was carrying a child, in or out of proper wedlock.

Minutes passed by. The sun grew hotter, and her back began to hurt badly.

"Excuse me," she told the children.

"Kiernan," Jacob began, but before he could stop her, she had turned around and burst into the officers' field tent.

A group of officers were huddled around a table covered with maps. She stared straight at the Yankee faces, framed by their fine plumed hats.

"Excuse me. But you gentlemen are not simply the enemy—invading my home, my state, my land—you are excruciatingly rude!"

Dead silence followed her arrival, then one of the men attempted to hide the maps. A gray-haired gentleman stepped forward. "Your pardon, madam. We *have* been excruciatingly rude. Why wasn't I informed of this lady's presence?" he demanded.

The soldier she had first met stepped forward, saluting sharply. "General, sir, the colonel said I was not to interrupt."

"Madam, just what is it that I can do for you? I'm General Jensen, and I wish to be at your disposal."

"I want to go home, General, and your troops are preventing me from doing so."

"Is it urgent that you get home?"

"My father is ill, sir."

A snort suddenly rang out, and a man stepped forward. Kiernan's eyes widened as she recognized Captain Hugh Norris, the cavalryman who had been so eager to burn down Montemarte.

"Norris, I demand a reason for your behavior!" General Jensen said sharply.

"She's a Miller, General."

"Meaning, sir?"

"That should be answer enough, General. Miller Firearms. She's part owner of the company."

"I see," the general murmured, stroking his chin as he surveyed Kiernan.

"And beyond that," Hugh Norris went on, "a number of men are convinced she was spying in Harpers Ferry. The Rebs over there eluded us any number of times."

"Those Rebs eluded you, sir, because they are far smarter than you," Kiernan told him sweetly.

For the moment she thought Norris was going to assault her. General Jensen, however, stood between them. Norris clearly hated her, and it was obvious the man wanted her blood.

She stared at the older officer. "General Jensen, I swear to you that I am not spying. My father is ill. I am desperate to reach him."

"Mrs. Miller," Jensen said with a weary sigh, "I will have to ask you to wait outside for a few minutes while I straighten a few things out. Private Riker, bring the lady a chair, and see if she'd like some coffee."

Kiernan's heart sank. Hugh Norris would have plenty to say to the major.

Riker, who was the soldier who had escorted her to the tent in the first place, took her arm to escort her back out. She knew she had to appear as sweet and innocent and harmless as she could for the moment.

"Please, sir," she told the general, looking back over her shoulder as Riker led her away, "I just want to get home."

"And where is home?"

"An hour's ride from Williamsburg," she told him.

"Give me a minute, madam," he said.

Having little choice, she lowered her head and allowed Riker to lead her out. Jacob seemed oddly exuberant—she had expected him to be at some Yank's throat by now.

She cast him a frown while Riker dragged out a folding field chair. Jacob looked like a cat who had swallowed a canary.

She wanted to demand what was going on with him, but Private Riker wouldn't leave them. She asked for coffee, but the coffee was right there, just beyond them at a fire. He stayed with them.

A soldier suddenly came running by them. "Message for the general, Private! Make way!"

The private stepped aside, and the soldier went in. Still, they waited.

An officer came out of the tent, and Kiernan leaped to her feet. "Sir—"

"I am sorry, ma'am," the man said. "The colonel's insisting that you stay."

"The colonel?" she said, wondering what colonel he meant.

"Have a seat. He'll be right with you."

She had just taken her seat again when she heard the clip of horses' hooves coming at them quickly. She leaped up, certain that animal was about to run her down.

Her eyes widened in amazement as she recognized the horseman.

Jesse.

He was the colonel who had demanded she be held!

He reined Pegasus in abruptly and leaped down. Before she knew it, he was before her, looking wilder than she'd seen him since Harpers Ferry.

But this was a different kind of wildness. He seemed to be absolutely furious.

His hair was totally disheveled, his black locks falling over his stormy eyes. He was hatless, and his high black boots were covered with the mud that had splashed him on his way here. His fingers, closing harshly around her arms, were hard and taut, almost brutal.

But his whisper, brief, desperate, was intended for her ears only. "Help me, Kiernan. Play along with me."

Instantly his manner changed. His words and his tone of voice matched the fever and fury of his touch. "Kiernan!" He spoke so harshly and so loudly that his voice carried into the tent. The general suddenly threw open a flap, came out, and stood before them. Jesse, incensed, seemed not to see him. "Yes, I heard of your condition, Mrs. Miller. But it never occurred to me that you would hunt me down across a warring countryside! Yes, I'll ask for leave to take you home, madam, but don't expect any more from me! I'll not marry you to save your honor! Who knows what you were up to with those Rebel friends of yours, coming in and out at all hours!"

Play along with me! Had she imagined the words, or had they been real? What was he doing to her? Everyone could hear his voice as he made a horrible mockery of her and everything that had passed between them. Her cheeks were surely bloodred, and despite his whisper, she was hurt and furious.

"What are you talking about!" she demanded.

"I won't marry you, Kiernan. I won't do it!"

She gasped, stunned. What could be bringing about this kind of behavior in Jesse? "I don't need to be taken home, and you're the last man I'd ever marry!" she cried out, shaken and enraged. Dear God, this couldn't be Jesse, with his eyes on fire, his hold so brutal, doing this to her in front of all these people— making a fool of her, and a bastard of himself!

Play along with me! he had said. Well, she hoped she was playing along as he wanted. She was confused and furious and miserable, and she wanted desperately to be away from him and every Yankee there.

"Let go of me!" she demanded. Wildly, she tried to kick him. He wrenched her hard against him, and she struggled more desperately. "Jesse, you bluebelly fool! I'm not in any condition—"

"Liar!" he charged.

In a minute he would hold her too close, and he would feel her abdomen, and he would know her condition for certain.

She was close enough now. Now he knew he was going to be a father soon.

But he was still playing some game.

"Damn you, lady! I won't marry you!"

This wasn't Jesse. Because of his upbringing and his sense of right and wrong, he would have demanded that the mother of his child marry him, no matter what his feelings for her.

At least, the Jesse she had always known would have done so.

She lifted her chin. *Play along with me!* What was this ruse? It was humiliating!

"Jesse, damn you! Let go of me!"

But before she knew it, he had ripped off her cape, and her condition was very apparent to everyone there.

Then General Jensen snapped out Jesse's name.

"Colonel Cameron!"

"Sir!"

Jesse swirled around, saluting sharply, as if he had only just noticed that the general was present. Hugh Norris was beside him, sniggering at Kiernan and Jesse.

"What in God's name is going on here?" the general insisted.

"It's personal, sir!" Jesse said.

"Colonel Cameron, with the lady in front of us all, it ceases to be personal. Is this child yours?"

Jesse stood very stiffly, taller than anyone, his feet firm on the ground, his stance entirely military. Static seemed to leap from him. "Maybe," he replied.

Kiernan gasped with fury and amazement.

"Maybe!" Hugh Norris repeated, laughing. "He took over the house! I told you, she's a spy! She has her way about her, but I was able to see through that, sir. Cameron here was duped."

"I was never duped, sir. She was a seductress and intended to do me in, but I was never duped. She was under house arrest."

"I have had enough!" Kiernan exclaimed in fury. "I am going home. I will walk if you confiscate my wagon, General, and I will keep going unless you choose to shoot me. And if you do, God will see to it that it is spread across every newspaper in the known world!"

But before she could turn around, Jesse stopped her. "You're not going anywhere!"

"Colonel!" General Jensen snapped. "Young woman, my men do not shoot women in the back."

Kiernan was at a complete loss to understand Jesse. Why was he making a scene? She loved him, she wanted him, no matter what—she knew that. But again the colors seemed to come between them—blue and gray—so vividly, so painfully. She just wanted to go home and see her father.

She wanted to have her baby.

Jesse's baby.

She straightened her shoulders and spoke with dignity to the general. "You bastard Yanks!" she said softly. "You invaded my house and used it as you would. You've threatened my life. You've killed my husband, and now you—"

"I'm about to rectify the situation, Mrs. Miller," the general insisted. "Union soldiers in my command are gentlemen. Is the child that you're carrying Colonel Cameron's?"

With everyone looking on, Kiernan wanted to deny it, to strike out at them all—and so she hesitated too long.

"Yes!" Jesse snapped out. "All right, yes! *I'm* sure that it is my child."

"Get Father Darby. They'll be wed right now," Jensen ordered. "Do you hear me, Colonel Cameron? Marry this woman immediately. That's an order! I will not have this army accused of peopling the South with bastards!"

Jesse was silent. His jaw twisted as if he were in a rage, and he seemed to be looking for some way to avoid marrying her. But finally he looked straight ahead and waited.

"Do you hear me, Colonel?"

"Yes—sir!" Jesse snapped at last, doing his duty like a man of honor.

"Wait!" Kiernan protested. She wasn't going to be married here and now—not when she couldn't talk to Jesse first! Not when she didn't understand what was going on! "Wait! I will not—"

Suddenly Jesse pulled her into his arms again and held her so tight against him that she thought she was going to pass out. His blue eyes bore into hers, bluer than the summer's sky, a piercing, vibrant, blade-sharp blue. His whisper, as his lips touched hers, was hurried and desperate: "Agree now, Kiernan!"

"Let me g—!" she began.

But his arms tightened, and his whisper came urgently. "I desperately need a reason to leave. I have to take you home. Daniel is here. He's injured. I have to get him out and hide him. Daniel's life is at stake!"

Daniel!

She went dead still, understanding at last. Jesse had been forced to make a big scene, to do this to them both, so that no one would question his leaving his company while battles were raging all around them.

The twins were standing together at a distance, deadly quiet. Jacob hadn't said a word in Kiernan's defense through all of this—feisty, proud Jacob—because he knew. Somehow, he had found out about Daniel.

Where was Daniel now? How badly was he hurt?

"Mrs. Miller," General Jensen said consolingly, a hand upon her arm and a hand upon Jesse's shoulder, "we will right this problem. The colonel is a fine man, and usually, he's even a gentleman. But let's get on with this, eh? Here's Father Darby. Father, Colonel Cameron stands there. Mrs. Miller, come—we'll have you right here."

Father Darby was a tall, lean man with a sorrowful face that indicated he'd brought far more solace to the dying lately than anything else. Being ordered to conduct a wedding under fire seemed to be quite a surprise for him.

"They must agree to be married," he said, seemingly puzzled as he studied Jesse.

"They agree!" General Jensen said.

"Jesse?"

"Yes," Jesse said with a long, exaggerated sigh. "I agree."

"And you, Miss . . ."

"Mrs. Kiernan Miller," Kiernan supplied, "and I—"

Jesse's foot slammed down on hers so hard that it brought tears to her eyes. Daniel was somehow at stake.

"I agree!" she exclaimed.

Before she knew it, Jesse was holding her hand.

Patricia and Jacob stood silently in the background, and Private Riker and Hugh Norris looked on, Norris sniggering all the while.

General Jensen gave her away.

In less than five minutes, she and Jesse exchanged their vows. Jesse's signet ring sat around her finger, heavy, too large, and Anthony's gold band was tucked away in her pocket.

Darby cleared his throat. "Well, Colonel, now is when I should tell you to kiss the bride. But you seem to have taken matters into your own hands. I needn't advise you to kiss her."

Jesse's eyes were on Kiernan's. "Ah, but Father Darby, I intend to have a kiss."

It wasn't a customary kiss. She was not pulled reverently into his arms, and she did not feel the gentle press of his lips.

Instead, she was swept into his arms and carried to the rear of the tent, away from the others, held tightly in his arms. Only then did his lips touch hers.

All the fire was there, a taste of heaven, a hint of the blaze of hell. She wanted to fight his touch, and she struggled against him for the disgrace he was bringing down upon them now that they were married. She fought hard . . .

But nothing could ever sweep away the magic of his kiss. Nothing could quell the burning deep inside. Nothing could take away the sweetness and the warmth, when he had been away again so very long.

Nothing—except Jesse himself.

His lips broke from hers just slightly and hovered above her own. "We have to leave!" he whispered fervently. "I have to bring Daniel through the lines secretly. Do you understand?"

She must have been slow to respond, for he shook her as he held her.

"Do you understand?"

"Yes!" she hissed back.

"Colonel!" Father Darby called, choking on the word.

Kiernan was suddenly on her feet, and Jesse was pulling her back before the general.

"Sir! Request leave to bring my wife home!"

General Jensen shook his head. "Colonel, we're in the midst of a major campaign. I can't let you go."

Kiernan wanted to slap Jesse's face as hard as she could. But she realized that he was in difficulty, and she knew that he would not be lying about Daniel, no matter what. She instantly realized how she could help.

He had once accused her of being a wonderful actress. Now it was time for her abilities to be tested.

"Oh!" she cried out. She fell flat upon the ground, doing her best not to jeopardize the baby. Jesse was instantly at her side, setting his arm around her shoulders, pulling her against him. "Oh, Jesse! The baby! Ohhhhhh!" she wailed.

"Colonel Cameron! Take your wife where she'll be comfortable!" General Jensen ordered.

"No!" she screamed. She struggled against Jesse's hold as hysterically as she could. "No, you despicable Yankees! You invade my home, you take everything! You ravaged my life, and now you expect me to have a child in a battlefield!"

Patricia stepped forward. "You cad!" she told the general indignantly.

Kiernan wailed again, moaning with true dramatic purpose. She would never have fooled Jesse with her performance. She had never fooled Jesse in all of her life.

But something more was at stake at the moment. She screamed as if she had been cut with a knife, then she grated out, "I want to go home!"

"What you want, Mrs. Cameron," Hugh Norris said flatly, "certainly can't matter! This is war!"

"I want to go home!" she wailed again. Norris! That bastard. He sensed that something was going on, and he seemed to hate Jesse almost as much as he hated her. "Please! I want to have my child at home!"

"Dear Lord!" General Jensen was a good man, and he was obviously very upset. "But your husband is here, Mrs. Mil—Mrs. Cameron!" the general tried to soothe her. "He may be a knave, but he's one of the finest physicians in the Union Army! You'll be in his hands—"

"I hate him! I want to go home! My father is ill, and I want to go home! I want my baby born at home! If you force me to have this child in a battlefield, I swear—"

"Yes, yes! Every newspaper in the known world will know about it," Jensen finished wearily. "You win, Mrs. —er, Cameron. Colonel, take your wife home. Madam, you've twenty-four hours to deliver that baby. Then I want you, Colonel, back in the field!"

Jesse saluted sharply. "Yes, sir!"

Hugh Norris narrowed his eyes and gritted his teeth, but there was nothing he could do. General Jensen had given his orders.

Jesse swept Kiernan up into his arms and carried her from the tent. Jacob and Patricia followed quickly behind.

There was no romance to his hold. As soon as they arrived outside, he slid her to her feet and barked instructions to the others.

"Get Tyne and the wagon, quickly, Jacob! Follow me and Pegasus around to the med tent. Kiernan, get in the wagon and look as if you're in agony."

She nodded briefly. A jagged pain swept through her, and she clenched her teeth very hard.

With amazement, she realized that she wouldn't be acting anymore.

Twenty-three

They traveled a good distance from the main camp to reach Jesse's field tent. Kiernan realized that the bulk of the army must have pulled in on a tactical retreat, leaving Jesse to take in the last of the wounded.

She didn't feel any more pain, low and deep in the small of her back, as they traveled to Jesse's tent. She began to think that she had imagined the sensation, but then it came again. She was tempted to scream and beg some assistance as panic nearly overwhelmed her. The baby was early, not due for another four weeks. She was suddenly terrified that in her desperation to reach her father, she had jeopardized the safety of her child.

She bit down hard on her knuckles and remained quiet. She still didn't understand quite what was going on, but Daniel's life was at stake too. Lacey had told her that first babies take forever to come—sometimes all day and all night and part of the next day too. She had to keep her silence. The pain finally subsided.

When they reached the tent, Jesse dismounted from Pegasus and called sharply, "Tyne, give me a hand! The rest of you, stay there."

Ignoring the order, Kiernan braced herself carefully on the wagon and stepped down from it. She hurried after Tyne, who had followed Jesse.

Jesse, realizing that she was there, spun around furiously. "I told you to wait in the wagon!"

Hot tears stung her eyes, tears she wasn't about to shed. "You've been telling me what to do and what you will and will not do ever since I've seen you!"

His hands fell hard upon her shoulders. "Daniel—"

"Yes, Daniel! His life is at stake, and if you had just told me from the very beginning, I wouldn't have felt so humiliated when you forced me to marry you!"

"I would have said more if I could. I asked you to play along with me! And don't you think it's convenient that I've married you?"

"I didn't have to be married for convenience!" Kiernan protested in a rush. "I can take care of myself very well."

"But maybe my child wouldn't have appreciated growing up a bastard!"

"This conversation isn't necessary now," Kiernan informed him coolly. "If you had just told me—"

"I couldn't have walked up and told you! I'd requested a leave earlier and been denied it. It was the only way."

She twisted from his hold, still wanting to scream. "I married you for Daniel's sake," she said stubbornly. "The least you can do is let me see him. He's in here, is he not?"

"Miz Kiernan," Tyne said, stepping around her diplomatically, "let's get Captain Cameron into the wagon, and then you'll see him fine enough."

"Yes, and we've got to hurry," Jesse said sharply. "Troops of every color are all over the place. I want to get him home." He started to turn away but came back and faced her, pulling her against him.

"I need you, Kiernan, I need you now! Say what you want to me. Leave me, if you want. I'm still everything that you hate and loathe in the world. But for the love of God, help me now."

She choked at the intensity of emotion that welled within her. So very much was at stake. "I want to help you—that's obvious, you fool!"

"I should be offended that my wife of a bare few minutes is calling me names," he told her. The words were soft and tender, his lip curling into a rueful grin as he spoke. "What we need, madam, is a truce. A separate peace. A cease-fire. Have we got it?"

She nodded. "Jesse, how bad is he?"

"I pulled the bullet out last night. It didn't injure any major organs. He's strong as an ox. He just needs to heal somewhere where the air is cool, where the breeze is clean. I can't let them take him to a prison camp. Do you understand?"

She nodded. In the filth of a prison, he would surely die. "Yes."

"You're with me? A truce?"

"A truce. A separate peace," Kiernan agreed.

"Kiernan," Jesse warned her tensely, "this could be the most dangerous thing any of us have ever done. The Yanks will be after Daniel, and the Rebs will be ready to shoot me down. Are you still willing?" His eyes were bright upon hers. Their differences would have to come between them later, not now.

"I was going through the lines one way or the other, Jesse. I'm going home. My father needs me, and I need him. Now Daniel needs me too. I'm not afraid, Jesse."

"You never were afraid," he said softly. "And that, my love, could be your downfall. Trust me. I'm afraid right now—damned afraid."

Startled, she looked at him.

"I don't intend to die before a firing squad," he said briefly.

Kiernan watched him, silent and still as Jesse walked by her. A second later, he appeared with Tyne and Corporal O'Malley, carrying a stretcher to her wagon. The figure upon it was swathed in a white sheet. "Make way!" Jesse called to Patricia, Jacob, and Janey, and the trio moved to allow the stretcher to be laid out on the wagon's floor. Kiernan stared at O'Malley, who surely knew that he'd had a Reb in his charge.

O'Malley, with innocence that would have stood him well in a poker game, tipped his hat to her. "Mornin', ma'am."

"Good morning, Corporal," she said.

"Nice day for a ride."

"I imagine so, Corporal. Are you coming with us?"

"No, ma'am, the colonel won't allow me to do that. I've got to see that the colonel's orders are carried on to the other surgeons."

"I see," she murmured.

"You look after the colonel, ma'am."

"I will."

O'Malley took a step closer. "Look after him well!" he said in a rush. "He's so all-fired determined to save his brother that he's risking his own life. For hiding a man in gray, his own side could shoot him for treason. And if the Rebs get hold of him, they may well shoot him for a spy. Lady, you're taking a treacherous journey!"

"Kiernan!" Jesse called to her sharply.

Oh, Jesse, she thought briefly, you are indeed a fool! Yet what else could he do? As he had chosen to fight for the Union, now he had chosen to fight for Daniel. She couldn't change him. His mind was set. But she loved him. Even if the circumstances of their marriage had enhanced their differences, she still couldn't change that fact.

"Kiernan!" Jesse called again.

"Yes, I'm coming." She stiffened, O'Malley saluted, and she hurried to the rear of the wagon. She looked up at Jesse for a moment and saw exhaustion in his features, tenacity, determination. She knew why she loved him, even if he was the enemy.

She lowered her lashes. She still knew little about Daniel's condition and wanted to see him for herself.

Jesse lifted her into the back of the wagon. A blanket had been arranged over Daniel, and the twins and Janey sat near him. "Kiernan, lean back so," Jesse instructed her. She nodded. His blue eyes met hers. His features were more tense and weary than she had ever seen them. "Don't let anyone see my brother," he said softly.

"I won't."

He was quickly gone, crawling up front alongside Tyne. O'Malley saluted sharply to Jesse.

"Thanks, Corporal," Jesse called to him.

"See you soon, Colonel!" O'Malley returned. Jesse flicked the reins, and the horses started off. O'Malley trotted alongside the wagon. "Congratulations, ma'am. The best to you and the colonel."

Kiernan waved to O'Malley, and the wagon, with Pegasus tied to the rear, moved away very quickly. They had begun the journey. Patricia looked at her with wide, frightened eyes. Jacob was still and stoic and silent, every inch the young man.

Kiernan tried to smile. She dared not think of the danger.

She thought of her circumstances instead. She and Jesse were married. It was what she had always wanted, it was right. They were about to become parents.

But nothing had changed. If anything, their world was a nightmare. Daniel was lying by her, seriously injured. He might be dead, or he might be dying, and she couldn't even touch him.

The countryside was combed with troops.

And Jesse was still a Yankee, a bitter enemy.

She closed her eyes as fear swamped over her. They still had hours to go. On the way, Yanks might well threaten Daniel.

And Rebs might well shoot Jesse down before asking any questions.

"Halt!"

Kiernan's heart began to hammer at the command. Jacob sat across from her. She couldn't see the road, but Jacob could.

"Reb or Yank?" she mouthed the words. How would she ever bear this? She clenched her fingers together so that they would not tremble. Lucky, lucky Daniel! He was either unconscious or sleeping, unaware of their situation.

"Yank," Jacob mouthed back.

Jesse was producing his pass, and she heard his easy drone as he talked to the man who had stopped him.

"Sorry, Colonel, we've orders to stop everyone," the man was telling him.

"Good to see you obeying orders, soldier!" Jesse responded. Kiernan heard him pick up the reins again.

Daniel moaned loudly from beneath his cocoon of blankets and covers.

"What's that?" the soldier demanded.

Kiernan tensed with every inch of her body. What if the soldier insisted on searching the wagon? Jesse might have no choice but to shoot the man. Would he be able to live with himself if he shot down an innocent man?

"What's what?" Jesse said casually. "My wife is back there with the children and the darkies. My leave is to take her home."

"It sounded like a man," the soldier said. "I could have sworn." He started around the wagon.

"Ohhhhh!" Kiernan cried out, drowning out Daniel's moan. The young soldier moved around the back and stared into the wagon. She covered her rounded abdomen with her splaying fingers. "Please, sir! We must hurry. Please!"

"Of course! Of course!" The soldier backed away. Jesse flicked the reins, and they were moving again, fast.

Thirty minutes later, she heard Jesse call a soft "Woah" to the horses. The wagon halted beneath huge shade trees, and she heard him leap to the ground. He appeared around the side of the wagon. "Janey, Jacob, Patricia—there's a stream down the embankment. Get yourselves some water." He looked at Kiernan, then pulled her to her feet, setting his hands upon her to lift her down beside him. He took her right hand within his own and kissed it softly.

"Whatever you think of me, Kiernan, or ever feel for me, I want you to know this. I will be eternally grateful for this."

"I love Daniel. He is one of my best friends," she said softly.

"Yes, I know. And that is why you agreed to the marriage. Not for our child —you would have allowed him or her to have been born a bastard. And not because you love me. Ah, no, you can't love me, can you? I'm the enemy." His voice had a bitter sound to it.

"Jesse, what do you want from me?" she cried out softly. "You are the enemy. I don't know what I think or feel anymore."

"You're my wife now. You've vowed to love me, Kiernan. Love, honor, and obey, until death do us part."

"And this war, Jesse. And death could come too quickly."

"And if it did?" he queried her softly.

She didn't know what to answer him. They were married, they were having a child together. And they were traveling a countryside that was laden with danger. She wanted to tell him that she loved him. Pride and fear kept her silent.

"I'm just wondering, will you ever be my wife in truth? Will you ever get past the fact that I chose to serve the Union? Or have I now condemned us both?" Cobalt blue and probing, his eyes searched out hers. She still had no answer.

"Never mind, you've been brilliant, and I am more grateful than you'll ever know," he said with a weary sigh.

Suddenly a pain, deep and cutting and sweeping away her breath, seared into her lower back as they spoke. She almost gasped out loud, but she would not let him know her condition, not at this moment. With sheer will power she kept from crying out.

"We've Daniel to worry about," she said.

"Indeed, we do."

He turned from her and leapt into the wagon, hunkering down by his brother's side. He pulled away the covers, touched Daniel's cheek, and then found the pulse at his throat. Daniel's eyes flickered open. "How're you doing?" Jesse asked him huskily.

Daniel nodded, and asked for water. Jesse was prepared, finding a canteen beneath the covering. He let his brother sip the water, then he set the canteen aside. "Let me just see to the bandage," Jesse said.

Kiernan clamped her teeth shut as she saw the bandage that wound around Daniel's gut. Red was slowly staining it.

Daniel was pale, but remained conscious. He looked at his brother and grinned. "It's a dangerous region for a man in blue."

"He's right!" Kiernan murmured. "Jesse, you should put on something of Tyne's—"

"As soon as I take off this uniform, I'm a spy," Jesse said. "I'll wear my colors, thank you. Kiernan, get some water so that we can get going. Refill the canteen, please."

She took it from him as he handed it over, and turned awkwardly and hurried to meet the children by the stream.

When she came back, Jesse lifted her up beside Daniel once again.

"You'll be all right with him?" Jesse asked her.

"Fine," she replied briefly. He took his seat in front with Tyne. The reins cracked, and they were moving again.

She thought Daniel was sleeping, his lids were so low. Then he grinned. "I'm going to be an uncle?" he said softly.

"Yes."

"Did he do the right thing by you?"

"Yes," Kiernan replied, then lowered her head to speak to him with mock anger. "Thanks to you, Captain! It was the only way to get you out of the Yankee camp. You'd best get well after all this!"

Daniel grinned complacently. "Well, hell. I managed to make Jesse do the right thing after all. You two could have been a little easier on me, though. I had to get gut-shot for you two to tie the knot!"

Kiernan's quick retort was ready, but they moved over a pothole in the road and Daniel winced. She curled her fingers around his tightly. His eyes closed. Moments later, they opened again.

"Kiernan, your father . . ."

Her pulse quickened as his voice trailed away. "Daniel?" Her fingers tightened. "Daniel, my father! Have you heard something else?"

His eyes opened, just barely. "No, no, I haven't heard. But make sure Jesse stops by your place first. I'll make it. He's already pulled the bullet out of me, and I'm on the mend."

"Daniel, you're bleeding."

"And I'll bleed again before it's over, no doubt. Your place before ours, anyway. We'll see how John is doing, and we'll be just fine."

Torn between her father and Daniel, Kiernan looked across the wagon at Jacob. He shook his head miserably, having no help to give her. To complicate matters, she felt another searing pain. She stiffened, bracing her hand against her back, and resolved not to alarm the others.

Janey, looking at her, was about to speak. She knew what Kiernan was going through. Kiernan shook her head fiercely, and Janey closed her lips with disapproval.

Kiernan leaned back and felt the breeze bathe her face. The wagon jerked to a halt, and she heard Jesse swearing softly. Jacob, across from her, called out, "Rebs!"

"Jesu!" Kiernan whispered in panic. Their worst nightmare was now upon them.

"Hey, it's a Yank!" drawled a thick southern voice. "A go'darned Yank! You, Yank! Get out of that wagon. What you got in it?"

Kiernan struggled to look. With alarm, she saw they were surrounded by a party of five Rebs. The one speaking had ridden forward and close and was sneering at Jesse. There were too many of them! Without daring to think, she launched into a reckless speech. "He's got nothing in it! Nothing but an expecting wife and an injured man! Please, sir, let us pass—"

"Kiernan, shut up!" Jesse demanded furiously. He stood on the seat, one hand lightly on the Colt in the holster by his side, as he looked at the five rough-looking men in gray surrounding the wagon.

She stared at him blankly. "But, Jesse, if they only knew—"

"If they knew," Jesse informed her flatly, "they'd still be deserters, Kiernan! Now shut up and sit down!"

"Deserters!" the leader of the Rebs said in an irritated cry. "Yank, what are you—out here all alone?" Kiernan shuddered, studying the man. He was unshaven, and his uniform was muddied and dirtied. She suddenly sensed that Jesse was right. The man smiled at her. "Well now, there's a comely lass for you, even if she is in the family way!" He looked back to Jesse. "She'll be some lively sport once you're dead, Yank."

"Son of a bitch!" Daniel hissed softly at her side.

The Reb grinned and aimed his Enfield rifle at Jesse. But he never had a chance. Jesse moved like lightning with the Colt. Then he spun around and caught the second man in the hand. The third managed to get off a shot that sent the Colt spinning from Jesse's hand.

Kiernan screamed, but Jesse ignored her, leaping from the wagon with his saber drawn. The third Reb deserter didn't have a prayer of getting in a second shot with his muzzle-loading Enfield. He turned the weapon to use the bayonet, charging at Jesse. Jesse instantly parried the first blow—and the second, and the third. The two were quickly embroiled in a lethal and deadly dance.

The fourth man, shaking, took aim at Jesse's back. Kiernan cried out, but a shot rang out from behind her. She spun around. Daniel was up, and he'd fired at the man.

And hit his target clean through the heart.

Then Kiernan saw another man emerge from the trees. She jumped from the wagon, hurrying to find the Colt in the dirt. Her fingers had just closed around it when a booted foot landed hard upon her hand. She looked up to see a man looming over her, laughing. "Come on, boys, get the hell out of here before they shoot us all down!" the man called out. To Kiernan's horror, three more unshaven and muddied soldiers came crashing out of the trees. Jesse was engaged with two of them, while Daniel fought to keep shooting from the wagon.

"Get up!" the deserter raged at Kiernan. He reached down for her with his hand. She twisted and managed to kick him with all her strength in his groin. He screeched like a banshee, doubling over, then pulled a pistol from his belt and aimed it straight at her.

But he never fired.

His eyes widened, and he swirled about. Kiernan realized that Jesse was behind him, the point of his sword in the man's back. "Throw it down!" Jesse ordered, indicating the pistol.

The deserter refused. He lifted his arm to shoot Jesse, a cocky grin on his face. But Jesse's sword waved in the air like silver lightning. The man spun around again. He stared at Kiernan, stunned. A red stain was spreading across his chest. He fell down dead on top of her. She screamed wildly, and Jesse quickly shoved the man's body aside, reaching for her.

"Jesse!"

She crushed herself against him, her head next to his heart. She felt the pounding of his pulse, the heat of his body, and the tenderness of his hands as he stroked her hair.

"Jesse, get down!" Daniel shouted.

A shot rang out. Kiernan and Jesse spun to see another deserter Reb fall dead to the ground behind them. Jacob had taken the man with Daniel's service revolver.

Jacob leaped from the wagon and rushed to Kiernan's side. He led her away from Jesse, who strode off to search out the nearby trees.

"Is it the last of them?" he demanded of his brother.

Pale, Daniel nodded. "I wasn't a hell of a lot of help," he said.

"Damned good for an unconscious man," Jesse told him.

Daniel grinned weakly.

Kiernan started toward the wagon, leaning on Jacob, then staggered at the worst pain yet took hold of her. She couldn't help but cry out.

Jesse swung back, startled by her cry. With his sword still in his hand, he ran to take her from Jacob's hold and support her weight.

"Kiernan!"

"I'm fine," she insisted, and started for the wagon. But as she did, a shot rang out from the trees.

Jesse let out an oath, spun around on the dirt road, and fell flat.

Daniel instantly returned the fire, and a man fell out of a tree, stone dead before he hit the ground.

But Kiernan barely noticed him, for her eyes were upon Jesse lying in the dirt, his eyes closed. She threw herself down upon her knees beside him. Blood stained his arm and his chest, where his arm lay flung over it. "Jesse!" Tears running down her cheeks, she lifted his head into her lap, cradling it. "Jesse! Oh, my love! Where are you hit? Jesse, open your eyes! Damn you, Jesse! Just live! I'll be your wife in truth, I'll love you, I swear, I'll love, honor, and obey until death do us part. Oh, Jesse, I do love you. You can't leave me. Jesse, please, I love you. I love you so very much. I want to be your wife, to love you forever—"

Her words choked off as he opened his eyes and smiled at her. "Really?"

"Really. Jesse, just live!"

"You'll love me forever?"

"Forever!"

"Swear it?" he whispered huskily.

"I swear it!"

To her astonishment, he sat up. He pulled her into his arms and kissed her, and it was hardly the kiss of a dying man at all. He kissed her in the dusty roadway with fever and passion and tenderness, so much that she nearly returned the urgency of it, nearly forgot where they were.

She jerked away from him, staring at him hard.

He grinned ruefully. "I was only nicked by the bullet. See? It caught my arm here. Just a little bit of blood on my chest—"

"Oh, you blasted Yankee scoundrel!" Kiernan accused him.

His smile broadened. "That's fine, just as long as I know you'll love me forever."

"Jesse!"

"Horses!" Tyne called out.

Jesse leaped to his feet, pulling Kiernan up and pressing her body behind his. Tyne jumped down from the wagon, making a dive for the Colt.

"Tyne! Give it to me! If it's Rebs, they'll shoot you for having that weapon."

"Master Jess, I'm willing to fight for you."

"No, dammit man, you won't hang for me!" Jesse snatched the weapon from Tyne. With his sword in one hand and his pistol in the other, he shouted to his brother, "Daniel, get down!"

"No, damn you, Jess, I'll fight with you too!"

"It's Rebs!" Jacob cried out. "Look!"

Kiernan looked. Horsemen were coming, Rebel horsemen. They broke upon the road, a bearded cavalry captain with a company of twenty or so.

The bearded man reined in and raised a hand to stop the troops behind him. He saw the gray-clad men on the ground, then looked hard at Jesse.

"Well, Yank, what have we here?" the Rebel captain asked. His gaze took in Jesse's medical insignias—and the weapons he held with such menace.

He dismounted from his horse. Kiernan felt Jesse stiffen, felt his hand tighten around his sword.

"It seems that I have a prisoner, one who might well meet with a firing squad. Who in the hell are you, sir? What in God's name is a Yank doing in this neck of the woods? Colonel, you are mine!"

"I'm afraid I can't let you take me, Captain."

The captain's brows raised. "Sir? I seem to have the greater number, since you are dealing with a boy, a girl, two darkies, and a lady very far gone with child, it seems. Ma'am, I'll ask you to move away now."

Kiernan shook her head fiercely. She tried to step around in front of Jesse to protect him.

"Kiernan!" he thundered, stepping back around her, his sword flashing. "Sir, I repeat, I cannot allow myself to be taken." He actually grinned a reckless grin. "And I beg to differ with you, sir. I am an extraordinary swordsman, and the boy in the wagon is one of the best shots in the world, I dare say. As to the lady, here, why, she may well be the most dangerous of us all."

He was teasing her still, Kiernan thought. Tenderly, gallantly teasing, when they could no longer wage battle and win, when the odds against them were overwhelming. He intended to fight these men, until he could fight no longer.

"Wait!" she pleaded.

"Why, it's Greenbriar!" Daniel's voice called suddenly, interrupting her. Holding his gut, he had managed to stand up almost straight in the wagon.

The captain spun around. "Cameron!"

"In the flesh," Daniel grinned. "I'd stand with more ceremony to greet you, Greenbriar, if I could. But I'm in a rather sad position here. And this Yank—who *is* an extraordinary swordsman, by the way—is my brother, Jesse. He's also the best surgeon in or out of Virginia. Colonel Jesse Cameron, Captain Nathaniel Greenbriar, Virginia militia."

Greenbriar stared from Daniel to Jesse, and back to Daniel again. "Captain Cameron—just what is going on here?"

"I was shot up keeping the Yanks out of Richmond. Our troops were gone, and I looked up, and there was Jesse. So he spirited me across the river, and then my sister-in-law here made a timely arrival, and Jesse's been trying to get me home ever since. Greenbriar, it isn't a spying mission, I swear it. He's trying to take me home. You can't take a man in for that!"

Once again, Greenbriar looked from Daniel to Jesse, and back to Daniel again.

"Sir!" one of the men said from behind him.

"Yes, Potter, what is it?"

"That's Shelley on the ground there, sir. He deserted last month, raided the Halpren estate last week, and was accused of a lot more. We've been trying to chase him down for ages. He shot down three men in cold blood when they were trying to arrest him. Seems like this Yank did us a bit of a favor."

"Is that a fact?" Greenbriar said. He scratched his chin.

There didn't seem to be a breath of movement on the roadway. The leaves didn't rustle in the trees, and the stillness seemed to last forever.

Greenbriar moved at last. He mounted his horse. "Let's ride," he told his men.

"What about the Yank?" Potter asked.

"What Yank?" Greenbriar said. He set his heels to his horse's flanks and rode by.

All the Rebels rode by, looking straight ahead and seeing nothing in their path. Potter held back and spoke quickly to Daniel.

"That Yank who isn't here had best be gone within the next few minutes. We'll have to come back to bury that riff-raff, and I'm afraid of what will happen to him if we get a glimpse of him on the road again."

"He'll be gone," Daniel said. Potter smiled and rode off.

When he was gone, silence reigned once again. Kiernan was aware of the tension all about Jesse and in the air—and then the sweet explosion of it as they all realized they were safe.

"Jesu!" Daniel exclaimed. "We've made it!"

"Thank the good Lord!" Janey breathed.

Kiernan wanted to laugh and to hug Jesse. She wanted to hug Daniel, and she wanted to thank the good Lord too.

But it was all suddenly too much for her.

The light paled all around her, and she felt herself falling.

"Oh, Jesse!" she whispered as she toppled to the ground.

He swept her up and walked fast. She fought the darkness descending upon her and opened her eyes to his.

"Why the hell didn't you say something?" he demanded.

"About what?" she said weakly.

"You're having the baby now."

"I can't have the baby now. You have enough medical emergencies at the moment."

"Whether I do or don't, Kiernan, you're having the baby. And you'll have it right here on the road if we don't get moving!"

"No," she told him, her eyes were wide, dazzling and emerald on his. "I'm having the baby at Cameron Hall!" she insisted.

But then darkness did descend upon her, and for the moment, she could argue no more.

Twenty-four

*K*iernan awoke as an excruciating pain tore across her lower back and curled around to the front of her abdomen, as tight as an iron band about her. She awoke to the sound of her own scream, for the pain had taken hold of her so severely, she hadn't had the awareness to fight it.

"It's all right, Kiernan. It's all right. Hold my hand, and it will pass."

Fingers curled around hers. She heard the soft, husky sound of Jesse's voice, and she looked up quickly into his eyes. He was with her, a rueful, tender smile curved into his lips. He placed a cool damp cloth upon her brow.

They were home, she realized.

They had made it to Cameron Hall.

It was her home now. She was his wife, and they had made it. The child would be born here. She was lying on the huge four-poster bed in Jesse's bedroom. Beyond the windows she could see the gardens and the slope of the lawn. If she moved just a bit, she would probably be able to see all the way to the river.

The pain was easing. Even as he spoke, the pain was easing.

"Jesse, how long have I been out?" she whispered. Her lips and her mouth were so terribly dry. She was no longer clad in her cumbersome travel clothing and cape. She had been changed into a cool cotton nightgown with fine embroidered sleeves and a smocked bodice. She recognized the gown vaguely, then realized it was her own.

It wasn't one she had brought with her in the wagon. It had been brought from her own home on the peninsula.

She jerked up, grabbing Jesse by the shirt collar. "My father! Jesse, my father! Have you seen him? Is he well?"

He caught hold of her hands, pushing her back down.

"Kiernan—"

"Jesse!" she cried, pushing against his hold. Then, exhausted, she allowed him to push her back down.

"Kiernan, you're very close to giving birth to our child. You must relax and save your strength."

"Jesse—"

"Wait!" he told her firmly.

He walked across the hall to the door and threw it open. "John!"

Once again, Kiernan jerked up. "He's here? Can he walk?"

"What do you mean, 'Can he walk'?" John Mackay's voice boomed out to her. A second later, he was brushing past Jesse and coming to her bedside. "Ah, Kiernan, it's glad I am to see you lying there awake and aware now. I was worried half out of my mind when you were lying there so still." He perched at her bedside. Scanning her father's face anxiously, Kiernan decided that he was slimmer and his face was pale, but his eyes were bright and filled with mischief, and his grip upon her hand was strong.

"Oh, Papa, Christa sent word that you were sick."

"Yes, I was sick. Miss Christa Cameron was a saint, she was, keeping up with me. They've something of the healing touch in this family. I had a fever for days and days, it seemed, but she was patient as could be. And I was beginning to feel just as right as rain—until Jacob rode up on that horse of Jesse's to find out how I was faring. Then I heard about you, young woman!"

Kiernan swiftly lowered her lashes. After all she had done on her own, she felt like a chastised child. She realized that it was because she loved her father so, that she did not wish to disappoint him.

"Why, I was ready to run for my old shotgun, daughter, until I found out that the man had done right by you."

"John!" Jesse protested calmly, standing behind her father, "I'd gladly have done right by her long ago, had she ever given me half the chance."

"Right," John Mackay agreed. His cloud-blue eyes were on his daughter's. "Daughter, you might have written me!"

"I didn't want to hurt you!" she said. "But I was coming home—I've been trying to come home."

John Mackay grinned. "Kiernan, you have come home. Still! You should have had more faith in your old father. I'd not have been angry with you, ever, Kiernan."

"I love you so much, Papa."

"And I love you, daughter. But you shouldn't have come across country like that. Jesse says the baby is early. We'll pray that the little one is well. You shouldn't have caused that on my account."

"But I had to."

"And if I heard things right, it's well enough that you did. Daniel is here safe too. And you're a married woman again." He leaned close to her and winked. "Married to a Yank—but legally wed, and my grandchild will have a name. Mackay's a fine enough name for any man or woman, but a child wants his own father's name, and that's a fact."

"Oh, Papa—" she began, but she broke off, breathless, tensing and bracing against the pain. It was coming, and it was getting worse and worse.

She fought the urge to scream, grinding down on her teeth. Her fingers wound like steel around her father's. She was able to best the urge to scream out with the agony that assailed her, wrapping all the way around her again, but a whimper did escape her lips, and her father was quickly upon his feet.

"Jesse! Do something for her!"

"Sir, she's in labor. There's very little I can do."

"She's your wife, son!"

"And she's in labor."

He smiled when he sat beside her again. His fingers, so strong, gripped hers. "Kiernan, don't tense so—go easy, it will be all right. Breathe, my love, you're turning blue. You'll manage. I'm here with you."

The pain was blindingly intense. Tears sprang into her eyes, and she felt as if she were being cut in two. It went on and on.

"It's all right, Kiernan," Jesse soothed her.

"Go to hell, Jesse!" she whispered.

"Jesse," John Mackay began in distress.

"John, you'd better leave me with her now," Jesse said, grinning. "The baby will come very soon. Send Janey and Christa in, will you?"

Kiernan closed her eyes tightly. The pain was just beginning to fade.

"Right!" John said.

Jesse eased his fingers from Kiernan's and ripped back the covers. She started shivering fiercely. The pain had ebbed, but she was miserably cold.

"Jesse, give those back!" she pleaded.

"Kiernan, I need you to sit up more."

"Oh!" she screamed, startled when the pain seized her again so quickly. The last pain had barely ebbed away, but already the new one was upon her. It was strong, sweeping from her back to her front with near-blinding agony.

She seized hold of Jesse, gasping as an overwhelming desire to push suddenly mingled with the pain. "Jesse, the baby is here!"

"Wait, Kiernan, let me see. If you push too soon, you'll injure yourself!"

She fell back, feeling her cheeks flood with color. She felt so wretched. She was in such terrible agony, and Jesse was seeing her so huge and ungainly, and so intimately, at such a wretched time.

He moved to examine her, and she wrenched her knees together tightly.

"Kiernan, I'm your husband!" he told her.

"It hurts!"

"Well, of course it hurts—you're having a baby."

"Jesse—"

"I'm a doctor, Kiernan."

"You've never had a baby, so don't tell me how it feels!"

"Kiernan, please!" he whispered with exasperation.

To her distress another cry escaped, and she was certain that in a few minutes she would be a fountain of tears, it hurt so much. But he was beside her again, holding her in his arms, cradling her. "Kiernan, I love you. I don't know how it feels, but I've delivered other babies. I'm nervous about delivering my own, but I'm also ecstatic, Kiernan, because in just a few more minutes we can both cradle our child. Our child, Kiernan. A beautiful, precious new life, something wonderful that came from love, despite all the horror of war. Something that is love and defies the fact that life would call us enemies. Kiernan, trust me. I love you, with all of my heart. And I am doing my best for you and for our babe."

Tears glittered in her eyes, but she went easy in his arms. He started to push her back again. Then he whispered mischievously in her ear. "Besides, I've been between your thighs often enough before."

"Jesse!" she cried out.

But he laughed, and despite her refreshed anger, she was filled with new-found strength. She gritted her teeth against his touch when he examined her, and when she cried out that the pain was coming again and that she had to push, he cried out in turn, "The head is here! Just the tip, but it's here, Kiernan. Dark as a raven's wing. It's fine, Kiernan, push!"

Christa was up by her shoulders supporting her, while Janey waited to take the babe. Kiernan pushed and pushed and pushed, and the three of them encouraged her. Exhausted, she fell back. She cried out that she was too tired, that she couldn't go any further.

She told them all to go right to hell.

Jesse called out, "Kiernan, the head is free, our child is nearly born. Push again—hard!"

She pushed. She felt the child expulse from her body, and she was relieved and exhausted and ecstatic all at the same time. "Jesse!"

Everyone was silent. There was no cry. She pleaded, "Jesse, is the babe—"

She broke off as she heard a little cry at last, and Jesse was at her side, showing her the child. It was dark, as he had told her, slick from birth. But its little arms and legs were moving madly, and suddenly the babe wasn't giving out little cries—it was screaming.

"Oh!" she gasped in gratitude. "Jesse—"

"A little boy," he told her. "Mrs. Cameron, you have given me a son. I thank you with all my heart." He cut the cord swiftly, coming around to her.

He kissed her, his lips warm on hers. He placed the screaming bundle into her arms, and her arms closed around her child. She looked into the squalling little face that she and Jesse had created, and love surged through her that was deeper than any she had ever imagined.

"We've a son!" she said softly. She protested when Janey reached to take him away.

"He's got to be bathed, Miz Kiernan."

"And we've got to finish with you!" Jesse informed her. "You've torn, Kiernan. You need a few stitches."

"But I feel so good, Jesse!"

He laughed, and she leaned back, and she listened to Christa describe the baby. She didn't feel a bit of pain or unease while Jesse delivered the afterbirth and stitched her up. Christa held her bundled son, while Janey brought her water to bathe her face and a new nightgown. There seemed to be so very much activity, but when she tried to hold tight to Jesse again, he forced her back down. "Sleep, Kiernan."

"Jesse, he's so beautiful."

He kissed her brow. "Indeed, he is."

"I want to see him. I can't possibly sleep."

But even as she said it, an overwhelming exhaustion laid hold of her. Jesse pressed her back into the pillows. "How nice. For once, my love, you don't have the energy to fight me!"

She smiled, her eyes closed, and she slept.

She was awakened soon after she fell asleep, it seemed. Janey had brought her son, and he was squalling furiously. "He's very hungry," Janey told her.

Kiernan fumbled with her gown, then marveled that instinct showed her how to bring him to her breast. The first little tug he made upon her nipple brought a gasp to her lips. Then a sensation of wonder filled her.

She had married her enemy, and they'd had a child together, she mused.

And she'd never known such a sweet sensation of peace.

After a while, Janey took the baby from her and tiptoed away as she drifted off again.

When she awoke again, it was morning. Birds were chirping wildly, and the sun was streaming through the windows.

Patricia was at the foot of her bed in a rocking chair with the baby.

"Oh, Kiernan, he's just beautiful!"

"Is he? I think he is, but is he really, to everyone?"

"Exquisite!" Patricia told her. Kiernan smiled, and reached for him. She set him on the bed and unwrapped his blankets and cotton breeches and looked at him.

"He has all his fingers and toes," Patricia assured her. "He's just a little bit small, but that's because he's a little bit early. Jesse says he's well developed, though."

That was what mattered, Kiernan thought. She smiled. Her new son was staring at her. His eyes, for the moment, were bright blue. His cheeks were perfectly rounded and flushed. His lips had a sweet pucker, and his hair, cleaned and dried, was raven black. "He's a Cameron, all right," Kiernan murmured. She looked at Patricia, feeling a twinge of guilt. But Patricia's warm brown eyes were filled with nothing but tenderness as she studied the baby. "He looks just like Jesse."

The baby's face screwed up into a scowl, and he let out a fierce scream. Kiernan laughed. "Sounds like him, too, doesn't he?"

"Are you casting aspersions on my brother?" a masculine voice asked.

Kiernan looked up. Daniel was standing in the doorway. He was pale, but he seemed stronger.

She let out a little cry and slipped from bed herself. She winced as she realized that it wasn't easy to walk, and he scolded her for getting up just as she scolded him.

"Daniel, you should be in bed!"

"Kiernan, you get back in there!"

They laughed, and then she hugged him carefully. He placed a kiss on her forehead.

"Daniel, are you going to be all right?" she asked anxiously.

He nodded. "I'm going back to bed. I just wanted to tell you that my nephew is beautiful."

She nodded, meeting his eyes, and bit her lower lip. "He's part Yankee," she said, "but I love him anyway."

"Yes," Daniel said with a soft sigh and a slow smile. "His dad is a Yank, and I love him anyway."

"So do I," Kiernan admitted.

Daniel grinned. "Good. Now get back to bed, and I'll do the same."

Kiernan did so. She and Patricia played with the baby, and Kiernan nursed her son again. Then Janey brought her breakfast. She was ravenous. Her father came to see his new grandson, and Jacob came, and even Jacob admitted that for a little thing, he was a fine-looking boy.

Everyone had come—except Jesse.

"Where is he?" Kiernan asked Christa.

"Oh! He was down in the office. I imagine he fell asleep down there. I'll go see."

"No," Kiernan said, "I'll go."

"Wait!" Christa protested. "He'll be furious that you're up."

"I feel very well, and I'll be good like Daniel and come right back to bed. But I want to see him now."

Christa worried that Kiernan might not be able to walk down the stairs, but

Kiernan insisted on brushing her hair and donning a clean gown. She studied her reflection in the mirror, watching Christa's secret smile as their eyes met in the glass.

She left the room and went to the portrait gallery. She smiled up at the handsome faces of the Cameron men and the beautiful faces of their women. "I really have come home!" she whispered. She smiled, and wondered if any of the Camerons past smiled in return.

Kiernan carefully descended the stairs. She was weak, she realized, and she would have to be very careful. But she was filled with a certain energy too. She had to see Jesse.

She passed the parlor and came to the door of the office and looked in. Jesse was indeed there, his feet up on the desk.

His head was back against the edge of the captain's chair, and his eyes were closed. His white shirt was open at the collar. He had bathed during the night, and he was dressed in civilian trousers and a simple cotton shirt.

He was sound asleep.

She bit into her lip, thinking that she should leave him undisturbed.

He had to go back to the war, and he needed his sleep. He'd certainly had enough family crises to deal with.

But he was going to go away again.

And because of that she had to have this time with him.

She stepped into the room, closing the door behind her. As she did, his eyes opened. He frowned when he saw her. "Kiernan! What are you doing up?"

She walked over to the desk and discovered that she was suddenly shy.

After all of this, she thought.

All the years, and all their times together.

And now, the birth of their child.

She stopped in front of the desk. "Jesse, I had to see you." Suddenly, she could say no more.

He stood, his boots falling hard on the floor. He walked quickly around the desk, sweeping her up into his arms. And he carried her back around with him, holding her tightly against himself as he took a seat in the captain's chair once again.

"Did I thank you sufficiently for my son?" he asked her softly.

She nodded. "Oh, Jesse, did I thank you?"

He laughed. "The pleasure was all mine."

She flushed, but laughed along with him. "Oh, Jesse!" She wanted to say more—there was so much to say. She set her fingers against the tight black curls where his shirt lay open against his chest. She whispered, "It all came out right! Daniel is home, and he looks wonderful. I know he's going to be fine."

This time, she thought. The war was still going on. But she was careful not to say it.

Like Jesse, Daniel would go back to it.

She refused to worry about it now. "My father is well, Jesse. And we've a son. He is small, but he seems so wonderful too." She was suddenly speaking very quickly. "I'm even glad he's a boy. Girls are wonderful children, too, of course, I've learned that with Patricia. Would you have minded a girl?"

"I'd have loved a little girl," Jesse told her solemnly. "Except that I suppose I am pleased we had a son." He smoothed her hair back from her forehead.

"We're still at war. I on my side, and Daniel on his. I'm pleased, for I know that my father would be glad, and his father. Since . . ."

His voice trailed away. "Since the Cameron name will go if you and Daniel are both killed?" Kiernan said, her voice breaking.

Jesse tightened his arms around her. "I love you so much, Kiernan. I've loved you for years. I've been thinking all night. I've always believed that I had to fight for what my conscience dictates to be right. But I love you so much, Kiernan, I'll resign my commission. I can't fight for the South, but we'll go to England if you want, or maybe we could head west, or—"

She pressed her fingers against his lips. Tears came to her eyes and fell. "Jesse, you would do that? For me?"

He smiled, slowly, crookedly. "I would lay down my life, my heart, my soul —everything."

She shook her head vehemently. "Oh, Jesse!"

"Can you love me, Kiernan? I am a Yank at heart, dressed in blue."

"I do love you, Jesse, so much. And once it worried me, that I could love a Yankee so thoroughly, so desperately, so completely. But a friend told me something once. He said that I don't love a Yankee, I love a man. And I do, Jesse, I love you. And the color that you wear can't change the man that you are. I love that man."

His lips found hers, and he kissed her. It was a long kiss, warm, flamed by passion, held in check by the depths of tenderness that overrode all else.

When he broke away from her, her eyes were dazzling upon his. She smiled. "I don't want to go west, Jesse. And I don't want to go to England."

He frowned, his blue eyes very sharp, his raven dark hair disheveled upon his brow. She smiled, loving him so.

"Jesse, you're a doctor, and a good one—no, you're the very best. You save lives, you don't take them. I know that you'd feel as if you'd betrayed your calling if you didn't go back."

"Kiernan—"

"I'm not changing sides, Jesse. No one can change their heart. The war will go on until someone wins it. And if you're posted in Washington again, I'll come there. I won't spy ever again—I'll promise you that. The other day, you asked me for a truce. A separate peace. And that's what I want now, Jesse. A separate peace."

He smiled, and once again he kissed her. He kissed her warmly and deeply. He kissed her with remarkable tenderness, and he kissed her so long that she grew dizzy, feeling a sweet delirium sweep over her. And at last his lips lifted from hers.

He stood up, holding her securely in the strength of his arms. Brilliant blue eyes blazed down into hers, and he smiled. "A separate peace, Mrs. Cameron, is so declared. Now, let's go to see to young Master John Daniel Cameron."

"John Daniel Cameron?" she queried.

"Do you like it?" he asked.

She leaned back in his arms, delighted, secure. "I love it," she assured him, and she curled her arms around his neck. "Just as I love his father!"

Jesse smiled again, tenderly, then turned.

They left the office behind, and Jesse climbed the stairs with her in his arms.

They passed by the watchful eyes of the Camerons in the portrait galley until they came to the master bedroom once again.

And there they doted upon the newest Cameron.

The cannons of war raged on, but Jesse and Kiernan had indeed found their separate peace.

And One Wore Gray

Dedication

As this is a sequel, I would like to dedicate it to those same people who were so helpful and kind when I began my imaginings for One Wore Blue—*Mr. and Mrs. Stan Haddan, Shirley Dougherty, Dixie, and the many wonderful people of Harpers Ferry and Bolivar, West Virginia. Also, the National Park Service guides who have been so helpful over the years, very especially those at Gettysburg, Harpers Ferry, and Sharpsburg.*

As this April marks my tenth anniversary with Dell Publishing, I would also like to dedicate this book to some of the very wonderful people there—to my editor, Damaris Rowland, who is simply wonderful in all things. To Carole Baron, for being both an incredible businesswoman and a more incredible human being. To Leslie, Tina, Jackie, and Monica, and to extraordinary art and marketing departments. To Barry Porter—who will always be "Mr. Romance." To Michael Terry and Reid Boyd—for having been there the longest! To Sally and Marty, thank you—actually, Toto, that was Kansas!

And very especially to Mr. Roy Carpenter, for being such a wonderful salesman, and fine gentleman.

And last, but never, never least! To Kathryn Falk on the tenth anniversary of Romantic Times*! Congratulations, and thank you, thank you, to Kathryn, Melinda, Kathe, Mark, Michael, Carol, and everyone at R.T.*

Prologue

CALLIE

July 4, 1863
Near Sharpsburg
Maryland

Beneath the light of a lowering sun, sometimes brilliant and some-times soft, the woman at the well beside the whitewashed farm house seemed like a breath of beauty. Her hair, a deep rich auburn, caught the light. At times it shimmered russet, and at times it was softer, deeper, like the warm sable coloring of a mink. It was long and free, and cascaded around her shoulders like a fall, framing a face of near perfect loveliness with its wide-set gray eyes, fine high cheekbones, and full, beautifully shaped mouth. A hint of sorrow touched the curve of her lip, and rose to haunt her eyes, but that very sorrow seemed to add to her beauty. Against the ending light of the day, she was a reminder of all things that had once been fine and beautiful, just like an angel, a small glimpse of heaven.

She stood there clean and fragrant, and though simply dressed, she seemed an incongruous bit of elegance as she watched and waited while they came.

And come, they did. Endlessly.

Like a long slow, undulating snake, they came, hundreds of men, thousands of men, the butternut and gray of their tattered uniforms as dismal as the terrible miasma of defeat that seemed to hover about them. They came on horses, and they came on foot. They came with their endless wagon train that stretched, one weary soldier had told Callie, for nigh onto seventeen miles.

They were the enemy.

But that mattered little as she watched these men now, for she was surely in no danger from them.

There was only one rebel who could frighten her, she thought fleetingly. Frighten her, excite her, and tear at her heart. That rebel would not be passing by. He could not be passing by now, for he had not fought in the battle. The war had ended for him. He awaited its conclusion behind the walls and bars of Old Capitol Prison.

If he were free, she thought, she would not be standing here, by the well, watching this dreadful retreat. If there had been any chance of his being among these wretches, she would have run far away long before now. She would have never dared to stay here, offering cool sips of water to his defeated countrymen.

He would no longer be the enemy just because he wore a different color. He would be the enemy because he would seek her out with cold fury, with a vengeance that had had endless nights to simmer and brew in the depths of his heart.

It was her fault that he lived within those walls and behind those bars and fences while his beloved South faced this defeat.

If he were free, it would not matter if she tried to run or hide. He had told her he would come for her and that there would be nowhere for her to run.

She shivered fiercely, her fingers tightening around the ladle she dipped into the deep bucket of sweet cool well water for each of the poor wretches who strayed from the great wagon train to come her way.

He had sworn that he would come back for her. She could still hear his voice, hear the deep, shattering fury in what he thought had been her betrayal.

Even if these men marching by were the enemy, they brought nothing but pity to her heart. Their faces, young and old, handsome and homely, grimed with sweat and mud and blood, bore signs of exhaustion that went far beyond anything physical. Their anguish and misery showed in their eyes, which were like the mirrors of their souls.

They were retreating.

It was summer, and summer rain had come, turning the rich and fertile earth to mud. By afternoon, the summer heat had lessened, a gentle breeze was stirring, and it seemed absurd that these ragged and torn men, limping, clinging to one another, bandaged, bruised, bloody and broken, could walk over earth so beautiful and green and splendid in its cloak of summer.

The great winding snakelike wagon train itself had not come close to Callie's farmhouse. Stragglers wandered by. Infantry troops, mostly.

It was the Fourth of July, and on this particular Fourth of July, the citizens of the North were at long last jubilant. Over the last few days, around a sleepy little Pennsylvania town called Gettysburg, the Union forces had finally managed to give the Confederates a fair licking. Indeed, the great and invincible General Robert E. Lee, the Southern commander who had earned a place in legend by running the Union troops into the ground in such cities as Chancellorsville and Fredericksburg and numerous others, had invaded the North.

And he had been thrust back.

"It were over shoes, mum," a Tennessee fellow had told her, gratefully accepting the cool dipper of water. He was a man of medium height and medium weight with thick dark hair on his head and a full, overgrown beard and mustache. He wasn't wearing much of a uniform, just worn mustard-colored trousers and a bleached cotton shirt. His bedroll and few belongings were tied around his chest, his worn hat sported several bullet holes. "We were on our way to attack Harrisburg, but we needed shoes. Someone said there were shoes aplenty in Gettysburg, and first thing you know, on the first of July, there's a skirmish. Strange. Then all the southern forces were moving in from the North, and all the northern forces were moving in from the South. And by nightfall on the third of July . . ." His voice trailed away. "I ain't never seen so many dead men. Never." He wasn't looking at her. He was staring into the bottom of the ladle, and his gaze seemed hopeless.

"Maybe it means that the war will be over soon," Callie said softly.

He looked up at her again. Reaching out suddenly, he touched a stray wisp of her hair. She jumped back and he quickly apologized. "Sorry, ma'am. You standing here being so kind and all, I don't mean no disrespect. It's just that you're nigh onto one of the most beautiful women I've ever seen, and it's just making me think awfully hard of home. Your hair's just as soft as silk. Your face is an angel's. And it's just been so long . . . well, thank you, ma'am. I've got to keep on moving. Maybe I will get home soon enough." He handed her the dipper and started walking again. He paused and looked back. "I don't expect the war will be over any too soon. Your general in charge—Meade is his name these days, I think—he should have followed after us. He should have come now, while we're hurt and wounded. Even an old wolf knows to go after a lame deer. But Meade ain't following. Give our General Bobby Lee a chance, and he runs with it. No, the war ain't going to end too soon. You take care, ma'am. You take great care."

"You too!" she called after him. He nodded, smiled sadly, and was gone.

The next man who passed her by had a greater story of woe.

"Ma'am, I am lucky, I am, to be alive. I was held back 'cause of this lame foot of mine here, took a bullet the first day. Comes July third, and General Lee asks us can we break the Union line at the stone wall. General George Pickett is given the order. Ma'am, there ain't another man in my company, hell, maybe in my whole brigade, left alive. Thousands died in minutes." He shook his head, and seemed lost. "Thousands," he repeated. He drank from the dipper, and his hands, covered in the tattered and dirty remnants of his gloves, shook. He handed her back the dipper. "Thank you, ma'am. Thank you most kindly, ma'am."

He, too, moved on.

The day passed. The long, winding wagon train of Lee's defeated troops continued to weave its way over the Maryland countryside. Even though Callie was appalled by the stories told her by each weary man, she still held her ground. She already knew something of the horror of the battlefield, for less than a year ago, the battle had come here. Men in blue and in butternut and gray had died upon this very earth.

And he had come to her. . . .

She dared not think of him. Not today.

She lingered by the well, but toward the late afternoon Jared began to cry, and she went into the house to tend to him.

He slept again, and she returned to the well, entranced by the flow of time.

Dusk came. And still the men continued to trickle by. She heard about strange places where battle had raged. Little Roundtop, Big Roundtop, Devil's Den. All places where men had fought valiantly.

Darkness fell. Since all who had passed her way had been on foot, Callie was surprised to hear the sound of horses' hooves. A curious spiraling of unease swept down her spine, then she breathed more lightly as she saw a young blond horseman approach. He dismounted from his skinny roan horse and walked her way, thanking her even before he accepted the dipper she offered out to him.

"There is a God in heaven! After all that I have seen, still I have here to greet me the beauty of the very angels! Thank you, ma'am," he told her, and she smiled even as she trembled, for in his way, he reminded her of another horseman.

"I can offer you nothing but water," she said. "Both armies have been through here, confiscating almost everything that resembles food."

"I gratefully accept your water," he told her. He took a sip and pushed back his hat. It was a gray felt cavalry hat, rolled up at the brim.

It, too, brought back memories. "Are you a southern sympathizer, ma'am?"

Callie shook her head, meeting his warm brown eyes levelly. "No, sir. I believe in the sanctity of the Union. But more than anything these days, I just wish that the war would be over."

"Amen!" the cavalryman muttered. He leaned against the well. "With many more battles like this one . . ." He shrugged. "Ma'am, it was horror. A pure horror. Master Lee was fighting a major one for the first time without Stonewall Jackson at his side. And for once, Jeb Stuart had us cavalry just too far in advance to be giving Lee the communication he needed." He sighed and dusted off his hat. "We wound up engaged in a match with a Union General, George Custer. Can you beat that? Heck, my brother knew Custer at West Point. He came in just about last in his class, but he managed to hold us up when he needed to. 'Course, he didn't stop us. Not my company. I've been with Colonel Cameron since the beginning, and nothing stops him. Not even death I daresay, because Cameron just plain refuses to die. Still—"

"Cameron?" Callie breathed, interrupting him.

The cavalryman started, arching a brow at her. "You know the colonel, ma'am?"

"We've—met," Callie breathed.

"Ah, then you do know him! Colonel Daniel Derue Cameron, he's my man. Never seen a fiercer man on horseback. I hear he learned a lot from the Indians. He's not one of the officers who sits back and lets his men do the fighting. He's always in the thick of it."

Callie shook her head. "But—but he's in prison!" she protested.

The cavalryman chuckled. "No, ma'am, no way. They tried to hold him in Washington, but they didn't keep him two full weeks. He was wounded at the Sharpsburg battle here, but he healed up and come right out, escaped under those Yankee guards' noses. Hell, no, ma'am—pardon my language, it's been a while since I've been with such gentle company. Colonel Cameron has been back since last fall. He has led us into every major battle. Brandy Station, Chancellorsville, Fredericksburg. He's been there. He'll be along here soon enough."

She felt as if the night had gone from balmy warmth to a searing, piercing cold. She wanted to speak, but she felt as if her jaw had frozen. She wanted desperately to push away from the well, and to start to run. But suddenly, she could not move.

The cavalryman didn't seem to notice that anything was amiss. He didn't realize that her heart had ceased to beat—then picked up a pulse that thundered at a frantic pace. He didn't seem to realize that she had ceased to breathe and then begun to gulp in air, as if she would never have enough of it again.

Daniel was free. He had been free for a long, long time. He had been in the South. He had been fighting the war, just as a soldier should be fighting the war.

Perhaps he had forgotten. Perhaps he had forgiven.

No. Never.

"I've got to move on," the cavalryman told her. "I thank you, ma'am. You've been an angel of mercy within a sea of pain. I thank you."

He set the dipper on the well. Bowed down and weary, he walked on, leading his horse.

Callie felt the night air on her face, felt the breeze caress her cheeks.

And then she heard his voice. Deep, low, rich. And taunting in both timbre and words.

"Angel of mercy indeed. Is there, perhaps, a large quantity of arsenic in that well?"

Once again, her heart slammed hard against her chest. Then she could not feel it at all.

He was alive, and he was well. And he was free.

He had been there a while, just past the fence, beyond the range of her sight. He had dismounted, leading his horse, a gray Thoroughbred that had once been a very fine mount but now resembled all the other creatures of the Confederacy —too gaunt, with great big haunted brown eyes.

Why was she looking at the horse?

Daniel was there.

He hadn't changed. He still towered over her, clad in a gray frock coat with a pale yellow sash looped around his waist, his sword at his side, buckled on by his scabbard. He wore dun trousers and high black cavalry boots, muddy and dusty boots that were indeed the worse for wear.

He wore a cavalry hat. It was rolled at the brim, pulled low over his eye, with a jaunty plume waving arrogantly from the top, laced to the hat at the narrow gold band around it.

She no longer gazed at his clothing, but met his eyes.

Those blue eyes she had never been able to forget. A blue framed by ebony dark lashes and high arched brows. A startling, searing, blue. A blue that penetrated her flesh with its fire, a blue that pierced into her, that raked her from head to toe. A blue that assessed, that judged, that condemned. That burned and smoldered with a fury that promised to explode.

They stared out at her from a face made lean by war, a handsome face made even more so by the lines of character now etched within it. His flesh was bronzed from his days in the saddle. His nose was dead straight, his cheekbones broad and well set. His lips were generous, sensual, and curled now in a crooked, mocking smile that nowhere touched his eyes.

"Hello, angel," he said softly. His voice was a drawl, a sound she had never forgotten.

She mustn't falter, she musn't fail. She wasn't guilty, though he would never believe her. It didn't matter. She simply could never surrender to him, because he did not understand surrender himself.

Breathe! she commanded herself, breathe! Give no quarter, for it will not be given you. Show no fear, for he will but leap upon it. He is a horse soldier, and so very adept at battle.

But still her fingers trembled upon the ladle. Lightning seemed to rake along her spine, and at first, it was not courage that held her so very still and seemingly defiant before him. She was simply frozen there by fear.

She had always known that she would see him again. There had been nights when she had lain awake, praying that when that time came, all that had gone so very wrong between them might be erased. Many a night she had dreamed of him, and in those dreams she had savored again the taste of the sweet splendor and ecstasy that had been theirs so briefly, once upon a time.

She would never be able to convince him of the truth. So very little had been left to her in this war. But she still had her pride, and it was something that she must cling to. She'd never beg.

Or perhaps she would, if it could do her any good! But it would not, and so she would not sacrifice her pride. The war, it seemed, had stripped all mercy from him. She wanted to be as cold as he was.

She wished that she had betrayed him. With all her heart, at that moment, she wished that she could hate him with the same fury and vengeance he seemed to send her now.

Angel, he had called her. With venom, with mockery. With loathing. Surely the word had never been spoken with such a tone of malice.

"Cat got your tongue?" he said, his tone still soft, his Virginia drawl deep and cultured—and taunting. "How very unusual. Weren't you expecting me?"

He seemed taller even as he stepped nearer to her, leading his gray horse. Despite his leanness, his shoulders seemed broader than ever, his size even more imposing, his supple grace of movement more menacing.

Run! Run now! Blind instinct warned her.

But there was nowhere to run.

He was a gentleman, she reminded herself. An officer, a horseman. One of the last of the cavaliers, as the Southerners liked to call their cavalry. He had been raised to revere women, to treat them kindly. He had been raised to prize his honor above all else, taught that pride and justice and duty were the codes by which he must live.

He had been taught mercy . . .

But no mercy lingered in his eyes as they fell upon her now. She nearly screamed as he reached toward her, but no sound came.

He didn't touch her but merely pulled the dipper from her hand, and sank it into the bucket. He drank deeply of the fresh well water.

"No poison? Perhaps some shards of glass?" he murmured.

He stood just inches from her. The world around her was eclipsed.

For a fleeting moment, she was glad. She had thought him in prison, but she had believed, always, that he lived. No matter what he thought, what he believed, she had desperately desired that he live. Swiftly, sweetly, in a strange shining hour that had passed between them, she had loved him.

No color of cloth, no label of "enemy," no choice of flag to follow could change what dwelt so deeply in her heart.

She had loved him through the long months of war. Loved him even while the belief of her betrayal found root in his heart, nurtured by the vicious months of war. She had loved him, she had feared him, and now he stood before her again. So close that she could feel the wool of his coat. So very close indeed that she could feel the warmth of his body, breathe in the scent of him. He had not changed. Lean and gaunt and ragged in his dress, he was still beautiful. Handsome in his build and stature, noble in his expression.

He came closer still. Those blue eyes were like the razor-sharp point blade of his sword as they touched her. His voice was husky, low and tense and trembling with the heat of his emotion.

"You look as if you're welcoming a ghost, Mrs. Michaelson. Ah, but then, perhaps you had wished that I would be a ghost by now, long gone, dust upon the battlefield. No, angel, I am here." He was still as several seconds ticked slowly past, as the breeze picked up and touched them both. He smiled again. "By God, Callie, but you are still so beautiful. I should throttle you. I should wind my fingers right around your very beautiful neck, and throttle you. But even if you fell, you would torture me still!"

He hadn't really touched her. Not yet. And she couldn't afford to let him. She squared her shoulders, determined to meet his eyes, praying that she would not falter.

"Colonel, help yourself to water, and then, if you will, ride on. This is Union territory, and you are not welcome."

To her amazement, he remained there, standing still. His brows arched as she pushed him aside and walked past him. Inwardly she trembled, her show of bravado just that—a show. But there was no surrender in this. That had long ago been decided between them. Regally, she walked on. She would not run. Head high, she continued toward the house.

"Callie!"

He cried out her name. Cried it out with fury and with anguish.

The sound of his voice seemed as if to touch her. To rip along her back, to pierce into her heart and soul and bring both fear and longing.

It was then that she suddenly began to run. She couldn't look back. She had to reach the house.

She picked up her skirts and scurried across the dusty yard toward the rear porch. She leapt up the steps, ran across the wood planks and through the back door. She leaned against it, her heart leaping.

"Callie!"

His voice thundered out her name again. She gasped and jumped away from the door, for he was hammering it down with the weight of his shoulders.

He had warned her.

There would be no place to run.

No place to hide.

She backed away from the door, gnawing on her knuckles. There had to be some place to hide!

He couldn't strangle her. It might be war, but Rebel soldiers didn't strangle Yankee women. What would he do to her?

She didn't want to know.

"Daniel, go away! Go home, go back to your men, to your army—to your South!"

The door burst open. He stood there staring at her once again, and there was no taunting in his eyes now, or in his smile.

"What? Are there no troops close enough to come to your rescue once you've seduced me into your bed this time?"

She had never, never seduced him!

There was a coffee cup upon the kitchen table. Her fingers curled around it and she hurled it at him. "Go away!" she commanded him.

He ducked, ably avoiding the coffee cup.

"Go away?" he repeated. "How very rude, Mrs. Michaelson! When I have waited all these months to return? I lay awake nights dreaming for a chance to come back to your side. What a fool I was, Callie! And still, I suppose I did not learn."

He stepped into the kitchen, swept his hat from his head, and sent it flying onto the kitchen table. "Well, I have come back, angel. And I'm very anxious to pick up right where I left off. Let's see, where was that? Your bedroom, I believe. Ah, that's right. Your bed. And let's see, just how were we situated?"

"Get out of my house!" Callie snapped.

"Not on your life," he promised. He smiled again, a bitter, self-mocking curl. "Not, madam, on your life!"

He strode toward her, and a sizzling fear suddenly swept through her. He wouldn't really hurt her, she assured herself. He'd never really hurt her. Not Daniel. He'd threaten, he'd taunt, but he'd never really hurt her. . . .

But she couldn't let him touch her. She couldn't want him again. She couldn't fall again!

"Don't!" she warned.

"This is one invasion of the North that is going to be successful," he warned her, his tone bringing shivers down her spine. He smiled, relentlessly coming toward her, his eyes ruthless as they fixed upon hers.

Callie knocked a chair into his path. He barely noticed.

"Don't, damn you! You have to listen to me—" she began.

"Listen to you!" he exclaimed. She heard the sound of his fury explode in his voice. "Callie, time is precious! I have not come to talk this night. I listened to you once before."

"Daniel, don't come any nearer. You must—"

"I must finish what you started, Callie. Then maybe I can sleep again at night."

He reached for her arm and the fire in his eyes seemed to sizzle through the length of her. She didn't know him anymore. Or had she ever really known him? In his eyes she could see the effect of his days in the prison camp and even the days beyond. She had not imagined that he might be so ruthless. She still did not know how far he could go.

"Daniel, stop!" she hissed. She jerked free of his hold upon her arm, turned, and ran.

He was on her heels, not racing, just following her.

Relentlessly.

She stopped and found a vase and tossed it his way. He ducked again, and the vase crashed against a wall. She tore through the parlor, looking for more missiles. A shoe went flying his way, a book, a newspaper. Nothing halted his stride.

She reached the stairs, and he was there behind her. She started to race up them and realized her mistake. He was behind her. She reached the landing. When she paused to catch her breath, his fingers entwined in her hair, and she was wrenched back and swept into his arms. Struggling wildly, beating her fists against his chest, she met his eyes. For a moment she was still, breathing hard, her breasts heaving with her exertion.

"Let's finish what we started, shall we, angel?"

"Let me go!" Callie demanded. Tears stung her eyes. He was alive; he held her again. So many days and nights of dreams and memories had passed her by. If only he could be made to understand, if only she could see his smile, hear his laughter once again.

If only he could believe her.

But he would never understand, and there was nothing left for her but the violence and the fury in his eyes.

"Let you go?" he repeated, his tone bitter. "Once I tried to walk away. To honor both North and South, and everything that we both held sacred. But you raced after me, angel. You could not bear to have me leave. You wanted me to stay here. Remember, Mrs. Michaelson? Here."

He walked again, carrying her into her room. A second later she found herself falling, cast down with very little care or tenderness onto the bed. She struggled to rise, her heart beating furiously. She wanted to fight him with a vengeance, and she hated the excitement that was snaking its way into her limbs.

Did it matter? Did anything matter when he was alive, when he had returned? When she could reach out her arms and hold him once again. When the night could sweep them into fields of ecstasy where there was no North and no South and where the sounds of roaring cannons and rifle fire could not intrude. Sweet, magical places where there was no black powder to singe the air, no pain of death, no anguish of defeat.

No! She could not hold him, she could give nothing to him, take nothing from him, for he sought not love, but vengeance. He had sworn once that he would never hurt her, and she had to believe in that vow, for in his present ruthless mood, she had no way to fight him.

"Don't!" she commanded. "Don't even think—"

But he was suddenly straddled over her, stripping off his mustard gauntlets to catch her wrists where she pressed against him.

"Just what am I thinking, Callie?" he demanded.

She lay silent, watching his eyes. There was no mercy within them. Hard and brilliantly blue, they impaled her where she lay upon the pillow. She had no choice but to fight him, and fight him with equal fervor.

"I don't know. What are you thinking?" she asked, gritting her teeth.

"Ah, if the Yanks but had you in the field!" he murmured. "Maybe you are recalling the last time we met. It was right here. I'll never forget, because I loved this room from the first time I saw it. I loved the dark wood of the furniture, and the soft white of the curtains and the bed. And I loved the way that you looked here. I'll never forget your hair. It was like a sunset spread across the pillow. Sweet and fragrant, and so enticing. Newly washed, like silk. I can't forget your eyes. I can go on, Callie. There's so much that I never forgot. I remembered you in camp, and I remembered you every moment that I planned and plotted an escape. I thought of your mouth, Callie. It's a beautiful mouth. I thought of the way that you kissed me. I thought of your lovely neck, and the beauty of your breasts. I thought of the feel of your flesh, and the movement of your hips. Over and over and over again. I remembered wanting you like I'd never wanted anything or anyone before in my life. Of feeling more alive than ever before just because I breathed in the scent of you as I lay against your breast. And when you touched me, I think I came closer to believing I had died and gone to heaven than I've ever done upon a battlefield. Damn you! I was in love with you. In the midst of chaos, I was at peace. I believed in you, and dear God, when I lay here with you, I even believed in life again. What a fool I was!"

"Daniel—" Callie said, desperate to explain.

"No! Don't!" he said coldly. His fingers shook as they grasped her wrists. She felt the terrible tension in his limbs as his thighs tightened around her. Her heartbeat lifted and soared further. "Don't!" he insisted again. "Don't tell me anything. Don't give me any protestations of innocence. I'll tell you what I've thought over all these months. I've thought that you were a spy, and that you deserved the fate of a spy. I thought about choking the life out of you." He released her wrists. His knuckles moved slowly up and down the column of her throat. She didn't move. She didn't dare breathe. In fascination, in dread, she listened as he continued to speak. "But I could never do it," he said quietly. "I could never wind my fingers around that long white neck. I could never do anything to mar that beauty. Then I thought that you should be hanged, or that you should be shot. Through long dark nights, Callie, I thought about all of these things. . . . But do you know what I thought about most of all?"

His face had lowered against hers. Taut, bitter, hard. She should have fought him then. Fought him while she was nearly free.

But she did not. She stared at him and at the eyes that held hers so fiercely and passionately. "What?" she whispered.

"I thought about being here with you. I thought about this bed. I thought about your naked flesh, and I thought about your smile when it seemed that you poured yourself upon me, heart, soul, and body. I thought about the way that your eyes could turn silver. I thought that all I wanted was to be back here."

His fingers moved suddenly upon the lace of her bodice. And still Callie didn't move. Not until he spoke again.

"I wondered what it would be like to have you when I hated you every bit as much as I had once loved you," he said softly.

At last, too late, she came to life. She tried to strike his face, but he caught her wrist. "Hate me, then, you fool!" she told him heatedly. "Give me no chance, no leave, no grace, no mercy—"

"Were I to give you more mercy, I might as well shoot myself, madam!" he swore.

"You self-righteous bastard!" she charged him. "Hate me and I will despise you. You were the enemy! You are the enemy! This is Union soil! God damn you for expecting more from me," Callie swore. Enraged beyond all reason, she managed in a fierce and violent burst of energy to twist away from beneath him.

He moved like lightning, dragging her back down. Gasping, struggling wildly, she fought him, until her breath left her, until she was caught and spent. She stared hatefully up into his eyes again.

Her situation was worse, for now the length of him lay against her, and all the fever and the fury and the heat that had burned and built so long within him seemed to encompass her.

"Here we are, Callie. You'll not leave me tonight. And you'll not betray me," he whispered fiercely.

"And you'll not have me!"

"I will."

"It would be—rape!" she spat out.

"I doubt it."

"Oh, you flatter yourself!"

"I've waited long and cold and furious nights, Callie. I will have you."

"You won't!" she cried to him. "You won't hurt me, you won't force me. You won't, because you promised! You won't, because of who you are. I know it, I know you—"

"Damn you, Callie! You don't know me. You never knew me!"

But she did. She knew the sound of his voice, and she knew the twist of his jaw. She knew the way he stood, and she even knew the way he thought. She knew the searing blue light in his eyes, and she knew both the tempest and the tenderness that could rule the man.

And she knew the raw passion that guided him now.

His mouth descended upon hers. His lips were hard and forceful. She could not twist or turn to avoid or deter him for his fingers threaded through her hair, holding her head still to his assault. She clamped down to fight him in any way that she could. She hammered her fists against his back, but he ignored her blows, and eventually they began to slow, and finally to stop. He robbed her of breath, and of reason, and of her fury. Her defenses were weak, and her enemy in gray was powerful. Even more powerful was the enemy of time, and that of loneliness, and even that of love. For there was more than determination in his kiss. Perhaps there was even more than passion.

Her lips parted to his as the thrust of his tongue demanded. Searing hot, liquid, demanding, seductive, he played upon her senses, tasted her mouth, the deep recesses, the curve of her lip. Touched and demanded that she give in turn, and seemed to reach within her, more and more deeply, fierce and volatile.

Her fingers ceased to press against him. She no longer tried to push away. She hadn't the power.

"Callie!"

She heard the whisper of her voice, fierce, passionate, spoken with anger, and spoken with anguish.

"Damn, I'll not let you sway me!" he cried out furiously. His eyes were fire as they touched hers. His fingers bit brutally into her arms.

At that moment, she did not know him. She didn't know if he would have her in anger and hatred, or if he would cry out an oath and jump from her side. She didn't know, and then it didn't matter.

Because there was suddenly another loud, fierce cry that came to fill the room. It wasn't a Rebel yell, nor was it any Yankee call.

It was a high, trembling, furious, and extremely demanding cry. And as it was ignored, it grew to new, hysterical heights.

The sound of that cry stopped Daniel flat, stopped him as Callie could have never done herself.

He sat back upon his haunches, his eyes narrowed sharply upon her. "What in God's name . . . ?"

Her breath caught. She strove for calm. She shimmied from beneath him and he made no effort to stop her. "It's—it's Jared," she said.

He was still staring at her blankly. Like a man trying to understand code when the code was plain English.

"That's a baby," he said.

"Yes! It's a baby!" she agreed. She managed to leap from the bed at last. She hurried down the hall to the nursery, throwing open the door.

Jared had kicked off his coverings. His hands and feet were flying furiously. His little mouth was open wide, and he was screaming with a demanding will.

Callie swept him quickly up into her arms.

Daniel stood in the doorway, having come behind her. He stared at her with amazement etched across his features. She realized that he wasn't looking at her at all, he was looking at Jared.

He strode across the room.

Instinctively, Callie held the child close to her breast, cradling him there. But Daniel ignored her protective hold and reached for Jared with a dogged determination. "Give him to me, Callie," Daniel warned.

Lest she hurt Jared, she had to let him go. Daniel meant to see him, and see him he would.

Daniel, ignoring Jared's squalling and the flailing of his tiny fists and feet, walked over to the flickering lamplight that filtered in from the hallway. Callie swallowed hard, feeling shaky as she watched him scrutinize the baby clad in his white cotton shirt and diaper. He stared from Jared's furiously puckered face to his perfect little feet. Daniel held the infant well, his hand and arm secure beneath Jared as he touched the long wild tuft of ebony dark hair upon Jared's head. Then Daniel's eyes—those distinct blue eyes, mirrored in the tiny face of the child—fell upon her again.

"It's my baby!" he exclaimed harshly.

She wanted to speak, but her mouth had gone dry. Then it didn't seem to matter to Daniel. He didn't need her to answer him.

He turned and started out the doorway.

With her baby. His baby. Their baby.

He couldn't—he wouldn't!—be leaving with Jared, she thought. Jared was just an infant. Daniel couldn't begin to care for him. Even he wouldn't be so cruel.

But his footsteps were retreating down the stairway.

"Daniel!" She found her voice and a frantic energy, at last. She raced after him, and this time it was she who accosted him at the foot of the stairs. "What are you doing? Give him to me! Daniel, he's crying because he's hungry. You can't take him from me! Daniel, please! What do you think you're doing?"

Daniel stood stone still, staring at her. "He's my son."

She didn't know what to do, and she blundered, frightened of his behavior. "You can't begin to know that—"

"The hell I can't. What a fool you are to try to deny it," he said softly, coldly.

"Daniel, give him back!"

"He doesn't belong here. He belongs at Cameron Hall," Daniel said stubbornly.

Callie's mouth dropped. "You can't take him! He's barely two months old. You can't care for him. Daniel, please!" Tears sprang to her eyes. She caught hold of his elbow and held on hard. "Daniel, he needs me. He's crying because he's hungry. You have to give him back to me."

A slow smile curved his mouth despite the baby's hungry screaming. "You didn't even intend to tell me about him, did you, Callie?"

She shook her head, the tears now brimming in her eyes. "Yes, I intended to tell you!"

"When the hell did you intend to tell me?" he bellowed.

"You didn't give me a chance. You came in here condemning me—"

"You knew that I'd come back. Maybe you didn't," he corrected himself bitterly. "Maybe you thought that I'd rot and die in that camp!"

"Damn you, Daniel, you can't kidnap my son!"

"My son. And he'll have my name," Daniel said. To her amazement, he started walking by her.

"You can't care for him!" she cried out. Of all the things that he might have done to her, she had never imagined this.

He stopped and turned back with a smile. "Oh, but I can, Callie. I can find a mammy to care for him easily enough. Within the hour."

"You wouldn't!" she breathed.

"He's a Cameron, Callie, and he's going south tonight."

"You can't take him away from me! He's mine!"

"And mine. Created under very bitter circumstances. He's coming home, and that's that."

"This is his home!"

"No, his home is south, upon the James."

No matter what had passed between them, no matter how bitterly he might have learned to hate her after the months that lay between them, she still could not believe it when he stepped past her again.

"I'll call the law!" she cried out.

"There is no law anymore, Callie," he wearily said to her over his shoulder. "Just war."

She followed him to the door. Jared was crying with an ever greater vengeance, furious that his meal was being denied him. The tears she had tried to hold back burst from Callie's eyes, and streamed down her face. "No! You cannot take him from me!" she thundered, and she slammed against him, beating her fists against his back.

He spun on her, his blue eyes fierce, furious, ruthlessly cold.

"Then you'd best be prepared to travel south, too, Callie. Because that's where he's going!"

She stepped back, stunned once again.

"What?"

"My son is going south. If you want to be with him, you can prepare to ride with me. I'll give you ten minutes to decide. Then we're moving. Who knows, Meade just may decide to chase Lee's army this time, though it seems poor Uncle Abe can't find himself a general to come after Lee. But I'm not waiting. So if you're coming, get ready."

South!

She couldn't travel to Virginia. Her heart had been set long ago, at the beginning of the war.

No . . .

She couldn't travel south because she was against slavery, but more than that, because she had understood President Lincoln's war from the beginning. The first shots hadn't been fired because of emancipation. The war had begun because the southern states had believed they could secede, that states' rights were supreme. Now the war was about so much more.

She couldn't go to Virginia because of Daniel Cameron. Because he was convinced she had betrayed him. Because he was determined to be her enemy with a far greater hostility than any northern general had ever felt for Bobby Lee.

She reached out her arms to him. "Daniel, give me the baby. Just let me feed him." He stared at her in an icy silence. She gritted her teeth. "Please!"

Daniel hesitated no longer. His frigid blue stare still pierced her condemningly, but he brought the baby to her. Jared was suddenly in her arms, warm, trembling, precious, still screaming. Callie shook, knowing that the baby meant more to her than anything in the world.

More than war. Far more than pride or glory.

"Ten minutes, Callie," Daniel said. "I'll be waiting on this step. For Jared, and you, if you choose to come. But Jared is coming with me."

"But we're enemies!"

"Bitter enemies," he agreed politely.

"I could betray you again, moving through this territory."

"You'll never have the chance again," he promised softly.

She met his startling blue gaze and then turned and fled up the steps with Jared. She ran into her room, her heart beating. She kissed her son's forehead, and distractedly pulled upon the strings of her bodice, freeing her breast for the baby to nurse. She touched his cheek with her knuckles, and he rooted for a moment before latching onto her to suckle strongly.

Love, enormous waves of it, came rushing through her. She rested her cheek upon her baby's head. She would never let Daniel take him from her.

No matter what had been. No matter how bitter Daniel might still be.

No matter what it was she had to face as a Yank in the South.

She closed her eyes. Daniel was wrong. Their son had been conceived in love.

Not even a year had passed since she had first seen Daniel Cameron.

So little time . . .

But oh, what a tempest that time had been!

She closed her eyes and remembered. . . .

PART 1

Enemy
Territory

One

September 1862
Sharpsburg, Maryland

Once Daniel fell, the reality and the dreams began to blend together.

They had come riding in with glory, a cavalry unit with extraordinary horsemanship, all of them handsome astride their fabulous mounts, swords gleaming in the late summer sun, their plumed hats flying like the banners of long-ago knights. Ah, but that's what they were, the last of the cavaliers, fighting for honor, for glory, for love, for the intangible essence that embodied a people. . . .

No, that was what they had been. The love was there still, as were the dreams of honor. He had been fighting far too long to believe any longer in the glory of war. And seen too close, he and his horsemen were not so splendid. Their uniforms were torn and tattered, their boots were worn, their faces were gaunt and haggard. Yes, they rode with their steel swords glistening in the morning sun, and when they let out with their Rebel cries, they were both fierce and beautiful, and awesome to behold. Riders of destiny, riders of death.

He had not lost his horse while engaged in battle. Not while locking swords with men in blue with faces he dared not look upon too closely.

It was the cannonball exploding just at his heels that had unhorsed him. For a few, brief, shimmering moments that seemed to waver between life and death, he had known what it was like to fly. It had all been so painless.

But then he had come crashing down, and the earth had embraced him ferociously. It was then that the pain came, searing and shooting through his temples even as the fragrant grass of the rich Maryland farmland teased his flesh. Then had come a sudden, stark darkness.

And then the dreams.

One moment, he could hear the horrible whistle of the cannons, could see the fires bursting against the beautiful blue of the summer sky. He could hear and feel the pounding of the horses' hooves, the clang of steel, and the horrible cries of men. Then it was all gone, as if a clean, clear breeze had come to sweep it away.

The James River. He could feel the breeze that came off the James, that sweet coolness, touching his cheek. He could hear the drone of bees. He was lying in the grass on the slope of the lawn at home, at Cameron Hall, staring at the blue sky above, watching as white clouds idly puffed by. He could hear singing, down by the smokehouse. Something soft, and sing song, a spiritual. A deep, low male voice rumbled, and beautiful female voices chorused around it. He didn't need to open his eyes to see the smokehouse, or the hall, or the endless slope of green lawn where he lay that stretched all the way down to the river, and the river docks and the ships that came to take the crops to market. Nor did he need to open his eyes to see the garden, bursting with bright red summer roses that wove enchantingly down the path from the wide, porticoed back porch of the hall. He knew it all, like he knew his own hand. It was home, and he loved it.

But he needed to get up. He could hear Christa's laughter. She would be coming up the slope with Jesse to get him. Pa would have sent them to bring him in for dinner. Jesse would be teasing her, and Christa would be laughing. They'd both be ready to taunt him for his daydreaming. Christa, still just a little girl, was so accomplished in the house. And Jesse always knew what he wanted. An appointment to West Point, a few years in a good medical school, and an assignment in the West. While he . . .

"Daydreaming, Daniel?" Jesse asked. His brother sat down beside him on one side, while his sister, her bright blue eyes as shimmering as the sky, sat on his other side.

"Nothing wrong with daydreaming, Jess."

"No, nothing wrong at all," Jesse said. He was the most serious of their family, and he always had been. He was the peacemaker, calm, decisive, and as stubborn as they came. There weren't all that many years between them and so they had always been the best of friends. They might fight, but let anyone else ever make a critical comment about either of the Cameron boys and the other brother would leap to his defense, willing to take on any fight. And no one had best ever find fault with Miss Christa, for both boys—though they might torment her endlessly at home—would instantly be ready for battle.

"Dreaming about what?" Christa demanded. She laughed, and the sound was like all the others that Daniel heard, the ripple of the river, the whisper of the breeze. It was a sound that belonged to the languorous days of summer, to childhood.

"Horses, I daresay," Jesse volunteered for him, and pulled his hat low over his head. The eldest of the threesome, he was always quick to speak his mind.

Daniel grinned. "Maybe. Christa is going to be the most beautiful and accomplished young lady in the country, you're going to be the greatest doctor since Hippocrates, and me, well, I guess I'm going to be a horse master."

"The best darned horse master this side of the Mississippi," Jesse promised him.

Daniel leapt to his feet, swinging an imaginary sword. "The best horseman, the best swordsman. I'll be just like one of King Arthur's knights!"

"And save damsels in distress!" Christa laughed, clapping.

"What?" Daniel demanded.

"Damsels. Fair maidens in distress. Well, it's what all the best knights are supposed to do."

"They're supposed to fight dragons."

"Or Indians," Jesse observed wryly.

"Everyone knows that you have to save the damsels from the Indians and dragons!" Christa insisted.

"Woah!" Jesse, always the voice of reason, warned them. "Give him time, Christa. Damsels tend to be interested in knights before knights tend to be interested in damsels. He'll get there. But right now, there's supper on the table.

Honey-smoked ham and sweet potatoes and new peas and fresh-squeezed lemonade.''

A shell burst in the sky. Jesse's memory disappeared. Christa's laughter dissolved into the shriek and whistle of a cannonball as it flew through the air.

He was no longer lying on the cool green grass of home. He was in the farmlands of Maryland. The grass was no longer green, it was churning to mud beneath him as horses pranced and dug up the earth, and men fell and spilled their blood upon it.

He had learned about saving damsels. He'd never really met a dragon, but he'd had his day with the Indians in the West.

And he'd met enemies he'd never imagined. His own countrymen. Yankees. Men he'd gone to school with. Men with whom he'd fought in the West.

His own brother . . .

How much better it would have been, had there been dragons!

He was bleeding himself, he knew. Not a new wound, but an old one, ripped open as he had flown through the air.

He couldn't feel the pain but suddenly felt the spatter of mud against his cheek.

He wondered if he was dying.

He tried to turn. If they'd been able to take him, his men would never have left him here. Unless they had been convinced that he was dead.

He couldn't continue to lie here. He was injured and bleeding. Eventually, surely, someone would come to this patch of earth again. Either the Yanks, or the Rebs. Battle could rage here again.

But he knew he could just as easily die here before anyone ventured near enough to help him. And it was just as likely that Yanks might come upon him as Rebs.

He blinked, moving carefully, looking about himself.

There was a house in the distance.

It wasn't Cameron Hall. It was a whitewashed farmhouse, and there were planters of summer flowers on the front porch. An old swing hung from a big oak.

The flowers had been mown down in a hail of bullets. The white paint was pockmarked with rifle fire.

Distantly now, he could still hear the cries of warfare, the crack of steel against steel.

His company had moved on. The battle had changed terrain. Dead men lay around him. Men in blue and men in gray.

He tried to raise himself and crawl toward the house.

The effort was too much for his remaining strength. The house began to fade. Blackness descended swiftly upon him once again. Let it come! he thought. Let it bring me back to the sweet grass by the river. . . .

When he opened his eyes again he thought that he was dreaming. He thought he had died, and somehow made it to heaven, for the creature above him could not be any part of hell.

She was beautiful. As beautiful as his dreams of the river, as beautiful as a clear summer sky. Her eyes were a clear, level gray and her hair was a rich, dark, abundant auburn. It framed delicate, beautifully chiseled features, a face shaped like a heart, full, delineated, rose dark lips, a fine straight nose, and high, striking cheekbones. She was bending over him. He could almost reach out and touch her. He breathed in the sweet scent of her, as fragrant and soft as roses.

Just as he could feel and reach and touch the slope of grass back home, hear the river, be brushed by the breeze! he thought in dismay. He was seeing things again.

But no, she was real. Perhaps an angel, but real nonetheless, for she reached out and touched him. Her fingers gently moved over his face like the coolest, softest breeze of spring.

She lowered herself down beside him. He wanted to keep staring at her, but he couldn't. He hadn't the strength to keep his lashes raised.

He felt her fingers moving around his head. And still her touch was so gentle. She cradled his head in her lap.

"You are breathing!" she whispered. He tried to open his eyes. Tried to see the wide, compassionate, dove-gray beauty of her eyes.

He could see her! His lashes were raised just a slit, but he could see her against the gray powder that sat in the air like an acrid mist. Her voice was low and soft and like a melody when she spoke.

Perhaps he was dying. Even when his eyes closed again, he could see her face, that radiant sunset burst of her hair.

"Alive?" she demanded.

"Yes." He tried to form the word. No sound came from his parched lips.

"Ma'am! Ma'am!" Someone was calling to her. "The shells are coming down again! This battle isn't anywhere near over. Get inside!"

"But, sir! This man—"

"He's a dead Reb, lady! A dead Reb officer, probably responsible for more'n half the dead Yanks lying around him. Why, he's practically a murderer! Get inside!"

A Yank! He needed the Yank to believe he was dead. Maybe he was so close to death it didn't matter. He couldn't keep his eyes open.

He thought that he saw those dove-gray eyes once again. Exotic, really beautiful, slightly tilted at the corners. That face . . . ivory, with a delicate blush upon the cheeks. Those lips . . .

"Ma'am—why it's you. Callie! Callie Michaelson! God in heaven, Callie, get yourself into the house."

"Eric!" Callie gasped. "My Lord, I hadn't expected to see a soldier I knew. This man—"

"This man is a dead Reb!"

The Yankee infantryman standing above him spit out of the side of his mouth, aiming for Daniel's feet. He hit the ground instead.

Ass! So that's why you fellows can't win this war, you can't even aim spittle! Daniel thought.

And you'd spit on a dead man, soldier! Pray God, sir, that I never rise to meet you in battle!

"Callie, my God, I'd never forgive myself if something happened to you. Gregory would be tossing in his grave. Now please, get in the house and quit wasting good time on a bad Reb! Jesu, Callie, I can't believe that you're even touching that man!"

But she was. He managed to raise his lashes. Her eyes met his. Those beautiful, entrancing gray eyes touched by silver, and those dark sunset lashes. Her hair was a halo of radiant dark fire. . . .

She jumped up, and his head cracked back down on the ground. Hard. The world went very dark. He fought to remain conscious.

He reached out for her in desperation.

Her delicate, black-shoed foot struck his fingers as she left him.

His angel of mercy was gone.

She had remained until she'd been reminded he was a Reb! he thought bitterly.

Perhaps it was for the best. A Yankee company was moving over the lawn now, and he did not want it to be known that he lived. If there was one fate he wanted to avoid, it was that of prisoner of war.

Best to let the Yanks think he was dead.

She was gone, and then the Yanks moving across the lawn were gone. The light before him seemed to be fading for real. He was losing consciousness again.

Perhaps it was a great kindness, for the shells began to burst once again. Riders came. Horses' hooves just missed him as they trod over the mud and the grass. There was no slackening in the fire. There were no moments of peace when each side came hastily for their wounded.

The dead could always wait.

He saw a flash in the sky, and then he saw nothing more. Not for a long, long time.

When he opened his eyes again, the world was nearly silent.

Incongruously, he heard the chirping of a bird.

He was alive. And he could move. He clenched and unclenched his fingers. He stretched out his legs. He closed his eyes and rested once again.

He was stronger than he had been before. He could swallow, he could open and move his eyes easily. His fingers followed every direction his mind gave them. His feet moved when he commanded them.

He closed his eyes and breathed deeply.

He was desperately thirsty. He opened his eyes again. His head still pounded, but the pounding was lessening. He tried to rise, and did so. He rubbed his neck, and moved slowly and carefully.

Sitting up, he looked around. The ground was littered with men. Men in blue and men in gray.

He looked toward the house. He had to reach it.

The battle was over, and he did not know who had won. Maybe neither side had seen a clear victory. But his men were gone. They would have returned for him, or for his body, if they could have done so.

That meant only one thing. They had to be retreating. He would have to get through Yankee lines to return to them.

He pressed his temples together hard for one long moment then managed to make it to his feet.

As he staggered, it seemed that he was alone in the world.

Alone in the world of the dead, he thought wearily.

He looked to the house, then remembered the woman. The one with the amazing gray and silver eyes and the flow of hair like a deep rich sunset.

He wasn't alone.

His Yankee angel was in there somewhere, very near. The sweet little beauty who had cradled him so tenderly until she had been reminded that he was the enemy.

Pretty soon, Yankee patrols would be around to search for their wounded and to gather their dead.

And capture any stray Rebs for their notorious prison camps.

His fingers clenched into fists. He wasn't going to any Yankee prison camp.

He looked back to the house, and his lips slowly curved into a smile, wistful, bitter—determined.

"Well, angel," he whispered softly, "it seems that we are about to meet!"

Slowly, silently—very carefully—he made his way toward the battered and bullet-riddled farmhouse. He kept low as he approached the porch. She might well have a loaded shotgun in there, and from the snatches of conversation he had heard, she was definitely on the side of the blue.

He'd best go in by the back. He'd need to take her by surprise, and to have her understand that he very much intended to stay alive.

He touched his head and winced. Had it hurt this badly before she cracked it down on the ground? And then kicked him?

She'd looked like such an angel. He'd been sure that he'd died and gone on to the hereafter.

He smiled wryly. His angel was going to keep him from the certain promise of hell!

Two

The last drumbeat had sounded. The shrill call of the bugle had ceased to blare. The battle was over.

It was over, all but for the acrid smell of powder and smoke in the air, all but for the wages of war left strewn across the once green and fertile and peaceful farmland.

For two days Callie Michaelson had sat down in her basement and listened to the horrible sounds of war. Once before she had heard the curious sound of silence, and she had ventured out, but there had only been a lull in the fighting, a shifting of the troops, and as she had been ordered, she had hurried back inside.

How strange it had been to discover that the officer concerned for her was Eric Dabney! He came from a small town about twenty miles northeast of her. He had stood up for Gregory at their wedding, and the two of them had always been close friends. She had lost track of him since the war. He'd gone to military school as a very young man, and with Lincoln's call to arms, he'd won himself a commission in the cavalry.

Union cavalry had died here, she thought pityingly. Just as Confederate cavalry had died. And the only thing she had been able to do was to wait down in the basement.

There had been nothing she could do for the men beyond her door. The men in blue, or the men in gray.

Not once had it come again. That sound that was even more horrible, the sound of silence.

But now, the battle was over. The ravages of war would be all that were left behind.

When she emerged from her basement at last, she was first aware that the black powder from the guns and cannons still hung upon the air, thick and heavy.

When she walked through her parlor and out on the porch, an anguish like nothing she had ever felt before came rushing around her heart. There were so, so many dead.

The powder stung her eyes as she looked around her yard. Standing there, she felt a chill sweep her, for she seemed such a strange being in the midst of the carnage. She was dressed in a soft blue day gown with a fine lace bodice and high neckline. Her petticoats, a snowy white that showed when she walked, seemed incongruous against the blood and mud in the yard. Even her hair, so fiery with its auburn highlights, seemed too bright for this late afternoon.

There, before her, hanging from the old oak, the big whitewashed swing miraculously remained. As if some spirit touched it, it drifted back and forth in the gray mist.

The oak itself, to which the swing was tied, was riddled with bullets.

Callie stepped from the porch. Her gray eyes were almost silver with the glistening of tears that covered them as she looked at the lawn, heavily laden with soldiers. She was horrified. She lifted her skirts and then swung around. It seemed that something had grabbed her hem.

And so it had. There lay a hand, upturned. And the hand was that of a very young Confederate soldier. His eyes remained open.

Atop him, as if caught in a last embrace, lay another soldier.

This one in blue.

Both so very, very young. Perhaps at peace, at last, entwined in blood and death.

Where was the soldier she had held so briefly before? she wondered, gazing around the yard. She knew that she had touched life, something warm and vibrant in this field of cold damnation. And it had seemed so important that something, someone, survive the carnage. Trembling suddenly, she remembered his face. It had been a striking one despite the smudges of mud and black powder on it. Ebony dark, thick, arched brows, and lines clean and stubbornly strong. In death, his very strength and masculinity had held a haunting and gallant beauty.

Perhaps the handsome cavalry officer lay beneath his fallen enemy, just like the two young soldiers near her feet.

"Oh, God!" Callie whispered. Shaking, aware that more than the powder was bringing tears to her eyes, she sank low upon the balls of her feet and tenderly closed the eyes of both soldiers. She fought for some words, to mouth a prayer. She felt numb.

She straightened and tried to look out across the mist of powder and the coming dusk.

Where once the fields had been covered with near sky-high stalks of corn, they now were cleared, the corn literally mown down by bullets and cannonballs and canisters.

Everywhere she looked, all over the beautiful, rolling countryside, there lay the lost. The strength and beauty of two nations—their youth. Their fine young men, their dreamers, their builders. All lost . . .

The sound of hoofbeats brought her swirling around again, her heart seeming to leap to her throat. Out of the mist emerged a horseman. Who had taken the battle? Who was coming now?

The horseman wore blue. Behind him rode others.

The man saluted her. "Captain Trent Johnston, Army of the Potomac, miss. Are you all right?"

She nodded. Was she all right? Could anyone stand in the midst of all this carnage and be all right? "I'm—I'm all right, Captain."

"Is there anyone else in the house?" he asked her.

She shook her head. "I live alone. Well, I've three brothers. They're all in the West."

"Union army?" Johnston asked her sharply.

Callie felt a wry curl come to her lip. Maybe it was natural. A lot of soldiers had little faith in the loyalty of Marylanders. There was tremendous southern sympathy here. There had been riots in Baltimore when Lincoln had come through on the way to his inauguration. But she resented her loyalty being questioned when she had just spent two days hiding in her basement, and when both her father and her husband lay in the family plot down by the creek.

"Yes, Captain. My brothers are with the Union. They asked to join up with companies fighting out West. They didn't want to fight our immediate neighbors to the south here."

The captain's eyes narrowed. He rose slightly on his horse, his heels low in his stirrups, and called out a command. "Jenkins, Seward, take a look at the men on the ground here. See if we've any Billy Blue survivors."

Two men dismounted and quickly looked to the fallen men.

Callie stared at Trent Johnston. He wasn't an old man. But time—or the war —had etched deep lines of bitterness into his face. His eyes were a faded color. Maybe they had been blue once. Now they were the weary shade of the powdery mist.

"Did the Union take the battle?" she asked.

Johnston looked down at her. "Yes, miss. From what I hear, both sides have been trying to claim the victory. But General Robert E. Lee has taken his men and pulled back, so I daresay the Union has taken the battle. Though what we've taken, I'm not so sure myself," he said softly. "Jesu, I have never seen so many dead."

He looked over to the two privates he had ordered down. They were still stepping around the men strewn across her yard, studying them carefully. Callie felt her nails curl into her palms.

Good Lord, she could not look at them so closely. She didn't want to see the saber wounds and the great holes caused by the minnie balls and the destruction wrought by the cannons and canisters.

There were no living men in her yard. Not one of them had moved. Flies created a constant hum beneath the warm September sky, and that was the only evidence of life.

"See if those Yank boys are breathing, men," Captain Johnston said.

Callie looked at the captain and then gazed upon the devastation on her lawn. "What if there had been a survivor in gray?" she asked softly.

One of the men on the lawn, either Jenkins or Seward, answered her gravely. "Why miss, we'd take care of him, too, right as rain, don't you fret none about that." His voice lowered, and she was certain he didn't want his hard-nosed captain hearing him. "I got kinfolk myself on the other side," he told her. He looked to the captain. "We would take care of a Reb, right, Captain?"

"Oh, indeed, we would," the captain said. He gazed hard at Callie once again. "Are you sure your loyalties are with the North, miss?"

"Yes. My loyalty is to the North," Callie said flatly, her teeth grating. But no one could stand here and see these men, these young men, enemies in life, so pathetically entwined in death, and not feel a certain pity for the other side.

"Sir!" Callie said, remembering Eric. "An officer I know went through here in the midst of the battle. Captain Eric Dabney. Have you seen him? Has he— survived?"

Johnston shook his head. "Not as yet, I haven't, ma'am. But I'm sure that I will by nightfall. I'll be glad to express your concern."

"Thank you."

The captain tipped his hat. "We'll be back with a burial detail shortly, miss. Seward, Jenkins, mount up."

With another nod to her, the captain turned his mount. Dirt churned as his company did an about-face, and he rode into the gray mist of the now quiet battlefield.

Callie closed her eyes. She suddenly felt very alone, standing on her lawn surrounded by the dead. Her fingers wound tightly into her skirts, and she fought the overwhelming feeling of horror and devastation sweeping through her. They would come for these poor fellows. They would be buried somewhere nearby, she was certain, and probably en masse.

And somewhere, far, far away, a sweetheart, a mother, a lover, a friend, someone would weep for their fallen soldier. And say a prayer, and erect a stone in memory, and bring flowers to that stone.

Just as she brought flowers to the stone that had been erected out back next to her mother's grave. Gregory's body had been returned to her in a coffin. She had awaited it at the railway station, cold, numb, and clad in black. But her father had fallen at Shiloh, far, far away, and all that she had received had been the letter from his captain. "Dear Mrs. Michaelson. It is my great misfortune to have to inform you . . ."

She had been lucky, she understood now. Officers no longer had the time to write to loved ones of their fallen men. Widows now discovered their status by reading their husband's names aloud from the lists posted in the nearest town, or reprinted in the newspapers.

It was no good to stand on the lawn. No good to feel the air on her cheeks, to feel the coming of the darkness, the whisper of the night. For these fallen men around her would never again feel the soft caress of a breeze, or the endlessly sweet nectar of the first soft kiss of the night.

She turned, anxious not to see the faces of the men as she hurried past them. The house, she realized, was riddled with bullets. Her front windowpanes were shattered. There was even a small cannonball lodged in the stone base of the left corner of the porch.

This was one battle Callie would never be able to forget.

She stepped back into the parlor. Her feet crunched over broken glass.

It was beginning to grow very dark and shadowy within the house, and she was anxious to light the gas lamps.

She started to move, but then her hand flew to her mouth and she tried desperately to swallow down a gasp. Fear, vivid and wild, came sweeping through her. She fought a growing sense of panic, biting down hard upon her knuckles.

She wasn't alone.

There was someone in her house. Someone who had come through the rear door, and into the kitchen.

From the parlor through the hallway, and to the door frame that led into the kitchen she could see him standing there. He was very tall, and his height was emphasized by the plumed hat he wore at a rakish angle over his brow. She could see little of his features, for the shadows of dusk hid them.

But she could see his uniform, and it was gray. Gray trousers, rimmed in gold. Knee-high black boots. A gray frock coat, also trimmed in the same gold. He was southern cavalry, she thought quickly.

The southerners had pulled out. That's what Captain Trent Johnston had said.

So what did this southerner want with her? She'd heard tales of what happened to lone women when men of an invading army came their way.

Don't panic, she warned herself.

But his mind was moving in the same direction, and his warning came down upon her like a hammer.

"Don't!" he rasped out sharply, before she had found the breath to scream.

She had to scream, she had to move. Quickly. Captain Johnston still had to be close by.

Callie spun around, ready to exit her house as swiftly as the wind. But even as her hand fell upon the doorknob the southern cavalryman fell upon her.

Her scream escaped her then, as his hand touched her arm, ripping her away from the door. "Stop it, damn you, ma'am, I am not spending the rest of the war in a prison camp!"

The voice was deep, rich, almost musical in its drawl. But it was also touched with an arrogant authority, a harshness, even a ruthlessness.

And his face . . .

He was the soldier she had touched! The one she could have sworn had lived.

He stared at her with eyes as sharp as steel blades beneath those imperious, high-arched, and deadly dark brows.

"No!" Callie screamed, finding breath at last. Her fingers clawed at the fingers that held her arm. She touched something warm and sticky. Blood.

She looked up into his eyes.

They were deep blue, nearly cobalt. They stared at her evenly and with a dangerous and determined warning.

"Let me go!" she demanded. Oh, Lord. She was a competent woman, she assured herself. She was not easily intimidated. She had lived here all alone since the war had begun.

She had never been so frightened before in all her life. This soldier looked at her as if he had some personal vengeance in mind.

"Let me go!" Her voice was starting to rise again. He was very tall, even allowing for the heels of his boots. He towered over her, and his frock coat emphasized the breadth of his shoulders. His jet dark brows framed his eyes, and hiked up high as he watched her. His mouth was set in a firm line within his square and unyielding chin.

"Miss, don't—"

"No!"

She wrenched free and made for the door again. "Captain Johnston!"

The cry rose high on her lips.

"Don't! Dammit, I do not want to hurt you!" He swung her around and planted his hands firmly on either side of her head against the door as his arms formed steel bands around her. She opened her mouth. One of his hands moved to clamp down hard over it.

She was forced to stare into those endlessly blue eyes. His face, she realized, was a strikingly handsome one. His features were cleanly sculpted, very well defined.

"Listen to me, ma'am. I do not want to . . ."

He broke off. He took a deep breath. Callie realized that he was struggling to remain standing.

"I do not want to . . ."

He blinked, ink black lashes falling over his cheeks. A wild bravado filled Callie along with her realization that he was barely standing. She thrust away his hand and pushed against his chest with all of her might. "Let go of me, Reb!" she demanded.

He fell to his knees.

And then he keeled over.

He lay flat on her floor by the door. For several seconds, she stared down at him. She prodded him with her toe to see if he would move. He did not.

Was he dead?

She wanted to swing open the door and shout for Captain Johnston, but she was certain that the horseman was long gone by now. And this Reb was no longer any danger to her.

Gingerly she bent down, trying to decide if he was dead or alive.

His hat had fallen aside, and she saw that he had a full head of near ebony hair, rich and waving just below his nape. He was handsome, and more, she thought, a sudden wave of pity sweeping over her. He had gained something more than beauty in his years. There was character to his face, something in the set of his jaw, in the fine lines etched about his eyes and his mouth.

He is the enemy, she told herself.

She saw a lock of damp, matted hair at his temple. She smoothed it back and saw that he had been grazed there by a bullet.

He was also bleeding from his side. There was no rip or tear in his uniform, but a crimson stain was appearing over the gray wool of his frock coat. She rose and hurried into the kitchen, soaked a towel with cool water from the pump, and hurried back out to the parlor. She bathed his forehead and determined that the wound was not bad. He might live.

She lay her hand upon his chest and waited, and then nearly jumped when she felt the beating of his heart. The blood staining his frock coat and shirt at his side disturbed her. She moved his coat back and then pulled away his shirt, gingerly pulling the tail from his breeches. A small pang struck her, and for the first time she didn't think of him as being the enemy. His belly was taut, his chest was tightly muscled, his flesh was handsomely bronzed. His skin was very hot to her touch. Yank or Reb, this was what war brought, the loss of such men, so handsome, so gallant, so beautiful, and in their prime.

Not so gallant! she thought with a sniff.

She brought her towel up to bathe away the blood at his side.

It was an old wound, she discovered. A slash above the hip, probably from a saber or a bayonet. It had reopened, and he lay bleeding from it.

She pressed against the towel. The flow of blood seemed to stop.

"You're going to live, Reb," she said aloud. "Maybe," she murmured. She wasn't convinced that Captain Johnston wanted any Rebs to live.

And both sets of soldiers, from the North and from the South, dreaded the horror of the prison camps.

Well, it wasn't her problem. Her house was decimated. Not far from where the soldier lay were the shattered panes of her windows. This soldier had invaded her very home. She couldn't care what happened to him after Captain Johnston took him away.

She bit her lip, curious. He wore the insignia of a Confederate colonel of the cavalry. Southern uniforms were often very haphazard—she'd heard that many of the great southern generals still wore their old U.S. Army breeches with jackets and shirts of their own design. But this cavalryman was well dressed in gray with yellow cavalry trim. He came from money, she thought.

There was a small leather wallet attached to the band of his scabbard. Certain that his eyes were still closed and that he remained unconscious, Callie delved into it. Hurriedly, she looked through the packet of papers she discovered within. There were a number of letters and an old pass. She glanced over the pass quickly. It had been issued to a Colonel Daniel Cameron, Army of Northern Virginia, by General J.E.B. Stuart.

Cameron. Daniel Cameron. So that was his name. She shivered, suddenly wishing that she did not know it.

The enemy should remain nameless, she thought. It made it easier to hate. But the enemy should have remained faceless too.

She had seen all those faces out on her lawn. Young faces, looking to heaven.

Stop, she commanded herself. This was war.

She thought she heard horses coming once again and relief filled her. She stuffed the papers quickly back into the wallet. All that she had to do was call Captain Johnston, and this enemy could be off her hands. She started to move, and discovered that she could not.

She looked down. Blood-stained fingers curled around the hem of her skirts. And sky-blue eyes, very much alive with a startling threat, were upon her.

He was very much alive.

She forgot that she had been feeling magnanimous toward her enemy as a swift new fear filled her. "Let go of me!" she commanded sharply.

Those blue eyes seared right through her. A lopsided grin touched his lips.

"Not on your life, angel. Not on your life," he promised her.

Three

The riders weren't coming to the house, she realized. Already, the sounds of their hoofbeats were fading.

To reach the Yankee horsemen, Callie would have to move quickly. She had to escape the Reb who had so menacingly come back to consciousness at exactly the wrong time.

"No!" she shrieked. She jerked firmly at her skirt, tearing herself away. She ran to the door. She nearly had it flung open when an arm snaked out from behind her and a hand encircled her waist.

An arm covered in gray. A hand reddened by blood.

Instantly, a scream tore from her throat. "Stop it!" he commanded fiercely. He swung her around. She tried to strike him again, growing more and more frantic. She jerked away from his arms and pounded against his chest.

But this time his arms encircled her, and they came crashing down on the floor together, rolling over. To her great consternation, when they came to a halt, he was on top, straddling her. She struck out wildly at him, her panic growing. Grimly, he caught her wrists. "Ma'am, I am trying damned hard not to hurt you. Can't I get through that thick Yankee skull of yours! What were you doing? Picking a man's pockets before he was quite cold?"

Her eyes narrowed. There was a tone of dead reckoning in his voice. He didn't want to hurt her, but he would do so if he had to.

"I was trying to help you—"

"Oh, just like you were helping me when you dropped my head out there and left me to die? I can see where the enemy stands with you!"

"I thought you were dead!"

"You realized that I was a Rebel!"

"You are the enemy!" she snapped out. "One of those fine, gallant cavaliers, fighting for your life of chivalry, right? Is this a sampling of your fine Southern gallantry?" she demanded.

"Darlin', I'll tell you, there's lots more chivalry you're receiving right now than I'm in the mood to give. It was one hell of a battle. I was down and wounded to begin with, and you, my dear, most courteous and proper Yank, made it all the worse with that kick in the head!"

"I did not kick you in the head!" she protested.

"You did! Right after you dropped me flat, bleeding and in torment, on the ground! And to think that I thought you were an angel!"

The sharpness of his stare seemed to go beyond her for a moment, and he winced. She didn't think it was his own pain he was feeling. She could see from the anguish in his eyes that he thought of the rows upon rows of dead in her yard.

But now his eyes were gleaming down upon her again. "I'm not going to pass out again," he warned her, his tone grating.

"Well, I am going to scream!" she threatened in turn, and she opened her mouth to do so.

He was so damned quick. His hand landed over her mouth again.

It was then that she heard a knocking on the door.

Her eyes widened as she stared up at the southerner. She was definitely victorious.

"Miss! It's Captain Johnston. We're out here to pick up our men!"

Callie squirmed furiously. She tried to sink her teeth into the Reb's fingers.

To her amazement, he suddenly pulled a knife from a sheath at his ankle and brought the razor-sharp edge to her throat. "Don't scream," he hissed at her.

He wouldn't do it. She was damned convinced that he wouldn't do it.

She didn't scream.

He was suddenly up, and pulling her to her feet. She still didn't scream. He still had his knife out.

He swung her around and prodded her to the door. She felt the point of the knife right at the small of her back. "Tell him fine. Tell him that you know that he's there, and thank him."

Callie stood very still.

"Tell him!"

"Go ahead! Stab me!" she hissed back at him.

His fingers suddenly threaded through her hair. "Don't tempt me!" he said.

He opened the door, standing behind her in the shadows, but keeping the blade of the knife against her all the while.

Captain Johnston stood on her porch. She opened her mouth. She meant to tell him there was a Reb in her house. She didn't give a damn about the knife. She wasn't afraid of the Reb, she assured herself.

She was never really sure why she didn't turn him in right then and there. Maybe it was Captain Johnston. She was so certain that to him the only good Reb was a dead one.

What did she care? Her husband lay dead and now long buried in the yard. Her father lay dead in a mass grave with hundreds of other Yankee soldiers. And he had fallen to a man like this one. . . .

"Yes, Captain Johnston," she said gravely. She didn't allow her eyes to flicker downward. She didn't want to see the Confederate or the Union dead.

"We should be out of here soon enough, ma'am. Can my men do anything for you?"

The knife jabbed closer against her flesh. "No, Captain, I just . . . I just want to be left alone."

The captain nodded. "You see any soldiers around here, you call for me. Someone will be around. I don't want to lose any strays. There just might be a wounded man or two separated from his company. I'll be close. Just down in the valley by the little offshoot of the Antietam stream."

"Yes, thank you so much," Callie said.

Johnston turned away. Callie almost called after him.

The door closed with a slam. Arms came around her, and she found herself sliding down to the floor with the Reb on her side.

"That wasn't bad," he told her.

"That was damned good, Colonel," she said icily. "If you stick that knife at me again, I will scream until the sun comes up."

"Lady, you do tempt fate!" he warned her roughly.

"What choice have I, cast into the company of so fine and chivalrous a cavalier!"

He gritted his teeth and exhaled. "I have to rejoin Stuart!" he told her.

"Well, you may just have to bleed to death first, Colonel," she said sweetly. "Will I?"

Feet suddenly came tramping up the porch. He drew her near again, his hand clamped tightly over her mouth. She could barely breathe. She struggled. It made no difference. He was built like Atlas. He might be dying here in her living room, but his arm muscles were still in very fine shape.

It seemed forever that he held her. A strange eternity, for she'd never been closer to any man, never held so intimately, so tautly, for this length of time, even by Gregory. She had never sought more desperately to escape, and she had never been so securely held. After a time, she closed her eyes. The darkness continued to arrive. She could still hear the tramping of feet. Then it seemed that they slowly faded.

She was almost passing out, or almost sleeping. Perhaps she had been nearly asphyxiated, she wasn't quite sure. But when the pounding came on the door a second time, he startled her until she nearly jumped out of her skin.

He was still beside her. He pulled her along with him to her feet.

Slowly, slowly, he eased his hand from her mouth. He turned her toward the door, and opened it.

Johnston was there again.

"We're through here, ma'am."

She looked outside. The bodies were gone. All of them. She felt as if she would fall for a minute.

All the poor young men . . .

"Miss? Are you all right?"

She nodded. Her mouth was very dry. She swallowed. Johnston wasn't such a bad man. Not if you were on his side.

"Yes. I, er . . . Thank you, Captain."

"Take care, then. If you need help with anything—"

"No, no, thank you. I don't need any help."

"Oh! I'm sorry, I forgot to tell you, miss. Captain Dabney did survive the day. He took a gash to his arm, but not a serious one, the surgeon says. Captain Dabney sends his regards, and his concern, but I took the liberty of informing him that you were very well."

"Thank you. I am so relieved for Captain Dabney!"

Johnston saluted, then turned away. She watched him as he walked to his horse. He mounted it, signaled with his hand, and shouted out an order. His company—the group of horsemen and the wagons that now accompanied him—began to move. Callie stared after him.

A slow smile curved her lip. The Reb hadn't held the knife on her at all, not once during the entire exchange.

The door suddenly closed. She was careful to let her self-mocking smile fade as she met the Reb's stark blue gaze again.

"Good," Cameron muttered. "You did well."

"That's because you have such a way with women, Colonel," Callie told him sweetly.

"And you ma'am, are pure sweetness and light!" He grinned slowly. He mocked her in return, but he was surprisingly, wickedly handsome.

"Colonel—"

"Who is Captain Dabney?" he demanded.

Her brows shot up. "A friend, Colonel," she said icily.

"A friend, or lover?"

Stunned, she felt her hand go flying through the air without the least bit of thought. He caught her hand before it could connect with his cheek, but it was no stay for her amazement and fury. "War or no war, sir, how dare you come up with a question—"

"Because I have to know if this Captain Dabney is going to come stepping into this house at any given moment!" he told her.

"You'll just have to wonder, won't you?" she said heatedly.

He smiled. "Ma'am, you are a Yank to match any Rebel I've known in all my born days. Ah, but with outrage like that, you're probably innocent."

"Innocent!" Callie exclaimed. She wanted to kick him. "Mark my words! I will assuredly be as dangerous as any man you might meet on a battlefield! And Colonel, I'd be much obliged if you'd step outside the door before closing it again," she said.

"I can't rightly do that, ma'am," he said, sweeping down to pick up his hat and set it upon his head. He seemed affectionately attached to that hat.

"Why?"

"I'm bleeding."

"Is that supposed to mean something to me?" she demanded, suddenly furious. "Men bled and died all over my property—"

"You must excuse us for dying. We don't do it on purpose," he interrupted dryly.

Callie ignored his sarcasm. "You insult me, you invade my property—"

"I invade it!" he snapped back. "Lady, if you think this is something, you should see Virginia! Your armies have ripped it to shreds. There are miles and miles where nothing grows anymore, where there isn't a horse or a cow to be seen, where the children are half-starved! And you're going to tell me about invasions!"

She stepped away from the pain and the passion in his eyes.

"I lied for you, Colonel. I kept you from a prison camp. Now you can go on to kill dozens more Union soldiers. You could even kill my kin."

He leaned against the door, suddenly very weary again. "I could kill my own kin," he said softly. Then his eyes shot open again. "I'm very sorry, but you are going to help me. I am not going to bleed to death on your property!"

He suddenly gripped her hand and dragged her along with him into the kitchen. At the sink he began to pump water. Callie gritted her teeth, but she reached for a clean towel and soaked it, and when she had done so, she pressed it against the wound on his side. "Hold this!" she snapped.

He did so, and she dragged a chair over by the sink and stood on it and delved into a cupboard above it. She found some clean linens and brought them down, and began to rip them. "Lift your shirt!" she commanded him, and he did so.

Once again, she was uneasy at the closeness between them as she wound the linen around his bronzed torso. "It seems that whoever sewed you up didn't do a complete job. And they slander our Yankee surgeons!" she muttered.

His fingers were suddenly digging into her arm, drawing her eyes to his as she gasped at the jolt of pain.

"A Yankee surgeon sewed me up, Miss Stars and Stripes. And a damned good one. He just wasn't expecting me to be riding quite so hard so fast. He did the best damned job he could for me."

Startled, Callie stared up at him. "Why, you're kind to our side, Colonel. Why should a Yank do the best damned job for you?"

"Because he's my brother," he said impatiently. "Are you done?"

"Your brother?" Callie said, startled.

"My brother," he snapped flatly in return. He didn't intend to be questioned about his words—or his family.

Perhaps she shouldn't have been so surprised. Her own brothers had asked to fight on the western front, just so that they wouldn't be expected to shoot their neighbors or friends from Virginia. Maryland itself was a state with totally divided loyalties.

"Are you done?" He nearly bellowed the words this time.

Callie jerked away from him. "You're—bound up the best that I can do for you. Now will you please leave?"

He pulled down his shirt and tucked it into his breeches, wincing slightly. He strode out to the parlor, his boots crunching over the glass. In the darkness, he opened the door and stared out over the fields. He stood there for the longest time, and she wondered what horrors of war he relived as he waited.

He finally closed the door and turned around, striding back toward her.

She moved away, but he didn't intend to touch her, it seemed. He strode in and pulled out a chair at the big oak table and sat. "Have you got anything to eat in here?" he asked her.

She didn't know why she suddenly felt so nervous in his presence. She wasn't afraid anymore. Despite his threats, she didn't believe that he would have really hurt her, no matter what she had done. Perhaps his chivalry was not the spoken kind. It had been in his eyes when he had looked out on the battlefield.

She wasn't afraid of him but she was becoming increasingly more aware of him as a man. Not as an enemy, not as a Reb. Just as a man. Aware of his height, his scent, his voice. His nearness. Even the way he sat with his long, booted legs stretched before him.

"Look, I've done everything that I can for you—"

"Right. There's nothing like a good kick in the head. You definitely owe me for that!"

"I did not kick you in the head!"

"I do beg to differ, darlin'. I felt it, that tender touch of your delicate foot!"

"I certainly didn't intend to."

"Then you would be merciful to your enemy, eh?"

"I've been damned merciful!"

He tilted back his hat. He watched her with heavy-lidded, curious eyes.

"But I am the enemy?"

She gripped the back of a kitchen chair. How dare he sit there in his gray uniform with his gaunt and haggard face and say such a thing to her.

"Yes! Yes, you are the enemy! And I don't owe you a damned thing! I've done far more for you than I should have done in all good conscience!"

"Why did you lie for me?" he asked curiously, his voice almost soft. A voice that seemed to reach out and touch her, moving like a warm breath along her spine.

"I don't know what you're talking about. You had a knife—"

"And you knew damned well that I'd never use it. I never even threatened you with it the last time."

"What difference does it make?" Callie asked impatiently. "Can't you just be grateful—and leave?"

He pulled the brim of his hat down very low, and it was a while before he answered her. "I'm starving. I haven't eaten or slept in hours and hours. And your Yankee patrols are going to be all over the place tonight."

Callie stood by the sink for a moment. She pursed her lips and reached over the sink for a match and lit a lamp to set on the table. She started down to the cellar, and he called her back sharply.

"Where are you going?"

"For food, Reb, if that's what it will take to make you leave."

She walked down the steps and found a large wedge of cheese and a smoked ham. She walked back up the steps and jumped when she discovered him waiting for her at the top.

"If I were going to turn you in," she told him, "I would have done so when Captain Johnston was here, Colonel Cameron."

One of his ink-dark brows shot up. "You know my name? Oh, of course! You discovered it when you were picking my pockets."

"I wasn't picking your pockets."

"Oh?" His brows arched high. "What were you looking for?"

She flushed despite the fact that she had every right to be furious with him for invading her house. "I thought you were dead," she said coolly. "I thought it might be provident to know your name."

"Oh," he murmured. He stepped aside, letting her pass. She set the cheese and ham on the table and was startled when he brushed past her. She didn't have a chance to give him a plate, she didn't even have a chance to cut him a piece of the cheese. He broke off a wedge of it, and wolfed it down.

"My, my, but they do teach good manners down in Virginia!" she said dryly. "He speaks with such eloquence and dines with such gentlemanly care!"

The gaze he cast her might have frozen fire. She determined to ignore it. She set a plate before him, and sliced the ham. "Colonel Cameron, I even have bread if you think you could wait—"

"No, I can't wait, but I'll have the bread too," he told her.

The loaf was much more than a day old, but Cameron didn't seem to notice as she set it on the table and he broke off a piece. An unlikely streak of pity swept through her. She had the feeling that the bread was probably amazingly fresh to this soldier, and that neither he nor his men had eaten much in a long, long time. He was right about one thing. So much of the war was taking place in the Shenandoah Valley and in the Virginia farmlands. It seemed that the North couldn't come up with the generals to best those in the South, but in time, it seemed, the South would be starved out.

It was war, Callie reminded herself. And it was probably one of the reasons that Lee had determined to bring the battle north for a change.

But while Southern soldiers endured endless days on small rations, they still managed to tear apart Northern soldiers. She owed this man no pity.

"What can I get you to drink, Colonel?" she asked with an edge to her voice.

"Whiskey? And coffee. Both would be wonderful."

"Of course."

She went to the cupboard and set a bottle of whiskey before him. "I'm sure you don't need a glass," she said. She lit the stove and measured out the coffee. When she was done, she discovered him staring at her. She discovered, too, that the plate he had ignored had been filled with food. For her. He pushed it across the table to her.

"Sit down." He thrust out a chair for her with his foot. "I'm sure you can't have eaten much."

She sat, staring at him. But she didn't touch the food.

"What's wrong? Can't you eat with a Reb?"

She shook her head. "I just can't eat yet," she said softly. The sarcasm was gone. They were both thinking about the battle.

He shoved the whiskey bottle across the table to her. "Take a swig. It will help you to forget. It's helped me a hell of a lot of times."

She started to shake her head again, but he said, "Take a swallow. A long swallow."

To her surprise, she did so. The whiskey burned. She choked, coughed, and swallowed again. The heat warmed her. And she did feel better.

She felt his eyes on her. They were fascinating eyes. They seemed as cold as ice, as hot as blue fire. They studied her as if they saw so very much of her.

"I think . . . I think the coffee is ready," she murmured. She stood up, found cups, and poured them both coffee. She sat down and set the mugs down, too. He topped off both of the cups with a measure of the whiskey.

"Relax, Miss . . . ?"

"What difference does my name make?"

"What difference does it make whether you tell me or not?" he countered.

"Callie. Callie Michaelson."

"Relax, Miss Michaelson."

"It's Mrs. Michaelson. And it is rather difficult to relax with the enemy in one's kitchen."

"Is it?"

"Yes."

"I'll be leaving before dawn. But then, of course, we do have the evening before us. And I need to get some sleep. Tell me, where is Mr. Michaelson?"

"Out in the yard," Callie said flatly. But if she expected to see some sign of fear or alarm in his eyes, she was disappointed.

"Dead and buried?" he asked.

"Yes."

"Where did he fall?"

"In a skirmish in Tennessee."

"When?"

"A little over a year ago."

"Well, Mrs. Michaelson, I was never in Tennessee, so I didn't kill your husband."

"I didn't suspect that you had."

"Ah. You simply hate all Rebel soldiers."

Callie swallowed down a gulp of her coffee and leapt to her feet. "I don't hate anyone. But you are the enemy. You just can't stay here any longer."

"I have to."

She turned around and strode out to the parlor. She heard him drink the last of his coffee and set down the cup. Then he followed her out. "You weren't thinking of leaving, were you, Miss Michaelson?"

"Frankly, yes. Since you're not."

"You can't go."

"Why?"

"I won't let you."

"But I haven't turned you in—"

"And that doesn't mean that you won't. I'm sorry. I'm really sorry. But I can't let you go."

She swore in exasperation. His dark brows shot up and he laughed. His face was really nice then. The enemy had charm.

But then he leaned against the wall by the broken windows and the once elegant parlor drapes. "What language for such a refined and sophisticated northern lass! And a beautiful one. Even more beautiful when you're swearing away in such a ladylike manner!"

There was a statuette on the table. A little statuette of Pan. Callie picked it up and hurled it at him.

It didn't matter much. Everything else in the house was ruined.

Her enemy ducked and laughed again.

"You really will be gone in the morning, Reb," she warned him. "Or I'll shoot you myself!"

"Will you?" he murmured, appraising her with interest. "Actually, you won't need to shoot me. If what you were out in the yard doing was helping me, you could just help me a little more, right into the grave. Would you really shoot me?"

"Yes! Oh, will you please leave then!"

"Oh, yes, I'll be leaving in the morning. I promise. And you'll be coming with me."

"What?"

Blue eyes, razor sharp, commanded hers. "You'll be coming with me, Mrs. Callie Michaelson. You're going to get me through the lines, and back to Virginia."

"You are insane! That is the last thing that I'm going to do! You had a nice meal, and you'll get a good night's sleep. I'll be damned if I'm going to be here when you wake up—"

"And I'll be damned if you're not!" he replied. With a sudden swift jerk he brought down the golden tassel and pull for the drapes. Before she knew it, the decorative rope was flung around her waist, and he was pulling her against him.

"What the hell do you think you're doing, Colonel?" Callie demanded, struggling fiercely.

It was all to no avail. She was swept up into his arms, and he was striding across the room to the stairway. "Going to bed. For that good night's sleep. And like it or not, Mrs. Michaelson, you'll be sleeping right beside me." Those blue eyes met hers once again. "Right beside me. You do owe me, Mrs. Michaelson. That's the way I see it, my angel."

"No, damn you, you Rebel bastard!" Callie swore. She tried to strike him. He held her closer.

He carried her up the stairs, heedless of her flailing arms.

"Yankee," he murmured softly to her, "it's going to be one hell of a night."

"Rebel bas—" Callie began.

But his arms slammed down hard on hers, and his eyes seemed to sear their blue fire into hers once more.

"One hell of a night!" he interrupted her. "I can promise you that!"

Four

The darkness at the top of the stairs seemed engulfing to Callie, but it didn't daunt her wayward cavalier in the least. He paused on the top landing for a moment, then headed for the closest doorway. Callie, breathless, exhausted, feeling the scrape of the wool of his uniform against her cheek, wondered desperately where he was finding his strength as they burst through the doorway into one of the bedrooms.

"What would your General Lee have to say?" she taunted. Lee might have been a Rebel commander, but he was equally famous in the North. He had been with the Union army when there had been no Confederacy, and Lincoln had once asked him to lead the Federal troops. But Lee's loyalties had been to his state, and when Virginia had seceded from the Union, Robert E. Lee had gone along with her. He was a man still known for his gallantry, for his ethics, and for his code of honor. Taunting this man about him was surely as damaging a blow as any she might throw with her fist.

"You just might have the opportunity to ask him, Mrs. Michaelson," Daniel Cameron replied, his deep drawl strangely intimate in the darkness.

A ripple of unease went sweeping through her. She should have been more frightened, she told herself. An enemy soldier was bearing her into a bedroom. It was darkly disturbing to realize that what swept through her was just as much a sense of excitement as it was fear. She wanted to do battle with this man. She didn't know if she wanted him to suffer for all that he was causing her, or if she had lived alone for so long that she was thrilled at the very thought of battle.

"Is this one your bedroom?" he asked suddenly.

She tensed. "What difference does it make?"

"None. I just want you to be comfortable."

"Comfortable?" Callie demanded. "How comfortable can I be, Colonel, caught in this vise against my will? And sure to suffer worse!"

His laughter suddenly rang out in the darkness, and she wondered if she had spoken too dramatically. In a second she was no longer held in any vise, he had set her down upon the bed. He may not have done so tenderly, but neither was he careless in his handling of her. He must have carried a matchbox, for in a moment there was a flare of light, and he saw the lamp upon her dresser and lit it. Hoisted quickly up on her elbows, Callie stared at him as he surveyed the room. He took in the fine white eyelet draperies on the windows, the braid rug on the hardwood floors, the polished mahogany dresser and wardrobe and washstand, and finally, the bed, with its beautifully carved headboard and footboard and white knit spread. It was her room, a warm, welcoming room, with imported tiles surrounding the hearth, and warm woolen blankets laid over the two rockers that sat right before the fireplace. Curiously, no bullets had strayed here. The soft eyelet drapes wafted lightly in the night breeze, untouched. She wondered if the Reb colonel thought about that fact as he surveyed the room, but his sharp blue eyes gave away none of his thoughts.

With the lamp lit, Callie could see the pallor in his handsome features. How was he still standing?

He started to unbuckle his scabbard, still surveying the room. Again, unease came sweeping through her system. What did he intend? She swallowed hard, and determined that she would fight to her very last breath for her honor.

He cast his scabbard and sword onto the side chair and sat for a moment. Then his gaze came down hard on her once again.

She gritted her teeth. Well, he was welcome to stay here. She would not do so.

She leapt up, praying that she might be granted speed and endurance while the weight of his injuries fell upon him at last.

But even as she sprinted for the door, he was up, and she went flying straight into his arms.

She cast back her head, and their eyes met. There was a certain amount of humor in his.

"You're not going anywhere, Yank. Sorry," he told her.

"Let me go. You've no right to hold me here at all."

"I have to hold you here."

"You're supposed to be gallant and fighting for the honor of the South! It's your duty—"

"I consider living through this one of my duties, too, Mrs. Michaelson. So you just might—"

"You can't stay here. In my room! With—me!"

His brows shot up suddenly. His hands on her shoulders were warm and firm. She felt his nearness with the length of her body. He smiled. Slowly. A handsome, lazy, compelling smile. Long ago, at some distant ball, while the whippoorwills trilled and the moss hung low over old trees, that smile must have melted many a heart.

Now it also held a little bit of bitterness, and even, perhaps, a shade of wistfulness. Here was a hardened soldier, an enemy long in the field, probably a veteran of nearly every battle in the eastern theater of this war.

He was amused. "Why, Mrs. Michaelson, just what are you afraid of? Me?"

"Certainly not. You are merely a very rude—and I might add muddy—Rebel soldier. I'm not afraid of you a single bit."

"Why not? Is there a Yankee in the wardrobe, waiting to protect you?"

She didn't know if he was taunting her, or if he was really suspicious of her.

"Perhaps there is a Yankee in the wardrobe," she returned swiftly. "Perhaps you should leave me be and run as swiftly as you can!"

"Hmm . . . Let's see, it's Captain Eric Dabney I need to fear, right?"

"Yes, you should be running just as fast as you can."

He started to laugh. "Ah. Captain Dabney has been biding his time in a wardrobe all these hours. He doesn't mind a Rebel dining with you, but now that you feel truly threatened by a member of the Confederacy, he's going to come jumping out."

"He just might."

Cameron ran his knuckles over her cheek, so softly that the touch might have been just the warmth of a nearby whisper. But she felt the warmth come sweeping into her, felt it spiral and curl and flow up and down the length of her spine.

"A damsel in distress," he murmured.

"Pardon?"

"Nothing," he said, then he smiled again, meeting her eyes. "If I'd been in your wardrobe, Mrs. Michaelson, I'd have been out of it long ago. I'd have had a sword to the throat of any man who came within inches of you. I don't think that Captain Dabney is hereabouts. And I do think that you're afraid of me."

"Well, I'm not!" But she was! Not so much of his violence, though there was violence in him. What she feared was the tenderness of his touch.

"Not a bit?" he taunted.

She tried to pull away.

"Not even a little bit?" he repeated. He laughed softly.

Her chin lifted, and her eyes met his. Her body was flush with his so that she could feel the beat of his heart.

And he could feel the frantic pulse of hers.

"Callie Michaelson, there is a pulse fluttering along your throat like wildfire. You've had it right from the beginning. Once upon a time I was taught manners. My mother was gracious and sweet, and she taught the three of us all about the feelings of others. And yet that seems so very long ago now. War does strange things to people. Did you know that?"

His hold upon her was tight. She felt panic creeping into her despite her sure conviction that he would never hurt her.

"Afraid yet?" he demanded, his eyes ablaze.

To her amazement, her passion and courage held out. "I'll never be afraid of the likes of you, you gray-bellied hooligan!" she swore.

His laughter rang out pleasantly. Before she knew it, he had turned her around by the shoulders. "Don't worry, Mrs. Michaelson. There is no reason for you to be afraid. I have absolutely no evil designs upon you."

She swung around again to face him. "I didn't think that you—"

"Oh yes, you did! And now you're indignant that I don't."

"I most certainly am not—"

"Oh yes, you are. Well, calm down. It isn't that you aren't beautiful. And I am assuredly entranced, and I imagine, once you set your mind upon it, you could seduce a saint."

"How dare you—" Callie began furiously. But he was still laughing, and very quick to interrupt her. "I'm merely trying to set your mind at ease!"

"The hell you are!" She swore, her hands on her hips.

Her language only served to amuse him further. "Mrs. Michaelson, they should have you on the field. You certainly do not retreat!"

"I don't retreat, and I don't lose, and I never, never surrender—" she began.

Before she could go further, a soft cry escaped her as his hands fell upon her shoulders again. This time he swung her around in a no-nonsense fashion and gave her a good prod. She went flying back down upon her bed, and quickly rolled to face him, ever wary once again.

"I don't want to hurt you or frighten you."

"Really?" Callie retorted sarcastically, her eyes narrowing.

"Really." He bent low over her, his arms like bars on either side of her as he braced himself over her. "Not that I wouldn't want you!" he whispered, and the sound was serious and deep and husky, one that seemed to sink into her body and leave her both hot and shivery. He spoke again, and this time he sounded exhausted. "I have to get some sleep. And you are a Yank, and I can't trust you. You're going to stay with me."

He pushed away from her. Her eyes widened with alarm because he had his belt off and was approaching her with it.

She opened her mouth to scream, amazed, thinking that he meant to beat her with it. But before she could even whisper, he was straddled over her, his finger pressed against her lip.

"Mrs. Michaelson, believe it or not, there is some sense of honor nesting in this Rebel bosom, and believe it or not, I've no real desire to cause you stress or pain. But I have to sleep, and I can't let you go roaming around on your own while I'm at it. Understand?"

She stared at him, still wary, uncertain whether to move or not. "Do you understand?" He asked the question in a softer tone.

She nodded, certain that if she didn't do so, he'd find a way of pressing his point.

"Good," he said softly. To her dismay, he looped the belt over her arm and then around his own. He looked down at her for a long, stern moment of warning.

Then he pitched forward, falling over her and coming to rest at her side.

For several moments, Callie lay perfectly still, feeling the beating of his heart and the frantic clamor of her own. Seconds passed, minutes. He didn't move, and neither did she.

He had passed out cold.

What tremendous strength of will he must have to taunt her so coolly, when he was so very close to total collapse!

For one frantic moment Callie was afraid that he had died. That she was tied in bed to a dead man. But then she felt his heartbeat again, felt the rise and fall of his chest where he lay beside her.

She closed her eyes, inhaling and exhaling slowly. She should have prayed for his death, for it seemed to be the only way that she would find her own escape. He was the enemy. Perhaps he had never been in Tennessee, perhaps he hadn't fought at Shiloh. He should have remained one of the nameless, faceless soldiers in gray who was her enemy.

She didn't want him to die in her house, she told herself. But if he had passed out again she needed to be quick and free herself from him. There still had to be Union soldiers in the near vicinity. This battlefield that had encompassed her home had been so littered with the dead and dying that it would surely take days to clear the bodies.

The thought made her ill, and she closed her eyes tightly. But even with her eyes closed, she kept reliving the horror of all that she had seen in her yard. She opened her eyes again, and turned carefully to view the Rebel face she was coming to know so well.

He was very pale, and his face was damp. He was probably far more seriously injured than he cared to admit and she could judge. If he was sent on to a prison camp, he most assuredly would die.

She couldn't allow that to be her problem, she told herself sternly. She had given her loyalty to the Union, and before God she knew herself right to have done so. She had not been influenced by her father, or her brothers, or even her own husband. All around her, in the state of Maryland, men had split on all the questions about the war. In the beginning it had been a question of states' rights —but that question had been there mainly because of slavery. Maryland was filled with slave owners.

Maryland had troops fighting with the South, and troops fighting with the North. The state had not seceded from the Union, but there was probably no other place where it was more likely for a father to face a son down the length of his rifle, or for a brother to come front to front with a brother.

She had weighed and judged all that she heard, listening to her father, her brothers, and her husband. In the end, she had concluded that they were one nation, and that the Union must be preserved. Though many of her neighbors owned slaves, she had asked Gregory to free the five hands that he had owned, and Gregory had obliged her. It was simply wrong to own a man, to keep him in bondage, to whip him, to abuse him, to strip him of his dignity. Though many slaves were well cared for—just as their master's pet hounds and finest horses were well cared for—Callie knew of few slaves who had been left with their pride and dignity intact.

She had made up her own mind about the war. Luckily, she had been in agreement with those closest to her. That meant that the Rebel lying beside her was indeed the enemy. And the war was far from over. The Rebels had battered the Union forces time and time again.

Rebel soldiers had brought about destruction. Just as they had destroyed her father and Gregory.

She twisted with discomfort and with a raw edge of anguish, thinking of her husband. Even now, she dared not dwell upon his death too long.

Colonel Daniel Cameron. She bit her lip, and she tried to pull her arm closer to herself. She needed to slip her arm free of the loop he had fashioned from his belt. She grit her teeth. She gently pulled at the loop he had made, and then more aggressively. She couldn't budge the knot.

She swore out loud. It didn't matter. Colonel Cameron wasn't moving.

Near tears, she continued to tug at the leather. The more she worked at it, the tighter it became.

She tried to slide the loop down her arm. Again, her efforts only served to bind her more tightly.

"You son of a bitch!" she swore out loud to him.

She could have sworn that even in his unconscious state he smiled at her distress.

But his eyes remained closed, and his breathing became more ragged.

She sat up, tugging upon his arm and the loop of the belt that tied him to her. The leather was tied from his wrist to hers, with perhaps fifteen inches between them. He had tied the knots so tightly she could not budge them. She fought urgently with the leather, breaking her nails. Tears of frustration stung her eyes. He had known what he was doing. He was the most adept man with a knot she had ever met.

Worn, desolate, she flung herself back against the bed. The lamp was burning low. The night had become cool, and there was no fire burning in the hearth. She lay still, her teeth grating, her mind working furiously.

She remembered his sword.

She sat up. It lay against one of the rockers by the hearth. If she could just reach it, she could sever the leather that bound them together.

She lay flat and reached for the chair, her arm outstretched. She could just touch the chair with the tip of her fingers. She bit into her lip, and tugged upon her captor. Nothing. She paused, breathing hard. She tugged again. It seemed that he moved, just a hair. But she came closer to the sword hilt too.

Silently, she began to pray, and in seconds, she was victorious. Her fingers curled around the hilt of his blade. She was startled by the weight of it, bearing down on her free arm, but she grit her teeth, determined. Suddenly, the blade came free from his scabbard, with such a force that she could not control it. It seemed to fly through the air, and then it struck down upon the braid rug beneath her bed with an incredible force and a snap that sounded like a sure hit by cannon fire.

She tried to lift it, and twist it again, and even as she did so, a startled cry escaped her.

The sound had awakened her weary Reb. Pale, drawn, tense—and seeming to breathe smoke rings of fury—he stared at her. With amazing speed and agility he reached over her, and snatched the sword from her grasp with an ease born of familiarity and skill. He was so angry that she cried out again, certain that he meant to let the blade fall upon her, slicing her in two.

He tossed the sword aside, and his staring eyes were as hard and cold and striking as the blade. "You meant to kill me!" he whispered.

"No!"

"Ah, you did not mean to kick me, but your foot connected fiercely with my head! And you did not mean to slay me—rather, my sword jumped into your hand!"

"I meant to free myself from you!" she cried.

"One way or the other," he suggested harshly.

"I want to be free!"

"Well, you can't! Not tonight!" With a jerk, he brought her hurtling back against him. She lay dead still and furious, dismayed that he believed with no uncertainty that she had meant to kill him if she could.

"Please, Mrs. Michaelson!" The whisper touched her ear. "Please, just go to sleep. Things will look better for both of us in the morning."

A startled gasp escaped her as she was pulled more closely against him. She was turned, and his arm came around her, a gray band against the very thought of movement.

A gray-clad leg fell over her own. She caught her breath. She could feel his hand, just below her breast. She could feel the length of him pressed against the length of her back and limbs.

She did not move again. She barely dared to breathe.

In time, she did as he had commanded. She slept.

Heat encompassed him.

It was summer, and they were lying on the slope above the river once again, Jesse, Christa, and him. He could feel the sun, and he should have felt the ever soft breeze that came in off the river, no matter how hot and humid the day came to be. But the breeze wouldn't come.

He knew why. The cannons were exploding. They were exploding all around him.

Suddenly, he and Jesse were alone, riding away from Harpers Ferry. They were both in blue, and coming away from the assault on the fire-engine house where old John Brown had holed up with his few surviving raiders. He could hear John Brown, shouting around them, again and again.

". . . blood, this land shall be purged by blood . . ."

He looked from his brother's wary face down to his hands, where they lay idly upon the pommel of his saddle.

His hands were covered in blood.

It seemed that more bombs exploded. He was back at Cameron Hall, and he was standing by the cemetery. Clasping Jesse. There were no words that passed between them. The rift that had driven apart the country had also driven them apart.

His brother was riding north.

Skyrockets seemed to burst and soar.

He heard crying. Christa crying, Kiernan crying. Jesse was going away.

The skyrockets were soaring over Fort Sumter. It was April 1861. The war had begun.

He tossed and turned.

He was riding hard. He always rode hard, for he was part of General James Ewell Brown "Jeb" Stuart's fantastic cavalry. They could ride circles around almost any army. They could move endless miles in unbelievable time. They saw action again and again and again, scouting, circling, carrying information vital to Jackson and Lee.

He shouldn't have been back with his troops. He'd been wounded when Union General McClellan had made his abortive attack on the peninsula, and it had only been because he had been found by his own brother that he had avoided a prison camp. Jesse had sewn him up, and Jesse had carried him home.

In his restless sleep, Daniel twisted and turned again. Hot, it was so hot. He was back at Cameron Hall again, looking out over the James. He heard the cry of a child, and smiled. War brought death, and war brought life. Jesse's son had been born, a strapping baby boy. So tiny. The baby's little fingers had barely managed to curl around his own.

Jesse had had precious little time with his child. McClellan's troops had retreated, and it was imperative that Jesse leave behind him the Rebel-held land where he had been born.

Once again the brothers had said good-bye, and Daniel had been summoned back to duty.

With General Thomas "Stonewall" Jackson, he had been part of the army Lee had split in half for this daring invasion north. They had captured the town of Harpers Ferry—now being called "West Virginia"—and the thousands of Federal troops that had been holding it. Then, with no sleep and precious little food, they had ridden hard to meet up with Lee in this tiny town of Sharpsburg, Maryland. Under special assignment to Lee, he had seen much of the battle. Too much of the battle. He had seen the area they were already calling "Bloody Lane"—the deep trench along the farmlands where the Rebels had dug in. Where they had held so fiercely until the line had been broken and the Federal forces had rained down upon them with shot. Where bodies were piled upon bodies that were piled upon bodies.

He tossed and turned. He looked up. She was there. His angel. The beautiful angel with the fantastic dove-gray eyes and wealth of deep flaming auburn hair.

She leaned over him. She smelled so sweetly. Like the summer rose. She should have belonged to the past. To the beautiful, lazy days along the river. To the great, porticoed back porch of Cameron Hall. She should have been dressed in muslins and hooped petticoats, and she should have sat upon the wicker swing. Breezes, soft and sweet, should have played over her hair. He could see her, a great straw hat shading her eyes, swinging, white gloves upon her hands. An angel, she would turn to him. Her laughter would be music, as beautiful as her wide gray eyes, framed by the black sweep of her lashes.

Yes, she was there. Home, where the river whispered its faint harmony, where the green grasses met with blue sky and green water. Where Cameron Hall stood with its grace and welcoming beauty. Where the oaks were covered in moss. She was there, running through the trees. He heard her laughter, soft, clear, delicate, like the sound of the wind chimes in March. Against an oak she paused, looking back, her laughter escaping her once again. It was contagious, and he laughed in turn, and ran after her once again. Upon the slope, above the river, where dreams were woven, he caught her at last, and laughing together, they rolled in the sweet scent of the rain-washed lawn while the river drifted lazily by. He stared into her eyes. So intriguing a gray, rimmed with deep dark blue. He touched her cheek and held his angel.

Angel! Yes, an avenging angel who wielded a sword.

Visions began to collide. The river no longer whispered. He felt the heat, the terrible heat. But she was still there.

She was speaking to him. He tried very hard to understand her.

". . . you must help me. You have to try to help me get free of this belt. Colonel, if I don't cool you down, you'll die. Don't you understand me?"

Cameron Hall faded clear away. He was drenched. He was hot, he was shivering. Lamplight flickered against the handsomely decorated room. He lay upon a white bedspread, and it was no angel, but his gray-eyed Yankee vixen who leaned over him.

It only appeared that those dove-gray eyes were filled with compassion. She had meant to slay him once. He was nearly at her mercy now. He could almost taste death, it seemed that close.

"Colonel, listen to me!" she pleaded with him.

"Can't!" he whispered.

"Please! I don't want you dying on me!"

He almost smiled. Her voice. So soft. So musical. It should have been an angel's voice.

"You'll turn me in." His words must have been very low, for she leaned against him to try to catch them.

"Colonel, you have to have some faith in me! Help me with this! I must cool you down. I swear to you, I'll not leave you like this—"

He fought for strength. He managed to wind his fingers around her arm. His eyes met hers.

"Honor," he interrupted her.

"What?"

"On your honor?"

"What?" she repeated. "Oh!" she breathed. She hesitated a moment. His eyes started to flicker closed. He was losing consciousness again.

"On my honor, Colonel! I'll not leave you. Set me free, and I'll not leave you."

"Unless I die," he commanded her.

"Don't—"

"Unless I die!" he repeated.

"Fine! On my honor, I'll stay with you. Unless you die," she said.

His fingers were shaking. He could scarcely raise his hand, scarcely control it. He found the loop on his wrist. For a moment, he fumbled. He didn't have the strength. He caught the leather with his teeth. He pulled with his last strength. She was free.

She was up in a flash. His last thought was that she had lied, that she had deserted him as soon as physically possible.

It didn't matter. The room spun and faded.

Cannons exploded. He was in the midst of a fire. Fire was all around him, engulfing him. . . .

It seemed to be much, much later that he first felt the coolness of the cloth against him.

He savored that coolness.

It touched his forehead, and moved over his shoulders. He no longer shook, but lay there, weak, disoriented. At first, all he knew was that sensation of coolness. Had he died at last, and gone to heaven? After all, how many times could he taunt death?

Was this a Yank prison? Did they heal him now, just to make his stay more wretched, until he could succumb to some other evil?

This was so tender, so gentle a touch.

He opened his eyes. They widened still further. She was still with him. Mrs. Callie Michaelson. His shirt was gone, he lay on his back, and she moved a cool, water-drenched cloth over and over his naked chest. She continued to do so for several long minutes before her eyes met his. She jumped, suddenly aware that he had been watching her.

"You're still here," he tried to say. The words were little more than a croak.

"I gave you my word of honor that I would remain," she said. Her hand had stopped moving. It lay upon the cloth just over his heart.

He willed himself to find some strength. His fingers curled around her wrist. "You'd keep your word to a Reb?" he asked her softly.

"My word, sir, is a vow—no matter to whom it is given."

He smiled slowly. "Well, then, I thank you, Mrs. Michaelson. You've probably saved my life."

She stood up, gently tugging her wrist from his grasp. Regretfully, still curious as he surveyed her fascinating eyes, he released her.

"Not probably, Reb," she told him. "I've most certainly saved your life. You were burning up. But it seems that your fever has abated. Let me get you some water to drink. I've barely managed to get a few glasses into you. Then I'll get you something to eat, and when darkness falls again, you can go."

She poured him a large glass of water from the pitcher at his bedside. Daniel sipped it at first. Then it suddenly seemed to be the most delicious thing that he had ever tasted. He swallowed down the whole of it in a matter of seconds. God, it was good.

She took the glass from him.

"Now, Colonel, you can rest, and I'll get you some soup. But I warn you, I do feel that my word to you has been fulfilled. You are the enemy. And I want you gone."

So battle was thus reengaged, he thought. Indeed, it was so, for there was a silver light in her eyes, shimmering, beautiful—and certainly something to reckon with.

He frowned suddenly, catching her wrist once more. He stared at her, a demand in his eyes. "You said, 'when darkness comes again'?"

"Yes, Colonel, you've come in and out of consciousness for nearly forty-eight hours now."

Two days! He had lost two full days.

She had stayed with him. She had not gone for the Yankee troops, and there must have been many Yankee troops in the vicinity.

Because of her word?

Once he had awakened to the certainty that she was trying to cut him down with his sword. But now she was still here with him. Because of her, he had survived another battle. But now she had warned him that he was her enemy.

"I have to get up," he said and started to throw the sheets back.

"No!" she exclaimed. "Colonel, wait!" For a few fleeting seconds her eyes seemed wide, alarmed. She stepped back demurely, her rich lashes falling over her eyes, but her manner entirely calm and regal. "You might not want to do that, sir."

"Why not?"

"Because you're buck naked beneath that sheet."

Stunned into momentary silence, Daniel stared at her blankly.

She sighed with impatience. "Colonel, I had to soak you in the coldest water I could find. I needed to cool down the length of your body for any hope of fighting the fever."

"So you—stripped me?"

"Don't sound so outraged, Colonel." Her words were slow and cool, and she lifted a delicate brow to a high and imperious angle. "I told you. I had no choice."

"What have you done with my uniform?"

"Your uniform was full of mud and blood." She smiled. "I burned it. My apologies. It really wasn't at all salvageable."

"It wasn't salvageable?"

"No more so than your lost cause, Colonel Cameron."

"Lost cause, ma'am? Why, it still seems to me that we Rebs are riding circles around you Yanks."

"You will not be victorious."

"I, ma'am, will be," he promised her.

"Then I must thank goodness, Colonel Cameron, that the war will not depend on one man alone."

Mrs. Callie Michaelson could be one very demure and confident woman, Daniel thought. He didn't know if he was outraged or not.

He smiled slowly, not knowing if he wanted to taunt her, or throw his arms around her and drag her down with him and show her all of the very real dangers of stripping down a man who had been at war as long as he had.

He'd never do such a thing. His sense of honor wasn't really half as tarnished as she seemed to think.

Actually, he wasn't sure that he had the energy left to drag her down beside him.

"Are you all right, Colonel?" she inquired. She knew she had the upper hand at the moment, and that he knew it. Those beautiful gray eyes were awfully smug.

"I'm just fine, Mrs. Michaelson. If anything, I'm surprised that a gentlewoman such as yourself would show such mercy as to strip down a Rebel soldier. I am amazed. How alarming it must have been for you! Such danger you cast yourself into!"

Her lashes swept her cheeks again, but he failed to draw a blush.

"Colonel, it seems to me that beneath the fabric, be it blue or gray, men do seem to be very much alike. I found nothing alarming about the act at all, and my dear Colonel, I must say, I hardly found you . . . dangerous."

With that she spun around and started toward the stairs.

Daniel's smile deepened. He closed his eyes. He had lost two full days. He didn't know what was happening, and he didn't know where he needed to get to rejoin his men or Stuart.

For the first time since the war had begun, he decided that he had to allow himself a certain period of convalescence. He had to get through the lines to get home. The cavalry would be awaiting him somewhere in Virginia.

But for the moment, he determined there was something else equally important.

He wanted Mrs. Callie Michaelson to know that he could be dangerous when he chose. Damned dangerous.

He rose, pulling the sheet with him and wrapping it around his waist. He paused for several minutes, finding the strength to stand. Life and energy slowly eased back into his limbs. He flexed his fingers and then his arms. He became certain that, weak as he was, he was not going to keel over with his first step.

With the white tail of sheet following him like a bridal train, he left the room and walked carefully down the stairs.

It was time to confront his enemy angel once again.

So there was no difference between men, was there?

She wanted battle? Well, battle was thus engaged.

She was about to discover that, indeed, there were very real differences between men.

Five

Callie wasn't at all sure she had managed to appear calm and completely unruffled in front of her uninvited guest. By the time she reached the kitchen, her palms were very damp and her heart seemed to be thundering at a thousand pulses a minute. She nearly splashed the stew she had been cooking all over her fingers when she went to stir the large pot over the stove.

She was so much more comfortable with him when he was unconscious!

No, God forgive her, she hadn't just been comfortable. She had actually enjoyed caring for him.

It hadn't been easy at first. He had been on fire, his flesh simply burning, and she had been powerless, bound as she was to him. No matter how he had kicked and thrashed and turned, no matter how hotly he had burned, he had maintained a fierce strength. She hadn't been able to free herself from the binds he had created between them and she hadn't been able to get through to him. Alone in the darkness she had imagined his dying, and herself bound to him day after day while his body decayed.

But she had known it had been more than the fear of being tied to a dead man that had so frightened her. She didn't want him to die. Cocky, arrogant Rebel that he might be, he had put something of challenge and vitality back into her own life.

And he was, in his masculine way, beautiful.

That was what she had enjoyed.

She'd not thought this at all at first. Once she had convinced him to free her, she had cut away his clothing because of the mud and the blood that matted his chest and his abdomen. And then she had been so busy soaking his flesh that she had paid it little heed. Tirelessly, she had run up and down the steps, fetching more and more water from the pump. She had opened all of the windows to cool the room, and then she had soaked him again and again.

It had been well into the day when she had known that she had succeeded, that he was going to live. He didn't open his eyes, he didn't speak—he gave her very little sign of life. But the awful heat began to cool, and his flesh was no longer so horribly dry to the touch. He breathed more easily. The fever was gone. He slept a sweeter sleep.

It was then that she dared to look at the man she had tended so long. From the handsome features that had so intrigued her from the beginning to the broad planes of his shoulders. His well-muscled torso and arms were taut and cleanly defined, making his skin smooth to her stroke now that the fever had broken. There was a wild profusion of dark hair upon his chest, hair as ebony as that upon his head, its course of growth just as defined as his muscle tone, swirling across his breast, than narrowing down to a fine little whorl at his navel. That fine lean line continued to his groin, where the wild nest of darkness flared deep again. Against it lay that part of him that brought a wildness to her heart, for even as he slept his maleness seemed to have a life of its own, veins pulsing vibrantly, his natural endowment both intimidating and tempting despite his restful state. She was absolutely shocked to find herself so fascinated to touch him, and very glad then of his sleep, for she must have blushed a thousand shades of purple. Indeed, she had turned him over so as not to find such a fascination with his anatomy, but then she had discovered herself admiring his back and, worse, his buttocks. From head to toe he was excellently muscled, so taut, so trim, so sleek and beautiful, like an exceptionally fine wild animal.

He wasn't a wild animal, she reminded herself. He was worse. He was a Rebel soldier.

But while he lay there unconscious, she needn't think of what he was, she told herself, or why she had worked so strenuously to save him. The breeze shifted, fall had come. Though the day was gentle and cool enough, she was suddenly made aware of the scent of death that still hung heavy upon the air so near the battlefield.

She closed the window and pulled the sheets up to his waist. She closed her eyes, holding her breath while memories assailed her. Once upon a time, not so very long ago, she had been in love. And she had been loved in turn. They had both been so young, at first exchanging shy, hesitant kisses in the fields, then exploring those kisses more deeply in the dark of the barn. They'd been very proper, of course, never dreaming of discovering any more of one another until their wedding night, but then that night had come, and love itself had led the way. Their first night had been awkward, but their love had let them laugh, and in the days and nights that followed, they had learned that their laughter was but an added boon. Callie had learned to cherish her young husband's kisses, to thrill to his touch, to awaken in his arms.

But Gregory Michaelson now lay out back, his young limbs decimated by war, his soul surely risen, but his body nothing more than food for the ever triumphant worms. When he had come home to her in a military-issue coffin, she had been cold. Her heart had been colder than death itself, she was convinced. She would never love again, she swore it.

And she had never felt tempted to love again. No matter what soldiers came passing through, no matter what friend her brothers brought by so quickly on their few days of grace from the army, she had never known the slightest whisper of warmth to come to her heart.

Her heart had not warmed now, she assured herself.

But something else had.

Since she had first seen his face, she had found it attractive. From the first time his startling blue eyes had fallen upon hers, she had felt faint stirrings within herself. She had never felt fear that had been greater than her sense of excitement around him.

She had known, from somewhere deep within her soul, that she could not bear him to die. Not because she feared being bound to a dead man, but because it was him.

And now, in caring for him, she discovered herself ever more attracted to him. She wanted to forget the war. She wanted to go back and pretend that it had never come. She wanted him to be Gregory, and she wanted to lie down beside him and feel the warmth of his body stealing into hers, know the sweet rush of excitement that could sweep away all sense and reason.

Shivering, she stared into the pot of bubbling stew. The war had come. It was very real. The young blond Maryland farmer she had loved and married was buried in the yard, and she was a widow. A respectable, moral widow. She should be shamed by the very thoughts filling her head. Shamed by the beat of her heart. By the nervousness that shivered through her, by the recklessness that haunted all of her being.

He would leave tonight.

"That smells wonderful."

She jumped, spinning around. He had followed her down the stairs and stood lounging comfortably in the doorway.

He was wearing her sheet. It was stark white against the sleek bronze of his torso. His nakedness had been imposing enough while he slept. Now the taut ripples of muscle against his lean belly seemed downright decadent.

"What do you think you're doing?" she demanded. She wanted to be righteously angry. Her voice was faltering.

He lifted his hands innocently. "What do you mean?"

"Colonel Cameron," she said with soft dignity, her eyes narrowing warningly upon his, "you come from a good home. I do believe, sir, that you come from a landed home, that you probably went to the best schools, and that you were raised to be a gentleman. So what are you doing in my kitchen in a sheet?"

"Well now, Mrs. Michaelson," he taunted, blue eyes flashing, "should I have dropped the sheet?"

"This from a man who lives and walks due to my mercy," she retorted.

He shrugged, walking across the kitchen, coming uncomfortably close to stir the stew and inhale its sweet aroma. "Mrs. Michaelson, from your comments, I assumed that you found me no more threatening in any state of dress or undress than you would find a toddling lad of two. And besides, you've burned my uniform. A grave injustice, I daresay, but as you've just reminded me, I must be grateful for your mercy. So what would you have me wear?"

"I'd have you back in bed, resting, gathering your strength, so as to leave this evening," she told him.

He smiled and went to sweep his hat from his head, then realized that he was no longer in dress of any kind. "Ah, well, the uniform can be replaced. I was quite fond of the hat. Was it necessary to burn it too?"

"Quite," Callie said.

"A pity."

"I think not. There are breeches and shirts in the wardrobe in my room. The fit may not be perfect, but I'm sure you'll manage."

"Union uniforms?" he asked her.

She shrugged. "I'm not sure, to tell you the truth," she said.

"I'm not escaping in a Union uniform, Mrs. Michaelson."

"I'm sure that you wore blue at some point, Colonel. You mentioned that your brother was a Yankee surgeon, so I find it quite possible that you were both in the military before secession and this war of rebellion came about. It'll not hurt you to wear blue once again."

"I prefer the sheet, thank you."

He stood by the pot on the stove, so intimately close to her that she felt the urge to scream. She fought for control, determined that he'd never best her. Perhaps that was part of the excitement. He made her determined to win. He challenged her on so many different levels.

She smiled sweetly, turning to stir the stew and managing to take a step farther away from him. "You plan to run through the Yankee lines in a sheet, Colonel?"

"Better a sheet than a Yankee uniform, Mrs. Michaelson." He took the ladle from her fingers, dipped it into the stew, and tasted it. His eyes came instantly back to hers, and he arched a brow, a slow smile curling his lip. "It's wonderful, Mrs. Michaelson. Really, Providence must have had mercy to have left me here, upon your doorstep."

"Providence was just wonderful," Callie muttered, snatching the ladle back from him. "Would you please go and put something on?"

He was quiet, watching her. She could feel his eyes just like she could feel the heat of a flame when a candle was too close.

"Truly, Callie, I cannot wear a Yankee uniform. I am not a spy, and would not be caught and hanged as one, unless I were, indeed, involved in some necessary subterfuge. I don't relish the thought of dying in battle, but in the line of one's duty, it is, at the least, an honorable way to perish. I'd not hang unless such a death could, in truth, do justice to my cause."

"Oh!" Callie murmured. She hadn't been thinking. It was true. If Yankee troops caught him in his own uniform, they would call him a prisoner of war. And he might waste away in a prison camp, but unless he came upon them with his sword swinging or his guns blazing, they'd not hang him. Spies were dealt with harshly in this war. Why, in Washington, they'd even imprisoned Mrs. Rose Greenhow, a lady who had once been considered a belle of the capital's society. There were many suggestions that even she might be executed, although Callie tried to convince herself that the poor lady would not come to such an end.

"Callie, surely you did not offer me so much mercy so very tenderly, only that I should be well when I was hanged?"

"I was never tender," she informed him.

"So, you did intend that I should be hanged."

"No, sir, I did not," she said irritably. She waved the ladle at him, taking a step forward, determined that he should retreat. "Colonel—"

He took the ladle back from her. "Really, Mrs. Michaelson, I have been attacked by swords and cannons and guns, but I am weary still, and haven't the heart to defend myself from a soup ladle!"

In exasperation she grated out a soft oath. "Colonel, surely your mama would be quite horrified to see her son in a young woman's kitchen garbed in nothing but her sheet!"

"My mother, ma'am, was a sage and careful lady and would surely have been as matter-of-fact as you yourself have been. She would be grateful that you had saved my life, however, and I'm quite convinced that she wouldn't even ask why I found it necessary to be clad in nothing but a sheet."

"Colonel, I am about to throw you out in that sheet!" she warned him.

"Cast me naked to the wolves, eh?"

"You forget, I am a Yankee. Those are but the wolves I run with myself."

"No," he said softly, "I do not forget."

A curious shiver swept through her as he said the words and as his gaze met hers with a startling blue sizzle. Since she was hardly a danger to him at the moment, she didn't understand the strange dread that filled her, almost like a premonition.

She took another step away from him. "Well," she murmured, "I cannot bring back your uniform. I did burn it. You'll have to find something. There should be enough civilian clothing to choose from." She stared him up and down. "My husband was not, perhaps, so tall, but . . ." She paused, then shrugged. "My father's breeches might well fit you. And my brother's shirts are in a trunk just down the hallway."

"I take it that I am not invited to dinner unless I am decently clad?" he said. His voice was light, a tone that teased. Were he not naked, he might easily have had the manner of the Virginia gentleman he surely once had been. The effect upon her was both sweeping and alarming, for she smiled quickly, wishing he were not capable of being quite so charming.

"You most certainly are not," she assured him.

He bowed to her in a courtly gesture. "Then I will return as decently clad as I can manage."

He turned with his sheet trailing. She watched him for a moment, then sank her teeth into her lower lip, fighting the sudden temptation to cry.

War had changed everything. It had stolen everything from her. And now it had brought the enemy to her doorstep, and even robbed her of the luxury of hating him.

She turned back to the stew, impatient with herself. While he was gone, she set the table. She had had precious little time to do much about the house while she had tended him over the last hours, but she had managed to pick up the kitchen and sweep up all the glass that had littered the living room. She wondered if she hadn't become obsessive, or partly crazed, for it seemed to her now that it was almost ridiculously important to behave as if life and the passing days were just as normal as any others.

Of course, the days weren't normal at all. Union soldiers had passed by this afternoon, still trying to collect all of the dead from the battlefield. A sergeant to whom she had nervously offered a dipper of cold water that afternoon had been near parchment-white when he had stumbled onto the porch. Before realizing that he was speaking to a young lady—and that manners dictated he take grave care to make his words delicate—he had told her about a trench the Rebels had been holding, and how, at the end, a New York regiment had broken their hold on it, and shot down the Rebs until they were piled two and three deep in death.

The gulley was now called "Blood Alley."

Fifty thousand men had perished in the one battle. More blood had been spilled here in one day than in any other battle of the war thus far.

No, life was not normal today. Not while soldiers still prowled fields where the corn had been mown down to the ground by bullets, and the blood of two great armies was still damp upon the ground.

Not normal at all. Out of twenty chickens, three remained out by the barn. Two of her goats were dead, three had just disappeared. For some miraculous reason, her horse had been spared both injury and theft, but her milk cow was long, long gone, along with numerous sacks of wheat. The garden had been trampled down to nearly nothing. Indeed, war had changed everything.

But there were certain things that she could do, she determined, and so she set the table as if she were sitting down to any meal with her family. She lit candles on the table and used the good English dishes and her mother's fine silver, and the Irish white linen tablecloth and napkins. She dug deep into the cellar to find a bottle of vintage wine, and she was just pouring it into her best crystal wine glasses when Colonel Daniel Cameron, C.S.A., made his appearance downstairs once again.

He had chosen one of her father's simple cotton work shirts and a pair of blue denim breeches. He'd found his boots, and they came up to his kneecaps. The whole ensemble should have given him the appearance of a farm boy, but instead he had the look of a pirate about him, dashing and dangerous, and intriguing.

"Will this do, Mrs. Michaelson?" he asked politely.

"Yes, quite," she told him. She indicated the table, untying the apron she had been wearing about her waist. "Do sit down, Colonel."

"Why, I thank you, Mrs. Michaelson," he told her. But he drew out a chair and stood behind it, politely waiting. Callie dished the stew into a server and brought it to the table. Once she had set it down, she allowed Daniel Cameron to seat her.

He did not seat himself immediately, but picked up the wine she had chosen. "Ah, how nice, Mrs. Michaelson. A French burgundy, 1855." With practiced ease, he uncorked the bottle, casually inhaled the scent of the cork, and expertly poured out the wine into their glasses. He lifted his to hers, tasted the wine carefully, and grinned. "An excellent vintage, Mrs. Michaelson. I must say, the hospitality here in the North is far more than this Rebel ever dared hope."

The smile that had just begun to curve Callie's lips faded. "Must you keep reminding me that you are the enemy?" she asked him irritably.

He grinned and took his seat at last. "Perhaps I should eat before I do so again, since this stew promises to offer an even sweeter treat for the senses than that given by the wine."

Callie stared at him gravely across the table. "You do have a gift with words, Colonel."

"Only when I mean what I say, Mrs. Michaelson. May I?" He reached for her plate, and spooned a fair portion of the stew into it. He set it down before her, then helped himself. He tasted a bite of the meat, then another. He was famished, she saw. He went through half the food on his plate before suddenly pausing, having realized that she had yet to touch her fork.

"Excuse me. I'm afraid that my manners have become atrocious as of late."

Callie shook her head. He'd had nothing but water in almost two days. She thought lamely for something to say. "My mother, sir, raised three sons, and she'd have been delighted to see any man who had been so ill enjoy a meal with such gusto."

She was startled to realize that his free hand had moved across the table, and that his fingers had fallen over her own. Warm, intimate. His touch sent a quiver tearing raggedly down her spine. "Callie, should all Yankees have your way, war might well have been averted."

The touch of his fingers, the sensual feel of his eyes upon her, were suddenly too much. She snatched her fingers back quickly.

"There you go again. You are the enemy. If you cannot remember that fact for a meal, then you really should eat alone."

He hesitated, then shook his head. "It's dangerous ever to forget the enemy," he told her.

"Meaning?"

He shrugged. "Did you know, Mrs. Michaelson, that soldiers trade? Time and again, my Rebel troops have been encamped on one side of a stream, with Federal troops encamped on the other. And all night they send little boats of tobacco and coffee back and forth, and sometimes they get to be darned good friends. Sometimes we're close enough to see their faces."

His voice was harsh, his words were bitter. Callie shook her head again.

"There, sir, goes a touch of humanity within this insanity we have set upon. Why should it disturb you?"

"I'll tell you why it should disturb me, Mrs. Michaelson. One of my young privates became very friendly with a boy from Illinois one night. And then he met his newfound friend on the field of battle the next day."

"And?"

"And he hesitated to pull the trigger. His newfound friend did not. My private died, Mrs. Michaelson."

Callie kept her chin high. Her lashes swept over her cheeks. "Colonel, you are not going to meet me on the battlefield, ever. Therefore, you need not worry about my status as an enemy."

"Ah—" he began, but then he fell silent, tense and still—listening. For a moment, Callie did not know what he heard. The sound of horses' hooves pounding against the earth came to her ears. Someone was riding up to the front door.

He was instantly on his feet, vibrant, filled with tension and with readiness for battle. She was suddenly very afraid for him, because she knew then that no one would ever take him easily, he would always fight until the very end.

"Don't you dare draw a knife on me again!" Callie warned him as he started to reach for her. Despite her words, he was quickly around the table, his fingers creating a vise about her arm as she stood. "Callie—"

"Let go of me!"

"I can't—"

"I've already kept silent about you for two days. I didn't mention a word about you when the soldier came by today."

"What?"

A certain tension gripped her as he shook her arm. "Soldiers have been crawling all over the place, Colonel. If I were going to turn you in, I would have done so by now."

Slowly, cautiously, he released her arm. Callie walked through the kitchen and the parlor, going to the front door. She threw it open and gasped. She wasn't startled to see a Yankee soldier at her door, but she was surprised to know the officer who came this time.

It was Eric Dabney, Gregory's friend.

"Eric!" she said.

"Callie!"

Disconcerted to say the least, Callie stared at the Union cavalry captain standing on her porch. He was a young man, in his early twenties, of medium height and build with warm brown eyes and a head full of thick brown hair. He had a sweeping mustache and well-manicured beard. He was an attractive man, Callie thought, but he'd often amused her because of his vanity. She wondered, upon occasion, just how he managed to get in much soldiering, because he was very proud of his mustache and beard, and Gregory had told her once that he spent hours grooming his facial hair.

But he was concerned for her, she knew. She should be grateful to see him on her porch.

As it was, she couldn't think of anyone she'd less rather see at the moment.

"Callie!" he repeated.

"Eric!" she said and fell silent.

He was certainly expecting more. She had to ask him in.

"Callie, I had to make sure for myself that you were all right. What with Gregory . . . gone." he said. He cleared his throat. "I have time for a cup of coffee."

"Oh, of course, you'll have to come in!" she spoke loudly. She hoped her Rebel guest heard her. She had no choice. She had to ask Eric in. She could tell he was already suspicious. She should have hugged him and told him how glad she was that he had survived the battle. She shouldn't have left an old friend on the porch.

What was she doing? There was an enemy in her house. She should tell Eric that this minute.

No. She had made up her mind long ago—maybe right from the beginning— that she was going to shelter this particular Rebel, wrong as it might be.

Besides, she wasn't sure that Eric alone would be any match for this Rebel, even if Daniel Cameron was wounded. There was a quality of strength about Daniel. He had grown very lean and hard. Callie was convinced that he was very adept with any weapon he might choose to use. He wouldn't have survived this far if he were not.

The only way to best him would be when he was completely down.

For Eric's sake, she needed to take grave care.

"I was worried through the whole battle," Eric said as he took a step closer to her. "As soon as I saw you outside in the lull, I was worried sick. I imagined us losing this ground, I was horrified about the Rebs coming in here and finding you. A woman alone . . ." He touched her chin, and then he drew her against him in a warm hug. "Callie, if anything had happened to you . . ."

She wondered if she was being watched. They were standing in the doorway. She wondered why she should care if her uninvited Rebel guest saw her being hugged by another man.

They were enemies, but Daniel owed her for her silence, and for the care that she had given him.

Still, the thought of his watching her now with Eric made her uneasy.

She broke away, taking Eric's hands and holding them, but creating some distance between them.

"I'm fine, Eric. And I thank God that you came through this horror alive."

"I thank the Lord too," he murmured. "But I mean to come out of this war all right. And I mean to come back here, Callie, for you."

"Eric, I promise, you mustn't worry about me!" She assured him as lightly as she could.

"Callie, it's my beholden duty to worry about you," he said. He patted her hand and started walking into the house. Her heart began to hammer again.

What would happen when they reached the kitchen? How would she explain two plates, two wine glasses?

And the Rebel soldier at the table?

"Gregory was more than my friend," Eric explained to her as they walked through the house. "He was as close as a brother. And, of course, there's more."

She barely heard his words, she was so worried about what they were going to find at the table.

They reached the kitchen, and she dared to breathe easily again. She wasn't going to have to explain anything. Daniel had disappeared along with his plate and wine glass.

"Callie, I care about you. Deeply."

"What!"

Eric had swung around suddenly. She was nearly trapped against the entry-way leading to the kitchen.

His eyes were dark and earnest. His voice had a waver in it.

"I know that this isn't particularly the time—"

"You're right, Eric, this is not the time!" she exclaimed. Where was her wandering Rebel? Watching the scene?

Eric moved closer. He reached out to stroke her cheek, his emotion naked in his face.

Oh, Lord!

"Callie, Gregory hasn't been gone long, but in this wretched and war-weary world, it has been time enough. We both loved him. Who better to care for you, to love you, in his absence? Callie, don't—"

"Eric!"

"What?"

"I—I can't talk about this now. I . . . coffee! Eric, sit down, let me give you a cup of coffee." She pressed her hands against his chest and quickly hurried by him. She took coffee from the stove, poured him a cup, and set it across from her dinner plate. "I have stew—"

"I've eaten, thank you."

"Army rations. Have something."

He shook his head and sat where she had set down his coffee cup. It was the same seat that Daniel had so recently vacated. "Callie, I came to see you."

She breathed in deeply and sat down. "I appreciate that, Eric, and I'm fine. Thank you."

He reached across the table, and his fingers curled over hers.

"Callie—"

She pulled her hand back. "Eric." She lowered her lashes, growing desperate for a way to make him stop without being entirely cruel. She even forgot that Daniel Cameron might still be moving stealthily about her house. "Eric, listen to me, please. It's simply too soon. I can't even think about anyone but Gregory. Please understand." She raised her eyes to his and smiled as sweetly as she could, giving a promise for a future that could never be. "Give me time. I'll pray for you; you will come back."

Eric swallowed down his coffee in a gulp, his eyes never leaving hers.

He set the empty cup back down on the table. Callie gazed at it.

The coffee had been hot. She hoped that his throat was scalded all the way down to his gullet.

Eric stood up, drawing her along with him. "Just think about me, angel. Please, just think about me. Callie—Callie, I will love you until my dying day!"

Startled, she blinked. She wanted to give him something to go away with, some sign of affection. She had never realized that he felt this kind of emotion for her, and she had never given any thought to her feelings for him. He had been Gregory's friend. She had loved her husband. His friends were her friends.

And if war had never come, no man would be acting this way. She would have still been clad in black, shielded from the passions and emotions of others.

Eric would face bullets and swords and bombs in battle. He could easily die before another month was over.

She brought a smile to her lips. "Eric, I care for you. You know that. For the moment, my heart lies out back with my husband," she said softly.

"Tell me that I can come back," he urged her.

"Eric, I will be praying that you are able to come back," she said. She meant that he must make it back through all the battles.

That wasn't what he heard at all.

His eyes lit up, and a smug, triumphant smile went sailing across his features. His mustache fairly twitched.

Callie sighed, ready to correct him, but then decided against it. Who knew what tomorrow would bring.

He drew her fingers to his lips, kissing the tips. "Then, Callie, I bid you good-bye. 'Till this cruel war is over!'" He quoted from the song that grew more popular daily.

Callie nodded. "Good-bye, Eric. Take care."

She walked with him through the parlor again and stood in the doorway while he moved past her.

He suddenly pulled her into his arms and kissed her.

It was probably a passionate kiss. On his part. It was merely a surprise to Callie. She pressed against him. He made no effort to be daring, he did not try to part her lips, but seemed happy enough to hold her. Just as suddenly as he had touched her, he released her. In the doorway, he saluted her sharply. He whispered her name, turned, and left her, hurrying down the pathway to his waiting mount.

"Oh, Jesu!" Callie whispered aloud. She closed the door and leaned against it, not knowing whether to laugh or to cry.

She rushed back into the kitchen. "Daniel?" she called his name, not whispering, but not speaking loudly, either. There was no answer.

She hurried back into the parlor. "Daniel?"

Again, there was no answer. She picked up her skirts and came running up the stairway. She hurried into her bedroom. The door was already open and she burst through the doorway.

"Daniel?"

He didn't answer. She sat down at the foot of her bed, then fell flat against it.

"Oh, thank the Lord! The Reb's gone south!"

But then the bedroom door, thrown against the wall, suddenly squeaked and started to swing. Callie leapt up to her knees, staring at the patch of wall now displayed.

There stood Daniel Cameron, grinning. "No, angel, not on your life." He walked toward her, his eyes alive with wicked flames of amusement. "He's going to love you until his dying day?"

"Oh, will you please shut up!" she snapped. "How incredibly rude. You were listening to every word."

"I wouldn't have missed it," he assured her. He stood over her, then reached down for both of her hands. He pulled her up so that she stood right before him. He stood so close their bodies touched.

" 'When this cruel war is over .'. .' " he murmured.

"I'm warning you, quit!" Callie threatened.

His smile broadened. The searing flames in his eyes seemed to catch hold of her heart. His face lowered, and the flames came closer.

And burned more hotly. All through her. Warming, searing her limbs. Sweeping along her breasts, her hips, invading her thighs. Taking root deep, deep within her.

"Don't wait for him, angel. Not unless he can do better than that."

"Better than that? Just what should he be doing, Colonel Cameron?" she demanded.

"I'll show you," Daniel whispered.

It seemed that the flames within her sizzled and soared, and then leaped to become an inferno.

His arms closed tightly around her, and his was a passion Callie couldn't begin to deny.

Six

*P*erhaps because he had taken her so very suddenly, Callie stiffened. And then, for the very same reason, she felt herself meld against him.

He knew, it seemed, just how to hold her. Just how to sweep the length of her against the length of him. He held her tightly, warmly, securely.

In his arms, she felt the quicksilver fanning of a heat that was deep and undeniable, seeping through her limbs, to her breasts, to her hips. She felt the thunder of her heart, nearly suffocating her, yet combining with the still stronger pulse of his.

There was the startling comfort of feeling that she belonged in his embrace. There was the strength of his arms when she had been alone for so very long.

She felt the touch of his eyes. So searing a blue. In that sweeping gaze, she felt anew the fire, the burning, the instantaneous warmth created by this man. All of this she experienced in seconds as he brought her against him, stared at her, touched her. He smiled slowly, lowered his head to hers, and kissed her.

Then came an entire new burst of sensation as she tasted his lips, felt the pressure of them against her own. He kissed her as if he had intended on kissing her for a long, long time. Kissed her as if he savored the very breath that came from her lips, as if he had desired just that touch with every bit of longing within him. She could not deny him, not when he held her so tightly and securely in his arms. He demanded her acquiescence, but he knew how to kiss, how to take, how to give.

He flooded her senses as he molded his mouth to hers, slowly parting her lips with a sure thrust of his tongue that entered more and more deeply into her mouth. It was just a kiss. But perhaps that was its true magic. He made her think of so much more. Made her long for more. The sinuous, undeniable stroke of his tongue brought with it a sweet ravishment of the whole of her mouth.

His mouth lifted from hers, leaving a breath of air between them. She reached up to him, and he kissed her again, open-mouthed, hungry, drawing her more swiftly and more deeply into his intimate swirl of desire.

A trembling began within her as she felt his fingers, gentle and determined upon her cheek. She felt the length of him against her and knew the growing pulse of his desire.

He felt good, and he smelled wondrous. She'd never felt such a burst of passion within herself, not even with Gregory.

Gregory!

The memory of her husband burst into the bubble of longing and sensation that had seized such sure hold of her, eclipsing everything else. Gregory! She had never imagined wanting another man until this Rebel had happened upon her. Why, in Eric's arms just moments ago she had felt nothing except for discomfort and the longing to escape.

She wanted this man, she cared for him. She loved the contours of his face and the light in his eyes and the sound of his voice. She had found him so very beautiful naked, and when naked, a man wasn't in blue, nor was he in gray or tattered Rebel butternut.

No! she told herself fiercely. This man wore gray, naked or clad. His cause was in his heart, and she could not strip it from him.

And she was a widow, betraying her own heart.

"No, please, no!"

She managed to twist from his touch at last. He had not forced her. He had held her, so firmly. He had demanded from her, so sensually. But he had not forced her.

His mouth lifted from hers. His gaze met hers. His arms remained loosely around her, and he waited for her to speak.

She shook her head, horrified by the hot sheen of tears that glistened in her eyes. "No! Please, I can't. I won't. I . . ." Words eluded her. Explanations eluded her. "You have to leave!" she choked out.

Her lashes fell, hiding the anguish in her eyes. She pushed against the arms that held her. He tensed for one moment. "Callie . . ."

"Please!" She pushed harder against him. And then she was free.

She backed away from him. "You have to leave!"

She turned and fled from the room, racing out the door and down the stairs. But not even that distance took her far enough away from him. She burst out the front door, closed it behind her, and leaned against it, breathing deeply of the night air.

What was she thinking? Her father was dead, her best friend, husband, and lover was dead, and all at Rebel hands. So many dead, her own home made into a battlefield. And none of it mattered a single bit when this man touched her.

Bless the night! The darkness closed around her, and the coolness seemed to steal away some of the dreadful heat that assailed her. He would leave tonight, and she would forget.

She closed her eyes. He was wounded. A horse soldier without a horse.

But his fever had broken, and the wound that had caused him the difficulty was an old one. Perhaps he was weak, but even weak, he was a formidable enemy. He was not far from Virginia. He would go now, she knew, because deny it or not, he was one of those southern cavaliers.

A sound in the night suddenly startled Callie. Her eyes flew open. She didn't see anything to mar the stillness of the night. She closed her eyes again and listened. She could hear horses' hooves. There were a number of them. She stiffened.

Slowly, she relaxed. The riders were not coming to the house. She heard someone call out an order. The words were clear, but distant.

"Captain! We'll form an encampment next mile south, by the old orchard. There will be two sentries per company, sir!"

"As you say, sir!" came a brisk reply.

The slow hoofbeats of walking horses continued to sound. The troops were moving on.

Thank God. No one else was coming to her house.

But they would be close! There in the woods and the farmlands and fields. So very easy to stumble upon.

"No!" she whispered out loud, her hand flying to her mouth. Tears stung her eyes once again.

She swirled around, swinging open her door again and flying into the house.

He was in the parlor, buckling on his scabbard. As she entered the house, his sword came free of its protective sheath. Those startling blue eyes pierced into her, as sharp and vibrant as any blade.

She backed against the door, catching her breath, staring at the glistening silver of the sword.

"Jesu, Callie!" he muttered irritably, sheathing his sword once again with a practiced movement. Hands on his hips, he stared at her, slowly smiling. "Callie, I've been tempted to do a few things, but running you through with this sword has not been one of them," he said more lightly. Still she didn't speak, but remained with her back against the door.

"Callie, I'm leaving," he said very softly.

She shook her head strenuously. "You—you can't."

His eyes narrowed. "Why can't I?"

"Because there are Yankee camps all around us tonight."

He shrugged. "I can move around the countryside very well," he said quietly.

"No man can move well enough to escape the number of men out there now."

He smiled slowly. "You don't want me captured?"

"You're still injured, you fool."

His smile remained in place. "But I'm much, much better now."

She stiffened. Damn him. She was worried for his life. She squared her shoulders, and lifted her chin imperceptibly.

"Had you allowed yourself to heal properly the first time, Colonel, it's doubtful that wound at your side would have reopened and caused you that awful fever. If you're all fired determined to go out there tonight, be my guest. It's likely they'll shoot you down in the darkness. If not, it's likely they'll take you prisoner."

"And you know enough about Yankee prisons to assume that I'll die there?" he inquired.

She stiffened. Both sides complained about prison conditions. They were bad in the North, she knew, from a number of articles and editorials she had read on the subject. Despite the war, and despite anything that Daniel might believe, there were those in the North who were appalled by the way that prisoners of war were treated.

Conditions in the South were far worse. Callie was convinced it was not done on purpose. Half of the southern fighting men were shoeless. Their uniforms were tattered, nearly threadbare. They fought on meager rations. They were half-starved themselves. Under those conditions, what could they spare for their imprisoned enemies?

Abraham Lincoln had been dealt many a defeat at the hands of the talented southern generals, but he understood his war. He had superior numbers. When his men died, they could be replaced. And they could be fed. The northern blockade was slowly but surely taking its toll upon the South. The war that tore up the farmlands was taking its toll upon the South. If they couldn't feed their own, how could they be expected to feed others?

But horror stories of the way that Union men starved in the South reached the North. And for every humanitarian who worked for better conditions, there was a bitter person who demanded that southern prisoners should not be coddled. There were widows and orphans who hated any man in gray. And for every respectable and decent jailor, there might also be a warped and angry commander, grown cold and heedless of human life. No one, northerner or southerner, wanted to face a prison camp.

Callie clenched her teeth. What should it matter to her what happened to this damned Reb.

She stepped coolly away from the door.

"You may stay, Colonel, if you so desire. And sir, you may leave, if you so desire."

She was alarmed by the rueful curve that came slowly, wistfully, to his lip. She was further dismayed by the quickening beat of her heart.

There was nowhere to go when he walked slowly toward her, then stopped just before her. He touched her chin briefly with the back of his knuckle.

"I can't stay, Callie. Because if I do, I can't give you any guarantees or promises."

Pursing her lips, she determined not to wrench away from him. "You may stay, Colonel. Because I am the one who can give the guarantees."

He arched a brow, and she thought that the curve of his smile was definitely wicked now. "Callie—"

She pushed his hand aside and walked past him. He turned to lean against the door, watching her wander over by the hearth as she spoke. "You have recovered very nicely, Colonel. Many men—most men—would surely have died from the type of wound you suffered. And if not then, they'd have surely died from the fever. You have done miraculously well. But how far would you test fate, sir?" she demanded, swirling around to face him again.

"I keep going, Mrs. Michaelson, because I must," he told her.

"What you need to do, Colonel, is go home. Rest. Heal properly."

"I cannot do that."

"And why not?"

"Because," he said simply, "I am irreplaceable."

"Sir—"

"We haven't the manpower," he said, and to Callie, he at last sounded weary of the war. "I must always go back. I should be back now."

"You are weak. And if you die you'll not go back," she stated flatly.

"True," he agreed.

Callie's eyes suddenly came alight. "Your brother!"

"What?" he demanded darkly, a frown quickly descending upon his face.

"I can go out! I can see what I can do about finding your brother. Perhaps—"

"No!"

"But if he's a Union surgeon—"

"No, damn you! I am well and fine enough. Jesu, I'll not have Jesse risking anything again! Do you understand me?"

She had seldom seem him so furious, even with all that raged between them. Irrationally, she felt the heat of tears burning at the back of her eyes again. She was doing her best to help the enemy, and the damned enemy wasn't cooperating in the least.

Let him go! she told herself. Let him go out, let the Union take him!

She turned away from him, determined that he would not see the emotion in her eyes. "Do whatever you choose to do, Colonel. I cannot be bothered with it any longer."

"Ah. You've ceased to care whether I am caught or not!"

She spun around once again. "At this moment, Colonel, I'd set the shackles around your wrists myself!"

He smiled. A cold, set smile. "Madam, that is something that you could never manage to do. I think you know damned well that—weak as I may be— I'm still far more than a match for one or two or maybe even three of your Yankees. And I think, Mrs. Michaelson, that one of the reasons you were so careful to rid this house of your dashing Yankee captain—the one who is going to love you until he dies"— The last was added in a curious tone, and Callie wasn't sure if it was a bitter one or one of amusement. But then his voice hardened as he continued—"is because you knew damned well that he might not be any match for me."

"You are extremely arrogant," Callie informed him. "You should just be grateful that I didn't call the whole Union army down upon you."

"The whole Union army isn't around anymore."

"Enough of it is."

"You were afraid for your friend," he insisted.

"I didn't care to have the inside of my house as well as the outside littered with bodies!" she returned sharply.

"Ah, a true tender heart!" he said, laughing.

"He might have slain you on the spot!" Callie stated.

"He might have. But I doubt it."

"My, my, sir, but you are pleased with your own prowess."

"I haven't been pleased with anything in a long, long, time, Mrs. Michaelson. And I've been out there for a very long time. There are few battles that I've missed. And even when I've fallen, I've brought down countless men before doing so." His eyes looked old and weary, his face drawn. "I'm not pleased at all, Mrs. Michaelson, I'm sickened. But I'm a survivor, and an officer, and I'm needed. And I'm good with a sword. It's very unlikely that I could be taken by one man. And you know it. You saved your friend's life by not mentioning the fact that you were harboring a Rebel."

"You are not just arrogant, you are insufferable," Callie muttered. She determined that she couldn't stand there any longer, and that it was one thing for him to guess that she hadn't wanted him to clash with Eric, and quite another to know it for certain. "Do what you will!" she told him. "Although, who knows? Perhaps I should tremble for the entire Union once you are loose upon it!"

She swung around a final time, heading back for the kitchen.

She didn't reach it. She felt his hand on her shoulder, spinning her around.

"Do you want me to go or don't you?" he demanded, his eyes dark, nearly cobalt, his features tense.

She jerked free from him. "Yes. No. No, I don't! I'm sick of the death and the pain. And God help me, I do not want your death on my conscience!"

"And what of those I may kill later?" he demanded.

She inhaled sharply, staring at him, stricken with the thought. God in heaven, who had invented this horrible thing called war?

"Better a Rebel soldier now, not scores of Yankees later, eh?" he asked softly.

Callie swallowed tightly as she continued to meet his steel-blue gaze. "Do what you will, Colonel," she repeated.

He shook his head. "No, I want to please you, Callie," he persisted.

"What?"

Dismayed, she tried to pull free from him. Damn him! He was too close again. She could feel the things she had felt when he had kissed her. She breathed in the scent of him, the clean scent of the soap she had bathed him with, the deeper, more subtle scent that was his alone, and part of the things that made him the man he was.

She didn't want to see his face so closely, see the fine set of his cheeks, the molding of his jaw. She didn't want to grow attached to this man. And she certainly didn't want to be held in his arms again, to feel the startling, overwhelming sense of desire that had risen within her. And most of all, she didn't want to feel as if she could fall in love with him, as if loving was something that could come all too easily, as if it might be something that had already begun.

"What are you talking about?" she demanded harshly.

"I want it to be your call, Callie. You tell me to stay, or you tell me to go. Thousands of men are dead, from both sides. Thousands more are going to die before it's over. Tens of thousands."

"Would you stop that!" she cried out, horrified. She backed farther away, afraid of the stubborn set to his chin.

He came toward her again, and she should have run from his touch but she did not. He cupped her chin and lifted it so that her eyes were caught in the charisma and determination of his.

"The call will be yours."

She didn't want him standing there. So painfully close again. So close that she wanted to forget everything.

Again, she jerked away—and retreated. "I don't want you to die," she said simply.

"Because I'm in your house?"

"Because I know your face."

"More than my face," he reminded her ruefully.

"Oh!" She let out an oath of impatience, curling her fingers into her palms. "Because you're no longer a stranger. You're not just a number." He still stared at her, waiting. "All right! Because I care for you!" she admitted, but when he would have walked toward her again, she set a hand into the air, stopping him. "I don't want you to die, but I don't want you near me. Do you understand?"

His smile was slow, bittersweet. "Yes, I think that I understand," he told her.

To her amazement, he walked by her. She was still for a minute, then she heard a clattering in the kitchen.

He was picking up the dishes that remained on the table. He ignored her when she stood in the doorway, bringing things to the counter and to the water pump to rinse them.

She watched him for a moment. "Did you—manage to eat anything?" she asked him.

"Yes, thank you. I ate just fine," he told her. He shrugged, glancing her way. "I took my stew upstairs. Remind me. The dish is still on the floor."

He seemed adept enough at picking up. Callie leaned against the door frame, watching him. "You're quite useful, so it appears," she told him.

He glanced her way, arching a brow.

"Well, you do come from a big home, right? A plantation. And I'll bet you grew up with lots of slaves—"

"Excuse me," he interrupted her, setting down the plate that he had just rinsed and putting his hands on his hips to face her. "I'm the younger son. Jesse —my Yankee brother—is the one who owns them. Or owned them," he corrected himself.

"You don't have slaves on your plantation anymore?"

"It's Jesse's plantation, the main house, anyway. But yes, they're still there. Most of them. They just aren't slaves any longer."

"Jesse freed them?"

"We freed them. The three of us. My brother, my sister, and I. In June. Jesse was home for a spell, and considering that he's a Yank himself and damned unwelcome in Virginia at the moment, it seemed the time to settle some family business. We knew then that the war wasn't going to be over in a few more weeks, or months even. We needed some things settled, what with Jesse going one way, and me going another. But don't go applauding us, Mrs. Michaelson. We didn't do anything spectacular. We freed our people because we could afford to do so. We can pay them. The good majority of them chose to stay on. God knows what will happen by the end of the war. I'm going to worry about some of them then."

"Why is that?"

"Why is that?" he repeated. He smiled. "Well, now, I don't take anything away from your Mr. Lincoln. Oddly enough, I rather admire the man. Maybe slavery—and the South's determination to cling to that institution—is why we got so fired up over states' rights to begin with. But Lincoln didn't go to war to strip the South of her slaves. Lincoln wound up fighting a war to preserve the Union. Maybe the outcome of this war will be hundreds and thousands of freed slaves. Then what? Will they all be welcome in the North? Welcome in New York City along with the thousands of immigrants that seem determined to flood these shores? I don't know. I do know that my people—whether they are owned or free—have work. And they have food. They have roofs over their heads. Not many of them live in the plantation house. But human life, black or white, has always been respected in my house. I just hope their lives will be worthwhile in the North, once this thing is over."

"Any price is worth freedom," Callie said.

"Well, now, maybe that's true, Mrs. Michaelson. I don't rightly know. Hunger can be a pretty fierce enemy."

Callie shook her head. "You said that you admire Lincoln. There's right, and there's wrong, he said. And it's wrong to own another person!"

Daniel Cameron lowered his eyes. She could see the small, secret smile that curved his lip. "Is that what he said, Mrs. Michaelson?"

"Well, more or less! Really, Colonel—"

"Callie," he said, raising his eyes to hers, "I'm not making fun of you. I'm admiring your passion! God alive, Callie, I wish it could be so simple for me! Many men have decried slavery. Thomas Jefferson wanted to abolish slavery when he was writing the Declaration of Independence! And he owned slaves! But it's not that easy. There's an entire economy based on slavery. There are men who insist that even the Bible condones slavery. Callie, I'm not God, I don't know!"

"So you're a Rebel!"

"I'm a Virginian. And Virginia chose to secede from the Union."

"But your brother—"

"My brother followed his conscience, Callie. I followed mine."

"So he is your enemy."

"He is my brother, and I love him."

"But you fight him!"

"Jesu, what is this!" Daniel exploded, throwing his hands into the air. "I didn't start this war! Sometimes, I don't even give a damn, except that it might be over. There are days when my only real hope is that Cameron Hall survives both armies, that it will be there for me to see when at long last that day comes that I can really go home. But a man has to be what he is, and do what his heart dictates to him! Virginia seceded, and my oath, my allegiance, is to my state! I'm a cavalry officer, and I serve the cavalry. I serve Robert E. Lee, a man of ethics, grace, and honor, and in return, I serve with all the ethics, grace, and honor I may possess in turn. I cannot walk away from the war because I am tired of it. I am what I am, Callie. A Rebel. Your enemy!" He exhaled a long breath, watching her where she remained silent and wide-eyed, in the doorway. "Oh, hell!" he muttered. Tense as a jackal, he spun around and strode across the kitchen to one of the shelves. There was a whiskey bottle upon it, and he grabbed it by the neck and walked angrily toward Callie.

There was such a leashed passion to his stride and taut features that Callie jumped back, unnerved by the way he seemed to be bearing down upon her. But long before he reached her, he paused, his mouth twisted into a bitter facsimile of a smile.

"I've no intention of harming you—or touching you, Mrs. Michaelson. But if the countryside is that packed with Yanks, then I will accept your gracious hospitality for the night. And since I dare not come near you, I'm going to go and lock myself in a room. And since I don't want to lie awake all night wondering just where you are and what you're doing, I'm taking the whiskey bottle. What a companion it will make!" He paused in the doorway and bowed very low to her.

He walked through the parlor and started up the stairs, the whiskey bottle tucked under his arm.

A moment later, Callie nearly jumped a mile as she heard the ferocious slamming of a door.

Indeed, it seemed that her Rebel was here for the night.

Seven

*I*t seemed to Daniel that he spent the majority of the night leaning by the window, staring out at the darkness.

He felt surprisingly well—almost too damned well. Because of that, he had decided not to remain in his hostess' bedroom, but had come down the hall to the second bedroom.

This room was every bit as impeccably neat as the first, but furnished with more of a masculine flair. There was a bed with a polished oak frame, a heavy desk, a large wardrobe, and a seaman's chest at the foot of the bed. He had come here before to find the clothing he was wearing, but he hadn't thought much about the room's occupant. Did it belong to one of Callie's brothers? Or had it been the private domain of her father?

Sitting on the windowsill in the darkness, Daniel took another long swig from the whiskey bottle. There was a beautiful painting of a horse that hung over the desk, and sitting on top of the desk was a fine antique compass. There was a Revolutionary War sword hung on the wall, a trophy passed down from generations before. There was a deck of cards in the bottom drawer at the base of the wardrobe—he knew that because the cards were just beneath the breeches he had borrowed. It seemed those cards had been kept there discreetly. Somebody was a bit of a gambler.

He'd probably like the fellow who was supposed to be sleeping here. They both had a passion for horses. And Daniel liked to gamble just as much as the next man. They shared an appreciation for the past, and . . .

They probably shared a passion for Mrs. Callie Michaelson.

Daniel swore softly and swallowed more of the whiskey. What was it that was so damned entrancing about her? She was a beauty, but he'd known many beauties, he'd admired them, and he'd even loved one or two. This was different. Seeing her was different, listening to her was different. Touching her was different.

What was it that made him want her so badly? The war, he tried to tell himself. The days and nights of nothing but dirty water and hardtack. The endless riding, the company of soldiers.

No.

Had he spent the last months in a whirl of socials, he would still have felt such emotion for this woman. She was unique. There was wisdom in her eyes. After all, she had been a married woman. But there was innocence in them too. There was something beneath the beauty of her lips, the silk of her flesh. Something that smoldered, something electric, something so alluring and seductive that being near her was nearly more than he could stand.

"Damn! So what am I doing here?" he murmured aloud. He looked out on the darkness beyond the house. He should have moved on. He was restless, and he needed to be back. He needed to find out just how many men had been lost by Antietam Creek, and he needed badly to let Jeb Stuart know that he was alive. His friends and superiors might well be mourning his loss this very moment.

But he couldn't allow himself to be killed, either. He'd be no damned good to anyone that way.

He flexed and unflexed his hand, then stood and looked out the window again. He really shouldn't let his guard down. How the hell did he know what really went on in her heart? She might care for him, but she might also have signaled that Yankee captain somehow. She hadn't wanted them to clash in her house because Daniel would have been forced to slay her friend. But maybe she had given him some message, some clue.

They could be surrounding the house right now.

No, he determined dryly. She hadn't given the man a message. She'd been too busy trying to dissuade him from his sudden turn of passion.

"I will love you till the day I die!" Daniel said out loud. He lifted the whiskey bottle. "Yes, Mrs. Michaelson, I can well understand the poor man's anguish. I pity my enemy, ma'am. And I pity your poor young husband, facing death, and knowing that he left you behind, angel," he murmured.

He looked outside again. No one was coming for him tonight. He needed to get some sleep.

She'd done a fine job binding his wound. When he stripped off his borrowed shirt, he looked carefully at the gash on his lower abdomen and side. The bleeding had completely stopped. It looked no worse than it had when he had entered into battle.

His head no longer ached, and his fever, he knew, was completely gone.

"Jesse, she's damned near as good as you are!" he murmured, speaking to the whiskey bottle he'd set on the desk. "And she's much, much prettier."

She wanted him gone.

She wanted him.

He stalked across the room, running his fingers through his hair.

That was the rub. She cared about him, she wanted him. There was all that sweet and wonderful and simmering passion within her, just waiting for him. Yes, for him. He'd watched her with the Yank. And he'd listened to her. She hadn't offered the Yank anything at all.

Life and love didn't work that way, Daniel knew. She didn't *want* to feel an attraction to him, she just did. When she came close, he sure as hell felt the depth of that attraction.

Damn. It was going to be a long, long night.

He stripped back the calico covering and white cotton sheet from the bed and lay down. He stared at the ceiling and reminded himself that he'd just recovered from a severe fever.

But he felt good. Really good. Strong. Ready to be up and about. To walk, to run . . .

To make love.

He groaned, rolled over, and pulled the pillow on top of his head. It could be so easy. They could both forget who they were and give in to temptation. Had he forgotten? She was a widow, but a respectable one. She should never have been kissed the way that he had kissed her. There were ways to act with a young woman, and ways not to act.

War made a mockery of propriety.

She had asked him not to touch her.

And so he would not.

Sleep. The Yankees are not coming tonight. She's given you back your life, your health. She's sheltered you from the enemy. She's fed you, and given you clothing. And she's cared for you.

He leapt up and went back to the dresser for the whiskey bottle. He swallowed a big draught, then fell back on the bed.

Colonel, you will sleep, he told himself. That's an order.

But he didn't sleep. Lying awake, he thought of home. Kiernan, Jesse's wife, was there now, with her new baby. His nephew. Daniel at last smiled, thinking of the big, lusty fellow with a fine temper to match any Cameron who had come before him.

His smile faded. That's where the future lay. With their children. What would the South be now, after this ravishment had gone on even longer? What world would they inherit?

He reached out in the darkness, almost as if he could touch some intangible beauty that might soon be gone. A very special world had been his. His, and Jesse's, and Christa's. Cameron Hall had provided everything for them. All of those lazy days by the river. All of the dreams that they wove and dreamt beneath blue skies and powdery white clouds, beneath the shade of moss growing thick on old trees. Maybe it had been a world of privilege, and maybe the privilege was about to be lost. He wouldn't mind that so much, he thought. Since the war he had become extremely self-sufficient, as there was little other way to be. But if they were to lose Cameron Hall, he was not sure he could ever learn to live with the loss.

Cameron Hall, or Christa—or Jesse. His brother, his enemy.

Daniel had understood when Jesse had kept his loyalty to the Union. Maybe because he knew his brother better than anyone else in the world. The first Cameron to come to America had left behind vast estates and wealth. He had turned his back on those riches and built in a wilderness. More than a century later, Daniel's great-grandfather had set his cap with the struggling new colonies, despite the fact that he had been an English lord. Win or lose, they had always been taught that a man had to follow his heart and the dictates of his soul.

The way that Daniel saw it, Jesse's soul had just told him to go the wrong way. But he understood. And he would never have asked Jesse to go against those dictates.

It had been hard to watch him walk away the first time, back in '61, right after Virginia had made its decision to leave the Union. He was the oldest son, the inheritor. Still, he had walked away.

They had not met in person again until McClellan had waged his peninsula campaign early in the summer.

Then it had become necessary for Daniel to find Jesse because he had to tell his brother that Kiernan was expecting his baby. Kiernan, who was as passionately southern as Jesse was determinedly pro-Union.

A smile crept slowly onto Daniel's face then. He'd been badly wounded in the battle that day. Jesse had found him and had risked a hell of a lot to bring him home to Cameron Hall, along with Kiernan, who had been trying to reach her own home. And Jesse's Yank friends had turned blind eyes toward Daniel, and a whole troop of Rebs had pretended not to see Jesse along the way.

Kiernan had married Jesse, and the baby had been born, and Daniel had healed up nicely in a few days. In that time they had almost brought back the magic. They had all played with the baby on the grass, they had lain back and listened to the river, and they had felt the heat of summer and the soft breeze of the night.

And then Jesse had ridden out again. A number of Yanks might have been dispensable, but not Jesse. He was a doctor, a good one. No army in this war could afford the absence of a good doctor and crack surgeon.

They'd stood by the old cemetery, surrounded by their long-gone ancestors, and in silence they had embraced once again. The silence had been broken by the sounds of Kiernan's sobs. She had discovered that she loved Jesse far more than any cause.

Kiernan was at Cameron Hall now, along with Christa, the baby, and Kiernan's young in-laws from her first marriage. The slaves had been freed, but most had remained. There was nowhere that they really wanted to go. So right now, it was still possible to dream of home.

He rolled over, wishing that his thoughts would cease to haunt him, that he might sleep.

But no thoughts of others could keep his thoughts from the one Yankee who now shared this house with him. If Kiernan had married Jesse in the midst of the conflict still raging, then all was possible.

It could be possible for him to touch his angel once again. She of the dove-gray eyes and dark-fire hair and swift, elusive tenderness. She was so near him. Just down the hall.

She had asked him not to touch her.

Asked him after he had already touched her once, felt the fever in her body, felt the shape of her, sensed the longing, known the taste of her lips.

He flung himself up, swearing loudly and violently. One more swig of whiskey. Hell, no, maybe the whole bottle. He had to do something. He was a wounded soldier, needed back in action. He had to sleep, to heal.

He glanced at his sword across the room and took another pull from the near-empty bottle. At long last, he slept.

* * *

The sound of something heavy falling awoke him from a deep, deep sleep. He jumped up, startled, instantly on the alert.

He was no longer drunk though he did feel slightly hung over. The more awake he became, the more his head hammered.

He stood shirtless and barefoot, clad only in his borrowed breeches, listening. The sound didn't come again. He narrowed his eyes, realizing that it had come from the bedroom to his left down the hallway.

Callie's room.

He reached for his hip, accustomed as he was to wearing his Colts and sword even as he slept. He didn't know what had happened to his guns, and his sword lay in its scabbard across the room. Silent on his bare feet, he strode across the room, sliding his cavalry sword from its scabbard. Still moving in silence, he slowly twisted the knob on his door and began to move down the hallway.

The door to Callie's room was closed. He was certain the sound had come from there. He clenched his teeth tightly together, hesitated just a moment, then twisted the knob, and thrust the door open in a single, fluid movement.

A startled "Oh!" greeted his arrival. He stood in her doorway, his sword at the ready, the tension in him rippling the muscles in his naked chest. His hair was in rakish disarray over his forehead from the night he had spent tossing and turning.

There was no enemy within the room to meet him, just Callie herself.

She was not ready to welcome him at all. Her eyes, enormous in the white heart of her face, flashed out a silver dismay. Deep auburn wisps of hair escaped a knot she had fashioned at the back of her head to trail damply about her cheeks and forehead. Her flesh, too, was damp, touched with little buttons of water.

She sat in a hip bath, her knees drawn halfway to her chest, the wooden tub itself barely blocking the length of her body from his view.

It was the most extraordinary torment. There was so much that he could see. The long ivory column of her throat. No woman had ever possessed a throat so beautifully long, so slim, so elegant. He could see the slope of her shoulders and the hollows of her collarbones. Lovely hollows, shadowed, dark, seducing, demanding a kiss or a caress. Beneath the shadows, he could just see the rise of her breasts. Full, fascinating, taunting.

He had to walk away. Fast.

But just then she nervously moistened her lips with the tip of her tongue. He didn't know if it was the wetness of her lips, or the glimpse of her tongue, but every bit of his control vanished, swept away in the mist that rose from her bath. He didn't move. He remained transfixed, his eyes upon her lips.

"What—what are you doing?" she managed to demand in a whisper.

He had to wet his own lips to talk. He couldn't quite draw his eyes to hers.

"I heard something."

"I dropped a kettle," she said defensively. Still, he didn't move. His gaze was slipping. Her mouth was fascinating, but so was her throat. And the lush hint of the fullness of her breasts.

He dragged his gaze back up to hers.

"I thought that the house was under attack," he said.

A smile flashed quickly across her features. "So I see. You were ready to defend yourself. So, Colonel, would you skewer me through?" Her voice was still almost a whisper. Husky, throaty. A voice that titillated, that sent hot spirals curving into his groin. If he hadn't felt the raw surge of desire searing into his body already, the sound of that voice alone would have brought him to attention like a bolt of steel. "What with your sword so raised, Colonel . . ." The hush of her voice trailed away all together. Her smile faded and a flush infused her cheeks as she realized the double meaning of her words. Indeed, both his "swords" were well raised and certainly at the ready.

"Cause you injury, madam? Never," he said gallantly. But had he really been gallant, he would have turned at that moment. But his feet were lead, and he could not leave. He remained, watching her.

"You are interrupting my bath!"

"I came rushing to your defense."

"I am in no danger."

"I could not know that."

"I take that back!" she cried. "I am in grave danger now."

Indeed, she was. "The danger, Mrs. Michaelson, was in choosing to bathe, I'm afraid," he murmured regretfully.

"Oh, damn!" she swore softly. "Damn! I could have bathed in the kitchen, but with you here, I did not! I dragged the tub and the buckets up the stairs, and . . . and . . ." She paused, staring at him. "And here you are, invading my privacy." She was really beautiful with her eyes flashing so. He'd never seen a color closer to true silver. Shimmering, haunting. So elusive, so seductive.

"I didn't mean to invade your privacy. Only—"

"Defend me, indeed," she murmured.

"I should leave now," he said.

"Yes, you must."

But he didn't leave.

Watching him there, Callie knew that there had been no conviction in her voice. Leave, yes! Walk away, she thought. But the words would not come. She had watched his eyes. She had felt their blue fire move over her. Felt them touch her own eyes, felt them slip lower. And where his eyes touched her, she felt a sweet fever, as if that mere touch could warm and excite her flesh. As if some exotic caress covered her shoulders, and skimmed her throat. She felt the desire, and feeling that raw passion deep within him ignited some essence within her own soul.

It was so wrong. She was a widow. She had loved her husband. She honored his memory. She never should have had a man in her house. She never should have allowed a man's eyes to touch her in this way.

But sweet visions of the past had faded away. All sense of propriety seemed to slip through her fingers like the water that she bathed in.

From the moment that she had seen him, she had felt a fascination with his face. From the moment that she had touched him, she had felt a growing affection for him as a man. From the moment he had first touched her, she had felt the overwhelming stirrings of desire that came now to haunt her heart and limbs and soul with a vengeance.

Tell him to go! she commanded herself.

But she could not.

She stared into his eyes, and then her own vision slipped. She was staring at his chest. At the sleek muscle there, so taut now, rippling with his every breath. At the dark whorls of hair that grew there. She wanted to touch that whorl, feel it spring beneath her fingers. He was so bronze. He had probably tanned in the rivers where he bathed while camped with his men. He had gained that muscle from wielding his sword, she tried to tell herself. But reminders of war meant nothing. Enemy or no, she liked the man she had come to know. Watching him now, she wondered if even that mattered.

She wanted him. Wanted him to come closer. And touch her.

"You have to go." She managed to speak the words. That was not at all the message in her eyes.

"I know," he said. But neither was that the message in his movement, for he had lowered his cavalry sword and was walking toward her.

Closer, closer, until he stood over her.

And then he smiled. Ruefully. Sensually. His fingers wound around the rim of the tub.

"I like my women to want me badly," he drawled softly, his blue gaze burning into hers.

"Ah, but I don't want you at all, Colonel," she told him smoothly. What a lie. In all of her life she had never wanted anything so badly as she wanted this man now. Her lips were dry again, despite the steam that rose from the bath. She could feel the swell of her breasts, the hardening of her nipples. And dear Lord, what she could feel between her thighs . . .

His smile had deepened. "I like my women to want me very badly, Callie. I like them just as hungry as they can get. I like my women—"

She crossed her arms over her traitorous breasts and raised her chin in a taunting challenge. "Ah, but Colonel, I am not one of your 'women.' I am the enemy, remember?"

"Indeed, Callie. But what a way to do battle!" he murmured.

"We cannot do battle."

"On the contrary, Mrs. Michaelson. I'm afraid that we must." He lowered himself down on his haunches, his eyes on a level with hers. "You are one Yankee to best me beyond a doubt, Mrs. Michaelson, for I could not leave this room were I threatened with Hell's damnation itself! To think!" he added softly, ruefully, "I mocked that poor fool last night, Callie, when I, myself, will want you now until I die."

He could not know what he did to her, how he made her feel, how deeply, how desperately she wanted him in turn. But how could she dare touch him, stroke his shoulder, taste the salt upon his flesh, lie naked beside him. . . .

Flashes of desire, like melting stars in the sky, caught fire and danced all through her.

"Callie!"

Her name on his lips was a caress. He stood above her once again, and still he had not touched her.

"Think!" she charged herself to say once again. "I am the enemy! Vile, fearsome—"

"Never, never vile!"

She drew her knees more tightly against her body. Sensations tore madly through her as he walked behind her slowly. To have him here, so close, where she could not see him! To know that soon he would touch her and then . . . She felt the blood begin to race through her body like wildfire and a raw, searing excitement bring shivers to soar up and down the length of her spine.

"Really. You have to go," she whispered. She was barely able to create sound. The words were a breath on the air.

He knelt down behind her. "I know," he said. But he made no attempt to leave. "Really. I have to go. Dear God, Callie, we both know that I cannot!"

Just when she thought she would scream with the waiting, with the anguish, with the denial, with the desire, she felt his lips at the back of her neck. Felt his kiss cover her flesh. Felt a searing, sensual heat that was so sudden and so startling and so welcome that it sent a burning ripping through her.

"Oh!" The softness of her cry escaped her. She nearly slipped beneath the water, but he was there. Lifting her up, pulling her into his arms. She fell against him. The water from her body formed rivulets that snaked along his. Her breasts were crushed against the dark hairs that had so fascinated her before, and now brought such a new rush of sensation to fill her. He held her still for one breathless moment, held her against him, feeling the mist-laden heat that fused between them. His hand stroked the side of her face. He cupped her jaw. And he kissed her. Kissed her again and again.

Deep, wet, hungry kisses rained down upon her. Kisses that raped and ravished. Kisses so tender that she strained and ached to have more. Kisses that again plundered and excited, kisses that left her both weak and hungry. As hungry as he might ever have desired her to be.

Her arms wound around his neck and he lifted her high from the tub. Water sluiced over both of them, and neither of them seemed to notice. He stretched her out on her bed, freeing her hair from its wound knot as he did so, and splaying it over the white covering on the bed. He watched his handiwork as he surveyed the dark fire and sable strands, then his gaze met hers.

He found her eyes full of wonder.

Once again, he kissed her. This kiss was soft and slow and achingly tender. Everything wild and raw and urgent was held tightly back, and his mouth very slowly caressed her. Liquid and effusive, his lips moved over hers, his tongue tasted them, his teeth grazed them.

She felt the movement of his hand upon the length of her, his fingers grazing over her thigh and her hip, her ribs, her breast. His knuckles grazed the lower side of her mound, then his hand cupped around it. She realized that he was no longer kissing her, his eyes were on her once again. His gaze lowered, focusing on her breast, and on a tiny bead of water on the hardened red peak. Once again, his gaze touched hers. His head lowered against her body and the tip of his tongue touched the droplet of water, and moved erotically over the very crest of her nipple. His mouth closed over that taut bud and the dusky rose areole, and began to tease and taste and savor, to suckle and caress.

She cried out at the strength of the sensations that seized a tight hold of her. Her fingers curled into his hair, and she heard herself calling out his name.

Deep within her body began a pulse, an urgency unlike anything she had ever experienced. She felt the power of his body over hers with every inch of flesh, with all of the searing fire now burning swiftly through her limbs. Her fingers moved in his hair, stroked down his neck, then down over his back. She stroked hard muscle, alive and vibrant. Flesh and muscle she had touched before, to cool, to heal.

And now she touched him, adding to the heat, adding to the fire.

When his gaze met hers again, she knew she was even adding to the healing.

"Should all the armies fall," he said softly, "I do not think that I could regret this invasion of the North."

She wet her lips, about to reply. He did not need one. He lowered himself against her again, just touching her lips with his. His mouth brushed briefly over her throat, against the hollow of her collarbone. His tongue teased the flesh at the valley of her breasts.

He inched himself lower, creating a searing liquid line of heat, slowly, surely, down her midriff, between her ribs to her navel. She wanted to cry out, she wanted to move. She wanted to fight the very force of the sensations he evoked. She could not. She lay still, feeling the tremors rock her body again and again.

His tongue moved leisurely upon her abdomen. Caressing, stroking, tasting. She tried to say his name again. The words would not come. She set her fingers once more into the rich mat of his ebony hair. She did not desist him in his purpose.

His kiss swept to her hip, and back to her navel. Fire, shooting, golden streaks of it, seemed to spring forth from the deepest, darkest, most intimate recesses of her desire as she felt the movement of his lips and the searing wet stroke of his tongue. He couldn't be intending to kiss her there . . .

Anticipation swept through her along with the protest that bubbled to her lips but went unspoken. Surely a flush covered the length of her body. The expectation was the sweetest agony. It was too intimate, too deep, too close to her soul. . . .

He shifted. He kissed all of her flesh, the sweep of her stomach, the top of her thighs. He moved all along them. He came everywhere but there.

And then he was gone. She was cold and bereft, and she was in anguish! How she needed him, wanted him. Her body moved, as fluid as water, seeking his touch in a subtle undulation. It was the sweetest ecstasy of wanting, it was sensation so strong that it was anguish.

What did he now intend? She didn't dare meet his eyes. The intimacy had gone too deep.

He lowered himself against her body, stroking her leg. His kiss fell upon the back of her kneecap.

And then that hot and molten trail of steaming moisture began to move up the length of her inner thigh once again. Higher and higher now until she trembled and writhed and waited.

She cried out, the breath escaping her, the very life seeming to escape her as he at last ceased to circle the velvet petals of her deepest desire and treasure them with his liquid caress. The world itself spun with the leisurely, supple movement of his intimate kiss. But it was swift, so swift, for the sweet, spiraling soaring was barely upon her before it burst into blackness, then came crashing down upon her in wave after wave of shimmering crystal, wracking her body with quivers. Words began to escape her then; if not words, then sounds. What she had done, what she had permitted—what she had felt!—came rushing in on her senses. Again she felt that the whole of her body must have blushed a vibrant red, and she was wholeheartedly eager not to have to meet his eyes.

"Oh, no!" she whispered, but soft laughter greeted her, words that she barely heard in her sudden and swift desire to hide away.

His eyes were above hers, deep cobalt blue, so hot and demanding still, so very alive with their startling blue fire. In his arms, she was reassured. In his arms, she realized that he wanted everything. His mouth found hers even when she would have twisted away. His lips parted hers, his tongue plunged and plundered past her teeth, capturing her own.

Just as his body at long last captured hers.

Ecstasy had come so swiftly before. It could not come again. But he intended that it should, and those startling eyes pierced and held hers as he began to move. He entered deeply into her. More and more of him became a part of her, until she thought that she would shriek, for he could go no further, she could give no more. But he could, and he would.

And she could, she discovered, give endlessly.

His eyes remained upon hers as he began to move. She gasped softly, realizing that she was moving again herself, undulating, writhing, grasping again for the elusive wonder. His eyes closed and he clasped her tightly into his arms, and a sound choked from her as he gave a total free rein to the strength of the desire he had restrained so patiently, so very long.

And then it was as if a storm swept through her, wild, reckless, violent, encompassing everything within its pass. The thunder and the size and power of him seemed to rock her to her extremities, seize her in tempest. She clung to him, her arms around him, holding tight. And he lifted her higher and closer, whispering to her, until her legs were also locked around his back, until tears of pleasure and pain stung the back of her eyes.

Until the world, and all the stars within it, suddenly exploded.

Night descended, eclipsing the room, eclipsing life itself. She wondered if she had died. She knew vaguely that she had not.

She opened her eyes slowly. She was indeed alive. A silver sheen of perspiration moistened her body, and her body remained entwined with his. A hot flush covered her cheeks as she felt him, still inside her, still filling her with the searing sweet nectar of his climax. His body lay limp, though his thigh was still cast over hers, his arms still about her. The desperate tension was gone.

He slept, pray God, he slept. With her passion spent, she suddenly realized just exactly what she had done.

She had made love with a stranger.

No, no, not a stranger!

She had made love with her enemy.

A choked cry caught in her throat and hot tears of shame nearly fell then from her eyes. She had betrayed everything that she had been taught, and she had truly betrayed the love she had once known.

But she had wanted him. She had seen the male glory of his nakedness, and she had felt his kiss, and she had known that she wanted him.

Wanting him was one thing. Having him was another.

She cared for him. More deeply than she could ever dare admit!

He moved his forefinger tenderly over her lip. She looked at him to discover the warmth of his eyes upon her and compassion etched deeply into the cobalt of his eyes. She shivered. Even while lying here ashamed of herself, she wanted him again.

She liked his face. Liked the character there, and the honesty, and yes, the honor, and both the tempest and the peace.

He appeared very much at peace at the moment. But he did not appear smug, or triumphant, rather, it seemed that his features were touched by concern.

Daniel *was* concerned. Now that the ragged fires that had threatened to incinerate his very soul had been somewhat quenched, he was worried about the very object of those desires.

She had given him so very much. She had surrendered herself to his every lead. Yet even while he had lain there, spent, amazed by the climax of desire when he was not an inexperienced boy, she had begun to withdraw.

He couldn't let her withdraw from him. Ever. Not now that he had felt the silken fire of her hair flow over his fingers when he held her. Not now that he had feasted upon the beauty of her nakedness, tasted the sweetness therein, known her, loved her. He was amazed still by the natural and fluid movement of her body, by all that she had brought forth in him. She was so alluring looking up at him with her dark lashes shielding those silver and gray eyes. Her lips, parted and moist and slightly open with the whisper of her desire, had sent him into new realms of need and pleasure, into a world he was suddenly certain he had never quite been before.

He held her when she would have turned away. "Callie, I am ever more entranced. Yet *you* look now as if you had truly come from battle."

Her eyes, soft gray now, flickered shut, then met his again. "A battle lost," she whispered.

"No, angel. A battle won. By North and by South."

She still seemed distressed, and he understood. It was one thing in this world for a man to want a woman. But in that same social world, her wanting him would be condemned, time and time again. Prim and proper madams would whisper, and all would swear that their daughter would never be so bold or promiscuous. Be she rich or be she poor, a woman should be chaste, so society claimed.

Daniel had decided long ago that society could be damned. What needs and emotions lurked in the hearts and minds of men and women could not be dictated by society. There were other reasons for Callie to have regrets now, when the flames cooled between them.

He was the enemy. One of the enemy who had taken her husband.

A husband she had loved.

Daniel wished that there were something he could say to convince her that there had been something special and unique between them. That no intimate action could be condemned when two people had been so strongly attracted to one another, when emotions had come so swiftly, when need had been so deep. There was nothing at all wrong because he loved her, he thought with a growing amazement.

He loved the gravity and emotion in her eyes, and he loved the way that they could fall upon him. The way that she spoke would remain in his memory forever, the softness of her voice, the beautiful tone of it. During long lonely nights ahead, he would dream of the perfection of her face, and he would remember both the thrill and the tenderness of her fingers upon him. He would remember, too, the steadfastness of her heart, her loyalty to her cause, right or wrong. He would remember the way that she had loved him, and he would know that, yes, he loved her.

Perhaps he couldn't tell her such a thing. Not now. She mourned a husband and lived in the midst of a battlefield. Perhaps all that he could do was hold her and let that be enough.

"I surrendered everything!" she said suddenly, fiercely.

He cupped her cheek and met her gaze, and smiled with all his tenderness. "No, angel. I surrendered everything."

He felt her trembling and hesitated to speak again. Her eyes widened with a sudden gratitude, then suddenly she pushed away from him, sitting up. Her gaze met his, a sizzling, shimmering silver. She lifted back a long, wild wayward skein of her deep flame hair, sending it sliding down the length of her back as she straddled over his hips and leaned closely over him.

"Want to fight again?" she whispered softly.

He grinned, knowing that she was going to be all right with her decision to lie with him.

Her head lowered, her lips touched his chest, the tip of her tongue seemed to singe it.

"Fire away, Yank," he told her, caressing her neck, cradling her head against him. "Fire away!" he repeated, and he wound his arms around her, sweeping her beneath him, as all the fires that had just begun to cool found a new and wild ignition with her touch.

The whole world could be damned, Daniel thought. Even as he lost himself within the musky sweet scent and taste and feel of her, he dimly marveled at the very idea.

He was falling in love.

With a Yank . . .

It was a strange war.

And a strange, strange battle.

Eight

"We call him 'Beauty.' Of course, we try very hard for the rank and file not to hear such terms. After all, we are military men. But Beauty he became, and so Beauty sticks."

"Is he really so handsome a man, then, so beautiful?" Callie asked, laughing.

It was night again. They had spent the day like newlyweds until dusk had fallen, and then Callie remembered the few animals that remained on the farm. Feeling more than a little guilty toward the poor creatures, she had enlisted Daniel's help to feed them.

It was interesting to watch him—not because she had discovered it was hard to take her eyes off him—but because he was so at ease with everything she asked of him. He knew what he was doing, whether measuring grain for Hal, her one remaining horse, or strewing out the grain for the chickens. Of course, a plantation was just a big farm—a very big farm—she reminded herself, but Daniel had been born and bred a child of privilege, of the southern aristocracy, and she had never imagined he would have such ease with manual labor.

Not that he had given her a chance to talk about it. Still barefoot, in her father's breeches and open plaid flannel shirt, he might have been the image of any farm boy. Against the setting sun, atop the gate of the barnyard door, his legs dangling, he seemed so very young. The lines had eased from his eyes while he chewed upon a blade of hay and entertained her with stories about some of the more infamous southern commanders.

"Is he really beautiful?" Daniel repeated, then laughed. They were talking about Stuart—General James Ewell Brown Stuart, "Jeb," as he was known. He was Daniel's immediate superior, but it didn't sound to Callie like Daniel gave that matter much thought at all. He called Stuart "Old Beauty."

Daniel shrugged, the light of laughter still in his eyes. "Beautiful, well, let's see. He is certainly gallant. And he loves to dress. He is flamboyant, he is courageous, and to Flora, I imagine, he is beautiful."

"Flora?"

"His wife," Daniel said with a grin. "But beautiful? The name was given him at West Point. I fear it was given him as a joke, for apparently, his classmates found his features not beautiful in the least."

"And what do you think?"

"Well, he is my superior officer."

"And you do not sound respectful enough."

"Well, I have known him forever, so it seems," Daniel admitted. "He's older than I by a few years." He was quiet for a minute. "He and Jesse were in the same class, but we were all Virginians, and were all assigned to the West together." He shrugged again, as if he didn't want to dwell upon the past any longer. "Beauty and I are friends, we are both avid horsemen, and we work very well together. In truth, I am very respectful, for I know of no cavalry commander more talented, dashing, or bold."

"Here, here!" Callie applauded, smiling. Then her smile faded, and she swirled about in the dust to cast more seed to the chickens. Dear God, how strange. He was speaking about the men who were grinding countless companies of the Union army into constant bloody defeats. The way that he spoke, she found herself smiling far too frequently, and anxious to meet such a man as Beauty Stuart.

"There was an occasion when the Federals under Pope managed to take Stuart's magnificent cape and his plumed hat," Daniel told her, his eyes twinkling.

"And?"

"And so we had to go after Pope—and get back his cape and hat."

"I don't believe you."

"It's true, and we succeeded nicely, thank you. You see," he advised her, his tone grave, his eyes alight, "we are entirely bold and dashing and daring, and there's nothing that can stop the southern cavalry."

It was often proving all too true, Callie thought. Northern horsemen had a difficult time keeping up with their southern counterparts. Too many of the South's men were like Daniel, born and bred to ride and hunt and master the slopes and hills and valleys and forests of their region.

"We are Lee's eyes and ears—" Daniel began, but he broke off, looking into the darkness of the night.

"What is it?" Callie asked him.

"Nothing," he said after a moment. He shrugged. "I thought I heard something." He stared at Callie again. "Cavalry was all-important in the battle here.

Lee's orders for the campaign were discovered by the Federals, and it was our scouting and riding around the Federals that brought back that information."

"Lee's orders were found by the Union?" Callie said. One point for their side. How unusual.

Daniel nodded, watching her. "Special Order Number 191," he said. "It advised a number of Lee's key generals that he was splitting the army, that Jackson would be taking Harpers Ferry. Someone was careless. There were seven copies of the order. One was found by Federal men in the grass at one of the campsites we had abandoned near Frederick, Maryland. It was wrapped around three cigars, can you imagine? It was an incredible gift to the Union—and a blow to us. But McClellan moved too slowly. Jackson managed to take Harpers Ferry, and to meet us here to do battle. And Lee was forewarned that McClellan knew about the order because we looped around to get the information."

"You didn't win the battle," Callie reminded him.

"Do you know that for a fact?"

Callie shrugged. "Union soldiers are keeping you here," she said softly.

"I wonder. I wonder if it is Union soldiers keeping me here," he murmured softly. He tore his eyes from hers, looking out over the night that settled around them. "Perhaps we didn't win. Maybe we didn't take the territory. But I don't think that the Union won either."

Callie didn't want to remember the aftermath of the battle. The bodies had been taken away from her lawn. More selfishly, she didn't want to give up the night, or this very strange time between her and this Rebel. He was anxious to leave, she knew. Now that she was anxious that he stay, he was feeling the hard pull to return to duty. She was very afraid for him to go. He wasn't strong enough yet, she had convinced herself. And the countryside was crawling with Union troops.

He wouldn't allow himself to be taken. Not easily. He'd die to escape, or he'd bring down more men to whom she should owe her loyalty and concern.

She smiled at him, dispelling the desolation that had intruded between them.

"So the southern cavalry can all ride," Callie said. "Watch it. The northern boys just might catch up."

"But we ride very well," he assured her with a grin.

"So might they."

"We ride exceptionally well."

"And you also excel in your humility," she said.

"The prim and proper Mrs. Michaelson, returned to me at last!" he teased.

Callie threw out a handful of seed to the chickens, which hurriedly pecked away at the offering. "I am very prim and proper, and you must keep that in mind," she told him. She didn't dare look at him to see the warmth of the smile that curved his lip. Perhaps she had been prim and proper once. But he had changed her. Irrevocably. He knew her more intimately than any man alive . . . or dead. He had demanded so many things from her, and he had given back so many. He had robbed her of old emotions, and given her new ecstasy—and anguish. She didn't dare dwell too closely upon it. She was falling in love with her enemy, and in this war, that was a very frightening thought.

She turned back to face him and met his gaze. He was looking at her with that blue fire kindled within his eyes once again. A fire that caught deep within her just because he glanced her way. A fire that evoked sweet longings and seemed to touch down upon her flesh with a dance of sweet little flames.

A fire from which she needed some distance.

"Let's hear more about these famous—infamous!—men in gray," she told him. "What about Lee? Is he really so great as they say?"

Daniel grinned. "There is no man greater." He slid down from the gate, leaning against it. "Imagine, Callie. He had a beautiful home in Arlington. It still sits there, high upon a ridge, looking over the Potomac, right in Washington, D.C. And it wasn't just his home, it was his wife's home. And she is—"

"Martha Washington's great-granddaughter, and the step great-grandchild of George Washington," Callie interrupted softly. Daniel looked at her with an arched brow. "So I've heard," Callie said. "Your General Lee is a legend here, just as he is in the South. Many people believe that the war would be over now if we had had him leading some of our troops. They say that he is a brilliant commander, and an extremely fine man."

Daniel smiled ruefully. "It's quite true; he is both of those things. And sometimes, when the war seems to drag on and on and I'm thinking of home with every breath I take, I think about Master Lee, as we sometimes call him, and his wife, Mary, and that beautiful home of theirs."

"And what of Mary Lee?" Callie murmured.

A slow, wry curl worked its way into Daniel's lip as he looked down at Callie. "Mary Lee loves her husband very much. And trusts in his decisions."

"It is her home that is lost," Callie said. "He is off riding around the countryside."

"Skedaddling Yanks," Daniel said lazily. She cast him a most condemning gaze and he laughed softly.

He leapt down from the barn gate and came toward her. "He's very, very good at it."

"Is he?" Callie said.

Daniel nodded. "Yes. All Rebs are. Look. All I'm doing is walking very slowly toward you. And you're already trying to skedaddle."

Her heart was thudding already. Yes, she was backing away from him. She just couldn't feel this warm, lusty wonder every time he looked at her. It was wrong, and she had created a fool's paradise. She had to learn to walk and talk and keep her distance from him, to regain her sense of propriety, dear God, to regain her morals!

But all that he had to do was beckon, and she felt the heat come simmering through her.

"I'm not trying to skedaddle," she assured him.

"Then stand still."

"But I'm not ready to surrender!" she said quickly. He was still coming. She dropped the bucket of chicken feed and veered around toward the paddock fence, making sure she kept her eyes on him all the while.

"How futile to battle when the war is already lost!" he told her.

"No, sir! The war is not lost. Battle after battle may be won, but that does not mean that the war is lost!"

"The enemy can be worn down."

"Not a determined enemy."

He paused for just a moment, his head cocked, a crooked smile playing into the corners of his mouth. "Have you ever made love in the hay, Mrs. Michaelson?"

Her mouth dropped, although she didn't know why anything that he should say or do should surprise her anymore.

He didn't wait for her answer, but came toward her again with his long, relentless stride. A sound escaped her as he came too close, and she made a beeline past him, slipping behind the barn gate and using it for a barrier between them.

"Colonel, things have happened very quickly here," she told him, "and I think that a measure of constraint—"

"The moment is constraining me to sheer distraction, Mrs. Michaelson," he said pleasantly enough. But then his hand touched the rim of the gate and suddenly he was leaping up and over it, and facing her.

"Daniel Cameron—"

"You never, never made love in the hay?"

She pushed away from the gate, backing away from him once again. "Well, it's hardly the proper thing to do—"

"Callie, Callie, Callie, making love is not supposed to be a 'proper' thing at all. And the scent of the hay is so delicious—"

"And it surely sticks into your flesh and tangles in your hair!"

He laughed, his blue eyes sparkling and alive, even in the darkness. "Come here, woman!" he commanded. He reached for her hand, pulling her to him.

She felt as if she were melting inside. Was this love? So quickly, so easily? Or was this the effect of war?

"You behave, Reb!" she informed him regally, and she jerked free from his hold, only to fall backward with her effort—and wind up right where he wanted her, in a pile of hay.

In seconds he had fallen down beside her, his arm about her, lifting a handful of straw to breathe in its scent. "It's wonderful, it's fresh, it's clean—"

"And one should be careful of cow manure!" Callie interrupted.

But his laughter rang softly around her, husky, seductive. She needed to protest, they were moving too quickly, he was the enemy.

He touched her lips with his own. She was well dressed for seduction in the hay, wearing nothing at all but a simple blue cotton day dress with a button-up bodice and full flaring skirt.

One by one, her buttons were coming open. In the darkness, she felt the stroke of his hand moving up the hem of her skirt.

Her bodice fell open, her breasts spilled free. Her skirt was shoved to her hips, and she felt the swift, sudden, and breathtaking weight of his body come boldly atop hers. His fingers stroked between her thighs, touching, probing, as he kissed her.

His lips moved from hers. He buried his face between her breasts just as he thrust his shaft deeply, firmly within her.

She gasped, and breathed in the hay. The scent was sweet and titillating, just as the feel of the earth around her and the raw scent of the man atop her combined to bring within her an explosion of wild and reckless passion.

He was not so tender a lover as he had been before. When he touched her, surrounded as he was by earth and night air, it was with a wild and reckless need that boldly mingled with the scent of the dirt and the hay. He did not tease or cajole, but his lips lay claim to a response, with no protest allowed her.

His body moved with the same hard passion, not tempting or eliciting a response but, rather, provoking one. Yet all that he did was what she craved. She did feel the hay against her naked flesh, and she did feel her body pressed low and lower into the earth. The scent of his body and the scent of her own then mingled with all those other earth scents, and as he moved so boldly between her thighs, she felt again a starting, wild thunder of passion seize hold of her. In seconds it seemed that the desires that sang so within her blood and coursed through her limbs were appeased with a swift and startling volatility. Hot honey filled the very center of her. She saw blackness and then light. She did not know if the cries she heard were sounds she emitted, or part of the words he whispered tensely to her, or if the searing nectar had spilled from herself, or from him. She only knew that she lay spent on the hay when he was done, exhausted, and still drifting in distant fields of beauty.

They were silent and it was long minutes later when she again felt the prick of the hay against her flesh. She smiled, and he was suddenly over her, wickedly grinning. "Mrs. Michaelson. There is hay in your hair!"

"Oh, you wretched Rebel!" she cried, laughing, and shoved at his chest. He did not intend to let her go, and so she laughed as they rolled over in the hay together. She managed to elude him, but just as she did so, she reached the edge of the hay, and shrieked as she went teetering over the two-foot pile to the ground below. His head instantly appeared above her. Tousled, blue eyes alight with laughter, he stared down at her. "There you go, Mrs. Michaelson! See what happens to wayward Yanks? I daresay—"

His voice suddenly broke off and his laughter faded. He reached down a hand to her, and his voice was suddenly grave. "Callie, give me your hand. Come back up."

He didn't want her to look to her side—she knew it instantly.

But like Lot's wife, she couldn't help doing so. She turned to her left, to stare at a spot where there were just a few feet between the hay pile and the rear wall of the barn.

It was dark in the barn. Shadows were intensified and increased because of the one lamp that illuminated everything from the spot where it hung near the door. There was a moon out, but its glow was pale and did little to illuminate the corners of the barn.

Still, she could see the man and see his face, with horror. A terrible scream rose in her throat. It choked there, and the sound that came from her was simply one of horror.

He leaned against the barn wall, his hand over his abdomen. His eyes remained open, his mouth was in an O, as if he were still surprised by his own untimely end. He was a young soldier boy, a sad, pathetic figure in deep, dark, haunting blue.

"Callie!"

She couldn't seem to move on her own. Strong arms enveloped her, and in seconds she was swept up and held tightly.

Daniel sat on the hay with her upon his lap, cradling her head against his chest, murmuring assurances. She couldn't even hear his words.

She had seen so many dead men. She hadn't thought that the sight of another could do this to her.

Perhaps that was it. There had been too many before. None of them had been like this poor soldier. Alone. He had crawled here, into her barn, to die. He didn't stink yet, so he hadn't been dead that long. He had holed up here, weak, afraid, dying. She had come and gone the last three days, feeding the animals, and she had never seen him. He had just lain there. . . . .

They had just lain in the hay, half-naked, entwined, whispering, crying out. And all the while the poor young soldier's sightless eyes had been open upon them.

"Oh, God!" she whimpered against Daniel's chest, and she was shaking again.

"Callie, it's all right. It's all over for him. He's at peace. Callie, look at me, will you."

She tried to stare at him. She tried to focus on him. Tears swam in her eyes and guilt riddled her.

She had spent those days tending to an enemy soldier, wanting an enemy soldier, making love with an enemy soldier. And this boy had been out here, dying.

She jumped up, pulling her bodice together. "Oh, my Lord, how could we—"

"Callie, stop it!" He was instantly on his feet, calmly belting his breeches.

She shook her head, feeling wild, as if she wanted to run and run until she made it all disappear—the hatred, the war, the guilt, the love. "No, Daniel." She backed away from him, but his hands were quickly on her shoulders, shaking her lightly. "Callie, we've done nothing wrong. It's not wrong to live, to survive! You cannot feel guilty for living!"

"I do not feel guilty for living!" she protested. "I feel guilty for—"

"For loving?" he inquired softly. She stiffened, trying to escape him, but he drew her to him, holding her very close. "Callie, we did not take his life—"

She jerked free again. "But you might have! You might have shot him down. And I might have allowed him to die by neglect!"

"Callie, I didn't shoot him. I fell in your front yard. And nothing that you did or didn't do could have saved him."

"How do you know?"

"He was gut shot, Callie."

"He didn't die quickly. He just lay there—"

"Unconscious, Callie," he assured her, advancing toward her.

"No!" she shrieked. "No! You are the enemy. Don't touch me, don't touch me—"

But he did touch her. He took her into his arms again, and she beat furiously against his back until her energy drained from her. Tears fell down her cheeks once again.

He didn't say anything else to her, he just held her. He smoothed back her hair, and rocked her. In time she felt the tremors that had seized her begin to fade. She sniffled raggedly, and then she felt the simple edge of exhaustion come over her.

She was dimly aware that he rose, and that he would take her back to the house. She stopped him.

"Daniel, we can't just leave him."

"You're right. We can't just leave him," he agreed. He set her down upon the hay, and cupped her chin, lifting her face so that he could meet her eyes. "Are you all right?"

She nodded. She wasn't all right at all. One moment she was freezing, and the next she was numb. She felt as if all the agony of the war had descended down upon her, and then it was as if she couldn't feel anything at all.

But she nodded again, trying to assure him.

He left her sitting on the hay. She heard him moving about the barn, looking for a shovel.

It seemed forever that he was gone. She waited on the hay, and then she remembered that she was alone in the barn with the young soldier with the dead eyes that still seemed to watch her. She leapt up and started to run out of the barn.

Daniel was just coming back in. He caught her shoulders. "I dug the grave in your family plot. You may want to send his things home; I'll collect them for you. Maybe his family will want to send for his body later too. But for tonight . . . tonight, we'll just lay him to rest."

She nodded, not realizing that she was clinging to him.

"Callie, I have to get him," Daniel reminded her softly.

"Oh!" She released him and walked on out to the small family cemetery. There were monuments to her mother and her father, and to Gregory. Farther back were the stones for her grandparents, and for her aunt Sarah, who had died as a child of six. There, by Gregory's grave, was a gaping new hole.

A moment later, Daniel reappeared. He had wrapped the soldier in an old horse blanket, but carried him as gently as if he were alive.

He just as gently set the body into the grave he had dug.

Watching him, Callie felt the cold close around her heart again. This poor boy, so far from home! None to mourn him, none to say a prayer.

But she was wrong. Daniel repacked the earth over the grave, and when he was done, he drew a cross in the dirt. And to her surprise, he began to speak.

"Dear Lord, this is Private Benjamin Gest, an artillery man. Brave, loyal, true, he gave his all for his cause. Into your hands, we commend his keeping. Ashes to ashes, dust to dust, earth to earth. Father, look gently down upon him, for he was just a boy. Be with his loved ones, God, and give them strength."

He stepped back from the grave, his hands dirty but folded, his chest still naked and streaked with dirt and sweat. His head bowed low, he was silent for several long seconds, and then he looked to Callie again.

She felt tears rising once more. She didn't want to shed them.

"Thank you," she said.

"It is the least that any man deserves."

"You knew his name."

"I went through his haversack. It's in the barn, with his personal effects. There's a letter in there for his mother. You might want to make sure that she gets it."

Callie nodded.

"Callie, go in. Go to bed," he told her.

"What are you doing?"

He shrugged awkwardly. "I'm covered in dirt. I'm going to clean up."

She felt the same herself, but she was suddenly so exhausted, she didn't know if she could stand much longer. He wanted her to go in. She didn't know where he meant to clean up, but she didn't ask. He obviously wanted to be alone.

She walked woodenly back to the house and up the stairs. In her room she discovered that she was desperate to wash up too. She poured out water and scrubbed her face and her throat and her arms and her breasts. She dug into her wardrobe and crawled into a white nightgown.

She caught sight of her reflection in the swivel mirror in the corner of the room. The gown seemed mockingly virginal.

She closed her eyes, and turned away, and crawled into her bed. But once she was there, she couldn't sleep. She lay awake, staring up at the ceiling and waiting.

She had assumed that he would come to her. But time passed, and Daniel did not come. A slow aching began to build inside her.

She got up and opened the door. She could hear him in the parlor below. Hurrying down the steps, she saw him before the fireplace, staring into the flames of a blaze he had just built against the chill of the late night. His arm rested against the hearth, his head against his arm.

"Daniel?" she said softly.

He looked up at her. Blue eyes meeting hers. She felt a special warmth grip hold of her heart. There was something very noble in the structure of his face, in the weary slope of his broad shoulders.

"You should sleep," he told her.

"I don't want to sleep alone," she said.

He smiled, understanding exactly the need that she couldn't quite voice aloud. He came up the stairs and lifted her into his arms.

He brought her back into her room and laid her down, then stretched out beside her. He took her gently into his arms, and smoothed out her hair.

She managed to close her eyes and to sleep.

All through the night she was warm and safe and protected from all the demons of war that had come to haunt her. Even in her sleep, she knew that he held her.

He might have been her enemy.

But she had never been kept more safely.

Nine

Callie slept late the next morning, and when she awoke she was alone. The bed beside her still retained a little warmth. She ran her hand over the sheets and then closed her eyes.

She had liked sleeping beside him. Feeling his arms, warm and strong, wrapped about her. Turning to rest her head against his chest. Feeling the even tremor of his breathing.

When he was gone, she would be bereft. It would be worse than it had been when she learned Gregory had died. She had learned to stand alone, and now she was going to have to learn that bitter lesson all over again.

He couldn't go, not yet. He was well enough to help with the animals, or in the house. He was certainly well enough to make love. But he was not yet recovered enough to make the dangerous and difficult trip through enemy lines. He had to see that.

But he wouldn't, she knew. It was time he made his move, whatever came of it. A feeling of dread settled over her.

Maybe she would still have tonight.

She slipped out of bed and walked over to her window and looked down into the paddock in front of the barn at the back of the house. He was out there, fixing a broken hinge on the gate. He moved as if he would lower his hat against the rising sun, and then he seemed to realize that he no longer wore his magnificent hat. She smiled, and bit lightly into her lower lip, wondering if she hadn't gotten just a bit carried away when she'd burned his hat.

After all, Beauty Stuart had ridden after General Pope's army just to retrieve his hat and cape. Daniel Cameron must have been very attached to his hat.

He looked up suddenly, as if he sensed that she was there. He waved to her. "Good morning."

"Good morning."

"The gate is all right now." He looked around and shrugged. "I replaced a few rails in the fencing for you, but there's not too much that I can do about all the bullet holes."

She looked down at him and lifted her shoulders in a small shrug. "No, not now," she said. "Would you like breakfast?"

"The coffee is already on," he told her. "I'll be right in," he added.

Callie stepped away from the window and moved back into her room. He was leaving. He was trying to repay her in some way for what she had done for him.

She dressed quickly, simply, in a muted blue plaid cotton that buttoned to her throat. The day might well be warm, but she welcomed the long sleeves on the dress, anything that might put some distance between them and give her the dignity she would need to let him go.

When she was dressed, she surveyed the length of her hair, thick and curling over her shoulders and down her back. She picked up her brush and worked through it vigorously, then twisted it into a severe knot, which she secured with pins. She was determined on a look of staid respectability.

He had not been here very long. Not quite a week. Why did it feel as if he had changed her whole life, as if things could never be the same again?

She heard the back door close, and she hurried down the stairs. He was in the kitchen, sipping a cup of coffee, ready to hand her one when she walked in. His eyes rode over her. Blue, endlessly blue. She thought that there was anguish in them, and despite herself, she was glad of it. He had torn her world in two. He hadn't made her question her own loyalties or her beliefs, but he had forced her to see the face of the enemy, and she realized all too painfully that they were one people. And that it was possible to love and agonize despite their differences.

"Callie—"

"You're leaving today," she said softly.

"Tonight."

She nodded, sipping her coffee.

"Last night, when we found that boy . . . ." He paused, shrugging. "Callie, they'll have reported me as missing by now. I don't want that kind of news getting back to Virginia. My sister and my sister-in-law would be devastated."

"And your brother?"

"It might take longer for the news to reach Jesse," Daniel said. He cocked his head, reflecting. "And then again, the news might already have reached Jesse."

"That's right," Callie murmured. "He and Beauty went to school together."

Daniel smiled. "That's right," he said softly. "Callie, I can't let them mourn for me, or go through the anguish of wondering."

"I know," she said.

"I've tried to—to do what I can around here."

"You don't owe me anything."

"Other than my life," he said lightly. He set his mug down, walking toward her. In seconds, he undid all that she had done to keep her facade of composure. He pulled the pins from her hair, letting them fall to the ground. The knot unwound into a wild mass. He lifted her hair from her back and spread it out over her shoulders, watching his handiwork as it streamed down her back. "What I do has nothing to do with owing you, Yank," he said very softly. "It has everything to do with not wanting to leave you."

She still needed to keep her distance. She stood still, not protesting his touch, but not giving in to it either. "Duty calls. I understand."

"My God, do you?" He demanded, suddenly fierce, his voice trembling. His hands locked around her shoulders and he shook her so that her head fell slightly back. She raised her eyes to his, cool still, as if she calmly awaited his words. She was anything but calm, her heart racing, her blood seeming to seethe and boil.

"You can't possibly understand. I would give everything to forget the war and stay here with you. I'm sick to death of dead men, of blood, of heroes in tattered jackets and bare feet. I'm weary of camp fires, and orders, and trying to learn new and better ways to kill my enemy. I would give everything . . . ."

His anger suddenly faded as she stared silently into his eyes. He shook his head. "I have to go back. I am fighting for something. I can't explain it to you. I'm fighting for the river. I'm fighting for the bricks and pillars of my home. I'm fighting for those hot days in summer when you can hear the chanting from the fields and quarters. For the rustle of silk, for the soft tone of a drawl. Maybe I'm fighting for a dying empire, I don't know. What I do know is that it's my empire, and right or wrong, I must defend it to the last."

She felt that she could move at last. She reached up and stroked his cheek. His lips came down upon hers, nearly brutal in all that he demanded. When he raised his head at last, she was shaking. Her lips were swollen from his passion.

Her heart was lost, her resolve shattered.

"You cannot go until nightfall," she whispered.

His eyes touched hers with their fire, and he swept her up into his arms. Callie reached up, winding her arms around his neck, meeting his gaze. He started for the stairway.

She rested her head against his chest. "I knew that you had to go. But I could not let you go. Not without being with you one last time."

"I could not go without having you one last night," he whispered huskily.

He started up the stairs, his arms tight around her. But even as his long-legged gait brought them upward, they were both startled from the intimacy of their private world by a hard knocking upon the door.

Daniel stiffened instantly. Panic swept quickly through Callie, then she managed to control it. "Let me down, quickly, Daniel."

To her amazement, he did so. She raced up the stairs herself, with him fast behind her. From the hallway window, she looked down, but the eaves over the house shielded their visitor.

The knocking sounded again. Tense, Callie held still. She could hear Daniel moving away from her now, walking toward her brother Joshua's room.

She knew that he was going for his sword.

"Frau Michaelson!"

She heard the deep, slightly accented voice and she let out a quick sigh of relief. Daniel was back in the hallway, watching her, his sword hilt held tightly in his hand.

"Who is it?" he demanded.

"It's all right," she said quickly.

"Who is it?" his voice was tense.

"It's just Rudy Weiss—"

"And who is 'just' Rudy Weiss?"

She hated his tone when it became so imperious. She hated him when he became so cold.

"He is my neighbor. A Dunkard."

"A Dunkard."

"He's one of the German Baptist Brethren who worship in the little white church that must have been in the middle of your battlefield," Callie said quickly.

"That could make him an ardent Yank or a southern sympathizer. Which is he, Callie?"

"He's neither!" Callie replied irritably. She lifted her hands with aggravation. "There isn't even a steeple on their church, these people believe in such a simple lifestyle. They want no part of the war, they don't want to hurt anyone. They lead very strict, religious lives. I'm not even sure that Rudy approves of me, but he is a caring man, and he knows that I am alone. He has come to see to my welfare, nothing more."

"Frau Michaelson?"

They heard the voice again, rising, concerned.

Callie spun around, heedless of Daniel's staring at her. She hurried down the stairs and opened the door.

Rudy Weiss, white-haired, white-bearded, a man who looked as if could have been close to one hundred years old, but still tall and agile and very dignified, awaited her with anxiety in his powder-blue eyes. But once she had opened the door, he smiled.

"So, you are well. I was getting very worried. The place, it was loaded with soldiers, jah?"

"Yes, Herr Weiss. There were many soldiers."

"You were not hurt?"

"No, no, I wasn't hurt at all."

"And none of the soldiers have disturbed you? If you are worried, we will take care that you are not alone."

"No, no, thank you," Callie said quickly, then she asked anxiously, "Your wife, your family, were any of them injured?"

"Nein, nein, we are well," he said. He continued to stand on her porch, then said worriedly, "There is a friend staying with you, then?"

Callie froze, staring at him. He lifted a hand, palm up, and explained. "Karl, my oldest son, saw a man feeding your chickens."

Callie exhaled, "Oh." She didn't know what to say. It didn't matter. She didn't have to say anything. She hadn't realized that Daniel had followed her down the stairs until he stood by her, offering his hand to Rudy. "Daniel Cameron, Mr. Weiss. Yes, I am a friend of Callie's."

Rudy nodded gravely, surveying Daniel. "Well then, perhaps you can stay on a bit longer, Herr Cameron." As Daniel frowned he continued, "There is a bit of news. Grave excitement in the North."

"The war . . . ?" Callie said.

"The war—it goes on," Rudy said. He slipped a newspaper from his pocket, handing it to Callie. "I do not usually bother with the affairs of others," he said to Daniel. "Mein frau insisted this might be important for Callie, for she lives here alone."

"What is it?" Callie said, for Daniel was taking the paper from her and scanning it quickly.

"President Lincoln has issued a . . . a preliminary e-man-ci-pa-tion pro-cla-ma-tion," Rudy Weiss said, speaking very carefully, and very slowly.

"Emancipation proclamation?" Callie repeated, trying to take the paper from Daniel. He wouldn't allow her to do so. He was avidly reading every word in the article.

"By God, he's gone and done it!" Daniel exclaimed.

"It frees the slaves," Rudy said.

Daniel swung around, laughing hollowly as he stared at Callie. "No, no, not exactly. It frees the slaves—in the states that are in rebellion! It frees the slaves in the South, not in the North, not in the border states! This is rich, really rich. Oh, God! Do you know what this means!"

Callie wasn't sure that she did know what it meant, not the way that Daniel seemed to understand it. He released the paper to her at last and sank down into one of the upholstered chairs in the parlor, staring straight ahead at nothing.

Callie looked back to Rudy Weiss, who remained on her porch.

"Your friend, Herr Cameron, understands," Rudy said softly. "The slaves are freed as of January third, next year. The slaves in those 'states in rebellion.' Herr Cameron knows. The southern men will not consider any proclamation of Lincoln's as law in their Confederacy. But the slaves will want to be free. They will begin to escape. Many of them will be hungry, and they will come north, looking for food, looking for jobs, looking for ways to be free. Many may become desperate. That is why mein frau is so anxious for you, Callie. She says that you must take care if these people come this way. Myself, I told her that you must take care with the soldiers too. Some men are good, and some men are evil, no matter what the coloring of their skin or their clothing."

Callie nodded, moistening her lips nervously. Daniel was watching Rudy, and Rudy, his old eyes very bright, was watching Daniel. Daniel rose and walked back to the doorway. "You take care, too, Herr Cameron," Rudy said quietly.

"I will. Thank you," Daniel said.

Rudy knew damned well that Daniel was a Reb soldier, Callie thought. And he didn't care. If he was a friend, he was a friend. And a friend who needed to be warned, it seemed, for Rudy turned then to leave, saying over his shoulder, "There's still a troop of soldiers camped just south of us, in a cornfield. They seem to be watching the roads." He stopped, and looked up at the sky. Then he looked back to Callie and Daniel. He wrinkled up his nose, then shook his head sadly. "There is still the stink of death about us; the creek still seems to run red with blood. It is a sad thing, this war. A very sad thing."

He left them, walking down the walk, then out and across the road and into the field that faced Callie's house.

Daniel watched until he was gone, then his fingers suddenly crumpled over the newspaper. "This is rich. Damnation, but this is rich! Your Mr. Lincoln is no fool, Callie." He threw the paper across the room with a sudden fury that brought Callie's eyes to his, wide with amazement.

"You told me that you'd already freed your own slaves!" She exclaimed. "If the South doesn't recognize Lincoln's authority, what difference does any proclamation make?"

Daniel turned his fury on her, swirling around with his teeth clenched. "I'll tell you what difference! Slaves will be escaping by the dozens, hundreds— maybe even thousands! And some of them will be dangerous. But that's not the crux of it. Don't you see what Lincoln has done?"

Startled and hurt that he could direct his fury so wrathfully upon her, she retorted with a sarcastic and passionate anger of her own. "Yes! Yes, I do! He's freed a lot of people who were in bondage! I see exactly what he's done!"

"He's done more for his war effort than any general he's ever had!" Daniel snapped back. "Don't you see? Europe will never recognize the Confederacy now. And England! England who takes our cotton by the balefuls but looks down her regal nose at our 'institutions'—she will side now with Lincoln, surely. There will be no help for us anywhere. My God, but I have always said that he is a painfully smart man!"

Callie felt a fluttering in her heart as she grasped the things that Daniel was saying. The Confederacy had hoped for supplies, for funding, from Europe. The Confederacy had been desperate for recognition. And perhaps the Reb government had almost achieved it.

But Lincoln had circumvented that. The English despised slavery. And Lincoln was no longer fighting a war just to preserve a Union. He had created a noble cause, a cause for humanity. The war had taken on another dimension. Passion everywhere would truly be aroused.

Daniel was laughing. "You'll note, Callie, that slaves in Maryland are not freed. President Lincoln would not dare test the loyalty of his border states any further. Oh, it is rich, I say. It is a death knell!"

He stared at her as if she had sounded that knell herself. She felt as if her breath were leaving her. He was challenging her, accusing her—awaiting some response from her.

"What would you have me say!" she cried out. "I do not believe in slavery. If Lincoln can bring the South to her knees and end this war with such a proclamation, then I must be glad!"

He exploded with an oath, his fingers clenching into fists at his side. "Do you know what he will do eventually in Maryland, Callie? He will see that the slaves are freed here, but it will be with some type of compensation for the owners."

"So he is not a stupid man!"

"No, he is not a stupid man at all!" Daniel spat out. "It is only to us—" He broke off, and she didn't miss the handsome but bitter twist that curved his lip. "I keep forgetting," he said softly. "There is no 'us.' You are 'them,' or 'they'— the enemy. And to think—I had almost forgotten!"

"Yes!" she cried passionately. "I am the enemy! And you should not forget it! You told me once that no man should ever forget his enemy. Your private died for hesitating before he could shoot a friend. Don't forget your own lessons, Colonel!" she reminded him. She gasped, backing away as he took a sudden, menacing stride toward her. "Oh!"

He stopped, his features taut, his shoulders and his body ramrod stiff. "Damn you!" he grated out. He turned about, straight as steel, and started for the stairs. He paused, his back to her. "Enemies, madam, until the day that we die. I will be out of your house as hastily as I can manage!"

Callie stared after him, furious, shaking. As he disappeared past the upstairs landing, she felt her anger begin to fade.

He was going to leave her when he was still so furious. They might never talk again. So much for love! So much for the hunger, the need, and all the passion that had flared between them. So much for his whispers that he could not leave without having her again.

Then damn him, her pride cried out. Let him go! If he wished to see her as the enemy, then so be it! She would not apologize if her side—after defeat and humiliation and death—was finally beginning to see signs of hope. She would not say that she was sorry for her beliefs when she knew in her heart that she was right.

Daniel knew, too, that slavery was wrong. No man, black or white, should be owned, body and soul, by another. He had freed his own slaves. He was angry because Lincoln wasn't just a 'long drink of water' as political opponents had labeled him. The backwoods lawyer from Illinois might prove to be one of the greatest men of their time. Daniel saw it, and he was angry because of it.

Alone upstairs, Daniel plucked a pillow from the bed and hurtled it across the room. It felt so good that he picked up the next pillow and threw it too.

He sank down at the foot of the bed, running his fingers through his hair. Damn Callie! Damn her.

No. Damn Lincoln. And damn the war.

If Callie had been born in the South, she might be on a different side. She had never lied to him. She had never pretended to be a southern sympathizer. She hadn't even tried to fight him. She had simply refused to back down.

He frowned suddenly, thinking he heard something from outside. He rose and looked out the window. It must have been Callie. If he wouldn't leave her house, then maybe she was planning on leaving it herself.

He shouldn't be so distracted, he thought vaguely. On the battlefield, it would be deadly to lose oneself so completely to emotion.

He was going to leave now, he decided. He rose and reached for his scabbard and buckled it around his hip. He pulled on his boots and clenched his teeth against the sudden onslaught of pain that assailed him.

He was in love with her. With the beauty in her dove-gray eyes, with the fire in her hair, and in her voice. With the passion of her heart.

The past half hour had proven them enemies. He had no right to stay longer. He was needed at home. And he had probably just cost them any chance of a tender good-bye with his irrational display of temper.

Walk away, he told himself. Make it easy on both of us, and walk away!

But as he started down the stairs he knew that he could not just walk away.

She waited in the parlor, her fingers wound into her palms, her palms held tautly at her sides, for what seemed like forever. Daniel didn't reappear. Tears stung her eyes. She refused to shed them.

He was angry, she realized, because he was losing his grasp upon his world. He was fighting with all of his heart and with all of his strength. He could ride, and he could wage battle, and he could best his enemy. But it wasn't enough. He couldn't be brave enough, he couldn't be daring enough, and he couldn't be loyal enough. The numbers were against him.

She knew then that she understood him, maybe better than he did himself. If she knew Daniel—and dear Lord, yes, she had come to know him—he would realize it all soon enough.

He had to go. He had to go back to his damnable dying cause, because if he didn't, he'd never be able to live with himself. But he'd never, never admit—not even now—that his precious Confederacy might really lose the war.

She moistened her lips and fought the tears that stung her eyes. She turned on her heels and walked through the house to the kitchen, and then out the door to the back. She walked down the steps, not knowing exactly where she was going, except that she was leaving the house—and Daniel—behind her.

But she did have a direction in mind, she discovered. Her footsteps took her past the barn, and far out back to the little family graveyard. She plucked a wildflower from a thicket and dropped it atop the new mound of dirt over the Yankee soldier they had buried just the night before. She stared down at the tombstones that honored her father and Gregory, and she felt as if a rain of tears suddenly fell upon her soul. How many? How many would have to perish in this awful contest? What price this honor that all the fool men of her acquaintance seemed so desperate to shed their blood for?

She sat down atop the grass that had grown over her husband's grave and closed her eyes, remembering. It seemed as if they had loved and laughed in another world. He had not died very long ago, but it seemed like forever since she had seen him. He had held her, laughing, in his arms. The war would be over in just a few weeks, he had told her, and he would be back. He had seemed invincible then with blond hair curling over his collar and his blue-green eyes solemn with both his cause and his duty. But he had been so certain. All that they had to do was give the surly Rebs a good lickin', and they'd come marching home.

Instead she'd met his body in the railway station, a lonely figure clad in black, awaiting a coffin.

She'd been so much younger before that day.

She started, hearing something by the house. She shaded her eyes and looked toward it. There was no one.

Sighing, she moved her fingers over her husband's tombstone. It was then that she heard a soft voice, Daniel's voice, coming to her gently from across the graveyard.

" 'He is dead and gone, lady,
He is dead and gone;
At his head a grass-green turf,
At his heels a stone.' "

Callie stood, dusting off her hands on her skirt, touched by the sad, haunting quality in Daniel's voice.

He seemed so far away, so distant from her. His temper had faded. Just as he had seemed to mourn the life of the boy who had died in the barn, he seemed to mourn her husband's life too.

"I'm sorry, Callie."

But she wasn't sure if he was apologizing for their argument, or if he was saying he was sorry Gregory had died.

He was ready to leave, she saw. His scabbard was buckled over his hips, and his fine cavalry sword with its menacing edge was situated in that scabbard. He was still in her father's breeches and cotton shirt, but he was clad in his high black boots once again, and curiously, he looked every inch the soldier. His ebony dark hair fell low on his brow, but his eyes were unobscured, and they were filled with a breath-stealing tenderness as they fell upon her.

"Shakespeare," she murmured softly.

"*Hamlet*," he agreed.

"Ophelia's words," she said.

"Yes."

She tried to smile. "You read fairly well, for a Rebel."

His smile deepened. "Yes."

She stared at him, over Gregory's grave, as the breeze rose between them, lifting her hem, playing a bit of havoc with the stray tendrils of her hair. The sky was blue, the day was pleasantly cool, the sun touched down upon them over a cloudless sky.

The scent of death was gone. There seemed to be just a hint of wildflowers on the air.

It was a beautiful day. Such a beautiful day to say good-bye.

She wanted to say his name, but no sound would come. A ragged little sound escaped her, and he stepped across Gregory's grave and took her into his arms.

His kiss was long and deep. It was filled with tenderness and with anguish, and it seemed that it lasted forever. When he raised his lips from hers, it seemed that it had lasted not at all.

He stared into her eyes as endless seconds ticked by. He was waiting for her to speak, but words would not come.

Maybe there were no words that could be said. He had to go. They both knew it.

Maybe he would return.

And maybe he would not.

He touched her cheek with his knuckles.

"Once I mocked a man for words that I heard him whisper to you. No more. For Callie, I, too, will love you until my dying day!" he told her quietly.

She tried to blink away the sheen of moisture in her eyes. Despite his words, he was building a wall between them, holding himself from her.

"And still I remain your enemy!" she cried softly.

"And I, yours," he reminded her.

"It isn't dark yet," she said stiffly.

"No, it isn't dark. Damn you, Callie, I can't wait for the dark. Lord in heaven, I'm trying hard for just a bit of nobility here. . . ." He pulled her close against his heart. She stiffened. No, she could not beg him to stay, she had to let him go! She could not plead, or seduce, for he was right, they had to part. God! Give her strength, give her pride!

"Ah, Callie!" he murmured.

He released her, then turned around and began to walk.

He skirted around the house, and she stared after him, unable to believe that he had really left so easily. Yes, he had to go. But not yet, oh not yet! They had to be together, they had to have their last moment.

She had to tell him.

Damn strength, and damn pride.

She had to tell him that she loved him.

"Daniel!"

She cried out his name and started to race after him. He was already around the house, starting out across the field, she thought.

"Daniel!"

She raced around the back porch and had nearly turned around the back corner of the house when suddenly fingers wound tightly around her arm, jerking her back.

She spun around astounded, gasping.

Her eyes widened with horror and alarm and she opened her mouth to call out a warning.

She came flying forward, jerked hard against her assailant. She choked and gasped, trying anew to scream, but she was swirled around and a hand clamped down hard on her mouth.

Her cry became a silent scream of anguish.

A whisper, furious, harsh, touched her ear.

"So you've been harboring the enemy right to your bosom, Callie Michaelson. And right over Gregory's grave! Traitor, witch!"

He paused, so furious that words failed him. "Whore! Well, you're going to pay for it, lady. Because you're going to get your lover back here for me, Callie, and you're going to render him vulnerable and harmless, or else you're going to watch him die!"

Ten

"*E*ric!"

Callie tried to fight his hold upon her. He held her tight, his fingers trembling with emotion. He didn't intend to let her go. She looked around wildly, trying to understand how he had managed to arrive at the house, with neither her nor Daniel aware of his presence.

She realized that he had probably come upon them very easily. He had probably ridden near and heard the argument ensuing in the house. Daniel was usually so wary. But he had not been so careful after Rudy Weiss had appeared and after he had read about Lincoln's emancipating the slaves. Neither had paid heed to anything around them once they had begun to argue. They had allowed Eric the perfect opportunity to approach the house.

And he wasn't alone, she saw quickly. Three of his men were flattened against the wall of the house.

Eric and his men had only had to dismount and leave their horses down the slope. Then all they'd had to do was slip around the house while she was out and Daniel was upstairs.

Why hadn't they attacked him already, she wondered? Chills sped over her spine. Why hadn't they just drawn their swords or attempted to shoot him down?

She opened her mouth to scream out a warning again, but was jerked back hard against Eric.

"Don't do it, Callie. I don't want to have to try to shoot him down."

"Why not?" she demanded, fighting his hold.

"Because I want him alive."

"So why haven't you taken him?"

Eric hesitated. She heard the grinding of his teeth. "Because he's carrying that sword of his."

"There are four of you."

Eric's lashes fell over his eyes, and when his gaze fell upon her fully again, it was bitter. "I guess maybe you didn't know just who you were entertaining, Callie. That's Daniel Cameron."

"I know his name."

"I'll just bet. I'll bet you know lots more about the man too."

She didn't want to flush or falter, but she felt the warm red coloring suffusing her cheeks despite her best efforts. Eric's fingers tightened over her arms like a vise. She bit down hard on her teeth to keep from crying out with the pain.

Meeting his eyes, she realized that he hated her. As much as he might have once coveted her, he hated her now. It wasn't because Daniel was a Confederate, she thought. It was because she had turned Eric down, and because she hadn't been able to stay away from Daniel.

She lifted her chin. For every second that they spoke, Daniel gained some advantage. But Eric knew that. A ragged fear swept over her. Seconds were ticking by quickly now. What did he want of her?

"Get him back here," Eric commanded, his eyes on hers.

She shook her head. "I can't get him back. He's gone. You saw the way that he left."

"Yes, I saw every poignant moment of it—you wretched little whore," he added softly.

She broke free from him, her fury stronger than his hold. She struck him, swiftly and hard. His face reddened where her fingers had touched it, and she heard the quick intake of breath by one of his men.

His fingers stretched out, entwining into her hair so tightly that she cried out, but softly. Daniel wouldn't have heard it. He would already be moving across the field by now.

Eric's taut grip upon her hair pulled her close to him, and his heated whisper touched her ear. "You're going to go get him right now, Callie. You're going to say something, anything. You will convince him that he can't leave until dark. You can promise him—" He hesitated, then lowered his voice even further to tell her exactly what she could promise. Shocked, Callie tried to whirl upon him and hurt him, but she could not. His grip upon her hair was too tight to allow her any movement.

"Bastard!" she hissed at him. "And to think that you were Gregory's friend—"

"To think that you were his wife!" Eric retorted.

"But it would have been fine if I had chosen you, is that it?"

"Captain," a young soldier interrupted, "Colonel Cameron is nearly across the cornfield yonder."

"Go get him. Bring him back here. To your room."

"Why the hell should I do it?"

"Because if you don't, I will kill him. I'll keep my distance from his sword, and I'll shoot him."

Callie swallowed hard. Eric meant it.

"You're afraid of him!" she murmured, "You're afraid of his sword. Four of you, and you're afraid to do battle with one Confederate—"

"Not a Confederate, ma'am," interrupted the young soldier who had spoken before. He cleared his throat nervously, looking at Eric. "Just that particular Confederate. We really don't want to hurt him, ma'am. We want to capture him. If we can capture him, he won't have to die."

"And he will die, Callie, if you don't go out there and get him," Eric said.

She wrenched free from his hold. To her surprise, he let her go. His eyes continued to condemn her as he watched her.

"What if I do manage to get him, and bring him back?" Callie demanded. "He'll still be wearing his sword."

"I'm sure you won't have any trouble getting that scabbard off him, will you, Callie? I don't think that you'll have any difficulty getting anything off him. How convenient for me."

"I never knew that you could be so despicable, Eric," she said icily.

"And I never knew that you could be such a hussy, but that's rather beside the fact, Callie. This is war."

"There's been enough death! Just let him go!"

"You're trying to kill time, Callie. Don't waste too much of it. If he goes too far, I'll risk any number of my best sharpshooters to take him down. He's not just the enemy, Callie. He's one of the most dangerous." She still couldn't move. They were going to try to kill Daniel, and because he had been so concerned with her, they had slipped past all his defenses.

If she didn't go after Daniel, they would kill him. They wouldn't give him a chance at all, because they did not dare do so. They would shoot him down, there in the field, and his blood would run with the blood of all the countless others who had perished there.

"If he's so dangerous, let him go!" she pleaded.

Eric's eyes narrowed on hers. His mustache quivered with the wry quirk of his mouth. "Bringing him in could give me the promotion of my career, Mrs. Michaelson. Damn you! Do you know how many Yanks he's brought down? Or maybe it just doesn't matter to you anymore. Maybe your father doesn't matter, maybe your husband has ceased to matter!"

"My husband is dead and buried. And nothing will bring him back!"

"Then realize this. You've got three seconds, and if you don't go racing across the field, I'll kill him. I'll have that field so alive with bullets that not even a blade of grass will survive. Do you understand?"

"Let me go," she told Eric coldly.

He released her instantly. "Run, Mrs. Michaelson," Eric hissed to her. "Run quickly, before he is too far gone!"

She backed away, staring at Eric. She would never forgive him for what he was forcing her to do. Because Daniel would never forgive her. She couldn't allow that to matter. As Eric had commanded her, she ran.

He had moved quickly and carefully.

There wasn't much left standing tall in the region—full cornfields had been mown down to stubble by the barrage of canister and bullets that had clashed over the gentle slopes of the region. Still, he had found a patch of still-standing corn in which to move. It would have been much better if he had waited until dark to leave. But if he had stayed, he would have wanted to say good-bye properly.

No, it would have surely been improperly. It would have been in a way that she could not forget him. No matter how long the war raged, no matter what came between them. No matter who else entered her life, she would not be able to love again, because she would feel that imprint, that brand. And then he would come back.

What a fool. He could not guarantee that he would come back. It was a wretched, bloodly, horrible war, and no man could guarantee his life. And when it was over, what would there be to offer her? A devastated landscape? Good God, no, Cameron Hall could never fall, he could not believe that it could fall. And still, when the last shots had been fired, would they be any the less enemies? One side would win, and one side would lose. What would there be for the victor and the vanquished?

He paused in the midst of the field of corn, closing his eyes, fighting the wave of pain that assailed him. He was in love with her. More deeply in love than he had ever imagined being. The feeling was supposed to be beautiful. It was wretched. It made him want to go back, just for an hour. Just long enough to hold her, really hold her, once again.

Memories for all the lonely nights to come.

Why had he left just now? Because the hours of waiting might have become more and more painful?

"Daniel!"

The call was faint at first. It might have come from deep within his heart or mind. But then he heard her calling him again, the sound louder, even frantic.

He frowned and started moving quickly back through the tall corn stalks. Green leaves rippled as he passed through the plants.

"Daniel?"

"Callie?"

He still couldn't see her. He began to run through the corn.

He heard his name called again, closely. He paused.

"Callie, I'm here!"

She stepped into the path, perhaps twenty feet away from him.

She stared at him, her hair wild and flowing down her back, touched by the sun and radiant. Her eyes were wide, dark in the distance, large and imploring, so beautiful and seductive.

Her breasts heaved with the exertion of her movement, and electricity seemed to sizzle in the air all around her, as if lightning had rent the sky.

"Daniel!" His name was a whisper on her tongue, ardent, soft, and still impassioned.

And then she was running through the corn again, trying to reach him.

He spoke her name again. It was a whisper on the air, as soft as the breeze. He ran, too, until he reached her, the stalks of corn waving just above their heads, the green leaves softly wafting, the smell of the earth and autumn as sweet as an aphrodisiac.

He lifted her into his arms and he spun beneath the sun with her. As he came around she sank slowly down against his body.

"Daniel, don't go!" she whispered.

"I have to go."

"Not now."

"Callie, we're only making this worse."

"No! No!"

She rose upon her toes, cupping his neck with her hand, reaching to kiss him. Her lips trembled, her kiss was sweet and ardent and impassioned. He tasted her tension and her hunger and, he thought, even the salt of her tears.

He broke away and stared into her eyes. They were luminescent, silver, wide.

"I have to go," he repeated.

"When it's dark. Daniel, when it's dark. Please, come back with me."

His heart shuddered and slammed against his chest. He had to move on.

But how much better in the darkness. How much better to leave when their own peace had been found, when he could move through these fields without daylight giving him away.

She lowered herself against him, her eyes upon him. He could feel the sure pressure of her breasts against his chest. And so softly as to be almost imperceptible, he felt the pressure of her hips. He closed his eyes. He wanted her one more time. With her hair spread out across the whiteness of the pillows, a deep dark flame to ignite a blaze between them.

"Callie!" He buried his head against her neck. "Dear Lord, but I should go!"

She pulled away and looked at him. By heaven above, he had never seen such a dark and seductive hue in such a beautiful set of eyes.

"Daniel, don't leave me. Yet. Come back now. Give me the hours until darkness falls. Daniel, for the love of God, come back with me!"

Her tone was urgent. Her fingers curled around his.

"Until darkness, Callie," he said. "It's all that I have."

She stared him straight in the eyes, her lashes barely flickering. "It is all that I need," she whispered.

She turned, her fingers still entwined with his. They started walking back toward the house.

They reached the road and the open lawn before Callie's house. Daniel paused, and Callie released his hand, stepping out into the road. She spun about, looking.

The rays of the sun seemed to touch every highlight in her hair. Her skirt spun about her along with the radiant fire waves of her hair. She seemed to move in slow motion, as though she had been captured here for all time. He would hold tight to this vision for an eternity.

She faced him again, reaching out to him.

"It's all right. Come."

He stepped forward. Without question, he stepped forward, trusting her.

They hurried across the lawn and into her house. When they had stepped through the door, he caught hold of her arm and pulled her back into his embrace. He kissed her, holding her close. His fingers ran through her hair. His open lips parted from hers and reclaimed them, his tongue running over that rose circle, his mouth finding the sweetness of hers once again.

She seemed strangely stiff in his arms. He raised his head, looking into her eyes.

"Callie, truly I'm sorry. For all that I said before. For my anger against you. I'm sorry."

She shook her head. "It—it doesn't matter."

"It does. I can taste it in your kiss."

She shook her head, and she suddenly seemed pained. "No . . ."

"Then come back here!" he urged her softly. Again, he kissed her, putting into this embrace all of his passion, his need, the sweetness of all the desire that had raged between them. His fingers moved over her cheek, his arms pulled her close.

Suddenly, it seemed that she was stiff again. Confused, he lifted his head and met her eyes. They were more silver than he had ever seen them, filled with her tears.

"Callie, I shouldn't have come back—"

"No! I needed you back."

"But—"

"Not here, Daniel. Not by the door. And not—not with your sword between us."

She was everything soft and feminine. There was a trembling in her voice, and a trembling in her fingers. She was so very beautiful.

"Callie . . ." he murmured. He kissed her temple, and he kissed the pulse at her throat. His fingers played upon the button at the neckline of her dress. She shied back from him, her cheeks suffused with a soft rose color. Her lashes fell over her eyes, and it was almost as if she feared they had an audience in their intimacy.

He laughed softly. "Callie—"

"Come with me, Daniel," she whispered. She looked up at him, and her eyes were deep pools of entreaty, of sweet silver seduction.

"Anywhere you wish to lead," he told her. His arms came around her, sweeping her up and off the floor into his embrace. She laced her fingers around his neck, those soulful pools of silver and gray staying fixed with his. He could not tear his gaze from hers.

They reached her room. She moistened her lips as he moved through the open door with her.

She pushed against his length, sliding to set her feet upon the floor. She placed her palms against his chest and offered him a quick and breathless kiss, then stepped back.

Puzzled, he reached for her. She smiled, shyly, ruefully.

"The sword, Daniel!" she murmured. She stepped forward, her fingers shaking wildly while she unbuckled his heavy scabbard from about his hips.

The weight of the weapon in the scabbard was more than she had been expecting. He took it from her, holding it while he watched her. She smiled, moistening her lips again. She stepped back, then twirled around and walked toward her bed. The bed with its beautiful white sheets and spread.

She stood by the bed, noting the narrowing of his eyes as he stared at her. She crawled atop it and lay back.

Her hair was spread across that elegant white, a fire, a flame, as endlessly seductive and appealing as he had dared to dream.

Her gaze met his. Radiant, shivering. She touched the rose of her lips with the tip of her tongue.

"Daniel, get rid of the sword, please." She moved her fingers over the spread, invitingly. She leaned up on an elbow. "Please, get rid of the sword. Come to me."

Circe had never sung so seductively upon the sea.

He was in love with this Circe.

He set his sword down on one of the chairs by the cold hearth, and walked to the foot of the bed. He paused, then unhooked the single button at the throat of his shirt and pulled it over his head.

He smiled at her and mouthed the words, "Angel, I love you."

He started to stretch down beside her.

He had scarcely begun to move when he heard the quick flurry of footsteps behind him. Instantly on the alert, he tried to swing around.

A fist caught him in the jaw.

The world seemed a blur, but it was a whir of blue he recognized well. Yankee soldiers! The room was crawling with them.

Far more startling than the pain that stung his jaw was the gut-wrenching agony that streaked through him.

Callie.

She had betrayed him. She had brought them here. She had seduced him like any fool, and God damn her to a million hells, he had fallen.

"Bitch!" he snarled. The blue clad arm with the fist attached was swinging again.

"Hell, no!" Daniel raged.

Then a sound filled the room. Callie, leaping from the bed to lean flat and miserable against the wall, nearly screamed with pure terror. She clasped her hands over her ears, aware that the sound had come from Daniel, and that it was the ear-piercing warning known as a Rebel yell.

Every man in the room blanched at the sound of it, just as surely as she did herself.

Shirtless, his naked shoulders and chest shimmering sleekly with his every movement, Daniel almost seemed to dance with an agile ease about the room. Eric's three subordinates fell atop Daniel one by one, and one by one, he fought them off with his fists. A slug to one man's jaw, a kick to the next man's groin. Then his fists flew again, and the sickening sound of those fists against human flesh filled the room.

"Rebel, be damned!" Callie heard Eric growl, stepping into the fray.

She heard a thud again, and Eric came rolling out of the huddle of the fight, clenching his bleeding jaw with his hand.

He drew his pistol.

"No!" Callie shrieked.

But no one was listening to her. Daniel's opponents at last managed a well-coordinated attack, one of them slamming a pistol on the back of his head just as he turned to face the two others. Gritting his teeth and holding the back of his head, he fell to his knees.

Before he could rise, Eric was behind him, the shining rod of his revolver set against the base of Daniel's skull.

Everyone in the room heard the cock of the trigger.

"Don't make a move, Reb," Eric warned. "Not a move."

Callie waited, praying.

She saw Daniel's eyes close, saw his teeth grate down harder. He opened his eyes again.

They were a different blue from any color she had seen before. Suddenly they fixed upon her.

They were the cold blue of hatred.

He was still as one of Eric's men carefully grasped his wrists and drew them back. Callie winced, trying not to jump as she heard the snap of steel.

They had set slave shackles around his wrists.

Eric caught hold of his shoulder, pulling Daniel to his feet. He was a tall man. Callie hadn't realized just how tall until she saw him rising an inch or so over Eric and his Federals.

Eric spoke to him, gloating. "How do you like the feel of them shackles, boy? It's just what you folks do to your people down there. Kind of puts a crimp on things, eh, boy?"

Daniel suddenly spun, and his feet moved in a flash. Shackled in steel, he was still a dangerous man.

His feet hit Eric dead in his middle. Stumbling backward and turning white, Eric clutched his wounded body and swore.

Freed for the moment, Daniel took the opportunity to stalk Callie. His long strides brought him quickly across the room until he was standing just an inch from her. She could see the sheen of sweat on his chest, feel the exertion of his rapid breathing. Feel the cold ice-fire of his eyes upon her.

She felt the blood drain from her face. A trembling like a palsy swept through her.

"Daniel—" she tried to whisper.

"This steel won't hold me forever, Callie. No chains and no bars can ever do that. And I'll be back. I promise you that. I'll be back for you."

"Shut up, Reb!" Eric called to him suddenly. "She was just a good Yank, turning you in. It was a damned good job, Callie."

She wanted to scream. A pulse ticked violently against Daniel's throat, and she knew that he believed the very worst, that she had planned on turning him in for a long time. It was your fool life I was trying to save! she wanted to scream. But there couldn't be any explanations, not here, not now. Not with Eric and three of his badly battered Union soldiers looking on.

She moistened her lips. She saw the mocking sneer that curled his mouth.

"Daniel, I didn't—" she began at last.

"Poor Yank!" Eric said. "She's a pretty piece, isn't she, southern boy? We have our weapons here in the North too. And she's a deadly one, isn't she, boy?"

He didn't turn. "It's Colonel Cameron, Captain, not boy," he said flatly. He smiled at Callie. A smile so cold that chills began to sweep furiously through her once again.

"I'll be back, Callie. And when I come for you, there won't be anywhere for you to hide. Believe me. I'll be back. It's a promise."

"That's enough!" Eric cried out sharply. "Take him, Corporal Smithers."

Smithers didn't move quickly enough. Daniel turned around, still smiling. They were all still afraid of his booted feet.

Callie flattened herself against the wall because Daniel was turning back to her. She could breathe in the scent of him, feel the slow, sure pounding of his heart.

And feel his eyes once again.

Eric brought the butt of his revolver down hard upon Daniel's head. Without a whimper, without a sigh, her passionate Rebel fell at last, black lashes closing over the blue hatred in his eyes.

PART 2

Captive Hearts

Eleven

*I*t was still daylight when the wagon carrying Daniel to Old Capital Prison in Washington, D.C., stopped before the building.

Daniel was able to see it clearly. There were no shadows of darkness to take away any of the squalor of the sight before him.

Dark, dank, decaying walls greeted him. A miasma hung over the place. High plank walls surrounded it, and iron bars covered the windows.

It was a building he knew well enough, as any frequent visitor to the capital would have. Before the war, Daniel had certainly been in Washington often enough.

He had always loved the city. It had been planned and built with the purpose of being the capital of a country. The vistas down the long mall were exquisite, the government buildings were handsome, and the wide streets and rich boulevards were inviting. In spring the river kept the scent of flowers fresh and clean, and in the fall, no place could be more beautiful.

But even here, a man could find the results of ill treatment and abandonment. At no place could that be seen more clearly than at Old Capitol Prison.

When the Capitol had been destroyed during the War of 1812, a brick building had been constructed for the temporary use of the government on 1st Street. Then the Congress had moved back to their permanent quarters, and the building, simply called "Old Capitol" the last time that Daniel had seen it, had begun to deteriorate.

It had been deteriorating ever since, Daniel thought wearily.

Someone prodded him in the back. "We're here, Colonel. Your new home in the North," his Yankee driver said with a snigger. "Get on up and out of there, now."

It wasn't easy for Daniel to do. His feet and wrists were still shackled. In fact, he'd lain on his side in the jouncing wagon so long that all of his body felt bruised and knotted and stiff, and trying to arise at all was difficult.

It had seemed like an endless journey from the Yankee encampment where he had first awakened to find himself so trussed. He'd been in pain from the first, aware that he'd been kicked and beaten by his captors even after he'd lost consciousness. His ribs were sore, his old wound was oozing a trickle of blood.

He hadn't been bothered by much at the encampment. He'd seen enough soldiers, though, all coming around to peek in the tent where he'd been taken as if he were some kind of circus animal. They all wanted to see Danny Cameron, the horse soldier with the rapier sword, brought down at last. Some of them jeered. Some of them asked how it felt to be trussed up like a pig for gutting. Some of them just stared gravely. One soldier said that it just wasn't any way to treat a man, any man.

A Union major had agreed, and before Daniel knew it, the onlookers were driven away, and he had been brought a chair to sit on and a blanket. None of it really mattered to him at the time because he was still living in a haze of pain. But the major seemed a fine enough fellow, determined that Daniel be given good, clean water and a decent meal. His own troops were eating well enough, it seemed.

Not even the major seemed to feel safe enough around him to see that his shackles were removed. It wasn't until Daniel told the young private assigned to look after him that he couldn't possibly eat the meal—or take care of any other human necessities—with his hands shackled that they were undone. The nervous private faced him with a rifle aimed at him all the while he ate and attended to other necessities. Then the irons were put back on him.

The major also demanded that his prisoner be treated with respect. They'd all been brothers once, and God willing, they'd all be brothers again. It seemed that this major knew Jesse, and was appalled that any West Point graduate should be treated so shabbily.

"Beauty himself chose to ride for his homeland," the major said wearily. "I'd not even have you cuffed so, sir, were I certain that you could not escape."

"Sir, it would be my duty to Beauty himself to escape at any possible opening," Daniel told him honestly.

He wondered about his damned honesty because the stinking irons remained. Night had come and he'd been left to sleep in his shackles, but had spent most of the night awake, cramped, bruised, and in pain.

He hadn't minded the pain, he'd rather welcomed it. It had kept him from thinking.

Thinking was dangerous. Every time he dared to think, a blind red fury settled over him.

He'd been such a fool. Half the Yank army hadn't been able to drag him down, but that little flame-haired witch with the silver eyes had only to crook her finger to do so.

Lying in agony, he'd seen it all, over and over again, every word that passed between them, his wanting to walk away, her beckoning him back.

The fury that raged in him was so strong, he wasn't sure he cared who actually won the war anymore.

Just as long as he could go back. For her.

He wasn't sure what he wanted to do to her. He just wanted it to last long. And to be unendurably agonizing. He felt his fingers jerk, and he thought that he wanted to wind them around her neck.

Too smooth. Too easy.

What then?

An ancient English torture maybe. Like the rack.

Not vicious enough . . .

Morning had come. His temper hadn't eased a wit.

Another day passed with the major being a decent enough fellow. Daniel hadn't known the man before the war, but apparently his reputation in the West before the start of the war had circulated through the night.

Maybe some of the Union soldiers hated him more for having resigned when Virginia seceded.

But for the most part, he thought that the men understood. Little things began to appear for him. A really beautiful red apple. A small flask of Irish whiskey.

That night, he played cards with the major, and it was then that he learned he'd be moved to Old Capitol in the morning.

"I'll see to it that your brother knows where you are, safe and alive and out of action," the major assured him.

Daniel winced. Jesse would start moving heaven and earth, and get in bad with his own side, to get Daniel out. Especially if he was worried about the wound. Jesse never stopped being a doctor.

"Thank you just the same, Major. Jesse's got his own war to fight, and he's busy somewhere patching up men. I don't want him informed."

"He'll find out soon enough."

"I reckon. But give it till then. I'm a big boy, and I chose my own side." He was quiet for a moment. "And I made my own fool mistakes," he added. He smiled to the major, just to assure him there were no hard feelings.

"I'd like to let you go, Colonel Cameron. But I can't. You're just too damned important. Maybe they'll exchange you. They're still trying to swap a private for a private, a sergeant for a sergeant—a colonel for a colonel. Sixty privates for a general. But I hear that our side is starting to say we've got to quit exchanging. Every time we put one of you Rebs back in the field, you just start killing Yanks all over again."

"It is a war," Daniel said politely.

"To our great sorrow, Colonel, yes. To our great sorrow." He sighed, and rubbed his whiskered chin. "I can't even make you more comfortable. If your wrists are free, I've got to keep the shackles on your ankles. They tell me you fight like a son of a gun. Where did you learn to fight like that?"

Daniel grinned. "Why, Major, I learned how to fight back home."

"Your pa bring in a professional to teach you?"

"No, sir. Jesse was bigger, and we'd disagree now and then, so I had to get tougher."

The major laughed. He shared the Irish whiskey with Daniel.

But the major wasn't there when the soldiers came to load Daniel into the wagon. These soldiers weren't interested in respecting their enemy in any way, shape, or form.

The driver who had prodded him shouted out an order.

"Move it, Colonel!"

Hands grasped hard upon his shoulders, wrenching him up to his feet. He was shoved hard from the open back of the wagon.

There was no way to gain his balance, not with both arms and legs shackled as they were.

He sprawled down into the dirt road, striking hard. Gritting his teeth, he stumbled up to his feet.

There was a handsomely uniformed Union lieutenant colonel hurrying toward him. The uniform didn't bear a single speck of dust, and the officer didn't look as if he was many months past his twenty-first birthday.

"That will be enough, soldier!" he said. The soldier snickered beneath his breath, but saluted. "Yes sir, whatever you say, sir!"

"Colonel Daniel Cameron, you are now a prisoner of war, here at Old Capitol. Be a model prisoner, sir, and we will strive to see that your stay isn't too painful."

"He means he'll try to keep you alive, Colonel!" someone shouted from one of the barred windows.

"Yeah, yeah, yeah," the soldier who had brought him said. He caught Daniel's shoulder. "Let's move him in, sir. He's a dangerous one."

It was obvious that a number of the guards considered him to be a "dangerous one." There was little chance of his harming any of them, what with the numbers they had on their side. Guards encircled the walled structure, and guards seemed to be in abundance within it. But though his hands were freed, they shoved him roughly into the large room with its heavy doors, trying to keep a distance from him.

And there he met a ragged band of Confederates.

They stood, gaunt and disheveled, some with bone-thin faces, some with fraying blankets around their shoulders. They wore all manner of uniform, a few with the colorful remnants of Louisiana Zouave baggy trousers, some in plain old washed-out breeches; some in proper militia uniform, and some in the butternut and gray of the regular army.

They watched as he was thrust in among them. Thrust so hard that he stumbled again, and fell to his knees. Squaring his shoulders, he rose painfully. His bare feet were bruised and bleeding. He'd been given a shirt, but it was torn and tattered now too. His hair was matted, his face was covered with the dust from the street where he had fallen before.

He might have been dressed in scarlet robes.

All around him, cheers rose up. Then a Rebel yell sounded, nearly shattering the prison walls.

"Colonel Cameron, sir!" his name rang out; he was saluted again and again, one by one.

The Yankee guard at the door swore softly. "I'm getting the hell out of this one!" he muttered.

The heavy door clanked shut. Daniel looked around him, greeting his countrymen as they greeted him.

"Your feet look bad, sir, cut up and swollen," said one young private with snow-blond hair and cornflower-blue eyes. He came up, setting down a pair of boots. "I've got kinfolk in D.C., and I got an extra pair of shoes, sir. I'd be beholden if'n you'd wear these."

"Thank you, son," Daniel said.

Another soldier stood before him. "My wife just knitted me a pair of socks, and the pair she sent before ain't hardly got a hole in them, sir."

Daniel smiled. Someone else brought him a blanket, and then someone brought him a thin little cigarillo, the likes of which he hadn't tasted in a long time. He thanked them all. He told them what he knew about the battle of Sharpsburg, and he laughed when they told him tales about his own exploits in the saddle.

"Well, are they true, sir?"

"It's like anything, Billy Boudain," he told the young man who had given him the boots. "Some is true, and some is the storyteller's relish for the story." He winced. Sitting against the cold stone wall had aggravated a crick in his neck.

"Colonel, there's a nice thick thatch of hay over yonder for you. Wish we could do more. Some of us have money and kinfolk near, and we can bribe a tiny bit of luxury, but not much."

Daniel stood, stretching. He inhaled on the cigarillo, enjoying the fine taste of the tobacco. He grinned at the young soldier again, unaware that the bitter curl of his mouth was extremely chilling.

"Don't worry about it, soldier. Don't worry on it a bit. I don't intend to stay long. Not long at all." He crushed out the cigarillo. "I've got business elsewhere," he said softly.

The ice-blue fury in his eyes belied the very softness of his words.

"You—you sound determined, sir," Billy said.

"Oh, I am. Nothing will stop me from getting out of here." He realized that his words had brought about a hush in the room, that the men were all staring at him, with maybe just a little bit of fear themselves.

"I thank you all," he said more softly, and he offered them a rueful grin. "I thank you very much. I am weary, though. Good night, men."

The pile of hay wasn't much. It didn't matter. He was surrounded by his own again.

He fell into it, and curiously enough, slept like a babe.

Fall was coming to the Maryland countryside. The leaves on the trees were just beginning to show the beauty of wild red and yellow and flaming orange.

Dusks were cool, with a cleansing breeze.

Callie sat out on her porch after a long day, anxious to feel that breeze. No matter how fresh or gentle it came to be, no matter how cooling, or how cleansing, it never seemed to blow away the feelings that had settled over her. She tried to tell herself again and again that she had done the only thing possible. It didn't help her. Daniel's voice still came to her in the night. His promise, spoken so bitterly, so hatefully.

"I'll be back. . . ."

But he would not be for a long while. They had taken him over to Old Capitol Prison in Washington, and he was a prisoner that the guards would watch well and warily. Eric had assured her so.

She shivered, remembering the end of the night once Daniel had been knocked out.

They had shackled his ankles just as they had shackled his hands. One of the officers had stolen his boots.

Eric's men had carried him off, and Eric had stayed behind.

She would never forget that night. The anguish of what had happened to Daniel and what had come after.

Eric had cornered her against the wall. She remembered him caging her in, his palms flat on the wall on either side of her face. She remembered the bitterness in his voice when he told her that all that he wanted was what she so blithely gave the enemy.

She remembered the awful choking horror of wondering if he would go through with the violence that he threatened.

She never knew what gave her strength. She smiled sweetly at him and slipped his revolver from his pocket as he moved in closer. When he would have pressed his lips to hers, she aimed the revolver right at his gut.

She warned him that she knew how to pull a trigger, and that she would do it without blinking.

He believed her. He'd stepped back so quickly it was comical. He'd scowled and sworn. Callie had told him to get out of the house or she'd be out riding hard to find his superior officer to let him know just what his cavalry captains were doing in the field.

Eric had left, swearing his own form of vengeance against her.

She had then sunk down in her corner against the wall, and cried. Eventually, she'd fallen asleep.

In the morning she'd realized that she had to go on. Daniel had not been in her life so very long.

But the time before he had stepped into it no longer seemed to matter.

The day after Daniel's capture, a different soldier had come by. Callie had kept Eric's fine revolver. She had six shots to use if she needed them.

But the man hadn't come by to threaten her. She was amazed to discover he had come to replenish some of the livestock that had been taken from her. There were now two pigs in back, two horses, two cows, the goat, and scores of chickens. The animals gave her plenty to do, as did the effort to restore her garden, although with winter coming on there was not much she could do.

There was definitely going to be a shortage of corn in the area.

She was glad of work, any work, for it helped to keep her mind off Daniel, and both the anguish and the splendor that had so briefly been hers.

She tried to tell herself that it was all for the best. Daniel was too daring, too talented, too able. If he fought on, he was sure to get himself killed. He was an expert with his sword, he was probably an amazing sharpshooter, and he could fight bare-handed with a vengeance. But no man alive was immune to bullets, and with his determination to lead his men straight into every fray, it seemed only a matter of time.

He was safe in prison.

But as she sat on the porch that dusk, watching the swing wave gently in the breeze, she knew that he would never see it that way. He dreaded prisons. Callie couldn't believe that Old Capitol Prison could be as bad as they said. It was right in Washington, D.C. There were any number of good citizens in Washington who despised the war, and who would demand fair treatment for the prisoners. After all, weren't the northerners fighting this war to prove that they were all one Union?

It didn't matter. Just remembering the look in Daniel's eyes made her shiver.

She closed her eyes, determined to forget. She had to get over everything that had happened, and get on with her life.

She still had a little unfinished business, she reminded herself sadly, and she stood, and walked back into the house. On one of the big plush parlor chairs lay the bedroll belonging to the young Union soldier who had crawled into her barn to die. She had to get those belongings back to his family.

She turned the bedroll, trying to compose in her mind a message to send to his family. "Your son died instantly, painlessly. He died a hero's death. . . ."

The truth. He died in terror and agony, lingering away in my barn.

No, she didn't have to write the truth. No one knew the truth about the soldier's death except for herself.

And Daniel.

Swearing softly, she started to untie the bedroll. If there were tobacco or pipes or playing cards within it, she would get rid of them. She was convinced that if a boy was big enough to go into battle and die, no one should care if he wanted a bit of tobacco or had taken to a fun game of cards on a quiet night. But mothers still looked for honor in their sons, and boys, she knew, still longed to please their mothers. So if this boy's mother had to receive the sad news of her son's death, Callie was going to see to it that she was spared all possible extra pain.

The minute she undid the bedroll the first thing to flutter out was the boy's letter. It had obviously been signed in quite a rush, and he had never had a chance to find an envelope for it, or a way to post it back home. He'd probably just finished up before he heard the bugle's blare calling him to battle.

Callie bit her lip and absently set her free hand against the small of her back. She stretched and wandered back out to the porch, sinking down on the steps to feel the night breeze while she read the letter.

Dear Mother,

Just a letter to tell you that I am well, and feeling fine. I wanted to write, because we're ready to go into battle. Some soldiers found an important order given out by the Confederate General Lee, and there's all kinds of excitement going on. Seems like we'll meet up with the Rebel forces real soon, and real big.

Well, Mother, I've just got to say that it won't be easy. Seems like it was just a week or so ago that we were down in Virginia—so close we could see Richmond—and just across the river from some of those Rebs. Ritchie Tyree —you know Ritchie, Mother, he grew up down the road by the dairy farm— he had some kinfolk over on the other side, cousins he was right close to, and so I promised him that I'd sneak across the river with him. I know that it wasn't right to go against my orders, but no one really ordered me not to go across the river. If a man doesn't owe his friends, then we can't have much of a country to fight for, right? Anyhow, that's the way I saw it, and I did weigh the decision real careful, just like you and Pa taught me to do. Ritchie and I slipped across the river that night, and we met his cousins Zachary, Tybalt, and Joseph. We sat around in the dark, gnawing on jerky we'd brought over, us having much more in the way of vittles than the Rebs. We talked about old times, and who had died, and who had been married, and it was a right nice night. We came back across the river, and we slipped into our tents, and no one was the wiser, so I was glad of the chance to embrace my enemy.

The only thing is, I started wondering in the morning just why those boys were my enemies. We knew a lot of the same folks, we spoke the same language, and Ritchie and Tybalt even look close enough alike to be near twins. We laughed just alike. And Mother, I tell you, we pray to the same God every night, we pray mighty hard, both of us praying to live, and both of us praying to win.

Well, Mother, I don't mean to burden you with my thoughts. I may question this war, but I swore my oath to my country, and I know my duty, and I will serve.

How is Sarah? Give my love to her. I write to her often, but I've so little time now, and I must write these words to you. God willing, I will come home, and Sarah will be waiting. And we'll wed, Mother, and though you've already lost Pa and Billy, I'll be the teacher in the old schoolhouse just like I've always wanted with Sarah there at my side and all manner of little ones belonging to me and Sarah to people up your life again.

It's going to be a big one, though. A mighty big battle. If God wills that I not return, Mother, remember me to Sarah. Tell her that I loved her, that she was often in my dreams. Know that I was ever your obedient son, and that I'd never bring dishonor upon you. If God so wills that I fade away, hold me with you in your heart.

There goes the bugle, Mother, calling me to war. God keep you, for you are ever the greatest lady. Your loving son . . .

                                                                Benjamin

The letter fluttered to Callie's lap. She hadn't realized that she was crying until the first of her tears splattered down on the paper.

Quickly, almost frantically, she blotted the tear with her skirt.

The boy's mother was going to receive this letter.

She started suddenly, realizing that she had become so involved with the letter that when hoofbeats had sounded, and were now coming closer, she had paid them little heed.

She leapt up, wondering if she should hurry inside for the revolver.

But the approaching rider had already arrived at the front of her lawn.

Her heart began to beat hard as she slipped back into the shadows of the porch. The rider hadn't seen her, and he certainly hadn't come furtively. He dismounted from his horse and walked across the lawn to the well. Callie couldn't see his face. His uniform was a regulation blue. His hat was plumed, cockaded at the brim with a large feather. She watched him for some moments, trying to read his insignias. He looked like cavalry, but some of the insignias on his shoulders were different from any she had seen before.

She must have made a move that made him aware of her presence, for he turned quickly, staring at the porch. She was in the light from the house; he was in the shadow. She still couldn't see his face.

"Good evening!" he called out. He had a low, cultured voice, but it still carried a touch of a drawl. "Please excuse me. I've just stopped for water, if I may. And I'd like to ask you a few questions, if you don't mind. I've not come to hurt anyone." He paused. Callie knew he had to be reflecting his position. Maryland was a border state in every sense of the word. There were "Maryland" troops fighting for the North and for the South. Even a lone Union soldier took a chance riding here.

"May I?"

He had lifted the dipper from the bucket of water that swung into the well.

Callie stepped out from behind the post, still holding on to it for moral support.

"Yes, of course. Any man is welcome to water," she said.

"Thank you kindly."

He sank the dipper into the water, and then drank from it deeply. Callie exhaled, realizing that she had grown so wary because of Eric, and walked the few steps down to the lawn.

This soldier could be a godsend to her. If he didn't mind waiting just a minute, she could quickly compose her note to the dead boy's mother and send his things on to her. Perhaps the poor lady did not want to learn that her son was dead, maybe she wanted to live on hope, knowing only that her son was missing.

No, there was nothing worse than the wondering, Callie determined. She needed to turn this letter over to this soldier, along with her own words of condolence. That is, if she felt that she could trust him.

He had just finished drinking, and he seemed to know that she had come down the steps.

"I'm looking for a man," he said, his back still facing her. "He disappeared somewhere around here in the recent battle."

The soldier turned around, and Callie stepped back, gasping. For a moment she felt as if she were going to faint.

His face was so familiar in the shadows it might have been Daniel.

His appearance so stunned her that she froze, unable to speak or to move.

He had the same very blue eyes and near-ebony hair. The handsome structure of his face was similar and yet different. This man was just a little bit older. He was perhaps a bit heavier in the shoulders and across the chest. There were a few more lines about his eyes; his face was fuller.

"Ma'am? Are you all right? I assure you, I pose no danger to you. I've recently discovered that my brother didn't return to his troops. If he didn't return to them, well, I know my brother, you see," he said huskily, and Callie thought, yes, he knows Daniel well. Nothing on heaven or earth would have kept Daniel from returning, unless he had been killed—or captured.

She still couldn't quite speak, and so her visitor continued. "I guess I should explain. This man isn't a Union soldier, but a Rebel. No one saw him killed, and he was rather well known, so I'm hoping that he is alive. He might have been injured. He shouldn't have been fighting to begin with. It's a strange story, ma'am, but his commander is an old friend of mine, and word just got through a number of the lines that he hasn't been seen or heard from since the battle. Have you seen anyone, or heard tell of any missing soldier, trying to move toward the South, perhaps?"

"I . . ." she paused, moistening her lips. She fought desperately for composure, determined to remain calm.

He strode across the yard to her quickly, hope filling his eyes. He gripped her shoulders, and when he touched her, she at long last felt a warmth dispel the chill that had assailed her.

"Have you seen him? Please, help me! Tell me anything that you can, I am so desperate!"

Her heart beating wildly, she stepped back. She blinked, then she found her composure.

"You met my brother!" he said urgently.

She smiled. "Oh, yes, we met," she said with irony. She extended her hand. "You must be Jesse."

"God, yes, I'm Jesse! And Daniel—"

"Is alive," she said.

"Thank God! Thank God in heaven! Where is he now? Has he headed back? Jesu, our lines are thick around here!"

She shook her head. "He isn't headed south."

"Then?"

"Daniel is safer than he has been in a long, long time," she said softly.

"I beg your pardon?"

"He fell here," she said, keeping the cloak of composure about her the best she could. "During the battle, he fell here, not far from where you're standing. He was deathly ill one night, but he roused himself quickly enough." She hesitated, forcing herself to breathe regularly, even as she stared into these blue eyes that were so very familiar. "Perhaps you should come in. I have coffee."

He watched her for a moment, obviously aware that there was quite a story behind her words.

"Yes, thank you, I'd like very much to come in. But if you're certain that Daniel isn't headed for home, where is he now, Miss . . ."

"Mrs. Michaelson, Callie Michaelson. Daniel is in Old Capitol Prison in Washington."

"What?"

"He's where he's really safe."

Jesse Cameron tilted his head. "Maybe, and then maybe not. You don't know my brother all that well, ma'am."

Oh, sir, you don't know the half of it! Callie almost cried. But his words made her uneasy. "What do you mean by that, sir?"

"I'll be happy to explain. And then, if you don't mind, I'd like to hear whatever else you can tell me about my brother. Coffee sounds right fine, Mrs. Michaelson."

Callie turned around quickly, heading up the steps. Jesse Cameron was right behind her.

Dear God, just exactly what was she going to tell him?

And what did he mean by saying that maybe Daniel was safe, and then maybe he wasn't?

"Do come in, sir," she told Jesse. He was right behind her by the door and she knew that she needed to go on with her story.

She lowered her lashes, and then she raised them. "Come into the kitchen, sir. I'll put the coffee on." Damn these Camerons, she thought. Those blue eyes were so intently on hers.

Twelve

*M*rs. Callie Michaelson was an incredible and fascinating woman, Jesse determined, sitting down to a cup of coffee at her kitchen table.

The coffee was the best he'd had in some time, even though he was lucky enough these days to spend time now and then where the shortages were few.

There was cream for it, a taste he'd gotten away from on the battlefield, but which, here in this warm and welcoming place, tasted delicious.

Watching his hostess, he wanted to go home.

She was beautiful. She had a soft, cool reserve about her that, joined with her gracefulness, added mystery to that beauty. The kitchen table reminded him of home; she reminded him of Kiernan, his wife, and suddenly the desire to be back where he really belonged was so strong he could scarcely stand it.

But he couldn't go home.

He would take this time to search for his brother. Sometimes, there were ways around the war. Beauty Stuart had gotten word through to him that Daniel hadn't returned after Sharpsburg.

His heart heavy with dread, he had come to the battlefield. He had asked every Union man left he could find about the burial places of the fallen Rebs, but he'd gotten no word on Daniel at all until he had met this woman.

A fair estimate of the body count was in. More blood had been spilled in one day at Sharpsburg than at any other battle. Looking for Daniel could have been a never-ending task.

Friends had tried to dissuade him from the search, shaking their heads sadly.

But he had believed that Daniel was alive, that he would know, somehow, if his brother had died.

So he had strayed by this little farmhouse, and this beautiful woman was calmly telling him about his brother.

When the coffee was poured, she sat, her hands folded in her lap, her lashes slightly downcast over her eyes.

"The best that I could see, sir, there was quite a skirmish going on here. Cavalry first, then infantry. At first, I believe the Rebels held the area, but then they were frightfully outnumbered and your brother's men were cut off. There was a lull in the fighting when I found him first, but an officer came by and told me Daniel was dead, and that the firing was about to start again."

She paused, her lashes rising. Her eyes were large, a fascinating, provocative gray. She was dressed rather primly, in blue cotton edged with white lace that buttoned to her throat. She wore a petticoat, but no hoop, and she should have appeared very much the demure young farm woman.

Her coloring, her radiance, were extraordinary. Her hair was a glory, a deep, dark red, and free as it was tonight, it cascaded like a river of haunting splendor. Her manners were correct, everything about her was correct, but there was still something deeper about her, something beneath the prim exterior, the soft, cultured voice. Tension radiated from her despite her demure calm. Were he not so in love with his own wife, he would probably be fantasizing about this woman. As it was, he thought wryly, the less he told Kiernan about Mrs. Michaelson, the better.

"Was Daniel seriously injured?" Jesse asked her.

She shook her head. That blaze of hair shimmered over her shoulders. "No, I don't think so. He was knocked unconscious. He must have received a good wallop upon the head. But that was not what made him so ill. He had an old injury, and it must have reopened with his exertion. I have nursed before, but I'm afraid that my experience has not been extensive. I knew that he had a very serious fever, and I worked to keep him as cool as possible. He pulled out of it, and he seemed fine."

Watching her, Jesse nodded. She had cared for Daniel, she had kept him alive. But he couldn't help it. He was curious.

"You did not turn him over to any of the Yankee patrols?" he said.

She shrugged. "There were enough dead men all around me," she said softly.

Jesse sat back in his chair, a wry twist touching his lip. "I've heard my fellow physicians and myself maligned greatly by the Rebs—and sometimes with just cause. But I've met an endless array of very good men in this war too. Yankee surgeons who fight as energetically for any man in gray as they would for those in blue."

"But sir, I did not know what manner of man I might be turning your brother over to," she said. "I knew he had a brother who was a Yankee doctor, but I'd have had no way of finding you. And besides . . ."

Her voice trailed away. Her lashes fell, sweeping her cheeks.

"Yes?"

"Well, I was his prisoner in my own home for a while," she tried to say lightly. "Once I knew how ill he had become, I swore that I'd not turn him in if he'd only release me. I gave my word, you see."

No, he didn't see. Jesse leaned over the table toward her.

"But he's in Old Capitol now?"

He thought that a slight flame made its way into her cheeks. Her gaze suddenly flew up to meet his. "Sir, I don't know if you're aware of it or not, but your brother has a rather deadly reputation among your soldiers. I was put into the uncomfortable position of watching them take him—*or watching them murder him,*" she said. Her eyes dropped again. The edge of a desperate tone entered into her voice. "They wanted him alive. They thought that bringing him in could mean a promotion. I'm sure that they kept him alive."

"Who took him in? Did you know the men?"

"Er . . . well, yes, one of them," she said, waving a hand vaguely. "A Captain Eric Dabney. Do you know him?"

Jesse frowned. Yes, he had heard of the man. He knew a lot about the cavalry troops fighting in the eastern campaigns because he had been cavalry himself until the Union had begun to build a separate medical corp. Captain Eric Dabney. An interesting man. He was known for being cautious with his troops. It was rather difficult to imagine him tackling Daniel.

Not if he had help. Lots of it.

Callie Michaelson looked at him with worry in her eyes. "You do think that . . . he made it to Old Capitol?"

Jesse nodded, watching her. She was very anxious.

And why not? He had learned in the many "hospitals" where he had worked to patch men up that the war hadn't changed a thing. Men were still men, some with honor, some without. Despite the fact that his wife Kiernan remained a Confederate, he had seen her be as tender to any young Yank as she might be to an injured Reb.

"I was so torn," Callie murmured suddenly, and that liquid gray gaze was on him again, beautiful, shimmering its special silver. "I—I truly had no choice in the matter. But when he was taken, I told myself that it had to be for the best. Because he's safe now. Or, at least he should be." Her voice was growing anxious again. "You're a colonel, too, are you not, Doctor Cameron? That's an impressive rank. If you were to stop by the prison, if you were to make sure that the people there knew he was your brother, maybe they'd be careful not to let anything happen to him. And if he's locked up, he won't be able to lead any more raids. He won't come charging into battle. They were so afraid of his sword. He's just so determined—" She saw the curious light in his gaze and quit speaking, then flushed again. "Am I wrong? Maybe he'll be safer."

"Maybe," Jesse said. He didn't tell her that he knew Daniel well and that Daniel would never stay in prison. He'd be looking at every single possible avenue of escape, and if a means was there, Daniel would find it.

Her eyes lowered again, and Jesse almost grinned. Leave it to Daniel. Daniel would never have fallen on the farm grounds of an old woman or a graybeard. No, Daniel would manage to fall here. With this beautiful, exotic woman. He was good with horses, good with swords, damned good with reconnaissance—and good with women.

He started suddenly, realizing then what the tension in her was all about.

She had done more than care for Daniel through a fever. Things had gone much farther between these two.

He sipped his coffee, anxious that she not see what he had discerned in her eyes. She was something, this Mrs. Callie Michaelson. Elegant, reserved, and so composed and well mannered.

It must have been interesting, Daniel, he thought.

He finished his coffee and set the cup on her table. "Don't worry, Mrs. Michaelson, I do intend to go by and see my brother. And the conditions under which he's being kept." He arched a brow at her. "You are on our side, correct?"

"Which is 'our' side?" she asked him dryly.

He grinned. "Well, I was talking about the North. But my home is in the South, as you must know. It is a bitter feeling, Mrs. Michaelson, not to be able to go home."

"I can well imagine, sir."

He shrugged. "I live for the day when it will be over. When I can ride back and see the house sitting on the river. . . ." He shrugged again. "Sorry, Mrs. Michaelson. I have a wife and a son back there."

"In Virginia?"

"Yes. A very old plantation. The cornerstone was laid in the mid-sixteen hundreds. It's very gracious and very beautiful, and sometimes I just pray that the house survives the war."

"It must be quite a place," Callie murmured.

Jesse watched her smooth her fingers over her skirt.

"Once upon a time it was a very rich estate. Fields lie fallow now—not enough people to work them. Daniel was the one who looked over the estate. He knew how to keep up the house, and he knew what to plant, and what not to plant, and where to sell, and when to hold. It will not be such a rich place once we return." He paused. "If we are ever able to return. I don't know, Callie. Some people say that you can never go home again. What do you think?"

"I think that you can always go home," she said softly. She looked up at him and tried to appear very casual once again. "Your wife and child are there, so far from the world you're living in?"

"Well, my boy is not very old. There is no place else where he could have been born, except for Cameron Hall. And Kiernan . . ." He smiled. "She's quite a Rebel. It's an interesting dilemma, isn't it? Well, I've taken enough of your time, as apparently my brother has also done. I'll leave you, but I promise I'll write once I've seen Daniel."

"Yes, will you please?"

He nodded. "I'd promise to try to come by, but the war being what it is, it's hard to make such promises. I will write, though."

"Thank you." Her eyes were downcast again. She was the perfect lady. She might not realize it, clad as she was in simple cotton, but Callie Michaelson was every inch a lady.

He hoped that Daniel realized it.

He hurried down her path to his horse, Goliath. Coming to the porch, she called him back.

"Doctor Cameron?"

"Yes?"

"There was a boy who died in my barn. A Union boy. He's—he's buried out back, with my family. But I have his effects, a letter for his mother, his bedroll, a few other things. I'd like to write a little note myself. Would you mind waiting just a minute and taking them for me?"

He shook his head. "Not at all."

She swirled around and slipped back into the house. She returned with the soldier's things, handing him a letter. Again, there was that anxious look to her eyes. "Would you read the note I've written, sir, and see if it will help?"

Jesse quickly scanned her words.

Dear Madam,
*   I am heartily sorry to inform you of your son's death, here before my home outside of Sharpsburg. Please know that he knew no suffering, that his death was instant. And know, too, that he died a hero, protecting the men around him even as he fell. We honored him when we buried him, and he rests by my husband's grave, and near a headstone to my father. May God be with you.*
*   Callie Michaelson*

Jesse glanced at her. "Is it the truth?"

She shook her head. "No."

"It's a beautiful note. I'll see that it reaches the proper party."

He took her hand. He was about to shake it, but he squeezed it instead.

"Good-bye, Mrs. Michaelson. Take care of yourself."

"God go with you, sir. God go with you."

He saluted to her and rode away. Turning back, he saw that she was still standing there, tall, beautiful, both proud and ethereal in the moonlight.

Daniel, you son of a gun, he thought. Now if I could just be sure that they could keep you in prison until the war ends!

He doubted it. He wondered if he'd even return soon enough to find Daniel in Old Capitol Prison if he rode straight through tonight.

He quickened his pace.

It was exactly what he was going to do.

Prison was sometimes an interesting place to be, Daniel thought. He leaned back on his straw, lazily chewing on a piece of it.

But his eyes were moving. Not that there was much to see right now. Four of the men were engaged in a game of cards, gambling little bits of tobacco and flasks of whiskey. Some were just sitting back, as he was himself. Old Rufus MacKenzie, the one real graybeard in their midst, was reading his Bible. They were all grouped together, twenty-four men, in the one big room. They had themselves one "necessary" pot built against the wall, and the stench could get pretty bad. Billy Boudain told him that you forgot about the smell after a while.

There were no cots, just beds of straw and whatever else the men could lump together. It wasn't so bad. It was just bleak. As bleak as the decaying color of the walls, as bleak as the cry of the rats that became daring and loud at night.

At least, he thought wryly, he was in the company of friends.

And he watched. Daniel watched everything. Over the past few days, he had watched all that took place. He'd watched the coming and going of food and supplies, and he'd watched the way that the prison worked.

The guards, most of them, were easy to bribe. Captain Harrison Farrow from Tupelo, Mississippi, had a sister married to someone in the Yank Congress, and she saw to it that he received all manner of goodies from home, from baked pies to blankets and extremely fine cigars. Some of the fellows didn't do so well. Private Davie Smith, a small-time farm boy from the Shenandoah Valley, didn't know a soul in the North. But like Daniel, he had been shoeless. Prison had a way of drawing out the best and the worst in men. Captain Farrow couldn't acquire enough from his sister to keep them all in the lap of luxury, but he had been careful to get Private Smith a pair of shoes. And Private Smith was one good-looking Southern lad who liked to flirt with the girls through the window bars as the young ladies passed by.

Every once in a while, Private Davie Smith managed to get one of those giggling young ladies—young ladies whose mamas would have them strung up if they knew their girls were fraternizing with the enemy—to give him an important piece of information.

It was through Private Smith that Daniel learned a lot. The Rebel troops—who had done such a daring and spectacular job of taking the Union garrison—had abandoned Harpers Ferry. Jackson was moving back into the valley again. Lincoln's Emancipation Proclamation was stirring up public sentiment just the way Daniel had assumed it would.

The Yankees were feeling mighty proud of themselves at the moment. They were claiming Sharpsburg a victory.

But so was the South.

Hell, anyone who had been there would just call it a disaster, Daniel thought, but he never said it aloud. He was the ranking officer among the prisoners, and it was up to him to watch out for morale.

As long as he stayed.

There were ways out of here. He had watched the supply wagons come and go, and he had watched the coffins come and go, and reflected on that as a means to escape.

A lot of coffins came and went. Daniel didn't think their warders were exceptionally cruel—except for one or two of the men. When those guards jeered the prisoners, the Rebs jeered them right back, usually asking what able-bodied men were doing watching over tattered and injured Rebs. "Afraid to be out on the battlefield, eh, Yanks?" they taunted back.

The food wasn't so bad. At least, it wasn't any worse than what Daniel was accustomed to eating in the field. A few more years, and he'd be able to convince himself that worms were the best part of meat and that "hardtack" was just that —so hard that the challenge for a man was not in managing to eat enough, but in managing to keep his teeth.

Old Capitol Prison was survivable, he determined, because he meant to survive. Every night, when he felt the cold dankness of the surrounding walls, when he heard his fellow prisoners hacking away with the coughs they acquired here, he thought about Callie.

He thought about her when he felt his straw crawling with all the bugs that were alive and thriving in it, and he thought about her every time one of the coffins came and went.

I will get out, he promised himself. But he meant to be careful. He didn't mean to get caught again, he didn't want to do anything rash or stupid. If he were caught again up here in plain breeches and white cotton shirt, he just might be considered a spy. If he was caught, he would likely soon be a dead man.

As he idly chewed his grass, he watched Billy Boudain and handsome young Davie Smith at the window. Billy was favoring his right arm, Daniel noted with a frown. He couldn't see anything wrong with it, since Billy was wearing a gray coat with red artillery trim.

"Hey, Billy!" he called, sitting up straight on the straw and beckoning to the young man. "Come here."

Billy crawled down from his post at the window, eyeing Daniel apprehensively.

"What is it, Colonel?"

"What's the matter with your arm?"

Billy shook his head. "Just a little piece of shrapnel I picked up at Sharpsburg, Colonel Cameron."

He said it lightly, as if the injury were nothing. "Let me see it," Daniel said.

"Colonel, it ain't nothing at all."

"Billy, that's an order. Take off your jacket and roll up your sleeve. Let me see your shrapnel."

Bland-faced, Billy did so. He tried damned hard not to wince when the jacket fell over his arm as he removed it. He kept trying not to wince as he rolled up the dingy white cotton sleeve of his shirt.

Daniel bit his lip so as not to cry out when he saw the wound. Billy was doing one hell of a job not to make a sound.

The wound was not just a little shrapnel scratch. Daniel was certain that something—some piece of metal or grapeshot—remained in the wound. All around it, the flesh was turning unnatural colors. It was mottled and oozing.

With a sinking heart, Daniel thought that Billy was going to lose his arm. If he wanted to live, he was going to have to lose it soon.

"Hell, boy!" Daniel muttered softly. "We can't just ignore this one!"

"We got to ignore this one, Colonel," Captain Farrow said, stepping up beside Billy.

"Ain't nothin' else we can do," Davie said.

Daniel shook his head. "Something has to be done, Billy," he told the boy bluntly. "You're going to die if you don't let them take off your arm."

Billy blanched, looking to Harrison Farrow for help. Farrow shifted from one foot to another. "Colonel, I imagine that Billy would just as soon die right here as under the knife with one of them Yankee sawbones."

Daniel looked back and forth between the two, then glanced at Davie. Davie looked away.

"They're not all murderers," Daniel said. He paused, looking at faces that politely hid their disbelief. "Billy, isn't your life worth a chance?"

No one answered. Apparently, they didn't think that Billy had any chance.

"Billy—" he began.

"Colonel, there ain't no hope that I could keep the arm?" Billy said.

Daniel hesitated. He wasn't the doctor, Jesse was. But he'd been around Jesse enough, and he'd been around enough maimed limbs. Maybe it could be saved, but he only knew one man who could do it, and that man wasn't around.

"I don't think so," he told Billy frankly.

Billy looked a little white around the gills. "Maybe I oughta just die a whole man then, sir."

"Damn it, Billy! You don't want to die! Hell, you're just a kid—"

"Then this war is being fought by a bunch of kids," Captain Farrow interrupted softly. Daniel stared at him. "Meaning no disrespect, sir."

"None taken," Daniel said. "But Billy, we've got to call the Yanks in on that arm."

"Ain't no way I'm going off with the Yanks—"

"Yes, there is. You'll go, because I'll go with you."

"What if they say no?" Billy demanded.

Daniel shook his head. "They aren't going to say no. Not unless they're planning on putting a gun right to my head."

"What the hell you mean by that, Colonel?"

"As it happens, I have a brother who happens to be a Union sawbones. He'll know soon enough where I am, and he'll have to come here. Every man jack out there knows it. So as far as playing fair with me, they're in a bit of a knot."

"You've got a brother who's a Yankee sawbones?" Billy said incredulously.

Daniel smiled slowly. "Yeah."

"And you're still speaking to him?" Billy said.

"Yeah," Daniel repeated. He lifted his shoulders. "He's my brother."

Billy still looked dubious. "That lieutenant colonel fellow in charge of the place when I came in didn't seem so bad," Daniel said.

"You mean Lieutenant Colonel Wadsworth P. Dodson," Captain Farrow said with a broad grin. "Our boy colonel."

"He does look a little wet behind the ears," Daniel agreed. "But sometimes that's good. Sometimes a young man is a good man. He hasn't had time to find out just how worthless it is to be good sometimes."

Farrow shrugged. The little group looked from one to another. "Billy, I'm going to call for him," Daniel said. "That arm is bad. You can't wait any longer."

At last, Billy nodded, biting down hard on his lower lip.

"But if you call, will they come?" Farrow demanded.

"You just have to be nice to them," Daniel assured him. He stood up and went to the door with its small barred window. "I need some help in here. This is Colonel Daniel Cameron, and I want a meeting with Colonel Dodson."

"Ah, take a nap in there!" one of the guards called out.

"I want Dodson!" Daniel demanded.

The guard came to the door. "I told you—"

Daniel slipped a hand through the bars, catching the man's collar and jerking him hard and flat against the bars. He twisted on the fabric, and the guard's face began to turn a mottled red. "I said, I want Dodson. Please. And if I don't get him, soldier, you'd best hope we never meet outside these walls!"

Daniel smiled complacently as he allowed the guard to break free from his grasp.

"See? You just have to be nice."

The guards eyes appeared between the bars. "I'll bring him along just as soon as I can. You stay quiet in there while you're waiting."

"Quiet as a church mouse," Daniel agreed pleasantly.

It wasn't long before Dodson appeared. Daniel noted with a certain amusement and a certain respect that the young man wasn't afraid of him—or the others. He walked right into their dank prison room, into the midst of his enemies. Dodson had treated them all well enough. He had nothing to fear.

Other men in the prison systems, North and South, might not feel so safe.

Dodson might have gotten his military rank and appointment at his young age because of who he knew, but he was sincere in his determination to be a fair warden.

"What is it that I can do for you, Colonel?"

"One of my men has a severe injury. He needs to see a doctor. I don't doubt Yankee physicians myself, but my young friend is afraid of them. I want to accompany Billy here to see a doc."

One of the guards snickered outside.

Young Dodson peered anxiously at Billy. "We ask every morning in the prison yard if any of the men needs to see a doctor."

"Colonel Dodson, we both know that there have been rumors out—on both sides—that the physicians claim they can kill more of the enemy than the generals in the field. But Billy is going to die if something isn't done about that arm. It's my order that he do something. And I want your guarantee that I can be with him to assure that he's going to be all right."

"This is highly irregular—" began one of the guards in the hallway. But Daniel fixed a cool blue gaze on him, and his voice died away.

Dodson watched Daniel. He looked to his guards. "Irregular or not, I can't see any harm in it."

"Cameron is trying to escape!" a guard said.

Dodson looked at Daniel. "Are you trying to escape, sir?"

Was he trying to escape? Hell, yes, he'd spent days watching for a way to escape. But this wasn't it. Not with Billy as a possible sacrifice.

"Sir, you have my word of honor that I will not escape when I'm in Private Boudain's company."

"A Reb word of honor—" the same guard began.

"The colonel's word is enough for me," Dodson said flatly. He looked to two of the guards, the one Daniel had threatened, and the older man who had been making the bitter comments.

"Palacio, Cheswick, you'll accompany these men to the hospital. Tell Captain Renard that I've given Colonel Cameron permission to sit in and"—he paused, looking at Daniel—"assist in whatever surgery is necessary. Is there anything else, Colonel?"

Daniel shook his head and smiled broadly to Dodson. "No. That about covers it. Thank you, Lieutenant Colonel Dodson."

Dodson nodded and left the room. Daniel slipped his hand beneath Billy's elbow. "Come on. Let's go."

"Hey, Billy, it's going to be all right!" Captain Farrow called out.

"Yeah, it's going to be just fine!" Davie agreed. "The girls will be waiting, Billy!"

"For a one-armed man?" Billy asked.

"Sure!" Davie said with a grin. "They like to be tender and sympathetic."

A sound started in the prison room. Low, and then growing. Billy was being sent off with a Rebel yell.

"Stop that caterwauling!" the guard Dodson had called Cheswick yelled. The sound just increased. Muttering beneath his breath, Cheswick led the way and Palacio followed behind.

They were brought to an anteroom and told to wait. Dr. Renard, a staid man with iron-gray hair and a rigid countenance, appeared shortly.

"Let me see the arm," he told Billy.

Billy looked at Daniel, and Daniel nodded. Billy showed the doctor his arm. Renard didn't even blink. "Yes, it will have to come off. You're going to be a lucky young man if the poison isn't already moving through your system." Renard looked at Daniel. "I hear, Colonel, that you want to clutter up my surgery. You've assisted before, I assume."

"Often enough," Daniel told him. He was certain that Renard knew Jesse.

Renard looked at Billy. "You're not going to suffer as you might have on the battlefield, soldier. I've got morphine, and a syringe to inject it with. Colonel, you're still going to have to hold him tight. Are we understood?"

Daniel nodded. They walked in to Renard's surgery. There was an operating table in the center and Billy was set up on it and given the morphine. His eyes met Daniel's all the while. The look in them was so trusting that Daniel was surprised to feel a chill sweep along his spine. This had to work out.

He smiled encouragingly. Billy's eyes began to close, and Renard began to assemble his instruments.

Renard took out a sponge to soak up the blood. Daniel's eyes narrowed. There were traces of his last patient's blood on that sponge.

"Wait a minute, Doctor Renard," Daniel said.

"What is it?"

"You can't use that sponge on Billy."

"And why not, Colonel? It's the same type sponge I use on every man, Yank or Rebel."

"I'm not accusing you of being prejudiced against a Reb, Doc," Daniel said. "But you can't use that sponge." Renard was still staring at him blankly. Daniel sighed, gritting his teeth. He didn't want to aggravate Renard, but he didn't want Billy dying in the next couple of weeks either.

"You need linen, sir," Daniel said. "Clean linen. And a new square for each man."

"So you think you're a doctor now, eh, Colonel? Well, I tell you, I spent my years in medical school—"

"Sir, I'm not questioning that. I imagine that this is fairly new. My brother told me he'd learned from a Rebel surgeon that the survival rate was much higher when clean linen was used every time."

"Well, Colonel, I'm not a Rebel surgeon!"

"But, Doctor Renard—"

"And I'm operating my way!"

"Then you're not operating on Billy!"

"This boy is going to die if I don't!"

"I'll let him die whole."

Determined, Daniel reached for Billy, ready to lift him over his shoulder.

"Put that man down, Colonel!" Renard demanded.

When Daniel failed to oblige him, Renard suddenly called out. "Guards! Get in here!"

Palacio and Cheswick were quickly inside the operating room. Daniel swiftly laid Billy back down. Cheswick came for Daniel first. Daniel ducked and swung, and flattened the man in a second. Palacio intended to be more careful. He circled around Daniel, looking to Renard. "Better get help!"

But two other guards were already rushing in. "He's trying to escape!" someone shouted.

Daniel barely heard him. Men were coming at him one after the other and he had to move like lightning to keep up with them. He watched his space carefully, managing to get a wall to his back so that he could put all his defense efforts forward. A fist connected with his jaw. He tasted blood, but he fought the sensation of dizziness. He kicked, and he swung, and he managed to avoid further blows while connecting his own fist nicely with the guts and chins of a number of his opponents. He was good, he reckoned, but he'd have been taken by now if the soldiers hadn't been so cautious.

"Get him!" someone called.

"You get him!" came the reply.

Suddenly, in the midst of the melee, a gunshot exploded. The room went still. Daniel, tasting blood on his lip, leaned back against the wall.

Two men were coming into the surgery. The first was Lieutenant Colonel Dodson.

The second man stood in shadow for a minute. Then the light touched his face.

It was Jesse.

Daniel closed his eyes, leaning back.

"What the hell is going on here?" Dodson demanded.

"He was trying to escape!" Cheswick excused himself.

"Renard needed us!" Palacio said.

"Were you trying to escape, Colonel?" Dodson asked.

"No, sir, I wasn't," Daniel said. He crossed his arms over his chest and tried not to grin. "Hello, Jesse."

Jesse, grinning, leaned against the doorway. "Hello, Daniel. In trouble again, I take it. Were you trying to escape?"

It was good to see Jesse. It had been several months since he had seen his brother. He never knew when they parted if he would ever see him again. Blue eyes so like his own met his. Jesse was aging with the war. Tiny lines of gray entwined with his ebony hair at his temples. Those were new. But his brother looked good. Damned good. It was almost worth having been taken prisoner to see him again.

"I gave Dodson my word that I wouldn't try to escape," Daniel said.

Jesse, the ranking officer among the Yanks, shrugged and looked to Dodson. "If he gave you his word, Colonel, then he was not trying to escape."

"Then what was going on?" Dodson asked.

Jesse looked back to Daniel. "What was going on?"

"Doctor Renard wanted to operate with a sponge. I asked him to use clean linen."

Jesse looked at Renard. "Since it seems to mean so much to the Rebs, couldn't you possibly oblige them, sir?"

Jesse was so pleasant. There was just the slightest edge of steel to his voice.

And Renard heard it. He answered just as pleasantly, with just a bit of an audible grate to his teeth.

"Perhaps, Colonel Cameron, you'd like to take on this particular operation yourself, since you are with us."

Jesse glanced to Daniel and cocked his head. "Why, Doctor Renard, thank you. I'd very much like to take this one on."

"Is that all right with you, Colonel?" Dodson asked.

Daniel grinned. "Yes, sir, it is." Billy didn't know just how lucky he was, Daniel thought.

Thank God. Jesse was here.

Thirteen

"*D*avie's been here a long, long time. Why, he was here all the time they kept Mrs. Rose Greenhow here." The last words slushed together, but Billy didn't seem to mind or even notice. "She was quite a lady, Davie said. The Yanks brought her here because of the Allan Pinkerton fellow. He suspected her of spying for the South, and of course, that's exactly what she was doing. She's the one that got the message to our General Beauregard about the Yankee troop movements before the first battle at Manassas. 'Course, Pinkerton's a damned fool, always telling the Yanks that we have twice as many men as we do. But he brought Mrs. Greenhow here, separated her from her daughter, and threatened to kill her, so Davie told me. She was incredible throughout her long ordeal, sir. The men here were gracious and supportive, giving her their full respect. I hear now she's in the South, far away from harm's touch."

Billy rambled on and on.

"Jeff Davis has sent her over to Europe to see what support she could drum up for us over there," Daniel told Billy with a touch of amusement. The operation was long over, but Jesse had warned that there would still be pain, and Billy was hugging a flask of whiskey as if it were a long-lost brother.

"Now, that cute little hussy, Belle Boyd—the one spilling all the information to old Stonewall—she kind of comes and goes here all the time. All the time, so it seems."

"Billy, she ain't no hussy!" Davie called over. He was seated against the wall. They'd all been listening to Billy ramble on for some time. Mostly, they just let him talk. Every once in a while, one of his comments brought a rise out of someone.

"Davie's in love with her!" Billy said, and he started laughing. "Davie's in love with Belle!"

"Colonel, make him stop that, won't you?" Davie demanded. "Order him to quit. Belle Boyd is a beautiful young woman, and a heroine to the Confederacy."

Daniel grinned, leaving Billy's side at last to rise and stretch. "He's got so much drugs and alcohol in him right now that about the only thing I could order him to do and expect a response on would be to smile."

Billy was smiling right then. A crooked smile that had reached his red-rimmed eyes. "She's a heroine all right, Colonel. A heroine with two of the biggest, ripest, juiciest tomato—"

"Colonel, make him stop!" Davie pleaded.

"—like cheeks I've ever seen. She's got the cutest little round face."

"Well, there's a little more respect," Davie said.

"And what a great pair of breasts!" Billy sighed.

"Colonel!"

Daniel laughed. "I don't think he means any disrespect with that one either, Davie. We all salute our sisters of the South, eh, gentlemen?"

A cheer rose up, and as it did so, Daniel had to fight to keep his own smile in place. To the women, yes, dear Lord, to the women. Of the North and South. Rose Greenhow had made fools of many men. She had been more valuable to the Confederacy than many a practiced general. Belle Boyd had proven herself a priceless gem to Stonewall Jackson. There were more.

But the North was not to be undone, Daniel thought bitterly. Maybe Callie Michaelson hadn't turned the tide of any battle, but she had surely done him in. Maybe she would move on to bigger things now.

He almost groaned aloud. It wasn't so much that she had betrayed him. It was that he had been such a damned fool to have fallen for her every step of the way.

But I'll get back! He promised himself.

"Someone's coming, Colonel," Captain Farrow warned. Daniel left Billy's side, walking across the room. He could already hear the key twisting in the lock. The door opened, and Jesse stepped inside.

Every southerner there stood. They stared at him for a minute.

Jesse saluted the group. They saluted in return. "Colonel Cameron and Colonel Cameron. Blue and gray. Don't that just beat all!" Captain Farrow murmured.

"If anybody else has got health complaints," Daniel advised quickly, "now's the time to voice them."

Davie Smith took a step forward. "I ain't got no health complaints, Doctor," he told Jesse. "But you saved Billy's arm, and we're all beholden to you."

"You don't need to be beholden to me," Jesse said. "I'm a doctor, and I took an oath. I drained his arm of all the poison and I pulled out the lead. But if he doesn't take real good care of it now, infection will set back in, and he'll be right back where he started. It's up to you all now. Make him keep dry and clean. I won't be around later to see to him." Jesse turned to his brother. "How's my patient doing?" he asked Daniel.

"Drunk as a skunk."

Jesse grinned and walked over to where Billy was lying on a pallet of straw. Billy smiled broadly for him. "Hello, Doc!"

"Hello, Billy. How are you feeling?"

"Like I could whomp the whole Yank army," Billy admitted, still with his grin in place.

"Well, I think that you'd better lay low on that for a little while," Jesse advised.

"Maybe. Till I sober up, at least."

Jesse unwrapped the bandaging, looked the arm over carefully, and then rewrapped his handiwork with a gentle touch. Billy watched him all the while.

"What are you doing on the wrong side, Doc?" he asked.

Jesse paused just a second, then went on wrapping Billy's arm. "Son, I'm not so sure there is a 'right' side or a 'wrong' side. There's just a point of view here." Finished with his task, he stood and saluted Billy. "Whatever, I hope to see you when this war is over."

"Yes, sir!" Billy saluted in return.

Jesse walked back to Daniel.

"You're leaving," Daniel said.

Jesse nodded. "I have to. You know that."

"Yes, I do."

"Come with me. I've permission to have a few minutes alone with you."

Daniel's brows arched high. "They don't think I'm too dangerous to be out with you?"

"I'm allowed to talk to you in an empty room across the hall." He knocked against the door, then saluted the entire room of men again.

"Colonel Cameron!" They said en masse, saluting him once again.

Daniel was surprised to see the faintest hint of a flush touch his brother's cheeks. "Watch it, fellows," he said gruffly. "They'll be in here accusing me of all manner of things. Gentlemen, take care."

With that, he slipped through the door that a guard had opened for him. It was a new man, Daniel noticed. A big one. He had to be almost as tall as old Abe Lincoln himself. He towered over Jesse and Daniel and they were both a very tall six feet two inches.

And he was built like a gorilla, with a flat, stupid face.

"He can fight like a lion, so they say," Jesse advised Daniel wryly.

"So he's in honor of me, huh?"

"I imagine. I was told to warn you."

Daniel grinned as they slipped into the room across the hall. It was very much like the room where he and the others were kept, but it was very small. He imagined that it was where the female prisoners were kept when they were housed at Old Capitol.

For a moment he and Jesse stood staring at one another. They'd seen each other in surgery, and they'd worked together over Billy's arm. Daniel was long accustomed to helping his brother when they'd both been regular cavalry out in the West. But there had been guards in attendance this time, and after the surgery was finished, Daniel had accompanied Billy back to their room. Jesse had suggested that Billy be isolated in a hospital bed, but Daniel felt certain that Billy would much rather be among his own people. At any rate, they'd never really had a moment to say anything personal, and standing here, they both started to grin. They embraced, holding tightly for a moment, then stepped back.

"Jess, it's good to see you. Damned good to see you. You came in the nick of time. Did the colonel reach you about my whereabouts?" Daniel asked.

Jesse shook his head, watching his brother curiously. "Nope. A certain young lady told me where to find you."

Daniel stiffened just like a poker. His words fell from his lips like cubes of ice. "So you met the little bitch."

"Brother, what a way to refer to the lady! She speaks so highly of you!"

"Yeah, I'll just bet," Daniel said. "Did she mention how I happen to be in here?"

"She more or less mentioned that she felt responsible."

"Oh, yes. She was responsible. I'm just curious. Did she mention just exactly what she did?"

"Why don't you tell me?"

"Let's suffice it to say that she used every last power known to women."

Jesse grinned suddenly. "She seduced you. And you fell for it."

Daniel felt a tightening rip through his muscles. A pulse that he could feel beat against his throat. "If you weren't my brother—"

"But I am your brother, and I told all the powers that be here that I'd be safe in your company. Who knows—maybe I can beat the tar out of you."

"And maybe you can't," Daniel warned.

But Jesse was still laughing. "Jesu, Daniel. She was glad because she thought that you were safe. Hell, it's drafty, the walls are dank, there are rats, but you're probably eating better than half of the Confederacy. I'd be just as glad if they managed to keep you in here for the rest of the war."

"They won't, Jess, you know that," Daniel said softly.

"God in heaven, Daniel, be careful! You push things too far, and they'll hang you, and there won't be a thing in the world that I can do about it!"

"Jesse, don't worry about me. I will be careful. I'm always careful. Damn you, you can't take on the whole weight of the war and the weight of worrying about me too!" Daniel told him.

"I'm not taking on the whole damned war, Daniel."

Daniel smiled ruefully. It was all so hard for him; it had to be harder for Jesse. "Jess, it's me you've got to quit worrying about."

"Do you ever stop worrying?" Jesse demanded.

No, he didn't. Daniel tried again.

"You know that I'm good, and you know that I'm careful."

"You know, she was right, your Mrs. Michaelson. You are better off in prison, Daniel."

"She isn't my Mrs. Michaelson. Is that what she told you?"

"Oh, I think she's yours, all right. And yes, I think that, more or less, she told me something like that. She was very impressive. She's got to be one of the most beautiful women I've ever seen—"

"Then there's your wife," Daniel reminded him politely.

"Yes, of course. Kiernan is extraordinary. But this Callie shines—"

"Just like a beacon," Daniel agreed. "Until you're right betwixt her teeth and she clamps down hard."

"What was that you were betwixt?" Jesse asked.

"Damn it, Jesse, I—"

"Seriously, she is fascinating, Daniel. When I leave here, I am going to try very hard to ride by and tell her that you're safely locked up. And that if we're both lucky, they'll keep you locked up—and alive—until the war is over."

Daniel slowly crossed his arms over his chest. Goddamn, if it wasn't so easy to see her in his mind's eye all the time. If she didn't haunt his dreams. If he didn't see those eyes with their captivating silver luminescence! Hear her voice, the whisper of her pleading.

And if he didn't remember what it was like to make love to her. To stroke the silk and softness of her flesh, drown within the flaming bounty of her hair.

Not again. She'd never seduce him again. Never.

But the dead-set determination could not erase the dreams. He clenched his hands. Yes, he was going back one day. They could finish what they had started. He could strangle her. Hang her up by her toes. Take a horsewhip to her. No, have her drawn and quartered . . .

Touch her . . .

"If you go by, Jess," Daniel said softly, "just remind her that I'm coming back for her. It may take some time. But I'll be back."

Jesse had never seen Daniel so heated with emotion. Not in all the years he had known his brother. His fingers wound into fists that still trembled while he spoke.

"Daniel, you can't hate her for being on the other side!"

"I don't hate her for being on the other side."

"Daniel, think about it. Things could work out. You have to remember how Kiernan hated me. I did everything that I could for the longest time—"

"Well," Daniel interrupted politely, "you could have changed sides."

"Other than changing sides," Jesse said dryly, "and she still hated me. But if you could just realize that *we're* not at war with each other—"

"That's just it, Jesse. We never want to realize it, you or I. But we are at war with each other. And I am—thoroughly and completely—at war with Mrs. Michaelson."

Jesse started to speak, then changed his mind. "Well, I've got to head out of here. Take care of your friend. And if you should get out and get home, give my love to Kiernan and to our sister and to my baby."

"Sure, Jess. And if for some reason you get there before I do, you do the same."

"Right."

"And Jesse."

"Yes?"

"Thank you for Billy. I'm grateful that I've got a Yank doc for a brother."

"I took an oath, and it's just like your word when you give it. I have to save life—any life—when I can."

"I know, Jesse. Hey, God go with you, brother."

"You too, Daniel."

They hesitated, still awkward with these partings. They embraced tightly for a moment and drew away. And then Jesse was gone.

Daniel stared up at the ceiling, fighting the wave of painful emotions that washed over him. But within a matter of seconds, the gorilla guard returned to escort him back to his prison room with the others.

Billy was sleeping. Or Billy was passed out in an alcoholic stupor. Daniel sank down on the floor by Billy's straw bed and closed his eyes wearily.

"Colonel Cameron!"

Captain Farrow was beside him, his eyes alive with excitement as he rubbed his stubbled cheek.

"What is it, Captain?"

"Something of grave interest, sir."

What could have happened in the ten or fifteen minutes he was out with Jesse?

"Well?" Daniel said.

Farrow sank down beside him and plucked at a stray blade of straw.

"Billy's Aunt Priscilla made an appearance."

"So Billy had a visitor, huh? Before or after he passed out?"

"No, sir, he was plumb out when she arrived. But you've got to meet Aunt Prissy. She's some girl."

"Sir, I don't—"

Farrow's voice lowered to something that couldn't even be called a whisper. "We've got a plan, sir. Seems Beauty knows where you are and he wants you out. 'Aunt Prissy' ain't really Billy's relative at all. She's a friend to us here."

"And?" Daniel said, feeling his heart slam against his chest.

"Well, sir, we think we've got a plan to get you and a few others out. General Stuart wants you back. Are you game, sir?"

Daniel grinned, leaned back, and closed his eyes tightly with gratitude.

"Sir?" Farrow repeated.

"Oh, yes, Captain! I'm game. You'll know just how game. Tell me about this plan!"

Luckily, Jesse had been ordered to report to Frederick, Maryland. It was close enough for him to take the time to ride back by the farmhouse where he had first seen Callie Michaelson.

It was midafternoon when he rode by.

He found her on the front porch of her house. Curiously, she didn't seem to hear him as he approached. Even more curious, she was just sitting there, barefoot, in a very plain gingham dress with a high collar. Very proper for the time of day, he thought with a slow nostalgic smile. It had been a very long time since he had lost his mother, but he could still remember the things she was so determined to teach his sister, Christa. "Never, never show bosom during the day, darling. Only after five may a lady wear a dress that is at all revealing, and then, of course, in the most fastidious taste!"

"Mother, I haven't got a bosom," Christa would reply. "Therefore, I can't show it at any time."

"Oh, but darling, you will have one, you will!"

"Yes, and Daniel and Jesse will grow hair on their chests. Maybe!" Christa would tease.

And their mother would sigh, and roll her eyes, and then she would laugh and swear that she was raising a family of ruffians who were just playing at being gentry. Maybe that was true, but his mother could be the first "ruffian" among them because upon occasion, she would lose her austere dignity and slip off her shoes and go running through the grass with the rest of them. They had all adored her. To this day, Jesse was convinced that his father had died soon after she succumbed to pneumonia because no matter how he loved his children, he simply could not bear life without her.

Maybe death was easier for them now. He wondered vaguely if they could look down from heaven and see that he and Daniel were on opposite sides.

They would understand, he thought. They were the ones who had taught their children about conscience and dignity and moral duty and . . .

Honor.

He smiled slightly as he approached Callie. Yes, his mother might well approve of her. Her collar was high, her feet were bare.

"Mrs. Michaelson." He called her name softly. He was nearly upon her at the steps to the broad porch and she still hadn't noticed him, despite the fact that her eyes were wide open. She seemed so lost and vulnerable and waiflike.

She gazed at him. Her eyes widened and a look of panic flashed through her eyes. She leapt to her feet nervously, almost like a child who had been caught with something that she wanted to hide.

"Colonel! Colonel Cameron!" she gasped.

He frowned, dismounting from his horse. "I'm sorry, Mrs. Michaelson, I didn't mean to frighten you."

"I'm not frightened."

She was lying. No, she wasn't, Jesse determined. She was very startled, but she wasn't frightened. She had been seriously caught off guard. By him—in particular. He wondered why.

"I didn't think that I could come back, but as it is, I have to report to Frederick. I thought that I'd stop by instead of writing. I wanted to let you know that, yes, Daniel is in Old Capitol Prison. He's well, and with any luck, he'll stay there."

"Thank you. Thank you very much." She still seemed unreasonably nervous, but her appreciation and concern showed in the beautiful gray of her eyes.

"It's nothing, really."

She regained her composure. She regained it so completely that he had to wonder if he hadn't imagined the lost look in her eyes just seconds before. Her voice became soft and very gracious. Her eyes were downcast. Her bare feet were hidden by the sway of her simple skirt.

"You've come out of your way for me, Colonel Cameron, and I appreciate it very much. Come in, please. Let me make you something to eat before you travel on."

"It's not necessary—"

"But it is. Please, Colonel Cameron. I'd very much like to have you here."

"All right then," Jesse said. "Thank you, Mrs. Michaelson." He hesitated on the step, watching her. What a miraculous change she had made. He suddenly felt like grinning.

So here was the woman to bring down Daniel at last. It was intriguing. It was amusing. It could be wonderful.

If they could just get through the war.

"There's just one thing, Mrs. Michaelson."

"What's that?"

"My name is Jesse."

"Callie, sir."

He smiled and walked up her steps.

She paused. "Did you mention that we had met? Did he say anything?"

Jesse reflected for a minute. Yes, Daniel had had his message for Callie. But Jesse wasn't going to deliver it.

"He wasn't very talkative. Do you know, a home-cooked meal does sound wonderful, Callie. Shall we?"

She turned, and he followed her into the house.

Surely, he decided, there was some little twist of evil in his soul. He couldn't wait to write to Daniel. He wanted to tell him just how gracious and beautiful Mrs. Michaelson was and what a wonderful meal he had had in her company.

He was composing the letter even as he followed her into the house.

It occurred to him that he had never seen his brother angrier than when he had been talking about Callie Michaelson. Maybe Jesse would merely be adding fuel to that fire.

Maybe Daniel and this woman would just have to fight their own battles.

And maybe, just maybe, find their peace.

"Now?" Daniel said.

Captain Farrow nodded solemnly. Daniel started to lift the vial to his lips, determined that his hand would not shake. But Billy Boudain—up and about and doing darned nicely—suddenly interrupted.

"Jesu, Colonel, is it worth it? What if the—er—what if the box don't go where it's supposed to go?"

"But it will go where it's supposed to," Daniel said wearily. All of the men were staring at him. It was night, and the prison was quiet. Every man in the room was up, tense, waiting. Daniel grinned, saluted—but then paused himself.

The drug had not been his companion's choice for his method of escape.

Daniel hadn't been able to tolerate the first method planned for him.

Aunt Priscilla had planned on acquiring a Union Colonel's uniform with all the proper medical insignia upon it, slipping it to Daniel, and boldly walking out of the prison with her arm slipped right through his, convincing the guards that Colonel Jesse Cameron was leaving after a quick visit to see to the welfare of his brother, and his recent patient, Billy Boudain. No one had realized just how alike the Cameron brothers were—not until they had been seen there together at the prison.

Daniel had refused point-blank.

"I'm not using Jesse."

"Colonel, if you're afraid of getting caught, I imagine that you've got a justifiable concern. If you're afraid of being hanged—"

"I'm not afraid of being hanged, although I admit, it's not the way that I want to go. I want to get out of here so badly, Captain, that I can taste it. I dream of it, night and day. But I'm not using Jesse. He saved Billy's arm—and his life. And if he hadn't, I still wouldn't use him. Damn it, don't you see, it just wouldn't be right!"

"But sir—"

"What are we fighting for?" Daniel demanded.

Captain Farrow had grown quiet, and the next thing Daniel knew, he was listening to a new and wilder plot. Aunt Priscilla could get hold of a drug. Foul-tasting stuff, but it would do the trick. Daniel would appear to be dead. The Union would try to hold his body, of course. They'd want to get hold of Jesse to see what he wanted done with his brother's remains. But Aunt Priscilla would appear with a woman swearing to be Christa Cameron and between the two of them, they would demand the body.

There would be no discernible heartbeat in Daniel's body. His breathing would have become so slow that the doctor would not be able to detect it. The effects would last approximately forty-eight hours, so all that they had to do was get Daniel safely into Aunt Priscilla's hands by then.

Aunt Priscilla, Daniel reckoned, must be quite a reader. There were fine shades of Shakespeare in this wild scheme. He just hoped that the Union officers weren't quite as up on their classics.

"Well, men . . ." he murmured.

He shook his head. He capped the vial and handed it to Captain Farrow. "Put it away."

Farrow frowned.

"Billy Boudain, Davie Smith, you're both with me." He clasped Farrow's hand. "Sir, you are a fine inspiration to the men. I'll see if I can't arrange for a prisoner exchange for you once I get back to Richmond."

"But, Colonel—" Farrow said, confused.

Daniel shook his head, grinning. "I'm walking out of here tonight, Captain."

"But—"

"Watch me, sir."

He strode casually to the doorway. "Hey! You—you, the gorilla out there. Come over here. I've got to talk to you!"

He saw the big man sneer. Everybody had been warned about Daniel Cameron. But this hulk thought he was just too big to be taken.

Maybe he was. Daniel had one chance. Just one chance.

When the guard approached, he moved like lightning. He reached through the bars, caught the man's collar, and jerked him as hard against the bars as he could.

Steel struck the man's balding temples. The crack was quite audible. Heavy as lead, he started to fall.

Daniel fought to keep him up. "Davie, get the hell over here! Get the keys out of his pocket before he falls. Quick."

Davie was shaking uncontrollably. "Is he dead, Colonel?"

"No, he's not dead. He is going to have one hell of a headache. He's going to wake up as mean as a bear. So we've got to move. Fast."

Shaking, Davie managed to get the keys. Twisting, turning—and making way too much noise and taking way too long—Davie at last managed to twist open the lock on the door.

Daniel flung the door open and dragged the body of the guard into the room. He slipped the guard's revolver from its hip holster and shoved it into the waistband of his breeches.

He saluted the others. Silently, they saluted in return.

He urged Davie and Billy Boudain through the door. Even as he did so, he began to wonder at his own intelligence.

Now what the hell was he going to do? There were still monstrously high walls around Old Capitol Prison.

More than that, there were still scores of Yankee guards surrounding it.

"What now, sir?" Davie demanded.

What now, indeed? There was still an army between him and freedom.

But he could almost taste that freedom.

He could almost taste revenge.

If only he hadn't loved her so much.

It seemed very late when Jesse Cameron rode away from the farm at last.

She had been good, Callie thought. She had been cool and calm and composed when she had longed to shriek and tear her hair out. But he had been such a gentleman. So handsome.

So damned much like Daniel!

Except polite. And kind. And courteous to a fault.

Once upon a time, Daniel had been tender.

Too tender. That was why she was in this mess!

Jesse had reined in his horse. He turned back, and she waved to him. Cheerfully. He turned again, and within minutes, he was swallowed into the darkness.

"Oh, God!" she gasped aloud, and she sank down to the porch step, hugging her knees to her chest. A sob escaped her. It couldn't be true.

How long had Daniel been gone now? Over three weeks. Almost four. She picked up a stick and drew out lines for the days. She tried to convince herself that she was counting wrong.

Yes, she was counting wrong. And she was imagining that she had been queasy several mornings last week and was downright sick every morning this week.

She felt dizzy. It was a good thing she was sitting. She might have fallen. It had struck her like a ton of bricks while she had been feeding the chickens, just an hour before Jesse Cameron had come riding up.

Jesse Cameron. With blue eyes just like his brother's. That captured and imprisoned Reb who had sworn to come back for her.

"Oh, God!"

She buried her face in her hands. She had dallied with the enemy. She was going to have the enemy's baby. Her brothers might very well come home and throw her out of the house. Her neighbors would turn their backs on her. She would be ostracized by everyone. It was horrible.

She leaned back. She wondered why she didn't feel so horrible. She was a fallen woman. She closed her eyes.

She had loved him. She still loved him. She ached nightly for the way that she had been forced to betray him. Seeing his brother had reminded her of so many fine things about the man. His courage, his valor, his charm. The sound of his laughter.

The harsh sounds of his anger, she reminded herself. And those blue eyes could turn as cold as ice.

He'd had no right to condemn her. He hadn't given her the least chance to explain.

There was nothing that she could have explained at the time.

He had judged her mercilessly. She should be as furious with him as he was with her. She should hate him just as fiercely.

But after a moment, a smile curved her lip. The baby would still be part his. And maybe have those extraordinary eyes. Or the fine bone structure of his face. She might convince herself she was angry with him, she might even hate him fiercely in self-defense . . .

But still, it was difficult to mind having him as a father for a child.

Except that she was a woman alone, having a child alone.

After a while, she stood up. Though it was dark, she found herself walking around the house in the moonlight to where her father's stone stood in the graveyard.

She pressed a kiss to her fingers and set them on Gregory's tombstone, but she smiled because she did not feel the guilt she should have felt. It was her father's ghost to whom she spoke softly, in the moonlight.

"I think I want this baby, Pa. Can you understand? Oh, Pa, I've lost you, and I've lost Gregory. And I came out here and I watched all those handsome young boys die. This baby is life. In all of this misery, perhaps he can be hope. I think that you'd understand. I know that you'd love me anyway."

She sat there a while, and then she was stunned by how easily she had managed to accept what was happening.

Perhaps the way that she felt would change in the morning, she warned herself.

She wanted the baby. After all of the death, she wanted the life.

But as she walked toward the house, she paused.

The baby would be Daniel's too.

A chill settled over her.

She had loved him. He had beautiful blue eyes, he was proud and tall and valiant and all manner of good things. . . .

And he wanted to throttle her.

Daniel . . .

She'd had enough for one night. She'd have to worry about Daniel in the morning.

Thank God he was locked up in prison!

Fourteen

The hallway was silent; the door was closed behind them. Daniel moved as quietly as he could along the hallway until they came along the next set of guards.

They were seated at a table, playing cards. Real Union greenbacks and gold coins were casually laid out on the table.

There were three guards and three of them. Pretty fair odds, Daniel decided. And they weren't expecting any trouble. They were playing loudly. A whiskey bottle sat in the middle of the table. Daniel was certain Lieutenant Colonel

Dodson would not be pleased to know that his men were imbibing while on duty.

He smiled, and then his smile faded. He didn't want to kill anybody. It was horrible enough to kill in battle, when an opponent was seeking his death. If this went smoothly enough, they wouldn't have to spill any blood.

He motioned to Billy, pointing to his boot, and to the man in the center, the one with his back to them. Billy was healing nicely, but Daniel still wanted to give him the advantage of complete surprise. Davie, watching Daniel's signs to Billy, quickly understood Daniel's strategy, and nodded when Daniel pointed to the guard that he would take on.

He raised his hand, then one finger, then another, and then a third. And simultaneously they moved, striding in as if they had every right to be there.

"Hey!" began the corner man, the first to see them.

It was all that he managed to say. Daniel had the guard's heavy revolver and he gave the man a good clunk on the head with it. He crashed over, just as Billy and Davie reached their victims and likewise dispatched them with good clouts to the head.

"Look at this, will you? This ole bluebelly here was sitting pat on a full house," Billy commented.

"And look at this one!" Davie exclaimed. "Why, the ace of spades is sitting up his sleeves."

"Leave it," Daniel advised. "They might wind up more interested in fighting over the card game than looking for us." He picked up the bottle of whiskey and began to liberally sprinkle it over all of their heads and the card table. He grinned at Billy and Davie. "If they don't tear into one another, Dodson will. It will buy us some time. Billy, get that Colt over there. What a handsome gun! Davie, there's another service revolver there in that Yank's holster. Slip it out and let's move on."

Although that Old Capitol was crawling with guards, they managed to move about the prison rather easily. Billy was hesitant—Daniel knew why. The Yanks weren't expecting any break like this. Not that they hadn't had a few already. But prisoners hadn't risen up en masse, and none had pulled any tricks recently. Live men sometimes went out with their dead companions in coffins, and Daniel should have been playing a dead man in a coffin by now himself. He was glad he wasn't. He'd heard tell of an infantry commander who'd gone out of a Chicago prison that way. And he'd been buried alive, just as planned. But communications had gone awry, and when they'd dug him up two weeks later, he was found glassy-eyed, his fingers shot through with the slivers he'd received trying to dig his way through the box.

Daniel, Billy, and Davie came down another hall. The exercise yard was ahead of them. It was small, and the high walls surrounded it. There were guards at the gates and guards all around the high walls.

"What now, Colonel?" Billy demanded.

They could brazen their way out with their guns, but they'd probably be gunned down in turn.

"I—" Daniel began.

But it was then that fate stepped in. Out in the street there was the sudden, deafening sound of an explosion.

Davie dropped to his knees. "Merciful heaven, what was that?"

For a moment, Daniel wasn't sure. Then he realized what had happened, and he grinned broadly. "A supply wagon exploded out there. It was probably carrying a ton of dynamite. Every man jack around will be forgetting his position and running out to see what's happened or if he can help. Let's go! Fast. Move, move, move!"

Heedless of being sighted, Daniel began to run. To the amazement of his two men, no one paid them the slightest heed. Everyone was running, racing toward the street. There were shouts of help.

The gates opened, and men in various stages of dress began to rush through them.

Daniel made it through the gate with Davie and Billie behind him. There was smoke everywhere, helping to screen their escape. But better than that, there were screams in the street and a wild mass of people in any manner of dress running in every possible direction.

Street lamps were lit, but they did little against the heavy, acrid smoke in the air.

"Close the gates!" someone shouted. But it didn't matter. Daniel and his men were out.

Billy kept running with the crowd. Daniel snatched him up firmly by the collar. "Jesu, Billy, we're trying to get away from those men, remember?"

"Right!" Billy said.

Daniel led them down a cold, dark alley. He closed his eyes, trying to think of what to do, or where to go now. He could hear horses' hooves thundering as fire engines hurried toward the street in front of the prison. It might be a long while before they were discovered missing. And then again, it might be too soon.

Huddled in the alley, their hearts pounding in equal rhythm to the thundering hooves, Daniel tried to think. Who did he know in D.C., where could he turn for help?

"There's Aunt Priscilla's," Billy offered.

Daniel stared at him. "You know how to find her?"

"Sure. E Street. Come on."

Billy led the way. Daniel felt like a snake, slinking along the buildings, falling flat against them any time they came across citizens out in the night. But bit by bit they moved through the city, and at last they stood in the alleyway behind a fine old Federal-style house of red brick with big Greek columns. "That's it," Billy whispered. "But I think that Aunt Priscilla is entertaining."

Through the shades they could see movement. A man and a woman, entwined. No, they were dancing, Daniel decided. No, they were just entwined. Her laughter rang out, and the characters caught in shadow on the drapes disappeared. A moment later, a light appeared from one of the upstairs windows.

"What do we do now?" Davie murmured.

"We go on in. Quietly. I'm not staying in this alley."

Daniel led the way across the yard, keeping a careful eye on the upstairs window and watching the downstairs too. They reached the porch, and moved carefully along it to a window. Daniel looked in. The room was empty. He slipped on in, motioning to the two others to follow him.

They did so. Then Daniel jumped, for he heard the soft cadences of a black woman singing. He motioned the others back and hurried to the hallway door. An attractive young housekeeper was just closing off the dining room, humming away. Daniel slipped back against the wall as the girl passed by the hallway. He watched as she hurried along to a back set of steps, the servant's stairway. She disappeared up the stairway, and Daniel stepped back, sighing softly.

Maybe they were safe for a spell. Maybe not. They needed to move. At the least, they needed a plan. By morning, their disappearance would definitely be noted.

He motioned to Billy and Davie to stay behind and started silently up the main stairway. It was beautiful, with a carved mahogany banister and red velvet runners. The runners silenced his footsteps.

He stood outside in the upper hallway, listening. He could hear a woman giggling again. He tiptoed closer to an open bedroom door.

A heavyset man with an iron-gray handlebar mustache sat up in his long johns in the bed. His uniform—that of an artillery commander—lay across the footstool at the bottom of the bed.

Aunt Priscilla stood before her mirror dressed in a set of some of the most outrageous undergarments that Daniel had ever seen. Brilliant orange lace frothed in between rows of black. Black mesh stockings barely covered her legs. A fine set of breasts were well displayed, popping over the orange-and-black lace at the top of the garment.

He saw that she had passed through many more years than her body gave hint to. Her hair was red, but not a real red. It was almost as orange as the color in her garment.

"Don't you worry your little head none about what old Abe's planning on doing with his army now. He'll think of something—"

"But you know what he's thinking, Louis, and I feel so much safer here when you talk to me!" she replied. She frowned suddenly, and Daniel realized that she had met his gaze in the mirror. He had thought to withdraw quickly. He did not want to embarrass this helpmate of the Confederacy.

But he didn't embarrass her at all. She smiled at him in the mirror, and moistened her lips. Her eyes were large and brown and fine, and she winked.

"Louis, I believe that I need just a touch of sherry tonight. I've a chill. If you'll excuse me—"

"Why, Prissy, I'll get you anything that your heart desires—"

"No, no, no, Louis! You stay right there! And stay warm, darling. I'll be back in just a flash."

She slipped a flimsy wrap around her shoulders, kissed Louis on his near balding pate, and hurried out of the room, closing the door behind her.

She leaned against it breathlessly. "You're Daniel Cameron," she mouthed softly.

He nodded. She gripped his hand and urged him quickly down the hall, pressing him into another room, and closing the door.

"You're supposed to be in a coffin!" she told him.

"I didn't want to do it that way."

"It's amazing that you haven't been caught!" she exclaimed. "You fool! You should have done things my way. I'd have found you and brought you here—"

"Well, I'm right beholden for that, ma'am, but I'm here on my own now—"

"They'll be looking for you!" she exclaimed.

"Well, yes, that they will. By morning."

"I wanted to keep you for a while!" she exclaimed.

Startled, Daniel took a step back. She wasn't an unattractive woman. She was perhaps ten years his senior, and in her way, she was very pretty. Her face was round, her eyes were intelligent.

Her hair reminded him of Callie's. Hair that was real fire, hair that he had swirled around his fingers, hair that had covered his body like a sweep of silk.

Hair I could string her up by, he reminded himself.

"You are just like him!" Aunt Priscilla said.

"I beg your pardon?" Daniel said.

"Your brother. You're just like your brother."

"You know Jesse?"

"Oh, of course. I move in all the right circles, very carefully. I wanted that brother of yours the moment that I saw him, Colonel. But I heard that he'd lost his heart to some little southern girl. Then I heard that he had a brother in prison who was very near his double."

Her voice trailed away suggestively.

Daniel didn't know whether to be amused or offended.

"I'll have to have you out of here by morning!" she wailed.

Daniel cleared his throat. "Ma'am, have you forgotten that you've a man in another bedroom?"

"Oh, Louis!" She waved a hand in the air. "I can dispatch him rather quickly." Her eyes opened very wide. "I do enjoy my work, Colonel," she said. "And I have been invaluable to the troops. General Robert E. Lee said so himself!"

Daniel tried to envision the exceedingly dignified Lee in the same room with this woman. He couldn't quite drum up the sight.

"Ma'am, I imagine that your services have indeed been invaluable," he assured her. "But please, don't dispatch Louis on my account."

"But I've waited—"

"And I have to move on, ma'am. I've two men with me. I want to be in Virginia by morning."

Virginia! No, he wanted to go back. To Maryland. He wanted to go back to Callie Michaelson's farmhouse, and he wanted to confront her there.

He gritted his teeth, suddenly realizing—or admitting—that he couldn't go back now. His first responsibility was freedom—for himself, and for Billy and Davie. He had to cross into the South, and he had to make his way back to Stuart's service as quickly as possible.

A time would come. Soon. There would be another campaign into the North again, he was certain. They'd have to attack the North for supplies. If they didn't attack the Yanks on their own territory, the Yanks would never see just how ugly war could be.

He would go to Virginia now.

"Colonel, you're not even paying any attention to me!" Aunt Priscilla complained.

"I'm sorry, ma'am. My mind is on my heartland!" he assured her dramatically.

She sighed, looking very peeved. "Colonel—"

He stepped forward, took her hand, and kissed it. "Alas, regrets, ma'am! But I do have to move on. And I'm sorry, but Jesse married that southern girl. I'm afraid you won't have any luck with him in the future either."

Once again, she sighed, and turned.

She could turn nicely. Everything about her seemed to move and sway.

He should have wanted her. It should have been an escapade, like some of the nights they had all spent out west long before the war.

His jaw clenched down hard. Callie. Damn her.

He wanted her. Wanted the flame of her hair, and the flame of her love. No other woman, strumpet or lady, could fire him the same way.

Damn her, he thought.

Priscilla stopped suddenly, saying over her shoulder, "Get your men, Colonel. There's a wagon out back in the barn. Harness the horses to it. Get yourselves in it and as soon as I get that old goat Louis off to sleep, I'll be out. I may even have something for you to bring to your commander."

She swayed out of the room.

He smiled. Maybe he should be flattered that she had been interested. After all, to most Rebs, Jesse looked like Daniel, and not vice versa.

Downstairs he found Davie and Billy, and they slipped just as quietly out of the house as they had entered it. The night seemed just about dead silent now, and there was only the sliver of a moon out. They found the barn easily enough, and the wagon. It was loaded up with hay and straw. Without even speaking, they set about choosing a team of horses, and hitching them up to the wagon as quickly as possible. The three men crawled in, covering themselves up the best they could.

Moments later, a dark-clad figure hurried into the barn. Daniel was startled to see that it was Priscilla, and that she had made a drastic change. She was in black widow's weeds, with fabric to her throat and a heavy black veil over her face. Curiously, Daniel found her much more fascinating in such apparel, for her eyes now wore a look of tragedy or pain that made them a mystery, one that deserved unraveling.

But when she spoke to him she was very business-like, and the interlude upstairs might never have happened.

"They're looking for you already," she told Daniel. "I sent my maid out. They discovered you gone after that awful accident with the dynamite. Luckily, they've no idea when you made your escape, and they've no idea at all where you might have gone. I'm going to take you over the Potomac. You'll be in Virginia when I leave you, but I warn you, the Federals are holding most of the extreme northern areas. There's a ring of forts around Washington. There's a farm over the river where I go regularly to buy my eggs. I'll get you there. If we're caught, I'll deny all knowledge that you were with me. I have to. Do you understand that?"

"We understand. We won't jeopardize your disguise," Daniel assured her.

"Thank you," she said.

She was about to crawl into the wagon. Daniel tapped her on the shoulder. She turned around. "Did Louis go nighty night?" he asked very politely.

She stared at him and then smiled slowly. "Just like a babe, Colonel. Just like a babe. Let's go now, before I change my mind about getting you there."

Priscilla crawled up to drive her wagon, and Daniel sank back into the hay.

The wagon began to rock and roll.

Covered with the straw and deeply nestled into it, Daniel could see little. Light became more prevalent as they came across busier streets. In his mind's eye, he tried to plot Priscilla's course, but beneath the hay, he lost his sense of direction.

All he knew was that the journey seemed endless. He could not see Davie or Billy; he couldn't even see his own hands. Sometimes there was a lot of light, sometimes there was a little. Sometimes the road was smooth, and then it was rough, very rough.

Sometimes the wagon stopped, and he could hear Priscilla's voice as she charmed her way past the city's guards. Each time his heart seemed to cease to beat. Then it would slam against his chest when the wagon began to move again. We owe this woman our lives, he thought.

He heard the clip-clop of the horses' hooves over the bridge, and then he felt that they had veered off on a rougher road.

Then it seemed that they stopped in no time. "Colonel!" she called softly in the night.

He crawled out of the straw, with Billy and Davie following suit. The moon was out a little more brightly, but they were alone. "Follow that road, sir, and it will take you down to Fredericksburg. There are patrols in this area, so watch yourselves. And—" She paused, then handed him an envelope. "Please see that this gets to General Lee."

"I'll do that." Daniel promised her. He frowned, looking at the envelope. "Priscilla, if we are killed or taken again—"

"Then I will be hanged," she finished for him. She smiled. "Don't get killed, Colonel."

He swept her a low bow. "No, ma'am. I will not get killed."

She lifted a hand in a salute. Daniel returned it, and Billy and Davie followed his lead.

The wagon began to clip-clop away, the sound seeming to echo in the stillness of the night.

"Well, boys, we are almost home free!" Daniel said. "Shall we walk?"

"Walking seems mighty fine to me, sir!" Billy told him.

"Yessir," Davie agreed.

Daniel paused suddenly. A breeze had picked up in the night. He turned to the northwest. Maryland. He wanted to go back. For a moment the ache was so strong he could scarcely bear it. And it had nothing to do with revenge. It had everything to do with wanting to touch her.

He swallowed hard, then grinned to his men. "Well, gentlemen, this is home for me." He started walking, the others behind him.

Twice in the night they heard the sound of horses' hooves. They melted into the trees, off the road. Yankee patrols rode by.

In the morning, they found a cove and slept. By afternoon, the pangs of hunger were tearing at them. Though Davie convinced Daniel he could catch a rabbit with his bare hands, Daniel convinced Davie that they couldn't light a fire. They had to settle on some wild berries.

By night, they walked again. With careful scavenging, Billy managed to slip an apple pie off the windowsill of a small farmhouse.

Some small boy was probably going to take a licking for a crime for which he wasn't guilty, Daniel reflected. They were in Virginia, but he wasn't ready to test the loyalty of the farmers yet. One day, he'd come back and pay for the pie.

They had been on the road for four days and nights when they heard horses' hooves and jumped into the foliage for what seemed like the thousandth time. Daniel tried hard to see through the brush. His heart hammered hard.

The uniforms were gray. Peering through the bushes, Daniel frowned. They weren't just gray. They were familiar. As were some of the faces.

"We've got to keep looking," an officer said. Daniel knew the voice. "Our intelligence is certain that they'll be coming this way, down toward Fredericksburg."

"What's that?" someone demanded.

Daniel stepped out of the bushes, grinning broadly, his hands raised. They weren't just cavalry men. They were cavalry men who had been in his command at one time. "Don't shoot, my friends. I believe we're who you're looking for."

"Daniel!" someone cried. A man slipped down from his horse. It was Captain Jarvis Mulraney, a neighbor from the peninsula, a good friend under Daniel's command since the war had begun. Red-haired, freckle-faced, he looked too young to be in the war, but he was the captain of a crack group of horsemen.

Daniel embraced him.

"Thank God, you're home!" Jarvis told him, beaming. "Jesu, we thought that we'd lost you for sure back in Sharpsburg!"

"No, I'm back," Daniel said. "And yessir, thank God. I'm home."

Men were dismounting from their horses all around him, embracing him. Harry Simmons, Richard MacKenzie, Robert O'Hara. He called Billy and Davie from the bushes and introduced them all around. It almost seemed like a party, right there in the road.

Yes, he was home, he reflected.

But there had been a piece of him lost for good back in Sharpsburg.

The days seemed to pass endlessly for Callie. October rolled into November.

She went into town for supplies, and she visited there with friends, but she felt strangely isolated, as if she wasn't really a part of the community anymore.

She received letters from all three of her brothers, Joshua, Josiah, and Jeremy, and she was grateful, for all three of them were alive and in good health. It seemed forever since she had seen them. She wrote to them frequently, but she never knew just how often they actually received the letters that she wrote.

She never mentioned Daniel. She wouldn't have known what to say.

She did tell them about the battle that had been fought in her front yard, and she carefully minimized any danger to herself. She was determined to be cheerful, and she told whatever stories about the antics of their neighbors that she could embroider upon.

The letters she received in turn were too much like those of the young man who had died in their barn. They all knew that they might meet death any day and they stressed emotions and feelings. Mainly, they stressed love, and the appreciation for the quality of the lives they had already lived.

On Thanksgiving, Rudy Weiss appeared very early at her door with his wife at his side. Surprised to see them, Callie stared at the pair for a moment, then quickly invited them inside.

Helga, Rudy's wife, a tall woman with a broad, ample bosom and truly apple-red cheeks, brought in a big basket and offered it to Callie with a shy smile. "Thanksgiving. And you are alone. You should not be alone. We have brought you a goose and corn and mein own apple sauce. It is good."

"Well of course, it's good! I'm sure it's wonderful. I thank you very much."

They stayed with her, and they shared the goose, and before he would leave, Rudy wanted to know if she needed anything done that she could not handle herself. She told him that no, she was fine. She'd had the windows repaned soon after the battle by glassworkers from town, and she felt that she was really in very good shape.

All of the Sharpsburg area was slowly healing. What remained of the corn was all in. Winter was coming to cleanse the rest of the landscape.

"Thank you for coming," Callie told them at the door when they were leaving. "I know that you—I know that it is important for you to remain with your own people, and so it is doubly good of you to come to me."

Helga clicked her teeth. "We are a plain people, not a mean one!" she assured Callie. She kissed her cheek, just like a surrogate mother, and she and Rudy quietly walked down the steps.

Callie wondered whether she might spend Christmas with Rudy and Helga, but just a few days before the holiday, she saw a soldier walking down the path toward the house, leading a handsome bay horse. Something about the way that he moved drew her attention, even while he was at a distance.

She dropped the feed bucket that she had been carrying for the chickens and started to run. She ran as fast as her feet would carry her, and then she threw herself into the soldier's arms.

"Jeremy!" she cried, delighted. The youngest of her brothers had come home.

"Callie, Callie!" He held her face between his palms, staring into her eyes, then he crushed her to his chest once again. "God, it's so good to see you! I've missed you so much! And home. Callie, I can't tell you what it's like to be away from home like this!"

"But you look wonderful, Jeremy, wonderful! What a mustache! That's one of the finest mustaches I've ever seen!"

And it was. Rich, dark red, full, well-manicured, and twirling nicely.

His eyes were silver-gray. Quick to burn, quicker still to sparkle, as they did now. "You like it, huh?"

"Well, it makes you look old. Very old."

"Old enough to be a lieutenant?"

"You've been promoted! Oh, how wonderful!"

He shrugged. "Callie, we have an atrocious death rate. It's horrible to say, but sometimes the Rebs are better fighters. Not many Yanks can deny that Bull Run was a 'skedaddle.' There have been lots of battles like that. We fare better in the West than they do in the East, but not much. Callie, those Rebs are fighting for their homeland. We're marching all over it, stripping everything from it. And they're killing us right and left. Promotions come quickly in wartime."

"Jeremy, I'm proud. And I know that Pa would be proud, and glad that he made you all go to military school, even if we are farmers. But I don't care about that right now, I'm just so glad that you're home. And on leave. You are on leave, aren't you? Jeremy! You didn't desert, did you? I heard in town the other day that desertions were pouring in from both sides, that men were trying to go home for winter. You didn't just pick up and walk off, did you?"

"No, no, I'm on leave. I have until the day after Christmas, and then I'll have to start back. But Josiah couldn't come now, and neither could Joshua. They're outside Vicksburg, Mississippi, and there aren't many leaves being given there. I reckon I'll have to report there, too, once I get back. Lucky for me, this promotion gave me Christmas."

"I'm so grateful!" Callie exclaimed.

The days that passed were wonderful for her. She loved all of her brothers, but Jeremy was her favorite. They had been closest in age. They had fought in the haystacks, they had tried to tear out each other's hair.

They had banded together against their older brothers, against their parents, against anyone who would dare say something ill of the other.

It was so good to have him home. Somehow the nights were a little easier. Her sleep was still plagued with dreams, but during the day she was no longer alone.

She wanted to tell him about Daniel, but she knew that she couldn't. She wanted to tell him that he was going to be an uncle, but she couldn't do that, either. She couldn't send him back to war upset or angry or worried about her.

On Christmas morning Callie presented him with a beautiful navy blue scarf that would help keep him warm in the brutal winter weather. It was a fine, handsome piece of clothing, and his gratitude for it showed in his eyes.

"I didn't have time to be anywhere near so creative, Callie," he told her.

"Your being home is gift enough, Jeremy."

He smiled. "I said that I wasn't creative. I didn't say that I didn't have anything at all."

He presented her with a box wrapped in silver paper. She opened it to discover a beautiful cameo. She stared at her brother.

"I bought it. Legitimately."

"From?"

"A lady in Tennessee," he said softly. "She had four children and a husband dead at Shiloh. She wasn't doing well feeding the children with her Confederate paper money. She wanted Union dollars. I gave her plenty of them, I promise you."

"But you took this brooch from her—"

"Callie, she didn't want charity. I told her about you. She said that she'd be happy if you wore it."

He took the pin, and carefully set it on her bodice. He stepped back, smiling. "Callie, I promise you, I paid her much more for it than it was worth."

Callie smiled. "I'm glad."

She hugged him, then pushed him away. "We have to get into town for church, and then I've got one of the biggest chickens for the fire that you've ever seen."

"And apple pie?"

"Of course."

They sat through the Anglican service in town. Callie kept her head bowed all through the service, certain that she should be praying and begging pardon for her sins.

Up by the altar was an old crèche. The Christ child lay in a cradle of straw, tiny arms outstretched. As she watched the crèche, she felt a warmth almost overwhelming her. She closed her eyes tightly. She could almost envision the baby, feel the softness of its flesh, see the tiny fingers, hear the squalling cries. Perhaps she had been wrong, perhaps she had sinned. A war was going on. The "war of the rebellion" as Jeremy was calling it—or the "civil war" as Daniel had referred to it. No matter what was going on, there could be no evil in a precious babe, and she was convinced of it. She felt like crying, and she felt incredibly happy.

She must have been crying, because Jeremy pressed a handkerchief into her hands.

When they left the church, Callie stepped back as Jeremy was greeted by the townspeople. The men shook his hand. Women kissed his cheeks. A few of the more brazen—or lonelier—of the ladies left behind were so bold as to kiss his lips. Callie just leaned back against the church building, watching and enjoying.

They headed back home at last.

Callie thought that she had been well over the sickness. She had felt wonderful for days before Jeremy had arrived home. But right in the middle of setting the table for their meal, she suddenly felt a violent upheaval.

Jeremy, putting out the forks, looked up at her strangely. "What's the matter?"

She wanted to answer him; she couldn't. She tore out the back door and leaned over the railing, then choked and spilled out the apple and the porridge she had eaten that morning.

"My, Lord, Callie!" Jeremy cried, concerned, his hands on her shoulders. He pulled her around. He touched her forehead. "No, no, you're not feverish. Come in and lie down. I'll hitch the wagon back up and head to town for the doctor—"

"No! I don't need a doctor."

"Callie, I won't leave with you being sick like this!"

"I'm not sick, Jeremy."

"I just saw you—"

"Jeremy, it was nothing. Trust me. I'm not sick."

She didn't know when something he had learned about women suddenly dawned in his mind.

"My Lord, Callie, you're—why, you're in a family way. Oh, poor Callie, with Gregory dead these many, many months—" He broke off, staring at her, his mouth gaping for a moment. "Callie, Gregory's been dead way too long."

She stared straight at him. She tried to feel the coolness of the breeze.

"The baby isn't Gregory's."

"Then whose baby is it? I'll find the man, Callie. He'll do right by you, I swear it."

She shook her head. "Jeremy, I don't want you finding anybody."

"It was a soldier?"

She hesitated.

"Why, those bloody bastards! Callie, you were"—he couldn't quite seem to spit out the word, and then he did—"raped?"

She shook her head again. "No."

He lifted his hands, at a loss. She'd never seen him more hurt.

"Callie, I can't help you if you won't let me."

"I don't want to be helped."

"Callie, any Union soldier would be proud to come back here—" He broke off, his eyes widening, then narrowing sharply. "My God, it wasn't a Union soldier. It was a goddamned Reb!"

"Jeremy—" She reached out a hand to him.

He backed away. "A goddamned Reb. Pa's dead, and Gregory's dead, and hell, you'll just never know how many others. You don't get to see your friends and neighbors explode daily! My God. My sister's having a Reb bastard. My own sister! Goddamned, Callie, I don't even want you in my house anymore!"

"Jeremy—"

"Don't touch me, Callie!" he snapped. He spun around and went stomping off the porch.

"Jeremy!" She tried to call him back, but he was gone. She leaned against the wall, and then she pushed away from it and made her way back into the house.

The chicken was ready. She had cranberry sauce on the table. And thick gravy, the kind Jeremy loved the most. The table was beautiful, and she'd been so very happy.

She leaned her face down upon the table, right against the linen. She was too weary and heartsick to cry.

It didn't matter. She'd fight for the baby. She'd fight Jeremy and Joshua and Josiah and the whole town.

She'd fight Daniel too.

But she'd lost her brother. There were more ways than death to lose someone, she realized. She bit her lip and closed her eyes. She couldn't cry, she couldn't. Not anymore.

Her eyes opened, for she felt soft fingers against her cheek. She opened her eyes again and her brother was there, kneeling down by her side. "I'm sorry, Callie, God forgive me, and I pray that you forgive me. I love you, Callie. I don't understand what you did, but I love you. And I'll love my nephew—or niece—I swear it. I'll be here for you."

She started crying, despite all her determination that she wouldn't do so anymore. She threw her arms around his neck, and he held her.

"Callie, I can help you still, if you let me. I can maybe find this Reb—"

"No," Callie said firmly.

"Oh Lord, he hasn't been killed already, has he?"

She shook her head. "He is, er, out of action for the moment. Jeremy, please, just leave me be. Maybe, when the war is over, if he survives it and I can find him, I'll let him know."

"Callie, damn it, he has a responsibility—"

"Please, Jeremy, please!"

He sighed. "Callie, I'm going to get the truth out of you if it takes me an eternity."

She smiled at last. "Well, I can't stop you from trying. But I want this baby. And the baby is mine. Anything else is for a far distant future. All right?"

Jeremy still wouldn't agree. He stood up, and he started to prepare their plates. He sighed. "Well, I've made supper a bit cold here."

"I can stoke up the fire again—"

"No, the gravy's still warm. That's what's important."

She smiled at him.

"Callie?"

"Yes?"

"Merry Christmas, sister. Merry Christmas."

She jumped up, because she just had to hug him one more time.

Fifteen

T he end of 1862 proved to be an especially brutal period for Daniel.
While he had been held in Old Capitol, Jeb Stuart had been managing another of his sweeping raids around the Yanks, going so far as to encircle the enemy in Pennsylvania. But by the time Daniel returned to active duty, it was necessary for the Rebs to begin a tight watch around the area of Fredericksburg, Virginia.

In the North, President Lincoln had given up trying to believe in his very popular general, George McClellan. Rumor had it that Lincoln felt sending reinforcements to McClellan was like "shoveling flies across a barn." McClellan was removed and General Burnside was sent in to take his place.

Daniel wasn't so sure about the wisdom of such a choice. They were calling a bridge over Antietam Creek "Burnside's Bridge" these days because the general had tried so long—and at such a great cost of human life—to cross that bridge.

Burnside was a good man, though. Daniel knew him by reputation, and knew that he was loyal to his cause. He knew that Lincoln was totally disgusted with the way that "Little Mac," as McClellan was known, had hesitated time and time again when he could have moved against the Rebels.

It would remain to be seen just what Burnside would do. Because there was one certainty about the South. The Rebs might be low in manpower, and they might not have industrial strength, and Lord knew they hadn't the sheer numbers of the North, but the South could boast some of the finest generals to come along in centuries. Lee would be careful, watching Burnside. Daniel still doubted there was any way Burnside could "out-general" Lee.

Still, it seemed apparent that the new Union commander was going to be making a strike toward Richmond. The North was growing more and more desperate to take the Confederate capital.

On the fifteenth of November, they skirmished with Federal troops at Warrenton, Virginia. By the eighteenth, General Burnside and his Army of the Potomac had arrived in Falmouth, on the banks of the Rappahannock River, across from Fredericksburg. Jeb's cavalry was positioned at Warrenton Station.

It was good for Daniel to be back with his troops. He was still with Billy Boudain, having managed to get the boy transferred into his cavalry regiment. Billy had been given a promotion to sergeant and was serving as Daniel's staff assistant. Although the cavalry prepared for heavy battle, they remained the "eyes and ears" of the Confederacy, and it didn't seem to Daniel that a single night passed in which he wasn't sent out to scout Union positions.

He didn't mind. He liked falling into his cot dead exhausted every night. Sometimes the exhaustion kept him from dreaming.

But sometimes he dreamed anyway. The dreams were sweet, and the dreams were cruel. Sometimes he'd be back on the river. He'd see the rolling landscape, feel the breeze. The river air would rustle the leaves in the trees and all around him the world would be rich with the sweet scent of the earth.

And she would be there. Her eyes so wide and gray, touched with shimmers of silver. She'd be whispering and in his arms. The feel of her flesh would be warm and velvet, the sweep of her hair like a caress of silk. She'd come closer, closer, whispering . . .

Then, from somewhere, would come an explosion of heavy artillery, and she would be gone.

It was war, Daniel told himself wearily. And there was nothing to be done but fight it.

And live. Yes, live. Because he had to go back. No matter how long it took him, he had to return to that small farm near Sharpsburg.

Sometimes when he lay awake at night, he wondered what he would do once he got there. It wasn't to be soon. On the thirteenth of December, the situation around Fredericksburg came to a head. Burnside's force of one hundred and six thousand men attacked the Confederates under Stonewall, a force of seventy-two thousand.

During the battle, the Yanks were forced to attack Marye's Heights. The slaughter was horrible.

By nightfall, it was clear the Confederates had taken the day. For Daniel, there was little other than a hollow feeling in his heart. He'd heard that one Union soldier had commented, "They might as well have asked us to take Hell!"

When the fighting had ended and the generals had conferred, a very weary "Master" Lee had said, "I wish these people would go away and let us alone!"

Dear God, yes, Daniel thought. By midnight he'd made his reports, he'd been to the field hospital, and he'd braced himself against the horror to be found there. Now his men were preparing to sleep, and he was free from responsibility until morning. He walked down to the river and looked out over the water.

Jesse would be busy tonight trying to put back the pieces of human beings.

Just leave us alone, he thought, remembering Lee's words. Lee had looked so weary of the war when Daniel had seen him last, delivering Aunt Priscilla's package to him. Daniel was sick to death of the killing, and there was so much more to follow. Why couldn't Lincoln just let them go? He didn't understand it.

But Jesse did. That's why he had stayed in the Union. "God in heaven, I am at war with my own brother!" He whispered aloud. He lifted his hands, suddenly remembering that he carried a package in brown wrapping. He had seen Harley Simon, a neighbor in the artillery, when he had gone through the hospital. Harley had been carrying the package with him for two months. It was a silver baby cup, a present for Jesse and Kiernan. Harley's wife had gotten it to Harley, and Harley had been carrying it in his haversack ever since, hoping he'd see Daniel soon enough. Jesse might be on the other side, but he'd always been the Simons' friends.

How could it be that they were all trying to kill one another, but they were still friends?

Daniel closed his eyes, then opened them. The moonlight glistened on the water. How many good, good friends did he have in the Union army, not to mention his brother? He didn't want to think about it. Jesse and Beauty. When the war was over, would they all be able to drink good whiskey and laugh over pranks again?

Would they survive the war? Would they be able to forgive one another?

Yes, he could forgive anyone. He had understood Jesse from the start.

Not Callie. He would never forgive her. She had betrayed him. He had fallen in love, and she had betrayed him.

And now his every moment, waking, sleeping, fighting, was consumed with her. Maybe if he could just touch her again.

Burnside retreated the next day, but Daniel was swamped with duty, being sent almost daily to observe his enemy. Christmas was approaching, and it seemed the action had somewhat quieted here in the East, although skirmishing did take place. The situation was different in the West. President Jeff Davis was furious with the happenings in New Orleans. Since the fall of that city, a Union general named Butler—"Beast" Butler, as he was being called—had been in charge. The women in the city had been so rude to the Union officers that Butler had issued a proclamation called his "Women's Order," in which he stated that any female acting rude to his officers would be considered a woman of the streets, plying her avocation, and be so duly treated in turn.

Jeff Davis wanted Butler executed on the spot if he could be captured. It was a strange turn of events, for once upon a time, when there had been only one country, Butler had been one of Jeff Davis's strongest political supporters.

Thankfully, despite strong support in the North, Butler was removed, and General Banks was sent in to take his place. Banks was far less objectionable to the citizens of New Orleans.

December wore on.

Three days before Christmas, Daniel was given ninety-six hours leave. When he heard the news, his heart began to thud with anticipation.

He was going to go to Maryland. He was going to find out just what he would do when he saw her again. He would wrestle with both the beauty and the beast that haunted his dreams, his days, and his nights.

But another Beauty got wind of his plans, that Beauty being Jeb Stuart. Beauty, dashing as ever in his flamboyant plumed hat and cape, came to visit him, carrying a bottle of a fine vintage wine and good-humored Christmas stories. As they sat there, Jeb suddenly ceased to smile and told him flatly, "You're not to travel north, Daniel. I need you too badly. You cannot risk capture now."

"I risk capture almost daily!" Daniel exploded. "How else does one encircle an enemy for intelligence?"

Stuart sighed. "Daniel, war is a danger. Bullets are dangerous! We cannot avoid either. But I'll not lose you again over something . . . unnecessary. Daniel, you've chosen not to speak about Sharpsburg, or your capture, or even your days in prison. I can't make you. But you've changed since then. Even the men have noticed it."

"I'm a damned good officer, and I never ask more of my men than I'm willing to give."

"I agree, the men would agree, and hell, yes, you must be a cat, you're so willing to lead into the fray rather than ask another man to do it. But Daniel, you can't go north now. I'll see that your leave is revoked unless you give me your word that you won't head into Maryland."

Daniel scowled. Anticipation had been so sweet. Seeing her, shaking her, touching her. It had all seemed so close he could almost taste it.

"Daniel, damn it, don't put me in a position to pull rank!" Stuart pleaded.

Daniel swallowed hard. "I've got to get back to Sharpsburg."

"I'll get you there. In '63 sometime. I swear it," Stuart promised him.

Daniel exhaled. It hurt. Almost physically. Stuart rose and stretched out his hand. "Your word, Daniel. I need you back here."

His word. His precious honor. Wasn't that what they were fighting for?

He gave Stuart his hand. Beauty turned and headed out of Daniel's field tent. He paused, his back to Daniel. "Jesse is just across the Rappahannock. Did you know that?"

"I figured he was still with the Feds, somewhere close."

"We're exchanging some prisoners right before Christmas. Anything you want to send him?"

"Yes," Daniel said quietly. "Tell him that Harley Simon sent him a gift for the baby, and tell him that I'll be taking it home to Kiernan. And send him his brother's warmest regards. Tell him that I've gone home for Christmas. And that we'll all be thinking of him."

"I'll tell him," Stuart agreed, then left the tent.

The next morning, Daniel started off.

From his position near Fredericksburg, Daniel needed the time to carefully skirt the Yanks and ride the distance, stopping overnight in Richmond, where he was able to attend an evening at the White House of the Confederacy with President and Mrs. Davis. The house, which had been donated to the city of Richmond and then to the Confederate government, was gracious and beautiful, but what made it more so, Daniel thought, was the South's first lady. Varina Davis was many years her husband's junior. Where Davis was known for being reserved and opinionated, Varina was all warmth and beauty. The cares of the Confederacy were etched in her features, but she had lost none of her warmth that Christmas season. Daniel came into the entryway with numerous other officers. He was led into the house, where all of the pocket doors had been thrown open to make one large space for all of the guests. The president and his lady were not elusive creatures, but hardworking individuals who strived to be available to friends and associates. Daniel had never known Jeff Davis well; still, the man was kind and concerned when they spoke. And Varina reminded him of everything that they were fighting for. Beautiful, vivacious, and still regal and dignified, she moved with a rustle of silk and a whisper of femininity. Watching her brought a warmth to him, until her movement reminded him of Callie.

He still had far to go, and so did not tarry long in Richmond. It was a careful day's ride out to Cameron Hall from the capital, since he didn't know if there might be any Union troops on the peninsula.

But coming home, he thought, when he first saw the drive leading down a length of oaks to Cameron Hall, was worth any care or danger. The house still stood, and stood regally with its huge white columns and wide, inviting porches. Seeing the house, he began to ride hard. Even as he neared the house, the large doors to the grand hallway were thrown open and a woman appeared on the porch. She was dressed in deep maroon velvet and her hair was darker than his own. She cried out, and was joined in seconds by another woman, this one blond, and dressed in deepest royal blue. The brunet was his sister, the blonde his sister-in-law.

"It's a soldier, Kiernan!"

"Reb or Yank, Christa?"

"Reb. It's—"

"It's Daniel!"

The two of them came flying down the stairs, running for him. Daniel felt the bitterness of the war melt from his heart, and he leapt down from his horse and began to run himself. Seconds later they were both in his arms, and he was swirling with them and holding them close. They each kissed and hugged him, and he returned the kisses and hugs, meeting his sister's crystal-blue gaze first, then Kiernan's entrancing emerald-green one.

"Oh, Daniel, you made it home for Christmas!" Christa said happily.

Kiernan was observing him more carefully. "I sent all kinds of things to you in Washington, Daniel. Jesse got a letter through that you'd been captured. But then I received another letter saying that you'd escaped before my goods ever reached you!"

He grinned. "Kiernan, you know I couldn't stay."

She shook her head, nervously biting her lower lip. "Oh, Daniel! I was almost glad! You might have survived very well up there."

He arched a brow to her. "Is my brother changing you into a Yank, Kiernan?"

She flushed, and he was sorry he had spoken. No one could be more torn than Kiernan. Her heart had been so completely for the Confederacy—and yet her love for Jesse had proven stronger than any war. She and Daniel had been friends all of their lives, good friends. But even as she greeted him now with warmth and tender concern, he knew she was wishing that another Yankee soldier was also coming home for Christmas.

"Never mind," Daniel said quickly. He slipped an arm around her shoulders and turned to his sister. "Christa! Will we be able to have a Christmas dinner?"

"Of course," Christa said, her head high, a smile still teasing her lips. "We've had no battles on the property, Daniel, nor even skirmishes. The closest difficulty has been in Williamsburg. So we've all manner of good things. I gave a number of chickens and several cows and numerous bales of hay to a group collecting for the cause the other day, but everything is running very well. Kiernan and I do quite nicely, really."

Daniel laughed. "Remember all the times Pa used to spend with Jesse and me determined we'd be very well-educated planters? Who would have thought you'd be the one to carry on with the family business!"

Christa grinned. "I have lots of help," she assured him, winking at Kiernan, and the three of them walked into the house.

It was good to be home. Jigger, the very dignified butler of Cameron Hall, was quick to see that Daniel was pampered during his stay. Some men had brought slaves or servants right to the battlefield with them, but neither Daniel nor Jesse had ever seen the right in dragging another man along in a fight that wasn't his. On the line, he took care of himself. Here at home, it felt good to let Jigger take charge of his life. That meant steaming hip baths with a brandy at his fingertips. Slippers ready to cushion his feet, soft cotton shirts to slip over his head. It meant coffee with rich heavy cream in the morning, and it meant eggs and ham and bacon. It meant fine tobacco. Being home was good.

Being home meant that he was even more amazed at how well the plantation was running. Kiernan and Christa could give him long accounts of everything that they had done, ledgers on planting and harvesting, sales of horses and livestock, the buying of carriages and equipment. Except for salt and sugar, they were almost entirely self-sufficient at Cameron Hall. They had lots of help, of course, because life at the house had really changed very little. Most of the slaves had stayed on as freemen, willing to work for wages, for the right to better their small cottages, and knowing that they could move on if they chose. Some had left. Several of their people had gone north and then come back, Christa told him. When he complimented her and Kiernan again, she was quick to remind him that Jigger ran the house, Janey had come back with Kiernan from Montemarte, and that Taylor Mumford, a freeman of mixed blood, ran the plantation just as he always had. Christa wasn't alone because Kiernan was there, Kiernan's father was nearby to advise them, and the children, Jacob and Patricia Miller, Kiernan's sister and brother-in-law from her first marriage, were always eager to help with the garden, or with making soap or candles, or whatever else might be necessary.

"And of course everyone dotes on the baby!"

The baby was his nephew, John Daniel Cameron, named for Kiernan's father and himself. Now six months old, he was creeping about the house with a thick thatch of raven-black hair and a pair of startling blue eyes and a set of lungs to defy any army. The very best part of being home, Daniel thought, was spending time with the baby. He liked to jiggle John Daniel on his knees after a meal while Christa, Kiernan, and Patricia amused him with the harpsichord and piano and all manner of songs.

It was just like old times; almost like old times. Walking with his sister by the river one morning, he looked back at the house, and a shiver seized him. He glanced back at Christa. She was growing older, and so very, very beautiful with her pale skin, ebony-dark hair, and crystal-blue eyes. There was a serenity and maturity about her now. In a yellow day dress, she was stunning. She was smiling at him. "What is it, Daniel?"

"I'm afraid every time I ride away."

She shook her head. "Daniel, we're safe here. The Rebs keep clear of us because it's your home. Even when the Yanks are on the peninsula, they stay away because it's Jesse's home."

"Yes," he said softly. "But, Christa . . . ."

"What?"

He shook his head. "It ought to be over," he said softly. "I've seen more men die, more men maimed, left limbless, emaciated. We fight better, but that Lincoln, he's a tenacious man. It's going to go on and on. And it's going to get worse. I've seen what happens when the battle actually comes to your doorstep. . . ."

He broke off. Damn. He was trying so damned hard not to think about her —Callie. He'd given his word; he hadn't traveled north. He'd come home.

Cameron Hall was a huge and magnificent plantation. Life here was complex, with ships still moving on the James, with the fields still bringing in an income, with meals an affair, with life rigorous but still played by the codes that Kiernan and Christa had learned as girls. And his sister and sister-in-law were still gowned in fine materials, with deep layers of petticoats, with hoops and stays.

While Callie survived alone. Serene, regal, she had come from a different life. She kept the farm running herself, in the hope that someone would come home. She'd survived in the very midst of battle, with windowpanes shot out and cannonballs in the very eaves of her home. Her clothing was not nearly so elegant.

Her beauty was every bit as deep.

And her mind just as cunning, for she had betrayed him so completely. He groaned, amazed that he could still feel the bitterness, the anger, the pain, so deeply.

"What is it, Daniel?"

"Nothing. I've just seen what happens when the battle hits home. Christa, if it comes to that, neither Yanks nor Rebs will care about our traditions. Both armies will be seeking food and supplies. Both will strip us bare. Both will burn the house to the ground if necessary. I want you to remember this, Christa. As much as we love it, this place is wood and brick. You and Kiernan and John Daniel and the others are what matter. Guard yourselves first, always. Promise me that."

"Daniel—"

"Promise me that!"

"I promise!" she said softly. Hand in hand, they walked back to the house together.

That night, they stayed up late, sipping cinnamon wine that Kiernan had made. The baby was put to bed, and Patricia and Jacob were encouraged to tell them all that they wanted for Christmas. Patricia wanted one of the new foals that had been born that spring, a little Arabian. Jacob wanted a sword and a uniform. "There will be time for that later," Daniel told him gruffly. The twins were sent to bed, and the three of them were left in the living room. "What do you want for Christmas?" Daniel asked Christa.

Kiernan laughed softly and answered for her. "His name is Captain Liam McCloskey. He was here on a reconnaissance ride out of Williamsburg soon after you and Jesse left last June. He's been back a few times since then. Buying grain."

"Really?" Curiously, Daniel looked at his sister. She was the shade of a tomato, but didn't deny anything. "How serious is this?"

Christa was looking at her fingers. "Well . . ."

"Well?" he said.

"Well, I believe he intends to find you when he can. He's asked me to marry him."

Marriage! Well, of course, she was all grown up now, and she was beautiful. It was such a huge step. Jesse should have been asked too. They should have done all kinds of checking up on this man, this captain. They should have known exactly where he came from and all about his family. Most of all, they should have known if he could care for Christa properly, if he could provide her all that she had grown up with.

But none of them would know, or could know. Who knew what would be left when the war was over.

I shouldn't say yes, I should meet him, Daniel thought.

But he loved Christa, and Christa was intelligent, and exuberant and beautiful and young, but she knew her own heart and he thought her a good judge of men. If she loved this captain, it was enough for him.

Daniel exhaled and then laughed. "I take it that you do want to marry him?"

"With all my heart. Daniel, have I your blessing?"

"Yes, with all my heart. I look forward to meeting this young man."

"That's all that I want for Christmas," she said softly. "What about you, Daniel?"

He couldn't say all the things on his mind. "I don't know. Let me think. Kiernan, what about you?"

She smiled. "That's easy. I just want to see Jesse."

He rose and kissed them both, and went on to bed. He stayed up half the night, looking out at the river.

Despite his lack of sleep, he rose very early. He walked out to the family graveyard where nearly two centuries of Camerons were lain to rest. For some reason, there was always peace to be had here. He walked back to the house and walked the length of the portrait gallery. Jassy and Jamie, the founders of the line, looked down upon him in their seventeenth-century finery. His great, great —he didn't know how many greats—grandparents. She'd had nothing when she had met Lord Cameron, so the legend went. Nothing but sheer guts and tenacity. Together, they had forged this place from the wilderness.

Dear God, let it stand! he thought.

But it wasn't so much a house that they had created, he thought. It was something intangible, something that had given him and Jesse the right to go their separate ways, and to love one another still. That something wouldn't live on in brick and stone and wood. It would live on in John Daniel Cameron, and Lord willing, in themselves.

He turned from the pictures and hurried down the elegant hall, rapping hard on Kiernan's door. She opened it, startled, her hair wild, her eyes wild, dressed in a white cotton nightgown with the baby on her hip.

"Daniel!"

He grinned. "You want Jesse for Christmas, eh? Well, I know where he is, and I'm going to get you to him. Get dressed, pack up, let's ride!"

She stared at him for a moment, then her face broke into a smile so beautiful he was convinced sacrificing the remaining days of his leave would be well worth this early trip back.

"Oh, Daniel!"

She kissed his cheek, then slammed the door on him, and he had to laugh. Within half an hour she had herself dressed, and Janey and the baby ready to travel.

It was difficult to say good-bye to Christa, but Christa was delighted for Kiernan.

It was difficult to ride away from home, because he wondered if he would ever come back.

They reached Richmond with little problem, and as they were there for the night, they once again attended an evening at the White House of the Confederacy. Many officers' wives were there, as were many officers, politicians, and socially prominent citizens. It was a curious war. Kiernan greeted old friends, some of whom snubbed her for being a Yankee's wife. One woman actually turned her back on her. But Varina took Kiernan's hand, mentioning that if she had time in the future, they could always use help at the hospital. Kiernan was surely experienced, having worked with such an excellent surgeon and physician.

The next morning they started out again. The roads were clear; the weather held. By late that night, they had returned to Daniel's encampment. The Yanks were right across the river.

"Welcome back, Colonel!" Billy Boudain called, seeing him approach his command tent. "What you got there, sir—oh, sorry ma'am!"

Daniel laughed. "I've got a Christmas present for my brother across the river," he said. "Billy, send out a messenger for me under a white flag. Ask the Yanks for a private rendezvous with Colonel Jesse Cameron, Medical Corp. I'll see him at the pontoon bridge."

"Yessir!"

That night at dusk Daniel rode down to the makeshift bridge the Yanks had used to cross the river. There were pickets—numerous pickets—on either side, and he was careful to call out that there was a meeting going to take place. He didn't feel like being shot by his own men, or getting Kiernan or the baby shot either. He left her in the shadow of the trees while he moved down by the water. A horseman stood on the other side.

"Jesse?"

"Daniel. I was hoping to see you. Merry Christmas, brother."

Daniel grinned. "I got a present for you, Jesse."

"You're living and breathing, Daniel. That's present enough."

Daniel shook his head. "This present is even better."

He turned back, and beckoned to Kiernan. She rode out from the trees, the baby in her arms. Slowly, she rode down to the river.

"Jesse?" Her voice, soft and feminine, touched the air.

"Kiernan! My God, Kiernan!"

She was off her horse, and running across the bridge. Jesse dismounted from Goliath and went running to greet her. Darkness fell over the moon, and they both disappeared in the shadows. Daniel heard their glad cries mingling in the night.

He smiled, and turned his horse away. He rode back to his tent, and gently refused the company of his men. He retired with a brandy bottle.

Later that night, Billy Boudain and some of the others arrived at his tent. He heard giggling, feminine giggling, and he knew they had arranged some companionship for the evening. In the pale light of muted camp fires he could see a woman's silhouette in his doorway. "Colonel, this is Betsy. She's heard a whole lot about you. She wants to wish you Merry Christmas."

Why not? Betsy was young, it seemed. Maybe even fresh at her profession. Hell, it was Christmas. It had been a long, long time.

In the shadows he could see the girl. She was small, slim, dark. Forget the world, forget the war, forget the night, he told himself.

But he could not. Visions swam before him. Visions of his own bronzed flesh entangled in silken hair that flamed like a fire run rampant. Of silver eyes that met his. Of a voice that whispered and caressed, beckoned and betrayed.

He could touch no other woman until he had found either his vengeance or his peace.

"Thanks, Billy," he said softly. "Young lady." He inclined his head to the girl. "I'm, er, well, I'm just in for the night. You all go on. Merry Christmas."

Billy was disappointed, but he had come to know Daniel, and he knew even his most polite tone of command. He bid Daniel good night and Merry Christmas.

Merry Christmas. Merry Christmas. Yes. Where are you tonight, Mrs. Callie Michaelson? Is your Christmas warm, is it full of wonder?

He did get through Christmas. And then into the new year.

And into more battles.

But even as the battles began to rage, he had no idea what 1863 would bring.

They were well into the year before he even heard of that little town in Pennsylvania called Gettysburg.

Sixteen

May 1863

"*L*ord God, he's down! Stonewall is down, he's been shot by his own troops!"

The agitated cry of a Reb horseman was the first that Daniel heard of the injury to Stonewall Jackson.

He was down, Daniel thought quickly, but that didn't mean that he wouldn't be up again. Men were frequently injured.

And injury frequently meant death.

He'd been in his tent, dictating his own current situation to Billy Boudain, who was proving to have a marvelous craft with letters. He was surely the finest staff assistant that Daniel had ever had.

The fighting was over for the day. Again, some of the fiercest fighting Daniel had seen. They were at Chancellorsville, and Jackson had just completed one of the most amazing feats of military agility ever accomplished.

The general had cut short a visit to his wife on the twenty-ninth of April when he heard that one hundred thirty-four thousand Federal troops—now under the Union General "Fightin" Joe Hooker—were crossing the Rappahannock on both sides of Fredericksburg. It had been the first time he had ever seen his infant daughter, but he had rushed back to take command. Splitting his forces, he had sent troops against Major General John Sedgwick's left wing, and then he had taken the majority of his men into the wilderness near Spotsylvania. Daniel's troops had been with him, and they had driven the Federals back to Chancellorsville.

The next day, Jackson and Lee split the army again. Lee and his men faced Hooker at the front; Jackson completed his wide sweep around Hooker's flank to attack from the rear, and on the morning of May second, they completely routed the Federals.

Now they were saying that he was down.

"Soldier!" Daniel called out, stepping forward. "It's true? Jackson is injured?"

"Mightily, sir. He's been taken to a nearby farm."

"God help him!" Daniel murmured.

"Indeed, sir!"

And well God should be on his side, Daniel thought, for Stonewall was a deeply religious man. A disciplinarian, strange to many, stoic, and sworn to duty.

And necessary to Master Bobby Lee, Daniel thought.

There was nothing that he could do for Jackson, but all through the night, messengers rode back and forth, reporting on the general's condition.

By the late hours of the night, his wounded arm was amputated. He could survive still, Daniel thought, and he couldn't help but think of Jesse. He could survive if it could be kept from infection. If, there were so many ifs.

And there were still the Federals to be fought. . . .

The battle continued through the third and the fourth of May. At the end, Sedgwick and Hooker were forced back, and the Army of the Potomac was withdrawn. Though it was a southern victory, the Confederates also lost, and lost sorely.

On the tenth of May, General Thomas "Stonewall" Jackson died, succumbing to the pneumonia that had set in following his surgery. He died in the company of his beloved wife, and he died at peace with the God he had so worshipped. But he died a soldier still badly needed upon the battlefield.

The entire South mourned, and mourned deeply, no one more so than Robert E. Lee. Daniel had seen death hurt General Lee; he had seen the pain in the man's gray-blue eyes at the death of any soldier. He had never seen anything like the expression that now haunted that gallant gentleman with the loss of Jackson.

And still, the war went on.

Lee had made the decision to carry the war northward once again. There were very good reasons for doing this, the main one being that while the fighting went on in the South, it was the South that was being stripped of her resources. It would be far better to have the southern armies stripping the North for food and sustenance.

Also, there were many northerners wearying of the war. McClellan—Little Mac—the general Lincoln had removed from command, was now moving politically against Lincoln. He was planning to run for president of the U.S. McClellan wanted to sue for peace. If Lee could just bring the brutality and horror of warfare north, more and more northerners might begin to side with McClellan, and look forward to a negotiated peace. Then the Confederate States of America could move on separately.

On the western front, Union troops were beginning to move against Vicksburg, Mississippi. It was imperative that Vicksburg be held—the Mississippi River was one of the lifelines of the Confederacy.

The Rebels needed the war to end.

Daniel felt a growing heat begin to move in his veins. They would soon be traveling through Maryland once again.

Beauty had promised him time. He didn't know when it would come; he just prayed that it would come soon.

Don't let her forget me, he prayed in silence to himself. Don't let her forget that I am coming. . . .

As always, the emotions knotted tightly within him.

Callie could not forget him.

And certainly not the very beautiful morning of the twenty-fifth of May.

It began as a morning much like any other for her, for she awoke very early, dressed, and hurried down to feed the animals.

She felt the first twinges in her back while she was doling out grain and hay, and the next came while she was throwing out feed to the chickens. She barely noticed the first, and the second only gave her a momentary qualm. It was really too early for the baby. He—or she—wasn't due until June. When June came she had planned on moving into town, near Doctor Jamison. He might not approve of her, but he was a good and kindly man and he'd not see anything bad happen to her or an innocent infant.

She still had so much to do. The vegetables in the garden were almost ready for jarring to see her through the winter. She was in the midst of making several little winter sacques for the baby, and she had recently gone into a frenzy of spring cleaning.

The cleaning didn't matter, the jarring didn't matter. In fact, very little seemed to matter when the third pain came streaking through her spine and around her middle like a bolt of vicious, clutching lightning.

She was in the back, by the paddock, and she staggered with the onslaught of it, reaching out for the fence. For a moment she was so startled that she didn't even think; then it slowly dawned on her that she must be having the baby.

The pain faded. It remained with her for a moment, then it disappeared so completely that she began to wonder if she hadn't imagined it.

Perhaps she had. She turned around and walked toward the well, drew up a bucket of water, and sipped a dipper full of it. She felt fine. Perfectly fine.

Still, perhaps she should lie down for a few minutes. She was here alone, with no one to care exactly what time anything got done. She very seldom received visitors from town anymore. Her condition was known, and on occasion, when she had gone in for supplies, old friends had actually turned their backs on her. It didn't matter, she had told herself, fighting back the first sting of tears. When the war ended, when her brothers returned, she would take the baby and she would leave. She'd heard marvelous stories about New York City and Washington D.C., and she dreamed of a day when she could go there.

After she had seen Daniel.

And what? Apologized for the fact that she'd sent him to a prison camp?

He was coming back for her. He'd warned her that he would.

She felt a quivering take flight inside of her and she tried to swallow her thoughts of the man. She was always trying to do that. To forget the excitement, and the love, and the fear. The color of his eyes and the slow sensual drawl of his voice.

"Stop!" she commanded herself aloud.

But it was impossible to stop thinking of a man in her current condition. When people turned away from her. When she was so heavy that she dragged herself about.

When she could feel the movement of life within her.

Damn them all, she thought. She loved the baby, loved it fiercely. A tiny creature who would need her, who would love her and trust her, who would not condemn her.

She started to walk away from the well. She felt dizzy. She should lie down.

But even as she walked toward the house, she felt a sudden onslaught of water. It was so startling, soaking her skirt and her petticoat and pantalets, seeming to come like a river. She had no experience with human birth whatsoever, but having lived on a farm her entire life, she was very much aware that she had lost her waters, and that the baby must come soon, or die.

"Oh, no!" she cried softly to the morning air. She had never felt more alone. Nor had she ever felt such fear. Women died in childbirth. Frequently. She wasn't terrified of death itself—too many people she loved dearly had already gone before her—but the idea of having her baby live with no one to find it or tend to it was terrifying.

She stood there a moment, drenched and freezing in the cool morning air. Should she try on her own to reach town? The birth could take hours, she knew that, perhaps she had time.

But even as she finally found movement and began to walk to the house, a pain was upon her again. It was so sharp and horrible that she screamed, heedless of the sound. She doubled over, shocked, stunned by the intensity of it.

This was going to go on for hours?

She grit her teeth against the pain, and then she tried to inhale and exhale with it.

She wasn't going to be able to go anywhere. She was going to have to move very quickly. She needed to sterilize a knife for the cord, she needed blankets, she . . .

She needed not to be alone!

She reproached herself furiously for not having taken into consideration the fact that the child might come early. She saw pictures of herself too weak to force out the child. Bleeding to death. Dying with no one to hear her screams, or to care for the tiny life inside of her that she loved so passionately.

Move! she commanded herself, and with the pain still tight around her, she hurried into the house and into the kitchen, seeking a knife to sever the baby's cord. Now she needed to gather fresh bedding and cloths to clean the baby and herself and tiny garments for the baby to wear.

She gripped the doorway as she left the kitchen. She was shivering like a blown leaf tossed in winter, trying to block her mind. But it was then that she saw a picture of Daniel. Laughing, casual, standing in the doorway, watching her. His smile so beautiful, his eyes so seductive. She could remember everything about him so clearly. The breadth of his shoulders, the bronze of his flesh. The feel of it, oh, the feel of it, so warm, so supple, so powerful, beneath her fingers. She could remember the way she had wanted him. Wanted so much she would willingly be damned for just one touch.

She remembered his anger, remembered his eyes.

She suddenly began to laugh. "Oh, Daniel! If you wanted revenge, here it is! No one could be more terrified than I at this moment!"

She started to laugh hard, but then once again, a pain came around her. Hard, tight, instant, growing.

She'd been to Doctor Jamison. He had looked down his spectacled nose at her, and he had been totally disapproving of her. But he had told her that the pains might come slowly, that they might last all day. That she would be near to time when the pains came very near one another. Most first births took a long time.

Of course, there were exceptions.

"Oh!" Her laughter became a scream, but she didn't care, there was no one to hear her. She was wet and freezing, and she didn't care about that either.

She waited for the pain to ebb, and then she pushed away from the door. She started to walk through the parlor, anxious to reach the stairs.

Another pain came, before the first had really faded. Panic seized her, and then an agony unlike anything she had ever imagined. She buckled down on the stairs, fighting the tears that sprang to her eyes, fighting to retain some control over the awful pain. It clutched like rivulets, like fingers, starting at her lower back, sweeping all around the circumference of her abdomen. She could bear it in the front; it was the agony at her spine that was so very vicious. How much could she stand?

Whatever came. She had no choice.

She started to rise from the stairs. It seemed that the pain came immediately. She cried out and fell again, and for a moment, there was blackness, the pain was so fierce. The blackness lifted, and she ceased to care for her own life, or for that of her child.

She just wanted someone to walk in and shoot her and put her out of her agony.

"Dear, dear, dear!"

Dimly, she heard a voice. A gentle, soothing, female voice. Then she heard a clucking sound, and soft, gentle arms were around her. She blinked and looked up.

Helga Weiss was there, and Rudy Weiss was right behind her. It was Helga who held her, Helga who spoke softly, giving her strength, giving her assurance.

"Poor child, poor child!" she clucked again. "All alone here and soaking wet and the babe on its way. Rudy, we must get her to bed. And into something dry."

Callie shook her head, tears suddenly streaming down her cheeks as she stared at the woman. "I'm going to die," she said.

Helga laughed kindly. "No, no. You are not going to die. Helga is here."

Helga tisked away as she and Rudy carried Callie up the stairs. Then Rudy was sent away, and Helga worked on her own. In minutes, Callie was in a warm gown. The pains still continued to assail her, but Helga talked her through them, and the panic that had seized her was gone. The pains remained very close together.

The closer they came, the more she wished that Helga would just shoot her instead of trying to talk to her.

No! Daniel ought to be shot. Prison wasn't good enough for him. He ought to be shot, and then she ought to be shot.

"Hold tight, it will be soon!" Helga told her.

Callie told Helga where she thought she should go.

But the kindly German woman never lost her gentleness, no matter how Callie tossed or screamed, or fought her assurances. Then, along with the pains, came a new sensation, the desperate desire to push.

"What do I do?" she begged Helga.

Helga competently looked into the situation and smiled at her, smoothing back her hair. "You push, Frau Michaelson. You push. Your little one is here."

It wasn't quite that easy. The pains remained savage, and she had to push and push and push. She thought that she passed out again, she strained so hard, but Helga was telling her that the head had been born and that they needed another shoulder, and another shoulder.

She heard the cry. Her baby's cry. Drenched in sweat and tears she cast her head back and began to laugh, and then to cry again, and the sensations seemed to overwhelm her. That cry! That pathetic little cry. It reached inside her and touched her heart, and filled her body with wonder. The tears, the laughter, both remained as she reached out to Helga. Helga, smiling like a saint, handed her the bundle of her baby, so tiny! And so, so beautiful! He was a little pinched, and very much a mess, but so beautiful. He screamed like a banshee!

It was a he!

"Helga! A little boy!"

"A son, yes. A beautiful, beautiful son."

Callie forgot all about the pain. She barely noticed as Helga cut and tied the cord, and she was heedless of all sensation as Helga reminded her that they were not done, that she must deliver the afterbirth.

Callie didn't care. She had already forgotten that she had wanted Helga to shoot her.

Her hands were on her tiny son. She was counting fingers and toes, and she was marveling at the exquisite beauty of her baby. Hers.

"Come, come now," Helga told her. "Into a new gown with you. And now, I must have the baby. You won't recognize him when I give him back. He will be so beautiful; you will see!"

Callie held him for a minute, then released him to Helga. She closed her eyes, overcome with wonder. Then, amazingly, she slept.

When she awoke, she was completely disoriented. She remembered her baby, and she bolted up, panicking.

But Helga was there, sitting in a rocker by a fire she had built against the coolness of the night. She was singing softly in German.

"May I see him?" Callie whispered.

Helga gave her one of her beautiful smiles. "He wants his mother. He has waited patiently, but now he is hungry."

Callie reached out for the baby and Helga brought him to her. He took one look at her and began to howl. Helga laughed, and Callie fumbled a little with her gown, then awkwardly tried to lead him to nurse. His mouth was so wide against such a tiny face!

But her son instinctively knew what he wanted. The wide but tiny mouth closed over her breast. The first tug that touched her as he suckled sent a new wave of emotion sweeping through her, emotion so strong that tears instantly rose to her eyes again and her heart seemed to warm there within her chest, beneath the little body. With trembling fingers she touched his head. It was covered with ink-black hair. She touched his hand, resting against her breast, and she was in awe of the perfection of the little fingers. Nothing that had come before could matter now. Nothing. People could turn their backs to her; they could damn her. None of it mattered. He mattered. This precious child. Her child.

"Jared?" She looked at Helga.

Helga shrugged. "It's a fine name. But perhaps he should be named for his father."

Callie lowered her lashes. "Jared was my father. It is a fine name."

The baby fell asleep, right against her flesh. Helga came to move him. Callie didn't want to release him. "You need something to eat," Helga told her. "You will need strength. For him."

Callie released the baby. Helga had made him a bed in one of the dresser drawers. She set him down to sleep. "I've made soup. I will bring it," Helga told her.

It struck Callie just how wonderful this woman had been to her. She reached out for Helga's hand. "Thank you. Thank you so much, Helga. You have been so good to me. And surely, in your eyes, what I have . . . done," she said lamely, "must be so very bad."

Helga smiled. "All around us there is death. Today, there is life. God has given us this beautiful life. What can be bad? You are good, Callie. You are good, and life is good. And God has let me be here." She squeezed Callie's hand. Callie smiled.

"Thank you so much!" she whispered again.

Helga hesitated. "You must find the baby's father."

"When the war is over," Callie said.

"He has a right to know about this child."

What rights did Daniel have? Callie didn't know. She felt the usual shivering seize her. All she really knew was that Daniel hated her, that he had promised to come back. She had never, never forgotten the look in his eyes.

"He's in prison," she told Helga. "When the war is over, I will find him. I promise."

She was still shivering. She had time. The war was nowhere near being over. Maybe Daniel would not care. Maybe he would not want to acknowledge the child.

Maybe he would want to strangle her, and take the child.

She moistened her lips. For the first and only time, she was grateful that the war was going on.

And that as long as the battles waged, Daniel would be safely locked away.

In the days that followed, Callie quickly regained her strength.

Helga and Rudy stayed with her nearly a week, but then she felt very well and she was anxious to get on with life in the way that she must learn to live it. It was not so difficult. Jared was demanding, but he slept frequently, and she was able to manage very well. She felt wonderful. She was so very in love with her child that she felt more exuberant than ever. She walked with a new spring to her step, and lived for the moments when she could just lie with the baby and inspect him over and over again.

By the time that he was three weeks old, his resemblance to his father was startling. It was more than the ink-black hair or the startling blue eyes. His mouth was Daniel's, his nose was Daniel's, the set of his brow was Daniel's.

Callie often lay on the bed with the baby sleeping beside her, seeing Jared, feeling the softness of his breath, remembering Daniel.

She had loved him so fiercely.

But he hated her. Hated her with as much passion as he had ever loved her. She had betrayed him. He would never let her explain. He would never believe that she had fought only for his life.

Every time she thought of Daniel, she began to shiver again. It was best not to think of him.

She couldn't look at Jared and not think of him.

And then came the rumors that the southern army was going to come north again.

Lee wanted to attack.

In Virginia, the armies were beginning to move.

On the eighth of June, Lee attended a review of Jeb Stuart's troops at Culpepper Courthouse.

Word reached them that on the westward front, the Yanks had reached Briarfield, Confederate President Jefferson Davis's home. They had burned it to the ground.

Two days later, Beauty Stuart's cavalry were able to pursue their anger at any and all insults, for Union cavalry met them at Brandy Station, Virginia.

The most furious clash of cavalry in all the war took place that day.

For Daniel, commanding his troops, it was a nightmare like none other. Horses trampled men and other horses, guns were emptied of their shot and used as clubs. Sabres slashed and rained down death, creating bright red streams of death.

And through it all, the cries of the animals and the men met and melded, and as the day progressed, Daniel could no longer ascertain whether it was a man or beast who screamed in ragged agony at his side.

Time and again, he just missed the blade of a Yankee sword; time and again he felt a bullet whiz by his cheek so close that he could hear the rush and whisper of the displaced air.

Time and again he wondered how he could live, how he could survive the awful mechanics of the day.

But he did survive; and the battle did end. The Yankees had come on reconnaissance, and perhaps they had learned something of the southern troop movements. But it was the southerners who had held their ground.

Brandy Station was theirs. For what it was worth. Brandy Station, littered with the dead and the dying.

In the dusk he looked over the death-littered terrain and shuddered. He set his fingers before him in the coming darkness. He hadn't sustained a single scratch.

He didn't want to think of the death he had wrought himself.

A shivering seized him. This battle was over. They were no closer to a certain victory than they had been before it.

But now they were really moving north. He'd been given partial orders already about moving his troops. The North had been testing their movements—now it was his turn to test the movements of the Yanks.

Through Maryland, on up to Pennsylvania.

Again, he felt the most curious trembling sweep through him. He closed his eyes tightly. It had been a long time. A long, long time since he had stepped foot on that Maryland soil.

A few days later, Jeb gave him their orders. They were to move ahead. Lee's ultimate goal would be Harrisburg, Pennsylvania. The cavalry was to move on.

As always, the horsemen were ordered to be the eyes and ears of the South.

"I want my time in Maryland," Daniel told Jeb. The words were almost cold.

"Not on the campaign north. You'll get your time on the return south. You've got my word."

Beauty's word was as good as gold. Daniel knew that he would see her soon, and the excitement and the bitterness and the fury and the passion all churned tightly within him.

There would be fierce battles in the North.

They didn't matter. He knew that he was going to live because he had to see her again.

He didn't know at that moment that his emotions would run even more deeply when he saw her again at last.

And he had no way of knowing that there was a city called "Gettysburg" to stand in his way.

At the moment, it was nothing more than a little speck on the map.

Seventeen

As it happened, Daniel and Stuart and his cavalry arrived late for the battle.

By the time they made it, a day and a half of bloody fighting had already occurred, fields were already strewn with the dead, and a great debate over what was going wrong was already in process.

Some said it was the first major battle Lee was having to fight without his right-hand man, Stonewall. Some said that Stuart, in his attempt to make another great sweep around the Union army, had ridden too far and deprived Lee of his eyes and ears.

In their journey north, the cavalry had become involved in battle again and again. Even after the inconclusive battle at Brandy Station, there had been skirmishes at Aldie, Middleburg, and Upperville. On the twenty-second of June, Lee gave Stuart discretionary orders, permitting the cavalry to harass the Union infantry. Stuart and his men were also to guard the army's right flank, remain in communication, and gather supplies.

They came close—very close—to the Maryland farmland where Callie lived. So damn close that he could almost reach out and touch it. So damn close that the thought of desertion touched both his heart and mind. At that, he had to convince himself she had become an obsession.

She might not even be there. Who knew? Perhaps she had turned from him to her Yank cavalry comrade, the damned Captain Dabney who had delivered the coup de grace once Callie had disarmed him.

Maybe she had married him.

It didn't matter. She could have married a hundred men, he was still going back for her. But not now. He could not give in to his desire and pursue her, even though they passed so near. His honor was at stake, he reminded himself dryly. Ah, yes, honor and ethics! Without them, what were they?

They rode very hard, and they rode very fast. On the twenty-seventh, late in the day, they crossed the Potomac. On the twenty-eighth they captured one hundred and twenty-five Federal wagons, but the capture was surely a mixed blessing, for the wagons slowed them down.

They rode all night toward Pennsylvania, slowed down by their wagons and their prisoners. Near Hood's Mill, they destroyed part of the Baltimore and Ohio railroad. At noon they rode on to Westminster, and there they were attacked by Federal cavalry.

They were victorious, repulsing the Yanks, but the Yanks, like the wagons, had cost them time. The next day they entered Hanover, Pennsylvania, and immediately, they were charged by another Union brigade. Once again, they repulsed the Federals, but only after a savage battle had been fought. When it was done, they rode on through the night, halting at Dover.

On the morning of July first, they rested and fed their mounts.

They had no idea that Lee's army, having heard nothing from Stuart, had stumbled into the battle of Gettysburg.

A message reached Stuart by late afternoon. It was then that he and Daniel and a few other officers rode hard ahead of the brigades to report to Lee at Gettysburg.

And Lee, the careful gentleman, the ultimate officer, looked hard at Stuart and said, "Well, General Stuart, you are here at last."

But the matter went no further; there was a battle to be fought. Daniel found himself quickly thrown into communications, surveying the landscape of the area. He was assigned a young captain from Tennessee to explain the current positions and situation. His name was Guy Culver, and he was an excellent horseman. Though he'd barely graduated from the VMI before the onset of war, he had a good sense of strategy, and was quick to give Daniel a good overview in one of the command tents.

"Can you beat it, Colonel, it all began over shoes! There was this big advertisement, you see, for shoes, in Gettysburg. So we have a brigade under Heth marching down the Chambersburg Pike and they're seen by some Union cavalry. Well, the Union cavalry commander must have decided that this place held strategic importance—it does, there's nine roads go through here—and he engages his cavalry with our infantry. Before you know it, both sides are calling for reinforcements, and now, the bulk of both armies are engaged."

He spread out a map of the area, and Daniel quickly acquainted himself with the layout of the area.

He spent what was left of the day riding from one area of carnage to another. Little Round Top, Big Round Top. Culp's Hill, Cemetery Hill, the peach orchard, the wheatfield, Devil's Den. The fighting was fierce, the battles were savage. At the end of the day, the fighting came to a halt with a last abortive Confederate assault upon Culp's Hill.

After two horrible days of fighting, Lee was still determined to hold. That night he laid out his plan for a direct assault against Cemetery Ridge. General Longstreet protested, but Lee was determined. The Union Army was under Meade now, but the Union had a history of dissolving quickly under pressure, and a reputation for retreat.

Stuart and his cavalry were to attack the Union rear from the east.

But Daniel was still assigned to communications. Few men, even among Stuart's fine cavaliers, could ride as fast or as hard as Daniel, and few seemed to have quite as many lives. While Jesse had managed to keep Goliath fit and well during these two long years of war, Daniel had lost at least seven horses from beneath him.

Lee did not want to be blinded again.

By noon, a seven-hour assault upon Culp's Hill was giving the Confederates no success. Lee decided to send eleven brigades against the very center of the Union line. Stuart would come from the rear; the other men, led by General George Pickett's fresh division, would charge straight across the field upon the Union line.

It was ominous, Daniel thought. Silence pervaded the field; dear Lord, it seemed like forever. It was only an hour.

Then the cannons began to roar. For two hours, Confederate gunners sent a barrage soaring across the heavens. The sky became sickly gray. The noise was deafening. Firestorms exploded.

And then, again, silence.

After that silence came the awful sound of the Rebel yell, and with startling, near perfect precision, thirteen thousand Confederate soldiers came marching out across the field. They were awesome; they were majestic. They moved like a curse of God, and they moved with a stunning courage and devotion to God and duty and state.

They were mown down, just the same.

The Federal artillery burst upon the men, and they fell. They fell with horrible screams; they fell, men destroyed. Canisters sprayed out their death.

And still, the men charged on.

There was no help from the rear assault, Daniel discovered, for riding around the action he found Stuart and the cavalry engaged in a fierce battle and gaining no ground.

Sweeping back around with his information for Lee, Daniel found the remnants of the charging Confederates limping, crawling, staggering back to their own line.

He found Lee, the grand old gentleman, there to greet them. "It's all my fault. It's all my fault."

Pickett's Charge was over.

Indeed, Gettysburg was over.

There was nothing to do but count the losses. That night, the estimates were horrible. Nearly four thousand Rebs killed, nearly twenty thousand injured, and over five thousand missing.

Then there was the battlefield. In all that he had seen, in all that he had witnessed, Daniel had never known a sensation like standing on Seminary Ridge and looking down over the fields of devastation. Men moved among the fields of bodies. Sad bodies, twisted bodies, destroyed bodies. Young bodies, old bodies, enemies embraced again in death.

Now the medics moved among them, and again, Daniel thought of his brother, and he knew that Jesse must be out there, that he must be up to his elbows in blood. He wished that he could be with him, that he could help him. It didn't matter to him that night whether the injured were Reb or Yank. War was horrible. And it would not end.

He looked down and saw one of their own regimental physicians moving about the wounded. He started down toward him, walking first, then running. The doctor, a Captain Greeley, looked at him, startled.

"Colonel!"

"Tell me what to do. I'm a fairly decent assistant in a surgery."

"But Colonel—"

"I am at my leisure, sir, at the moment, if such a thing can exist on such a night. I am not a doctor, but I know something of medicine. God knows what lives I have taken. I wish to help save those that I might tonight."

Greeley still seemed unnerved that a cavalry colonel was offering assistance in such a way. But he shrugged, and he asked Daniel to pick up a young man he had found still breathing by a tree stump. "We've not enough stretchers. We've not enough doctors. We've not enough anything," he finished lamely.

"Then any hands will help," Daniel said, and he scooped up the private with the blood-spattered uniform.

For the next hour, he served by searching out the living. There weren't enough stretchers. He found a few of his men to help, and he knew that they had made a difference while the hours wore on. Greeley stopped him before he could make a return trip, asking him then to help in the surgery.

He had done it before. Yet nothing made it easy.

He helped hold down the men while Greeley removed limbs. He tried to talk to them; there was nothing to stem the cries. All that could help a limb so shattered was its removal.

He didn't know how many men he had assisted with when an orderly brought in a figure he knew well.

It was Billy Boudain.

"Colonel!"

Billy's handsome face was pinched and gray. He smiled nonetheless. "They let you ride in to surgery, eh?"

Daniel didn't like the look of Billy. He was too gray. He smiled in turn anyway, knowing how important the will to live could be.

"Hell, you know I have some acquaintance with what I'm doing, right, Billy?"

"That I do, sir. That I do."

"What did you do, Billy? Get too close to one of those Yankees?"

"Hell, sir, I wasn't close at all. Something exploded by me, and I just woke up a few minutes ago, it seems."

"It's going to be right as rain, won't it, Doctor Greeley?"

Greeley had peeled back Billy's cavalry shirt. His face lifted to Daniel's, and Daniel instantly saw in his eyes that there was no way at all. Daniel glanced down to Billy's chest. Bone and blood were shattered and mingled.

He almost cried out. He felt tears welling behind his eyes, stinging his lids, and he fought them, furious with himself. Officers could not cry, and Camerons never gave way, and by God, he would not be weak, especially not now, not now when Billy needed him so much.

He curled his fingers around Billy's hand. "Just hold tight and breath easy, Billy."

"I'm going to die, Colonel."

"No, Billy—"

"Don't tell me that I'm not, sir. I can feel death. It's cold. It—it doesn't hurt."

Daniel choked, then knelt down by Billy. "Billy, you can't die on me. I'm going to take you home with me to Cameron Hall. Billy, you've never seen anything quite like it. The grass is as green as emeralds and it rolls and slopes down to the river. The trees are tall and very thick, and there's always a breeze, so they sway there. And there's a porch, Billy, a broad, wide porch, and you can just sit there and feel the breeze—"

"And sip on a whiskey, eh, sir?"

"Whiskey, brandy, julep, whatever you've a mind for, Billy. We'll get back there."

Billy's fingers tightened around his. "The grass is like emeralds?"

"Just like."

Billy coughed. Blood spilled from his lips. "Pray for me, Colonel. Someday, we'll meet again. In an Eden, just like Cameron Hall."

"Billy—"

Billy's hand tightened, and then went limp. Daniel's fingers curled around him. He grated his teeth hard.

"He's gone, Colonel," Greeley said softly.

Daniel nodded.

"We need the table."

"Yes."

Daniel lifted Billy in his arms, and walked out of the surgery with him. He walked into the night, and found a tree, and sat down beneath it, still cradling Billy in his arms.

He sat so for a long time. Tall cavalry boots appeared at his side.

"A friend, Daniel?"

Stuart, worn, haggard, and weary, sat down beside him. He didn't seem to notice that his friend cradled a corpse.

"You've got to let him go, Daniel."

Daniel nodded. "He wouldn't be here if it weren't for me. I brought him out of Old Capitol."

"God decides what happens to all of us, Daniel. And God knows, I failed Lee these last days!"

"We've lost a big one," Daniel agreed.

"Armistead is dead; Pickett has sworn that he will never forgive Lee. And what can any of that matter to all the boys, Union and Confederates, who have gone on from here. Hell, Daniel, any of us can die at any time. But it's God's will, not mine, not yours."

They were both silent for a minute.

"We begin a retreat, you know." Stuart motioned to someone. A soldier walked over and saluted Daniel sharply. He reached for Billy's body.

Daniel gave it up.

"Yes," he said to Stuart.

"We're going south, through Maryland once again. We'll be a long time regrouping from this one. I'll give you your time now, if Meade doesn't follow us. If Meade does follow us, God alone knows what will happen. But if the Union does not attack, you may have the time I promised you. Do whatever it is that you're so desperate to do in Maryland. I'll give you until the end of the month. Then report back to me."

Daniel looked at Stuart.

Maryland.

Yes . . .

It was time to see her again.

Callie could see the movement of part of the armies as they headed north.

They didn't travel a path that led directly by her farm. They remained at quite a distance, and it was only with her brother Josiah's glass that she was able to see them clearly at all, and that from her bedroom window.

From the first moment she saw a gray uniform and the straggle of poorly clad men around it, she knew that the Rebels were advancing again.

Her heart seemed to leap to her throat. Rebels. Coming here, coming after her.

No. There was only one Rebel who might be coming after her, and he could not possibly be doing so. She was so grateful. She'd heard about the huge cavalry battle in Virginia, and she'd had to sit down and hug her knees to her chest, grateful that Daniel could not have been part of it, that his name could not have appeared on the list of the dead.

Now the Rebels were heading north again. She closed her eyes, and prayed. Prayed that the battlefield would not be her front lawn again, that she wouldn't have to see the awful horror of war.

Her eyes flew open and she prayed simply that they would not come her way at all.

There were more and more deserters these days. From both armies. Some of these men could be dangerous. She hadn't only herself to worry about anymore.

She had Jared.

Fear drove her to the room she had set up as a nursery for her son. He was sleeping, but she slipped him up into her arms anyway and held him close. She'd die before she'd let anyone harm him in any way.

She squeezed him so tight that he awoke and let out a cry of protest.

"My love, my little love, I'm so sorry!" she said softly. He quieted, studying her with his wide blue eyes. He let out a little cooing sound and pursed his lips, and she laughed. Well, she had woken him up. He thought it was time to eat.

She carried him to the old rocker in his room and sat with him, rocking while he nursed. She ran her fingers over his silky ink-black hair, and when she closed her eyes, she couldn't help but think of Daniel again, and her thoughts were torn. Thank God he could not reach her. Dear God, but she had to reach him. One day.

He'd merely want to throttle her. Perhaps he wouldn't want anything to do with the baby.

Perhaps he would want the baby and nothing at all to do with her.

Her pulse beat too quickly with just the thought. Guiltily she realized she had been thinking once again it was a good thing the war raged on.

No, no, Lord, I did not mean that!

The war was horrible. Jeremy and Josiah were outside of Vicksburg, Mississippi. Jeremy had written to her about the awful battles they had fought, and how they were trying to starve out the population of Mississippi. There were those who managed to get in and out of the city, and Jeremy's letters were full of pity for the citizens who were living in caves in the hills—and dining upon rats when they were lucky enough to catch them.

No, no, God, let the war end! she prayed fervently.

She heard the sound of a wagon. A sizzle of fear ripped through her, and she jumped up, holding Jared tightly to her.

She looked down from the window and breathed a sigh of relief as she saw that the wagon below carried Rudy and Helga Weiss.

"Callie!" Rudy called to her, standing up in the wagon.

She looked out of the window. "Hello! I'm here."

"Thank the Lord!" Helga muttered.

Curiously, Callie watched as Rudy helped his wife from the wagon. She hurried down the stairs, the baby still in her arms.

She met the two of them at the back door. Helga burst in, sweeping the baby from her arms, and murmuring to him in soft German. Callie looked at Rudy, her brows lifted.

"You are all right? You haven't been disturbed?"

She shook her head. "I'm fine."

Rudy sighed and sank into a kitchen chair, mopping his brow.

"They came through our place, they did."

"Who?"

Rudy grimaced. "First a Confederate major. He left us a wad of his Confederate money, and took almost everything that moved on the property, goats, chicken, cows. Then, not long after, another soldier comes by. This one is all dressed up in a blue uniform. He lays another wad of money on the table, and cleans us out of everything that the Rebels forgot to take!"

"Oh, Rudy!" Callie murmured. She sat down across from him. "Did they take your grain and everything else too?"

"Everything."

"Well, then, you must help yourselves to what I have here."

"Nein, nein! We did not come to take from you—we came to be certain that you were all right. Our people need very little, and we look after one another."

"But I don't need all that I have. You would help me if you took some of the animals."

"Perhaps the armies will still stumble upon you," Rudy said wearily.

"Then they might as well stumble upon me with half of what I have, right?" she said cheerfully.

Rudy argued, Helga argued. But before she would allow them to leave, she had a goat tied to their wagon and a dozen chickens within it, along with several sacks of grain and numerous jars of her preserves and pickled vegetables.

A few days later, Rudy was back.

"Callie, you must be careful. Come home with me."

"Why?"

"The battle has been fought. A big, horrible battle. They say that between both sides, near fifty thousand men were killed or injured."

"Oh, my God!" Callie gasped.

"They are coming home. The Rebs are coming home. They will come limping and worn and hurt. And many will pass by here. Come home with me."

Callie shook her head. She felt an awful dread, and an awful anticipation.

Her heart was beating too hard once again.

He couldn't be among them. He was in prison. Thank God, she had really done something good. She had kept him from the horror, from the death, from the blood.

He would never see it that way.

"Callie, come with me!"

She shook her head, feeling an awful fascination. Pity filled her heart, and the startling certainty that she had to stay. She had to offer them water on their long journey homeward, if nothing more.

Perhaps there would be someone who knew him.

Someone who could tell her that he was still in Washington, that he lived, that he was well.

She shook off the awful shivers that seized her. "Rudy, I cannot come. I must stay here."

"Callie."

She didn't understand it herself. "I must stay, Rudy. I—I simply must. Maybe I can help. Maybe I can do something."

Rudy shook his head. "These men . . . these men are the enemy."

"A beaten enemy."

"This war is not over."

"I will be all right, Rudy. I need to see these men. I need to hear what has happened."

He argued with her, but she would not be budged. She simply could not fight the compulsion to stay.

Eventually, as Rudy had said, the men began to come back. Slowly. Beaten, ragged, weary.

And Callie found herself down by the well.

And it was there that she stood when Daniel Cameron rode into her life once again.

Rode in worn, weary, ragged.

And furious still!

"Angel . . ."

Interlude

DANIEL

July 4, 1863
Near Sharpsburg
Maryland

*P*erhaps, after the long months of waiting, of dreaming, of seeing her in his sleep, of hearing her voice even in the midst of shells, he had not believed that she could be as beautiful as he had remembered.

But she was.

Daniel watched as she offered his officer water. Watched her move, listened to the musical flow of her voice. Even as he did so, he felt his fingers curling into fists, felt a sizzling heat of fury and bitterness come sweeping through him. He had to hate her. She had used her beauty, used the softness of her voice, the fiery flow of her hair against him.

And still, she enchanted. Enchanted every man who passed her way. The word came to the lips of these men as easily as it had once come to his. Angel. God alone could have sculpted such a face. Created the color of her hair, the pools of her eyes.

This sweet creature from heaven!

And seductress born of Hell, he reminded himself, swallowing hard. Looking at her a man could forget that she had so sweetly coerced and lured him, forget the irons about his wrists, the days in prison, the cold dampness of Old Capitol, the misery, the humiliation.

By the gate, he dismounted from his horse and watched her.

Damn her. Was betrayal perhaps her business? Had other soldiers stumbled her way, had she seduced them, and seen them turned in, just as she had done with him?

God, he was weary! But no weariness could take away his fury at this moment! Had she but turned old and haggard, had she not been so unbelievably beautiful still! But there she stood. His angel. Their angel. Her dress so simple that it enhanced the perfection and loveliness of her womanhood.

Did she remember him?

Ah, but she would, he swore.

As the last of his cavalry soldiers passed by, Daniel came in to greet her by the well.

"Angel of mercy indeed. Is there, perhaps, a large quantity of arsenic in that well?"

She didn't move, but just stood there. The slight breeze lifted her hair, and in the coming night it seemed to burn with a dark fire. She seemed to gaze about him, and then her eyes fell on his, wide, gray. Did they dilate, perhaps? He felt the grinding of his teeth, the tearing emotion sweep through him. If she was afraid in the least of his revenge, she showed no sign of it. She stood like crystal, no, porcelain, still and perfect, the perfect heart of her face an ivory softly tinted rose at the cheeks, her beautiful lips as red as any long forgotten rose, her eyes, as always, silver orbs that shimmered and taunted the soul.

He smiled suddenly. She certainly wasn't going to cower. She was, as ever, ready for battle.

"Hello, angel!" he said softly.

Still she was silent, proud and silent. Yet at last he could see the rise and fall of her breasts with the uneven whisper of her breath; he could see a pulse at her throat, beating there in fury. Why? he wondered. Was it fear at last? Did his angel realize that a man cast into hell came back by far the worse for wear?

The heat was ripping through him, tearing through his limbs, spiraling around his chest, and tightening low in his groin. Well, here he was at last. Standing before her as he had dreamed so often, as he sometimes felt he had survived to do. His fingers itched. Yes, he wanted to strangle her.

He wanted her. He wanted her with a blind fury, with a desperate desire. He wanted to hold her tightly and shake her, and he wanted to feel the softness of her flesh. He wanted to hear her cry out his name, and he didn't give a damn if it was with anger or despair or love or hatred. He wanted revenge, but most of all he wanted to cool the heat that imprisoned and embraced him, slake the thirst that lived with him day and night, through days of battle and days in the saddle, through rare moments of quiet, and even in the midst of the shrill shrieks of guns and cannons and men.

"Cat got your tongue?" he asked. Damn, it was hard to talk when his teeth were grating so. A slow, bitter smile curved his lip. "How very unusual. Weren't you expecting me?"

He didn't dare touch her. Not yet. He took the dipper from her fingers, lowered it into the bucket, and raised the water from her well to his lips. It was cool and sweet. It did nothing to ease the fire burning ever more brightly throughout his limbs.

He could see that she was wondering just what venue his anger would take. That pulse against the ivory white column was beating ever more rampantly.

"No poison? Perhaps some shards of glass?" he murmured.

He moved more closely toward her. His voice was husky, low and tense and trembling with the heat of his emotion. "You look as if you're welcoming a ghost, Mrs. Michaelson. Ah, but then, perhaps you had wished that I would be a ghost by now, long gone, dust upon the battlefield. No, angel, I am here." He was still as several seconds ticked slowly past, as the breeze picked up, as it touched them both. He smiled again. "By God, Callie, but you are still so beautiful. I should throttle you. I should wind my fingers right around your very beautiful neck, and throttle you. But even if you fell, you would torture me still!"

At last she moved, squaring her shoulders, standing even more tall against him. Her chin hiked up, her eyes shimmered, and her tone was soft and entirely superior to any of his taunts.

"Colonel, help yourself to water, and then, if you will, ride on. This is Union territory, and you are not welcome."

The back of her hand touched his chest. Head high, she was pushing him out of her way and starting for the house.

"Callie!"

Perhaps the extent of his rage was in his voice. Perhaps there was even more than that in the simple utterance of her name.

She began to run.

"Callie!" He shouted out her name again. Every restraint within him seemed to fail. The bitterness of nearly a year ripped wide, and he didn't know himself what he intended to do.

He followed her.

She had slammed the back door on him, bolted it against him. He hurtled his shoulder against it. It shuddered. He slammed against it again.

It began to give.

"Daniel, go away! Go home, go back to your men, to your army—to your South!"

The door burst open.

She stood staring at him.

Again, he felt a taunting curl touch his lips. He hadn't known what he would do when he saw her again. He still didn't know.

But he was going to touch her.

"What?" he demanded, taking a stride into the kitchen. "Are there no troops close enough to come to your rescue once you've seduced me into your bed this time?"

He ducked quickly. Her fingers had curled around a coffee cup, and hurtled it across the kitchen at him.

"Go away!" she commanded him.

"Go away?" he repeated. "How very rude, Mrs. Michaelson! When I have waited all these months to return? I lie awake nights dreaming for a chance to come back to your side. What a fool I was, Callie! And still, I suppose I did not learn."

He swept his hat from his head and sent it flying to the kitchen table. "Well, I have come back, angel. And I'm very anxious to pick up right where I left off. Let's see, where was that? Your bedroom, I believe. Ah, that's right. Your bed. And let's see, just how were we situated?"

"Get out of my house!" she charged him.

"Not on your life," he promised. "Not, madam, on your life!"

He strode toward her.

"Don't!" she cried out instantly.

Her denial seemed to touch him inside and out, adding fuel to the fire that raged so viciously inside of him. Dear God! Where was everything he had learned through a lifetime? Where was restraint, forgiveness, mercy?

He remembered the chill on his naked back when the Yanks had taken him. He remembered being in love with her. Damn her, but he remembered trusting her.

"This is one invasion of the North that is going to be successful!" Indeed, yes. Let it be a battle.

A battle that he would not lose.

He began to walk toward her once again. Maybe his intent was clear in his movement. Or perhaps she saw it in the cold hard glimmer of his eyes. Some sound escaped her, and she knocked over a chair in his way.

It wouldn't stop him. Not tonight.

"Don't, damn you!" she cried out suddenly. Her breasts were heaving more swiftly now with her growing agitation. Angel, you can falter and fall, and so beautifully. For a moment he almost paused. For a moment it was there again, the silver softness in her eyes, the sweetness in her voice. The plea, the seduction. "You have to listen to me—" she began.

The seduction. Yes, damn her.

"Listen to you!" he exploded. He was shaking. His flesh was on fire. His fingers twitched.

"Callie, time is precious! I have not come to talk this night. I listened to you once before."

"Daniel, don't come any nearer. You must—"

"I must finish what you started, Callie. Then maybe I can sleep again at night."

He reached for her arm and the fire in his eyes seemed to sizzle through both of them.

"Daniel, stop!" she hissed. She jerked free of him and ran.

But tonight, there was nowhere for her to run. He followed her.

She stopped and found a vase and tossed it his way. He ducked again, and the vase crashed against a wall. She tore through the parlor, looking for more missiles. A shoe came flying his way, a book, a newspaper. Nothing halted his stride.

She reached the stairs, and he was there behind her. She started to race up them and realized her mistake. He was behind her. She reached the landing.

He caught her by her hair. He thought that she cried out, but he didn't care. All that mattered was having her.

He swept her into his arms and strode the last few steps to the bedroom, the bedroom where she had lured him once before.

"Let's finish what we started, shall we, angel?"

"Let me go!" Callie demanded. Her fists were flying; she struggled wildly.

"Let you go?" He heard the lethal roar of his own voice, and it might have belonged to someone else. He'd never let her go. Not now. His words tumbled from his lips. "Once I tried to walk away. To honor both North and South, and everything that we both held sacred. But you raced after me, angel. You could not bear to have me leave. You wanted me here. Remember, Mrs. Michaelson. Here."

He strode to the bed, and tossed her heedlessly upon it. She rose up on her elbows instantly, head proud, chin high, and watched him.

"Don't!" she commanded. "Don't even think—"

He straddled over her. Her eyes widened. He glowered at her.

Her hand connected with his cheek, but he stripped off his mustard gauntlets to catch her wrists when she struggled against him.

"Just what am I thinking, Callie?" he demanded.

He heard her teeth grinding. Felt the defiant flame of her gaze as it met his.

"I don't know. What are you thinking?"

"Ah, if the Yanks but had you in the field!" he murmured. "Maybe you are recalling the last time we met. It was right here. I'll never forget, because I loved this room from the first time I saw it. I loved the dark wood of the furniture, and the soft white of the curtains and the bed. And I loved the way that you looked here. I'll never forget your hair. It was like a sunset spread across the pillow. Sweet and fragrant, and so enticing. Newly washed, like silk. I can't forget your eyes. I can go on, Callie. There's so much that I never forgot. I remembered you in camp, and I remembered you every moment that I planned and plotted an escape. I thought of your mouth, Callie. It's a beautiful mouth. I thought of the way that you kissed me. I thought of your lovely neck, and the beauty of your breasts. I thought of the feel of your flesh, and the movement of your hips. Over and over and over again. I remembered wanting you like I'd never wanted anything or anyone before in my life. Of feeling more alive than ever before just because I breathed in the scent of you as I lay against your breast. And when you touched me, I think I came closer to believing I had died and gone to heaven than I've ever done upon a battlefield. Damn you! I was in love with you. In the midst of chaos, I was at peace. I believed in you, and dear God, when I lay here with you, I even believed in life again. What a fool I was!"

"Daniel—"

"No! Don't! Don't tell me anything. Don't give me any protestations of innocence. I'll tell you what I've thought over all these months. I've thought that you were a spy, and that you deserved the fate of a spy. I thought about choking the life out of you." He released her wrists. His knuckles moved slowly up and down the column of her throat. She didn't move. Those silver-gray eyes met his. Wide. Luminous. Beautiful still. Haunting him. The eyes of an angel.

"But I could never do it," he said quietly. "I could never wind my fingers around that long white neck. I could never do anything to mar that beauty. Then I thought that you should be hanged, or that you should be shot. Through long dark nights, Callie, I thought about all of these things. But do you know what I thought about most of all?"

She was so still. He moved more closely against her.

"What?" she whispered.

"I thought about being here with you. I thought about this bed. I thought about your naked flesh, and I thought about your smile when it seemed that you poured yourself upon me, heart, soul, and body. I thought about the way that your eyes could turn silver. I thought that all I wanted was to be back here."

He had to touch her. He had to finish what they had started.

"I wondered what it would be like to have you when I hated you every bit as much as I had once loved you."

She moved swiftly. Her eyes grew instantly dark, and she swung at him with a wild fury, but he caught her hand. She lashed out at him with venom in her voice. "Hate me, then, you fool! Give me no chance, no leave, no grace, no mercy—"

"Were I to give you more mercy, I might as well shoot myself, madam!" he swore.

"You self-righteous bastard! Hate me and I will despise you. You were the enemy! You are the enemy! This is Union soil! God damn you for expecting more from me!"

She was so furious, the force of her anger was great enough to dislodge herself. But not for long. He hadn't known what he would do. Now he did.

He had wanted some proof of innocence. He had wanted her to plead, to profess her innocence. He had wanted to believe in her.

God damn you, he raged inwardly. He caught her hard, and dragged her back down. He used the length of himself to subdue her when she fought and struggled wildly. He felt the fluid movement of her body, and he wanted her with an ever greater hunger. She was so warm against him. He felt her heart and her breath. Felt the curve of her hip, the length of her thigh. Even the curve of her breast. Her body seemed etched against his. He could feel all of her heat, and against the growing swell of his desire, he could feel the subtle movement at the juncture of her thighs.

In all the heat and tempest there was the pulse of something beside her anger. She wanted him.

"Here we are, Callie. You'll not leave me tonight. And you'll not betray me."

"And you'll not have me!"

But he would. He'd be damned if he'd be a gentleman. He would have her. Now. And in any way.

"I will."

"It would be—rape!" she spat out.

"I doubt it."

"Oh, you flatter yourself!"

"I've waited long and cold and furious nights, Callie. I will have you."

"You won't! You won't hurt me, you won't force me. You won't, because you promised! You won't, because of who you are. I know it, I know you—"

She didn't know him. Not anymore. He didn't know himself.

"Damn you, Callie! You don't know me. You never knew me!"

His lips descended upon hers. With hunger, with passion. With all the longing that had tormented him through the never-ending months. He kissed her with a startling violence, demanding, parting her lips and tasting their sweetness, marveling at the feel of his tongue upon them.

She fought him. Fought his touch; fought the invasion. Fought the sweep of his tongue, the taunt and the fury of it. And then, somewhere within this fury she ceased to fight.

His kiss gentled. His fingers moved upon her. Ached to touch her. She seemed to give. She trembled beneath him.

"Callie!" he whispered her name. Her gaze touched his. Did she plead for mercy still? Did she seek only to be freed? Was she, ever and always, the ultimate actress? Did she spy for the Yanks, had she done more for her cause than just her capture of him?

"Damn, I'll not let you sway me!" he roared. His fingers bit into her arms. Nothing would stop him, nothing, he swore.

But something did.

A loud, fierce cry suddenly tore through the air between them.

A baby's cry.

He sat back. "What in God's name . . . ?"

"It's—it's Jared." She slipped from beneath him, and he let her go. He stared at her, amazed.

"That's a baby."

"Yes! It's a baby!" She leapt from the bed and disappeared into the hallway.

He followed her down the hall. He watched her pick up the tiny bundle of an infant. Hers. He knew immediately that it was hers.

If the child was hers, who knew how many men she had betrayed. There was the Yankee captain who had taken him, once Callie had disarmed him. How many others, friends, enemies?

He strode across the room.

She hugged the child to her breast, staring at him with the first real fear in her eyes.

He reached for the child. "Give him to me, Callie."

She wanted to fight him; he could see it in her eyes. But she wouldn't hurt the baby. She released him.

Daniel watched with amazement as the baby squalled, little fists and feet flying. He was beautiful. He was amazing. He was perfect in every way. And loud. His screams defied any Rebel yell that Daniel had ever heard.

He was beautiful, perfect, sound. Something welled up inside of Daniel. The fiercest urge he had ever known to protect someone. It was warm. It was all powerful. He looked into the little face. The face of his son. I love you, he thought, amazed at his own emotion. We've never met, until this moment. You are incredible.

And indisputably, my boy, you are a Cameron.

Daniel stared at Callie. Did she intend to deny it? She'd certainly made no effort to tell him about the child. Had she done so, she would have learned that he had been out of prison for a long, long time.

"It's my baby!" he exclaimed harshly.

She didn't answer him. Damn her. She would do so. He turned and started out the doorway.

"Daniel!"

She caught up with him at the foot of the stairway. For once, she was learning how to plead. She was desperate. Tears touched her eyes, making them sparkle an incredible silver. "What are you doing? Give him to me! Daniel, he's crying because he's hungry. You can't take him from me! Daniel, please! What do you think you're doing?"

"He's my son."

"You can't begin to know that—"

"The hell I can't. What a fool you are to try to deny it."

"Daniel, give him back!"

"He doesn't belong here. He belongs at Cameron Hall."

He'd never seen her so stunned. She must have just realized how deeply he felt.

"You can't take him! He's barely two months old. You can't care for him. Daniel, please!" Tears sprang to her eyes. She caught hold of his elbow and held on hard. "Daniel, he needs me. He's crying because he's hungry. You have to give him back to me."

A slow smile curved his mouth despite the baby's hungry screaming. "You didn't even intend to tell me about him, did you, Callie?"

She shook her head fiercely. "Yes, I intended to tell you!"

She was lying. She was still beautiful, and he was still in love with her. No, in hate with her. He didn't know which.

"When the hell did you intend to tell me?" he bellowed.

"You didn't give me a chance. You came in here condemning me—"

"You knew that I'd come back. Maybe you didn't," he corrected himself bitterly. "Maybe you thought that I'd rot and die in that camp!"

"Damn you, Daniel, you can't kidnap my son!"

"My son. And he'll have my name," Daniel said. He realized then that he did intend to take the baby. With or without Callie.

Or maybe he was taking the baby because by doing so, he would take Callie too.

"You can't care for him!" she cried out.

But he could. And he was determined to do so. No, he couldn't be a mother to his son. But Jared was coming to Cameron Hall.

He stopped and turned back with a smile. "Oh, but I can, Callie. I can find a mammy to care for him easily enough. Within the hour."

"You wouldn't!" she breathed.

"He's a Cameron, Callie, and he's going south tonight."

"You can't take him away from me! He's mine!"

"And mine. Created under very bitter circumstances. He's coming home, and that's that."

"This is his home!"

"No, his home is south, upon the James."

"I'll call the law!" she threatened.

"There is no law anymore, Callie. Just war."

She was following him as he strode for the door. Did she know that he was waiting for her? Waiting to see what she would do next, when she would swallow her pride, when she would plead to come with him?

Was this the great cruelty, the revenge he had imagined so many dark nights?

If so, it was not sweet, as revenge should have been.

"No! You cannot take him from me!" she thundered, and she slammed against him, beating her fists against his back.

He spun on her, blue eyes fierce, ruthlessly cold.

"Then you'd best be prepared to travel south, too, Callie. Because that's where he's going!"

She stepped back, stunned once again.

"What?"

"My son is going south. If you want to be with him, you can prepare to ride with me. I'll give you ten minutes to decide. Then we're moving. Who knows, Meade just may decide to chase Lee's army this time, though it seems poor Uncle Abe can't find himself a general to come after Lee. But I'm not waiting. So if you're coming, get ready."

She didn't answer him, but he knew that she believed him—knew that she had only one choice, and it was a simple one. Her lips were trembling.

She reached out her arms to him. "Daniel, give me the baby. Just let me feed him." Her voice rose to a cry. "Please!"

He placed the baby in her arms.

"Ten minutes, Callie," he warned her. "I'll be waiting on this step. For Jared, and you, if you choose to come. But Jared is coming with me."

"But we're enemies!"

"Bitter enemies," he agreed politely.

"I could betray you again, moving through this territory."

She was still threatening him, he thought with amazement. Daring him. Defying him. But he wouldn't be taken in by her again. Ever.

"You'll never have the chance again," he promised her.

She stared at him, her eyes a tempest of her inner conflict. She turned and fled up the steps with Jared.

He watched her go.

He looked down at his hands. They were trembling. In all this horror and bloodshed, here was something incredibly fine and good, a child. His. Callie had betrayed him, and he had lived with the rage and the bitterness building within him for nearly a year.

While she had lived with Jared.

It was astonishing how deeply he felt about this tiny babe. He hadn't even known that the boy existed and now he loved him. Instantly. Completely. He was more important than anything in the world.

Daniel leaned back wearily, and his gaze followed the path that Callie had taken up the stairs.

He loved him. Jared. He loved him with the same deep passion with which he hated his infant's mother.

Hated, loved, which was it? He wasn't sure that he knew himself.

Perhaps he would discover the truth soon enough.

It might be a long, long ride back home. A very long ride for a Yank and a Rebel. And the child born of the tempest between the two.

PART 3

Bittersweet Revenge

Eighteen

When Callie made her final decision and came down the stairway, she found Daniel sitting in the parlor. His arms were spread out over the back of the settee and his booted feet were stretched out before him, resting on the fine cherry-wood occasional table. He appeared entirely relaxed. Rudely so. She was certain that he would never sit so in his own parlor.

She was equally certain that his posture was a definite statement of his opinion of her.

But then again, maybe it was just a bone-deep exhaustion brought on by the war. Yet his eyes were on her like those of a hawk.

"You've been far more than ten minutes, Mrs. Michaelson," he informed her.

"And you're still here, Colonel," she commented in return.

"I told you that I wasn't leaving my son," he said flatly.

"Yes, well your son needed things for the journey," Callie informed him coolly. She wondered why her stomach was winding into such vicious knots. How could she wonder? Daniel was back.

She was suddenly aware that she was still very much in love with him. No matter how condemning his eyes, or how furious she was with him. He was back, and he was in her parlor. The same man who had ridden into her life before, in the same gray uniform. A uniform the worse for wear, ragged, frayed, and even torn in spots. A wealth of unbidden tears threatened to spill from her eyes. She clamped down hard on her jaw.

But no matter how ragged or worn the uniform, the man within it was Daniel. And nothing could change the fact that he wore it well, that he was strikingly handsome in his cockaded and plumed hat, and that when he stood, he was tall and regal in the uniform.

Regal—and menacing, she decided. Against her will, Callie took a step back. He had been an extraordinary lover. Now he would prove to be an exceptional foe, she was certain. He would never believe that she had really been innocent of betrayal. She had no proof to give him. The only proof could come from his heart, and that heart was sealed hard against her.

He stood and walked toward her. She backed away again, warily. She couldn't let him touch her. If he wanted to wage war, well, war it would be.

He smiled, aware that she had backed away from him. She couldn't begin to read what lay in his mind. He ceased to move and contemplated her as if she were a stranger he had been sent to escort south.

"I reckon then, Mrs. Michaelson, that you are accompanying me?"

"I reckon, Colonel, that you've given me no choice," she replied politely.

"There are always choices, Mrs. Michaelson."

"Well, I choose for you to ride on, Colonel, but it doesn't appear to me that you are going to do so."

"Not alone."

"Then it seems that I have no choice. But I wonder, Colonel, if you know quite what you're taking on?" she asked, raising her chin.

His challenging smile deepened. "Mrs. Michaelson, I regret to inform you that I am well acquainted with infants."

"Really? Well then, you must understand the collection of clothing and diapers that are necessary! And I'm ever so delighted that I shall have help along the way!"

"Where's the baby?" he asked her.

She hesitated. "Sleeping. I set him in his bed so that I could collect his things." Something was at war within her. She was so sorry for his appearance. He looked so exhausted. His handsome features were gaunt and strained. He was thin. The battle he had left had gone so badly for the Rebels. She'd been hearing the tales of it all day from the soldiers in retreat. She wanted to hate him. She wanted to be mad enough to scratch his eyes out.

She also wanted to hold him in her arms, to smooth away the lines of care that haunted his eyes. She wanted to scrub away the dust and grime of battle from his back.

"Daniel, everything has been taken by one army or the other, but I've still some soup left in the cellar. If you want to rest a night I could clean your uniform and you could take a long bath—"

"And you could seduce me and the Yanks could come and take me again. No thanks," he informed her icily.

She felt her back stiffen just as if a rod of steel had been set in it.

"Fine! Go hungry. Go dirty. Be miserable! I never seduced you."

"You did."

"I had no choice."

"Poor Callie. You never seem to have choices. How is Captain Dabney, by the way?"

"I certainly don't know," Callie said.

"Really?" He arched a brow. "I thought you knew one another very well."

Callie took two steps toward him and struck out as quickly as she could. He caught her hand—but not before it connected with his cheek, bringing with it a sharp, startling sound.

Once he had her hand, he pulled her against him, hard. His gaze glittered as it touched hers. "Watch it, Callie. The war has taught me lots of nasty habits. When I'm attacked, I attack back."

He was so hot. Like a fire. And so furious. So many emotions seemed to churn in the searing blue force of his eyes. She wanted to cry out. She could not. She had to keep the battle waging, for it was better than surrender.

"When *I'm* attacked, Colonel, I attack back."

"I asked you a question."

She shook her head vehemently. "No, you haven't asked me a question! You've cast accusations at me, and I find them offensive."

"I found what happened to me here offensive."

"I'm sorry for that. But you don't believe me, so there's nothing more I can say."

"Yes, there is. I've asked you about Dabney. How is he? Is he still roaming the area? Has he ever managed to bring his company into a real battle?"

"I did answer your question! I don't know!" His grip was tight around her wrist, and she was still held close against him. The warmth, the vibrancy of his body seemed to wrap around her own. She needed to break free from him.

She jerked hard on her wrist, backing away once again. "I don't know! I haven't seen him."

He turned away from her. "I want to leave, Callie. Now. Shall I get the baby?"

She felt the blood rushing from her face. She had known that he meant it. Then why did she feel so frightened now?

Because he was taking her away, and this was home, despite the enemies who had trampled over her land. She didn't know exactly where he was taking her, or how she would manage once he brought her there.

He wanted the baby. He didn't want her. And they were going south. She had brought up the law. Surely no judge would allow a soldier to take a child from its mother. But she didn't know for sure. Perhaps Daniel would take her to a place where the Camerons owned the judges, where her child could be taken from her.

She clenched her fists hard at her sides and took a step back from Daniel, lifting her chin, praying that her voice would not waver.

"I won't leave him, Daniel. I don't know your intentions, but I won't leave my son. I don't care what you try to do."

He stared at her, perplexed, as if she had suddenly lost her senses.

"If you were intending to leave him, Callie, I don't imagine that you'd come with me now."

"No! I didn't mean that. I mean that you—you won't be able to get rid of me."

"Oh, Mrs. Michaelson, I didn't intend to get rid of you," he said, and something about the depths of his voice sent shivers racing along her spine. "I think it's much safer to know exactly where you are at all times. I spent time in a northern prison," he said softly. "Perhaps you're about to spend time in southern incarceration."

She kept her chin high. "Just so long as . . ." Still, her voice broke.

"As what?"

"You don't intend to—force me away from him."

Her voice was a whisper. Soft and desperate on the air. Maybe it touched something within him at last.

"I said that I was taking him home. I told you that you had ten minutes to decide. What are you talking about now?"

She lowered her eyes. "You're taking him to your home, Daniel. This is my home. His home."

He was silent and she raised her head at last. He studied her intently.

"His home is Cameron Hall, Callie. He will be welcome there."

"And what about me? I won't be welcome. Will I even be abided?"

"No one has ever been made to feel unwelcome in my family's house."

"Right. I'm sure your slaves were always welcome."

"I don't own any more slaves, Callie. But if you're interested in your own private shack, it's a very big plantation."

"You're going to put me in a shack—"

"I said you were welcome to one if you want one!" Daniel barked back.

"But what do you intend for me?"

"How prim, how sweet, how innocent!" he responded.

"It's a legitimate question!"

"What do you intend, Callie?" he demanded harshly.

"You are impossible!" she gasped, her fingers curling into the cotton of her skirts.

"No, Callie, I'm not impossible. But I'll never, never be taken in by you again!"

"Taken in! You needn't worry, Colonel Cameron. You'll never touch me again, I swear it!"

"It's far safer to touch a rattler."

"Then how will we live, what will we do?" she demanded.

"What are you talking about?"

She was going to falter soon, she knew. "This is foolish, what we're planning—"

"We aren't planning anything," Daniel said flatly. "I'm taking Jared to Virginia. You're coming with us."

"But we live in a certain society. North or South."

"Society will wait, madam. At the moment, I'm wondering if we'll survive this trip, if I won't waken to find the Yanks at my throat, if I haven't taken a sweet viper to my breast once again."

Scarlet flamed across her cheeks and she felt the simmering growth of fury deep within her. "Sir, I would rather travel with an entire band of Apache Indians!"

"Pity the Indians!"

"Daniel, damn you! How will we live? How can we do this? Are you thinking of this child at all that you're so determined to have—"

"Jesu, enough questions, Callie! I don't intend anything right now. Except to get Jared home!"

"Daniel, don't speak in circles!"

"What do you want from me, Callie? I was chained like an animal because of you!"

"And I have been ostracized because of you! What do you think? That this has been easy? My husband, a good Union soldier lies dead in my yard. When I should have still been clad in black, I was carrying a Rebel's child! Don't you see? You've no right to him at all—"

"I have every right!"

"You don't!"

"Well, I'm taking him."

"How can you just—"

"Callie, I am much bigger and much stronger than you are, that's how. Now, shall I get the baby?"

He didn't wait for an answer. He stared at her for a moment, then started for the stairs.

She raced after him. She was afraid to let him have Jared until they were well under way. "I'll get Jared. I've packed Pa's old saddlebags with his things. If you'll get them . . ."

She let the words trail away, and she hurried up the stairs past Daniel. She hurried into the baby's room, swept him gently up into her arms, and swirled around. Daniel was behind her. As she had asked, he picked up the saddlebags and threw them over his shoulder.

Oh, how she hated him at this moment! And still . . . . She looked at him. He was so tired, so worn. Like a lean, hungry wolf. For a moment she forgot the passion of her hatred and her anger.

"You really should eat something—" she began.

"Not on your life. Let's go."

"Fine. Starve. Don't expect me to be nice to you again."

"The last time you were nice I wound up in chains."

"What you belong in," she informed him evenly, "is a muzzle, Colonel."

She turned around, head high, and started down the stairs. He came behind her.

She walked through her parlor with her shoulders straight. Tears threatened to spill from her eyes again. She was going to walk away from her home. A home she had kept so long and so industriously, waiting for the day when her brothers would come home.

She stepped out on the porch. She didn't look back. She didn't dare. She would see in her mind the warmth and comfort of the parlor, the settee where Daniel had awaited her. She would see the little marble side table with the paintings of her parents, and of Jeremy and Joshua and Josiah. She had never left it before, except for short trips to Washington. Even when she had married, they had come back to this house because there had been more room for them here.

It was where her family lay buried.

She stood on the porch, feeling the slight breeze of the night stir by her. To her surprise, Daniel carefully locked the door behind them. She smiled.

"What?" he demanded.

"Two armies have come and taken what they want. The windows have been shelled, and there are still cannonballs in the wall. Yet you lock the door."

"Yes." He walked by her, approaching his gaunt horse, a tall roan that waited by the well. He turned back. "Have you any animals? If so, we need to leave them somewhere, though certainly with all these soldiers coming near, anything that walks on four legs will quickly become a meal."

"I've no animals left. Your soldiers have already come through."

"Then let's go."

He strode across the yard to where his roan horse waited. He turned back to her. "Let's go," he repeated, looking at her before tossing the saddlebags over the roan's haunches.

It had grown very late. Despite the heat in the summer days, the night had grown cool, perhaps because of the rain that had made mud of so many of the roads.

In the darkness, near and far, they could see the light of camp fires.

Yanks and Rebs were camped all around them.

Callie swallowed hard. The going would be rough.

"Do you really want to ride out tonight?" she whispered.

"This minute," he informed her.

Reluctantly, she stepped forward. Before she reached the roan horse he turned. His hands spanned across her waist as he lifted her and Jared, setting them both up atop his mount. With an easy swing he was up behind her, and a moment later, he was urging the horse on, into the night, into the darkness.

She was aware of him as she had never been aware before. Aware of the rough wool of his uniform coat, of the heat and movement and muscle play of his body beneath it. His arms were around her, and around their sleeping child as they started off at a slow walk.

Callie wondered if the roan could take more than such a slow pace.

"There are troops camped all over," Callie said softly.

"I know."

"You're worried about my bringing the Yankees down upon you—"

"I know that there are Yankees out there," he said lightly. "It's when I don't expect to find them that they're so dangerous."

He was silent for a second, and she winced when he continued.

"I didn't expect to find them in your bed."

"They weren't in my bed."

"Damned close."

She bit her lip, determined not to make an effort to explain things to a man who would not listen.

The baby began to whimper. She cradled him more tightly against her, and he fell silent once again. She was tempted to try to turn around, to look back.

The sight of the farmhouse would be fading away.

"Oh!" she exclaimed suddenly.

"What?"

"There is something that I need to do. Could we stop—"

She felt his arms stiffen instantly. He would always be suspicious of her, she thought.

"Rudy and Helga Weiss. They'll worry when they find that I'm gone. They might look for me. At a hardship to themselves. Please. Their place is not far off the road."

"And you want to stop? You've become good friends with the Dunkards?"

"The Dunkards became my friends," she said softly. She didn't add that they had done so when no one else seemed to care if she lived or died. "I have to tell them that I'm leaving. There's no treachery involved, I swear it."

"I'll stop, and you may have five minutes to speak with them. I'll keep the baby."

"Helga delivered him for me—"

"I'll keep the baby. It's my last offer. Take it or leave it."

Damn him. She managed to keep her mouth closed, very aware that nothing could deter him when he spoke in that tone of voice. She pointed the way down the road to Rudy's small farmstead.

As he had said he would do, he stopped a certain distance from the house. He dismounted from the roan, and his hands circled around her waist once again. He lifted her down, but once her feet had touched the ground, he released her. The warmth of his touch was gone.

He took Jared from her arms. He did so easily, with no awkwardness. He didn't even waken his sleeping son.

"Say good-bye to them, Callie. Quickly. For all I know, you could be planning on having them send someone after us. I'm warning you. If I have to run, I'll run with Jared. And I'm good at getting where I want to go."

"I'm not warning anyone about anything," Callie said irritably. "I'm saying good-bye to people who were very good to me. And to your son."

She didn't wait for his reply, but hurried toward the small, simple house. She knocked quickly on the door. Rudy answered it, crying out when he saw her. "What's wrong? What has happened? Where is the baby? Are you all right, Frau Michaelson?"

"Yes, I'm fine, and the baby is just outside. I'm—I'm leaving the area for a while. I just came to say good-bye. And to thank you. Thank you so much for everything."

She could see past the plain entryway and into the house. It was barren of decoration in any form, and still it was warm. A fire crackled in the hearth, and simple wood furnishings were set around it. From the kitchen, Callie could see Helga hurrying out to greet her.

"Callie! Where's mein kinder?"

"Jared is just outside. I'm leaving for a while. I'm taking Jared south."

"South!" Helga exclaimed. "But there is so much danger in the South—"

"Helga!" Callie interrupted, smiling. "Twice we have been in the path of a battle here! I don't think that I can find a place with greater danger!" Impulsively she hugged the older woman. "I'll be all right, I promise. I just came to say good-bye, so that you wouldn't worry about me."

Helga hugged her warmly in return. "I will worry about you anyway, child. I will miss you."

"I will miss you, too, Helga. I thank you so very much for all that you have done for me."

"What we have done? Bah. We have all looked out after one another, yes?"

"You are going with the child's father?" Rudy said disapprovingly.

"Rudy! She must do what she feels is right. And surely, it will be right. God will see to it, soon enough. You go, and you take care of yourself." She smoothed her hand tenderly over Callie's cheek.

Rudy sighed. He still didn't like the fact that Callie was leaving. "I will look after the farm, Frau Michaelson. I will look after it carefully."

"Thank you. But you musn't make yourself too much more work."

"Work, what work?" He threw his hands into the air. "There are no animals left to work for!" He took her from his wife's arms, and hugged her warmly. Callie stood on her toes and kissed his cheek. "I'll come back," she promised. "When the war is over."

She turned and fled, amazed at how attached she had become to the elderly couple. It was worse than leaving her own home. She didn't dare take any more time, though. Daniel was waiting.

When she came back into the yard, Daniel was nowhere to be seen.

Fear stormed into her heart, stark and vivid. She swirled in the pale light that radiated from the Weiss home, looking feverishly about her.

He had warned her that he would take the baby. He had threatened to take the baby if she didn't return quickly enough.

No! Oh, God, no! This couldn't be his revenge!

"Daniel!" She shrieked his name, heedless of the sound, heedless of the night. Tears sprang to her eyes and she started to run in the darkness, tearing for the road. "No, oh no, oh no, Daniel!" Her breath came raggedly, desperately. She swirled around in the road again, unable to see him anywhere.

"Daniel!"

She almost fell, doubling over with panic and pain.

She heard hoofbeats, and then the sound of his voice.

"I'm right here, Callie! Would you hush? You'll wake the dead Yanks nearby as well as the living ones!"

She straightened, and blinked away her tears. He had emerged from the side of the road, Jared in his arms, leading his horse. Jared, miraculously, still slept.

Callie rushed to Daniel's side and looked down at her sleeping son. She itched to snatch him back from his father, but she refrained.

She felt Daniel's fingers on her cheek, and met his gaze, startled. There was a gentleness in his touch. Almost a reassurance.

"You really love him," he said softly.

"More than life," she agreed.

He handed the baby carefully back into her arms. She was silent as his hands slipped around her waist and he lifted her back onto the roan horse. Silently, and with perfect agility, he leapt up behind her. Once again, the lean horse bore them down the trail.

"You said your good-byes?" he asked her.

"Yes."

"And you won't look back?"

"I'm not looking back."

He fell silent. They plodded along.

The night was dark. There were few stars in the skies. It was cool, with the promise of rain, and then it seemed to become hot and muggy with the same promise.

They moved very slowly. Daniel stopped time and time again, listening.

Sometimes he reined in and paused, rising in his stirrups, looking around them. Callie didn't know what he saw. She could see nothing at all, except for the stygian darkness.

They rode on.

Callie grew tired. Jared's weight seemed to grow with each heavy plod of the horse's hooves. She felt her eyes closing, and she fought to keep them open.

She felt herself easing back against Daniel. She didn't want to do so. She wanted to ride with her back straight and her head high. She couldn't quite manage it. She leaned against the warm living strength of his chest, and the warmth and comfort there became more and more inviting. Her eyes began to close. She couldn't sleep, she warned herself. She might drop the baby.

No, Daniel would never let her drop the baby.

A curious sensation swept along her spine. She wasn't alone anymore. There were two of them concerned for Jared.

She blinked hard. She shouldn't sleep.

Daniel reined in. She tried very hard to open her eyes. The darkness remained.

"Where are we?" she whispered.

"We're still in Maryland, Mrs. Michaelson," he said softly. "We'll sleep here tonight."

She tried to open her eyes more widely. "Here? Where are we? We're nowhere."

He dismounted from the horse, and reached for her. "We're in the wilderness, my love. And this is where we shall sleep tonight."

He set her down upon the ground, then immediately turned and began to unbuckle the girth on the horse. "Go ahead and find a tree. Curl up."

Callie stared at him blankly. He turned around, the saddle in his hand, and laughed when he saw her forlorn face.

"Come here, Mrs. Michaelson."

He carried the saddle in his one hand, and with the other, he led her along. From nearby, she could hear the soft sounds of a bubbling brook. Daniel dropped the saddle by the base of an old oak tree. He released Callie and headed back to his horse, brought down the blanket and both his saddlebags and the ones Callie had brought, and led the horse to the side of the road where rich long grasses grew.

He tethered the horse loosely to a tree, and returned to Callie's side once again.

"We needed to leave my house quickly so that we could come and sleep here?" she said.

"There's a beautiful sky for a roof, grass for a bed, sweet air to breathe," Daniel told her. "And there are no Yankees here. None to have to keep an eye on."

"You're wrong," she reminded him. "I'm a Yankee."

"Excuse me. There's only one Yankee here," he said. He touched her chin. "And I will keep my eye on her," he said, his voice husky.

She turned away from him. He tossed her a blanket and she did her best to stretch it out and maintain her hold on the baby. Daniel made an impatient sound and came and stretched it out for her.

She lay down, her back to him, easing Jared to her side. She stretched a protective arm around him, as if he could roll away in the darkness.

She felt her baby moving. Felt the subtle rise and fall of his little chest. Her fingers moved over the ink-dark hair. He still hadn't awakened. She touched his cheek. She felt the always overwhelming sense of love for him invade her.

She closed her eyes. She was so weary. It had been such a long night. They had ridden so far.

He had come back into her life.

She hated him. She loved him.

The darkness seemed to close in around her. She started to shiver, cuddling Jared even closer. Summer days were hot. It was amazing that night could be so cold.

Her shivers increased. She was shaking so violently that she started to fear she would wake the baby.

She started to rise, but suddenly there was warmth all around her.

Daniel was stretching out beside her. "Dammit, Callie, what is the matter?"

"I'm cold!" she cried softly.

He brought her back down with him, his arm around her, warm and secure.

His hand, so large and bronze and powerful, rested protectively around her and on top of the blanket bundling their son.

Callie's shivers slowly ceased.

A smile curved her lips. She slept, as easily, as sweetly, as Jared.

Nineteen

*T*he journey southward was long and tedious.

Despite the very late hour at which they had stopped, Daniel woke Callie early. Not long after she had finally fallen asleep, the baby had awakened, hungry, and so she had spent time up with him. She was very tired when Daniel woke her. She had a headache, her throat was dry, and her hair was in a wild tangle. She could barely struggle into a sitting position, bringing the baby up with her.

It didn't help any that Daniel laughed at her when she turned reproachful eyes his way.

"Up!" he commanded her. "If we get going now, I'll make coffee a little way down the road."

He reached for Jared, and Callie surrendered the baby to his father. To her surprise, the baby was awake. He wasn't crying—he watched both her and Daniel pensively.

"There's a creek right down there," Daniel advised her, inclining his head down the slope from the road. With his free hand, he helped her to her feet.

Callie searched through her set of saddlebags for her brush and toothbrush, both of which were showing sad signs of wear, but then again, in comparison to the supplies that Daniel carried, they seemed to be in exceptionally fine condition.

She bit into her lip, not wanting to look back at Daniel. She could too clearly remember the imprint of his body next to her own as they had slept. With the morning's light, she was once again reminded that no amount of wear or tear really seemed to tarnish her wayward cavalier. He had shaven before he had awakened her, scrubbed his hands and face, and doused his ink-dark hair. The hollows in his cheeks were deeper than she had remembered. More tiny lines were etched around his eyes. And still, she loved his face. More gaunt, it merely appeared more noble.

She walked down to the creek, branches catching at her skirt, wondering again how it was possible to hate and resent someone so very much and also love him all the while.

There was little she could do for her own appearance, but the cool water felt good, and she took the time to brush out her hair. When she reached the road once again, Daniel was ready to ride.

The morning passed silently. When she would have spoken, he shushed her. When the baby cried at last, Daniel urged her to quiet him quickly. Lee's entire army might be heading this way, but there might well be Yankee patrols following in its path. Skirmishing was sure to take place, and Daniel was determined to avoid either army.

Biting into her lower lip, she loosed the buttons on her bodice to feed the baby while they rode. She had promised herself that she would demand her privacy in all things. This decision was quickly falling apart. But Daniel seemed heedless even of her presence as she fed the baby. He merely grunted his approval when she whispered later that Jared slept once again.

He had promised her coffee, but she was certain that it was at the very least late afternoon when he reined in on the road and dismounted. He did so easily. When he lifted her down, she staggered and would have fallen with Jared if Daniel hadn't supported her. She was not accustomed to hour after hour in the saddle.

Her stomach was growling. She'd had soup the night before—Daniel, she was certain, had paused for nothing on his way to reach her. How could he go so long and so far on nothing?

The war, she thought. As always, these days, it seemed that the answer to any question was the same.

He had stopped where she could hear the nearby gurgle of a creek once again. When she could stand on her own he led the horse through the trees to reach it, and Callie followed behind with the baby. The water looked delicious and she quickly sat down beside it. Holding the baby close against her chest, she cupped one hand to scoop up the cool liquid.

She looked behind her to discover that Daniel had cleared a spot of ground on which to build a fire. Quickly and competently, he drew coffee and a tin pot from a saddlebag, took water from the brook, and set the coffee to brew.

"Are you hungry?" he asked Callie.

She nodded, aware that he had really forgotten that people usually ate three times a day, beginning with breakfast.

He dug further into the bag, and came out with a pair of heavy square biscuits. He handed her one. Hardtack, she thought. A soldier's staple. But even as she looked at the biscuit, a tiny worm crawled out from it. Then another, and another.

She swallowed hard, allowing the biscuit to fall.

"Sorry," he said huskily.

She shrugged. "I've seen worms before. Just not—just not so many," she finished. She handed him back the biscuit. "I'm really not that hungry."

He stared at the biscuit, then seemed suddenly furious. He tossed it away in a wide arc.

"Jesu! This is what we're reduced to!" He inhaled and exhaled raggedly. "It won't be like this at home. The river is teeming with fish. We've livestock in abundance. So many ducks you can hardly imagine them, and enough chickens for an army—"

He broke off, twisting his jaw. They both knew that if any army had been through the peninsula—even Daniel's own army—there was probably nothing left at Cameron Hall either.

Jared opened his wide blue eyes and smiled at his mother. He didn't seem to care about the food supply. He didn't need to care, not yet, Callie thought. But a few more days of nothing, and she might well fail in her efforts to feed him.

Daniel was watching the baby. Jared flailed out with his tiny hands and Daniel suddenly reached over. Little fingers curled around his larger one. Daniel smiled, much like his son. Callie felt a tug at her heart as she realized that Daniel had never decided to take the baby for revenge. He loved Jared. Maybe he couldn't love the baby the same way that she did. He hadn't borne him, hadn't held him from the very start. But he loved him, nonetheless.

"I think that the coffee's ready," Callie said.

His gaze met hers. Blue. Speculative. "So it is," he said. He went over to the pot, and a moment later he was back with a tin cup. Callie laid the baby in her lap, and took the cup from Daniel. The coffee was curiously good, or else it was simply delicious because it was a different taste from water, all that she had had. She sipped it, savoring it. She looked at Daniel, who was watching her.

"You're not having any?"

He shrugged. "A soldier's mess carries only one cup," he said.

She flushed, passing it back to him.

"There's plenty of coffee in the pot. Finish that."

She did so, then passed back the tin cup. He left her, poured himself a cup of coffee, drank it, then immediately began to put out the fire and return his belongings to his saddlebag. Callie watched him, then realized that he wanted to start riding again and roused herself. "I need to change the baby," she told him, and dug through her own belongings for one of the diapers she had made for Jared. Daniel had moved so quickly, and she tried to do the same. Finishing with the baby, she paused, but just briefly. She set him into Daniel's arms to hurry down to the creek to rinse out his old diaper. It could dry while they rode.

Daniel handed her back the baby, set her on the horse, and they were on their way once again. She realized that they were going very slowly, but as nightfall neared, they had reached the Potomac River.

Daniel halted, staring out over the river. She followed behind him. Despite the war, the view was still beautiful, the mountains rising high over the water and the valleys, the colors of summer so rich and green and blue.

But Daniel wasn't seeing the beauty of it.

"The Yanks must be holding Harpers Ferry again," he mused. "This bridge is out. The water is swollen from all the rain. We'll have to find somewhere else to ford the river."

Callie nodded, but shivered. When night came, so did a chill, despite the fact that it was summer.

"Cold?" he asked her.

"Yes."

"I can't build a fire. It could too easily be seen by night," he told her.

She nodded, understanding.

"You must be very hungry."

She shrugged. Hungry? She was famished.

"You must be hungry too."

He grinned. "I'm accustomed to hunger. I barely hear the growls or feel the claws anymore." He watched her in the fading light. "I can't light a fire by night. In the morning, we'll snare a rabbit or catch some fish. We'll—we'll rest a few hours."

Callie nodded and turned away from him. He passed her by, striding to the horse. "We'll sleep on the other side of the river, over there. There's a feeder creek for water," he told her.

Callie didn't answer. She followed along with him. Daniel left the road behind, leading the horse deep into the trees and down by the creek bed. Jared was starting to cry. She held back as Daniel led the horse onward to drink from the creek.

Finding a tall oak, Callie sat down before it, loosed the buttons of her bodice, and swept her shawl around herself and the baby as he nursed. She felt the familiar tug of his tiny mouth against her breast and closed her eyes, still so grateful for him. Nothing, no horror or war, no comment or fury from Daniel or anyone else, could change the fact that Jared was beautiful, a true gift from God.

The Lord did move in mysterious ways. Helga had assured her that it was so.

She opened her eyes and jumped. Daniel was back, standing before her. He was caught in shadow, and she could see nothing of his face. All she could see was his silhouette, the tall cavalier in his high black books, his frock coat a cape over broad shoulders, his sweeping plume jaunty against the night.

He watched her.

But then he turned away and spoke to her over his shoulder. "The blanket is laid out over here. Get some sleep so that we can rise early."

He walked away from her. Hungry, weary, and very sore, Callie decided that there was little else for her to do. She held the baby over her shoulder, waiting for little burps, and then she rose and walked over to the blanket.

Daniel was still standing there, looking out over the creek.

"What is it?"

"Someone is near," he said. He pointed in the darkness. Callie strained her eyes. She could see the flicker of a camp fire.

"Who—"

"I don't know. Fires don't wear colors," he told her. "Go to sleep. We're safe enough here for the night."

"But you—"

"Damn it, Callie, I'm staying up awhile. Take the baby and go to sleep."

She spun around and took the baby and laid down with him by the tree. But she didn't sleep. She lay there, awake and waiting.

Finally, when it seemed that hours had passed, she dozed off. She woke, time and again, shivering.

Then she slept soundly. She awoke again because Jared was beginning to fuss.

Daniel was with her at last. The warmth of his body had entered into hers, and that was why she had slept so easily.

She kept her back to him while she fed the baby. She kissed Jared's forehead, pleased that he had slipped back to sleep with his little mouth still moving.

She slipped back to sleep herself.

When she awoke in the morning, she was alone. She looked around and saw that Daniel had gathered the makings for a fire, but it seemed that he was waiting to build it.

Perhaps he was off finding something to eat.

She hoped so. The pain in her stomach was sharp and cruel now.

Jared made a gurgling sound, and she glanced at him, smiling as she laid him down on the blanket. She whispered silly words to him, rubbing his tiny nose with her own, watching his smile spread across his face. His arms and legs wiggled and flailed and she laughed. He started to stare at something above her and she realized that he was fascinated with the leaves on the trees. Smiling, she left him and hurried to the water. She was desperately thirsty.

She leaned down and buried her face in the cool creek. The water was cold in the early morning, but it was delicious. She raised her face, and opened her bodice to splash the cool water against her chest. She drenched her gown, but it didn't matter. The sun was going to rise hot and high, and it would dry her.

She reached into the water again, and then she paused.

She could hear movement across the creek.

Frozen, she watched as men began to move toward the river. There were at least ten of them, and all in Federal blue uniforms. Yankees. Her own side.

Her heart seemed to freeze.

She stood quickly, trying to back away from the creek in absolute silence.

She backed against something and almost screamed out loud. She felt hands on her shoulders, spinning her around.

Daniel was back. He held a finger to his lips. His eyes held all manner of warning.

"Don't scream, Callie."

"I wasn't going to scream!" she whispered back furiously. "I was going to warn you!"

She didn't know if he believed her or not. His eyes were cobalt and entirely enigmatic.

They heard voices carrying across the creek, and Daniel pressed on her shoulders, pulling her down low on her knees beside him.

"She can't have gone too far. The old man said that she was traveling with a baby. That will cost our Reb friend some mean time."

Callie's eyes widened with dismay and disbelief as she stared across the creek.

It was Eric Dabney again. He'd stripped off his uniform shirt and was in the creek in his blue breeches, underwear shirt, and suspenders, and he was talking to the man beside him.

"Lieutenant Colonel Dabney, sir!" a soldier called out from the bank. "There's the remains of a camp fire to our immediate east, sir!"

"Lieutenant Colonel," Daniel murmured bitterly into Callie's ear. "So he did receive a promotion out of me." He turned to Callie and stared at her. "And you," he added softly.

She wanted to shout at him, to strike him, to hurt him in some way.

It wasn't the time.

"I think there are about twenty of them," she warned him quietly.

"Yes, I reckon you're right," he agreed. He was still staring hard at her. "And you didn't know anything about them. Or him. And you didn't leave a message with the old folks, your Dunkard friends, when we left?"

Callie gaped at him, incredulous. Her jaw snapped shut with fury. "I could have screamed right now, you fool!" she hissed. "I could have brought every single one of them down upon you—"

"Except that I'm armed now, right, Callie?"

She wrenched free from his touch. To her amazement, he let her go. "You are incredible!" she stammered. "There are twenty of them. One of you."

"Those are the odds we Rebs always did pride ourselves on."

She shook her head furiously. She was so mad she wanted to spit.

She was also afraid. What was he planning on doing?

"Ten to one, Colonel. I've heard all the boasts. The Rebs always claim that one of them is worth ten Yanks. Not twenty." She grit her teeth, still staring at him incredulously. "Do you have a death wish, Cameron?" She demanded harshly.

He smiled, reached for her, and jerked her close to him so that they were hunched down on the creek bank on their knees. His eyes seemed to sear into hers like the heated steel of a sword. His arms were hot, the length of his body was hot, electric, tense, and poised for battle.

"And you're innocent this time, right, Callie? You really haven't seen this Eric Dabney in all this time. He just happened along here today?"

Callie grit her teeth. Obviously, Eric hadn't just "happened" by. He must have gone by the farm. And he must have found Rudy and Helga, and maybe Rudy had thought it in Callie's best interest to say something.

She tried to keep her chin high. "Innocent or guilty, I am condemned in your eyes," she said bitterly.

"You're so treacherous, Callie, and so beautiful," he said softly, and she was startled when he stroked her cheek. "Perhaps you could not be the one without the other."

"I had nothing to do with this!" she insisted.

His reply was a grunt; his eyes were on the Yankees across the creek.

"Would you stop it!" she hissed to him. "I could scream right now if I chose to do so."

Instantly, his eyes were back upon her. Speculative, sharp.

"If you would just trust me—"

"Never. Never again," he said flatly. A startled cry nearly escaped her, for suddenly she found that his hand was clamped over her lips, only to be quickly replaced with his yellow uniform bandanna, tied tight around her mouth even as she struggled against him. Her eyes widened with alarm as she wondered if he had forgotten the baby, lying peacefully beneath the tree. She fought him like a wildcat then, but he ignored her eyes and the fire of her flailing fists. He even ignored the solid punch she managed against his chest, and the sounds of desperation that sounded too quietly in her throat. He twirled her around, lacing her wrists together behind her back with his uniform sash.

He jerked her back against him, his whisper stinging her ear. "Give me any trouble now, Callie, and I'll take the baby and the horse and ride. I'm damned good at riding. Alone—alone with Jared, that is—I can move like lightning."

She went dead still in his arms. Holding her, he dragged her backward with him from the creek until they were out of view of the Yanks. He brought her back until they were beneath the oak where Jared lay.

He slept. While the world rocked around him, the baby slept, his face as peaceful as that of an angel beneath the sunlight that flickered through the leaves of the trees.

Daniel set her beside him and rose, and she knew that he intended to leave her there.

She was suddenly very frightened.

She tried to make some sound to stop him. Fighting her fury and her fear, she stared at him with imploring eyes.

To her amazement, he paused. His fingers moved gently over her cheek. "Scream now and I really might throttle you," he warned.

He slipped the bandanna from her mouth.

"Daniel, you have to let me go!" she whispered. "What if Jared awakes? He'll cry out—"

"If his mother hasn't done so first."

"I won't. I swear it." She hesitated. "On his life, Daniel, I swear it."

He hesitated only a moment longer, then roughly turned her about. A second later she was free.

She had no chance to say anything else to him. By the time she twirled around, he was gone.

Nervously, she knelt beside the baby and looked past the brush and tall grasses to the opposite side of the creek.

Her hand flew to her mouth as she saw Daniel behind the Yankee troops. One by one, and with a silent agility and speed, he moved from Yankee horse to Yankee horse, freeing them all. The company of Yanks, involved with their thirst and their desire to douse themselves in the cool water, were making a fair amount of noise.

None of them noticed Daniel.

Callie's heart seemed to hammer against her chest. As he neared the end of the line of horses, Daniel held on to the reins of the last pair. Both were tall bays, and both looked healthy, and well fed. Far more so than the pathetic roan they had been riding.

He was coming back around for her with the fresh horses, she realized. She started to rise, but maintained a low position on the balls of her feet. She watched Daniel as he moved far to the rear of the Yankee soldiers, circling them widely. He was well down the creek before he crossed it once again, and then she lost sight of him.

She was still searching for him when she felt his hands on her shoulders. She nearly jumped, but his whisper quickly touched her ear. "Get the baby. I'll get our things."

She did as he told her, quickly scooping Jared into her arms and against her shoulder. She hurried after Daniel in time to see him throwing the saddlebags over the haunches of one of the Yankee mounts, a tall bay that glistened in the early morning sunlight.

"Here!" he called to her softly. She hurried over to him. His hands were on her waist and he lifted her quickly, setting her upon the first horse. She balanced the baby tightly against her chest as she reached for the reins. For a fleeting second his eyes touched hers. "I'll be right behind you," he warned.

She didn't answer him. He didn't deserve an answer.

A moment later, he was mounted himself on the second horse. The Yanks still hadn't noticed that their entire line of horses had been released. Some of their mounts wandered to the high grasses near them; some had ambled clean away.

"Go!" Daniel urged Callie.

It was just then that Jared chose to awake, letting out a lusty and hungry wail.

Callie's gaze met Daniel's once again. "Go!" he roared. Riding up behind her, he slapped her horse hard on the rump. The animal leapt forward, then began to race in a long, clean gallop. It was all that Callie could do to hold the baby and the reins. Foliage slapped her and tugged hard at her flesh and clothing and hair. She was blinded by the branches that tore at her, desperate to shield Jared from danger.

Even as she left the embankment behind, she realized that Daniel raced after her. Her horse, spurred on by the sounds of his behind it, raced on at a frantic pace. They reached the road, and a small bridge that crossed the creek farther down from the bend where they had spent the night.

Her horse tore over the bridge. Daniel followed. She heard him shouting "Woah!" and he reined in his horse.

She brought her own mount under control and turned it around. Daniel had paused on the bridge, she saw, because two of the Yankee soldiers had managed to capture their horses and come in pursuit of her and Daniel.

Daniel drew his sword from its scabbard. A Rebel cry, a sound so frightening it even brought chills to her spine, tore from his lips, and carried hauntingly on the air as he charged his enemies, his sword swinging.

He didn't need to slay either of them. The men were so unnerved by his charge that they backed their horses too close to the edge of the bridge. Callie watched as men and horses went plunging over it amidst the sounds of their own screams. The horses quickly staggered up; the men, drenched and demoralized, barely made it to their knees.

Daniel spun his mount about and started to race toward Callie. There was one more horseman coming up behind him.

"Daniel!"

She shouted his name in warning.

He twirled his mount around once again. The grace of his horsemanship was so fine and deadly that it held a rare and chilling beauty.

The Yankee coming his way reined in.

It was just a boy, Callie thought. He couldn't even really be eighteen, she was convinced.

He faced Daniel and Daniel's very lethal cavalry sword.

No! Callie cried out in her heart. No, please.

But if the boy came after Daniel, Daniel would have to slay him. To defend himself, and her, and Jared. She closed her eyes. She couldn't bear to see it. She didn't want to see Daniel slain, but neither did she want to see this boy fall beneath his steel.

"Stop, son!"

She was startled to hear Daniel's voice, and her eyes flew open. He was sitting still atop his new mount, staring at the boy.

"Come no further."

"Sir, you are my prisoner!" the young Yank said in a wavering voice.

"Sir, like hell I am!" Daniel replied. "Go back, boy, save your fool life!"

But the lad, quivering as he might be, drew his own sword and faced Daniel.

"Daniel, no!"

She didn't know she had intended to cry out until she did so. And then she was terribly afraid. Daniel didn't turn, but apparently he had heard her.

"Oh, the hell with this!" he muttered.

She watched in horror as he pulled out his Colt pistol with his left hand. The boy's eyes widened in fear; his face blanched.

Daniel shot at the bridge, his bullet lodging into the wood barely an inch from the Yank horse's hoof.

The horse screamed and reared, and the boy went catapulting from it.

"Ride!" Daniel commanded Callie.

She turned to do so, giving her horse free rein to gallop down the road.

Daniel was behind her once again. Despite the pounding of her own horse's hooves, she could hear that he followed her.

And again, she knew when he paused.

She knew, once again, that they were being followed.

She reined in even as Daniel did. Closing in on them was Eric Dabney himself.

Eric's horse's reins lay idle over the saddle.

Eric held a rifle aimed their way. Callie wasn't at all certain which of them he intended to hit. Her heart thundered hard. He would kill one of them.

She heard the explosion of a shot and a scream ripped from her lips. But Daniel didn't fall, and neither did she. Jared shrieked, but she quickly ascertained that he had not been hit.

A shout of pain and fury reached her ears, and she saw Eric Dabney fall from his horse to the ground. He rolled, and came to his knees gripping his arm.

Callie realized that Daniel had drawn his Colt once again, and that miraculously, he had beat Eric to the trigger.

"Bastard Rebel varmint!" Eric shouted in a rage. "You'll pay, Cameron! I swear, you'll pay for this!"

"Go!" Daniel commanded Callie, and once again, he gave her mount a firm slap upon its hindquarters. Her horse leapt into flight.

And this time, as Callie raced with the wind, no one followed.

No one except Daniel.

She was running with her enemy.

Twenty

*A*fter the incident by the creek Daniel drove them harder than ever. He was too smart a horseman to race the horses forever, but he didn't let up on a continuous movement. They paused only to water the horses once they had cooled down, and then they rode, relentlessly.

It was night before he allowed them to rest, and by then, Callie's stomach was truly grumbling. The day had been hot, and then it had rained, and then it had become hot again. She was exhausted from the hours in the saddle, worn ragged from the heat and the dampness.

When Daniel dismounted at last and came to set her on her feet, she nearly fell over. The look in his eyes, however, kept her standing.

"You—varmint!" she exploded. "You really think that I had Rudy Weiss send someone after us!"

He didn't answer her. He turned away and reached to take the saddlebags from his horse's haunches.

It was the wrong side of enough for Callie. Her limbs found new life. With Jared cradled strongly in one arm, she marched on Daniel and sent a fierce punch into his back with her free hand. It must have packed a certain wallop, for he spun on her with his eyes wide and his teeth clenched. "Bastard!" she hissed.

"And you must think that I sat there and pinched my own baby to make him cry out when it appeared that the Yanks might not stop us! I enjoy a reckless gallop across the countryside with my infant in my arms! Arrgh!" The sound escaped her, a cry, a growl, an emission of her deep-seated rage and resentment. She smashed her fist against his chest with the same fury.

"Stop it, Callie!" he cried in turn, catching her wrist, twisting it, pulling her against him. Her gaze met his, still in a rage. "Stop!"

"You stop!"

"Give me one good reason to trust you!"

She wrenched free of his hold, amazed that she could be so angry and feel the flash of tears burning in her eyes.

"One good reason? All right, Daniel, I'll give you the best. You should have trusted me, no matter what, because I loved you."

"Love is a word, Callie. One you know how to use well."

She inhaled sharply. "I was trying to save your life, you fool Reb!"

"By sending me to a Yankee prison camp?"

"You're not invincible, Daniel. They would have killed you."

He took a step toward her. There was a deep tension etched into his features. "Would that I could really believe that, Callie. Would that I could trust you."

The tears that had burned her eyes threatened to spill over. Maybe she had planted the seeds of doubt within his mind, but he still didn't believe her. Maybe he couldn't. Maybe the war had made him too mistrustful, too bitter.

But she had told him the truth, as simple as it was. And she wasn't risking placing her heart beneath his feet any longer.

She backed away from him, rubbing her chaffed wrist. "Don't bother to put yourself out on my account, Colonel. You must be a bitter man, dragging me through enemy territory. Don't ever forget, Daniel, that I am a Yankee. I believe in our cause. If you must mistrust me, go ahead and do so. I've never lied to you about my loyalties."

He stared at her. In the night, she couldn't fathom the emotion in his eyes. Perhaps there was none.

She spun on her heel, and walked away from him. Exhausted, heartsick, and bone weary, she sank down by a tree. Jared was fussy. She tried to feed him and crooned to him softly. She was so hungry herself perhaps she wasn't making decent milk for him anymore. She closed her eyes. Even the extent of her anger was fading. Everything was fading except for the pit of hunger at the bottom of her stomach.

She didn't realize that Daniel had left her until she began to smell something with an aroma so sweet and tantalizing that she thought she had to be dreaming. What a dream. She smelled something fresh-baked, like a pie crust. There was meat in it. Maybe even beef. It had that rich, wonderful scent of beef and gravy.

There was no beef to be had. Daniel hadn't caught and cooked anything because he didn't want to light a fire by night.

But oh, what a dream!

Her eyes flew open.

She wasn't dreaming. Daniel was hunched down before her with a fresh meat pie in his hands. Steam wafted above it, and it was the steam that brought the incredibly sweet and wonderful scent to her nose.

She stared at him, amazed.

He produced the fork from his mess kit, and handed it to her. She kept staring at him.

"Eat slowly, or you'll get sick," he warned her.

"But how—where—?"

"A farmhouse window, a good mile down the road. There were three of them. I only took one."

"You stole this?"

"I confiscated it."

"Stole it."

"Do you want to eat it or not?"

She did. She started to raise Jared to her shoulder, but Daniel reached for his son. The baby began to cry, but for once her hunger was stronger than her maternal instinct. It had been Daniel's idea to drag him through the countryside like this. And Daniel had claimed to be good with babies. He was welcome to be good now.

And he was. He walked away from her, gently rocking the baby on his shoulder, talking to him. Callie couldn't hear his words. She worried for just a second, and then she worried no more. She dived into the meat pie.

The first bite was heaven. The second bite was even sweeter still. She tried to warn herself to slow down, but the food was so good that she began to eat faster and faster. The food hit her empty stomach. Had she been standing, she would have swayed. She bit down hard, fighting a wave of nausea. Slowly, it passed. She looked down at the pie again. She had eaten more than half of it.

She waited a minute, assuring herself that she could stand, and that she wouldn't be sick. Then she rose, and walked the pie slowly over to Daniel.

She wanted to clobber him, but she felt compelled to apologize about the food. She did so, regally, trying to dredge up the best of her prewar manners.

"I'm so sorry. I believe that I've managed to consume a great deal more than my share."

There was the first light of humor in his eyes as they met hers.

"It's all right."

"It's not all right, sir! I had no—"

"Callie, you're feeding a baby. And we're not at a barn dance, or in someone's parlor. It's all right." He exchanged the baby for the pie, plucking the fork from her fingers. She had a feeling he would have lit into the pie with just his fingers if that meant saving some of the juices.

She would have done so herself.

He walked away from her, calling to her over his shoulder. "There's water, just down through the embankment over there. It's a creek, but it's running pretty deep, and there's plenty of rapids and falls along it. Be careful."

She nodded and turned away from him. She found a clean diaper for Jared and one of the few clean sacques she had along for him. She hurried down to the water.

It might be dangerous, she thought, but it was breathtaking. There was a moon out, and it was glittering down on the water that rushed over rocks, creating tiny falls. The creek ran straight to the river, she was sure, and it had some of the scope and power of the Potomac. The water seemed to dance in the moonlight, beautiful, magical.

She set Jared down on the soft shoulder, changed him and cleaned him, talking to him all the while. He smiled and gurgled in turn. She rinsed out his old clothing and diaper, and set them to dry on a rock. They probably wouldn't do so overnight, but in the morning they might.

She drank deeply, and splashed the water over her face and throat and arms. It felt so cool, so clean, after the long day. Days, she reminded herself. She had never felt so sweaty, so dirty. She glanced out over the creek, longing to dive right into it.

Some slight sound came from behind her. She swiveled around on her haunches.

Daniel was behind her. Leaning against a tree, he watched her. She wondered just how long he had been there. He walked down to her and fell on his knees beside her. He swept off his hat, then buried his own face in the water. He rose with it falling from him in splatters and waves. He cupped his hands and drank deeply. Then he eyed her, speculatively. "Good night, Mrs. Michaelson," he said softly.

He rose and walked slowly up the shoulder. He didn't go very far. She saw that he had led the horses to a nearby tree and tethered them. He had set the blanket down under the shade of a heavy old oak. He stretched out on it, adjusting his hat over his face to cut out the moonlight.

Well, she wasn't going to curl up by him. Not tonight.

She picked up Jared. She whispered to him, playing for a while, and Jared smiled and cooed and played back. He became fussy, and Callie fed him, and in time, he fell asleep at her breast. She adjusted her bodice and turned at last. There was another large oak near Daniel. She could spread her shawl out there for the baby to sleep on.

She did so, curling up beside him. The ground felt very rough and gritty. And dirty.

It was supposed to be dirty, she reminded herself. It was dirt.

But she began to wonder what crawled in it, as she never did when she slept beside Daniel. When she heard the hoot of an owl, she bolted up, nearly dislodging Jared.

Daniel was up, too, instantly alert. He stared at Callie in the moonlight.

"What the hell are you doing?"

"Trying to sleep."

"Why are you over there?"

"Because I don't care to sleep that close to you!"

He arched a brow. "Oh, I see. Fickle. Eat my pie, but eschew my bed!"

He was laughing at her, she thought. She turned her back on him, stretching out to try to sleep again.

He sighed. "Get over here, Callie."

"I will not."

"Get over here."

"I will not sleep beside a bloody Reb who won't even trust me!"

"You've warned me that you're a Yank through and through. I don't dare trust you completely. Now, are you coming over here?"

"No, I'm not!"

He was on his feet, striding her way. She bolted warily to a sitting position. "Are you planning on apologizing?" she asked him.

"No!"

"Then I am not coming over!"

"Give in, Callie."

"I will not. You give in."

"Hell no! I don't give in. It's all we Rebs have got."

"Well then, sir, we are at a stalemate, and no one wins!"

He paused, directly above her. She shrieked out as he reached down and plucked her up into his arms. His hold was tight. His eyes were fierce.

"No, Callie!" he corrected her as she stared at him, lips tight, body tense. "I win."

"Why the hell do you win?"

"Because I'm bigger. And stronger. And because you're going to sleep where I put you, that's why!"

He turned around, heading for the tree. "Daniel, don't you dare—Daniel, the baby!" she reminded him.

"I'm going back for him," he assured her, depositing her none too gently on the blanket beneath the tree that he had chosen. As he promised, he turned back for Jared.

A minute later her sleeping child was pressed back into her arms.

She kept her back stiff and hard to him all through the night.

Toward morning he awoke briefly, as she did, when Jared began to cry with hunger. Callie was very aware of him behind her, but she kept silent, her back stiff even then. She felt Daniel lie down beside her again.

She never went back to sleep after that point. She lay there for a long while, just watching as the first faint streaks of dawn began to peek softly through the leaves of the tree overhead. She closed her eyes, and she could hear the light chirping of the birds, and the soft rush of the water in the brook so near them. She opened her eyes again. The light that slowly began to flood around them seemed colored itself, pink and gold and orange and even crimson. It flickered gently, beautifully, over the trees, the earth, and the bubbling water. The earth smelled rich with the coming of the morning. From where Callie lay, it might have been a little stretch of Paradise, rather than a piece of border land, deeply divided between North and South.

For once, it was hard to think of the war. Callie sat up, watching how the light of dawn played over the water. The colors were truly glorious, dancing, playing on the foam that jumped and bubbled over the rocks.

She glanced at Jared. He slept soundly, his little mouth open, his tiny limbs splayed. She smiled. Her smile fading, she glanced at his father. Daniel, too, it seemed, slept peacefully.

Carefully, so as not to arouse either of them, she rose. She walked down to the creek bed. The water was so clean and enticing. And she was so dusty and sweaty and miserable.

She glanced back at the sleeping men in her life. She shed her shirt and bodice and her petticoat and pantalets. She shivered as the morning air hit her, clad only in her long chemise. She wanted to strip it away, too, but she didn't. She glanced at Daniel again nervously, but then she didn't care. The temptation to soak herself in the cool clean water was overwhelming.

She stepped into it. She nearly screamed as the cold first struck her, but she swallowed down the urge. She moved farther across the creek, grateful that it grew deeper, deep enough for her to sink into it to her waist, and filled enough with rock so that her toes didn't sink into squishy mud. She shivered violently at first, but as she came down into the water, her shivering ceased. It was beautiful. It seemed to cleanse away the days of riding, the mud and the dust.

She found a low, flat rock beneath a craggy rapid and sat upon it, delighting in the water that cascaded down upon her head and hair. She scrubbed her face with it, and rubbed it over her shoulders. She stretched out, allowing it to fall over her breasts and belly and thighs. She opened her mouth, and drank it, and she cupped it into her hands and sluiced it over her throat once again.

She looked to the embankment.

Jared still slept.

Daniel did not.

Barefoot and in his uniform breeches only, he was standing on the embankment. He had cast off his frock coat and shirt to bury his torso in the water, it seemed, but then he had seen her. He watched her now, the sun glistening over the bronze muscles of his shoulders and chest, and the lean ripple of flesh that led down to his belly.

His eyes met hers.

She had kept on the chemise for modesty's sake. How foolish. For it was sheer and pale, and it was plastered against her, and it hid nothing of her body. It accented it, she thought, clinging to every curve and angle. Puckering over her breasts. Molding tight to the triangle at her legs.

She needed to do something. To sink low into the water, to cover herself.

But as she watched him, she discovered that she couldn't move.

Daniel had no such problem.

His eyes held hers. With a slow stride, he started across the rushing creek. The water waltzed and danced and rushed around his gray pants legs. It shimmered in droplets on his shoulders and chest. He had grown lean, she thought vaguely. Lean, but hard, harder than ever. A pulse ticked against the cord of his throat, and muscles constricted and rippled as he moved.

Leave, she told herself. Push away from the rock, and leave. Walk by him. He will not stop you.

But she didn't leave. She stayed there, watching as he came. Feeling his eyes burn into her. He came close, closer still. The heat and power of his body became tangible.

And still, she didn't move.

He stood in front of her in his taut, soaked breeches. She raised her chin, to better look into his eyes. She moistened her lips with the tip of her tongue against the dryness that so suddenly and so fiercely plagued them.

He was watching her mouth. He was going to kiss her.

He did not.

He suddenly dropped to his knees in the shallow water, his hands bracing her hips. She should have moved. She should have cried out. She should have denounced him for the way that he condemned her.

She did nothing. She was electrified, caught in his hold, in the staggering heat of his body.

And in the kiss that finally touched her. Not her lips. Her belly. Through the thin fabric of her chemise, she felt his lips. Then felt the ragged, searing fire of his tongue as it moved in a staggering path across the plane of her stomach.

Touching her navel, lowering to tease and taunt in an ever closer pattern to the heat and pulse that had now begun to throb between her thighs.

Cry out, stop him! she warned herself. She opened her mouth, but no words would come, only a choking, breathless sound. He stood, rising before her. His hands moved possessively over the length of her. Touching her, warming her. His mouth, his lips, his kiss, focused on her breasts. Closing over the fabric, heedless of it, no, using it. The movement of cloth and the heat and dampness of his mouth upon her nipple were nearly more than she could bear. He tugged gently, then suckled hard, drawing her into his mouth, easing his hold, playing his tongue upon her again. He must taste the baby's milk, she thought, her face flaming, but if so, then he was fascinated by it. For his intimate touch moved over her breasts again and again.

At long last, his lips found hers. Found them, and held them. Moved upon them frantically, demanding more and more. His mouth parted hers, his tongue delved deeply, plundered, and caressed once again. She began to shake and shiver wildly, not from the cold of the water, but from the heat of the man.

His mouth closed over her shoulder, his teeth nipped lightly, his tongue bathed her. His kiss trailed down the sodden valley of cloth between her breasts. He created a line with his tongue. The line began to burn.

And to travel farther and farther down.

It seemed to lazily sear the length of her. Touching her navel again. Forming a distinct trail beneath it. Coming lower and lower and then finding the very heart of the throbbing between her thighs. Touching upon soft and intimate places with the fabric still between his mouth's caress and the tender and sensitive and secret regions of her flesh. Had fire been set to dry kindling, no sensation could have been more explosive. Sweet honeyed ripplings of pleasure burst through Callie, and she cast her head back, trying not to cry out with the sheer sensual pleasure that filled her, but emitting soft moans despite her best efforts.

And he kept on and on until she was shivering anew, filled to the bursting point, scarcely able to stand. Perhaps he knew his own power, for the very moment she would have fallen, he was up, scooping her into his arms, carrying her to the embankment. In seconds his breeches were shed, unleashing the ardency of his desire to spring to life before her. She closed her eyes, shivering, wanting him.

He lowered himself upon her. She was barely aware of the earth and sky and the rush of the water, and then again, she had never felt them so keenly. She felt her back, moving over the earth, she felt the hot touch of the sun, she felt the cooling sensation of the water.

She felt the hard burning entry of the man, felt a spasm of pain at first; she almost fought him. But his words were there, as silken and seductive as the movement of his fingers over her bare flesh. "It's the baby, Callie. You've had a baby. It will ease."

She bit into his shoulder, and he moved again. Slowly. Fully. Desire rushed through her again, easing away the pain. Within moments, it was gone.

Blessedly so, for his desire seemed even greater than the other hunger that had plagued them so. He was ever a considerate lover, then consideration fell away. He was the sun itself, burning with a fire not to be quenched. He moved like the impetus of the brook, cascading in a rush upon her. He was as rich, as full, as redolent as the earth around her. But most of all, he was storm,

thundering against a windswept shore, and sweeping her into the ardent whirlwind of his deepest needs.

Even as she soared and seemed to slip into some netherland of near darkness,
he shuddered violently against her, again, again, and again. She felt the ripple of
muscle, the sweet expulsion from his body filling her own, and then slowly, the
heat of his weight, descending upon hers. For long moments their breath mingled, their heartbeats thundered and finally slowed together. For long sweet
moments she felt encapsulated by warmth, by intimacy, by tenderness.

He held her, his face wet and slick against her throat and breasts.

"Callie!"

She thought she heard his whisper and that something remained in it of the
love they had once shared that seemed but a distant memory now. It seemed as if
something might be salvaged, as if he might believe in her again.

He rolled from her, breaking the band of heat and the aftermath of tenderness. He lay with his arm cast over his forehead as he stared up at the sky.

Callie felt the cold breeze sweeping around her. His warmth was gone from
her. And she realized that although he might be feeling a few doubts, he still
didn't trust her. Maybe he wanted to.

But he hadn't really forgiven her. He had come to her because he had wanted
her. He had come to her because of the deprivations of war. Just as a hungry
man would dine on any meal.

Tears, as hot and vibrant as her passion had been, rushed to her eyes. She
would never shed them before him, she swore swiftly. She twisted far from his
touch and rose, rushing back into the water.

"Callie!"

He, too, was on his feet quickly, heedless of his lack of dress. She ignored his
call, sinking into the water, glad of the cold, grateful even for the discomfort.

"Callie, damn you!"

He caught her hands and wrenched her up. "What in God's name is the
matter with you?"

"Nothing. Will you get away from me, please?"

"Why are you running from me?"

"I'm not running. I'm trying to bathe."

She saw him stiffen. Felt it in his fingers. "Trying to bathe away my touch?"
he asked softly.

"You tell me," she replied, her tone as light, "Have you decided that I didn't
warn the Yanks? That in that, at the very least, I am innocent?"

He didn't answer. She saw the shadows cover his eyes, the hard subtle twist of
his jaw. "You're trying to tell me that you didn't bring me back to your house to
be disarmed and taken by your friend, Captain Dabney?"

"Yes! I brought you back! I didn't want them to kill you. You don't want to
understand—"

"No, you're wrong. I want desperately to understand. I'd like to understand,
too, why Dabney reappeared," he said politely. Something was different. Maybe
he did doubt himself. Maybe he was afraid to do so.

She stared at him, frustrated, furious, wishing that she could slap him—and
then jump up and down on his fallen body. "Bastard!" She shoved against him
so hard that he stumbled.

Trying to pull her drenched chemise down as she moved, she ignored him and started to stride from the water.

His hand fell upon her arm, swinging her back. "I've been the target for enough Yanks, Mrs. Michaelson. Don't push me any further."

"Push you!" she hissed. "Push you! I'd like to take a buggy whip to you!"

"Careful—" he warned, his eyes narrowing.

"Careful be damned! You despise me, you mistrust me, yet you're willing to drag me across the country. Your hatred seems to have little to do with your desires."

"Really, and what of yours?"

"I didn't accost you—"

"Accost?" he interrupted coolly. "I don't think that what I just did could be misconstrued in any way as an attack or an act of force."

Her cheeks flamed. "It surely was not my idea, you Rebel—rodent!"

"Rebel—rodent?" he repeated, just a shade of amusement touching his voice, bending his lips. The amusement vanished. His eyes were intense. "Sorry," he said softly, "I didn't hear the protests."

"Well, hear them now, Colonel Cameron. Stay away from me."

He stared at her, then reminded her quietly, "There was a time, Mrs. Michaelson, when you didn't seem to mind so very much. There was a time when you went out of your way to openly seduce a man. Today you were far more subtle."

"What?" Callie gasped.

He smiled, a casual, taunting smile. He would have tipped his hat, had he been wearing it. And still, not wearing anything at all, he managed a swaggering arrogance as he passed by her.

"Today you were a vision in white, Mrs. Michaelson. From the moment I awoke. White that lay like a second skin over your bare flesh."

"I needed to bathe!" she cried out indignantly.

He walked by her. The assumption was left that it had been her fault. That she had seduced him before, and tried to do so again now.

"Oh!" she screamed out her exasperation and fury. He didn't stop. She stooped down and grabbed some of the mud from the floor of the creek. She sent it flying across the creek to slap hard over his naked back.

It brought him to a standstill. He whipped around, and seeing the look on his face, Callie was ready to run again. She spun, but the creek bottom was slippery. She hadn't managed to take a single step before he catapulted his length against her, bringing them crashing back down into the water.

She struggled to free herself from his hold. He straddled over her, holding her tightly. Panting, she paused and found herself staring up into his eyes again. He was laughing, and suddenly she discovered that she was laughing too.

But then their laughter died away, and once again, a warmth swept through her, one always created by his touch. The cold shadows had slipped away from his eyes and his passion rode hot within them again.

"Tell me that you didn't want me, Callie!" he charged her heatedly.

"I did not set out to seduce you!" she cried. Dear Lord, what did he want from her? "Daniel, let me up, let me be! All right! I wanted you. But this can't happen anymore!"

"Why, Callie? If you're so damned innocent, why is it only all right when the Yanks are around?"

"Stop it!" she charged him. "That's exactly why it's so wrong."

His hold on her suddenly loosened. His fingers moved gently over a wet tendril of hair. "Help me?" he whispered suddenly. "I want to believe! Callie, you do seduce, so help me God, you seduce. You are beautiful. And what if you're telling the truth? I'm still a Rebel. You're a Yank. Not just by geography —by conviction, Callie, I . . ."

His voice trailed away. He started to speak again, but they were suddenly interrupted by a loud and furious cry.

Jared.

Callie shoved at Daniel. "I have to get the baby."

He didn't move but stared hard at her. She shoved him again. "I'm begging you, leave me be!" she cried to him passionately. "Leave me be."

He rose, caught her hands, and jerked her to her feet. "If only we can leave one another be!"

She heard the baby's plaintive wail. And still they stared at one another.

She spun around, heedless of his meaning. She rushed back to the river bank to sweep her son into her arms.

If only they could leave one another be.

Twenty-one

Three days later, they managed to cross the Potomac. They were back in Virginia, but it was dangerous territory, and the going was rough. They could stumble upon more troops from either army at any given time.

It was difficult, for they both had little to say to one another. The tension grew between them as the long days and nights passed.

Finally, eight days but a true eternity since they had set out, they reached Fredericksburg. Callie could immediately see the change in Daniel when they reached the city, for it was held firmly in Confederate hands.

It was a beautiful old city, Callie thought. She knew that George Washington's family had lived here and kept property near the Rappahannock. Under better circumstances, she might have enjoyed the travel.

But war had come here and too many times. Many buildings were riddled with shot, and the people bore the haggard look of tenacious but weary fighters.

Callie hoped that they would stay, at least for a few days. She longed for a bath with steaming hot water and for a soft bed beneath her at night. But Daniel was determined to push on. He was able to buy some food, some bread and ham at exorbitant prices, and he procured a wagon so that Callie could ride awhile with the baby sleeping in back. But he was dead set on reaching Richmond, and then his home.

At last they passed by all the sentries and came into Richmond, the Confederate capital, the heart of its existence.

Daniel was driving the wagon with the horses hitched to the rear when they first approached the city from a slight ridge. Callie looked down on it. It was large and sprawling with the beautiful capital buildings visible in the sunlight. She could even see the statuary before it. Handsome buildings and beautiful churches surrounded it. It was a busy place, with people moving at a hectic pace.

"Well, you are home," Callie said softly.

He glanced her way. "Not home, but close."

She bowed her head. She was so weary. She prayed he didn't intend to keep riding on tonight. Yet she was afraid to let him know just how exhausted she was. It hadn't seemed that she had slept, really slept, in an eternity. She and Daniel had taken to sleeping at a distance, and the ground—to which it seemed he had grown so accustomed—was hard and cold to her, sending chills into her body every night. And every night she lay awake, wanting the warmth he could give her, more furious with each passing day that she could still desire someone who taunted her so, condemned her so.

She loved him still. As much as she hated some of the things that he said and did, there were other things that reminded her why she had first fallen in love with him. When she watched him with Jared, she knew that he loved the child, that he was the best of fathers, that he would have been this caring with or without the war. He had tried very diligently to see to her welfare, managing to procure more and more food for them as they came closer and closer to Rebel territory. He would never take a portion of food first; he would never even take a sip of water first when they came to a stream. Her cavalier was tarnished and tattered, but underneath the fraying gray, the gentleman remained, no matter what the circumstances, no matter what his anger or his emotion.

Callie's only defense against Daniel were her pride and strength, and both were at a low ebb now.

She sat stiffly, determined that she would not break down and beg for anything at this late date. Perhaps she could make a casual suggestion.

"Have you friends to see in Richmond?" she asked him, feigning a yawn as she did so.

She felt the force of his blue gaze. "Yes, Reb friends, of course," he replied politely.

"People you need to see?"

He laughed softly. "You don't give a damn if I need to see anyone, Callie. You just want a bed for a night."

She gazed at him coolly. "Is that so bad?"

"Not if you come right out and ask for it," he told her. He clicked the reins over the horses' flanks and the wagon began to move more briskly. "Yes, Callie, I have friends here. And we'll stay for the night."

It wasn't quite that easy. By the time they moved into the city streets, Callie saw that they were filled with people hurrying along their way. There were lines in various places where people were trying to buy goods. Inflation was high; the Yankee blockade was doing its damage to the Confederacy with far more efficiency than any of the troops in the field.

A footless soldier in a ragged uniform limped by them on a pair of rude crutches and Daniel drew in the carriage, calling out to him, "Soldier, do you know of any rooms available?"

The man saluted sharply, then came toward Daniel. "Sir! I'm afraid I know of none." He glanced Callie's way. "How do you do, ma'am." To Daniel he said, "Bringing your wife and child into safety, eh, sir? Well, I'm sure the army can see to something. And you, ma'am, you musn't worry. We won't let the Yankees into Richmond. Ever. We've fought 'em time and time again. Don't fret none."

Callie remained silent. Within another hour, though, Daniel was swearing softly. He'd tried every rooming house and hotel he knew, and all were filled to the hallways. Refugees naturally seemed to flock to Richmond. Once their farms were destroyed, they had to seek some kind of employment. As the war continued, their numbers were growing.

"We should have just ridden home," he muttered.

Callie, with Jared in her arms, stretched her aching back. "I thought that you had friends in the city," she said.

"I didn't think you would want to meet them," he returned.

Of course. His friends would know he didn't have a wife.

"Hell!" he muttered suddenly. "If we're going to go that route, we'll do it from the top."

"Daniel, what are you doing?" she demanded.

He refused to answer. Ten minutes later they were pulling up before a beautiful and gracious white house with a wide porch and huge white columns. There were horses and carriages all around, soldiers standing on duty, and a great deal of commotion.

"Daniel, where are we?" Callie demanded.

"At a friend's house," he said tersely. He caught her hand. "Come on."

"I can't go in there!" Callie said, tugging on her hand nervously. "I haven't bathed, it's been as hot as blazes, the baby's clothes are as filthy as my own. Daniel, let me go—"

But he didn't let her go, and his hold was fierce. Apparently he was well known here, for soldiers greeted him not just with salutes but with warm greetings as they hurried to the entry.

"Daniel, where are we?" Callie persisted.

"They call it the White House of the Confederacy."

"And—and Jeff Davis is your friend?" she nearly shrieked.

"Actually, I know Varina much better," he told her. She blanched. She wanted to hit him, she wanted to run.

"Let me go, Daniel."

"Not on your life."

"You're bringing a Yank to see Jeff Davis?"

"You said you wanted a bed. Varina will find one for me."

"You'd better let me go! I could do horrible things in there, Daniel. I could start singing the 'Battle Hymn of the Republic.' I could—"

"Open your mouth just once at the wrong time, Callie, and you'll be singing it hog-tied in the wagon!" he warned her.

The door opened. A handsome black butler stood there, his face split into a grin. "Why, Colonel Cameron." His smile faded slightly, and his voice dropped to a whisper. "Colonel, I'm mighty pleased to see you alive, sir. We heard all about that battle in that Gettysburg place, sir, yes we did. It's taken a hard toll on my folks in there, what with Vicksburg falling on the Fourth of July, just like a plum into the hands of them Yanks. But you come on in now, ye hear. Lawdy, yes, Colonel, you come on in. And a little one! My, my, you've gone done and got yerself hitched, Colonel Cameron!"

Daniel didn't reply. The butler was now taking a closer look at both of them, staring at Callie's worn shoes and getting a full view of a dusty, travel-stained skirt. He swallowed. "Yessir, you and your lady come on in."

Daniel thanked him and they came into a handsome foyer with statuettes in niches on either side of the main entry into the house. The fine hardwood floor was covered with a thick paper matting in an attractive pattern, set there to protect the floor from the hundreds of feet that must surely pass over it every day. The walls were covered with a beautiful papering that made them appear to be marble.

The butler disappeared ahead of them. A doorway to the right, slightly ajar, led to an immense dining room. The doorway to Callie's left was closed, but the main doorway before her suddenly burst open, and a beautiful woman with haunting dark eyes came through.

"Daniel!"

Her voice was soft, gracious, melodious. She was not a young girl, but a mature woman, probably in her middle to late thirties, Callie thought. She had seldom seen a woman more beautiful.

Or clean, she added, in comparison to herself.

Her skirts rustled with her every movement. Her day dress was demure, cut nearly to the throat. It was a dove gray and shimmering silver, enhanced by rows of fine black embroidered lace. Her hair was neatly confined to a net at the back of her head, and despite the heat of the day, she appeared remarkably cool and poised.

She hugged Daniel. He caught her hands and kissed both of her cheeks.

"Daniel, you've come back from Gettysburg!" she whispered. "Was it as horrible as they say? Oh, dear Lord, what am I asking you? Of course it was horrible, wretched, terrible. But my poor old Banny, so many don't see it, but he dies just a little bit with every soldier out there! Now Vicksburg has fallen too."

Her voice trailed away as she looked past Daniel and saw Callie. If she thought anything at all of Callie's pathetic appearance, she was too well bred to give any sign. "I am so very, very sorry!" She broke away from Daniel and stretched out her hands to Callie. "I am Varina Davis, child, and you appear exhausted. And you've a baby! Please, may I take him?"

The beautiful woman in her crisp elegant clothing swept the baby into her arms, not seeming to notice that his bundling was as dirty as everything else about Callie and Daniel.

Varina Davis took one look at the baby and then not even her immense poise could hide her surprise. "Daniel! Oh, but the war does strange things to people. You've married and had this precious child!" Jared started to whimper and Callie had to fight the impulse to snatch him back. She didn't need to. Varina Davis laughed and set him over her shoulder, patting his back, and he quieted. "Daniel, you must be trying to get your baby and bride home."

Callie waited, holding her breath, wondering if Daniel would blithely mentioned that he hadn't bothered to marry his child's mother.

She thought about mentioning it herself. She opened her mouth to do so, thinking that Daniel deserved whatever she chose to say.

But her mouth closed, for she discovered that no matter what her anger for

Daniel, she was entranced with Varina Davis. The lady was truly the heart of the Confederacy, Callie thought. And if the Rebs were her enemies, no one could be more so than this woman, wife of the Confederate president. But she was charming, and she was caring. In her voice was all her passion for the men who had died—and all of her concern and empathy for her Banny. Just a few short years ago—before the war, before secession—Jefferson Davis had been the secretary of war for the United States, and he had been a fairly well-known man. His reputation was that of a cold, hard, unyielding man, one with little charm. And yet, if this woman loved him so deeply, there had to be something good, something warm, about him.

"You all look exhausted and famished!" Varina said. "I've some ladies from the hospital league in the drawing room; come in, please, and join us. They'll all be so delighted to see Daniel, and soon I can be alone—"

"No!" Callie gasped. She realized quickly how rude she had sounded, and she apologized quickly. "I'm so sorry, it's just that we really can't come in." She moistened her lips. That her simple homespun cotton could never compare with the elegance of Varina's dress didn't bother her. Before the war, her family hadn't been rich, but they hadn't been poor, and Pa had always told them that the measure of a man or a woman wasn't in the gold in his pocket, but in the way he felt inside. She had never been intimidated by silk, satin, or wealth.

She was somewhat intimidated here, though. Not by Varina's elegance, but by her poise and her heart. She had never felt more shabby in her life.

"Mrs. Davis, truly, I couldn't possibly come farther into your home than I am now."

"I'm desperate for a room, Varina," Daniel told her. "Richmond has gone insane, it seems. I cannot get a room anywhere."

"Of course!" Varina murmured. "Stay here, I shall be right back."

She smiled, surrendered Jared back to Callie, and disappeared into the parlor for a minute.

"How could you bring us here!" Callie hissed to Daniel.

"You said that you—"

"But to bring us here!"

"Sad place for a Yank, eh?" he murmured. He bent closer. "Jeff receives his official visitors upstairs. If there is anything you wish to plan against the Union, that's the place where you should be."

"It would serve you right if I were a full-fledged spy!" she retorted.

"I must admit, I have given the idea some thought," he said with a slight bow.

She would have replied, except that Varina was returning, stepping back through the doorway into the foyer. She smiled radiantly at Daniel. "Well, Daniel, we're all set. Lucretia Marby is in the parlor and just as I thought, her sister's house is empty, what with Letty and her husband striving so diligently for our cause in England. You know the place, Daniel, it's the brick Gunner Estate. And you know the people, of course. Gerald and Letty Lunt. You've been there for parties, I'm quite certain. Ben, Letty's house servant, is there, and will see to your needs." She passed Daniel a note. "Just hand him this note. He does read, so you'll have no difficulties."

"Thank you, Varina," Daniel told her. "Very much."

He kissed her cheek. She smiled again. "I'll expect to see you before you leave. And that beautiful baby of yours." She took Callie's hand. Her grip was warm and firm. "It's been a pleasure, dear. If you grow weary at that old plantation of Daniel's, come back to Richmond." She sighed softly. "We'll put you to work!"

"Thank you," Callie told her. Varina withdrew, and she turned as Daniel took her elbow and led her back out of the foyer. People were hurrying down the walk to reach the house even as they left it; women who nodded cordially, men who tipped their hats.

They reached the wagon and Daniel lifted her into it. "You were very well behaved," he told her pleasantly.

"Spies need to be," she told him sweetly. He arched a brow, but didn't take the bait. When he was seated again, and flipped the reins, she studied him. "Do all Confederate colonels know the president and his wife so well?"

He glanced her way. "My mother was from Mississippi. From near Varina's home. Their families were friends. But the door to the house is nearly always open. They entertain frequently. Jefferson is not nearly so rigid as he is often made out to be; he is an excellent husband, an adoring father. And Varina . . ." He paused for a moment. "I think that she is the greatest lady I have ever met."

Callie listened to the gentleness in his voice, to the note of reverence in it. He would never, never speak so kindly of her, she was certain, and for some reason, she was hurt.

The wagon turned a corner. "Here we are," Daniel commented.

They had come to a large, Federal-style brick house with a broad porch. Daniel reined in the wagon and lifted Callie down with the baby, and urged her up the walk and steps. He knocked quickly at the door, and it was answered by a very tall black man in gold-and-black livery. A bright white smile quickly lit across his features. "Why, Colonel Cameron."

"Hello, Ben," Daniel said, passing him the note. "We've come for the night. I hope we're not too great an inconvenience to the household."

Ben looked from their weary faces to the note, quickly scanning it. "You didn't need no note, Colonel. You know you're always welcome in this house," he chastised. "Colonel, Mrs. Cameron, please come right in. You just tell me what you want, and it's yours."

They entered an elegant, marble-floored foyer with ceilings that seemed to touch the sky.

Callie stared about, awed despite her best intentions. This was a room for the night?

"What would you like, Callie? A nap?" Daniel suggested.

She looked at Ben. "A bath. With steaming water. Please."

"Just as you say, ma'am. It will steam like a kettle, I swear it! Cissy!" Ben called out. He smiled at Callie. "Cissy sure does love little ones. She'll bathe him and fix him up right as rain, with your permission, ma'am."

Cissy entered the room. She was round and plump, with a broad smile. Callie wished that she could curl into the woman's arms right along with the baby.

"I don't need long—" Callie began.

"Oh, he's a precious one!" Cissy crooned. "You go right on, ma'am." Cissy turned to walk away with the baby. Ben clapped his hands and a few boys appeared, tall, wiry youths. He quickly ordered that Miz Letty's big tin tub be filled upstairs in the guest room, then he told Callie that he would show her to the room. Daniel excused himself, saying that he was going to the den, and would help himself to brandy.

After the days on the road, the house was like a buffer of soft cotton. Following Ben up the stairway, Callie was afraid to touch the bannisters. She hated to walk on the crimson carpeting.

When she reached the guest room, her eyes went first to the huge bed with its beautiful quilt. She would sleep on that tonight, she thought, and the very idea of it seemed to be a promise of heaven.

The tub arrived in the room, and then bucket after bucket of steaming water. A young black girl arrived with soap and a cloth and a heavy bath sheet. At long last, she was left alone. She touched the water, and it was steaming, so warm it almost scorched the flesh. It was just what she wanted.

She peeled away her clothing with haste, heedless of where it fell, and crawled into the tub. She almost cried out, but the warmth evened out, and it was delicious. She waited a moment, then sank low into the water, soaking her hair.

She breathed in the soap, then scrubbed it furiously over her body, working the lather into her hair. She rinsed, soaped herself and her hair again, and then sank back, resting her head on the rim of the tub, and simply luxuriating in the feel of being clean.

She could have lain there forever.

Downstairs, Daniel poured himself a large brandy from Gerald's desk-side bar. He swallowed the first one quickly, then poured himself another. This he sipped, slowly savoring the taste. He rolled the glass in his hands. Despite the blockade, the Lunts seemed to be faring well enough. He had heard that Lunt had financed a blockade runner, and that while the ship was bringing in its share of medicines and the more necessary implements of a war-torn society, the ship was also bringing in fashions and colognes and soaps from France from which a tremendous profit was being made. Wars could break men. They could also make them rich.

He set the brandy glass down, noticing that his fingers weren't quite steady. At the moment, he was grateful that Gerald Lunt was doing well. He was desperately hungry, and someone was in the kitchen fixing him a dinner of fried chicken, potatoes, turnip greens, and black-eyed peas. Callie had wanted a bath first. He'd wanted to eat. He'd been so careful never to let her see how hungry he had been while they traveled.

He sat back in a leather armchair. He still wanted to throttle her. Now more so than ever. But he hadn't been able to stand watching her in any physical distress. It had hurt to see her hungry; it had hurt worse to watch her shiver in the night. Especially once he had discovered that he dared not go near her.

Dear Lord, he wanted her still! Nothing had been quenched by touching her.

Was she as innocent as she claimed? Maybe his anger had seized hold of his mind. He still couldn't trust her completely, but doubts as to his own righteousness had set in.

Why was he so damned torn, thinking one moment that he cradled a viper to his breast, and finding the very next second that he could still think of nothing but her. Maybe she was innocent—and he was a fool. He dreamed now night and day of touching her again, dreamed of the way she had looked rising from the water, droplets gliding along the curves of her body, that sheer garment of hers hugging everything that he longed to touch. He hadn't thought that morning, not for a single minute. He had just walked out to take what he wanted.

She was the greatest glory he had ever known.

He raised his brandy glass again. "Angel!" he whispered.

The door opened. Ben brought in a plate of food. The aromas were mouth watering. The tray, with its steaming coffee and well-seasoned food, was set before him on Gerald Lunt's cherry-wood desk.

"How's that, Colonel?"

"Well, I'll tell you, Ben, I don't think that I've seen anything quite so wonderful-looking in my whole life."

Ben laughed. "Get on with you, sir! Why, that little boy of yours has to be the most wonderful thing you've ever seen. He's your spittin' image, sir, that's what he is."

Daniel looked up sharply. "He is, isn't he?"

"A boy to be proud of, sir!"

Yes, he was. Jared was wonderful. Daniel drummed his fingers over the desk, watching Ben. "How is—my wife?"

"Sir, she seems just as pleased as if she's gone to heaven with all the angels! She's a right fine lady you've found yourself, Colonel."

Daniel grunted.

"And she sure done give you one beautiful boy, sir!"

Yes, she had done that. It seemed that she hadn't even intended to tell him about Jared, but that didn't really matter. Not now. He had his son.

What were the laws on the child?

More importantly, what were his responsibilities to her?

"Enjoy your meal," Ben said, and grinned. "Good thing you married her, sir, before she could get away. I'm not so sure I've ever seen a more beautiful woman, white or black! Some other man would have been along for her real quick, that's darned certain, if you hadn't a married her, Colonel!"

Daniel forced his face into a grin. "Right, Ben."

Ben left him. He tried to bite into the chicken that had smelled so damned good just a few moments before.

What about Callie? Did she hate him now, did she fear him? Sometimes she felt the same things he did. He had held her when she quaked within his arms and had flown the ultimate bounds of passion.

She was always fighting him. But she had carried Jared, and she had been determined to come with Daniel when he had said he was taking his son.

He had to marry her. His father would have said so; his mother would have been shocked. Jesse would definitely find it his sworn duty—especially since Daniel had been the one to warn his brother that he had best marry Kiernan quickly if he wanted his son born in wedlock.

It was the only honorable thing to do. And she said that she had loved him. Had. Past tense. Even if those words were true, so very much lay between them. Their worlds were at war.

What were his feelings for her? His real feelings? Just the thought of her made him warm, made him tremble.

He groaned aloud and set down his fork. Once upon a time, he would have known that it was the only right thing to do, no matter what. But once upon a time he had lived in a beautiful gracious world where men and women knew all the rules, and both lived by those rules. It had been a beautiful time, before hunger, before this awful loss of innocence had befallen them all.

Jesse! He thought suddenly of his brother. His best friend. His companion. The steadying voice in his life for so many years. If only he were here.

But Jesse wore blue. He couldn't be here to listen, to advise.

Daniel leaned back, and the hint of a wistful smile played at his lips. "I do know what you would say, brother. I believe that I do. And maybe that doesn't even matter. I cannot risk losing my son. You should see him, Jess. God, is he beautiful."

His voice trailed away.

He wondered if he wasn't just a little bit afraid of losing *her* now that he had his hands upon her.

Maybe reasons didn't matter at all. Only the deed.

He rose, strode across the room, opened the door, and shouted for Ben. He was going home with a wife.

"Yessir, Colonel?" Ben was quickly before him.

"Ben, I have a little problem with my wife."

"What's that, sir?"

"She isn't my wife."

Ben drew back, shocked. Daniel hid a smile. Even the old-world servants knew that the world had rules. And they insisted their masters know them and live by them.

"Well, it ain't my place to say nothin', sir—"

"Ben, I'm trying to rectify that situation, but I need some help. Could you find me someone very, very discreet, who could arrange to marry us?"

"Here, sir? Now?"

"Right now. Well, say, in thirty minutes."

Ben grinned broadly. "Well, now, sir, I—I'll do my best!" He stepped back, frowning. He started to walk away, shaking his head. "Brandy, that was easy," he muttered. "A meal, that's easy, too. A bath I can manage quick as a wink. But a minister . . . folks, they just want everything these days!"

"Ben—one more thing. Could I scare up some clean clothes? I can arrange a new uniform at home. Civilian dress would be just fine. And I need something for Callie."

"Yessir!" Ben said. "Yessir." He turned again, shaking his head as he hurried away.

Daniel smiled. With his mind made up, he found that he was famished once again. He sat down to his meal. He'd just eaten the last piece of chicken when there was a tap on the door. Ben entered with a large box.

"Colonel, I got here a white muslin with fine little flowers embroidered into it."

Daniel's brows shot up. Ben had worked quickly. "Is it Letty's?"

He shook his head. "No sir, I didn't think that Miz Cameron—that your lady —would be too cotton on taking a handout for her wedding. I bought it from a young lady down the street who's heading back to Charleston to stay with her family. Her man's just been killed at Gettysburg and she's wearing black, so she's no more need of this."

"That's fine. I've not much money on me, Ben, but I'll get the cost back to Gerald as soon as I reach Cameron Hall."

"There's no need, Colonel. I bought it with your horse."

Daniel laughed. "That's fine." The Yankee bay cavalry horses were worth quite a bit. Especially now. But he was going home. No place on earth bred finer horses than Cameron Hall. "What about the ceremony?"

"I went on down to the Episcopal Church, and I didn't know where to start, so I just set the whole thing right in Father Flannery's lap. He said that it was all highly irregular, that's what he said—irregular—but seeing as how you were a hero in the cause, he could understand how maybe you and the lady were delayed a bit in the sacrament."

Daniel lowered his head. He was certain that he might also need to make a bit of a contribution to the church.

"When's he coming?"

"Within the hour, Colonel. He promised."

"That's good. I thank you, Ben. You're a good man. You ever get tired of working here, and there will always be a place for you at Cameron Hall."

"Lawdy, Colonel Cameron, you know I can't go nowhere, never. I'm Mr. Lunt's personal property."

"Not according to Lincoln," Daniel muttered.

Ben shrugged. "But Mr. Lincoln, he got to make those northerners win the war first, right? And you must own your own houseman, Colonel Cameron."

Daniel stood up. "I don't own any man, Ben." Ben looked at him curiously.

Daniel clamped him on the shoulder. "It's a strange damned world, isn't it, Ben?"

"Yessir, Colonel. And getting stranger by the minute!"

Callie stayed in the water quite some time. Nothing had ever felt so good.

But as the water cooled, she felt the stirrings of hunger. The miraculous thing was that she could eat. Here, in this household, wonderful things like beds and baths and food seemed to be hers for the asking.

She just needed to rouse herself.

She opened her eyes and almost screamed. She wasn't alone in the room anymore.

Daniel had come in silently, as if it were his right. He stood there watching her, a large dressmaker's box held idly in his arms. His sweeping hat was gone, but he still wore his tattered uniform. The fire that could make him so exciting burned in his eyes. He stood straight, shoulders squared, yet still casual.

And still arrogant.

She swallowed hard, narrowing her eyes. "What are you doing here?"

"How very rude of you," he replied.

"Get out."

"Can't, I'm afraid. It's my room too."

"Your room—"

"Well, you haven't protested being called Mrs. Cameron. They've placed us here together—my love."

"Don't call me that!"

"Is it so disturbing?"

"It's hypocritical."

"Just practicing."

"For what?"

He pulled out his pocket watch. "There's an Episcopal priest coming in about twenty minutes now. If we're lucky. I need the tub. Out."

"What?" Callie's fingers gripped the rim of the tub.

"He's coming to marry us."

Her fingers curled more tightly. Someone was coming to marry them. Daniel was joking. He was speaking too blithely to be joking. And he seriously wanted her out of the tub.

Her heart seemed to catch in her throat. Of course she wanted to marry him. The hope had always been there, she had just never let it rise from the depths of her heart, because she hadn't begun to imagine that he would marry her, not even for Jared, not after what had happened when she had turned him over to Eric Dabney.

She couldn't breathe, because suddenly it all hurt very much. She wanted to marry him because she loved him. She should have stopped loving him. She should have been able to make her anger into a real hatred and make that hatred stomp out the love.

But she hadn't managed to do so. All that she had managed to do was play a part. What did she want then, she asked herself. Easy, she wanted him to love her.

She bit into her lip, watching him as he stood there, the dressmaker's box in his arms.

She turned her gaze from him to the linen washcloth she had been given.

"No."

"What?"

"I don't care to marry you."

The box went flying onto the bed. She shivered as he strode across the room to glare down at her. "What the hell do you mean, no?"

"I mean 'no.' You haven't even asked me. You're rude and obnoxious. I hate you. You are truly—"

"A Rebel rodent?"

"Precisely," she said pleasantly. "Why should I marry you?"

"Because you have borne my son out of wedlock, madam, and because of him, I am willing to marry you."

"Well, I'm not willing to marry you."

She heard him sigh. "Well, I hope you're willing to receive my hand across your posterior anatomy."

She glanced at him quickly, suddenly afraid of pushing him too far. She had come to know the tone of his voice very well, and he meant the threat.

"Why are you marrying me? What will you tell your family? Am I a suitable wife for a Cameron?"

To her surprise and alarm he knelt down by the side of the tub. She moistened her lips quickly and hugged her knees to her chest.

"I'll tell my family that you were buck naked and I was overcome," he said flatly. "I fell down on my knees and asked you to marry me. It will be the truth."

"No—"

"It will be the truth. You're going to marry me, Callie."

"No! You haven't asked me!" she cried. "You just keep telling me. And you still hate me, and I'm still a Yankee, and you condemn me for what wasn't my fault—"

"All right. Will you marry me?" he said impatiently.

It certainly wasn't what she had in mind for a proposal. She swallowed hard. "I—I can't."

"Why not? You prefer being an unwed mother? On your own?"

"I can make it on my own, Daniel."

"But do you have the right to do it to Jared?"

She looked ahead of her. Her lashes skimmed over her cheeks. She loved him. And she had to believe that underneath it all, he loved her. "I'll marry you, Daniel. For Jared. But I . . ."

"You what?"

"I can't . . . I mean . . . I don't want—"

"Spit it out, Callie. I haven't seen you shy yet."

"I want you to leave me—alone." He stiffened. His movement was barely perceptible. Had she hurt him?

He started to laugh, and it was a very dry, hollow sound. "Madam, I want my son. Legally. And you might want to recall—I've never forced you into anything. At the moment, you're welcome to any privacy you desire. I give no guarantees for the future—should we have one."

Her fingers moved idly over the water.

"I don't know," she began.

His startling blue eyes met hers. "Take a gamble. You should be pleased. I'll be returning to the war almost immediately. I could very easily be shot or run through with a sword. You'd have all my money and my name and your freedom."

"Yes, that could happen," she said coolly. God, but the water had gotten cold! She was starting to shiver. The cold she felt went beyond anything she had ever known.

He stood up. "Your dress is on the bed. I'm afraid we haven't time for any false modesty now. The priest will be here very soon, and even if this water is stone cold, I need a good dousing in it." He stretched out the towel to Callie. She rose to take it.

It dropped to her feet before she could grab it and wrap herself within it.

"Sorry," Daniel said idly.

Like hell he was sorry.

She swept the towel up from the floor. She started to walk away and nearly lost the towel again.

"One more thing, Callie," he called after her.

He was stripping off his dirty frock coat, watching her.

"What?"

"I don't call any man property—you know that we freed all of our slaves."

"Yes, you told me."

He smiled. "Well, I just want you to know that I do consider a wife a man's property. You'll be mine."

"We'll just have to see, won't we?" Callie said sweetly in reply.

But as she turned to dress, she was still shaking.

Twenty-two

The dress was beautiful. It was unlike anything she had ever owned before.

It came with exquisite undergarments, made especially to enhance the gown. There was a huge hoop and a petticoat with row after row of bristling taffeta. There were fine white hose, shimmer-thin pantalets, a silky soft chemise, and an ivory corset, embroidered with the same tiny red flowers that patterned delicately over the dress itself.

Despite the fact that she was clad in nothing but the giant bath sheet, Callie had to pause to stare at the gown before she could even think of putting it on. Her fingers trembled as she touched it.

"Is something wrong?" he asked her from the tub.

"No," she said quickly. Her back to him—and trying to keep the bath sheet around her back—she began to dress. It was difficult. She managed everything but the corset. It was incredibly difficult to try to tie it on by herself.

She stiffened as she felt his hands on her. "Suck in," he ordered, and she did so. "Oh!" she gasped. He had it pulled taut and looped and tied in a matter of seconds. His touch definitely spoke of experience.

She pulled away from him, spinning around. She turned around quickly again because he was as naked as a tiger in a jungle and seemed just as dangerous.

"What's the matter?"

"You're extremely competent with women's—clothing," she told him over her shoulder.

"Am I?"

She ignored him, reaching for the elegant dress. She slipped it over her shoulders. It fell about her softly, like angel's wings. She struggled to adjust the back, to fluff the skirt out over her petticoat.

Once again, she felt his touch, his fingers at her back. One by one, he did up the tiny hooks, then shook the skirt out over the taffeta petticoat. He stood back to study her.

"Would you please put something on?" she hissed.

That drew a smile. "You've seen me often enough. Now that we're about to make this legal, you're going to find offense?"

She was determined to ignore him. She snatched the skirt from the adjusting touch of his fingers and strode to the long swivel mirror near the door. Her breath caught at the sight of the gown. It had been made for her. It was exquisite. The bodice hugged her breasts. It was not at all decadently low, but it left bare her collarbone and the first hint of the rise of her breasts. The puff sleeves also bared her shoulders. It was cool and sweeping, a perfect dress for the heat of summer. Her hair was nearly copper against the white, damp as it still was.

Her eyes were very wide and her cheeks were flushed. She actually felt beautiful, dressed in the gown.

There was a sharp rap on the door. She jumped as Daniel strode across the room to open it. He had wrapped her discarded bath sheet around his hips. Ben was there with an outfit for Daniel. There were charcoal-gray pinstripe trousers, a red vest, a gray suit coat with elongated tails. There was a frilled white shirt, a cravat, and even a pair of shining black shoes.

"These should be all right, Colonel Cameron," Ben told him. "They come from Miz Letty's oldest boy, Andrew, and he grew to be right near as tall a man as you, Colonel."

"Thank you, Ben. I'll see that they're returned in as good a condition as you've given them to me."

"Colonel Cameron, sir, that won't matter none. He was killed back at Sharpsburg. His folks would be right proud to hear his clothes were of use to you."

"Thank you, then," Daniel said softly.

"Oh!" Ben said, a grin splitting his face once again. "Why, Father Flannery is downstairs. I showed him into the den, and he's having himself a brandy now. His niece is with him, to witness the ceremony."

"We'll be along immediately," Daniel promised.

He closed the door.

Callie realized that she was really going to get married. She looked at her fingers. They were shaking.

Daniel was already halfway dressed. He needed no help. In seconds he had his cravat tied, his vest buttoned, every piece of his outfit perfectly adjusted. He winced as he slipped on the shoes. "A little small," he murmured. "But then . . ."

He stared at Callie. She had been watching him in the mirror.

"Callie," he nearly growled, "we need to get down there."

She glanced at her own reflection in the mirror again. Her hair was still damp against her head. She couldn't possibly dry it in time, but she could at least brush it.

She turned quickly to find her shoes, but when she did so, she paused, biting her lip. They had been good shoes, serviceable shoes. But now they appeared as rough and worn as burned lumber. They seemed a travesty against the beauty of her dress and the white silk stockings.

"Shoes!" Daniel moaned. "I forgot all about shoes." He shrugged. "Forget them for now. No one will see your feet." He strode quickly across the room, plucking a brush from a dressing table. Before Callie could move he was behind her again, pulling the brush through her hair.

"I can do it myself!" she protested, and he gave her the brush. She could still see him in the mirror. Maybe she couldn't do it herself. Her fingers were still trembling. He was dashing in the civilian dress clothing, so lean, so dark, so fluid still in his movement. The gray, black, and red enhanced his dark good looks. The outfit might have been tailored specifically for him.

"Give it to me!" he commanded, taking the brush back from her fingers, and making quick work with the length of her hair.

"You're awfully good with hair too," Callie commented.

"Experience," he said briefly.

She inhaled swiftly, nervously longing to slap him. His eyes were sharp when they met hers in the mirror. He tossed the brush back to the dresser and took her elbow. "Let's go. We can't keep Flannery waiting."

He was walking so swiftly it seemed that he dragged her along. "Slow down!" she commanded.

"Move faster," he replied.

She stubbed her shoeless toe on the first step. She wasn't accustomed to the huge hoop, and she had difficulty just managing to stay on the stairway with him.

But Father Flannery, white haired and very grave, was awaiting them now at the foot of the stairs, a young, brown-haired girl at his side. Callie refrained from making any comments to Daniel.

"Father, thank you for coming," Daniel told him.

"Well, Colonel, I must tell you, I disapprove of this haste. I understand, however, sir, that you have been delayed by battle after battle, and so here I am. Sir, you are, I fear, at least better late than never."

"Right," Daniel said briefly. "Shall we get started." He looked at Callie. "My love?"

"Of course. If both parties are of age and entering into this sacrament willingly?"

Callie suddenly couldn't speak. Daniel squeezed her fingers so hard she nearly yelped. "Yes. My love," she squeezed out. Father Flannery turned to give them all room at the foot of the stairs. Callie stared at Daniel. "Bastard!" she hissed.

He smiled serenely. His grip was still upon her and he pulled her close, whispering. "The bastard you are about to promise to love, honor, and obey."

"I don't love you."

"I'm merely shooting for two out of three, and the last two will do nicely."

"Is there a problem?" Father Flannery demanded, turning back to them.

"Not at all," Daniel said. "Would you like to begin?"

Flannery gazed at them both sternly, then sighed. "All right, then. Your name, young woman."

"Calliope McCauley Michaelson."

Daniel swung around and stared at her. Flannery began flipping the pages in his book.

"Calliope?" Daniel whispered.

She shrugged. "My father was very fond of the circus."

He was smirking. She was about to get married, and the groom was smirking.

Flannery settled on a page in his prayer book and began to read from it. She heard the words—they seemed to drone on and on. It was a good thing that Father Flannery had never desired to make his life's vocation drama, she determined, for she had never imagined anyone could make a wedding service more dull or dry.

Perhaps it was her. Her fingers were ice cold. She felt numb from head to toe.

She wasn't sure that they could really be doing this. It was a wedding. When it was over, she would really be Daniel's wife.

Even so, she would know how he felt. Property. A wife was property. He would do whatever he chose. And she would, indeed, be trapped in a southern prison.

"Callie!"

They were all staring at her, waiting. She was supposed to speak. To give her vow. She couldn't do it. She loved him.

He nearly broke the bones in her fingers once again. She must have shrieked out something that sounded like "I do!" because Flannery was droning on and on again.

Then Daniel was slipping his pinkie signet ring over her middle finger, and Flannery was pronouncing them man and wife.

It was done. There was a flicker of fire in his eyes, and she realized that the bars had, indeed, just closed upon her own private hell.

His lips touched hers. Briefly. He turned from her and thanked Flannery and promised that he would send support to the church as soon as he reached home. Ben managed to produce champagne, and Flannery seemed willing enough to share a glass with them. He allowed his young niece a glass, too, and then announced that the papers had to be signed. Callie found herself writing out her name, and then realized that it was different again.

She was a Cameron.

And theirs was, indeed, a house divided.

She managed to write out her name. Just as she finished doing so, she heard a wailing and swung around, feeling a tingling in her breasts. Jared! Ben was bringing the baby forward. He'd been bathed and dressed in a fine bleached white cotton shirt.

For the first time in his short little life, she had forgotten her son.

Forgotten him for the wedding that was taking place because of him.

"Thank you, Father Flannery," she said hastily. Ignoring her husband of a matter of seconds, she took Jared gratefully from Ben, and ran up the stairs with him to the bedroom that had been given them.

She closed the door and sat at the foot of the bed with the baby, struggling with the tight gown to free her breast. Once the baby was situated, she began to tremble again, thinking about what she had done.

She had married Daniel. She was committed to him now. No, she had been committed to him since she had decided to follow him home. No, that had been a commitment to Jared.

He had made her no promises. What would their marriage be? She had asked to be left alone. He would never leave her alone. She was property; he had said so.

She shivered and realized she shivered because she did not know what she wanted from him. Yes, she wanted him to demand everything from her.

But she wanted something too. His love, unconditional. The kind that would allow him to trust her.

There was a tapping on the door. She jumped, staring at it. Daniel? Would he knock? Or would he merely burst in?

"Callie, we'll leave here in ten minutes for supper with Varina. Be ready, please."

It was Daniel. He had spoken politely. It had also been with an implacable authority.

It was the way he had always spoken, she told herself.

No, something was very different. He had married her. And he expected two out of three. Honor and obey.

Jared suddenly sputtered and coughed. Callie swept him up on her shoulder and stood, walking nervously with him as she patted his back. He let out a startling burp for such a tiny being, and she laughed and sat again, stretching him out on her lap. "Just what can he really expect, my love, eh? He married a Yankee. And really, I haven't 'obeyed' anyone since Pa . . ." Her voice trailed away.

She leapt up. Her ten minutes had to be just about up.

She paused, feeling the hard wood beneath her stockinged feet. She still had no shoes.

Well, it was summer; her feet wouldn't freeze. But there was so much mud and dust in the road.

"Callie!"

He called her from downstairs. Her old shoes were too worn and filthy to possibly be on her feet while she wore this dress. She bit into her lip once, then went flying out of the room.

He was waiting for her at the foot of the stairs. His eyes swept over her and he let out a grunt, as if voicing a grudging approval.

"Let's go. Ben will be taking us in the Lunt's carriage." He hesitated. "You could leave Jared with Cissy."

She shook her head vehemently. "He might—need me," she said. Actually, that night, she needed Jared. And she hadn't come from his kind of money. She wasn't accustomed to leaving her baby behind.

It was a brief ride back to the White House of the Confederacy. Night had come, and the house was lit against it and seemed very beautiful as they approached. There were other carriages arriving, and guests coming on foot. Once again, they came in by the pleasant foyer. Varina, gracious and beautiful, greeted them. This time they moved through that central door into a very gracious parlor.

The women there seemed to dazzle, Callie thought. They all sat so beautifully, or stood with such grace, their hair swept up, their fans moving like hummingbird's wings against the heat of the night.

They all seemed to know one another. And Daniel.

They flocked around him, talking about the war, demanding to know about this battle or that, then whispering that, of course, they didn't really want to hear.

They were ladies, after all.

They spoke softly, with lovely, cultured drawls, ignoring Callie at first, then trying very hard to appear well bred and not stare too pointedly once Varina had managed to introduce her as Daniel's wife.

Callie felt as if her teeth had been permanently glued into a mask, but to Daniel's credit, he seemed totally unaware of the adulation that had come his way. They were quickly parted, but each time she looked across the room, she found his eyes upon her, cool and speculative.

"Why are you staring so?" she whispered when she had a chance.

"I'm just hoping that no one spills any of the big secrets of the Confederacy while you're here," he whispered back.

"How very amusing."

"It's not amusing at all. At the moment, it seems that we're doing a very good job of losing the war without your help."

He moved on. A blonde caught his arm. She felt a strident pang of jealousy.

A dashing young man with a sweeping mustache, dressed in uniform that had surely never seen any duty, struck up a conversation with Callie, assuming that she knew all about Daniel's Tidewater home. She smiled and murmured now and then, and that seemed enough.

One buxom brunet cooed over the baby, but a moment later Callie heard a whisper behind her back that such an infant should have been left with its nanny. Callie didn't care as long as Varina seemed so delighted with Jared.

Daniel introduced her to two men in uniform, a Major Tomlinson and a Lieutenant Prosky. When she turned, she heard the major speak to his wife.

"My Lord, but he did find a stunning bride!"

"Find? But that's just it dear, where did he find her?" his wife replied. "I know nothing of her, or her family. Does anyone know anything about her?"

Callie felt as if her ears were burning. Daniel had been swept away by the lieutenant. She had never felt so very alone, surrounded by so many people.

And all of them Rebs.

The crème de la crème of Rebs, at that!

A soft hand fell on her arm, and she was looking into the warm and beautiful eyes of Varina Davis. "Come, Mrs. Cameron, let me show you the house. The dining room is there, of course, to the left of the foyer. Now, these rooms here you see, the one we're in and the one to the right, can be separated by those doors. Pocket doors. They're so very clever, don't you think? We can break the house up when we're alone, and open it up like this for such an occasion as tonight. It's a wonderful house. We were so grateful that the city should give it to us. I've enjoyed Richmond and the Virginians tremendously. Jeff was inaugurated in Alabama, of course, but I've very much loved this place."

"It's very beautiful," Callie agreed.

Varina smiled. "You'll like Virginia."

"I'm not from so very far away," Callie murmured. "Maryland."

Varina studied her. Maryland. A state more split than the country itself. It seemed that Varina sensed that Callie had come from a home with Federal leanings, no matter where that home stood. But she didn't seem to despise her for it. She seemed to understand.

"It is a very hard war," she said softly. She reached out and stroked Jared's dark hair, for the baby slept against Callie's shoulder. "Come, follow me," she said, leading Callie to a small room that sat straight to the right of the foyer. "If you want privacy with the baby, you must bring him in here. There are a few of Jefferson's books here and my sewing, and a nice comfortable chair. You will not be disturbed."

"Thank you," Callie told her. She hesitated. "I'm sorry. I didn't—I don't— have a nanny. He has always been with me."

"That's very special," Varina said. "Children are precious. Perhaps we forget that too often." She smiled, and started to lead the way back. When they returned to the main parlor, Callie was immediately struck by the tall thin man with the haggard face standing by the mantle, conversing with the major. His hair was graying, but he stood with a striking dignity. There were heavy lines about his eyes, and he appeared a man wearied by a great sorrow. He listened to the major, but as his eyes caught Varina's across the room, it seemed that the weariness he wore like a heavy cloak was somewhat lightened. He smiled vaguely. His gaze rested upon Callie, and his brows arched.

Varina caught her hand. "Come, you must meet my husband, Mrs. Cameron."

Her palms went wet; Callie nearly pulled back. She had just married Daniel, and now she was about to meet the president of the Confederate States.

How could she ever explain it to her brothers?

But there was nothing that she could do—short of shouting out that she was a Yankee and probably finding herself facing half a dozen swords.

She had to go forward.

But Lord, how had she wound up here, a very part and parcel of the beating heart of the Confederacy.

"Daniel's wife, my love," Varina said. "Mrs. Cameron, my husband, President Davis."

She extended her hand. Very much the gentleman, the president leaned over it with all gallantry. "Mrs. Cameron. You grace us with your presence."

And that was it. Dinner was announced, and now Daniel's hand was on her arm again. In the large dining room, they were seated across from one another. Despite efforts for the conversation to be led along light lines, there could be no conversation that did not include the war.

The gentleman to Callie's left complained about inflation. But the president, helping himself to meat from a platter, did not seem to hear the words. "There have been cavalry skirmishes all the way down, Daniel," he said. "Lee brought the bulk of the army over the Potomac on the fourteenth. Meade is following, so I am told. But he failed as those men always failed—he has not managed any assault on our main army."

"Lee is a wily commander, sir."

"Were it only that all my commanders were so able."

"Yessir."

Davis set his fork down. "Dear Lord, but we are in dark days now. This horrid battle . . . Gettysburg. And the loss of Vicksburg."

"They can't break our spirit!" Varina said softly from the other end of the table.

He lifted his wine goblet to her. "No, they cannot break our spirit," he agreed. He looked to Daniel again. "Nor can those northern fellows best our brave fighting men, like our fine Colonel Cameron. Sir, you will be back with your unit as soon as possible, won't you?"

Callie was startled to sense the slightest hesitation on Daniel's part. Perhaps she had imagined it.

Yet when Daniel spoke, she thought there was a deep weariness in his voice, despite the words. "Yessir. I shall be back as soon as possible." His eyes, deep, brooding, touched Callie's across the table. Yes, he would be gone. Soon. And she would be free of him.

Except for her vows.

"To our brave boys in fine butternut and gray!" someone called out.

The guests stood. Wine glasses clinked.

Callie took that opportunity to flee, excusing herself swiftly to Varina, finding the sanctity of the sewing room where she could be alone.

Yes, Daniel would be gone.

It was truly a world gone mad. She closed her eyes, rocking with Jared. It hadn't been so long ago that she had lived on a little farm and had wanted nothing more than to stay there, with the mountains always in view, for all of her life. Day in and day out, her cares had been the same. She had buried her loved ones, her grief sustained by the firm belief that they had died for something that she believed in deeply—the sanctity of the Union and freedom for all men. A freedom promised in the Constitution of a great nation, but a freedom not yet realized. Still, it had been a simple life.

Now here she was, in silk and taffeta, married to the enemy. And dining with the president of the enemy nation.

She swallowed hard, then pressed her hand against her hot cheeks. She could not stay here forever.

Daniel might well believe she was tearing apart the president's house in search of some vital information.

Jared slept. She rose with him and started out of the little room.

The pocket doors to the right side of the parlor had been pulled over. She could dimly hear the voices still coming from the dining room.

She wasn't alone.

She stopped short, seeing the tall, lean president of the Confederacy slouched by the mantle, his forehead in his hands. Etched into his face was a look of such utter misery that Callie could not help but find a burst of pity swelling within her heart.

He sensed her there and turned.

"I'm—I'm so sorry," she murmured swiftly. "Mrs. Jefferson said that I might use her sewing room. Well, it's your room, too, of course." She sounded so very awkward. "I'm sorry. I've intruded terribly, and I did not mean to do so."

He watched her gravely, then a slow, sad smile touched his lips. "You are welcome here in this house, Mrs. Cameron. Wherever it is that you choose to be."

"But I have disturbed you. I—I'm sorry," she said again. "The look on your face . . ."

"You mustn't worry so. I was merely thinking of the men."

"The men?"

"Those who have died. So many. I read the death lists and I see so many friends have gone on." His gaze met hers suddenly. "From both sides, Mrs. Cameron. The men I fight are often the men with whom I worked for years and years before this all began."

"The lists of the dead hurt us all."

"They must, Mrs. Cameron. Have you still kin in the Union army?"

How did he know? She was certain that Daniel had not announced her status. "Yes, sir. I do."

"It is very hard to pray for men, Mrs. Cameron, when the ones you love might well face one another. Daniel must face his own brother. And now, perhaps, he will face your kin too. My heart is with you, Mrs. Cameron."

"Thank you," she said swiftly. He was gentle and kind. She didn't want him to be so. She wanted him to be stiff and cold, the president that the northerners so frequently mocked. She didn't want to like him, or feel this empathy with him. "I am sorry that I disturbed you," she said. "The baby—"

"Yes. What a lovely thing to see him with you. May I?"

To her amazement, he reached for the baby. Callie hesitated, then walked across the room. Davis took the child from her gently. Jared didn't protest. He stared up at the tall man in black.

"He's a very beautiful child, Mrs. Cameron. My congratulations."

"Thank you."

A curious, small bubbling sound of laughter came to them. Callie swirled around. From the hallway, where there was a beautiful winding stairway to the upper floors, there was movement.

"Who's there?" The president demanded. He sounded very stern.

But his voice didn't bother the pretty child who suddenly appeared. She stepped out, her eyes alight, her hands behind her back.

She was in a long white nightgown, and she looked very demure at first, then she pelted across the room to come to a swift halt in front of the president.

"Margaret, my eldest," he explained to Callie, and his face softened tremendously, even as he tried again to be stern.

"Young lady, you are supposed to be in bed." His voice was meant to be stern. It was not quite so hard as it might have been, and Margaret, who knew very well she should have been in bed, lowered her lashes, then gave him a beautiful, imploring smile.

"But, Father, what a lovely baby! May I see him?"

"You must ask Mrs. Cameron." Davis said. Callie could not help but think that here was a man, a very powerful and important man, and like all others, North and South, he was blessed or cursed with an Achilles' heel where his children were concerned.

Margaret had wonderful, deep eyes. She was as charming as her mother as she turned to Callie. "May I, Mrs. Cameron? Just peek at him, please?"

Callie smiled. "Of course."

Davis went down on a knee, holding Jared. Margaret touched his cheek, and the baby offered up a coo. "I'm very good with babies, Mrs. Cameron. Truly, I am. I am the eldest, you see."

"And now, back to bed! Before your mother catches us!" Davis said, rising with the baby.

Margaret gave him an impish grin, and turned to flee back toward the stairway. She paused before she reached it, turned and bowed very prettily to Callie. She disappeared once again.

"Perhaps I haven't a heavy enough hand," Davis mused.

"She's a lovely girl, sir."

"Thank you." He crossed the room, returning the baby to Callie. "Perhaps we had best return. My wife will be worried for my state of mind. And your husband will be worried, for surely he must worry every time you are out of his sight."

Yes, that was probably true enough, Callie thought wryly. Daniel would be worried about the state of his beloved Confederacy.

The president took her elbow to lead her back to the dining room.

"I am sorry that you must find yourself here, dear, in enemy territory. It is so very complex, this war. My enemies are so often my friends. Perhaps, eventually, you will be more a Virginian than anything else. Whatever, you must not think yourself an enemy to this house. Come visit when you may, and know that the door will be open to you."

"Thank you!" Callie said. They had reached the dining room, and Daniel's eyes were on the doorway, as they must have been since she had first left the room.

Those sharp blue eyes narrowed the moment he saw her entering upon Davis' arm.

He stood up, walking around the table to seat Callie himself. He stared at her, in question, in warning.

She smiled demurely and dinner continued.

It was a subdued night, because of the battle losses. And because Meade, with his whole army, was moving after Lee's. Sluggishly, perhaps, but still, the Union army would be raping the Virginia countryside once again. Virginia herself was now already long split, with the western counties having voted to join the Union and the Union now having taken them on as a state. Some said that especially in Harpers Ferry, the people had voted to secede from Virginia and the Confederacy because there had been Yankees all around with rifles, watching the voting.

No one really knew.

But it seemed the South had reached a darkest hour, and that was evident tonight.

Yet it was equally evident, Callie thought, that no essence of their spirit was dead. These people were proud, they were honorable. She felt, as she sometimes did with Daniel, that intangible thing they were fighting for. It held them together against loss. It—along with the talent of their generals—kept them strong in battle when the northern numbers should have been overwhelming. It sustained them against loss.

And she thought, it would hold them together as a people when this great conflict was long over.

Despite the losses now coming the Rebel way, victory might still be theirs. Not so much on the battlefront, but in the political arena.

The war had changed dinner conversation. No one suggested that the present situation not be discussed in front of the ladies.

And so Callie listened to the talk and speculation.

McClellan, Little Mac, the general who had so often infuriated Lincoln by refusing to move against Lee, was moving now—into the political arena. If he were elected president of the United States, he wanted to sue for a negotiated peace.

But the elections were still a year off.

Lincoln now had a few great victories behind him.

The South would rise again.

The South would always rise again.

Callie looked up. Daniel's eyes were steadily upon her.

"Tell us, what do you think, Mrs. Cameron?"

Startled, she drew her eyes from her husband's. Down the hall, the young lieutenant in uniform was speaking to her. He continued, "How can we lose, when we have such dashing cavaliers, such splendid horsemen as your husband! He's been known to cover well over fifty miles in a single day, to ride circles around the Yanks! We cannot lose! What do you say, Mrs. Cameron?"

All eyes on the table were upon her. The war was suddenly sitting in her lap.

Once upon a time, she might have engaged in battle. Not tonight. Tonight her enemies were truly flesh and blood. They were people with graciousness, with kindness, with exceptional honor and pride.

They were people who loved their children.

She smiled gravely, and then her eyes touched Daniel's once again.

"I say that, indeed, my husband is a splendid horseman."

Pleasant laughter rang out. The moment passed. Conversation continued.

Daniel's eyes remained upon her, grave, intent.

Perhaps there was even the slightest flicker of approval in them.

She had neither surrendered nor taken up the sword. She was somewhat startled to realize that perhaps, just perhaps, it was all that he wanted of her.

Dinner broke; the men had brandy and cigars, the ladies closed the pocket doors and sipped a supply of English tea which had come through the blockade as a special gift from one of Varina's close friends. Thankfully, they did not tarry long, for Callie was uncomfortable again, aware of the very curious stares that came her way when her back was turned.

But no one was rude now. The ladies, even as they speculated about her, passed Jared from one to another, heaping all manner of advice upon her.

At last, it was time to leave. Varina managed to hold her back until the last of the guests had gone other than she and Daniel.

Even then she pulled Callie back into the little sewing room on the pretext of showing her something.

On the floor lay a pair of red satin slippers. They matched the tiny flowers in her dress beautifully.

"The moment I saw your dress, I thought that you must have these to go with them!" Varina said.

Callie flushed. "Oh, but I can't take your shoes. Oh!" She gasped, aware that she had been in Varina's house all night, shoeless, depending upon her skirt to hide the fact. "I'm so sorry—"

"Please try these on. Our men go barefoot in the field, I am told, and I am heartbroken that I can do nothing for them. At the very least, I can see a pair of slippers on the wife of a dear friend and cavalryman. I shall be truly upset if you do not take them."

Callie stared at her, then tentatively placed a foot in a slipper. It fit her comfortably.

"But I can't—" she began.

"Of course you can! A wedding present!" Varina told her.

She could protest no more, for Varina had opened the door to the foyer, and Daniel was there with the president.

Davis was giving him stern warning. "I am ever on the alert, lest the times grow dangerous, indeed, and it is necessary to evacuate Varina and the children. If you must go home, you must take grave care. It seems we never know when the enemy is upon the peninsula."

"I'll be careful, sir."

"You could leave Mrs. Cameron in Richmond," Varina suggested. "She could travel with me farther south, should it become expedient."

"I'm not sure that would be such a good idea," Daniel said, eyeing Callie. His tone was pleasant. His wry glance was something only Callie could really understand. He turned then to Davis. "Well, good-bye, sir, and thank you immeasurably for the evening. We'll be leaving quite early, and with any luck, sleep in Williamsburg tomorrow night, and reach home the next day."

He kissed Varina's cheek, and shook Davis' hand. Both of them bid Callie good night, both of them kissing her cheek.

Out in the night air Callie and Daniel hurried to the coach. Ben had come for them.

They were silent for a few minutes. Callie sat far to her own side of the carriage, wishing that she could not feel the speculative heat of his gaze so constantly.

He spoke to her dryly. "My, my, Mrs. Cameron, but you were on good behavior this evening!"

She hated the tone of his voice. "The better to steal Confederate secrets," she said pleasantly.

A mistake. She could almost feel the sudden burst of fury within him, despite the fact that he in no way touched her.

He replied softly enough. "At the very least, madam, you were polite."

"Dared I not be so?"

"Of course not." Even in the darkness, she felt the cobalt stroke of his gaze. "Had you been anything less than entirely pleasant, I would have merely excused myself and taken you for a foray into the barn and a lesson with a buggy whip!"

Tremors assailed her. She was suddenly very ready for battle. "Oh, I do think not, Colonel Cameron! Why, every man there would have been totally appalled by your lack of manners and good breeding!"

"They might have been startled, but they would have pitied me, thinking that the hardships of the war were costing me my mind at last."

Callie drew herself very straight in the carriage. "Say what you will. You'll not threaten me."

"I don't really care to threaten. And you need never fear me—my love—action will come far before any words of warning!"

They had reached the house. Callie held Jared close to her and leapt from the carriage before either Ben or Daniel could give her any assistance.

"You fool!" Daniel called after her. "You could have tripped! You could have injured the baby!"

She spun around at the door. "I have become very accustomed to caring for him under any circumstance or physical handicap!" she retorted. "After all, his father chose to drag him through war-torn country."

She hurried into the house and began to race up the stairs. She would reach the guest room, slam the door against him, and bolt it quickly. Surely, not even Daniel would dare to break down another man's door.

She shouldn't have bothered to elude him. Daniel caught her on the upstairs landing.

"What!" she cried.

He dropped her arm. To her surprise, he offered her an elegant—if mocking —bow.

"Actually, madam, I had meant to thank you for your manners this evening in the proximity of your enemies. Perhaps we will change you to our side after all."

She stared at him, at the evocative blue fire in his gaze, at the ebony lock that now dangled rakishly over one eye.

Her husband was indeed a splendid horseman.

A splendid man. She wanted to reach out to him and to be held by him.

They had just been married. It was their wedding night. She should have been able to cry out and fall into his arms.

And whisper, beg, that he make love to her, and in doing so, erase the fact that they were enemies. She wanted so dearly to be held against the darkness!

But by morning's light, they would be enemies again.

"I cannot change sides," she said softly. Neither could she lie at that moment. "I cannot change sides, for you are wrong, sir. And you know it, Daniel. You know that owning another man—be he black, white, or purple—is wrong. Jesu, Daniel! In his will, George Washington freed his slaves! He was a *Virginian*, Daniel. *He* knew slavery was wrong!"

He stared at her. Tall, straight, as proud as the southern cause itself.

He bowed again, graceful and agile.

"Good night, madam," he said simply, and left her.

She didn't have to close or bolt a door against him.

It was their wedding night and he walked away from her.

Twenty-three

*N*othing that Callie had ever seen before prepared her for her first sight of Cameron Hall.

It was twilight when they came upon the house, and it seemed to sit atop a glittering hill, the last rays of the sun shimmering on the elegant white pillars. The house was large, rising into the blue and crimson sky, with gentle acres of lawn sloping off from its height. A long, wide, curving drive led to the large steps that ended at the huge sweeping porch. Back upon the porch were massive double doors with brass knockers that, even from this distance, gleamed.

Daniel had reined in the remaining Yank horse and Callie, mounted behind him, leaned around to see his face. He was staring hard at the house himself. For the last several miles, he had been exceptionally tense.

He had seen to it that Ben awakened her at the crack of dawn the day before. If she thought he had ridden hard to reach Richmond, she had not imagined just how anxious he could be to reach his home. He had barely spoken to her the length of the long road home.

He had ridden carefully, always aware that there could be danger on the roads, but he had ridden quickly. She had wondered if he meant to ride through the night yesterday, but he had stopped in Williamsburg, taking a room at an old inn.

Williamsburg had seemed very quiet, depressed. The war had touched the town, and it was obvious. The young men were all gone. There was no bustle in the streets. Fresh Confederate graves lay behind the old Episcopal church. Fields were empty.

The inn, though, was pleasant enough, exceptionally clean, and the innkeeper was a charming man. Callie, exhausted, had eaten and taken Jared up to bed, falling asleep with the baby at her side.

Daniel had known a number of the older men down in the tap room, and found two old friends who had been badly disabled, one without a left hand, and one minus his right leg from the knee down. It had seemed to Callie that they all overindulged in whiskey, yet she had been far too weary and heartsick to care. Lying awake she realized that her stomach was in knots because she would soon reach Daniel's home. Though she had met Jesse Cameron and knew him to be a kind gentleman, it would not be Jesse she would be meeting, but his household, a Rebel household. How strange, though, that she could live there, and Jesse could not.

She was uneasy about the women she would meet, for Daniel had been so curt with her that he had described them very little. There was Kiernan, Jesse's wife, and Christa, their sister. There was a man named Jigger who ran everything in the house, and a woman named Janey who had once belonged to Kiernan, but who was now a free black. They still grew cotton and tobacco, and so far, had managed to survive numerous battles in the near vicinity. The house was very old, he had told her, the cornerstone having been laid in the early sixteen hundreds.

Having awakened later in the evening, she wondered what made him so certain that she would stay once he had returned to war. She felt a set of chills assail her. If she left, he would come after her. As he had told her once, there would be no place where she could hide. He would find her.

She had to write to her brothers, to pray that her letters would reach them wherever they were. She would have to make them understand why she was suddenly living in the heart of the Confederacy.

She would leave out the part about having dined with President and Mrs. Davis!

Though Jeremy, at least, might understand.

She punched her pillow, and tried hard to sleep again. She could hear the laughter from below. Damn Daniel. Well, they would have a late morning of it!

She didn't want him here! she reminded herself. She didn't want him demanding any rights. She bit down on her knuckle, remembering the sweet ecstasy at the creek that had been so cleanly swept away from her when she had seen the look on his face. He didn't love her; he had wanted her. Forgiveness was the farthest thing from his mind.

She didn't want forgiveness. She hadn't betrayed him. She wanted understanding. She wanted trust.

She tossed and turned. She would fight him tooth and nail now if he touched her. Yet he made no attempt to come near her. He gave her no chance to tell him what she thought about his conjugal rights!

Exhaustion overwhelmed her and at last she slept. Sometime deep in the night, Daniel came to the room. When he awakened her next morning, she was certain that he had slept on the other side of the bed, on the other side of Jared. The pillow was indented, the sheets were warm.

He was in breeches only, reaching for the white cotton shirt he had left at the foot of the bed. "Get up. I want to get going."

They had started out with the wagon. They hadn't traveled very far before a Confederate sentry warned them there were rumors of a Yankee company moving down the main road.

Daniel decided to leave the wagon to travel through the forest paths.

They had left everything with the wagon. She had left the beautiful white dress with the tiny red embroidered flowers.

She didn't know exactly why, but leaving the dress hurt. Daniel had commented on it.

"I won't be stopped over a gown, Callie."

She had shrugged. "You, sir, are the one bred to wealth. There is nothing that I need," she had told him regally.

But it hadn't been true. The dress had meant a lot to her. It was the first really elegant piece of clothing she had ever owned. And it was matched so perfectly by the red slippers that Varina Davis had given her.

It didn't matter. They had deserted the wagon, and she had cradled Jared into her arms, and mounted behind Daniel on their remaining horse. They were both back in the near rags they had worn from Maryland to Virginia, clothing that had at the least been cleaned and mended during their short stay in Richmond. To Daniel, it didn't matter. He was in uniform again and he was going home.

Along the way, riding through the forests and close to the river, they had come upon the ruins of two great houses. A stairway still extended from one of them, leading straight up into the blue sky. Daniel had paused, stared hard, and then ridden again.

And at last, Cameron Hall seemed to burst and blaze before them.

And Daniel, at long last, seemed to draw in an even breath.

"This is it. Home," he told her briefly. He urged the horse forward, bringing them down the path. When they were still a good fifty yards from the house, he flipped his leg over the horse's haunches and leapt down from the mount. "Christa! Kiernan!" His voice rang out and he went running.

Seconds later the double doors burst open. Callie allowed the horse to amble forward at a slower pace as she watched as Daniel was greeted by the two women.

One with deep, raven dark hair, the other a blonde with sun-bright reddish streaks. The dark-haired girl was in a sunburst yellow gown, and the blonde was in midnight blue. Their gowns were beautiful and elegant, even if they were just day gowns. They were trimmed with fine laces, and both women wore hoops and petticoats.

And both were young, and fresh, and very lovely.

And both were very loving.

Callie felt very much the intruder as she watched the scene upon the grand porch. One by one, the women kissed and hugged him. And one by one he swept them up, swirling them around. There was laughter and chatter and so very much happiness.

The horse was still plodding forward. Callie pulled back on the reins, determined to go no farther for the moment.

But it was just when she did so that the blonde caught sight of her.

In the beat of several seconds, Callie just stared at her, and couldn't help but feel a peculiar little flutter of fear.

She didn't belong here.

But then the blond woman smiled a broad, entrancing smile of greeting. Her eyes fell from Callie's to the bundle in her arms.

"A baby!" she exclaimed. "Daniel, you've brought a baby!"

She came running down the steps, moving as if she glided across the expanse of lawn to reach Callie. "Hello! Welcome! I'm Kiernan Cameron, Daniel's sister-in-law."

"Hello," Callie said softly. "I'm Callie . . ."

Her voice trailed away. She'd never spoken her married name; she still couldn't quite grasp that it was really hers, and she knew that she couldn't form the words to explain that she was Daniel's wife.

She didn't need to. Daniel spoke dryly from the porch. "Callie is my wife."

"Wife!" the brunet gasped. But she quickly regained her composure. "How wonderful! And that means that this is your baby, Daniel. But you were just home before Christmas and you didn't mention—"

"Christa!" Kiernan interrupted quickly. She hadn't lost a bit of her composure or poise. Callie was sure that her cheeks were growing pink despite her very best efforts. "Let's get Callie and the baby in, shall we?" She smiled brilliantly. "Daniel has always been full of surprises."

Daniel left the porch, and now strode up to the horse, reaching up to lift Callie down.

"The baby!" Kiernan cried.

"We're quite accustomed to him," Daniel told her.

But when Callie's feet touched the ground, Kiernan was reaching out for Jared. "May I?"

She didn't really expect an answer; she swept the baby up and pulled the cotton bunting from his face. "Oh, you're beautiful!" she murmured to the baby. She glanced up, smiling at Callie and Daniel. "My Lord, Daniel, you would recognize this child anywhere as a Cameron. And he's so young! Callie, how old is he now? Two months old?"

"Yes, just about," Daniel replied before Callie could speak.

"Oh, is he precious!" Kiernan said.

"But Daniel, you were here last fall and you never mentioned a wife. Oh—" Christa began. She cut off her own words, flushing. Of course, it had to be painfully evident to them both, Callie thought, that if she and Daniel were actually married at all, the ceremony had to have taken place long after the baby's conception.

"Oh!" she repeated quickly. "Where are my manners? You've had a long trip. You must be tired."

"And famished," Kiernan added, "and very thirsty. Daniel, bring your wife in." To Callie she added, "We've done our best to aid the war effort, but we've also been very lucky. We've had friends burned out, but the Yanks haven't trod this way yet. Of course, my husband is a Yankee—maybe that's kept some of the companies from our doorstep—but that's another story, and a very confused one. Come in. Just leave the horse, Daniel. Jigger will have him seen to."

Kiernan had the baby bundled in the crook of one elbow. She linked her free arm through Callie's and started leading her up the steps. "I don't imagine that my brother-in-law will be home very long?"

The affection in her voice was warm and genuine and Callie found herself answering softly. "I don't think so. He has to return as soon as possible to his command."

"Well, then, we shall have to make the best of this time for both of you. Christa and I will not intrude. Still, first things first!" She had pushed open the doors to the house. Callie was met by a massive wide hallway with doorways leading to rooms on either side of the house. There was a wonderful grand stairway leading to a landing where, even from here, Callie could see a gallery filled with pictures. Embroidered love seats lined the great hallway, and the matching rear doors, the ones that faced the river, had been thrown open. Far beyond the house Callie could see the beginnings of a rose garden.

"Janey, Jigger!" Kiernan cried out. A doorway to the left burst open. A tiny whirlwind of energy in very small breeches came bursting through first, racing toward Kiernan.

"Mama!" he cried.

"Oh, dear!" Kiernan laughed, scooping down to pick up the little boy. Callie was startled at the boy's appearance, for surely she was looking at her own son, one year from now.

"John Daniel," Kiernan said, "this is your aunt Callie. And your cousin. What is his name?"

"Jared," Callie said.

"This is your cousin, Jared."

"Kiernan, he isn't in the least interested in a cousin, yet!" Daniel said. He came around to sweep his wriggling nephew from Kiernan, holding the little boy up in the air so that he shrieked with laughter. "My goodness, John Daniel, you're getting big!" He glanced at Kiernan. "Has Jesse seen him lately?"

She shook her head. "Not since Christmas. We discussed the idea of my moving up to Washington, but he knew that I would hate it there, and it probably wouldn't help much, he never seems to get any time away." She breathed quietly for a moment, looking at Daniel. "He's back in Virginia, I've heard. In the valley somewhere, with Meade's army."

"Perhaps I'll see him," Daniel said lightly.

"Oh, Daniel, I pray not! When you see him, it is so frequently because you're injured or in some place like that horrible prison!"

"Yes," Daniel muttered, and despite herself, Callie felt herself flushing again. Well, it seemed evident enough that he'd never mentioned her to his sister and sister-in-law before. But she couldn't tell by his manner just what he intended to tell them now that they were here.

He wasn't going to say anything now, for there was suddenly a cackle of glee. "Master Daniel, you've done come home!"

"Jigger!" Daniel said happily, striding across the hall to hug the tall, lean black man who had just come in, running after little John Daniel Cameron. The boy, caught between the two men, squealed with delight.

"You look wonderful, Jigger. The rheumatism's not too bad, eh?"

"No, sir. The summer weather is kind to my bones! But you, sir, you are looking by far the worse for wear!"

"Well, that's because I do feel so well worn," Daniel said.

Jigger was frowning, looking at Jared, still held in Kiernan's arms, then glancing at Callie, and glancing at the baby again. "Oh, Lawdy! Why, you done brought home a missus, sir. And another little one." He rolled his eyes. "This is going to be one busy household, sir, that it is!" He suddenly stood very straight, and offered Callie an extremely dignified bow. "Miz Cameron, welcome to Cameron Hall!"

"Thank you, Jigger," she said quietly.

His gaze moved quickly over her travel-worn dress. "First things, first, I think. The new Miz Cameron must surely be wanting a bath."

"Of course!" Christa said suddenly. "And you couldn't possibly have carried any of your things. I think we're of about the same size. I hope you won't mind taking a few dresses and things from me?"

"I wouldn't mind at all," Callie said. "But you needn't—"

"Here's Janey!" Kiernan interrupted. A very tall, extremely attractive black woman came walking in from the rear porch.

"Well, I'll be . . ." she began. "Master Daniel!"

A grin broke out on her face, and she ran down the hall to greet him. Callie suddenly felt warm. He was loved here. Dearly loved by his family. He could not be a cold or a cruel man and have earned this love.

She had loved him herself. He was hard, he was a blade honed razor-sharp by the years of war. But she had known that he was admirable, and that was why she had loved him.

Loved him still.

No! Only a fool would love a man who felt such a contempt for her as Daniel did for Callie.

"What!" Janey gasped, listening to something that Daniel had said. She, too, swung around to stare at Callie. "A wife! And a baby! Another boy? Miss Kiernan, when is someone in this house going to produce us a little girl to dress up and pamper."

Kiernan laughed. "Don't look at me, Janey. I haven't seen Jesse since Christmas. Perhaps we can look to Daniel and his bride."

Callie gritted her teeth. If she flushed just one more time here, she was going to scream. Don't look at us! She almost cried. We hate one another.

But, as she had discovered, that very often had little to do with the production of a child. No promises, Daniel had told her. She had agreed to become his wife.

He stared at her now, watching her reaction. Gauging it?

Or mocking her all the while?

She didn't know.

"Let's give the poor woman a chance to breathe," Christa said, laughing. "A bath first! Janey, can you see to it, please?"

"Surely," Jane said. "I'll just take that child for you—"

"No, you will not!" Kiernan protested, holding tight to Jared. "John Daniel has gotten far too big to hold and love like this. I'm going to become acquainted with my new nephew. Daniel, perhaps you should take a walk with yours! Christa can see to whatever you may need, Callie, and then supper should be ready soon enough. How does that sound for everyone?"

"Fine," Daniel said. "Young John Daniel, you and I are going for a walk."

John Daniel wasn't old enough to have much of a vocabulary, but he seemed to like his uncle well enough. "Walk!" he agreed, chubby little fingers winding around Daniel's neck. Without a backward glance, Daniel started out through the back. Kiernan offered Callie a radiant smile. "I'll just take him into the study."

"He might need new—pants," Callie said.

Kiernan laughed. "Why, Mrs. D. Cameron, I'm certainly experienced with changing a baby's pants. Get away with you now!"

Then she was gone, and Christa had taken Callie's arm. They walked up the long winding stairway, with Christa talking all the while, softly, warmly, as sweetly as if she had asked Callie to her home herself.

Callie paused in the portrait gallery at the top landing, intrigued by the portraits. Some of them were very old. All of them were oil paintings, except for one at the end of the gallery.

It was a photograph, a picture of a family. A handsome man and woman sat on a sofa, with Christa, perhaps at fifteen or sixteen, between them. Behind the sofa stood both Jesse and Daniel. Both were dressed in the dark blue of the Union cavalry.

"It's nice, isn't it?" Christa said softly. "It was taken several years before the war. I've heard that it was one of Mr. Brady's finest. Ma and Pa were still alive then. And Jesse and Daniel were both in the U.S. Army. I love this portrait. It means so much to me. Especially when day after day after day goes by and I don't know exactly where either of them might be . . ." Her voice trailed away. "A bath! I know that it is the first thing that I would desire, and I'd desire it with all of my heart!"

Christa led her to a room. Wonderful full-length windows looked out on the garden and the river beyond. Against the inner wall was a cherry-wood sleigh bed, and to the left was a huge fireplace. A desk was situated before the windows to catch the light, and two plush chairs were drawn close by so that someone sitting in them might look out on the beauty of the view. There were also two huge armoires in the room, and a large trunk at the foot of the bed, and a washstand to the left of it.

It was an attractive room, a welcoming one. It was also a definitely masculine one.

Daniel's.

The tub had already been brought, and a golden-colored little servant boy was dumping in a huge bucket of water.

"Just let me get you some things, and then I'll leave you in peace," Christa told her.

She was as good as her word, bringing in a supply of soap and towels, and then being joined by Janey, who helped her carry in all manner of petticoats and pantalets and stockings and gowns. There was such an array of things that Callie began to protest, but Christa ignored her. "There's nowhere for me to wear all of these things anymore! I'm afraid I was terribly frivolous before the war, so I'm grateful now that I can think perhaps it was destiny I was so sadly greedy!" She laughed, and then she was gone, and Callie was alone.

The first thing she thought when she sank into the water was that it was not going to be nearly so terrible as she had imagined.

She leaned back, then bolted up again. This was Daniel's room. She didn't know when he would come back to it. She bit her lip, looking around, noticing the little things she hadn't seen at first.

There was a set of crossed swords on the wall, old swords it seemed, from the Revolutionary War. There was a tintype of Daniel. He was in a Union uniform, and he appeared very young. She wondered if it had been his graduation from West Point.

In the stand beside the bed were several books. Books by Shakespeare, by Defoe. She strained her eyes. A copy of Chaucer's *Canterbury Tales*. There were a few other books. A small handbook on military maneuvers, and one on animal husbandry. On the desk was another photograph. It was one of Daniel and Jesse, arm in arm, in front of the house.

She closed her eyes. The water was growing cold.

How would they bear it here if either brother died?

Don't go back, Daniel, she thought.

But it was wishful thinking. Even if he loved her, even if he adored her, he would not shrink from returning to the war.

I love him, she thought.

No! He would not believe you; he would hurt you worse. Maintain your distance, keep your heart safe and hold on to your pride. And then he will be gone.

But what if he doesn't come back?

With that question continuing to plague her, she rose from the tub. She dried herself quickly, then looked through the array of Christa's gifts. There was a silver-gray day dress, with cream and black lace edgings. She ran her fingers over it, then began to dress. Christa had supplied simply everything. She found stockings and garters and pantalets, and everything fit. She awkwardly tied herself into a corset, then slipped the dress over her head and shoulders, and let it fall. It was beautiful.

She still wished she had the white dress back. It had meant so much to her. She didn't know if it was because it was the first thing that Daniel had given her, or because she had been married in it, or because of the little red slippers Varina had given her to go with it.

No matter. It was gone. And she was surrounded by more luxury than she had ever known.

Christa had supplied her with shoes as well. And with a silver-handled brush.

She finished dressing, aware of the silence in the house. She tentatively stepped into the hallway and walked down the stairs. A door toward the back of the house was open. She could hear voices coming from it and walked toward it.

She paused, for she could hear Kiernan and Daniel.

They were talking about her.

"Daniel, truly, I've no wish to intrude in your life, but . . . ?"

"What is it, Kiernan?" he asked dryly, but a warmth and humor remained in his voice. "Please go ahead and intrude now, because eventually you're going to do so anyway."

"All right, where is she from?"

"Maryland."

"Are you really married?"

"Yes."

"Does she want to be here?"

"No."

"Wonderful. You're going back to war and leaving us with a woman who despises us all!"

"She doesn't despise you all. Just me," he said. There was a deep, underlying bitterness there. Callie bit her lip. She had no right to be eavesdropping in the hallway. She needed to make her presence known.

"But that baby . . . Daniel! You didn't—"

"I didn't what?"

"Force her into anything, did you? I mean you didn't—"

"Rape her? Kiernan! How the hell long have you known me?"

"I'm sorry, Daniel. But this baby! He is so beautiful! All that black hair—and the eyes. Beyond a doubt, they are Cameron eyes!"

"Yes, I know."

"Daniel Cameron, you forced her down here because of this baby!"

"He's my son."

"But he is hers too!"

"And she's my wife, Kiernan!" he said, and sounded impatient.

"But—"

"Kiernan, Lord knows how many marriages are arranged with the bride and groom scarcely knowing one another. So ours is not a love affair. She is still my wife."

"Well, you did acquire a striking woman, Daniel. She is probably the most beautiful woman I have ever seen."

Daniel sniffed loudly. Callie could hear the sound all the way into the hallway.

He spoke softly. "Yes, she is beautiful. And she knows how to weave a spell and use that beauty. My wife can be as treacherous as she is lovely, Kiernan. Remember that."

"Where are you going?" Kiernan said.

He must have been rising. Panicked, Callie ran out to the porch.

It was dark now. She flattened herself against the wall. She was breathing far too quickly. She closed her eyes, willing her heart to beat at a more sensible pace.

She opened her eyes. Daniel was standing before her.

He had bathed and shaved elsewhere. His hair was damp, his cheeks were clean and alluring, the fullness of his mouth was twisted in a wry, rueful smile. In the darkness, his eyes were obsidian. His scent was clean and raw, and as he moved closer to her, she nearly cried out.

"Well, well, good evening, Mrs. Cameron. Fancy finding you out here."

She lifted her chin, and hiked up a brow. "Oh? Was I to have been confined to the house, sir? If that is the case, then you should have advised me so."

"Careful, Mrs. Cameron, you'll find yourself confined to your room."

"I haven't a room. It is your room."

"I keep a lot of my personal property in my room," he said casually.

She tried to kick him. He stepped out of the way, laughing, then he caught her arms and suddenly wrenched her toward him.

"I'm going to have one dinner in this house, madam. And it's going to be a pleasant one."

"Perhaps I should beg a headache, and then you needn't fear any disruption."

"No, my dear wife, for if you were so distressed, I would consider it my duty to be with you. And we'd be locked together all of those endless hours."

"Dinner sounds divine," Callie said sweetly.

He took her arm. Warmth danced along her spine.

The moon suddenly appeared, shining down on them both. "You are extraordinarily beautiful," he told her softly.

She swallowed. She wanted to say something. She wanted to beg for a truce.

"Am I?" she whispered wistfully.

"Indeed. We've one night, my love. Just one night."

The warm, dancing shivers assailed her once again.

She didn't know if the words were some kind of a threat or a promise.

Twenty-four

*S*ometimes, Daniel reckoned, it was possible to forget the war.

Sometimes he could almost half close his eyes, sit back, and imagine that they had gone back to a time when the army rations weren't always riddled with worms, when he didn't have to look at shoeless men in rags day after day.

Sometimes there was a return to events so warm and sweet and gracious that he forgot the screams of the dying as they echoed in his head.

Like tonight.

The older children, Patricia and Jacob Miller, had determined that they weren't going to eat with the grown-ups, but that they'd be responsible for entertaining John David until his bedtime.

Christa had determined they wouldn't sit at the regular dining table, for it was far too large for an intimate dinner of four. The large oak table had been set far down the room, and a small square table from the kitchen had been brought in and covered with a snowy cloth.

The Cameron's best silver was on the table, and their glittering Irish cut crystal. Between the women of the household and Janey and Jigger, they had created a banquet. The meat was only ham, but there was an array of summer vegetables and fruit to tempt even a well-fed palate, let alone Daniel's. He held an orange with amazement, but Kiernan cheerfully told him they'd had a blockade runner tied up at their dock just the week before, picking up raw produce from the plantation in exchange for all manner of commodities. The captain had just been down to Florida, and the fruit he had brought back had been exceptional.

He saw that Callie, too, studied an orange with a certain awe, and he was startled by the depth of feeling that suddenly shook him, a combination of shame and admiration.

Perhaps he really had had no right to drag her through the lines the way that he had. He'd put her through danger, and massive discomfort. She'd never once complained.

He bit into his ham, chewing hard. She'd always had courage. He'd admired it from the start. That was why he had fallen so swiftly and so completely in love with her. That was why he had followed her out of the cornfield that day.

It was why the Yanks had beaten, subdued, shackled, and imprisoned him.

But perhaps she had done it to save his life. If it weren't for the damned war, perhaps he *could* trust her. He wanted to.

She had created the fabulous creature now being rocked by Janey in the kitchen. Jared Cameron. His son. A healthy, beautiful baby boy.

His stomach turned. Who could have ever imagined that it would feel this wonderful to be a father? He'd always liked children; he'd had some time with John Daniel as an infant to learn what they were like. And he'd loved his nephew dearly, just as he loved Jesse and Kiernan.

He'd never imagined what he would feel, looking into Jared's sky-blue eyes, feeling those tiny fingers close around his own.

They were all here now. He'd wanted his son home. The idea probably hadn't even been rational at first. But he hadn't been about to leave the boy with Callie.

Revenge?

Maybe. Or maybe he had just wanted her here. And maybe he hadn't wanted to marry her because that would hurt her too. She had come with him anyway. She had never suggested marriage. He had.

He sat back. They were all so beautiful. Most men in his position would be convinced they had died and gone to heaven. His sister was striking with her ivory skin, coal-dark hair, and startling, deep-blue Cameron eyes. Even as a child Kiernan had been a beauty, with her classic features and wheat-blond hair, just touched by streaks of strawberry and sun.

Callie sat between them to complete the picture. Delicate, elegant, with the perfect shaping of her face, the large pools of her haunting gray eyes, the lovely bow of her mouth, and the shimmering auburn blaze of her hair to defy even the shade of a perfect sunset. She was dressed in silver this evening, silver-gray, a color that met and matched her eyes, and made them even deeper, darker, more elusive.

She truly was beautiful, he thought, extraordinarily so. In this dove-gray and silver, and in the white gown with the embroidered red flowers that Ben had procured for their wedding.

She'd been upset when they had left that gown behind. It had probably been the first gown of such elegance that she had ever owned. She had come from a small farm. Even the white wedding dress she had certainly worn to her first wedding had probably not been of the same quality.

He could never accuse her of seeking riches of any kind. She seemed to stand up well against any calamity, be it flying bullets, poverty, hunger, hardship.

But this was the same way that he had been made the fool before, believing in her, loving her. She had the face of an angel.

She caught him studying her as she handled the orange and she flushed, placing it back on the table. She sat very stiffly, so quickly on the defensive.

And why not? Do you ever say anything even remotely kind to her? he taunted himself.

What is there to say? Tell her the truth? I love you, Callie, I love you with all of my heart. I want it just to be Jared, but I need you, I want you. So many times I have longed to bring you close beside me, to speak all that is in my heart.

But then I hear your whisper, feel the softness of your flesh. . . .

They were all talking. His sister and Kiernan, who truly loved him, and Callie, who they were artfully drawing into the conversation. He watched as she became animated, talking about her brothers.

Her smile was beautiful; the sound of her laughter was contagious.

He wanted to love her so badly. But he was afraid. Afraid that he had killed the love between them. Afraid that he could never really trust her, not while the war raged on.

He pushed back his chair. Three pairs of startled eyes were drawn his way.

"Excuse me, ladies," he said with an extravagant drawl. "I think I'll go out on the porch for a cigar."

He bowed abruptly and turned to leave them.

"But Daniel—" Christa began. "Ouch!"

Kiernan must have kicked her beneath the table, Daniel decided wryly. His sister was hurt, he knew. He had so little time with them, and it seemed that he was trying to escape them.

He leaned over the porch rail and looked over the rose garden, beautiful, haunted in the moonlight. Far down the slope of the lawn, the ivory glitter of the near full orb in the sky fell upon the river, the ever moving river. It was beautiful. It was peaceful. It was his home, and he was loath to leave it again.

Far across the yard he saw the old family cemetery, and beyond, the summer cottage. He paused, struck a match to his boot and lit a thin cheroot he had taken from the huge accounts desk in the den. He puffed on the fine tobacco.

He wandered down the steps and began to walk.

Summer was hot and humid. But here, by night, no matter how bad the day had been, nightfall brought a balmy breeze that seemed to caress and envelop him. Had it always felt so good just to walk in the darkness? Or had he learned the beauty of his home once he had been forced away from it so many great lengths of time?

Traditionally, the house would come to Jesse. Cameron Hall had always been inherited by the eldest son. But Jesse had always been more interested in his medicine, and Daniel had been the one who knew the acreage and the livestock. There had never been any reason to worry about who actually owned the place. They both loved it. And the family owned more houses than they might ever need. His mother had hailed from Mississippi, but his grandmother had brought a plantation into the family, a place called Stirling Hall. Kiernan had her own home, too, just up the river, and a doting father with no one to leave the place to except to his daughter and her children. Yes, they were all rich in houses and land.

Now they were rich. But the war would eventually strip them all. So far they had been lucky. Maybe they would stay lucky.

Maybe some Union company that didn't give a hoot about a colonel named Cameron might come along and burn down the place.

And any company, Reb or Yank, could come by and rob it blind, "confiscating" for the troops. Just as they had confiscated through Pennsylvania and Maryland.

He had reached the graveyard. The shadowy silver light of the moon fell upon the white tombstones. A low heat fog lay on the ground, and marble angels seemed nearly to dance.

Daniel walked through the little gate and wandered to his father's grave, and his mother's beside it. "Who's right, Pa? Jesse and Callie, so convinced on the one side, and Kiernan and Christa and I, ever rebels at heart!" he whispered to the night. He sighed and continued to speak out loud. "Maybe slavery is wrong, Pa, but isn't it equally wrong for one set of people to tell another set how to live? Given time, the southern states might have begun to free their slaves—they might have voted it out. I hear tell that Vermont abolished slavery some time ago. Hell, Pa, Thomas Jefferson couldn't deal with the question when he was writing the Constitution. The founding fathers actually left us in a bit of a bind here. And we're killing one another over it daily now. I had to go with Virginia, Pa. That's the way I saw it. Just like Jesse had to go north."

And then there's Callie, he thought, silent once again.

His father would have liked her. He would have liked her poise, and he would have liked the way that her eyes met the world, wide and steadfast. He would have liked her strength under duress, and he would have liked the beautiful smile that curved her lips every time she looked upon their son.

"Yes, then there's Callie!" he said aloud. "How do I know what's true within her heart and soul, Pa? How do you learn to trust someone again? I want to believe her, but then I'm afraid. I hurt her, and God knows, I hurt myself. And if she really cared for me once I've managed to turn that love to dust!"

He paused in the moonlight, then smiled suddenly and turned away from the graves. He didn't know what he had expected to find here, but he had found a curious determination.

He walked past the smokehouse and the laundry and the rows of slave quarters until he reached the barn. Quietly and quickly he walked among the horses, talking to them as he passed them, looking them all over one by one.

The Yankee bay had been a decent enough mount, but he was wasn't taking it when he rode back to war. He wanted one of the saddle horses he had bred and trained himself.

He paused, wincing, thinking of the horses that had been killed beneath him. He chose a tall black named Zeus, patting the animal's nose. "Maybe we'll have better luck this time, eh, boy?" he whispered, stroking the fine neck. Zeus was half Arabian, and he had the deep dish nose and flying tail of that breed. He was a large horse, standing nearly seventeen hands high. "The Yanks might be after me just to get their hands on you, boy, but what the hell, sir, they'll be after us no matter what. We'll worry about that tomorrow. Tonight, well, tonight we're out for a ride."

He saddled and bridled the horse, and when he was done, he mounted up and began to ride.

The moonlight was all the guide he needed.

He rode over the plantation, impressed again with the manner with which his sister and Kiernan—and the twins—had managed to keep things going. He rode slowly, determined to drink in the sights and scents and the richness of summer here along the river before he would have to ride away.

But he did not ride idly. He knew where he was going.

An hour or so out he came upon the rough wagon they had abandoned on their ride in. There, in the darkness, he looked through the belongings they had deserted on their trip home.

He found the box with the white dress and its embroidered red flowers, crooked it under his arm, and mounted up once again.

He returned to the barn, watered Zeus and brushed him down well, and strode slowly back to the house.

The house seemed very quiet as he entered it through the back porch. He glanced in the dining room, but it was empty.

Curiously, he walked up the stairs, still carrying the dress box. He strode the few steps from the portrait gallery to his room. He tried the doorknob and scowled, a bolt of fury ripping through him like lightning.

The little witch. She'd bolted the door against him.

He nearly slammed his shoulder against it then and there, determined to break it down.

He hesitated. No, not yet. If she was lying awake, let her brood for a while.

And hell, he wanted to get his temper back under control.

He strode back down the stairway and went back into the den, drew the chair out from the desk, sat down, and propped his feet up. He leaned back, closing his eyes.

He had one fool night home, and he had spent it in the saddle, where God help him, he'd be spending his nights from now until who-knew-when!

And now she'd bolted the door against him. No matter. He'd made her no promises, and he didn't give a damn what the household might think. It was his room. He'd give her a few minutes. But then he was going in.

"Daniel?"

The soft whisper startled him. He glanced up. Kiernan was in the doorway.

"Come in," he told her.

She did so. He'd known her his entire life. She wasn't shy with him.

She sat down across from him, folding her hands in her lap. He smiled. That surely meant he was in for it.

"What, Kiernan?"

"That was rather rude."

He shrugged. "Kiernan, I assure you, my wife would far prefer your company to mine."

"Are you so very certain?"

"Entirely."

"Daniel—"

"Kiernan, I love you dearly," he warned her softly, "but you are treading on dangerous ground!"

"Hmmph! And I used to think that Jesse was the difficult one!"

"He is. You just don't see enough of him to truly appreciate his difficulty anymore," Daniel teased.

"Daniel—"

"Kiernan!"

She sighed. "Oh, all right! But just in case you're wondering about your wife, I'll tell you. She kept up a tremendous front, trying not to appear embarrassed that her husband had but one night with her and his son and disappeared in the midst of dinner despite it. She was in a difficult position, but I daresay she held her temper fairly well the first hour. Then she excused herself, saying that she was exhausted, which I'm sure she is, although I imagine she is presently torn between sleep—and the burning desire to skewer you through."

Daniel arched a brow at Kiernan. "I wasn't wondering about my wife. I know exactly where she is. But thank you, Mrs. Cameron!"

"You don't intend to apologize?"

"No, madam, I do not! I told you," he added more softly. "I don't think she missed my presence. In fact, I can almost guarantee it. And I will be going up. Soon."

Kiernan rose. "Well, I think that you're being as pigheaded as a mule. But still, I want you to know . . ."

"What?"

"Well, I've put both the boys to bed in John Daniel's nursery. John Daniel has graduated from his cradle, and it's just right for Jared. They're both sound asleep. I thought that you should know. Just in case."

It was good to know.

"Thank you," he told her softly.

"Good night, Daniel," Kiernan said softly. "I love you, you know." She came behind him, hugging his shoulders. She kissed him on the cheek.

He held her hand, where it lay against his shoulder. Then he turned slightly and kissed it. "I love you too."

She left him, and he stared broodingly across the room.

He'd married her. He'd brought her home. She was upstairs in his own room, and he was her husband, and he had every right, and he was about to ride away to war. . . .

There was a sound outside. He narrowed his eyes.

Maybe she was bringing the war to him.

But it wasn't Callie.

There was a slight tap on the door, and then Christa poked her head in.

"Daniel!"

"Come in," he told her.

She smiled and came in. "How about a brandy for your sister?" she asked.

Placing his feet on the ground, he pulled out the brandy carafe and glasses. He quickly poured the amber liquid. He didn't comment that a lady shouldn't be so determined on drinking at this hour of the night.

A lady shouldn't be working the way that Christa did to keep a place together, either.

He walked around the desk, handing her a brandy. "To the real Cameron among us, Christa! The one keeping the home fires burning."

Christa smiled. "You've three women keeping the home fires burning now, Daniel! Even if you are atrociously rude."

He sighed. "Must everyone comment on my affairs?"

Christa lowered her head. "No, I won't. Not anymore, not tonight. You're my brother, and I love you."

She stood up abruptly, careless with her glass as she suddenly hugged him, hard and tight. "Oh, Daniel, it's so good to see you, and so hard to know that you'll ride away so quickly again. Every time one of you leaves I feel that more of my heart is torn away. Jesse hasn't managed to come home in more than a year now!"

He hugged her in return, smoothing back her hair. "Shhhh!" he told her softly. "It's all right."

"Sometimes. And sometimes, I'm so scared, Daniel! It will never be the same again. Never, never."

"No, it will be the same! We'll be the same, Christa. Nothing has ever managed to touch the fact that we're a family, that we love one another, that we have one another! We need to hold on to that."

"Yes, of course. Except that Jesse is so far away. He might as well be across an ocean, the chasm is so deep!"

"Christa!" He lifted her face by her chin, searching out her eyes. "What—"

"Daniel, I want to get married. I can wait a few more months, but not forever! I love Liam McCloskey so much, and I'm always so afraid! With—with your blessing, we've set June for a wedding date. I pray that the war will be over. I pray so desperately that it will end! But if it doesn't, Jesse will be far away! Oh, Daniel, he should be there—"

"Hush, Christa, maybe he will be."

"Kiernan can go to Washington. She can see Jesse there and let him know."

That probably wasn't such a good idea. Kiernan had to be very careful, moving back and forth across enemy lines. Too many Yanks knew that Jesse's family was all Reb, including his wife. The war itself was like that. Families were divided.

But spying was dangerous, and though Daniel knew that Jesse had suspected his wife of spying at one time, they had come to a truce of their own.

"There will be a way to let Jesse know," he assured her. "I'll see to it."

"He won't say no, will he?"

Daniel grinned. There were some things war couldn't change. Christa wanted Jesse's approval. It was only right.

But after their own hasty marriages, Daniel couldn't begin to see either Jesse or himself dictating anything about propriety to Christa!

"He won't say no."

She leaned against his shoulder. "I'm just so tired of it all. Daniel, there was an explosion in Richmond at the munitions factory—someone grew careless— and there were over sixty people killed." She pushed away from him and her eyes welled with tears. "They were mostly women, Daniel, working because the men were all gone to war. So now the ladies die as well as the gentlemen, and still, a generation of boys will be dead when this is done! Are we wrong, Daniel? Have we brought on this bloodshed for nothing?"

"We didn't bring on the bloodshed, Christa. Not you, nor I, nor Jesse. We were swept up into the midst of it, and we all did what we thought we had to do, and that's all that any man—or woman—can do. I pray that we're not wrong, I pray that daily. It's all I can do when I watch men fall, and bleed, and die. And walk barefoot in the snow, looking to me for a guidance I find it harder and harder to give."

"Oh, Daniel, I did not mean to distress you!"

He smiled and touched her cheek. "You never distress me. At least, you don't anymore. You were, upon occasion, a tremendous little hellion years ago."

She grinned. "I've seen to it that you've a fresh uniform to wear back to the front, Daniel. I've sewn on your insignias and bars just today. And I've knitted you a wonderful sash, and Patricia went out to find new plumes for your hat."

"Thank you."

She kissed his cheek. "Good night, Daniel. And don't forget, you must come home next June to give me away for my wedding just in case Jesse can't make it."

"Will your groom be home?"

"Of course. I'm giving you both ample notice."

She blew a kiss to him and disappeared. Daniel sat back down and picked up his brandy glass, swallowing down the contents instantly.

Poor Christa. She could give them all the time in the world, but neither he nor Christa's beloved captain could dictate the course of the war.

Please God, let it be over! he thought.

It didn't seem that God had answered many prayers lately.

The brandy was good. It burned. He poured another quickly and swallowed it down just as fast.

He had a good head for brandy. But he wanted the haze tonight, something to blunt the edges.

What the hell was he going to do? Sit here as the hours passed and want her, ache for her, long to wake her and shake her . . . and have her?

He caught his breath suddenly, for he could see her through the slit at the doorway. The door to the den stood ajar.

She was coming down the stairs. She seemed a wisp of cloud at first. Ethereal, magical. She moved like a sprite, reaching the foot of the stairs.

She moved swiftly and furtively across the hallway. Still, she seemed to float, in that elusive cloud of beauty, her hair a clean and brilliant fire, the sheer froth of whatever she was wearing swirling with her at every step.

She was wearing something of Christa's.

And Christa had beautiful things.

This concoction of silk and fluff was in softest gray, a color that caught hold of the moonlight well, that shimmered and moved beneath it. It seemed to dance hauntingly along with the swift, graceful glide of the woman. When she paused, it hugged her form, delineating each curve and plane and fascinating hollow.

Everything within him tightened and constricted. Still, he sat motionless in his seat, watching her. What was she up to?

He knew. She had come down to assure herself that he had chosen to sleep elsewhere, that she might find herself in peace for the evening. He sat back, watching, brooding, as she looked into the dining room. She peeked quickly in and quickly out, a wraith in the shadows of the darkened house.

He rose at last, silently leaning against the doorway, watching her still as she moved along the great hall. She turned and started to hurry back to the stairway, and that was when she discovered him standing there, arms crossed over his chest, awaiting her.

"Good evening, Mrs. Cameron."

She stopped dead still. "Good evening," she replied coolly, spinning to skirt around him, having decided, it seemed, that retreat might leave her to battle another day.

Not tonight.

He caught hold of her arm, swinging her back around. "I believe you were looking for something?"

"Yes," she said quickly. "I thought that a sherry might help me sleep."

"No, you didn't. You don't want anything to drink, and you weren't looking for anything to drink."

She jerked her arm free. "Well, the same doesn't seem to be true of you!" she informed him smoothly. She wrinkled her nose as if she were the grandest dame to have ever set a foot on Virginian soil.

"Why, yes, Mrs. Cameron, I have had a drink or two. But rest assured, I am not drunk." He bowed deeply to her. "A southern officer would never over-imbibe."

Callie didn't know if he was drunk or not; she only knew that he was danger-ous at that moment.

If she came too close, he might touch her. She couldn't allow him to do so. Her pride still seemed ravaged by what he had done tonight, walking away from his own family in order to walk away from her.

"So, just what are you doing?" he asked her.

She felt his tension, felt an anger as great as her own. An uneasy thought struck her. Perhaps he had come upstairs and he knew she had locked the door against him.

"I told you—"

"You didn't come down for anything other than the hope that you would find me sound asleep in a desk chair. I imagine you were hoping I might be well gone into oblivion!"

"Don't be ridiculous," she said. "It is immaterial to me where you choose to sleep."

He smiled, striding toward her. It was probably the moment to run. She couldn't quite do that. He had her angled against the door, and suddenly she was pinned there, his hands on either side of her face.

"Then why was the door locked?" he demanded.

"Oh, did I lock it?"

"Indeed, madam, you did."

His gaze was sharp, glittering in the moonlight. Callie felt the tension that ripped through his body, and she was suddenly more furious than ever.

"Yes, I locked the door! I locked it against the rudest Rebel bastard I've ever met, and I'd do so again."

She slammed her fists against his chest, shoving past him. For a moment he was still, and she thought that she might make the stairway in one piece. If she could just reach the room, she could lock the door against him again. He wouldn't break down a door in his own house.

She didn't dare look back. She fled, running up the steps one by one on bare feet. She burst into the room and turned to close the door.

But he was there. He had followed at her own speed, in silence. She tried to throw the door shut.

He caught the door as Callie tried to slam it against him. He slammed it back open with both palms. The door shuddered and reverberated and Callie won-dered if the sound couldn't be heard throughout the entire house.

"You've no right!" Callie hissed suddenly. "No right whatsoever in here—"

She broke off, crying out, spinning to leap away as he strode for her. His fingers knotted into the beautiful silk-and-lace nightgown that Christa had given her. He jerked her back around to face him.

His eyes touched hers, and to her deepest dismay, she felt the fire from that blue stare leap into her trembling frame. He held her shoulders, held them taut. And then he kissed her.

Deeply. With no desire to seek acquiescence, his mouth bore down on hers. He forced her lips to part. She felt the sure sweep of his tongue within her mouth, and each liquid caress seemed to steal more resolve from her pride and soul.

She tried to wrench free, beating her hands against his chest. She turned, but a piece of the gown caught in his hands, and she heard a rip. Startled, she paused, and turned back. She met his gaze again.

This night, he had determined, was his.

And God help her, seeing him stand there, the hot blue resolution in his eyes, the granite determination in the contours of his face, she felt a burst of near desperate desire come sweeping through her once again.

"The gown is Christa's!" she snapped at him. "You've no right to destroy it."

"Then get it off."

In a fit of fury she drew the exquisite piece of fluff and lace over her shoulders, tossing it on the floor. Naked, she lifted her chin.

"We haven't begun to discuss this—"

"And we're not going to discuss it!" he told her curtly.

She backed away with his first stride toward her. "Oh, yes, we are! Don't you ever think that you can just burst into places and behave this way. At the very least, you could have pretended—"

"Pretended what?"

"You're only here this one night! You could have pretended that we had a normal marriage. That if we weren't madly in love, at the least we didn't despise one another. That there was something we each wanted from one another. You know very well what I mean and you have no rights with me whatsoever and you will not—"

"Oh, but I will! Rebels do what they choose, Mrs. Cameron," he assured her.

"No! I won't be—"

"I keep forgetting! This play is to be reserved for those moments when they might suit you well—when your fine noble Yanks are waiting in the closet. Should I look? Have I someone in my bedroom closet already?"

Callie stopped backing away. She struck him across the face instantly, just as hard as she could.

It was all that she could do to keep from crying out, for she was lifted up into his arms and thrown down upon the bed. Dazed, she lay still for a moment. He strode toward the bed. She thought that he was unbuckling his scabbard, but when she tried to rise from his bed she discovered the truth.

He had drawn his cavalry sword.

The point of it lay between her breasts, the steel cold against the bareness of her flesh.

"It's a pity, Callie, that I can't simply split you in two." The steel lifted. Just a whisper above her flesh now, it moved. Along her ribs, low over her abdomen, lower. It rose again. "Tear away the flesh and the outer beauty, and see into the very depths of your heart. I would dearly love to see what lies there. Maybe I should try it. Sever you into two pieces . . ."

He let his words trail. She glared at him shivering.

What would you find, my love? That I want you now, that I love you, that I have so little to cling to when you fight a war against me more bitter than that you wage against the men of the North.

Damn him.

He would never really hurt her. Whether he hated her or no. She had learned that much about him.

She shoved the sword away from her face, and told him exactly that. Then she told him what she thought he ought to go do with himself.

His laughter rang out. His sword, his scabbard, and his clothing fell to the bedside.

"Don't you dare think that you're coming to this bed, Daniel Cameron! If you do—"

He did.

Naked, hot as fire himself, he came upon her with the grace of a great cat, covering her body with the length and breadth of his. She squirmed beneath him, feeling the flush, the fever, seize her. His chest pressed to her breasts, his thighs were hard upon hers.

And his sex, immensely hard and erect and insinuative, lay directly against the apex of her thighs.

"If I do, you'll what?" he demanded, his lips directly above hers, his fingers moving into the wings of her hair at the sides of her head.

"I'll scream."

"Scream."

"I think that I really hate you, Daniel!"

His reply was bitter, but the words startled her. "I wish that I really hated you, Callie." Still, his lips were just above hers in the near darkness. The whisper of his words caressed her mouth. The pulse of his desire lay very naked against her, and she had never wanted him more.

"Well, will you scream?" he murmured.

"Bastard!" she whispered in return.

His mouth touched hers again. This time she did not fight him. She molded her mouth to his; she arched against the imprint of his body, feeling a liquid like lava sweep through her, creating an arousal and a passion both beautiful and painful.

His mouth caressed hers. Savored, touched, licked. The touch came sensually over her shoulders, her collarbones, her breasts.

He moved, still agile, quick, flipping her over in the bed. She felt his lips against the line of her spine and still close to her ear.

"You wanted to pretend. Let's pretend. Let's pretend that you love me. That your heart aches to see me leave. Let's pretend . . ."

Dear Lord, but he knew how to kiss and caress. Straddled easily over her, his hands swept her shoulders and her back, his fingers caressed the sensitive sides of her breasts.

His lips continued their sweet assault upon her senses as he spoke, whispering against her flesh, following the trail of her spine.

"Let's pretend that I am a soldier, going off to your own cause. That you will pine away the hours that I am gone. That you will love me now with all your heart and soul, touch me to remember me, in all the long days that will come to pass."

His kiss fell very low against her buttocks. His fingers swept her flesh. She shivered, alive, quaking with the desire he had so deftly lit and stoked.

He flipped her over again, and his gaze met hers.

"We needn't pretend on one thing, my love. For I do want you. God, yes, Callie, I want you."

His dark head buried itself against her breasts. Against her belly, against the juncture of her thighs. She cried out softly, trying to rise against him, tugging at his dark hair. She brought his lips to hers, and she kissed them in turn, kissed and savored his lips and his mouth.

She rose against him, her fingers tracing patterns over his shoulders, her lips against the muscles of his chest, her teeth nipping at them, her tongue running elusively over every tiny touch. She stroked his body and knelt before him, then dared to let her hands fall. Her fingers curled around the hard, pulsing rod of his sex. His body nearly jackknifed. She grew bolder and bolder, stroking, touching.

His arms were suddenly around her and they fell into the depths of the bed together. Soft, clean, fragrant sheets seemed to reach up and take her in, a contrast to the blinding heat and demand of his body, now part of hers. She bit into his shoulder as he thrust deep inside of her. Deeper. His body moving. A startling, soaring rhythm.

Stars burst, the darkness was broken, and then it fell again. She felt the sweat-slickened weight of his body hard against hers, and lay there in silence, still touching him, feeling his touch. It was good to lie here so, sated, entwined, as if they loved one another.

Moments later, she gave in to temptation. She crawled atop him, legs straddled over his hips. She leaned low against him, her hair teasing his flesh, trailing against it.

"Let's pretend," she whispered softly. "Let's pretend that you love me. That you crave this night before you ride away to war. That you will hold me into the darkness, and into the light. That my name will be upon your lips when you fight a thousand battles. Daniel, let's pretend . . ."

She paused, her eyes meeting his in the near darkness.

"Pretend, my love," he whispered in return.

His arms wrapped around her. He swept her beneath him, and she cried out softly again with the volatility of his assault upon her senses, his kisses roaming where they would, his touch demanding every intimacy.

He was part of her again, one with her. No darkness of war could enter then within them, for they soared above any matters of the earth. This time she reached a pinnacle so high it seemed she lost touch with even the pale moonlight, and then she was gently, gently falling again.

She wanted to speak, but her eyes were so heavy. She wanted to say things, but she didn't want to break the spell. She lay upon his chest, touching him still, her fingers lying easily upon muscle and the crisp dark hair that grew there.

And he held her tight.

Her eyes were so heavy. She closed them.

He awoke with the first pink streaks of dawn. For a moment, he started, and then he felt her against him. He held his breath and studied her.

The auburn hair, more than a match for those radiant streaks of dawn. Her face, now surely that of an angel, so delicate, so beautiful, half hidden by the profusion of her hair.

The length of her. Ivory beauty as she lay curled against the sheets—and him. Each supple curve seemed both innocent and evocative this morning. Angel.

She slept so peacefully.

He rose, careful not to waken her.

In his wardrobe, he found the clean uniform that Christa had seen to for him. He would be very well clad and well shod, compared to the rest of his troops.

He buckled his scabbard around his waist, and stood at the foot of the bed. He wondered if he should wake her and apologize for being a horse's ass.

Sorry, Mrs. Cameron, but maybe we southern gentlemen do overindulge upon occasion.

No.

He wouldn't awaken her. Their world of pretend was far too sweet.

He hurried downstairs and into the den, finding the box with her dress. He came back up and hesitated. No, he could not wake her.

He had to touch her, though. He bent, smoothed her hair away, and kissed her forehead. Still, she didn't rise.

And so, regretfully, he left her.

Down the hall, he entered the nursery. He was tempted to sweep his tiny son into his arms, but he refrained from doing so.

Like his mother, Jared slept peacefully.

Janey came in to tell him that she had food ready. He nodded absently and said that he would be along.

The sun rose higher.

It was time to go.

It was several hours later when Callie awoke.

She did so abruptly, with a jerk, instinctively reaching out for Daniel.

He was gone.

The white dress with embroidered red flowers lay spread across the foot of the bed.

PART 4

When Johnny Comes Marching Home Again

Twenty-five

$\mathcal{D}$uring the fall of 1863, Daniel felt as if they played a game of cat and mouse with the Yankees, covering a great deal of Virginia, pushing forward, being pushed back, skirmishing.

Both sides were becoming quiet once again.

As always, silence was ominous.

Daniel hadn't been back long with his regiment when a lull in the fighting brought him a visit from a tall cavalry captain with the Virginia militia. Daniel was busy with a group of maps when the man stepped into his tent and saluted sharply. Daniel gazed at him, thinking that he somewhat resembled George Custer, for he had long blond hair, a curling mustache, and a neatly clipped beard. He was young, in his early twenties, and for a moment Daniel stared at him blankly, wondering just who he was and why he was disturbing Daniel when he was so engrossed in the geography of the area they were trying to hold.

"Colonel Cameron!"

"Yes?"

The man was stiff and straight, and seemed somewhat nervous. Odd, for he looked like a strong fellow, one quite confident in himself. Daniel gave him his full attention, noting that he would probably be considered a very handsome lad by the ladies, and that he also seemed determined.

Daniel sat down behind his field desk. "Yes, Captain. Just what is it that I can do for you?"

"My name is Liam McCloskey, sir. I have been trying to find you for quite some time. I . . ." He took a deep breath, then spoke in a rush. "I wish to ask for your sister's hand in marriage, sir. I understand that you are not the eldest male member of the family, but since that man is a member of the enemy's army, I have come to you."

Funny, he didn't like to hear Jesse called an enemy. Even if it was true. But the look on the young man's face was so earnest that Daniel bit back a retort.

"Ah, Liam McCloskey." He rose and came around his desk, offering the man his hand. He studied him carefully once again. The earnestness remained.

"I meant no offense, sir. Christa has made it quite plain to me that she loves her family intensely, and I have assured her that whatever my mind concerning the North, my thoughts will be kept to myself should the Yank Colonel Cameron and I manage to meet. Truly, Colonel, I mean no offense."

"None taken." Obviously, there were no split loyalties within McCloskey's family. He was suddenly reminded of what Jeb Stuart had told him he'd written to a family member when he heard his father-in-law was determined to stay with the Union. "He will regret it but once, and that will be continuously."

But Jeb had also said upon a number of occasions that he would rather die than lose the war.

He had been so furious with his father-in-law that he had renamed his son, since the boy had been named after his grandfather. Philip St. George Cooke Stuart became James Ewell Brown Stuart II.

Daniel was no longer certain what he felt. He'd never hated Jesse. He'd never even been angry. He'd often seen Jesse's side.

In the long days and nights, Daniel could too often remember Callie's words, telling him that he knew slavery was wrong.

The North had made it a question of slavery. He believed with his whole heart that he and the state of Virginia were fighting for states' rights.

But he had to admit that the southern states were fighting for the right to keep their way of life.

And that way of life meant slaves.

"Sir?"

"Yes, yes, I'm sorry."

"I believe that Christa might have mentioned—"

"Indeed, sir, she did."

"Colonel, I must tell you that I hail from a decent-sized farm down Norfolk way. I'm never quite sure of what is going to be left of it once this thing is over and the Yanks are beat back, but I can promise you this—I will love her with every breath in my body, from now unto eternity!"

Daniel lowered his lashes quickly, not wanting the very passionate young McCloskey to see his amusement. Yes, he did love Christa. He seemed to embody all the right virtues for a young man.

And Christa loved him.

"I'm glad we've met, Captain. Christa has expressed a desire for a June wedding."

"Yes, sir. With your blessing, sir."

"You've got my blessing, Captain. I've promised to do my best to be there to give my sister away."

"Thank you. I've requested my leave for June fifteenth, just in case we don't get a chance to whip the Yanks by then, sir. Again, I thank you so much." He saluted and turned sharply, striding out of the large field tent. He paused at the flap. "Rest assured, sir. I do love her!"

The words were so soft and so fervent Daniel couldn't help but smile as the young man left at last.

For days, the fervent passion in McCloskey's voice haunted Daniel and left him thinking of his own wife again. Sometimes speculating, sometimes hurting, and always wishing that he could get home again.

The skirmishing dragged on, the Yanks and the Rebs skirting one another.

On the western front, great armies clashed at Chicamauga and then at Chattanooga, and southern casualties were high. Those losses brought further weight down upon the laboring shoulders of the Confederacy, and yet few men spoke of a true defeat.

Daniel's forces battled fiercely at Bristoe, then the armies shifted again.

By December 1, the Union army moved across the Rapidan.

Southern commanders were wary, and Daniel knew there would be no way he could take another leave to go home for Christmas.

He managed to get a letter through to Jesse, assuring him that his wife and child were fine, and telling him about Christa's wedding plans. "She would dearly love to have you there, but God alone knows when this war will end. I believe she knows her own mind and is determined upon marriage now. Don't risk yourself."

He had not heard back from his brother, and he was worried.

He ached for home.

Or maybe it wasn't home that he pined for anymore. He lay awake each night and relived every last moment he had spent with Callie.

He had tried to write to her but his notes never sounded quite right, and so he had given up the effort, addressing his letters to all three of the women in his household and keeping them as light as he could.

She did not write in return. Christa wrote, and Kiernan wrote, and sometimes when he was lucky, mail came through.

But Callie did not write.

She remained at Cameron Hall, and must have been resigned to life there, for Christa and Kiernan both mentioned her and the children constantly. John Daniel was speaking more clearly daily, and Jared was tearing around the house on his knees. Ships were still managing to come and go on the river, despite the Yankee blockade. They hadn't heard of any troops anywhere near them for quite some time.

On Christmas morning, Daniel was in a command tent along the Rapidan River when one of his sergeants made an appearance before him.

"Yanks across the river, sir!"

"Yes, I know," he said dryly. "They've been there for quite some time. I don't think they're planning on any hostilities today. It is Christmas day." Sometimes fighting did break out on Christmas. Both sides tried to avoid it.

"No, sir. They aren't planning any hostilities. Come on out, sir. I promised that I'd bring you down to the river."

Curious, Daniel rose, buckled on his sword, and followed his sergeant.

Far across a new layer of snow and ice-clogged water, he could see a detachment of mounted soldiers, Yankee cavalry.

One of the mounted men raced forward, close to the glistening river, and shouted out.

"In your honor, sir! Your brother, Colonel Jesse Cameron, has recently heard of your marriage, and the birth of your son. He—and many other officers with whom you studied at West Point and rode with in Kansas—now salute you, sir! Also, sir, Colonel Jesse Cameron sends his love to his wife and his sister, and congragulates the latter on her upcoming nuptials, sir!"

And there, on Christmas day, guns exploded into the air and a series of cries went up.

Daniel grinned broadly, shouting back to the Yank across the river. "Tell my brother, and the other gentlemen, thank you, sir!"

They both saluted. The Yankees rode away, disappearing into a haze of snow.

"Well, Jess," he murmured to himself, "at least I know that you are alive and well."

Daniel turned, startled to discover that he was more weary than ever and returned to his tent.

It was Christmas. A dark day for the men and women of the Confederacy.

With a new, dark year stretching before them.

As yet, they couldn't guess how dark that year would be.

* * *

Christmas came to Cameron Hall.

By that time, Callie was very comfortable in her new home and with everyone in it.

During the long fall, she had earned herself a place there, startling both Kiernan and Christa with her abilities with both the plantation lifestock and the garden planting.

She didn't know anything about cotton at all, but that didn't matter because both Christa and Kiernan did, as did the very able ex-slaves who had served the Camerons for years.

Christa told her that there had been a time when she had worried deeply about running the place herself, because a number of their freed people had determined to move to the North.

But a large group of blacks from Cameron Hall had been in New York when the draft riots had exploded in mid-July of '63. In a period of four days, mobs had burned the draft office, the offices of the *Tribune,* and other buildings. The violence had turned toward the blacks—held to be responsible for the war by many of the northerners. White men had died, too, but it had been mostly blacks killed, and in that four-day period, nearly a thousand people had died or been wounded.

It had been a dark day for the North.

But it had brought a number of Cameron Hall's freed slaves back to work her fields, and Christa had been relieved to have them return.

Before the war, there had been nearly a hundred field hands at Cameron Hall. Now there were only thirty-eight, but before the men had made their way back from New York, there had been a scant twenty-two.

In November they had acquired some more help, in the form of Joseph Ashby, a Confederate soldier honorably discharged after he lost his left leg at Gettysburg. Joseph was as cheerful as the day was long—still convinced that the Yanks would never win—and the best overseer any plantation had ever seen. With Joseph up every morning at the crack of dawn to hobble along on his wooden leg, life became much easier not just for Christa, but for all of the Cameron women. Not that Callie had ever minded work—work kept her mind off the future—but Jared was constantly changing now, learning new things, and she cherished her time with him. The household could also be fun, with John Daniel running about everywhere, and Jared now trying to keep up on his knees.

Callie discovered that she liked both of her sister-in-laws very much. They were both headstrong, and determined, but also very kind. While Callie could make a garden grow under the most difficult situation, Kiernan and Christa knew every little nuance of proper dress and society, and even in the midst of war with her own inner conflict almost always raging, Callie learned that her sisters-in-law could make her laugh, exaggerating the proper way to hold a teacup, to walk, to laugh, to flutter eyelashes, to lift a chin imperiously, in short, to charm a man—or stop him cold.

They lived for the days when a letter would come through, brought more and more often by passing friends or even strangers as the war disrupted regular mail service. Letters came most frequently from Daniel, but they were never addressed to Callie alone, and she tried to hide her feelings of both embarrassment and desolation that he would not make a special effort to write to his own wife.

Two letters came through from Jesse, and they were for Kiernan alone, although she assured both Christa and Callie that he had sent them both his love. After the first, Kiernan had seemed strange for a day or two, and then she had come to Callie's room one evening to ask just how Callie had come to know Jesse.

Callie explained that he had come by after the battle of Antietam, when he had been looking for Daniel. And that she had known, of course, where daniel was.

Kiernan watched Callie as she spoke, then she exclaimed softly, "That's it! Daniel thinks you were responsible for his being in prison!"

Callie looked down at her hands. "I was responsible," she said quietly.

Kiernan gasped. "Dear Lord, I could have sworn that you cared something for him!"

"I do," Callie told her. She shrugged and added, "I love him. That's why I did what I did." She tried very hard to explain everything that happened. She couldn't quite meet Kiernan's eyes when she told her almost exactly what she had done, but she stuttered through a story very close to the entire truth. "They would have killed him, Kiernan. I didn't want him to die."

Kiernan sat beside her and hugged her tightly. "Oh, Callie! But if you've explained things to Daniel the way that you've explained them to me—"

"I've tried, but I don't think he believes me. Maybe he can't believe me. And maybe it's just the war that now makes enemies of us."

"And maybe he ought to be smacked right in the face," Kiernan said determinedly.

"I've tried that too," Callie admitted, smiling ruefully.

"Perhaps if I were to intercede—" Kiernan began.

"No," Callie told her. "Kiernan, don't you see? He has to believe in me again, or nothing will ever be any good. The fates don't seem to be looking on me very kindly. As soon as we started heading for Virginia, the same Yankee came after us again. He's Lieutenant Colonel Dabney now—he received a promotion for bringing Daniel in. What's worse, he was a friend before the war. I had asked Daniel to stop to say good-bye to the people who had helped me when I was alone. Dabney came after us because one of the Weisses—concerned for my welfare or that of the baby, I'm sure—told him where I had gone."

"I see," Kiernan murmured.

"And there's more, of course."

"What's that?"

"*I am a Yankee,*" Callie said. "Oh, Kiernan, I'm sorry, I know how you love your South! But I believe in the Union, I believe that as a whole we can be great, I—"

"Wait! I've heard it!" Kiernan interrupted her. She smiled. "You forget, I've a Yankee physician for a husband. Callie! I've seen Virginia ravaged, I've seen men die—God, help me! I've assisted in removing their limbs. I cannot bear what has happened here, the rape of the land, the cruelties that exist. But I have discovered more than ever that the war has brought out the best in good men, and the worst in those less noble, North and South. I don't want to see this, my home burned, nor my father's home burned. What I want, more than anything, is for the war to end."

Callie smiled, and hugged Kiernan fiercely. "It's what I want too."

Kiernan sat back, studying her. "Daniel does love you, you know."

"Once, I think that he did. Sometimes now I'm convinced that he hates me."

"No. I've known Daniel all my life. I have never seen him so intense before, so passionate, so torn. Don't you see, Callie, if he did not care, his manners would be far better!"

Callie thought of the beautiful white dress with its red flowers, left at the foot of the bed.

Let's pretend . . .

"But I can't tell him that I love him—he does not trust me. And I try so very hard to keep my distance, because I am lost if I ever surrender—"

"I agree! You can never, never surrender to Cameron men," Kiernan assured her. "But you can sue for a negotiated peace."

"Perhaps," Callie agreed.

"Time will tell."

"And the war will end!"

But the war didn't end.

Christmas day brought the three Cameron women outside, despite the cold. They sat on the porch, watching the drive, all praying that a loved one would come to them.

No soldiers came home that day.

Callie prayed for safety, for Daniel, for Jesse, for her brothers on some distant front. She wrote to them time and time again, but so far, had received no replies. Maybe her letters had never reached them. Maybe they didn't know where she was. She could only pray that they were safe.

In early February, Kiernan received a request to come and help one of the matrons at the military hospital on the outskirts of Richmond. Again, she sought Callie out at night, reading the letter.

"I know, dear, that some of our Richmond ladies have been less than kind since hearing of your marriage to the Cameron who turned his back on his people, but as I knew your heart to be strong and true—and at the utmost, loyal—I am begging you to suffer their slings and arrows, as it were, to come give me some assistance here. Supplies are woefully low, and the men are dearly in need of good cheer. I have heard from a young man your husband assisted (an officer injured and imprisoned and exchanged) that you are an excellent nurse, with better qualifications gained at your husband's side than many a man who titles himself 'doctor.' Please come. But take extreme care. Yankees are ever trying to reach our dear capital!"

"What will you do?" Callie asked her.

"I will go, of course."

"I'm coming with you," Callie determined suddenly.

"To save Rebel lives?" Kiernan asked her.

"To save human lives."

Kiernan grinned. "Good! I was hoping you would come!"

* * *

Yankees were very near the capital.

At the end of February Daniel was summoned to a meeting. A courier had arrived with dispatches warning of the discovery of a planned raid on Richmond. Federal General Judson Kilpatrick and Federal Colonel Ulric Dahlgren were leading forces that would separate, meet, seize the capital, distribute amnesty proclamations, and free the Federal prisoners in Richmond.

Daniel, who knew the countryside like the back of his hand, was ordered to leave his troops to ride communications for the troops who would defend against these raiders.

By nightfall of the first of March, Dahlgren and his men were within two and a half miles of the capital. Daniel was there with the Confederate forces who fought him.

Riding around Dahlgren's forces, Daniel discovered that he had ordered a retreat.

The next day, the Confederates pursued him. Late that night they set up an ambush. In the fighting that followed, Dahlgren was killed.

The raid might have been considered a minor incident in a war in which thousands sometimes died in a battle, except for the fact that startling documents were found on Dahlgren's body.

There were orders to his men—signed by Dahlgren—that they must burn Richmond, "the hated city," to the ground.

A second paper, unsigned, said that they must find Jeff Davis and his cabinet, and kill them.

Daniel returned to his command with the couriers carrying the photographic copies of the letters to Lee. Word was out about the letters, and emotions were running high against the Union. Southerners, on the field of battle and off, were outraged.

Lee sent copies of the letters to Meade. In turn, Meade replied to Lee assuring him that the United States government had never sanctioned such orders, had indeed, sanctioned nothing but what action might be necessary by war.

Whether it was a cover-up or the truth, no one knew.

Beauty Stuart had summoned Daniel when the reply came in. He showed him a copy. "Well, what do you think?"

"I think it's a good thing that Dahlgren did not succeed with his raid," Daniel said.

"And what of our one-time friends in the North?"

"I cannot believe that they would condone murder."

Stuart shrugged. "Perhaps not." He gazed at Daniel sharply. "Well, did you see your wife in Richmond?"

"What?" Daniel demanded sharply.

"I'm sorry, you didn't know? Flora mentioned in a letter to me that she had heard both your sister-in-law and your wife were working at the hospital. You know that I'm not a man to take leave often, and that I don't appreciate time taken by my officers. But as you were so close . . ."

Daniel gritted his teeth. He hadn't known that Callie was in Richmond.

Callie didn't write.

But he hadn't heard from Kiernan, either.

"As we are still so close," Daniel said, "when you feel that I might be spared again, I would highly appreciate just a day or two to see to her welfare, and that of my sister-in-law and son."

Beauty acquiesced.

Once again, Daniel bided his time.

Winter was fading; spring had come. With warmer weather, the fighting would intensify.

He wanted to see Callie. Soon.

Callie's first days in the hospital seemed to bring her from one horror to the next.

She had seen men die before. She had seen them die all over her yard. She had nursed Daniel when he was wounded, and she had feared for her life.

None of it had prepared her for the hospital.

There were not enough drugs, and now there was barely enough whiskey to be prescribed for the patients.

Amputations were the order of the day. By the end of her first week, Callie couldn't count the number of operations in which she had assisted. At first, she had nearly passed out. Kiernan had warned her to pinch herself, and thus save herself such an embarrassment.

There was much more to helping in the hospital than the horror of seeing whole men lose their limbs. Some soldiers tried to bring their whole families in to sleep, and she had to part clinging wives from their soldier husbands and insist that the hospital was for the sick. She read until she was hoarse, and she wrote endless letters.

She wrote letters for men who died before they finished dictating them.

She and Kiernan and Janey had rented a small row house right by the hospital for themselves and the boys, and while Kiernan and Callie put in their endless hours with the wounded, Janey minded the boys and did what she could to put food on their own table.

Callie couldn't have said that she was happy. To live in the midst of such pain and misery could not make one happy.

But she felt useful.

She was also, upon occasion, able to visit Varina Davis. One evening she and Kiernan both stripped off their worn work gowns and attended one of Varina's receptions. Kiernan tried to tell Callie that she was really not very welcome because of her marriage to Jesse, and Callie commented that it was very strange that she—the one who was the Yank—seemed to fare better than a full-blooded Confederate like Kiernan.

"I'm afraid it's a man's world," Kiernan said. "And we are judged by our men." She grinned. "You, at least, are thereby a national hero."

"I don't think that Daniel would agree."

"But you must take advantage of his situation, right?"

It was impossible not to come to love Kiernan dearly, and Callie was very grateful for her. No matter what other women might be saying about Kiernan, Varina was, as always, the ultimate hostess.

Varina was expecting another baby that spring, and despite the lines drawn into her beautiful face by the tensions of her position, she seemed to hold a special beauty.

"You manage to be happy, despite it all," Callie told her.

"And you seem to serve us well, even if your heart lies elsewhere!" Varina told her. She smiled a beautiful smile, even if her slender face seemed drawn. In her way, Varina was happy. She loved her husband, and she loved her children. She was willing to ride out any storm with him, to rise to the heights, to endure any hardship.

Callie was suddenly very envious. She could suddenly see clearly what she wanted more than anything in the world.

A love so simple, and a love so complex.

It might well be something she could never have. She and Daniel might never come to an understanding. He didn't trust her; there was the possibility that he never would.

It was a division every bit as deep as the Mason-Dixon line.

Kiernan had told her that Daniel did love her. Maybe in time.

She smiled ruefully and told Varina, "I'm glad to be at the hospital. Well, I think I am. It's terrible to watch the men suffer. Sometimes, it's pure agony to write their letters, and help them say good-bye, telling their mothers or wives or children that they love them so. But when they're in the hospital, it doesn't seem that they are Yankees or Rebels anymore, it just seems they are men, God-fearing and all alike."

"And once we were," Varina murmured. She flashed Callie a smile. "I have a wayward child slipping down the stairway once again. Excuse me!"

Callie laughed. Through the open foyer doors she could see a dark-haired little boy with a brilliant smile to defy any mention of warfare, inching down the elegant stairway.

Again, she felt a little tug of envy for Varina Davis.

The world, it seemed, was crumbling down around her. But she had her "dear old Banny," and her beautiful children.

Callie and Kiernan enjoyed the evening, but retired early.

Richmond was crawling with refugees. Even in the late evening, the streets were filled with people. Many of them were living on the streets, Callie had heard. They had been burned out of their homes, or were in the way of a northern army determinedly destroying any source of supply it could.

The Yankees were very close. And still, the southern spirit was a determined one.

The Yankees might come close, but they wouldn't take Richmond.

Working in the hospital again, Callie discovered that more and more of the injured men were coming in from skirmishes extremely close to the capital. She was startled to discover that she was hanging on every word that the soldiers told her.

She began to hear about her husband. He was close with his flamboyant commander, that dashing cavalier Stuart, and they were keeping close tabs on Union General Custer's troops now.

Callie felt her heart beating quickly as she cooled fevered foreheads and tried to make men more comfortable. She realized that she was longing to see Daniel again. But as Kiernan had said, she could not surrender. But she could sue for a negotiated peace.

But war gave no quarter to the wants and desires of the contestants locked within it.

Daniel remained on the battlefield, and Callie remained in Richmond, praying that he would come for a day, an hour.

Deeper tragedy struck.

On April 30, the precocious little boy with the beautiful smile, Varina's Joey, fell from the porch of the Confederate White House.

A servant brought news of the awful event to Callie at the hospital. An old, gaunt black man, tears running down his face, told Callie the tale.

"Miz Varina, she had just left the children playing in her room, and she done bring some tea or some-such into the president. Next thing we all know, that boy—her very pride and joy—why he done crawl up on a bannister and then . . . then he was on the ground and there was all manner of screaming. Miz Varina, why, she done reach her child mighty quick, and he died in his mother's arms. She was overcome. Just overcome. But the army, ma'am, it had dispatches coming in for the president all the time, even as he was kneeling there, bowed over his son in grief. He done told them at last that he had to have one day with his child. And there she is, Miz Varina, expecting another babe, weeping over this one, and trying to hold up her husband all the while. She's strong, Miz Cameron, but Lawd almighty, how strong can a woman be? She sets a store by you, ma'am, and I thought that maybe . . ."

"I'll come right away," Callie promised him.

And she did.

It seemed that there was so little that she could do. The Davises were closeted with their grief.

Callie tried to help with the weeping babes who were so lost and confused at their brother's death, and she tried to greet the mourners who came to the door. She sat numbly as she saw the small boy dressed out for his burial, and she could think of no words to say when Varina was before her.

There *were* no words to atone for the loss of a child. Callie thought of how recently she had seen little Joey with his beautiful smile.

And after all the death she had witnessed time and time again, she turned away and wept.

The thunder of cannon fire could be heard as the little boy was laid to rest.

Within days, the Union and Confederate forces were engaged in fierce fighting in the Wilderness. Callie had never seen anything more terrible, for the forests caught on fire, and men brought into the hospital were sometimes little more than charred corpses. And no one knew if their uniforms had been blue or gray.

Then came the battle of Yellow Tavern.

A little less than two weeks after the death of little Joe Davis, the thunder of cannon fire could be heard again as Callie stood in Hollywood Cemetery, eyes glazed as she watched another burial.

James Ewell Brown Stuart, the flamboyant, defiant, passionate, dashing cavalier, was dead.

He had been mortally wounded in battle with General Custer's forces. An ambulance had been found to bring him back to Richmond.

Jeff Davis had come to his side; some old friends and comrades had come to do the same.

They had sung "Rock of Ages," his favorite hymn. He had asked the doctor if he might survive the night, just long enough for his wife to arrive.

But Flora Stuart had arrived to a house of silence, and no one had needed to tell her that her husband was dead.

The Yankees were so close that there was no local militia to form an honor guard—the city's forces were all out fighting for the city's defense.

Callie attended the church service, her heart heavy. She'd never met Stuart—she had known that he had meant a great deal to Daniel. Stuart had known he was dying; he had ordered his officers not to follow him to his deathbed, but to see to their duty.

So Daniel must be seeing to his duty, collecting bullets. Like Stuart. Like Stonewall Jackson. Like so many others.

Callie didn't hear the service at the cemetery. She heard the burst of shells, a not too distant sound. She saw the slopes and curves and sections of the cemetery, and she gazed at the place where Jeb's little daughter—Flora, for her mother—had been reinterred just a year ago. He had accepted his death, they said, because he whispered that he would be with his Flora again.

Callie looked at the sky, and she thought that soon it would rain. She couldn't pray for the man being buried.

She could only fervently pray for Daniel. He would never falter if asked to lead a charge. All these years, he had been in the thick of things. The fighting was growing more and more fierce daily.

Dear God, don't let him die.

She could hear Flora Stuart, sobbing softly.

He wouldn't die, she told herself. Not now, not today. Little Joe had died, and Jeb was dead, and no matter what his general had ordered, Daniel had thought the world of Jeb Stuart. He would leave the front lines; he would come home to be here now. She would close her eyes, and open them, and Daniel would be there, across the crowd.

She closed her eyes, her lips moving in prayer.

She opened her eyes.

But Daniel was not there. He was not coming. He was still in the battlefield, where he had been ordered to stay.

The minister finished the service.

The sky suddenly seemed to burst open, and it began to rain.

Twenty-six

June 7, 1864
Cold Harbor, Virginia

*S*ince the third of June, Daniel was certain that he had done nothing but listen to the moans and cries of the wounded.

They were mostly Yanks out there now, but since battle had been engaged here, the Union man in charge, General U. S. Grant, had refused to seek any parley to remove his dead and wounded from the field.

Perhaps it was because the commanding general who asked first to bring his wounded from the field was customarily the general admitting to defeat.

Grant had been defeated here, whether he wanted to admit it or not. In these days of almost constant battle, from the Wilderness to Yellow Tavern to Spotsylvania, and now here, at last, to Cold Harbor, Grant had been defeated. Richmond, once again, had been saved.

Grant's forces were still in their trenches and so were Lee's. The southerners watched carefully, wondering just what Grant would do next.

Riding in back of the curiously quiet lines, Daniel wondered why he felt no exuberance.

Perhaps there was none left to feel.

Beauty was dead, dead and buried. Daniel still felt numb when he thought of it. Stonewall a year ago, Beauty now, and so many others in between.

Now they had beaten back even Grant, but Grant didn't retreat. His men lay on the field, screaming and dying, but he didn't admit defeat.

The Confederates had brought in a number of the Union wounded with their own, risking forays out into the field of battle. To listen to the men scream was torture; it was no hardship to bring them in, be they Yanks or rebels.

Everyone seemed to be waiting.

Daniel reined in. He still smelled like soot and ashes, he thought, and that from the Wilderness.

Never had he seen anything like it, or imagined anything like it. Smoke and fog so thick that Union troops fired on Union troops and southern troops did the same. Then the forest burst into flames, and then again, the horrible screams of men and horses trapped in fallen foliage or wounded too severely to try to escape the lapping flames of the fire.

So much bloodshed in so very few days.

The problem was that they could lick the Yankees. They had licked them time and time again. But more of them came. No matter how many they battled and how many they killed, there were always more.

They were outnumbered and outgunned.

"Colonel Cameron, sir!"

A young soldier on horseback came riding up to him. "We've stopped a conveyance on the road, sir. There's two ladies, two children, and a black woman in it."

"Yes?"

"Well, the women claim to be kin of yours. Your wife and your sister-in-law."

His heart suddenly slammed against his chest. Callie, here?

He was instantly torn in two. He had wanted to see her so damned badly for so very long!

They couldn't possibly be such fools, riding around the countryside with battle waging like this!

"Where is this conveyance, soldier?" Daniel asked. He called to one of his lieutenants to take charge of the forces directly beneath him, and he rode swiftly behind the soldier back to the main road. The Yankees were well to the other side of it, but the fighting here had been so fierce and so vicious that he felt ill thinking of Callie and Kiernan stumbling upon it.

With the children!

It couldn't be the two of them. Surely, Kiernan would not be so foolish.

But it was them.

He reined in his horse and leapt down from it at the road, staring at the wagon.

Callie and Kiernan were both in the front, waiting. Daniel was startled at their appearances, for though nothing could take away the extent of their beauty, they were far different from the women he had last seen at Cameron Hall. Both were in black, the color of mourning. In honor of Beauty, or perhaps in honor of little Joey Davis. They were minus their hoops, their gowns were simple, and they were both very thin.

"Jesu!" Daniel breathed. His eyes fell upon his wife, and only his wife. His stomach and heart seemed to catapult together. His fingers were shaking.

No black costuming could take away the radiance of her color. Silver-gray eyes fell on his, and warmth surged through him. Dear God. It had been so long since he had seen her.

Pretend that you love me!

He had pretended through all these awful months of warfare. Dreamed of her through the nights when he had managed to sleep through the screams of the dying.

And she was indeed before him now.

All he could think of was the dangerous mission they had set upon, and how she dared risk herself so!

There were Yanks everywhere!

She was a Yank!

It wasn't so much that she might have run into Rebels or Yankees, it was the fact they might have stumbled upon deserters, as they had once before, in nearly this same place, and at nearly this same time, years before.

Before he had met Callie, before he had loved her.

Temper! he warned himself. For those silver eyes were on him, brilliant, beautiful. He wanted to crush her into his arms, and hold her so tightly.

But he didn't embrace her; he was shaking too hard to do so. Long strides brought him to the wagon.

"What in God's name do you two think that you're doing?" he thundered.

He reached for Callie, grabbing her around the waist, and bringing her down against him. The warmth of her body seemed to explode against him. Her toes touched the ground, and he met her angry eyes.

"We're trying to get home," she informed him.

She had called Cameron Hall her home.

"What?" he said incredulously. He looked from Callie to Kiernan, and back again. "Haven't you heard? The fighting has been constant here!"

Callie was still against him. She'd made no attempt to fight his hold. He looked down into her eyes again. She smiled suddenly.

Smiled, and the anger faded from her eyes. The silver light was in them once again. Without conscious thought he touched her face, his thumb tracing over her cheek. She really had the face of an angel. She was hatless, and her hair streamed down her back in all its glory, the deepest, richest fire imaginable. I love you, he thought. I have loved you for years now.

"You could have been killed, you little fools!" he murmured.

"Daniel, Kiernan and I must get home. Christa is going to be married, remember? And . . ."

"And we didn't know if you or Jesse would manage to get there, and so we decided that we had to," Kiernan finished from the wagon.

"Jesu! Christa would understand. We're in the midst of a war!"

"Mum?"

A sound from the back of the wagon suddenly distracted Daniel. He looked around the rough wood exterior and jumped.

His son was standing, holding on to the wagon. Bright blue eyes looked at him with no recognition. A second pair of blue eyes stared at him, too, as John Daniel leaned up to see what was going on. Except for the difference in their ages, the little boys might have been twins.

Like Jesse and I, he thought. And then emotion seemed to rush in on him. My son is standing, maybe walking. He forms words now, and he doesn't know who I am. He has gotten so big, and I haven't been there to see him stand, to take his first steps.

This was war. He could still remember Beauty's strong feelings on the subject. Duty came first. House and home came later.

Still, how could a man make house and home come later when his family was sitting in front of him, and the war itself was all around them?

He decided that he didn't give a damn about the war for the moment. He left Callie's side and walked around to the wagon.

"Hello," he said softly to the boys.

"Mum," Jared repeated.

"He doesn't say very much," John Daniel advised his uncle. "He's just a little over a year, you know."

Daniel grinned, tousling his nephew's hair. "And you're just over two, young man!" He reached out to his son. Jared observed him with wide blue eyes. Don't shy away from me, he thought. Please, don't shy away from me!

For a moment, he was certain that Jared would. Then the little boy reached out with his chubby little arms and Daniel swept him up, hugging him fiercely.

Callie had come around the wagon. He saw her over his son's dark head. She watched him gravely, and he wondered for a brief moment just what it might be like if they could only have a normal relationship, if they could only have a life! She was so beautiful. And she had given him this child, and so far she had cared for his child alone, and she had done so in his home, or in Richmond.

"He's big now," Daniel told her softly.

She smiled. She'd never seemed to begrudge him Jared, or to begrudge him any of his son's affections. She'd been so independent, but she'd bowed to him in so many things. Yet, he'd been stronger, he'd had the ability to take Jared and make her come south.

But he'd never forced her to stay, yet she had done so anyway.

"Very big," she agreed.

"Why in heaven did you come to Richmond?" he asked her.

She shrugged. "They needed help at the hospital."

"So you came to Richmond to patch together Rebs."

"Rebels, Yankees, whoever came in," she agreed.

He buried his face against his son's throat. "You were there for little Joe's funeral?"

"And Jeb Stuart's," she said softly. "We could hear the cannon through it all."

"What did you two think that you were doing, riding out with the children like this?"

"Daniel, I'm not afraid—"

"Callie, you should be afraid!"

He gritted his teeth. They hadn't been so far from here a little over two years ago. Was it two years ago? It felt as if he had been fighting forever. He had been injured, Kiernan had been expecting the baby, and the ride home had seemed endless. We're going in circles! he thought, feeling they were back to that time. Somehow, he had to get them home. Grant's forces were quiet at this hour, but that could change anytime.

He handed Jared to Callie. "I'll ask for time to bring you home," he told her.

"Daniel, we are capable—"

"Callie," he snapped roughly, "you're taking my son and my nephew through battle lines!"

She stiffened. Dear Lord, why was he always yelling? What little ground they had made toward one another in a year of absence and a smile seemed suddenly to be swept away.

"I have never risked our child!" she said. He thought that the brilliance in her eyes might be that of tears. "But take time, Daniel, yes, please, take time! It's a way to get you out of the front lines of this war!"

She sounded bitter, ironic.

Almost as if she had missed him.

He turned away from her and mounted his horse, anxious to find his superiors. Had it been just two days before, he knew he never would have been given any leave to travel.

But now Grant was ominously silent.

He was able to find both Wade Hampton—Stuart's successor with the cavalry —and Fitzhugh Lee, Robert E.'s talented nephew. Both thought him insane at first, but the explanation that his wife had simply appeared in the road was taken well by both men, and he was granted leave to escort his wife and son back to Cameron Hall.

Signing a pass so that Daniel could move unharrassed through any Confederate lines, General Hampton warned him, "Make haste. It seems that the Yanks have started terrorizing all of the countryside, and I must have you back. On your honor, sir!"

He left his lieutenant in charge, and begged his men to obey him as they would himself, promising to return swiftly.

He came back to the wagon, tied his horse to the back, and urged Callie to move over so that he might take the reins.

He met Kiernan's eyes over Callie's. They both remembered the last time they had taken such a ride. They both remembered the dangers they had met along the way.

He urged the horse forward. "Home, horse!" he told the nag. And they started off.

They rode for miles in near silence, Janey in the back with the boys; Daniel, Callie, and Kiernan in the front. No troops accosted them.

The cannons were quiet. Along the lush and beautiful countryside, they heard no sound of guns. Summer had come to the land beautifully. The foliage was brilliantly green, and there was a soft breeze as they rode. Upon occasion, they passed a burned-down house, or a field stripped of any good supply it might have carried. Only then did it seem possible that there was a war.

How quickly the land made up for the things that befell it! Daniel thought. For once they passed by such a place, the deep forests took over once again.

By nightfall, he moved into one of the forest trails, glad that he was in a place he knew so well. He was determined not to go into Williamsburg, but to skirt around it, and thus come home that way.

He jumped down from the wagon, and reached up for Callie. She hesitated, then set her hands upon his shoulders and allowed him to lift her down. He released her quickly, though, and reached for Kiernan.

"We're staying here tonight?" Callie asked.

He nodded. "You two and Janey can sleep with the boys in the back. I'll keep watch now. Try to get some sleep. I don't know if I can stay up the whole night. If not, the two of you will have to stay up together. Can you do it?"

Callie nodded. "Yes, of course we can."

"Then get some sleep."

He sat down before the wagon, and loaded his guns. He had two Colts, and a Spencer repeating rifle that he had taken from the ground at the Wilderness.

The gun hadn't saved its previous Yank owner from the fires of hell, but Daniel prayed that now it could keep them all safe.

Callie didn't go to sleep right away. He was startled to find her by his side, offering him a cup of water and some bread and dried beef.

Rations had been more than slim since their last campaign had begun. He didn't hesitate, but took the water and the food from her.

While he ate, he watched her. She seemed to have acquired a composure and a serenity since he had seen her last. Her eyes met his, then fell, rich sweeping lashes creating shadows on her cheek. She sat close to him, nearly touching him. The sweet feminine scent of her was nearly more than he could bear.

He touched her cheek. Her eyes, gray and silver and luminous, came to his once again. "How have you been, Callie? Tending to the sick and wounded, how have you been yourself?"

"Well," she told him. She poured more water into his cup. "Except when we read the death notices. I always knew that I would not find your name on the list. I felt certain that I would hear if you had been injured, if you had been . . ."

"Killed?"

"Yes," she said flatly.

He caught hold of her wrist. "I'm not going to die, Callie. I'm good, I'm careful."

"No. You're a colonel. I know you're probably reckless! I . . ."

Her voice trailed away, for his eyes were so hot upon her.

He watched her mouth, and suddenly, he could bear it no longer. He leaned forward, pulling her into his embrace, and kissed her. He touched her lips with his own, ground down upon them. He parted her lips with his tongue, and he felt her give to him. He filled her mouth with his kiss, tasting, savoring, needing. She gave fully to him. Their tongues met, wet, hot, touching, dancing, needing more.

Then out of the near darkness, he heard a warning cry.

"Daniel! There's someone on the road," Kiernan cried from the wagon.

He pressed Callie from him, leaping to his feet. Kiernan was right and he should have heard it. There was a horseman coming nearer and nearer. He backed behind the tree that blocked the wagon and tried to look around it. Darkness had come, and there was very little moon. What there was seemed to be behind a cloud.

The cloud moved and he saw a Yankee horseman coming.

Daniel strode quickly down the road, keeping to the shadows. He shimmied up the trunk of a tree just in time to see the shadowed rider pause.

The rider had heard him. The rider had sensed danger.

He urged his horse forward, closer.

Daniel leapt from the tree and onto the horseman. He swept the rider from his horse, and together they rolled and rolled on the dark ground, both grunting, both breathing hard. An elbow caught Daniel in the ribs. He nearly cried out. He shoved a fist into a muscled gut.

He briefly obtained the upper hand, straddling over his enemy.

The cloud moved completely.

"Jesse!"

"Daniel, Jesu, you scared the damn hell out of me!" Jesse swore.

"You're lucky I didn't shoot you!" Daniel stood quickly, stretching down a hand to his brother. Jesse stood. For a moment they stared at one another in the moonlight. Then they stepped forward and embraced. "How the hell did you come to be here?" Daniel demanded.

"Mutual friends," Jesse said dryly. "I heard that my wife had passed by Cold Harbor, and that my brother was taking her home."

"And you got leave?"

Jesse shrugged. "There weren't many wounded left alive after Cold Harbor," he said bitterly.

The two went no further in their conversation, for they were suddenly interrupted by a shrill, glad cry. They started and turned, and Kiernan came leaping out of the darkness, running like a bat out of hell to reach Jesse.

She catapulted into his arms. Daniel stepped aside as the two of them greeted each other with one of the most tender and passionate kisses he'd ever witnessed. A throat cleared softly, and he realized that Callie was on the other side of the entwined pair, a child in either arm.

Jesse and Kiernan split apart. Daniel could hear his brother inhale sharply. "John Daniel and Jared, is it?" He took his son from Callie, staring at the little boy. "John Daniel . . . you've gotten so big! Do you know who I am?"

John Daniel surveyed him studiously. "He's Uncle Daniel. You're my father."

"That's right," Jesse said. He hugged the boy, and he glanced at Callie again, grinning. "Welcome to the family," he told her.

"Thank you," Callie replied. She glanced nervously at Daniel. "If Jesse came upon us so easily . . ."

"Then we need to be very careful, because anybody could. I'll take the first watch, and Jesse can take the second," Daniel said.

"Who are we watching out for now?" Callie asked softly. "The Yanks or the Rebs?"

"Either," Jesse and Daniel answered together.

"All of you, go and get some sleep," Daniel said. He glanced at Callie. He could still taste her kiss. It had been sweet, so much so that if Kiernan hadn't been on guard, he wouldn't have heard Jesse coming.

"Everyone, go to sleep," he persisted. "I'm best on guard by myself."

Callie turned away, hugging Jared to her.

Kiernan's eyes still shimmered as she looked at Jesse. The two of them, with John Daniel between them, walked away.

Stiff as a poker, Daniel sat down to keep guard.

There were no other interruptions. He sat awake and alert for hours, but nothing moved but the breeze through the trees. At about three, Jesse came and tapped him on the shoulder. "Go get some rest. I'll take it from here."

Daniel nodded. He rose, stretched, and yawned, and started for a tree. "Over there," Jesse directed him.

Daniel looked where Jesse pointed. Callie was there. She was sound asleep, but she had stretched out a blanket that was plenty large for them both and Jared.

Jared was in his mother's arms. Daniel stretched out at her back and held her tenderly. It wasn't exactly what he wanted. Not when the scent of her was so intoxicating. It was good to hold her. To hear her sigh softly and curve against him, even as she slept.

When Callie awoke, she felt his hand on her upper arm. She started and turned, and found his enigmatic blue gaze upon her. "We've got to go," was all that he said. He had slept with her, she thought. He had held her through the night, given her his warmth.

Pretend that you love me.

He was quickly on his feet and reaching a hand down to her. She accepted his help to rise, then turned for Jared, who was still sleeping. Daniel leaned past her, picking up their sleeping son. He nodded toward the wagon. Jesse and Kiernan and Janey were there, waiting for them.

"I'll ride on ahead and scout the road," Daniel said.

"I can do it—" Jesse said.

"It's still supposed to be Rebel territory," Daniel reminded him. "I'll go." He handed Jared to Callie, then untied his horse from the back of the wagon and mounted up. Callie watched him ride ahead.

There was a difference in the brothers now, she thought sadly. Jesse's uniform was in sound shape. Daniel was in near rags again.

Yet no matter how tattered his uniform became, there was still something majestic in his appearance. The plume remained high in his hat, his shoulders were broad. He still seemed a part of some sweet chivalry gone past. She wanted to reach out and hold on to that chivalry.

"Let me help you up," Jesse told her. "Kiernan, ride with me up front?"

"Of course," Kiernan said softly.

Callie was still tired, and Janey seemed weary herself. Callie lay in the back of the wagon with Jared, closed her eyes, and dreamed.

It had been something to see Kiernan and Jesse as they had spotted one another. Something to watch their every step as they moved toward one another. Something to watch their kiss.

She wanted Daniel to love her that way. Wholeheartedly, with no reservations. Without the terrible mistrust that always stood between them.

She must have dozed, for she could see the long, long drive to Cameron Hall. Daniel was coming down that walk, her tattered cavalier. She saw him, and he saw her. His eyes lit up as his brother's had done for Kiernan. Her hand flew to her throat, her heart quickened. Suddenly she was running, running . . .

He was running, too, to greet her. He reached her, and she was in his arms, and then his lips were on hers, and he was spinning with her, spinning beneath a beautiful, red setting sun.

She awoke with a start. Janey was sitting up in the back of the wagon. She looked at Callie and smiled. "Home, child. We're home."

Christa came running out to the steps. Daniel was dismounting, and she threw herself at him, hugging him first. She went on to Jesse, and then to Kiernan, and then she came to the rear of the wagon. "Oh, you came! You all came, every one of you. Give me the boys, Callie, one by one. There we go, you scamps. Janey—"

But Daniel was there, lifting Janey out, then reaching for his wife. She slipped into his arms, watching his eyes as he slid her down to the ground, his movement slow, his touch warm.

"Let's get in," Christa said. "We don't want any of the neighbors to notice Jesse."

Their nearest neighbor was acres away, but it seemed they all believed that Christa had a point. Callie found herself back in the house, greeting Jigger once again, and Patricia and Jacob Miller. It seemed that they all talked forever, avoiding the war, and then Daniel rose, saying that he was going to go and find their new overseer.

Callie watched him rise and impulsively asked Patricia to take Jared, and she followed her husband out.

He wasn't in any great hurry to find the overseer. He had headed straight for the old family burial ground, and was standing broodingly by the fence. He heard her coming, and his back was still to her when he spoke. "What is it, Callie?"

She paused, then kept coming. "You tell me, Daniel," she said softly. "What is it?"

He turned and stared at her hard. "What do you mean?"

She lifted her hands, tears making her eyes glisten silver. "I came here, I married you. I lived here, among all my enemies. I waited for months. I served the enemy. I mourned for you, Daniel. For Joe, for Beauty. Jesu, Daniel, what more do you want from me? Why can't you—"

"Why can't I do what, Callie?"

"I love you, Daniel. I've tried to show you that in every way that I know how. Why can't you love me?" she said softly.

It seemed he stared at her the longest time, his gaze nearly cobalt.

"I do love you," he said, the words so quiet they might have been a rustling in the trees overhead. His voice was deep when he continued, "I love you more each day this wretched war keeps me from you."

Stunned, she heard the words tumbling from her. "But you hold me at arm's length! You don't really believe—"

"Callie, I was hurt. It takes time to heal. To believe."

"I swear, Daniel, I only ever wanted to save your life. I love you. I loved you then. I never stopped."

"You denied it well!" he whispered.

"Pride," she admitted ruefully.

"Come here," he murmured. She couldn't move. He caught her arm, and he pulled her close against him. He gazed down deeply into her eyes, and his fingers threaded into her hair. His lips touched hers, softly. Yet they spoke of a deeper passion, of a hunger. They stirred and stoked and kindled sweet fires and hungers deep within her. She parted her lips to his kiss. Tasted it. Savored it.

Callie thought she would die with the sweetness of his kiss. Then suddenly, he broke it. He stared off around the corner of the house.

"Daniel, what is it?"

His eyes focused on her. "You don't know?" he said sharply.

"What are you talking about?" she demanded, confused.

He shoved her forward. "You love me, yes! And the damn Yanks are heading straight for the house!"

"What?" she said incredulously.

"There was a man in a Yank uniform who just stepped onto the front porch."

"Daniel, damn you, it's probably Jesse."

"I don't think so."

He was staring at her, hard. She trembled. Could he doubt her still? "You said that you loved me," she reminded him harshly.

He nodded, still watching her. "I do. But, Jesu, Callie, why is it that every time you whisper words of love, I am plagued by blue uniforms?"

"I'm telling you—"

"I do love you, Callie."

"Daniel—"

"Get to the house!" he thundered, shoving her forward. She tried to swing around, to protest. It was too late, Daniel was gone. She didn't know which way he had disappeared, but he had slunk into the forest, and she was very afraid.

Jesse. She had to reach Jesse. Maybe he could make some sense of this. Her feeling of danger was acute.

She went racing full speed back to the house. Maybe the man in the uniform was Jesse. Maybe he had gone back outside for some reason.

She burst through the back doors and stared around the hallway. Christa was just walking back toward the den and she stopped, startled by Callie's appearance.

"There's a Yank in the front. Is it Jesse?"

"What?" Christa said.

Callie shook her head, racing down the length of the hallway, throwing open the doors.

There was a Yankee soldier there. A cavalry officer. He was bent over, dusting the dirt from his boots. "A Yank!" Christa whispered. "You're right! My Lord, I'll get my gun."

"It could be Jesse—"

"I know my own brother!" Christa cried.

Callie gasped suddenly. "No, no! You can't get your gun."

"I'm telling you, it's not my brother!"

"But it *is* mine!" Callie told her. She cried out, "Jeremy!"

The soldier stood and smiled and came hurrying toward her.

Within seconds she was in his arms, laughing as he swung her around the porch.

Then her laughter was suddenly caught short as Jeremy's circle brought her around to face Daniel as he stepped from behind a pillar, his hands on his hips, his eyes as sharp as razors.

"Excuse me, Mrs. Cameron, but just what is going on here? Do I pour brandy, or draw my sword?"

Twenty-seven

Callie felt Jeremy tensing beneath her fingers. Daniel looked as if he were ready to explode.

Suddenly Christa Cameron was out on the porch. "My Lord, Yanks are just springing up all over!"

"You're on my porch in southern territory, Yank," Daniel stated. "And worse than that, sir, you've got my wife. You've about five seconds left for an explanation!"

"Me!" Jeremy exclaimed. Callie could feel her brother's temper beginning to seethe. "Insolent Reb! You came north and kidnapped—"

"Kidnapped!" Daniel exploded. He was about to draw his sword.

"That's right," Jeremy stated.

Daniel let out a warning oath. Steel was going to flash any second.

"Wait!" Callie cried, pushing away from Jeremy, and standing before Daniel. "Daniel, stop! This is my brother!"

Daniel gazed from Callie to the stranger on his porch, then back again.

"Brother?" Daniel said.

There was chaos on the porch, with everyone talking, and everyone wary.

"Did he really marry you, Callie, or is he talking through his teeth?"

"Don't you dare accuse my brother of lying, you northern varmint!" Christa put in.

"Christa, please, I told you, he's my brother—"

"Your *brother*? Really?" Daniel demanded.

"Yes, I have three of them, you know that."

Everyone fell silent. Jeremy and Daniel were still looking at one another suspiciously, and Callie thought that with the drop of a hat they could be at one another's throats.

A new, amused voice interrupted them.

"I think that brandy might be a good idea." Jesse had come out to the porch.

Jeremy swung around and looked at him. He saw the colonel's blue uniform from the medical corps, and he instantly saluted, then dropped his hand.

"My Lord, he's a Yank!" Jeremy stared at Callie. "Who is he?"

"*My* brother!" Daniel offered, then brushed past them all. "If I'm not drawing my sword, then I'm pouring the brandy. Anyone care to join me?"

"Indeed, sir, I would!" Jeremy announced, following closely behind him. Callie started to follow the two of them. Jesse caught hold of her arm, gently pulling her back.

She stared at her brother-in-law. "Jesse, they'll kill one another."

He shook his head, and smiled. "Give them a chance."

She looked to Christa for help. Christa shrugged. "Daniel is hotheaded, but you know that, you married him. You ought to know, too, that he's not a murderer, and that he's sick and tired of death and violence. He'll be all right." She paused. "What about your brother?"

"He's not a murderer!" she said quickly, indignantly. "But they've both been shooting people in uniforms just like one another's for three years!" Callie added miserably. "Are they going to know the difference now?"

"Give them a chance," Jesse told her. He released her and opened the door for her, following her into the main hallway.

Down that hallway, the door to the den was closed.

She walked down to it, and stood very still. She could hear nothing.

She glanced to Jesse, but he shrugged and grinned.

Callie began to pace the hallway.

Inside the den Daniel was beginning to wonder how he had ever missed the fact that this man was Callie's brother, except that his wife was so beautifully feminine it was, perhaps, difficult to transfer her coloring and attributes to a man.

This soldier was tall, his own height. His eyes were so similar to Callie's eyes only a darker gray. His hair was an even deeper auburn than Callie's, and his features were more ruggedly hewn. But he was a striking man, just as Callie was a beautiful woman. Nor did he seem afraid of Daniel, or of the fact that he was facing an enemy in enemy territory. Maybe it was because he had already seen a fellow countryman in uniform, as unlikely as such a presence should have been at this southern plantation.

Daniel poured brandy and handed one to Jeremy. So far they hadn't exchanged a word.

Daniel asked one question, and the words began to flow between them like wildfire.

"Why did you come here?"

"To bring her home. I heard that she had been spirited away—to the South."

"Well, she wasn't spirited away. I came after her. And my son," he added softly.

"Where the hell were you when she was expecting that son?" Jeremy demanded heatedly.

Daniel arched a brow. "In Old Capitol Prison," he said briefly.

"Oh," Jeremy murmured. "Well, then, perhaps . . ." He shrugged. "She is my sister, sir. My father is dead. Her welfare is my concern."

Daniel smiled suddenly and lifted his glass. "Sir, I see your point, truly, I do. And I assure you, we are legally wed." Yes, they were wed, but was Callie where she wanted to be? He hadn't actually kidnapped her, but then again, he had given her little choice.

"I think, sir, that we must ask Callie where she wants to be," Daniel said softly.

Jeremy arched a brow, watching Daniel. But Daniel frowned suddenly.

"How did you know where to find your sister if you heard only that she had been spirited away?"

"That was easy enough. An old friend of the family did some research for me, Eric Dabney. He knew who you were, and he found out where you lived."

Dabney!

"You know the name?" Jeremy said.

"Oh, yes." Daniel ran his finger around the rim of his glass. "I know the name well. Lieutenant Colonel Dabney was responsible for my stay in Old Capitol."

"How curious!" Jeremy said. "I was always convinced that Dabney was in love with Callie himself. He was close to her husband, but you could always see that look in his eyes . . ." He shrugged. "I'm surprised he would want to make her miserable. Maybe he didn't know that there was a relationship—"

"He knew," Daniel said flatly. He rose to pour Jeremy another shot of brandy. "Excuse my curiosity, sir, but it has been some time since Callie and I left Maryland. Why has it taken you so long to come here?"

"I've been on the western front of this war, under Grant. When Grant was ordered east, I received papers soon after to come this way. I didn't want to fight here," he said regretfully.

"Because?"

"Because I've too many good friends in Virginia and Maryland companies—fighting for the South."

Daniel nodded wearily, taking up his seat behind his desk. "I understand," he said.

Jeremy grinned. "So the Yank out there is really your brother?"

"Yes, sir, he is."

"And you're still speaking to one another?"

"Any time we come across one another, which seems to be about once a year."

Jeremy grinned slowly. "How interesting."

"Too interesting," Daniel said softly. "You're regular cavalry, aren't you?"

"Yes," Jeremy answered. His grin faded. Jesse was with the fully established medical corps now, he would never face Daniel in battle.

Jeremy very likely could.

"Jesu!" Jeremy breathed. He started to speak again, then the door suddenly burst open, and in came Callie, breathing hard, her eyes silver and as wild as her hair. She stared at them both. "I'm—sorry!" she murmured. She tossed back that wild mane of hair. "No, I'm not. I was worried sick about the both of you!"

Daniel walked around and leaned on the edge of his desk, watching her. "Why would you be so worried?" he asked her.

Jeremy, in turn, stared at his sister. "Indeed, Callie! We're both quite civilized."

Civilized! They were so civilized she wanted to smack them both.

Where was the brother who adored her, who should have gone to battle for her with a vengeance?

And where was her enemy, her husband, who had brought her here? If the love between them had all been pretend, at least the passion had been real.

Wives were property, he had told her!

Would he fight for the plantation before he would fight for her?

What was the matter with her? Did she want a fight between Daniel and Jeremy?

No. She just wanted Daniel to care.

"I was worried," she said quietly.

Daniel stared at her. She'd have given anything to read what lay behind the brilliant blue fire in his eyes. What emotion lay within his heart?

Fight for me, dammit! She thought. Fight for me as you do for this place, as you do for those other things in your heart that mean so very much to you.

Ebony dark lashes fell over his eyes, and then he was staring at her again. She could still read nothing in his eyes.

"Your brother came to rescue you, you know," he told her.

"Oh?" she murmured, looking at Jeremy.

"He seemed to have been under the impression that you were kidnapped."

She didn't respond; she didn't move. What in God's name was Daniel doing?

"I thought that I should give you the choice, Callie. I don't want you to be miserable here, in the South. Or with me." The last was spoken so softly that she wasn't even certain that she heard him correctly. Did he want her to stay, or did he want her to go? What was he doing? She wanted to cry out, and she wanted to scream and beat against him.

She stood silently at the door, returning his stare, trying to keep her chin very high. She had told him that she loved him. She had given him everything.

"Callie?" he said.

Pretend. Pretend that you love me.

She opened her mouth, but she never had a chance to speak. The door opened again suddenly and Kiernan, smiling brilliantly, stuck her head in.

"We've a supper on, of sorts, gentlemen, Callie. Janey and Jigger—and I, of course, would be delighted if you'd join us." She extended a hand to Jeremy. "I'm Kiernan Cameron. Welcome to this house, just in case the other residents have neglected to say so. I'm sure you're anxious to meet your nephew. He's right out in the hallway here."

"Supper sounds fine to me," Jeremy said, rising and bowing very politely to Kiernan. He gazed at Daniel. "If I'm truly welcome in this house."

Daniel threw up his hands. "The odds, as always, are against me. We've two men in blue tonight, to one in gray."

Kiernan lowered her lashes, hiding a grin. Jeremy followed her out. Daniel kept studying Callie. "Well?" he said softly.

He never gave her a chance to answer. He took her elbow and led her toward the hallway. "I'm sure Jeremy can be convinced to stay the night. And—" He paused slightly. Callie heard a note of bitterness in his voice. "I'm equally certain that we'll all be riding back to war in the same direction very soon. We can all give it until tomorrow, don't you think?"

"Daniel—"

"No! I don't want you to say anything now." His hand on her elbow, he led her out into the hallway.

Jeremy was busy meeting Jared, and Kiernan was still trying to usher everyone into the dining room. Jesse and Jeremy arrived in uniform blue, Daniel in his tattered gray, Kiernan and Callie in their mourning black, and Christa a burst of summer in a dazzling yellow gown. Patricia and Jacob Miller were also at the table, scrubbed and clean, nearly fourteen now. They'd grown accustomed to Jesse, but Jeremy was a new Yank, and they eyed him very cautiously.

Callie wondered how the meal would go when, before they even sat down, Jesse told Jacob how big he was getting and Jacob stated that he was near big enough to be going off to war. He didn't make any comments about killing Yanks, he cared too much about Jesse to do so, but it was plenty clear just whose side Jacob was on. Kiernan told him he was nowhere near big enough to go off to get killed.

"Soon. Another year, maybe," Jacob said, setting his jaw stubbornly. "There's boys younger than me out there fighting, isn't that true, Daniel?"

It was pathetically true. The South was drawing deeper and deeper into her reserves, though by law, no boy Jacob's age should be fighting. But when the enemy neared Richmond, time and time again it seemed that the soldiers marching out from the city were growing both older and younger—the graybeards came out, and then the boys who couldn't quite grow whiskers yet.

"Jacob, don't go making Kiernan unhappy tonight," Daniel warned the boy. "There's no need for you to be coming to war for some time, and God knows, it has to end soon enough."

"But Daniel—"

"Jacob, see to the young ones at that end of the table, will you?"

The older children watched the younger ones, but Jigger, trying to serve the meal, grinned from ear to ear. "It's near like before! A party this size. And we have excelled, yes, we have!"

"It's certainly the finest meal I've had in some time," Daniel assured him.

And it was. The table was filled with vegetables, string beans, peas, turnip greens, summer squash, sweet potatoes, and tomatoes. There was a smoked ham, rich with the taste of hickory, and there were several fat chickens, too, for someone had decided that this would be a real feast.

As if a prodigal son had returned home.

Which was the prodigal, Callie wondered, Jesse or Daniel?

Conversation flowed easily throughout the meal. The men seemed to be all right about the color of their uniforms, even if the blue at the table didn't seem to set well with Christa. Still, there was laughter at the table. More than Callie had heard in a long time.

She saw Jesse looking at Daniel. "I understand that Jeff Davis passed a suspension of habeas corpus a while back. We could all be in trouble here."

The adults all grew silent.

"What does that mean?" Patricia Miller demanded.

Jesse hesitated, then answered her. "Men—and women—are granted certain rights by the constitution. Your constitution, and our constitution," he added. "You have the right to privacy, and no one should be able to arrest you without proper cause. But in the case of war—"

"Lincoln suspended the right of habeas corpus very early on in the north," Daniel commented.

"But what—"

Daniel set down his fork. "It means we're in trouble if we're all caught," he said flatly. "It means Jesse and Jeremy could wind up in Andersonville, and it means that I could be arrested for consorting with the enemy."

"We could all be in trouble for having dinner?" Patricia said incredulously.

No one answered her. She stared at Jesse. "The South isn't wrong, the North isn't wrong—the war is wrong!" she exclaimed.

Everyone around the table had grown very tense.

A pea suddenly sailed across it. It smacked Jeremy right in the face and he jumped.

Startled, they all looked down the table. John Daniel grinned at them happily, and sent another missile flying.

"My Lord!" Jesse exploded. "The war better end quickly! I've a child with no table manners!"

Callie couldn't help it. She burst out laughing when a third flying green missile caught Jesse square in the left cheek.

"John Daniel!" Kiernan cried in dismay, leaping to her feet. But by then, Jared, entranced by his cousin, was attempting the same feat. He hadn't really the coordination to balance the pea in his spoon, so he merely toppled over his entire dish, stared at them all with deep pleasure, laughed, and offered the table a beautiful grin.

"Jared!" Callie moaned and jumped up too.

Christa laughed. "Really, why be so distressed? The two of them at least know they are supposed to be hurtling their shots at Yanks!"

"Christa!" Daniel exclaimed.

"Never mind, Daniel. I shall get the children and myself away from this meal! Patricia, care to join me? Do excuse me, all of you!" She said the words sweetly, but her eyes were afire. Patricia, serene and mature far beyond her years, rose and grinned. "I'll take the young masters Cameron out into the kitchen with Christa," she said. "Please, enjoy dinner, all of you."

When she was gone, there was silence at the table. "I shouldn't be here," Jeremy said.

"Jesu! This is our home!" Daniel exploded. "I'm calling a truce, North and

South, for tonight. Let's eat, shall we? We've no time, we've never any time. We're all here now, for the love of God, let's enjoy what we have."

"Yes," Jesse agreed. "Kiernan, sit. Pass the peas, please."

"The normal way, if you would, please," Daniel suggested.

Kiernan sat, laughing, excusing her son's bad manners to Jeremy.

Callie watched them all in silence, so very aware of Daniel across the table from her.

They ate. The conversation was polite. There was a silence again until Jesse asked Daniel, "When are you going back?"

"Tomorrow," Daniel said briefly. He shrugged. "We don't seem to know quite what Grant is doing, and we need to keep a close watch on him." He paused. "When are you going back?"

"Tomorrow. I don't know what Grant is doing either, but he's giving me plenty of wounded, that's for certain." He hesitated, looking at Daniel. "What about Christa's wedding? We're just days away. Liam McCloskey should be arriving any time."

Daniel exhaled slowly and miserably. He shook his head. "There's nothing I can do," he told Jesse softly. "Kiernan will be here. And Callie . . ." He paused again. He had given Callie permission to leave in the morning if that was her desire.

He suddenly determined that it wasn't going to be her desire.

Or if it was, she wouldn't be able to forget him once he had gone.

"Jeremy?" Daniel said suddenly.

"Sir, I'm on leave, but I hardly think that your sister would want me attending her wedding!"

"No, no, that's not what I meant," Daniel said. "I'm glad that you're on leave. You can stay the night," Daniel said. He rose suddenly, walking around the table behind Callie's chair. "My sister will see to a room for you. Now if you'll all excuse the two of us . . ."

Callie's chair was abruptly pulled back. He had her hand, and she was on her feet. She felt a flush flaming her cheeks, and she wanted to protest his sudden and so obvious command, but she had a feeling that she'd be leaving the room one way or the other. If she went out hectoring she'd risk a duel between her brother and her husband once again.

But she did protest as soon as they reached the hall. "Daniel, what do you think you're doing? We were in the middle of a meal—"

"I ate, thank you."

"We weren't alone!"

"Ah, but we're going to be."

"Daniel—" She paused, tugging back on her hand. He paused, but only to scoop her up into his arms and head for the stairway.

"What are you doing?" she demanded angrily.

"What do you think I'm doing?" He cross-queried almost savagely, his eyes cobalt as they touched hers.

She knew what he was doing. His eyes, and his touch, both were so explosive when circumstance had again separated them for so very long. Rivers of excitement began to stream within her. She clenched down hard on her teeth, trying to understand him. Not an hour ago he had been telling her that it was her choice if she wanted to leave him. And now . . .

"Daniel, put me down."

"No."

"You were just saying that I could leave—"

"Not now. In the morning."

"Well, if you want me to leave—"

"I don't want you to leave."

"But you said—"

"I said that it would be your choice."

His long strides had taken them up the stairs now and below the portrait gallery. Long-gone Camerons looked down upon them. Some of them sternly, some of them with mischief in their eyes.

Eyes as blue, as startling, as deep and dark and demanding as those that focused upon her now. "You said that you loved me."

"And no matter what I say," she challenged him heatedly, "you never really believe me, you don't fully trust me!"

They had reached his room. He shoved open the door with his foot, and walked into the darkness.

She wanted him more than she had ever imagined that she could. In the darkness she felt electric. His calloused hands upon the bare flesh of her arms seemed to light swift burning fires just beneath her skin. They raged down the length of her, they tore into her. Sweet, wonderful. He could do this too easily to her.

And leave her so swiftly when it was done.

"Daniel!" she cried. Not tonight. There could be no "pretend" tonight. She wouldn't allow it to be so.

He dropped her down upon the bed. She felt the fall of his weight beside her and then she felt his fingers moving impatiently upon the topmost button of her gown.

"Stop it!" she cried and tried to twist away.

"Callie! We've one night!"

"One night!" She moistened her lips. "Do you believe me?"

"Does it matter so much?" He paused in the near ebony darkness, and all that she could see of him was shadows and a silhouette. She loved that silhouette, the plumed hat gone, the soldier tall and straight as he stood now, looking down at her. What did he see in the darkness? she wondered.

Did any of it matter? If only he would lean down and touch her lips, and make the world go away.

"Yes, it matters!"

His lips came close to hers. She felt the warmth, the whisper of them in the night. "You are a Yank. *Would* you betray me now?" he asked softly.

"Daniel—"

"Callie—"

"Daniel, no!" She found an extraordinary strength, pushing him aside and leaping to her feet. She stared at him, trying to discover something of his features in the darkness. "No, Daniel, I would not betray you now! I would not have betrayed you before, except that I was desperate to save your life. I've told you," she cried out, "that I love you. What more would you have from me, Daniel? I've lived here, without you, all this time. I went with Kiernan to Richmond to be near you. I learned to love my enemy so well that it broke my heart to see that poor child, Joey, die, and still you ask these things of me! I've loved you from the beginning, Daniel. I never ceased to love you. But now! Well, sir, I have had it! I have—"

She gasped, her words breaking off, for he had come for her. Hands upon her upper arms, he dragged her against him. His mouth bore down on hers in a fever; his body, touching hers, was electric. His hands were upon her face, his lips seeming to devour hers. His lips touched her throat, her cheek, her lips again.

"Daniel—"

"I love you, Callie," he said softly.

"But—"

"And I believe you. Forgive me. I was afraid to believe you, but I do. And I love you."

"Oh, Daniel!"

"Make love with me, Callie?"

She paused, her arms around him, meeting his eyes. "There are Yanks downstairs, you know."

"Are there any in the wardrobe?"

She smiled and shook her head. "The only Yank in the room stands before you, waiting."

"Kiss me, Callie?"

"Seduce you?" she queried. "You'll not blame the Yankees being in Virginia on me?"

His fingers threaded into her hair and gave a little tug. She cried out softly but his lips found hers, hungrily, eagerly.

"I said," he whispered just above her mouth, "that I believe in you. And I love you, Callie. More than you'll ever know. More deeply than I'll ever be able to say."

She had never heard words so sweet. She was barely aware when he kissed her again.

"Try . . ." she murmured, smiling, when his lips lifted from hers.

"I love you more than life, more than limb, more than heart or soul . . ." he began, and kissed her again. He began to speak once more, but only slowly did she become aware of his whispers, for she was so acutely aware of his touch upon her clothing.

He whispered of how he dreamed of her in the long nights away. How he closed his eyes and saw her in his dreams, walking toward him. He whispered of how he had longed to believe.

So many times she was there with him. With the breeze from the river lifting her hair, the gently rolling water lying far below them. Honeysuckle was lightly on the air, and there in the rich green grasses, she would shed her clothing and lie down beside him.

In the darkness, the black dress she had worn was suddenly at her feet. She felt her own fingers moving, trembling, upon his scabbard. His weapons were set aside.

The tattered gray uniform lay on the floor.

For a moment they stood together, naked, and the moon came out at last, casting a dim and ivory light over the room. Callie felt the touch of his flesh against the whole of her body, and then she pressed him toward her. Her love . . .

He was tautly muscled and lean. More so every time that she saw him. She pressed her lips against his collarbone, then against the rigid muscle of his breast, then against the bone of a rib. The sleek touch of his hands moved up and down her arms. Whispers, kisses, pressed into her hair. She rubbed her face against his belly, her lips pressing there. She came lower and lower against him until his hoarse cry would allow her no more. She was swept up again, into his arms, and laid down upon the bed in a tempest.

Within seconds he was a part of her, and their magic had begun. The emptiness of lonely nights was filled, just as the thrust of his body filled her own. Hands, limbs, whispers, and kisses entwined as each strove for more of one another, hungry, near bursting, longing for the pleasure—and the love—to go on and on.

Daniel felt the fierce shuddering of her body, the tightening of her slick passage as it grasped his sex. His hands moved deftly over her shoulders and arms, caressed and grasped her buttocks. Climax, sweet and violent, flooded through him and from him and he held her very close, feeling her heart, feeling his own. Her breasts continued to rise and fall. He laid his head against them and touched them tenderly.

At last he rose and kissed her lips. She smiled and quivered. He pulled away. In the moonlight, she was exquisite. Naked ivory flame, her perfect face encompassed by the shimmering auburn of her hair. Hair that waved and tangled around her, beneath the curves of her body, her beautiful breasts, her hips, her thighs. Her eyes were as silver as the moon, and he suddenly found himself shaking.

All these long months of war. He had dragged her here. He had cast her in among her enemy. And she had stayed. She had come to Richmond. Her heart had never faltered in her belief in the northern right, and yet she had cast it aside for him.

All this time he had hurt her so badly with his doubt.

He trembled and laid his head against her breast again. "Forgive me," he whispered.

She rose up next to him, throwing her arms around him, holding him again. "Oh, Daniel!" She leaned back. The darkness had been dispelled. Their shadow land was really magical. "Oh, Daniel, I love you so."

Entwined, upon their knees, they began to kiss one another again. He told her that she was beautiful, and she laughed and whispered that he was beautiful too.

"Rebel soldiers are not beautiful," he told her.

"Oh, but you are!" she protested, and despite his indignation, she began to tell him about the time when he'd had his fever. "I had to cool you down. I had to get rid of your uniform. I hadn't been a widow long enough then, but I was so fascinated with your shoulders." She stroked them. "And I needed to . . . to taste you!" Her lips touched down on his flesh. Her eyes met his again. "You were beautiful. Very male and very beautiful. I thought that you had the most beautiful shoulders I had ever seen, the leanest, tightest belly, the trimmest hips. The most beautiful legs . . ." Her voice trailed suggestively. She leaned close and wickedly whispered precisely how beautiful the extraordinary piece of his anatomy that lay between them was, too, and how she had longed to touch that . . .

She had him laughing, and then she had him on fire again.

In the ivory light, they were both very beautiful, he decided, and he made love to her with a driving, desperate passion once again.

And so went the night. They dozed, they awakened, they made love, they dozed.

For the first time, Daniel was truly bitter that he would have to return to the war.

They were losing it. No, it was already lost, he decided. They could hold the Yanks from Richmond. Maybe they could outfight the Yanks. They were naturally better horsemen. So many of them had military educations. But the Yanks weren't cowards, they never had been. And there were so damned many of them. The South would be starving soon. She was nearly in a death grip now. There would be no help from Europe.

I have admitted that I am losing, but I will go back, I know that I will, he told himself.

His arms tightened around his wife. Dear God, let me come home. Let us survive this. Let us live.

She moved against him. Slowly, erotically, she began to make love to him. Sensual, seductive in her every movement, she rose above him. She bent to kiss his lips. She began to move, oh, so slowly. Like a dance engaged . . .

Until the flames caught, and he could give her the lead no more, but became the aggressor, until he fell beside her, spent once more.

He held her very close, breathing in the fragrance of her hair. He trembled, thinking of how deeply he loved her.

It was morning. The first rays of light were just beginning to streak into the room.

Daniel frowned suddenly, certain that he had heard something outside.

Callie slept. Naked, he slipped quietly from the bed and strode to the window. Carefully, he pulled back the drape and began to watch.

Callie awoke with a start, aware that he was no longer beside her. She sat up, running her hand over the bed where he should have been.

"Daniel!" His name formed on her lips, but something had warned her, and she barely voiced it aloud. She saw him. Naked, silent, he was by the window, looking down. He saw her, and pressed his finger to his lips.

"What is it?" she mouthed.

He walked back to the bed, looking down at her. "Yanks," he said softly.

Yankees. Not her brother, not his brother. Every time he trusted in her, every time he made love to her, the enemy appeared.

Callie leaned up to him, gasping. "Daniel, I didn't—"

"Hush!" He pressed his lips to hers. With sadness, with regret? With a poignant bitterness? "Get dressed, Callie, quickly." He was already dressing. Even as he spoke again, he was pulling on his cavalry boots and reaching for his sword and guns. "I've got to rouse the house, and I've got to get out there."

"Get out there? Daniel, you need to stay in here! Jesse can speak with them, he can—"

"Callie, these aren't friends of Jesse's. These men are definitely the enemy. They're trying to fire the house," he said softly. "I've got to stop them."

"But how—"

"Callie, your old friend, Eric Dabney, is down there. I saw him. Now get dressed. Hurry."

With those last words, he turned and left her.

Twenty-eight

Callie managed to dress quickly. With her blouse barely buttoned, she ran out of the bedroom and raced down the hall, determined first to see to the children.

Janey, her beautiful silk-black flesh paled to an ashen shade, was standing guard over the cribs where the youngest Camerons were sleeping unaware of any danger.

"They're fine, Miz Callie. No one will touch these boys, by my life, I swear it!" she promised.

Callie felt as if she were choking. "We may—we may have to move them out quickly," she advised Janey. "Where has my husband gone?"

"He's gone down, Miz Callie. Move soft, and move quiet, he's got to take them by surprise."

Her heart slammed hard against her chest. Eric Dabney was here. Trying to burn down Cameron Hall. And it was her fault. He had come because he hated Daniel and that hatred was because of her.

She hurried out into the hallway again. Maybe she could speak with him. Maybe she could ride back with him. Maybe she could do something!

She gave Janey a fierce hug. "Please, Janey, please, do watch out for the boys!" she said, and she hurried out.

She reached the portrait gallery. All those long-gone Camerons seemed to look down on her with reproach.

At the foot of the stairway, she nearly cried out as she crashed into a tall, rocklike body. Arms gripped her. But they weren't Daniel's. They were her brother's.

"Jesu, Callie, that's Dabney out there!"

"I know," she whispered miserably.

"I'll talk to the son of a bitch!" Jeremy exploded.

"It won't do any good," a voice suggested softly. Daniel emerged from the shadows in the hallway. "Jeremy, how many of them have you counted?"

"At least a company. There won't be many of us against them—"

"*You* can't shoot at them," Daniel said flatly. "Neither can Jesse."

"But—"

"Unless we kill every man in that company, the two of you could be hanged as traitors at a later date, assuming you survived the fighting."

"Sir—" Jeremy began. He was interrupted as Christa came running down the stairway with a large, lethal-looking revolver in her hands.

"Daniel! There are dozens of them out there!"

"Not dozens," Jeremy corrected, his eyes raking her length. He looked to

Daniel. "I know Dabney; I knew him before the war. He has a company, but no more than twenty. He can't seem to keep much of a command around him. His men ask to be transferred. And they die. Frequently."

Daniel nodded. "Thanks," he told him.

"Wait!" Jeremy said. "This is my fight too!"

"Jeremy, it can't be your fight. And Christa, have some faith in me! Put that damned gun down until I tell you that I need it."

"There's Yankees inside, and Yankees out!" Christa protested. "I wonder what happened to the overseer!" she cried. "He would have warned us if he could; he would have fought them . . ." She broke off, biting into her hand, misery clear in her features.

Jesse Cameron came hurrying down the stairway, loading a cartridge into his revolver. Daniel stared at his brother and then whispered, "What the hell do you think you're doing?"

"They're attacking my home!" Jesse said flatly. "And I know damned well they haven't been ordered to!"

"You can't shoot at them! They're still Yanks! Someone will have you court-martialed if you fight your own kind."

Jesse Cameron was going to ignore his brother. Callie was glad of it—there was no way that Daniel could take on a company by himself, and she was becoming more and more aware of the furtive intruders herself. She could hear the creaks on the porches, hushed whispers near the windows.

Daniel was striding toward his brother.

"Jesse!" he said suddenly.

Jesse looked up. Daniel caught him in the jaw with a clean right hook.

Jesse Cameron slumped down to the floor.

At the top of the stairway, Kiernan cried out softly. She came running down the steps. "Daniel!"

"Jesu, Kiernan, I had to! He could be shot for what he was intending to do!"

"If we survive this!" Kiernan moaned. "Daniel, they're preparing to light fires out there. They mean to burn the house down."

"I know," Daniel said. "I'm going to take care of it."

"It's twenty to one out there!" Callie cried to him. "Don't be a fool, you can't—"

"I can't have my brother hanged, Callie, and I will not have you and Christa and Kiernan endangered. And I'd just as soon not see your brother hanged either. For the love of God, will you all have some faith in me?" he demanded. "Stay here!"

Christa had found herself a position at one of the windows. The revolver was still in her hands. She was as ready to defend the place as her brothers.

"Kiernan, get that damned gun from Christa, will you? If I don't come back, Dabney will have what he wants, and you won't need to defend yourselves."

"Daniel!" Christa protested. "We're the Rebels! And you can't knock me out like you did Jesse."

"I would," Jeremy muttered.

Daniel cast them both warning stares. "Leave me to this, damn you, both of you! Christa, put the gun down! If I am killed, don't you go trying to shoot them! Jesse can negotiate something for you."

"No!" Christa protested.

"Cameron, whatever your plan is, I'm going with you. Damn it, if Dabney is here now, it might well mean that he followed me, and that I brought this on," Jeremy insisted.

"I brought it on!" Callie said softly.

"If you want to help me, keep an eye on my sister," Daniel told him.

"What?" Christa demanded, indignant, incredulous, and furious.

But Daniel paid her no heed. He was staring at Callie. Suddenly, he wasn't there at all anymore. He had slipped through the door.

"What is he doing?" Callie demanded desperately.

Kiernan, holding Jesse's head in her lap, sighed softly. "He's gone to war," she said.

"He can't fight them alone!" Callie said.

Christa still had her gun. "He isn't alone," she murmured.

Callie bit her lip and moved toward Kiernan. She curled her fingers around Jesse's gun. "I'm going with him!" she whispered.

"The hell you are!" Jeremy growled behind her. He grabbed the gun from her, and sighed, looking at Jesse. "They can sure punch, huh?"

"Yes," Kiernan agreed.

Jeremy tried to lift Jesse to something of a sitting position, but it was true, Daniel knew how to knock out a man.

After all, Jesse had taught him just how to do it.

"He's going to wake up madder than a hornet," Jeremy said. He pressed a finger to his lip. They could both see a shadow by the window in the dining room.

There was silence, then a big thump.

Daniel was out there, all right. But what was he doing? Callie wondered.

Jeremy's eyes met hers. He winked.

Then her brother was off to join her husband, and she was left behind.

To worry. To wait. She gazed at Kiernan and Kiernan at her.

"Oh, dear God, please!" she whispered aloud. The tension mounted.

It was not difficult surrounding his own house in a sure, silent movement. Daniel knew the exact placement of every small bush and trellis.

He stayed low on the porch, moving on the balls of his feet to come around to the north wing of the house. Two men were busy by a dining room window, stuffing straw against the base of it. Daniel rose and padded softly to them.

"Hey!" he said.

They turned to look at him. He caught the first with the butt of his gun in the jaw. He brought the second down with the return thud of the barrel.

He paused long enough to look them over well, stripping them of their weapons. One of them was carrying a Spencer repeating rifle. Daniel acquired that as his own.

He began to inch around the house again. In the rear were three men, setting dry twigs. It seemed that Dabney still considered himself safe from sight. Or maybe he thought Daniel was the only male in residence. That couldn't be true, if Jeremy was right, and Eric Dabney had followed him out. No, Dabney had to think that he had been quiet enough so that the household still slept. That was to Daniel's advantage.

He dropped down below the porch level to the ground, coming around the back. He waited for one of the men to near the edge, then he jerked him over by a foot. The flailing man cried out. Daniel belted him in the jaw, and he crumpled like a puppet. But he'd been heard.

"Jace, what's going on down there!" someone hissed. Footsteps came to the edge of the porch. A wary soldier looked over.

Daniel jerked him down too. This fellow fell with a crunch to his arm. Daniel heard the bone snap.

He didn't have to hit the fellow. The soldier opened his eyes once, stared at Daniel with alarm, and passed out cold.

Daniel looked up. The third Yank was staring at him. He was going to have to pull his gun and shoot. He hadn't wanted to make that kind of noise and alarm the others.

But he didn't pull his gun. To his amazement, the soldier's eyes flew open wide and then closed, and the man toppled over the porch.

He looked at the fallen man, then looked up. Jeremy McCauley was grinning down at him. "Want a hand up?" he mouthed.

It seemed there was no point talking sense to Yankees. Daniel reached for his hand, and Jeremy helped him leap up to the porch.

He tensed as he realized that someone was coming around the corner. He started to cock his Colt, then realized that it was his brother.

Jesse was rubbing his fist, as if he'd just given somebody a good knocking with it.

"Can't talk sense into Yankees, and can't knock it into them, either!" Daniel complained.

"I'm going to knock some into you, little brother, when this is over," Jesse warned him.

"Christ among us!" Daniel complained. "I'm trying to keep the two of you from a hanging!"

"Fine," Jesse said. He hunkered down low, rubbing his sore jaw. "There were two on my side," he whispered.

"Two on the north side, three back here," Daniel said.

"Seven," Jeremy murmured.

"And the rest . . . ?"

"The barn," Jesse suggested. "It will burn like a hellhole!"

It would, Daniel thought quickly. He rose. "If you're with me, come on!" he told his brother and brother-in-law.

They started to move off the porch. It was then they heard a shot fired and then a bloodcurdling scream from the front of the house.

Christa was by the front door, sunk down by the narrow strip of etched glass on the side of it. Kiernan stood on one side of the great hall, watching the dining room windows, and Callie stood on the other side of the hall, looking out through the parlor.

"I hear . . . something!" Christa whispered.

Both Callie and Kiernan hurried toward her. Callie stared out, searching the frozen scenery, feeling as if her heart had lodged permanently in her throat. Kiernan was beside her, and the three of them searched the front in the morning light that grew ever brighter.

Callie felt something cold and sharp at her spine. She swallowed down a gasp, turning around.

Eric Dabney was there, holding a pistol to her. He had come in from behind them. Instinctively she looked toward the stairway, praying that no one had reached the children.

He saw the way that her eyes moved. He smiled, his eyes bright, amused.

"I haven't been up there, Callie, not yet. And I won't go up there. Maybe I won't even burn the house. Not if you come with me. And not if you help me bring in Daniel Cameron."

"Help you?" she queried, fighting desperately to remain calm. "There are any number of you here, Eric. Daniel is out there alone. You need my help?"

"He isn't alone," a man behind Eric said, and Callie realized that he had entered the house with two of his soldiers. "Why, we got men down—"

"Get away from Callie," Christa interrupted the man, aiming at him.

"I'll get her—" Eric's man began, taking a single step.

"Stop!" Christa warned.

But he didn't heed her. Christa fired her gun and Callie heard a long horrible scream. No, it was two screams combined, for the wounded man had screamed, and so had she. The second of Eric's soldiers hurtled himself toward Christa, wrenching the gun from her grasp before she could fire again. Christa swore savagely, something not at all ladylike.

"She's killed him," the man said to Dabney. "She's done killed Bobby Jo."

"He's not dead; he's still breathing," Dabney said. He stared at Callie, twirling the fine end of his mustache. Heedless of the fallen man at his side, he grinned slowly, having seen Callie about to reach for Christa's fallen weapon. He took careful aim and a shot exploded by the gun, which forced her to wrench back her hand and stare at him furiously.

"Come here, Callie. And say thank you, will you? I've come to bring you home."

"I am home," Callie told him. "So you can just get your men—"

"I'm taking Daniel Cameron again, Callie. Dead or alive. Preferably dead. He tore up half my company the last time we met. Cost me good horses."

"Cost you a promotion again too," the man holding Christa supplied.

"Shut up, fool!" Dabney hissed. "This time, Callie, that Reb is going to die."

"You didn't best him before, and you won't best him now!" Callie told him heatedly.

He kept his gun trained on her and walked to the window where his man now held Christa in something like a death grip.

"What have we here?" Eric asked softly.

Christa spit at him. He laughed. "Why, Callie, after I finish with you, I just might have a talk with this little lady. . . ."

"Touch my sister-in-law," Kiernan warned, "and my husband will see to it that you hang."

"And just who might your husband be?"

"Colonel Jesse Cameron, Army of the Potomac," Kiernan enunciated sharply.

"Well, Mrs. Cameron, I imagine that he's far, far away—"

"He's right outside with his brother," Kiernan said.

"There's another Yank with the Reb too," Eric's man muttered.

Eric looked at Callie. She smiled grimly. "Jeremy's out there too, Eric. You're going to war against him?"

Eric Dabney's handsome face seemed to darken. "Why, damn you, Callie! You've made a traitor of your own brother. You deserve to pay and pay dearly!"

He caught hold of her, swirling her out in front of him. Before she was aware of what he intended to do, she was staggering to her knees, taken unaware by the force of his blow. She swallowed hard, determined not to cry out. But then his fingers entwined in her hair, wrenching her back to her feet, and a cry did escape her lips.

Fury ignited within her. She swirled, despite her pain, kicking him with all of her strength and managing to draw a groan from his lips. But it was to no avail, for too quickly he had her hair again, and she was wrenched so tight against his body that she could scarcely scream.

"You and that damned Rebel! You turned me away to bed down with him! Well, that's all over now, ma'am. This hellhole of traitors is going to light up the sky, and Daniel Cameron is going to die. I'm going to cut his throat in front of you, Callie. I'm going to let you watch your hero beg for mercy."

Callie bit her lip. "You're sick!" she told him.

"Maybe I am." He turned around, suddenly taking careful aim at Kiernan. Her eyes widened, but she didn't let out a sound. "I'll shoot her, Callie. I'll shoot her right now unless you start being a little helpful."

"If Daniel doesn't kill you, you're going to hang," Callie promised him softly.

"Maybe. Let's go. You come with me now, and these two ladies will have a chance to save your brats before the flames become an inferno."

"Light the fires!" He bellowed out the order.

Nothing happened.

Callie smiled, hating him, and wondering what could have gone so wrong with his mind that he could hate her so.

"Don't look at me like that!" he ordered her. He jerked her close against him. "It's you, Callie, always you! From the beginning. You wouldn't look at me because you had to have Michaelson! Well, lady, place that at your feet too. No battle killed him."

She stared at Eric and gasped with horror. "You killed him! You murdered your best friend! Dear God, you bastard—"

"Just so long as you know there is nothing I won't do, Callie," he interrupted softly. His voice rang out again.

"Light the goddamn fires!" Eric exploded. He jerked on her hair again. "In a moment, Callie, you'll smell the smoke."

But there was no smoke. No sound, no fire.

"Let's go out and get your husband, shall we, Mrs. Cameron?" Eric said to her.

Callie felt ill. She could scarcely stand. All these years she thought that she had been fighting the South.

But during all these years, it had been Eric who had declared war on her. He had killed her husband.

And now he wanted Daniel.

"Eric!" she cried suddenly. "Forget this! Forget the house, forget Daniel. Let's forget the whole war. I'll go with you. I'll ride with you—"

"Too late, Callie," he said softly. "It's too late now. I've got to kill him." Eric dragged Callie to the doorway. He stroked her cheek with his gun.

"Keep quiet, and I may let you live. Jensen, you stay here, and keep your gun on these two." He indicated Kiernan and Christa. "The others will be out in the barn. I'll get help once I've gotten Cameron."

Dragging Callie tightly along with him, he threw open the front door.

"Call your husband. Tell him that you need him."

His fingers were tight on her upper arm. In a moment he would force her to do something.

To betray Daniel again. . . .

No, Daniel would understand this time.

If he lived.

Callie couldn't risk his life. She closed her eyes for a moment. It might not just be his life. It might be Kiernan's and Jesse's and Christa's and her brother's and John Daniel's and . . .

Jared.

She twisted her head, sinking her teeth hard into Eric's hand. She didn't care about the rifle in his hands—she just bit down. As hard as she could.

Eric screamed out. But he didn't release her.

She cried out, "Daniel, don't come! It's just what he wants you to do. Daniel, stay away—"

She saw Daniel. He had moved around the house, sneaking up on Dabney's men, one by one. They littered the area around the house, some slumped over, either unconscious or dead, and several of them tied up like hogs.

Now he stood just below the porch in plain view. His gun was trained on Eric.

"Let her go. Now," Daniel commanded, his tone deathly quiet.

"I'll kill her first," Eric said. "You drop the gun. Then she lives."

"No!"

Callie kicked him hard, and he lost his grasp.

"Callie, no!" Daniel shrieked to her.

But she had to reach him.

She ran.

She heard simultaneous explosions of gunfire. There was a sting, high up on her temple, just like that of a bee.

She reached for her face, and her fingers came away red. She tried to turn. She didn't need to run anymore. Eric was dead. Daniel had taken him down even as she had burst away from him. Sightless now, Eric Dabney stared up at the sky.

Callie stumbled. She looked before her.

Daniel was running to her. His blue eyes were suddenly naked. Brilliant with color. She wanted to smile; she wanted to touch him.

She had never seen such concern. Such love. In all of her dreams, she had never imagined him looking at her as he was looking at her now.

She couldn't quite touch him. Her fingers were numb.

"Daniel!"

She called his name again, and then she felt herself falling into his arms.

"Callie, Jesu, Callie! You're hit!"

"There's another man in there, Daniel. He has Christa and Kiernan—"

"Shh," Daniel said softly, still holding her. But Callie realized that he was taking aim, that the soldier had brought Christa and Kiernan out to the porch, and was trying to use them as shields.

He fired. The man fell. Christa shrieked as he nearly dragged her down.

"Callie!" Daniel said. She could hear him, hear his voice, but he seemed very far away. She touched his cheek. It felt as if it was wet. She marveled at the feel. He did love her.

In the distance, she could hear the sounds of more gunfire. It was coming from the barn, she thought.

"I'm all right," she told Daniel. She tried for a smile. "Flesh wound." She grabbed onto him. She managed to stand.

"Callie!" Kiernan was there, and Christa was at her other side.

Callie forced a smile to her lips, praying that she could stand long enough to convince Daniel that she was all right. "Go."

"I can't—" Daniel began.

"Daniel, you must!" Kiernan urged him. "It's Jesse and Jeremy against how many?"

Anguished, Daniel kissed Callie's forehead, and left her in the tender care of the other women.

He dashed off toward the barn.

"Can you stand?" Kiernan asked Callie.

"No!" She laughed. "Oh, God, Kiernan, what's going to happen now?"

"Now there are three of them, against ten," Christa said miserably. "We should go—"

"I can't walk!" Callie told her.

"Jesu, but are you bleeding!" Christa murmured, and she tried to dab at Callie's forehead with her hem. She ripped up her petticoat, creating a bandage. "Jesse will see to it!" she said, worried. "As soon as he comes back!"

The firing was becoming far more fierce at the barn. Dabney was dead, and they still might lose, Callie realized. There were just the three of them, Daniel and Jesse and Jeremy, and there were Eric's men, entrenched in the barn, with rapid-fire weapons and plenty of ammunition.

They heard the sound of a bugle. Troops were coming.

"My God," Christa whispered. "Are they ours?"

Callie wondered if it mattered. She closed her eyes, fighting to remain conscious.

For a moment, the firing increased, then all was silence.

"Oh, Kiernan!" Callie cried, and holding tight to her sister-in-law, she watched.

Moments later, Jesse, Jeremy, and Daniel were marching her way. Her brother and her brother-in-law in blue, her husband in gray.

Behind them rode a small group of Confederate horsemen.

Daniel was alive; Eric was dead. Rebels were here now, and so were Jesse and Jeremy.

"Colonel Cameron!"

The bewhiskered head of the Confederate soldier called to Daniel. He didn't pause, not until he reached Callie. He put his arm around her, then turned back to the Confederate militia captain.

"Colonel Cameron, just what is going on here?"

"They attacked our house. We fought them," Daniel said simply.

"But what about—these two?" the man demanded. "I'll have to take them with me, sir—"

"No," Daniel said firmly. "Not unless you want to arrest me too." He hesitated. "Captain, these men chose a different side, but this was a private war."

The captain stared at Jesse. Obviously, he had known him at some earlier, different date.

"Colonel Cameron, have you—become a Reb?"

Jesse shook his head. "No, sir. I can't say that I have. But these men attacked my house. I fought for it."

"They attacked my sister," Jeremy exclaimed.

"Well, then—" the captain began.

"Sir," Daniel said, "On my honor, nothing was exchanged here. No information. Nothing. We brought down twenty Yanks. You can bring them all in. But couldn't we just pretend that you didn't see these two? On my honor, sir, I'll have them back with their own armies by tomorrow!"

"On my honor, sir!" Jeremy said.

"On my honor," Jesse agreed. "We'll be gone. Sir, we were fighting for my home!"

The captain, still confused, sighed.

At his left, one of his men murmured, "This is highly irregular, sir—"

That comment seemed to make up the captain's mind. "I have never doubted the word of a Cameron, ever. Be he my countryman, or my foe. Gentlemen!" He turned to his troops. "We'll clean up here and leave these people be!"

A cheer went up. A Rebel yell. Callie smiled. "Oh, Daniel!" she whispered.

The darkness she had fought so strenuously came crashing down upon her. Despite her very best efforts, she fainted in his arms.

Minutes later—or eons later?—she opened her eyes. A pair of brilliant blue eyes met hers, but they weren't Daniel's. They were Jesse's.

She was no longer on the ground in front of the house. She was lying on a plump sofa in the parlor.

"There, I told you! She's back with us," Jesse said.

The room ceased to spin. She hadn't died, it wasn't heaven.

It was the next best thing. It was Cameron Hall. Still standing. And there were faces within it. Faces that stared down at her with grave concern. Kiernan's face, and Christa's face, and her brother's and Janey's. Even Jigger was there, watching over her too.

She tried to smile. Where was Daniel?

Behind Jesse. Jesse suddenly moved, and Daniel was there, sitting beside her.

She stared into those eyes searchingly. He bent low and kissed her forhead. "Jess said it was just a flesh wound. It scared the hell out of me, all right."

"Daniel . . ." She whispered.

"She's going to be fine, trust me," Jesse told the others. "She needs rest." He cleared his throat. "That means you, too, Daniel."

Daniel nodded, but he didn't move. The others cleared out of the room.

"Daniel . . ."

"Don't talk."

"I love you, Daniel."

"I know that you do. I love you too."

She smiled, feeling her eyes flicker shut again. "It doesn't really matter what we are, does it, Daniel?"

His fingers smoothed more hair from her forehead, and he smiled tenderly. "What we were today mattered," he told her softly. "We were a family, all of us. Brothers again, not enemies, Jesse and I. Even Jeremy. Protecting the house and those we love."

"But it's my fault that he came here—"

"No more than it was my fault for bringing you here, Callie."

She shivered, violently. "No, Daniel, you don't understand! Eric hated me. Because I spurned him, I suppose. I didn't even realize it. Daniel, he—he killed my first husband!"

"Shh. I know. Kiernan told me."

"You could have lost Cameron Hall."

"I could have lost you."

"I nearly lost you! Daniel, you went after so many of them—"

"But my brother stood with me. And your brother stood with me. And it's going to be all right. Sleep."

Tears touched her eyes. "I can't sleep. You're going to be leaving too soon."

He hesitated, wishing that he could lie to her. His fingers curled around hers. "I have to go back, Callie." He hesitated another moment. "Callie, you're right. I've always known that slavery was wrong. But I also believe that each state should have decided upon emancipation, that we should have managed it with our laws—"

"It wouldn't have happened, Daniel."

"Hear me out, Callie, please. I want you to understand. I have to go back. I have to see the war through. There are men beneath me, and men above me, and I owe them my loyalty and my service. I have to, Callie. To the bitter end."

She was blinded again. Not by blood, by tears.

"Callie, don't you see? If I don't remain loyal to my cause, to my country, I will never be able to be the father that Jared deserves?"

She nodded. She did understand him.

"Sleep, Callie."

She shook her head. "No! You're leaving!"

He kissed her forehead. "I will wait. One more day will not win or lose the war any faster."

She closed her eyes, believing that he would stay. He had said that he would. He had given his word.

Daniel was glad that Callie slept. As Christa had assumed, their overseer had been killed by Eric's men, shot in his bed before he'd ever awakened.

Daniel, Jesse, Jeremy, and Christa saw to it that he was buried in the family cemetery in the back.

The Yanks, the living and the dead, Daniel turned over to the Rebel captain.

He spent the early afternoon with Jesse, and it was damned good just to talk with his brother again.

They were going to stay another night. Kiernan was awaiting her time with her husband, so Daniel excused himself on some pretext or another. Despite the fact that he was leaving, he couldn't bring himself to wake Callie.

He had been too terrified when he had seen the blood on her forehead. And now she needed rest.

In the late afternoon, he left the house. Daniel came to the slope of grass by the river, his favorite place on the plantation. It was where they had come as children. It was where the grass grew the richest, where it was such a dazzling green it was extraordinary.

It was summer, but the breeze, as always, was soft. The river gave the breeze that brush of velvet. The roses from the garden made it redolent and sweet. Far up on the mound, he could see Cameron Hall, still standing. White, stunning, beautiful in the sunlight.

He smiled. None of it mattered, he knew. None of it. He could live in the snow, in the desert, if he lived with Callie.

But this had been the dream, he reminded himself.

He had lain in the grass, felt the soft kiss of the breeze, heard the endless rush of the river. And then he had seen her. A slow smile on her face, coming toward him. Her hair, catching the sunlight. Her eyes, a silver dazzle.

He blinked.

She was there.

Her hair was pure fire, caught by the last rays of a setting sun. And indeed, her eyes were silver. Her face, her angel's face, had never been more beautiful.

She smiled, standing above him. She lowered herself to her knees. There was a white strip of bandage across her forehead. But her color had returned, and his heart raced as he realized how very well she looked. There had been those awful moments when he hadn't known how seriously she had been injured, trying to keep him from danger.

He smiled, tossed aside the blade of grass he had been chewing, and reached for her. "Come down here, angel!"

She knelt down before him.

"This is a dream, you know," he told her.

"Really?"

He nodded. "In the middle of countless battles, I would see this place with you. Right here. By the river."

"And then?"

"Then you stripped off all of your clothes, and we made love."

"Like this?"

She was all seductress, slowly loosening one button after another.

"Mmmmm," he agreed, but frowned, determined that two could play a game.

"What's wrong?"

"The bandage wasn't in the fantasy," he said.

"Oh! Well, you Rebel varmint!" she began. But by then he was laughing, and he swept her into his arms.

The kiss was far better than any fantasy, any dream.

The sun set, lower and lower. Rays of gold and crimson streaked out over the river and over the grass.

And still, Daniel held Callie in his arms. As he had done as a child with Jesse and Christa, he now spun dreams with Callie.

"When the war is over . . ." he began.

She turned to him, fiercely, passionately. "Oh, Daniel, yes, please God! Let it be soon! When the war is over!"

"My love, our war is over," he whispered and kissed her in return.

But in the morning, he kissed her again, and rode away once more to battle.

At the end of the long drive, he embraced his brother and said good-bye to him.

He turned back and looked to Cameron Hall. "When the war is over, please, God, yes! Let it be soon!"

Twenty-nine

The war would not end that soon.

In the North, George "Little Mac" McClellan lost his bid for the presidency, Lincoln was reelected, and hopes for an end to war by a Union peace effort perished.

Just as thousands more soldiers perished on the fields.

Liam McCloskey never appeared for his wedding—he was killed at Cold Harbor. His name didn't appear on the lists of the dead for weeks, but from the moment that he failed to appear at Cameron Hall, Christa knew. Kiernan and Callie comforted her the best that they could, but there was little to be done. She cried once, then never again, turning her sorrow into supplying the Rebel troops with the very best that she could.

In Richmond, Varina Davis gave birth to a baby girl. She was named Varina for her mother, but they called her "Winnie," and to many she was the "daughter of the Confederacy," for she brought life and hope to a time of loss and desolation.

Spring brought new life and hope to Cameron Hall. On March 14, Kiernan gave birth to a second son. Five days later, Callie had her second child, a little girl.

She was the most beautiful infant Callie had ever seen, she was convinced. More beautiful than Jared, but Jared, of course, had been handsome. Her daughter was born with a full mop of deep red curls and brilliant blue eyes.

And the face of an angel, Callie thought.

She prayed ever more fervently that Daniel would live to see her.

For Daniel was with the battle to the very end, with Lee at Petersburg.

And the South tried. She fought hard, she fought valiantly, she fought with the life's blood of her sons and daughters.

It wasn't enough.

Grant surrounded Petersburg, and the city was under seige.

Sherman moved steadily forward on his "march to the sea," destroying everything in his path in Georgia.

The Confederacy staggered and fell. She struggled to her feet again. Rebel cries resounded in battle, and some men never gave up.

But in the end, none of it mattered, for the South stumbled and went down again, and this time she was on her knees.

Petersburg fell, and Lee had to warn President Davis to flee from Richmond.

They circled around their enemy. Lee planned to make a last stand near Danville, joining his army with that of Johnston, moving northward from the Carolinas.

But desperately needed supplies did not arrive. Unlike many of his predecessors, Grant could move quickly. One quarter of Lee's men were captured; he was left with a ragtag force of thirty thousand while Federal forces blocked his only avenue of escape.

On April 9, Lee tested Grant's line. It was far too strong to break through.

And so they came to a little place called Appomattox Courthouse.

On the afternoon of Palm Sunday, Lee met with Grant at a farmhouse. It was a curious place, for its owner, a Mr. McClean, had moved to Appomattox Courthouse when his first home had been in the path of some of the opening shots of the war at Manassas.

Lee rode to the meeting upon Traveler, straight and poised in his saddle.

Silent groups of men awaited the outcome.

For all practical purposes, it was over.

Lee didn't formally address his troops until the next day. He told them that he had done his very best for them. And he told them to go home. He told them to be as good citizens as they had been soldiers.

Daniel watched the man he had followed for so very long, and his heart was heavy. The war had taken its toll upon him. His marvelous face was lined with sorrow and with weariness.

The great Army of Northern Virginia was done. There were other forces in the field, still fighting. But they couldn't last long. It was over.

Some of Daniel's men shouted that they would fight on and on. One of them called out to him in dismay. "He's done surrendered, sir! What are you going to do?"

Daniel mulled it over and then smiled with a bittersweet curl to his lip. "I'm going to find my brother. I'm going to embrace him. And I'm going to go home."

It wasn't that easy, of course. The formal surrender of the troops came on the following Wednesday, April 12, 1865. Neither Grant nor Lee was in attendance. The surrender was to be accepted by Major General Joshua Lawrence Chamberlain, a man who had held his positions at Gettysburg, who had been wounded time and time again.

And a gentleman without thought of revenge.

For as the conquered troops moved by him to lay down their arms, Chamberlain ordered his men to salute them.

And salute them they did.

The men were allowed to keep their horses or mules and their side arms.

They were allowed to go home.

Daniel was promoted to brigadier general in the final days of conflict. It was not so easy for him to leave as it was for his men, and there would be all manner of things that he must clear up, but he knew that Jesse was with the Union troops, and Daniel was anxious to see him.

It was Jesse, though, who found him. Daniel was bidding Godspeed to a young major from Yorktown when he looked past the man to see Jesse standing there, waiting silently for him to finish.

Daniel grinned and strode the distance between them, pausing just a second as his brother saluted him.

He saluted in return.

He grasped Jesse, and the two held tight for a long moment.

"I'm sorry, Daniel."

"So am I. Can you get leave?" One good thing about losing, Daniel decided, was that you didn't need permission to go home anymore. Jesse was still in the military.

"Yes, I've already arranged it."

"Good," Daniel told him. "We rode away separately. I'm glad to ride home together."

"Congratulations on your daughter."

"And on your son."

"And we haven't even seen them," Jesse murmured.

"Soon enough, we will."

Jesse held him tight one more time and left him. Daniel returned to the command tent to finish with the business of losing.

His heart should have been heavier. There were still forces in the field. He'd heard that Jeff Davis and the cabinet were in hiding, trying to decide whether to surrender themselves, hide out and fight on with guerilla warfare, or try to escape the country.

Daniel was sorry for all of them, but as Lee had known, to go on was foolish. Lincoln had already been in Richmond. It was over.

And he wanted to go home.

Janey brought the paper with news in it to Kiernan, handing it to her in silence. Kiernan quickly scanned the sheet, then sank into an armchair with it. "We've lost," she said softly. The paper fell from her hands and wafted to the floor. She put her head in her hands, and she began to sob.

Christa walked over to the parlor window and stared out in silence.

Callie thought of the hundreds of thousands of men who lay dead, and she thought of the devastation of the countryside. Kiernan wasn't sorry that it was over—Callie knew that. It was just that intangible thing, that essence, that something that had been the cause itself, a way of life, of acting, of being, was over. Never to come again. She understood. They both understood.

She walked over to Kiernan and put her arms gently around her sister-in-law. "Kiernan, it means that they'll be coming home now!" she told her. "They'll be coming home."

Shocking news reached the country by the morning of April 15. Abraham Lincoln, the greatest single force behind the Union victory—and the sanctity of the Union—was dead. He had been assassinated at Ford's Theater, shot in the back of the head by a man named John Wilkes Booth—an actor, a southern sympathizer, a man who had attended the hanging of John Brown all those years ago at Harpers Ferry. There had been a conspiracy, and officials were in a fury to arrest anyone involved.

Booth had escaped, but he was soon hunted down, and killed.

Daniel, hearing the news, mourned Lincoln's death as deeply as any northerner could.

Lincoln had been as dedicated to repairing the great schism in his country as he had been to preserving it. The Rebels could always claim that they had produced some of the greatest generals to ever live.

The North could claim one of their country's greatest men, for the rail-splitting lawyer from Illinois had proven with tenacity, dedication, and wisdom to be just that.

With Lincoln gone, who knew quite what would befall the South?

That all remained to be seen.

Daniel just wanted to go home.

Early on a late April morning, he rode out into a field of mist and he waited. Minutes later, another horseman appeared. Jesse.

They *were* going home.

Christa was the first to see them. She started screaming from an upstairs window.

Callie heard her and rushed to the porch. She could see them both, the Cameron brothers.

The one in blue.

And the one in gray.

They had dismounted from their horses, and they were walking down the long drive together toward the house, weary, arms linked, leaning upon one another.

Callie cried out.

Daniel lifted his head, and he saw her. A broad grin touched his face. He turned to Jesse, said something, and broke away from him.

And then he was running to Callie.

And she left the porch behind, running to him.

The distance was not far. It seemed forever. Her feet moved so fleetingly over the earth.

Once upon a time she had dreamed of this. Of seeing Daniel before her, so hungry to meet her, to touch her. Once she had dreamed that she could run to him, with all her love naked in her face.

She catapulted into his arms. She felt them surround her. She caught sight of the blazing blue of his eyes. Then his lips were on hers.

His kiss was eternal. So hot, so sweet, so hungry. A touch that tore away, and fell again. Trembling. Deep. Lifting once again so that he could meet her eyes.

"Jesse! Oh, Jesse!" Callie was dimly aware that Kiernan had raced on by her. Farther down the lane, another sweet homecoming was going on.

But now Daniel was before her.

"Oh, Daniel!" she whispered softly. "I am so sorry!"

He pressed his finger to her lips. "Hush. I am not, Callie." His finger rimmed her lips. "I've a son to raise, a daughter to see. Oh, Callie!"

His mouth seared down upon hers once again. Fierce, poignant, giving, seeking. His eyes rose to hers once again.

"I love you, Callie. The war is over, but"— He smiled, a crooked, rueful, tender smile—"my life is just beginning," he told her.

And arm in arm, they walked back to the house.

And to a new life, together.

And One Rode West

This one is dedicated to some of the heroes in my own life.

In memory of my father, Ellsworth D. "Dan" Graham, who gave me wings with which to dream and fly. As long as I live, I will cherish his memory.

For my father-in-law, Alphonse Pozzessere, for being the kindest, sweetest man in the world, and having been there for us, so consistently, all these years.

For my stepfather, William Sherman, a gentleman beyond measure. Mom, you got lucky twice!

For my husband, Dennis, for keeping the love, the passion—and the conflict!—so fresh throughout all the boundaries of time. The years just make things better!

And for my three sons, Jason, Shayne, and Derek. I cannot imagine life without them.

Prologue

Late September, 1865

$\mathcal{S}$lowly rousing from a restless doze, Christa became aware of the man. Her heart seemed to fly to her throat, ceasing its beat, then pounding furiously.

He was tall, and he filled the entryway to the tent. His shoulders were broad, and cast against the darkness of the velvet, stormy night, he was touched only lightly by the blood-red blaze of the low-burning fire in the center of the tepee.

Terror filled her in those first few seconds. The red and gold light made him appear like some ancient pagan God of this wild, raw land, some indomitable being, created of muscle and sinew and vengeance.

Dear God! Who was it? Standing in the firelight and shadow, she knew he had come for her.

It must be Buffalo Run, she thought, coming to take his revenge. He would have what amusement he could find from her—and then he would have her scalp. She knew the Comanche sometimes tortured their captives, cutting their tongues out if they screamed in the night.

And when she died, her scalp, with a long black tress waving from it, would be stuck upon a pole high atop a plain's butte for some other traveler to discover.

Just as they had found that blond scalp themselves, not so very long ago. The blond scalp that must have belonged to a young woman, as Robert Black Paw and Dr. Weland had determined.

Dear God, no!

Jesu, sweet Jesu, let her open her eyes again and see that the man at the entry was gone! That she had imagined the towering figure of a man there in the darkness, touched only by that flickering light! Once it might not have mattered so fiercely. But it did now. She wanted to live. She wanted to live for her child. She wanted to live for the life that they might share together.

She opened her eyes. Her heart seemed to shudder. He was still there. He stared at her in the firelight, and she saw he had the advantage, for he was cast against the blackness of the night while she was bathed by the golden flames. She swallowed hard.

She didn't show fear, Jeremy had told her once, and that was, perhaps, the one thing he admired about her. Lying in their tent beneath the stars one night, he had admitted with a bitter tone to his voice that she was no simpering belle, no matter how she liked to play the part of the grand dame. Had she been in the midst of the fighting, Grant might never have taken Richmond.

She knew how to fight! But could she fight now? She had fought her way right into the middle of this disaster. Now the red and gold fire lit up the tepee from its center, casting some objects into amber light and some into crimson shadow. How menacing those dark shadows seemed.

How menacing the man who stood between that ominous play of light and dark!

Her heart slammed, seemed to cease its beat, then began to pound with a fury to rival the drumbeats.

The man cast in the light began to move. He took a step forward into the tepee.

Outside, it had been storming. Now, the rains had stopped. Only the chill wind remained. Anguished moans turned into tearing howls, cries that haunted the landscape. She could still hear the endless monotony of the drums as she watched that towering figure come toward her.

The night was savage. So seemed the man.

She placed a hand above her eyes, trying to see him. All around her, the pulse of the drumbeats continued as the seconds ticked by.

What did those drumbeats mean, she wondered desperately. Was she to become a sacrifice to a pagan god? Did each beat spell her doom?

Jeremy would know. He knew the Comanche ways well, just as he knew the Apache, Cheyenne, Pawnee, Ute, and the other tribes along the long trail west. To some of the soldiers, they were all just savages. But Jeremy knew them individually. He had taken the time to do so.

And he had warned her often enough about the Comanche. They could be savage, indeed. But there was more to it than that, he had warned her often enough. They were fiercely proud. They were independent.

She felt a scream rising in her throat. Instinctively, she cast the back of her hand against her mouth, praying that she might choke it back, then wondering why she even cared.

Maybe there was a chance. Comanche sold their captives too. Raped them and sold them to the Spaniards in Mexico, making sure that they only traded soiled goods.

It was warm within the tepee, she realized dimly, despite the pelting rain that had fallen, despite the howling cry of the wind. The Comanche knew how to keep their portable dwellings secure from the rain and the cold. They knew how to live off of this hostile land. They knew how best to torture captives.

She shivered fiercely. He was just feet away from her. In seconds, he would reach the center of the tepee. She would see him bathed in the red-gold glory of the fire, and she would see his eyes, and she would know why he had come.

"You!" she gasped.

He reached the fire. She blinked and her mouth went dry. She could scarcely move, could scarcely believe.

Indeed, the golden glory of the fire touched him. Touched his majestic height, played upon the fine breadth of his shoulders. Touched his eyes, and she saw the jeweled gleam of them. She saw the burning of emotion, but just what emotion, she could not determine.

He reached down his hands to her, catching her wrists when she continued to stare incredulously at him.

He wrenched her to her feet and brought her crashing hard against him.

"Tomorrow, madam, I may die for you," he said. His voice was rich and deep, his words harsh. The emotion that burned in his eyes brought fire to his fingertips, a touch of steel to the way that he held her. He brought her closer against him. His fingers stroked and cupped her chin, tilting her face, forcing her eyes to his. His fingers threaded into the wild tangle of her hair. His eyes traveled the length of her, assessing her for damage, so it seemed. His fingers, entangled at the nape of her neck, held her head steady as his lips lowered until they hovered just above hers. His grip was forceful. The length of him seemed to shake with electric energy, be it passion or fury.

He continued to whisper, the warmth of his breath bathing her lips and her face.

"Tomorrow I may die. Tonight . . ." He paused just briefly. She felt the fire in his eyes once again, and the tension of the blaze that burned within his body, as crimson and gold as the flames that lit the tepee. "Tonight," he continued raggedly, "tonight, my love, you will make it worth my while!"

His lips descended upon hers, hard, questing, demanding.

And bringing all that fire within her.

"Jesu!" she whispered when the bruising force of his lips left her mouth at last. The fire coursed throughout her body. It felt like electricity, moving through her limbs and heart and womb. Her eyes searched his out. God, yes, she had wanted him before. Deeply, passionately. But never like she wanted him this night, with the wind crying beyond the buffalo-hide walls, with the pulse of the drumbeats never ending.

He had come.

She threw her arms around him, clung to him. His fingers moved over her hair, reveling in the length of it. He drew her away from him, the fury, the passion, still alive within him.

"Life—and death. Make them both worthwhile," he told her harshly.

She stared at him, and then he swept her up into his arms, and bore her down to the furs upon the ground.

"Love me!" he commanded her fiercely.

For a moment his handsome face hovered close over hers. She wanted to reach and touch him, yet she felt as if her limbs were frozen. He stood briefly, casting off his shirt, shedding his clothing, then coming down to her, sleek and naked upon the fur. The length of him was bathed in the fire-gold beauty of the flames. His hands were upon her, stripping her of the fine doeskin tunic the women had given her to wear.

And then she was against his burning, naked flesh.

The corner of his lips twisted into a self-mocking smile.

"Give in to me!" he commanded her. "Everything, Christa, everything."

Staring at him in the dancing light, she felt a pain like death steal over her heart.

She had given in to him—long ago. He knew that he had brought about her surrender.

But perhaps he didn't know just how completely he held her heart.

If she said it, he would never believe her. He would assume that she was deliriously grateful that he was here.

She had fought her battles all too well.

She had disobeyed him. In fact, she had betrayed him. Her reckless determination had brought them here, brought on this disaster.

And still, he had come for her.

He straddled over her, his naked thighs like oaks, the ripple of muscle in his arms and chest gleaming gold and bronze. From head to toe, he was tension, passion, and determination. She began to tremble, wanting him.

And knowing that she loved him.

She reached out her arms to him, her eyes wide and luminous. She moistened her lips to speak, and her words quavered.

"I will give you everything!" she vowed, and added in a vehement whisper, "And well, well worth your while will it be!"

He groaned softly, capturing her lips again with his hunger, a callused hand stroking and cradling the fullness of her breast.

Fire exploded.

And the words almost left her lips.

I love you.

What words to cry when there might be no future to prove them, she thought with anguish.

For fierce, fiery moments, it ceased to matter. His kiss claimed her and burst into her. The fire of need burst and spread rampantly. His touch encompassed her. The hardness of his body against hers aroused and awakened her to a fever pitch. She had sworn to make it real. She parted her lips to his kiss, and felt his tongue rake the insides of her mouth. His touch seemed to be all over her. Fingers touching her breasts, caressing her hips, stroking her thighs. His lips rising from hers, his mouth forming over the hardening peak of her breast, lapping sweet fire. His hands upon her inner thigh, his fingers touching, stroking, finding her cleft, diving within her. Soft cries escaped her. She shifted and undulated beneath him, and he stopped all but that touch, watching her in the golden red light. She heard his whisper.

"Death holds no threat, my love. Indeed, you have made it all worth my while!"

He would never see the flush that rose to her cheeks against the fire's glow. Perhaps he sensed it. Perhaps he would brook no hesitance or modesty on her part this night. He fell atop her again, kissing, stroking. She fought his touch, hungered then to give what he gave to her. Upon her knees, she kissed his shoulders, her fingers biting into flesh and muscle. She kissed his lips, his chest, dazed to be with him again. He caught her hand and guided it to the fullness of his sex, and she trembled, still awed by the size and vitality of his passion. Yet even as she stroked him, he cried out. He swept her up into his arms, then laid her flat against the hides and fur of the bedding. He caught her ankles, spreading her legs. He hovered over her, his lips ravaging hers again, his eyes seeking her own. He would take her now, she thought, for they were both well starved for one another. But he did not. He could not seem to have his fill of the touch and taste and scent of her. Again, his lips covered hers. He kissed her breasts, then bathed her belly, and even as she cried out, his lips and his tongue stroked and teased her in an incredibly bold and intimate fashion. The fire glistened, her body throbbed. She thought that she would black out from the force of her emotions. Within her a climax began to build unbearably. She whimpered and twisted, and then he rose above her again, his eyes on hers.

"Jesu!" It was his turn to whisper.

He scooped her into his arms and thrust into her hard. The force of his passion was breathtaking.

There was no subtlety now, just the hunger, let go at last to run rampant. Her arms entwined around him, she was near to sobbing as he thrust and stroked, as she strove to meet him, as the blazes burst high and climbed and soared around them. Senseless, she registered only the physical feelings. The buff color of the buffalo-hide walls. The never-ending gold and red of the fire. The feel of the furs and hides beneath her on her naked skin. The man above her. His muscles were slick with sweat now and glistening with every bit as much fire and gold as the blaze. Rippling, tense, constricted, easing.

His eyes, so demanding, hard upon her own. The planes of his face, both rugged and handsome. Fine lines, beautifully and harshly drawn. The feel of his flesh against her. The feel of his sex enclosed within her, slick, wet, hot.

She shrieked out, holding fiercely to him, limbs locked around him as her climax exploded fully upon her at last. She heard him whisper something, but she didn't know what. She drifted, aching, trembling, spent, delicious, still throbbing.

Seconds later, she was aware of the sudden, steel-hard constriction of his body. A long, harsh groan escaped him, and he shuddered, coming within her again and again. And more gently, just once again.

He held her, then sighed. He eased his weight from her and scooped her into his arms. He held her, stroking her hair.

I love you!

The words were there again.

But she couldn't say them. He had brought her to the plains of heaven. But that was only an illusion. The tepee was real. The fire was real. The threat of death was real.

She started to speak.

"Sh!" he said softly. "We have the night."

The night. They had the night.

Perhaps no future. Only a past.

Sometimes it seemed the past they shared had begun forever ago.

Sometimes it seemed as if it had been just moments ago when he had come to her, galloping up upon his horse.

An unwilling cavalier. One who wore the wrong color.

And one with whom she had made a devil's bargain.

It had been forever ago . . .

No, it had been just a few months ago, with a lifetime of living in those months.

The war had ended at the beginning of summer.

And their private battle had begun.

A Conquered Nation

The day was so hot that the sun seemed to shimmer above the ground, making the fields and the land weave in a distorted manner. The humidity was as high as the day was hot.

Christa Cameron suddenly stood straight, bone-tired from the heat. She arched her sore back and dropped the small spade she had been using to loosen the dirt by the tomato plants. She closed her eyes for a moment and then opened them.

If she looked to the river, it was as if the past years had never been. The river flowed on just the same as it always had. The sun shimmered above it, too, and the water seemed blue and black. At this distance, it seemed to be standing still. Pa had always said that summer in Virginia could be like summer in hell. Hotter than it was even down in Georgia or Florida, or way out west in California. The river might make it a spell cooler by night, but by day it didn't seem to help at all. Still, the heat was something she knew well enough. She'd lived with it all her life. The house had been built to catch every little breeze that might go by.

Turning around, Christa stared up at it. While the river gave away nothing of the tempest of the past four years, the house told it all. Peeling, cracking paint, loose boards, that one step from the back porch still missing. There were a few bullet holes in it from the day that the war had come right to them. Staring at the house, she felt ill. For a moment, she was dizzy. Then her anger and bitterness came sweeping down on her and her fingers trembled.

She should have been grateful that the house was still standing. So many other fine homes had been burned right to the ground. In so many places lone chimneys could be seen, rising up like haunting wraiths from the scorched earth around them. Her house still stood. Cameron Hall. The first bricks had been laid in the sixteen hundreds. The building was a grand lady if ever there had been one. Down its middle ran a huge central hall with broad double doors on the front and rear porch, all of which could be opened to welcome the breezes, to allow a host of beautifully dressed men and women to party and dance out to the moonlit lawn if they so desired.

Even the lawn was ravaged now.

The house still stood! That mattered more than anything. The graceful columns that rose so majestically from the porches might need another coat of paint, but they stood. No fire had scorched them, no cannon had leveled them.

And though the paint was chipping and three-fourths of the fields were lying fallow, her home still stood and still functioned because of her.

The Yanks had been ordered to leave the place alone because of Jesse. Jesse was the oldest male heir, so the place legally came to him. And Jesse had fought for the Union. But the Rebs had left the place alone because her brother Daniel had fought for the South. Once, the Yanks had nearly burned it, but for a few bright shining moments her family had all managed to band together, neither Yanks nor Rebs, and fought to preserve it.

They had all fought for it, but she had saved it. She had stayed here while Jesse had gone north and Daniel had gone south. She had learned to keep the garden when so many of their slaves—freed by an agreement between her brothers—had begun to wonder what they could do with their lives in the North. She had watched them go—and she had watched some return. She had learned to garden, she had learned to plant. She had plowed, she had picked cotton. She had even repaired the roof when it had begun to leak in Jesse's study. She'd had help from her sisters-in-law, but they'd both been busy with their babies. Jesse, the Yank, had married Kiernan, the Reb, and Daniel, the Reb, had married Callie, the Yank, and so they'd all had each other.

Christa had had the house.

The softest whisper of a cooling breeze suddenly swept up. She lifted off her wide-brimmed straw hat and held it before her.

It might have been different. She might not have had to love a house—brick and wood and paint and shingles—if it hadn't been for the war. Once upon a time she'd been in love. And it hadn't been awful, like it had been for her brothers, loving women who were their enemies. She had been in love with a Confederate officer, Liam McCloskey. They'd spent what hours they could together, dreaming and planning and building a better world, one they could live in when the war was over, the brand-new and liberated Confederate States of America. They would have had a half-dozen children, and they would have raised them along with the cotton and tobacco that had built their world, that had made it rich.

But they wouldn't raise anything now. Her fair young officer was dead, fallen upon the field of battle. His uniform was his funeral shroud; the bare dark earth of his homeland, the Confederacy, was his coffin.

She and Kiernan and Callie had all worked endless hours, sewing beautiful beads and lace onto a white taffeta bridal gown. The war had raged around them, food had grown more and more scarce, and a pair of stockings had become a great luxury. But they had created a stunning gown for her to wear for her wedding.

But though she had dressed in the beautiful white gown, Liam McCloskey never arrived for his wedding. When Liam did not arrive by the time night fell, she had known with a sinking surety in her heart that he was dead.

They had taken the beautiful wedding gown and had dyed it black. Dressed in her mourning, she had gone to the train station to claim her lover's remains. All she'd received was word that his body had been buried with countless others in a mass grave.

At least he had died in Virginia.

Christa swallowed hard and lifted her face to the sun, her eyes tightly closed. She had ceased to cry. So many were dead. She had grown numb against the news of death. Both Jesse and Daniel had survived, and she was deeply grateful for that, but they had come home to wives with open arms. She had watched her brothers, one in blue and one in gray, coming home together. She had started to run to them herself, but then she had remembered. They had wives to run down the long road to meet them. She could not run, for the man she should have run to, ragged and worn in his gray, was no more than a memory now. He would never walk down any trail toward her, never smile his slow, warm smile, never open his arms to her again.

And so she had watched.

Now she was like the house. When the war had begun, they had both been beautiful, vibrant, full of life.

The house needed paint and repairs.

She needed her youth back. She had been so very young before it had all begun! The hostess of Cameron Hall, her father's daughter, her brothers' pride. Men from across the country had vied for her attention at parties and balls. She was known as the "Cameron Rose," for they joked that she was the beauty between two thorns, Jesse and Daniel. They'd all been blessed with the Cameron eyes, eyes that were near cobalt-blue, and the Cameron hair, a deep dark shade that was nearly as black as ebony. In those days her face had been ivory with just the right touch of rouge in her cheeks. She had been so quick to smile, so quick to laugh.

Maybe now she needed a paint job too.

Her big floppy hat hadn't kept the sun from her face. She had burnt, she had peeled. No matter what lotions Janey had given her for her hands, they had callused and grown rough. She'd acquired startling muscles. Very unladylike.

But Cameron Hall still stood. She had done it. Despite war, despite devastation. She had kept the hall standing, and she had seen to it that they all ate while they waited and prayed.

Now the war was over, and she was still out here working with the tomato plants.

It wouldn't be long now. She was alone with the house again because Jesse and Kiernan were in Washington on business and Daniel and Callie were in Richmond trying to help sort out some of the confusion of getting wounded Rebs back south from northern prison camps while returning wounded Yanks to their homes. The babies—her three little nephews and one little niece—were all gone with their parents. The Millers' twins, Kiernan's young sister and brother-in-law from her first marriage, were also in Washington. Janey had gone with them, just as Jigger had determined to go along with Daniel to help him and Callie with their little brood.

And so now it was just her again, her and Cameron Hall. She wasn't completely alone. Jesse and Daniel had agreed to free their slaves long before any emancipation proclamation had been written. Many of their slaves had left, but many had returned.

Many had stayed even at those times when she'd had nothing to pay them with but worthless Confederate scrip. Big Tyne, the huge, handsome black man Kiernan had brought home with her from Harpers Ferry, was with her, but his cottage was down by the stables.

She was alone in the house she had been born in.

She suddenly wondered if she was destined to grow old and die here.

She'd be Aunt Christa—a maiden relative. Living on the fringes. She could almost hear the children at some later time, telling a visitor about her. "Ah, yes, that's our aunt, poor dear! She is wrinkled and withered now, but once upon a time, she was one of the greatest beauties in all of the South. Men flocked around her like daisies in the summer. Her fiancé was killed in the war, but she's —well, she's been with us always, keeping up with us as children, making delicious little things to eat, knitting, sewing . . ."

Hanging on. Hanging on to other people's lives, Christa thought.

She should marry sometime.

There wasn't anyone left to marry. Far more than the devastation of buildings and land had been the devastation of human life. So many men, in the flower of youth, cut down to bleed, like her beloved Liam, that blood feeding the land they had fought for, died for.

It wouldn't matter if there had been a thousand men left to marry. Christa had been in love. She had buried her heart in that unknown mass grave along with the tattered remnants of her lover's body.

What was left? Cameron Hall. It had kept her going through the war. She had clung to one of the tall proud pillars while her sisters-in-law had rushed to greet her brothers. And there were those long empty years ahead when her nieces and nephews would say, "Yes, that's Aunt Christa, and there was a time when she was beautiful, when she was young."

She bent down again, pressing the soft dirt around her tomato plant. A faint trembling in the earth caused her to look up quickly.

Just around the corner of the house she could see the long elegant drive that led up to it. She frowned, seeing that an unknown rider was coming along the drive at a hard lope. She squinted to see better. The heat of the sun shimmered above the drive and the rider and horse seemed to weave and wave even as they moved.

The man on the horse was wearing a Yankee uniform. Her heart beat fast for just a moment, and she wondered if it was Jesse returning for some reason without Kiernan. But within seconds she knew that it wasn't her brother. There were no medical insignias on the uniform, nor was this man wearing a plumed hat the way that Jesse always wore his.

Nor did he ride anywhere nearly as well as either of her brothers, Christa decided matter-of-factly. This was a Yankee, and Yankees just didn't ride as well as their southern brethren.

The war was over. She wasn't going to be afraid of this Yankee. She dusted off the dirt from her fingers on the plain green apron she'd been wearing over the gingham skirts of her day dress and started to walk around the house to meet the man at the porch. A trickle of sweat ran down the back of her neck, then it seemed to turn cold, and a chill of unease swept along her spine. What did this man want?

He reined in, trotting up the drive. Christa began to hurry, catching up her skirts and running. As she neared the front porch, she could see that the Union soldier had dismounted. He had some kind of a flyer in his hand. He stared up at the house, then dug in his saddlebag and found a hammer and a nail, it seemed, shook his head, and started up the great sweeping steps to the porch. At the front door, he began to hammer in the notice he had carried.

"What do you think you're doing?" Christa demanded breathlessly, having arrived at the foot of the stairs.

The Yank turned to her, arching a slow, curious brow. He was a big, furry fellow with broad shoulders and a paunchy gut, sideburns and a full beard and mustache. His curious brow began to wiggle licentiously as he looked her up and down, and somewhere, in the midst of all that fur on his face, he began to smile.

"Well, how-de-do, ma'am! I heard tell there was a Rebel lived out here, but they didn't tell me it was a Rebel gal, pretty as a picture! It's right nice to meet you, girly. Right nice. And we're going to get along just fine!"

Christa ignored him. "What are you doing?"

"Uppity little miss, ain'tcha? Well, you'd better be nice to old Bobby-boy here. I'm slapping an eviction notice on this place."

"An eviction notice!" Christa exclaimed. She felt her temper flaring. Damn, if it wasn't one thing after another! She'd loved Jesse all through the war, even though he'd been a Yankee. He was her brother. She'd had to forgive him his confusion.

When the war had ended, she had tried to understand why it seemed to him that the sanctity of the Union had been so all-precious important. She hadn't really minded digging in the garden, and she hadn't even minded learning to fix the roof. But she did mind the scalawags, carpetbaggers, and downright trash that the Union had been sending down upon them now that the war was over!

"That's right, little Miss Uppity. An eviction notice. For crimes against the United States of America by one Colonel Daniel Cameron."

"Crimes!" Christa echoed incredulously. "He was a soldier, fighting in the war! You can't evict him for that!"

The soldier walked toward her, peering intently down upon her. He looked toward the house, then back toward her. "You Cameron's wife?"

"Who I am is none of your concern!"

"You a servant, then?"

"I'm Miss Cameron," she informed him, exasperated.

"His sister," old Bobby-boy said knowledgeably. "Well, where is he?"

"In Richmond—helping sick and injured people get back home where they belong! Rebs—and Yankees. The war is over, and you can't evict people anymore, and I don't think what you're threatening is legal to begin with! The house isn't really Daniel's—it's Jesse's. Who is your authority?" she demanded.

Bobby-boy was grinning. "My, my. Ain't you something. Whew! A wild one. I like that!" the soldier announced. He came down the steps toward her. Christa wasn't a tiny woman. She was slim—the war seemed to have made almost everybody more so, except for this furry soldier here—and nearly five feet six inches tall. Though this fellow was no giant, his girth was excessive, and despite the muscles she had acquired gardening, she suddenly felt another chill of unease sweep through her.

"I'll take this up with someone who actually has authority," she said. "For now, just state your business and get the hell off of my land!" she warned him, her hands on her hips as she took a single step back.

"Your land?"

"Yes!" she hissed. "It's Cameron land, and I'm a Cameron!"

He grinned again. "Yep. Even all kind of starved-up looking, Miss Uppity, you are a right fine portrait of southern womanhood! I hear tell that demure southern ladies get real fired up underneath all that magnolia blossom innocence. You could be nice to me. Real nice. Then, if you were nice enough, I could probably make things better."

He reached out and touched her, running his fingers over her cheek.

Christa didn't even think. She recoiled, furious. She lashed out in a flash, striking him in a slap that turned his cheek crimson with the imprint of her fingers. She hit him with such strength that he staggered back, his hand flying to his face with surprise.

"Why, Miss-Uppity-Southern-Bitch!" he murmured in a long twang, staring at her with eyes like little twin points of fire in the midst of all the fur on his face. "You just made yourself a mistake. A real mistake."

A mistake? Christa couldn't begin to see it that way. She stared him down, her own eyes sizzling. "You get your fat Yankee carcass off my land right now or—"

"Or what?" the soldier demanded in a voice that had grown very ugly. He took a step toward her, then another. He was smiling again. "All alone, eh, Miss Uppity? You got this nice great big old house, and you think you come from some goddamned kind of southern royalty here, huh? Well, you and your kind have been beaten, lady. You ain't no royalty no more and you're putting your nose up real high for a gal dressed in clothes just as tattered as this here paint job."

"Take one step nearer to me and I'll scream to blue blazes!" she warned.

He stopped for a moment, then his grin deepened. "Why, honey, even if you've got darkies lingering on here now that they've been freed, they ain't gonna raise their hands to help out the white woman who made them all slaves. Hell, honey, they'll just cheer me on!"

"Don't be a fool, Yankee. Our hands are all good people, and they know white trash when they see it."

"Well, you know what I think? I think there just ain't no one around at all. And you know what else I think? I think we're going to have a good time, and you're going to get your comeuppance."

"If you touch me—"

"I'd just say that you were willing, Miss Cameron. Willing to do anything at all to bargain for this old house of yours! You tried to seduce a Union soldier."

Despite his threats, Christa was amazed when his beefy hand reached out, his sausage-shaped fingers actually grabbing the folds of her bodice. He jerked her toward him. She smelled the scent of stale whiskey on his breath and realized that he was probably some lackey who sat around town all day drinking and whiling away time in the South. Reconstruction! This was it. Men like Bobby-boy.

They all said that it might have been different if Lincoln had lived. But Lincoln was dead.

And the powers in the North wanted to keep the South on her knees.

Bobby-boy was touching her now and the smell of whiskey on his breath was so bad that she was feeling queasy when it was important that she think and fight.

Fear suddenly coursed through her. Deep, gut-level fear. Tyne was here, but God alone knew exactly where. Tyne would kill the Yankee, but with emotions being what they were, someone would see that Tyne hanged for killing a white man. Old Peter was down in the smokehouse, but his hearing was all but gone and if he tried to help her, that fine old man would suffer the same fate as Tyne.

She stared into the soldier's leering eyes, feeling his hot, fetid breath upon her cheeks, feeling his pudgy fingers curved over her flesh.

The war was over. All those awful years were behind her.

Why was this happening to her now?

"Let me go, you repulsive gorilla!" she hissed, trying to strike out again.

He didn't let her go. He lifted her cleanly off the ground with one hand, then dropped her flat on the porch, crawling over her.

Christa's heart hammered at a furious beat. In disbelief, she began to fight the man in earnest, twisting, striking, kicking, scratching.

This couldn't be happening.

She grit her teeth, blinking back tears. Once, she had been so desperately in love. She had planned with Liam, waiting for the first possible moment for their wedding.

She remembered being in love, remembered his kisses. Remembered his touch, and remembered wanting more. But they had both been strictly disciplined. She would have been a bride in white, in love, waiting to be awakened.

They had waited to become man and wife. But bullets had severed the dream.

She had held back from the sweetness of desire, to come to this. Honor and innocence would be taken by this burly, bitter bear of a wretch in the dust on the porch of her very own house!

For a moment the fur-covered, pock-marked face rose above hers. She'd gotten in her digs, she realized. Bloody scratches tore his face. There was spittle on his lips and Christa inwardly recoiled again. "Hold still! You'll like it, I promise, girly!" he told her.

"I don't believe this!" Christa shouted. "They'll shoot you! They'll court-martial you. Rape is a crime—"

"A Yankee—against a Cameron? Why, honey, my commanding officer would give me a medal!"

He shoved her skirt up. Christa realized that she was really fighting a desperate battle. "You're insane!" she cried. "You and your commanding officer! My oldest brother, Jesse, is the legal master of this place. He's a colonel in the Yank army. He'll have your hide if you so much as breathe my way again—"

"Hold still, you wily she-devil!" he ordered, and punched her right in the stomach.

For a moment, her breath was swept away. Stars seemed to shoot in a black sky before her. Stunned, Christa lay still. Then every fighting breath in her body returned in a maelstrom. She cracked her knee up into his groin and sent her nails raking across his cheek. He howled and she twisted, managing to crawl from beneath him. On her hands and knees she escaped to the porch steps and then ran down them.

But he was behind her. He caught her arm and threw her down to the ground. Her hands clawing into dirt and grass, she tried to drag her way across the lawn, her heart beating in a fury, her breath coming in quick gasps. She kicked out with all her strength, blinded by the dust in her eyes.

She made it to her feet again, but fell upon the tangle and fullness of her skirt. She felt his hand around her ankle. "No!" She glanced back. He was about to pit the bulk of his weight against her again. She closed her eyes against the dust, crying out again. "No!"

Suddenly, she felt a violent rush of air. He was no longer touching her.

Bobby-boy seemed to fly up, as if he had been plucked away from her by some gigantic hand. He grunted, landing hard, several feet behind her.

She was free.

What in God's name . . . ?

She gasped in a great rush of air, trying to ascertain what had happened. Bobby-boy was reaching out a hand. Was he trying to reach her again, or was he protesting some new threat? She shrieked, still in a wild panic, backing away from him.

She crashed against something hard.

A body.

A man.

Someone else was with them. Someone who had the power to rip Bobby-boy off her and send him flying across the yard.

She twisted around to see that she had backed her way to a pair of shiny black boots. Cavalry boots.

"Touch her again and you're a dead man!" a deadly male voice warned Bobby-boy.

Gulping in more air, Christa allowed her gaze to rise. She was shaking.

This man, too, was in blue.

And it wasn't Jesse.

But like Jesse, he wore a regulation Yankee cavalry uniform. Blue pants hugged long muscular legs. A scabbard and sword clung to a taut waistline and hard narrow hips. As she lifted her head still further, the brilliance of the sun blinded her for a moment. All she saw was that the man was very tall, and that he wore a plumed hat. Leather-gloved hands were upon his hips as he surveyed the situation.

The sun shifted, and she saw the man's face.

Deep, rich russet hair framed handsome features tanned to a bronze color despite the rakish angle of his hat. Arched russet brows framed steel-gray eyes, eyes of a color so like quicksilver that it could change like lightning, being as stormy as a tempest one minute, and light as a mist the next. Gray like steel, silver like a glint beneath the sun. Eyes that touched her now, and flicked quickly past her.

Him.

Bitterness plunged through her heart. She didn't realize for a moment that she was safe, that she had been saved from rape. She thought only that he was here.

Him.

That Yank of all Yanks.

Jeremy McCauley.

Two

*H*ell, what a mess, Jeremy McCauley thought wearily, looking from the puffed-up soldier to Christa. Her brilliant blue eyes were on him. He couldn't read quite what emotion was in them, but he knew Christa, and he doubted, even under the circumstances, that she was glad to see him.

A shudder ripped through him, and despite Christa, a wave of anger washed over him. Jesu. The war was over! The damn thing wouldn't seem to end, though.

He'd seen too many instances now when the victors were acting like conquerors. We won the war! he wanted to shout at the soldier. We didn't win the right to rape and murder and plunder. And how the hell dare he touch Christa Cameron?

It startled him to realize that he felt like ripping the man's throat out for having touched Christa. They might be enemies, but Christa was Callie's sister-in-law, and so in a way, Jeremy determined, he was kin.

Christa was still down on the ground, staring up at him. Christa on her knees was a view to begin with. But even with her clothing disheveled and covered with dust, she was a stunning woman, proud and defiant.

Maybe she hadn't needed his help. Maybe she could have whipped Bobby-boy all on her own. It was possible. She hadn't his strength, but she had a raw willpower to match any soldier Jeremy had ever met.

She was still staring at him, and he suddenly found himself annoyed that she could be such a disaster—and still be so beautiful. Her hair was a tangle, falling down her back in blue-black waves. Her eyes were that uncanny color to rival a summer's sky. Her features were incredibly classical and beautiful.

And for just a moment he saw a flash of emotion in her eyes. She might still hate him. She might still blame him for the whole damned war, it was hard to tell with Christa, but she had been scared. For once in her life, she'd had the sense to be scared, and she was glad that he had come.

He remembered the first time he had seen her. He'd been standing on the porch just feet away from where he stood now. Callie had come out to throw her arms around him, and when he had looked over Callie's shoulder, he had seen Christa standing there. Tall, slim, regal, stunning, with an exquisite face and beautiful coloring. He had thought for an instant that she was the most beautiful woman he had ever seen, even more beautiful than Jenny.

He had felt like a traitor, and he had been furious with himself. She had muttered something about Yankees being everywhere and Daniel Cameron had accosted him. Jesse had appeared and it had been mayhem on the porch until Daniel had brought him into the office for the two of them to settle things between them.

Of course, he'd seen much more of Christa that trip. The very elegant Miss

Cameron had begun to dine with them that evening, but she had chosen to take the children to the kitchen rather than sup with another Yankee.

Now here was Christa again, on the ground before him.

"Get up, Sergeant!" he commanded Bobby-boy sharply. He was just itching to touch the man again, to send him far across the yard.

"Now wait a minute, Colonel, sir!" he gasped out quickly. He looked still to be smarting from Jeremy's having plucked him off Christa and thrown him to the ground. "Colonel, I don't think you rightly see the situation—"

"You've got two seconds or there'll be pieces of you flying all over this grass, Sergeant!" Jeremy warned him, his voice low but deadly.

The man was quickly on his feet, keeping a safe distance from both Jeremy and Christa.

Jeremy reached a hand down to Christa. Her eyes were still on him. She was probably damned surprised to see him. He hadn't written, hadn't told anyone his intentions of coming down here. But he'd made some decisions in Washington just last week, and it had seemed important to come down and say good-bye to Callie. He wasn't quite ready to head out to his new post, but he didn't know if he'd get much time to come south again, and so it had seemed imperative to come here now.

Christa stared right past his hand, and he was certain she was trying to pretend she didn't see it.

She wouldn't want to take a Yankee hand. Though General Lee might have decided a surrender was in order, Christa had certainly never done so.

Christa, my dear Miss Cameron, he thought wryly, you are a witch! Maybe I should have rescued the soldier here from you.

Witch or no, she was a stunning young woman. And she was his kin. He'd just as soon see this soldier's face broken in a million pieces than see him dare to touch an inch of her again.

He arched his brow to Christa as she got up, then turned his attention to the errant soldier. He was tired. Tired of the North and tired of the South. He wanted no more of it, but if there were a problem here, he was honor-bound to solve it if he could.

"Who in blazes are you and what in the Lord's name is going on here?"

"Eviction!" the man said quickly. He was panting harder than Christa. "Any living folk are to clear out of this place. It's to be burned to the ground tonight."

"Burned!" Christa raged. "They're evicting us to burn it to the ground?" She wanted to scratch his eyes out at that moment. She took a step toward him furiously.

Jeremy McCauley caught her shoulders and jerked her back against him. His chest was rock hard, the grip his fingers formed was a forceful one. She grit her teeth, unable to fight him.

"This house is owned by Colonel Jesse Cameron, United States Medical Corp," Jeremy said over her shoulder.

"That's not what the records say. Seems the house was put in Daniel Cameron's name when these people wanted to keep it from being burned by the Confederates. Hell, it's real hard to tell just who is and who isn't the enemy, eh, sir? Or maybe these people just did whatever was convenient. Anyway, the house is down as having belonged to Daniel Cameron, Colonel, in that rebellious army that used to call itself Confederate."

"Convenient!" Christa choked out, wrenching away from Jeremy. How dare this stinking Bobby-boy say such a thing? Her family had been split and torn, and it had all been anguish. "Jesse is the oldest in the family and he never left the United States military, never!"

"It will burn for Daniel Cameron!" Bobby-boy said, a pleased grin on his face. He saw Jeremy's expression and the grin quickly faded.

Jeremy spoke softly. "You'd better explain this and explain it fast, Sergeant. You are going up on charges as it is—the war is over, and even if it weren't, soldiers do not resort to rape—"

"Ah, sir, she was asking for it, I swear!"

"Asking for it!" Christa exploded furiously. "Being mauled by corpses could not disgust me more!"

"Sergeant, I daresay that the lady was not 'asking for it,' " Jeremy stated flatly. He continued in the same dispassionate tone. "I know Miss Cameron. She might be guilty of many things—but never 'asking for it' from a man in a blue uniform."

"How gallantly you do rush to a woman's defense!" Christa murmured, irritated.

Jeremy didn't seem to notice. His attention was on Bobby-boy.

Bobby-boy seemed to have realized just how serious his situation was with Jeremy. His eyes remained glued upon the man. "I could see to it that you were court-martialed—"

"You'd take her side against a Yankee soldier—"

"Damned right!" Jeremy said softly. "Now tell me what's been going on here."

Bobby-boy was silent for a second, shuffling his feet. "All right," he muttered after a moment. "Well, it don't rightly seem as if it should be legal, and I don't really know just what is going on!" he said sourly. "Someone big, someone up top, wants this place razed. And the last taxes that were paid were paid in Confederate scrip, and the last persons to sign any bills were Daniel and Christa Cameron. So if Jesse Cameron is the real owner, he'd best get his Yankee body—and his Yankee dollars—down to the courthouse in Williamsburg by nightfall, else the place will be taken, lock, stock, and barrel, and burned. There's a new owner waiting to take over. And the new owner is waiting for the legal time limit to be up to take the place down."

"New owner?"

"Well, the party who intends to buy the place at sunset."

"And that's tonight," Jeremy said sharply. "Who's the new owner, and how come this notice just reached the house?"

Bobby-boy shrugged. "Maybe somebody didn't want it to reach the house until tonight. I'm just a soldier, just a messenger!"

"Who's the party intending to buy the place?" Jeremy demanded sharply.

"God as my witness, Colonel, I don't know. Lieutenant Tracy in Williamsburg gave me the order to nail the notice up this morning. He led me to believe that the house was a bed of rebellious vipers, just like the kind of folk what decided to kill Lincoln."

Christa hugged her arms tightly against her chest, staring from Jeremy to Bobby-boy. She shook her head, looking at Jeremy. "It can't be legal! What new game are you filthy, stinking, scalawagging, carpetbagging Yankees playing down here?"

"See there, Colonel? 'Filthy' Yankees. And you say that she isn't asking for it!"

Jeremy took a menacing step forward and Bobby-boy shrank back. "She may ask for a lot," Jeremy said, his eyes like a flash of steel, "but she most assuredly isn't going to get anything from you. Now you hightail it on out of here and fast. And if I ever hear tell that you've even been near this place I'll forget that I'm a Yankee officer and I'll hunt you down and rip you limb from limb. You got it, Sergeant?"

Pale as a sheet beneath the fur on his face, Bobby-boy nodded. On quaking legs he turned and hurried for his horse. He mounted and quickly rode away. In silence, Jeremy and Christa watched him go.

She felt a strange, cool breeze touch her. She was alone with Jeremy. Even though she had learned to love her sister-in-law, Callie, she'd never managed to accept Callie's brother in their home.

She'd never known quite what it was between them. Maybe it had been the war. Maybe she'd just been too bitter to accept any Yankee other than Jesse by the time that she had met Jeremy. But from that time when she had first seen him on her doorstep, she'd felt as if the air were charged with lightning anytime he was near her.

They'd been bitter enemies from the moment they had met.

Maybe she thought that he had never understood her. Perhaps he'd been expecting a very sweet and ladylike belle. Maybe she'd even been one once. But the war had forced her to take care of her house and her home.

And it had forced her to take up arms against the enemy.

She hadn't felt in the least obliged when Daniel and Jesse had determined to let Jeremy in because he was Callie's brother.

Admittedly, Jeremy had been caught up in a fight to save Cameron Hall once before. When unauthorized troops had come against him, Jeremy had fought alongside both of her brothers to save the place.

She hated being grateful to him. Hated to be obliged.

But there didn't seem to be a choice. If he could help her now, she was going to have to accept that help.

Sweet Jesu. She'd accept help from the devil himself to save Cameron Hall.

He was already caught up in this mess, so it seemed. He turned to Christa as soon as Bobby-boy was out of earshot. "Where's Jesse?" he demanded.

"Washington," Christa said quickly. "There's no way that he can be back here before nightfall. Even with the railroads all working, I'd have to reach him, and then he'd have to get back here. He'd never make it." She forgot for a moment that she needed his help. Feeling desperate and bitter, she lashed out, "McCauley, tell me that this can't be real! Not even you wretched Feds can come sweeping down here like a horde of conquerors—"

"We *are* the conquerors," he reminded her softly, but there was a silver fire in his eyes as he stared at her. She wondered at his thoughts as her temper flared.

"Ah, yes! Hail the conquering heroes! Bastards!" she spat out.

His jaw set. There was something different about him. She realized that the last time she had seen him, he'd had a mustache and beard. He was clean-shaven now. His jaw seemed even more square and determined.

"Christa, do you want to fight with me? Or do you want to solve this mess?"

She lowered her lashes, wishing that she didn't feel so compelled to battle Jeremy. She did need his help. "How can this be?" she cried out. "Aren't there supposed to be some laws?"

His silver gaze was assessingly upon her. What he saw in her, she couldn't quite fathom. The only thing she knew about Jeremy was that he seemed to have the ability to see right through her.

At the moment, he seemed nearly as disturbed about the house as she was. He sighed. "This shouldn't be possible, and who would do this except—"

"Except?"

Jeremy shrugged. "Someone acquired an enemy. An enemy with power. And then . . . well, then anything can be done."

"Because the North wants the South on her knees!"

"Christa! Some men are good, and some are bad. And some bad men do get into situations of power!"

She lowered her head again. She didn't want to fight with him. Not now.

He paused a moment, then turned his back on her, walking along the drive to where a big, handsome bay horse awaited him. He turned back to her as he mounted the bay. "I take it my sister isn't here? Daniel can't be."

"No, Callie is in Richmond with Daniel. How did you know that he wasn't here?"

"Because if Daniel had been here, that sergeant would have been a dead man," he said. "All right. I'll find out what's going on."

"I'll come with you—"

"No!"

"Dammit, it's my house, my home—"

"And you're very likely to get it burned before nightfall with your gracious way of addressing us conquerors!"

Christa braced herself, wanting to smack his handsome face.

He was all that she had at the moment. "Hurry. Get back here immediately."

He tipped his cavalry hat. "Yes'm, Miss Cameron. Let me see, save you from rape, and the home from demolition, and do it fast. I'll do my filthy Yankee best."

She felt her cheeks coloring. "Just go!" she hissed.

He inclined his head in a bow. Christa watched him race away on the bay, her teeth clenched bitterly. She hated to admit it, but he was one Yankee who could ride almost as well as her brothers.

An hour later she was pacing the steps before the house when she heard the sound of hoofbeats once again.

Her heart slammed against her chest as she rushed to one of the pillars, holding it for strength as she peered down the drive.

It was Jeremy, returning. Christa ran down the steps, ready to greet him when he dismounted from his horse.

"Did you do something? Did you stop it?" she asked anxiously. She saw from the storm-cloud gray of his eyes that nothing was resolved.

Tears welled in her eyes, but she wasn't about to shed them. She knotted her fingers into fists and slammed them against his blue-clad chest. "Damn you! You should have let me come! This isn't your home. You didn't fight hard enough. You don't care—"

"Shut up, Christa!" he commanded harshly, catching her wrists and jerking her close to him. Her head fell back, ink-dark hair cascading over the length of her spine as her eyes met his. "Don't you think I would have done something? Hell, I was on Jesse's side! My sister is married to Daniel. It's her home too."

"Then—"

"I found a friend in the courthouse, but not even Lieutenant Tracy knows who's after the place. A General Grayson is the one who gave the order that the house be confiscated, and he went about it all legally—at least, on paper it looks like it's legal. The notice was supposed to have been on the house thirty days ago."

"Supposed to have been!" Christa reiterated bitterly, trying to pull away from him. He wasn't letting her go. His jaw and his voice hardened as he continued.

"Well, Grayson must be playing dirty politics. Taking bribes. But the only thing I could do would be to call him out, call him a liar to his face. Then I'd have to shoot him, and then I'd be court-martialed and hanged."

He still wasn't letting her go. Christa swallowed hard, afraid that she was going to start crying in front of him. "Would that save the house?" she asked him.

He shook his head, his eyes narrowing. "No."

"Then don't bother!" she whispered miserably, pulling away from him and starting up the steps, her shoulders drooping.

"There's only one way to stop this. They need a signature before dark," he called after her.

She spun around. "I'll sign anything!" she whispered, still fighting tears.

"No, Christa, that won't do. A Yankee signature, that's what they want. If Jesse were just here!"

"If Jesse were just here, this would never be happening!" Christa said.

"You're most assuredly right," Jeremy said evenly. "But Jesse isn't here. And I've just walked into the middle of something that I don't understand. And though I know you'd like me to shoot every Yank in town, I just don't know who to shoot! Whatever is going on isn't my fight."

"Some dirty, lying vulture—"

"Yes, some dirty, lying vulture, sweeping down from the north," Jeremy finished for her evenly. "But I don't know who, Christa. And I'm not going to try to shoot every man in town, not even if you're still convinced it's your due!"

"It's our due!" she cried out. The tears were stinging her eyes again. She'd been to town. The blue uniforms were everywhere. She was damned sure that most of the men in town had never fought, they'd just seen the South like a wounded and dying creature, and they'd come just like a pack of jackals, sniffing opportunity. There were free blacks to exploit, starving women to proposition, near-slave labor in desperate straits, orphaned urchins—and there were houses to pick up for a song!

But whoever wanted Cameron Hall wanted to burn it!

She would never let it happen.

"There has to be something that can be done," she said vehemently.

"They'd even take Callie's signature," Jeremy told her. "Along with the money." He sighed. "Except that I'm not sure she ever swore any kind of an oath to the Union. Think, Christa, maybe there is someone. Some relation. You need a Cameron, or a Cameron spouse, who has sworn an oath to the Union."

"What?"

"You need a hundred and fifty dollars, but I can loan you a bank draft for that. What you have to come up with is a Yankee with a serious connection to this house." She was staring at him, too desolate to go to war with him at the moment. He stared at her, waiting for her to say something.

"I don't understand this. It can't be legal without warning—"

"Christa, don't you understand? They're saying at the courthouse that they've put up numerous flyers and warnings and that you've just ripped them all down."

"My God! It's a lie! It's a horrible, filthy Yankee lie—"

"Christa, dammit, whether it's a lie or not, it's what they're saying." He hesitated, staring at her. "And hell, Christa, like it or not, the South was beaten! Your word is just about worthless right now!"

She grit her teeth tightly together. She wanted to run down the steps and pummel her fists against his chest. She wanted to hurt him.

"I need a brandy," she announced tonelessly. She turned her back on him once again and started into the house.

No.

She paused a moment.

She could not lose it. Not after all this. Not after all these years. She could not lose the Hall. She had lost Liam. This was all that she really had left.

Jeremy followed behind her. She walked straight through the hallway to Jesse's desk and pulled out the brandy bottle. When she started to fill the entire glass, he jerked the bottle out of her hand. She swirled on him, staring at him hatefully. "How dare you! You're not my brother, my father, my husband—"

"That's right, Christa, I'm no one but a filthy Yank. And you're going to turn into a southern lush if you're not careful!"

She stared at Jeremy. He was too tall and too damned superior with his cockaded hat sitting low on his brow and his eyes flashing at her with silver scorn. She had never felt more bitter. Maybe that was why she longed to slap him all the more.

But she was careful with Jeremy McCauley. She had come to know a little about her sister-in-law's brother. He had a certain quality about him that might make someone else want to call him a gentleman.

He was extremely well built, with arms like iron and a hard, muscled chest. He was quick, and could be ruthless. He had no patience with her, and wouldn't even pretend to play any chivalrous games.

Not that she had really attempted to play any games with him. She'd tried to keep her distance from him.

He'd been fighting a war for a long time too.

And in an all-out battle with him, she wouldn't win. He was accustomed to snapping out orders, and he was always quick to give them to her. He must have known damned well by now that she would never obey him. He wasn't her brother! And most certainly wasn't her—

Husband.

A deep, searing chill came sweeping through her and her knees went weak.

She took the chair before Jesse's desk just as Jeremy sat himself, watching her with narrowed, speculative eyes as he poured himself a brandy.

"What?" he demanded in something that sounded like a growl.

She moistened her lips. She couldn't do it. Not even for Cameron Hall.

She'd do anything for Cameron Hall.

"You're trying to tell me that this has all been done legally? Or, at least, what you Yankees are calling legal these days?"

"Christa—"

"Someone hates either Jesse or Daniel. Probably Daniel—he was the loser here, right? Hates him enough to have gone through all kinds of machinations to burn this place to the ground."

"Christa—"

"Is that it?"

"Yes, dammit, that's it. So let's try—"

She leaned forward. "Wait. I need one hundred and fifty dollars and the signature of someone connected with the hall who has sworn an oath to the Union. And whoever is doing this must know that Jesse is in Washington. Jesse could stop it, but he can't get here in time. Someone knows that I'm alone here, and that I haven't any Yankee relations nearby."

"That's about the gist of it," Jeremy said. He tossed down the whole of his brandy, staring at her with his silver eyes. Then he sighed. "I'll stay here, Christa. I'll try to stop what's happening, but somewhere along the line, one of your brothers made an enemy. A big enemy. I don't know who. And I don't rightly know what I can do, but I'll try whatever I can."

"You can sign the paper," she said in a rush.

"Christa, I don't own Cameron Hall. I don't even have a real connection with it. Callie does, not me."

"But you would, if—"

"If?"

Why did he have to stare at her the way that he was staring at her now? He was a Yankee to the core with that hard-edged face of his and those flashing eyes. And that voice that could sound like a whip-crack.

How the hell did she do this?

She stood suddenly, trying not to appear as nervous as she felt. She had to sound offhanded. As if it were certainly no major task she was asking of him.

She folded her hands before her and sighed in what she hoped was a very mature and very matter-of-fact manner. "We'll have to be married," she said. "Very, very quickly, of course."

Maybe he would understand. It would just be something done on paper. It might be complicated to undo, but once they had saved the house, it could be done. Maybe, just maybe, he would understand, and make it easy for her.

"What?" he exploded, leaping to his feet and towering over her.

Then again, maybe he wouldn't understand.

And he sure as hell wouldn't make it easy for her.

It didn't matter. He was going to have to do it. And she was going to have to convince him.

"Jeremy, it's necessary."

He came closer. She had to lift her chin and lean her head back to attempt to stare him down.

She didn't like the disadvantage.

Her fingers curled around her glass and she tried to keep her gaze level with his. "Oh, you don't have to take it seriously. We can do something about it later, I'm sure. But we'll have to be married, and fast."

He sank down into the chair behind Jesse's desk again, a dark auburn brow arched high. "Oh, you think so, do you, Miss Cameron?" he demanded.

"Yes."

His brow arched still further as he stared at her incredulously. "Just like that?" he said softly.

"It's not such a big thing—"

His eyes narrowed sharply. She had come too close to him. He reached out, plucking the brandy glass from her hand, setting it on the desk. Then his fingers were suddenly wound around her wrist, and she was afraid of the strength in them, and afraid to fight him. Before she knew it she had been pulled down on her knees before him. "It's not such a big thing, eh, Miss Cameron? Ah, no, not for you perhaps. Liam McCloskey is lying dead in a battlefield and you don't give two figs for any other man living or dead."

She tried to free herself. "That's not true!" she cried out. "I care! I care about many people. I love my brothers—"

"And you love a hunk of bricks! Brick and mortar and glass and wood!"

She managed to jerk her hand free, lowering her head. "You don't understand! It's not a pile of brick! It's my family, it's history, it's—it's been here for centuries! It's not just a house!"

For a moment he didn't say anything. Then he ordered her, "Look at me, Christa!"

She did so. She wanted to be defiant. Maybe that would be the wrong ploy. In a way, Jeremy knew her well. He knew the gracious games that she could play, but he also always seemed to know what was in her heart.

"Christa, no."

"Damn you!"

She wanted to hurt him. To scratch and strike out and hurt him. He was the conqueror. She had already lost, and she was about to lose more.

Don't fight him! she warned herself. Play it softly, softly!

"Please!" she whispered, and she tried to give him a beseeching look.

"Don't bat your lashes at me, Christa. I know you hate the very sight of me," he said flatly.

Anger flashed through her eyes, making them brilliantly blue. "Then do it for your sister! Do it for your niece and your nephew. Do it because you goddamned filthy Yankees owe us something for this war!"

"Ah, with such a declaration of undying love and devotion, how could I possibly refuse you!" he retorted, a hard curve to his lip.

"Then you'll do it?"

"I already said no!"

"Oh!" she cried out. She freed her hand. She swung it at him with all her strength.

But he caught her wrist. "Christa! You have to stop fighting. You have to worry about—"

"I don't care! I don't care about anything. There won't be anything left to care about."

"Christa—"

His voice had changed. Just a little bit. She looked up into his eyes. They were pure silver now. Burning harshly within the handsome planes of his face.

"Christa, you hate me! And I must admit, you are not on the top of the list of my favorite Rebel women! You can't marry me."

"I'd marry that disgusting fur-face fleabag old Bobby-boy to save this place."

"You can't mean that!" he told her incredulously.

"I don't know what I mean! All I know is that I can't let it go!"

He pushed her away from him, furious. "It's a pile of bricks!" he roared.

Tears touched her eyes again, glazing them. "I'd do anything."

Before she knew it he was suddenly up again, his hands on hers as he wrenched her forcefully up before him. His eyes touched her like fire. "Anything, Christa?" he said. "Anything? What you're asking me to do is a mockery. So *you* had best mean it. You would do anything to save this place. You'd marry that white trash. You'd marry *me.*"

She opened her eyes wide, gasping. "You mean—you'll do it?" She couldn't believe it. He seemed angrier than ever with her.

And furious with himself.

"Miss Cameron, you are quite something, you know. Marriage doesn't mean a damn thing to you. You don't, in the least, mind selling your own soul for Cameron Hall. But what of mine? What if I were in love with someone?"

She grit her teeth, meeting his eyes. She felt a trembling inside of her. It was quite possible. He was a very handsome man. She wasn't blind and she wasn't stupid. He was tall, trim-hipped, broad-shouldered, lean, and muscular. His face was both ruggedly masculine and classically cast, with high cheekbones, startling eyes, and striking, deep russet, high-arched brows. He was a war hero. There might well be a woman waiting for him in the North.

"Are you in love with someone else?" she said.

"Would you really give a damn, Christa?"

She was afraid of his answer. "No!" she cried. "I care that your kind are threatening to tear this place down when I've worked my fingers to the bone for it, when it's all that I have left . . ." Her voice trailed away. "Damn you, Jeremy! Will you do it, or not?"

He stared at her long and hard. She felt the sizzling heat of his eyes rip into her, and then he turned away from her as if he were more furious still. He was going to refuse her! His back was as stiff as steel.

"You have sold both our souls, Miss Cameron. But yes, I'll do it. And we'd best hurry. We've just hours left before sundown and Richmond is a long hard ride from here."

"I would ride to hell!" she said.

He mocked her with a sweeping bow. "Perhaps, Miss Cameron, it is exactly where you are going!"

"Don't threaten me, Jeremy," she told him, lifting her chin, alarmed at the trembling that had begun within her.

"Don't worry, Christa, I would not dream of bothering with a threat," he responded quickly, silver eyes flashing, his fingers tightening upon her arms until she was afraid she would cry out. "To say that you have cast us into hell, my love," he murmured, his voice low and harsh, "is most assuredly not a threat."

"Then—"

"It's a promise. And I vow that I will keep it!"

Three

To Christa, it seemed the strangest wedding imaginable. The Episcopal priest agreed to marry them when the case was truthfully put before him. They were both obliged to swear that they meant to uphold the sanctity of their union before God. The words were spoken, and two choirboys witnessed them.

She had imagined once that when she did marry she'd be dressed in white, not in the cotton day dress she'd been wearing to dig in the garden. She'd have curled her hair. She'd have been surrounded by her family and friends.

She would have been marrying a man who loved her, and a man she loved deeply in return.

But the white gown had been dyed black and it was now a mourning dress. Her family was nowhere near, thus the forced wedding. Her friends, or very many of them, lay dead in battlefields and graveyards across the country.

The man she had loved lay buried along with the rest of the South.

She shivered, then mentally braced herself. She glanced at Jeremy, standing beside her. Once committed to her cause, he had done very well. He had explained the expediency of their need to the priest. Christa wondered what thoughts were passing through his mind. He looked so harsh beside her. What memories came to him as he agreed to this arrangement?

But he didn't mean it, she was certain. It was just to save the house. Once that was done, they could go their separate ways.

She looked around. They were being married in an empty church on the outskirts of Williamsburg. Cannonball fragments were lodged in the outer brick of the church. Some of the stained-glass windows were still cracked and broken from shots.

Christa barely heard the priest's words as he droned on and on. She heard just bits and pieces of the ceremony. Love, honor, and obey. She was supposed to vow to do so.

She would have agreed to anything.

She looked up during the ceremony and saw the large crucifix hanging from the altar.

Forgive me, God! she cried inwardly. She had to look away. God had to understand. He had let this happen.

He had let the Yankees win the war.

She heard Jeremy's vows. Surprisingly, his voice was strong and level. Perhaps it was not so surprising. His voice was laced with his anger. He had agreed to help her. But he was furious with her and himself for having done so. He was going to make her pay somehow for this, she knew. She tossed her hair back. She didn't care. She'd fight him from now until eternity, just as soon as her home was safe.

The priest cleared his throat. The ceremony was over.

"You may now kiss the bride, Colonel McCauley."

Jeremy's lips barely touched her forehead. Yet where his lips touched her, her flesh seemed to burn. And where his hands held her, she felt a riddling tension and a frightening pulse.

The wedding certificate was produced. Her fingers trembled so, she could barely write. McCauley. For the moment, her name was McCauley. She had given up the Cameron name to save her Cameron birthright.

The priest's wife managed to produce a little glass of sherry for them each. She chatted. She wanted to believe that it was a love match.

Jeremy tossed down the sherry, tipped his hat, paid the priest, and grabbed Christa's hand. They mounted their horses and raced like the wind into the town and down the street to the courthouse.

There, Jeremy produced their wedding certificate with the ink scarcely dry. He paid the hundred and fifty dollars and signed his name. A harried clerk assured them that the property could not be touched. Jeremy had gained a certain reputation as a cavalry commander. No one could deny that he was a stalwart Yankee.

Christa stood by his side tensely waiting as he filled out several documents.

Then he straightened.

It was over. Christa turned and hurried out of the courthouse into the yard, Jeremy following.

They stood in the yard and he stared at Christa, his silver eyes hard and enigmatic.

"Are you happy now?"

"Of course."

"You've lied under oath." Why were those eyes of his so damned condemning?

She tossed back her hair. "I would have wed the devil for the Hall," she told him coolly. "And I am going to hell when I die. You've already told me so."

He shook his head, his lip curling into a small, mocking smile. "Oh, no, Christa. I didn't say a thing about death. You're going to live in hell right now. But let's see, you would have married the devil—or old fur-faced Bobby-boy," he reminded her. "But I think fur-face might have been preferable to me. In your eyes, madam, you have married the devil, haven't you?"

"A Yankee devil," she agreed. It was already done. Why was he torturing her now?

"A Yankee devil," he repeated smoothly.

She lowered her lashes quickly, reminding herself that she was supposed to be grateful.

"I—I'm sorry," she managed to mutter. "I truly appreciate your help."

Her gaze was lowered, but she felt his, silver and steel, burning over her.

"My, my!" he murmured. "You're sorry that you called me a devil—or you're sorry that you married one?"

Her gaze rose quickly to his. He laughed with true amusement. "Never mind, don't answer that. Well then, let's see, the wedding is over and done with.

Cameron Hall is free and clear from all liens, and cannot be sold to anyone for any reason. No one can torch it. So, where does that leave us? Dinner, I think."

"I'm not—really hungry," she murmured. She wanted to get home. To Cameron Hall—and away from him.

"I am. I'm starved."

She looked down at the ground. All right. They were here, he was hungry. She'd have to have dinner with him.

"Fine. Let's find somewhere to eat," she said, attempting to be gracious.

Her impatience was still clear in her voice. Jeremy seemed amused. He didn't give a damn if she was impatient or not.

There was a small inn down the street. Jeremy was determined to annoy her, telling their waiter that they were newlyweds, ordering champagne and the chef's special roast beef.

Christa forced herself to keep a dry smile on her lips. She wasn't going to let Jeremy's mockery disturb her.

"Let's see. To you—Mrs. McCauley." He hadn't addressed her so as yet. He rolled the words on his tongue bitterly. Still, he raised his glass to hers.

She lifted her glass in return. "To Cameron Hall," she retorted sweetly.

He tossed back his champagne. "And to all that we have done in its sacred honor!"

"Be that way, then!" she whispered fiercely across the table. "I don't care!"

"Just so long as I came in the nick of time, right?" he asked her, pouring more champagne.

She arched a brow to him. For the first time in the long day, she was suddenly curious as to how he had happened to be there at just the right time.

"What are you doing in Virginia?" she asked him, trying to sound polite and interested.

He set his glass down, watching her. "I came to say good-bye to Callie."

"Good-bye?" she said. "Where are you going?"

He waved a hand in the air. "West," he said simply.

She frowned. "But the war is over—"

"Yes, the war is over," he said, leaning back. "And my neighbors are all maimed, my fields are filled with decaying corpses in blue and gray. Your brothers fought on different sides. You should understand. Maryland's loyalties were split in two. Maybe some people can go home. I can't. Not yet, anyway."

She was startled to feel a certain empathy. Just how well did she know the man? It had been a long war. Like Jesse and Daniel, he had been in the first fighting, and in the last. He sounded bone weary. For a moment, she understood.

She picked up her champagne glass again. She suddenly determined that they could, at the very least, manage to get through one dinner together.

"You'll stay in the military?" she asked him.

"I was always regular army, so I'm retaining my rank. Some promotions were only valid while the war was going on, but I'll remain a colonel. So for the time being, I have determined I'll stay, yes. I'm bringing a regiment to one of the forts in the western territories. There's a lot of land to be had in the West."

"Indian territory?"

He nodded.

"You'll be going to war again."

"I hope not."

"But the Indians are all savages."

"Not all of them. Some of them are quite civilized. Especially when compared with . . ."

His voice trailed away.

"With Rebels?" she inquired icily.

His gaze settled on her. "No, Christa, that's not what I was about to say."

"What were you about to say, then?"

"That they are quite civilized when compared with some white men—and I wasn't thinking white northern men or white southern men—just white men."

She looked down at her plate. She had hardly eaten. Actually, she was hungry. She had been hungry a long time.

"You need to eat more," he commented, his gaze steadily on her as he poured more champagne.

For some reason, the comment hurt. Was she that gaunt? Was he implying that she was a skinny shell of an old maid? She smiled. "Maybe I do. But we southerners are accustomed to starving. Just as you Feds are accustomed to wolfing down our food," she said politely.

He set down the champagne bottle. Something that had begun to glow warm in his eyes turned chill once again. "Truly, Lord, I have been blessed!" he stated, and continued, "Starve then, Christa, if that's your pleasure."

She lowered her lashes again. She didn't mean to strike out with so much venom so quickly. She had been fighting too long. She had spent too many years fearing all blue uniforms other than Jesse's.

"I—"

"What?" he demanded.

"I'm sorry."

He was silent for a moment. Again, she felt him watching her. Currents of lightning seemed to riddle the air between them again. She had to quit being so antagonistic. Maybe he hadn't wanted to help her, but he had done so.

She was startled when his fingers curled over hers. "It was a damned long war, wasn't it?"

There was gentleness in his tone. She didn't want to hear it. She snatched back her hand.

"I would really love to get back to the house," she murmured uneasily. "I'm exhausted."

"It's a long ride back. We should stay here."

"No! Well, you can stay, Jeremy. I can't. I've got to go home. To make sure —to make sure it's still standing."

She felt Jeremy looking at her. He made no comment. He called for their bill and paid it. Christa watched in silence as he doled out the Yankee bills.

Dear God, but the world had changed quickly! Not so very long ago they had all mocked the Yankees.

Now even the southerners were scrambling for Yankee money, using their Confederate bills for the fodder and tinder they were worth!

She rose when he pulled back her chair, straightening her shoulders. "If you'd rather stay in Williamsburg for the night, I'll understand."

"No."

"I'm perfectably capable of riding home—"

"No."

"Really—"

"Christa, dammit, if you were a bare acquaintance, I'd see you home. And you're not a bare acquaintance. I'd hardly let my wife travel the night road alone."

She thought that she might be safer alone than with him. She wasn't quite sure what she had done to start his temper seething, but his mood seemed to be growing darker.

"Suit yourself," she told him.

He led the way back home. It was a long, hard ride. They rode it in near silence.

Halfway along the trail Jeremy glanced back, wondering with some concern if she had fallen asleep, if she was in danger of falling from her mount.

But Christa was in no danger. They raised horses at Cameron Hall. She'd probably ridden before she had walked and she was an excellent horsewoman. She sat easily in her saddle, but her lashes were low.

It had been one hell of a long day, he thought. And now, to finish it. He had a day or two before reporting back in Washington. He'd wait until he could get word to Callie to say good-bye, then he'd be on his way. He was sure that Christa could manage to get a divorce or an annulment. It might take some time, but then he didn't really care. He'd be in the West, and though Christa couldn't possibly know it, he'd buried his own heart in the ashes of the war. She was more than welcome to take her time ending their mockery of a marriage.

Suddenly he remembered the wedding ceremony. Remembered her vows, remembered his. Why had he agreed to this? She was his wife. Legally. It was an entanglement that would take years to end. And all of his life, he had imagined that marriage would mean love and commitment for a lifetime.

He locked his jaw. She'd done it for a house. And whether she really realized it or not, the house was Jesse's.

It would serve her right if I held her to her vows! he thought. She was always so damned determined to have things her way.

They came upon Cameron Hall in the moonlight. He reined in absently. It was a beautiful place. The red brick and the white columns rose majestically in the glowing light. It sat atop its knoll before the James like a castle.

Maybe that's what it had been, Jeremy speculated, before the war. Christa had ruled here like a goddess. People had attended to her every whim. Her older brothers adored her. And most certainly, young men had swarmed around her. She was probably accustomed to having her every wish obeyed. She had certainly expected *him* to do as she wished with no objection.

Marriage!

The word chilled him for a moment and he felt his temper rising. Ah, yes, Christa liked to pull strings. She'd pulled his, all right.

He didn't know why it suddenly sat with him so poorly. She hadn't said a word along the ride, but he had felt his temper start to grow at the restaurant.

"It's standing!" she said with relief. Behind him, she suddenly nudged her horse, and went galloping down the drive. She rode like the wind, one with the horse. He grit his teeth, then followed her.

She had already dismounted from her horse when he reached the front of the house. Yes, the house was still standing. She twirled before him, as smooth as silk, as pleased as a cat with a bird. "Thank God!"

"Indeed."

She didn't seem to notice his tone. She dropped her horse's reins. "Jeremy, why don't you see to the horses!" she commanded rather than asked and went tearing toward the house.

"Yes, ma'am!" he murmured. His voice was low. There was an edge to it, and she heard it.

Catching up her skirts, she suddenly turned toward him.

"The guest room is always kept ready for company," she said hurriedly. "You know where it is, right? Third room down the hall to the left."

"I know where it is. I stayed there several times," he told her, dismounting from his own horse. By then, one of the stable hands had appeared, and Jeremy quickly turned the horses over to the lad.

"Rub them down good, will you? They've had a hard ride," he told the boy. Christa was starting up the stairs. He realized that she intended to leave him out here in the moonlight.

Cameron Hall was standing. She seemed to have forgotten all that he had done to keep it that way.

His teeth grated. What was he going to do?

He was tired of being called a Yank and tired of being used. She could have things her way, but she was going to pay the price. He'd never forced a woman into anything, and he knew that Christa would fight him like a wildcat.

Maybe he wanted the fight tonight.

He didn't want to take anything from her. He just wanted her to know that she couldn't enter into any bargains—especially not with him, dirty Yank that he was—without paying some price.

"Christa!" he called after her. "I think you'd best wait a minute," he told her. He wasn't tired in the least. He was angry. Maybe if she had managed to be grateful he wouldn't feel quite so irritated. He just felt as if he wanted to shake her, and the longer she looked at him as if he were the hired help, the more irritated he became.

"Jeremy, I'm very tired," she said. It was definitely a "mistress-of-the-house" type voice she leveled at him. He had done his duty. He was dismissed.

Not so easy, Miss Cameron.

His fingers knotted into fists. Yes. Let it be that easy. Say good night.

He didn't want to hurt her.

But neither did he want to let her walk away. Jesu! She had forced him into a marriage.

She stood regally beneath the moonlight, aware that he was watching her again, his hands on his hips.

Christa stared at him in turn, wondering at the twist of his jaw. "Oh!" she murmured. "Thank you, Jeremy. Really. And good night," Christa said and started for the house.

But when she started walking, Jeremy caught hold of her arm, spinning her back in such a way that she plowed right into his arm, her fingers splayed upon his chest while his hold then encompassed her. Her eyes widened with protest, but before she could speak, Jeremy did so, tauntingly. "No, no!" he warned softly. "Where do you think you're going?"

"I—I'm tired. I'm going to bed."

"Just like that?"

She stared at him and shook her head blankly. "It's over now."

"Over? It's just beginning! You're not going anywhere."

"I don't know what you're talking about. I'm going to bed."

He smiled slowly, shaking his head. "I don't think so."

Christa pursed her lips, feeling her temper flaring. "Who the hell do you think you are? You're not my brother, or my father—"

"But I am your husband now!" he snapped. "Dammit, don't you even remember what you did? You married me!"

So this was the way that he wanted to play it. She'd cajoled him into it, and he just wasn't going to be a gentleman about the whole thing. He wanted to make her suffer. Somehow. It was payback time.

Her temper flared. She was ready for battle again. "If I choose to go to bed, sir, I will do so!"

"Always the princess!"

"I'll do what I damned well please!"

"Have it your way, then," Jeremy said softly, and his eyes seemed very silver, cutting into hers like sword blades. "You will go to bed, Christa. But not alone."

"What?" she whispered in return, stunned. "What?" she repeated, both her amazement and her fury clearly discernible in her tone.

"Lady, you forced me into this. You were willing to sell everything, both of our souls, for Jesse's house. Well, we saved it. Jesse will come back to claim it. But you forced me to be a husband. Now, Mrs. McCauley, I'm afraid that I'm going to have to force you to be a wife!"

Her eyes widened still further. She wanted to strike him. Slap that taunting, mocking curl from his lip, the hard silver glitter from his eyes.

She pressed with a greater fervor against his chest. "Don't be absurd!" she hissed. "You can't mean—"

"Oh, but Christa," he interrupted her. His voice was low and husky and filled with a ring of steel. "That's exactly what I mean!"

Suddenly his fingers were threaded through her hair, pulling her head back, forcing her eyes to his. She saw the hard, handsome cast of his face, the rock-firm set of his jaw, and a sudden chill seized her.

"You married me, Christa. Marriage! It was a serious step. I warned you. As the saying goes, madam, you've made your bed. You're going to lie in it. You understand what I mean, Christa. I know you do."

She shook her head violently, freeing her hair from his fingers. Yes, she knew. She just couldn't believe what he was saying. Leave it to a Yankee! He couldn't just be pleased that they had saved the house. Oh, no. He wanted a real marriage. It was impossible. For many reasons—not excepting the fact that they could scarcely stand being in the same room with one another!

She swallowed hard and grated her teeth. "Leave it to a no-good Yankee varmint of a man to try to take the term 'husband' literally!" she whispered furiously. "This has to be a marriage in name only. I accept Jesse because he's my brother, but on the whole, Jeremy McCauley, I can't abide Yankees, and even if you weren't a Yankee, I'm not so sure I could abide you! All that aside, you're still in the cavalry. You'll be riding west."

"Then, Christa, my dear wife—and, yes! I do take that term literally!—then you will lie with me in the West." His face lowered toward hers, the silver gray of his eyes alive in a taunting sizzle. "I have a bad time abiding certain Rebels, Christa, and I'd have to say that you're right there among them. But this isn't going to be a marriage in name only."

She stared into his eyes and something hot raced through her. Something that seemed to touch her inside and out. Something that made her knees feel weak and her lips go dry. He meant to touch her. To have her. To do all the things that husbands and wives did together. Tonight. She was quite certain that she hated him, but suddenly she was imagining his bronze hands against her bare flesh. That hard, taut-muscled body against her own. Those curving, sensual lips pressed to her throat.

She couldn't breathe. Her heart beat painfully, and fire seemed to rage throughout her. She caught his gaze upon her, and suddenly she knew that he felt it too. It was hatred, it was anger, she thought.

It didn't matter what it was, it was explosive and it was frightening.

She shook her head again, desperate to find words. "No!" It should have been a cry of defiance and of rage.

But she hadn't the breath for it. It was a whisper. Barely a protest.

Because those silver eyes were on her. He spoke again in a voice that was shiver soft, and with an underlying current of rock. "Let me remind you. You did this. You begged, pleaded, and cajoled me into marrying you. I have done so. You said that you would pay any price. Well, my love, it's time to pay that price!"

She found her strength at last. Found strength and courage.

"You must be insane!" she hissed. "I am not bedding down with any Yankee vermin!"

"Even the vermin who saved your precious house?"

"The war is over!" she said desperately.

"No." He shook his head. There was challenge in his eyes, a wry grin that bitterly mocked them both curling into his lips once again. "No, Christa, you insisted on drawing fire. This war has just begun!"

Before she knew it, he had swept her into his arms. He carried her up the steps of the porch and burst through the front door. He reached the grand staircase leading to the second-floor bedrooms before she realized that he really intended to carry her up.

"Put me down!" she gasped, trying hard to struggle within his arms. "Dammit, I don't know what is the matter with you Yankees. You're done, you're finished, don't you understand!"

Done and finished? Jeremy wasn't really sure what he had been intending himself. Just a delivery to her bedroom door, perhaps. But suddenly all the anger that had been simmering inside all day came swiftly flying to the surface with her curt dismissal. All he knew at the moment was that Christa wasn't walking away from what she had done by throwing a blanket at him.

He was dimly aware that they passed the portrait gallery at the top of the stairs. Generations of Camerons looked down upon him. If he could have thrown a blanket somewhere, he would have liked to toss it over those faces.

He didn't need to hesitate in the hallway. He'd been a guest here three times now. Jesse and Kiernan's room was at the top of the stairs. Daniel and Callie's was farther to the right. The nursery was down at that end.

Christa's door was to the left.

Her fingers were burning into his arms as he kicked the door open with a boot. She was struggling so fiercely that he felt as if he was carrying a squirming greased pig.

She was going on and on, with every single word she uttered feeding fuel to the flames of his temper. She called him a small-time farmer, no-account white trash, and of course the very worst of them to her—a Yankee. "Who on earth would even think—oh! Leave it to a Yankee! Leave it to a Yankee!"

He didn't need light in the bedroom. The gas light poured in from the hallway, and a full moon was still up, casting a golden glow upon everything in the room. It was the first time he had actually entered the regal sanctity of Christa's room—the first time he had ever thought to do so.

It was beautiful. The bed was canopied with a white curtain and spread. There were huge wingback chairs by the sheer drapes that fluttered by the windows. A beautifully polished cherrywood writing table gleamed in the moonlight.

He walked her across the room suddenly aware that she had been pummeling and clawing him all the way. He tossed her down on the bed, leaning over her and pinioning her there.

Her eyes with their glittering blue fire and ice met his with a wild fury.

Her mouth was opening. She was going to say something about Yankees again.

"What?" he thundered before she could speak. "Rebels don't sleep with their wives, is that it, Christa?"

Her eyes widened. For once she seemed tongue-tied.

But only momentarily.

"You're no better than that fur-faced blue-belly who came here—"

"The one you said you'd be willing to marry?" he demanded quickly.

Even in the moonlight, he saw the flush steal over her face.

"If you don't let me up—"

"Oh, you're going to get up," he assured her. His hands were on her waist and she was on her feet. He spun her around, his hands on the tiny hooks at the base of her spine. "I just sold my soul. I want to see what great and outstanding Rebel beauty I've achieved for my efforts."

He wasn't sure exactly what he wanted, and he wasn't sure himself exactly how far he meant to go with her. Maybe he had just intended to remind her that she was living now on his bounty, and that if she was lucky, he would be magnanimous.

But he never had a chance to be magnanimous.

She jerked violently away from him. It was her mistake. The worn fabric of her day dress ripped with a loud tearing sound and came away in his hands. She hadn't been wearing any of her multitude of petticoats that day, nor a corset. Her torn day dress slipped down the length of her one undergarment, a soft chemise left over from the days of glory. The fabric was cotton, elegant, sheer cotton. The straps were wispy and it was ribbed with lace. It molded her breasts, a garment that was soft, elusive, sensual, clinging to her waist, then flaring free— and sheer—to the floor. It did little to shield the rouge-colored crests of her nipples, nor did it do anything other than add mystery to the ebony-dark triangle at the juncture of her thighs. It emphasized her slender beauty in the glow of the moon. For a moment he stood still, looking at her.

It was impossible not to want her. She might have indeed been a goddess, created to be desired.

He started, drawn instantly from such retrospect as her hand cracked hard across his jaw. The sound echoed and echoed in the night.

Even Christa seemed surprised by it. She backed away from him, stumbling over the dress that had fallen to the floor.

"I—I—" she gasped, then she cried out, "You are a detestable Yank! Even married couples use dressing screens. Men turn their backs for their wives to change. They maintain decorum—"

"Decorum!" Jeremy interrupted. Despite the nagging pain that still stung his cheek, wry amusement tinged his anger. "You think that your brother makes love to my sister with decorum? For her sake, I hope the hell not!" With those words, he traveled the two steps between them. He didn't know what he was after.

He caught her shoulders, drawing her to him. He lifted a hand to her chin, cupping it.

His lips touched hers.

You may now kiss the bride.

The words echoed mockingly in his mind, then faded away. Christa protested. A strangled sound escaped her. She struggled against the rock-hard hold of his body.

In all his years of warfare, he had never felt more merciless. She'd married him. She could damn well kiss him.

But that wasn't why he had touched her. And it wasn't why he kept touching her.

Her lips were full and beautiful, the taste of them was sweet. More than that, the passion that filled her trembled there, within her lips, her mouth. Maybe it was the passion of hatred. That didn't seem to matter. Maybe it was the passion of his own anger. That didn't matter either. He wanted to kiss her, wanted to taste that sweetness. He didn't give a damn if she was protesting. His fingers curled into her hair, holding her to his will. His tongue broke through the restraint of her lips, forced her teeth, discovered the fullness of her mouth. Still the taste was so sweet. It seemed the smothered protests were being swallowed away as he held her.

Maybe it was more than her lips that spurred him on. The first time that he had seen her, he had been startled by her beauty, perhaps even a bit captivated by it. He could remember just staring at her and forgetting where he was and what he had come for.

Once again, he discovered himself startled, captivated.

Beneath the sheer fabric of her ribbed and laced chemise, he could feel the sensual curve and shape of her body. Full breasts crushed against his chest. Despite them, he could feel the wild pounding of her heart. Her legs were long and shapely, nearly entwined with his. He could feel the flatness of her stomach, and even the rise of her femininity, for he had crushed her very hard against him. The taste, the scent, the feel of her, all were suddenly blinding.

And suddenly so arousing that he could think no more. Her hair was silk to his touch. Her body was fire. He could forget pain touching her. He could forget the war. Forget love, and the dreams that had been cast to ashes. No matter that it was a passion born of anger, Christa seethed with it. She was raw and exciting to touch. More than her beauty made her arousing. The electricity that shimmered from her and around her evoked a shattering burst of desire within him. It made him long to drink and drink of her lips. To savor the sweet taste of her mouth. To delve further and further within it. As the seconds passed it seemed that she ceased to protest. Perhaps her body yielded to his. Perhaps her lips surrendered, parted of their own accord.

Let her go! he warned himself.

His mistake. He should have never come so far. Kissed her so. Taken her so into his arms.

She broke away from him suddenly. The back of her hand flew to her swollen lips. Her blue eyes were liquid as she gazed at him.

"You've no right!" she choked out.

He shook his head. "No, Christa. You had no right to slap me. I have every right to be here. You married me, remember? You insisted on it."

She bit her lower lip. Blue flames seemed to leap from her eyes. He crossed his arms over his chest. He might have been amused if he didn't feel as if he were suffering all the torments of hell.

"But you can't mean—"

"I don't know what I mean. I just want to see this incredible piece of southern fluff I've acquired."

"How dare you—"

"Take care, Christa. Get to know the enemy you've harnessed. I dare quite a bit. Let's go. I'll have the chemise—*Mrs. McCauley.*"

If she'd had a gun at that moment he was quite sure she would have shot him.

"Why, you—" she began.

He shook his head, his lip curling with dry humor. "Watch it, Mrs. McCauley."

"Why should I bother?"

"If you act the dutiful wife, I might decide to go away."

"And if I don't?"

"Well, the dress is in tatters. The chemise can follow the same route."

Her eyes narrowed. "You wouldn't."

"Want to try me? I am a Yank, after all. You need to keep that in mind."

She lifted her chin. "You can talk that way tonight, but if Jesse or Daniel were here—"

There was nothing she could have said to quite test his temper so far. His hand shot out, his fingers winding around her wrist. In a second she was in front of him again. "Don't threaten me with your brothers, Christa. Ever. Not unless you like the thought of more bloodshed. You married me. I warned you that you were selling both our souls to the devil. Jesse and Daniel are your brothers. Your name is McCauley now. I'm your husband. And so help me, Christa, you caused it, you'll remember it!"

He didn't mean to hurt her. He didn't mean to be destructive. His fingers gripped the bodice of her chemise at the cleft between her breasts. Alarmed, she tried to wrench free again. The fabric began to tear and she stopped, furious, shaking. She wrenched the garment over her head, throwing it at him.

"Bastard!" she cried. "Take the damned thing!" He was blinded by a cloud of white fabric as she started by him.

He threw it savagely aside, long strides bringing him to her. He caught hold of her elbow, swirled her around, and swept her into his arms. He cast her, naked, defiant, and trembling, onto her bed. Before she could think to spring to her feet he had straddled her, his weight bearing her down.

She was pure rebellion, staring up at him. A flush of color had risen to her cheeks, but her eyes were wild and furious and challenging.

Pure rebellion—and beauty. Her hair spilled about her like a black cloud, her lips were still red and moist from his kiss. Her coloring, even in moonlight, was glorious. Her naked breasts and flesh were radiant and beautiful. Heat cascaded from her in great waves. It seemed to touch him. To sweep into his body, constrict his muscles, quicken his pulse. The heat entered into his hips and his loins, and he was stunned by the savage and volatile way in which he wanted her.

He clenched his teeth hard together. He could walk away from her. Damn her, he could walk away from her!

She started to struggle. "Stop!" he warned her with a roar. He pushed back while she seethed, trying to remain still, her lower lip caught between her teeth, her breasts rising and falling with her exertion, her eyes alive with fire and vengeance.

He allowed his gaze to flicker over her. Not too slowly. A quick assessment.

"Well?" she flared. He could hear the grating of her teeth beneath the word.

He leaned close to her. "I think, Christa, that you are well aware of your own attributes. But are you payment enough for the price of a soul?" he murmured.

He felt her begin to tremble more fiercely. He pushed away from her, furious with her and with himself. He rose. He saw her eyes widen with amazement. She inched up quickly, grabbing for the coverings on her bed. He bowed to her. "My dear."

"You're leaving?" she said quickly.

"For the moment."

"But what—" She paused, moistening her lips. He could see her pride battling with her absolute relief that he seemed about to let her be.

"You'll do, Christa. But hell, I think I need a drink!" He turned and started for the door.

To his amazement, he was hit by a pillow. "Oh, you bastard!" she cried as he spun around. "This whole thing was just to torture me, to humiliate me, to strip me of my modesty—"

He walked back to her quickly, catching hold of her even as she shrieked, pulling her back up into his arms. "Christa, I can't strip you of what you've already given up. You said you would have married the blue-belly who would have raped you, so don't ask me to think too highly of your modesty. Maybe I did want to torment you." And God alive! I tormented myself! he added silently. "But there's more to it than that. You married me. You didn't care to first find out what it would mean. Well, it's done now. And you're going to find out that it does mean something! But for the moment, good night!"

He set her down. She sank back to the bed, her eyes spitting fire.

But when he left her this time, she was silent. Hatefully silent. Even as he walked away, he could feel the fire in her eyes.

Just who had taken whom tonight, he wondered.

For Christa might well lie awake worried.

But he was suffering the tortures of the damned.

Four

*J*eremy came down the stairway with tense, heavy footfalls, trying once again to ignore the numerous Camerons who seemed to be still staring at him from their frames with silent reproach. He didn't want to see any more Camerons. The memory of Christa, naked and furious, seemed to be branded within his mind, and she was enough Cameron for him at the moment. He could still feel the sparks that had seemed to leap from her, like streaks of electricity. Christa in all her glory. All that magnificent black Cameron hair streaming down her back, every curve and nuance of her perfect young body.

Her eyes. Those blue fire-and-ice eyes. Revenge? Indeed, he'd had a taste of it. And it was sweet.

Then why was he the one so aflame now, the one suffering the pain of the damned? What a fool. How the hell could he want her so badly now? When there was nothing but hostility between them, after this travesty of a marriage, how could he have come to this position?

He reached the Camerons' study and burst irritably into it, lighting the gas light above the desk and sinking into the chair behind that desk. He poured himself a brandy from the decanter on a side table, then leaned back in the chair, swallowing it down, wincing at the fire that seared his throat. He didn't dare close his eyes, and he didn't dare open them. He saw her either way.

Christa. Naked. Maybe emotions didn't mean anything after so long a war, and so long a time since emotions had meant something. Maybe the wanting was just enough. Christa was perfect. Tall, slim, a little bit too thin, but not even the war could have taken too much a toll upon the natural dips and curves of her body. Her naked flesh was a beautiful ivory shade and it had the sweetest scent and the most inviting appeal.

He exhaled on a long groan.

He should have left her the hell alone.

He didn't know what force or demon was driving him tonight, he knew only that she had goaded him to a point where she was going to pay a price for what she had forced upon them.

If Christa Cameron thought it was an easy thing to twist and bend people to her will at her convenience, he was damned sorry, but she was going to have to see that her actions had serious repercussions.

Marriage. It had come so easily to her. Just a slip off her tongue. No more than a trip into town, an afternoon's escapade, easily done, easily forgotten.

In truth, she hadn't cared. Hadn't given a damn about his situation, just so long as she had gotten what she wanted, to protect the sacred halls of Cameron Hall.

Not that he resented having done something to salvage the place. Perhaps Christa had been right about one thing. The Hall was history. It was beautiful, gracious, a monument to centuries of a family that had found roots and flourished in a new world. Now Cameron Hall had weathered revolution and civil war, and all the trauma in between. It deserved to stand. He could understand her desire to save it, even if he was infuriated by the way she was willing to use him to do so.

Although he had fought all the long years of the war, although there had been times when he had watched his men fall and die and in his heart he had hated all things Rebel, he was disgusted with the way things were being handled in the South. Power was being put into careless hands. Lincoln had wanted peace. But Lincoln was dead, and Johnson's administration was determined not on peace but on punishment. Elections were being rigged, and half the men who had been in politics before the war—those who were still living—were being barred from office for having served with the Confederacy. Daniel Cameron had yet to receive a pardon from the United States government because of his high rank in the military service, and as things stood now, some men wondered if Jeff Davis might yet meet a hangman. But beyond the blatant abuses of power, there were smaller struggles going on. Officials—many of them opportunists who had come down upon the South like locusts—were taking all manner of bribes, selling out to the highest bidders. Such had been the case with Cameron Hall.

Jeremy liked his brother-in-law, Daniel Cameron, just fine. Daniel had been a Virginian born and raised, and there hadn't been a lot of help for the fact that he'd been a Reb. He'd just followed his own conscience. The war hadn't given them a lot of time to deepen their acquaintance, but from what they'd come to know of one another, they shared a common way of looking at the world, at responsibility, at life. And Jeremy's sister, Callie, loved Daniel. That said a lot for him, right there.

Jeremy was glad to have done anything that might have helped Daniel.

He lifted his brandy glass. "To you, Daniel!" The first time he had come here, looking for Callie, he had wound up in this room, drinking brandy with Daniel Cameron. It had been a strange day. He had come here ready to do battle for his sister's sake. He had come here an enemy. He had left here his brother-in-law's friend, even if neither of them had changed his colors.

Then there was Jesse Cameron. He'd had several occasions to get to know Jesse—they'd fought on the same side. Jesse was the finest physician and surgeon he'd ever come across. The war had taken a hell of a toll on him as he'd patched up his friends and old acquaintances—from both sides of the fighting field. In the regular cavalry, Jeremy had ridden in by the hospital tents often enough to see his sister-in-law's elbow deep in the wounded, that anguished look on her face that Jeremy could read too clearly.

Jesse Cameron was always afraid that someone would be bringing his brother in to him.

But the war had ended. Jesse and Daniel had both managed to stay alive.

Jeremy liked them both. It didn't matter which side they had fought on, he had no problem with the Cameron men.

It was the Cameron woman he longed to throttle.

Christa!

Damn her. Men knew how to fight, and they knew how to surrender. For Christa, the war would never be over.

Nor, he thought soberly, would she ever realize that she wasn't the only one to feel that she had lost a love, lost everything, in the carnage. For a moment the pain returned to him, though he thought that he had learned to suppress it a long, long time ago. It returned, harsh, brutal, tearing into his heart.

It had been one thing to see soldiers die. That had been anguish enough. But sometimes fire went awry. Sometimes cannonballs tore up far more than fortress walls or other cannons or fighting men . . .

Sometimes fire killed the innocent. Old men, children.

Women, trying to shelter little ones.

He grit his teeth. Jennifer Morgan had been killed during the long, awful shelling of Vicksburg, Mississippi. It had been over two years ago now. He could still remember how he had found her when the ragged, bone-thin little blockade-running urchin had brought him to her when the city had fallen into Yankee hands. She'd been in the caves beneath the hills. They'd folded her hands over her breast, and she might have been sleeping except for the clot of blood he found at the base of her skull when he'd tried to move her.

Jenny. He hadn't known her a year. He had first met her when his troops had encamped on her farmland and he'd gone to make what restitution he could for the destruction that his men were causing with their tents and multitude of horses. He had expected a haggard farm wife, but that wasn't what he had discovered at all. Jenny had been beautiful. Blond, green-eyed, delicate, and lovely. So very proud, but so sweet and soft-spoken. Three little children had clung to her skirts, and all were threadbare and thin-looking.

Jeremy hadn't just paid for the damage to her crops. He managed to pay her a small fortune for a broach she had. He was going home, and he had needed a gift for Callie.

Callie would take good care of the gift. And with his Yankee dollars, the widowed Mrs. Jenny Morgan—whose husband had been killed at Shiloh— would be able to buy food and clothing for her growing young brood.

Christmas had come and gone.

Jeremy had come back to Mississippi. He'd remained on her land while Grant determined to dig in until Vicksburg fell, no matter what the cost. Grant was the one damned smart general the Union had. He didn't retreat every time a southern force came near him. He knew that he had more of one important thing than any southern general out there—manpower. The Rebs couldn't afford to keep dying. The Union could keep replenishing her fallen forces.

But the war hadn't really mattered between them. They had never been at war with one another.

He didn't know when he had fallen in love with her. Maybe it had been one of those nights when he had stared at her windows so long he hadn't been able to take it anymore. He had mounted up and ridden over, and he had discovered that Jenny Morgan waited up nights for him. The hours of darkness became magic.

Jenny didn't have much interest in politics. But she had been born a Mississippian and she cared deeply about what was happening to the people around her. Jeremy never knew that she intended to go into Vicksburg along with her children *despite* his words of warning while the Union continued its siege of the city. She could help with the soldiers in the hospital.

Jeremy explained the futility of her wishes, and she listened to him. While war pounded on around them, they formed a curious domesticity. The children loved him, and loved to pick his pockets when he came. Jeremy and she were on different sides of the upheaval, but Jenny, though she wouldn't say the words, didn't believe that the Confederacy could win the war.

Jeremy was ordered to take his company on a reconnaissance ride around the perimeters of Vicksburg. As it happened, the maneuver took them days. When he returned, Jenny was gone, leaving behind a note that she loved him and that she'd marry him as soon as the siege at Vicksburg was over. She was expecting their child in autumn.

When she was gone, he realized just how much he loved her. He tried to get word into the city to make sure she was all right. There were Union spies moving in and out, so it wasn't very difficult to discover her whereabouts. She was with many other citizens of the city, living in caves below the hills because so many of the houses had been hit with cannon and shell fire. The caves were the only place to avoid fire.

It was a terrible ordeal for the citizens of Vicksburg. The Union spies who returned shook their heads wearily at his questions. There was no food to be had in the city. Those who remained were cooking the rats that scurried among the refuse.

His heart sickened and he wrote her a long letter, begging her to come out. Yes, he wanted her. Yes, he loved her. He wanted their child, and he wanted to be a father to her other children. He didn't want her in Vicksburg. She needed to take the children, marry him, and find somewhere to live safely.

Somewhere where neither army came.

Days passed. A spy brought a letter back to him. He was grateful. He knew the man had put his life at risk. The letter was filled with Jenny's words, with her enthusiasm and empathy for all men, with all the beautiful things that had made him fall so completely in love with her.

She was unique. He hadn't lived so very long—he'd just turned twenty-four at the start of the war—but he'd put some mileage into those years. He came from a family of hardworking farmers. They were not rich but his father had earned a wealth of friendship and respect in his dealings, and he'd seen to it that all his sons had gone to West Point.

Once he'd graduated, he'd served some time in the West, riding hard on the Santa Fe Trail. He'd seen some action, enough to test his mettle under fire. He'd been initiated into battle fighting Indians, and he'd come to know a fair amount about a number of the tribes, from the civilized and fascinatingly cultured to the very savage and warlike.

He'd seen some other action in the West with the camp ladies who managed to trail behind any army. He'd even been growing serious about the daughter of an army major, but something had been lacking and so he'd backed away.

Once he realized just how deeply he cared for Jenny, he learned what had been missing. Love. She was, indeed, unique. Sweet and dignified. And strong, too, he realized. She pretended to bow to him in all things, then she went her own way.

She would not come out of Vicksburg. She had learned how to meet one of the blockade runners on the river, and she was determined to be of help to the citizens in the city. She could bring in food and morphine for the children.

She had been dead a long time now.

He had come in the very day the city had fallen. He had watched the women weeping in the streets as the blue-clad forces had marched through. He had felt the southerners' hatred.

He had ignored them all, demanding directions to the caves.

He had found her. She had been struck by a stray bullet just two nights before the surrender of the city.

She had died within twenty-four hours.

No one in the cave had said anything about his blue uniform. Maybe his grief had been that naked. Jenny's beautiful blond children had offered him more comfort than he had offered them. He had taken her into his arms, held her dead body. He had laid his palm over her belly, where their child had died with her. He had not wanted to give her up.

A woman like Jenny had stood in the entry to the makeshift home in the cliffs. He had looked up, his eyes glittering with his pain. "I can take the children. I'll adopt them if they'll have me, I'll find some place—"

"Sir, Vicksburg will be safe enough now," the woman said. "We've surrendered. The children will be safe with me. I'm Jenny's sister, and I've lost my husband and my only boy."

He could remember nodding. He could remember stumbling to his feet, still holding Jenny's body.

"She did love you," the woman told him. "And she knew that you loved her. She was happy about the new one, and it didn't give her any mind whatsoever that it was a Yank fathered her babe, she loved you that much. You put her down now. We've got to bury her."

Jenny was buried; Vicksburg was secured. Jeremy was transferred back to the East, whether he wanted to fight there or not. Grant was determined to trap the wily Lee, and it didn't matter what it took. He would lose battles, and he would lose men. He'd fight again, and he'd draft more men.

There was one benefit to being assigned back to the East. He'd have a chance to see Callie. He had been so angry with Callie when he'd first discovered she was about to have a Reb's child, and she was not married to that Reb. He might well have fathered a southern child himself. It opened a wealth of understanding. He had been so anxious to see her.

But he discovered that Callie had been spirited down south by that Reb and so he had come to Cameron Hall for the first time. He had come to know Daniel and Christa. The beautiful blue-eyed witch upstairs. The one who had married him, condemning him, hating him.

"To you, Christa!" he murmured, swallowing down another two-finger swig of brandy. He was certain she had sat at this very desk often enough, sipping brandy—or swigging it down—just as he was now. It was a fine old office with the massive desk and rows of books. The ledgers and all the books were kept here. And once, Jeremy was certain, gentlemen would have retired here in the midst of a party for brandy or whiskey and cigars and talk. Politics. Animal husbandry. Things in which the women wouldn't be interested.

Until the war had taken away the men and left the women.

For a moment, a heartbeat of pity slipped its way into his heart. She had managed well enough. She had a right to love the place. Working like a field hand, she had kept it standing. And she had fought for it. When Eric Dabney's Yankee raiders—out to bring Daniel in dead or alive—had come sneaking around the place, Christa had been armed and ready. She had shot a man in defense of herself and Kiernan and Callie. She hadn't killed him, but she hadn't hesitated to pull the trigger when she had been threatened. She was a fighter.

Pity. Because she was going to lose the place. The house belonged to Jesse.

He smiled suddenly. He *should* make her come west with him. She was a fighter; she had magnificent courage.

And she was beautiful. And desirable.

He set his glass down, sobering. The western plains were really no place for a woman, any woman. Some of the men did bring their wives, but those wives loved their husbands.

The West was wild, primitive, dangerous, savage. Then again, Christa was all those things too! Heaven help the Indians she got her hands on.

Somewhere in the house, a clock struck. He counted the chimes. Midnight.

It was his wedding night. He had imagined it so differently. He'd imagined laughter and caring, and making love deep into the night. He'd imagined sleeping with golden blond streams of hair tangled all over his naked flesh. He'd imagined her smile and her welcome, touching her stomach to feel their child grow.

"Anything! Anything but sitting alone in the Camerons' plantation office, sipping brandy."

It probably wasn't what Christa had imagined either, he reminded himself. Maybe it was worse for her. She'd been engaged, she'd waited.

Callie had written Jeremy when they'd all heard the news that Liam McCloskey was dead. She had told him how they had all dyed their wedding finery black. Christa hadn't mentioned her fiancé's name today, not once.

He stood up suddenly.

She wasn't going to sleep alone. One didn't marry an ebony-haired enchantress and sleep in the guest room—even if she was a shrew!

He took one more swig of brandy. He sighed out loud, lifting his glass again to the air. "To all of us poor wretches!" he said. He smashed the glass against the fireplace, left the room behind him, and started up the stairs.

The damned Camerons looked at him again from the portrait gallery along the upper stairway. This time he paused and looked back.

"Not a damned word out of a one of you! She's my wife."

The word sounded so damned strange in connection with Christa.

He walked purposefully past the portraits and to her room. The door was closed. He entered the room and closed the door behind him.

Moonlight streamed in on the canopied bed. He walked to it and looked down at her.

She had fallen asleep. Another woman might have cried herself to sleep, but he doubted that Christa had done so. She lay on her stomach, and the covers were pulled just to the small of her back. The beautiful curve of it was plainly visible in the moon glow. Black hair spilled all around her, and her fingers were curled just below her chin. Her lashes swept her cheeks. He reached out and touched her face, wondering if he didn't feel just a bit of dampness there, just a hint of tears.

"But this is it!" he said to her softly in the moonlight. "This is what you wanted!"

He sat at the foot of the bed and pulled off his boots. She must have been really exhausted—she didn't even stir. He watched her face all the while that he stripped off his uniform, folding it neatly, piece by piece, and setting it upon her dressing table. He crawled in beside her, not touching her. He stared up at the ceiling, then swore silently at himself once again.

He knew damned well he'd never intended to rape her in her sleep, so what the hell did he think he was accomplishing by being here? He was on fire again, from head to toe. He had tried to pull the covers over his body, and now the damned sheet was rising, just as if there were a ghost down in the center of the bed. It was impossible to lie beside her and not want her.

Remember Jenny! he told himself fiercely. Remember what it should have been. Remember Christa's words. The way that she says "Yankee" as if it were the filthiest word in the English language.

It didn't work. He was as hard as a poker, and with the sheet flying up he felt like a flagstaff.

Well, he wasn't getting up. They were married, and whether there was anything between them or not, he was suddenly determined that they were going to sleep like a married couple tonight.

She was his enemy, as no man had ever been.

But she was also soft and supple. Her flesh was silk, and he could just feel the whisper of it against his own. He turned slightly and her hair teased his nose, smelling like roses, feeling like a swatch of velvet.

He turned his back on her, making sure that their flesh didn't touch. He slammed his fist against his pillow.

He started to count sheep.

It was damned funny.

No, it was torture.

But thank God for brandy, for long endless days, for total exhaustion. Toward morning, he slept at last.

He usually awoke easily, at the slightest sound. All those years of sleeping on the field in tents, alert to the slightest danger, had done something to his ability to sleep deeply.

But that night he slept as if he were dead.

And oddly enough, he had beautiful dreams. He was in some meadow, somewhere. Maryland, probably. He had always loved his home, where in the distance around him the land began to roll majestically and the mountains rose blue and green. The trees were rich and beautiful, draping over the trails in natural arbors. He was coming home. He was running because he could see her. Jenny. Delicate, feminine, her hair a cloud of sunshine around her, she ran down the trail toward him, her arms outstretched. He began to run. He could feel his heartbeat. He could feel the muscles constricting in his legs. The war was over. It was time to come home. She was reaching out to him.

Then the vision of her began to fade. In the dream he knew that she was dead.

Vaguely, from the deep, deep recesses of that dream, he began to hear a noise, and he realized that the noise was coming from the real world of consciousness.

"Christa!" It was a soft, feminine voice. Then there was a rapping on the door. "Christa . . . ?"

He opened his eyes, fighting the last vestiges of sleep, pushing himself up.

He glanced to the right. Christa was just struggling to awaken. He was startled at just how quickly he found himself aroused at the sight of her. Her back was beautiful and sleek against the bedding that was falling from it, her hair was pure ebony against the snow-white coloring of the sheets. It fell in wave after wild wave down her back, and despite himself, he found himself making comparisons. Jenny had been so delicate, so ethereal. Blond, pale, soft. Christa was as slender, perhaps more so, but even slender she was richly curved, and she was not in the least ethereal. She was passion and fire and sensuality.

He wanted her.

"Christa . . . ?"

Someone was directly beyond their door. With his present feelings, he couldn't help but feel a malicious pleasure in the fact that Christa seemed so truly alarmed at the prospect of being discovered with him in her bed. She glanced at him with absolute horror in her beautiful blue eyes.

"What in God's name are you doing there?" she hissed. "You've got to get up, you've got to get out of here."

He leaned back against the bedstead, studying her, shaking his head slowly. He crossed his arms stubbornly over his chest. "I don't think so, Christa."

"That's Kiernan! She and Jesse have come back. If my brother finds you here, he'll kill you."

"Christa, I'm married to you. Remember? And what a pity! Jesse's back? Just think, for a matter of less than twenty-four hours, you've had to con me into marriage!"

She flashed him a furious look. "You're a horrible person, Jeremy McCauley. No less than I'd expect—"

"From a Yank. Yes, I know."

She flashed him another of her regally condemning glares, then started to push up from the bed determined to find clothing even if he wasn't going to do so.

He reached out quickly, sweeping an arm around her, and drawing her back down.

"Jeremy, let me go—"

"Cover up, my love. Someone's about to burst through that door."

And he was right. He'd barely brought the covers up over the two of them when the door did burst open.

A loud gasp sounded.

Kiernan stood there. And Jesse was with her.

But they weren't alone.

Daniel and Callie were beside them.

The foursome stared into the room, jaws gaping. "Oh, my God!" Kiernan breathed.

Five

Beyond a doubt, they had quite an audience. Jesse, still in the military, was in his blue uniform, a signature plume in his cockaded hat. Kiernan, at his side, was elegant in a yellow-and-mustard day dress that emphasized her blond beauty. Daniel had retired his butternut-and-gray uniform. He was dressed in fawn breeches, a black frock coat, white shirt, and red cravat. Callie wore a blue dress with modified petticoats and a velvet bustle. Her gray eyes were very wide with surprise, and he might have smiled at her expression—if the room were not so filled with combustible tension.

Beside him, Christa groaned. He kept his arm around her, wondering how—with this audience—he could still be so aware of her, of the feel of her hair tumbling over his shoulders and chest, of the silken feel of her naked flesh beneath his fingers. She was trembling.

He was certain that not one of the Camerons facing them intended to be so rude, filling the bedroom with their presence, gaping at them, slack-jawed and stunned.

"My God, how can you possibly be here?" Christa demanded, staring at the group. "I—" she began again, but she was cut off.

"Jesu—it's McCauley!" Daniel said. There was a raw edge of anger in his voice. Well, that could be expected, Jeremy thought. Daniel was more hot-headed than Jesse and fiercely protective of his sister.

How the hell do you think I felt about mine? Jeremy wondered in silence.

There was a long stretch of silence.

Then Daniel spoke again. "McCauley, if you've—"

Callie jumped to Jeremy's defense. "Daniel! That's my brother!"

"And my sister!" Daniel grated out.

"All right, all right!" Jesse lifted a hand, stepping into the breach. "Let's try to sort this out—"

"Dammit!" Daniel shook off Callie's restraining arm. "She's your sister, too, Jess—"

"Yes, and I'm sure we're not making her feel very wonderful, standing in here and staring at her like this. Jeremy, there is an explanation, right?"

Christa opened her mouth, about to speak. Jeremy tightened the pinioning arm he had around her. "You know, Daniel," he said smoothly, "you do, sir, have a hell of a nerve questioning me with such a damned note of accusation when I came home in the middle of the war to find my sister expecting a baby. And then to find that she'd clean disappeared, kidnapped south by some Reb the next time around!"

"I married your sister—" Daniel began heatedly.

"Whoa!" Jesse warned, coming to stand between them. Not only did they have an audience, Jeremy thought wryly, that audience was coming closer and closer. "Daniel, Jeremy, you made your peace about Callie a long time ago!

Daniel, Jeremy fought with us to save this place. Let's have some reason here." He paused, then stared hard at Jeremy. "All right, McCauley. Just what the hell *are* you doing in bed with my sister? I need an explanation, and a good one!"

"There's a damned good one," he said lightly, addressing Jesse but his eyes narrowing on Daniel. "She's my wife."

"Wife!" Kiernan gasped.

"Christa, is that the truth?" Daniel shot quickly to his sister.

"Yes, I—"

"You married him?" Daniel said incredulously.

Callie cleared her throat. "Daniel, it's not so amazing that someone would marry my brother!" There was an angry emphasis on the last two words. She stared at Jeremy. "You married Christa?"

"Callie!" Daniel snapped.

Once again, Jesse stepped into the fray. "Let's not create offense where none is intended," he said flatly. "If we state surprise, Callie, it is merely because we never imagined Christa and Jeremy carrying on a civil conversation together, much less marrying one another. But it is the truth, right?"

"It's the truth," Jeremy said. "And I'm more than willing to explain it all, if you'd be so good as to excuse us long enough so that we can dress?"

"Oh! Yes, of course," Kiernan said. She started for the door. No one else was moving. She cleared her throat. "You all! They're naked and in bed and we're just staring at them!" she said in exasperation. "Jesse, come on. Daniel, Callie?"

"Oh," Jesse said quickly. Callie lowered her head and followed behind him. Daniel was the last to leave. "I'll see you in the study—" he began. But Jesse had his arm.

"Come on, Daniel. They'll be down in a minute!"

And Daniel, too, disappeared through the door. It shut with a small bang.

"Oh, my God!" Christa breathed. She leaned forward, burying her face in her hands. "How on earth did they all get here so quickly? Not just Jesse, not just Daniel. It will be so hard to get out of this now!" She leapt up, too distracted at first to realize that she was swirling around the room in all her naked glory as she searched for her clothing. The tangled fall of her hair was wild and sensual. The contrast between the rich color of her hair and the ivory of her flesh was exotic and tempting. He realized that she had two small dimples at the base of her spine, one over either buttock.

She wrenched open one of her drawers. "We'll have to try to explain it to them," she murmured, not even glancing his way.

Jeremy rose more slowly. He walked over to stand just behind her back. She found the pantalets she had been searching for. "I know that there's something we can say—" she started.

But he took hold of both of her shoulders and stared into her eyes. "No."

She shook her head. "What do you mean, no? I forced you into this, remember?"

"You forced me—and I did it. Well, now it's done. We're not getting out of it."

Her breath quickened. He was gazing into her eyes, but he could see the rise and fall of her breasts with his peripheral vision. Jesu. A part of his anatomy started to rise right along in response.

Christa's gaze slipped from his. A gasping sound escaped her and she tried to elude his hold, her chin rising, her eyes narrowing. "My brothers are home now, Jeremy. If you even think to touch me, I'll scream!"

He could hear the grating of his own teeth, the comment made him so furious. He jerked her hard against him. "Christa, this isn't a garden party any longer. Can't you understand the seriousness of what you've done? You'll scream?" he hissed. "Then you'll just have to go ahead and do so because I'll touch you when and how I like. They're your brothers. You married me. And unless you're really fond of bloodshed, you had best bear that in mind. Now, I'm sure you wouldn't mind in the least becoming a widow, seeing my Yankee carcass slipped into a shroud. Your brothers are good, damned good, but don't underestimate my abilities. I managed to stay alive through four years of fighting at the front too. So if you ever think about doing anything so stupid as causing a further friction between us, just remember that."

She had grown very pale. She no longer resisted his hold upon her. Her lashes, so long and rich a black, fell over her eyes. "Will you let me go, please? We do need to give them some kind of an explanation."

Instantly, he released her. She turned her back on him and stepped into the pantalets. He strode across the room and picked up his own neatly folded clothing, dressing quickly. He could hear the splash of wash water from the pitcher to the bowl as he buckled his scabbard in place. With his back to her, he waited for her.

"You can go down without me," she told him. Damn, how she wanted him gone! More time to plan a story for her brothers? Why a story, when the truth explained it all so clearly?

"You want to send me down to face the lions alone?" he drawled, turning to watch her. She was in the process of slipping into a dress. Christa certainly had enough gowns. This was another day dress, a handsome blue-and-gray plaid taffeta with black lace trim. It was elegant and very demure.

She dressed with care for every occasion. She stared at him, trying to do the hooks. He walked around behind her, impatiently grabbing her about the waist and pulling her back to him when she would have avoided his touch.

"My brothers are not lions," she said. "And I thought that you didn't give a damn about them."

"I'm not afraid of them," he told her. "I never said I didn't give a damn about them. There's a big difference." He rubbed his chin. He needed a shave. It would have to wait. The Camerons downstairs—including his sister—did deserve some kind of an explanation.

He was going to let Christa give it.

"Shall we go, Mrs. McCauley?" He offered her his arm. Christa ignored it, spun around, and started for the door. He followed on her footsteps.

Christa walked down the hallway through the gallery, painfully aware of him behind her. This could have been so easy. If Jeremy had behaved like a gentleman and kept his distance.

She suddenly felt a rush of blood rising to her cheeks. She could remember waking beside him. It had been almost like a dream. Being curled against him had been nice. She had felt the warmth of his body and the muscled length of him. She had also felt the hardness of him, warm and pulsing against her bare flesh. It hadn't been horrible at all, it had been fascinating, sensual, nice. She had wanted to turn around and curl against the strong male body. She had wanted to be held.

It's what it would have been like to wake up married.

She was married.

According to Jeremy, they were really married. She stopped short suddenly in the portrait gallery.

Camerons stared down upon them.

"What are we going to say?" she asked him.

"Let's see. I know. I rode by, you were swept off your feet, we couldn't wait a minute, you married me."

"How amusing," Christa murmured.

"How pathetic," he responded softly. He had dressed in his full uniform, down to his hat. It was a cockaded cavalry hat, just like Jesse's. Jeremy wore two plumes in his.

With the hat pulled low over his forehead, his eyes were barely discernible in the shadows of the hallway. He seemed exceptionally curt this morning, even for Jeremy. As if he were totally impatient with her now, and as if he truly regretted all that he had gotten himself into.

Except that he didn't seem willing to help get them out of it! He was a tall man and she felt again the disadvantage of looking up to him. His hair was still slightly askew beneath the brim of his hat, falling rakishly over his forehead. Her heart took a hard thud. He was a handsome man, but a very hard and unapproachable one at the moment. He leaned against the banister and casually studied her. "They're your brothers, Christa," he reminded her. "What's the matter with the truth?"

"I just don't want them to . . ." she began, but her voice trailed away.

"What?" he demanded sharply. She didn't have an answer for him—at least not one that she wanted to give. It didn't matter, Jeremy had the answer.

"Let me see, maybe I can answer this myself. You don't want them to know that you did something so desperate as to marry a man you despised to save a house. That you sold yourself for a pile of bricks."

She was itching to slap him, but he must have known it because he caught her wrist before she had barely made a move. "No, Christa," he warned her huskily.

She didn't want him as close to her as he was. She didn't want to feel the husky tenor of his voice, nor the heat of his body. She was very disturbed to realize that there were things about him that fascinated her. The size of him, the feel of him, the strength of him, the look of his bronzed hands with his long fingers and blunt cut nails against the pale ivory of her flesh. Something inside of her responded to him, whether she liked it or not.

She looked up into his eyes. They were steel gray with warning. His jaw was set at a hard-edged angle.

"Then quit being so horrible!" she charged him.

"All right." To her great unease, she was closer to him once again. He drew her very close, and whispered to her with his mouth just inches above her own. "We tell them that, yes, it was a matter of expediency. But the more we thought about it, the more wonderful it was. We're not really enemies at all, not now that the war is over. And of course, they're both home now. You don't need to guard the place anymore. You have your own life to lead. You're coming west with me."

She gasped. "I can't come west!"

"Whether you do or don't doesn't really matter at the moment, it's just something to say."

She stared at him. She wanted to wrench away from him, and she wanted to tell him that she'd never, never come west with him. But he was right—it didn't matter at the moment. She just had to get through today.

"Are you ready?" he said impatiently.

She moistened her lips. No, she wasn't ready. But he took her hand and started down the stairway, dragging her along with him.

The others were in the parlor to the right side of the entryway. Christa could hear their hushed voices as they came down the stairs. She bit her lower lip. She could hear Callie's voice. Though she couldn't hear her sister-in-law's words, she knew that Callie would be defending Jeremy. Then she heard Daniel, and she knew that he was concerned.

Then she heard Jesse. And though she couldn't make out a single word he was saying, she sensed that he was damning himself a thousand times over, certain that it was his fault that she had felt so forced to do something desperate.

"Well?" Jeremy arched a russet brow to her at the double doors to the parlor.

"Go on," she said.

"Oh, no, my love! After you."

She cast him a scathing glare and pushed open the double doors.

Four pairs of eyes turned to them instantly—and very guiltily.

Jeremy paused at the doors, closing them behind him, then leaning against them and watching Christa.

She was a wonderful performer, he determined.

She walked into the room with a beautiful smile—a Madonna's smile—on her lips. "It's so wonderful! I can't believe that you're all home—together. Where are the children?" She kissed both her sisters-in-law on the cheek, then gave Jesse a big hug and turned to Daniel.

Daniel accepted the hug stiffly. The silence in the room was deafening.

Christa didn't let it bother her. She spun around, the perfect hostess in her own home. "How on earth are you here?" she asked.

Jesse, an arm on the mantel, arched a brow. "A little matter of the house, Christa," he said sternly. "A friend of mine in Washington heard that there was some dirty politicking going on here and that someone had made sure this house would go for back taxes. We picked up Daniel and Callie on our way through Richmond, and here we are." He paused, walking across the parlor to reach her. "I thought that we were going to be too late. I had this awful fear in my heart that we were going to get here to find the house burned to the ground." He took both Christa's hands. "What happened, Christa?"

Maybe it was time to jump in, Jeremy thought. No, not yet.

"Umm . . ."

All right. She could fume later. It seemed time to jump in and save her for the moment.

"Something was going on, Jesse," he said, eyeing the eldest Cameron squarely. "I came down to see Callie before being reassigned, and I happened on a slovenly misfit tacking a notice on this place. We had until sundown to do something about it." He walked across the room, setting his arms around

Christa's waist and pulling her against him. Her hair just teased his chin. "The best solution in the world came to us," he said huskily. "Marriage."

"But you loathe one another!" Callie gasped out.

Jeremy smiled, amazed to discover that he was as good a performer as Christa. "Well, now, maybe that's what it seemed. But I swear to you, Christa wanted to marry me. More than she's ever wanted anything in the world, right Christa?" His arms tightened around her.

"Right!" she gasped out.

The Camerons still weren't convinced. "Dammit," Jesse swore suddenly. "This is my fault. I shouldn't have let them order me back to Washington. I should—"

"Hell, Jesse, it wasn't your fault," Daniel said bitterly. "I was the Reb, remember? The enemy to cause all this."

"Daniel, I'm the eldest. It was my responsibility—"

"Wait!" Christa cried out softly. "Will you two stop, please?" She leaned back against Jeremy, running her fingers tenderly over the arms that held her against him. "There's no fault here! My Lord, Jeremy and I are so happy! What's the matter with you all? We should be having a toast, you should be wishing me well!"

There was silence again. Jesse cleared his throat. "Jeremy, could I see you alone in the study?"

He released Christa, bowing his head in acquiescence. Jeremy opened the door to lead them out. Callie was on her feet in a split second. "Alone," Jesse said.

Callie sat. But Daniel was following him out.

"She's my sister too," he reminded Jesse.

Jeremy preceded the two to the study where he had overimbibed on Cameron brandy the night before. This morning he stood by the door, arms crossed over his chest, as he faced the two of them.

Jesse wasn't pouring brandy. He had the whiskey bottle out, even though it was still morning. "Jeremy, hell, I owe you," Jesse said, passing him a tumbler full of whiskey. He was quiet for a minute, and Daniel was silent behind him too. "I owe you for fighting here long before the war was over when the place was threatened by that misfit, Eric Dabney."

"Dabney was threatening my sister too," Jeremy reminded him. "You're not in my debt, Jesse. Neither is Daniel. Not now, not ever."

"Then what the hell happened yesterday?" Daniel demanded.

Jesse looked at his brother-in-law. The accusing tone was gone. There was anguish in his voice. Daniel adored Christa. He knew the feeling. Knew what it had been like to come home and find Callie gone.

He could have reminded Daniel of that now. He decided not to.

"It happened like I told you," he said. He set his glass down, leaning across the desk to talk to them both. "Look, I swear, I'm legally married to your sister. I've the certificate in my saddlebags. She would have liked you all to have been there, but it didn't seem to be worth the house being burned down to wait on the right kind of ceremony!"

Quick glances flickered between Jesse and Daniel. "We are in your debt," Daniel said. Jeremy knew that it must have been damned hard for him to say it. The Confederacy had lost the war, and Daniel accepted it, ready to go on. But some things were hard for him, like being in the debt of a Yank other than his brother, even though that Yank was now his brother-in-law. He inhaled and exhaled. Despite their differences—despite even the fact that they were both cavalry, that they might have met anytime in battle—they had formed something of a friendship. But this—this was hard for them all.

"Hell, Jeremy, it's just that Christa is our only sister!" Daniel said. "If you intend to divorce her—"

"I don't intend to divorce her," he interrupted quickly.

It was the truth. He hadn't really realized it until now. He hadn't known what to look for in the future. Now he knew. They might have no love lost on one another, but he didn't intend on a divorce. He had no heart left. Neither did she. Maybe they were made for one another.

He had discovered that he wanted her. Desperately. Maybe that was enough. Maybe it was much more than some had.

"You don't?" Jesse said.

He shook his head. "I admit, it was all rather sudden. I have to report back to Washington, and I have orders to head west. Maybe she'll come with me, maybe she'll stay here. There's a lot to decide about the future. But I don't intend on a divorce." He was silent for a moment, feeling them both watch him, feeling the relief that seemed to grow within them like something tangible. What else could he say with conviction? A wry smile touched his lips. "She's probably the most beautiful woman I've ever met. Why on earth would I want a divorce?"

Looks were quickly exchanged between the brothers once again. A slow grin broke out across Daniel Cameron's face. "Well hell, then, welcome to the family!" he said. He reached out a hand.

"Hell, nothing!" Jeremy murmured. "You already joined the McCauley family," taking the hand that was offered to him.

Jesse clapped him on the back. "That's between the two of you. For my part, congratulations."

"Don't worry," he heard himself saying. "I swear to you both, I would die for her."

Well, that much was true. He'd put his life on the line many a time for a man, woman, or child put under his care.

Yes. He'd die for her.

"The ladies must be chewing their nails to the bone in the parlor," Jesse commented. "Think we ought to rejoin them?"

They did so. When they came back to the parlor, three sets of feminine eyes stared at them nervously. "I don't even know anymore," Jesse said. "Have we got any champagne in the house, Christa?"

She had been sitting on the love seat, next to Kiernan. She leapt up nervously. "In the cellar, I think. I'll—"

"No, Jigger is here. He'll run down. He won't mind."

Jesse called to Jigger. Jigger was delighted to run down for the champagne. Everyone drank a toast.

Janey came back with the children. Christa delighted in playing with the whole brood of her three nephews and one niece while Jeremy looked more curiously to the two who belonged to his sister.

Her son, Jared, was the spitting image of his father. Blue eyes, black hair. The little girl, Annie, had McCauley coloring, almost as if it had been evenly divided. She had a riot of russet curls and huge silver eyes.

This is what our children would look like, he thought. Christa's and mine.

They couldn't have children, he mocked himself. They had never made love.

Yes, but they were going to. Maybe that would be his part of this bargain. Christa would have her house—Cameron Hall. May it stand forever.

He could have a son. Or a daughter. Maybe a girl as beautiful as Christa. But gentle, with eyes that grew wide with wonder at the world, with lips that turned easily to laughter.

His nephew toddled over to him and pulled at his pant leg. He reached down and picked up the little boy and held him close.

Soon after, Janey came in with a tea tray for a light supper. She promised a big supper for everyone by nightfall.

The afternoon passed quickly. Jeremy was glad to be with Callie, Christa was delighted to have everyone home. He was even drawn into conversation with both Daniel and Jesse about his new orders to ride west. They'd all been assigned to Kansas once, before the war.

Over lunch and dinner they discussed the Santa Fe Trail, the Indian lands, the civilized tribes, and the not-so-civilized ones.

But then dinner ended, and the entire family headed back to the parlor for coffee and brandy.

Christa quickly caught hold of Jeremy in the breezeway, before he could enter the room again.

"What?" he asked her impatiently.

She swallowed slowly. "I—I wanted to thank you."

He relaxed somewhat, watching her. It was nice to watch her squirm a little. "I don't know what you said to Jesse and Daniel but—thank you."

He nodded. "My pleasure."

"What did you tell them?"

"That I'm not filing for a divorce."

She inhaled quickly, watching him.

"And I'm not a liar, Christa. I'm a man of some honor, even if it's 'Yankee' honor. So be prepared. It's a real marriage. You do know what I mean."

She looked as if she wanted to slit his throat. He smiled. "You do know what I mean?"

"I know damned well what you mean!" she retorted angrily.

"And?"

Her eyes narrowed. "Camerons always pay their debts!" she whispered fiercely. And miserably.

She walked into the parlor. He held back, breathing deeply. It was going to be a real marriage.

He wanted children.

And he wanted Christa.

He went into the parlor. The children had been put to bed, the grown-ups were left alone. Jesse drew out some of the maps he had from his days in the West. He, Daniel, and Jeremy began to study them.

Kiernan excused herself first, saying that she was exhausted. Christa went next —right after she had fiercely hugged her brother and given Jeremy a very dutiful and wifely kiss. After a while Jesse excused himself. Jeremy and Daniel talked on a while longer, then Daniel suggested to Callie that they should retire too.

"I'll be right up," Callie promised her husband. When Daniel had gone, she turned to Jeremy. "You may have fooled them all," she said softly, "but I don't believe a word of it."

Callie stared at him with her wide silver eyes, and he found himself lifting his hands. "Callie, what do you want out of me?" he asked, rising, running his fingers through his hair, then leaning against the mantel. "They were going to burn the house down."

She stood and came over to him and began to speak softly in a rush. "It's just that you don't know Christa like I do, Jeremy. She's proud, yes. And she can be very stubborn, and she can fight harder than a catfish. But you don't know what it was like being here for the whole war, not knowing if and when the house would be taken—" She broke off, because he was looking at her, smiling.

"Callie, you're my sister, remember. I don't intend to do anything evil to Christa. She wanted to become my wife. That's all that I intend to ask of her."

Callie came up on her toes and kissed his cheek. "I'll pray for you both!" she promised. "Jeremy, you are my brother, and I do love you, and I want you to be happy."

"I'm going to be very happy," he promised her softly. "You'll see."

She smiled wanly, then walked to the door. "Good night, then. Don't stay up too late. Christa will be waiting."

He nodded. "I won't be long."

Callie left him. Yes, Christa would be waiting. Yes. Camerons always paid their debts.

Fine. He was going to collect.

He started to pour himself another brandy, then decided against it.

He left the parlor behind and started up the stairway. The floor in the upper hallway creaked beneath his footfalls.

She was in the bed when he entered the room. She was in some kind of an all-encompassing nightgown, and her back was to him. He was certain that she was feigning sleep.

He didn't care. He closed the door behind him with a definite click. He paused for a moment. Let her wait, let her wonder. Let the blood begin to flow too quickly through her veins. He knew damned well that she was awake.

He strode across the room to the bed. Once there, he methodically took off his clothes. When he was naked, he drew back the covers and crawled in beside her.

He wasn't going to make her wait any longer.

He put an arm around her, rolling her around to her back. Her eyes were tightly closed.

"Christa, I know damned well you're awake," he said.

Her eyes flew open. Burning blue in the night.

He ran his fingers around the beautiful embroidery and lace at the high collar of her nightgown. "Off with it," he told her flatly.

"You are a son of a bitch!" she told him heatedly.

He nodded. "A Yankee son of a bitch. One you're going to remember when I'm gone."

"You're leaving?" she said quickly.

He nodded. He had decided it just this minute, but it was probably the best thing for everyone involved. "First thing in the morning. I'm going back to Washington until the final order to head west is given."

He could almost feel her relief. It was not particularly complimentary.

She wasn't getting out of the night ahead of them. "Christa, get the damned thing off."

"But—"

"You can take it off, or I can rip it off. Either way, it goes."

Next thing he knew she was hissing that he was a Yankee bastard and scalawag, but she sat up and nearly ripped the gown herself, wrenching it over her head.

She didn't scream. She even cursed him just as quietly as she could manage.

She threw the gown furiously on the floor, then she sat there, naked beside him, seething and trembling, her eyes downcast. They rose to meet his, liquid and blue and shimmering. She threw herself back on the pillow. "Go ahead, then! Do whatever you've got to do!"

He was hard put not to laugh out loud. He leaned down on an elbow at her side, tossing all the covers back as far as they could go, then running his hand down the length of her body. How had she been created so damned perfectly? Moonlight fell over the rise of her breasts, and added mystery and shadow to the clefts at her hips and the dip between her breasts. At first he just touched her, running his fingertips lightly over her flesh. He felt her inhale sharply as he paused, running his palm over her nipple. Her breasts were perfect, firm and rounded, the peaks large and deeply rouge in color. Tempted, he leaned over her, running his tongue slowly around the aureole, then encompassing the whole of her nipple. She shifted beneath him. He felt the slam of her heart, the quickening of her body. He cupped her other breast with his hand, then rose, meeting her eyes before lowering his head to take her lips.

She didn't intend to respond to him. She didn't exactly fight him, but neither did she simply allow her lips to part to his. He intended to persist. He threaded his fingers into her hair, and with a growing passion he forcefully invaded her mouth, bathing her teeth with his tongue, then plunging deeply into her mouth. He could still feel her heartbeat. And he could feel the trembling that still riddled through her.

There was so much passion within her. If he could only reach it, touch it.

Her mouth was sweet. The taste and feel of it seeped into his system, adding to the hunger that had begun for her, creating a harsher throb of desire within him. She no longer protested the kiss. Perhaps she did not aid him, but she did not resist him either.

He lifted his lips from hers. Her eyes were open and on his. Her breathing came quickly and shallowly. Was she afraid? Christa Cameron, afraid?

She'd kissed a man before, he was damned certain. She'd been so in love with Liam McCloskey. Just how much else had she done? How much was innocence? And how much was hatred?

"You've never done this before?" he queried.

"Oh, you oaf!" she cried out, struggling then to free herself from him.

He laughed softly, pleased, and not at all sure why. He caught hold of her cheeks and kissed her again, deeply, hungrily, giving her no chance to protest.

The heat surged swiftly to his loins now. He tasted her lips and tasted them again. He rose above her.

"I will try to be very gentle," he told her.

She didn't answer him. Her eyes were closed. She lay, her beautiful face pale against the ink-dark cloud of her hair. He kept his eyes on her as he lowered himself against her. He caressed her breasts once again, feeling the pulse within her, feeling the heat. He lowered himself still, burying his face against the dip of her belly. Then lower. He brushed his fingers over the triangle between her thighs. Stroked her lower and lower. Forced her thighs apart.

He stared up at her. Her eyes were still closed. There was so much inside of her! he thought. He had felt the quickening in her when he touched her breast. He felt the rampant trembling within her now.

But she wasn't going to give to him. No matter what, she was determined to deny him.

Still, he didn't want to hurt her. He slid his thumb through the silk ebony of her pubic hair, and then into the damp softness of her sex. He felt again the trembling. Slowly, sensually he stroked her. He lowered his mouth to the tender, intimate regions of her flesh and began to tease her thus, moistening her at the least, if he could not arouse her.

But he did arouse her, he was certain! For scarce had he touched her before she jerked and surged. Her fingers tore into his hair. Whispered protests flew from her lips, but he ignored them all, delving deeper and deeper within her, bathing her, savoring her. She began to shake. Hunger gnawed raw and painfully within him, a surge of heat came like a rush of anguish.

He rose over her at last. And at last, those magnificent blue eyes were on his. He said nothing more but seized her mouth once again, taking her lips just as he took her body. He tried to take care, tried to go very slowly. She hadn't lied in her earlier protest—she had never made love with young McCloskey. Her body protested the invasion of his; she cried out briefly at the pain, catching her lower lip between her teeth to keep from letting out any other sound. He forced himself to stop completely, gritting his teeth against the will of his body as he awaited the acceptance of hers. Then he began to move with her slowly. Filling her with the length of his shaft, feeling the hug of her body around him. Dear God, it was good to be within her, sheathed by her. Even if she bit her lip. Even if she damned him for all eternity.

She had been made for this! he thought. For despite her protests, she gave to him, her body beautifully encompassing his. He thrust slowly at first, very slowly, bracing his arms at his sides, watching her face. But her eyes remained closed, her head to the side—her teeth upon her lower lip. Yet as he moved, she began to move with him, instinctively, naturally. The subtle undulation of her hips quickened the drive within him. He closed his own eyes, clenching down hard on his jaw, fighting for control. He maintained it as long as he could. Then his rhythm came faster, his drive stronger. He slipped his hands beneath her buttocks, molding her to him, and he gave free rein to the voracity of his hunger, taking her then with a volatile and fierce passion. Again and again he drove into her. Perspiration broke out in a fine sheen on his skin. He stiffened and thrust once, and once again, hard and deep within her, and his climax burst fiercely upon him, spilling his seed within her.

His weight was upon her, and his sex remained within her. She struggled beneath him, and, somewhat ashamed, he quickly lifted his weight from her, rolling to her side. Instantly she turned her back on him, like some creature deeply wounded. A rush of anger and impatience came to him. Dammit, she was his wife. And if he only saw her every five years or so, he intended to see her in bed.

He set an arm on the shoulder she had set so defensively against him.

"Christa, I'm sorry if I hurt you. It's fairly natural, I understand, for a woman to cry the first time—"

"I am not crying!" she whispered.

But he thought that she was. He wanted to comfort her. He ran his hand down her beautiful, sleek back. "Christa—"

Her back stiffened like a poker. "You've had what you wanted. Now, please, leave me the hell alone!"

He withdrew his touch as if he had been burned. He laced his fingers behind his head and stared up at the ceiling. Liar! he wanted to charge her. She could have responded if she wanted. He had felt the response of her body. She was beautiful, passionate, sensual, and he could feel it all. Feel it in her hunger for life, in her will, in her spirit.

Even in her hatred.

Hate me then, he thought. But you will respond to me, Christa, you will.

He let her lie there, fuming, stiff, and keeping her distance.

Then he reached for her again.

He saw her eyes. Blue ice and blue fire. Rebellious, furious, she stared at him.

"It's over—" she cried.

"It's just begun," he corrected. This time he swept her into his arms. From the very first touch of his lips to hers, he was filled with a force and passion that brooked no resistance. He kissed her until her lips were wet and swollen, then tasted her earlobes and her throat. He suckled her breasts, one then the other, taunting them with a slow rubbing motion with his thumbs, then suckling them again until she cried out. His hands, his lips, were everywhere. Hers flew about in protest, but he merely moved on. He rolled her onto her stomach, teasing the line of her spine with the caress of his fingers and tongue, nipping her buttocks, then rolling her over once again, parting her thighs, and having his way between them. When he took her again, he was so fiercely hungry himself that he could scarcely believe it. He should be sated with her. He wanted more. He knew her from head to toe. He had touched her, tasted her, from head to toe. But she moved, whether she wanted him or not. She writhed, and trembled, and created an ever greater fire. And it burned. Burned so that he stroked and drove until he was nearly mindless himself, and then amazed at the force of the climax that seized him again. She shuddered as he filled her. But no sound escaped her, no surrender even came in a whisper from her lips.

He fell to his side. Once again, she turned her back to him. Frustrated, he stared at her in the moonlight.

"Christa—why?" he demanded.

"I don't know what you're talking about," she replied.

He touched her again, stroking her back whether she wanted his touch or not this time.

He grit his teeth. "Christa, you're my wife. Why won't you give in to me?"

"I don't know what you're talking about."

He rose up on an elbow. "Yes, you do. You're flesh and blood, and you're very much a woman. And you're doing your damned best to deny me."

"I didn't deny you anything," she said.

"You did, and you know it."

She was silent for a second, then burst out. "I don't owe you anything. You take what you want. There's nothing else that should be yours. You're not—"

She broke off suddenly.

He caught hold of her shoulder and rolled her around once again. He met her eyes, those blue eyes that were brilliant with tears that she would die before she shed.

"I'm not what, Christa?" he demanded harshly.

She shook her head.

"Answer me. No? All right, I'll answer for you. I'm not Liam McCloskey. Well, my dear Miss Cameron, you're not the woman of my dreams either. But you are my wife. Liam is dead, lady, and you're going to let him rest. Do you understand me?"

She bit her tongue, staring at him. But then her lashes fell over her eyes. "Hail the conquering heroes!" she whispered vehemently.

"Damn you, Christa," he said quietly. "Fine. Have it your way. It's a conquered nation, Christa. Consider yourself beaten."

Her eyes rose to his again. "The South lost the war. I have never been beaten."

"Oh, I don't know. You'll surrender. I'll see to it. I promise it," he told her.

She wrenched herself from his touch once again, presenting him with the long line of her back. He lay back, staring at the ceiling.

He should have been feeling pretty wretched.

Oddly enough, he smiled.

It was there, somewhere inside of her. Something tangible to hang on to, to make a life with. Something made up of passion and spirit and glory, and all manner of hot and wonderful things. She might spend a lifetime hating him, but at the very least, they would have an interesting time of it.

He just had to discover the key to reach inside of her, to forge past the power of her will.

It would be something to think about in all the long nights to come.

Six

Christa arrived at Sterling Hall well ahead of the others. She observed the house as she patted her mare's neck, thinking that it was a very beautiful place and it was a pity it had been neglected so long. The majority of the construction was brick, and much of that had been plastered over so that the edifice seemed to be a large white building with symmetrical columns. It was very much like Cameron Hall, and like the age-old family estate it was still equipped with all its outbuildings, smokehouse, laundry, kitchen, and slave quarters. There were no longer any slaves but a lot of the household servants intended to come along with Daniel and Callie. Numerous Negroes—and poor lost white souls too—needed work and a place to live. Things would never be quite the same, and they'd probably have to sell off a lot of the land. Still, her brothers would manage both places well enough. Jesse wanted to resign his military commission soon and come home and practice medicine. Daniel was the natural-born planter and horseman. He could manage both estates.

And where would she live, she asked herself. As close as Jesse and Daniel were, they had both wanted their own homes. Sterling Hall had been in their family since the Revolutionary War when their great-great-grandmother had brought it into the list of family holdings. They hadn't worried about it much during the war years, but luckily neither had either of the fighting armies. Maybe that was because it had been cloaked by the overgrowth of shrubs and trees. The house was still standing, and except for the overgrowth and what some carpentry, paint, and a lot of cleaning would do to improve it, it was in very good condition. Callie would certainly make a very beautiful home of the place.

She slipped down easily from her horse and walked up the steps to the porch. With her hands on her hips she surveyed the place, trying to imagine it brought back to grandeur.

It had always been the family plan that Daniel would come here. The house had been willed to him. Cameron Hall for Jesse, Sterling Hall for Daniel. No home for Christa, since she would, of course, marry properly. A fine southern boy from a fine southern home she would take over as chatelaine when the time came. It was the way it had always been. The natural order of things. The Camerons had always prospered—more of the natural order of things. The very first Cameron had been a titled aristocrat, seeking more adventure than riches in the new world. Their great-great-grandfather had given up the title to cast his lot with the rebels in the Revolution. Through that rebellion they had prospered.

Now those who had rebelled had been beaten.

She had brought saddlebags full of things to start to build a household for Callie. Instead of bringing them in, she wandered along the porch and took a seat on the broad railing. She leaned back against one of the structural pillars and closed her eyes.

It had been so bitter for them to see Jesse ride away in his blue. Kiernan, in love with him then but not yet his wife. Daniel, the brother he had been as close to as his own conscience his whole life. And Christa, the baby sister he had halfway raised and lovingly protected. She hadn't understood Jesse's reasoning when he had sided with the Union. But not even the war had divided them. She had watched him go, loving him fiercely no matter what the dictates of his heart.

Still, not one of them had imagined that, eventually, they would all be grateful that Jesse had chosen to fight for the North. They had property left because of that decision. And they had Yankee dollars.

Actually, she reminded herself, they had property left because of her.

And Jeremy McCauley.

She grit her teeth, suddenly feeling the breach between them and the worlds they knew to be incredibly great. Angry feelings were very high at the moment. With military occupation and harsh Congressional Reconstruction taking place, men and women were hostile enough. The lost cause of the Confederacy, and her failure to split from what she thought had been a voluntary union, was becoming something sacred. It lived with tremendous pride in the hearts of the vanquished southerners. Perhaps they could be physically beaten, but in the depths of their souls they would never give up.

Yet newspapers—North and South—had been filled lately with accounts of the execution of the "Lincoln Conspirators." Callie had read of the assassination of Lincoln and everything that had followed. John Wilkes Booth, the actor who had killed the president at Ford's Theater, had been shot and had died himself. But on July seventh, Mary Surratt—the first woman ever executed by the Federal Government—was hanged along with others involved in plotting first the president's kidnapping, and then his assassination. Some said that Mrs. Surratt was guilty only of association with the killers, others that she had been as set on assassination as anyone else and that she had deserved to die. Mrs. Surratt's son had been involved to some extent, but he had escaped. The conspirators had been tried by a military tribunal that some considered to be a mock court. It was difficult to find the truth, Christa thought. Lincoln had been horribly murdered, and although many southerners had considered him an awful tyrant throughout the war, they now felt that he had been the one chance for a decent reconciliation. Booth had thought himself a hero but he had died despised by many of his own people.

The executions, just like the assassination, made public sentiment run high and volatile. Tempers flared, fights ensued. And chasms seemed to grow ever deeper, old wounds to bleed afresh.

Christa stood up, stretching her hands against her back. The lower part by her spine had been giving her trouble lately. It was because of this move, she thought. She and Callie and Kiernan had already been inside Sterling Hall, all scrubbing away with Janey, the ex-slave who knew her business like nobody else.

When it was done, what was she going to do?

For all his threats and promises, Christa had yet to see Jeremy again.

He wrote volumes to his sister.

He kept up appearances for Christa.

He was still in Washington—not so very far away. There were great upheavals in the army. Men staying in, men mustering out. New companies to be formed and assigned. Jeremy's command was being delayed. Since he really had nothing to say to her, he sent her newspaper clippings on the West, books by explorers, botanical articles, and the like. Occasionally he actually wrote a few words to her. Wonderfully tender, husbandly-type words like "Thought this might interest you" or "Pass on to Daniel."

She pressed her hand to her forehead, frowning, then shaking her head against a moment's dizziness that seized her. It was the sun. Or the fact that she hadn't been sleeping very well.

She sat again.

It was Jeremy's fault, she was certain.

He'd been gone a little over five weeks now, and she wished fervently that she didn't think of him. At first she'd been so delighted to wake up and discover that he was gone. On that morning she had been exhausted and sore from head to toe, and she had wanted nothing more than time in which to convince herself she had healed her wounds.

But days had passed. And when she thought about him, and that night between them, she had alternated between moments of deepest humiliation . . . and fascination.

Thinking of it now, she nearly groaned aloud, raising her knees to the rail and hugging her arms around them. Liam should have remained in her dreams. She should at least have fantasies of what might have been.

But thoughts of Jeremy preoccupied her too much now, when she was awake and when she was asleep. There was no denying the war-sharpened strength of the man, the size of him, the sleekness of his power. She tried to close her eyes and her mind from such thoughts, but they came to her again and again, unbidden. She could see his steel-gray eyes, warning her that his will was law. The rakishly tousled auburn hair, the naked length of him, stalking her, touching her.

Then all manner of heat began to rise in her, and her cheeks bloomed crimson and she swallowed down the thoughts. Thank God he was gone. She didn't have to submit to any wifely duty.

Or feel that shameful tug to surrender, the desire to reach out, to touch something sweet and magical and elusive.

She leaned her head back against the pillar, opening her eyes to watch the sky around her. It was so very blue today. The dead heat of summer was leaving, and fall was beginning to come upon them. It was such a beautiful time in Virginia. The air would be wonderfully cool, the sky still so beautiful, and then the leaves and trees would begin to change and the green landscape would be carpeted in color. She did love her home. Passionately.

She sighed, watching a spider build a web. Eventually, Jeremy would make the trip west. What then?

She bit her lower lip. She had caught Jesse watching her so frequently lately. And she had seen a heartsick expression in his eyes.

He wasn't going to play along much longer with the story that they had entered willingly into marriage. And then he was going to feel guilty the rest of his life, certain that he had caused her hardship by not being there when he should.

He had already torn apart half of the government offices in town trying to discover what had happened. But not even Jesse had been able to find out the truth. Everything had been in order on paper. There should have been plenty of time for Christa to reach Jesse, for him to have come home and straightened things out. Reconstruction staff had come and gone, men knew what they had been ordered to do, and the truth had eluded them all. The buyer who had been so frantic to buy the place and burn it down had disappeared without a clue.

So Cameron Hall still stood. And it was still her home. But Daniel and Callie were moving out with their children, anxious to set up housekeeping on their own. She would be welcome either place.

She rose, having forgotten the feeling of dizziness, and walked back to the brick pathway before the house where her mare was standing. She reached up to take down the saddlebags with their precious cargo of silver dinnerware and napkin rings. When she lifted the saddlebags down, the dizziness seized her once again. She swore softly—having learned some very colorful language during the war—and hurriedly set the bags down on the steps. She was startled by a sudden surge within her stomach. She leaned a hand against a pillar and paused for a moment. She'd felt queasy a few mornings ago, but she had swallowed hard and the feeling had passed. It would do so again.

She waited. The feeling didn't pass. To her astonishment, it worsened.

There was a well around the side of the house and Daniel had just tested it the day before. Cool water might help. She walked around quickly to the well and pulled up a bucket of water, drinking deeply from the ladle.

It didn't help. She clutched her stomach, and found herself being sick into the midst of a honeysuckle vine. She straightened, dismayed, wondering what sort of strange disease she might have caught. She ladled out more water, bathing her face in it, washing out her mouth, trying to swallow more down. It stayed. Maybe she was going to be all right.

The petticoat she wore was a very old one. It had already been ripped up once, the day Eric Dabney had tried to burn Cameron Hall down with his renegade forces. She had made bandages from it for Jesse to treat the wounded. It didn't seem much of a loss now to rip another panel of cotton from it to dip in the water and continue to cool her forehead. She soaked it, then leaned against the well, her eyes closed as she set the cloth against her face.

As she did so, she felt a curious feeling of unease slip over her, as if she were being watched.

She pulled the cloth from her face and stared across the weeded and overgrown yard.

A horseman had come upon her. A Yankee horseman. Jeremy.

As usual, he seemed to be in excellent condition. From his shiny black cavalry boots to his Union blue jacket and plumed hat, he was handsomely attired. When he dismounted from his horse and walked toward her, she noted that he hadn't lost a whit of his sleek muscled tone or suppleness. His hat was pulled low over still-relentless silver-gray eyes and neatly clipped russet hair. He was clean-shaven, and his features seemed exceptionally striking against the precision of his uniform.

Damn him. He had a habit of coming upon her when she was less than at her best. Last time she had been in the dirt, fighting off Bobby-boy. Now she was in old, worn clothing, her hair was damp and her cheeks were flushed, and she had just been wretchedly sick.

The closer he came, the more fiercely her heart began to pound.

"Want a hand?" he offered. "Are you going to faint or fall?"

She stiffened instantly. "Of course I'm not going to faint or fall. I—"

"You're a Cameron, right? And Camerons never falter." He paused, his hands on his hips, his head cocked at an angle as he watched her. Why did he make it sound like such a bad thing that she was determined to stand alone?

She stared at his face, and despite herself, she felt a slow flush coming to her cheeks. He was back. And despite herself, emotions seemed to be racing through her.

She turned quickly back to the well, using it to brace herself. "How long have you been there?" she whispered.

"Long enough."

"How did you—find me?"

"I've been by Cameron Hall."

She nodded. Needing something to do, and feeling so ridiculously flushed, she dipped her ripped piece of petticoat into the water again, pressing it against her forehead. "I'm sorry, I must be catching something. Perhaps you should stay away."

She was amazed at the crooked smile that slid easily onto his lips.

"You think that you're ill?" he queried her, an amused glint of silver in his eyes.

She threw up her hands. "Well, McCauley, I'm ever so glad my misfortune amuses you."

"I'm sorry to disappoint you, but no misfortune of yours would amuse me. I just don't think that you're ill."

"Then—"

"Christa, my sweet innocent!" he said with exasperation, making her sound anything but sweet or innocent. "Hasn't it even occurred to you that you might be expecting a child?"

Perhaps she had flushed red before. Now she felt every drop of blood seem to drain from her face. No! It never had occurred to her! She'd been busy, she'd been torn, she'd been wretched.

And she'd been queasy. Morning after morning now. If she'd given the least attention to the time that had elapsed she might have noticed that . . .

"Have you missed your monthly?" he demanded frankly.

The blood came surging back to her face. "How—how dare you speak to me about such things! A gentleman should never, never—"

"Jesu, Christa, spare me this!"

"You shouldn't even know about such things!" she charged him.

His smile was back. He was keenly amused once again. "Do forgive me. Christa, we both grew up on farms—be it true that mine was ever so humble while yours was ever so grand! And it's rather difficult for a man to have reached my age with a total lack of knowledge."

"I don't think you're lacking anything," she charged him miserably. She was going to be sick again. She couldn't be so. Not with him here right on top of her, asking such personal questions. "Could you please just go away?"

"Christa, I want to know—"

"Don't, please!" she whispered miserably. "Maybe you know such things, but you shouldn't talk about them!" She placed the rag against her forehead, suddenly wishing him away.

He didn't go away. "Christa, turn around. Look at me."

She shook her head. Damn Jeremy. He never just let her be. His hands were on her shoulders and he was turning her around. The glint of silver amusement was gone from his eyes. Before she knew it he was at her side, sweeping her up into his arms.

"I'm not going to fall!" she protested irritably. If she was lucky, she wouldn't be sick again.

He walked her around to the porch, sitting upon the steps where he could brace his back against a pillar. With his left arm supporting her, he used his right hand to gently press the cooling rag over her forehead and cheeks. She closed her eyes, most certainly unaccustomed to such a show of care.

It felt curiously soothing. Maybe because she was just worn out. He seemed a very strong protector at the moment, and it seemed especially nice not to feel the need to fight. His arm was very strong, his chest secure. His touch was gentle if not tender. He smelled nicely of clean soap and sweet tobacco, leather and brandy, all scents that she had known and loved all her life.

But they came with Jeremy McCauley, she realized suddenly. And if he was right, she was going to have his child. From that one wretched night when he had determined that it was going to be a real marriage, that he wasn't going to politely go away.

Well, maybe he couldn't have done so. Maybe he had salvaged something for her with Jesse and Daniel. Maybe she had owed him.

But not this much!

Her eyes suddenly flew open. His were on hers, deep gray, intense. "It can't be!" she whispered. "There was only the one night!"

Something seemed to shield his eyes. "Christa, it certainly can be—from only one night."

Something about his voice was very irritating, and she was suddenly frightened. She wasn't ready for this kind of responsibility. There was too much else to worry about!

No, not anymore. She didn't have to worry anymore.

He was watching her. "Oh, you'd like that, wouldn't you!" she snapped. "You'd get to feel wonderfully puffed up and arrogant and proud of your male prowess!"

He sighed, his teeth grating. "Christa, I wouldn't feel a thing. Jesse could explain it to you better than me, if you haven't raised your horses long enough to know about breeding! If it was the right night for you to conceive, it was the right night, and it would have damned little to do with any magnificent prowess on my part."

Her lashes fell quickly, covering her eyes. She was sorry she had snapped at him. Really, he managed to behave much better than she did upon occasion.

But he wasn't going to have a baby!

She opened her eyes again and met his. She didn't know if he was pleased or displeased or still amused. She swallowed, suddenly trembling from his touch and feeling as if she needed to escape it. "I'm sorry," she murmured quickly. "I'm all right now."

She was pushing away and so he helped her up, standing along with her, one booted foot on a step as he did so. He looked up at her on the porch. "Really," she said. "It may just be nothing, you know. The heat—"

"It's not very hot today," he said politely.

She couldn't be having his child! He was still a stranger, still the enemy, even if they'd fought alongside each other upon occasion.

Even if he had touched her. Made her feel . . .

She lifted her chin. "You act as if you know something about women expecting . . . babies. As if—" She broke off, some startling intuition coming to her. "You've had a child. I mean—you've fathered a child!"

It was an accusation. She certainly didn't expect the dark fury that constricted his features. After all, she was legally his wife. He was the one who should be apologizing, coming up with a quick explanation.

"I've no living children," he stated coldly.

"But—"

"I've no living children. Drop it, Christa, now."

The sudden cold from him seemed to wrap around her. Fine. She lifted her chin. "So what are you doing here? What has brought you back? What do you want?"

"What do I want?" he echoed, and he smiled again, but with no humor.

"Why, I want my wife. My final orders have come at last. It's time for me to head out west."

The world seemed to drop from beneath her. Her knees felt weak, as if she couldn't possibly stand. She wouldn't reach to him for support right now.

Her horse. She started down the steps past Jeremy, anxious to reach her mount. He watched her running toward her mare until she spooked her, and the animal raced off toward Cameron Hall.

Home! Christa thought, her eyes stinging with sudden tears. Blindly, she reached out in the horse's wake.

He came up behind her, swinging her around, his arm about her in support. "Come on, we'll take my horse."

"I can't go west," she said tonelessly.

"We'll see."

She stumbled. He lifted her again, walking her around the side of the house to where his very well-trained cavalry horse awaited him. Her arms slipped around his neck, but she protested still. "I can't leave. I did everything. I kept it standing. I planted crops myself. I fixed the roof. I shot at a man once! I—I—"

"You performed the ultimate sacrifice!" he said, peering down at her. "Alas! You married me!" He set her up on his mount. She looked down at him, moistening her lips. She shook her head. "You don't understand."

"Christa, *you* still don't understand. It's Jesse's now."

She looked up, hearing the rumble of a wagon arriving at last. Around the corner of the building she could just see Daniel and Callie arriving.

Her sister-in-law jumped down from the front of the flatbed they were using to haul large belongings. "Christa!"

She started to reply, but Jeremy looked up at her, putting a finger to his lips. She didn't know why, but she obeyed his silent command.

Christa could see Callie on the steps, spinning around to meet Daniel as he walked up to meet her. "Daniel, the saddlebags are here on the porch, but Christa is nowhere to be seen."

"Jeremy must have found her."

"Yes, yes, of course."

There was just a moment's silence. Callie spoke again, softly, huskily. "Daniel, Kiernan and Jesse have the children. And we're alone—"

"And Mrs. Callie Cameron," Daniel finished. "Think of it! This is our threshold. Our very own threshold. It would be nicely fitting if I were to sweep you up into my arms and carry you over it and—"

"Oh, I like the 'and' part! Very much!" Callie whispered.

Christa could see them both—her brother, so tall, dark, and handsome, and Callie, beautiful with her rich red hair, slim figure, and beaming face. They'd waited so long for the war to end. They'd weathered everything that had happened since.

Christa closed her eyes. Suddenly, she heard Callie shrieking. Her eyes flew open. Jeremy was still just staring up at her. "He's hurting her!" she blurted out.

"Oh, Jesu, Christa! She's my sister. If he were hurting her, I'd have been in there with the speed of lightning. Don't be a fool. She loves him! And some women do enjoy being intimate with their husbands."

Crimson flooded her face now. Yes, she knew that Callie loved Daniel and

Daniel loved Callie, and what a fool she had been! She knew, too, that her brother would never hurt Callie.

That fact was plainly evident in just seconds. They could hear Callie's voice again. Very soft, very low, and very intimate, whispering her husband's name.

"Daniel . . ."

The name was followed by a combination of sigh and laughter that gave no doubt as to the pleasure of her mood.

Jeremy was still staring at Christa. "Clearly," he murmured dryly, "she is in no pain!"

"Quit!" she whispered down to him furiously. Her cheeks were still flushed and she was painfully embarrassed. They had no business being here, listening.

Jeremy leapt up on his horse behind her. His arms encircled her. "I wonder. Can you say my name like that?"

"Must you always make a joke of everything?"

"Sadly, my love, I was not joking."

He nudged the horse quickly to take them away from the house—and from Callie and Daniel's chance to be alone.

They had ridden for several minutes before he spoke to her again.

"So, Christa, let's see, you can't go west. So which of your brothers are you going to grace with your presence in his home?"

"Stop it!" she whispered.

"Poor Christa! You worked for it all, you bled for it. And you married me for it. But it isn't yours anymore."

"Stop mocking me."

"I'm not mocking you. I'm pointing out the truth."

"I don't know why you're so concerned. I don't know why you're doing this. You don't like me. You don't like a single thing about me, and you can't possibly want me with you."

"There's where you're wrong, Christa. I admire your courage very much. And your strength. I think you'll make an exceptional cavalry wife."

Her head was pounding. Ah, there was something! He thought she was capable, at the very least! Just like an experienced field hand!

Within a matter of minutes, they had ridden the distance back to Cameron Hall.

Christa slipped down from his horse without his assistance. Her skirt caught on the saddle and he had to release it for her.

"Accept it, Christa. You're coming with me."

She tugged at her skirt, then looked up at him desperately. "Why? Because I might be useful? Just how much help can I be if—"

She broke off, lashes lowering, biting her lower lip.

"If you are expecting my child?" he asked softly. He leaned low, slipping her hem from his stirrup where it had snagged. "Well, there's one reason right there. Every man wants a son, Christa."

"Yes, and then I have callused hands and I know how to shoot and—"

"And at heart, Christa, you always were and always will be a pampered little belle!"

She gasped, jerking away. "Then—"

"Then there's the reason that, although I very much hate to admit it, to add any more flattery to that defiant Rebel head of yours, I do find you very beautiful. Exceptionally so. And . . ."

"And?" she whispered, startled by his last words.

"And you're my wife, and I've determined that you'll accompany me."

"I—I can't!"

"But you will. So prepare yourself, Christa. Willing or no, my love, you're riding west."

Seven

*J*eremy stood by one of the wide windows in Christa's room overlooking the maze and the garden. From this vantage point, he could see the graceful slope of lawn that rolled all the way down to the river and the dock. It was beautiful country, rich country. And the Camerons were the royalty of it, he knew. The place was Christa's heritage.

His gaze fell from the distant dock to his wife's head. She was to the right of the house. She had walked out back a while ago with Jesse.

She hadn't asked him for time to be alone. He'd made it a point of telling her he'd had something to do. Maybe he needed time himself. It wasn't that Christa would have to find herself instantly swept away—on the contrary, she had some time. He'd had a long discussion with Jesse to work out the arrangements. He had to return to Richmond right away, and from there on to Washington where he'd be taking the railroad as far as Illinois. Once there, he'd be taking steamers down to Little Rock. Some of his troops would be accompanying him from Washington, and some would be assigned to him at Little Rock. He was glad to be going ahead, and he would be glad to arrive early enough in Little Rock to ride out into the countryside alone before leading his men and some of their wives across it. It was always good to know the lay of the land. He had been assigned to the West before, and there were dangers there.

Christa would join him in Little Rock. Jesse had assured Jeremy that he could extend his leave of absence even further, and escort his sister as far as Little Rock. Christa was upset, convinced that Jesse shouldn't leave his wife and children again, but Kiernan and Jesse had looked over her head to Jeremy. They all knew that Christa should not be traveling through the Reconstruction-era South alone, nor through some of the northern cities now either. The war was over, Kiernan insisted. She didn't mind seeing Jesse ride away one more time. And Christa had to have time to pack her household belongings as well as her clothing, and make all the arrangements to bring one of her favorite horses too.

Jeremy would return to Little Rock two weeks after his own arrival in the area, for Christa. Then they could begin their westward journey from fort to fort, camp to camp, together.

She wasn't saying good-bye to Cameron Hall for good today, but it felt as if she were doing so.

There was certainly no turning back for her now.

For a while he had heard the low murmur of voices on the back part of the hall's wraparound porch. But then the two, arm in arm, had walked down to the family cemetery that lay halfway between the house and the river. He couldn't hear what they were saying anymore, but he could see them. They were handsome people, these Camerons. Jesse, tall, with that ebony-blue of his hair, just now beginning to show a hint of silver at the temples. The war had brought on that silver early, Jeremy was certain. Jeremy had felt the division of the country very clearly—few states had been quite so wretchedly torn as Maryland. But until Callie had met and married Daniel Cameron, he'd never had kin fighting on the other side. It was a wonder Jesse wasn't solidly gray by now. Jeremy wondered how he had ever managed to walk away from all this never knowing if he could come home or not.

A soft tinkle of laughter rose up from below. It was faint, for Christa was at a distance, but it evoked all kinds of nostalgia and wonder within him. How had they been back before it had all begun? They would have been quite remarkable here, he was certain. Jesse, Daniel, Kiernan—in love with Jesse but not yet his wife—and Christa. Christa, so very young back then, the pampered pet of both brothers, uncontested mistress here since her mother's death. She must have been sheer elegance and beauty in those lighter days, allowing that spill of laughter to fill the halls, to brighten the days and nights of all their guests. She laughed so seldom now.

He closed his eyes. For a moment he could almost hear the clang of harness, the churn of carriage wheels. People would have gathered here from all corners of Virginia. Dignitaries had surely traveled down from as far away as Washington upon occasion. Ladies in their silks and satins. Men in their finest dress uniforms and most elegant civilian attire. Musicians would have played well into the night, and Christa would have tapped her feet and danced the night away.

What were they saying, those two Camerons below him? His eyes were sharp, and he could see her face, even as she turned to her brother at the gate before the ancient cemetery. She was smiling at him. Her head was tilted back, her hair, free and lustrous as the blue-black wing of a bird, flowed in rich waves and curls down her back, catching the sunlight. She laughed at something he said, threw her arms around him, and hugged him fiercely. Someone called from across the yard.

Daniel was back. He walked out to join his brother and sister. He slipped an arm around Christa. For a moment, the three of them were posed there, arm in arm, in a continuing triangle. Tall and handsome and beautiful and entwined by love—and that sometimes irritating Cameron honor!

He sighed, catching hold of the rise of his temper. He didn't begrudge her her brothers, or the love or loyalty between the three of them. It was something precious to her, something that he hoped they had forever. Things weren't so terribly different in his family. At least, not with his remaining family. The war had taken his father early. Their oldest brother, Josiah, had been reported missing in sixty-four. They'd discovered later that he'd died in some little skirmish in Tennessee. The second eldest in his family, Joshua, was back home now tending to the farm. He'd married his childhood sweetheart—who had waited out the war for him—and at least, for the two of them, there had been a happy ending. Josiah might be gone, he thought, but he and Joshua still loved Callie fiercely, and if they had been as close to the events in her life as Daniel and Jesse were to those in Christa's, she might have had a very wretched time, indeed, trying to explain Daniel Cameron. The war had kept Jeremy from her until she'd had her baby and come south and been duly wed—he never had found out just exactly in what order it had all happened!

His eyes narrowed as he watched Christa. She was so alive, so exuberant, so vivacious! Her spirit was as deep and bewitching as her vibrant coloring. Her passions ran so very deep.

But not for him.

How would it feel if she were ever to set her eyes upon him like that? So sparkling, so brilliantly blue, so tender? And that smile . . .

Ah, never in a thousand years!

Heaven help him, he decided dryly, if she did. He needed a strong guard against Christa Cameron. Her will was as strong as steel. If she ever felt that she really had any power over him, she would do her best to break him. She'd be free from him, taking what she wanted on her way!

He leaned back against the wall, closing his eyes for a moment. Maybe he judged her too harshly. Maybe he spent too many hours mourning a gentle blond woman who had never even thought to disagree with him. No, Jenny had been blessed with her own kind of strength. She hadn't needed to spend endless hours fighting him tooth and nail. But he was married to Christa, and unless he missed his guess, he was expecting another child.

They were going to make it work.

Every time he saw Christa, he found himself doing things he had never intended to do. He had never intended to marry her. He had never meant to order her to come west with him. He had actually come back to say good-bye and perhaps discuss the possibility of her joining him. But once he had seen her, the order had just come out. Once he had issued it, he realized that he had meant it.

He was a married man. He didn't intend to live without his wife, cold in the night. She might not be much of a willing partner, but she was beautiful. And in all the long nights he had been away from her, he had dreamed about her, and he had wanted her.

A slight sound from outside attracted his attention, and he took up his vigil at the window again. Jesse and Daniel were leaving her by the cemetery. She watched them go, smiling. But when they had come up the knoll leading to the house, when she felt herself sheltered by the foliage between them, she turned back to the graveyard. He saw her shoulders hunching over.

He knew that she cried.

She leaned against the cemetery fence, then slipped slowly against it to her knees. Her shoulders shook. She did not cry, she sobbed, in great, gulping waves. He clenched his teeth, torn by a wave of sympathy.

"Actually, I don't think it's all just because of you!" he heard.

He turned. Callie stood in the doorway. His sister was really beautiful too. There was an added luster about her. Callie was blessed. She was a woman deeply in love and, perhaps, more deeply loved in return.

"Thanks for such a vote of confidence. And from my own sister!" he reproached her mildly.

The others might have been well fooled, but Callie? Never.

He crossed his arms over his chest, leaning against the wall. "What brought on such a comment? What does she say about me?"

"Never a word. Even when I ask her outright. She stares me straight in the eye and reminds me that you're my brother, and that truly, I should understand what she has come to see in you. Then she very innocently and very sweetly, I assure you, reminds me that sometimes oil and water do mix, and that passion, hatred, and love are separated by very narrow lines, and surely I, of all people, should understand that!"

"Does she now?" he murmured. He shouldn't have been surprised. Christa would never give herself away. Not to Callie. Not to anyone.

"You forget, I know her well, Daniel. I came here uncertain, and she—and Kiernan—were wonderful to me. She gave me the clothing off her back—"

"Hardly off her back," he commented wryly. "Christa has enough clothing to open a fashion shop."

Callie waved a hand in the air. "She shared everything she had with me."

"I grant you, in some things, she has a generous nature."

"But not in others?"

"Callie, there are certain things that are simply none of your business."

She flashed him a quick smile and came into the bedroom, slipping her arm around his waist and staring out the window with him. "I know what she's thinking."

"You do?"

He felt Callie nod slowly. "She's thinking of everyone that they've lost. Not just her parents. She's thinking about Anthony Miller, Kiernan's first husband. And about Liam. About little Joe Davis, Jeb Stuart, so many old family friends and acquaintances. Young, dashing, proud! A breed of cavaliers. The death toll was terrible, Jem."

"Callie, my God!" he said hoarsely. "We lost our father and our brother!"

"I know, but we won the war. They lost. You have to try to remember that!"

"It's tough," he told her, adding dryly, "Camerons don't surrender!"

"Don't I know it!" Callie laughed.

Christa had risen. As he watched, she came around the corner of the little cemetery and disappeared into a cover of trees.

"Where in bloody hell is she heading now?" he demanded, then realized his language, and remembered that once upon a time he would have never thought to have been so crude in front of any lady, much less his own little sister. He closed his eyes. "Sorry, Callie—"

"It's quite all right, I've most certainly heard it," Callie said, then asked, "Why are you so angry with her?"

"I'm not angry!" he denied. But Callie was right. Fine, Christa had her wonderful Cameron pride. She wouldn't cry in front of him.

But she was sobbing blue blazes behind his back and he wanted to shake her. He wasn't forcing her into a life as a scullery maid.

No, just into a life with him.

"Where has she gone?" he repeated.

Callie sighed. "The summer cottage. You can just see a corner of it through the trees right there. See, it's all whitewashed. I understand it used to be furnished quite elegantly during the summer months before the war. It overlooks the water, and if you open all the shutters the river breezes pour right in. There used to be a time when the ladies sipped mint juleps and lemonade while the male guests were offered stronger refreshment. There's not much there now. I think Christa had an old chaise brought down there last June. She told me that they all used to go there when they were children and in trouble. It's a habit that stayed with them all. Everyone knows it's off limits once another member of the family is in it. She'll come out of it soon enough, Jeremy."

"That's right, she will," he murmured. He started from the window, long legs carrying him quickly from the room. He was down the long stairway before Callie seemed to have found the energy to come after him. "Jeremy!" she called his name, but he pretended not to hear her. By the time he had left the porch behind him and passed by the extensive maze of rosebushes, he heard his sister reach the porch herself. But she was stopped there.

Daniel came beside her.

"Let them be," he warned her.

"He's angry, Daniel."

"They'll solve it. Callie, you keep reminding me—he's your brother. I can call him out and one of us can kill the other, and the one left alive can be arrested for illegal dueling."

"Daniel, don't be ridiculous—"

"Then leave them be."

The voices faded behind him. He came to where Christa had stood, to the low whitewashed fence that surrounded the graveyard. He'd come here before. Admittedly, the Cameron heritage had fascinated him, and on his first trip here he had come to the graveyard while awaiting a little time to say good-bye to his sister alone. That time he had been heading back to his troops in the field. He'd been transferred east along with General Grant, and he had left here with the very real possibility that he and Daniel might meet in combat. But they never had. In a cruel war God had, upon occasion, shown his small mercies.

He stared at the graveyard. There, in the far corner, were the first of the Camerons. Jamie and his Jassy. The tombstones were dated sometime in the late sixteen hundreds. The slate stones were very old, but the family had kept them all up and the writing remained clear. It was an oddly beautiful place, haunting, ghostly, but beautiful too. Magnificent angels hovered over some Camerons, while virgins cast their serene gazes down upon others. The funereal art was exquisite, history in itself, were there no beautiful house to grace the grounds. But of course, this meant so much more to Christa. Her parents lay within the gate. Her grandparents. Aunts, uncles, and cousins and "greats" who had lived through two centuries of Virginia's history.

He walked around the cemetery at last. Through the foliage he could see the summer cottage. Like the main house, it seriously needed paint.

He came around the front. The door was closed but not locked and he came through it. There was a main room with a large fireplace.

With a smile he wondered if the cottage hadn't been used frequently in winter. He could just imagine how it would feel being here, a blaze snapping warmly from the hearth, cold winds blowing beyond, and a landscape carpeted in snow.

He walked through the room, not intentionally coming in quietly.

But Christa hadn't heard him. She was curled on a green brocade-covered lounge that looked out over large windows with a river view. The river rolled by, dark today, but enchanting. Its color, its slight turbulence, warned that fall was nearly upon them and winter was coming.

Some sound or instinct alerted her to his presence, for she turned, somewhat alarmed.

Women, he thought, didn't look good when they cried. Their eyes usually got all puffy and their faces became a blotchy red.

But not so with Christa!

Her cheeks were damp and flushed and her eyes remained crystal with the wetness of her tears. But as she stared at him she brushed her hands over her cheeks, and the wet glimmer of tears became that of defiance. He'd never seen eyes more vividly, beautifully blue. He'd been so sorry, so touched by the pain that she had been feeling.

But seeing the mercury-quick change in her, he felt his resolve concerning her stiffen.

Her pride was greater than any emotion within her heart.

"What are you doing here?" she whispered.

He lifted his hands. "Have I entered some sacred domain?" he asked.

She turned back around, staring at the river. "Of course not," she said. "It's a cottage on the grounds, nothing more."

He remained behind her in silence. His presence must have disturbed her though, for she was quickly up, swinging around to meet him as if she feared to have him at her back. She stared at him, and he must have betrayed some surprise at her movement, for she flushed slightly and strode toward the mantel. Her feet moved silently over the flooring. There was a handsome oilcloth on the floor, painted to look like marble. It was old and fraying now, but it had once been grand. Over that, before the hearth itself, was a rich stretch of fur rug, warm and very inviting. Christa was glancing at the fur, too, he saw. She caught his gaze, then turned away very quickly.

"I think I know why you're doing this," she said. She was suddenly very prim, her hands folded before her, her eyes steady on his.

He took up a military "at ease" stance, legs slightly apart, his hands together at his back. "Oh?" he said politely. "And what am I doing?"

"Making me come with you."

"Why?"

She waved a hand in the air, unable to continue meeting his eyes. "It has something to do with Daniel and Callie. I believe you're trying to get even with him in some way." He was dead silent, and she continued in a sudden rush, "For taking Callie from Maryland. Well, for what happened between them in Maryland, and for taking her away. Perhaps you're not even aware of it. But if you stop to think—"

"If I stopped too long to think," he interrupted her at last, struggling to keep a cap on his rising temper, "I'd be tempted to wring your neck. Then your brothers would be obliged to come out and shoot me, but that's all right, my love, we'd expire in marital bliss!"

She didn't flinch. Her eyes narrowed and she stared him down in her very regal manner. "I didn't think that you'd begin to understand. I—"

She broke off because he was striding across the room to her. He caught hold of her elbows, lifting her, swirling her around.

"Let's get this straight right now, Christa. I said everything I had to say to your brother about Callie back then, but if you want to know something, my love, I'll tell you. Once I met him, I never felt much bitterness or anger toward your brother. It was too painfully clear that he was very much in love with Callie, and so damned obvious that Callie was in love with him. That makes up for a hell of a lot of sins, Christa. And just for the record, I'm not a Cameron. I have faltered and fallen upon occasion. But whether you believe it or not, we heathen Yanks raised in the Maryland farm country were brought up with a certain code of ethics too. I'd never use any animosity I had against Daniel against you in any way."

"Then—"

"No, no, no, hear me out. My turn, my way. This is between us, Christa."

"I see," she said coolly, staring at her arms where he touched her with a scornful command that he release her in her eyes. "All your animosity is strictly toward me."

He released her. He'd break a bone if he didn't.

"This isn't hallowed ground!" he told her.

Her lashes fluttered. She started to turn away. He grasped her back with a force that sent her spinning hard against him. "This is why you're coming with me!" he said sharply. He did what he'd been itching to do since he'd first seen her. He raked his fingers through the soft wealth of her hair, and kissed her. Touched those lips that were so quick to curl against him with his own. Hunger and dreams bubbled to the surface. He kissed her hard, ruthlessly, determinedly. Tasted the sweetness of her mouth, the mold of her lips, the very indefinable femininity about her that was so very elusive and so very beautiful and seductive.

Perhaps he took her by surprise. Perhaps he had been so forceful so that he left her no room to protest. A single sound escaped her; her arms rose between them, falling against his chest once, and then no more. His arms encircled her while his lips molded to hers. He sank down to the ground with her.

They were upon the fur.

He'd never meant to do this. To disappear such a length of time, then return and take his unwilling bride on a cottage floor.

But he continually discovered himself doing things he didn't intend in the least with her.

Her lips were parted to his. Perhaps she was not so willing a participant in the kiss, but she did not deny it. She made no effort to twist from him. He kissed her and kissed her, and her breath came too quickly and her heart hammered. When he brought her down, her arms laced around his neck. To keep her from falling, of course. But still, there was no protest.

She was laid down upon the floor, her hair spread across it, ebony blue. He leaned over her, aware of her eyes again and the sweeping richness of her black lashes. He stretched out beside her, cupping her breast beneath the fabric of her gown. Her lashes fell, her cheeks found color. He covered her mouth with his own once again, his hand tugging upon her skirt and petticoat. Damn women. They wore so much clothing. He was impeded further by the lacy pantalets she wore, but he impatiently found the tie to the garment and freed it. His palms moved over the naked flesh of her belly. He massaged it and slipped his fingers between her legs.

He heard the first rumble of sound from deep within her throat and ignored it. Touching her, feeling the silky hair of her triangle, the tender, damp flesh of her sex, added fuel to a fire that had tormented him all the time that he had spent away from her. He had sworn it would be hell. It was indeed his own hell, for he burned in it, wanting her. Now the flames were flaming to a peak. He wedged his weight between her thighs, fumbling quickly with his cavalry trousers. Some sense of sanity within him cautioned him that she was still new at this game, and not exactly an avid player—no matter the torment of his own desire. He touched her again, seeking erotic zones to tease, to arouse. To his surprise he was at the least rewarded with a startled gasp. He rotated his touch, moving more deeply inside her. She tried to clench her thighs against him but his body cleanly divided them and she was certainly at his mercy. Another sound escaped her as she felt the first thrust of his sex, just at the very vulnerable portals of her own. He could feel the charge and friction, the heat of his own desire. Her fingers bit into his blue-clad shoulders, she buried her face against his neck. He lifted his hips and thrust deeply and cleanly within her, feeling her arms tighten about him as he did so. He expected a cry, of pain or of protest. No sound escaped her. Slow! he warned himself. And he tried. But the dreams blended with reality. The sweetness of her scent pervaded his blood. The hunger he had lived with since he had left her gnawed with a burning ache for fulfillment. The flesh of her buttocks and thighs was like satin beneath his touch, and being within her, clothed and sheathed by the hot liquid heat of her body, touched off depths of desire he had scarcely known existed. As unwilling a bride as Christa might be, she was still, as she so often said herself, a Cameron. And her passions were all Cameron, wild and exciting. Whether she meant to give to him or not, she did. Perhaps she merely rode the storm. As the intensity of his need rose in a sweet and merciless spiral, he locked her into his embrace and rhythm. He forced her hips into a liquid smooth undulation. He swept her into his tempest, until it burst upon him, wonderful and volatile. He drifted downward, amazed at the sensations she created, at just how damned good it was to have her. Nothing had ever seemed quite so fierce or quite so sweet before.

Imagine! he mocked himself, if she were just willing!

She was quiet, breathing hard, her eyes downcast. She tried, which was futile with him still half atop her, to straighten her knees and bring down her skirts.

He bit his lip, rolling from her. He'd done well, he taunted himself. Let's see, he'd invaded her place of peace, then taken her nearly fully clothed on the very floor of her sanctuary. Now she was trying to cover a slim, shapely leg and to his annoyance, he was discovering that he could be aroused again himself by just such a sight.

Jenny would have taken a look at herself and giggled. And she would have whispered in his ear. "Well, that was fun, but really, Jeremy, shouldn't we shed our clothing this time?"

But, no! This was Christa, with her flaming blue eyes and midnight hair. And the sweet passion that simmered beneath everything, driving him to distraction. Making him want her more than he had ever wanted Jenny.

No.

Yes.

But denying him still.

She was uncomfortable, he realized. And she'd been in love once, yes. But she'd never married her Reb, never taken a chance on learning what it was to be in love and make love.

He rose, adjusting his trousers. He walked to the back window and looked out over the river before gazing back to her.

"I'm sorry," he told her quietly. It took some effort.

She didn't answer him. She was sitting up, her black hair a fall over her face, hiding her eyes. She was still trying to straighten out her attire. Her shoulders were squared. "It's really to be expected—" she began.

In that voice of hers. In that regal southern belle voice that set his nerves on edge.

He was back beside her in a number of seconds. He didn't touch her, but he hunkered down before her furiously. "All right, Christa, I'm not sorry. I'm not in the least damned sorry. You're my wife. This is what married people do!"

"Actually, most married people are completely polite and respectful of one another," she said smoothly, tossing back that mountain of hair. "They don't just couple like—"

"Jesu! Christa, you cannot be so blind! What do you think Daniel and Callie were so excited about this morning, sharing a cup of tea? Come, my love. Where do you think that damned fur came from in the first place?" He inclined his head toward the fireplace and the fur rug before it.

She was gracefully on her feet in seconds. "So why bother to apologize?"

He stood, hands on his hips, facing her. "I won't do so ever again, Christa, I promise." He smiled icily, remembering her secret torrent of tears over the fact that she was to come with him. He hadn't the least control over the malicious twinge that came to him when he reached for her, pulling her close once again. "Never. And so much—truly decadent, by your standards—lies before us. There is the dirt on the floor of a soldier's tent, and there's the dirt of the wide open fields! There are streams galore out there, abandoned Indian dwellings, wonderful, savage places to couple just like a pair of wild animals! And with my willing, imaginative bride, I just can't wait!"

She jerked her hand free. Her chin was high, her eyes blazing. "If you're trying to shock or frighten me, Jeremy, you can go to hell. I survived the war. And I'll survive you. I—"

"Yes, you are a survivor! No one fights so damned well, Christa. Had you just been in the damned field, Grant would have never stood a chance of taking the Rebs. I'm sure the goddamned Indians would be quaking in their buckskins if they knew you were coming."

She threw back her full mane of ebony hair, her eyes sizzling, her hands on her hips, the whole of her trembling. Actually, he'd never seen her quite so vital, so passionate, so wild.

So beautiful, sensual, and appealing.

"You sorry excuse for humanity!" she lashed out. "You can just stop it, or I'll—"

"You'll what?" he taunted. "Call in big brother? Tear me limb from limb?"

A cry of fury brought her flying across the room against him. He had goaded her on, and still, he hadn't quite been ready for her. She nearly knocked him flat. He caught his balance just in time. He caught her fingers just seconds before she could bring her nails raking across his face.

Husky laughter spilled from him then, even though he gave himself an inward warning. She was someone to reckon with.

"Christa—"

"Let go of me!" She kicked him hard, right in the shin. It hurt like hell.

"Christa!" He jerked her around so that her back was flat against his chest and her arms were tightly locked against his hold over her breast. She tried to bite him. He wrenched harder on his hold and she went dead still, rigid as steel.

"Don't raise a hand against me. And no more kicking. Or biting."

She remained still. And trembling. She tossed back her head. "Or what?" she whispered vehemently in turn.

He lowered his mouth against her ear. "Or I'll make you sorry, I promise."

He knew, from the feel of her, that she longed to tell him he didn't begin to know what sorry was—not yet. She'd see to it that he did.

But she was quiet for a long while. Then words seemed to explode from her. "I'll best you yet, you Yank!"

"Ah, yes!" He pushed her from him. When she spun around quickly to face him again, he swept her a low bow. "You're a Cameron! God has nothing on you, my love!"

"How dare you—"

"How dare I? I've no choice, do I? I've wed into the Holy Family."

"That's blasphemous as well as despicable. Leave it to a—"

"Yankee bastard. Yes. Well, I do apologize for disturbing your peace. Jesse intends to accompany you into Richmond to see me off, but we don't need to start until sometime tomorrow. I'm interested in some of the books in your brothers' library, so, should you find yourself pining for me, you'll know where I'll be. You can have hours and hours to yourself to go cry over your tombstones. Enjoy yourself!"

With another exaggerated and courtly bow—certainly as well executed as any given her by a prewar beau—he left her.

But as he walked toward the house, his shoulders squared, a tempest of anguish seethed within him.

Jesu! He was sorry. Sometimes it seemed that the war was all that he had ever lived. He had despised the fighting of it, he had hated seeing his family, friends, and neighbors die, no matter which side they had fought for! It had been agonizing to watch the fall of Vicksburg.

A Marylander, he understood Christa, understood her pain and all that she had lost. But understanding hurt too. He didn't want to be crude with her. Or cruel. He kept finding himself wanting to put his arms around her. Soothe her.

And she would just as soon be soothed by a rattlesnake, he was certain.

He stood still, suddenly wincing. Damn her! Her pride, and her courage, and her beauty, and all the fire that spilled from her soul! Even before the strange day of their wedding, he had been touched by that fire. But he'd been able to keep his distance then, avoiding the fact that most of his hostility stemmed from desire.

Even now, he wanted to go back. Take her into his arms. Tell her that things would work out.

But no, because then she'd want her own way again!

He had to take care. He couldn't let her know just how much he understood all that she felt. Couldn't let her know how he dreamed of her, wanted her.

Damn! He stiffened and gave himself a mental shake. Yankee fool! he accused himself.

He would not weaken. And he wouldn't fall in love with her.

Unless it was too late already.

Eight

"They're vast lands out there," Christa heard Jesse saying when she came to the house at last. She didn't know where her sisters-in-law were, but she had heard the murmur of male voices coming from the parlor, and she moved toward the doorway, hesitating as she listened to the men speak. "It can be dangerous territory," he said.

"Especially approaching the Comanche and the Apache tribes," Daniel added.

Christa looked silently through the doorway. The three of them stood in the center of the room with a map spread out on the table before them.

"Up around Little Rock, the Indians are all fairly civilized," Jeremy was pointing out.

"Some more so than some of the white folk I know," Daniel agreed, grinning.

"If you're referring to Yankees, remember that you're outnumbered," Jesse teased.

"Only some Yankees," Daniel responded easily enough. Christa leaned back against the wall, biting her lower lip. Daniel was coming to grips with the fact that they had lost. Maybe it was easier for him. He'd told her once that by the time it had come to the end, he just hadn't given a damn. All that he'd wanted was for the dying to stop.

Jeremy was speaking. Because of his words Christa imagined that he was pointing at the map again.

"Once you enter the Great Plains, you're in the hunting grounds, and you can come across just about anyone there. Southern Cheyenne, their allies, the Shoshone, or the Snakes. Here we've got Kiowa, Kiowa Apache—"

"And Comanche," Jesse said softly.

"Is Christa going to be safe?" Daniel demanded. "Jesu, Jeremy, I'm not at all sure you've any right to be taking her out there." Christa smiled. Daniel was so blunt. Jesse would be far more diplomatic.

"Military wives often follow their husbands," Jesse said. "But Jeremy, it is a frightening thought. And if Christa is expecting a baby, it's more dangerous still."

"All right, Jesse, you tell me. Just from that standpoint. Do you think it would be dangerous to take her?"

Jesse hesitated. "No," he said at last. "I have always found that women who are more active during pregnancy do much better in labor."

"Will there be a company surgeon?" Daniel asked.

A match was struck. Someone was lighting a cheroot. Christa held her breath.

"Major John Weland," Jeremy said.

"John?" Jesse's pleasure at the name was obvious.

"You've served with him?"

"He was with me until the last year of the war. He is an excellent physician and surgeon."

Well, Jesse was not going to be worried about her medical welfare, Christa decided bitterly.

"It's still dangerous territory!" Daniel insisted. "You know that, Jeremy—you were just reading to us from Colonel Cralton's letter to you." She heard a rustle of paper, and then Daniel's deep voice as he began to read. " 'The twelve men were apparently attacked by hundreds of Sioux. Each had been pierced by at least fifty arrows. Their ears and genitals had been lopped off; the genitals were found stuffed into the men's mouths.' " The paper floated down. "Jesu!" Daniel exploded.

Christa swallowed hard, leaning against the wall. She felt as if she were going to pass out. No, she never passed out. She never even pretended to do such things. But the pictures Daniel's reading had evoked in her mind . . . She clamped her hand to her mouth. A wild panic seized her.

"And those men were on a search mission," Jeremy said. Christa heard the clink of glass. Obviously, everyone had seen mental images of the twelve unfortunate soldiers. "Sent out by a fool to look for a fool," Jeremy commented. "I intend to keep my regiment together."

"And you have a certain rapport with the Comanche, so I've heard," Jesse commented.

"No one really knows the Comanche," Jeremy said. "There are dozens of bands. But yes, I know Buffalo Run, and he does exert some influence."

"Enough to save Christa?"

"I don't intend to lose her." Jeremy sighed. "Listen, it isn't a perfect life. But I'll be in command of Fort Jacobson, we'll be just north of Texas, and I'll also be receiving a thousand acres of land. Yes, I chose to go west. Just like I chose to fight on the western front when I was given the option at the beginning of the war. I didn't want to fight my Reb friends from Maryland and Virginia. And now —well, hell, now we've won. And I've seen Johnson's idea of his great Reconstruction! Crooked politics, carpetbaggers, swindlers, and chaos. That's what's here for Christa if she stays. I chose the West before, and I'm choosing to go farther west now. Hell, yes! I prefer the Indians!"

Christa closed her eyes, bracing herself against the wall. There was silence for a moment. Then she heard her brother speaking softly. "Well, maybe you've got a point," he murmured. "Still, I wonder what Christa will think. Will she be afraid of the Indians?"

Yes! Terrified! She wanted to cry out. But she didn't.

Maybe Jeremy sensed that she was at the doorway listening. Maybe he even realized that she might be enjoying a moment of feeling just a little bit smug. "If I know Christa, she'll do well enough," he said. "It's the Comanche we'll have to worry about, I think."

"What—" Jesse began, but by then Christa was swirling into the room, her skirts rustling around her as she entered, her chin high. She smiled, although it felt like her smile was chiseled of plaster. Jeremy had seen her skirt, she realized, from his vantage point behind the map. He had known that she was there.

No matter.

She headed straight to the whiskey decanter, determined to ignore Jeremy if he should give her a look that insinuated she was being in the least improper.

So much for manners and mores. She poured out two fingers of whiskey, then stared at Jeremy. He didn't appear shocked. He seemed amused.

So that was to be her fate in life. To amuse him at every turn! She pushed the whiskey aside. Her stomach was churning. She didn't want it anymore.

"Well, what do you think, Christa?" Daniel asked her.

"You should think about this, seriously," Jesse said.

It was her opportunity. Her golden opportunity to tell Jeremy to play cowboys and Indians all on his own. She'd stay home. Her brothers would protect her.

But her brothers were, at long last, getting a chance to lead normal lives with their families. And, yes, she could stay. They loved her. She would have a place . . .

A place on the fringe of life.

Jeremy moved around the table, away from the map, fingering his whiskey glass. He strode over to Christa and added a new shot to his glass, his eyes probing hers, silver and steel.

"They're really fascinating, you know. We whites, especially here on the eastern seaboard, have a habit of grouping Indians together. Their societies are so unique. Take the Choctaw and the Cherokee. Christa, you'll meet several. They have excellent systems of justice, and their tribal laws are impressive. The Arikara, along the Missouri, tolerate such curious practices that their neighbors on the Missouri have moved away. They choose to live in earth lodges, keeping all their garbage between them. They practice incest, and spend the winter chasing one another's wives. The Cheyenne are famous for their chastity. The wives often belong to guilds, and brag about their domestic abilities with greater pride than the bucks brag about their hunting prowess."

"Then there are the Sioux, the Apache, and the Comanche," Jesse reminded him.

Jeremy was intending to shock her, she realized. Did he suspect what she had already heard? She wouldn't show him that she was afraid. Ever.

She smiled, determined that she would not crack.

"Tell me about the Comanche," she said pleasantly.

"Christa, maybe you shouldn't—" Daniel began.

"Oh, no! I'm just dying to hear anything that Jeremy can tell me!"

"They tend to be small and bandy-legged. They are the horsemen of the plains—no man rides better than a Comanche. They are inordinately proud of their stealth." He walked around her, his voice coming husky. "They say that a fellow named Walking Bear stole a Texan's wife away while he was sleeping right beside her. They are fond of taking captives, and sometimes they are fond of torturing them. At night, if their cries are too loud, they are fond of cutting their tongues out."

"Good Lord, Jeremy—" Jesse started to protest.

"Jesse, it's quite all right," Christa said quickly. "This is going to be my life. I should know about these things."

"You'll start a new life frightened and miserable!" Daniel warned her. "Perhaps you should stay home. Until the baby is born, until Jeremy is established, at the very least."

Here it was again—her golden opportunity.

"But Christa is never frightened, are you, my love?" Jeremy queried.

She spun around. His eyes were sizzling out a challenge. Or maybe he was goading her into doing his will. One or the other, it didn't matter. He was going to win.

She spun around to smile broadly at her brothers again. "My, my! I've married a Yank. How on earth could I ever be frightened of a short, little Comanche?"

"They tend to be short," Jeremy said suddenly. She spun around. His fingers were now tense around his glass, and his eyes seemed to blaze into hers. "Some are tall. And smart. And great forces to be reckoned with. They can be passionate, and very fierce. Perhaps you should stay home."

Even Jeremy was saying it now. All she had to do was speak.

But she didn't speak, and the moment was swiftly gone. He lifted his glass to her. "But Christa Cameron, the great Rebel, is coming west. I say that the Comanche, Apache, Kiowa—all—had best take care. Right, my love?"

"Certainly," she replied, and lifted her glass in kind. "After all, I shall have the great Colonel McCauley at my side. No brave would dare to steal his wife, I'm sure."

"Let's hope not," Jesse murmured. His eyes were darkening with concern. She could sense that Daniel was about to jump in and there was only so much that Jeremy could do to keep peace in the family.

"I know that I will be just fine!" she said enthusiastically, her eyes rising to Jeremy's. Damn him! He seemed to want her to back out now, to cause some problem. What was the matter with him? He had, at the least, helped her with her brothers before.

He sighed suddenly, reaching out for her. She remembered the last time that he had touched her, and a sizzle of burning heat came sweeping through her. But he merely slipped an arm through hers and led her back to the map. "Let me show you the way you'll be coming to join me. The train will take you from Richmond to Washington, and from Washington you'll pass through to Illinois, and then come south again down the Mississippi by steamer—"

"Washington?" she said, dismayed.

"It's the best way," Jesse explained to her.

"I'm going to travel north to arrive southwest?"

"Christa, half the railways in the South still need repairing," Daniel told her. She sensed just the slightest note of bitterness in his tone. "And even if they didn't, that's your best route. Honestly."

She nodded, staring at the map. It was going to be a long, long journey.

She looked up. Jeremy was staring at her again. She looked quickly back to the table. It was one of Jesse's old maps, one he'd acquired in Kansas before the war. There were no marks on it that drew lines between the North and the South.

There was no North, and no South. It was all one big country once again.

And here was a map with broad stretches in the West with names like "No-man's-land."

It would be wild and untamed. And it might even be free from the heavy hand of Reconstruction.

"It should be a fascinating journey," she said. Her head was pounding. There were more words on the map. Words that broke the big territory down into smaller, more frightening areas.

The words were Indian names: Shoshone, Cheyenne, Choctaw, Sioux, Blackfeet, Crow, Apache, Comanche, and more.

They were all looking at her now. She could feel their eyes on her. Jesse was worried. Daniel was growing hostile.

What was Jeremy thinking? Had he decided that he had been roped into this misery, but that she really wasn't worth the effort anymore? He might have decided that she simply wasn't enjoyable enough material, as far as a wife went.

To her astonishment, she felt a prickling of moisture at the back of her eyes. It was the baby, she thought. It was the exhaustion she so often felt.

There were so many things she felt for her husband. She could not forgive him—not so much for winning the war, but for being so damned certain that he had always been right. She hated him sometimes. Most men went out of their way to be charming to her, while Jeremy wouldn't give her the courtesy of believing in the smallest feminine lie. She hated him, yes, and she wanted to best him. She wanted to prove to him that southern "belles" had always been made of sterner stuff. She wanted to prove to him that she wasn't afraid, that she could do anything a northern girl could do, and better.

And she was intrigued. By his eyes, gun-metal gray one minute, silver the next. And she was fascinated by the hard-muscled grace of his body. She was determined to deny him, and equally determined that he would never lose his desire to have her.

She had married him, and she was going to have his baby. Her fingers trembled.

Twelve men had been found with fifty arrows apiece protruding from them. Their ears and their genitals had been cut off. Stuffed into their mouths. Comanches liked to cut out the tongues of their victims.

"My love?" Jeremy murmured, watching her.

She was going to travel west.

She ran her finger over the map. "I've never really traveled very much," she murmured. "Well, let's see, I came to West Point to visit you and Daniel that winter, Jesse. And I've been to Washington and down south as far as Savannah, but this . . ." She looked up, her chin high. "This will be quite different. How long will it be before I meet up with you in Little Rock, Jeremy?"

He smiled. Another of his taunting, amused smiles. Yet she thought that there was a glitter of admiration in his silver eyes. "Not that long, my love. Assuming you're ready to leave in another two weeks, the journey will take you about two weeks. We won't be parted more than a month. That shouldn't be too distressing, should it?"

"Oh, I shall just pine every day!" she murmured. She spun around suddenly, feeling as if she were choking. She wasn't about to let him know that she was feeling ill again—he might mistake it for cowardice.

"Gentlemen, do return to your whiskey and conversation. If you'll excuse me . . ."

She didn't give a damn if they excused her or not. She needed to escape.

In her wake, she was certain that she sensed Jeremy's silent laughter.

As they rode into Richmond late the following afternoon, Jeremy watched Christa's face and became heartily sorry that he had ever suggested that she ride in with Jesse and say good-bye to him.

Maybe they had all become hardened—he, Jesse, Daniel, and others. Maybe they'd just all seen so much battle that the aftermath couldn't seem too terrible.

But it was.

The streets of Richmond were filled with maimed and broken men. Amputations had saved thousands upon thousands of lives, but watching the results now was painful.

On every street they passed, there were men. Some were walking, some were just sitting. Half of them were missing some part of their bodies. Many were still clad in their uniforms, or pieces of uniforms. Tattered gray shirts covered scrawny chests. Many were unshaven, dirty.

But the worst of it was the look in their eyes. They looked as if they had lost everything.

They had. And the hopelessness was more difficult to see than death in battle. Death was sometimes merciful.

This endless anguish was merciless.

And there were more than just the tragically maimed, wounded, and lost to fill the streets of the city. Whores strode freely and boldly where the most chaste and modest of women had once strolled. Brazen, red-lipped and red-gowned, they shouted to any able-bodied man they saw. Soldiers in Union blue walked here and there, some on business and in a hurry, some off duty and strolling about, some saddened by the loss of humanity, and some pleased that the blasted Rebels had been broken.

Then there were the moneylenders and the businessmen. Garish folk, dressed in bright shirts and striped trousers, standing up on soap boxes. Mostly they promised the lost and wandering slaves wonderful riches for working for them. Paid labor from the first streaks of sunup to the last whisper of light in the sky. But they would work as free men for a pittance—not enough to feed the families now looking to them for food and sustenance.

He hadn't lied to Daniel or Jesse yesterday. He was heartily sick of Reconstruction.

Christa, attired in a maroon riding habit and actually riding sidesaddle and looking very composed today, reined in suddenly. He realized that they had come upon the large dwelling that had once been the White House of the Confederacy.

Through the long years of the war, the Jefferson Davises had resided here. Varina, gracious and beautiful, had entertained, always seeking to keep up morale, her husband's staunchest supporter no matter what his difficulties with the North—or with his own generals. In northern camps, the men may have poked fun at Jeff Davis before their campfires but Varina had earned a reputation that had made her the envy of many. Poor Mary Todd Lincoln was said to be part crazy, and now, with Lincoln murdered, the poor lady was in sad shape, indeed. She had never been popular with the northern troops.

Now, men in blue uniforms hurried in and out of the White House of the Confederacy. Christa stared.

"Christa!" Jesse said her name softly. She didn't seem to hear him.

"Christa!" Jeremy said more harshly. "Ride on by! It will be easier!"

She rode. She spurred her horse and rode on ahead of them. Jeremy glanced at Jesse. She didn't have any idea of where she was riding.

They both spurred their horses, hurrying to catch up with her. Christa was well dressed; her mare, Tilly, was an exceptional Arabian. Alone, she could be inviting trouble.

They rounded a corner where merchants were in the street selling goods for exorbitant prices. Yankee prices. Southern pride might remain, but no one wanted southern money. There was a stand where tomatoes were going for two bits a piece. Milk was sky high, meat almost untouchable.

As they rode by the booths, a high, venomous female voice called out.

"Yankee-loving whore!"

A missile came hurtling toward them. Realizing that it was aimed toward Christa, Jeremy instinctively moved his horse forward. He stretched out a hand to catch the flying object. It seemed to explode in his hand, spewing red, like blood, around them. Someone had thrown a tomato at Christa.

He pulled off his glove, shaking the tomato from it. Christa stared at him in horror.

"By God!" she breathed. "So very dear, so expensive, and she was willing to throw it at me!"

"Stop!" cried another woman, apparently calling out to Christa's tormentor. "You'd have a Yankee, too, you old crone, if a Yankee would have you."

"Let's go on," Jesse suggested wearily.

But Jeremy started to dismount, determined to find the guilty party.

"No!" Christa cried. Jeremy looked at her. "Please!" she whispered. "Let's just go!" She flapped the reins over her mare's neck.

Once again, he was hard put just to follow her alongside Jesse. "I think maybe you'd best take her to the hotel, Jesse, right away, if you don't mind," he said to his brother-in-law. "She's not going to like seeing the people around the government buildings."

"I'll catch her," Jesse promised, riding ahead hard. Jeremy reined in. He watched them ride on, wishing with all his heart that he'd said good-bye to her at Cameron Hall. It was a bitter world. Maybe it was best she learned that now.

He reported in to a General Babcock, and was delighted to learn that he had a company of men waiting to travel with him, including a number of friends from his old regiment. He had barely left the general's office behind when he felt a tap on the shoulder. He turned around to see a very old friend standing there, a tall, lean black man. His name was Nathaniel Hayes, and he had never been a slave. He'd been born a free man in New York City, and from Jeremy's Indian days long before the war, Nathaniel had been with him. He'd carried firearms in the West, and he'd been dismayed to discover how many northern white men were against his carrying a gun against the Rebel forces; captured black men— free or not—did not fare well as southern captives. Especially if they'd carried firearms. So Nathaniel had just served Jeremy. He'd never carried a firearm, but he'd written many messages for Jeremy and he'd managed to attend to his every need.

"Nathaniel! You came all the way down here just to travel with me?"

Nathaniel grinned broadly. "Colonel, sir, I was delighted to come down. There's a number of the old regiment from the days we spent in Mississippi before you were sent east with Grant!"

"Tenting just outside the city?"

"That's right, Colonel. Waiting to travel with you. Are you joining us tonight?"

He shook his head. "My wife is with me."

"Traveling with us now, sir?"

He shook his head. "She needs to pack household belongings if we're to make a go of it out in the wilderness. She'll join me in Little Rock. You'll like her, Nathaniel," he heard himself saying.

He nodded. "Certainly, sir, that I will. She's a southern girl, I hear."

He nodded. Yes, she was that. A southern girl, very bitter at this moment that someone would hate her enough to throw a tomato at her—when tomatoes were so costly.

"Will you bring her tonight, sir? There's to be something of a barn dance. We've some young ones, new recruits, and they've managed to attract some of the young ladies hereabouts. With your permission, sir!"

"Permission granted," Jeremy assured him. "And yes, I'll come to see to my personal equipment, and to introduce my wife to the men."

As it turned out, Christa was not particularly interested in meeting his men. When he reached the hotel at last, he found her alone in their room. He unbuckled his scabbard, watching her as she sat staring silently out the window.

"Where's Jesse?"

"Bathing," she murmured absently, still staring out. She was so still and straight and miserable he wanted to offer her some comfort. She wouldn't want his comfort, though. It was because of him that someone had thrown a tomato at her and called her a Yankee-loving whore.

"There's to be a party, a barn dance of sorts, out where the men are tenting tonight. We're going to attend."

She shook her head. "You attend. I haven't the heart for it."

"We'll attend, because you're my wife."

"I don't feel well—"

"You're lying."

"I'm expecting a child!" she flared up.

"And you're feeling just fine."

She stood up, fingers clenched into fists at her sides, and accosted him. "If you were any kind of a gentleman at all—"

"If I were a southern gentleman, you mean, I would allow you to lie whenever it suited your convenience. Well, I'm not, and I won't. My men are eager to get a look at you. They've all heard that I married southern royalty. We're going to give them a good look. Make sure you wear something really lavish. They'll enjoy it."

He stalked out of the room, slamming the door behind him. How had he wound up fighting with her, when all that he had wanted to do was put an arm around her?

Easy. She'd insisted that he marry her but he'd insisted they make it real, that she accompany him. Why? Because he wanted her. He wouldn't have married her, not even for Cameron Hall, not for Jesse, Callie, or anyone, if there hadn't been something there.

He swallowed, grit his teeth, and went down to the taproom. It was a southern establishment, one Jesse had known well before the war. Its proprietor had a way about him—he was a man willing to roll with the times.

Jeremy was the only one in the public room. The innkeeper served him whiskey, then left him alone. Jeremy sipped it slowly, determined to give Christa more time alone.

What would he do if she flatly disobeyed him? Could he drag her along anyway? And what about Jesse? Right or wrong, he would have leapt to Callie's defense against Daniel if he hadn't been engaged in battle when the two had met.

When he'd sat with the whiskey long enough, he rose and returned to his room. To his surprise Christa was dressed, and beautifully so. She was in emerald-green taffeta and velvet, an off-the-shoulder dress that displayed the delicate beauty of her shoulders and the rise of her breasts. Her black hair was pulled into a riot of curls at her nape.

She sat by the window again, looking down, even though the night grew dark.

He held still in the doorway, watching her. Then he entered the room, closing the door behind him. To his surprise she turned to him at last. "Isn't this flamboyant enough?"

He discovered himself swallowing like a schoolboy. "It will do nicely," he said, then cleared his throat. "You're extremely beautiful."

She lowered her head. "For a Yankee's whore," she whispered.

"For his wife!" he reminded her harshly.

There was a knock at the door. He turned around. Jesse stood there. "Are we going to dinner? If you two would prefer to dine in—"

"No, no, Jess, thanks. We're going to something like a barn dance, and I think you'll enjoy it. You may know some of the men in attendance."

Jesse was agreeable. If he noted that his sister was pale and wan he must have thought it had something to do with her missing her husband once again.

Pray God we leave it that way! Jeremy thought. He didn't know what Christa would do once they reached the camp.

To his surprise, she did very well. She met Nathaniel first, and the two seemed to like one another immediately. He saw her eyes widen with surprise when Nathaniel first spoke, and he realized that she'd probably never met a black man without a southern slur to his voice. Jesse struck up a quick conversation with Major Weland, and Christa somehow wound up on Jeremy's arm. They joined the two physicians, and Weland assured Christa that he would see to it that she was safely delivered of a beautiful baby, no matter where they might be.

"I'll be—darned," Jesse said, looking across the large canvas mess tent where they had gathered for the dance. "Excuse me," he told the others. "That's Jules Larson. He's just turned twenty, I believe, but I thought he was fighting for the Confederacy at the end of the war. His family's from the peninsula."

Major Weland looked around Jesse. "The boy was a Confederate. He's joined on with the U.S. Cavalry again. Lots of southern boys will be doing so, you mark my words. A horse soldier is a horse soldier. The war is over. We've new worlds to conquer. The West is the future!"

There were a number of ex-Confederates who were going to be in his regiment, Jeremy learned. When the dance wound down to the final moments, the cavalry band decided to pay a tribute to them.

The last song played was "Dixie."

Jeremy watched Christa. She stood very tall and straight, and listened. She lowered her head, and he thought that tears must have sprung to her eyes.

But they had not. She lifted her chin. He thought that she had decided that she would cry no more for her homeland.

Pride was not such a terrible thing, he told himself. It had sustained many a man, many a time. If it would bring her west, so be it.

But she was so silent on the ride back to the hotel that he began to wonder again. He had determined that he would not press her that night, that he would leave her be.

But he could not bear to keep with that conviction. She had trouble with the hooks on her gown and he had to help her. When she stood in her corset and petticoats, he felt the familiar thudding of her heart, the ache in his groin. It would be their last night together for quite some time. He pressed his lips against her shoulder and inhaled the sweet scent of her. He didn't know if she issued a protest or not, but he swept her up, petticoats and all, doused the lights with a snuffer, and made love to her.

There was nothing different. She did not protest, she did not respond. Frustrated, he lay in the darkness and wondered if he hadn't made a horrible mistake. Then he leaned on an elbow and gazed at her. Her eyes were closed, her lips were damp, slightly parted. Her breasts rose and fell and her body carried a beautiful sheen, highlighting its perfection.

No, it could not be a mistake. She was his. They had cast their fates together.

But he thought of her in the wilderness. A fear gripped his heart. Did he have the right to drag her through savage country?

Her eyes opened suddenly. She flushed, reaching for the sheets as she caught him staring at her.

He closed his hand over hers. "Leave it. We'll be parted a long time now."

She didn't reply. Her lashes lowered. He sat up, then sighed. "Christa, don't come. Stay in Virginia. You don't have to join me."

Her eyes opened again. She looked at him. "I—I don't want to stay here!" she said softly.

He frowned, puzzled. "But—"

"I don't want to stay. I don't want—I don't want to see those maimed, hopeless men! I don't want to see the bastard scalawags tormenting the freed blacks and the whites who have been left with nothing. I—" She broke off. "I can't stay here!" she whispered.

He leaned low, watching her once again. "So you would escape—even if escaping means facing the Indians with me. Aren't you afraid?"

If she was, she wasn't going to tell him.

"I'm tired," she said.

He watched her for a moment. Then he slipped an arm around her and pulled her close. She stiffened instantly, but he merely smoothed her hair back.

"You're tired," he said irritably. "Sleep."

In a moment, she relaxed. And he held her, thinking that she was incredible.

So taut and wounded, proud and fierce—and so infinitely beautiful and precious. His enemy, his love.

He didn't sleep that night.

They breakfasted at the crack of dawn, for he was to ride to the train station at the head of his troops. They moved so swiftly that there was no more time to talk, even though he could suddenly think of a dozen things to say.

They rode to the camp together, then he kissed her briefly, shook Jesse's hand, and prepared to take his leave. He was at the head of his troops, the bugler was calling them all in and they were ready to ride.

He turned upon his mount to look down at Christa one last time.

She returned his stare. She hesitated a moment, beautiful, elegant in her white gown with the lilac flowers. She began to move, hurrying toward his horse.

They were about to move forward. He reined in instead. She continued to come. Then she hesitated.

He leaned down, sweeping her up into his arms. She seemed startled for only a moment, her arms instinctively curling around his neck.

He lowered his head and kissed her.

And for the first time she kissed him back.

He tasted the marvelous sweetness of her tongue, felt the gentleness of her lips. Felt the subtle movement of her body, the brush of her fingers against his nape. Heat rushed into him, suffusing his loins, his thighs, his chest, his arms. He could have held her forever, kissing her, tasting her, holding her.

She was kissing him.

Because she would miss him?

Or because he was actually leaving, and she had gained another month of freedom?

It didn't really matter. A burst of applause rang out. His troops were certainly entertained. No matter what she was doing to his system, he had to ride.

Regretfully, he lifted his lips from hers. He searched out her eyes. They were fathomless. He set her down gently upon the ground and tipped his hat to her.

"Take care, my love!" he said. She stepped back, her fingers against her lips. She raised a hand as he lifted his own, moving his troops out.

Within minutes, she was a beautiful blur in the background with Jesse at her side.

Yes, that was it. It was a show for her brother.

But she had kissed him back.

Damn her.

The heat would haunt him all the long days until he saw her again.

Nine

Autumn, 1865

I have now been on the road (a steamer isn't exactly on the road, and I have traveled forever by steamer, so it seems) for ten days, and as Celia Preston has suggested, I am going to keep a journal. All good cavalry wives do so, for future waves of women and men who come this way and enter into the wilderness. Keeping a journal, so Celia tells me, is a quite popular thing to do, and as it is also a way to keep abreast of events when writing home, I have decided to set my hand to it. And so thinking, I will go back ten days, to the day I said good-bye.

I had help in preparing to leave. Although I couldn't take everything that had been acquired for my "marriage chest" throughout the years, Jesse warned me that I would need my good dishes and silver and table linens— Jeremy would be expected to entertain along the way, and no one can know who might come to visit. So when the day came to depart, I was literally surrounded with trunks. It was Daniel's time to then assure me that Jeremy wouldn't be in the least alarmed, that there would be plenty of ambulances to convey all these things. Yes, ambulances. That's the way frontier military wives travel, they both assured me. The vehicles are fitted out to carry the sick and wounded—and officers' wives. I have to admit the idea of seeing the countryside is beginning to intrigue me. And I have to admit, privately to my journal, that the idea of certain Indians terrifies me. But the die is cast —there is no looking back now.

As I stood in the entryway at Cameron Hall I thought of what lay before me. Although the weather was beginning to turn cool, both sets of breezeway doors had been thrown open for all the coming and going that took place as my things were being packed. I felt that touch of Virginia air, and I stood where my ancestors had stood for over two centuries. I looked up at the portrait gallery, at Jassy and Jamie who began the construction of Cameron Hall, and at Ma and Pa, and at the picture taken just before the war of the three of us, Jesse, Daniel, and me. I thought that not even Jesse's determination to be a Yankee had split us up, but now with the war over at last, we were surely being torn apart.

I looked away quickly. I love Cameron Hall with all my heart. It is Jesse's, it is Kiernan's. I must leave it to them.

Yet it wasn't the Hall that so broke my heart. I kissed the children and set them down. John Daniel was quite old enough to understand what was going *on, and there were huge tears in his little eyes. Callie was crying and Kiernan was crying, and I kissed and hugged my sisters-in-law fiercely. No one, not Jesse or Daniel or Jeremy, will ever understand how close we became. The men fought battles together. We survived together.*

And, of course, it was saying good-bye to Daniel that broke my heart the most fiercely. Jesse is still with me; I dread our parting. I had sworn I would not cry, but when I embraced Daniel knowing not when I would see him again, if ever (life being so precarious a gift as it is!), I felt the tears burning at the back of my eyelids. "Little sister," he told me. "You kept the home fires burning for us for years. Before God, Christa, we will always keep them burning for you!" He hugged me so fiercely that I thought I would break, and still, I could have clung to him forever. But Jesse plucked me away before I burst into a torrent of tears, and so we drove away, waving merrily. Yet, if my heart did not shatter in those moments, I know that I can brave what the future will bring. If I can only brave Jeremy!

Christa frowned, then scratched out the last sentence. She would be seeing him soon enough. Her stomach was knotting, and she was increasingly nervous.

If the Indians did get hold of her, she didn't want him reading in her journal that she had been afraid of him! And she wasn't afraid of him. Sometimes she didn't understand what she felt at all. Oddly, she would wake up nights and reach out, and feel empty to realize that she was alone. She would remind herself fiercely that she would be sleeping with him soon enough, in the rain, in the snow, in the elements. And being Jeremy, he would reach for her whenever the notion swept him.

And she would fight the onslaught of sensations that always seized her.

Why?

She bit her lip, determined that she wouldn't think about it, or Jeremy. But she paused again. There were times when she missed him, and she didn't understand why. She came slowly to admit that she liked the deep sound of his voice, and she liked the way that he wore a uniform—even if it was a blue uniform. She liked the strong feel of his arms, and she even liked the way, at times, that he could look through her. There was no pretense with Jeremy. She admired his raw determination, and she could never fail to be touched by the silver and steel in his eyes. Thinking of him holding her again made her breathless. She hated him for taking her away, and yet she was glad of him for that very reason. He made her furious, he made her weak. He always touched some deep emotion, some passion, within her.

What of Jeremy? He'd had weeks now to ponder all that they had done. Did he regret the marriage? Of course he regretted it. He had never wanted it. But he had insisted that she come with him. Was he sorry now? He could seem so bitterly disappointed in her. Or perhaps she would be better than nothing at all along the trail.

She wasn't going to think about it.

She looked back to her journal.

Coming through Richmond again was horrible, seeing all the wounded and maimed and lost souls upon the streets. No one hurtled anything at me, even though Jesse has accompanied me in uniform as he is carrying dispatches for

several of the forts out west. He'll hand them—as well as me—over to Jeremy.
Jesse has tendered his resignation. He is ready to set his hand to being a
gentleman farmer and country doctor and live a peaceful life with Kiernan
at Cameron Hall. It will take some time, however, for him to actually
manage to leave the military.

Anyway, onward. A lot of rebuilding is being done. It is sad to see the
burned and gutted houses, it tears at the heart. Yet rebirth is also going on.
Fields are full, as there are no longer armies to tramp them down. One
minute you can see a house that is nothing but a shell, smoke stains upon it
and cannonballs within it. Then just along the road comes the scent of fresh
lumber, the sounds of hammers against nails, and new structures can be seen
going up. The South is repairing herself. Everyone says, "If only Lincoln had
lived!" We all hated him for so long for his determination to keep the country
together! But everyone knew of his gentle plans for the South to return to the
Union, and everyone has seen that President Johnson is not nearly so mag-
nanimous! Perhaps the nation will heal. And perhaps the West is where the
schism may come together at last, for I am traveling there with quite a
mixture of people.

I met Celia Preston in Washington, where we switched trains for Illinois.
She is very young, very pretty, and very frightened. She is a northern girl,
traveling west to be with her James. Apparently James and Jeremy have
served together before, and Celia is quite certain that the sun rises and sets in
Jeremy. I have refrained from telling her that it is otherwise. I do intend to
make an exceptional cavalry wife. I'm sure that Jeremy is expecting me to
arrive all froth and lace, the very stereotypical southern "belle," and I in-
tend him to know that few of us were ever so flighty as men seem to wish to
believe. Running a plantation was hard work. From sunup to sundown.
There were always candles and soap to be made, meat to be smoked, linens to
wash and change, and even if a household did keep slaves it was up to the
mistress of the house to see that it was all done, that hundreds of people were
fed, that things ran so smoothly that the master of the place could come in at
any moment, set his feet up, and call upon his beloved for a brandy, never
realizing what she had accomplished.

Those days are over. I have come upon an easy lot in life. Jesse assures me
that there will be a company cook, and that men often come up from the
ranks to cook specifically for the officers' wives. Also, we will be followed by a
host of laundresses.

All that I shall have to do is try to assure the other wives that we will not
be eaten by cannibalistic Indians.

Actually, that is not fair. None of the tribes I have heard about is a
cannibalistic one. They are just murderers, savages, and thieves.

She paused again, chewing upon the nib of her pen. She couldn't write all
negative things about the Indians. She was traveling with an Indian. His name
was Robert Black Paw, and like James he had served with Jeremy before. He was
a Cherokee. A tall man who could move like air. His eyes were very dark and
serious. He wore Union issue navy trousers with a deerskin shirt and hide boots
that laced up to his knees. He was soft-spoken and his English was excellent.
Whenever she needed something, he miraculously appeared. When she wished to

be alone, he just as miraculously disappeared. He and Jesse had seemed to hit it off very well and they spent a great deal of time together.

Robert was a Cherokee. Cherokee were among the Five Civilized Tribes. Jesse had told her that actual companies of Cherokee had fought for the North —and for the South. She knew that Jesse considered the Cherokee to be at least as civilized as the white man—Jeremy probably considered them to be more so.

Back to travel. It seemed difficult for me to go through Washington, but actually it was far easier than seeing Richmond. Nothing was bombed, nothing was burned. We had some time before the train was to leave and Jesse already had his dispatches, so we went for a ride. My mare, Tilly, and Jesse's horse will now be pent up in a railway car again for a long stretch, so it seemed only fair to exercise them. But then we came upon the very sad part of that journey, for Jesse rode toward Arlington House, General Lee's old home.

He and Daniel had been General Robert E. Lee's pupils at West Point. To this day they both adore Lee, as does a countryside now, it seems. (Other than that awful General Pickett who blames the entire disaster of Gettysburg upon Lee.) Even Daniel admits that Stuart did not have the cavalry where it should have been and so failed Lee. And with Stonewall so recently deceased, Lee was so alone! Do I defend him too rashly? Yes, perhaps. Stuart is gone now along with Jackson and so many others; Lee has aged ten years for every one in which he fought the war.

"He can't come home," Jesse told me. And I saw in his eyes that he was remembering all the times that he had come there in happier days. The moment Lee agreed to serve the Confederacy, the Union seized his home. They could not afford him his little mount that overlooked the city of Washington. The house still stood. The house where Lee's wife, Martha Washington's great-granddaughter, had grown up and raised her own family. It had been a home to the Lees as precious as Cameron Hall is to all of us.

Lee cannot come home, for the government still has the place. The grounds are filled with the bodies of innumerable Union soldiers. Someone once thought that it would be a fine retaliation against Lee to bury Yankees on his grounds. Jesse told me that there was talk that the place might be made into a national cemetery, like the grounds in Gettysburg, but at the moment it is all in the air. Perhaps Lee's family will try to get the property back or demand some recompense. Bitterness remains, although Lee himself has said that the war is over and that he is determined on healing—a healing as quick as can be accomplished.

We rode back from Arlington House and saw that the horses were boarded and then found our own accommodations. I have a beautiful sleeper to myself. The upholstery is velvet, the furnishings are mahogany. Jesse is traveling on my one side, and Celia on the other. There is a handsome dining car just beyond us, and beyond that a smoking car for the men. Jesse has refrained from spending much time there, as he is so tenderly determined to share what little time we have left together.

Celia is lovely, Robert Black Paw is fascinating. There is one more army wife with us, and she is not quite so lovely. She is Mrs. Brooks, wife of Lieutenant Brooks, and I do not know her first name because she has not offered it. She raised a huge stink that we must all stop and observe the Sabbath properly. She was furious with some of the men—enlisted men—in the far cars because they dared to use profanity in her proximity. Of course, I'm certain the poor fellows had no idea they were anywhere near her. She has assured me that she will insist my husband do something about it since I refuse to be concerned. Where is my proper respect and belief in the Lord?

I was so stunned by her that I'm afraid I took several moments to reply. I assured her that my God was still busy collecting souls from the battlefields, which brought a gasp from her. She huffed herself around and left and I haven't seen her since, so I'm quite sure she will complain to Jeremy. I don't care. Jesse was behind me, and he was amused and assured me that Jeremy would probably be too. Of course, Jesse doesn't know how Jeremy really feels about me, but I do hope that he'll support his men over that harpy. I walked to the rear of the train, stood out by the rail, and watched the countryside. We were traveling through the mountains and their beauty, captured in so many colors, was awesome. I wondered what had happened to so many of our own convictions. When we were young, we never failed to make Sunday church services. But then the war came and all men, Yanks and Rebels, prayed to the same God. I don't think that I have lost Him entirely. Perhaps I shall find Him again in the West, alive in the savage wilderness.

We left the mountains to travel through Cincinnati, Ohio, and I saw just a bit of the bustle of that city. It is so untouched by the war. The next day brought us to Odin, Illinois, where I was startled when Jesse insisted I not leave the station. "They call it the hellhole of Illinois," he informed me, and really played the big brother. I chafed at the bit, of course, and saw all that I could through the windows. In the dining car I managed to pick up quite a bit of gossip and was heartily sorry that I could not see the place, for it is truly reputed to be a den of iniquity. I could see some of the women in the streets, and certainly some of them were engaged in "the" profession, for their clothing was loud and garish and their faces were very painted. One young lady was wearing black stockings that could be seen beneath a rise in her skirt— which was crimson! She seemed a happy-go-lucky thing, and I imagined that she was probably much more down on her luck than evil in any way. Of course, there was more to be seen. Drunkards careening down the street, gamblers in very fancy black. Oh! There was a gunfight! Not that I could be a Cameron and be unaccustomed to guns, but this was quite different from anything in my experience. The two men were wearing slovenly long railway frocks, teetering about, and calling one another out. Fortunately—or unfortunately—they were both so drunk that they missed one another several times.

Jesse pulled me in from the window and warned that I had best watch out —they were such poor shots they might well catch my nose since it was protruding so from the train. I cuffed him soundly on the arm, then started to laugh, and he laughed, and then I was nearly crying and in his arms, but I sobered quickly. I will not cry again.

From Odin, Illinois, we came to Cairo and caught a steamer that would take us down the Mississippi. I was delighted with my beautiful stateroom, though that delight was somewhat dampened when the captain, a kindly old bewhiskered fellow, assured me that there would be nothing less than the finest for "Colonel Jem's" wife. I tried not to think about the future too much, for the steamer is a fine southern vessel and there is a certain feeling about *heading down into Dixie again. There are several ex-Confederates aboard. None of them seems to bear a grudge. Jesse has come across some old friends, and Rebel and Yank alike, they are all interested in a game of poker. Being Jesse's friends, they were more than willing to allow his sister to play, and Jesse thought it was all right since I would be in his company and the stakes would be very low. Mrs. Brooks is, of course, quite horrified, and I'm certain she is going to find a way to inform Jeremy fully about his wife's outrageous behavior. Well, she will just have to do so. I am enjoying myself tremendously, and I am very afraid that far too soon a noose will slip around my neck.*

I had been sick mornings. Jesse had been afraid that the steamer would make me doubly so, but oddly enough, I feel very well now.

In Memphis we left the steamer and caught a new one headed down the White River. The ride became fascinating, for the scenery was haunting and mysterious. Swamps and deep, submerged forests surrounded the river. Darkness descended quickly, it seemed, yet sunsets and sunrises were glorious. There was the constant hum of insects at night, and though it seemed somewhat dismal, it was also very beautiful.

Four days out of Cairo and we reached DeVall's Bluff, which is a teeming, busy port. Not even the war seems to have changed that here. Ships were coming and going, goods were piled high on the docks, and people bustled about with purpose, busy with their lives. It was wonderful to see.

I am, however, growing very nervous. We leave here on the noon train, and will reach Little Rock by five. My heart is racing, I cannot breathe very well. Women, especially women in my "condition," are supposed to have such difficulties, but I don't think that this has anything to do with my health. I think that it has everything to do with my husband, and I cannot, for the life of me, begin to understand it. We are enemies. It is more than the color of his uniform, for from the day we first met we were natural enemies. A fire would grow hotter if he entered a room, a clear soft day would seem charged with the force of a storm. Now, things are assuredly worse for he seems to think that this marriage business has made him lord and master. Perhaps there is some sense to that, for I am here, the old life falling behind like clothing that has been shed, the new life stretching before me, frightening and wild.

We are approaching Little Rock. My fingers are trembling and it is difficult to hold the pen. I look at what I have written and am amazed— these words be but for my eyes only! Any minute, I will be with him again. I am so very nervous! I will end here.

Five forty-five. I will not, after all, end here. We've just received a message that Jeremy moved out into Indian territory with a small company of men on a search mission. He has left word asking Jesse to bring me down to his regiment's encampment outside of Fort Smith. We will leave by boat again in the morning.

I have just read over my last entry. I wish that I might have enjoyed Little Rock more. Jesse was wonderful, taking me out for a delicious steak dinner at a very nice restaurant, joking and warning me that I must now be prepared for life in the field and that I should embark upon that life well fed. It was an interesting evening, for I met the matronly wife of a colonel just coming in from the Indian territory, and she has been wonderful. She warned me that, yes, I must have crinolines and petticoats for special

*occasions, but that if I were to be a truly respectable cavalry wife, I must dress
the part. Simple cottons and, with the colder weather coming on, warm
underclothing, nothing frilly. There will be occasions when one must dress up,
but on a day-to-day basis the simpler the better. A bonnet is a must if a
woman is to have any skin left whatsoever upon her nose. The dust will be
horrid, the cold will be bone chilling, and the rain will come in torrents. But
she assured me that she valued every minute of her experience. I hope that I
can be like her. She is charming and bubbling. Her interest in the flowers
and plants and the beauty of the scenery is contagious. Most of all, I am
delighted because, thanks to this dear lady, Jeremy will not be able to find a
bit of fault with me. He will meet the perfect cavalry wife. However else I
may fail him, in this I will succeed.*

*We left Little Rock early the next morning. The steamer seemed excessively
slow, and though the days should be turning cool, the ride seemed very hot. I
could not seem to still the onslaught of nerves that had assailed me, and all
because of Jeremy. I am afraid to see him, I am afraid of Indians, and I am
afraid of the unknown. I cannot be afraid of any of these things—especially
Jeremy. I am also anxious. The blood seems to race through my veins. Though
Jesse assures me that blood moves through the body at a constant rate, this is
different. I lay awake last night, almost all the night, and I thought that it
might well be the last time that I lay alone. Then I am anxious again,
because he does strange things to me, things that I can't combat, things that I
must surely combat.*

*I haven't thought of Liam in days. I loved him, but Jeremy seems to have
overpowered that loss, and if I let myself think about it I will be glad to have
him beside me, glad to feel his arms, for he does give me that feeling of
belonging. He is fascinating to me, and I am compelled by him nearly as
much as I am infuriated.*

*We have reached the camp. I am in Jeremy's tent. I think that I am quite
ready for a ride across the plains. I have folded up my crinolines, my dress is
simple (I learned a great deal about simple clothing while picking cotton
and tomatoes!), and I am trying to be very composed. Jeremy was still not
available when we arrived, but his aide, Nathaniel, the curious black man I
met in Richmond, has been very kind and efficient. My trunks are all arranged within Jeremy's tent. It's a large one. Even his bed, a folding appara-
tus, is large. The weather is fair, the flap is lifted, the insects are at a low,
Nathaniel has assured me, and I have been supplied with a bottle of sherry, a
small writing desk of my own—facing Jeremy's larger one—and I really
think that I am doing quite well. Nathaniel has assured me that there is a
hip tub that was ordered especially for my use, and that he will be delighted to
fill it for me if Jeremy does not return by mealtime. He has been gone several
days, but they expect his return very soon.*

*Camp is a very busy place. Jeremy is commanding a regiment of eight
companies, with each company consisting of eighteen to twenty-four men.
Each company has its own captain, with various sergeants and corporals,
and there are usually four lieutenants beneath Jeremy, but sometimes officers
come and go, and there are others among them not necessarily accountable to
any particular group of men. Dr. Weland, or Major Weland, is here and has
already come by to see to my comfort. Celia is settled—and I'm assuming*

that Mrs. Brooks is settled, too, eagerly awaiting her chance to leap on Jeremy with tales of my evil deeds. She may go right ahead and do so. When he returns he'll find me well composed—the sherry will see to that. I'll be tremendously prim and proper with my hair pinned and my clothing plain, and hopefully he'll have no complaint.

As it happened, her hair wasn't pinned up and she wasn't wearing clothing at all when he reached her.

But he certainly had no complaint.

While Christa was coming down to the encampment, Jeremy was busily engaged in a painful discovery.

He had come out to find an earlier company that had been headed for Fort Union had lost its regiment and bogged down somewhere in the vast country in between.

He knew the country and he had known where to look.

The Great Plains drew many tribes seeking the hunting grounds, the bountiful water, the rich grasses. Many of the tribes were peaceful, many were settled in reservations, and many were still at war.

He had come upon a place where they had dug into trenches. They had built up a wall of small rocks and mud to one side, and trenched in on the other. It had been a good maneuver to outsmart and outfight a band of horsemen. Some of the Indians had had rifles, but only a few. The others had been armed with bows and arrows.

But oh, how they had used them.

He could see the battle even as he walked around the trench of dead men.

The Indians had encircled the the cavalrymen. The cavalry had first used their horses as shields, forming a circle with their backs toward the middle, every man shooting as the Indians rode around them. It was the natural, textbook way to fight. It was perhaps the only way, under the circumstances. Perhaps night had then fallen. The men had dug in. The Indians had come again, but they had discovered that the white men were so well dug in that they were losing far too many braves with each encounter.

So the Indians had used different tactics, finding a distance from which to shoot their arrows. They had staked out the area with feathered shafts that remained to mark the grave the men had dug themselves. Someone had called out the order to fire—just like an artillery officer might have done in any battle of the war. Then adjustments had been made. A little to the left, a little to the right. Dead straight closer, perhaps a little farther. And so the arrows had flown. Perhaps twenty-five at a time. Once, twice, again. Until the men all lay dead.

"My God, Colonel! This is a sorry picture!" Captain Thayer Artimas of Company G told him. "Jesu, sir, but the poor fellows never had a chance."

Jeremy stepped forward, pulling the arrow from the heart of a very young private with wide open, staring blue eyes. He knelt down and closed the boy's eyes. He looked at the arrow. "Comanche," he said softly. "They've come in quite far east. They don't usually ride in this far."

"They've been hot to fight lately, sir," Captain Artimas said.

"I imagine they've been attacked a lot lately," Jeremy murmured dryly.

Artimas shrugged. He looked around himself uneasily. "Think we ought to be moving onward, sir?"

Jeremy nodded. Night was coming. Comanche seldom attacked at night, but he wanted to be out of the area. He had only twenty-five men with him and he didn't want another massacre.

"Let's get a burial detail going here!" he called to his men. But even as he said the words, he felt a peculiar sensation stirring at his nape. The wind seemed to have picked up. There was a trembling in the ground.

"Dismount and circle!" he ordered quickly. Jesu, it could be the same thing! Even as he gave the order, he heard the first war whoop of the Indians. They were coming around the scruff of trees that stood over the one hump of dirt near them that might be construed as a hill. He narrowed his eyes against the rising dust, trying to count. It was a small party—perhaps twenty or so braves.

He shoved his horse's rump, aiming his rifle, calling to his men. "Wait to shoot, then shoot straight. We have to take them the first time, we can't give them a chance to come back. Understand? We'll be trapped like these poor fellows here if we make a mistake."

There was no answer except for the rise of the war whoops on the air. The Indians were bearing down on them quickly. They were in buckskin breeches, only a few of them wearing shirts despite the fact that the nights were growing cooler and cooler. The paint on their faces, the feathers in the hair, all denoted them as a war party. They had come to kill.

Jeremy took careful aim at the warrior who seemed to be in the lead of the group. He squeezed the trigger and the man flew from his horse. He took aim again, steadying his nerves. He had learned long ago that no matter how difficult it was to stay still and take aim while Indians were bearing down on him, it had to be done. Steadily and quickly.

He fired again and caught a second warrior. At his side, Captain Artimas was also firing and firing fast. Private Darcy, an exceptional sharpshooter, was reaching for his carbine in his saddle. Indians were falling quickly. Darcy brought down another.

Jeremy noted Willy Smith, a new recruit, standing straight and staring at the coming promise of death with wide-eyed horror. He looked just like an animal caught in a sudden bright light.

He was a target as big as the side of a barn to the Comanche.

"Get down!" Jeremy shouted, leaping toward the boy. He brought them both flat on the ground, not daring to look at Willy again but keeping both eyes on the horses that pounded surely toward them.

He kept shooting, emptying the six chambers of his revolver. He released Willy as he hastily filled the chamber again as the Indians raced around them in a complete circle.

"I'm all right now, Colonel," Willy choked out. "I'm all right. I can shoot pert near as good as Darcy, and I won't lose my senses again, sir."

"I'm sure you won't," Jeremy told him.

Dust rose, choking them.

Willy Smith took aim. He fired. A shrieking brave came flying from his painted pony, landing dead just in front of Willy. The boy stared at the dead Indian a second, then took aim again.

They were doing well. They had downed at least ten of the warriors in the first go-round.

"Injured, dead?" he shouted.

Artimas called out for an assessment. No one dead yet. Two wounded.

"We have to take them all this time around!" he called. "Else we'll be sitting ducks for target practice!"

"Right, Colonel!" Darcy called and grinned. "I'm going to get me the first one this time, Colonel."

"You do that."

As he had expected, the remaining warriors began to circle again. They were lucky. If the Indians had thought to pin Jeremy's troops down in the same trenches, they might have done better. Except that Jeremy wouldn't have stayed in the death trap—he would have charged the Indians.

The circle began again with the braves crying out their horrible war cries.

Darcy caught the first of them, just as he had promised. Jeremy began to fire. Aiming, squeezing, aiming, squeezing, faster, faster. He caught one, lost one, caught two. His men were good. By the time the second circle was completed, only five of the braves were left to ride away.

"Mount up! We've got to stop them before they bring more warriors against us!"

He leapt upon his horse, spurred the creature into motion, and started after the retreating Indians. Darcy and Artimas were right with him; the rest followed at a gallop behind. Darcy aimed his carbine and brought down one Indian. Jeremy caught two more in rapid succession. Artimas caught the fourth, and a man from the ranks brought down the last of them.

"Let's leave them where they fell!" Artimas said bitterly, after dismounting by the first of the fallen Indians. The brave was half naked, his chest and face painted, his lance, still curled in his fingers, decorated with several scalps, some white, some Indian from other tribes.

"No. We'll bury them all. Maybe that will delay their discovery for a while, and buy us some time."

Darcy had already started digging with his gun butt. He looked at Jeremy. "Colonel, sir, what's going to happen when we ride this way with the whole regiment?"

"They won't attack the regiment, Darcy."

"Why?"

"Because they haven't the numbers to do so."

"Why, Colonel, sir, there's hundreds of them stupid savages out here—"

"First lesson, Private! They're not stupid. See how they planned the artillery arrow attack that did in these men from Fort Smith? Second, don't go causing a big war by assuming they're all savages—we're very friendly with a number of tribes."

Near his side, Sergeant Rodriguez, a Mexican-born soldier who had served most of his life in the West, spit out a big wad of tobacco. "*Madre mío, niño!* Some of them are much more clean and smart than lots of the gringo riffraff we get in the West, eh Colonel, sir?"

Jeremy smiled. "Right," he said. But his smile faded quickly. It was growing darker, they were miles and miles from camp, and they still had lots of burying to do.

"Let's get to it, shall we?" he ordered.

This was a new company for him. Darcy had served with him just briefly before the end of the war and he knew that the man was a tremendous sharpshooter. He was grateful to have him.

He wondered if Darcy didn't hear Rebel yells in the Indian whoops when he shut his eyes, just as Jeremy had.

He suddenly broke out in a sweat. God help him, but this was easier. Easier than shooting at men in gray uniforms and wondering if he might be aiming at his brother-in-law.

They finished with the burial detail, dusting over the Indians, packing down the trench dirt over their own dead. In the midst of it, a groan had been heard, and they had discovered one man just barely alive. They had gone back to thoroughly look over every dead man to be sure that he was dead before finishing with the burying. The survivor had an arrow in his upper back, but they had managed to extract it without further injury, get some water into him, douse the wound with whiskey, and bandage it well. Jeremy was certain that the young man would make it.

He had survived this far—he could go all the way.

He forced his own men to ride until the moon was high in the sky. They rode for over seven hours and they rode hard, but they covered nearly fifty miles. He knew they would not be attacked if they camped on the plains.

He lay beneath the stars, watching the sky, exhausted but anxious for morning.

Christa should have arrived. He stared at the sky, but he saw his wife's face. Beautiful, delicate, refined.

Passionate, alive, stormy, disobedient, and defiant, her blue eyes flashing.

He winced. What would it be?

Well, she would learn a few lessons in the West, he thought. She'd probably pass out from the weight of her petticoats on the first day!

Whoa, don't be malicious there, sir, he warned himself. But she did have a few lessons to learn.

He inhaled deeply. So did he.

Jesu, he couldn't wait. All the long nights without her he had lain haunted by her memory. What was it with Christa? What tore at his body and emotions so deeply? He had longed for her to arrive, then he had berated himself for ever suggesting that she come. This was no place for Christa.

But dear God! He wanted her. He didn't give a damn how he found her when he returned. He felt torn by the pain and waste of his discovery on the plains, and he wanted nothing but comfort.

Christa? he thought, bemused. Comfort? She was like a little tigress, a wounded animal, proud, fierce, and ever on the defensive.

Yes, maybe they were both like wounded animals. Maybe time would heal some of the lacerations.

He closed his eyes tightly. Maybe he was falling in love with his wife. Maybe he had always been just a little bit in love with her.

Aroused yes, but more. She infuriated him, but there was more. Christa would not be beaten. And he could not help but admire her for that. Exactly what were his feelings? He didn't know.

He did know that he wanted to see her, no matter what her mood. Whether she was pleasant or furious because she'd realized just what a life he had brought her to!

He smiled, and pulled his hat low over his eyes. Tomorrow he would cleanse away the sight of the men in the trench. He would do so in her arms.

He didn't know how he would find her—clinging to Jesse perhaps, or sitting in his tent with her toes tucked under an elegant gown.

But as it happened, he found her in a more delightful manner than he had thought to imagine. She was in his tent, in the hip bath, surrounded by a froth of bubbles. She didn't hear him when he first came and he paused, unable to resist the temptation to watch her for a while.

Where had Nathaniel gotten hold of those bubbles?

They were wonderful. They covered her body, they popped, and then they no longer covered her. She leaned back, surrounded by bubbles. She lifted them and smoothed them over her shoulders. She seemed as sleek and luxurious and sensual as a cat, deliciously enjoying the feel of the hot water and the bubbles. Her hair was drawn up in a loose tie. Tendrils escaped, damp and curling, framing the delicate, perfect beauty of her face. Her eyes were half closed. Ink-dark lashes fell against her cheeks.

Suddenly, she sensed that he was there. Her eyes flew open and she stared at him. God, they were blue. Bluer than any sky in deepest summer, richer than any sea.

She was definitely startled by his appearance. Obviously, she hadn't intended to be discovered so.

He smiled slowly, crossing his arms over his chest. "Hello, darlin'!" he murmured softly.

"You're—you're here!" she whispered, dismayed. A flush rose to her cheeks.

"It is my tent," he pointed out. "You did come here to join me, remember?"

"Yes, of course. I—it's just I intended to be in the perfect plains garb! I meant to be ready for you," she murmured, her lashes sweeping her cheeks again.

It seemed that all the wicked fires of hell came bursting to flame within him. "Christa!" he promised her hoarsely, "trust me! At this particular moment, there couldn't be a more perfect garb for you to wear—nor could you appear to be the more perfect wife!"

And with that, he took his first, swift steps toward her.

Perhaps she wasn't ready for him.

He was more than ready for her.

Ten

*S*o much for being entirely dignified upon his return, Christa thought quickly. Her fingers curled around the rim of the tub as he swiftly approached her.

She hadn't realized how anxious she had been for the sight of him. She studied him avidly, noting every little thing about him. There was a slight stubble on his cheeks and he needed a hair trim. His eyes seemed very dark, gray as storm clouds. His hair was tousled when he tossed his plumed cavalry hat aside. He was usually so impeccable in his uniform; today he was covered in a light coating of dust. He seemed taller than ever, broader in the shoulders. His cheeks seemed just a bit gaunt, but they added to the hardness of his rugged good looks. Her heart seemed to slam and scamper. She hadn't realized just how anxious she had been for this moment, just how hungry she had actually been for the sight of him.

It frightened her.

And just what was his intent? Did he mean to dive, uniform and all, into the small tub with her? A stray lock of deep auburn hair fell over his forehead, giving him a rakish look. As he came nearer she searched frantically for something to say, but no words came to her lips.

She shrieked out softly, discovering his intent. He didn't crawl into the tub with her, he reached inside of it and plucked her out. She felt absurdly faint for a moment, clinging to him. His arms felt incredibly hot and incredibly strong. He held her and long strides brought them quickly to the bed. He laid her down upon it and paused, taking a long look at her. Then he was beside her, wrapping her into his arms, and his lips were upon her naked throat, touching, tasting, licking away the drops of water that lay there. She began to tremble, feeling an overwhelming urge to simply give in to it all. But words came tumbling from her lips because he was always so quick to take her, and always so distant when the fire was quenched!

"How was your journey, Christa?" she asked herself out loud, trying to ignore the masculine lips upon her nudity. "It was fine, thank you. And the babe? Fine, too, I believe. Were you ill at all? Just a bit. Amazingly, it ended aboard the steamer, and I did very well from then on. How have you found the camp? The men, for Yanks, have been as pleasant as can be expected. How—"

She broke off. She had caught his attention at last. He leaned upon an elbow, staring down at her. His eyes were silver with laughter and appreciation now, even if it was a dark silver, and none of the determination or intent had left them.

"I had intended to get to all that," he assured her.

"Well, you hadn't done so!" she whispered. "All this time since we've seen each other, and you just grabbed me up and brought me to the—"

"All this time! That's quite the point, Christa. All this time! My love, believe me! This is the first act to be expected of any loving husband!"

Any loving husband, she thought.

He did not love her, but if she closed her eyes at that moment, she might well believe that he did. His lips were against her earlobe and his words were hot and evocative. "You smell so sweet, taste so sweet . . . Jesu, all of you!" He moved like quicksilver. One minute his lips were upon hers, the next second his tongue stroked her breast, and a spiraling began deep in the pit of her belly. Words of protest bubbled in her throat, but she did not issue them. Her fingers fell upon his waving russet hair, but briefly, for he was moving again, touching all of her, whispering more feverishly against her flesh. Her fingers fell upon his shoulders and she felt the dust upon him.

"You're covered with dust!" she whispered.

"Sorry!" he apologized briefly. Moving back he stripped off his jacket and shirt. She closed her eyes quickly, alarmed at how pleased she was at the sight of his chest, how fascinated she would be to touch it. When she opened her eyes again, he had stripped naked and was coming for her, and it seemed the devil's dance had begun within her, all at the sight of his nudity and the protruding hardness of his arousal. When he crawled atop her again, she noticed a streak of red running down his neck and she cried out in earnest.

"You're injured!"

"I'm not."

"Let me tend to it!"

"If it's anything, it's a scratch, and I'd far rather you attend to other things at the moment!" he cried in frustration.

He had other things on his mind.

But she didn't mind. He was always, even in his most fervent moments, a considerate lover. And there was a curious sense of rightness when he was with her so, when she felt his body blanket her own.

When she felt his body enter her own. Taking her, making them one. Moving. Even as she twisted her head, biting into her lower lip, feeling the rugged heat and rhythm of his motion, she discovered that deny it or not, she was pleased that he did want her so. Her fingers rested on his shoulders, and she felt the tremendous tension in the rise and fall of his muscles, felt the hunger building and building within him.

She had imagined something like this. But she had never felt this with Liam, never sensed that this could come.

Her breath caught with the sudden force of his movement, and she very nearly felt something exploding within her, something promised, something wonderful. Then she was washed in the rich expulsion from her husband and felt the shuddering that shook through him again and again.

She bit her lip hard, something inside telling her that it was wrong to deny him, that perhaps she could give them both a chance if she could quit denying him. But they had been apart too long. She didn't know his feelings, and she certainly didn't know his mood.

He fell to her side and was silent for a while. She curled to her side, not facing him, but not moving away from him. His fingers moved idly over her back.

"Liam McCloskey is dead," he told her. The words were soft—she still thought that there was a note of anger to his voice.

Her lashes fluttered over her cheeks. "I know that very well," she murmured. Darkness had fallen since he had come. Just dusky at first, then darker and darker. Outside the tent, the stars would be dotting the heavens. The moon would be rising. She had slept here last night alone, but she hadn't felt the wilderness so keenly.

Neither had she felt so truly alone then, for she had been waiting for him. But now she felt his withdrawal. He rolled to his back. She thought that there was now a note of grave disappointment in his tone, more jarring than the sarcasm of his words. "Liam is dead, the war is over, but you're still fighting. And you may look as sweet and southern and delicate as magnolia blossoms but we both know that you're no simpering belle! It's a pity, my love, a true pity, that you were not in the field. No matter how many had died, you'd not have allowed Lee to surrender!"

She stiffened, stunned that tears could suddenly burn so hotly behind her eyes. "All this time we've been separated," she charged, "and you're being exceptionally cruel!"

"All this time! And you're still as cold as ice. Well, my love," he said wearily. "You may not believe this, but I do not *try* to make you so wretchedly miserable."

She frowned, glad of the darkness. "I'm—I'm not wretchedly miserable," she said softly.

The tent had grown very dark. She felt him looming over her again. "No?" he queried. "You don't hate me, or"—she felt his slight hesitation—"this?"

Even in the dark—and even after the incredibly intimate things they had just shared—she felt herself blushing. "No," she murmured. "I—I don't hate this. I mean, I don't find you physically detestable. I mean—"

He laughed. She wasn't sure if he was amused or if the sound was entirely ironic. His lips touched hers again briefly. "Welcome to camp life, my love," he murmured. "My fair, sweet cavalry wife!"

He rose from the bed. "You need to dress quickly, Christa. I want a bath, but not one filled with rose-scented bubbles. The men might find it difficult to take me seriously if I smell too sweet."

He lit the lamp on his camp desk. Soft light flooded the room and Christa looked away from his nakedness, but he quickly drew his trousers back on and walked to the flap of the tent, lifting it to call to Nathaniel. Christa dived beneath the covers as he did so. She opened her mouth to warn him that she needed some time, but the words died in her throat.

There was something in the bed. Something very warm and furry. Something that moved.

She shrieked out, jumping from the bed. Jeremy stared at her, astounded.

"There's something hairy in there! That moves!"

"Thank God it isn't me!" Jeremy murmured, then ripped the bedding aside. Christa gasped again as two little creatures leaped up, flew from the bed to the ground, then raced wildly in opposite directions, finding the way out at last. She stared in astonishment and horror. Jeremy was doubled over in laughter.

Her eyes narrowed. "What—"

"They were just two little polecats, Christa!" he assured her.

Polecats. They wouldn't have hurt her.

"Sometimes the men keep them as pets. Lots of Indians do—they eat them when they're done being entertained by them. They say polecat can be very tasty."

He was still laughing, watching her in wry amusement.

Ah, yes. The girl from the plantation. The foolish little spoiled creature.

"I was startled," she said coolly. "It will not happen again."

He must have realized that he had offended her. He slipped his arms around her and she was reminded that she had jumped up naked. "I rather enjoyed your reaction," he told her.

She pushed his arms away. "Your man is going to be returning any minute." Freed from his touch but not from his gaze, she hastily found the very plain and sensible dress with the split skirt she had chosen for their first days of travel.

"How *are* you feeling?" he asked her.

"Fine," she said curtly.

"No more sickness?"

"No."

"You can still barely tell," he murmured. "Except that your breasts are larger."

Christa swung around. "You are outrageous!" she charged him.

He grinned, boyish and very appealing at that moment in his trousers and nothing more.

"Colonel?"

He was called from outside the tent. Nathaniel had come. Jeremy quickly asked for new water for the bath.

"It was a bad one, Colonel, eh?" Nathaniel asked.

"Yes," Jeremy said simply. Nathaniel tipped his hat to Christa, then went about his business.

"What was bad?" Christa asked.

"Nothing. I don't want to talk about it."

She grit her teeth. "I'm here. I have a right to know."

"All right, maybe you should know. Never, never wander away alone. One of the companies from another regiment did so. And they were wiped out by the Comanche. Are you afraid?"

She felt weak.

"No," she lied.

"Well, you had better learn to be very afraid. Never, never go off alone!" he warned her.

"What about—your men?" she asked.

"My Yankees? A few were wounded." He relented and added, "No one was killed. Is that what you meant?"

"Yes," she said softly. "I'm—I'm very sorry for those who were!"

"Are you?"

"Yes." She turned to him, eyes blazing. "Don't you believe me?"

"Yes, I believe you," he said tiredly. Maybe he was being wretched to her because he was still haunted by the sight of all those men dead in the trench they had dug.

He turned away from her. Nathaniel called out again, and entered with two other men to empty the tub and fill it again with water heated over a fire. When they were gone, all tipping their hats to Christa, Jeremy climbed into the tub. He winced suddenly, touching his neck. "I was nicked!" he muttered. "Want to come over here and take care of it now?"

"No!" she muttered. But she came toward him, fascinated. She picked up the washcloth and dabbed at his throat. "An arrow came that close?"

He caught her hand. "A bullet, I imagine. That close—you were nearly widowed. What a tragedy."

"You're a fool," she informed him coolly.

"Be tender. Take care of it."

She smiled. "I will. I'll get Jesse and he'll give you a stitch or two."

He shook his head. "Scrub my back—and tell me more about the trip out here."

"Ask me nicely."

His silver eyes touched hers. "All right. Please scrub my back and tell me about the trip."

She smiled, and tossed the washcloth his way. "No!"

"All right, you little southern vixen," he warned. "Scrub my back or—"

"Or what?"

"I'll climb out of this tub, drag you back into it, and scrub yours."

She bit her lip, picked up the cloth, and gingerly scrubbed his back. She liked the feel of it.

She even liked the intimacy of it. It seemed like a good time to warn him about a few things. She talked idly about Washington and the train. Then she told him, "You have a Major Brooks in your command."

"Yes?"

"He has a wife."

"Lots of men do."

"She, er, she traveled with us."

"Tell me about her."

"Oh, I think she's going to be much happier telling you about me."

"Oh?"

He turned around, staring at her. "What's she going to tell me?"

"Well, she was being rather self-righteous, I thought. I think I said something about my God still being on the battlefields picking up lost souls, and she went huffing off because we weren't observing the Sabbath properly. And then she didn't like the fact that I was playing poker—"

"With Jesse?" he said sharply.

She sighed. "Of course with Jesse! Oh come, Jeremy, had you sent me with the Virgin Mary, I couldn't have had a more proper escort!"

She thought that he smiled. His dark lashes fell and he leaned forward. "Down a little. Did you win?"

"Pardon?"

"Did you win at cards?"

"Yes, as a matter of fact, I did. I'm a—"

"Cameron, yes," he murmured. "And Camerons don't like losing."

"I wasn't doing anything wrong—"

"Then you don't have anything to worry about, do you?" He leaned back suddenly, and he looked very tired. "Go on and find your brother. I've hired a woman, Bertha Jacobs, to come along with the laundresses specifically to help with whatever we might need. She and Nathaniel will be serving us a private dinner here tonight." He hesitated a minute. "I saw your brother coming in. He's leaving in the morning at the same time we pull out from this camp."

Christa felt the blood drain from her face. Suddenly, she could care less about Mrs. Brooks. Jesse would be leaving her. Tomorrow. She stood up, and hurried from the tent, anxious to reach him, to hold tight to every minute they had left.

Jesse had to go home. He had a wife and children. She had borrowed him for as long as she could.

She wasn't going to be able to bear to watch him go.

They had a decent dinner, Jeremy thought. He and Jesse had become good enough friends, and Christa was always on her best behavior when she was with one of her beloved brothers. Weland stopped by for coffee which Christa had made herself over a fire after the meal. He smiled, thinking of her screaming over the polecats, then tilted his hat down, watching her. She was very sensibly dressed for the plains, no frills, just comfortable, durable cotton. Her face was flushed as she worked over the fire, and he felt a peculiar pounding in his heart. She would succeed. He could mock her all that he wanted, she would succeed. Even in the wilderness, as simply accoutred as nature deemed wise, she would still be beautiful.

If only he could reach her.

Jesse was watching her, too, Jeremy realized. And Weland was watching Jesse.

"I promise you, Jess," Weland said, "I will see to it that Christa has care almost as tender as that you'd give to her yourself!"

Christa, startled to be the sudden subject of conversation, looked up. "I wasn't worried," she said. Was she lying, Jeremy wondered. What woman wanted to have her baby in the wilderness?

But Christa stood, walked over to Jesse, and set her hands upon his shoulders. "Dr. Weland, I helped deliver my last little nephew and my niece too. Jesse and Daniel were still—" She broke off.

"At war," Jesse finished for her. He caught her eyes and patted her hand. She offered him a tender smile. One that dazzled. Were she to look at a lover that way, Jeremy mused, he would be smitten for life.

Were she ever to look at him that way . . .

"She won't mind labor," Jeremy heard himself saying. "She will mind the urge to scream, right, my love?"

The look she cast him was one of daggers. "My husband is so concerned!" she murmured.

"Your husband is very concerned," he said, rising. "And that's why I'm going to insist on you getting some sleep. We break camp tomorrow. It will be a hard ride."

Her eyes widened. "But—"

"We'll have time in the morning," Jesse said, rising too. "Christa, you do have to get some sleep."

"Jesse, Dr. Weland, may I offer you brandy and cigars beneath the stars?" Jeremy suggested. He caught hold of Christa, drawing her unwilling figure to his. He kissed her on the forehead. "My love, that way you may retire undisturbed and at your leisure!"

She cast him another look with eyes of shimmering blue fire, but Jesse kissed her good night and Weland thanked her for the delicious coffee. The three men then walked beneath the stars, seriously discussing the western question. Jeremy was sorry that Jesse was going to leave; he liked his brother-in-law more and more and felt he had very intelligent attitudes about the Indians and the western expansion movement.

When he returned to his tent, Christa was curled up in bed. He didn't know if she pretended sleep or not, but he quelled the urges the very sight of her created within him. It had been a long day for her. Tomorrow would be longer.

He kissed her gently upon the forehead and let her sleep.

The day began with rain.

The bugle sounded with the dawn and men were quickly up and preparing to ride, breaking down the tents, packing the equipment. All of his and Christa's personal and household items were packed into the ambulance he had outfitted for Christa to ride in when she chose. It was soon packed with their trunks, with his hunting guns, with his dress saber, with pots and pans and lanterns. There was a long bench where she could sit and where they could carry wounded men, if need be. The regiment was outfitted with several other ambulances, and the men who had been wounded in the Indian skirmish on the plain would ride in one of them.

He wasn't sure he trusted Christa with wounded Yankees just as yet!

He was busy that morning, but if he hadn't been, he would have found some way to stay away from her. She breakfasted alone with Jesse. They had several hours together. But still, the time came when they had to part. The regiment was ready to go west.

Jesse was ready to start the long journey back east.

Jeremy found them by an oak tree, and so he stood in the drizzling rain watching as she said good-bye to Jesse. She clung to him and he held her tenderly in return. There were no words between them. Maybe they had all been said already. Christa's eyes were closed. Her face lay against her brother's chest. At long last, Jesse pulled himself away from her. She wasn't crying. The effort not to do so was etched clearly into her face, and the sight of her trying so very hard not to give way to tears was far more heartbreaking than had she shed buckets of them.

Jesse's eyes met Jeremy's over Christa's head. "We have to go, Christa," he said quietly. She nodded. She still didn't release Jesse. Jeremy walked to her at last, taking her by the arm. She was wooden as he pulled her to him.

He offered his hand to Jesse Cameron, and Jesse took it. "Take care of my sister," Jesse said huskily.

"I certainly intend to look after my wife," Jeremy replied with a slow grin. "Give my best to *my* sister, and Kiernan and Daniel."

"I'll do that. You know, you will always have a home in Virginia," Jesse said.

"I know that, and I'm grateful," Jeremy told him. "I know we'll be back, for a visit at least, soon enough."

Jesse nodded. He reached out and lifted Christa's chin. "I'll see you, Christa. Take care now."

"You too, Jesse."

He nodded. He stroked her cheek one last time, then turned to walk away, a tall and striking man with his dark hair graying slightly at the temples, his posture straight and sure. Christa watched him for a moment.

"Jesse!" she cried out. She broke free from Jeremy and went running after him. He swung around, caught her, and hugged her one last time.

Then he set her firmly upon her feet. He said something to her and she nodded. Jesse walked on. She waved from where she stood.

She had never looked more forlorn. She stood very straight, her shoulders squared. Her chin was high and her eyes were damp. Her fingers were knotted tightly at her sides.

Jesu! He wanted to go to her, to put an arm around her in comfort. But she didn't want him now. He was the damned Yank who had brought her out here.

"We have to go, Christa," he said firmly. "Will you ride Tilly, or do you wish to start out in the ambulance?"

She didn't answer him. She was still staring after Jesse.

"Christa!"

She swung around. "What!"

He repeated his words. He had wanted so badly to be gentle, but there was a terse note to them now.

"I'll ride Tilly," she said. She started to walk past him. He caught hold of her arm. She stared at him furiously, and he saw that she was still fighting tears. "You take Tilly, you stay behind the front of the line, do you understand me?"

"I'll do—"

"You'll do as I tell you!"

She wrenched her arm free and saluted him sharply. "I'll do as you tell me. Now leave me be!" she hissed. He let her go.

She did not want his comfort. With a sigh, he strode down the line of horses and men until he reached his own mount. He yelled to the bugler to call the men to their horses. In a moment, he was swinging up on his horse. He had a hand lifted in the air. It fell, and the long column began to move.

He rode back, seeking Christa.

She sat upon Tilly, watching Jesse mount his horse to ride in the opposite direction.

"Christa!"

Jeremy called her name.

She looked at him, then spurred her horse and cantered by him.

He followed her to very near the front of the line. She fell in as he had commanded.

She didn't look at him.

But neither did she look back again.

Eleven

Christa did not have much time to brood over Jesse's departure during the next three days. The rain that had begun that morning continued to plague them, and she was quickly initiated into the cavalry life full thrust.

She rode the first day on Tilly until even she was exhausted, but the regiment was not stopping to camp for the night until they reached higher ground. So she traveled on in her ambulance for some time, watching the pots sway over her head, a lamp and kettle dance, and Jeremy's dress saber clash against the edge of the canopy. There was a litter of crying pointer pups in the wagon with her, along with their mother, Pepper, and she amused herself for a while trying to keep the pups quiet.

She became bored after a while, and the constant sway and jiggle of the ambulance felt even more miserable than riding, so she took to Tilly again. She saw Jeremy briefly, barely recognizable in his rain gear. He was telling James Preston that it was amazing to be able to cover over fifty miles in one day when he was riding with one company, but not quite manage to make ten when he was riding with the whole of the regiment. He seemed neither impatient nor frustrated, and she realized that he was very accustomed to this way of life.

She was not, but she would become so.

She scarcely saw him that first night. It was nearly dark when they stopped for a meal. They had reached high ground and the order was given not to pitch the tents, they would move out with the dawn. Men slept on their saddles.

Christa slept in the ambulance—tossing about as she listened to the whining puppies. She wondered if Jeremy's determination to drive the men so hard had been to avoid her. Since she had said good-bye to Jesse, he hadn't seemed to want any part of her. Thinking about it, she tossed and turned all the more. He must truly be regretting not just his marriage, but his determination to bring her out here.

The following morning was a wretched one. She had hardly slept; she felt as if she were twisted up like a pretzel. She didn't see Jeremy, but Nathaniel directed her with his slow beautiful speech to the creek nearby so she could wash, and he brought her coffee and some bread and porridge from the main mess pots. It was barely light before they started off again. She rode Tilly and kept abreast with Lieutenant James Preston, Celia's young husband. He told her stories about the territory they were traveling, about the Indians in general, and then cast her a quick glance, apologizing profusely.

"It's all right!" she assured him. "I'm here—I need to know things."

He shook his head. "I don't tell Celia anything. She is afraid of her own shadow. I'm very grateful that you've befriended her so. She's already having a horrible time of it, back in her ambulance."

"I'll see to her," Christa told him. She rode back down the long column, moving along slowly in the endless drizzle until she reached Celia's ambulance. She tethered Tilly to the vehicle and spent time in the wagon with her. She was heartily entertained. Celia knew many of the northern officers who were little more than names to Christa. She had Christa laughing with her stories about George Armstrong Custer, the brash young cavalry officer who had given Stuart such a nightmare of a time at Gettysburg.

"He is much, much more attached to his hounds than he is to poor Libby!" Celia laughed. "I've heard she can scarce fit in bed with all of his pups!" Then she sobered suddenly. "How unkind of me!" she said in horror.

"Oh, Celia! She's not about, and I don't intend to repeat a word. And we have to get through all of this somehow, don't we?" She grit her teeth as she finished, for they had hit another horrible rut in the road and the ambulance swayed so precariously that she was afraid they were about to go over. "Ugh!" she said, making a face for Celia. Celia smiled wanly, but Christa told her a story about burying the family silver while planting tomatoes and she had Celia smiling again in a few minutes. When the rain stopped, Christa left Celia's ambulance and rode along behind it with Nathaniel for a while.

By the end of the second day, they had traveled twenty-two miles. They set the tents up that night, but Jeremy never came to theirs. At midnight Christa still lay awake, oddly miserable that he did not come. She closed her eyes and told herself it was because no matter what, it hurt to feel unwanted.

They left Camp Creek at dawn, and managed to travel nearly fifteen miles. The rain had stopped. They encamped by another beautiful creek and there were wonderful wildflowers everywhere. Christa took a walk into one of the open fields beside the array of army tents. She was picking something with delicate little bulbs when she sensed someone behind her. She turned, and nearly screamed.

Two Indians stared at her. The man wore pants that looked like old army issue clothing, but the woman wore a loose buckskin dress with intricate embroidery. The man said something, and she shook her head, looking toward the camp. She had been warned not to wander away, but she had done so. Now she was facing these two Indians. The man spoke again, thrusting what he held in his hands toward her. Her heart started hammering.

"Two bits," the man repeated insistently.

"He wants you to buy his berries," she heard. She swung around. Jeremy had come up behind her. His hands were on his hips, the low slant of his hat covered his eyes. "Two bits?" he said to the Indian.

The Indian nodded, and said something in his own language. Jeremy replied, then produced the right coin from his pocket, and the Indian woman hurried forward with the basket the man had been carrying. The pair turned around and disappeared across the field.

"Did they frighten you?" Jeremy asked.

"I—no, I just—"

"They should have," he said curtly. He looked in the basket. "Dewberries. I told you not to wander off!"

She swallowed hard. "They were—Comanche?"

He shook his head. "Choctaw. They're a very civilized people."

"Then I had nothing to be afraid of."

"But you didn't know that. You wouldn't know a Comanche from a Seminole."

She stiffened. "But I will know the difference," she told him. "I learned to plant cotton, McCauley. I can learn to know one Indian from another too." She lifted her chin and walked back toward the tents, leaving him standing in the field. He didn't follow her.

That night she met Bertha, who was a plump, wonderfully pleasant Irish woman. She'd lost her husband back home years before to the potato famine, then she had lost two sons to the war. Now she was traveling to Santa Fe where her grandson was just starting a family of his own. She was a cheerful soul, a great believer in the will of God, and Christa was grateful to know her.

Later, Nathaniel brought her a freshly shot quail. "The colonel took her down, Mrs. McCauley. He says he's bone tired and hungry as a wolf. He'll be finished for the day in about an hour, and if you don't mind, he'll have dinner with you."

Christa was certain that Jeremy could care less whether she minded or not. She was being put to a test tonight.

She smiled sweetly. Did Jeremy have the audacity to think she'd never had to pluck a chicken before?

She smiled. "Thank you so much, Nathaniel."

"If I can help in any way—"

"Just get me a good fire started, if you'll be so kind. I'll manage from there."

She did manage. There were several cows among the animals trekking along with them, so she had fresh cream for the berries. She spitted the quail and seasoned it with their supply of salt and pepper. There were large bales of potatoes that the cooks had bought from the Cherokee encampments down the trail, and so she peeled and sliced and boiled them along with some salt and pepper and butter. By the time that Jeremy returned, she had finished cooking and eating, and had left his meal on his desk, covered by a silver tureen. She'd even seen to it that a glass of wine sat before his place where she'd folded the napkin elegantly. Determined to ignore him, she gave her attention to her journal, describing the prairie around them and the Choctaw who had sold her the berries.

She felt him staring at her when he came in, then he inquired, "Aren't you eating?"

"I've had quite enough, thank you."

"Who cooked for you?"

She looked up at him, her brow arching high. "I cooked myself. If things aren't to your liking, however, you shall certainly not offend me if you choose to take your meals elsewhere."

"I could eat horsemeat right now," he told her, and sat, throwing off his hat to land at the foot of their bed. She pretended to continue giving her attention to her journal, but she glanced at him now and then. He was hungry and he ate quickly. But all the while that he ate he was sketching on paper. He pushed his plate aside when he was done, not giving her the least attention.

She rose at last and cleared away his dish, washing it in a bucket of fresh creek water Nathaniel had brought. "Is there anything else you'd like?" she asked at last, annoyed. He could have said something.

She continued to stand there. Finally he looked up, frowning. "What is it?"

"Nothing."

A half smile curved his lip. "I'm sorry. I didn't realize that we had been gone so long you might crave even my Yankee company."

"I don't," she informed him coolly.

He watched her for a moment. "Then go to bed. It's going to be another hard day tomorrow."

"And you're making them harder and harder because of me, aren't you?" she demanded.

His brow hiked up in surprise. "Actually, no, I'm not. I just want to get settled in at Fort Jacobson before we start hitting really bad weather. And before some fool out there has a chance to cause us some really serious Indian problems." He looked back to his paper and began writing again. Christa clenched her teeth together and moved past him. Keeping her back to him, she changed into a warm flannel nightgown and curled into bed. She hated to admit it; she was exhausted.

She was also confused and hurt. He hadn't said a word about any of her efforts, and he'd made no effort to come near her. Not that she wanted him near her.

But she did. She wanted the comfort of being held.

She stayed awake awhile, but then her eyes closed and she slept. When she was very deeply asleep, she began to dream that she was being very gently kissed and caressed. Slow, sensual circles were being drawn over her back, lusciously brought to her buttocks, her hips, her belly, her breast. Sweet wet whispers touched her earlobe, her nape, her throat. She woke up, startled, and very aware that she wasn't dreaming because he had thrust within her from behind, and was not so gentle anymore but making love to her with a raw, wild fervor. Her fingers curled over his, holding tight, while the storm thundered. He went taut, then slackened. His arms remained around her, but she sensed that he lay awake. She wondered why she was so determined to keep something of herself from him. Maybe it was just all that she had left.

His temper was somewhat better in the morning. He rode with her for a while, pointing out some abandoned Indian huts as they passed them, reminding her again that the tribes could be very different. Here they often lived in these huts with land about them that they cultivated, growing potatoes and beans and corn and other vegetables.

"Soon, we'll be on the plains. You'll see some of the tepees of the nomads."

"Nomads?"

He glanced at her. "The Indians who follow the buffalo. In winter the buffalo go north. We'll still see them now along the trail we're following." He hesitated, then continued, "And the Comanche usually only travel just so far north. Their territory tends to be Texas down to Mexico, west into Arizona and New Mexico."

"You all talk as if the Comanche are the only Indians you worry about."

Jeremy smiled, glancing up at the sky as if he weighed its color. "Oh, no! There are lots of Indians to worry about. Apache can be terrifying. The Sioux can be extremely fierce. But when we get to Fort Jacobson the Comanche will be our nemesis. They are noted for being some of the most savage warriors ever to ride the plains." He reined in his horse, pointing across the landscape. "There are more Choctaw homes over there. They're bringing in some of their harvest, see?"

She nodded, seeing the neat little row of huts, the Indians busy in their fields.

"Choctaw," she murmured. She felt him watching her, but when she turned to him again, he was already looking forward once more.

"I'm riding on ahead. I want to make up some mileage today."

They rode hard that day, and she fell into bed exhausted that night. Very, very late, he woke her again. She didn't mind because it meant that she slept held in his arms.

It was clear and beautiful, growing slightly cooler, the next day. She rode with Jeremy for a while and with James for a while, and spent time with Celia in her ambulance. She was coming to know a few other wives. In those first days she became very aware that they talked about her all the time, and she became very aware of certain attitudes. Some of them were fascinated by the very fact that Colonel McCauley had plucked her off a southern plantation. Some of them were glad that the war was over and anxious for peace. Some of them were bitter, and, Celia admitted, hated her for being a Confederate. "Just as you hate the Yankees," Celia told her.

"I don't hate the Yankees. I don't hate all Yankees," she amended. She sighed. "One of my brothers was a Yankee all through the war."

"And then, of course, there's the colonel!" Celia said, a touch of awe in her voice. "Any of them who have anything to say at all are just as jealous as can be. He's such a handsome man with that thick red hair and those piercing silver eyes of his! And you are beautiful, Christa, you must know that, and you're both so wonderfully brave and full of life!"

Christa blushed. She wondered what Celia would think if she knew the circumstances of their marriage. She bit her lip, tempted to confide the truth, then determined not to do so. She didn't want any of the wives within the regiment to know that they were anything but the absolutely perfect couple.

That night when they camped on the Sans Bois, she walked down to the water and looked across it. The land was beautiful here, very green. It was very broad, and the area was deeply forested, which made her wonder about the name given the creek. With twilight falling, she felt a sudden, fierce twinge of nostalgia. She fought the urge to cry, the desperate yearning for home.

Jeremy came upon her. His hands fell on her shoulders. "We're about forty miles from Fort Arbuckle," he told her. "We'll be into buffalo territory soon."

She nodded.

"What are you thinking?" he asked. His voice was soft, his whisper near her ear.

"I was thinking that this particular area right here reminds me of home."

He was silent, and for a moment she didn't realize that her words had sounded like a reproach. His hands fell from her shoulders.

"It won't for long. The prairie can be dry, the grass scruffy, and when the buffalo come stampeding over a ridge, you'll know you're west and far from home."

He left her there. She stared after him and felt a fierce pain suddenly stab into her heart. Despite herself, she remembered Celia's words about him. Yes, he was a striking man with his deep russet hair and unique, silver-and-steel eyes. Besides the appealing cut and angle of his face, there was the broadness of his shoulders, the strength and heat in his arms, the taut ripples in his belly, the tightly compacted muscles of his buttocks and . . .

She straightened her shoulders, trembling suddenly. She had to be so very careful! But suddenly she wanted to talk to him and tell him that she didn't mind so much being away from home. She missed Virginia, God help her, she missed Daniel and Callie and Kiernan and Jesse and her nephews and her little niece. But the West was wonderful. The flowers were beautiful. The Choctaw, the Cherokee, and the Creek were fascinating. She couldn't wait to see a buffalo or dozens of buffalo grazing on the plain. Things were new and exciting every day —even if they were frightening.

She hurried back toward the encampment, but when she reached their tent she found Nathaniel sorting papers on his desk. "The colonel went on to the headquarters tent, Mrs. McCauley."

"Oh." She hesitated. "I guess I shouldn't disturb him."

Nathaniel shook his head. "You'd be fine and welcome. He's just received some army dispatches from a messenger, a Captain Clark, whom he hasn't seen since the second year of the war. I'm sure they'd both welcome you."

She hesitated. Would he welcome her if he was visiting with an old friend?

She thanked Nathaniel, then walked idly through the tents to headquarters. Along the way she heard a group of young privates discussing the battle of Antietam, arguing over whether they'd won or lost. A little farther on, she could hear shrieks of female laughter, softly muffled.

A number of the laundresses were tending to needs other than that for clean clothing, she determined, hurrying on by. She wondered if Mrs. Brooks knew what went on when the men were at their leisure for the night. If she did, she'd demand that Jeremy get the whole regiment down on its knees to cleanse them of their sins.

A few minutes later she saw the grouping of the command tents, the medical tent next to the headquarters tent. With the weather fair, the large headquarters tent stood with its flaps lifted high, the night breeze moving through. Dr. Weland was there along with Jeremy and the visitor. Jeremy was deep in conversation with the man, but Weland saw Christa coming, said something softly, and the three men quickly stood.

"Christa, how nice of you to join us," Jeremy said. She didn't think that he was finding it nice at all, but she smiled and turned curiously to the visitor. He was tall and sandy-haired with a sweeping mustache and full beard. When he greeted her, she thought there was just the slightest hint of a southern slur to his voice.

"Captain Clark, it's a pleasure," she murmured.

"No, Mrs. McCauley, the pleasure is all mine," he assured her.

"Sherry, Christa?" Dr. Weland offered.

"Thank you." He poured her the sherry from a portable leather bar. She accepted it, taking the camp stool Captain Clark was quick to offer her.

"How are you finding the trail?" he asked her.

"Intriguing."

"She's quite a trooper," Weland said. "Mrs. McCauley is in, er, a family way, and still enduring all the rigors without a blink."

"Another baby, how wonderful!" Captain Clark said.

Christa frowned. "Another—?" she began, but Captain Clark was sitting back, tilting his head curiously. "I hail from an area that's now West Virginia, and I would swear, Mrs. McCauley, that your accent is a Virginian one. But I remember distinctly your husband telling me years ago he was marrying a girl from Mississippi."

Christa's gaze shot quickly to Jeremy. She'd never seen him appear quite so tense or pale. His jaw was tense as if he were in great pain.

"I'm from Virginia, Captain Clark. Right from the heart of the Old Dominion." She sat back, still staring at Jeremy. "Darling, do you have another wife from Mississippi?" she asked lightly.

Captain Clark evidently—and far too late—realized the error of his ways. "Oh, I am so sorry. I beg you both, forgive me. It's just that—"

"It's all right, Emory!" Jeremy said, exasperated. He carefully controlled his annoyance, determined to make his visitor at ease once again. "I was to have married a girl from Mississippi. The fall of Vicksburg changed that. Christa is the queen of Virginia, Captain, beyond the shadow of a doubt. Perhaps you knew some of the same families?"

Jeremy was the one to start them comparing notes, Christa would remind him later.

At that moment though, he was hard put to curb his temper as the two of them leaned forward, talking a blue streak. Yes, they knew several of the same families. He had known the Millers, frequent guests at Cameron Hall. Kiernan had been married to Anthony Miller before he had died at Manassas, his younger sister and brother were still her charges. Emory talked about the dances, the estate, the sad shape of Harpers Ferry now that the war was over. Christa reminded him that at least the new state of West Virginia, established in 1862, didn't have a Yankee sent down by President Johnson to be governor of the state, and Emory laughed and told her that any governor would be a Yankee governor.

His Yankee jokes made her laugh.

They began talking earnestly about Reconstruction. "Of course, Lincoln meant to be far more magnanimous!" Emory declared. "Numerous members of Congress were furious when he so arbitrarily declared his will on the southern states. But dear Christa, you must remember! Many northern mothers lost their sons; wives lost their husbands. Some are very bitter, and yes, they do want the South to pay. What if the South had won, Christa?"

She sighed. "Don't you see? It was a cause! A bid for freedom—no different from the American Revolution! Had we won, we wouldn't have caused any hardship to the North. We'd have merely gone our separate way."

"It wasn't meant to be," he told her. "I don't even know why. There is something special, something grand, about this Union."

"You sound like my brother, Jesse," she said.

Weland was sitting back, watching the whole thing.

"Her brother fought for the Union," Jeremy explained, smiling over his grating teeth.

"One of them did, one of them didn't."

"They both came home?"

"Yes."

"You were very lucky."

"I know!" she said fervently.

Jeremy had had enough. He stood. "Well, we're riding hard tomorrow, and Emory will have a very long ride back to Fort Smith. We'd best call it a night."

Christa rose, wondering at the tone of his voice when he was the one who had so much explaining to do. Emory Clark leapt quickly to his feet, and Weland followed them all, rubbing his chin. Emory took her hand and kissed it, and told her what a pleasure it had been. He turned to Jeremy, saluting him and telling him he was glad to have him in the West, and very glad to be serving in a messenger capacity beneath him again.

Outside, Emory went on to his assigned quarters for the night. Weland tipped his hat, smiled curiously, and headed for his bed in the medical tent.

Jeremy took hold of Christa's arm and steered her toward their own quarters.

"It's amazing just how much you can like Yankees when you choose, Christa!" he told her. His escorting of her through the tent flap was much more like a thrust.

A lantern had been lit for them. Nathaniel, always seeing to their welfare, Christa thought.

She spun around, facing Jeremy. "Me? You have a problem stomaching Rebels, but apparently you were very fond of one in Mississippi. Why didn't you marry her? Did you change your mind? *Do* you have another child? What is it, Jeremy, a girl or a boy? Do you at least send the poor woman some sort of—"

She broke off with a gasp because he was striding toward her looking murderous. He paused just before he reached her, his eyes closed tight, his teeth nearly bared. She heard them grating. "Don't you ever question me about my past again!" he hissed, turning away from her, unbuckling his sword belt.

A trembling shot through her. She moistened her lips as he stared at her again. He had started this, not she. She just wanted the truth, even if she was going about it the wrong way.

"Then perhaps you should refrain from commenting on me!" she whispered fiercely.

He spun around to face her. "I wouldn't comment on your past. It's the present I couldn't quite help but notice! You might have been sitting on the lawn at Cameron Hall tonight, the queen-of-all-she-surveyed, the damned belle of the ball, flirting as if every swain in twelve counties was after her."

"How dare you!" Christa began, her voice low and throaty and dangerous. "When you've been running all over the South procreating!"

She cried out because he held her shoulders in an awful vice. "I have no children, madam. None. The lady is dead, the child with her. And I don't care to hear about it from you again, are we understood?"

"Yes!" she cried out. "Just let me go!"

He loosened his hold, and she wrenched herself away, turning her back to him. Angry, hurt, frightened, she found words flowing from her. Words that would hurt.

"I was trying to be pleasant to your friend!" she said. "And he was very much a gentleman. He might have been a Yankee, but he reminded me of—"

"Jesse?"

"No . . ."

"Who, dammit?"

"Liam!"

"Ah, yes! The wondrous Liam!" Jeremy said. He sat down on the foot of the bed and wrenched off his boots. "Well, that is one thing I can promise you. I will do my best never, never to remind you of Liam!"

He was usually so meticulous with his clothing, but tonight he nearly ripped every button from his cavalry shirt as he stripped it off. Christa moved away from him, unnerved by the depths of his temper.

She recalled the timbre in his voice when he told her that the Mississippi girl was dead. He loved her still, she thought.

"What the hell are you doing!" he snapped out suddenly. He was up, shedding his trousers, then standing naked in the lamplight, his hands on his hips.

Again, in the midst of all this anger, she thought of Celia's words about him. She swallowed, trying not to allow her eyes to roam down the hard-muscled length of his body.

"I'm keeping my distance," she murmured.

"Get in bed."

"I am not getting in bed with you when you're in this mood!"

Two long strides brought him across the tent before she could retreat further. "You're getting in bed with me no matter what my mood!" he informed her. He swung her around, undoing the buttons on her dress. She felt a trembling begin in her and she started to move away.

"I'll rip it into shreds," he warned, and she stood still.

"If you think—"

"I think I'm getting some sleep!" he announced.

He spun her around again, shimmying the dress from her body, then picking her up in chemise and pantalets and setting her down on the bed. He blew out the lamp on his desk and joined her.

She waited.

Waited for the touch of his fingers, for the heat of his desire.

They did not come.

An hour later when she knew that he slept while she was still lying there awake, she wondered if he dreamed of a dead girl.

And if he compared Christa with the sweet Mississippian of his past.

And if he didn't find Christa to be lacking in comparison.

He had been up some time before she rose the next morning. Nathaniel called her from outside the tent to warn her that they were nearly ready; the tent needed to be broken down, she needed to be ready to ride herself.

She started to rise, then stared down the bedding at her blanket.

There was a creature on it. A spider. Not just any spider. A huge, massive, hairy spider. Step by step it came crawling up her blanket.

She felt a scream rising in her throat. She fought it. The spider was moving slowly enough.

"Nat—Nathaniel!" she cried. It should have been loud. It came out like a whisper.

"Mrs. McCauley? What is it?" She could sense his confusion. He couldn't come bursting in on her. Then she heard him calling to someone, saying that something was wrong.

She was staring at the thing when the flap flew open. Jeremy burst back into the tent.

"Just stay still," he told her. He slipped a glove from his hand and slapped the thing from her blanket to the ground. He crushed it with his boot. She heard a strange crackling and popping sound and felt ill for the first time in ages.

She moistened her lips. "Was it—lethal?"

He shook his head. "It was a tarantula," he told her. "The bite can make you very sick, but it's seldom lethal. Are you all right?"

No! She wasn't all right! She hated spiders, especially big brown ugly spiders like that! She hated polecats in her bed, and most of all she hated feeling alone, the way that she had felt last night.

"Yes, I'm all right," she told him.

For a moment, she thought that he would come to her. Hold her. But he didn't. "Come on, then. Get up. We've got to move," he said softly.

Then he was gone.

She dressed quickly, fervently shaking out her clothes. Nathaniel brought her coffee. He tried to tell her that she might well have scared the spider more than the spider scared her. "They're really mighty curious creatures, Mrs. McCauley. They can build little trap doors for their nests that open when they leave and close tight when they come back. They spin webs finer than any silk cocoon you can imagine!"

"That's wonderful," she told him.

"I'll look things over real good tonight, I promise, Mrs. McCauley."

She smiled, then gave his arm a quick squeeze. "You're a godsend, Nathaniel. Thank you."

He managed to cheer her up, being so considerate and in a very good mood himself.

"We're out on the prairie today, Mrs. McCauley. Beautiful country with high plains and deep ridges. Wild things as far as the eye can see! We might even see a buffalo or two today."

"You think so?"

"I think so. If the critters haven't headed too far north by now!" he said.

Robert Black Paw came riding by. "Are you riding in the ambulance, Mrs. McCauley?"

"I think I'll take Tilly this morning," she told him, her hand over her eyes, shielding them from the rising sun.

He nodded. "I'll bring her up."

Robert was as good as his word. She had just finished packing the last of the overnight gear when he returned with Tilly, saddled and ready to ride. She didn't see Jeremy when they started out, but two hours into the day he rode back to her at last, tipping his hat to her.

"You've survived?"

"Yes, so it seems."

"If we don't come upon a buffalo we can take today, we'll take out a hunting party tonight. We'll stay close to camp, but we'll find fresh meat."

She nodded politely.

"If you're frightened because of the spider—"

"I'm not frightened," she said irritably, "and you needn't strain yourself to be nice because of a spider!"

She regretted the words as soon as they left her mouth. She bit her lower lip, but it was too late. He tipped his hat to her. "If you'll excuse me, then . . ."

He galloped on ahead, moving to the front of the ranks.

It wasn't much after that that Nathaniel rode back to her. "There's been a buffalo spotted up ahead!"

"Really?"

She started to ride forward with him, but then she suddenly felt a curious shifting in the ground.

It came again and again.

She saw Nathaniel's dark eyes widen. "God above us!" he whispered.

Then someone else shouted out. "It ain't a buffalo! It's hundreds of buffalo!"

"Jesu!" came a cry. "Jesu—stampede!"

Twelve

"Stampede!" someone yelled again in warning.

The earth didn't tremble—it shook.

Christa knew the feel of cannon fire and the feel of shot. She even knew the feel of the earth when hundreds or thousands of men were marching over it.

She had never felt anything like this. It was as if the whole world was giving away. The noise of it began to rise. It had started off sounding so low that she had barely heard it, and then it grew and grew. It was becoming a whirl, a cacophony of rhythmic pounding, a force that knew no bounds.

She was so absorbed with it that she was startled when Tilly suddenly reared high, letting out a snort of terror. She just barely brought the horse under control, her eyes meeting her husband's. "You!" His finger leveled at her. "I told you not to be riding in the front!"

"I—" she started to argue, but she could see them coming now, just over his shoulder.

They were horrible, they were magnificent. They came in a wave of brown and black, in a cloud of dirt and earth they kicked up in their frantic run. They looked like a swarm of locusts descended upon the plain, except that they were massive. Such strange creatures! Their heads so large, their shoulders huge, and their legs seeming so spindly to hold that bulky weight! But hold it they did. The creatures raced. Their great heads downward and butted forward, they ran with amazing speed and amazing dexterity. Beneath them and around them the earth continued to move. Great billowing clouds of dirt and dust rose and rushed before them, around them, and in their wake.

Indeed, they had changed the very landscape! It had been a simple plain, dry and dusty, with tufts of grass here and there, low, lonely foliage, and a blue sky overhead. The plain ran flat except for a ridge here and there, such as the one they stood on. Undulating only slightly, with that soft roll beneath the sun and blue sky, the place had seemed secure, serene.

Until the buffalo had begun to move.

More dangerous than any storm, more merciless in their mindless rush. The sky had turned gray; the sun was gone. The sound was becoming deafening.

Nothing could move them! Christa thought. Nothing could stop or move them. And anything caught in their path would be brutally, horribly crushed and broken beneath them. A man or woman would be left in torn and bloody pieces.

She moistened her dry lips, her eyes wide when she glanced at Jeremy again.

He wasn't in awe of the creatures—he was angry with her. Sitting atop Gemini—the well-trained cavalry horse who had carried him through the duration of the war—he rode with his customary easy grace, barely aware of the animal beneath him. This was his command.

The massive animals charging toward them were his concern.

"Get back!" he ordered her, his eyes blazing silver. "All the way back where you were told to ride!" He turned from her, a yellow-gauntleted hand raised to the whole of the company behind them.

"They'll be over the rise in a matter of minutes!" he called. His arm was moving in a circle, ordering the company back against its left flank. "Major Brooks! Hold the lead steady here, I'll bring in the rear. Not a horse, mule, or beast forward!"

He nudged Gemini and the experienced war horse moved forward. Christa hadn't had a chance to move; she had that chance now. Jeremy caught hold of Tilly's reins. He pulled her along behind him as he rode down the length of the ranks, shouting out his orders. Christa felt like a punished child, being dragged along.

But she also felt the keen edge of fear. All around her the noise of the stampede grew. Hundreds and thousands of buffalo were coming their way, climbing over rises, dipping into valleys. The air was already filled with dust and dirt, and the earth continued to tremble and shake as if it would disintegrate at any moment.

They galloped down the line of the men. Jeremy was making no attempt to move the whole of his column of men, horses, and wagons. Instead, he lined them in a narrow band just beneath the butt of the ridge, hard to the left flank. At the tail end of it, he released her reins, jumped down from his horse, and lifted her from Tilly. He thrust her toward Robert Black Paw, who, with Nathaniel, was helping calm a pair of mules.

Robert took her instinctively. "Get her below the ridge!" Jeremy commanded.

He leapt back up atop Gemini. Christa pulled from the Indian's hold, dismayed by the fear that surged through her. "Jeremy—"

But he had turned his horse and was riding hard down the line again at a full gallop.

"What's he doing?" she demanded miserably.

"He's going to see that the lead animals steer clear of our line," he told her.

"He's going to go out there? In front of them? That's insane! He'll be killed." She started to struggle.

Robert Black Paw held her back. "No! Come, Mrs. McCauley, down below the ridge."

She had no choice. Robert Black Paw dragged her stiff body down beneath the knoll of the rise and close against it. She was sheltered here from the swirl of dust and dirt. But the noise of the buffalo's pounding footfalls seemed all the more increased. Horses were screaming now in panic; the men were shouting, trying to hold them, to calm them.

Jeremy continued to ride straight toward the stampeding herd.

"My God, let me go! What is he doing! He's got to come back!" she cried, struggling against Robert.

He held her politely, but firmly. Robert Black Paw took his orders from her husband well, Christa thought bitterly. If he'd been shot dead, he'd die holding her tight!

But he was a good man, too, she knew. And if his hold was rigid, his words were gentle and reassuring. "He knows what he's doing. He's ridden these trails before."

"He's not a rock! A buffalo will crush him—"

"Watch!"

Robert pointed a finger past her nose. Over the ridge of earth at her side she could see the path that the buffalo were running. Their narrow line offered the buffalo a wide path. They were beginning to arrive, with just a few of the strays edging to the side. Then she saw Jeremy. At the least, he wasn't alone. Two of his officers were with him. They were waving brightly colored blankets and making almost enough noise to be heard above the stampede.

Christa's heart seemed to fly to her throat. One of the massive creatures had veered Jeremy's way. To her astonishment, Jeremy started to ride down on it, hard, headed for a collision.

A cry escaped her.

But at the last moment the creature turned and ran toward the clear path, and those behind it followed suit.

She sank back against Robert. She hadn't felt ill in a long time now, but she was suddenly afraid she was going to lose everything she had consumed for the last two weeks.

She heard a shot and jumped in panic, leaping away from Robert.

"What is it? What's happened now?" she cried out.

Smiling, Robert Black Paw set his hands on his hips. "There'll be fresh meat for supper tonight, Mrs. McCauley. Your husband brought down one of the last of them." He hopped up the short distance to stand atop the ridge again. He reached down a hand to her.

As she crawled atop it, the world around her seemed to be split by a cacophony of noise once again.

The buffalo were gone. The earth was still trembling slightly, as if the aftermath of some great cataclysm. The buffalo were still running, but far past them now. In their wake gray dirt and dust followed them like a windstorm.

Closer to her immediate vicinity, the noise was caused by the pick-up measures necessary after the stampede. One of the wagons had fallen over and a group of soldiers was righting it. Some of the horses had run off and Jeremy was now giving orders to men to go after them. The columns were re-forming. Sergeant Jaffe—Jeremy's favorite among the company cooks—was busy supervising men over the buffalo carcass.

Robert Black Paw, his duty to her ended, was leading a pair of mules and a wagon back onto the trail. Jeremy was still riding around giving orders. Christa saw that Tilly had held her head and remained nearby, and was now eating up little pieces of grass from the stampede. Christa caught hold of her reins and mounted her horse. She cantered over to the buffalo.

She felt sorry to see the great creature down. Close up, the head seemed even more ridiculously large in comparison to the body. Except that its eyes were tiny in that huge face, and part of the reason the head seemed so big was that it was covered with shaggy fur. Alone and downed it didn't seem such a menace. A streak of pity danced through her. It was an ugly beast, but in some curious way it was beautiful, too, by simple virtue of its magnificent size and power.

"Now, don't go feeling sorry for it, Mrs. McCauley!" Sergeant Jaffe told her. "Rations can get mighty lean out here, and the way I see it there ain't nothing like starving through winter! God put these creatures out here to feed us all. Don't you go turning up your pretty nose at buffalo meat!"

From her seat atop Tilly, Christa shook her head. She could have told him that she had watched a whole nation almost starve, but she kept her silence.

"I'm sure the meat will be wonderful," she murmured. "It's just—rather sad, for some reason!"

"Yes!" Jaffe said, cocking his head toward her. "It's always sad to see something so damned strong brought down. Don't know quite what it is myself, but I understand what you're feeling." He grinned. "Still, when it's either him or me, then I'm mighty glad it's him!"

She shivered suddenly, inching Tilly toward him. "Sergeant Jaffe, do stampedes happen often? We must be moving more deeply into buffalo territory and—"

"Don't you worry your pretty little head none, Mrs. McCauley. We keep our eyes open. It's strange though. You can ride up on a ridge and see a few buffalo grazing on the plain just as nice and peaceful as can be. Then you can see one or two of them running and you don't know if you've come across a couple of strays, or if you'll have a couple hundred thousand racing at you in a matter of minutes!"

"I'm sure my wife will rest well after that!"

Christa swung around. Jeremy had come up behind them. His hat was low over his head. She couldn't see his eyes. She was certain that he was still angry with her.

After last night, she felt as if a wall had risen between them, higher than ever before. Upon occasion, it had seemed as if they just might broach the barriers between them. Now those barriers seemed more insurmountable than ever.

On top of that, she thought wryly, she had disobeyed his orders to ride behind the front of the line.

She tore her gaze from his, determined to ignore him. He'd have his chance to chastise her as soon as they were alone.

Jaffe was apologizing profusely. "Didn't mean nothing by that, Mrs. McCauley, except that we keep our eyes open and our ears to the ground."

Jeremy led Gemini close to the fallen buffalo. "How are we going to make out with this one, Sergeant?"

"Right fine. We'll have buffalo stew and buffalo steak! Dried buffalo and smoked buffalo! We'll make out right fine. Good shot, Colonel."

"Thanks. See to it that my wife has some tender cuts. We've got a general riding in with an escort of officers, and I think we'll do a little private entertaining in my tent. And if you don't mind, Sergeant, she might need a little instruction. We'll be laying over for a few days, making camp, so you'll have some time tonight to deal with the kill. So will my wife."

Christa felt a soft wave of color touch her cheeks. He was making it sound as if she were the most worthless of fluttering belles. How could he! He knew damned well she'd managed with all manner of meat and meals before. The war had taught her an amazing array of crafts. She'd done just fine with his quail.

But then again, "the general" was arriving? This was the first she had heard of it. What general? Captain Clark must have brought the message that someone was coming.

What in God's name made Jeremy think she was about to entertain any Yankee general? She had done exceptionally well, she thought, living with

Yankees up to this point! She'd been polite, she'd even been friendly with Celia and James, Robert Black Paw and Nathaniel—and Captain Clark.

Jeremy didn't intend to give her any explanations now. He wagged a finger at her. "You'll ride at the back, with Robert at your side. If you don't, I'll take Tilly and set you into an ambulance and that will be that. Do you understand?"

She saluted him sharply. "Yes, sir!"

Gemini pranced forward. Jeremy adjusted his sweeping cavalry hat. "You are quite all right, I take it?"

"Fine."

"Then perhaps you'll be so good as to see to some of the other wives. Celia is shaking like a leaf, they say, and her husband is at his post."

"Yes, sir, Colonel, sir!" she responded. Jeremy didn't give a damn about her sarcasm. He didn't care how she obeyed his orders, just so long as she did. But the sarcasm in her reply was not lost on Sergeant Jaffe. He looked at her rather sorrowfully when Jeremy rode away, convinced that his order would be obeyed this time.

"I'll make you a cloak out of this here hide!" Jaffe told her. "Why, you just wait and see! It'll be the most wonderful warm thing you've ever owned, Mrs. McCauley."

"That's very kind of you, Sergeant," she told him. She didn't know if he meant the words or if he was just trying to make her feel better.

She smiled, waved a hand to him, and rode from the scene of the buffalo kill. Jeremy had asked her to see to the other wives. She cantered along the line until she came to Celia's ambulance. The young girl was shaking away and her husband, at her side, was looking very helpless, loath to leave her.

Christa dismounted and came to the rear of the conveyance. She offered Lieutenant Preston a reassuring smile.

"Celia, look who's here. Mrs. McCauley."

Celia released her death grip on him at last. Lieutenant Preston leapt down from the ambulance, thanking Christa with his eyes.

"Celia, come on now!" she said. "It's all over!"

"It was terrible!" Celia moaned. "Why, the ambulance almost turned. I saw your husband—oh, how could you bear it!"

"It's all right now, Celia, I swear it!" her husband said.

Christa was startled by the tug of envy that touched her. Preston was so tender, so caring of his wife!

She gave herself a mental shake and reminded herself bitterly that it was all right for Celia Preston to be a fluttering little female. She was a Yankee.

"Celia, come now!" she said impatiently, as her husband strode for his horse. "It's over!"

"Oh, Christa!" Celia said miserably, "I'm such a failure. He shall hate me!"

Christa sighed. She assured Celia she was no failure. Then she told her what a marvelous meal they would have that night. "And we're making camp for a few days, Jeremy said so. We'll be stationary for a few days. It will be fun!"

Celia was slowly mollified. Christa rode down the rest of the line seeing to the other ladies, but by then, though many had been shaken, they were all fine. Mrs. Brooks informed her that the Lord worked in mysterious ways against those who did not properly respect him. Christa smiled sweetly, her face feeling like wood, and told the woman that the Lord had chosen to protect them all from the buffalo—and to supply them with buffalo stew, so perhaps they were all respecting Him properly after all.

They made eight miles that day. Christa rode in the back of the line with Robert as she had been ordered. She wanted to hate the journey, she was so angry with—and admittedly hurt by—Jeremy, but it was difficult to do so. The landscape was still so different from anything she had ever known. With the buffalo gone, the sky was incredibly blue once again with just a shadowing of puffy white clouds against it. The land seemed so barren, but little flowers grew here and there. The day remained pleasantly cool, their path unobstructed, and the ride was not a hard one.

When the spot Jeremy had chosen for their camp was reached, a young private took Tilly from Christa, promising to rub her down well. The men, busy and competent, immediately started to raise the tents. Christa wandered over to where Sergeant Jaffe was making supper for the hundred and twenty-three men in the command. He talked to her about the value of good seasonings and gave her a sip of buffalo broth. It was sweet, she thought, but good. The taste was like beef, but different. It had more of a wild, gamy taste to it, but still the sweetness was inviting. Perhaps this buffalo was a little tougher than some of the steak she had had, but in the end she decided she liked the taste very much.

"It'll be stew in a matter of minutes, Mrs. McCauley. We'll have a big dish over for you and the colonel soon enough."

"That's very kind of you."

He shook his head. "I never did understand much how the officers' wives felt so obligated to cook for their husbands when there's so much food being prepared for the enlisted men."

"Well," Christa pointed, "because sometimes the men do cook at their own fires."

Someone cleared his throat behind her. It was Nathaniel. "Mrs. McCauley, your tent is up. Since we'll be here a spell, I've seen to the arrangement of your belongings to the best of my ability. I hope you'll be satisfied. And I've taken the liberty of bringing in the hip tub for you. Some of the boys are boiling water and filling it now. We figured that a lady like you—what with the buffalo dust and all —might be wanting a bath."

"How very, very kind of you!" Christa told him. She walked to him and took his hand, shaking it. She smiled at him as well. "How very thoughtful and gracious you all are to me! I should be learning about the tents and doing these things myself."

"We're always so proud of our cavalry wives, ma'am, braving buffalo and dirt and Injuns! We don't mind a bit what we can do," said Sergeant Jaffe.

"Well, I'm afraid I'm not much of a cavalry wife!" she admitted. "But I thank you both from the bottom of my heart. Nathaniel, a bath!"

His grin split his dark face handsomely. "Come, Mrs. McCauley, I'll show you to your tent."

"Mrs. McCauley!" Jaffe called after her. She turned around.

"You're wrong, you know. You make a right fine cavalry wife!"

She smiled. "Thank you."

Nathaniel led her to her tent. It was pitched some distance from the field of smaller tents, yet not far from some of the larger tents that had been pitched for Jeremy's officers. She was also quite near one of the large supply tents.

Maybe that had been done on purpose, she thought, if Jeremy was entertaining a general. Who? she wondered.

Then she ceased to care. Nathaniel had opened the flap to her tent. She cried out with a little sound of delight.

He'd fixed it beautifully. Jeremy's camp desk and her own smaller one had been set up on opposite sides of one of the structural poles. Their bed had been set up and made with the sheets and blankets arranged in a very inviting way. Their trunks had been set conveniently by the bed. Brandy and whiskey had been set out, and even the boxes with her china and silver had been thoughtfully supplied, ready if she should need them to entertain.

Best of all, a tub sat in the tent and the water that rose from it was definitely steaming.

"Bless you, Nathaniel!" she cried, clapping her hands together.

Again, he smiled broadly. "Someone will be near, Mrs. McCauley. You needn't worry about being disturbed." She flashed him a smile of gratitude. He disappeared outside the tent.

Christa thought of nothing but the heaven the water in the hip tub would offer her. She quickly stripped off her blouse and chemise, and then her boots, riding skirt, and pantalets. She shivered until she sank into the water. The heat wove its way into her tired muscles, feeling wonderful.

After a moment, she sank all the way in, soaking her hair, allowing the water to close over her head. She came up, eyes closed, reaching awkwardly for the trunk near the tub where her soap and cloth and the vial of her lavender-scented shampoo had been left.

Her hand came in contact with something that she hadn't expected.

Flesh.

She sat back, her eyes flying open. Jeremy was standing beside her. It was his hand she had touched. She stared at him balefully.

It had been such a beautiful moment for him to interrupt.

"My, my! You do have a knack for finding luxury, my love. Even in the wilderness."

She ignored his tone. He was going to yell about the fact that she had disobeyed his orders. She didn't give a damn. She wasn't wasting her hot water.

"Would you hand me my shampoo, please?" she said icily. "And then if you don't mind . . ."

He dropped down beside her, the vial in his hands. He poured out a portion into his palm. She pursed her lips, staring forward. A second later, his hands were moving in her hair. She closed her eyes. The movement was gentle, mesmerizing. She didn't want to enjoy it, but she did. She closed her fingers over the rim of the tub, clenching them. Then they eased their grip.

And just as soon as she was at ease, he spoke. "You pull a stunt like that again, and I'll take your horse away from you. You'll spend the rest of the trip in your ambulance. Do you understand?"

Her eyes flew open. "I'm not one of your men, Jeremy McCauley. I'm here under duress. And you're not acting like this because I was too close to the front of the line. You're still furious with me over last night. I—"

"All right, Christa. Yes, I'm still angry over last night. But you're truly a little fool if you think that has anything to do with my determination to keep you safe. You'll do what I say!" he told her sharply. "I'm not writing home to tell your brothers that you were mauled by buffalo or picked off by a Comanche scout, his arrow having found your heart since it was right there in perfect shooting range!"

She ignored him, sinking into the water once again to rinse her hair. It took her some time. When she came up again, she realized that he had stripped off his boots and cavalry jacket and that he was undoing the button at his shirt's cuff. Her eyes went wide with amazement. "You're not coming in here."

"I am."

"Then—"

"Nathaniel used to see to my needs. But now he and the others are always running themselves ragged to tend to the needs of my fragile little bride. I want some of that water while it's still hot."

She gripped the edge of the tub. "You're not doing this!" she whispered vehemently. "You always think that you can yell and scream and snap out your orders and then just—just do whatever you want with me! Well, it doesn't work that way. It—"

She broke off for a moment because he hadn't paid her the least heed. He had stripped naked and was striding the few feet toward the tub. For a moment she was taken aback by the sight of him, even though she had seen him hundreds of times.

He was startling to look at. His flesh was so bronzed. His movements were so supple. Quick, silent, powerful. His easy strides belied the knots of muscle that formed him, the breadth of his chest and shoulders, the tautness of his hips and belly, the bulge of his arms and rock hardness of his thighs and buttocks. She felt as if the water suffused with heat all over again just because he approached it.

"Jeremy, I'll get out—"

"The hell you will," he growled.

And he was behind her, his back against the tub. He pulled her back against him as some of the water sloshed over to the ground. She felt his chest and his hair-roughened legs. And between them, just teasing her back and buttocks, his sex.

"You'll get nothing from me—" she began.

"I never get anything from you, Christa," he said flatly. "Worrying about your mood doesn't result in a hell of a lot. But rest your sweet head. At the moment, I want the warmth of the water. You, my love, are like hugging ice, and I think I may be too weary for such an encounter tonight."

She stiffened. He ignored her, finding the soap and sudsing the washrag between his hands before her eyes. "Let's get back to where we were. I won't have you disobeying orders."

"Me!" Miserably torn between comfort and agony by his hold, she bit her tongue. "Of all fool things to do, you go racing right at a buffalo! Riding into the things, for God's sake! It was—"

She broke off.

Suddenly, he went tense behind her. "It was what?"

"It was foolish!" she charged. "You might have gotten yourself horribly trampled!"

He was quiet for a moment, then she felt the warm whisper of his breath as he spoke softly near her ear. "I'm the officer in command. It was my duty to see that the fool creatures turned away. And I do know what I'm doing. I've been out here before. But how nice. It sounds as if you might have been concerned."

"Of course I was concerned!"

"Why? If I had been trampled, you would have been free. You could have returned to your beloved Dixie and your precious Cameron Hall."

"What an awful thing to say!" she charged him, trembling. "How could you?" she whispered. "After all the years of death and destruction I witnessed, how could you even mock me so!"

She whirled to face him the best she could within the confines of the tub, his chest, and legs. There was nothing to be seen in his gray eyes other than speculation. One dark russet brow was slightly raised, and there was a curious, small curl to his lip. For a moment she remembered him riding out, reckless, fearless, precision perfect in his uniform, rugged and striking in his appeal. They were so intimately close. Warmth spread through her. She'd always admitted he was a handsome and appealing man. He had courage, and his own sense of honor. She'd never really realized until this moment that she admired him very much. He was many things, daring, bold, determined, sometimes reckless, but always aware of his responsibility for others.

No, he was not Liam. In many ways, he was very, very different.

She was coming to care about him. Deeply. She didn't mind him so much anymore. Not even his intimacies. Being with him grew more and more exciting. The men admired him very much. The women sighed when he passed by, and envied her.

Maybe, if he just hadn't been such a diehard Yank?

"Do I take that to mean that yes, you would have been distraught had anything happened to me?"

"Oh, stop it!" she murmured, twisting around, suddenly very anxious to be free of him. She tried to rise but his arms wound around her bare midriff, pulling her back down against him. She felt his fingers beneath the fullness of her breasts and she was startled by the streak of sensation that swept through her.

Her heart was beating hard as he pulled her closer against him.

"It was a terrible thing for me to have said, Christa. I'm sorry," he told her.

She didn't reply right away. He was idly running his fingers over her midriff in the warmth of the water. To her amazement, the feel of those fingers shot through her. It seemed to sizzle and burn its way right to the apex of her thighs.

She tried very hard to ignore the growing heat within herself. "It was horrible," she murmured softly. "And you might discover that I am capable of understanding things when you explain them instead of just bellowing out orders! If you could just be polite upon occasion—"

"Polite!" he murmured, his whisper very close to her ear, his tone amused. He seemed to think it over. "Well, I have considered it upon a number of occasions."

"And?" she persisted.

He moved his cheek gently against her temple. The warmth flamed more deeply within her. The gesture made her feel both very comfortable and stirred.

"Do you remember the very first time we met?" he asked her softly.

"Vaguely," she said. "You were ready to hang my brother. You were looking for Callie. What does this have to do with being polite?"

"I wasn't ready to hang your brother. I had to find out what had happened to my sister. Now—"

"You were a Yank deep in Rebel territory." She reflected on that for a minute. "Definitely an idiot," she told him frankly.

"Maybe. Callie is my only sister. We were always close. But that's beside the point. The very first time we met, you were ready to shoot me."

"Daniel wouldn't let me," she said regretfully.

She felt his smile.

"Let me see," he continued. "I think it was the same occasion when you left the dinner table simply because I was at it."

"There was a war on," she reminded him. "And we might have all been shot as traitors for entertaining you."

"Jesse was there."

"It was his house."

"Not during the war."

"What is your point?" she asked him, not really seeking an answer. For once, it seemed nice just to be with him. His touch upon her was easy, light. She felt secure in his arms, almost like a sleek cat being very nicely stroked. She closed her eyes. Maybe it was a time of truce.

"The point," he said, and again the hot whisper of his words touched her earlobe, sending little shivers down her spine, "is that there was always something between us."

She shifted slightly, smiling incredulously. She wanted to see his eyes. They were very silver. Amused. Tender. "The fact that I wanted to shoot you meant that there was something between us?"

His smile deepened. He nodded. She arched a perplexed brow, but eased back against him when his arm encircled her, pulling her back. "Anger, hostility —but sparks. Anyway, once in a while, I've wondered what it would have been like if I'd met you before the war."

Christa hesitated a moment. "Perhaps, if I hadn't met you as the enemy you would have been quite tolerable."

He laughed. "But then again, I might not have been all that tolerable. I can just imagine the type of occasion when I might have met you. Your brothers and I never met at West Point, but just say we could have. Jesse might have brought me home for one of your big barbecues. There would have been fellows all over the place, just tripping over themselves to get near you. Daft fellows with stars in their eyes. They would have been begging for dances, dying to bring you some punch, standing on their heads just for one little smile."

"Jeremy—"

"And there I would have been. Some poor farm boy from Maryland!"

"McCauley, we never judged any man by his money—"

He laughed, his knuckle running over her cheek. "No, I'm certain that you didn't," he assured her, and she bit her lip, pleased, because he seemed to mean it. "But you're not seeing the picture I'm painting! All those fine young strapping fellows! They would have all been as nice as was humanly possible! And you would have twirled every single one of them around your little finger. You would not have listened to a word any of them had to say. You would have thumbed your nose at any one of them who might have even thought of telling you what to do! And they would just have kept on being nice, begging and pleading and falling in love like a pack of fools—and never, never once managing to get you to do a thing by being polite!''

She shifted again, meeting his eyes. "Well, you are mistaken, McCauley!" she said with her nose just a bit in the air. "I always responded politely in return—"

"You were nice as can be—and went about doing just as you damn well pleased. I can't always afford to be nice, Christa. And heaven help me, I certainly can't afford to act like those poor boys so mesmerized by your beauty and your smile!"

"We didn't meet before the war—" she began.

He interrupted her with soft, husky laughter once again. "If we had, Christa, you wouldn't have given me the time of day!"

"If you had been nice—"

"I would have loved being nice," he whispered. "Very, very nice . . ."

His lips touched her damp shoulder. His teeth slightly grazed it, his tongue bathed the region. His kiss moved closer to her ear. Little raindrops of sensation danced through her flesh. She gripped the rail of the tub tightly. His palm was fully against her breast now. Cradling it. Tenderly cupping its weight, the center of his hand going round and round her nipple.

Her breath caught.

"Jeremy, it's not even supper yet," she breathed. "Sergeant Jaffe is sending buffalo stew. It's even light out. It—"

"It will wait," he told her. "Believe me, no one will disturb me now. Robert Black Paw is aware that I have joined my wife at her bath. If the Comanches raided, he would fend them off."

Perhaps the last was an exaggeration, Christa wasn't really sure.

And she wasn't sure in the least if she cared. She was always fighting him. This afternoon she was weary of the fight.

And she was so very aware of the way that she was feeling. Sweetness and fire seemed to pervade her to the depths of her soul. She was amazed that the tip of his tongue could create such havoc all through her. She didn't mind just lying back, feeling his arms, feeling his caress.

She felt his arousal hardening against the base of her spine, hotter than the water, exciting. She closed her eyes, catching her breath. She wanted him. She'd felt the sweet promise before. Now something golden and wonderful seemed to stretch before her. He had made comments enough about her refusal to give in to him.

Maybe this time it would be different.

She closed her eyes. He was stroking her, his touch sliding through the water, down along the flesh of her inner thigh. Closer and closer to intimate places. Touching her there. She froze, afraid to breathe, then exhaled in a gasp. She heard a soft groan behind her. He buried his face against the wet hair at her nape. "This is wonderful, but I think my body is breaking." He balanced her weight and stood, crawling from the awkward tub before reaching down to sweep her up, dripping.

"Do that again," he murmured.

Her arms locked around his neck as he held her. "Do what?" she whispered.

"Sigh. Softly. As if you wanted me too."

Color touched her cheeks, and he laughed. There was something different in his expression. Something anxious and pleased as he watched her.

She lowered her lashes. A drop of water came trickling down the center of his chest. She wanted to lean against him. Taste it with her tongue. Panic seized her suddenly. She couldn't surrender to him, no matter how sweet the feelings. Her distance was all that she had left of her pride and heart. Daily, she forgot more and more the look and feel and texture of Liam's face.

And daily, she came to discover more about Jeremy and his feelings toward her. He must have resented her heartily when he had married her. He had been in love before. He had been expecting a child. She'd been a southern girl, so he must have loved her very much. And he must surely lie awake beside her at times, feeling that bitter disappointment with her that he did, and wonder why God had chosen to take the woman and the child he had wanted, and saddled him with Christa and her baby.

"I . . . there's so much we need to discuss," she said.

"There's suddenly so much to discuss?" he said, laughing. "I don't think so. I don't want to talk," he said, walking her over to the bed. He pulled back the blankets that Nathaniel had so meticulously prepared for them.

"Jeremy, Nathaniel spent a lot of time—"

"Nathaniel would certainly forgive me," he said, laying her down flatly. His kiss touched her upper breast. Then covered the fullness of it. Amazing sensations began to seize hold of her. His tongue licked over her nipple. She clenched her teeth so as not to cry out. Her fingers fell into his damp hair. "It's—daylight still. Jaffe is coming. Because of the general. Remember, a general is coming!"

"Umm."

Maybe he knew just how close to surrender she was at that moment. Maybe he even sensed that she wanted him. Really wanted him at that moment, for the first time. He didn't intend to be dissuaded.

His tongue skimmed down the valley of her breasts, rimmed her navel. An ache was burning between her thighs. She was dying for him to touch her.

In anguish, she pulled upon his hair. "Jeremy!"

He came up against her. His smile was sensual. The silver gleam in his eye was wicked. Luxuriously lazy. "I can't believe it. My little ice maiden so warm. Trembling."

She moistened her lips, shaking her head. His smile remained. He stared at her mouth and then seized it in a sweetly savage kiss. She loved the feel of his mouth and the taste of it. Loved the way that he raked hers with his tongue, filling it, again and again. She was breathless when he broke from her. Breathless and staring at him. Her hands were upon his shoulders. She hadn't even realized it. She was stroking his arms. Her heart was thudding at a frantic rate. Her nipples were taut and hard, teased by the hair on his chest, delicate, taunting pinpoints against him. She flushed, the length of her feeling the hard pulse of his arousal.

His knee urged her thighs apart. He held himself above her. She trembled with a surge of anticipation for the silver in his eyes, a fire unlike any she had seen before. The feel of his hardened sex pressed against her own was dizzying. "Jesu!" he whispered, both tender and urgent. "Damn General Sherman! Were he due in ten minutes, my love, I could not leave you now!"

He pressed his lips to her throat, thrusting smoothly into her body.

Sherman!

The name went off like a burst of cannon in her head.

"Sherman!" She gasped it aloud.

The feeling of desperate desire that had been so strongly aroused in her slid from her like bathwater sluicing from her body. She braced herself, trying to deny him. It was too late. She had so nearly been the seeking force in this tempest. She clenched her teeth, twisting her head to the side. Tears stung her eyes and she held herself rigidly against him, not protesting, not even hating him, but becoming once again his ice queen. She closed her eyes. In time she felt the hardness of his constriction, felt his body tense rigidly from top to bottom. The warmth from him spread into her and she bit her lip, longing to run her fingers through his hair, to cradle his head.

But he had uttered the enemy's name.

"Sherman?" she repeated coldly.

He groaned, falling wearily to his side. Damn. What an absolute idiot he had been. So seduced and so enchanted that he hadn't even thought of what that name meant to her, he had spit it out just as if he were one of her prewar beaux, tripping over his own tongue in his desire for her.

He'd come so damned close!

"Jesu, you couldn't have waited to discuss this?" he demanded irritably.

"*You* brought up that name!" she cried, coming up on an elbow.

But he didn't look at her, and he didn't seem to care to have her staring at him either. He rose angrily and walked back to the tub and used the water to strenuously wash his face. When he was done he grabbed her towel and wiped his face and body and began to dress impatiently. Christa watched him, her anger growing.

"Sherman?" she said again, her teeth grinding.

He buckled his scabbard on, swinging around to meet her. Oh, God, no. This was going to turn into another battle. A serious one. He should have been more prepared.

Sherman hadn't gone into Virginia. But that didn't matter. He'd come through her precious Confederacy and had definitely done severe damage.

Dear Lord, he didn't *want* to hurt her and he did understand her feelings. But she was going to have to deal with them. She was going to have to accept the man. Sherman was his superior officer and they were both military men. He had no choice but to entertain the man when he came to the camp.

"Sherman," he said flatly. He didn't dare give her even an inch of leeway.

"As in William Tecumseh?" she demanded.

"The very same."

She leapt up, heedless of her nudity. She flew at him, slamming her fists furiously against his chest. He caught her wrists. She grit her teeth. "You expect me to entertain General Sherman?" she nearly screeched.

"Dammit, Christa, you should be used to Yankees by now!"

"Yankees, yes!" she spat out. "But not Yankees like Sherman! He ravaged the South! He raided it, raped it, destroyed it. He made women and children starve and freeze—"

"He fought an all-out war to win. He had a 'scorched earth' policy and it worked. And he did his damnedest to give Confederate General Joe Johnston the best surrender terms possible. He was called a traitor by Stanton for the terms he tried to offer—"

Christa could hear him. "How dare you!" she gasped. "How dare you even think that I will entertain that man."

"Because you're my wife, that's why!" he thundered. "I am the commanding officer here and you're my wife!"

"No! I won't do it."

"You will!"

"I won't!" she vowed, breaking his hold on her. "You can't expect this of me! I've done everything that you wanted. But I won't, I mean it, I won't have Sherman to dinner!"

"You will." He reached out for her, bringing her hard against him. His fingers were taut, he was shaking her and her hair tumbled down her back. Tears stung her eyes and she began to laugh.

"I will not do it!"

"Jesu! You will!"

"You can beat me black and blue—"

"I'm not beating you!"

"You're damned close!"

He stopped. He stared at her, his eyes silver and narrowing like daggers. He swept her up and deposited her back on the bed. "Damn you!" he cried. His eyes swept over her and he inhaled sharply. "And damn me for a fool!" he added. He turned on his heels and left the tent behind him.

Thirteen

Jeremy didn't return to his tent until it had grown very late.

Sergeant Jaffe had seen to it that his buffalo stew made its way around the camp and so there was no reason for him to go hungry. He ate with Celia and Jimmy Preston, then made his escape because Celia couldn't say enough about his prowess against the buffalo and Jimmy just couldn't quit shaking his head with wonder at the magnificent way Christa could handle herself in any situation.

For a while he walked along the river, glad of the spot he had chosen for their camp. There were two things the army needed when they camped for a stay of any duration—water and grass. He'd found both here in abundance. The river ran strong and pure here, surrounded by endless plains where the grass was deep green, rich, and abundant.

It was beautiful out here. The air was dry and cool, the horizon seemed to stretch for miles while mountains rose in the distance. It was a rougher place than his home, perhaps. Maryland was so very green, shaded with blues and purples. Out here, the landscape was tinged with earth hues, golds and tans, deep burnt oranges and scorching reds.

This was Comanche land, he reminded himself. He was in Buffalo Run's territory. It could be as wild and savage as the Comanche themselves, and as strangely beautiful.

He paused, listening to the run of the river at his side and looking back at the low burning fires of his camp. A sentry saluted him and he saluted in return. Fourteen men were on guard watching the perimeters of their camp. In four hours they would switch with others. They were spaced fairly tightly together, and they were wary.

Jeremy had been warned by his superiors at Little Rock that Buffalo Run was on the warpath.

But he knew Buffalo Run. He had met the Indian when they had both been quite a few years younger. Buffalo had not yet risen to become the great war chief that he was today. He had just been one of Gray Eagle's many sons, a handsome Indian, sleek, lean, as cunning as a fox, as strong as a bear.

Jeremy would never forget the first occasion he had met the Comanche. Cavalry and Indians had met in a skirmish just north of the Texas borderline. The cavalry had been doing well enough, until their commander had realized that they were running out of ammunition.

They had made a break for it. Jeremy had been bringing up the rear. They'd raced long and hard, losing the majority of the Comanche following in their wake. But then Jeremy's horse had suddenly and silently dropped beneath him and Jeremy had gone plunging into the dry dirt. Before he had much managed to catch his breath, he'd been attacked by a man like a five-armed creature out of hell.

He'd managed to dislodge the knife that nearly slit his throat from the Indian's hand, but the fistfight that had followed between them had gone on endlessly. It had felt like hours.

They very nearly killed one another, but when the sun went down they were both still breathing. Jeremy looked over to see that the Indian had closed his eyes. He picked up a large jagged rock and came up on his knees, ready to strike the weapon against his enemy. For some reason he held still, unable to kill such an enemy in such a way.

He dropped the rock and began to walk away.

It was a good thing that mercy had tempered his decision. The Indian opened his eyes. The two of them stared at one another for a long while. Then Jeremy felt a creeping feeling at the nape of his neck. He turned.

Around them were grouped five Comanche braves who had come for Buffalo Run. Jeremy was certain that he had breathed his last. His scalp tingled.

But Buffalo Run called out to them and stood slowly and painfully. He spoke again and someone trotted up with a paint pony. The pony was offered to Jeremy. Hesitantly, Jeremy took the reins, still staring suspiciously at the Indian.

"You can go, white man," the Indian said in well-enunciated English.

Jeremy frowned, surprised by his excellent English, and more surprised by the mercy he seemed to be receiving.

"Just like that, I can ride away?"

"I am Buffalo Run. Remember my name."

"And if I mount this horse and turn my back to you, I will still live to remember your name?"

"You would be a dead man now if I chose it so. Maybe you will even choose to understand. We are raided, and so we raid. Our lands are ceded to us and then snatched away, so we seek to take them back. You fought a brave battle. You would not kill a man who could not see his death. You will not die by my hand, white man. Ever." He suddenly extended his buckskin-clad arm, then pushed up the sleeve. Jeremy stared in fascination as one of the other young bucks brought up a sharply bladed hunting knife. Buffalo Run slashed his arm deeply and offered it up to Jeremy.

Jeremy had heard of the custom. Blood brothers. It meant they would fight no more. He took the knife and ripped up his cavalry sleeve. Buffalo Run's slash had been deep. He made his equally so, looking at the Indian, taking great care not to flinch even as he felt the pain. He melded his arm to Buffalo Run's.

"Go back. Tell them to leave me in peace."

"They will not believe that a Comanche seeks peace."

"Tell them anyway."

"I will try."

"We will meet again."

Jeremy didn't think so. The rumble of war was already growing deeper back home—he knew that the government would start sending troops eastward very soon. He'd already determined that he'd do his best not to fight in Maryland or Virginia, but he knew he'd soon be sent back to a battle line.

He mounted bareback the paint pony he had been given. He didn't turn around. He knew that no arrow would pierce his back, no shot would be fired, no knife would fly.

As it happened, he did see Buffalo Run again. He was sent with a commission to visit Buffalo Run's father. Jeremy sat in the Comanche village, fascinated. He had come to know the people of many Indian tribes, especially the Cherokee, members of the "Five Civilized" Tribes! Their manners were gracious, their desire for learning was a deep thirst.

The Comanche were different. They were a warlike tribe, and the chief's tent was decorated with many war drums, across which stretched animal sinews that held any number of human scalps. Many were Indian scalps. The Comanche went to war against the Apache and other Indian tribes, as well as the white man.

Tonight, they were invited guests. No one commented on the scalps—few of them could. White men in the West were sometimes as quick to take them as Indian braves. There was also a rumor that the taking of scalps had spread west from the East—that the first white settlers had started the custom by scalping Pamunkey Indians. Jeremy found such a thought difficult to stomach, but in his heart he knew that he had met both white men and Indians capable of taking scalps, and so he could not discount the rumor completely.

Buffalo Run greeted him with a nod. He spent a day in the sweat lodge with Buffalo Run and his father and brothers and other cavalry, and he sat for hours around a fire listening to the singsong of the shaman's chants. The medicine man threw powders from his bag upon the fire, causing it to flare up. They drank some concoction the Indians had brewed, and Jeremy saw—as the Indians had suggested that he would—many things in the flames.

It was an interesting occasion for Jeremy. He knew that many white men felt the only good Indians were dead ones, but he had seen many commendable things even among the savage Comanche. They were a fiercely loyal people, protective of their own and fearless when they were threatened.

He inadvertently received a valuable lesson that night too. When the cool night breeze soothed his flesh after the hours of the sweat lodge, Buffalo Run told him that the Comanche had been watching. They had watched the tribes come west of the Mississippi. They had watched Andrew Jackson try to strip Florida of the Seminole, they had seen the Cree taken from Georgia. Then they had seen the white man lick his lips and try to shove the Indians ever farther west.

"None can be believed," Buffalo Run told him. When a white man sees an Indian village and destroys it, he tries hard to murder the children for they will grow to be braves. And he tries harder to murder the women, for they will carry the future generations."

"Not all white men!" Jeremy protested. He pointed out that Indians were known for equal cruelty. In fact, part of the reason they had come was for the return of a young Texan girl.

Buffalo Run told him that neither did all Comanche choose to kill young people. Young white boys could grow to be fine braves, and young women the mothers of fierce warriors.

His mother had been one. The white man had come to rescue her, and she had refused to leave Buffalo Run's father. "The choice was hers. She saw the two worlds, and she knew."

"I find your tribe admirable," Jeremy told him.

They parted that night, intrigued with one another. They met up one more time on the plain, right before Jeremy came home. Buffalo Run was amused. "They mock us that we are all alike, and that Indians make war upon Indians. Now you will go home and fight your brothers." He pointed to Steven Terry, a friend of Jeremy's from Alabama. "You will fight one another. Shoot one another. Take your swords and bleed one another."

"It doesn't give us any pleasure," Jeremy said. He felt forced to explain. "We are fighting for ideals. For the whole of our nation."

"You will band together, all you different tribes, on either side of a line. One day, white man, you should take care. The Indians might well band together too."

When he had headed back east, he had spent much of the journey thinking about Buffalo Run. He understood many of the things that the Indian had said to him. For one, the whites were always overestimating the number of Indians. Some chronicler had written down that there were twenty thousand Comanche in Buffalo Run's territory. There were, perhaps, four hundred.

But Buffalo Run had given him fair warning too. The Indians could band together. The Comanche could band with the Kiowa and the Apache and others, and then they would indeed be a powerful force. Perhaps the alliance could spread north and farther west. Navaho and Hopi could join in, and Cheyenne and Black Feet and Oglala Sioux.

Someday, if the Indians were pushed too far, it could happen.

But then Jeremy had come home. He'd had a long leave to be with his family. They'd all been home, he, Josh, Josiah, and Callie. There had been long sweet days when he had gone back to an earlier time, tilling fields with his brothers, listening to his father read into the night, even indulging in a food fight when they put together a picnic on the lawn, laughing when they'd all managed to miss one another completely and catch Callie right on the nose with a blancmange. She'd managed to pay back the lot of them with a meringue pie, and then they'd all been sorry that they lost out on dessert. Their father had indulged them, smoking his pipe, watching with knowing eyes.

They'd all been there to see Callie wed to Michaelson, beautiful in her white, and then they'd all been together one last time to say good-bye and then leave Callie all alone as they traveled off to join their companies in distant fields.

Their father had been the first to fall. Then Michaelson, then Josiah. Their losses had been great. Yet all that was behind them now. The war was over. Callie had found Daniel—or Daniel had found Callie. Men and women struggled to understand, to come to grips with the war.

Admittedly, some men struggled still to see the South pay for all that had happened. It was said that Sherman's men had gone into South Carolina with an especial vengeance.

Some Yanks, like Christa's carpetbaggers, would take advantage of the South's defeat. Those in high political places would take their revenge against the men they held captive, like Jefferson Davis. Some Rebels would never surrender, like those he had heard were heading for South America to form a new Confederacy there. Like Christa herself.

He sighed, ready to kick himself again. He'd had her right where he wanted her. In so many things she was the dutiful wife, not because she gave a damn about being dutiful to him, but because she was determined to prove that a Cameron could do anything. She was an extraordinary cavalry wife. Hell, tarantulas hadn't sent her screaming, they had intrigued her. Buffalo hadn't brought about the first flicker of fear in her eyes.

She had faced Yankees. Nothing else compared to that ordeal.

She slept with him every night because she was his wife. She never protested his touch. But night after night he felt the passion simmering there, felt that she could be magnificent, that he had only to coax her surrender.

And that was it, of course, in a nutshell. Christa was not about to surrender.

Yet he had come so close. There had been a languorous look in her crystal-blue eyes. She had leaned against him so softly, she had sighed, moved so sweetly. The slightest smile had curved her lips, and even the promise that she might return the least of his desire had sent a near-maddened longing to his senses. He must have been insane. He had said the hated name. Sherman.

Dammit, he mentioned Grant's name all the time. He had served almost directly under Grant during most of the war, having been his aide-de-camp for a few months before he had been ordered directly to logistics. He talked about Sheridan. They talked about battles around the campfires sometimes, and Christa had never reacted so violently.

Maybe because his men were gentlemen for the most part, he thought, especially his officers. In all this time, there had never been a negative comment made about the Rebs. The North had won. His men were willing to speak the truth. The Rebs had been damned fine fighters and their leadership had been extraordinary. Jackson and Lee would go down in the history of military annals, just like Stuart with his magnificent, lightning cavalry raids. So many men were dead, blue and gray. It seemed the kindest thing was to offer them up a salute for their honor and let them rest. In her way, he thought, even Christa saw this.

Damn. He just couldn't wait until later to mention Sherman's name.

The fires were burning lower. The air was beautiful, but growing colder. He stared back at the camp. All was well. A horse whinnied from somewhere. The scene was peaceful.

Somewhere out there, he knew, Buffalo Run watched his movements.

And tomorrow he had Sherman and his party of officers arriving. It would be a very long day.

He set his jaw, his teeth grating. He was the ranking officer. He'd be expected to entertain Sherman. Christa would have to swallow hard and accept it.

But what if she didn't?

He determined that he'd best be prepared for the worst.

Jaffe, he thought, would be doing the cooking for the general's arrival.

He started back along the water, through the myriad tents of the enlisted men, and finally to his own.

Robert Black Paw, silent and nearly blending in with the shadows of the tent, saluted him and slipped past him. His vigil was over.

When Jeremy slipped inside, he found that she had doused the kerosene lamp on his desk, making it difficult for him to move about in the darkness. He would manage.

He crawled into their camp bed, wondering for a wild second if she would be there. Yes, of course, she would. Though she didn't know it, Robert always kept vigil, and if she had thought to go somewhere, Jeremy would have known it long ago.

No, she was there. As his eyes adjusted to the total darkness, he realized she was bundled from throat to toe in a flannel nightgown. She was as far to her side of the bed as she could manage and her back was to him. She was awake, he was certain. She was lying there too tensely to be asleep.

He leaned close to her. But before he could say a word, she whispered fiercely, "Touch me, and I'll scream until every man in this camp is awake!"

"My love, I am far too weary to touch you tonight. You should know that I don't give a damn if you scream until you're hoarse. In fact, princess, I have a word of warning for you. Be courteous tomorrow. Be courteous, or I will tan your hide. I will do so with an audience of dozens of men, and I will not care in the least what a single one of them has to say. Am I understood?"

"You wouldn't—"

"Dare. Yes, I would. But don't worry about your precious solitude this evening. My pillow offers far more comfort and warmth! But take care tomorrow!"

He turned on his own side. He didn't touch her. The inch between them lay like a great chasm.

General William Tecumseh Sherman arrived with a small party of officers and their wives, some who would now be joining Jeremy's ranks, and some who would be moving on with the general.

He arrived early and was greeted with a bugle salute. The men not on guard duty presented him with a show of their horsemanship.

Christa was not with Jeremy. He had slipped from bed while it was still dark to dress, and he had mounted his bay to ride out with James Preston to meet the approaching party as soon as the messenger had arrived to announce the imminent appearance of the great general.

He was an interesting man. A ruthless one in his way, Jeremy thought, but not an exceptionally cruel one, and certainly not cruel by choice. Like so many others, Sherman showed the wear of the war on his face. It was deeply lined, never a really handsome face, but now one with haggard cheeks beneath a full beard and mustache and with soul-weary eyes that looked upon the world with a weary wisdom.

He was accompanied by a Lieutenant Jennings and his wife, Clara, Captain and Mrs. Liana Sinclair, Captain and Mrs. Rose Claridge, and two bachelor officers, Captain Martin Staples and Captain Dexter Lawrence.

The younger women, Liana Sinclair and Rose Claridge, were both charming and sweet, if somewhat wide-eyed and ill-prepared for the rigors of the western roads. Liana giggled a bit excessively for Jeremy's taste, and Rose shivered every other minute. Yet both ladies seemed pleasant enough.

Clara Jennings, however, was a virago.

Jeremy had been in their company for not more than ten minutes before she had managed to complain about the ruts in the road, the dirty taste of the water from the streams, and the awful way they had been bumping along since coming into Comanche territory. Jeremy chanced a glance at Sherman and realized that the general was going to be overjoyed to leave the woman behind.

Through the presentations and ceremonies, Sherman was polite and cheerful due to the presence of the ladies. Despite a generally stern nature, Sherman could be a very polite and pleasant social companion when he chose to be.

But toward midafternoon, the ladies were escorted to their newly erected tents, and when he and the other officers sat around the field tent drinking coffee, he was much more blunt.

"Colonel McCauley, there is going to be trouble ahead for you. It's as clear as day, the handwriting is on the wall. Comanche."

"I've heard that Buffalo Run is on the warpath. They warned me about him in Little Rock. Has something else happened?"

Sherman waved a hand in the air. "A great deal has happened, sir. Some regrettable. Some, perhaps, unavoidable. Captain Miller, in charge of Company B of the Third, raided one of the Comanche villages. I understand that his men panicked and that it turned into a slaughter. It's been said that Buffalo Run promised retaliation. Now, you know my stand on the Indian issue pretty much, I think."

"Yes, I think I do, General." Sherman was a soldier, first and always. He didn't mind the Indians who behaved—those who bowed to the white decree and obediently went to live on their reservations. But he intended to be hell on those who were determined to go their independent way. Sherman knew that Jeremy felt far more sympathy for the Indians and the loss of their way of life than he did, although he didn't agree. From some of the things that Sherman had written and said, Jeremy was certain that he actually favored extinction of the tribes who continued to be warlike. Sherman was a man who tended to resent the point of view of another man, especially when it disagreed with his.

Lieutenant Jennings, the middle-aged man saddled with the harridan, Clara, made a sound and pointed his pipe at Jeremy. "Colonel, I believe I saw some of his work not an hour's ride from here. We couldn't detour much from our path with the ladies present, but I saw smoke rising and I rode out a bit. If I'm not mistaken, I saw smoke. I'm not sure where off the trail, but I'm sure that some mischief was afoot."

Jeremy was damned sure of it. He'd heard of Captain Miller. The man hated Indians, he'd had a brother killed in a prewar clash with them. Buffalo Run was sure to be on the warpath if one of his villages had been raided, if the innocent, women, children, and the aged, had been killed.

"I wish you had mentioned it earlier," Jeremy commented. It was too late to send his men out tonight. He'd send a party out with Robert Black Paw in the morning. If anyone could find the faint embers of a dying fire, it would be Robert.

"Gentlemen, perhaps we should retire for an hour. Sergeant Jaffe has taken it upon himself to create an excellent dinner, and I believe that Celia Preston is arranging entertainment. She determined to drag her spinet out to her husband's new post. We've also a fiddle player and some of our men are talented harmonica players. After everyone has freshened up, we can meet again at the officers' mess tent."

Jeremy rose and the others joined him, filing out. Sherman was watching him. "I look forward to this evening. It's my understanding that you have wed one of the most beautiful women to reside on either side of the Mason–Dixon line. I regret that I've yet to meet her."

Don't regret it! Jeremy thought. He smiled stiffly. "My wife is very beautiful. She is—she is with child. In the early stages, sir, but you know women and their moods."

Sherman laughed, rubbing his beard. "I know she's a Cameron, and a Rebel one at that. I imagine it will be a lively evening."

"Sir—"

"You mustn't expect too much of her, Colonel. It was a long, bitter war. Few people understand that I bear no rancor toward our southern brethren. A 'scorched earth' policy is the fastest way I know to win a war. It gave me no pleasure to hurt people."

"I know that, sir."

"I'll try to tell your wife," he said lightly, and winked. "But, yes, I think it will be a lively night!" He walked out.

You don't know how lively, Jeremy thought with an inward groan.

He hadn't gone near her himself all through the day, but he had asked James to see to her whereabouts now and then, and he knew that she had spent the day with Celia. She was in camp. Presumably, she would at least show up at the dinner table. He thought that he had made his threat strong enough for that.

When he returned to his tent to shave and change for the evening, she was nowhere in sight. She had been there recently, for the hip tub had been brought in for her use and the water in it was still tepid.

Whatever she intended to do to Sherman, she intended to do it clean, he thought wryly.

He hadn't intended to bathe, but the water was there, and so he made use of it, shivering when he rose—it wasn't quite as warm as he had thought and the night was growing chill. He dressed and shaved quickly, and came out in search of Christa.

Sergeant Jaffe stopped him, presenting him the full menu for the evening. They would begin with a buffalo broth soup. There would be a mixed vegetable platter composed of the yams and fresh greens they had purchased from the peaceful group of Choctaw the week before. He'd arranged for the best buffalo steaks. And one of the messengers had brought with them some strawberries from St. Louis last week, so they would be able to have a fine dessert with fresh cream.

"Very commendable, Sergeant."

"And we'll be eating on your wife's fine plates, sir," Jaffe said happily. "I think we'll do you proud, sir."

"I'm sure you will. She helped you today with her plates and silver?"

"Oh no, sir. She trusted us with the boxes. She's been busy with little Mrs. Preston all day. I'm sure they're planning a delightful entertainment for you."

"I'm sure," Jeremy agreed.

When he came past Jaffe, he nearly tripped over a dozen of the hunting hounds that accompanied the troop. He swore beneath his breath, then realized she was definitely getting the best of him.

He strode into the officers' mess tent. Nathaniel was in the corner, softly playing the fiddle. Officers in their finery were standing by their ladies, definitely decked out in theirs.

But there was no one there so striking or beautiful as his wife.

Christa was engaged in conversation with Jimmy and Celia. A delicate champagne flute was in her fingers, and he imagined that the glass had traveled with them from Cameron Hall.

Christa had eschewed her usual trail clothing for the most elegant wear. She was in a gown of rich blue taffeta with velvet and black lace trim. The gown had a slightly high collar at her nape, but the handsome edge work was cut low across the bosom. It hugged her upper body, and the skirt fell in elegant folds down to the ground, the rear caught up in a bustle at the back. Against the rich coloring of the gown her hair had never appeared more midnight black, nor her eyes so endlessly blue.

She had dressed for the occasion, he thought uneasily. She had drawn out her plates, her silver—and her own finery. Magnanimous. And frightening.

He strode across the tent, acknowledging the men and women as he did so. The company was not a large one. Tomorrow there would be an officers' picnic to which all the officers and their wives would be invited to meet the newcomers. Tonight was a smaller grouping, just the general, the newcomers, Lieutenant and Mrs. Preston, and a few others.

Christa's eyes rose to his. She studied him for a moment, her eyes grave, and he wondered what went on within her head. He tried to convey his own warning to her through his eyes.

Coolly, she looked away.

He came beside her, slipping an arm through his. "Evening, Jimmy, Celia."

"Colonel!" Celia always had a smile for him, even when she was frightened of something and her smile was wavering.

"Has he arrived yet?" he asked Jimmy.

"Just coming in now, sir."

Freshened, smiling, Sherman came through the entry, Lieutenant Jennings and Clara right behind him. His eyes fell instantly upon Christa. Naturally. He was intrigued with her.

Naturally. She was exquisite. Every man in the tent had looked her way.

"Ah, the elusive Mrs. McCauley at last!" Sherman said. He strode to them, ignoring the salutes of his officers. "McCauley, so here she is. No wonder you hide her. She is a treasure."

He reached for her hand and kissed it. Jeremy saw the blood drain from her face. She snatched her hand back quickly. "General Sherman," she murmured.

"I know of your brother, madam," Sherman said. "Men who should have died considered his skill a rare gift from God."

Her eyes narrowed. "Jesse is quite talented, sir. Have you heard of my other brother?"

"Daniel Cameron? Indeed." Jeremy waited. Every eye in the place was on the two of them. Tension rose. Sherman continued, "Time and again, Mrs. McCauley, we shook our heads at his exploits. Had he and his like but been on our side, the war might well have been won much earlier."

It was a gracious comment. Christa said nothing.

"I believe myself, General, that had Christa but been on our side, the war might have been won much earlier."

A burst of laughter rose. Christa still didn't reply, but the tension had been broken. Jeremy tightened his fingers around her arm. "Suggest we sit, madam!" he hissed to her.

She freed herself from his touch. Short of creating a disturbance, he could hardly pull her back.

"We need some dinner music," she said, walking over to Nathaniel and whispering something to him. Jeremy grit his teeth.

"Shall we sit?" he suggested himself.

As it happened, Christa was on his right—and Sherman was on her right. He was sure that Christa hadn't planned it that way—perhaps Sherman had. Sherman had been designated a seat beside Clara Jennings.

Maybe that was why his seat had been changed so that he was placed beside Christa.

Whatever the reason, Jeremy inwardly braced himself for the coming storm.

It arrived within minutes.

Sherman politely complimented the soup, and Christa assured him she'd had nothing to do with it. The subject of fine dining came up, and then the subject of dining on the trail.

Wine was served. A Bordeaux that they had carefully packed with them for special occasions. To Jeremy's surprise, Christa drained her glass immediately.

It was refilled. The men were serving them without a flaw.

"Mrs. McCauley," Sherman complimented Christa, "you have done remarkably well with practically nothing to work with here in the wild."

She was sipping her wine again. She smiled sweetly. "Well, I've years of training! I am a southerner, sir, very accustomed to doing the best one can with nothing! And even that nothing was so easily snatched away!"

"She should have been in the field," Jeremy said pleasantly, his fingers curling tightly over hers. Their eyes met. Christa flushed, snatching her fingers away.

Once again, silence fell over the table. Sergeant Jaffe and his crew served the main dish.

Christa's wineglass was refilled. She wanted to drain it once again. She was a Cameron. Southern belle or no, she had shared wine—and whiskey—with her brothers on plenty of occasions.

Since the baby, it made her ill. She needed it tonight. She couldn't do more than sip at it.

Jeremy asked the general to join him in a whiskey, and it was brought.

"Lord, but whiskey is in plenty out here in the wilderness! And to think it was not so long ago there were places we had none and soldiers screamed beneath the amputation saws!" Christa said.

It was shocking dinner conversation.

"She's so accustomed to her brother being a doctor!" Jeremy said, slipping an arm around her. His fingers threaded tightly into her hair. He smiled icily while turning her beautiful face toward his. "Beat you, eh?" he whispered softly. "I'm going to tan you to within an inch of your life!" he promised.

She smiled, gritting her teeth against the pain of his hold.

"Of course, it's true," she told Sherman sweetly. "We did survive much better in my part of Virginia than did those who lived off the land farther south. All of that deprivation, in comparison, makes the trail much, much easier to endure!"

Jeremy started to step into the breach, but inadvertently Clara Jennings did so.

"Well, I don't think that I shall ever be happy on the trail. The bugs! The rain. The terror of the Indians!"

"All trials the good Lord sends for us to endure, so that we see to the error of our ways!" Mrs. Brooks advised.

"Ah, well. The good Lord seemed fond of sending us southerners many trials!" Christa murmured, with a smile that seemed to make light of her comment. "We were ever afraid of Yankees invading, especially after having heard that our good General Sherman was on the march. Having lived with that fear so very long, I cannot worry too much about simple heathens like Comanche!"

"But as you said, you are a Virginian, Mrs. McCauley. I cut my path through Georgia and Carolina."

"We were ever in sympathy with our more southernly sisters!"

Her eyes were wide. Her tone was innocent. Christa knew how to cut to the bone. Sherman might long to strike her, Jeremy thought.

But apparently, the general had taken her on as a challenge. He leaned closer to her, speaking softly. "I swear to you, Mrs. McCauley, I fought a war the best, and oddly, the most merciful way I knew how. I offered generous terms of surrender. So generous that Secretary of War Stanton slandered me, calling me a traitor in numerous publications. I renegotiated with Joe Johnston as I was ordered, ma'am, but I was ever sorry that my original terms did not stand, for they were right, honest, and good."

Christa appeared just a little bit pale. Maybe Sherman had managed to touch something inside her.

"I'm a soldier, Mrs. McCauley, not a politician. It's up to the politicians now to reconstruct state governments. It is to the sorrow of all good men when those chosen for such tasks do not prove themselves equal to them."

"Reconstruction is a bitter thing!" she said.

Jeremy stood, thinking that this company would be fool enough to stop him if he did set his fingers around her throat. He dragged her to her feet nevertheless.

"We've music. Shall we dance while the plates are cleared and dessert is served?"

The suggestion was well met. He pulled Christa along with him over to

Nathaniel. "Nat, how about a jig on that fiddle for me, please. A lively dance tune."

Nathaniel nodded. A private who had been standing in the shadows behind the spinet piano stepped forward and took a seat.

The music was coming a little early. It didn't matter. Nat and the private broke into a lively rendition of "Turkey in the Straw."

Jeremy held Christa in his arms, whirling her through the song. Beneath the cover of the music, he gave her fair warning once again.

"One more thing, Christa. Just one."

Her eyes were blazing. The wine was giving her courage. She tossed her hair back. "And what?" she challenged. She didn't let him answer but rushed on. "You had no right to do this! No right at all to expect me to meet that man—"

"He's been exceedingly gracious. He's made every attempt to be pleasant—"

"And that atones for what he did to my people?" she said incredulously.

"Christa, the war is over!"

He felt a tap on his shoulder.

Sherman.

There was nothing to do but relinquish his wife to the general.

He did so, then stepped back, watching the pair. They talked animatedly throughout the dance. What was being said?

The music ended. Sherman led Christa back to him. Just as she reached him, her back went very stiff.

The men were playing a new tune in honor of their guest.

It was called "Marching Through Georgia."

The company began to sit. Christa's eyes were on his. He led her back to her chair, but she didn't sit.

"I think that I shall help with the entertainment," she murmured, pulling away.

He watched her walk to the spinet and speak with the private. He rose, and she sat.

She started off gently. As strawberries and cream were served, Christa played and sang.

She sang "When This Cruel War Is Over," a song so heart-wrenching that many commanders had ordered that it not be played in camps, for desertions often followed its playing.

It went well enough. Both troops embraced the song. She went on to "Amazing Grace." She had a beautiful voice, crystal clear, sweet, and pure, and she played just as beautifully.

Of course she played beautifully. She'd been bred and trained to play beautifully, to sing like a lark, to flutter her eyelashes, to rule like a queen. She'd spent years learning all the subtle arts so as to marry a man like Liam McCloskey, to supervise his household, to entrance his guests.

Perhaps she had prepared more for a military life than she had ever intended. The whole tent seemed enraptured. They were seldom treated to such a lovely display in the wild. She was doing it all on purpose, he knew.

She had them all!

She slipped into a song called "Southern Girl," a song in defiance of the Union, and went on to "I'm a Good Old Rebel," a song for those Rebels determined to die in rebellion. To make absolutely sure that no one could miss just where her loyalties lay, she broke into a soft, heartrending edition of "Dixie."

A wondrous finale. He couldn't say a word about it. Lincoln had ordered it played in honor of the South before that fateful night at Ford's Theater. Jeremy's own troops had played it before they left Richmond.

While the last echoes of the music remained on the air, Christa rose from the spinet.

Celia Preston began the applause.

General Sherman seconded it mightily.

Christa bowed low in a mocking curtsy. She rose and her eyes met Jeremy's. He could have sworn that for a moment she was very still, and that a slight tremor swept through her.

"Gentlemen, ladies, you will excuse me?" she pleaded politely, offering one of her beautiful smiles to the whole group. "I tire so easily!"

They all tripped over themselves to excuse her!

Jeremy awaited her at the exit from the tent, arms crossed over his shoulders. A flush suffused her cheeks as she looked up at him. Her lashes quickly lowered. "Excuse me."

He caught hold of her arm. To anyone viewing them, he might have been whispering the sweetest endearments.

"They might have excused you, my love. But be forewarned. I most certainly do not! When I get my hands on you, Christa . . ."

He let the warning trail away. She pulled away from him, her eyes blazing. She was flushed. Was it the wine, was it her temper, or the heat?

"Good night, Colonel." Her words were definite. Mistress of Cameron Hall definite.

He smiled, his fingers itching to touch her. If she had been determined to single-handedly destroy his career, she was well on her way tonight. It was good that Sherman, remarkably, had a sense of humor.

He still blocked Christa.

"I said, good night, Colonel," she enunciated carefully. "The night is over!"

His smile deepened. "Oh no, Christa," he assured her. "The night has just begun for you."

She pulled away from him and exited the tent. He let her go.

He would find her in time.

She had nowhere to go.

Fourteen

Christa did find somewhere to go.

Jeremy remained with the company of officers and their wives while Nathaniel began the strains of "Beautiful Dreamer." A number of the ladies patted their fans and assured him that they understood Christa's exhaustion.

He refrained from telling them that Christa had spent perhaps three weeks with some discomfort, but since then had seemed to feel more healthy than most of his men. He listened gravely to Sherman's warnings about the Indians, and he danced with a number of the women including Clara Jennings, a feat that did not in the least ease his temper.

By the time he left, he'd heard half the company cluck over what a beautiful and brave figure his wife was, poor child, always doing her best to make do.

That didn't improve his temper much either.

He was not far from his own tent. When he had said good night to the last of the guests, he strode the few feet to it, angrily jerking open the flap.

She wasn't there.

Fear drove into his heart, and while it did so he tried to assure himself that nothing could have happened to her. They were too large a camp, too well armed for the Comanche to attack.

He spun around, nearly crashing into Robert Black Paw. "She is by the river, some distance from the tents. I left Private O'Malley to guard her. I didn't know whether to bring her back or not. She is beyond the circle of our night guard. I'm afraid she strays too far."

"I'll bring her back myself, Robert. Thank you."

The scout nodded and disappeared into the blackness of the night. Jeremy started the long walk down to the river. Near its edge, he found Private O'Malley and sent the young man back to camp. He walked through the trees himself, amazed that Christa would have come here, so far from the camp. He saw her, standing with one foot upon a log, staring into the cold black water. The folds of her skirt fell elegantly about her, her hair cascaded down her back like a wing of the night. If any young Comanche brave had come upon her so, he would have thanked the gods for his incredible good fortune.

The thought spurred his anger, and he thrashed on through the trees, his eyes narrowed on her. She heard him coming and spun around, her eyes wide. The look on his face must have been as savage as his temper because she turned to run, when there was nowhere to run. She had barely taken a step before he was upon her, swinging her around and against a tree trunk.

"Get your hands off me!" she commanded him quickly.

"What the hell do you think you're doing?"

She interrupted instantly. "Jeremy, your swearing is excessive—"

"And you can swear with more ferocity than any mule driver I know. I repeat, what the hell are you doing?"

"Looking at the river. I needed some fresh air."

"So you just walked away from the camp?"

"All right, I needed to be away from you. And your Yankee company!"

"And you didn't give a damn that I'd come back, worried sick, wondering if the Comanche hadn't walked off with you?"

"I—" She faltered for just a second, then lifted her chin. "I thought that you'd be occupied, impressing the great general! The man who won a war by starving innocent women and children."

"He's not a monster, Christa! Jesu, madam, he did his best! Stanton tried to have him barred from riding at the head of his army when it passed the review stands in Washington because of his efforts! He risked his own career, and was as angry, I've heard, as a caged lion when Washington forced him to renegotiate his peace with Joe Johnston. Hell, Christa, if you want to crucify someone, let me try to get Phil Sheridan out here! He's a firm believer in a 'scorched earth' policy!"

"What difference does it make who you get out here?" she hissed. "We'll never agree. I just decided that I needed to take a walk."

"A walk! In the dead of night? In Indian territory?"

"I needed to be alone—"

"Like hell. You were hoping that I wouldn't find you. That I'd give up and go to sleep before you came tiptoeing back. That I wouldn't strangle you over what you did."

"I will never be afraid of you!" Her chin was high, her words scornful. Maybe the wine she had drunk was giving her an added boost of bravado. She still seemed flushed. "Never!" she repeated.

His eyes narrowed on her. "You'd best be—tonight."

She was breathing hard, both defiant and uneasy. He wished that wanting her, aching for her, desiring her so desperately would not plague him so when he longed to shake her. He couldn't keep his hands off her, despite his most stalwart efforts. He shot out, gripping her wrists, wrenching her toward him. It might have been a mistake. He could feel the trembling in her now. Her eyes were luminous with her fury. Her hair tumbled about her shoulders and fell down her back in a wild disarray. Her scent was sweet against the rich, earthy smell of the river and the breeze and the embankment.

"You let go of me, Jeremy!" She jerked free from him and started to walk away. She stumbled and caught her balance. Was it a root in her path, or a reminder of the wine she had drunk.

"Get back here!" He jerked her back into his arms. Her eyes went wide. Maybe she wasn't frightened.

"Let go of me!" she insisted.

He smiled crookedly. Let her go? Never, not tonight. He wasn't quite sure what seized hold of him, but he knew he would never let her go. Not tonight. Maybe it was her defiance, her passion, maybe it was even the depths of the hatred she seemed to bear him. But it felt as if an inferno had suddenly found roots within him, streaks of the blaze tearing throughout his body. Tonight? He wouldn't let her out of his sight again.

"You're not afraid of me, remember?"

"Jeremy—"

He lifted her up, flinging her over his shoulder despite her outraged shriek of protest. He instantly started his way back to camp.

She pounded fiercely against his back. "Put me down! Your friends might still be awake. What would they say, what would they think?"

"One, I don't give a damn. Two, any friends of mine would probably want to thrash you as well after that marvelously stirring rendition of 'Dixie.' "

She thudded his back again. She started to bite his shoulder and he gave her a sound whack on the buttocks, certain that he hurt the bustle—and her pride— far more than he hurt her. They had reached the outer rim of the tents.

"Damn you! Put me down!" she whispered fiercely.

"Soon enough, my love."

She fell silent, braced against him as he strode his way to their tent. In seconds he had set her down hard on the bed. He tried to walk away from her. He spun around. She lay there in the blue gown, her face flushed, her eyes flashing, her hair a magnificent spill around her, her breasts heaving over the velvet bodice of the gown. She sat up, then stood quickly, her hands clenched into fists at her sides. "I won't stay here, Jeremy. I can't. I told you that I couldn't be expected to entertain Sherman—"

"You did nothing, in fact. I took no chances on your cooking for him, lady. He might well have left here poisoned. And I never asked you to entertain the man. You took that on all on your own!" He stripped off his dress military frock coat, then removed his cuff links. " 'I'm a Good Old Rebel'! My God, you do have bravado, ma'am, I'll grant you that!"

She started to walk past him. "I have really tried to be an excellent wife—"

He interrupted her with a loud snort.

She stood still, stiffening. Her eyes were blue fire. "Since it appears you are determined to sleep here tonight, I shall find other accommodations."

"Oh? And where will you go?"

"Elsewhere!"

"I see. Perhaps that dear charming Captain Clark—who reminds you so much of your poor deceased Liam—will be willing to take you in."

"Perhaps I'd even prefer the Comanche tonight!" she hissed back furiously.

He caught hold of her wrist, throwing her back toward the bed. "Sit down. You sure as hell aren't going anywhere tonight."

She lay flung atop the bed, watching him, catching her breath. She wasn't about to stay down. Not yet.

She sprang up easily again, determined on walking out of the tent. She was no fool. He could see her weighing her options. Since the opportunity to best him was probably not going to come her way, she was seeking her ever majestic lady-of-manor dignity to use against him. She inhaled, as if with a great deal of patience. "I will not stay here and listen—"

"Sit down," he repeated, stripping his shirt over his head.

She swallowed hard, gritting her teeth. He knew she was fighting to think of some way around him. He was far stronger.

She tossed back her hair, smoothing it down. Her words were polite enough, but he heard the grate of her teeth that preceded them. "Perhaps this thing can be discussed at some later date. If—"

"It will be discussed right now. I warned you to be courteous, Christa. I warned you."

She stood once again, her chin up, her hands folded before her. He hated the stance. It was her lady-of-Cameron-Hall stance, and it was so damned superior. "You've had a fair amount of whiskey with your Yank cronies—"

"Oh, that's rich!" he exclaimed. "From the delicate belle who was downing wine like water? No, Christa. That won't work. I've had some whiskey, but I'd need a hell of a lot more to forget your performance this evening!" He kicked off his boots and pulled off his cavalry pants.

She seemed to pale somewhat. She was accustomed to the sight of him naked. Tonight it seemed to disturb her.

She pressed a hand dramatically against her temples. "I have a tremendous headache and you're making it far worse. I'm leaving!" she said flatly. "You'll just have to pretend you're capable of being a gentleman for once. I mean it, Jeremy. It was a wretched night!"

"Christa! The war is over!" he growled. "You're married to a cavalryman, and my future is at stake here. Did you ever think about that?"

Maybe she hadn't. For a second, she was silent. "I'm not terribly worried about your future, Jeremy. From what I understand, you're an excellent swordsman, you know the Indians better than their own mothers do, and you're even a friend to the buffalo! You'll rise high—with or without me being decent to Sherman."

"How amazing! I never knew I had such a vote of confidence from you. Especially after following in the wake of such men as your sainted brothers!"

"Don't you dare speak about—"

"Madam, leave it be!"

"Yes, leave it be!" she whispered. "Let the great Indian hunter have the last word! And the war is over, is it? Daniel still hasn't received a pardon, carpetbaggers are passing themselves off as politicians in Richmond, and the entire South is being run by Yankee riffraff opportunists! Don't tell me the war is over!"

"Christa—"

He moved toward her, at that moment wanting to comfort her, no matter how angry he was himself about the evening. But she backed away quickly. She was still too upset to accept anything from him. She jerked back. "Touch me and I'll scream. I'll scream and scream—"

He reached out with such a vengeance that his hold upon her sleeve tore the gown. She glanced down where the sleeve and bodice gaped from her body. "How dare you . . ."

He'd never meant to hurt her, or to rip her gown. The damage was done.

She wasn't going anywhere, and she wasn't going to threaten him with screaming ever again, he determined fiercely. Eyes on hers, he caught the fabric once again and ripped harder. She gasped as the whole of the garment began to fall from her, exposing her corset and petticoats. She tried to slap him and he caught her wrist. "I gave you fair warning, Jeremy, I'll scream—"

"Then start screaming!" he advised. She gasped out instead, her fists slamming against his chest as he plucked her up and threw her down on the bed, straddling over her. "Despicable Yank!" she hissed. "You'd rape me—"

"Not on your life, lady."

"Then—"

"Buck naked, darling, you might decide to stay in the tent!"

He flung her over on her stomach, trying to loosen her corset ties. The petticoat resisted him and he ripped it impatiently, only to be greeted with another flurry of her venom. "You're wrecking my things! You're—"

"Christa, for a poor vanquished Reb, you've still got more clothing than most birds have feathers! And you're damned lucky I'm ripping fabric, and not your irresistible, delicate, wonderful southern flesh!"

She stiffened, going dead still for a second. He used the opportunity to untie her pantalets. When she choked and began swearing again, fighting to unseat him from his perch atop her, she afforded him the chance to strip off the last of her garments. She lay facedown and bare, still fighting. Her back was sleek, her hips and rump rose smooth and delectable—and tempting.

"Despicable Yankee bas—" she began.

"One more word, my love, and—"

"And!" she cried in desperate challenge.

He tensed, swallowing hard. He didn't want the battles. What could he do when it seemed that something from the past always arose to come between them? Tonight, it was Sherman.

Damn Sherman. Couldn't he have traveled to some more northern Indian district this year?

Christa was shaking. Never, ever ready to surrender, never ready to call a truce. He bit into his lower lip and pressed a gentle kiss against the small of her back.

He might just as well have burned her with a branding iron. She shrieked out with rage, bucking against him and turning beneath him. Tears of fury stung her eyes. Her fists landed against his chest. Very suddenly, she went still. He became aware that he was straddled over her now with his sex laid low against her stomach and it was aroused and hard against her softness.

Her eyes narrowed on his. She moistened suddenly dry lips. "I hate you, Jeremy. I hate you for Sherman, and I hate you for the war. I—"

"Listen to yourself, Christa! You *hate me* for *Sherman*!"

Tears stung her eyes. "Can't you understand?"

"I can't change the past. And I'm not sorry that the North won, that slavery is dead and the Union preserved!"

"Get—"

"Christa! You don't hate me—"

"Trust me, I do!"

He shook his head again vehemently, his eyes dark and intense. "I don't really believe that. And I want you, Christa. I want to touch the spark of magic that is always there, just below the surface. So let's pretend that you don't hate me tonight. Lie still beside me. You claim that you are such an excellent wife. Be one for me."

"Jesu!" she rallied. "I ride the trail, I sleep in a tent. I have encountered tarantulas and buffalo. I lie with you night after night—"

"You are here, yes!" he continued for her. "And you refrain from protesting when I exercise my matrimonial rights. Dammit, Christa! The fire is there, I can feel it! I can nearly touch it. But you deny me and yourself, again and again!"

"I don't know what you're talking about!" she cried.

He pulled her up by the shoulders, searching out her eyes. "But you do, Christa, you do! You fight me, you fight yourself. You could taste the sweetness of fulfillment, but you deny yourself the chance. It's there within you, I know it. You possess a rare passion. Why fight me so?"

Her eyes were liquid. With emotion, with anger? "Perhaps I do not fight you!" she whispered vehemently.

"I know that something rich lies locked within you!"

"Perhaps, Yank, you haven't the key to unlock it!"

He eased his weight back, holding her still, shaking his head slowly. "No, Christa, it's not me. Maybe I'm not your Rebel lover. Maybe I am your Yankee husband. But in every way, I swear to you, I've sought to give what I would take. And I know that I've touched your senses. You hold back because you would continue to wage war in our bed. But I tell you, my love, no more. No more, after this night!"

"Don't—" she began.

"Jesu, Christa! Give me a chance, give us both a chance!"

"Jeremy—" she began anew. But he was done arguing.

His lips touched hers. For a moment, he felt her resistance, tasted the salt of her tears. Her fists banged against his shoulders and she tried to writhe out of his hold. No! He could not let her go!

"A chance, Christa!" he whispered, lifting his lips just a breath from hers. His voice was low, rich, deep. Demanding, pleading.

She inhaled on a ragged little sound.

He touched her lips once again. Tasted them, pressed past them, felt the desire in him flame wildly as he took in the sweetness and warmth of her. He wanted her so badly. She was in his arms, and he could have her. They'd waged this battle before. All he need do was take her. Ease the hunger.

He lifted his lips from hers. Thought himself insane. Her sky-blue Cameron eyes were on him, her lips were damp from his touch, still so tempting.

He smiled ruefully. "Your choice, Christa."

"What?" she whispered, amazed.

"I will not force the issue."

He rolled beside her. She quickly turned her back on him. He ran a finger seductively down the length of her back. Up again, down again. What was the matter with him? What if this didn't work?

It had to work!

The most seductive touch he could manage, down the bareness of her back, caressing the very base of her spine. Softly, gently, over the rise of her hip. The fullness of her buttocks. He drew circles with his fingertips.

Pressed his lips to her back. Followed the touch of his fingertip down her spine. Up again.

Jesu . . .

Please, God . . .

She swung back around on him.

"You said—" she began to accuse him, her eyes wild.

"I said your choice!"

"It's not my choice when Sherman—"

"Jesu! Christa! Could we please get Sherman out of this tent tonight!"

"Let's get him out of the camp!" she challenged.

"We'll start with getting him out of our bed!"

"But—"

His fingers threaded into her hair. His lips silenced her protest.

She still tried to keep up the fight, shaking her head slightly when his mouth rose above hers. "Christa, do you know what you're doing to me?" he groaned softly. "If the war were still on, I think I'd be willing to change sides at this point!"

Despite herself, she smiled. But she was ever determined. "You said—" she began again stubbornly.

"Your choice," he finished on a breath.

But he couldn't really leave it that way. Not as things stood. She still needed some persuasion.

He swept an arm around her, bringing her fully against him. The length of his body shuddered. He found her lips. Caught them, held them. Stroked the rim of them with his tongue, parried between them. She would fight him now.

To his astonishment, he heard a soft moan rumbling in her throat. Her hands pressed upon his shoulders, then went still. Her fingertips dug slightly into his flesh.

Holding him. Not pressing him away.

He took her tightly into his arms, afraid to let her go. He kissed her lips, stroking her back softly, feeling the sensual curves and planes. He broke from her lips to touch them again, his tongue tracing the shape of them before slipping deeply into her mouth again. He caressed the silky skin of her back, sweeping the length of it, creating sensual swirls once more at the base of her spine with his fingertips, stroking the curve of her hip, the rise of her buttocks.

There was a difference tonight. She hadn't returned his hunger as yet, but the pulse was there, as was the heat. The promise was in his arms.

Determined to discover it, he trailed his kiss to her earlobe, along her throat. He lifted the mass of her hair and kissed the nape of her neck, then shuddered, sighing deeply, burying his face within the ebony cloud of her, enjoying the scent and silken feel of it. He moved her about, shifting the fall of her hair once again and pressing a kiss against her upper spine. He bathed her shoulders with his caress, then moved lower against her spine, his fingers stroking fire while his lips delivered their liquid heat, down to the very small of her back, over the rise of her hip. He paused, sensations sweeping through him in a staggering manner from the taste and feel of her, as she suddenly sighed and shuddered.

He held her in his arms once again. Her eyes met his, very wide, soft, dazed.

Perhaps she hadn't really expected this. To feel the burning inside, the need like raw hunger. She shook her head wildly again. "No!" she mouthed.

"Yes," he insisted, both tender and determined. "Tonight, my love, we have twisted the key already."

"It's the wine!" she whispered. "You're taking advantage of my confusion."

"Damn right!" He laughed huskily. "I take every advantage that I can get. And it isn't the wine so much, because I've noted that you barely touch the stuff since you've been carrying our child."

"I tell you—"

He pressed his case, capturing her mouth, and feeling at long last the duel of her tongue with his own. Hunger seared through him. His hand moved fervently over her breast, discovering the peak pebble hard. He delivered his kiss there, teasing the peak, savoring the sweetness of it, suckling upon the fullness of it. She shifted beneath him gloriously. Even as she did so longing gripped his loins tightly, a savage heat swept through him and he moved against her, his hands never still. There was a greater demand to his touch now, an urgency that filled his body.

She could always arouse his desire. But tonight, she was a breath of magic. Perhaps hatred was close to love, perhaps the passion of anger danced narrowly close to that of desire. Maybe they had just been building to this.

But she was moving too. She was liquid and supple in his arms. He stroked her breast, and she rose against him, and he whispered soft words to her. "Feel the touch, my love. Here, and here . . . feel it become a heat that begins a swirl inside of you, deeper and deeper, here." He stroked her upper thigh, set his palm over the rise of her ebony triangle. "Here," he whispered, then slipped a finger deep and hard inside of her. "And here . . ."

She gasped and trembled massively against his touch, and shifted as if she would deny it. If the fires were not sizzling through her then, they were running rampant within his own body. Still, he took his time. She was stretched out on her back. Her flesh was damp with an exotic sheen, touched by the gold lamplight. Her hair was a tangle. Her limbs were long and beautiful and her breasts were rising and falling in a rush. Her eyes were soft glazed as if he had taken her quite by surprise. Perhaps he had. And perhaps it had been building as he had said, and tonight he had finally bridged the last of the walls of her defenses.

An anguish tore through him. He wanted her, then and there. But he wanted more tonight, too, than he had ever wanted before. He wanted those blue eyes to fill with the passion he knew lurked behind the midnight shadow of her lashes. He wanted to feel the bowstring quivering of her slender form, the ardent rhythm of her hips. It wasn't time to seize hold of her, not yet.

He rose above her and gently touched her lips with just the breath of his own. He drew a pattern between the valley of her breasts with his finger. He followed it with his tongue. He lowered himself slowly against her. Wherever he caressed her, he kissed her. Lower and lower until he lay between her legs. Touching her, parting her, caressing her, kissing her.

A soft, fervent cry escaped from her. Her fingers tugged upon his hair. He caught her hands and held them firmly within his own. She moaned softly. Her head began to toss, her body to writhe.

If it was the wine, then bless that wondrous fruit of the vine! Perhaps they lay in the wilderness, but magic surrounded them. Beyond the canvas of their tent, the night breeze stirred, making their flesh seem all the more searing. In the endless sky the stars rode the heavens. They seemed to also dance within the tent. They rained down upon him in bursts of radiant light. Jesu, she was beautiful, alive with her passion.

He smiled wickedly. All the torments of hell could take hold of him now and he would endure them gladly. He found the tiny bud of her greatest sensuality and played mercilessly upon it, laving, teasing, demanding with the caress of his lips and tongue. She began to shudder, and the golden gleam of light upon her began to shimmer with the growing undulation of her hips. "Please!" she whispered suddenly. "I can take no more!"

And she could not! What had happened tonight, she wondered. Why couldn't she fight this fire?

It mattered not, she could not, and that was simply that. She couldn't think, the sensations were so strong.

And it was wonderful, erotic, and sending her into such a sweet spiral of sensation that she couldn't fight. He was whispering things to her and in her mind's eye she was seeing things of startling beauty. A rosebud, so dark and rich a pink, flowering beneath a radiant heat, stretching, growing, parting to burst into an open beauty. Even as she saw the image of the rose she was aware of the very graphic reality around her, the camp bed, herself, the glow of light that touched them, the bed beneath them. Jeremy. The power of his hands, his fingers locked around hers. The taut muscled feel of his body. The weight of him between her legs. The way that he touched her. The things that he did. The tension grew inside of her, hot, warm, wonderful, painful, and sweet. It grew until it was anguish, until she was arching wildly against him. Until sounds filled the night, soft, desperate, breathless. Sounds that she was making herself.

Then something seemed to explode. Sweet, so achingly sweet! It burst with wonder over her, with light, and then with dark. With stars across a velvet sky.

Like a million shots firing into the night. It was the sweetest thing she had ever imagined, like a taste of honey burning throughout her system. It was so, so good. She floated with it. Saw the light, saw the darkness.

Then he was atop her. His eyes silver and wicked in the gleam of light, his naked body slick and hard and muscled and fascinating still. She cried out softly, closing her eyes, trying to turn away from him. He wouldn't have it. His body slid into hers hard. "Oh, no," she whispered.

"Oh, yes," he corrected.

Her fingers fell upon his shoulders. She shifted, amazed that he could feel so wonderful within her so swiftly. Even denying it, she had liked the feel before.

Tonight, the spiral began again. The heat deep inside of her. Curling, deepening. It couldn't come again. The velvet black, the bursting of light, the liquid stars bursting warmly throughout her body, so sweet, so delicious, so wonderful. It couldn't come again.

But the spiraling, the hunger, that led to it were so easily coming alive again. She was achingly aware of him, as if all sensation of her flesh had become heightened. She felt his hair-roughened legs and chest, the hardness of his arm muscles, the rock of his hips, and him, inside of her. The fullness of the movement, the thrust . . .

She gasped. The spiraling was rising again. She arched to meet him. She dared open her eyes. His blazed into hers, and she bit her lip, her lashes falling. His face remained so taut, his length so vital yet rigidly hard. He moved, demandingly. His arms held his body above hers. He thrust into her. And into her again, his eyes locked with hers. He moved faster and faster, his face fraught with tension. She cried out, unable to deny the quickening within her. Her hands fell upon his shoulders. Her fingers raked across them. She was pulling up to him, meeting his thrust with a rhythmic arch of her own. Her lips fell upon his shoulders. She covered them with ardent kisses. Her fingers played upon his back, massaging, digging, clinging. She felt him thrust incredibly hard against her just as the sensations seemed to split and explode within her in a wild frenzy of fire and hunger. She gasped, clinging to him, as she felt the force of the climax that seized her. Darkness fell. Light burst. The liquid stars seemed to rain down upon her once again. For a moment she was so absorbed with the shimmering feel of ecstasy that she did not realize that he remained above her, that the heat spilling from his body was just filling her own.

He fell to her side, slick with sweat, breathing hard.

She shuddered, turning to her side as sudden tears warmed her eyes. Dear God, she'd never imagined such a piece of heaven.

But yes, she had. She had known that Jeremy could bring her to it, and she had been fighting it fiercely. Why? Because it was wrong that it should be Jeremy when she had once loved so innocently and so sweetly? When Liam lay cold and buried. When all her world lay in ashes.

She had married Jeremy.

She could say what she wanted, to him, to herself. He was not so detestable. He had seized hold of her life. He had shaken her in the midst of defeat.

He had given her something more.

She bit her lip.

She cared for him. Cared far more than she wanted to know. They were enemies who had clashed head-on, but they were enemies, too, because they were both strong, determined, willful.

And he was honorable. She had demanded that he marry her, and he had done so. He had read her heart and eased the way with her and her brothers. He had brought her with him, and he had forced her to live.

He was beautiful, whipcord strong and lean in his physique, rugged and handsome in his face. Indeed, he held the key. He had touched her and found all that he had demanded of her.

He stroked her shoulder gently. "Madam, I take it back!" he murmured. "You are an excellent wife."

Was he gloating? She had certainly given him all that he wanted, whether willingly or not. Every word that he had spoken had been true. She had teetered on that precipice night after night, tasting the wonder, refusing to let it come to her.

Yet tonight it had been undeniable. It had taken her in a flood.

"Excellent . . ."

He was gloating. Yankees. Once they won, they just didn't let up. That's why it seemed tragic to surrender.

"It was the wine!" she whispered.

"Was it?" he murmured.

She started to stiffen, not sure if he mocked her or not. But then something miraculous happened. She felt something. Not wild and magical and excit-ing . . .

Different. She inhaled sharply.

The baby. Deep, deep inside of her the baby was moving. It was just a flutter. So curious. So light. Then it came again.

She gasped.

"What is it?" He was over her instantly.

She shook her head. "The baby."

"My God!" His voice was harsh, rasping. "Is it all right? Did—"

"No, no! It's fine. He's moving! I can feel the baby. It's so strange!"

His palm moved over her abdomen. "I can't feel it!" he said.

She shook her head again. The darkness cast shadows over them both. "No, you can't feel him, not yet. It's just inside. I think it takes time to feel the movement from the outside. But—oh, there again! He's alive, he's moving, he's kicking, he's . . ."

"He's what?" Jeremy said. His palm still lay gently against her flesh.

"He's real!" she breathed. "He's real, he's going to be born, he's going to live."

His hand went rigid. He pulled her back against him. "Go to sleep. Tomor-row is going to be a long day."

His body enwrapped hers. The comfort was there.

But she wondered if he thought of another unborn child. And of that child's mother.

Fifteen

"Christa. Christa. You have to wake up. Now."

She came awake from a deep unconsciousness. There had been a strange cocoon of comfort in her sleep. Last night, she had given in to him. She had given in to far more than duty. She had felt so very weary, and even in her surrender she had discovered a certain peace.

But now, awaking, she felt a tinge of fear encroaching upon her comfort. She had given too much. Surrendered too much.

She had tried to tell him that it had been the wine. Now all that she wanted to do was crawl beneath the covers and not have to face him until she was ready. Until it was dark again. Until forever. She didn't know which.

She shook her head, trying to pull the sheets tightly around her. "Leave me be!" she pleaded.

"Christa!" His voice had been fairly gentle. Now that old snap of command was back in it. If that weren't irritating enough, she felt the palm of his hand fall sharply upon her derriere.

Indignantly, she opened her eyes, staring at him with all the evil reproach she could muster. She turned her back on him again, murmuring. "Please, just—"

"Up!" he repeated, catching her shoulder and rolling her over to face him. He had apparently risen some time ago. He was fully clad in his dress uniform. She heartily resented the fact that he could appear so striking in the cavalry dark blue, and that most women would find him a handsome figure indeed.

Yes, he was a striking figure. Yes, he had done things to her that she had never imagined. Yes, now when he touched her, she remembered and grew warm.

She hugged the sheets tightly, determined to stare him down—even after last night. "Jeremy—"

"You have to get up."

"You did tell me a wife belonged in bed!" she snapped.

A smile curved his lip and he leaned against her. "I do like you there, Christa. Very much so. And I would dearly love to join you again. Especially after last night. You were wonderful. Extraordinary." He started to stroke her cheek.

A flood of color rushed to her cheeks. "It was the wine!" she whispered.

"The wine! And I thought it was my devastating charm! Ah, Christa, are you sure that it wasn't? Perhaps I should cast duty to the winds and crawl back in to discover the truth!"

"Trust me!" she murmured, inching herself against the rear of the bed. "It was the wine—"

She didn't want to remember how completely she had surrendered, how desperately she had wanted him.

And there was still the Sherman matter between them!

"If you'd please just leave me be—" she began.

But she broke off. She swallowed hard, shrinking back as he suddenly pinned his arms on either side of her, bracing himself as he studied her eyes. "Christa, I won't go back," he said softly. "Everything I longed to find was there within you. I won't let you deny it again. I never meant to press my point with as much anger as I did last night, but hell, who knows? Maybe the only way to ever get anything from you, Christa, is to take it by force."

She felt a trembling deep within her. She didn't want to have the surge of emotion that flowed through her. She didn't mean to be so hostile to him. There were times now when it seemed that he was trying to find peace, break down the wall between them.

This morning, she needed the wall. She was suddenly very afraid. Afraid for her own heart.

"Don't talk to me like that!" she said heatedly, and she saw the silver in his eyes glitter and harden but she couldn't seem to stop. "I'm not one of your privates to be ordered about. And don't think yourself such a great commander! You're only a colonel because the Rebs managed to kill so damned many Yankee officers that they had to scrape the bottom of the barrel to fill their ranks!"

His brow arched. His lip curled. She wondered fleetingly whether he was amused or furious. She hadn't meant to say the words. She was sorry that hundreds of thousands of Yanks were dead as well as Rebs. She was sorry for the whole damned war.

And she was heartily sorry that she kept finding herself fighting it again and again when it should have truly been over.

"I'm a colonel because too many Yanks are dead," he said softly. "And you're my wife because too many Rebels fell. And it's all a travesty, but it's the way that it is, my love, and you had best get used to it. I found there does exist a match to strike the fire within you. By God, Christa, I swear I'll not let that flame go out."

"I told you, it was the wine—"

"Then perhaps we shall have to douse you in the stuff nightly."

A sense of panic was rising within her. He could hurt her all too easily. It seemed best to strike out first.

"Have it your way, then! Dead Yanks, dead Rebs. But a few too many glasses of wine and you're no longer a Yank. You're a Reb officer, a ghost come back to life—"

She broke off with a little cry of protest as his fingers wound around her upper arms, lifting her from the bed and hard against him. "We'll have to see to it that next time, Mrs. McCauley, you are well aware that you're not sleeping with a corpse!"

The tension within him was suddenly frightening her. She wanted to cry. Last night had begun with anger, yes. But they had come so close to something being right between them.

Daylight always seemed to bring back the war.

"Let me go!" she cried. "If you even think about touching me tonight—"

"I'll think and do whatever I please, Christa. But cheer up—perhaps you're not so all damned alluring as you seem to believe. Maybe I'm weary of sleeping with someone who seems to be one of the walking dead herself at times. For now, just get up. Or stay there. My staff sergeant is due here any minute. Maybe you'll give him the entertainment of his life, lying there naked. The picnic for the officers and their wives is at eleven. You'll be there and you'll behave politely. And you won't sing a single note under any circumstances!"

He was balanced upon their bed on one knee, his fingers tightly vised around her arms. She should just give in, she thought.

But she wouldn't lie and promise that she'd behave any differently if General Sherman made an appearance.

She narrowed her eyes at Jeremy. "Will he be there?"

She almost cried out. It seemed impossible, but his hold upon her tightened. "What difference does it make?"

"All the difference in the world."

He released her so suddenly that she fell back, unprepared. Her hair spilled over her shoulders and breasts, and the covers fell away from her. He stepped back, his hands clenching into fists at his sides, then unclenching again. "The war *is* over!" he exclaimed. He stared at her and she was startled by the depths of the passion in his eyes. She wondered if the burning emotions within him then were hatred or desire, or perhaps a combination of the two. Despite his anger, despite his harshness, she wanted to cry out, to reach out to him. To tell him that she wanted it to be over! I just don't want to have dinner with George Tecumseh Sherman!

But she didn't cry out. He had turned and was walking away from her, ready to leave their tent. Before lifting up the flap he paused. His back to her, he spoke again. "Sherman will not be there. He is reviewing troops farther along the trail." He turned back to her. "I'm not asking you to like Sherman or anyone else. I'm not asking you to forgive the war. All I want is for you to extend whatever courtesy you can manage to our guests in this godforsaken land. Will you be so kind?"

She tried once again to assemble some dignity about herself, flipping back her wayward hair, tugging at the sheets once again to cover her breasts. "I tried to be courteous last—"

"Try harder. I'm warning you."

"Oh? And if I don't?"

He smiled, and doffed his hat politely. "My love, you will *please* try harder!"

When he turned to leave this time, he did so without another word. Christa threw herself back on the bed, fighting a new rise of tears behind her lids. He didn't understand. She didn't hate the cavalry wives. She felt sorry for so many of them! She, at least, had been forced to raise her own food. She'd smoked meat and made soap and baked bread. She might have been raised a lady, but life had already taught her hard lessons.

Little Celia Preston had been practically raised in a nunnery. From her home in Maine, she'd scarcely known that a war was on! An Irish maid had doted on her all her years, and she had come here totally unprepared for the hardships that faced them.

It was just Sherman.

How could any Reb be expected to tolerate the man?

She rolled over with a groan, her face against the sheets. As she lay there she became aware that there was a faint smell of her husband about the bedding. It was rich, pleasant, masculine. It reminded her of the night that had passed between them. She'd never imagined such a night. Not even when she'd been young and in love with Liam. Maybe a few previous occasions had hinted at such glory, but she'd been too naive to imagine what incredible physical sensations could be reached. Jeremy had known, of course. He had known long before he had known her.

And yet she had to give him credit where it was due. No matter what her protestations he had always been determined to sweep her into his fire. He had been a giving—if a forceful—lover. Because he had wanted her surrender.

He had wanted her to know the richness of sensation and emotion that could be reached. Any time that he had touched her with lovemaking in mind, he had been determined to teach her the sweetness and the beauty of the act.

She grit her teeth. She did not want to appreciate or admire the man.

Or love him.

A sigh escaped her and she shivered suddenly. The bed had grown cold without him. Her head was aching. She was tired and she suddenly wanted very much to close her eyes and go back to sleep. She wanted to forget the world.

Her lashes fluttered closed. Then they flew back open. Jeremy's staff sergeant was due any minute.

She flew up, dragging the covers with her. Jeremy had already brought in wash water. She bit her lower lip. He had left her a clean pitcher and bowl and towel. He was, she thought, always courteous in such things.

She hurriedly washed and more hurriedly dressed. She wanted to be out of the tent before Jeremy or his staff sergeant arrived. She needed some time alone if she was going to appear calm and poised—the subjugated and polite Rebel—for Jeremy's officers' picnic.

He hated to admit it—even to himself—but there were moments when Jeremy wondered if Christa would defy him so far as to refuse to show up for the impromptu social event, much less assist with it.

But when he had finished the morning business with Staff Sergeant William Hallie and then spent an hour being briefed on recent Indian events along the westward trails by Jennings, he came around to the center of the clustered tents to discover with definite relief that Christa was already there busily preparing plates and offerings alongside Bertha and Nathaniel. She glanced up briefly at his arrival, then looked quickly back to the chore at hand. She was busy twirling fine white linen napkins into silver holders.

Indeed, the camp tables that had been stretched out on the grass were covered in the same white linen. They were using Christa's china and silver, and even here in the wilderness she had made an elegant scene of the buffet table.

There were benefits to marrying a southern belle, he told himself wryly.

Her eyes rose to his again. Beautiful, as blue as the summer's sky. She hadn't wound up the bountiful wealth of her ebony hair but rather left it loose upon her shoulders. She was probably the most fascinating woman he had ever seen and the most beautiful. He felt a flash of heat come searing through his body, and he knew that the one benefit to the marriage had been Christa herself. No matter what words passed between them, no matter what gulf separated them, he ached for the nights. Even when she lay stiff. He had felt sometimes that he lived through the day just to touch her by night.

He lowered his head, determined not to let her see his smile. It wasn't amusing. It was painful to want his wife the way that he did.

But there was something special deep within her. A passion sweetly strong, feverish, dynamic. He had sensed it, felt it, longed for it. And now he had touched it. Briefly. For one night. And as he had suspected, there was nothing in the world like making love with Christa when she made love in return. Nothing. It was dangerous to remember last night, because it made him forget everything else that he was doing.

Night would come again.

He had to keep a smile from curving his lip once again.

Poor thing. Sherman, it seemed, had caused another southerner to fall.

She would certainly not see the amusement in it. And if she spoke today anything like she had spoken yesterday, they could all be in for a fall. He sobered quickly, determined to make his gaze a warning one as he watched her finish with the table.

Even as she did so, a number of the officers began to arrive with their wives. James Preston came with his lovely young Celia on his arm. Then Major Tennison with his wife, Lilly. Several of the captains came, some with their wives, some alone. Nearly all the invited men had made their appearances when Major Paul Jennings arrived at last with his wife, Clara.

Jennings wasn't a bad sort, Jeremy had decided. Sherman seemed to think highly enough of him. But though he liked Jennings well enough, he wasn't particularly fond of the man's wife.

Though most of the men on the trail, the officers and the enlisted men alike, were eager to see to the welfare of any of the ladies along with them, Clara Jennings was proving to be something of a harridan. She was a good companion for Mrs. Brooks. Since her arrival she hadn't done much other than complain. She had imagined they would be given real officers' quarters, not a canvas tent.

There were no real quarters, Jeremy explained. Clara didn't understand. Real quarters should have been built.

But they would soon be moving on.

Clara didn't seem to care.

She kept the men moving throughout the night, bringing her blankets, warming bricks for her bed, brewing her a cup of tea.

Now, as the others laughed and chatted and enjoyed the picnic, Jeremy noted that Clara was having difficulties again. She was complaining to Bertha about something.

Jeremy excused himself from the young captain he had been speaking with and placed himself strategically beside an oak that looked onto the buffet table and the scattered camp chairs and tables that had been set out.

Christa had finished preparing and serving and was leaving the rest to Bertha, who remained contentedly behind the tables. Christa, he noticed, was actually smiling. She was standing with James and Celia and Emory Clark, and Emory was saying something that pleased her. She laughed out loud.

Jeremy wondered at the rush of resentment that filled him. Why was she so quick to smile for Emory? Hell, he was as much a Yank as any man here. Maybe it was Celia, he tried to tell himself. Christa liked Celia. But then, who could help but like the young woman? She was small, delicate, lovely, with an innocence and wide-eyed wonder as big as the West. She had instantly formed an attachment for Christa, and not even Christa could find fault with her.

Christa was blushing, laughing at something that *Emory* was saying.

Emory. Who reminded her of Liam.

Jeremy tightened his lips. His attention was momentarily drawn away from his wife when there was a commotion at the buffet table.

"Oh! I'm afraid that it's sickening, just sickening! I can't possibly eat this meat! I need something quickly!"

It was Clara Jennings. She was waving her handkerchief before her nose.

Bertha, alarmed, had hurried around the table to her. "Mrs. Jennings, what can I do?"

"Some bread, please! That will help, I think!"

"Nathaniel, Nathaniel, please! Get Mrs. Jennings some bread."

Nathaniel was circulating around the tables, picking up plates as the men and ladies finished with them. As Bertha called him, he hurried over to the table.

Clara Jennings saw him for the first time. She watched as he cut her several slices of bread from the loaf.

"Oh, dear, you don't mean for him to give it to me after he's touched it, do you?" Clara Jennings said, horrified.

A silence fell upon the gathering.

Nathaniel, in the act of cutting the bread, went dead still.

Clara felt the silence. She waved herself with her handkerchief profusely. "Well, the man is a Negro!" she said defensively. "And he's touched the bread!"

Jeremy saw Nathaniel's face. The face he had known and trusted so long. A face he had come to care about greatly.

And he saw the weariness and the hurt on it.

He had to say something. As politely as possible, the woman had to be put in her place.

But he didn't have a chance to speak.

"Excuse me!" came a feminine voice with a ring of steel.

Christa stood up and came beside Nathaniel, slipping her arm through his. "Nathaniel, please, would you be so good as to go back to my tent for my shawl?" she asked him quickly.

Proud, wounded dark eyes touched hers. "Please, Nathaniel?"

"Yes, Mrs. McCauley. Yes, right away."

Jeremy could have spoken then, but he was too curious to see what his wife intended to do next. He leaned back against the oak, watching her.

Her back was very straight. Her hands were folded in front of her. Her chin rose as she stared coolly at Clara Jennings. "It always seems to me to be such a curious thing that so many northerners fought such a passionate battle as abolitionists when they were so ignorant of the people they longed to free. Mrs. Jennings, Nathaniel was born a free man. He's received a finer education than most white men I know. I don't know if that matters to you or not. I come from a family that owned slaves at one time. Black people fed me and bathed me as a child, and they stood by me as an adult while the world around us crumbled. I'm lucky. I know that they have hearts and souls—and that the black of their skin can be very beautiful, and that it isn't something that comes off when touched! Perhaps I was one of the wretched southerners holding a people in bondage. At least we knew that they were people. Now, if you'll excuse me, Nathaniel is my friend. I think that I need to see to his welfare."

She had never appeared more the great lady, Jeremy thought, his gaze keenly upon her as she swirled around. For a moment, her eyes touched his. There was an instant of wariness within hers. She thought that he would chastise her for rudeness to his associates again. But she didn't care. There was the slightest trembling to her lower lip, and then her jaw tightened. Her lashes lowered, and she walked by him.

He felt a smile tugging at his lips, but he suppressed it.

"Well, I never!" Clara Jennings stated indignantly once Christa had gone. She flounced around in her chair, staring at Jeremy. "Colonel, I demand that you say something to your wife about this matter!"

He bowed deeply to her, doffing his hat. "Indeed, Mrs. Jennings, I do intend to speak with my wife!"

"Hmmph!" Mrs. Jennings said, somewhat mollified.

"I intend to tell her that I found her speech most touching and admirable. Nathaniel, you see, is my friend too. He grew up in the North, but I want to reassure him now that most northerners do not share your sentiments—and that we are heartily glad that we fought and won a war for the Union and emancipation."

He bowed again and turned to leave the gathering. As he walked away, he could hear Clara Jennings again.

"Well, I never! Never, never! Paul, I—"

"Shut up, Clara," her husband warned her.

Jeremy followed the trail that led down to the river, certain that Nathaniel would come to his "thinking log," a place he sought when his emotions were in an uproar. When he reached the break in the trees before the river, he paused.

Nathaniel was indeed there, as was Christa. They faced one another across the log. Christa was speaking.

"I hope you won't let her words hurt you, Nathaniel. She's a dreadful woman."

"Yes, ma'am, Mrs. McCauley. She is that."

"She's too stupid to know what she's saying—"

"It's the way a lot of folks feel, Mrs. McCauley."

"Not good folks, Nathaniel."

"I thank you for what you did, Mrs. McCauley," he told her, standing very straight and tall. "I heard what you said when I left, and I appreciate it. But there's no cause for you to go getting in trouble with those other army wives, ma'am. I've been called 'dirty nigger' half my life. It's not something you have to suffer over."

"It's not something that's right, either," Christa said. "Just because it's something that has happened."

Nathaniel grinned broadly. "Maybe southern folk aren't so bad."

Jeremy watched as Christa lowered her head, then raised her eyes back to Nathaniel. She sighed. "Nathaniel, I don't know how to judge this world anymore. Far more than half the southern boys who went to war never owned a slave in all their lives. Some who owned them were very decent to them." She hesitated. "There were cruel men and women too. Men who overworked their people. Who shackled them. Who beat them. I can't—I can't defend slavery."

Nathaniel walked toward her. He reached for her hand. It was very small and pale against the ebony coloring of his own. "You do know, Mrs. McCauley, that the black doesn't come off like dirt. That means a lot to me."

She smiled at him. "However it came about, Nathaniel, slavery is over. We just have to convince some people that we're all human."

Nathaniel's handsome jaw twisted. "It's a nice thought, Mrs. McCauley. But a hundred years from now, we'll still be trying to convince some people of that fact. You shouldn't worry about those people who call us dirty niggers, Mrs. McCauley. We have our ways of getting back."

"Oh?"

"We just call them 'white trash.' And that's what they are. That's what they are. I—" He broke off. Jeremy realized that Nathaniel had seen him standing on the trail watching them.

Nathaniel frowned, about to tell Christa that Jeremy was there.

Jeremy shook his head, warning Nathaniel that he didn't want Christa to know that he had been there. Nathaniel nodded, and Jeremy turned and walked away.

Sixteen

*J*eremy couldn't return to the tea-time gathering on the lawn. Their guests would just have to get along without his or Christa's being present.

He had decided to double the guard—he was certain that Robert Black Paw would not return with any good reports about the smoke seen on the trail.

If Major Jennings was right, Buffalo Run was in a rage again, and though Jeremy's troops hadn't been guilty of any crimes against the Indians, it wouldn't matter. Just like some whites felt about Indians, Indians felt the same way about whites.

Jeremy could never guarantee that there wouldn't be a raid or attack against them. Not when they were in Comanche territory. He felt confident that his troops were capable of fighting the enemy, but he didn't want any surprises. Especially not now. There were far too many women present.

If Clara Jennings felt squeamish about a black man cutting her bread, just what would she feel about a red man whisking her away?

Actually, it might be total justice, Jeremy thought, a grin teasing his lips. He could just imagine the red-faced, corpulent Mrs. Jennings reduced to being a slave for some demanding Comanche squaw. The situation did have its humorous side.

But only in the imagination, Jeremy reminded himself somberly. The Comanche tortured their captives sometimes too. He knew that a number of officers in the West kept ammunition set aside to kill their own wives and children before letting them fall captive to the Indians.

A shudder ripped through him.

What of Christa?

No. He could never put a bullet through her heart. Christa was young and strong and beautiful. If the Indians took her, they might well make a slave of her, but the hope for freedom would always be there. She was a fighter. He would not take the chance for life away from her.

Besides, Christa's sentiments were just about the opposite from Clara Jennings's. To Christa's way of seeing things, she'd already bedded a Yankee. What worse could happen to her?

He paused in the trees for a moment, straightening his shoulders, stiffening his spine. God Almighty, what had he done to them both? Why in hell had he ever dragged her away from her precious Cameron Hall, her hallowed Virginia? How in hell had he ever made the stupid, stupid move of falling so deeply in love with her?

"Colonel!"

He gazed down the roadway as he emerged from the trail. Robert Black Paw was making his way toward him on his paint pony.

He saluted in return. "Robert. Did you look into the smoke that Jennings saw?"

Robert nodded gravely, throwing his leg over the horn of his saddle and slipping lithely to the ground. "It was a Comanche raid on a single wagon. Ranchers, I think, from near the Pembroke homestead. There were two men on the ground, both dead. The wagon was lit—that was the source of the smoke and the fire."

"Any sign of the Comanche?"

Robert shook his head. "I think it was a quick hit-and-run raid. In retaliation for the village that Captain Miller struck last week."

"Damn Miller!" Jeremy muttered.

"Yes, sir. Damn Miller. That kind of thing will start up some heavy wars with Buffalo Run. You know him, sir."

"Yes, I know him."

"The funny thing is, Colonel, I think that half-breed Comanche actually likes you. I think he believes you want to leave him and his people in peace. But if men like Miller keep on killing old men, women, and children, there isn't going to be anything that anyone will be able to do."

Jeremy clenched his fingers into fists at his sides. Robert was right. What the hell could he expect out of the Comanche when white men brutalized their people daily? Not that they weren't a warlike tribe—they were. But Buffalo Run seemed to know a hell of a lot more about making a treaty—and keeping his word—than the United States government.

"Damn Miller!" he repeated furiously.

Robert remained silent—there was nothing either of them could say on the matter. "All right," Jeremy said. "We'll have to take greater care. No small hunting parties heading out. I'll speak to the men, all of them. I think I'll ride out to the site myself." He started to walk away, then paused. "Keep a careful eye on my wife until I return."

The Cherokee nodded, placing a hand over his chest. "I'll guard her with my life."

Robert was his man, Jeremy knew. Fiercely loyal.

But he seemed to be falling under Christa's spell too. Don't love her too deeply, he wanted to warn the man. Don't let her hold your heart because she is clad in some prickly armor, and the knives she carries will cut and hurt you and you'll be bleeding before you even know that you were struck.

"Thank you," he told Robert. He strode away, calling for Staff Sergeant

Hallie to bring around his horse. He called up Company B and ordered the men to prepare quickly. They were going to ride.

Nathaniel had gone about his duties, leaving Christa alone by the river, sitting wearily on an old decaying log, when she first heard the bugle calls.

At least one of the companies was leaving the camp. She jumped up and started for the trail.

Jeremy wasn't necessarily leaving, she assured herself.

It might be a very good thing if he was leaving. If he did she wouldn't have to face him for quite some time, and that would surely be a relief.

But she didn't really want him to go. If something were wrong, Jeremy would be looking into the matter himself. And he would take all manner of risks because he was the senior officer.

She bit into her knuckle, wishing suddenly that she could run to him, warn him that he must take care. But, of course, if she hurried to him he might not want to see her. He was probably ready to throttle her over the things she had said to Clara Jennings. He had warned her not to make trouble.

She started along the path anyway, determined that she would at least discover what was going on. But even as she hurried along the trail she suddenly stopped, aware that someone else had stepped onto the trail.

It was Robert Black Paw, the Cherokee. Tall and usually quiet, he was an interesting figure. Today he wore his long ink-black hair in twin braids, and his regulation cavalry trousers along with a white shirt and a heavily decorated doeskin shirt. His features were not handsome, but they were chiseled like hard rock, giving him an exceptionally striking appearance. She didn't know his age; he seemed as old as time. Wherever Jeremy was going, Robert Black Paw would know.

"Robert, my husband—"

"He will return before dawn," Robert said. She stared at him, then started to hurry past him. "Mrs. McCauley," he said, stopping her. She looked back to him.

"He is already gone."

"What is it? What's going on?" she asked him tensely.

"There is nothing for you to be afraid of."

She kept hearing that. All along this trail. But there were things to be afraid of, and she knew it.

There were Comanche.

"Has he ridden out against a war party?"

Robert shook his head gravely. "He will be back before dawn. You are safe. He is safe."

She realized suddenly that Jeremy could have found her if he had wanted to. He could have given her this message himself.

He hadn't wanted to see her. Maybe he hadn't trusted himself with her. Maybe he didn't want his officers and their wives to know that he was itching to throttle his wife.

This was all for the best. She could pretend to be sleeping whenever he returned. With any luck, she wouldn't really have to talk to him until he'd had a chance to cool down a bit.

I'm not afraid of him and I was right, she cried inwardly.

But something felt hollow and empty inside her. She was worried, worried that something could happen to him. Her heart beat too strongly. She pressed her palm against it. She couldn't bear to lose him.

How had she become so entangled? She could not love him! But perhaps she did.

Robert Black Paw watched her with that seemingly ageless wisdom in his dark eyes. "Thank you, Robert," she told him, and walked by. She skirted around the camp. She had no desire to return to the scene of their picnic. Bertha would lovingly tend to the beautiful silver and china that she had brought along with her from what had once been her hope chest.

She skirted around the campsite with its endless array of A-frame tents to come to their own much larger canvas structure. She entered the flap and closed her eyes, then opened them again. Home away from home. She had made their camp bed that morning, but she had done so quickly. Someone else had been in to clean behind her. Jeremy's desk was next to one of the center support poles, his papers neatly stacked. The smaller secretary with her own writing instruments and her books was across from it.

Just as if it were all laid out for a loving couple. One that could spend an evening together, silent but bonded by the emotions between them, each set upon his or her own task.

For a home in the wilderness, it was so very domestic! Her trunk lay open with one of her cool cotton skirts stretched across it. A clean cavalry jacket lay folded over Jeremy's. The beautiful quilt that Callie had made them was folded over the foot of the bed. The washstand, pitcher, bowl, and mirror were set to one side of the tent, while a small squat folding table that held the bottles of brandy, wine, and whiskey lay invitingly near the desks. Christa bit her lip, staring at it. Ah, the downfall of the wine.

Ah, the downfall of her own heart!

What would his feelings be when he saw her again? He had been so furious with her after their evening with Sherman! Would he return angry enough to half-kill, and would it turn into a tempest again?

Or perhaps it might be as he had said when she had warned him not to touch her. Perhaps she wasn't so special. Perhaps she would bring him to a point where he wouldn't care at all any longer.

She paced the tent, wishing that he hadn't ridden away. They should have had it out by now.

"Christa!"

Someone called her softly from outside the tent. She lifted the flap. Celia Preston stood there, tiny, delicate, so pretty in her silver-gray day dress.

Beyond her, Christa saw Robert Black Paw was standing watch over the tent. She lifted a hand to him in salute. He nodded gravely.

Celia slipped into the tent, swirled around observing it, then plumped herself lightly down upon the foot of the bed. She smiled. "What space you have here! Of course, our tent is larger than most since Jimmy is a lieutenant, but this"— she broke off laughing, her velvet brown eyes wide—"this is sheer elegance in the wilderness." Her smile faded. "Oh, Christa! I'm so nervous. Jimmy rode out with Colonel McCauley and Company B. What's going on? What's happened?"

Christa shook her head. "I don't know. But everything is all right, Celia. The men are just very careful, you know that."

Celia nodded. "I hope you'll forgive me for intruding. I was just so nervous . . ." Her voice trailed away, and then she smiled again. "Oh, Christa! Did you give that virago what for this afternoon! You were wonderful. She's still so indignant she's about to pop! She and Mrs. Brooks haven't stopped buzzing about you! May I have a glass of wine? Will you join me?"

"Yes, of course, I'm sorry, I should have offered you some already," Christa said.

"Join me?"

"Er, I think not," Christa murmured. She poured Celia a glass of the burgundy, handed it to her, and sat down beside her.

"How do you endure this awful waiting?" Celia said.

"I haven't had to endure it often," Christa murmured. Celia was staring at her again. She realized she had the young woman's total—and perhaps awed—admiration.

"You're so strong, so wonderfully strong!" Celia said. "And you manage with everything, no matter what happens! Jimmy tells me how wonderful you are all the time!"

"Maybe I will have a glass of wine," Christa murmured. She felt so guilty. She didn't deserve any admiration. She did everything that she did just so that her husband would never see her falter in any way, just so that she wouldn't betray the slightest weakness. That was hardly noble.

"I wish I could be like you," Celia said.

"Jimmy adores you."

She smiled. "Oh, I hope so. But you see, you manage to be beautiful and the perfect wife."

Christa swallowed down a long draft of wine, fiercely reminding herself that she needed to go slow, that she mustn't drink too much.

She had, after all, become an excellent wife at last because of it.

"Celia, trust me. Jimmy finds *you* to be a wonderful wife." She hesitated just a second. "And believe me, my husband does not often find me so perfect as you claim."

Celia stood, her pretty mouth curving into a small smile. "How can you say that!"

"Easily. I assure you that he wasn't very pleased with anything I had to say to General Sherman. Nor can he be very happy about today."

Celia giggled. "I think that the 'Dixie' was the finishing touch with General Sherman! But, Christa! You're very wrong! It's a pity you didn't stay this afternoon. I can't remember his words, but he assured Clara Jennings that he had far more to say to her than he might to his wife! Christa, the colonel applauded your words to her! Why, surely, all of the men and ladies present—other than that shrew herself!—were in sympathy with you!"

Christa felt as if her heart skipped a beat. Jeremy had defended her? Against Clara Jennings? Was it true, or was Celia trying to make her feel better about the disaster of a social?

Celia leapt up suddenly, setting her wineglass down upon the little table. She gave Christa a quick and startling hug. "Oh, if I just had the courage to speak as you did! You were wonderful. I try every day to be more like you!"

Christa shook her head. "Celia, don't say such things. Your husband loves you just the way that you are. You don't want to be hardened, believe me. I'm just the way that I am because I was . . ." She broke off. She didn't know how to explain the war, or the things that had happened after the war.

"A Rebel!" Celia supplied for her. Her brown gaze was still filled with affection and admiration. "Christa, I'm so sorry for you. For all the things that happened. I was so very far away. The war was just something I read about in the paper. Until I married Jimmy, of course, and he was assigned to Washington. Then the war was over before I ever found out that he had been with the troops sent in at the last. I can't even imagine what it must have been like to live in Virginia, with the battles going on constantly, with kinfolk involved, with the enemy swarming everywhere. I would have never survived it."

Christa smiled wryly. "We survived, Celia, just because it's natural to do so. And—" She paused again. "It is all over now, isn't it?"

Celia nodded happily. "I'm so grateful, because I just don't know how I'd endure this without you!" She sighed, then hurried toward the flap. She stopped and looked back. "Thank you, Christa."

Christa shook her head. "No, thank you, Celia."

Celia beamed. "I want to be there, waiting, when Jimmy comes back. Good night."

"Good night."

Christa watched her go. She sat for a while, wondering if it could be true, if Jeremy had really defended her.

A while later, Robert Black Paw called to her. He had brought her some of the buffalo stew left over from the ill-fated picnic.

She thanked him, but she wasn't hungry. She left it to sit upon her writing desk. He asked her if she wanted anything else and she hesitated, then asked him if he thought some of the soldiers would mind heating her some water and bringing in the ladies' camp tub. Robert assured her the men would be glad to serve her, and it seemed that they were. In less than thirty minutes she had her bath.

She used a few precious drops of her rose-scented bath oil and soaked and scrubbed until she felt wonderfully, squeaky clean. In the middle of her bath, she realized that she was doing it all for her husband. Tonight she felt that she owed him a certain debt.

Camerons always paid their debts. She had told him that once.

He could still return furious with her. He might have defended her just to save face.

Still, tonight she would wait up for him.

She dressed in one of her flannel nightgowns and sat down in the chair behind her desk. She brushed her hair a hundred strokes, then curled her toes beneath her and sat, waiting. Through the white canvas of the tent she could see the fire Robert Black Paw had built burning brightly. He was out there, warming his own meal, brewing dark rich coffee.

She watched the play of the flames.

The night drew on. She watched as the fire burned lower and lower.

Her eyes grew heavy. She slid more deeply into the chair, then rested her head on the desk and closed her eyes. She wasn't going to fall asleep. She was far too nervous to do so.

But she closed her eyes.

And she slept.

When she woke the tent was dark. She was stretched out and comfortable. There was a remarkable warmth at her backside.

Disoriented in the darkness, she slowly became aware that she was no longer in the chair.

And she was no longer alone.

Jeremy had come home.

She stiffened. He had picked her up and brought her here, to lie beside him. But he wasn't touching her. He was drawn to his own side of the bed.

"What's wrong?" She heard his voice, deep and low.

He wasn't sleeping. He had sensed her slightest movement.

She didn't answer him. Her heart was suddenly thudding and she was afraid. She wanted to feign sleep.

He wasn't going to allow her to do so. "What's wrong?" he repeated.

"I—"

"Jesu, when the hell did you become afraid to speak your mind?" he demanded impatiently.

He still wasn't touching her.

He had said that morning that she was half-dead herself.

She bit her lip. It was really difficult to thank him for anything.

"I didn't mean to offend anyone this afternoon. It was just that when that woman started on Nathaniel—"

"You didn't offend anyone."

"I didn't mean to make you angry."

"Well, that's new," he murmured wryly.

Her back was still to him. She was glad. She was glad for the darkness too. He certainly had no intention of making anything easy for her.

She inhaled quickly and spoke in a rush. "I understand that you—that you defended my position. Perhaps you thought that you had to. I just wanted you to know that I really didn't mean to antagonize you, that I simply couldn't stand what she was saying about Nathaniel. I didn't want you to be angry—"

"I wasn't angry, Christa."

"I—"

"I know, Christa. My God, what kind of a wretch do you think me? Nathaniel has covered my back for years. He's one of my best friends. Did you think me so low that I wouldn't defend him myself?"

"But it wasn't just for Nathaniel. It was for him and for Tyne and Janey and for so many other people. I've never heard anything so incredible as her attitude! She's a northerner—"

Hell, yes, Jeremy thought, Clara Jennings was a northerner. Christa didn't understand that many of the men and women in the North had never seen Negroes, just as many men and women in the North didn't understand that more than half of the southern boys in the Confederacy had never owned a slave in their lives.

"The war has been won," he said quietly, staring at the dark canvas above them, "but real peace and freedom will probably take decades."

"Jeremy—"

She broke off.

Jeremy rose up on an elbow. She was trying to apologize, and to thank him. It was a unique experience.

And if he reached for her, she might even respond. Out of gratitude.

But tonight he was weary. Riding out to the scene of the Comanche raid had sickened his spirit, and he was tired.

And he wanted more than gratitude from his wife. He didn't want her paying off any imagined debts. He wanted magic again. The kind he had touched last night.

"Go to sleep, Christa," he told her.

He sensed the stiffening within her once again. He turned his back to her, closing his eyes tightly.

She smelled like roses, sweet and delicious. Her hair fell in a cascade of ebony silk, enough to entangle him straight to hell and back. When he had come in, she had been so incredibly beautiful, curled upon the chair, innocent in her sleep, all her defenses down. She had appeared so vulnerable. He had wanted to take her into his arms. Cradle her. Love her.

The scent of roses still teased his nose.

He clenched his eyes more tightly shut. Not tonight. There would be no battles fought, no peace discovered. He did not have to have her. He had warned her that she was not irresistible.

Then why did her scent haunt him so? Why did he long to turn to her? Bury his face against her neck and the sweet-smelling silk of her hair and forget the frontier and the death that stalked it.

He grit down hard on his teeth.

Who am I taunting? Her? Myself?

The answer was easy. He was the one in torment.

But then, he was the one who had so foolishly fallen in love, lost his heart.

And still he lay there, angered by his torment, his back to her.

Pride. What a foolish vice. She lay beside him. She had waited for his touch. And just last night, it seemed, they had evoked the angels when they had made love.

Damn his pride. He would hold her again.

At last he turned, yet when he did, it seemed that she slept again. He felt her breathing, slow, deep, and easy. It was very dark. He smoothed some of the hair from her face and felt her cheeks.

They were damp.

Christa crying? She didn't cry. Camerons didn't cry. The men or the women. She had told him so. She had cried wretchedly and alone before leaving Cameron Hall, but not a tear had appeared in her eyes since. She was fierce, she was strong.

"What in hell is this we have made for one another?" he whispered softly aloud. He slipped his arms around her and pulled her close against him, holding her as she slept. His hand fell beneath her breast. Her back lay against his chest, his hips curved around her derriere.

The ache of his desire was not eased.

But something within his heart was. She slipped beside him so easily. Curved against him naturally.

It was good just to hold her.

Last night she had felt their child moving. There would be a new life created. He shuddered, remembering Jenny.

Jenny had died. With all his strength, he had to protect Christa. He had brought her to Indian territory. He should send her home.

But he could not send her away. He could only keep her safe. By his life, he silently vowed to do so.

He pulled her more tightly against him. He smoothed back her hair.

The night passed on.

Somewhere, a wolf howled.

In time, he slept.

Seventeen

*L*ong, seemingly endless hours of rain and very hard travel kept Christa from seeing much of Jeremy over the next several days. Despite the rain they held a steady pace, and although he seemed not to choose to share any of his important decisions with her, James Preston was polite enough to always keep her abreast of what was going on. Captain Clark had moved on, being one of the messengers of the West, so he was no longer around to entertain them. But many of the other men were very kind, and despite her words with Sherman, they didn't seem to hold anything against her. Sergeant Jaffe had pointed a few men out to her, and to her surprise she learned that they had been wearing gray uniforms until just a short time ago. "Oh, we've an interesting army out here now, ma'am, that we do. A tough one! Half of these fellows have just spent four years shooting at other white men. They aren't going to bat an eye when they raise their guns to shoot at red men."

Christa didn't find that much of an encouraging thought. From the little that she did know about her husband, she knew that Jeremy was often appalled by the way his own army dealt with Indians. She knew that the reason he was so determined to move on was that he wanted to reach, occupy, fortify, and hold Fort Jacobson before harsh weather fell upon them.

For three nights they found high ground by the river when it was very late. The tents were not set up, and Christa spent the nights with Celia—and a parcel of the pointer puppies—in their wagon. By the fourth day the rain had abated. They passed a reservation of Indians, and Jaffe told her that they were Caddo Indians. They were "half-civilized" according to the sergeant, and Christa dismounted from her horse, intrigued and determined to buy whatever they were selling. One of the women was wearing a long cotton dressing gown in very pretty cotton. One of the men was adorned with a brightly colored kerchief about his head. A little child—very little, Christa thought, perhaps just a bit more than a year old—came running out and crashed into her legs. She laughed, a pain touching her heart as she thought of how he reminded her of her nephews and her niece. She scooped up the little boy and swung him around as she had once done so often with John Daniel and the others. The child, like any child—white, black, or red—let out a peal of laughter. The Caddo woman smiled slowly. Christa returned the child, and with Jaffe's help pointed out what she

wanted to buy. They would soon be into an area where the majority of the
nearby Indians would be Comanche and Kiowa, and neither tribe was an agricul-
tural one. They followed the buffalo and made war upon their enemies, and
supplemented their diets with berries and forage off the land. From the Caddo
she bought numerous vegetables.

A number of the men were there, too, buying what they could. Thanks to
Jaffe and some of the other cooks, Jeremy's men ate well, but army rations
themselves were still rather sparse. A private in the army was paid thirteen dollars
a month, Jaffe had told Christa. He was also allotted a weekly issue of salt pork,
dry beans, green coffee beans, brown sugar, soap, and wheat flour. They were
supposed to receive fresh meat twice a week, but since they had been hunting
quite successfully—and since the buffalo kill—they had done much better than
that. As far as fresh fruit and vegetables went, they were on their own. Even a
number of the men who were known to gamble their pay before they received it
were carefully buying up corn and greens from the Caddo.

They had started up on the march again long before Christa heard from Celia
that Mrs. Brooks and Mrs. Jennings were back in Mrs. Brooks's ambulance
praying for Christa's soul. "They're very upset about the way you played with
the Indian child," Celia told her.

"You'd think they'd complain about the snakes and tarantulas instead of me
for a while!" Christa muttered.

"Oh, they complain about those too!" Celia assured her, and laughed.
Christa was glad of Celia's amusement. She had taken to the hardships of the last
days very well. She was becoming a very well-adjusted cavalry wife.

They traveled well over twenty miles that day and camped on the Washita
River. Nathaniel and Robert Black Paw had set up her portable home, and she
was brewing coffee just outside the tent when she paused. It was dusk, but she
could see that a cavalry officer had come into the encampment leading a group
of three Indians.

There was something different about them, and it gave her pause. She rose
slowly from the campfire, staring at the newcomers.

The night was cool yet they wore no shirts. They were dressed in high skin
boots and breechclouts. There were paintings upon their horses in red, and their
faces were also streaked with the color. The lead rider was wearing a headdress
created from the head and horns of a buffalo. There was nothing civilized or
tame about them. The very way that they rode seemed to speak of their freedom
on the plains and of their fierce determination to cling to that freedom.

"Robert—" She turned quickly to her husband's Indian scout.

"Comanche," he said softly. He had been watching the newcomers too.

Her heart seemed to slam against her chest. "Why are they here? Were they
captured? That can't be, the way that they are riding. How do they dare ride into
the camp like that?"

Robert shrugged. "They've come to see the colonel. For now, they've come
in peace. You do not need to be afraid."

She nodded. The Indians dismounted from their horses in front of the headquarters tent and disappeared within it.

Christa tried to settle into the tent but she couldn't do so. There was little for
her to do. Robert had caught a prairie hare for their supper and quietly told her
that he would tend to the meal himself. The bedding was arranged, the tent was

comfortable. Celia was alone at last with her beloved James, and she certainly wasn't going to go pay a visit to Mrs. Brooks or Mrs. Jennings. Some of the other wives were very nice, but she only felt really close to Celia.

Nathaniel and Robert, ever concerned about her comfort, saw to it that after the long days of rain and mud the hip tub was brought in. She did relish her bath; she had felt almost as caked with mud as the earth itself.

She almost wished that Jeremy would come in while she was in it, since finding her in a bath tended to give him an urge toward action rather than conversation.

She was sure that she wanted to be held. To give in once again. To touch that shining pinnacle of paradise that came even here, in the wilderness.

She was so nervous about the night to come, because she had barely spoken with Jeremy since he had returned from his ride out on the plain. He hadn't touched her that night, and with the hardships of their ride, he had been a stranger since. It seemed that all she could remember was that he had called her "half-dead," but she had surely given him all that she had to give.

She left the bath, dressed, paced the tent, then sat at the edge of the bed. Jeremy still hadn't come. She leapt up suddenly. He was usually angry with her anyway—it didn't matter much if he wanted her with him or not now that the Comanche party had come. She was longing to see the Indians who kept even the most seasoned soldiers on edge.

She threw a shawl around her shoulders and left her own tent behind, heading straight for the headquarters tent. Private Darcy was on duty outside of it.

"Ma'am—" he began, ready to stop her.

She waved a hand his way. "It's all right, Mr. Darcy. I'm sure my husband won't mind."

Her husband would mind, but short of holding her back physically, there was nothing Darcy could do since she was on her way into the tent. She paused just inside the flaps, surveying the scene.

Captain Clark was the white man who had ridden in with the Indians. He was standing to the right of and just behind Jeremy. Two of the braves stood to the side of the desk. One of the Indians was speaking with her husband, and in an excellent English.

"It was just months ago when we gathered, thousands of us, Comanche, Apache, Kiowa, Pawnee, and more, on the banks of the Washita, hearing about the things that would be offered to us by the Great White Father of the Confederacy."

Christa's eyes widened as she realized that the man was talking about Jeff Davis.

Jeremy, seated behind the broad traveling desk that could be so easily transported to a wagon, nodded sagely to the man before him.

"The emissary from the Confederacy spoke to you in all good faith. But even as he was speaking, the government of the Confederacy was folding. Buffalo Run knows—"

"Buffalo Run knows that things happen—like the massacre at Sand Creek. He was glad when he learned that you were coming, for he remembers you well and he feels that you are, perhaps, the only honest white man he has met."

Jeremy leaned forward. "Eagle Who Flies High, I am pleased that Buffalo Run feels that we can negotiate. I have been very distressed. It was not long ago that I rode out here with a company from my regiment to discover that a stranded company of men from another regiment had been annihilated. And just days ago, I came across dead men on the plain. Is this Buffalo Run's message of good faith to me?"

"Just as you do not control all white men, Buffalo Run does not control all Comanche braves."

"Ah, but Buffalo Run can exert influence," Jeremy said.

The Indian before him—a man of medium height but with a solid, muscular build—inclined his head. "So he will speak with you. And his brothers Setting Sun and Walks Tall will await here in equal good faith."

"I am agreed," Jeremy said simply. He stood. The meeting had evidently been completed.

The Indian turned. He had been about to walk from the tent but he stopped, standing dead still as he saw Christa. Jeremy, who had been involved with his exchange with the man he had called Eagle Who Flies High, saw her too. His eyes narrowed, his jaw tightened. Christa felt a flush suffuse her as the Comanche studied her thoroughly from head to toe.

"My wife, Eagle Who Flies High," Jeremy said. The Comanche didn't really acknowledge Christa, he nodded to Jeremy.

"She is a fine wife." He studied Christa again in silence, turned back to Jeremy and bowed, then proceeded out of the tent, nearly brushing by Christa as he left. The other two braves followed him in silence, their dark eyes studying her with the same blunt appraisal.

When they were gone, Jeremy's wrath exploded. "What in God's name are you doing here?" he demanded, his tone low but shaking with the effort to keep it so.

"I just—"

"Colonel, sir," Emory Clark said, "surely it can't be Mrs. McCauley's fault to have stumbled upon us in the midst of—"

"Emory, I'll thank you to mind your own business!" Jeremy snapped, rising. He started toward Christa. "And you! You need to learn to stay out of business that does not concern you!"

"But it does concern me!" Christa retorted, wishing that she had never come, and miserable for both herself and for poor Emory. "The Comanche—"

"The Comanche are very fond of taking female captives!"

Emory cleared his throat. "He's concerned for your welfare, Christa—"

"Emory! I'll speak to my wife myself, thank you!"

"Yes, sir." Emory saluted. He didn't look pleased. He strode out of the tent.

"You didn't need to be so rude!" Christa cried.

"And you don't need to behave so stupidly!"

She stiffened, swung around, and strode out of the tent almost blindly. She nearly tripped over Private Darcy.

"Christa!"

She heard him, but she looked right at Private Darcy and pretended that she didn't. Furious, she strode on through the field of tents until she reached her own.

He was right behind, catching her by her shoulder, spinning her around. "Christa, don't walk out on me like that again!"

"Then don't yell at me like that again!"

"I'm just concerned—"

"Then you shouldn't have yelled at Captain Clark."

He threw up his hands. "Right. I wouldn't want to yell at the poor dear fellow who so resembles Liam McCloskey!"

"Oh!" she cried, and threw up her hands in aggravation. "You're right! He is poor Captain Clark. He will forever have to pay because of that!" Angrily, she pulled the pillow from the bed and threw it at him, hard. He caught it and tossed it to the bed, advancing on her. She backed away quickly, but found there was nowhere to go. He was nearly upon her when she began talking. "My God, I didn't mean to cause you difficulty!" she hissed out. "I didn't know if you were staying out all night or coming in. I merely wished to see—"

"You wished to see the Comanche!" he said.

She turned away quickly, trying to keep her fingers from shaking as she poured him a brandy, handing it to him quickly. To her surprise, he took it from her fingers. His eyes were still hard, silver and gun-metal gray. She quickly tried to ply her advantage.

"I've seen many of the Indians," she said.

"Not the Comanche."

"Yes, but they're important to you. There's so much that I don't understand. What was he talking about? What was the Sand Creek Massacre?"

"The Sand Creek Massacre," he repeated. He walked around his desk, pulled back the chair, and sat in it, his eyes remaining on her sharply. "You never heard of it?"

She shook her head. "There—there was a war going on."

"Yes," he murmured, looking away. "All right, you want to know. War came, and half the men out here resigned to go with the Confederacy. More men were pulled back to fight on the front. Once there was a fairly decent man named Wynkoop at a place northwest of here called Fort Lyon. Under terms, some Arapaho and Cheyenne Indians had put themselves under his protection. Wynkoop was too decent a man. Somebody decided to get rid of him and a Major Anthony came out to take charge. Governor Evans of Colorado and a militia colonel named Chivington wanted a war. Anthony managed to get the Indians to move away from the protection of the fort—he could attack them then. And he did. Chivington had given his men orders to attack all the Indians, to kill and scalp the big ones and the little ones because nits made lice. And so the men went in and killed, raped, maimed, and destroyed. A Captain Silas, a regular from Anthony's army, refused to follow the order. He was murdered in Denver soon after. Anthony and Chivington tried to make it sound like a noble battle, and still the truth got out to whites and red men alike. Buffalo Run is not a fool. He has seen the past, and by that, he sees the future. He doesn't trust many men."

Christa didn't think that she could blame Buffalo Run, not after the story Jeremy had told her. He didn't describe the slaughter in detail, but in his tone she could almost imagine what had happened and it had surely been horrible.

"It seems that Buffalo Run trusts you."

Jeremy shrugged. "He tolerates me—more than he is willing to tolerate most white men." He leaned forward suddenly, wagging a finger at her. "His men should have never seen you."

"But—"

"They are a polygamous society. Buffalo Run has several wives and probably wouldn't mind having another one."

"But—"

"The Comanche can move like the wind. They like to travel down to Mexico and trade with the Spanish. They trade women just like they trade buffalo meat and hides. They like to rape their female prisoners first so that they give the Spaniards a woman who is soiled. It's a way of being superior."

A chill was slipping over her. "But Jeremy, I came to the headquarters tent! I didn't wander out into open territory."

"But you've done so before," he reminded her tautly.

She felt a chill seeping into her. "I won't do so again," she said uneasily.

He was up suddenly, hands folded at his back, pacing the space between them. "See that you do stay close in!" he commanded. He stopped in front of her, his voice sharper than she had ever heard it to one of his soldiers. "Over the next few days, until my return, you must stay with Robert Black Paw. Always, always have him in sight."

"Until your return?" Christa said, startled.

"I am going with Eagle Who Flies High tomorrow to visit the place where Buffalo Run is keeping camp."

Christa gasped. "You're going—right into a Comanche camp? But you can't!"

"I've been in his camp before."

Christa shook her head. "But—how can you trust him? He kills people, he has his own set of rules, you just told me that!"

"I have to go, Christa. And I trust him more than I do most men, no matter what his color."

"If you trust him so much, why are you so angry with me?"

"Damnation!" he seemed to roar. "I've been trying and trying to make you understand!"

"Stop swearing at me like that!" she countered, her teeth gritting. "Mrs. Brooks will be in to get you!"

To her amazement, he paused. He sat down at the foot of the bed, staring at her incredulously, then smiling slowly.

"I have to go, Christa."

"But—"

"Will you miss me?"

Color touched her cheeks. "Jeremy, really—"

"Come now! Surely, you'll miss me just a little. I'm another body to fight off whatever threats may come!"

"You're a fool, marching into a hostile Indian camp!"

"Come here," he said suddenly.

"I—"

"Come here. I've got tonight. Then I've got to ride. I will not spend tonight arguing."

"You won't argue. No, you'll just yell and then expect me to jump at your beck and call."

"Fine!" He stood, strode the distance to her, lifted her high, and set her down upon the foot of the bed. "I'm not being a fool, Christa. Buffalo Run has sent two of his own brothers to be hostages here until I return safely. He and I are blood brothers. The Comanche are a very free people. There are many bands, usually created of family connections. Any Comanche is free to come and go from his band and a brave is certainly free to think for himself, but they all respect certain matters of honor among one another. Two minutes after I return here hostilities might break out. But while I'm under his promise of protection, I will be completely safe."

"Fine!" she said, repeating his words.

"You!" he said, pointing a finger at her. "I will never feel safe about you."

"But—"

"But! Will you miss me?"

She moistened her lips. "Perhaps."

His laughter was throaty.

"It will pain me every second that I am away."

"You are a liar!" she accused him.

"It's God's truth."

"Well, it's hard to tell. You do manage to keep your distance when you choose."

"And then I am furious with myself. There will be no distance tonight, Christa. When the night has passed, you will surely miss me. Whether you do with pain or pleasure, I can't be certain, but you will surely be aware of my presence tonight, and that it is gone tomorrow!"

A heat rose within her. She lowered her eyes quickly, avoiding his.

"What, no protests? No fury?"

The lamplight was very low and very soft. She stared down at her hands, studying them. No matter how she fought it, she felt a wave of crimson coloring rush to her cheeks and her words were soft and breathless. "You're mocking me. I truly don't know what you want! I surrendered everything the other night, everything. And you seemed pleased enough at the time, yet uninterested when you returned from your ride."

"I have never been uninterested!" he said, and he came down upon one knee, taking her hand from her lap to slide between his own. "Never."

"You said that I was half-dead."

"Because I wanted to shake you into the realm of the living."

She inhaled, feeling the fire of the silver in his eyes as they sought to impale her own. She refused to meet his gaze, shaking her head. "I did give in!" she murmured. "I swear, I ceased the fight! I—"

"You told me it was the wine," he reminded her. "I was palatable—because of the wine."

She lowered her head, wishing that he were not so close, so very demanding. "Perhaps it was. Perhaps it wasn't. I still don't understand what it is that—that you still want of me."

"More, Christa. I will always want more. But mainly, I want you to come to me. Not because I might defend you. Not because Camerons always pay their debts. But because you want me. Would that be so very difficult?"

She shook her head, swallowing hard. Her eyes met his at last. She tried to speak, moistening her lips with the tip of her tongue, seeking words, unable to find them. Perhaps he understood her dilemma, perhaps he knew exactly when to push her, and when to come to her rescue. He released her hands, his arms slipping around her. He rose, bringing her to her feet along with him. His mouth descended ardently down upon hers, seizing her lips in a fierce, hungry kiss. But one that gave so much more. One that teased, one that coerced. One that was hot and fervent, one that elicited fires to burn deep in secret places she had so recently discovered within herself.

Those fires seemed so quickly fanned! In the fierce sweetness of his kiss she swiftly understood more of what he sought from her, and with the honeyed excitement sweeping through her she dared to do those things she had dreamed before. Her arms slipped around his neck. Her lips parted more willingly to the pressure of his kiss, and tentatively at first, but more boldly with each passing second, she teased and taunted and elicited in return, her tongue playing with his, thrusting into his mouth, rimming it. Her fingers stroked the hair at his nape, caressed his cheek, curled into the muscles of his shoulders and arms. She felt the rampant beating of his heart, a hardness, a quickening within him. He lifted his head from hers at last, silver glistening in his eyes as they touched hers. "Jesu!" he whispered, and she smiled, unaware of how dazzling and beautiful the lights in her eyes could be. But he did not meet them long. He spun her around, his fingers impatient on the hooks of her gown. When the material fell from her shoulders, he spun her again, his lips touching down on her flesh, searing and wet, causing her breath to catch, and the flame within her to sizzle and soar. He eased her dress downward, and it fell in a pool at her feet. His fingers caught at the tie of her pantalets, and when they fell, she stepped from them. The lamplight seemed so gentle that night.

He sat, pulling off a boot. She knelt before him, taking off the other boot. She paused for a moment, aware that he was quickly shedding his shirt. Her eyes met his again and the searing spark of desire within them sent a flutter cascading from her heart to the center of her womb. She rose slightly, curling her arms around him. Her lips just brushed atop his, then pressed to his throat, to his collarbone, and trailed slowly across his shoulder. She teased his flesh with the tip of her tongue, tasting the salt there. Her fingers moved over the bronzed length of his arm, testing the ripple and feel of muscle. She sat back, watching with fascination as she brought her hands down over his chest, her fingertips dancing lightly over the crisp whorls of dark red hair upon it. She came close again, kissing his chest, testing with the hot tip of her tongue, finding a rich, rising excitement in the intrigue of his body.

"Christa!" He whispered her name huskily, rising suddenly, bringing her with him. Crushed against him, she grazed her knuckles over the length of his back, savoring the ripple and pull of his muscles. The soft sensations aroused him further. She stood on tiptoe. Her lips caught his, left them. Again she stroked his back. Lower. The evocative brush of her knuckles covering his buttocks. A husky groan escaped him, startling her. She found herself swept up and laid back upon the bed, dizzy with the sweet feel of her own commitment, so alive and vital, anticipating the wonder of what was to come. Yet when she saw that his cavalry pants were off him, she did not wait. He had said that he wanted her to want him. And she did. Her flesh burned. Ached for his touch on the outside.

And on the inside . . .

The fire of her flesh was now searing inside of her, and the longing was deep and rich. Even as he walked toward her, she rose again. With a little cry, she raced toward him. She found herself swept up again. Her legs locked around his back as he spun with her, kissing her. He held still. She slid down the length of him. Fingers and lips covered his chest. Stroked his naked buttocks. Her eyes found his, questing, blue. "This . . . ?" she whispered.

A deep, guttural groan gave her sweet reply. "This!" he said. "This, this . . ."

Against the softness of her flesh she could feel the hard arousal of his sex. Her heart hammered. She didn't dare—she couldn't. She closed her eyes, leaning her forehead against his chest. She teased him first, inadvertently, with the brush of her knuckles. She felt his breath catch, his heart thud. She closed her fingers around him. An exclamation exploded from him. She grew bolder, stroking the hardness, exploring beyond, her hands touching the softness of his sac, coming against the sheer hardness of desire. Whispers fell from his lips that she scarce understood, yet she did not need to hear the words, for the desire and approval were so rich in his tone. She was lifted suddenly again and found herself breathless as she lay flat. She cried out softly, for he was within her and the feeling was delicious.

Her legs locked around him, holding him close. He brought her soaring to the very crest of a pinnacle, then withdrew. She felt his lips upon hers, upon her shoulders, upon her breasts. So sweetly upon her breasts, teasing, bathing, suckling, first one and then the other. She was whispering frantically herself, demanding that he cease the torture and come to her. But he did not. He stroked, caressed, and bathed the length of her with his kiss, with his demand. When he was done, he lifted her over him, drawing her slowly down, his eyes impaling hers even as his body did the same. He taught her to move, his eyes fully upon the lush fall of her hair, the sway of her breasts. His hands curved strongly around her buttocks, and he guided her until the natural force of her desire brought her hungrily against him, sweeping them both into a maelstrom that exploded into an ecstasy beyond all that she had ever imagined, sweet, volatile, and violent, and bringing her crashing down against him at last, entangling him in the wild fall of her hair even as it seemed that the world burst into brilliant sunlight, fell to darkness, and burst into a beautiful array of stars once again.

She slipped to his side, still amazed. His arm came around her and he held her tight against him. The feel of his flesh was still hot and slick and wonderful against her own. She lay still, grateful for the warmth that surrounded them.

She heard his whisper, deep, husky. Mocking perhaps, but yearning, too.

"Will you miss me?"

"Jeremy—"

"Will you miss me?"

God, yes! she might have cried out. I'll miss you like the sun, like air. More than I've ever missed anyone in all my life, more than I missed my brothers in the awful years of the war. I loved them but I love you. Oh, my God, yes, I love you.

"Jesu! If it takes that long, you're not convinced!"

A gasp escaped her. She was suddenly, fiercely, in his arms again.

He made love to her, slowly, fervently, thoroughly. He erased all thoughts from her mind, other than the hungers and the beauties of human sexuality. When she lay panting at his side once again, he repeated the question.

"Will you miss me? If not—"

"Yes!" she gasped.

And the sound of his laughter was warm, as were his arms when he pulled her gently within them.

"My love, I'll miss you too!" he vowed softly. "Dear God, but I will miss you too!"

Eighteen

he days that Jeremy traveled to Buffalo Run's camp—accompanied by James Preston along with a few other men—moved slowly. Although Major Jennings and Major Brooks had more western combat experience, Jeremy had left the regimental physician, Major Weland, in command. Christa knew that both Mrs. Jennings and Mrs. Brooks had their noses cleanly out of joint, and she couldn't help but feel a little smug about it. She also saw the wisdom in Jeremy's choice. Weland held a comparative rank, and though he was their physician he was also a curious man with an open mind, fascinated by people, far quicker to think than he was to take up arms.

She had promised Jeremy that she would miss him and she did, desperately. She was amazed to discover that she lay awake night after night, aching for him physically and within her heart and soul. She wondered if there would ever be a time when she could tell him the truth of her feelings. Still, she lay awake sometimes in agony, wondering at all the secrets he kept locked within his own soul, wondering about Jenny, wondering about the child she had lost.

Though Jeremy and his men traveled slowly, they moved ever westward.

On the third day after Jeremy's departure, Weland invited her to the command tent to sup with him, and she was delighted to discover that he had a letter for her from home. A messenger had found their encampment that afternoon and come through with a great deal of mail. The letter was for her and Jeremy, and there were bits and pieces in it from everyone in the family—including a scrawl from the oldest of the next generation, Jesse and Kiernan's son, John Daniel Cameron. Callie, Kiernan, and Jesse wrote little bits of cheerful news about everyday life. Daniel, who had always been the best correspondent in the family, wrote more. She bit her lip, reading that he and Callie had taken a trip to Fort Monroe, where Jeff Davis was being held. Varina had been so good to them when times had been different in her life, they had been determined to see what they could do in return. There was little. The Union didn't know what it wanted to do with Jeff Davis yet. There had been rumors that he should be hanged, but even Daniel was certain that such a thing would never come to pass.

I think they will incarcerate him for a while, and then let him go. Perhaps they are afraid that the South shall rise again. It cannot do so. We are the lucky ones among our countrymen, for our land is in good repair, our house stands tall, and we have weathered it well. Still, to travel the nearby country-side! Building takes place daily, but wherever one goes it seems there are still the remnants of once great manors to be seen. Fields lie fallow or are overgrown, and at times it seems—in truth—that locusts have descended. I am not yet pardoned, but we have been encouraging Jesse to seek public office. Someday, this madness will end. The government of the southern states will be returned to the states. It seems that some of our most fervent Confederates are now dedicated to the task of sewing up the rip in the country. Perhaps we can start that here. It is sad and bitter to imagine that it will take years and years for all of the land to return to its bounty, for homes to rise again free from bullet holes and cannonballs, but it cannot begin at all unless we set our backs to the task.

She let the letter fall into her lap, imagining what home would look like now. The autumn foliage would be upon them. The landscape would be alive in crimsons and yellows and oranges.

"Homesick?" Weland asked her.

"A little bit."

"But it's not so bad as it was at first?"

She shrugged, then smiled slowly. "I admit, the travel is fascinating."

"The wild, wild West!" Weland murmured. "It will become more fascinating still."

"But at home they're rebuilding the South," Christa said softly.

Weland stood, coming around behind her, and gave her a paternal squeeze upon the shoulders. "There are great things happening!" he told her. "So many men and women have seen the downfall of the Confederacy as the end. Christa, we are entering upon a new age. We have battled ourselves at last. Now we can look to the future. The West will explode. The South will rebuild. It is an exciting time to be alive. It makes the choices all the more difficult."

"What choices?"

He came back around the dinner table, smiling at her. "Whether to explore the new world, or rebuild the old. Will your home be in Virginia, or in the West?"

She shook her head. "I don't think that I have any choices," she said ruefully. "Jeremy is a cavalry officer. I will go where he—" She paused. She had almost said "commands." "I will go where he goes."

Weland smiled. "Home has always been where the heart is. That is what you must discover. In time you will." He shook his head. "It is the poor Indian I pity!" he said.

Christa's eyes widened. She heard enough descriptions of what the Indians could do to wonder how Weland could speak so broadly.

"They are the true losers!" he told her. He spread out a hand. "Day after day, more wagon trains come now. The war kept us from this expansion. But now Americans, from the North and the South, will head here in droves. They'll settle and they'll force the government to break more and more treaties." He leaned forward. "Why do you think the Comanche hate the Texans so much?"

"I didn't know—"

"They hate the Texans! Why, they don't even think of the Texans as Americans. Other settlers are other settlers. But the Texans—the Comanche feel the Texans already stole all their land."

"Did they?"

"Sure did." Weland lit his pipe and winked at her. "That's progress for you!"

She smiled. She liked Dr. Weland. He always made her feel comfortable and as if she belonged. As if she was wanted, loved, cherished.

"Well, now. Will you have more coffee?" he asked her. She shook her head and thanked him. "I'm going to go and write back to my family," she told him. She wished him good night and returned to her tent.

As she walked back, she could hear some of the men singing soft songs to get them through the long hours of camp life. She didn't hear footsteps following her, but she sensed them. When she reached her tent, she paused. "Good night, Robert Black Paw!" she called out softly.

There was silence. Then she heard, "Good night, Mrs. McCauley."

Feeling curiously happy, she slipped into her tent, wrote a long letter home, and went to sleep. She only stayed awake awhile, staring at the canvas of the tent.

Jeremy had said with conviction that he would be safe. He would return.

The troops moved onward while awaiting his return. The country they came upon grew more and more intriguing. They were upon the Canadian River, Nathaniel told her, at a place near the line dividing Indian territory and the upper part of Texas.

The river was fascinating, being full and broad sometimes, then seeming to disappear. Nathaniel showed her how the water ran beneath the surface.

In the afternoon they came upon the "Antelope Buttes." They amazed Christa, being high tables of rock with the tops apparently perfectly flat. The sides of the buttes sloped precariously steep. The way that they dotted the land-scape seemed so unique to her that she spent long hours staring at them once they had camped for the night.

It was because of this that when the sun ceased to sparkle so brightly against her eyes, she saw the pole sticking out of one of the buttes.

Curious, she rode Tilly to the headquarters tent. Weland was deep in conver-sation with Jennings and Brooks, charting their course for the next day, and no one noticed her at first.

"We are dragging our feet enough as it is!" Major Brooks said gruffly. "Col-onel McCauley was the first to want to make haste. If he doesn't return tomor-row, we must push on harder!"

"Gentlemen, I have followed his orders precisely, and see no reason to change my course of action," Weland argued in return.

"Except that you can't trust that Comanche half-breed, Buffalo Run!" Jen-nings insisted wearily. "Major Weland, if the colonel doesn't return tomorrow, I'd say it's very likely that he and the other men might well be dead!"

Christa didn't realize that she had cried out until all three men stared at her. Weland was instantly on his feet. "Major!" he declared. "What a way to speak!" He rushed to Christa's side. "And the colonel's lady with child here in the wilderness. You should be ashamed of yourself, sir!" He forced Christa to sit. She saw him wink and shrugged.

"Oh, I do feel faint!" she moaned.

Jennings was quickly up, the poor henpecked man. "I'm sorry. So sorry, Mrs. McCauley! It's just that we have the whole of the regiment to worry about."

"Jeremy said that he'll come back. He will," she insisted.

"Yes, Mrs. McCauley," Jennings said. He cleared his throat and twirled his mustache. "Well then, I'll be on my way! Brooks?"

"Yes, yes, I'll be joining you."

The two majors left hastily. Christa burst into laughter watching them go. She smiled at Weland. "You were wonderful."

"No, you were wonderful—getting them out of my hair like that!" His smile faded. "You are feeling all right? I promised Jesse a healthy nephew or niece, you know. And of course, if I let any ill come to you, Jeremy would simply hang me."

"Oh, he would not!" Christa protested.

He stared at her, then smiled. "But he would! Well, never mind that now. Did you come to me because you were feeling sick or social—or both?"

She shook her head. "There's something up on one of the buttes."

He frowned. "What?"

"I don't know, but I'll show you."

He accompanied her out, calling to a private for his horse. He rode with Christa to the last tent, from where they could see the pole that seemed to extend from one of the buttes."

"I'll have Robert Black Paw see to it," Weland said. "I'll ride back and have him sent for."

Christa smiled. "Oh, there's no need to do that!" She raised her voice, whirling Tilly around. "Robert! Robert, where are you?"

Weland glanced to her, his brows arched, as Robert sheepishly rode out from behind one of the tents. He pointed to the pole. "Do you think you can reach the top of the butte?" Weland asked him.

Robert Black Paw nodded, but he looked to Christa. "I'll climb the butte. But—" He paused.

"I promise that I won't leave Major Weland's side until you return," Christa told him.

That satisfied him. With a few other men, Robert started out for the butte. Weland and Christa paid a visit to Celia, trying to cheer her up. Then they returned to the headquarters tent and waited, engaging in a game of chess.

Weland took so long to move at one point that Christa sat back, staring at him.

"Robert knew what was on the pole," he said.

Startled, Christa raised a brow. "Do you know?"

"I'm afraid I might."

She didn't have a chance to ask him what he knew. He was staring over her shoulder. She looked back to see that Robert had returned. He carried nothing with him, but stared at Weland.

"Whatever it is, say it, please!" Christa demanded.

"Christa, I don't know if you should—"

"Oh, please! You both know that I will not pass out or go into fits of hysteria!"

"A scalp?" Weland asked.

"Yes, a scalp. A white scalp."

She didn't get hysterical, she didn't pass out, and she didn't shriek.

But she did panic. Cold, black fear filled her. She felt the first taste of bile and terror rise to her throat. "A white scalp. Oh, my God, Jeremy—"

"No, no! Christa," Robert Black Paw said quickly, forgetting his customary manner and using her Christian name. He knelt down beside her. "It is a woman's scalp. The hair is long and light."

"Oh!" She locked her fingers together in her lap, holding them tightly.

"And how was it found?" Weland asked.

"Stretched out on a hoop, secured to the pole by sinew ties."

"You think it's a warning?"

"Perhaps."

"Do you think that Jeremy is safe?" Christa whispered.

"Buffalo Run gave his word of honor. Jeremy will be safe," Robert said flatly. Weland didn't say anything at all.

Christa leapt up. She felt so nervous. She had to be alone. "I—I think I'll go to bed then. We'll probably rise early. I'm—I'm very tired."

"Christa!" Weland said.

She paused, looking back at him.

"Jeremy will be all right."

She nodded. Fear had begun to live within her. She could not control it.

In her own tent she paced up and down.

She felt the baby moving and bit her lip, wondering if Jeremy might have been able to feel the strength of the movement if he had been with her. She sat on the bed, remembering how he had withdrawn from her the night she had said the baby was moving.

He hadn't told her then, but of course he had been remembering. Remembering Jenny and the child who should have lived.

She pressed her fingers to her cheeks. She was in love with a man whose thoughts were with someone else.

No. He had said she was the perfect cavalry wife. Her cheeks colored when she responded to him. She didn't think she could do anything but respond now.

She stood up, poured herself just a touch of brandy, and sipped it. It warmed her.

She dressed for bed in warm flannel, then curled up on her pillow. She could see the campfires burning beyond the canvas. She had to sleep. She turned down the lamp.

The fires burned low. She had to sleep, for the baby. For their son or their daughter. A child who would grow in the new world. In Weland's age of discovery. Sympathetic to the misfortunes of the South, sympathetic with the ideals of the North.

She closed her eyes and dozed.

Something was moving. She tried to awaken. All that she could see in the mist between wakefulness and sleep was the rise of the butte. And the pole upon that butte.

She could hear drums, she thought. War drums. She could see warriors, Comanche warriors, dancing to the rhythm of those drums.

Jeremy was there, staked out upon the dry earth. One of the Comanche braves, his face painted red, was bearing down on him with a razor-sharp knife aimed at his skull.

She awoke, gasping for air, leaping from her bed. There was someone within the tent. A scream rose in her throat. The Indians had come!

Arms encircled her in the near darkness. "Christa!"

It was Jeremy. She gasped, trembling. She forgot that he had ever been her enemy. "Jeremy! Oh, Jeremy! You're back! You've returned."

He was startled by the vehemence of her greeting. He smoothed back her hair, determined to enjoy her welcoming of him rather than analyze it.

"I told you that I'd come back."

"Yes, but they found a scalp!"

He didn't tell her that many, many a scalp could be found in the West—and many, many of those Indian scalps taken by white men.

"I heard. I've seen Weland," he told her. Still holding her, he tossed his hat from his head. She didn't seem anxious for him to let her go. In the dim light he tried to study her eyes, but they were shielded by the darkness. Still, darkness couldn't shield everything. Every time he left her and returned to her, he was struck anew by her beauty. Her skin was flawless, her face so delicately, classically, beautifully molded. And the softness of her! Her breasts were very large with her pregnancy, her belly just beginning to round with it. She was sweetly warm in his arms. He could hear the ferocity of her heartbeat, feel the unsteady rhythm of her breath.

"So you missed me?" he said lightly.

"I—" She paused, remembering the way that they had parted. "Of course I missed you," she murmured. "You left me here alone with those horrible Brooks and Jennings people!"

He laughed, familiar with the slightly tart twist of her voice. She may have claimed to have surrendered. But she had never done so. He might be battling all his life.

His smile faded. He didn't mind that. He didn't mind the skirmishes, nor did he ever mind trying to win.

If only he could rid them of their ghosts!

If only she could love him in return. But he didn't place his heart on a platter before her.

Camerons, among other things, could be ruthless.

"Well, I'm back now," he told her softly.

Her smiled eased. She slowly withdrew her arms from about his neck. "Well, how did things go with the Comanche, with this Buffalo Run person?"

"I don't want to talk about Buffalo Run or the Comanche at this moment."

"Oh. Then, I . . . would you like wine? Brandy? A whiskey."

"No, thank you." He unbuckled his scabbard, casting it aside.

"I could make you some coffee—"

"There is only one thing I want," he said flatly.

Even in the darkness, he could see the color that rushed to her cheeks.

"Oh."

"Well?"

"Well?" she whispered.

"Am I being offered that for which I truly hunger?"

Her lashes fell. "You know that you can always take what you want!"

"That's not what I asked you."

Her lashes rose. There was a flush of fury in her eyes. "Why do you do this to me?"

"I wasn't aware that I was doing anything to you. Yet!" he added with a smile. He touched her chin, lifting it. His eyes searched hers again. "You were all that I thought about the hours I was gone. I should have been concentrating on the importance of words spoken between Buffalo Run and me, but my mind kept wandering. I would close my eyes and see you here, naked, the fall of your hair about you, a sheen upon your flesh, the slightest curl of a smile to your lips. What have you done, Christa, bewitched me? Are Camerons so talented?"

She gazed at him, her eyes widening. She didn't reply, and he pressed his point. "I'm hungry, Christa. Starving for the touch and taste of you. Tell me, do you offer yourself up as freely as you would pass out whiskey or wine?"

"I can't play these word games!" she whispered.

He caught her arms, pulling her against him. "No games, Christa. Tell me! Will you come to me?"

"Yes!" she gasped. She truly couldn't say anything more. But tonight, the darkness and her own hungers were her shield. She slipped her arms around his neck. She rose on her toes and kissed him. The long hours of worry and waiting added to the savoring hunger of her kiss, and he marveled at the feel of her in his arms.

He lifted her up, thanking God in heaven, and brought her to their bed. She said nothing more and he forced nothing more from her.

He had no desire to break the fragile magic.

It lasted through the night.

He felt her get out of bed. Still drowsy himself, he watched her with half-closed eyes. She was so graceful and supple, sliding from the covers in the pale dawn, tall and naked and elegant, no matter that slight rounding of her stomach. He enjoyed watching her when she thought that he slept, dousing her face in wash water from the pitcher on the trunk, shivering fiercely, then dressing as silently as she could, determined not to wake him.

He tried not to smile, certain that she would go out and start the morning coffee, then come back to him. At the moment, he didn't care what time the regiment started moving. He'd earned his rest.

He watched her slip out of the tent and luxuriated in the comfort of his camp bed after the nights spent sleeping on the ground with his saddle as a pillow. She would return soon enough, bringing him coffee. The morning would be sweet.

He rolled over, glad to keep his eyes closed for a few minutes longer as he mulled over his days with Buffalo Run.

There were numerous bands of Comanche. They were all still friendly with the Wind River Shoshone, the tribe from which they had sprung and with whom they shared a common language. They had formed alliances with the Kiowa to create bigger raiding parties, but they fought the Utes—with whom they also shared their language. They acknowledged no central tribal chief or government, but each band recognized its own chief who might also hold some sway with the chiefs of other bands.

Buffalo Run was such a chief.

He was an intelligent man, a half-breed, a renegade. Many people thought that the Comanche were responsible for a majority of the white deaths in the West, but Jeremy didn't feel that Buffalo Run enjoyed the spectacle of death.

He had simply watched what happened with white men and learned from the misfortunes of others. When Jeremy had sat with him in the four-poled conical dome of his tepee, he had listened to Buffalo Run and admitted that he was listening to a history that placed a dark cloud upon his own people.

"Think on this, McCauley!" Buffalo Run had said, waving a hand in the air to create a picture. "It was just eighteen forty-six when your General Kearny took Santa Fe, until then the capital of Spanish and Mexican New Mexico. Navaho raiders stole some of his beef and went on to raid the settlements. Yes, white settlers were killed. Yes, the Navaho stole thousands of sheep, cattle, and horses. But General Kearny began a campaign against the Navaho that ended with over eight thousand of their number becoming prisoners at one of your white forts. Since eighteen sixty-four they still reside there."

"Perhaps it was Kearny's way of warning other tribes that they mustn't raid and steal."

"Perhaps it is his way to trick other tribes into submission. I tell you Mc-Cauley, I have seen the white man's ways. Your people will not be happy until they have annihilated mine."

"Your mother was white," Jeremy reminded him.

Buffalo Run smiled. He was a striking Indian. Despite his white blood, his eyes were an obsidian black, his features strong, bronzed, and clean-cut.

"I have never minded a white woman or child who lives with the *Numinu*," he said, using the Comanche's own term for the tribe. It meant "the people." "They learn our ways and they become one with us."

Jeremy had sat back then, still wondering why Buffalo Run had determined to have him come to his camp. He had been greeted as a friend. Buffalo Run's three wives, two of them sisters and the third a cousin to the other women, had seen to it that he had been brought the best of their buffalo meat, clean water, and a bottle of good Irish whiskey—one that had been traded for or stolen, he didn't want to know which. He was an honored guest, but he was certain that Buffalo Run wanted something.

He did. "I've not brought you here to make promises that you cannot keep, nor can I give you promises when the Comanche are a free people."

"Why am I here?"

"White men in gray uniforms have taken my youngest wife's sister. I have promised to take her in as one of my own. I am a powerful man, able to care for many women."

Jeremy nodded. A Comanche might take as many wives as he desired—and could handle.

Personally, Jeremy was certain that dealing with one vixen was enough.

"I hear that you have acquired a wife," Buffalo Run said.

"Yes." He didn't know why he felt so uncomfortable.

"Eagle Who Flies High tells me that she is a very beautiful woman."

He nodded again. "Yes." He hesitated. "We are expecting our first child."

"May you have a son."

Jeremy refrained from telling Buffalo Run that he did not care if his child were a son or a daughter—he cared only that his child be born alive and that Christa endure the labor with her life and health intact. "Thank you," he told the Comanche chief. "I still don't understand—"

"I want my wife's sister returned to me. I want you to go after the men in gray, and I believe that you will do so."

"Men in gray must be Confederate soldiers. Turned outlaw perhaps," Jeremy said. "I don't know what I—"

"They stole Morning Star," Buffalo Run interrupted, "and I would kill them, but they are armed with the Colt revolvers the Texas Rangers are so fond of using against us. I would lose many men. My braves are not afraid—to die in battle is the honorable way to die and a way to join one's ancestors."

Jeremy understood that. The Comanche believed in an afterlife—but that afterlife was denied men and women who died in the dark, who were strangled, drowned—or scalped. Burial ceremonies were important and sacred among the Comanche, and to die in battle was always the way for a warrior to fall.

"Then—"

"These men also held up the trading post just this side of Indian territory. They killed Joseph Greenley who was your friend, I understand. Eagle Who Flies High followed them. They also attacked a Union pay wagon, and slit the throats of the men who threw down their weapons."

"I would like to find them."

Buffalo Run nodded. "There is more. The men carried off Comanche arrows when they took Morning Star. They have made their acts look like the work of Comanche. They have left these arrows with their victims, and they have scalped the men and cut their tongues from their mouths."

Jeremy nodded again. Buffalo Run had asked him to come to his camp as a gesture of true friendship. He was being given the honor of bringing these men in.

Back in his own tent, he punched his pillow and laid his head back down on it. He could smell the coffee Christa was making. In a matter of minutes she would bring him a cup and he would take it gladly. Maybe they would share it. Then he would have to find a way to convince her to take off her clothing even though it was early morning.

She was coming in. Carrying a tin cup of coffee, just as he had known she would.

She walked to the foot of the bed. He anticipated the light tones of her voice, the rich taste of the coffee, the softness of her flesh.

"You—bastard!" she hissed.

He jumped up just in time to avoid the heat of the coffee spraying over tender parts of his anatomy. The cup nearly hit him on the head.

Her hands were on her hips, her hair was wild, her eyes were a blue glistening fire. She didn't seem to care in the least that she had nearly endangered the prospect of a sister or brother for their unborn child.

"You, you—bastard!" she spat again, furious.

The end of magic, he thought.

Christa had seen the Confederate prisoners.

"Madam, may I suggest you cease," he warned her harshly, "unless you would share their fate?"

"Gladly! Imprison me with them, tie me up, do your worst! How dare you! They are lost, they are beaten, and you would cage them like animals! How dare you! How—"

He jumped to his feet. His hand clamped over her mouth. "Shut up! You test me too far, Christa! All of the camp can hear you when you rage like that, and I won't—not even for you—become the laughingstock of an entire regiment! I have my reasons for what I've done, and I'll be damned if I'm going to endure this outburst before you know what my reasons are. Now, shut up!"

Slowly, warily, he eased his hand from her mouth.

"Yankee bastard!" she hissed out.

He suddenly felt exhausted, worn down by forces he couldn't fight.

"That's right, Christa, Yankee bastard. Then, now, and always. Christa, I am sorry!"

Her eyes were glittering. Were there tears within them? He wanted to put an arm around her, he wanted to hold her close, to explain.

She would never let him touch her now.

She tried to jerk free from him. He held her firmly, clenching his teeth.

Then he freed her.

She turned from him and ran.

Nineteen

*C*hrista hadn't been sure at all how a morning that had begun so gloriously could have darkened so quickly.

She had awakened so relieved to have him back! To have him at her side, his sun-bronzed hand so dark where it lay over the ivory flesh of her hip, his hair-roughened leg casually tossed upon hers. It had felt so good, so sweet, so secure, just to lie with him.

But when she had risen and dressed to start the coffee, she had seen the Confederates.

Someone had rigged together a ramshackle stockade in which to hold the men. There were four of them, worn, thin, tired, and weary looking, still wearing their uniforms. Stunned at the sight of them, she had found herself hurrying toward them.

Private Ethan Darcy had been guarding the group. She knew he was an excellent sharpshooter and could bring down a man or a beast at a tremendous distance. Her heart quickened, and despite herself she felt her temper rising.

Why were they being so cruelly held? There was little over their heads to shield them from the elements. They'd been provided with nothing to sleep on, and they were huddled before a waning fire.

"Mrs. McCauley, you need to be leaving these prisoner fellows alone now," Darcy warned her.

She shook her head at Darcy, studying the men. One wore a captain's insignia, one a sergeant's, and the other two appeared to be privates. She had never seen a sadder-looking group of men, so lean, so hungry-looking. They were the losers of the war, she thought, and they looked it. Emaciated, tattered, pathetic.

"My God!" she whispered. "Why are they being kept here like this? Who ordered this?"

"Mrs. McCauley, maybe you'd better speak with your husband," Darcy told her.

"He's taken the word of an Indian over a southern white boy," the man with the captain's insignia on his shoulders told her. "We're suffering for it, ma'am. Your colonel doesn't seem to know that the war is over."

She moved closer to the man. His beard was unkempt, his hazel eyes were watery. She didn't think that she'd ever felt quite so sorry for a human being, and she suddenly felt ill.

She gasped suddenly. There was the caked blood on the arm of the man's uniform.

"You're injured!" she cried.

He shrugged. "It's just a scratch, ma'am. But I admit, I would take kindly to any small mercy."

Last night, Jeremy had come back. She had been so glad to see him. He hadn't wanted to talk. She had been so glad to hold him. She had lain with him in warmth and ecstasy while he had been doing this to these men. She had been so deceived.

"I'll get the doctor out here," she said. She stared hard at Darcy. "They need better shelter! A warmer fire. What are you doing treating men like this?"

"Mrs. McCauley, we're just keeping a watch on them. We'll be moving into Fort Jacobson sometime very soon, and they'll be taken care of from there."

"I'm going to see to it that these men are treated better now," Christa said firmly.

She turned around to start back to her tent. Darcy called to her softly. "Ma'am, your husband is the one who brought these fellows in. And he was right firm when he did so. I don't think you understand—"

"I don't think that you understand! Jeremy has to treat these men better! The war is over."

"That's not it, ma'am. Mrs. McCauley, he's not going to bend on this matter—"

"Then I'll see to it that certain things are done!" she said firmly.

This time, she left Darcy behind, shaking his head. She clenched her eyes tightly together as agony ripped through her. She had fallen in love with him. She had greeted him with such heat and fever, and all the while these men had stood out here starving and wounded. He had told her that he didn't want to talk.

"Oh, God!"

She stopped in front of her tent, then looked down at the coffeepot and at the fire before it. With shaking hands, she poured coffee into Jeremy's tin mug and stepped back into the tent.

He was so damned comfortable, sprawled out with his long limbs, his skin so bronzed and healthy, his muscles corded and powerful. He was the picture of health.

"You bastard!" she swore and threw the tin. She didn't really intend to scald him; she hadn't really thought about what she was doing at all. Once she had seen the prisoners, she had felt only that somehow he had used her and betrayed her. He had said that the war was over. It was not.

He was up, of course, being too alert and agile a man to lie still while she hurled missiles of coffee at him. Then, of course, he started railing at her like the supreme commander, cold, distant, harsh. Warning her that she had best stop before she share the prisoners' fates.

She wasn't sure exactly what she said. She only knew that she was furious and very hurt. Yes, she would share their fate! She was a Rebel, just like those men. But she had spent the night comfortably, lying with a Yankee.

He shook her and held her in his merciless grip. She felt her teeth chattering in her head. He wouldn't take this rage from her. She could feel the searing anger and strength that radiated so freely from his naked body to hers, and she hated herself again.

How could she care so much? How could she have fallen so completely? How had she ever let him make such a fool of her? How had she loved him?

She couldn't break his hold. He released her at last, and she ran. Ran from his touch, from the strength of his hold. From the heat of him. From wanting him.

When she was free of that touch, she could think again.

She snatched up the coffeepot and a tin mug from her own fire and marched back to the makeshift stockade with it. "Darcy, let me in!" she commanded.

"Ma'am, I don't know—"

"Darcy, I have just come from my husband. Let me in. I've brought coffee. These men need to be warmed. Has it become our policy to sit judge and jury on those who have lost a country? Let me in to tend to these men!"

Darcy, very displeased, did so.

The captain took the coffee cup from her with shaking fingers. He paused to smell the brew before sipping from it, then offered it to the other men. "Thank you, ma'am. Thank you, right kindly. Do I take it you were a southern sympathizer, ma'am, or merely an angel straight from heaven?"

"I'm a Virginian," she murmured, looking to the rest of his band. One of the privates was a boy, no more than eighteen or nineteen.

That hadn't been so young in the last stages of the war, she reminded herself. Drummer boys and buglers far younger had perished. "Where are my manners, ma'am?" the captain said. "I'm Jeffrey Thayer. Sergeant Tim Kidder there, and my privates, Tom Ross, Harry Silvers."

Christa nodded to each of them in turn.

"Why—why are you here?" she asked.

"Some fool Indian told the Union colonel we were guilty of his own outrages!" Thayer said indignantly.

"Don't that beat all?" Sergeant Kidder asked. He'd drained the coffee.

"There's more," Christa said hastily. "I'll get you some food too. And Darcy can stoke up the fire. My God, and your arm, Captain! I'll get the doctor here."

"You are an angel!" Jeffrey Thayer said.

She shook her head. "I don't understand—"

"There's lots of ex-Confederate boys heading south from Texas," Jeffrey told her. "We were on our way to be among them."

"South?" Christa said, confused.

"Right on down to South America. We're going to start a new colony down there, ma'am. A rebel colony. You're right welcome to come now, if you wish. It'll be a place where Yanks don't come and burn down every food source in sight! Where the old ways can live again." He grit his teeth suddenly, clutching his arm. "My, my, but this does hurt."

"Good thing the colonel couldn't aim," the young boy, Tom, said.

She heard a sniff from Darcy. "Don't fool yourself, kid!" Darcy called. "Colonel McCauley hit the captain right where he aimed. If he'd have been aiming differently, the captain'd be pushing up daisies right now."

"Private Darcy!" Christa admonished. She looked up to the sky. It was barely dawn. John Weland would probably still be sleeping. She didn't care. She was going to wake him up. "Captain, I'm going to see about someone to help with your arm."

She started to turn, but he clutched her hand. His eyes were damp, his fingers trembling with emotion. He spoke in a whisper. "Ma'am, we've survived so much fighting. If there's anything you can do to get us out of here, I'd be beholden for life! They're going to hang us for what heathen Indians did. They're going to hang us just because they hate us still. They didn't kill us during the war, so they're going to do it now. Lady, please . . . !"

Shaking, Christa disentangled her hand from his grasp. She couldn't. She didn't have the power to help them escape. And if she did she wouldn't dare.

She closed her eyes, swallowing hard as she remembered the scalp they had found on the butte. The Comanche were savage and brutal. Jeremy couldn't really believe anything they might tell him about someone else! Jeremy had gone to see Buffalo Run. Buffalo Run had surely given Jeremy some lie to make up for an atrocity he had committed himself.

And Jeremy was willing to believe him! Because these men were in gray uniforms!

"I'll get the doctor," she said. She whirled around. As she made her way through the tents, she saw that only a few of the men were beginning to rise.

Jeremy didn't need to worry about men having heard her tirade against him.

They all seemed to have slept through it, she thought wryly. The few who were awake greeted her politely and courteously, making way for her. She reached Weland's tent and hesitated. "John?" she called softly.

"Christa?"

"May I come in?"

He wasn't really dressed, but he had on his long johns and his trousers and suspenders. He lifted the tent flap and let her in.

"Jeremy brought back prisoners—" she began.

"So I heard."

"What?" she said, amazed. "Then, John, why didn't you tend to the wounded man?"

"It was a scratch, or so I heard. He said he just nicked the man to get him to stop."

"He's in pain. Major Weland, please. For me, would you come look at this man's arm?"

A light suddenly seemed to shine in his eyes. Christa thought that he was a lot like Jesse. When it came time to heal the sick, Weland was ready to go.

"Let me get my shirt."

He did so and picked up his surgical bag and followed her out. They walked through the encampment until they came to the stockade at the far edge.

Private Darcy was still standing guard. Christa looked at the landscape beyond them and understood why their precautions against escape could be so lenient.

There was nowhere for the prisoners to go. Not on foot, and not in Comanche territory. With horses, yes, they could escape.

"Go on in, John, please," Christa encouraged him. "I'm going to go to see what I can find for them to eat."

"Sergeant Jaffe will be bringing them something—" Private Darcy offered.

"I want them fed now," Christa said firmly.

She found Jaffe, and to her relief he was already preparing food to be brought to the prisoners. She returned behind him and leaned upon a fencepost, pressing her cheeks against the cool wood as the men ate.

They had been near starving. They ate like animals. Even Doc Weland had stopped his treatment of the captain's arm to allow them to eat. When Jeffrey Thayer had finished, Weland set to bandaging his arm again. When he was done, the doctor stood with Christa while Thayer spoke. "I don't mind dying. Me and my boys, we stood in battlefields so long that death is like a long-lost cousin. But it just beats all that your colonel is going to see to it that we hang for some awful business done by a pack of savage Comanche."

Christa glanced uneasily at Weland. His face looked a little pale too.

"Did you—did you try to explain the truth to my hus—to the colonel?" Christa asked.

With a pained expression, Thayer nodded. "God's my witness, ma'am. I tried. But it seems that savage Buffalo Run has some kind of crazy influence over the man. And we're—"

"What?" Christa pursued.

He shook his head. "Same old story, angel. We're Rebels. A Yankee just can't believe a Rebel."

Christa turned away and walked some distance from the stockade. A second later, she felt a gentle touch on her shoulder. She spun around. It was Weland.

"Are you thinking of helping them escape, Christa?" he asked her.

She started to shake her head. "I—I—"

"Well, I am," he said bluntly.

She gasped.

"Shush!" he warned her quickly. "Come on. Let's get to the med tent. We don't want to be heard."

She stared at him in amazement, at the misery in his eyes, then nodded quickly. He was like Jesse. He couldn't stand the suffering.

And for Weland, the war was over.

She followed him hastily to his tent, nodding good morning to the men they passed, barely daring to breathe. When they reached the medical tent, she burst through the flap and spun around. Weland quickly came in behind her, pouring her a sherry from his stock on his camp desk.

"It's too early in the morning!" she whispered.

"You need it. And keep your voice down!" He began to pace. Christa decided that he was right and she swallowed the sherry down. He stopped pacing and stared at her. She knew that they were both thinking of the scalp on the pole on the butte. How could Jeremy have believed the Comanche over the emaciated men in his stockade?

"What are we going to do?" she whispered.

He sank into a chair. "I could be court-martialed for even thinking this way," he said with a groan.

"Then you can't do anything. I've got to do it."

He looked up at her, studying her. "Christa, you are the only one who can do anything."

Her fingers started to shake. Her knees went weak and she sank down to the foot of his bed. "How, what?"

Weland ran his fingers through his hair. "Well, we should have ridden into

Fort Jacobson today but I think Jeremy planned to camp over, tie up some loose ends with the men, write some dispatches. He should be busy in the headquarters tent all day. Not that they could possibly escape during daylight . . ."

"The dawn?" Christa said.

Weland nodded. "And they'd have a day's rest. Jeff Thayer's arm could heal a bit. They'd have some food in their bellies. What a pathetic lot! How could Jeremy . . ." His voice trailed away and then he looked at Christa guiltily. "I'm sure he had his reasons, of course."

Yes. The men were Rebs.

"I can see to it that some of the horses are tethered near the stockade for the night," Weland continued. "If you could just slip out very early, before dawn, and do something about Darcy."

She nodded. "Distract him?"

Weland nodded. He stood. "It wouldn't be so difficult. Because, you see, it would be impossible for them to escape from here without help, so no one will be worried very much. And when they do escape . . ."

"I won't ever let anyone know that you were involved, I swear it!" Christa promised him fervently.

He shook his head. "You have to play innocent too, Christa."

"I doubt if Jeremy will believe I'm innocent," she murmured.

He slammed his fist against his hand. "But is it the right thing to do?" he demanded suddenly. He answered himself. "It has to be. I can still see that scalp, stretched out, dried . . ."

"Stop, please!"

He swung around. "You must be careful. Very careful. Jeremy will see that you're very upset."

"Oh, he knows that I'm upset," Christa murmured. "I'll just stay away from him during the day. I don't think it will be difficult."

Weland stretched out a hand to her. "Oh, God, Christa! I can't believe that we're conspirators—against Jeremy!"

"I never meant to be!" she whispered.

"Nor I. You mustn't let him suspect, Christa. And you have to keep him in his tent through the night, so that I can casually see that the horses are moved around."

"Yes," she said flatly, staring at him. Keep Jeremy in the tent? They weren't even speaking!

"They will die if we don't help them," he said. "They'll hang."

Christa nodded, her fingers digging into her palm.

She turned and fled Weland's tent, grateful that he was first and always a humanitarian.

It wasn't difficult to keep her distance from Jeremy during the day because it seemed that he had no desire to see her.

She knew that he would be in the headquarters tent all day and that he was busy with correspondence. She tried to spend time with Celia so that she wouldn't stay too near the prisoners, but she couldn't even be near Celia without betraying her emotions.

Jeremy didn't come to their tent for supper. Robert Black Paw informed her that Jeremy was dining with Majors Brooks and Jennings and sent his apologies.

Ah, yes, he was sorry!

The hour grew later and later. She couldn't eat, and she certainly didn't dare sleep.

Keep him in his tent . . .

She couldn't even get him here, she thought.

But as the hour grew very late, she heard him coming back at last. He paused to speak with Robert Black Paw outside their tent, and she went into a sudden swirl of motion. She stripped to the flesh and lowered the lamp to a shadowy, soft glow. Before he entered the tent, she plowed beneath the covers and pulled them to her chin.

She felt his eyes on her when he came in and listened to the movements that had become so familiar. He removed his scabbard and sword, and she heard the clink of metal against his desk. She felt his weight on the bed and heard the soft fall of his boots beside it. Then the sounds were just whispers in the night as he shed the rest of his clothing and crawled into bed beside her. She opened her eyes just a slit, certain that she would find him lying there awake, his fingers laced behind his head, his eyes on the canvas above them.

His eyes were hard on her. He had known she wasn't sleeping.

"Christa, stay away from the prisoners," he warned her.

"I don't want to talk," she told him coldly.

"Christa—"

"I don't want to talk!"

"Well, maybe I do."

"You didn't want to talk last night, I don't want to talk tonight."

Aggravated, he started to toss the covers back and sit up.

But with the covers drawn back he noted her state of nudity and inhaled softly, his eyes riveted to hers. Silver, glittering, they spoke a silent demand.

"I—I said that I didn't want to talk," she whispered. She didn't really know how to play this game.

Yes, she did, she realized. She didn't want to talk. She was furious with him. She was heartsick over what he had done.

But, she realized with the pounding of her heart, that didn't change certain things. She wanted him. Perhaps she was even afraid that it might be the last time she would ever have him. Maybe after tonight, they would never be able to forgive one another.

She had to keep him in his tent.

It was not going to be so hard a task.

"Christa—!" His voice was harsh, rough-edged. She came up quickly, leaning over him, draping the length of her hair about his shoulders and chest. She pressed her lips to his shoulders, sliding the length of her body against him, her breasts brushing the dark hair and muscle of his chest, her body warm against his. She let her kisses fall where they would, her tongue teasing his flesh. She rose against him, her tongue sliding over the small hard peaks of his nipples, sweeping over the muscled structure of his chest. She moved against him again, the softness of her hair brushing where her kiss had just been. She pressed her face against the ripples of his belly, bathing him again with the warmth of her tongue.

She moved lower against him. Nipping at his hip, always allowing the soft flow of her hair to sweep around him. She felt the pulse of him. The powerful trembling of his fingers as they moved into her hair. She heard his tense whisper.

She felt the hard, searing shaft of his desire beneath her, and allowed her touch to fall all around it. Then she took him into her hands, into her caress, and bathed him with the slow, luxurious slide of her tongue.

Impassioned words exploded from him. The force of his desire sent longing and excitement sweeping into her. She gasped at the violence with which he clutched her, lifting her, bringing her atop him, impaling her there.

She could not meet his eyes, could not meet the bold hunger in them. She closed her own and felt him. His fingers curled around her buttocks, guiding her. She gasped, her head falling back as he thrust more deeply into her. The night seemed to take flight, the rhythm exploded, and she became aware of nothing but sensation, the force of her own desire to touch the peak, to reach out and feel the stars cascading, to feel the ecstasy and the splendor he could create.

She rose and rose, soared so high. Yet when she would have cried out, she suddenly found herself beneath him. She was devastated, for he had withdrawn. Then she gasped, feeling the rise of a greater fever as he touched and caressed her. Teased and tormented her flesh, touched her with the searing liquid fire of his kiss, stroked her with the evocative draw and thrust of his fingers and caress. She thought that she would die if the sweet anguish went on any longer, yet just when she reached that point, he was with her again, moving in the darkness, in the night.

And then it came, that honey-sweet explosion of the stars, of the world, of the velvet of the night. Shattering, violent, delicious, leaving her to cling to him while she trembled.

He fell beside her, his arm flung back, his breathing still harsh, his body hot and wet despite the coolness of the night. She closed her eyes tightly, thinking of the depths of her betrayal.

"Christa—" he began anew. The sound of his voice still seemed harsh. She didn't want to hear it! He would chastise her again about the prisoners. She reminded herself that she had to hate him for what he had done, taking sides with Comanche just because the men had been in the Rebel army!

"I don't want to talk!" she said fiercely.

"Damn you—"

"I don't want to talk!"

She heard his teeth grating in the darkness. "Fine. Have it your way, my love. Don't talk!"

And so he said nothing more, but minutes later she felt his hands in the darkness again.

It seemed hours later before he slept. The dawn was finally coming.

Christa bit her lip, threw back the covers, and rose. He stirred, but she turned her back to him, dressing. He knew that she was up.

But he never suspected her of this treachery, she was certain. She washed and dressed and headed out of the tent, looking back.

Her heart seemed to plummet. He lay at rest, his hair a rich dark red against the snow white of the covers, his face so handsomely defined. She stared at the hard, sinewed length of him, and a trembling seized her. How could she lie with him as passionately as she had, and do this?

How could she love him as she did, and do this?

Because he didn't understand. Even Dr. Weland realized Jeremy didn't understand. He had fought men in gray uniforms for so long that he couldn't let it go. He was being deceived by a Comanche. She wasn't doing this to hurt him. She was doing it to save her countrymen.

Christa slipped from the tent.

The rest of the camp lay sleeping. Mist was all around them. She hurried through it to the makeshift stockade where Ethan Darcy was once again on duty in the early-morning hours.

"Good morning, Private Darcy!" she called to him softly, walking over to him. "Don't tell me that they keep you here all day and all night!"

"No ma'am, Mrs. McCauley," he said, watching her warily. "Lennox and Fairfield were on duty before me. We stand guard in shifts."

He turned around, following her. Christa nearly allowed her eyes to widen and betray her as she saw Weland coming up silently behind Darcy. He brought the butt of a gun down hard on Darcy's temple.

Darcy never knew what hit him. He crumpled to the ground.

Christa stared from the fallen soldier to Weland. "Will he be all right?"

"Of course," Weland said softly. "Hurry now. I've the horses around here. Let's free the men."

He hurried around and slipped the slide bolt from the stockade. Jeffrey Thayer stepped out immediately. The others didn't follow.

"Come on!" Thayer commanded.

"I—I ain't going back out into Comanche territory," Tom Ross said.

"It's an order!" Thayer told him.

But Tom Ross was stepping back.

"Leave him!" Weland commanded.

"I—I ain't going either," Sergeant Tim Kidder said.

"Harry!" Thayer barked to the last of his men. "Are you coming or have you turned on me too, boy?"

"I ain't going to turn you in, but I ain't going with you," Harry said.

"I don't understand—" Christa began.

"It doesn't matter, let's just get this going!" Weland said. He caught hold of Christa's arm and led her along with Thayer to the horses. "Ride out with him a ways—if the sentries see you, they won't stop him!" Weland commanded her.

She shook her head. "John, I can't do that—"

She broke off in sheer amazement. He was aiming his gun at her. The same gun he had used to knock Darcy senseless.

"Get up on that horse, Christa," he commanded her.

"John—"

Someone suddenly interrupted them. She heard a low, dangerous voice. "What are you doing?"

She spun around. It was Robert Black Paw. She was never far from his sight, she remembered.

But that wasn't going to help her now. She cried out as Major Dr. John Weland took careful aim and shot the Cherokee scout.

No sound escaped her because Jeffrey Thayer had a bony but powerful hand wrapped tightly over her mouth. "Get her out of here—fast!" Weland ordered. "And see that she doesn't come back. Trade her to the Indians. Strangle her! Just see that she doesn't come back. It's your price for freedom."

Christa bit the hand covering her mouth. Thayer swore savagely, jerking her back against him. "When I get you alone, angel, are you going to pay!" he drawled.

She inhaled for a long, high-pitched scream. It never left her mouth because Weland had aimed his gun at Darcy. "One word, Christa, and I shoot Darcy too!"

Furious, she demanded, "Why? What did I do to you? What did Jeremy do to you?"

Dr. John Weland, her friend through so much, smiled. He tried to stroke her cheek, and she wrenched her head away. "It isn't you, Christa. I really like you."

"Then Jeremy—"

"And it isn't that proud husband of yours, Christa. Pity you wouldn't listen to him. You played right into my hands. I had myself assigned to this division purposely. I've spent months—no, years—planning this revenge. I had a better method of torment devised, but you ruined that."

"I don't know what you're talking about!" she whispered. If she could just stall for time, help might come. She was always being watched.

By Robert. And Robert was bleeding on the ground.

God! What had caused this?

"You married McCauley," Weland said quietly. "I could have had the house. I made a lot of money, putting in with those fool southern blockade runners! Not the noble boys. Fellows like Thayer here who knew how to make a dollar out of a war."

She gasped. "But—why?"

"Jesse Cameron," he said simply.

She was feeling faint. She couldn't begin to comprehend what was happening. The house! That seemed so long ago now. Yet, even when she had been about to lose it, she had been convinced that the enemy must have been Daniel's enemy.

"Jesse?" she repeated, stunned.

"Jesse Cameron," Weland repeated. "The one, the only, the majestic, the wonderful. The great healer, second only to Christ!" He spat on the ground suddenly. "The man given every promotion I should have had."

"You'd kill—because of that?"

His eyes had been distant. Now they were riveted on her. "He was the great healer. Until it came time for him to operate on my little brother. Then your goddamned sainted brother couldn't do a thing. Gerald died screaming on the operating table. They said that he'd been a coward. That he'd been running away from the battle when he was hit. It was a lie. But your brother killed him anyway. He opened him up and he killed him."

"You're wrong!" Christa said. "Jesse would never let anyone die if he could stop it, never, for any reason." She spoke very quickly. "I thought that you were like him! I thought you were a doctor just like Jesse, so concerned with healing! You believed in men's right to live, whether they were red or white or black. You—"

"I thought that seeing Cameron Hall burned to the ground would wound him forever. But this is better," Weland said. "He'll never know what happened to his precious sister. Whether the Comanche have you and rape and mutilate you daily, or whether some renegade, murdering Reb kidnapped you down to

South America to serve his comrades. He'll never know and it will hurt him all his life. It will cut like a knife. I hope he lives a long, long time."

"You're sick—"

"And I'm going to hang with those other fools if I don't get the hell out of here!" Jeffrey Thayer said.

"This is a sick man!" Christa tried to tell him.

"I don't care if he's a raving lunatic! He's set me free. And you're my way out. Let's go!"

"Go with him. Or I'll shoot Darcy right in the head. As a matter of fact, let me get Darcy up on a horse. Then Thayer can shoot him the minute you give him a word of trouble!"

Thayer jerked her around while Weland threw Darcy's prone body over one of the four horses brought for the Rebels' escape.

"Get up!" he commanded her.

She stared at him. "You are a murderer, aren't you?" she asked. "My husband believed the Comanche because the Comanche was telling the truth."

"Get on the horse. I've killed before. But there's a lot I'd rather do to you than kill you, angel. So keep quiet and—"

"I'll see you hang!" Christa promised.

Thayer smiled, the kind of smile that showed her, too late, what kind of man he was.

No matter what the color of his uniform.

"You want that private dead on your account?" Thayer asked, indicating Darcy.

She swallowed hard, then walked to one of the horses and mounted it. She stared at Weland. "They'll hang you too!" she promised.

He lifted a brow complacently. "I won't give a damn."

"Ride, angel," Thayer commanded her.

Just then they heard music. Someone was singing a hymn. "Onward Christian soldiers . . ."

"Christ Almighty!" Weland groaned. "It's that holier-than-thou Brooks woman!"

Mrs. Brooks had come upon them with her Bible, ready to read a sermon to the erring Rebel prisoners, Christa was certain.

Now the plump and proper old harridan stared at them all, openmouthed.

Weland turned, aiming his gun at her. "Mount up, Mrs. Brooks. You're going for a ride."

"Her!" Thayer protested. "Shoot her! Just shoot her!"

"Jesus, no!" Christa cried.

"What in the Lord's name—" Mrs. Brooks began.

"Just mount up! Mount up!" Christa urged her.

"I will not!" Mrs. Brooks said indignantly. "I will not be a part of this treachery—"

"He'll shoot you, Mrs. Brooks!" Christa cried. She leapt down from her own animal, prodding Mrs. Brooks toward one of the mounts. "He'll shoot you!" she hissed, trying to show the woman how serious the look was in Weland's eyes —and Robert Black Paw on the ground, blood oozing from his chest.

"Oh! Oh, Lord Almighty! I'm going to faint—" Mrs. Brooks began.

"Get on a horse!" Christa ordered her. Mrs. Brooks was heavy. With a strength she didn't know she had, Christa boosted her onto one of the horses.

If they could just ride, they could escape Thayer. He'd be on his own without Weland behind them.

When Mrs. Brooks was mounted at last, white-faced and wavering, Christa leapt up on one of the horses again.

"Good-bye, angel," Weland said. He stared at Jeffrey Thayer. "If she survives and comes back, you're a dead man."

Thayer started to laugh. "She'll be with me—until death!" he swore.

He slammed his heels against his horse.

And all four mounts—his, Christa's, and the beasts carrying the unconscious Darcy and the blubbering Mrs. Brooks—began to race across the plain.

The first pink streaks of dawn were just beginning to show on the eastern horizon.

Twenty

*I*t was still dark when he opened his eyes. He didn't stretch his arms out over the covers—he knew that she was gone.

How strange, he thought, to have had a night so sweet and spectacular, and to awaken now, feeling so pained and miserable! She still wouldn't let him speak. She didn't want to hear the truth. She wouldn't believe anything ill of a man dressed in a Confederate uniform.

He punched his pillow bitterly, wishing he could gain just a few more minutes' sleep. But thoughts of her plagued him, and he couldn't close his eyes. He jerked up suddenly. He had heard something. Not Christa. He didn't smell coffee brewing. In fact, he hadn't heard her since she had so silently risen and left the tent.

"Jesus!" he gasped out leaping off the bed, for a bloodied hand was reaching up, dragging the covers off him.

Robert Black Paw, huddled, broken, bleeding, had come to him. Crawled upon his belly to reach him.

Jeremy cried out again, shouting for help. He lifted the Indian scout who had been his friend and companion for so long, trying to find the wound. It was in his chest. Blood was pouring from it. He ripped up the sheets, packing the wound to stop the flow.

"Jeremy—" Robert was trying to speak.

"What the hell happened? My God! Someone get in here—"

Nathaniel rushed in. His eyes opened wide at the sight of Robert, and he exhaled quickly. "I'll get Doc Weland—"

"No!"

Robert found the strength to rise. Shaking his head vehemently, he fell back.

"Clamp down on the wound!" Jeremy ordered Nathaniel, reaching for his clothing. He slipped into his trousers, speaking to Robert at the same time. "Robert, don't die. Damn you now, don't die! I'm going for the doctor—"

"No!" The Cherokee thundered out the word again despite his wound. He beckoned to Jeremy to come close to his lips and he whispered quickly, knowing that his strength was failing him. "Weland—in on it. Something to do with your wife's—brother. Thayer loose. With Christa."

There was blood everywhere. Jeremy felt as if it drained from his body.

"Christa?" he whispered.

Robert's bloodied hand reached for him. "She thought—him innocent. Didn't know. Weland—hurt her." He tried to speak again. He fell silent.

"Robert! Robert, damn you, don't you die!" Jeremy cried.

Nathaniel looked at him. "He's still breathing. If I can just stop the blood—it seems the bullet made a clean hole through him."

"Nathaniel, if you can, save his life!" Jeremy commanded swiftly, reaching for his sword and scabbard and guns. He tore from the tent. Christa!

Damn him, what a fool he had been! Why hadn't he seen it? Yes, she had been furious. She hadn't forgiven him a thing, she hadn't missed him. She'd seduced him to go and set the Confederates free.

But Weland had something to do with it. Why would Weland want to hurt Christa, or Robert? It didn't make any sense.

He passed by one of the young buglers just staggering from his tent. "Call the men to arms!" he commanded quickly. "Get help down to the stockade!"

He rushed on and burst onto a scene he hadn't begun to imagine.

The gate they had so hastily rigged when they'd brought in the prisoners was down. But three of the men remained.

Dead.

Three of the soldiers were strewn about the ground, bright red bloodstains oozing out over the tattered gray of their uniforms.

John Weland stood in front of the stockade, staring at them, shaking his head.

"Jeremy, thank God!" Weland said. "It was the damnedest thing! Christa—I'm sorry, Jeremy, really sorry, but you, well, you know your own wife. She was determined to free these fellows. She got Thayer a gun somehow. Robert came after Christa, and Thayer killed Robert. Then he turned his gun on his own men!"

Jeremy stared at Weland. Everything was going mad here.

And Christa was gone. All that mattered was that Christa was gone. She was heading across the plains with a merciless cutthroat who had killed heedlessly already.

He watched the doctor cautiously. The man he thought he had known.

He strode into the fenced yard where the dead Confederates lay. The first was definitely gone. There was a bullet through his head. He moved onward. The second was dead too. Jeremy didn't think he'd ever seen so much blood. The bullet must have pierced him right through the heart. He moved on. He thought he saw the slightest movement. He knelt down.

It was the sergeant, the man named Kidder. His lips were moving. His eyes opened.

Jeremy could just see Weland through the fence. Weland didn't seem worried.

Because he was innocent?

Because he was certain that the dead could tell no tales?

He leaned closer to the sergeant. The man was whispering. "Your Yank's a traitor, Colonel. The bastard killed me."

A cold shiver ripped through Jeremy. More horrible than anything he had known through all the years of warfare. Weland. He had coldly shot Robert Black Paw and these men.

Why?

He stood, looking at Weland. "I'm sorry, Jeremy, there's nothing I can do for any of them. Or Robert."

"Robert isn't dead," Jeremy told him.

John Weland's eyes flickered. "Not dead? He's right over there on the ground! I found him first. I—" He turned. He saw that the Indian wasn't there. He stared back at Jeremy.

He was caught. They both knew it.

"Well, it really doesn't matter. There's nothing you can do. Thayer will see that she lives and dies miserably."

"Why?" Jeremy cried out incredulously. Weland just stared at him. Jeremy swore suddenly, fists clenched, teeth grating. It didn't matter. It couldn't matter now. What mattered was Christa. He had to find her.

He knelt quickly down to the Reb still breathing. "I'll get help, son."

The boy's eyes opened. He was trying to talk again. "I didn't never want to kill no one, sir, honest. I didn't take the Indian girl and I didn't shoot any cavalrymen at that pay wagon." He moistened his lips. "Thayer is going to head for Texas, so he can get to South America. I couldn't go. Hell, I'd rather be hanged than have the Comanche get me any day." He started to cough. A fleck of blood appeared on his lips.

"I'll get help," Jeremy said.

The boy clutched his hand. "Be careful. Thayer has the man who was guarding us, Darcy." Something almost like a smile touched his bloody lips. "And some battle-ax of a lady who sings psalms."

"Mrs. Brooks?" Jeremy said incredulously.

"That's how Thayer's going to keep your wife in line. She—she didn't know, sir. She just thought that we were ex-Rebs, unfairly treated."

Jeremy nodded. "Don't talk anymore. The men will see to you." He started to rise.

"Watch it, Colonel!" the young sergeant cried.

He swung around. Weland was at his back, his gun aimed. Jeremy instinctively reached for the Colt at his side. Even as he fired, he felt the flesh tear at his arm.

John Weland had missed his target.

Jeremy didn't.

He walked across the stockade yard. Weland was on the ground, dead, his eyes wide open and staring. Jeremy still didn't understand.

He looked up. Men were filing out. He saw Lieutenant Preston. "Saddle up, Company D! Five minutes, men," Jeremy commanded. "James—get Morning Star to ride with us. And somebody, dear God, get some help for this poor Reb!"

He strode past them, anxious to reach his horse.

Dear God, Christa was out there somewhere, in Thayer's hands.

They rode desperately hard until Thayer realized he would kill the horses if he pushed them any further. By then, Darcy was just beginning to come around, and Mrs. Brooks was finding her voice once again.

Jeffrey Thayer gave them all fair warning. "I need the whole set of you right now. If the cavalry starts closing in again, I can drop you back one by one and buy myself a little time. Except for you, angel," he told Christa, smiling. "You come with me. All the way."

"You're out of your mind," she told him.

He aimed his Colt, another gift from Weland, straight at her heart. "What? Have you lost your devotion to your cause? Angel, you were willing enough before!"

"I was willing to see you freed instead of hanged when I thought you were an innocent man," she told him.

"Honey, we had some fun with one little Indian maid. And I killed a few Yanks. Hell, I killed them by the dozens during the war. What difference does a few months make?"

"A world of difference," Christa told him. "You are nothing but a murdering bastard."

He grinned. "You'll get to like me. I like you. And I'm going to like you a whole lot more."

"Take her! Just take her!" Mrs. Brooks cried out. "We're far from camp now. Just leave me here alone, and I'll tell her husband that she wanted to go with you, she's always been a Rebel, she'll always be a Rebel, so take her, and the devil can have the two of you—"

"Mrs. Brooks!" Darcy cried feebly. Christa ignored both Mrs. Brooks and Jeff Thayer and turned her attention to Darcy. They had stopped by a creek to get water for themselves and for their horses. She ripped up her petticoat and soaked it and came over to bathe Darcy's face. "Jesu, Ethan, I'm sorry!" she whispered.

He caught her hand. "Weland hit me?"

She nodded.

"Why?"

"It's a long story."

"Come on, you're taking too long!" Thayer warned them. "I want to get started again. You, Miss Christa-belle, one false move and I put a hole the size of Richmond through the Bible bitch or your Billy Yank, understand? And you—" he warned Darcy. "No heroics. Or the noble little Reb gets to ride and bleed at the same time."

They all mounted up. Darcy looked woefully at Christa. "He has to sleep sometime!" he whispered hopefully to her.

She nodded. Would they get to that?

They started out, riding hard once again. They reached an outcrop of rock. To Christa's surprise, Jeff Thayer suddenly seemed uneasy.

She began to feel it herself. The sensation of being watched.

She turned around. Her heart flew to her throat.

They *were* being watched.

Atop the ridge behind them, silent as statues, Indians had appeared. Six of them. Painted in red, some bare-chested, with designs upon their flesh. All armed with rifles or bows and arrows and incredibly long lances, decorated with feathers and . . . scalps.

"That son of a bitch! Buffalo Run! He had McCauley followed, wanting to make certain the Yank executed me!"

"What are you talking about?" Christa demanded, staring at him.

"If you've got an extra gun," Darcy said, "for the love of God, give us all a chance—"

"You're on your own!" Thayer shouted. He spurred his horse cruelly. The animal leapt into the air, then started to race. The other horses, without cue from their riders, did the same.

Terrified, Christa leaned low against her horse's neck, praying as the dirt of the plain flew up at her.

To no avail. She sensed the colors of the horse and men at her side long before she heard the first wild war whoop. Her horse was forced to the side, slowly made to come to a halt as the Comanche rode a circle around her.

Darcy and Mrs. Brooks were being held in the same circle, she realized.

Jeffrey Thayer was not within it.

She stared in front of her, awed and horrified.

The ex-Reb had been forced from his mount. He tried to shoot the Indian bearing down on him.

Thayer screamed. The Indian's lance went thrusting through his middle, followed by a rain of arrows.

Each Comanche had shot at the man. The arrows pierced him. His legs, his arms. His eyes. Yet sounds were still coming from him.

An Indian knelt down beside him. Thayer was still barely alive. The Indian began to cut away the man's scalp.

Mrs. Brooks began choking and gagging. Behind Christa, she was sick. Even Darcy let loose with a little sound of terror.

Christa was too horrified herself to make a sound or to move.

The last of the Indians mounted up again. She instinctively slapped her reins over her horse's shoulder. The horse bucked and bolted and started to race once again.

But before many minutes had passed, a Comanche was riding at her side, their horses brushing sides.

He leaned over and was almost off the horse he was riding. He reached out for her, grabbing her while his animal eased into a canter. Christa cried out, grasping for something to hang on to.

Comanche could bring about a terrible death, she knew. She had just witnessed one, and death could be worse out here. But instinct assured her that she would not be trampled to death beneath the horse's hooves.

She needn't have feared. Her Comanche captor did not intend to release her. He was a strong man and rode his horse effortlessly, keeping her atop it as he did so. The animal raced across the plains easily, and it seemed to Christa, forever. She was not alone, though. Other Comanche had seized Mrs. Brooks and Darcy.

She thought about the way Jeffrey Thayer had died. Then she thought about Weland. She still couldn't grasp how the man, after failing in his effort to take

Cameron Hall and burn it, had managed to get himself assigned to Jeremy's regiment.

Jeremy! She had betrayed him. She might lead Jeremy to death, and she definitely might kill their child.

She had already been hungry and weakened from her sleepless night of love-making. The constant slap of her body against the animal and the roughness of the endless ride quickly sapped what little strength she had left. During the long harsh ride, she must have blacked out.

Such a merciful condition! It ended too soon. She came to as she was dragged from the haunches of the horse, warm brown hands powerful and insistent upon her. She struggled to free herself from the hated touch of the warrior, staggering as she tried to swirl away. A choked cry escaped her as he reached for her, dragging her back, tying her hands together with rope. Another of the braves came up to the warrior she faced, saying something to him in his own language.

Furious and terrified, Christa lashed out. "You wait! You just wait until the cavalry comes. They'll slice you into little pieces! They'll fill you with bullet holes. They won't leave enough for the buzzards to eat!"

To her amazement, the Indian smiled. He spoke to her in perfect, unaccented English. "Will the cavalry come for you, do you think? Why would they think to rescue you—when you were so determined to free a murderer?"

She gasped, blinking. He knew that she had freed Jeff Thayer.

"My—my husband will come," she responded quickly. Maybe she was wrong, but she was determined to defy this Comanche. "You have taken another man's wife as well—"

She broke off. The other Comanche was saying something in his own language again. The one she faced started to laugh.

"What?" she cried out, wanting it to be a demand but feeling her knees shake.

"My friend has suggested that this other woman's husband might pay us a ransom not to return her."

Mrs. Brooks was still carrying on, screaming, crying, screaming again. Christa couldn't blame her. She felt much like doing the same herself.

When their captives made too much noise, Comanche sometimes cut out their tongues.

"Let her go, then!" Christa suggested suddenly. "Let her go back to camp. Maybe they won't come after you then. Maybe—"

"Your husband will come," the Indian said flatly. "I know him, and he will come. And then we shall see."

"You know my husband," she murmured. Of course. It all made sense, the fact that this Comanche spoke English so well. "You're Buffalo Run."

"I am."

She remembered Jeffrey Thayer's curious words just before he had been killed.

"This party—did you ride out to see that Thayer was—killed by the whites?"

He indicated one of the other warriors. "It was Eagle Who Flies High's war party. He advised and I listened, and he was right. Your husband has never betrayed me. But it seems you have betrayed him."

He turned and the rope he held jerked her along. She nearly tripped but was determined not to cry out. This was different from what she had expected. This man understood her. She felt that he was still the worst savage she had ever come across, but he did speak her language. There was hope that he might reason.

Yet what did she have to reason with? He knew the truth that was so horrible to face herself.

He jerked upon the rope, then caught her when she nearly tripped a second time. "You're carrying his child?" he said.

"Yes!" she said swiftly. "Yes!" Would that buy her some mercy from this man?

He grunted and turned again. He walked her to a brook of fresh running water and released her leash long enough to allow her to drink. She was desperately thirsty, yet even as she drank she tried to think of some manner of escape.

He didn't intend to allow it. He caught hold of the rope again and, dragging her along with him, tethered her to a tree near the water. Then he left her, conferring with the other warriors. She waited miserably, her back to the tree, her wrists chafing before her. They had ridden most of the day. Now there was minimal light, for beneath the moon they had lit only one fire. She determined that they had decided to camp there that night under the stars.

What was to be her fate, she wondered.

Dear God, she didn't want to think about it.

Some instinctive numbness in her mind kept her from it. Oddly, she had nearly dozed again when Buffalo Run approached her, offering her a dried strip of meat. She was starving and she took it from him, not caring in the least that she should, perhaps, have clung to her pride and refused anything from the Indian. He watched her eat. As he did so, she suddenly heard a screaming again.

Mrs. Brooks.

The dried meat stuck in her throat. She looked at the Indian. "Don't kill her. Dear God, please don't kill her!"

"Because she is your cherished friend?" he inquired politely. She knew that the Comanche was mocking her.

"Because it will be my fault if you do kill her," she said honestly.

"They are not killing her," he said.

He did not tell her what they were doing to her—that was left to Christa to wonder, and she did so wretchedly.

He rose and watched her again beneath the moonlight. He was very tall, far taller than the other Comanche warriors. His eyes were dark, his hair long and smooth and almost ink black. His face seemed a little bit narrower than some of the other braves and Christa remembered that Buffalo Run was a half-breed.

Not in his heart, she realized. In his heart, this man was all Comanche.

"Are you going to kill me?" she asked him.

"Not tonight," he told her, and turned and walked away.

Mrs. Brooks's screams slowly faded. The Indians talked around their fire for a long while. Christa wondered what Jeremy was thinking, what he was feeling. She leaned her head back with misery. He had to hate her for what she had done. She had been so self-righteous about the poor wounded cavaliers of the Confederacy that she hadn't had the sense to realize that there were rotten apples in the ranks of Rebels.

And she hadn't given Jeremy the least opportunity to explain anything about his captives. Now she knew, and knew too late. Jeremy had taken the men instead of allowing the Comanche to take them. Jeff Thayer had played upon her sympathies and made a fool of her.

She couldn't hate Jeff Thayer for what he had done. She couldn't hate anyone who had died the way that he had. She could only despise herself for her stupidity.

Jeff Thayer had paid the ultimate price.

Oh, God! There had been Robert Black Paw! Ever there for her and for Jeremy. Teaching her and caring for her.

Dying for her.

"Oh, please God!" she whispered. She could well die herself.

She couldn't die. Not with the baby. But she didn't feel any movement, and she thought of all that had happened in the last twenty-four hours. She prayed that she hadn't killed her child.

Jeremy's child.

If only she had managed to tell him that she loved him! If only she hadn't been so proud, so stubborn.

She might have listened to him. She might have seen the truth.

She lowered her head, fighting the great wash of tears that threatened to cascade from her eyes. She had fallen in love with him, but she had been too proud to forget her past, and too proud to give either of them a real chance. Now she might never see him again.

And she had, perhaps, cost him another child.

He will come for you, Buffalo Run had told her. Was that the truth? Did the hostile savage know her husband better than she did herself?

Perhaps Buffalo Run couldn't begin to understand that her husband had never courted her, that she had forced him to marry her for a house, for bricks and stone and wood, for something that meant nothing out here. She hadn't even been willing to meet him halfway, not until something had turned somewhere within her heart, not until she had discovered that she could do nothing other than admire him, respect him, and love him.

Perhaps he would come. Perhaps his honor would dictate that he must. Perhaps he would come for their unborn child.

And perhaps, her heart seemed to whisper, perhaps he would even come for her!

But if he came, would he be risking his own life? What was he thinking at this moment? Was he hating her for what she had done? Thinking that she had brought this upon herself and that she deserved whatever happened to her? Was he missing her?

"Dear God, Jeremy! I'm sorry, so sorry!" she whispered out loud. "I love you, loved you. I—"

It didn't matter. It was too late.

Twenty-one

eremy dismounted from his horse and knelt down by the bloodied and battered body on the ground. It didn't take more than a few seconds, despite the condition of the corpse, to recognize the Confederate Jeffrey Thayer. His gray coat was blood spattered and stuck with a half-dozen arrows. The man's face had been slashed, his scalp expertly taken.

Jeremy felt his muscles tensing, the whole of his body quickening with anguish.

He no longer had to fear what the ex-Reb planned to do with Christa. Jeffrey Thayer wouldn't be doing anything with anyone ever again.

"Comanche?"

Jeremy turned. Jimmy Preston was watching him unhappily.

Jeremy nodded. "Search—" he began. He had to pause. In his heart he had to believe that the Indians wouldn't harm Christa. "Search the area for other bodies," he said. James stared at him, swallowed hard, then turned around and called out the order.

Company D dismounted from their horses. Jeremy walked across the dry plain and stared across it. Buffalo Run, he thought. He'd come to see if the whites were going to handle the matter of the murdering Reb.

Buffalo Run had taken down Thayer himself.

"You fool!" he hissed to the body of the dead man. He wanted to feel compassion for any man so brutally killed. But Thayer had murdered unsuspecting, innocent men. Red men, white men. He had, perhaps, come to his just reward.

"And you used my wife, you goddamned son of a bitch!" he swore savagely, fighting the temptation to kick the corpse.

"There's no sign of anyone else," James reported to him.

"Not Darcy, or Mrs. Brooks?"

"Or Christa," James said quietly.

Jeremy stared off across the plain. "It was Buffalo Run, then," he said.

"There are many bands of Comanche," James warned him.

"But only Buffalo Run would kill Thayer this way and take the others." He was quiet a moment, then said, "I'm going to have to go to him alone."

"My God, you can't go alone! You could run into other hostiles and get killed before you reach him."

"You'll accompany me with Company D until we reach the outskirts of his camp," Jeremy said.

"Even then—"

"James, if I were to take the whole regiment against him, it would be an even match. The death toll would be terrible. And the Comanche might kill the captives immediately on principle. If I go alone, I've got a chance. I won't be entirely alone," he said. "I'll have Morning Star."

"Colonel, sir!" one of the men called.

Jeremy looked back at the twenty-three enlisted men of Company D.

Private Jenkins was staring at him awkwardly. "Do we bury him, sir?"

Jeremy's throat seemed to constrict. He'd tricked Christa, and Jeremy had been too damned angry and proud to try to explain things. God knew just how far Thayer intended to go with her.

Let the buzzards eat the man! Jesu, he was in anguish! He knew the Comanche well. And he knew Christa well. Don't fight Buffalo Run, Christa, don't fight him.

And please God, don't let him hurt her.

"Sir, do we bury him?"

"Dammit, yes, go ahead. Hurry, we've got to ride!"

There was so much at stake. They had to make haste. He was responsible for Darcy and Mrs. Brooks. He had to reach the Comanche before they could kill any of their captives.

He could die going for Christa. But if he couldn't bring her back, he didn't know if life would be worth living. He had been in love before, but he had never known the passion of emotions he felt for Christa. Perhaps they were like the pieces of the country, torn and bruised, suffering bitterly for all that they had done to one another. Yet nothing but broken fragments without one another. He had married her under duress, but nothing in the world could have forced him to do so if he hadn't been willing somewhere in his heart. He had been determined to bring her with him, to demand that their marriage be whole. He had forced her to live it. In his way, he had tried to give her life. And she had given it to him in return.

Night was coming in all around them.

He looked to the darkening sky. Against the night were curious, winged shapes. Buzzards were circling over him. They'd been seeking a meal of Thayer. He prayed that he would not see them circling in the sky again.

He leapt up on his horse and shouted to James. "Let's ride!"

They would have to stop soon enough. The Comanche before them would have to stop in the ebony darkness too.

In the morning, Buffalo Run untied her and directed her down through a scruff of trees and foliage to a narrow creek below them. For a moment she felt the incredible wonder of her freedom, then realized that her hands were still tied together before her and that he had given her freedom only to perform the most necessary of human tasks. Yet as she came along the trail, she caught her breath, trying not to make a sound. She had come upon Private Darcy.

Like her, he had been bound to a tree. She wondered why they hadn't killed him yet, then she feared that he was dead, and she wondered why they hadn't taken his scalp. His eyes opened, slowly, miserably. He saw her. It looked as if he was going to cry out, but Christa shook her head, turning around to look at the camp.

The Indian braves were gathered around the fire. It seemed that they were exchanging stories about their exploits.

For the moment, she and Darcy were not noticed.

Christa quickly moved into the shadow of the tree and knelt down by Darcy.

Trickles of blood had hardened along his neck. She bit her lip. "Are you injured so that you can't rise, walk, or ride?"

His eyes, filled with pain and weariness, found hers. He shook his head. "They nicked at my ears and scratched my throat. They know how to keep a captive alive and in pain and terror a very long time," he told her.

Christa, with her hands bound together, struggled with the knots that held him to the tree.

The Comanche also knew how to tie very good knots, she realized. Her fingers began shredding before the rope did. Darcy started talking swiftly. "Pull up my pant leg. There's a small sheath at my ankle and I think my knife is still in it."

It was awkward, the way that she was tied, but Christa found the knife and managed to pull it out. A fine sheen of perspiration broke out on her forehead despite the coolness of the morning. She managed to balance the knife between her hands, and in a matter of minutes she had Darcy freed.

He leapt to his feet, quickly cutting her bonds. "We might have just signed your death warrant," he said.

"And yours."

"I was already a dead man," he assured her. "We've got to get horses."

"And Mrs. Brooks!" Christa said.

He stared at her as if she had lost her mind. "And Mrs. Brooks," he said.

She looked back up the trail. The horses were to the left of the fire and small encampment. Mrs. Brooks was somewhere to the far rear.

"You go for the horses," Christa told Darcy. "I'll go for Mrs. Brooks."

"If she opens her mouth just once," Darcy warned her. "Leave the old witch!"

Christa nodded. She slipped around the trail. Apparently, the Comanche seemed assured that their captives weren't going anywhere. The six braves remained around the fire, and though Christa couldn't understand a word that they were saying, she found them surprisingly similar to their white counterparts, probably telling tall tales around a campfire.

Mrs. Brooks had been very quiet during the morning, and Christa felt a surge of fear rise to her throat. The Comanche had cut out her tongue.

But when she found the woman, her eyes were closed. And she had been silenced with a gag made out of her petticoat. Christa, with Darcy's little knife, began sawing at the ropes that bound her to her tree. The woman awakened, her eyes flying open in terror. Christa pressed a finger to her lips.

For once in her life, Mrs. Brooks had the very good sense to keep silent.

Christa reached down for the woman. It seemed for several minutes that Mrs. Brooks wasn't going to find the strength to stand, she wavered so. "Please!" Christa whispered to her. Mrs. Brooks seemed to realize that they were dealing with life or death. She had no remonstrations for Christa; she looked at her with eyes as appealing as a child's.

"Come on. Quietly. Carefully."

She led the woman the long way around the braves once again, feeling as if she died a little with every step. They reached Darcy, who had untethered three of the horses. Between them, she and Darcy lifted Mrs. Brooks onto one of the horses before leaping atop mounts themselves. Darcy loosed the others from their tethers so that the horses would be gone when the Indians came after them.

Darcy swallowed hard and nodded to her. They broke away from the group slowly and carefully.

Then Darcy cried, "Ride!"

As if the flames of hell themselves were in pursuit, the three slammed their heels against their Indian mounts. Darcy knew his way, and Mrs. Brooks and Christa followed. She didn't know just how long they had ridden before she heard a cry behind them.

The Comanche were alerted at last.

Darcy leaned low over his horse and looked at Christa. The expression on his face warned her that they were all dead.

She looked back. Only three of the Indians were following them. Only three had managed to recapture their horses after Darcy had loosed them.

"Split!" she cried to Darcy.

"Jesu, Christa, no!" he warned her frantically.

But there was no choice. They could all die. Or she could lead the Comanche away. They might follow her.

They would kill Darcy now. Maybe they wouldn't kill her.

She reined in slightly and quickly before she could lose her courage. Darcy and Mrs. Brooks went racing by her. She turned toward a more northerly course and slammed her heels against her horse.

She raced the beast cruelly. Her heart beat with the same awful rhythm as that of the horse. Dirt and dust spewed up around her, yet despite the terrible pounding of her horse's hooves, she felt the tremor of the ground when another mount came in pursuit.

She turned slightly.

The Indians were in pursuit of her. One of them was nearly upon her. She could ride, and ride well, but the man coming after her was surely one of the most talented horsemen on the plains.

Buffalo Run.

She cried out as he bore down upon her. When he reached for her, she was certain that she was dead, for he would send her spilling down to the earth at their frantic pace.

But he did not. He pulled her from the horse and across his own, slowing his gait. In moments they walked. He made a curious sound with his tongue against his palate, and in a few minutes the other racing horse returned to him.

Miserable, beaten, Christa lay across his horse tasting dirt, animal hair, and sweat.

Buffalo Run's horse began a jolting trot. In another few minutes they were back with the other Indians. Buffalo Run shoved her from his horse and she fell into the dirt. She scrambled quickly to her feet, looking around. She was surrounded by Indians.

There was no sign of Darcy or Mrs. Brooks. The two had escaped.

Because Buffalo Run had come for her. She had gambled, and she had been right. She was the greater prize.

She backed away uneasily because the Indian was coming for her. He struck her hard on the cheek and she fell to the dust once again, reeling from the blow. He reached down a hand for her. She tried to shimmy away from him in the dirt, but he caught hold of her firmly, jerking her to her feet. He called out an order to the other men, then lifted her over his horse. They still had plenty of mounts, their own six Indian horses, hers, and Jeffrey Thayer's mount. But they weren't trusting her to ride alone anymore.

They started out slowly, allowing the horses a chance to breathe.

Buffalo Run rode behind her, a creature composed of flesh and steel, she thought dully.

"Are you going to kill me now?" she asked him.

"Not yet."

"Jesu!" she breathed out. "Then let me go!"

"It's never that simple. Not with the Comanche. Has no one warned you?"

Yes, she had been warned!

"Why don't—"

"You not only cost me two horses and two captives, you nearly killed the animal you rode so hard and those we rode to catch you!"

"Then—"

"I may still kill you!" he warned her. "And I may cut you up in bits and pieces to feed to the buzzards first."

"Yes, I cost you two captives!" she informed him, thinking herself a fool. "And two horses. And nearly four more! So do what you will—"

"The horses truly grieve me," he said roughly. "And if you wish to keep your tongue in your head, keep it still!"

"My husband will come for you. He will cut you into little bits and pieces!"

"Shut up."

"The cavalry will—"

"I will slice your tongue out myself if you do not take care!"

He meant it, she knew. A trembling seized hold of her.

Jeremy! She would never be able to tell him that she loved him.

"Please!" she began.

"One more word and it will be your last!" he said.

So warned, Christa fell silent.

The whole of Company D was still riding with Jeremy when he looked across the rolling plain to see the two riders.

He saw them from quite a distance at first, and he had to blink to assure himself that they were appearing before him. Because his vision was very sharp or perhaps because of instinct, he knew right away that the riders were connected with him, and he called out a warning to James. He then spurred his horse and went racing over the plain. There were only two. Mrs. Brooks and Darcy.

His disappointment when he neared the two—who had broken into a gallop at the sight of him—was difficult to conceal, and he swallowed it down with bitterness. He didn't have much chance to speak as he dismounted from his horse, for Mrs. Brooks threw herself into his arms, screaming and talking gibberish all at once and sounding something like a Comanche herself.

Darcy was far clearer.

"It's Buffalo Run, sir, I'm certain—"

"Christa!" he said hoarsely. "Darcy, where's my wife?"

"I know she felt responsible, sir. And I don't think that the Indian knew quite what he had on his hands. He loosed her to go to the stream. She managed to free me and go back around for Mrs. Brooks. Then we all started to race out of there but the savages were on our heels. Mrs. McCauley suddenly cried out that she was going to split up and I couldn't stop her, sir. She knew that they'd let us go and follow her. Sir, you don't know the half of it! Colonel, Doc Weland went mad on us! If he's still back there, he's dangerous, sir. He—"

"He's dead," Jeremy said flatly.

His heart sank. Christa was still with the Comanche. She had caused trouble and Buffalo Run had caught up with her again. She might still be fighting him.

No, Christa, no. They'll hurt you! I've warned you about the Comanche. I don't know if he'll remember that he's my blood brother or not, or if he'll see only that I was responsible for Thayer and that he was riding free. Christa, don't fight him.

Move, fool, he warned himself. He was still at the very least a day's ride from the encampment. Time might well be of the essence.

He turned to James, thrusting the wailing Mrs. Brooks upon his lieutenant. "I'm going on alone from here. I can ride faster."

"It's dangerous territory—"

"It's Buffalo Run's territory. If he sees me coming in with a company, he might decide to slaughter us all, and that will do Christa no good."

"We can go back for reinforcements," James said.

Jeremy shook his head. "If they were to see us coming, they might kill Christa and any other captives on the spot. We might annihilate half of them, but they'd do a damned good job on us too. I've no right to risk the entire regiment, although I'd do so if I thought it would save her life. But it won't. I have to go in alone. I have to bargain with Buffalo Run."

"Colonel, sir, I'll come with you—" Darcy began.

"Darcy, I guarantee it—you'd be a dead man. You and Mrs. Brooks hurry straight back to the encampment."

"Yes, sir, but I'd be willing to come with you, just the same. She was the bravest woman I ever saw, Colonel."

"She's a Reb," Jeremy said softly. "She learned how to fight with some of the best." He mounted his horse once again. "James, you're in command here. Bring them all back. Jennings is in command at the encampment. He knows to move the men into the fort."

James swallowed hard. "If you find her, sir—"

"If I find her, I'm going to do my best to convince her that the fighting is over," he said. He tipped his hat to the company.

He turned away from them and rode on alone, only the Comanche girl, Morning Star, following behind him.

Twenty-two

They came to Buffalo Run's encampment late that afternoon. It was a curiously peaceful sight. Perhaps two dozen tepees were set up along a slowly moving stream. Children were at play in the water and dogs roamed the camp. Women dressed in cotton shirts, skirts, and buckskin clothing were busy with their tasks, some sewing skins with large bone needles, some at work with what looked like mortars and pestles, and others working on skins that were strung across long frames by the sides of the tepees.

As they moved into the encampment, an old Indian with a broad, brown, and heavily leathered face came toward them, a wool blanket about his shoulders, his still pitch-black hair hanging in braids down his back.

Buffalo Run spoke to the old Indian with deference. The old man nodded, observed Christa where she sat before Buffalo Run, and nodded again. He raised his hands and spoke. The women, who had come running in when they had seen the braves returning, now milled around.

"Now you are with the Comanche!" Buffalo Run told her. He lifted her and set her down in the midst of the women.

They began shouting and poking at her. Some of them carried sticks. She tried to back away but she was encircled by them. She swirled, trying to see her tormentors, shouting at them in return.

There was a white girl among them, a long scar down the side of her left cheek. The lobes of her ears were missing. But whatever torture she had met at the hands of the Comanche, she was one with them now, shouting at Christa. She shoved at Christa so hard that she fell.

Christa rose and turned around. A very tall Comanche woman had joined in with the tormenting. Her eyes were obsidian dark, her words a singsong with a curious roll to the R's that was almost melodic.

Christa nearly fell again, her knees shaking horribly, when she saw the newly arrived, tall Comanche woman.

She, too, had been mutilated. The tip of her nose had been clipped off. It seemed to have made a very vicious woman of her. While the others chanted and laughed and poked at Christa, the clip-nosed squaw struck her again and again with her pointed stick. Christa cried out, trying her best to fight off the woman.

There was a sudden, sharp roar of command. The women backed off. Christa found herself facing Buffalo Run again as he walked into the melee surrounding her. He called out orders and the women melted away, murmuring. Buffalo Run took her by the arm, shoving her into a tepee. She stumbled into it, then gained her balance, swirling back around, ready to face him. She was dizzy, and so terrified. All of the things that had been told to her about the Comanche came bubbling to the front of her mind.

She backed against the rear of the tepee, watching Buffalo Run warily. It was horrible to be so terrified, to be living with such terrible images of death in her mind, and to know that she had to keep some sense of dignity about her or lose all hope for a future.

"All right, we're here now!" she said. She wanted her words to be so commanding! They were barely a whisper. After all, she had seen Jeff Thayer die. "What are you going to do with me?" she demanded.

He smiled, arms crossed over his chest. "You think that we are an exceptionally savage people, do you?"

"Yes," she admitted flatly. "There is a Comanche woman out there with most of her nose cut off. She is one of your own. What should I think?"

"Basket Woman knew the consequences. It is the Comanche way."

"The way for what?"

"She lay with another warrior."

Adultery. It carried a heavy fine, Christa thought.

"You are savage to your captives!" she whispered.

"The white man has been savage to us," he replied. "But perhaps we're not the worst of the tribes," he said, walking around the low-burning fire in the center of his tepee. "The Pawnee have an interesting ceremony—carried out with a captive man or maiden. It is a religious ceremony, a sacrifice to the god Tirawa. The Pawnee may take many captives and welcome all but one into their tribe. That one captive is given the finest food; if it is a man, women are sent to dine with him. He is treated with the most respect and deference. But then he is taken naked and tied to cross poles. The Pawnee who captured him shoots an arrow through him, in his one side, out his other side, while a fire is lit beneath him. Every male in the tribe then shoots an arrow into him, and the fire builds until he is burned to cinders. The tribe prays to Tirawa, especially the warrior who took the captive, so that he knows that a human life was taken. When this is done, the tribe has good fortune with its crops and does well in its wars. The captive can be a woman. The Pawnee hate to sacrifice their own. Perhaps I could trade you for many horses!"

"You're not going to give me to the Pawnee," she said. "And if you are going to kill me, why don't you get it over with?" Christa asked. She wasn't going to be able to stand much longer.

"We are masters of torture," he told her.

She heard a soft voice speak suddenly, the R's rolling, the whisper very gentle. She spun around and saw that a young Indian woman was curled down on a bearskin bed against the edge of the tepee. She hadn't been sleeping, she had been waiting, sewing a shirt, and she watched now.

Buffalo Run answered her angrily at first, then seemed to soften. He looked back to Christa. "My youngest wife, Little Flower," he said. "You will serve her and do as she says. It was her younger sister, Morning Star, who was taken by the outlaw soldier."

"What?" Christa asked quickly.

"The white man we killed kidnapped and raped Morning Star, Little Flower's sister, whom I meant to take for my fourth wife. They also killed the cavalry soldiers guarding a pay wagon and a white trader called Greenley. He deserved to die."

He turned and started to leave the tepee.

"Wait!" Christa cried out, and she was startled by the plea in her voice, and then more startled that he seemed to hear it and take pity upon her. He paused and turned back slowly.

"I—I didn't know. I didn't know until it was too late what kind of a man Thayer was. I'm sorry that he hurt Morning Star."

Buffalo Run grunted.

"Please—what is going to happen to me?" she asked.

"That we will see."

"But I—"

He seemed to relent, just barely. "You are my captive," he told her. "Because you are my blood brother's woman, I have already granted you mercy. The women will leave you be. You will serve Little Flower. And if you do not anger me, then you will live—until your fate is decided."

"And that—"

"That will depend!" he said angrily.

"On—?"

He walked toward her. She forced herself not to shrink back. "It will depend on McCauley, and it will depend on you. If McCauley dies, perhaps I will take another wife, if Little Flower and the others find you acceptable. Then, perhaps we will sell you to the Apache or the Spaniards—when we are done with you. It is not decided."

He turned and left the tepee.

Christa, aware of the Indian girl but heedless of her, gasped in a breath of air. She could stand no longer. She sank to the ground.

To her amazement, she felt a very gentle hand touch her hair. "You needn't fear," the girl said. Christa looked up. Her eyes were huge and dark and expressive. Her English was far more hesitant than Buffalo Run's, but it was very good. "Buffalo Run does not like to hurt captives. He is against some of our ways."

Christa looked at the girl and swallowed hard. "I just saw women out there who—"

"The white girl was not his captive. And Basket Woman was not his wife."

She needed to take comfort in that, Christa thought. She needed to take comfort from anything that she could—it was the only way she would maintain her sanity.

Little Flower, she thought, studying the Indian. The name was fitting, for she seemed as gentle and tender as the petals of a rose, as soft, as beautiful. Christa was amazed to realize that she was still discovering all that had really happened.

"I am really so sorry that your sister was hurt. Is she—is she all right now?"

"I don't know. She had strayed from her work by the stream. We found the basket of clothing she had been washing. We found some of her things, torn from her. But Morning Star was missing. Perhaps McCauley found her. We don't know."

"He will think I deserve to be hurt!" Christa murmured.

"He will be patient. He will not let others hurt you," Little Flower said.

Christa hugged her knees and shivered, grateful at last to be able to show some of her fear. "But he may! It's my fault he lost two other captives and two horses."

Little Flower was silent for a moment. "Perhaps he feels that he was at fault himself for carelessness? But that doesn't matter."

"What does?"

"Your husband."

Christa buried her face in her hands, fighting the savage wave of pain that streaked through her. Jeremy. Even when he wasn't with her, he was protecting her. Just by being the man that he was, the man she hadn't wanted to see for so very long because of the color of the uniform he wore.

"I don't know if he will come," Christa said dully. But she gripped the girl's arm fiercely. "Little Flower, your English is so good—"

"Buffalo Run taught me," she said proudly. "If I am to best whites, I must understand them, while they cannot understand me!"

Christa nodded. Buffalo Run could be an extremely intelligent man. "Little Flower, I'm going to have a baby—"

"Yes. McCauley told Buffalo Run."

Jeremy had discussed her with Buffalo Run?

She inhaled and exhaled, praying suddenly that at least the baby was still all right.

"Little Flower, I know that my baby isn't due for months, but if you have any influence with him and they should decide that something is going to happen to me, would you try to see that the baby is born first, that—that it is given to my husband?" she whispered.

Little Flower arched a dark brow. "That is what you wish?"

"It's what I wish."

"Then I will try. And I will try to help you while you are with us too. If you learn to work, you will be tolerated."

"I can work," Christa said simply. And she could. She had learned to work well on the plantation, and long hours and back-bending labor meant little to her now.

In the few days that followed, with help from Little Flower, Christa quickly learned about the Comanche way of life and tepee etiquette.

When the flap was open, a guest might enter directly. When the flap was closed, a guest announced his presence before being invited in. Guests invited to dine brought their own bowls and spoons—it was extremely rude not to eat everything offered. Guests did not pass between the fire and those seated around it, but around those seated who leaned in to afford room for movement.

Women did not sit cross-legged as did the men—they sat on their heels or with their legs to one side. Christa hated bowing down to Buffalo Run on any principle whatever, but she was too grateful to be alive and unharmed to fight with him—or even let him notice her—over such a small detail. All of society followed certain rules. Tall Feather was the peace chief, and in matters that did not concern warfare he was highly respected. He called his warriors to council and he looked to Buffalo Run for much of his advice, but all of the warriors had a say in things, and any one of them could initiate a raid or a battle. Young men did not speak unless they were invited to speak by an elder. Although some Indian societies were matriarchal, the Comanche society was dominated by the males.

She was expected to work with the women, and as long as she stayed with Little Flower she was glad of the tasks that lasted throughout the day. She quickly learned that the Comanche did not eat fish, nor did they, as did some of the Indians, eat dogs or coyotes, for one of their gods was a dog-god. They cooked fresh buffalo meat right over an open fire, suspended from a tripod, and they made stew from buffalo meat by making a cooking pouch from the lining of the animal's stomach and dropping hot stones into it. They were never wasteful, drying strips of the meat into jerky and making sausages from it flavored with wild onions and sage. They made pemmican from the jerky, pulverizing the jerky into powder with a stone maul, then mixing it with dried berries and fat. The pemmican was stowed away in parfleches, or rawhide cases, where it could preserve food for the winter months when hunting might be scarce.

The night was another exercise in misery, for she was kept in Buffalo Run's tepee. Besides Little Flower, Buffalo Run had two other wives and a growing family of children. His other two wives were sisters, Dancing Maid and Running Doe. Running Doe had a babe that was just a few weeks old, and Dancing Maid had a child Christa estimated to be about six months.

Throughout the night, the babies cried or gurgled off and on, or made suckling noises as they nursed. At night she could also hear Buffalo Run with Little Flower. She lay with her teeth clenched, her face flushed. She was horribly embarrassed—and cast into a realm of memory, thinking of her own husband. Thinking of him, tall and naked and sleek, coming for her, sweeping her into his arms.

But the cries in the night were not hers.

When he finished with Little Flower, Buffalo Run prepared to sleep. His eyes caught Christa's, open in the dim firelight. He looked her way and smiled slowly, then laughed out loud.

She knew that he was aware that she was afraid he might decide she would do for an evening's copulation, and he enjoyed tormenting her.

Christa couldn't understand the lack of jealousy among wives, but Little Flower seemed very adapted to the lifestyle. In the morning she tried to explain it to Christa. "We each had our time alone with him when we were wed," she said. "Dancing Maid and Running Doe are now busy with their infants. My time will come, and I will tend to my child while they tend to Buffalo Run. And if he takes you on as a wife, you will have your time."

"Oh, God!" Christa whispered. They had come to the stream to bathe. Little Flower, she had discovered, loved water. She didn't mind that it was very cool. Christa had been terrified to part with her clothing, but Little Flower convinced her that the Comanche respected one another's privacy.

She so longed to bathe. She had ridden so long, through so much dust and mud. And though none of the violence had actually touched her, she had felt as if she were covered in blood. Robert Black Paw's blood. Anguish filled her. His death would lie forever on her conscience.

If she was with Little Flower, she tried to assure herself that she was safe. She had to change her clothing, for Little Flower told her that her dress had offended Dancing Maid, and as she was the first of Buffalo Run's wives, she had the right to want their slave dressed as she pleased.

Dancing Maid wanted the dress, Christa was certain.

But Christa didn't mind if Dancing Maid took her clothing. Not so long as Christa got to keep her nose, earlobes, and health intact. She meant to keep her peace with Dancing Maid. She had also discovered the doeskin she had been provided with to be very soft, and she knew it would be very warm against the coldness of the night.

Oddly enough, she also discovered that none of Buffalo Run's wives really seemed to wish her any harm. She was careful to work as hard as the women did, no matter how exhausted she became. And it was easy to care for the babies. They didn't know that they were Comanche, or that she was white, and Christa had long ago discovered that an infant was an infant, black, white, or red, and ready to love and trust anyone who offered it love and tenderness. Because she was so good with their children, Dancing Maid and Running Doe were more tolerant of her. She knew that if Buffalo Run decided to take her on as a wife, his wives would not protest. There was a great deal of work for a Comanche woman to do—less if she shared it. And since warriors died in battle so frequently, the Comanche would have found it foolish for a young woman of childbearing age not to have a husband. Christa would have been the only one to feel abject horror if Buffalo Run decided that he would have her.

Little Flower frowned at her. "Buffalo Run is a fine war chief, and an excellent hunter," she told Christa. "He is half white himself. He was taken into one of the forts for several years when he was small. That is where he learned to speak English so very well."

The water seemed to have grown very cold. She hugged her arms around her chest. "He is a fine warrior. It is just that—" She paused, feeling the anguish sweep over her. "It's just that I love the husband I already have."

Little Flower nodded. "He is very handsome and noble, especially for a white man."

Christa turned away from her, hugging herself against the chill as she climbed up the embankment to find her clothing. Before she could reach the doeskin dress and boots, she paused, feeling the hair rise at her nape. Chills danced down the entire length of her spine.

An Indian brave blocked her way. He was the next tallest of the warriors to Buffalo Run. His breeches were made of animal skin, his shirt was cotton, covered by a fringed vest with beadwork. His long black hair was in braids, and a kerchief interlaced with rawhide was tied around his forehead.

Eagle Who Flies High, she thought quickly. She remembered the night when Jeremy had been so angry because she had made an appearance in the tent when he was there.

He'd been angry because the Indian had seen her. Eagle Who Flies High had initiated the war party to come after her and Jeff Thayer.

Now he was staring at her, blocking her path. She didn't move, but felt her nudity more keenly with each passing second.

"Little Flower . . . ?" she whispered.

The Comanche girl came from the water, her soft voice full of reproach, her language swift and intriguing with its rolling R's.

But it did no good. Eagle Who Flies High answered her curtly and angrily. Little Flower argued back, but the warrior seemed to grow angrier by the minute.

"What is he saying?" Christa asked nervously. Surely, he couldn't hurt her. Only Buffalo Run could hurt her, if he chose. Unless Buffalo Run were to be killed.

Then she might be sold, or traded, or given away.

"Little Flower!"

"He says that he saw you first. That by right, you are his captive. He says that Buffalo Run really has no right to you, that he has pampered you, that he has scorned the Comanche ways. He says that you should be his slave, and that he intends to take you."

"Jesu, no!" Christa cried. Eagle Who Flies High took a step toward her, and she didn't care if there were nothing but desert and dust and death if she ran from the encampment, she would not stand still and wait for this man to attack her. She spun around, naked still, and shrieked with terror. She raced across the water and started to run through the scruffy foliage on the other side of it. Brambles and branches tore at her flesh. Rocks bruised her feet.

He was slowed by the water between them. Christa continued to shriek and scream as she ran, but she wondered if she could be heard, and if she were heard, would anyone help her?

The calf-high boots that had slowed Eagle Who Flies High as he made his way through the water became his advantage when they were both on solid ground. She couldn't run over the rocky terrain the way he could. Pain seared into her foot and she cried out, holding it, as a jagged rock tore the bottom.

And even as that cry left her mouth, another formed inside her, for the Comanche had caught up with her. She went spinning around and fell flat to the ground. With deadly serious eyes he started to lower himself upon her.

Christa struck out, kicking him with all the vengeance and desperation inside her. She must have struck thoroughly and well, for the warrior who never betrayed emotion showed signs of the pain she had inflicted. His bronzed features tightened, his teeth grated loudly. He fell away from her, rolling to his side. Words of fury escaped his lips, directed toward her. She leapt to her feet, certain that were he to set his hands upon her now, she would be brutally raped, mutilated, and perhaps, if she were lucky, killed.

She started to run again. She screamed as fingers wound into her hair.

But before she could be dragged back to the ground, a bullet exploded, splintering a rock near her feet. She shrieked and spun about, just as Eagle Who Flies High did.

Buffalo Run had come. Christa was certain that Little Flower had gone for him. The shot he had fired from a U.S. Army issue Colt—surely taken in some raid—had been meant as a warning one.

Angrily, Buffalo Run began speaking. Eagle Who Flies High responded in kind. Christa didn't wait for the argument to finish. She shot back toward Buffalo Run, hiding behind him. Little Flower was there, awaiting her with a blanket. She wrapped Christa in it.

Others from the tribe had come around by now, but they all remained quiet, listening to Buffalo Run and Eagle Who Flies High. Tall Feather, the peace chief of the band, had come. He began speaking and the others listened.

"What are they saying?" she asked Little Flower.

But this time, there was no chance for Little Flower to answer her. Buffalo Run turned around angrily and caught her by the arm. He brought her back to the camp, dragging her along.

"I didn't do anything!" she cried out. "Please, tell me what is going on!"

But Buffalo Run wasn't going to explain anything to her. She felt a new rise of fear as he dragged her past his own tepee. He stopped before one that had been erected near his own. It had belonged to a warrior named Eagle Claw who had been killed in a recent raid. His young wife, childless, had returned to her father's home. She was being imprisoned in a neutral territory, she realized.

He threw her into the tepee. "You!" he charged her. "You are nothing but trouble!"

"But I didn't do anything this time! He just came after me—"

"This time! You freed the other captives, you cost us good horses. You were captured yourself to free the gray soldier." He spat on the ground. "The gray murderer! For McCauley, I have kept you from punishment. Your nose should have been clipped! You wouldn't have created such a lust in Eagle Who Flies High!"

"But I—"

"Stay here! I will come for you soon enough. You are a dangerous prize— someone will pay the price for you. And tonight—you will pay yourself!"

Furious, shaking, he turned and left the tepee. Terrified, she tried to come after him.

Basket Woman waited outside, grinning cruelly. She held a knife, and quickly raised it to Christa's throat.

The woman would gladly kill her, Christa knew.

She moved back into the tepee and sat. A few minutes later, she heard a soft whisper. Little Flower had brought her clothes. She came in and hastily started a fire, speaking as quickly as she could. "I cannot stay. There is tremendous trouble now, over you."

"What will happen?"

A blaze started up in the center fire. "You will be warm at least."

"Little Flower, please—?"

"I don't know! We have never had such an argument before. I don't know how it will be solved. Eagle Who Flies High says that he will use you as a captive should be used if Buffalo Run will not do so, as you should be his captive by right. Buffalo Run told him that Morning Star was to have been his wife, so you are his captive in exchange. He also says that he snatched you from your horse. There is great trouble, so something must happen. But now, in the midst of this there is more. I don't know quite what happened myself, but Tall Feather and Buffalo Run and Eagle Who Flies High have all gathered with—"

A sharp command came from outside. Basket Woman was warning Little Flower to come out.

"I don't dare stay longer! Their tempers are so high! Someone, I think, must die—"

Another roaring command came from the outside. Little Flower jumped up, stared at Christa, then hurried from the tepee.

Christa dressed and sank down upon a pile of furs, trying not to shake. Jesu, she should just die and end this agony!

But then, just as the thought came to her, she felt movement.

The baby was moving again! After everything. The baby was alive inside of her. She had to live. No matter what happened to her, no matter what was done to her, she had to live. If nothing else, she meant to see to it that she delivered her baby. If Buffalo Run had any sense of honor, and he did, he would see to it that Jeremy received their child.

She lowered her cheeks to her knees and fought the tears that threatened her. What would come now? Maiming, torture at the hands of Eagle Who Flies High?

Or would Buffalo Run return. He had said she should have had her nose clipped. Perhaps he would only rape her.

It was then that she heard the drums. A slow, steady beat. Continuous. Threatening. They seemed to go on for hours and hours. Hours in which she thought that she would lose her mind. Thump. Thump. Thump. They beat on. Warning of dire things to come.

What things?

Jeremy would know.

Tears, unbidden, slid from her eyes. She wiped them away.

It was then that she looked up, and terror struck her heart once again.

Someone was there. Tall, indomitable. Filling the entrance to the tepee.

A scream, silent and terrible, welled in her throat as she watched him come into the tepee.

Twenty-three

*H*e hadn't traveled much beyond the point where he had parted from Company D when he began to feel the sensation of being watched.

He was, indeed, in Buffalo Run's territory.

There was something so unnerving about the feeling, that he was upon occasion tempted to turn his horse about and race as hard and fast as he could in the opposite direction. He could never do that. Even if the desperate, all-consuming need to find Christa should suddenly and inexplicably fade, he could not turn and run.

He was being watched. He was close to the encampment and Comanche warriors were watching his progress.

He wasn't alone. Morning Star was with him.

Thankfully, when he had come upon the ex-Reb outlaws, they had been so busy with old Joseph Greenley's money and trading goods that they hadn't had time to give much attention to Morning Star. She was just a girl, younger than her sister Little Flower, but by Indian standards she was certainly old enough to wed, and it would not be at all unusual for Buffalo Run to take her into his household, where he would then have two sets of sisters, and those sisters cousins with one another. Morning Star was quiet, with a curious wisdom far beyond her years. He'd tried to talk with her, but there was very little she would tell him. She was grateful to be with him. She had known him from Buffalo Run's encampment, and she had come to him when he had seized the outlaws with an implicit trust that had been both frightening and endearing. "McCauley bring Morning Star home," she had told him, and of course she had been right. No matter what happened, he would see to it that she was returned to Buffalo Run and the Comanche encampment.

But he didn't imagine that he would be riding into the territory in the company of one small Indian girl. Nor had he ever imagined that she would be part of his bargaining power when he asked for the return of his own wife.

Moments later, he saw a warrior on the wave of ridge he approached. As he moved closer, a second warrior appeared, and then a third.

Within a few minutes, the Indians had slowly encircled him. No violence was offered. They kept their distance as an escort, bringing him the rest of the way into the camp.

He hadn't quite reached the first pathway through the tepees when he saw an old Indian step out, barring his way. For a moment he felt his muscles tensing, then he relaxed.

It was Tall Feather, the peace chief. The Indian lifted a hand in greeting to him.

"McCauley," he said.

Jeremy dismounted from his horse, walking the few feet that remained between them. "I've brought back the girl, Morning Star," he said. "And I've come for my wife."

"You wish to trade women?" Tall Feather said.

He shook his head. "I would have brought Morning Star home no matter what. If my brother Buffalo Run seized my wife, I wish to think that he would bring her home to me—no matter what."

Tall Feather lifted his arm, indicating his own tepee. "There is some trouble over your wife," he commented.

Jeremy felt his heart careen against his chest. He tried to still the panic rising in his breast and followed Tall Feather into his tepee. A good guest, he entered carefully to the left and sat with his legs crossed.

Tall Feather spoke to one of his wives in his Comanche tongue. Jeremy couldn't follow all of the words, but he knew that he sent the woman for Buffalo Run—and for Eagle Who Flies High.

Tall Feather produced one of his pipes. It was an exceptionally fine pipe, made with a stone bowl polished with buffalo grease. The stem was decorated with beads and horsehair, and Jeremy knew it was the old chief's best pipe, which was an encouraging sign. The Comanche respected him and wanted to remain his friend. Also, no serious business could possibly be done without the smoking of a pipe between men.

Jeremy tried to conceal his fear and impatience, inhaling deeply on the pipe before returning it to Tall Feather. "What is this trouble with my wife?" he asked, his heart pounding. All manner of horrors raced through his mind. They had punished her for freeing the other captives. They had slashed her legs or her face. They had clipped her nose or ears. "As Buffalo Run is my brother—"

"Buffalo Run does not refuse you your wife. He has been waiting for you to come."

"Then—"

"Buffalo Run said that we must leave the problem of the outlaws to you. They were white men trying to commit crimes as Comanche. He knew that you would believe us. But Eagle Who Flies High gathered the force to ride to your encampment to see that the white men had been taken. They found that the white man was escaping, and they passed their own judgment."

"I know that," Jeremy said. "I found the man."

Tall Feather nodded sagely. "We hear many things, so we know that your wife was with the army of the men in the gray coats." He leveled his finger at Jeremy. "A man should have control of his own home."

At that particular moment, Jeremy's fingers itched to slide around Christa's neck. "I bow to your wisdom, Tall Feather," he said to the Indian.

The tepee flap moved. Buffalo Run and Eagle Who Flies High entered, came around the left, and accepted the pipe so that they could be involved in the business at hand. Buffalo Run stared levelly at Jeremy. Eagle Who Flies High seemed to be staring above him. Jeremy realized that the man who had come to him before as Buffalo Run's emissary was gaining an equal footing with Buffalo Run as a war chief.

"She is well," Buffalo Run assured him, and Jeremy wondered just what of his fear he had given away. "For my part, my brother, I give up my rights to her, as you have returned Morning Star to me."

"Then I may take my wife and leave—" Jeremy began.

"No," Eagle Who Flies High said.

"There is the matter of which man here has the right to the captive," Tall Feather told Jeremy. "Eagle Who Flies High was the warrior to lead the raid. Before we knew of your coming today, they had disagreed about her. Eagle Who Flies High challenged Buffalo Run, and they agreed to meet with knives to settle the dispute."

"I will not give her up," Eagle Who Flies High said flatly. His eyes met Jeremy's at last. "It was not my woman you returned. I owe you nothing."

"I will not leave without my wife!" Jeremy insisted softly.

"Then Buffalo Run must be taken from this dispute," Tall Feather said. "And you, McCauley, must be ready to meet Eagle Who Flies High in his stead. Is your wife worth this?"

She is worth everything, he might have said.

But he had to take care. "She is mine. And I will leave with her."

"Or die in the trying," Eagle Who Flies High said with quiet menace.

It was more than just keeping Christa from this brave, Jeremy realized. It was a power struggle within the tribe.

"Or die in the trying," Jeremy said.

"It is settled," Tall Feather said. "You will meet in the morning with knives. The fight will be fair, between two warriors, in our fashion. The tribe will be witness."

"If I win," Jeremy said, "it is agreed, on your honor, that I leave here in peace with my wife?"

"It is agreed. You leave with our gratitude, for Morning Star is returned."

Tall Feather started to knock the burned tobacco from his pipe—a clear sign that the meeting was ended. It was time for them all to rise and leave the tepee. Jeremy, though he knew the etiquette, sat still.

"I will fight in the morning. I want to be with her tonight," he said.

"That I will not agree to—" Eagle Who Flies High began.

But Buffalo Run protested before Jeremy could. "The woman is McCauley's wife. And has been. And carries his child. He may well die. There are matters to solve between them. I say that he should have the night." He looked to Tall Feather.

Tall Feather nodded. "This is only just. We have kept our two good war chiefs from meeting one another and injuring one another when all braves are needed, when we can trust so few of the white soldiers and settlers. Neither will Buffalo Run and McCauley, who are brothers with mingled blood, meet one another. The fight will be good and fair, the outcome just. Buffalo Run, you will see that your white brother reaches the woman. And you will tend to his needs for the fight to come in the morning. Eagle Who Flies High—you will wait until then."

They all rose. Jeremy could feel the heat and fury emitting from Eagle Who Flies High. He knew the Indian longed to slit his throat then and there, but his tribesmen had spoken against him, and to retain face he must wait for the fight.

And win it.

That gave Jeremy the night. The night, if nothing more.

They walked through the camp. Here and there, Jeremy was greeted with a call by those who knew him. But mostly the Indians paused and stared at him. They all knew that Christa was in the camp.

They knew about the trouble over her, and now knew that he had come. A white man walking alone amongst them.

Buffalo Run came to a halt in front of a tepee not far from his own. "You must leave her at dawn," he said. "You will come to my home. I'll see you are dressed properly, and Dancing Maid will cover you in bear grease, so that your opponent will not have an advantage."

"Thank you."

"You are a rare white man, McCauley. You have always kept your word with me. I hope that you live to do so again."

Jeremy smiled. "So do I!" he said. Buffalo Run nodded and left him.

The battle-ax of a woman keeping guard in front of the tepee moved aside for him. He unpinned the flap, leaving it open, and stood there for a moment trying to see in the darkness. His heart started to pound suddenly, his loins to quicken. Christa. Buffalo Run had said that she was unharmed.

A fire was burning low in the center of the tepee. He could just make out a shape beyond it. He strode into the tepee anxious, fury and fear suddenly mingling within him along with the simple desperation to hold her. She wasn't moving, he realized. She was frozen as still as ice. He heard her shifting her position, inhaling sharply.

"You!" she cried.

He heard her startled gasp and realized that she hadn't known until that moment that it was he who had come upon her.

She was against the hide wall of the tepee, curled as close as she could come to the skin. The fire played over her, and he saw that she was dressed in soft skins, that her hair was free and long, flowing down her back. Her eyes were huge in the firelight, her face pale. She was terrified, he thought, and trying very hard not to show it. He was suddenly afraid himself. Not afraid of meeting Eagle Who Flies High in combat; he had fought too many times in hand-to-hand combat against white men in the midst of screaming cavalry horses to feel himself incapable of fighting Eagle Who Flies High.

He was only afraid that he had found her at last, only to lose her still to death —his own.

Christa, damn you, he thought. Why couldn't you believe in me? Weland was a traitor to us all, but you let him use you to thwart me!

He felt his hands shaking. He was so glad to see her safe and unharmed. Suddenly, if he was going to die, he wanted to do so with the memory of the sweetness of her kiss on his lips, not with the bitter taste of betrayal in his heart.

He reached down his hands to her, catching her wrists when she continued to stare incredulously at him.

He wrenched her to her feet and brought her crashing hard against him.

"Tomorrow, madam, I may die for you," he told her. He didn't mean to sound so harsh, but the depths of his emotion and hunger combined to give his words a rough-edged quality. His fingers were tense upon her, making his hold a rough one. He brought her closer against him. He wanted to touch her, all of her. From the soft planes of her face to her fingers and toes. To see that she was really unharmed.

He stroked and cupped her chin, tilting her face, forcing her eyes to his. His fingers threaded into the wild tangle of her hair. His eyes traveled the length of her. He held her head steady as his lips lowered until they hovered just above hers. His grip was forceful. The length of him seemed to shake with electric energy, be it passion or fury. And hovered there, continuing to whisper, the warmth of his breath bathing her lips, her face.

"Tomorrow I may die. Tonight . . ." He paused briefly, seeking out the shimmering blue beauty of her eyes. Yes, her arms were around him. Yes, dear God, she was glad of him tonight. The last time he had seen her she had seduced him to trick him. Sometimes she had been his because she had felt her debts deeply, and sometimes because he had learned to fire her passions. Yet, he realized, none of that mattered. Tonight, she would love him because the drums were beating, because he would live or die for the glory of her touch.

Tension seemed to burn in his body, hotter than the bluest streaks of flame within the fire. "Tonight," he told her. "Tonight, my love, you will make it worth my while!"

His lips descended down upon hers, hard, questing, demanding.

And bringing up all that fire within her.

"Jesu!" she whispered when the bruising force of his lips left her mouth at last. Again her gaze met his. Bluer than the sky, than the sea, deeper than the earth. The fire within him had touched her. The sound of the drums had entered her blood.

She threw her arms around him and clung to him. His fingers moved over her hair, reveling in the length of it. He drew her away from him, the fury, the passion, still alive within him.

"Life—and death. Make them both worthwhile," he told her harshly.

She stared at him. He swept her up into his arms and bore her down to the furs upon the ground.

"Love me!" he commanded her fiercely.

She was silent as he stripped, her eyes on his, waiting. Then he was down beside her, his hands upon her, stripping her of the fine doeskin tunic the Comanche had given her to wear.

She lay against his burning, naked flesh. He could feel the length of her, and he began to shake, certain at last in his heart that she was all right. They had not touched her, had not maimed her. He had come in time.

She would keep nothing from him, he decided. She wouldn't fight the sensations, she would do nothing but surrender. He whispered harshly to her. "Give in to me! Everything, Christa, everything."

He straddled her. Her flesh was beautiful, ivory and gold in the firelight. Her breasts were so large now, full, evocative, the nipples nearly crimson, hardened. He could just feel the slight rise of their child in her abdomen, and he prayed suddenly, fiercely, that they all might live. Beneath him she began to tremble, and he didn't know if it was with fear or with desire, or if the endless incantation of the drums had entered them both.

She reached out her arms to him, eyes wide, luminous. She moistened her lips to speak, and her words were soft, quavering, yet filled with a passion that touched his heart, soul, loins.

"I will give you everything!" she vowed, and added in a vehement whisper, "And make the night well—well worth your while!"

Tonight was different from all others. Tonight the words, the accusations, the anguish, the whispers, all hovered within his body, locked within his soul. He loved her. He didn't know how long he had loved her so fiercely, maybe it had been forever. For all else paled beside this. No love he had known could be so deep, no hunger could be so shattering.

He found her lips. They trembled beneath his and parted. Heat rippled and burst between them, spreading rampantly. His hands moved swiftly, circling the heavy fullness of her breasts, rounding over the rise of her belly, touching her.

The softness of her body seemed to meld to his. She twisted and turned, accepting his touch, wanting his touch. Soft sounds escaped her, sounds that sent desire rocketing more deeply into his mind and body.

"Death holds no threat, my love. Indeed, you have made it all worth my while!" he promised her.

He felt the urgency of her touch, pressing against him. Holding his breath, he let her have her way. Upon her knees she kissed his shoulders, her fingers biting into the flesh and muscle. She kissed his lips, his chest. Swept into a newer, even sweeter fire, he caught her hand and guided it to the fullness of his sex.

A ragged cry escaped him. He swept her up into his arms, then laid her flat against the hides and fur of the bedding again. He caught her ankles, spreading her legs. He hovered over her, lips ravaging hers again, eyes seeking her own.

His body screamed that he must have her then.

But something within him knew that he could not for he had to touch her more, had to feel her, see her, kiss her, touch her, taste her.

Again, his lips covered hers. They covered her breasts. They bathed her belly, and even as she cried out, his kiss, his lips, his tongue stroked and teased her inner thighs, the throbbing sweet cleft between them. A cry escaped her, then whispers and gasps. She urged him to her, near sobbing as she brought him into her arms.

"Jesu!" he cried out.

He felt so alive, so volatile. So damned, desperately hungry. He scooped her into his arms. Sensations sheathed and sheltered him as he thrust himself into her. Her limbs wrapped around him tightly, the liquid fire of her body accepted and encompassed him. He moved and let the thunder of the drumbeats call his rhythm, for he was far beyond reason, feeling the incredible rise of his climax. He fought the explosion, savoring the feel of his wife beneath him, the sleekness of her flesh, the undulation of her body, rising against his and meeting him. He felt the ragged rise and fall of her breath, the pure thunder of her heart.

But the splendor that night seemed as savage as the beat of the drums. Desire soared within him, then burst in a violent climax. He felt her shuddering beneath him, felt the explosion within her. "My love . . ."

The words escaped him. He didn't know if she heard him or not. It didn't matter. He grit his teeth, feeling the final thrust of his body, the last of the little explosions that shook him.

For a long while he held still. Felt the satiation fill his body. He lay down beside her, sweeping her damp, cooling body into his arms.

She started to speak.

"Shh!" he said softly. "We have the night."

She curled against him. She touched his cheek, but her eyes would not rise to his. "I can't!" she whispered. "I don't think it's possible to forget this fear long enough to . . . make love."

He smiled. "Give me a chance!" he said softly, and they both remembered another night he had made such a request.

She rose up, trying to see him in the flickering gold light. "Jeremy, I know that I betrayed you. I have no right to ask you to understand, but you can't know the whole of it. Dr. Weland—"

"Is dead," he told her flatly.

She inhaled sharply. There was a glaze of tears in her eyes. "Then you know? He killed Robert Black Paw."

Jeremy hesitated. "Robert may still be alive. It's possible."

"Oh, God!" she whispered. "Oh, God! I pray that he is!"

Her words were fervent, and he knew that they were honest. He prayed himself that the man who had been his good and loyal friend through so many things might still be alive.

But Robert seemed distant now. The cavalry encampment might have been a million miles away. The real world was here, in this tepee, with the sound of the drums all around them, the flickering fire bathing them in its gold light, and the promise of the violence that would come with the daylight.

"Jeremy—"

He reached up to her, threading his fingers through her hair, amazed himself that he could want her again, so desperately, so quickly.

It might be all that he would have.

"Come here," he whispered, pulling her head down to his. His lips just a breath from hers, he told her, "We haven't that long." He rose, pressing her back down to the furs. But she moaned deep in her throat, protesting, tossing her head. He released her captive lips, and she looked up at him, her eyes wide and incredibly blue, her hair wild and entangling them both.

"Jeremy, you said that you might die. I don't understand—"

"I am to meet Eagle Who Flies High in the morning. We will fight for you. With knives."

She gasped, and a tremble shot through her. "You—you can't meet him. He could so easily kill you—"

"Thank you for the vote of confidence!"

She shook her head raggedly. "Oh, my God, Jeremy, it's just that he's an Indian, a savage—"

"He is a savage? Jesu! You should have seen the way your friend Jeff Thayer killed poor Joe Greenley and the Union soldiers on the pay wagon!"

She swallowed hard, her lashes falling over her eyes. "I didn't know, Jeremy—"

"It doesn't matter!" he said roughly. "Not tonight."

He tried to capture her lips again, but she was speaking quickly. "Don't you see, it does matter?" she whispered. "Damn you, Jeremy, I don't want you to die for me! I don't want you to die for honor, not for my sake. I forced you into marriage, I—"

"Christa! You're carrying my child!" he reminded her.

She fell silent, inhaling, her lashes once again covering her eyes. She stared at him. "Before you came, I asked Little Flower to make sure that the baby was brought to you in the event of anything happening to me. She would have helped me. She—will help me get the baby back to you if you choose to leave now—"

"Christa, if I wished to, I couldn't leave now. My honor is at stake here, my credibility. I cannot go."

"But—"

"Christa! The night is short, the hours wane. Dawn will come soon enough."

"Dawn?" she whispered miserably.

"I have to prepare."

"Then you have to sleep!" she cried out fervently.

"I will sleep," he said. He threaded his fingers forcefully through her hair. "I will sleep soon enough."

"I—"

"Shush, Christa!"

She had no chance to disobey for his lips seized hers firmly, and the kiss was deep and demanding, stealing the breath from her.

When he finally dozed, she stared down at his face, biting her lip, feeling tears form and fall. She jerked back, lest her tears hit his flesh.

If something happened to him tomorrow, she wouldn't want to live. Once she had loved Liam, but never like this.

"Don't die!" she whispered. "Please, don't die! I cannot live without you!"

At long last, she lay down beside him, certain that she would never sleep.

Yet she did.

Jeremy awoke with the first light of the new day. He stared down at the woman entangled with him. Her flesh was so ivory and soft against the brown fur, her hair so black and richly cascading, her face so beautiful. Her abdomen seemed more rounded this morning; in the midst of this chaos, their child grew.

He leaned low against her and reached out and touched her cheek. It was damp. Tears lay upon it.

Tears she had been shedding for him.

He kissed her forehead, then silently drank in the beauty of her curled before him once again. He placed his hand upon her belly and wondered in sudden awe if he had actually felt movement. Life. If he were to die, he prayed God that Christa and his child might live. Gently, tenderly, he pressed his lips against the flesh of her abdomen, and then he rose. He hastily gathered his clothing, then left the tepee, moving on to Buffalo Run's home so as to prepare.

When Christa awoke, she heard the chanting and the cheers. She lay staring into space for a moment, and then she remembered.

She leapt up and found her doeskin dress and shimmied into it. She was afraid that Basket Woman would be waiting just beyond the tepee to stop her, but she was too desperate to care. She burst out of the tepee and found that she was not going to be stopped at all.

It seemed that all of the Comanche, Basket Woman included, were attending the fight.

She raced through the line of tepees until she came to a spot before the river where a circle had been drawn in the earth. The men were both there, surrounded by the tribe.

She hardly recognized her husband at first. He was dressed in a simple breechclout and nothing more. His flesh had been so rubbed with bear grease that it seemed nearly as dark as Eagle Who Flies High. When Christa reached the gathering, they were parted by a medicine man who danced between them, chanting and sprinkling herbs upon the ground. He carried a bear paw. He called something out and Eagle Who Flies High stepped forward, presenting his back to the man. The shaman brought the bear claw tearing down the Coman-che's back. Bright streams of blood appeared. Eagle Who Flies High stepped back. He hadn't made a sound, nor had he flinched. He appeared smug and well pleased with himself.

Jeremy stepped forward, turning his back to the shaman.

Christa cried out.

A hand clamped upon her arm. Dancing Maid was beside her, shaking her head. Christa opened her mouth to speak and then fell silent. She closed her eyes, feeling a numbing terror steal over her. She heard the Comanche give out a roar of approval and she opened her eyes. Blood was streaming down Jeremy's back. Her knees grew weak.

"Oh, God!" she whispered. "Please don't let him die, please don't let him die . . ."

A drumbeat sounded. The shaman left the circle.

Knives in hand, Eagle Who Flies High and Jeremy slowly began to circle one another.

Twenty-four

The two men lunged at one another simultaneously. There was a curious sound as their greased bodies smacked together. For a moment, they hovered in the air, then they were down on the ground, rolling. A streak of blood appeared on one arm, and for a moment Christa couldn't figure out to which fighter the arm belonged. She cried out again. The blood was dripping from Jeremy.

"You mustn't cry out so!" a voice suddenly warned in her ear. Little Flower was at her side. "Please, Christa, you will distract him."

She bit her lip. She wanted to go back to the tepee, she wanted to look away. She couldn't bear to do so, but neither could she bear to look.

The two men tore away from one another. Once again, they were up on their feet. Circling. Stalking.

Jeremy was a cavalry officer, she thought. Trained to fight from the saddle. He was excellent with a Colt and with a saber. But the Yanks and Rebs hadn't fought their battles with greased bodies and razor-sharp knives.

Jeremy and Eagle Who Flies High appeared to be evenly matched. Both men were superbly muscled, agile, and alert to the slightest movement from the other. Jeremy was slightly the taller of the two, Eagle Who Flies High was stockier. Christa bit her lip, praying that the Comanche's added weight would not make the difference in the end.

Eagle Who Flies High made another flying lunge at Jeremy. The two men went down.

The Indians gathered tightly around the circle. Christa couldn't see anything. She tried to burst through the crowd. "Dear God, dear God, please! I'll do anything, I'll tend the sick, I'll work for the poor—I'll be nice to Yankees everywhere. Oh, God, please, I'll never ask another thing of you, just let him live, please, please, let him live . . ."

She weaved her way through bodies, but was blocked again. She tried to twist through, and fell to the ground, plowing through the dust to land at the edge of the circle where the men were fighting.

A gasp escaped her. Tears welled into her eyes. Jeremy was down. A red gash had been cut across his chest; another sliced his shoulder. His eyes were closed; he lay on his side, prone, in front of her.

"Dear God, no!" she cried in pain and anguish. "Jeremy . . ."

From some distant fog, he heard her call his name. He fought the pain that seared through him. Fought the exhaustion. So much blood was draining from him now, it was making him weak. He had made a few strikes too. Eagle Who Flies High had to be hurting. Jeremy had cut him soundly about the hip and struck deeply into one leg.

But still, he hadn't been able to fight the dizziness. Death had not seemed so horrible until he had heard her voice.

He could see her, yes! Christa thought. He was not dead!

His lip curled suddenly. "I won't fail you, Reb!" he whispered.

He pulled up to his knees. Christa suddenly felt herself wrenched to her feet. She was being held back by one of the braves. She wasn't going to be allowed to come close anymore.

"Please!" she cried. But the brave did not intend to release her. She could see the men moving again. Circling, coming closer and closer to one another.

A war whoop shook the air. Someone had lunged once again. She could see the bodies entangled upon the earth. Flailing, fighting, one man gaining an advantage, then losing it.

Damn! The bear grease made fighting nearly impossible. Every time Jeremy thought he had a good hold on Eagle Who Flies High, the man slipped between his fingers.

But then, the grease worked to his advantage just as well. He saw the warrior's dark eyes on him, sizing him up as they both paused.

Jeremy grit his teeth. They were both losing blood. The blood dripping into his eyes from the wound on his forehead was blinding him. He had to win. He could see many things in Eagle Who Flies High's eyes. The Indian hated him. Hated that he had come to him in peace so many times. He could be a war chief now. As powerful as Buffalo Run. This fight was over many things, with Christa the main prize. And the Comanche coveted the woman.

Eagle Who Flies High had chosen the weapons. He had known his own expertise with the knife. Just as he knew that most cavalrymen were adept with their swords and guns. He had known he had the weight advantage. He had known he was a proud, fierce, good warrior, a strong fighter.

But he hadn't realized that weapons wouldn't matter, that fear wouldn't matter, that nothing would except Christa.

Love could be the strongest weapon of all.

He would not die.

"McCauley!" the Comanche taunted. "Come, McCauley, taste my steel. Taste it deep in your throat!"

He shook his head. "No, Eagle Who Flies High. You have chosen. You must taste my steel."

For the last time, the two of them lunged for one another, knowing that it must now be to the death.

There was a jarring, sickening crunch as steel met flesh and blood and bone.

One wearied fighter fell.

The other, severely wounded, staggered back.

Christa couldn't see them anymore. She heard an explosion of sound from the crowd of Comanche, and hands rose and struck the air, lances were raised, and loud cries sounded fiercely all around.

One of the combatants was down.

Down and dead, or dying.

She could not see which man.

"Please!" she shrieked, trying to tear away from the warrior who held her. He didn't release her, but the squaw in front of her moved.

She saw the bronzed back of a man. He lay with his face in the dirt. He was covered with blood and grease. The hilt of a knife protruded from the side of his rib cage.

"No!" she whispered. She started to fall. It was Jeremy and he was dead and she really didn't care what happened to her anymore. Her knees were too weak to allow her to stand, and she would have fallen if the Comanche warrior hadn't held her upon her feet.

"Tall Feather! Buffalo Run!" She heard the words, and she gasped. It was not Jeremy who had fallen. He was alive, and he was speaking, and the Comanche who held her so rigidly was at last moving forward.

He was alive but just barely. He was covered in as much blood as he was covered in grease. Standing seemed difficult for him, but he was determined to do so. He was addressing the chiefs, Tall Feather and Buffalo Run, his friend and his brother.

"I am sorry that it came to this. I am sorry for the life of a fine opponent. I ask that it be the end. We have all been betrayed by men we thought to be our friends. And in this, Tall Feather, and my brother, Buffalo Run, we have all learned that there can be honor among our enemies. I have met Eagle Who Flies High in fair battle, man to man. The gray-coat, Jeffrey Thayer, is dead. Even the man who betrayed me, who sought to bring down my wife's family, is now dead. I want to take my wife and bring her home. We can't stop the great tide of violence that goes on between our peoples. We can remember the honor in one another. Let me take my wife and go."

Christa felt the warrior's hold upon her tighten as he awaited word from the head men of the band. Buffalo Run and Tall Feather exchanged glances. Tall Feather looked at Jeremy a long while, and then nodded. He lifted a hand.

The brave released Christa. Suddenly, she was free.

With a soft cry, she raced the distance to her husband. The impetus of her weight against him almost caused him to keel over. She straightened quickly, made painfully aware of how he had been cut and injured. She tried to support his weight upon her shoulders, yet he would not lean upon her.

"McCauley," Buffalo Run said. "You are right. There can be honor among enemies. Take your woman and go home."

Christa inhaled a ragged breath, looking to Jeremy. He smiled and took a step forward.

But they weren't going home. Not quite yet. Jeremy took a step and fell flat into the dirt. Christa cried out, falling to her knees beside him.

Little Flower was quickly at her side. "Bring him!" she told the men gathering around. "Bring him quickly. We must stop the flow of blood."

When Jeremy opened his eyes again, Christa knelt by his side. He heard the tinkle of water and realized that she was bathing his wounds and his forehead again and again.

He blinked, trying to see her. Her face was very white and drawn. He tried to smile, but the effort seemed too much. He tried to rise. There was powder on his chest. He frowned, trying to dust it off. She caught his hand. "Leave it!" she said softly. Her gaze wandered elsewhere in the tepee, then returned to his. "It's all right. I really do know quite a bit. Before the war, I helped Jesse a lot, and he told me that a lot of Indian medicinal herbs were really very good. This is just a salve of yarrow, fine for cuts and bruises."

He nodded. He wanted to talk to her. The effort seemed too much. He closed his eyes.

When he awoke again, he felt much stronger. There was warmth at his side. He half rose. Christa slept there.

But they were not alone. He heard a soft whisper, and saw that Little Flower had come to him. She brought a bowl of a thin-looking gruel. She smiled, offering it up to him. "It will give you strength," she promised him. He sipped the substance. It was something made from buffalo meat, he was certain. He downed it all, determined that he would get his strength back.

She took the bowl from him. "Thank you, McCauley."

"For what?"

"For Morning Star."

He nodded.

"It was only fair that you should have your wife in return. That is why the gods smiled on you."

"Is it?"

"You should leave with your wife in the morning, McCauley. You mustn't stay too long."

"I'm not welcome here any longer?"

"You're always welcome here. But our worlds are not the same, and there is more bloodshed to come. And you need to take her home and have a healthy child."

"Yes, I will take her home."

Little Flower smiled. "She has waited for you. She loves you very much."

She disappeared. Jeremy lay back down, wishing he were still unconscious. They had survived. He closed his eyes. She was so warm beside him. He reached out, putting his arm around her, pulling her closer.

He slept again. When he awoke, it was morning. Christa was awake and watching him again, setting cool cloths on his head.

He sat up. "We have to go."

Alarm touched her eyes. "You shouldn't ride yet. You were seriously wounded."

He touched his forehead and his arm and chest. He was well bandaged with strips of cotton from Christa's old plain petticoat.

"We have to go," he insisted. He staggered to his feet. She followed along with him, supporting him. He stepped outside of the tent. Buffalo Run stood just outside with Tall Feather.

"Thank you for your hospitality, my brother," Jeremy told him. "We are ready to leave if we can take just the horses I came with."

Buffalo Run nodded gravely. Dancing Maid brought up the two horses. She said something in her own language and Buffalo Run nodded. "There is jerky in the saddlebags and a canteen of water. It will take you some time to ride home. Your men will be at your Fort Jacobson now, won't they?"

Jeremy nodded. "Yes. We will be there for the length of the winter."

Buffalo Run nodded. "Perhaps it will be a peaceful season." He reached out a hand to Jeremy. Jeremy grasped it.

Buffalo Run set Christa up on the army horse which Jeremy had brought Morning Star back on to the Comanche camp. He assisted Jeremy onto his own horse. Then Buffalo Run grinned and saluted. Jeremy saluted in return.

Following Jeremy, Christa slowly rode from the camp. She looked back. Little Flower was watching her.

"Thank you!" Christa called.

The Indian girl smiled. Christa turned again to continue following Jeremy. She didn't look back.

They rode for several hours, not racing, but plodding along. Christa, worried, hurried up alongside Jeremy.

"You need to rest!"

"I need some distance between us and the camp."

"But we've been freed—"

"I want more distance," he said stubbornly.

A while later she tried to talk to him again. "Thank you, Jeremy."

He didn't reply.

"Thank you for coming. Thank you for risking your life for me."

"Christa, dammit, you're my wife. You're carrying my child."

"I'm grateful—"

"I don't want you to be grateful!"

She fell silent and allowed her horse to fall back.

He was a very stubborn man and a very determined one. They rode until it was twilight. He dismounted from his horse, wincing at the movement. But before she could leap down from her own mount, he was beside her, reaching up to her.

She allowed him to ease her to the ground, but then she quickly broke away from his touch. Tears stung her eyes. How could they have come from the searing, intimate passion of just two nights ago to this?

They had stopped by a beautiful, bubbling little stream that was shaded by tall trees. Christa unrolled a saddle blanket and spoke to Jeremy behind her. "Sit, please. I'll get some water and the jerky."

He stood for a moment, but then he obeyed her. She brought him water in the cup from his saddlebag, then returned for more, drinking what felt like half the brook herself before coming back to him. She produced the jerky and he ate it hungrily, wincing when his back moved against the bark of the tree.

She stood and walked away from him.

Jeremy watched her. He realized that the pain from his wounds wasn't half as great as that which now seared his heart. She was standing so proudly. Trying to talk. But what was there for her to say?

She was a Cameron. Camerons always paid their debts. But he didn't want her owing him anything.

He wanted more.

"Jeremy, I don't know if you can forgive me or not, or even believe me, but I'm sorry."

"It doesn't matter."

"It does matter!" she cried suddenly, passionately. She fell silent, then spit out, "All right! If it doesn't matter, I'm going home. Home to Virginia just as quickly as I can, and I will not let you stop me!"

Agony seemed to sear into him. His head was pounding; his flesh hurt.

His heart was tearing in two.

"You're not going home."

"I'm going home because of all that has happened—" she began, but he cut her off furiously.

"Dammit, Christa, it doesn't matter!" he said fiercely. The scratches on his back were driving him crazy. He wanted to sleep, to ease the pain. The last thing he wanted now was another fight. His hands were trembling. What in God's name was this over now?

He thought that he knew. The Comanche had really frightened her. She wanted no more part of Indian country, and maybe she was right. Maybe he should send her home just as quickly as was humanly possible.

"All right!" he snapped out harshly. "I understand. The Comanche frightened you. And if the hatred in your heart is too much—"

"Hatred!" she exclaimed. She had been standing by the stream, her back to him, a very noble pride to her stance, her hair free and falling down the length of her back, as if she were an Indian maid herself.

But now she spun around, staring at him. He knew he was having some difficulty with his vision, but he must also be losing his mind, for he was certain there were tears in her eyes. "You stupid, stupid Yankee!"

"Christa, I am in no mood for Rebel abuse at this moment—"

"Abuse! I don't want to go because I hate you! I want to go because *I love you*. And I don't want you being honorable anymore, or having to suffer for the things that I do—"

"What!" he exclaimed. Painstakingly, he got to his feet. He must have thundered out the word because she looked frightened for a moment, as if she would back away from him.

"Little Flower said it," he told her. "Little Flower said that you had been waiting for me, that you loved me. But I didn't dare believe. Tell me!"

"I—" she began, and faltered.

He took a step toward her, fighting for strength. His fingers suddenly curled around her arms, exerting a power he hadn't known he possessed. "Tell me!" he exclaimed raggedly.

"You shouldn't have had to come for me. You shouldn't be bleeding and injured now. You shouldn't—"

"Not that!" he thundered, shaking her, pulling her closer into his arms. "The other!"

Her eyes widened. She moistened her lips nervously with just the tip of her tongue. "I might well have ruined your career with Sherman—"

"Damn Sherman. Go on!"

"I—"

"Say it, Christa! Dammit, was I imagining things, or did you say that you loved me?"

"I—" She paused. "I said it!" she whispered.

"And you meant it?"

She lowered her gaze and then her head. "I meant it." Then her gaze rose to his again, blazing blue. "It's not that I mean to take anything from you, Jeremy. I just don't want to stand in your way, or cause more horrible grief. I know that you would never have really wished me dead rather than someone else, but I've lain there some nights and wondered if you didn't wish that I were your Jenny—"

"Oh, Christa! Christa!" He closed his eyes tightly, wrapping her tenderly in his arms. "Christa, she was fine and sweet and gentle, and yes, I loved her, and dear God, yes, I'm sorry the war killed her, just as I'm sorry the war killed so many! But Christa, I have never wished that you were anyone but you, and I have prayed only that our child might survive. If you haven't read my heart, Christa, then you are a stupid, stupid Reb as well!"

She jerked away from him, her gaze crystal and doubting.

He smiled. "You stubborn, wayward little fool!" he charged her, glad to see the sizzle of anger touching her eyes. It was the Christa he knew—and loved. "From the moment I was legally able to get my hands on you, I was obsessed. I wanted you so badly, Christa, that it didn't even matter if you wanted to close your eyes and pretend that I was Liam at first."

"I never—"

"I never wanted to let you, but it wouldn't have mattered. More than anything in the world, I wanted you to respond to me."

"I was afraid to!" she whispered. "Because I knew that once I did, I would have to admit to myself that I did love you. Oh, Jeremy! It is horrible in a way. I never, never wanted to love a Yankee!" She smiled ruefully. "It was one thing to have one for a brother, but to fall in love with one . . . ." Her voice trailed away. She looked down to the ground once again. "Jeremy, I'm so sorry. I didn't even think when I was so determined to release the Rebel prisoners. How can you forgive me?"

He lifted her chin. "Christa, I forgave you long before I came for you. I was furious with myself for not having understood how you would feel. I should have talked to you. If I had talked with you all along, you would never have doubted me. I never wanted you to know that I was afraid, but I was worried about you and about our child. Sometimes I was furious with myself for what I had done, forcing you out on the trail. And then I knew that I couldn't let you go. That I couldn't live without you anymore. Christa, we've been such fools, going in such ridiculous circles. I felt that I was competing with a ghost. And so much more. The past. The present. The war, and even peace!"

"Oh, Jeremy!" she murmured suddenly, searching out his eyes. "I could never understand it, all those years, watching Callie and Daniel and Kiernan and Jesse. It was so tragic for them. To love the enemy—"

"I'm not your enemy, Christa!"

"But, oh, God, Jeremy, you were for years! I used to fear the sight of blue uniforms horribly. Every time I saw a soldier in blue I prayed fiercely that it was Jesse. Jeremy, you have to understand. The Union soldiers came onto the peninsula to burn and destroy."

"They had to reach Richmond!" he said softly. His strength was suddenly failing him. He'd been so swept up by her words, so torn, so anguished.

And then so awed. Watching her speak now, watching her eyes, still so wet with tears, he knew that everything she was saying was the truth. She loved him. He didn't know if it was the blood that he had lost or the simple miracle of those words, but he could stand no longer. He started to fall.

"Jeremy!"

Supporting him, she lowered them both to the ground. He leaned against the tree, his eyes closed. He opened them. Tears were damp against her cheeks. He touched them tenderly.

"Camerons don't cry."

"Oh, my God, Jeremy!" she whispered. "Don't you die on me, please, don't you die on me!"

He smiled very slowly. "I wouldn't die now for all the promises of heaven!" he said.

She caught his hand and kissed it. "You need to rest."

He nodded, then shook his head sadly. "My God, Christa! What a miracle. You've just said that you love me. We're all alone in some of God's most beautiful country, sweet green trees, a bubbling brook, and I can't even stand!"

She exhaled on a shaky sigh, her fingers curling more tightly around his hand. "You are going to live, I think!" she whispered. She sat beside him, leaning her head against his. He was silent for a minute.

"Christa, it's still going to be hard. There is so much bitterness. Most southerners do hate northerners. There's equal hatred in the North. The hatred will live for years. For generations. The difference, of course, is that—"

"The difference is that you won!" Christa interrupted.

"Right. The difference is that we won." He shifted, tilting up her chin. "Can you live with that?" he asked her very softly.

She smiled, lowering her lashes, resting her head against his shoulders. "Yes."

"You're certain?"

"I can live with anything, if I'm living with you."

"But I'll still be surrounded by a lot of Yankees."

"It doesn't matter," she said.

"You don't hate Yankees anymore?"

She turned, smiling ruefully. "I still hate lots of Yankees," she admitted. "It's just that—it's just that I love you far more than I hate them."

"You hate them so passionately!" he stated.

Her smile deepened. "Right. So just imagine how very, very deeply I love you."

He leaned back. His fingers moved in her hair. Branches stirred and rustled over them. The brook bubbled by. "Christa!" he murmured.

"Yes?"

"You are, in every way, the perfect cavalry wife." He mustered all of his strength together and turned, taking her into his arms. He planted a very tender kiss upon her lips. "And I adore you!" he whispered.

Then, his strength spent, he leaned back against the tree and slept.

She stood in the stream, stripped of her doeskin, doing her best to scrub her flesh as the Indians did, with the clean rocky sand from the shallow water. A sudden noise alerted her and she looked up quickly. She had imagined that they were so deeply in Indian territory that they wouldn't be disturbed by any casual passersby.

It was no casual passerby. Jeremy was up. He had shed the uniform he had so carefully donned over his wounded flesh. Ripped and bruised, he was beautiful still, she thought.

No. More beautiful than ever. The long red gashes had been gained in his quest for her. Some of them would scar. Maybe it was good. She would remember for all time just what he had sacrificed for her.

"You shouldn't be up!" she whispered to him.

He stopped before her in the water. The sunlight was playing upon it, mirroring both of their images. They were both, she thought, rather beautiful at the moment. Naked and glistening in the sunlight, as natural as Adam and Eve.

If the Comanche were near, she thought, they would never disturb them now.

It was the wild, wild West.

It was almost Eden.

He walked toward her. No, maybe not Eden. They were not so perfect as Adam and Eve. Despite his rippling bronze muscles, he was torn and wounded. And she was beginning to round more daily now.

But maybe that was why now they were so especially beautiful to one another.

He came before her and took her into his arms, kissing her with a slow burning fever and passion. "You're injured," she reminded him.

"Oh, no, I'm feeling much, much better now. And I don't care if every gash in my body breaks open, I can't wait to make love in a new way."

"A new way?" she asked huskily.

"With you whispering against my kiss that you love me, and with me crying out those same words every step of the way."

"Oh!" she said simply. He began to kiss her. Her lips. Her throat. Her shoulder.

"Jeremy."

"Yes?"

"I love you . . ."

Winter seemed very slow and domestic after all that autumn had brought.

On October fifth, a treaty was signed with the Comanche, among other Indians. Christa had thought that Jeremy would have been pleased, but he didn't seem to have much faith in it.

"I don't think that our side really intends to keep with it," he told her frankly. But winter and cold came to Fort Jacobson, where they had finally settled with Jeremy's regiment, and there were no disturbances over the long months.

There were miracles.

Robert Black Paw survived. Once she returned with Jeremy—and was greeted like a heroine by all the men and women, including Mrs. Brooks—she tended to her husband first, then to Robert, seeing to their wounds with the doctor they found stationed at the fort, Remy Montfort.

Dr. Montfort was a civilian. He had been in the Indian territory for the duration of the war, and he claimed he had never taken sides. Christa didn't know if that was true, but he was a lively old codger with twinkling blue eyes, and she liked him very much.

When Jeremy and Robert were fully on their way to healing, she let him know her own fears about the baby. "Life is miraculous," he assured her. "And wee ones are far stronger than we imagine. You wait and see. Things will come along just fine."

They did. On the morning of Saint Patrick's Day, she awoke with startling pains in her back. She didn't say anything at first, because Jeremy was expecting a company from a fort along the Canadian and she didn't want to disturb him if it was a false alarm. She went over to Celia's cabin where a number of the women had gathered to knit booties—Celia was expecting her own baby in the early summer. An hour later, she felt a pain so strong that she jumped.

"Christa McCauley! You've been in labor some time, haven't you, young woman?" Mrs. Brooks demanded.

"I—I don't know, Mary," Christa said. Now they all knew that Mrs. Brooks's Christian name was Mary. Jeremy had seen to it that the fort had been supplied with a likable young reverend, and Mrs. Brooks had been so pleased that she had actually learned to smile. Maybe the Comanche had changed her.

"I've never done this before!" she said. The pain came again, almost on top of the other one.

Clara Jennings jumped to her feet.

Things weren't perfect. Clara was still awfully hard to swallow upon occasion. But even she had changed. She had taken it upon herself to teach Nathaniel French.

Nathaniel didn't particularly want to learn French, but in the interest of interracial relations, he had determined to do so. "There's a great difference between a man like Nathaniel and a field hand!" Clara had announced.

"The difference is in the learning," Nathaniel had told her.

That had seemed to go over her head. But it didn't matter, not to Nathaniel. He was a wise, peaceful man who knew that changes could take a lifetime. Maybe several lifetimes, he had told Christa.

"I'll go for the colonel!" Clara said.

"No, no, please! I do know that this will take lots of time," Christa said.

"Now, Christa, how—"

"My brother is a doctor," she reminded them. She bit her lower lip for a moment. "He was probably the finest doctor in all the Union army!" she said. But then she gasped because the pain had come again, very quickly.

"Oh, dear!" Celia was on her feet, too, but it didn't matter, because Mary Brooks hadn't waited. She had taken the initiative and gone for Dr. Montfort. "Well, well, so this is it, eh, Christa McCauley? Let's get you back to your own bed in your own quarters, young lady. When did you first feel the pains?"

"Early this morning. Before six. But still—"

"This young one could come at any time, Christa! You've been as active as a worker bee all this time, and that often speeds things along."

"What can I do?" Celia asked quickly.

"Why, boil water, of course!" Dr. Montfort said, his eyes twinkling. "And maybe somebody had best go for the colonel!"

Dr. Montfort said that the baby did come incredibly quickly. Christa supposed that it did, knowing how long it sometimes took other women.

But in the time that it took the baby to come, she was assuredly wretched enough!

She grit her teeth against the awful pains and she tried hard not to cry out. But after Montfort told her that the babe was almost there, she felt one pain so tearing that she could not keep quiet, and she cried out.

She was surprised to hear a soothing voice. Fingers curled around her own. She opened her eyes. Jeremy had come. They had told him to wait outside, in their parlor in the fort. He hadn't done so.

"This is it, Christa. Bear down now, push!"

She pushed, and she fell back exhausted. She pushed again. She was certain that she nearly broke Jeremy's fingers. Montfort chuckled, very pleased. "The baby's head is here, Christa, now just one more . . ."

And the baby was born. Her baby. Jeremy's. "It's a boy!" Jeremy cried out. He stood beside her and kissed her, and she smiled, exhausted as she was, and reached for the little bundle.

He was beautiful. No, he was red and wrinkled and screaming furiously, his little fists batting away.

Jeremy kissed her forehead, marveling at their new creation along with her. "I think that noise he's making is a Rebel yell," he teased.

"Nonsense," Dr. Montfort told them. "He's simply too young to announce politely that it's a very frightening new world and that he'd like some warmth and sustenance, please!" He arched his brow at Celia and Mary, who were still in the room. The three of them quietly left the new parents alone. Just a bit awkwardly, Christa loosed the nightgown she was wearing to feed the tiny bit of new life in her arms. She gasped, startled, at the first fierce tug, then laughed. "Oh, Jeremy, I was so frightened so often for him! Yet he seems so strong!"

Jeremy drew a finger down the baby's downy cheek. "Oh, of course, my love. He's outstanding. Look at his parents. And that was a Rebel yell. My God, look at that hair. Pitch black. And his eyes are blue—"

"I think most all babies start out with blue eyes," Christa told him.

"Well, we'll see," Jeremy murmured. "He needs a name."

"Josiah!" she said quickly. She leaned her face against the baby's soft, damp hair. "Josiah, for your brother."

"Christa, it isn't necessary—"

"He was your brother, and Callie's brother, and you two loved him very much. Both of my brothers came home."

"He was a Yankee."

"I know." She nuzzled the baby's head. "But his father is a Yankee, too, and I love him very much. Josiah first, for your brother. James for a half-dozen Camerons."

"Josiah James McCauley," Jeremy said softly. He kissed Christa's forehead. "Thank you. And thank you for my son. He is exquisite! Like his mother."

There was a tap at the door. Dr. Montfort stood there, clearing his throat.

"Let's take the little one, shall we, Colonel? Your wife really needs some sleep."

Jeremy nodded.

"She came through it fabulously, Colonel!" Montfort added proudly.

Jeremy smiled. He smoothed back Christa's hair and spoke softly to her. "I knew you would do fabulously. After all, my love, you are a Cameron."

Her hand slipped into his, seemingly so fragile and so feminine. He remembered what Darcy had told him. "She was the bravest woman I ever saw." The bravest, the finest. Despite her delicate beauty, she was incredibly strong. She had survived so very much to come to this day.

Her fingers squeezed his. She was exhausted, but her eyes were brilliantly blue and very beautiful, and her smile was soft and enticing.

"I was born a Cameron," she told him. "But I am a McCauley now."

His smile in turn was miraculously tender. He leaned low and kissed her lips. "Mrs. McCauley, my dearest Reb, I do love you! This Yank has surrendered most willingly to the South."

Epilogue

June 1866
Cameron Hall
Tidewater Region
Virginia

Christa sat upon the window seat, draped in the long sleeves of Jeremy's white cotton shirt, her knees up, her elbows resting upon them, and her chin resting upon her hands. They were in the summer cottage, staring back out over the cemetery and onward to the lawn and porch and gardens beyond.

She looked something like a waif in the oversized shirt, but even as a waif, Jeremy decided, she was elegant. Christa, with her fine, beautifully sculpted features, sky-blue eyes, and jet-black hair. Even the way she curled the trim length of her body was elegant. She reminded him of a cat, sleek, glorious, and at the moment, purring.

He sat behind her, lifted the full rich sweep of her dark hair, and brushed his lips against her shoulder. She moved back against him, her arms falling upon his as they encircled her.

"You're happy to be home, aren't you?" he asked her.

He felt her smile and he felt her hesitate, careful with her answer. "Of course I'm happy to be home. It's nearly summer, and everything is growing so beautifully. The grass is so green, the air still just cool enough, the sun radiant. Virginia is beautiful in summer."

"And in spring," Jeremy agreed.

"And in fall, too, of course," she murmured. She twisted and her eyes danced with a blue fire as she continued, "Then, of course, I'm glad to be home because it's wonderful to see Callie and Kiernan doting over Josiah. I confess, I adore my son, but I'm grateful for the time we've managed alone here."

Jeremy felt his eyes drawn back to the furs upon the floor before the fire. He was feeling quite grateful himself. There were two half-full wineglasses awaiting them. And he had to agree, it was very nice to be alone. He'd found the invitation to the summer cottage beneath his breakfast plate this morning and he'd been delighted to find his wife there before him, without the child he too adored. The long miles home had been worth it for just those moments.

But, of course, the journey was worth it for so many more reasons. The sense of belonging here was wonderful. Daniel and Callie and their little ones had been at Cameron Hall almost constantly since they had arrived. Christa had been watching her brothers and their wives and the Cameron toddlers—and their own little bundle in his cradle—out on the lawn from the window for the last several minutes. The Camerons were all here. But the homecoming was even richer than that. Joshua McCauley and his young wife, Janis, had been invited down as a surprise for Jeremy just as soon as Callie had known when they were arriving.

Since the southern household had been filling with Yankees, Jesse had suggested that Kiernan's father, John McCay, come spend time with them too. The Joshua McCauleys were home now, and John, too, had returned to his own house. But for a while the household had been tumultuous with children everywhere and the discussions both serious and laughable.

Daniel and Callie and their brood were still at Cameron Hall, and it was those two Christa watched now, along with Jesse and Kiernan and the children. They were wonderful to watch. Kiernan and Callie were stunning in their gowns, sipping cold drinks on a swing and rocking the baby while Jesse was down on the ground and Daniel was directing the children, one after the other, to climb atop his back. Then Jesse was standing, insisting that it was Daniel's turn to play cavalry horse. Then Callie stood up, always the peacemaker, but before she could chastise them she shrieked as Daniel brought her down—elegant day dress and all—onto the lawn. The children couldn't let Kiernan be the only dignified one among the adults, so they dragged her onto the lawn too.

Jeremy and Christa couldn't really hear the words from where they were, they could only hear the laughter that occasionally floated to them, making them both smile.

"Think they know where we are?" Jeremy asked Christa.

She nodded, smiling. "Well, they know I'm here, so I'm sure they know you're here! But it's always been a private place. When we were children and we were in trouble, we used to come here to bind our little wounded souls! We all knew to stay clear until that someone reappeared. Then . . ."

"Then?"

Her lashes fell and she smiled. "Then . . . well, I'm quite certain that Kiernan met Jesse here before the war, before they were married. I carried messages for them now and then, and one of them was about fur . . . and well, you've seen how it's furnished!"

He laughed. "Minx! Spying on your brother!" he chastised her.

"I certainly never did such a thing!" she protested, but she leaned against him still smiling. "Oh, Jeremy! Look out there. It's almost like it was before the war!" Christa said softly.

"Because the war is over. Really over," Jeremy said, and he threaded his fingers through hers, lacing them together.

She sighed, leaning her weight against him. "But there's still so much that isn't healed!" she said. "Carpetbaggers and riffraff are still half of the ruling force. Daniel's had to ask another pardon—and it doesn't sit well with him, I assure you! The schism has remained."

"Yes, in a way," Jeremy agreed. He smoothed back her hair. "Christa, you can't take something as agonizing and devastating as the War of Rebellion—"

"The Civil War," she corrected.

"We Yanks do call it a War of Rebellion," he continued patiently, "and think that it can be over because the firing has ended. Christa, it may take years, it may take decades. Our country is just a pup when you compare it with others. The war has come and gone, and we've made it as a union! Maybe you can't see it yet. But it's time for growth again. Men and women are looking to the West, they're looking to the cities, they're searching for opportunities—searching for ways to live, and in living we'll heal the breach. In little ways, first. Like we've healed the breach here!" he said very softly. "We've found our peace. Others will find theirs. And a hundred years from now, maybe the Camerons living here will know that the war had to be fought, and had to be lost, for the whole country to be strong."

She looked up at him, smiling, her blue eyes radiant. She stroked his cheek. "I love you, Jeremy."

He caught her fingers and kissed them. He cleared his throat. "I love you, too, Christa. More than I could ever say. And I've lain awake nights lately, thinking about it."

She arched a brow. "I thought that love made you sleep well. When Josey isn't busy waking us up, that is."

He smiled. "Yes, but I've been thinking."

"Oh, dear! Yanks are so dangerous when they think!" she teased.

He ran a finger down her nose. "I'm going to tell you what I've been thinking despite that comment, Mrs. McCauley!" He paused just a second, then continued. "Jesse wrote me while we were still at Fort Jacobson—"

"Jesse wrote you?"

"Yes, your brother wrote me privately!" he teased, then sobered. "He wanted me to know that your father had left him instructions about a certain parcel of land. It was to be yours if you ever wanted it, once you were married and settled. I imagine Jesse was afraid it might cause a dispute if you had wanted to come home, and I had wanted to stay in the West."

"The two of us? Have a dispute?" she said, wide-eyed.

He grinned. Since the day he had taken her from Buffalo Run's encampment, neither of them had ever denied the depths of their love or would ever do so again. But they had learned that not even love curbed hot tempers completely, and that the making up from their inevitable disagreements was a wonderful thing.

"Well, my love, Jesse did grow up with you. He knows, of course, all about your temper."

"My temper!"

"Errant Rebs seem to come with them," he teased. She smiled, but then her smile faded. "Oh, Jeremy! I was so grateful for the way that you handled things last night!"

She had made him promise that they would never tell Jesse that John Weland had been seeking revenge against him. The danger was all over, but Jesse, being Jesse, would hound himself about it endlessly.

At dinner they had been talking about traveling, and Jesse had cleared his throat and commented that he was still afraid of being away from home too long —since someone had nearly succeeded in burning down the place just a year ago.

Jeremy had apologized profusely for not having told Jesse earlier that he had come in contact with a man who told him that he knew who had been after the Cameron estate, and that it had been a deranged major who had, since that time, passed away.

Jesse would never know the truth.

And they would all breathe more easily feeling that Cameron Hall was safe.

"You were wonderful!" Christa told him. She kissed his lips, then lay back in his arms, studying him. "You were always wonderful. Even when I was being incredibly rotten, you were considerate of my family."

He brushed a kiss onto her brow.

"You were quite good to my sister when she came here, too, you know," he reminded her.

"I loved her right away. Even for a Yankee, she was a sweetheart."

"Well, I admit, I was partial to your brothers from the start."

"Even the Reb?"

"Especially the Reb."

She smiled, leaning against him again, luxuriating in the quiet time and the rare solitude they were enjoying.

"Well?" he said softly.

She opened her eyes wide. "Well?"

"Christa—" he said, then he paused, swallowing. "Christa, when I married you, I dragged you away from here. I took you from everything that you loved, from your family, from your home. I forced you out west, to hardship, to danger. I had no right—"

"You had every right!" she corrected him. "I forced you to marry me, remember?"

"If I hadn't been willing, no one could have forced me," he said softly.

"And no one could have forced me west!" she replied.

He disentangled himself from her for a moment, pacing before the fire. Christa, watching him, hugged her knees more tightly and felt a rush of warmth sweep through her. He was naked, and very comfortable and natural that way.

And excessively handsome and alluring, too, so tall, so tautly muscled and sleek, so bronze, touched by the fire that took the chill from the air.

She swallowed and watched his eyes, reminding herself primly that he was trying to talk to her.

He came back to her, a foot upon the window seat, and he stared down at her. "Christa—"

"Out there," she interrupted him, "in the graveyard, are many of my Cameron ancestors."

"I know, Christa. That's the point—"

"The first Camerons to come here were Jassy and Jamie. He was a lord. She married him—"

"I've heard this story from Jesse," Jeremy warned her. "Jassy was a bit of a tart who married Jamie for his house and holdings in England. But he brought her here—"

"Precisely!" Christa whispered softly. "She was a bit of a tart! But she was strong-willed and determined, and she built this home with Jamie and stayed with him here. Because she fell in love with him, you see. And do you know what else?"

"What else?"

"He had to rescue her from Indians too. They were the Pamunkeys, I believe. And they roamed all this land. They're mostly all gone now." She flashed him a rueful smile. "Except, upon occasion, you meet a tall blue-eyed, very blond man or woman who happens to be a descendant of Pocahontas and John Smith! Is that what will happen out west, do you think?" she asked him.

He shook his head. "I don't know. But we do seem to be a gluttonous people. The railroads will go farther soon. We'll continue to call them savages while we kill their food supplies and steal their land. Maybe one day there will be a peace. I'm afraid that there will be tremendous loss with it. But there's so much only time will tell."

She smiled, watching him, feeling a warmth sweep around her. She loved him so much, yet it seemed that she loved him more daily.

She touched his russet hair, marveling at the color and the thick rich feel of it. "The point of this story," she told him, "is that Jassy gave up what she thought she wanted so much—"

"It was my understanding that he told her she was coming or he would see to it that she did so by force."

Christa waved a hand in the air. "The point is that she discovered that she loved him with her whole heart. And they came to love this land together, and they built their home here."

He took both of her hands. "So we will build a home here," he said.

She shook her head. "You're not paying attention to me. It doesn't matter where, Jeremy," she said.

"There's still tremendous danger in the West," he told her. "The Indian problems will not be solved for years!"

"There's danger, yes, but tremendous excitement and beauty too!"

"There's beauty here."

"There's so much to explore and build in the West," she argued.

"And there's so incredibly much to rebuild here, in Virginia," he said. "I—I brought you from your home. But then discovered how much I loved you. Christa, you and Josiah are my life. And love is far stronger than any need for honor or glory in the West! You hold my heart in your hands. Carry it tenderly, my love. But carry it with you wherever you would go. The future is yours to decide."

Her eyes widened upon his as she realized just how serious he was.

"But you're up for promotion again—"

"Christa, there's a great deal I could do here too."

She started to tremble. She threaded her fingers through his hair. "Oh, my God, Jeremy!" she whispered. "I love you!"

He caught her hand and kissed her palm tenderly. "Christa—"

"Oh, Jeremy! How strange, and how very sad and curious! That's one thing that John Weland told me once."

"Weland!"

She nodded. "He told me that home was where the heart was. And it's very true. Don't you see, it doesn't matter. It doesn't matter where we are at all. In your arms, I'm home."

He rose, and lifted her into his arms. She stared at the glittering silver in his eyes.

"So?" she whispered.

"So . . ." he said. He whirled around with her and lowered them both before the fire and onto the fur. He came upon his knees and drew her up likewise against him, entwining their fingers together.

"So?"

"So . . ." He paused and kissed her. Kissed her long and leisurely, savoring the taste and touch and feel of her lips, the brush of their bodies just barely touching one another.

"So?" she repeated one last time.

He smiled, his mouth just a breath away from hers. "So we will worry about it later. As wonderful as Josiah's aunts are, he will want his supper, and soon. And for now—though I would deprive my son of nothing—I'm afraid I want his mother too. And so I must take my time now."

"And the future?"

"It will come tomorrow. It always does."

She smiled. And then her smile was captured in the heat of his next kiss.

The fire raged high and golden around them. The summer cottage enveloped them, a haven for their love, providing them sweet secrecy and enchantment.

Somewhere nearby, the river drifted ever onward. The breeze stirred over the James. Timelessly.

Life went on.

The war was over, Christa reflected. Wherever she was, the war had ended.

They might ride westwardly once again. There was so much to be done in the years to come, the expansion would be tremendous. The frontier was opening as it never had before. There were so many ready for war with the Indians in the West, ready to decimate them. Men like Jeremy—men of peace and strength—would be needed.

They might build here. There was so much needed in the South too. A lot had been done. The land itself was beginning to cover over some of the scars of war. But so much more would be necessary. And yes, it would take years. Decades, maybe. But like a phoenix rising from the ashes, a new South would form. Different. They would be entering an age of progress, of learning, of growth. The South needed good men and women too.

Which would it be for them?

She didn't know. They needed time. To think, to dream, to talk.

And, she thought, meeting the silver of his gaze and smiling slowly in the comfort of his arms, it didn't matter.

Just as she held Jeremy's heart in her hands, he held hers within the tender grasp of his own.

He stirred, holding her close, kissing her forehead.

She smiled within his embrace. It had been a long, long road. A long time since she had stood by the gates of the family cemetery, feeling that she was being torn from her roots, from all that she loved. From all that Jassy and Jamie had built.

But she knew now that Jassy and Jamie would most certainly understand.

Truly, it didn't matter where she was.

She had finally come home.